Archie
1000 PAGE COMICS COMPENDIUM

Archie

1000 PAGE COMICS COMPENDIUM

Publisher / Co-CEO: Jon Goldwater
Co-CEO: Nancy Silberkleit
President: Mike Pellerito
Co-President / Editor-In-Chief: Victor Gorelick
Chief Creative Officer: Roberto Aguirre-Sacasa
Chief Operating Officer: William Mooar
Chief Financial Officer: Robert Wintle
Senior Vice President – Publicity & Marketing: Alex Segura
Director of Book Sales & Operations: Jonathan Betancourt
Production Manager: Stephen Oswald
Lead Designer: Kari McLachlan
Associate Editor: Carlos Antunes
Editorial Assistant / Proofreader: Jamie Lee Rotante

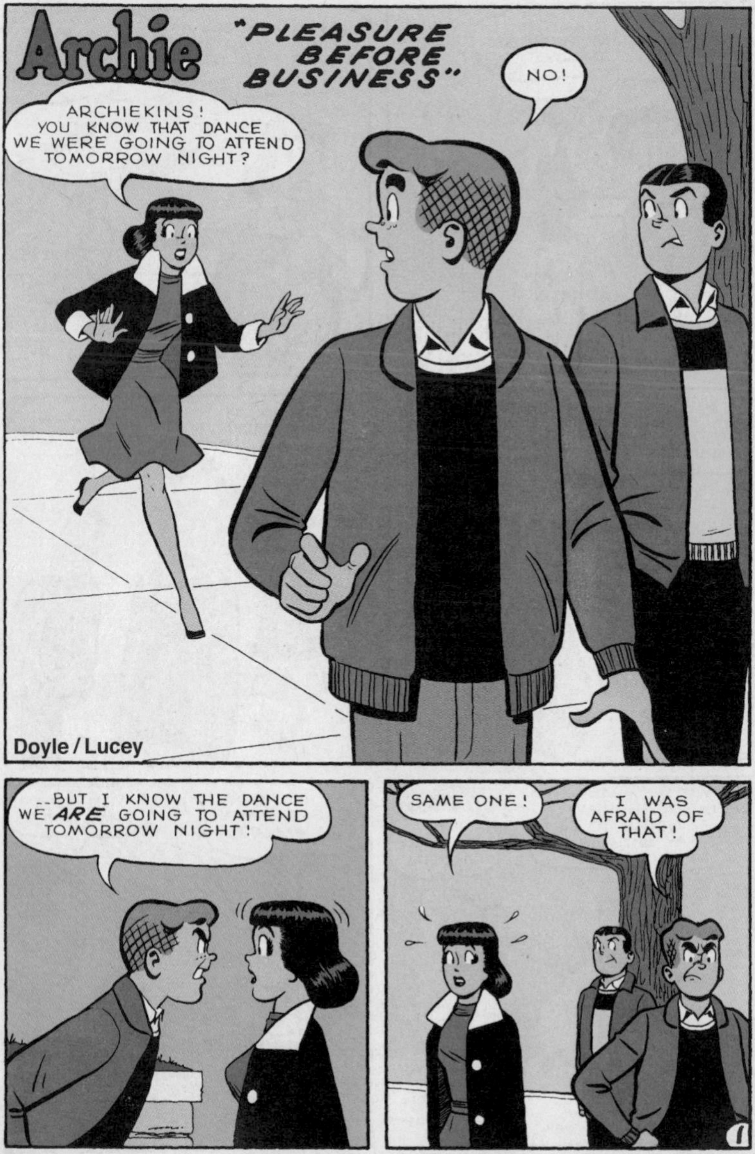
Archie
"PLEASURE BEFORE BUSINESS"
ARCHIEKINS! YOU KNOW THAT DANCE WE WERE GOING TO ATTEND TOMORROW NIGHT?
NO!
Doyle / Lucey
..BUT I KNOW THE DANCE WE ARE GOING TO ATTEND TOMORROW NIGHT!
SAME ONE!
I WAS AFRAID OF THAT!
1

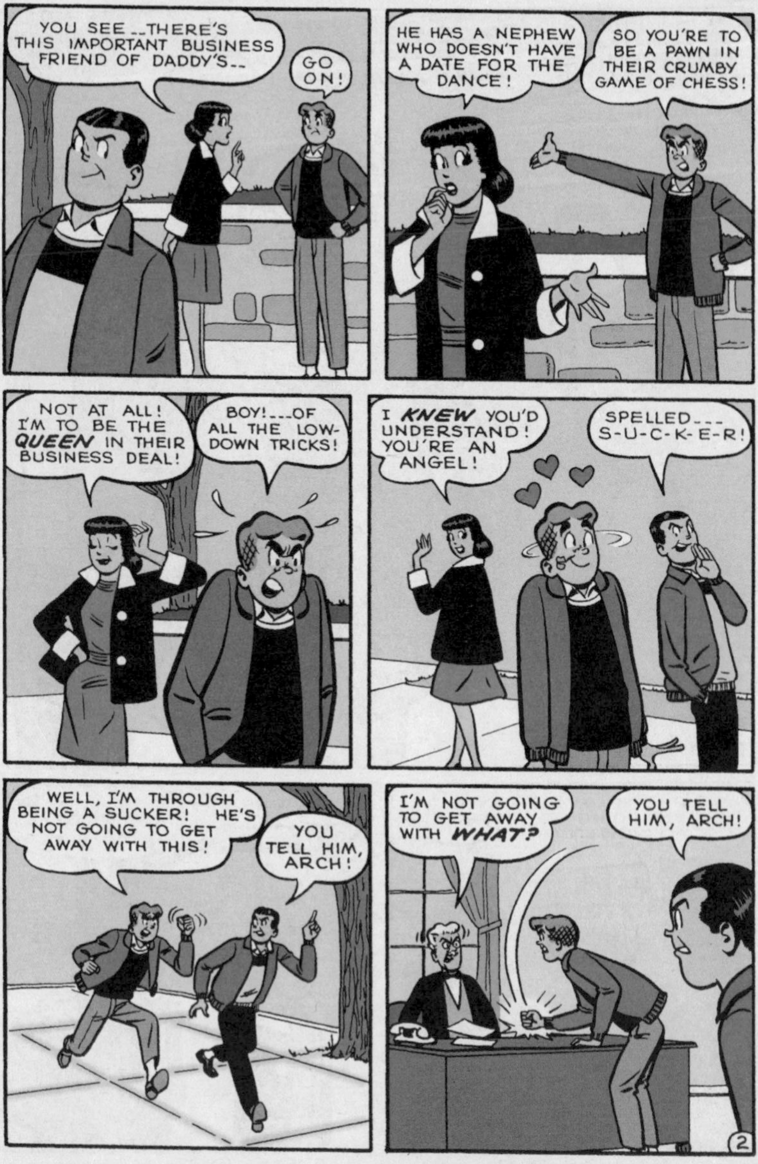

YOU SEE--THERE'S THIS IMPORTANT BUSINESS FRIEND OF DADDY'S--
GO ON!
HE HAS A NEPHEW WHO DOESN'T HAVE A DATE FOR THE DANCE!
SO YOU'RE TO BE A PAWN IN THEIR CRUMBY GAME OF CHESS!
NOT AT ALL! I'M TO BE THE QUEEN IN THEIR BUSINESS DEAL!
BOY!---OF ALL THE LOW-DOWN TRICKS!
I KNEW YOU'D UNDERSTAND! YOU'RE AN ANGEL!
SPELLED--- S-U-C-K-E-R!
WELL, I'M THROUGH BEING A SUCKER! HE'S NOT GOING TO GET AWAY WITH THIS!
YOU TELL HIM, ARCH!
I'M NOT GOING TO GET AWAY WITH WHAT?
YOU TELL HIM, ARCH!
2

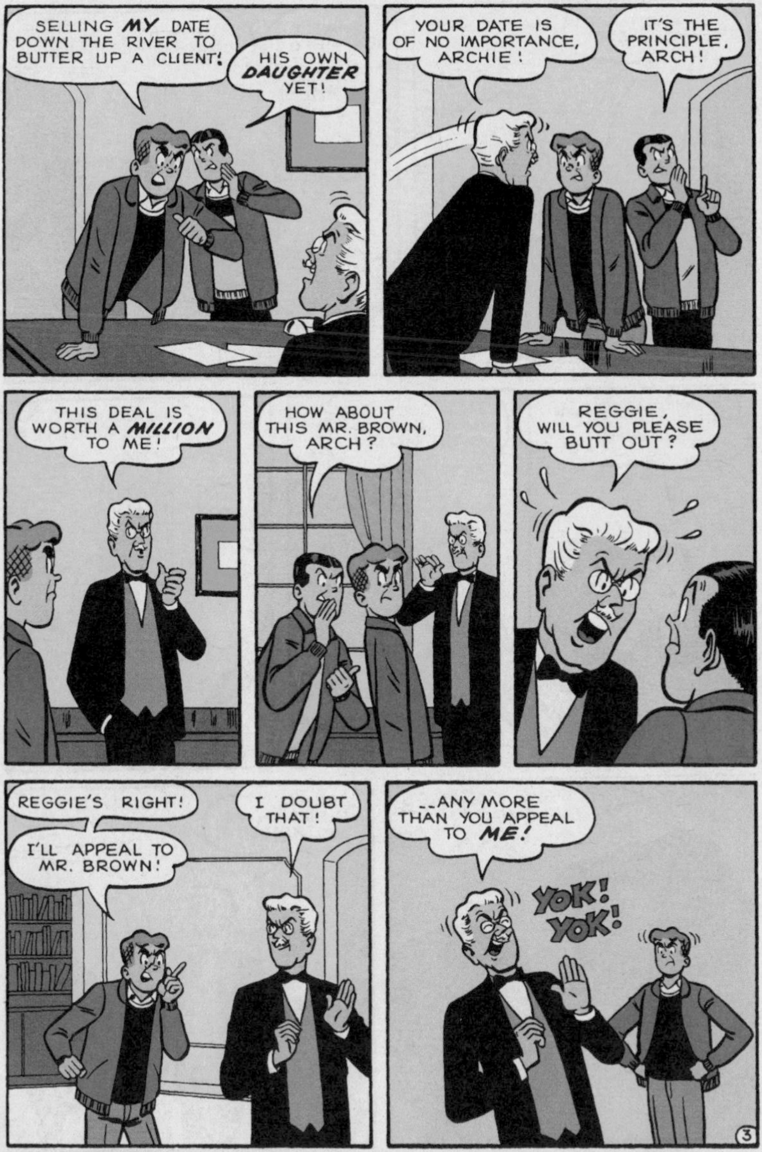
SELLING MY DATE DOWN THE RIVER TO BUTTER UP A CLIENT!
HIS OWN DAUGHTER YET!
YOUR DATE IS OF NO IMPORTANCE, ARCHIE!
IT'S THE PRINCIPLE, ARCH!
THIS DEAL IS WORTH A MILLION TO ME!
HOW ABOUT THIS MR. BROWN, ARCH?
REGGIE, WILL YOU PLEASE BUTT OUT?
REGGIE'S RIGHT!
I'LL APPEAL TO MR. BROWN!
I DOUBT THAT!
..ANY MORE THAN YOU APPEAL TO ME!
YOK! YOK!
3

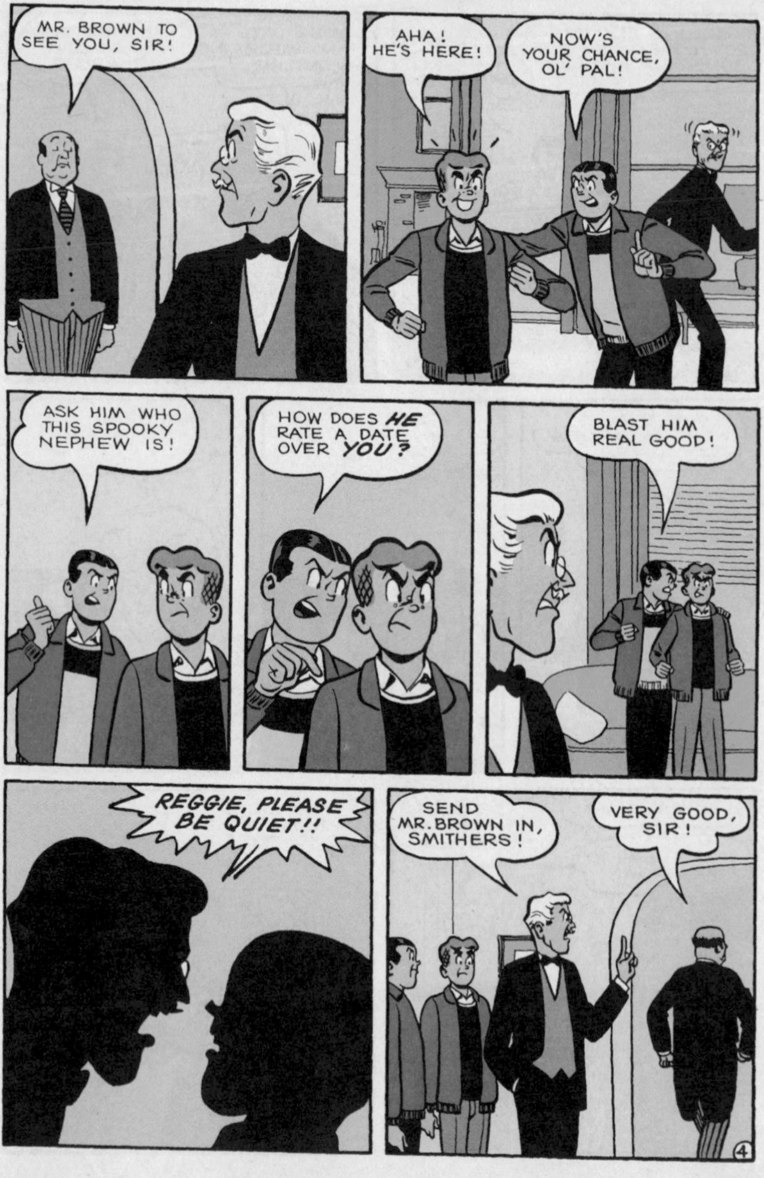
MR. BROWN TO SEE YOU, SIR!
AHA! HE'S HERE!
NOW'S YOUR CHANCE, OL' PAL!
ASK HIM WHO THIS SPOOKY NEPHEW IS!
HOW DOES HE RATE A DATE OVER YOU?
BLAST HIM REAL GOOD!
REGGIE, PLEASE BE QUIET!!
SEND MR. BROWN IN, SMITHERS!
VERY GOOD, SIR!
4

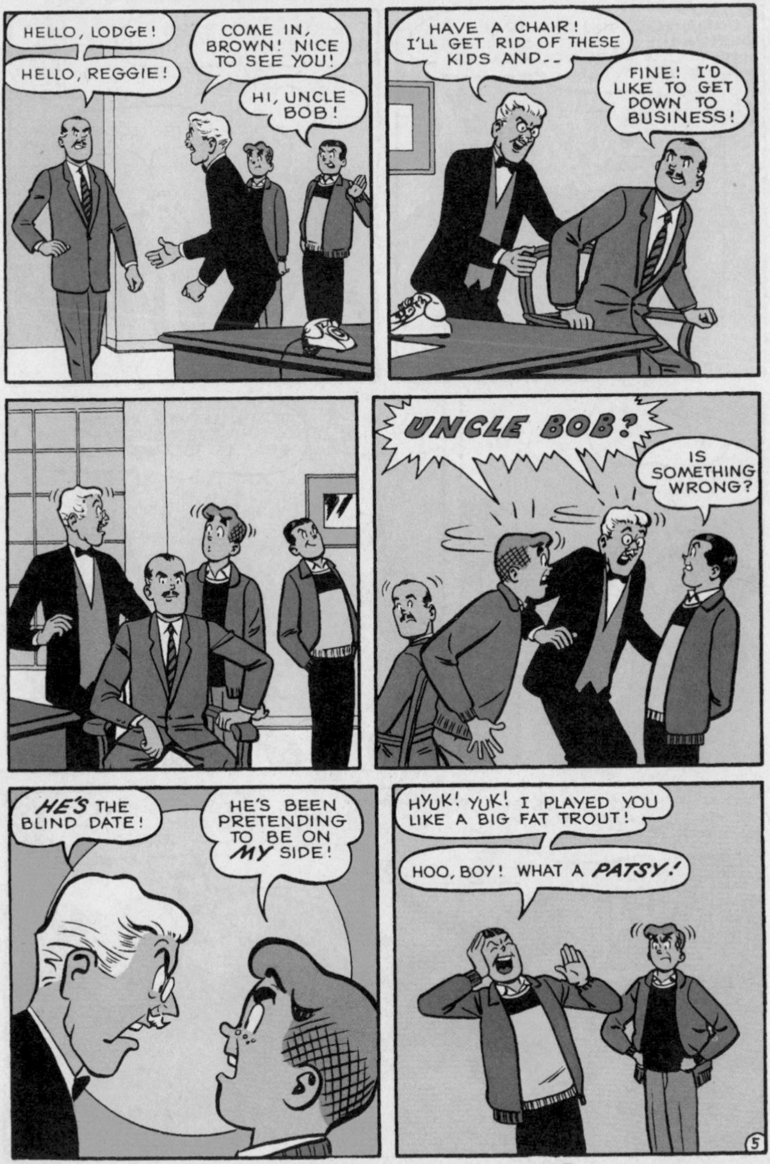
HELLO, LODGE!
HELLO, REGGIE!
COME IN, BROWN! NICE TO SEE YOU!
HI, UNCLE BOB!
HAVE A CHAIR! I'LL GET RID OF THESE KIDS AND--
FINE! I'D LIKE TO GET DOWN TO BUSINESS!
UNCLE BOB?
IS SOMETHING WRONG?
HE'S THE BLIND DATE!
HE'S BEEN PRETENDING TO BE ON MY SIDE!
HYUK! YUK! I PLAYED YOU LIKE A BIG FAT TROUT!
HOO, BOY! WHAT A PATSY!

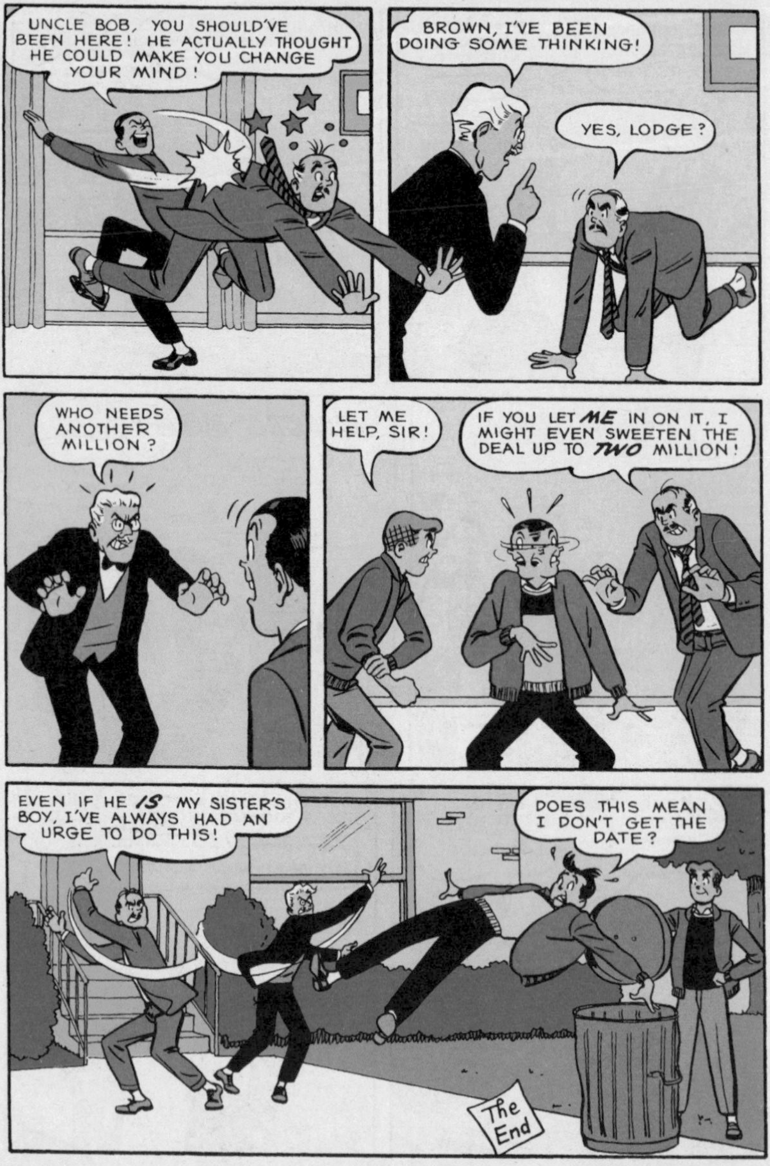
UNCLE BOB, YOU SHOULD'VE BEEN HERE! HE ACTUALLY THOUGHT HE COULD MAKE YOU CHANGE YOUR MIND!
BROWN, I'VE BEEN DOING SOME THINKING!
YES, LODGE?
WHO NEEDS ANOTHER MILLION?
LET ME HELP, SIR!
IF YOU LET ME IN ON IT, I MIGHT EVEN SWEETEN THE DEAL UP TO TWO MILLION!
EVEN IF HE IS MY SISTER'S BOY, I'VE ALWAYS HAD AN URGE TO DO THIS!
DOES THIS MEAN I DON'T GET THE DATE?
The End

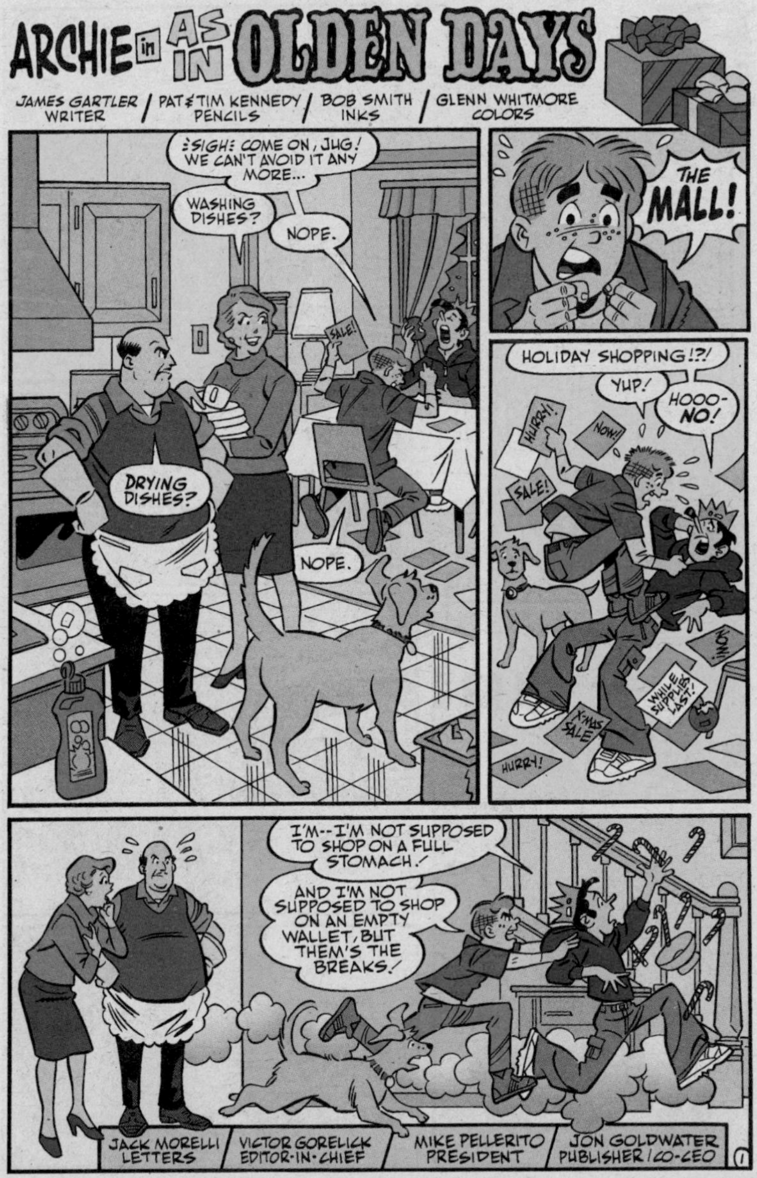
ARCHIE in AS IN OLDEN DAYS
JAMES GARTLER WRITER / PAT & TIM KENNEDY PENCILS / BOB SMITH INKS / GLENN WHITMORE COLORS
:SIGH: COME ON, JUG! WE CAN'T AVOID IT ANY MORE...
WASHING DISHES?
NOPE.
DRYING DISHES?
NOPE.
SALE!
THE MALL!
HOLIDAY SHOPPING!?!
YUP!
HOOO-NO!
HURRY!
NOW!
SALE!
NOW!
WHILE SUPPLIES LAST!
X-MAS SALE
HURRY!
I'M--I'M NOT SUPPOSED TO SHOP ON A FULL STOMACH!
AND I'M NOT SUPPOSED TO SHOP ON AN EMPTY WALLET, BUT THEM'S THE BREAKS!
JACK MORELLI LETTERS
VICTOR GORELICK EDITOR-IN-CHIEF
MIKE PELLERITO PRESIDENT
JON GOLDWATER PUBLISHER / CO-CEO
1

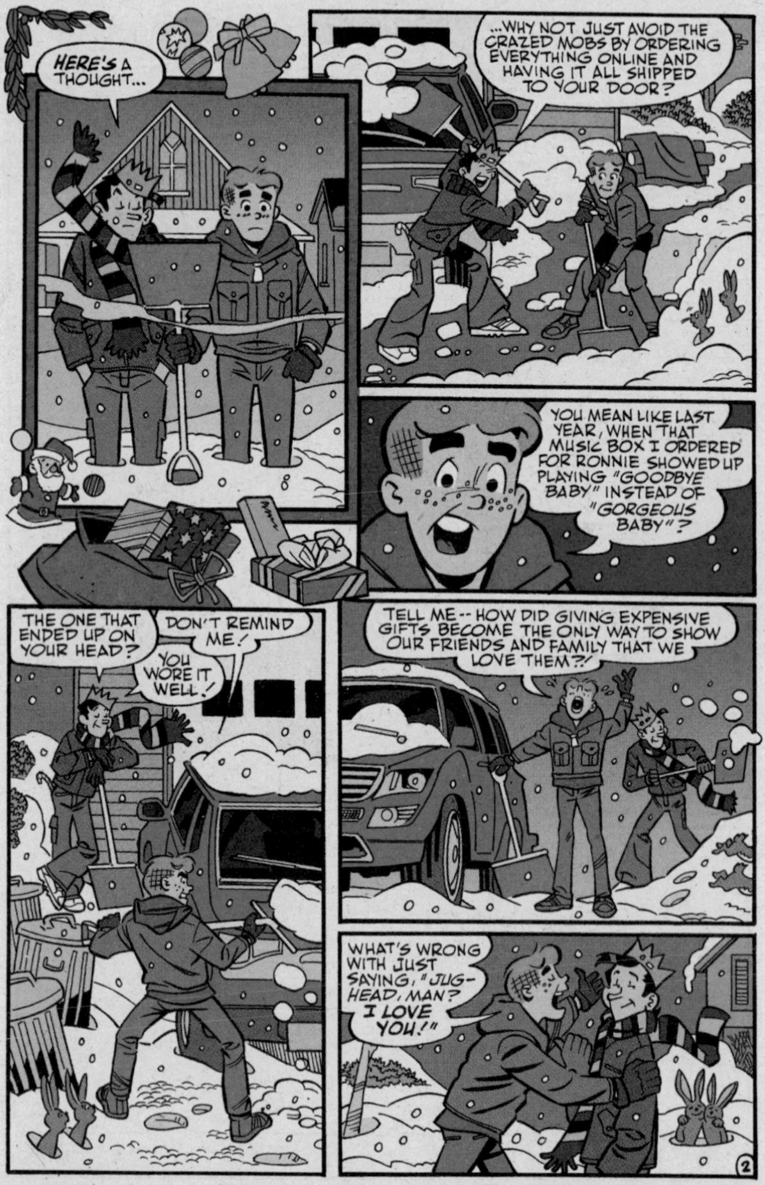
HERE'S A THOUGHT...
...WHY NOT JUST AVOID THE CRAZED MOBS BY ORDERING EVERYTHING ONLINE AND HAVING IT ALL SHIPPED TO YOUR DOOR?
YOU MEAN LIKE LAST YEAR, WHEN THAT MUSIC BOX I ORDERED FOR RONNIE SHOWED UP PLAYING "GOODBYE BABY" INSTEAD OF "GORGEOUS BABY"?
THE ONE THAT ENDED UP ON YOUR HEAD?
DON'T REMIND ME!
YOU WORE IT WELL!
TELL ME-- HOW DID GIVING EXPENSIVE GIFTS BECOME THE ONLY WAY TO SHOW OUR FRIENDS AND FAMILY THAT WE LOVE THEM?!
WHAT'S WRONG WITH JUST SAYING, "JUG-HEAD, MAN? I LOVE YOU!"

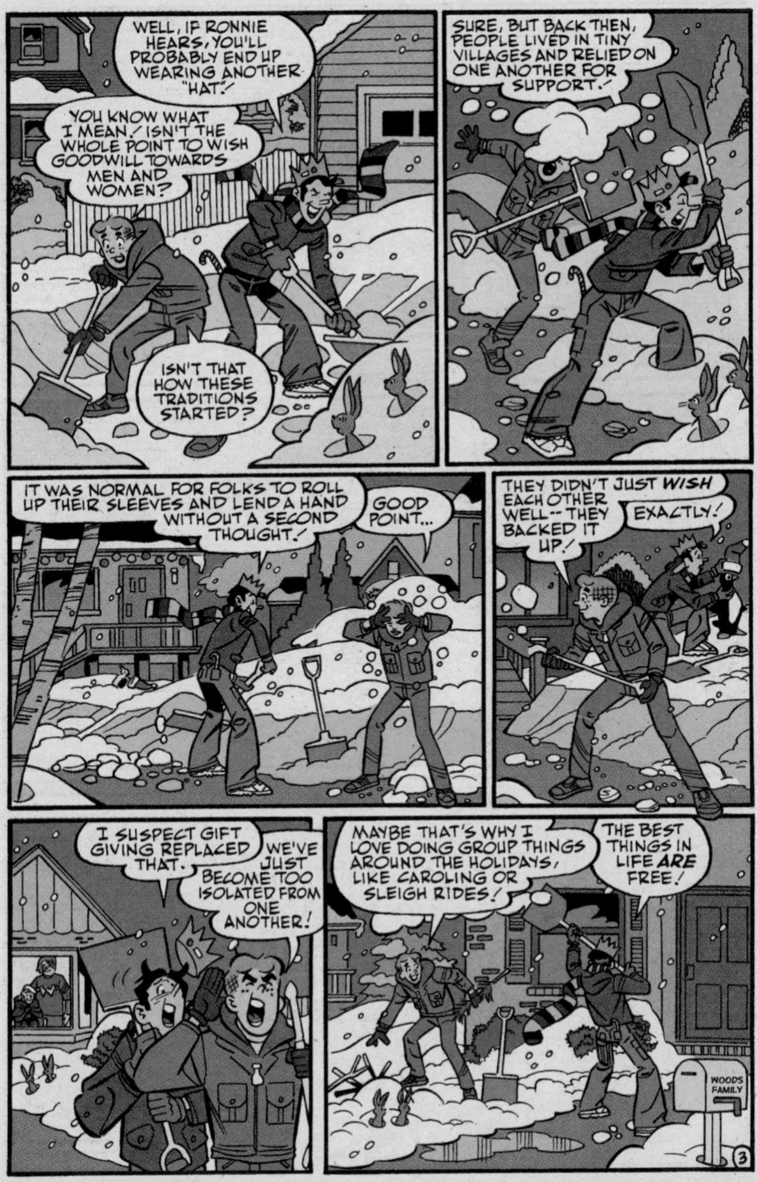
WELL, IF RONNIE HEARS, YOU'LL PROBABLY END UP WEARING ANOTHER "HAT"!
YOU KNOW WHAT I MEAN! ISN'T THE WHOLE POINT TO WISH GOODWILL TOWARDS MEN AND WOMEN?
ISN'T THAT HOW THESE TRADITIONS STARTED?
SURE, BUT BACK THEN, PEOPLE LIVED IN TINY VILLAGES AND RELIED ON ONE ANOTHER FOR SUPPORT!
IT WAS NORMAL FOR FOLKS TO ROLL UP THEIR SLEEVES AND LEND A HAND WITHOUT A SECOND THOUGHT!
GOOD POINT...
THEY DIDN'T JUST WISH EACH OTHER WELL -- THEY BACKED IT UP!
EXACTLY!
I SUSPECT GIFT GIVING REPLACED THAT.
WE'VE JUST BECOME TOO ISOLATED FROM ONE ANOTHER!
MAYBE THAT'S WHY I LOVE DOING GROUP THINGS AROUND THE HOLIDAYS, LIKE CAROLING OR SLEIGH RIDES!
THE BEST THINGS IN LIFE ARE FREE!
WOODS FAMILY
3

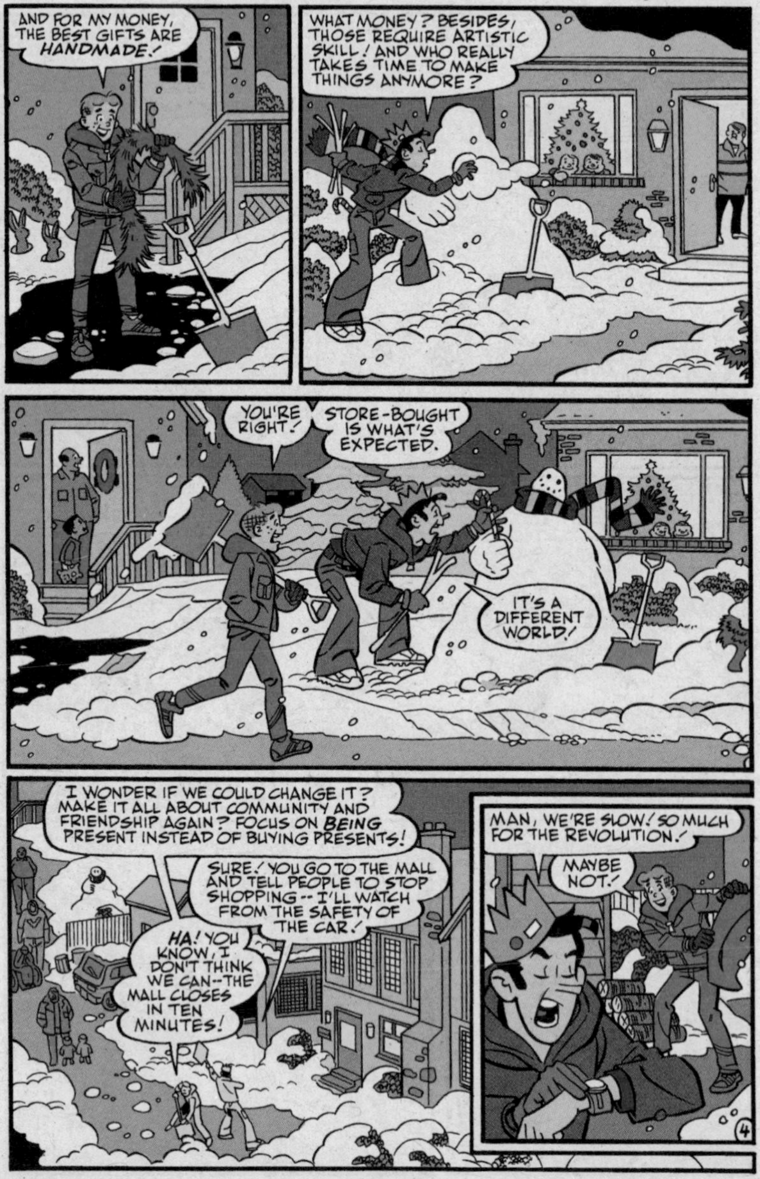
AND FOR MY MONEY, THE BEST GIFTS ARE *HANDMADE*!
WHAT MONEY? BESIDES, THOSE REQUIRE ARTISTIC SKILL! AND WHO REALLY TAKES TIME TO MAKE THINGS ANYMORE?
YOU'RE RIGHT!
STORE-BOUGHT IS WHAT'S EXPECTED.
IT'S A DIFFERENT WORLD!
I WONDER IF WE COULD CHANGE IT? MAKE IT ALL ABOUT COMMUNITY AND FRIENDSHIP AGAIN? FOCUS ON *BEING* PRESENT INSTEAD OF BUYING PRESENTS!
SURE! YOU GO TO THE MALL AND TELL PEOPLE TO STOP SHOPPING -- I'LL WATCH FROM THE SAFETY OF THE CAR!
HA! YOU KNOW, I DON'T THINK WE CAN--THE MALL CLOSES IN TEN MINUTES!
MAN, WE'RE SLOW! SO MUCH FOR THE REVOLUTION!
MAYBE NOT!
4

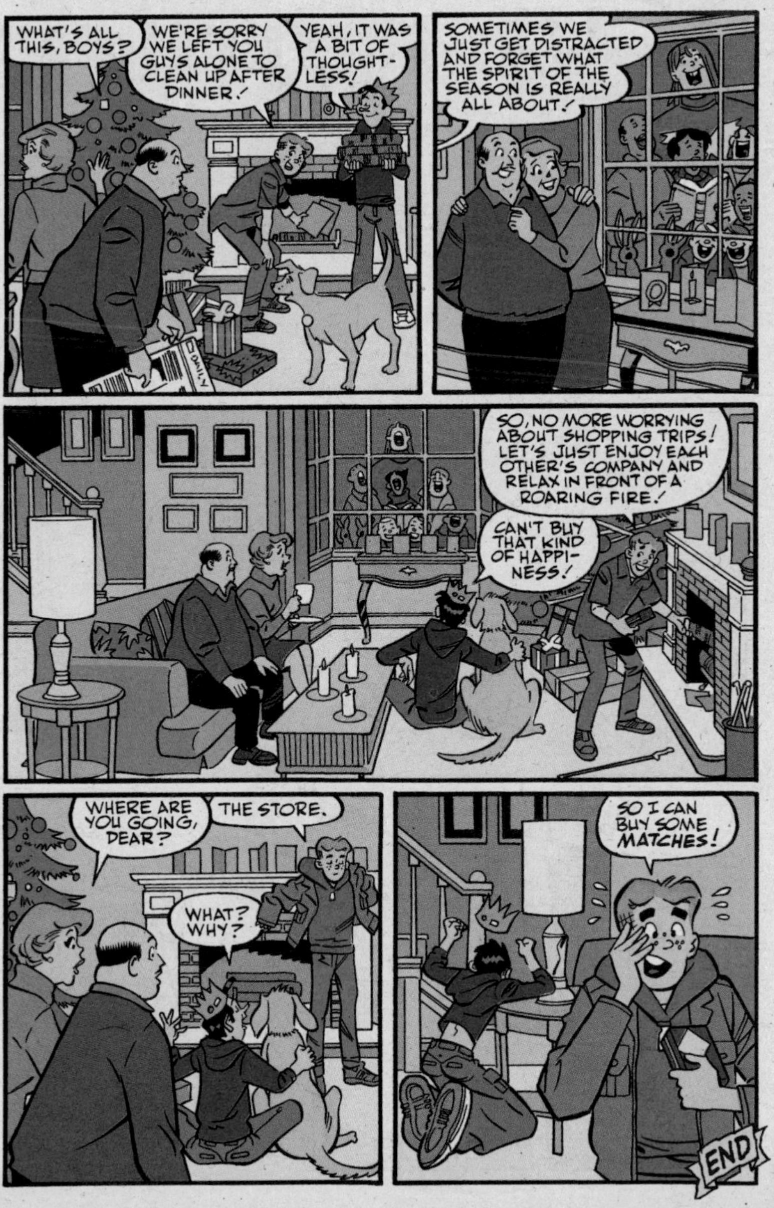
WHAT'S ALL THIS, BOYS?
WE'RE SORRY WE LEFT YOU GUYS ALONE TO CLEAN UP AFTER DINNER!
YEAH, IT WAS A BIT OF THOUGHT-LESS!
SOMETIMES WE JUST GET DISTRACTED AND FORGET WHAT THE SPIRIT OF THE SEASON IS REALLY ALL ABOUT!
SO, NO MORE WORRYING ABOUT SHOPPING TRIPS! LET'S JUST ENJOY EACH OTHER'S COMPANY AND RELAX IN FRONT OF A ROARING FIRE!
CAN'T BUY THAT KIND OF HAPPI-NESS!
WHERE ARE YOU GOING, DEAR?
THE STORE.
WHAT? WHY?
SO I CAN BUY SOME MATCHES!
END

Archie in LOCKET LUNACY

Script & Pencils: Fernando Ruiz / Inks: Jon D'Agostino / Letters: Bill Yoshida

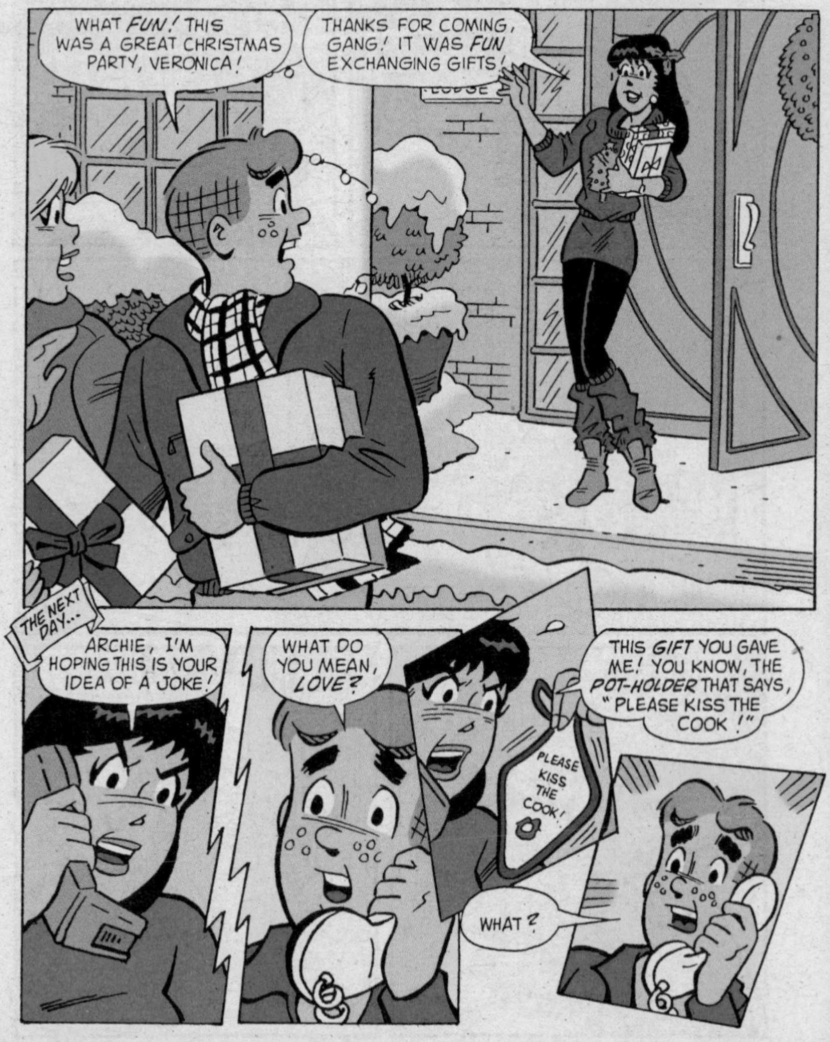
WHAT FUN! THIS WAS A GREAT CHRISTMAS PARTY, VERONICA!
THANKS FOR COMING, GANG! IT WAS FUN EXCHANGING GIFTS!
THE NEXT DAY...
ARCHIE, I'M HOPING THIS IS YOUR IDEA OF A JOKE!
WHAT DO YOU MEAN, LOVE?
THIS GIFT YOU GAVE ME! YOU KNOW, THE POT-HOLDER THAT SAYS, "PLEASE KISS THE COOK!"
PLEASE KISS THE COOK!
WHAT?

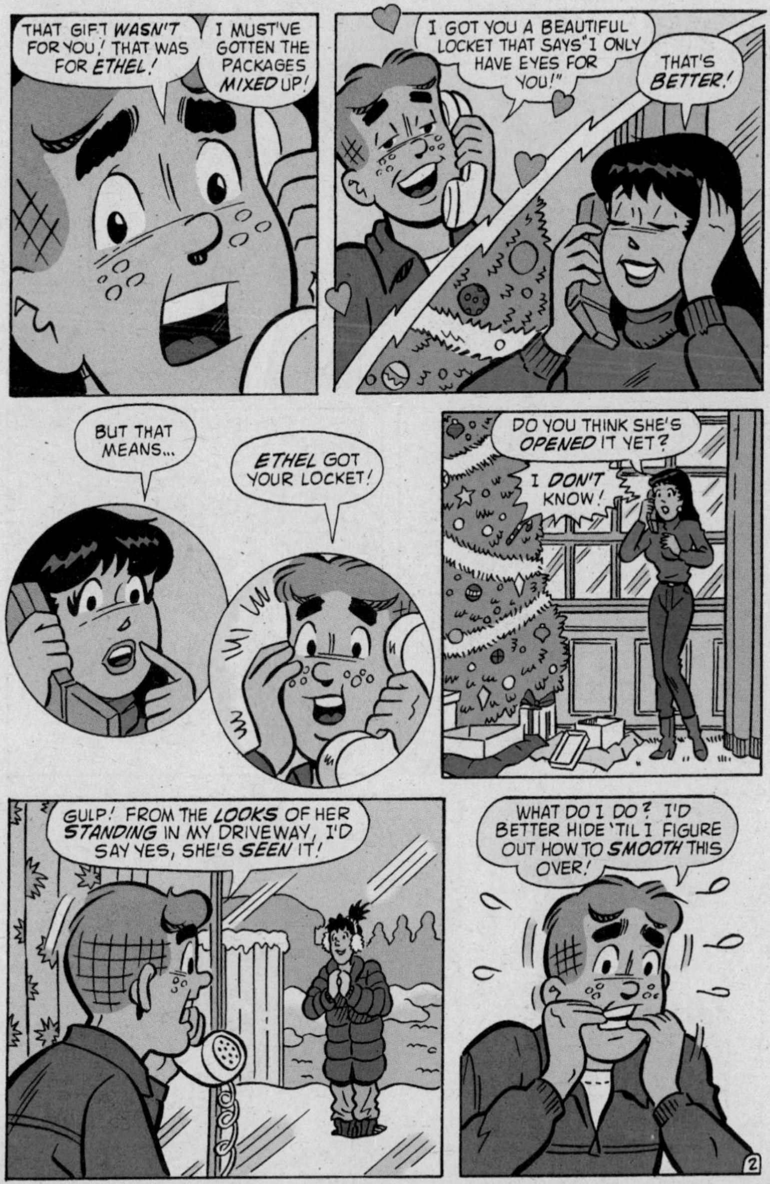
THAT GIFT WASN'T FOR YOU! THAT WAS FOR ETHEL!
I MUST'VE GOTTEN THE PACKAGES MIXED UP!
I GOT YOU A BEAUTIFUL LOCKET THAT SAYS "I ONLY HAVE EYES FOR YOU!"
THAT'S BETTER!
BUT THAT MEANS...
ETHEL GOT YOUR LOCKET!
DO YOU THINK SHE'S OPENED IT YET?
I DON'T KNOW!
GULP! FROM THE LOOKS OF HER STANDING IN MY DRIVEWAY, I'D SAY YES, SHE'S SEEN IT!
WHAT DO I DO? I'D BETTER HIDE 'TIL I FIGURE OUT HOW TO SMOOTH THIS OVER!
2

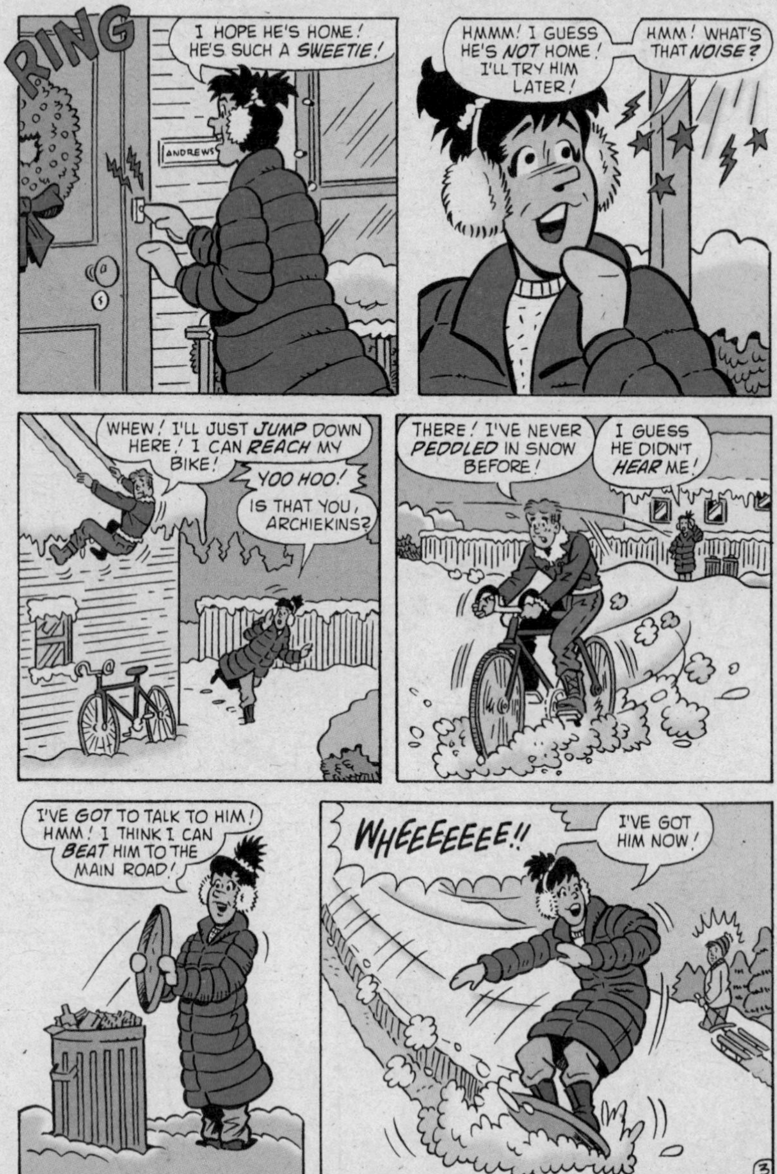
RING
I HOPE HE'S HOME! HE'S SUCH A *SWEETIE*!
ANDREWS
HMMM! I GUESS HE'S *NOT* HOME! I'LL TRY HIM LATER!
HMM! WHAT'S THAT *NOISE*?
WHEW! I'LL JUST *JUMP* DOWN HERE! I CAN *REACH* MY BIKE!
YOO HOO!
IS THAT YOU, ARCHIEKINS?
THERE! I'VE NEVER *PEDDLED* IN SNOW BEFORE!
I GUESS HE DIDN'T *HEAR* ME!
I'VE *GOT* TO TALK TO HIM! HMM! I THINK I CAN *BEAT* HIM TO THE MAIN ROAD!
WHEEEEEEE!!
I'VE GOT HIM NOW!
3

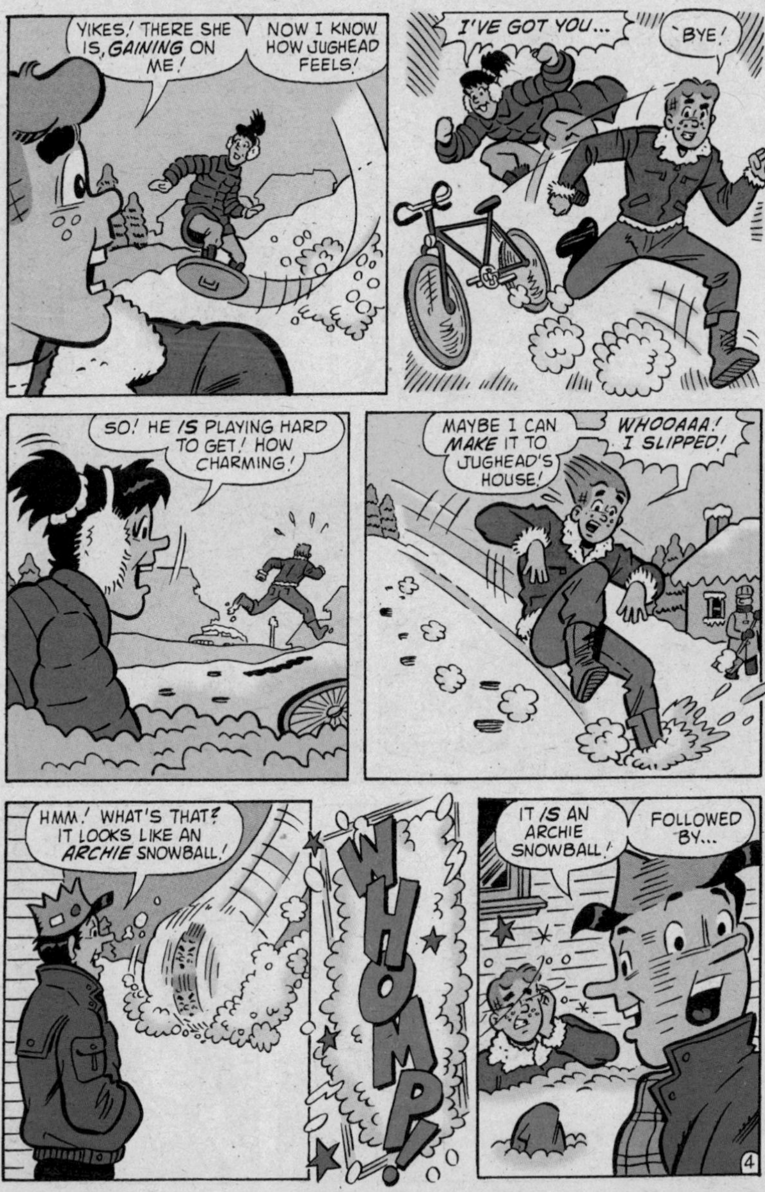
YIKES! THERE SHE IS, GAINING ON ME!
NOW I KNOW HOW JUGHEAD FEELS!
I'VE GOT YOU...
'BYE!
SO! HE IS PLAYING HARD TO GET! HOW CHARMING!
MAYBE I CAN MAKE IT TO JUGHEAD'S HOUSE!
WHOOAAA! I SLIPPED!
HMM! WHAT'S THAT? IT LOOKS LIKE AN ARCHIE SNOWBALL!
WHOMP!
IT IS AN ARCHIE SNOWBALL!
FOLLOWED BY...
4

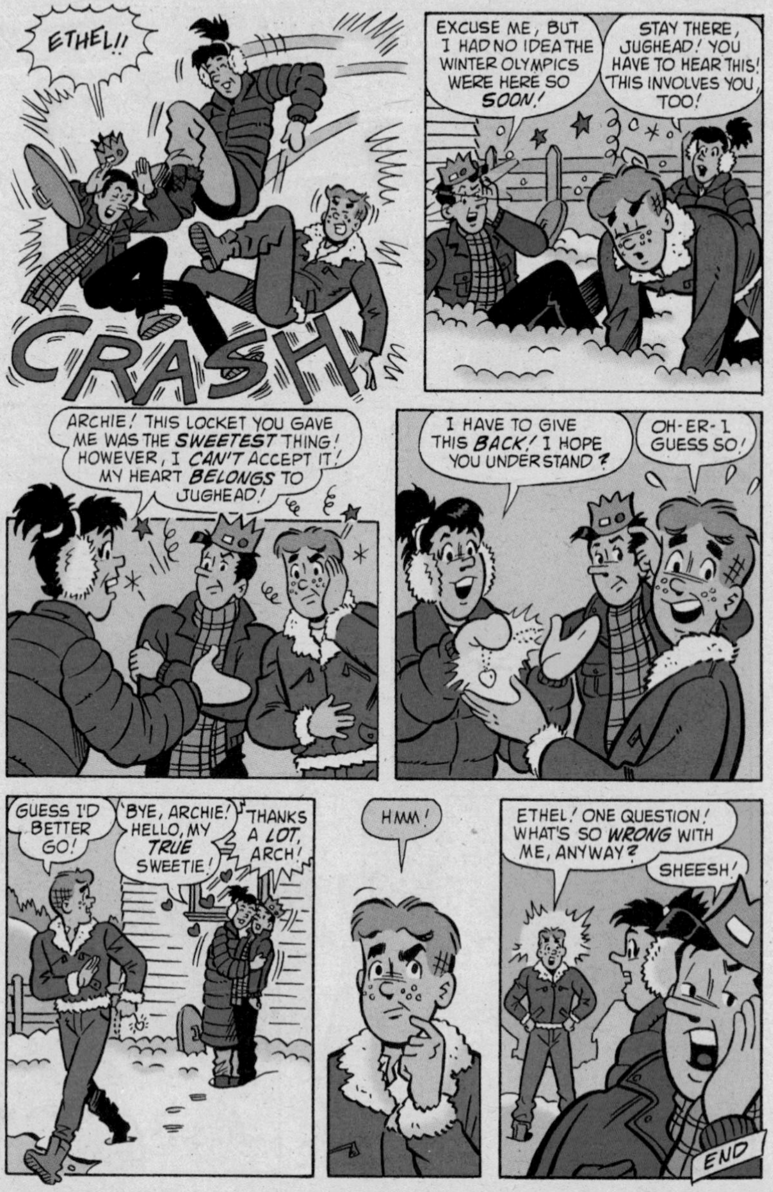
ETHEL!!
CRASH
EXCUSE ME, BUT I HAD NO IDEA THE WINTER OLYMPICS WERE HERE SO SOON!
STAY THERE, JUGHEAD! YOU HAVE TO HEAR THIS! THIS INVOLVES YOU, TOO!
ARCHIE! THIS LOCKET YOU GAVE ME WAS THE SWEETEST THING! HOWEVER, I CAN'T ACCEPT IT! MY HEART BELONGS TO JUGHEAD!
I HAVE TO GIVE THIS BACK! I HOPE YOU UNDERSTAND?
OH-ER-I GUESS SO!
GUESS I'D BETTER GO!
'BYE, ARCHIE! HELLO, MY TRUE SWEETIE!
THANKS A LOT, ARCH!
HMM!
ETHEL! ONE QUESTION! WHAT'S SO WRONG WITH ME, ANYWAY?
SHEESH!
END

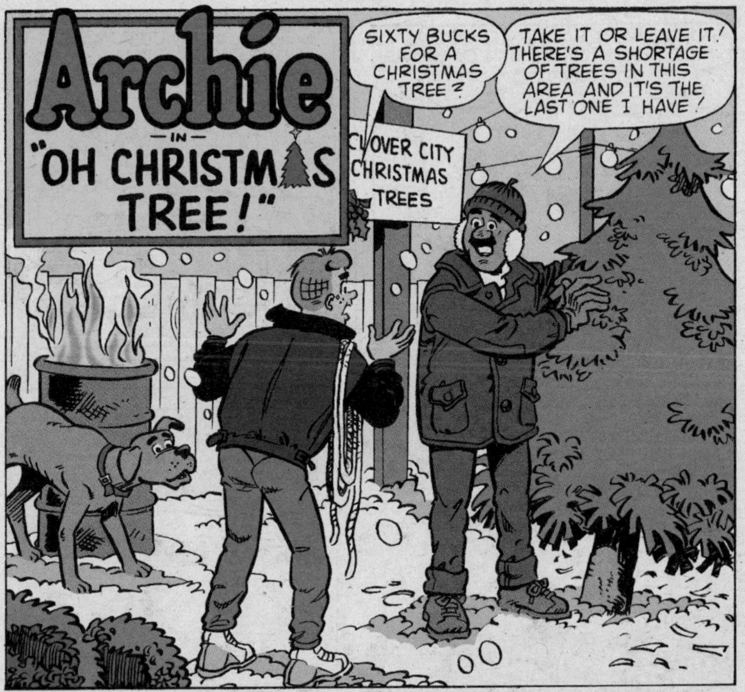
Archie
-IN-
"OH CHRISTMAS TREE!"
SIXTY BUCKS FOR A CHRISTMAS TREE?
TAKE IT OR LEAVE IT! THERE'S A SHORTAGE OF TREES IN THIS AREA AND IT'S THE LAST ONE I HAVE!
CLOVER CITY CHRISTMAS TREES

Script: Mike Pellowski / Pencils: Stan Goldberg / Inks: Jon D'Agostino / Letters: Bill Yoshida / Colors: Barry Grossman

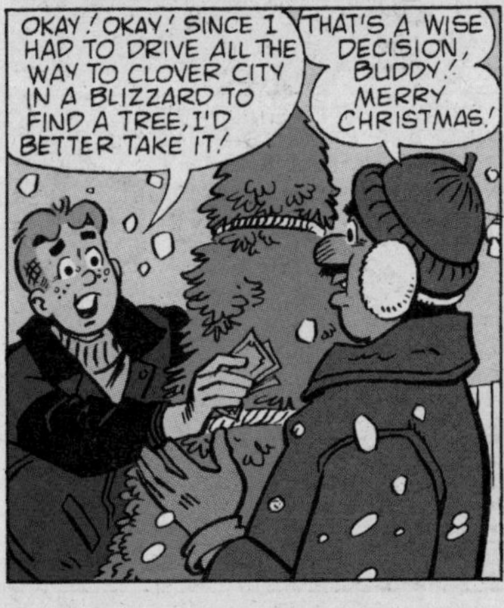
OKAY! OKAY! SINCE I HAD TO DRIVE ALL THE WAY TO CLOVER CITY IN A BLIZZARD TO FIND A TREE, I'D BETTER TAKE IT!
THAT'S A WISE DECISION, BUDDY! MERRY CHRISTMAS!

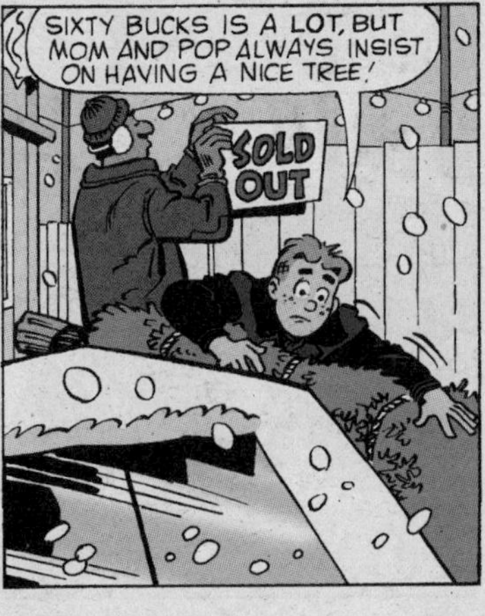
SIXTY BUCKS IS A LOT, BUT MOM AND POP ALWAYS INSIST ON HAVING A NICE TREE!
SOLD OUT

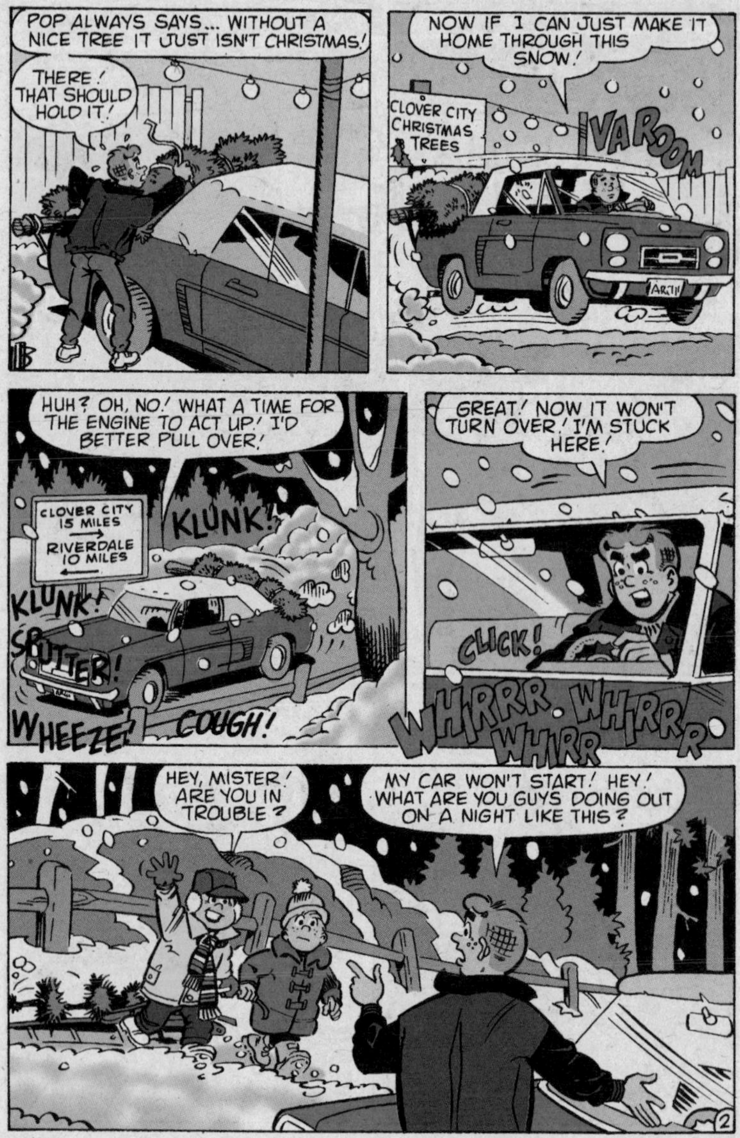
POP ALWAYS SAYS... WITHOUT A NICE TREE IT JUST ISN'T CHRISTMAS!
THERE! THAT SHOULD HOLD IT!
NOW IF I CAN JUST MAKE IT HOME THROUGH THIS SNOW!
CLOVER CITY CHRISTMAS TREES
VAROOM
HUH? OH, NO! WHAT A TIME FOR THE ENGINE TO ACT UP! I'D BETTER PULL OVER!
CLOVER CITY 15 MILES
RIVERDALE 10 MILES
KLUNK!
KLUNK!
SPUTTER!
WHEEZE!
COUGH!
GREAT! NOW IT WON'T TURN OVER! I'M STUCK HERE!
CLICK!
WHIRRR WHIRR WHIRRR
HEY, MISTER! ARE YOU IN TROUBLE?
MY CAR WON'T START! HEY! WHAT ARE YOU GUYS DOING OUT ON A NIGHT LIKE THIS?
2

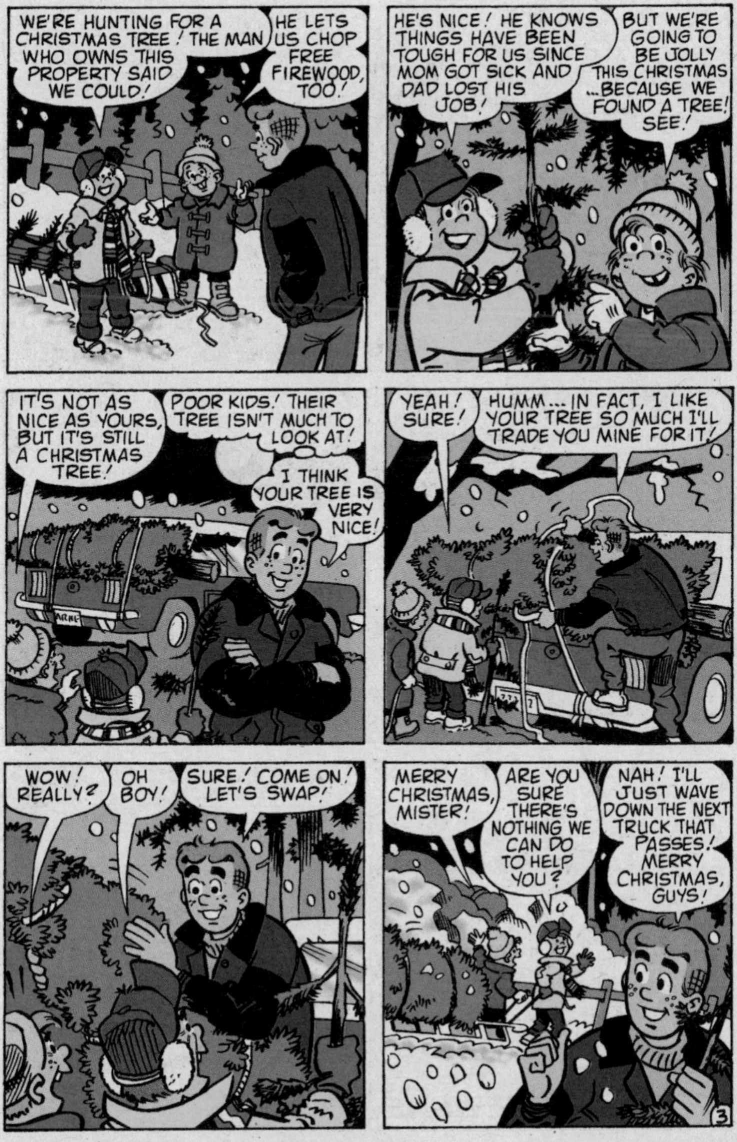
WE'RE HUNTING FOR A CHRISTMAS TREE! THE MAN WHO OWNS THIS PROPERTY SAID WE COULD!
HE LETS US CHOP FREE FIREWOOD, TOO!
HE'S NICE! HE KNOWS THINGS HAVE BEEN TOUGH FOR US SINCE MOM GOT SICK AND DAD LOST HIS JOB!
BUT WE'RE GOING TO BE JOLLY THIS CHRISTMAS ...BECAUSE WE FOUND A TREE! SEE!
IT'S NOT AS NICE AS YOURS, BUT IT'S STILL A CHRISTMAS TREE!
POOR KIDS! THEIR TREE ISN'T MUCH TO LOOK AT!
I THINK YOUR TREE IS VERY NICE!
YEAH! SURE!
HUMM... IN FACT, I LIKE YOUR TREE SO MUCH I'LL TRADE YOU MINE FOR IT!
WOW! REALLY?
OH BOY!
SURE! COME ON! LET'S SWAP!
MERRY CHRISTMAS, MISTER!
ARE YOU SURE THERE'S NOTHING WE CAN DO TO HELP YOU?
NAH! I'LL JUST WAVE DOWN THE NEXT TRUCK THAT PASSES! MERRY CHRISTMAS, GUYS!
3

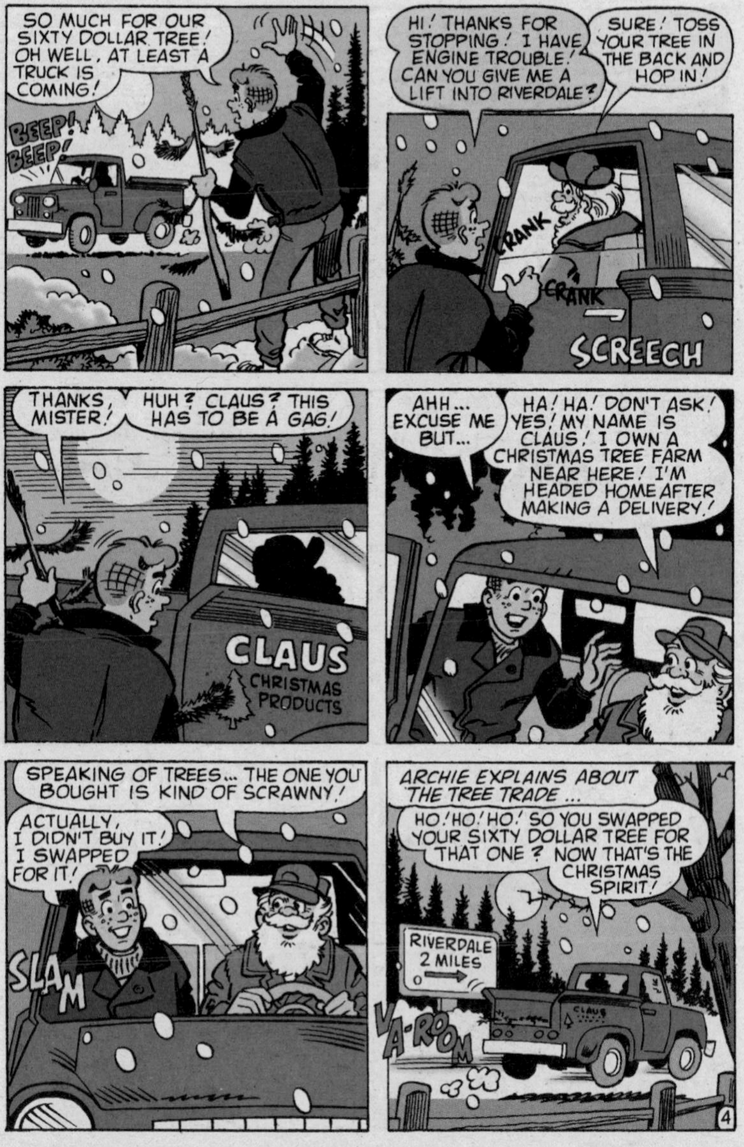
SO MUCH FOR OUR SIXTY DOLLAR TREE! OH WELL, AT LEAST A TRUCK IS COMING!
BEEP! BEEP!
HI! THANKS FOR STOPPING! I HAVE ENGINE TROUBLE! CAN YOU GIVE ME A LIFT INTO RIVERDALE?
SURE! TOSS YOUR TREE IN THE BACK AND HOP IN!
CRANK
CRANK
SCREECH
THANKS, MISTER!
HUH? CLAUS? THIS HAS TO BE A GAG!
CLAUS
CHRISTMAS PRODUCTS
AHH... EXCUSE ME BUT...
HA! HA! DON'T ASK! YES, MY NAME IS CLAUS! I OWN A CHRISTMAS TREE FARM NEAR HERE! I'M HEADED HOME AFTER MAKING A DELIVERY!
SPEAKING OF TREES... THE ONE YOU BOUGHT IS KIND OF SCRAWNY!
ACTUALLY, I DIDN'T BUY IT! I SWAPPED FOR IT!
SLAM
ARCHIE EXPLAINS ABOUT THE TREE TRADE ...
HO! HO! HO! SO YOU SWAPPED YOUR SIXTY DOLLAR TREE FOR THAT ONE? NOW THAT'S THE CHRISTMAS SPIRIT!
RIVERDALE 2 MILES
VA-ROOM
CLAUS
4

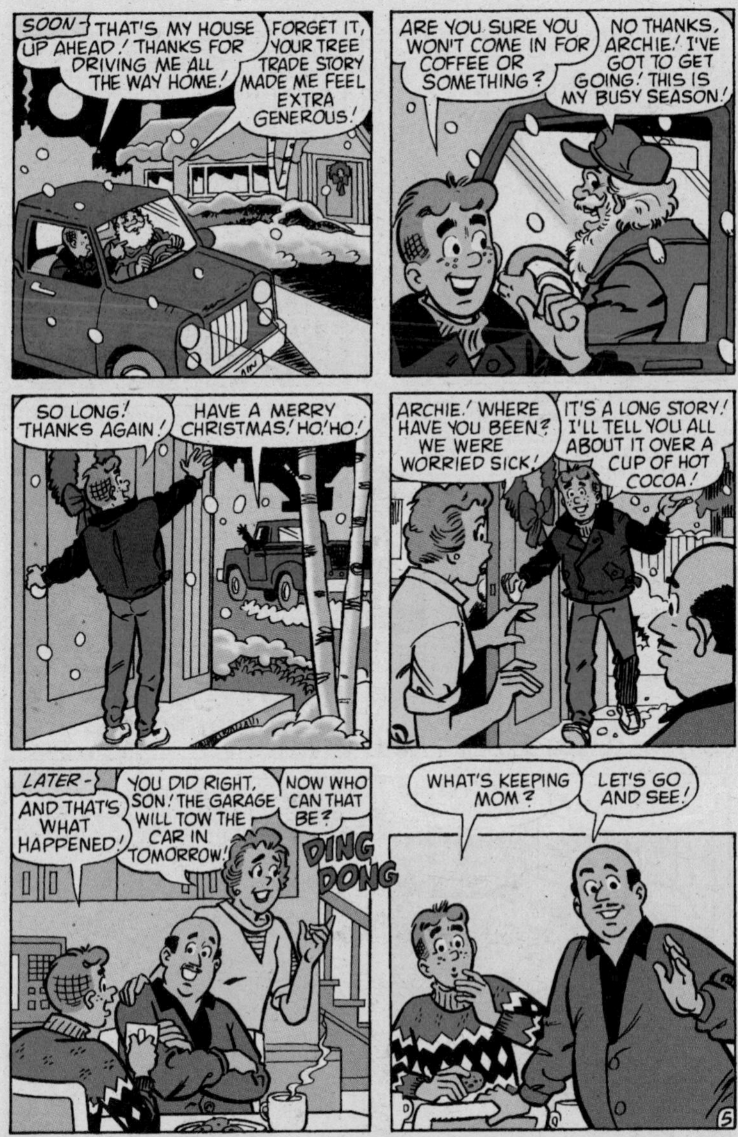
SOON-
THAT'S MY HOUSE UP AHEAD! THANKS FOR DRIVING ME ALL THE WAY HOME!
FORGET IT, YOUR TREE TRADE STORY MADE ME FEEL EXTRA GENEROUS!
ARE YOU SURE YOU WON'T COME IN FOR COFFEE OR SOMETHING?
NO THANKS, ARCHIE! I'VE GOT TO GET GOING! THIS IS MY BUSY SEASON!
SO LONG! THANKS AGAIN!
HAVE A MERRY CHRISTMAS! HO! HO!
ARCHIE! WHERE HAVE YOU BEEN? WE WERE WORRIED SICK!
IT'S A LONG STORY! I'LL TELL YOU ALL ABOUT IT OVER A CUP OF HOT COCOA!
LATER-
AND THAT'S WHAT HAPPENED!
YOU DID RIGHT, SON! THE GARAGE WILL TOW THE CAR IN TOMORROW!
NOW WHO CAN THAT BE?
DING DONG
WHAT'S KEEPING MOM?
LET'S GO AND SEE!
5

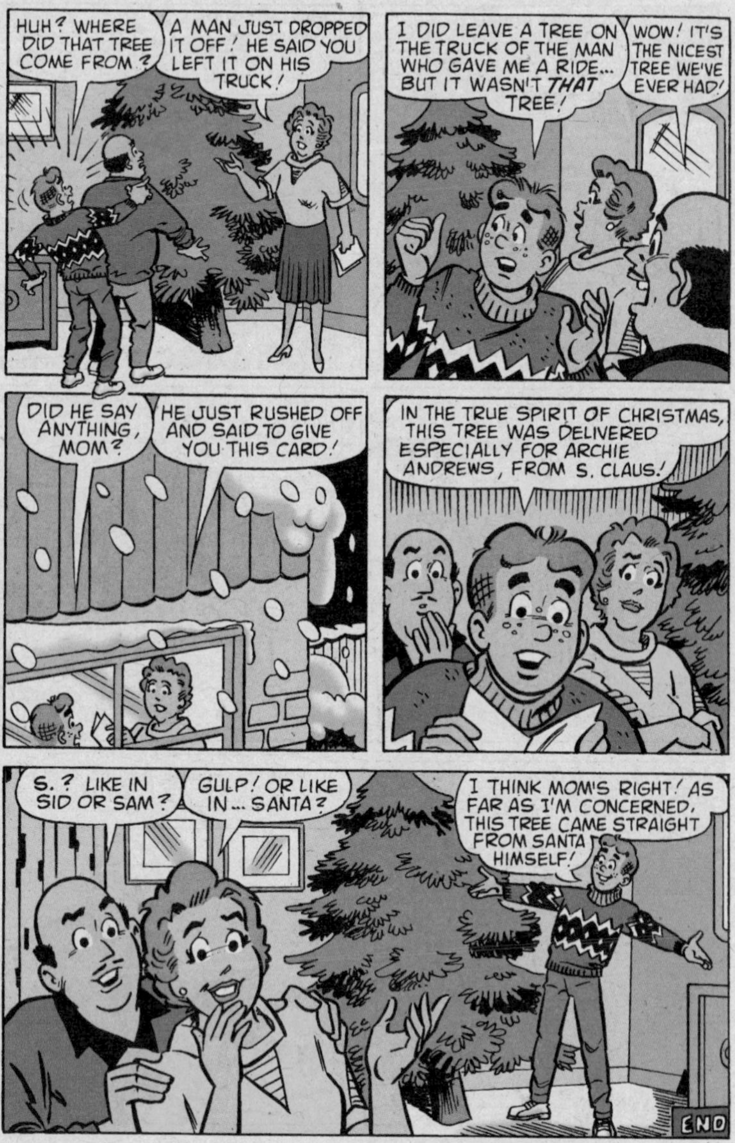
HUH? WHERE DID THAT TREE COME FROM?
A MAN JUST DROPPED IT OFF! HE SAID YOU LEFT IT ON HIS TRUCK!
I DID LEAVE A TREE ON THE TRUCK OF THE MAN WHO GAVE ME A RIDE... BUT IT WASN'T THAT TREE!
WOW! IT'S THE NICEST TREE WE'VE EVER HAD!
DID HE SAY ANYTHING, MOM?
HE JUST RUSHED OFF AND SAID TO GIVE YOU THIS CARD!
IN THE TRUE SPIRIT OF CHRISTMAS, THIS TREE WAS DELIVERED ESPECIALLY FOR ARCHIE ANDREWS, FROM S. CLAUS!
S.? LIKE IN SID OR SAM?
GULP! OR LIKE IN... SANTA?
I THINK MOM'S RIGHT! AS FAR AS I'M CONCERNED, THIS TREE CAME STRAIGHT FROM SANTA HIMSELF!
END

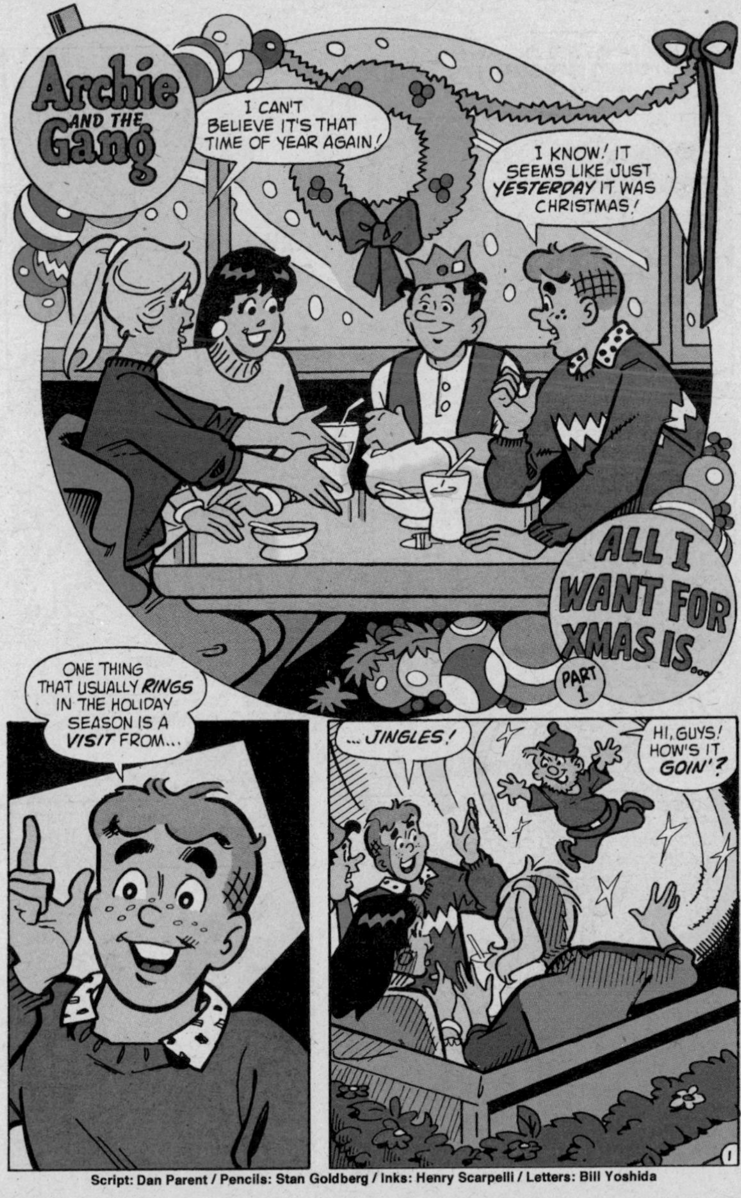

Archie AND THE Gang
I CAN'T BELIEVE IT'S THAT TIME OF YEAR AGAIN!
I KNOW! IT SEEMS LIKE JUST YESTERDAY IT WAS CHRISTMAS!
ALL I WANT FOR XMAS IS...
PART 1
ONE THING THAT USUALLY RINGS IN THE HOLIDAY SEASON IS A VISIT FROM...
...JINGLES!
HI, GUYS! HOW'S IT GOIN'?
1

Script: Dan Parent / Pencils: Stan Goldberg / Inks: Henry Scarpelli / Letters: Bill Yoshida

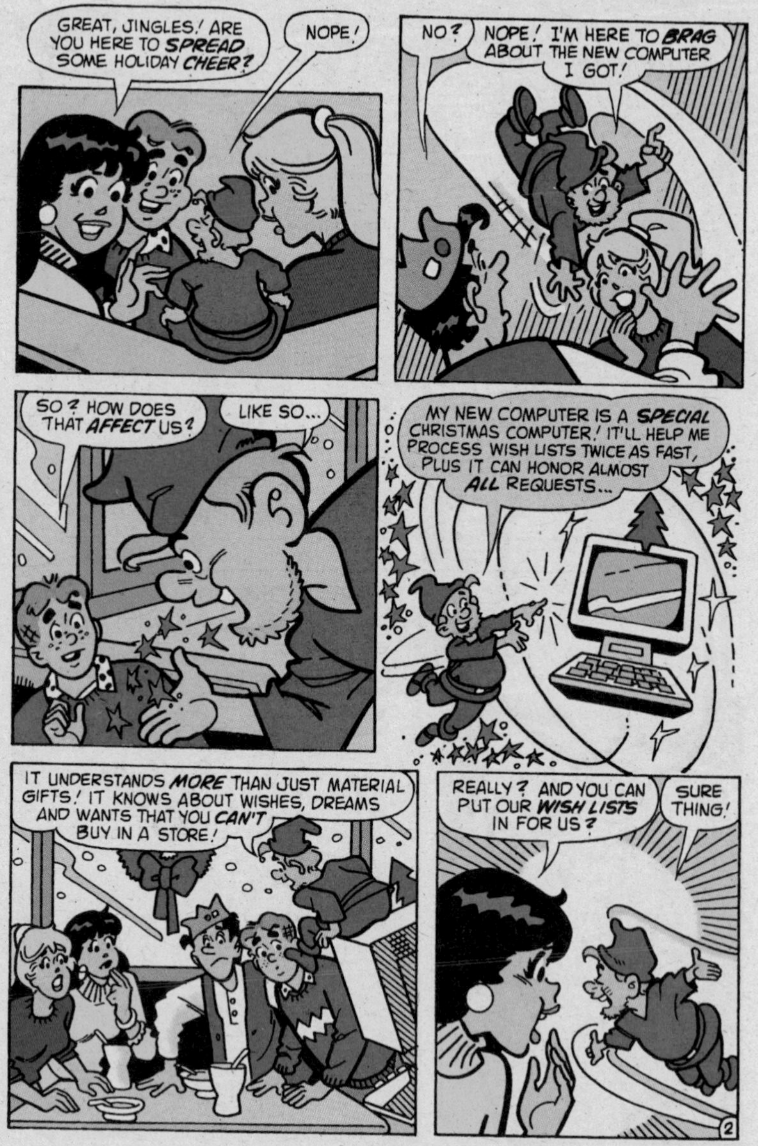
GREAT, JINGLES! ARE YOU HERE TO SPREAD SOME HOLIDAY CHEER?
NOPE!
NO?
NOPE! I'M HERE TO BRAG ABOUT THE NEW COMPUTER I GOT!
SO? HOW DOES THAT AFFECT US?
LIKE SO...
MY NEW COMPUTER IS A SPECIAL CHRISTMAS COMPUTER! IT'LL HELP ME PROCESS WISH LISTS TWICE AS FAST, PLUS IT CAN HONOR ALMOST ALL REQUESTS...
IT UNDERSTANDS MORE THAN JUST MATERIAL GIFTS! IT KNOWS ABOUT WISHES, DREAMS AND WANTS THAT YOU CAN'T BUY IN A STORE!
REALLY? AND YOU CAN PUT OUR WISH LISTS IN FOR US?
SURE THING!

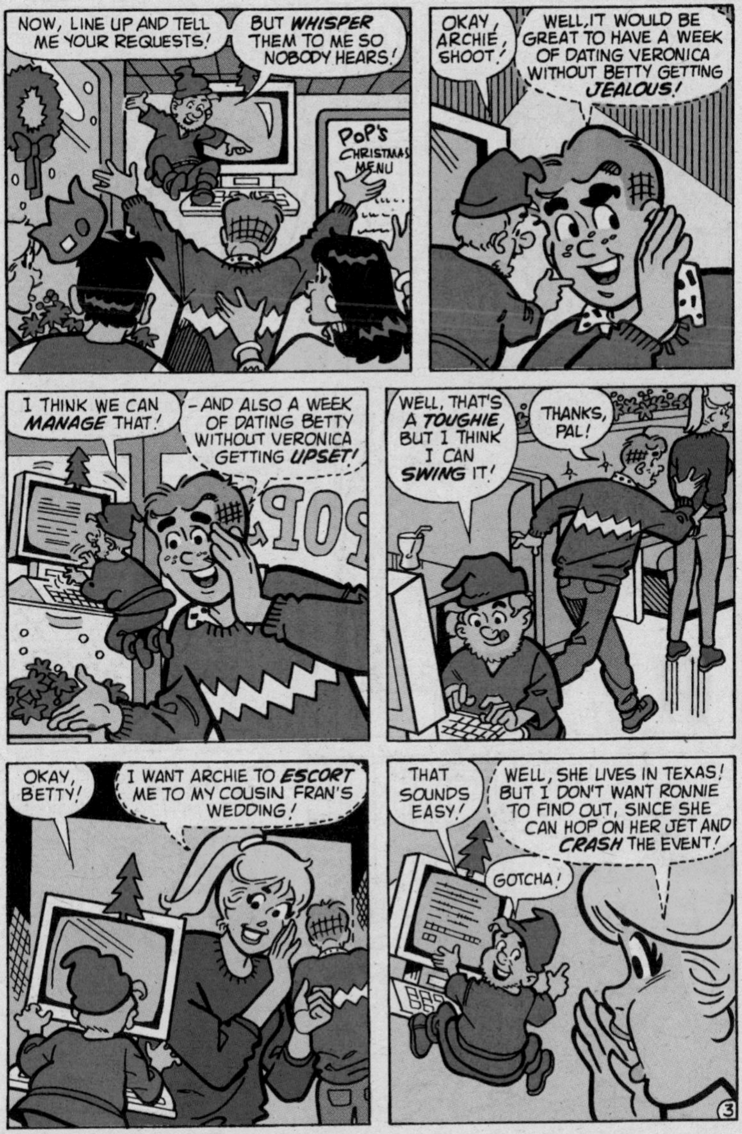

NOW, LINE UP AND TELL ME YOUR REQUESTS!
BUT WHISPER THEM TO ME SO NOBODY HEARS!
POP'S CHRISTMAS MENU
OKAY, ARCHIE, SHOOT!
WELL, IT WOULD BE GREAT TO HAVE A WEEK OF DATING VERONICA WITHOUT BETTY GETTING JEALOUS!
I THINK WE CAN MANAGE THAT!
-AND ALSO A WEEK OF DATING BETTY WITHOUT VERONICA GETTING UPSET!
POP
WELL, THAT'S A TOUGHIE, BUT I THINK I CAN SWING IT!
THANKS, PAL!
OKAY, BETTY!
I WANT ARCHIE TO ESCORT ME TO MY COUSIN FRAN'S WEDDING!
THAT SOUNDS EASY!
WELL, SHE LIVES IN TEXAS! BUT I DON'T WANT RONNIE TO FIND OUT, SINCE SHE CAN HOP ON HER JET AND CRASH THE EVENT!
GOTCHA!
3

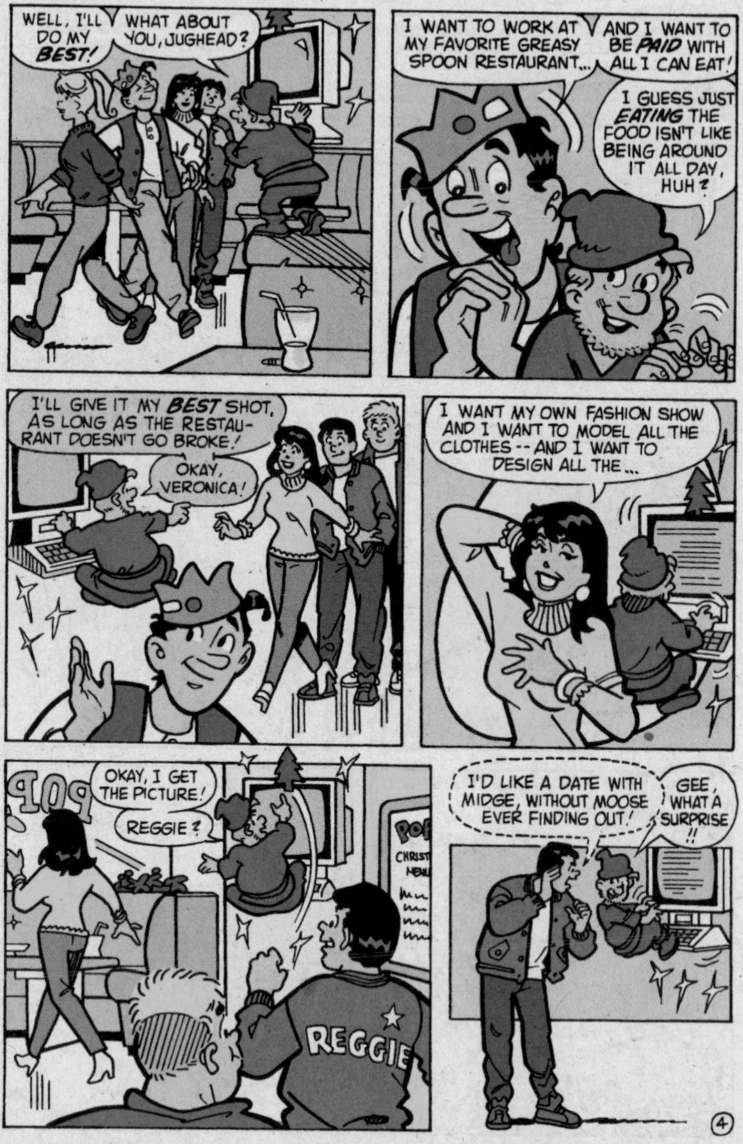
WELL, I'LL DO MY BEST!
WHAT ABOUT YOU, JUGHEAD?
I WANT TO WORK AT MY FAVORITE GREASY SPOON RESTAURANT...
AND I WANT TO BE PAID WITH ALL I CAN EAT!
I GUESS JUST EATING THE FOOD ISN'T LIKE BEING AROUND IT ALL DAY, HUH?
I'LL GIVE IT MY BEST SHOT, AS LONG AS THE RESTAURANT DOESN'T GO BROKE!
OKAY, VERONICA!
I WANT MY OWN FASHION SHOW AND I WANT TO MODEL ALL THE CLOTHES -- AND I WANT TO DESIGN ALL THE ...
OKAY, I GET THE PICTURE!
REGGIE?
POP
REGGIE
I'D LIKE A DATE WITH MIDGE, WITHOUT MOOSE EVER FINDING OUT!
GEE, WHAT A SURPRISE !!

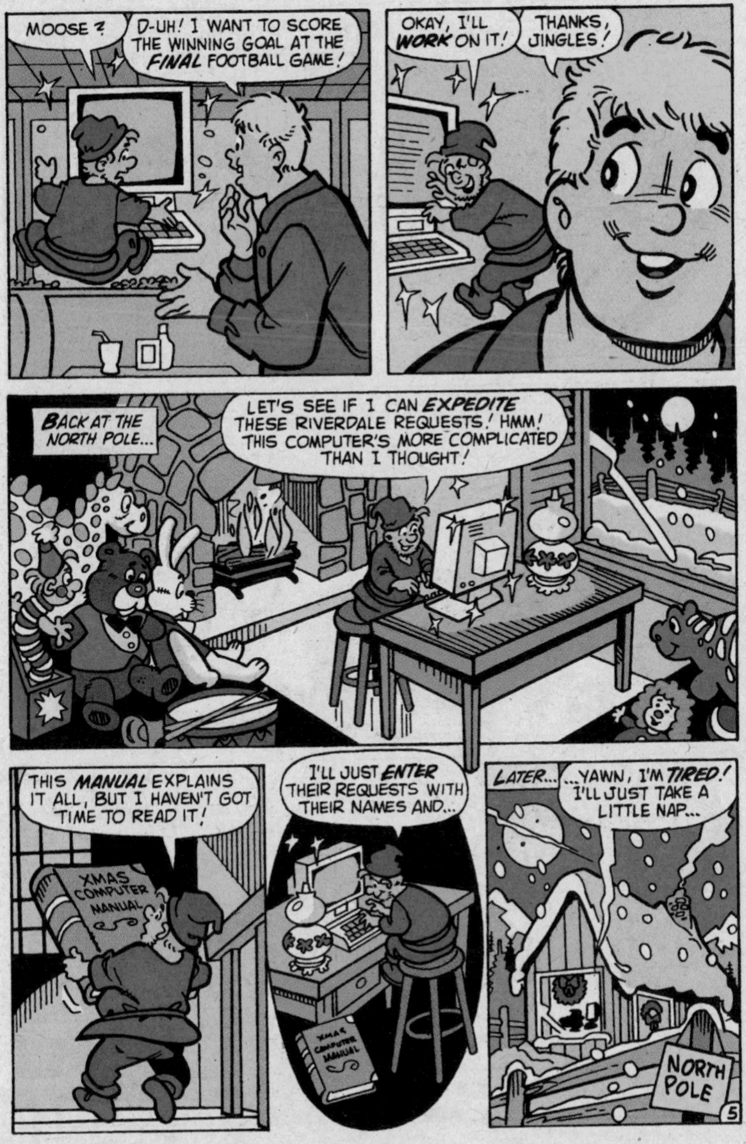
MOOSE?
D-UH! I WANT TO SCORE THE WINNING GOAL AT THE FINAL FOOTBALL GAME!
OKAY, I'LL WORK ON IT!
THANKS, JINGLES!
BACK AT THE NORTH POLE...
LET'S SEE IF I CAN EXPEDITE THESE RIVERDALE REQUESTS! HMM! THIS COMPUTER'S MORE COMPLICATED THAN I THOUGHT!
THIS MANUAL EXPLAINS IT ALL, BUT I HAVEN'T GOT TIME TO READ IT!
XMAS COMPUTER MANUAL
I'LL JUST ENTER THEIR REQUESTS WITH THEIR NAMES AND...
XMAS COMPUTER MANUAL
LATER...
...YAWN, I'M TIRED! I'LL JUST TAKE A LITTLE NAP...
NORTH POLE
5

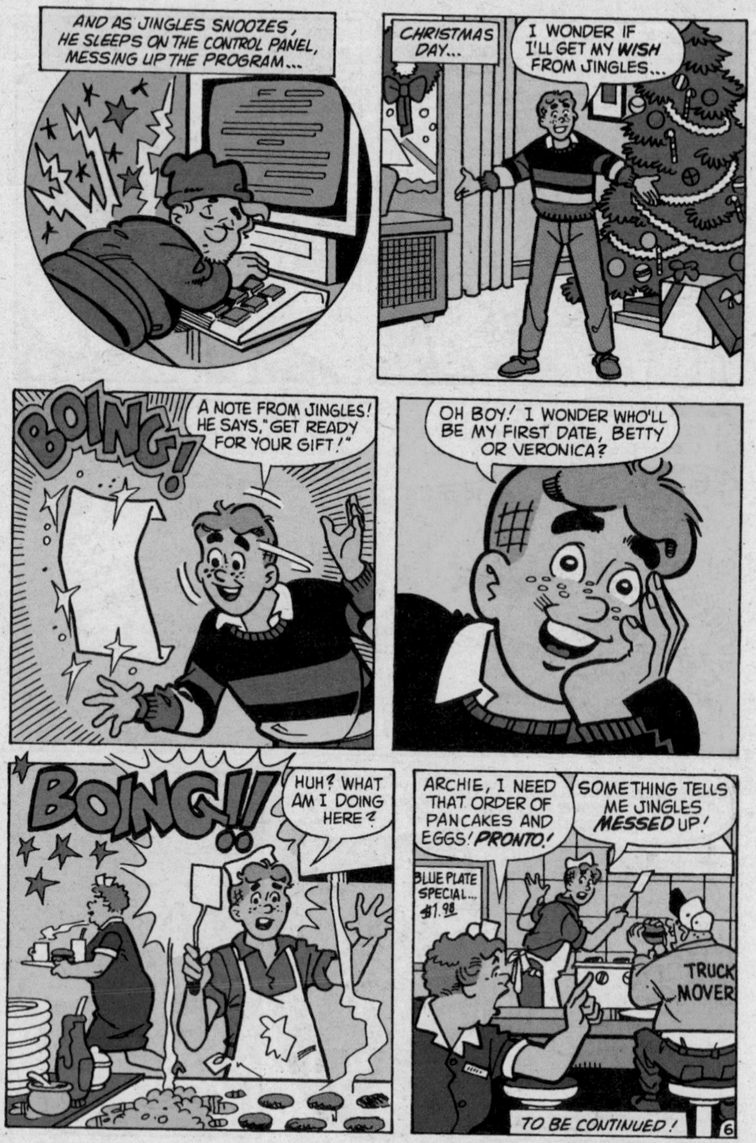
AND AS JINGLES SNOOZES, HE SLEEPS ON THE CONTROL PANEL, MESSING UP THE PROGRAM...
CHRISTMAS DAY...
I WONDER IF I'LL GET MY *WISH* FROM JINGLES...
BOING!
A NOTE FROM JINGLES! HE SAYS, "GET READY FOR YOUR GIFT!"
OH BOY! I WONDER WHO'LL BE MY FIRST DATE, BETTY OR VERONICA?
BOING!!
HUH? WHAT AM I DOING HERE?
ARCHIE, I NEED THAT ORDER OF PANCAKES AND EGGS! *PRONTO!*
SOMETHING TELLS ME JINGLES *MESSED* UP!
BLUE PLATE SPECIAL... $1.98
TRUCK MOVER
TO BE CONTINUED!
6

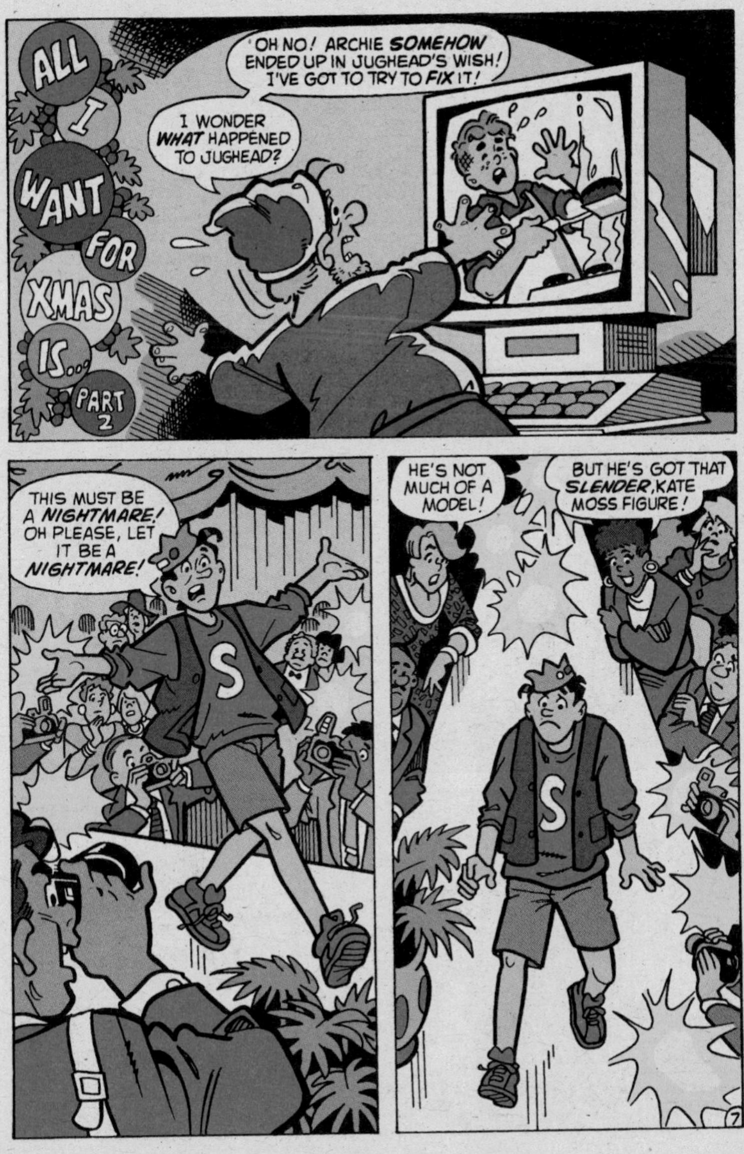
ALL I WANT FOR XMAS IS... PART 2
'OH NO! ARCHIE SOMEHOW ENDED UP IN JUGHEAD'S WISH! I'VE GOT TO TRY TO FIX IT!
I WONDER WHAT HAPPENED TO JUGHEAD?
THIS MUST BE A NIGHTMARE! OH PLEASE, LET IT BE A NIGHTMARE!
HE'S NOT MUCH OF A MODEL!
BUT HE'S GOT THAT SLENDER, KATE MOSS FIGURE!
7

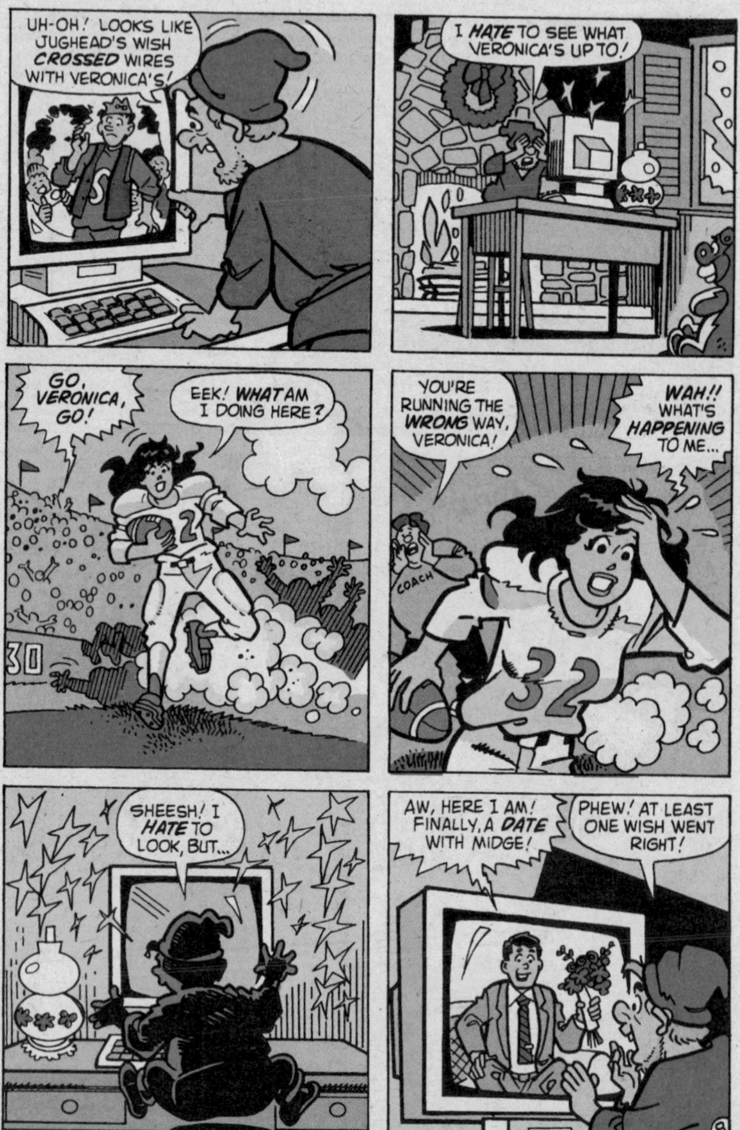
UH-OH! LOOKS LIKE JUGHEAD'S WISH CROSSED WIRES WITH VERONICA'S!
I HATE TO SEE WHAT VERONICA'S UP TO!
GO, VERONICA, GO!
EEK! WHAT AM I DOING HERE?
30
YOU'RE RUNNING THE WRONG WAY, VERONICA!
WAH!! WHAT'S HAPPENING TO ME...
COACH
32
SHEESH! I HATE TO LOOK, BUT...
AW, HERE I AM! FINALLY, A DATE WITH MIDGE!
PHEW! AT LEAST ONE WISH WENT RIGHT!
8

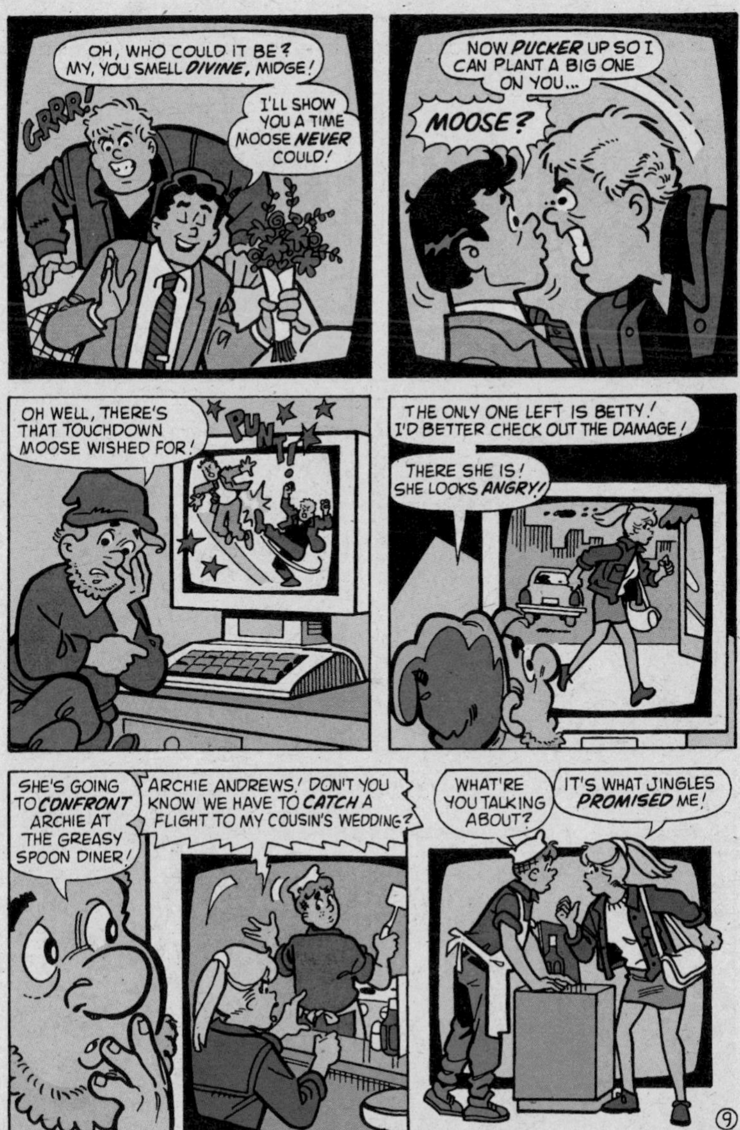
OH, WHO COULD IT BE? MY, YOU SMELL DIVINE, MIDGE!
GRRR!
I'LL SHOW YOU A TIME MOOSE NEVER COULD!
NOW PUCKER UP SO I CAN PLANT A BIG ONE ON YOU...
MOOSE?
OH WELL, THERE'S THAT TOUCHDOWN MOOSE WISHED FOR!
PUNT!
THE ONLY ONE LEFT IS BETTY! I'D BETTER CHECK OUT THE DAMAGE!
THERE SHE IS! SHE LOOKS ANGRY!
SHE'S GOING TO CONFRONT ARCHIE AT THE GREASY SPOON DINER!
ARCHIE ANDREWS! DON'T YOU KNOW WE HAVE TO CATCH A FLIGHT TO MY COUSIN'S WEDDING?
WHAT'RE YOU TALKING ABOUT?
IT'S WHAT JINGLES PROMISED ME!
9

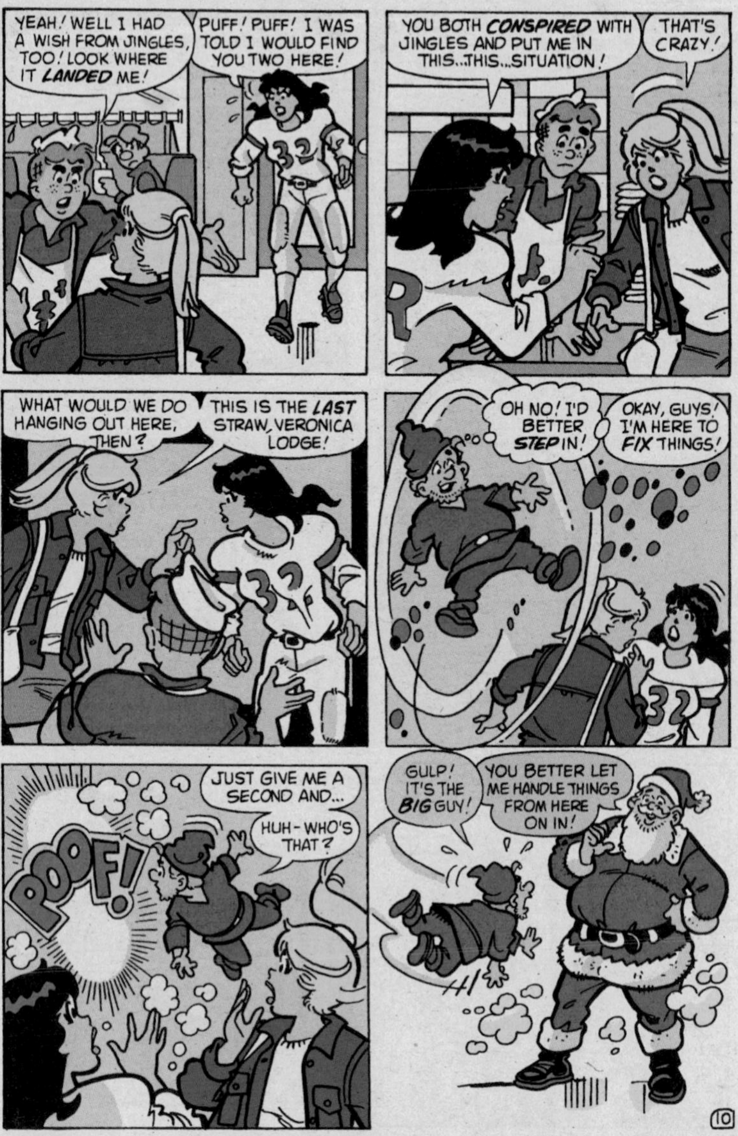
YEAH! WELL I HAD A WISH FROM JINGLES, TOO! LOOK WHERE IT LANDED ME!
PUFF! PUFF! I WAS TOLD I WOULD FIND YOU TWO HERE!
YOU BOTH CONSPIRED WITH JINGLES AND PUT ME IN THIS...THIS...SITUATION!
THAT'S CRAZY!
WHAT WOULD WE DO HANGING OUT HERE, THEN?
THIS IS THE LAST STRAW, VERONICA LODGE!
OH NO! I'D BETTER STEP IN!
OKAY, GUYS! I'M HERE TO FIX THINGS!
POOF!
JUST GIVE ME A SECOND AND...
HUH-WHO'S THAT?
GULP! IT'S THE BIG GUY!
YOU BETTER LET ME HANDLE THINGS FROM HERE ON IN!
10

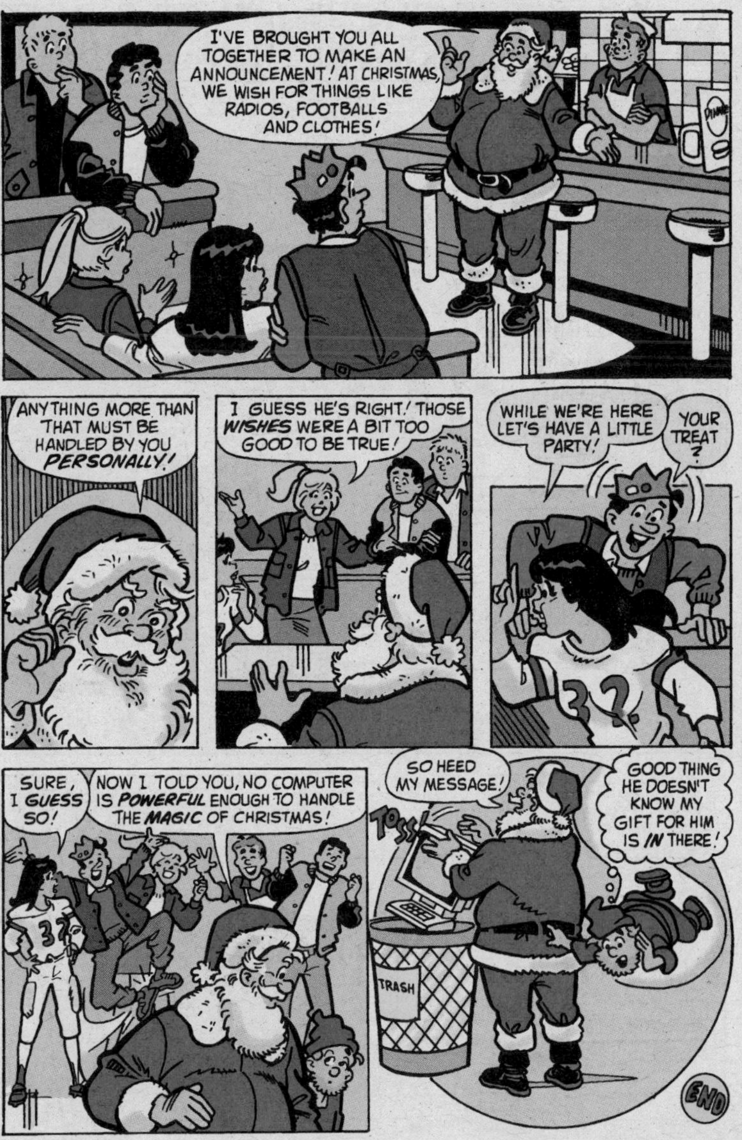
I'VE BROUGHT YOU ALL TOGETHER TO MAKE AN ANNOUNCEMENT! AT CHRISTMAS, WE WISH FOR THINGS LIKE RADIOS, FOOTBALLS AND CLOTHES!
ANYTHING MORE THAN THAT MUST BE HANDLED BY YOU PERSONALLY!
I GUESS HE'S RIGHT! THOSE WISHES WERE A BIT TOO GOOD TO BE TRUE!
WHILE WE'RE HERE LET'S HAVE A LITTLE PARTY!
YOUR TREAT?
SURE, I GUESS SO!
NOW I TOLD YOU, NO COMPUTER IS POWERFUL ENOUGH TO HANDLE THE MAGIC OF CHRISTMAS!
SO HEED MY MESSAGE!
TOSS
GOOD THING HE DOESN'T KNOW MY GIFT FOR HIM IS IN THERE!
TRASH
END

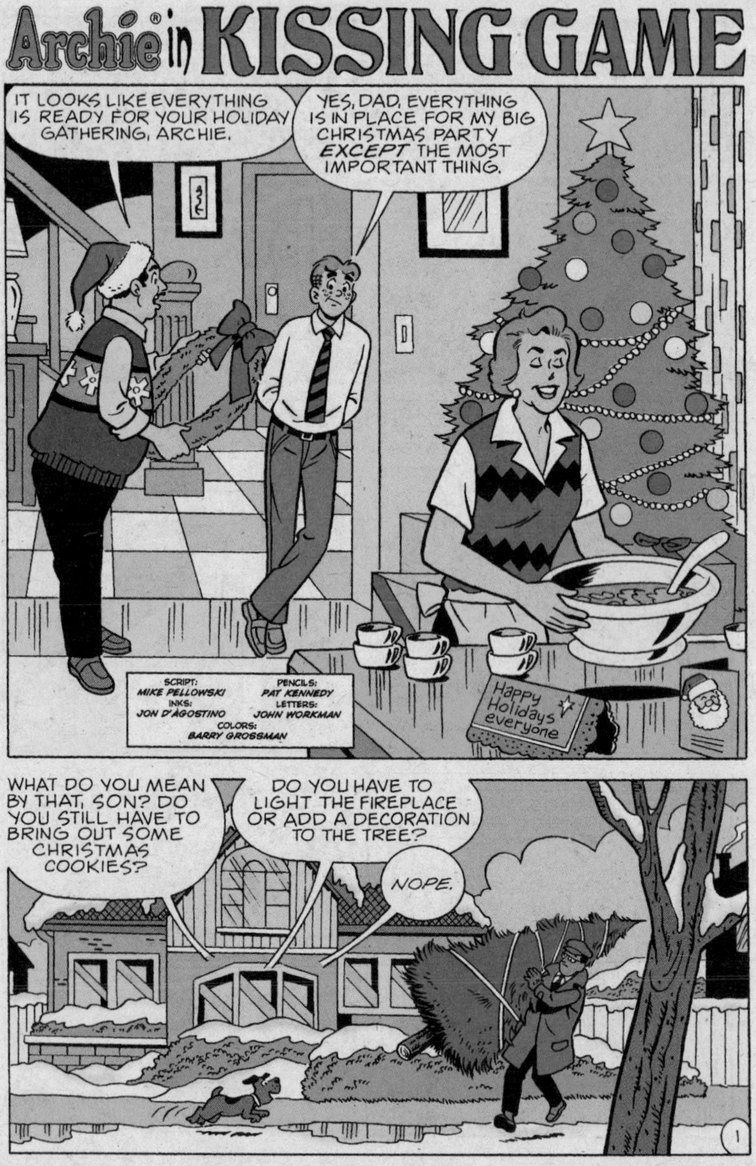
Archie® in KISSING GAME
IT LOOKS LIKE EVERYTHING IS READY FOR YOUR HOLIDAY GATHERING, ARCHIE.
YES, DAD, EVERYTHING IS IN PLACE FOR MY BIG CHRISTMAS PARTY EXCEPT THE MOST IMPORTANT THING.
SCRIPT: MIKE PELLOWSKI PENCILS: PAT KENNEDY INKS: JON D'AGOSTINO LETTERS: JOHN WORKMAN COLORS: BARRY GROSSMAN
Happy Holidays everyone
WHAT DO YOU MEAN BY THAT, SON? DO YOU STILL HAVE TO BRING OUT SOME CHRISTMAS COOKIES?
DO YOU HAVE TO LIGHT THE FIREPLACE OR ADD A DECORATION TO THE TREE?
NOPE.
1

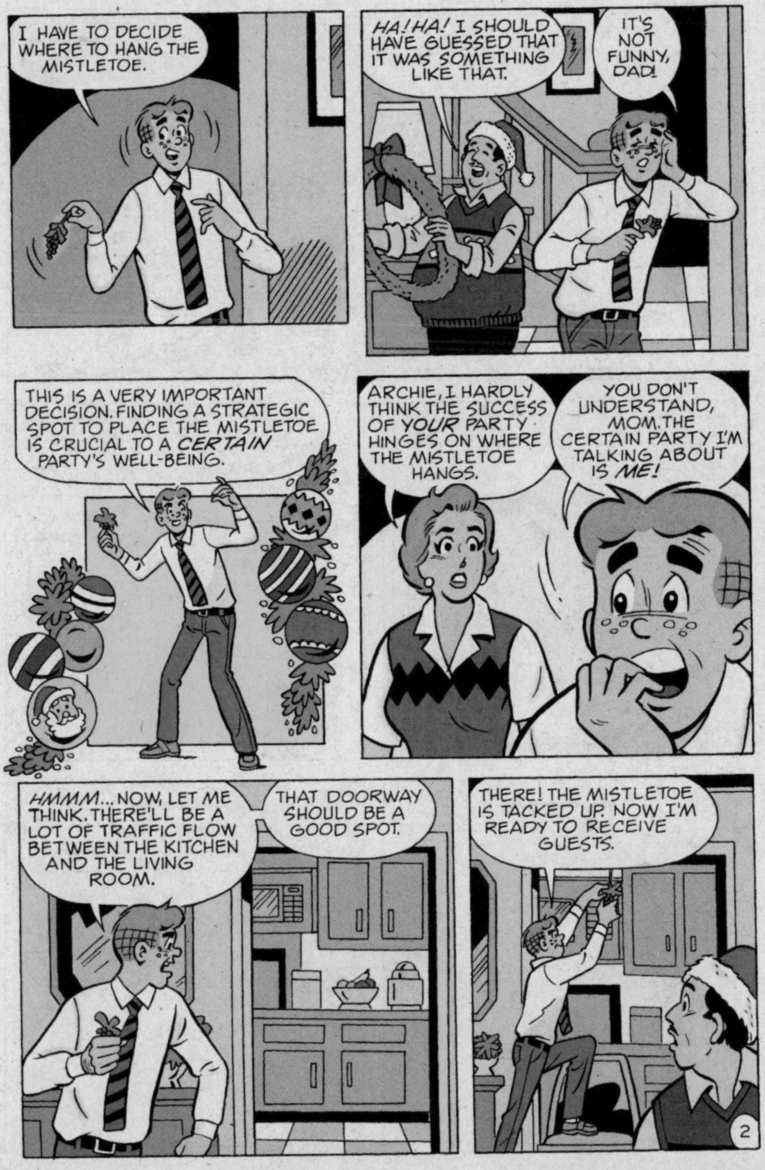
I HAVE TO DECIDE WHERE TO HANG THE MISTLETOE.
HA! HA! I SHOULD HAVE GUESSED THAT IT WAS SOMETHING LIKE THAT.
IT'S NOT FUNNY, DAD!
THIS IS A VERY IMPORTANT DECISION. FINDING A STRATEGIC SPOT TO PLACE THE MISTLETOE IS CRUCIAL TO A CERTAIN PARTY'S WELL-BEING.
ARCHIE, I HARDLY THINK THE SUCCESS OF YOUR PARTY HINGES ON WHERE THE MISTLETOE HANGS.
YOU DON'T UNDERSTAND, MOM. THE CERTAIN PARTY I'M TALKING ABOUT IS ME!
HMMM... NOW, LET ME THINK. THERE'LL BE A LOT OF TRAFFIC FLOW BETWEEN THE KITCHEN AND THE LIVING ROOM.
THAT DOORWAY SHOULD BE A GOOD SPOT.
THERE! THE MISTLETOE IS TACKED UP. NOW I'M READY TO RECEIVE GUESTS.
2

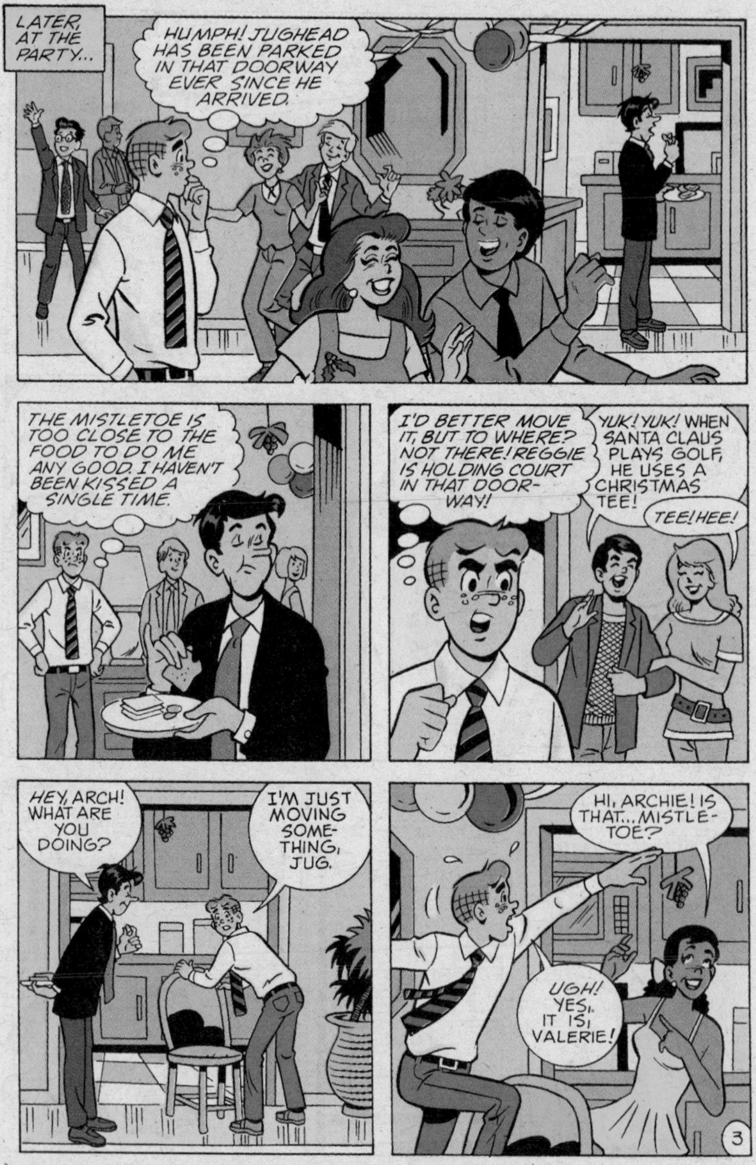
LATER, AT THE PARTY...
HUMPH! JUGHEAD HAS BEEN PARKED IN THAT DOORWAY EVER SINCE HE ARRIVED.
THE MISTLETOE IS TOO CLOSE TO THE FOOD TO DO ME ANY GOOD. I HAVEN'T BEEN KISSED A SINGLE TIME.
I'D BETTER MOVE IT, BUT TO WHERE? NOT THERE! REGGIE IS HOLDING COURT IN THAT DOOR-WAY!
YUK! YUK! WHEN SANTA CLAUS PLAYS GOLF, HE USES A CHRISTMAS TEE!
TEE! HEE!
HEY, ARCH! WHAT ARE YOU DOING?
I'M JUST MOVING SOME-THING, JUG.
HI, ARCHIE! IS THAT... MISTLE-TOE?
UGH! YES, IT IS, VALERIE!
3

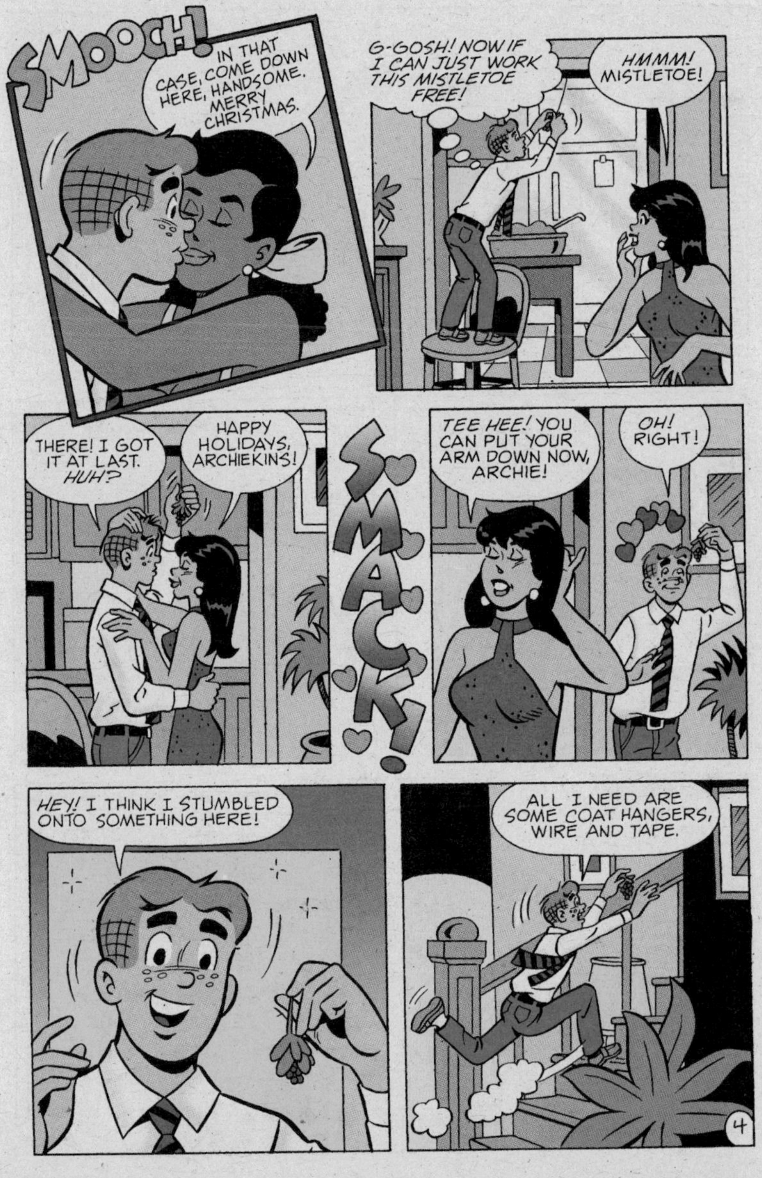
SMOOCH!
IN THAT CASE, COME DOWN HERE, HANDSOME. MERRY CHRISTMAS.
G-GOSH! NOW IF I CAN JUST WORK THIS MISTLETOE FREE!
HMMM! MISTLETOE!
THERE! I GOT IT AT LAST. HUH?
HAPPY HOLIDAYS, ARCHIEKINS!
SMACK!
TEE HEE! YOU CAN PUT YOUR ARM DOWN NOW, ARCHIE!
OH! RIGHT!
HEY! I THINK I STUMBLED ONTO SOMETHING HERE!
ALL I NEED ARE SOME COAT HANGERS, WIRE AND TAPE.
4

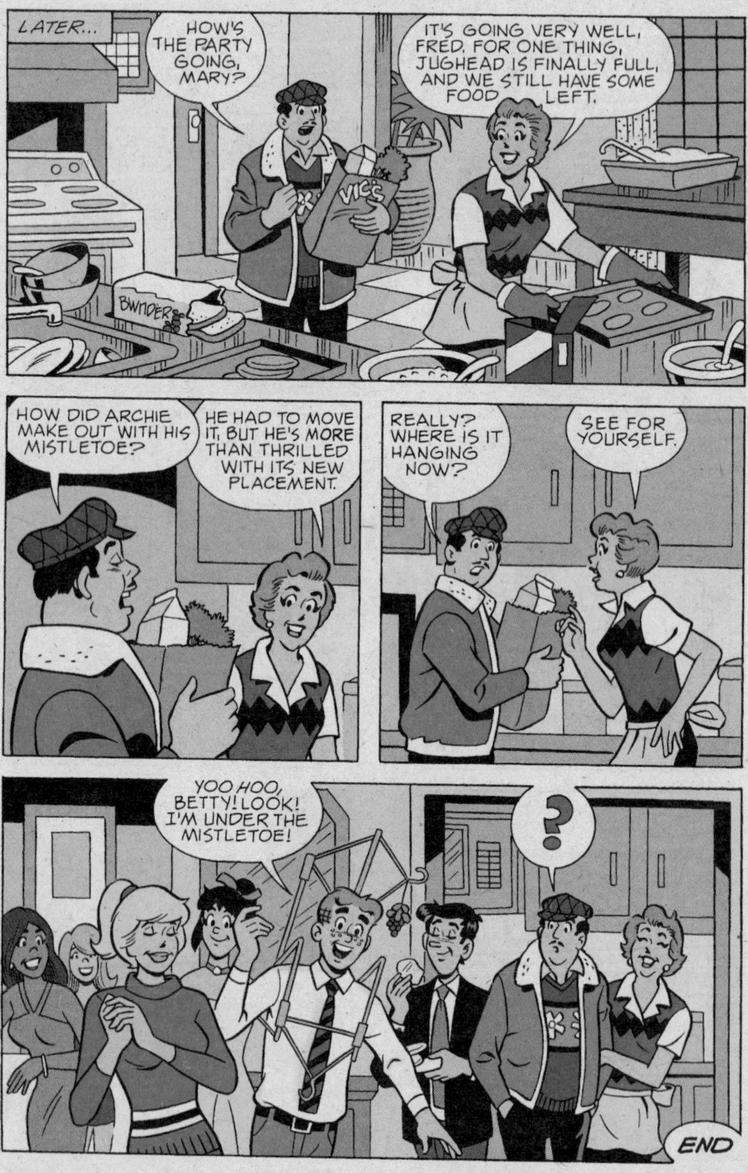
LATER...
HOW'S THE PARTY GOING, MARY?
IT'S GOING VERY WELL, FRED. FOR ONE THING, JUGHEAD IS FINALLY FULL, AND WE STILL HAVE SOME FOOD LEFT.
VIC'S
HOW DID ARCHIE MAKE OUT WITH HIS MISTLETOE?
HE HAD TO MOVE IT, BUT HE'S MORE THAN THRILLED WITH ITS NEW PLACEMENT.
REALLY? WHERE IS IT HANGING NOW?
SEE FOR YOURSELF.
YOO HOO, BETTY! LOOK! I'M UNDER THE MISTLETOE!
?
END

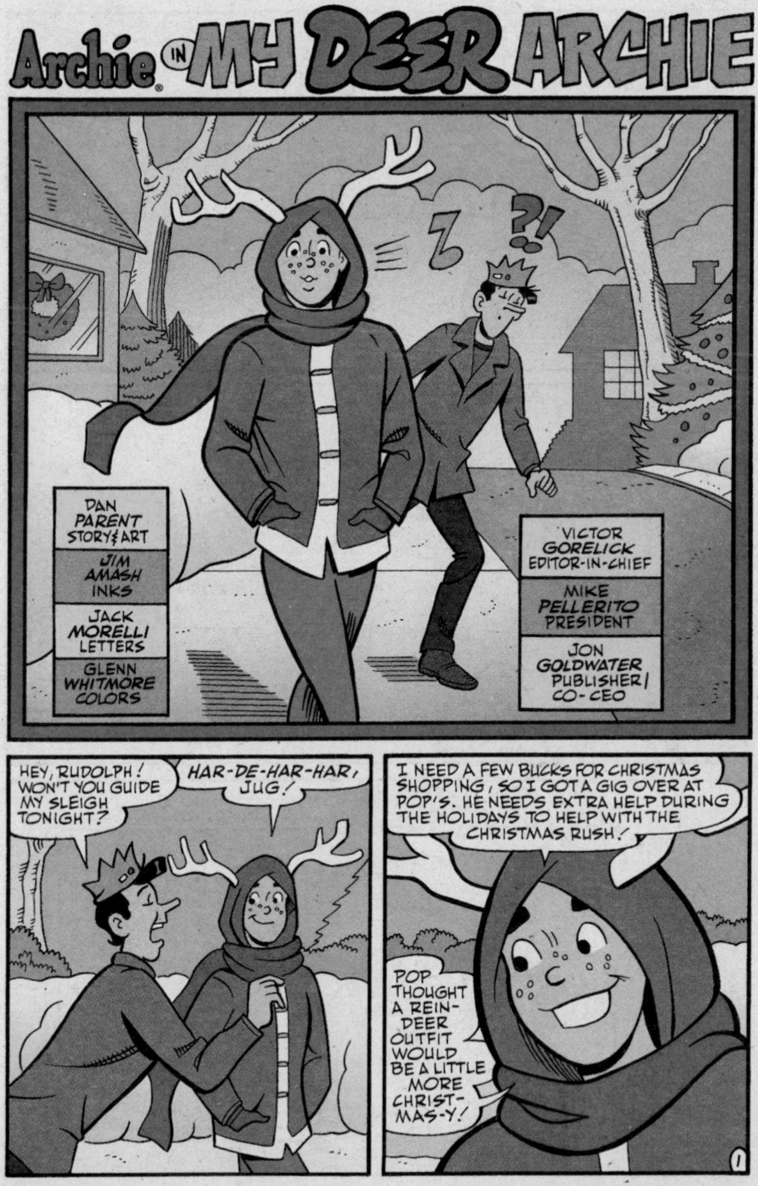
Archie IN MY DEER ARCHIE
Z
?!
DAN PARENT STORY & ART
JIM AMASH INKS
JACK MORELLI LETTERS
GLENN WHITMORE COLORS
VICTOR GORELICK EDITOR-IN-CHIEF
MIKE PELLERITO PRESIDENT
JON GOLDWATER PUBLISHER/ CO-CEO
HEY, RUDOLPH! WON'T YOU GUIDE MY SLEIGH TONIGHT?
HAR-DE-HAR-HAR, JUG!
I NEED A FEW BUCKS FOR CHRISTMAS SHOPPING, SO I GOT A GIG OVER AT POP'S. HE NEEDS EXTRA HELP DURING THE HOLIDAYS TO HELP WITH THE CHRISTMAS RUSH!
POP THOUGHT A REINDEER OUTFIT WOULD BE A LITTLE MORE CHRISTMAS-Y!
1

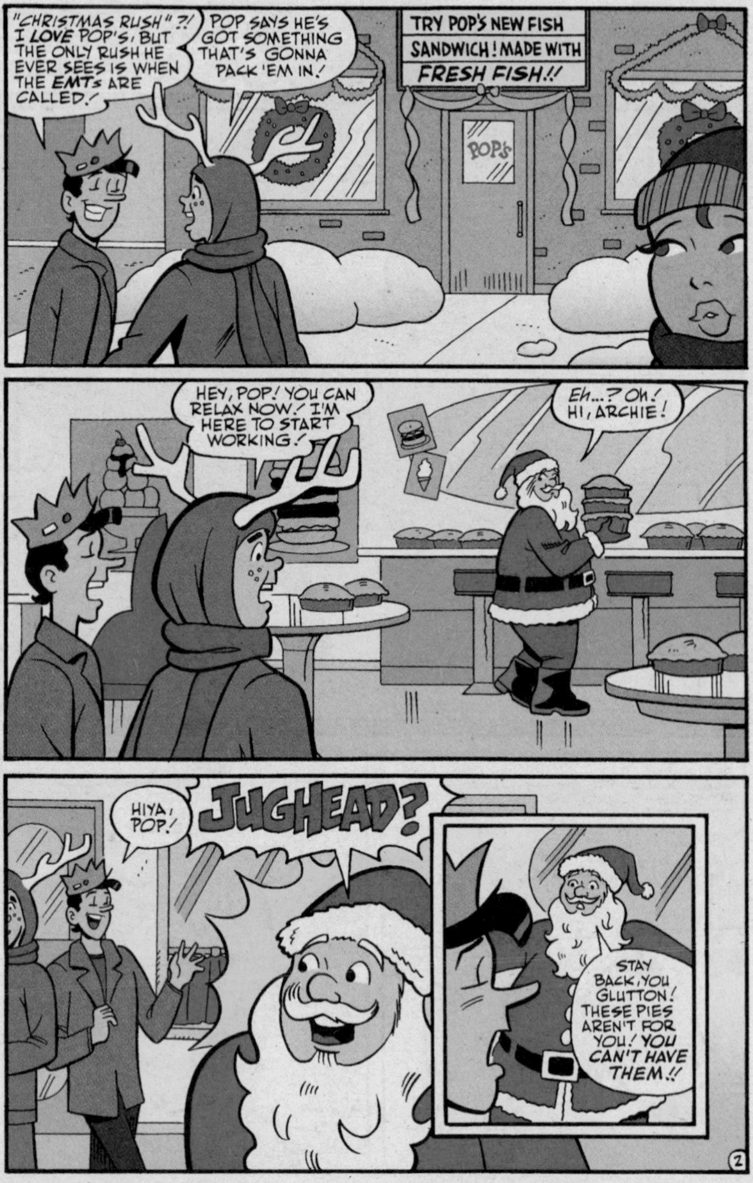
"CHRISTMAS RUSH"?! I LOVE POP'S, BUT THE ONLY RUSH HE EVER SEES IS WHEN THE EMTs ARE CALLED!
POP SAYS HE'S GOT SOMETHING THAT'S GONNA PACK 'EM IN!
TRY POP'S NEW FISH SANDWICH! MADE WITH FRESH FISH!!
POP'S
HEY, POP! YOU CAN RELAX NOW! I'M HERE TO START WORKING!
Eh...? Oh! HI, ARCHIE!
HIYA, POP!
JUGHEAD?
STAY BACK, YOU GLUTTON! THESE PIES AREN'T FOR YOU! YOU CAN'T HAVE THEM!!

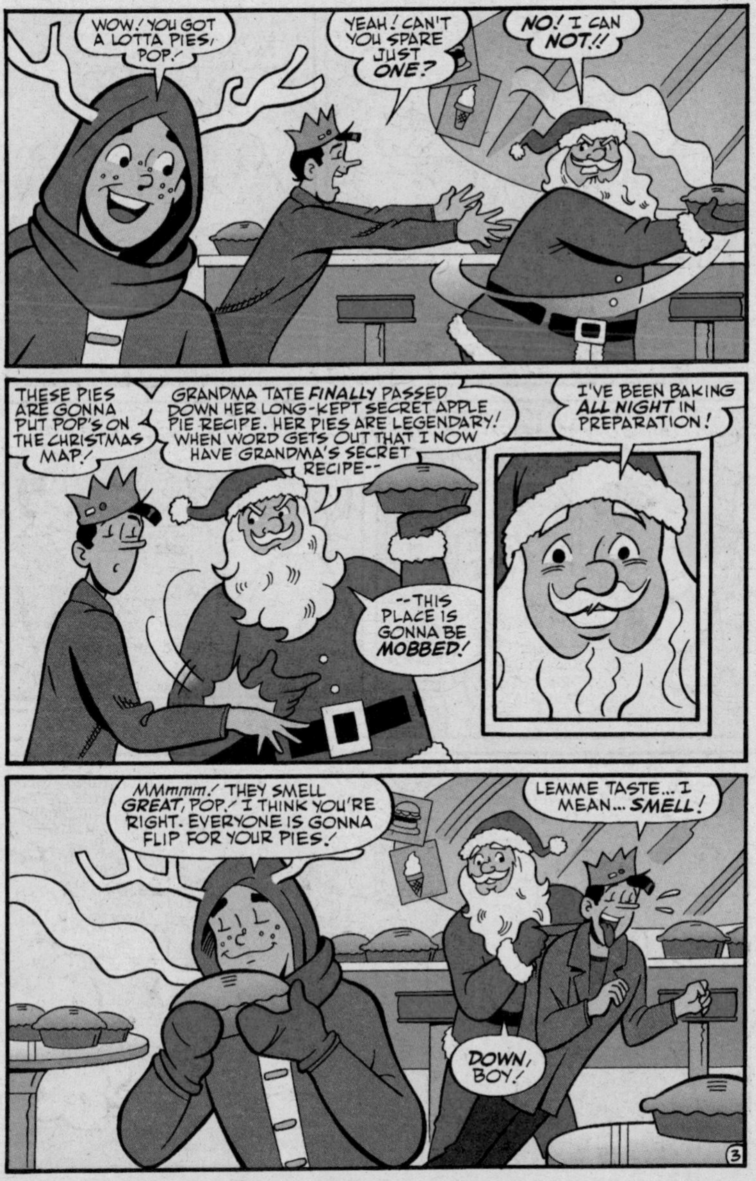

WOW! YOU GOT A LOTTA PIES, POP!
YEAH! CAN'T YOU SPARE JUST ONE?
NO! I CAN NOT!!
THESE PIES ARE GONNA PUT POP'S ON THE CHRISTMAS MAP!
GRANDMA TATE FINALLY PASSED DOWN HER LONG-KEPT SECRET APPLE PIE RECIPE. HER PIES ARE LEGENDARY! WHEN WORD GETS OUT THAT I NOW HAVE GRANDMA'S SECRET RECIPE--
--THIS PLACE IS GONNA BE MOBBED!
I'VE BEEN BAKING ALL NIGHT IN PREPARATION!
MMmmm! THEY SMELL GREAT, POP! I THINK YOU'RE RIGHT. EVERYONE IS GONNA FLIP FOR YOUR PIES!
LEMME TASTE... I MEAN... SMELL!
DOWN, BOY!
3

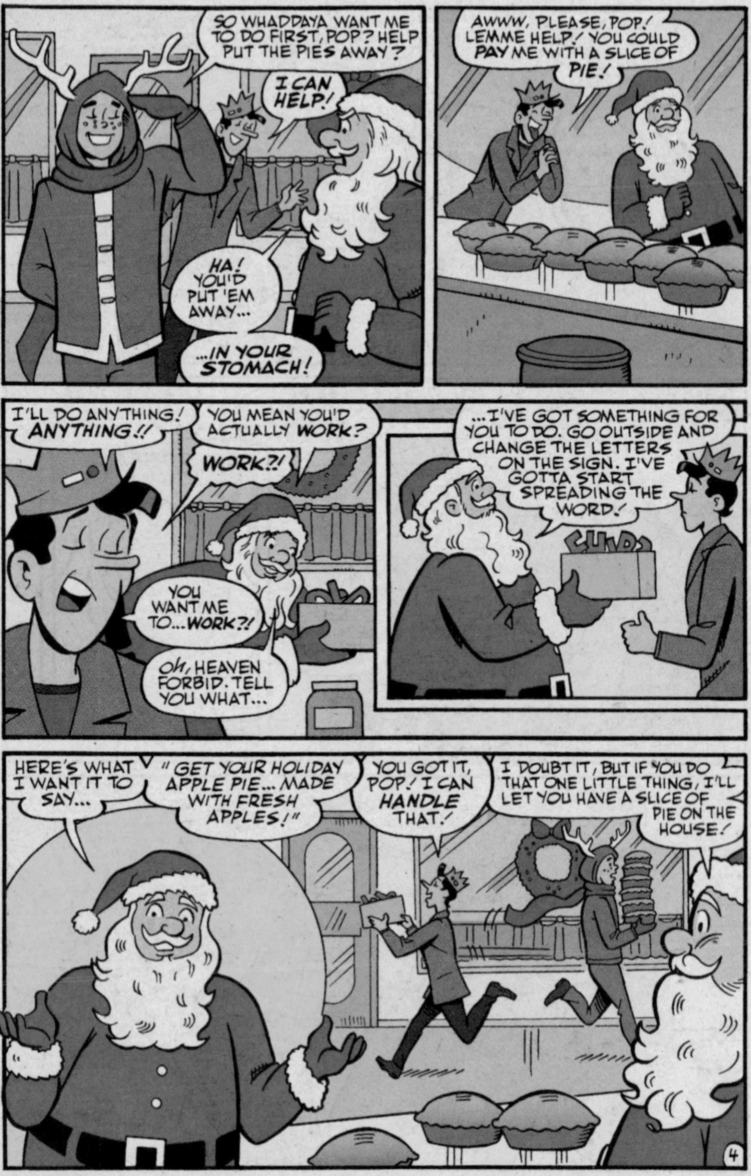
SO WHADDAYA WANT ME TO DO FIRST, POP? HELP PUT THE PIES AWAY?
I CAN HELP!
HA! YOU'D PUT 'EM AWAY...
...IN YOUR STOMACH!
AWWW, PLEASE, POP! LEMME HELP! YOU COULD PAY ME WITH A SLICE OF PIE!
I'LL DO ANYTHING! ANYTHING!!
YOU MEAN YOU'D ACTUALLY WORK?
WORK?!
YOU WANT ME TO...WORK?!
OH, HEAVEN FORBID. TELL YOU WHAT...
...I'VE GOT SOMETHING FOR YOU TO DO. GO OUTSIDE AND CHANGE THE LETTERS ON THE SIGN. I'VE GOTTA START SPREADING THE WORD!
HERE'S WHAT I WANT IT TO SAY...
"GET YOUR HOLIDAY APPLE PIE... MADE WITH FRESH APPLES!"
YOU GOT IT, POP! I CAN HANDLE THAT!
I DOUBT IT, BUT IF YOU DO THAT ONE LITTLE THING, I'LL LET YOU HAVE A SLICE OF PIE ON THE HOUSE!
4

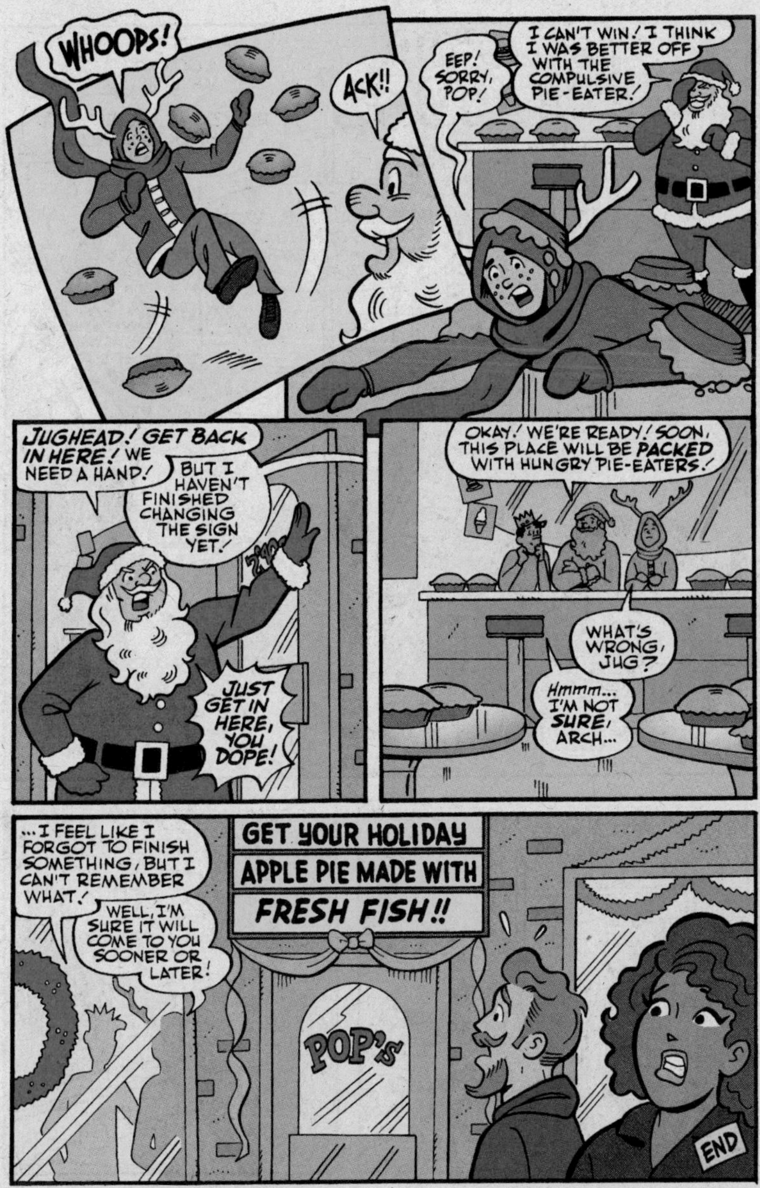
WHOOPS!
ACK!!
EEP! SORRY, POP!
I CAN'T WIN! I THINK I WAS BETTER OFF WITH THE COMPULSIVE PIE-EATER!
JUGHEAD! GET BACK IN HERE! WE NEED A HAND!
BUT I HAVEN'T FINISHED CHANGING THE SIGN YET!
JUST GET IN HERE, YOU DOPE!
OKAY! WE'RE READY! SOON, THIS PLACE WILL BE PACKED WITH HUNGRY PIE-EATERS!
WHAT'S WRONG, JUG?
Hmmm... I'M NOT SURE, ARCH...
...I FEEL LIKE I FORGOT TO FINISH SOMETHING, BUT I CAN'T REMEMBER WHAT!
WELL, I'M SURE IT WILL COME TO YOU SOONER OR LATER!
GET YOUR HOLIDAY
APPLE PIE MADE WITH
FRESH FISH!!
POP'S
END

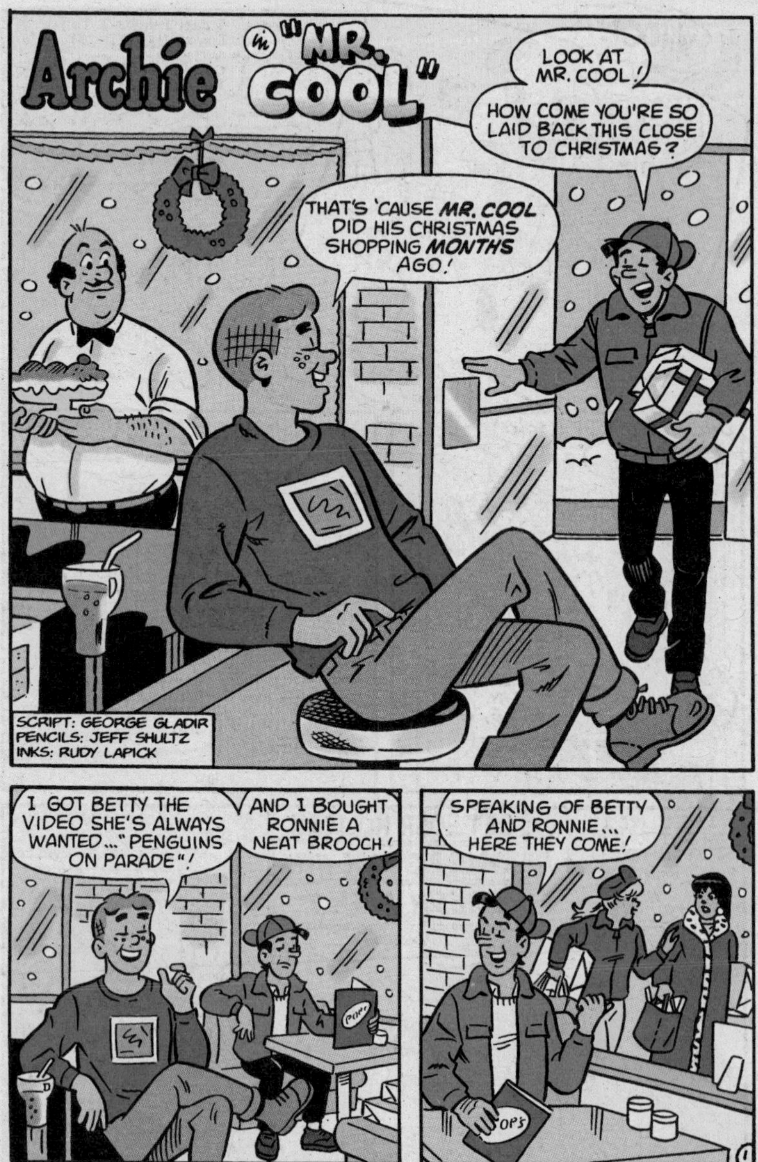
Archie in "MR. COOL"
LOOK AT MR. COOL!
HOW COME YOU'RE SO LAID BACK THIS CLOSE TO CHRISTMAS?
THAT'S 'CAUSE MR. COOL DID HIS CHRISTMAS SHOPPING MONTHS AGO!
SCRIPT: GEORGE GLADIR
PENCILS: JEFF SHULTZ
INKS: RUDY LAPICK
I GOT BETTY THE VIDEO SHE'S ALWAYS WANTED..."PENGUINS ON PARADE"!
AND I BOUGHT RONNIE A NEAT BROOCH!
SPEAKING OF BETTY AND RONNIE... HERE THEY COME!
1

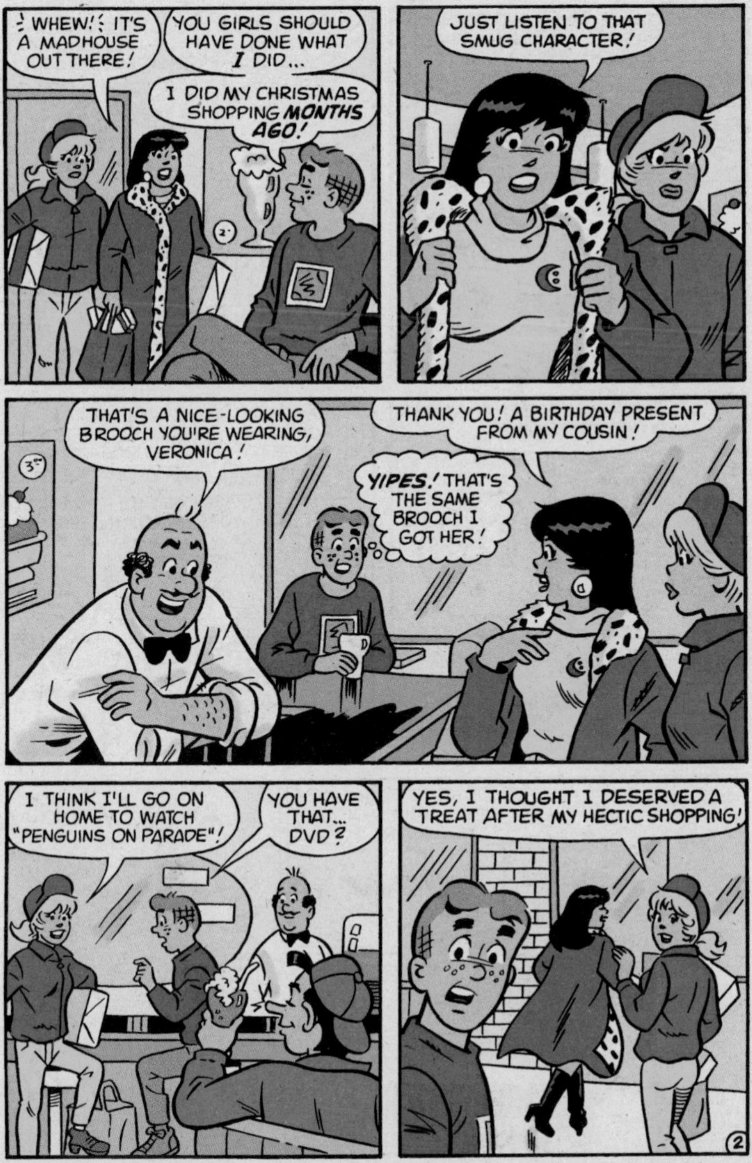
WHEW! IT'S A MADHOUSE OUT THERE!
YOU GIRLS SHOULD HAVE DONE WHAT I DID...
I DID MY CHRISTMAS SHOPPING MONTHS AGO!
JUST LISTEN TO THAT SMUG CHARACTER!
THAT'S A NICE-LOOKING BROOCH YOU'RE WEARING, VERONICA!
THANK YOU! A BIRTHDAY PRESENT FROM MY COUSIN!
YIPES! THAT'S THE SAME BROOCH I GOT HER!
I THINK I'LL GO ON HOME TO WATCH "PENGUINS ON PARADE"!
YOU HAVE THAT... DVD?
YES, I THOUGHT I DESERVED A TREAT AFTER MY HECTIC SHOPPING!
2

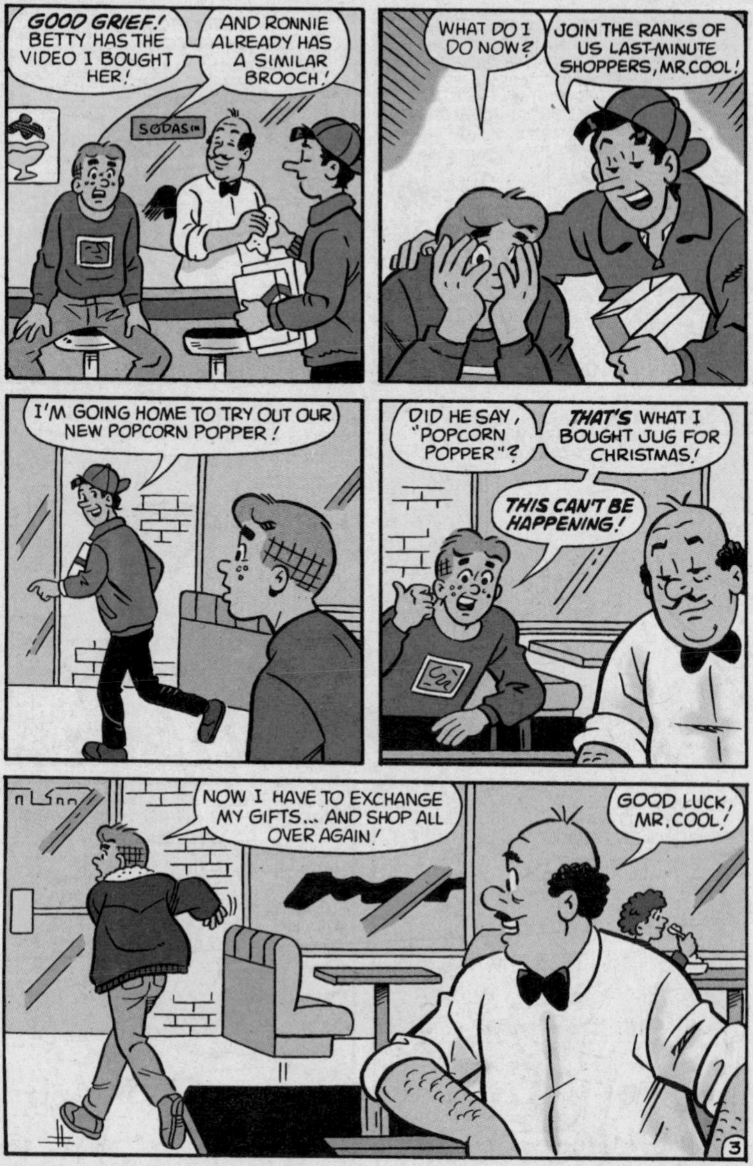
GOOD GRIEF! BETTY HAS THE VIDEO I BOUGHT HER!
AND RONNIE ALREADY HAS A SIMILAR BROOCH!
SODAS
WHAT DO I DO NOW?
JOIN THE RANKS OF US LAST-MINUTE SHOPPERS, MR. COOL!
I'M GOING HOME TO TRY OUT OUR NEW POPCORN POPPER!
DID HE SAY, "POPCORN POPPER"?
THAT'S WHAT I BOUGHT JUG FOR CHRISTMAS!
THIS CAN'T BE HAPPENING!
NOW I HAVE TO EXCHANGE MY GIFTS... AND SHOP ALL OVER AGAIN!
GOOD LUCK, MR. COOL!

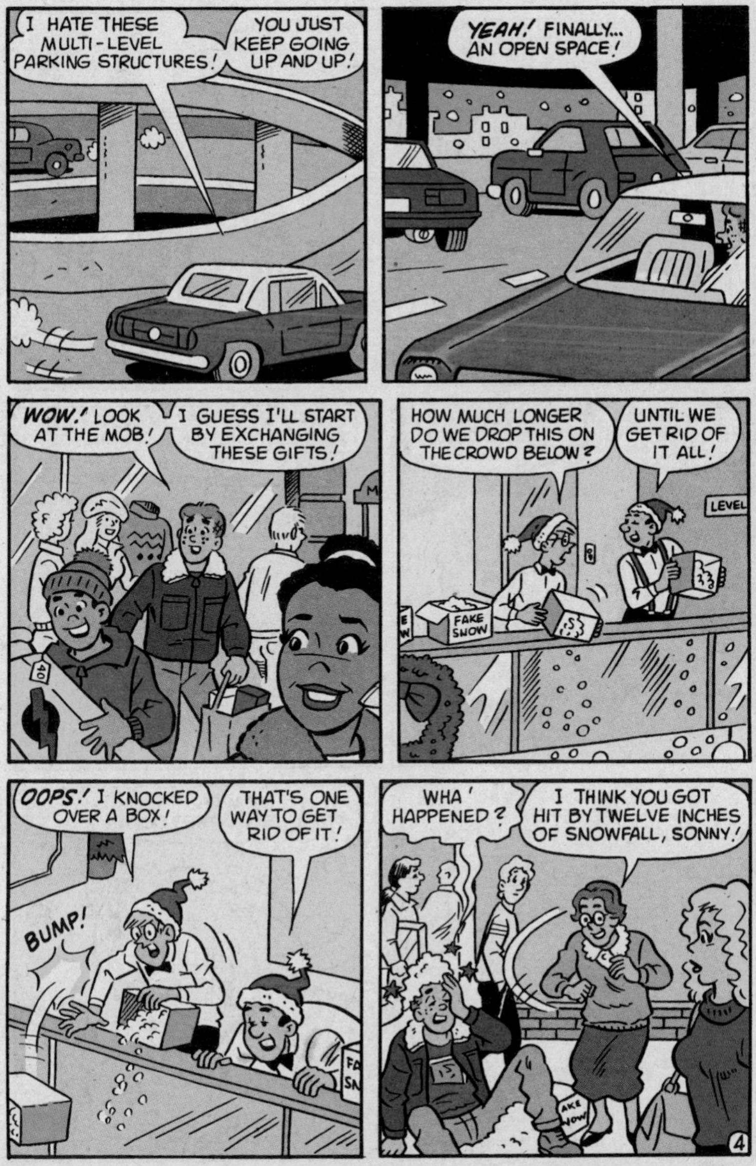
I HATE THESE MULTI-LEVEL PARKING STRUCTURES!
YOU JUST KEEP GOING UP AND UP!
YEAH! FINALLY... AN OPEN SPACE!
WOW! LOOK AT THE MOB!
I GUESS I'LL START BY EXCHANGING THESE GIFTS!
HOW MUCH LONGER DO WE DROP THIS ON THE CROWD BELOW?
UNTIL WE GET RID OF IT ALL!
LEVEL
FAKE SNOW
OOPS! I KNOCKED OVER A BOX!
THAT'S ONE WAY TO GET RID OF IT!
BUMP!
WHA' HAPPENED?
I THINK YOU GOT HIT BY TWELVE INCHES OF SNOWFALL, SONNY!
4

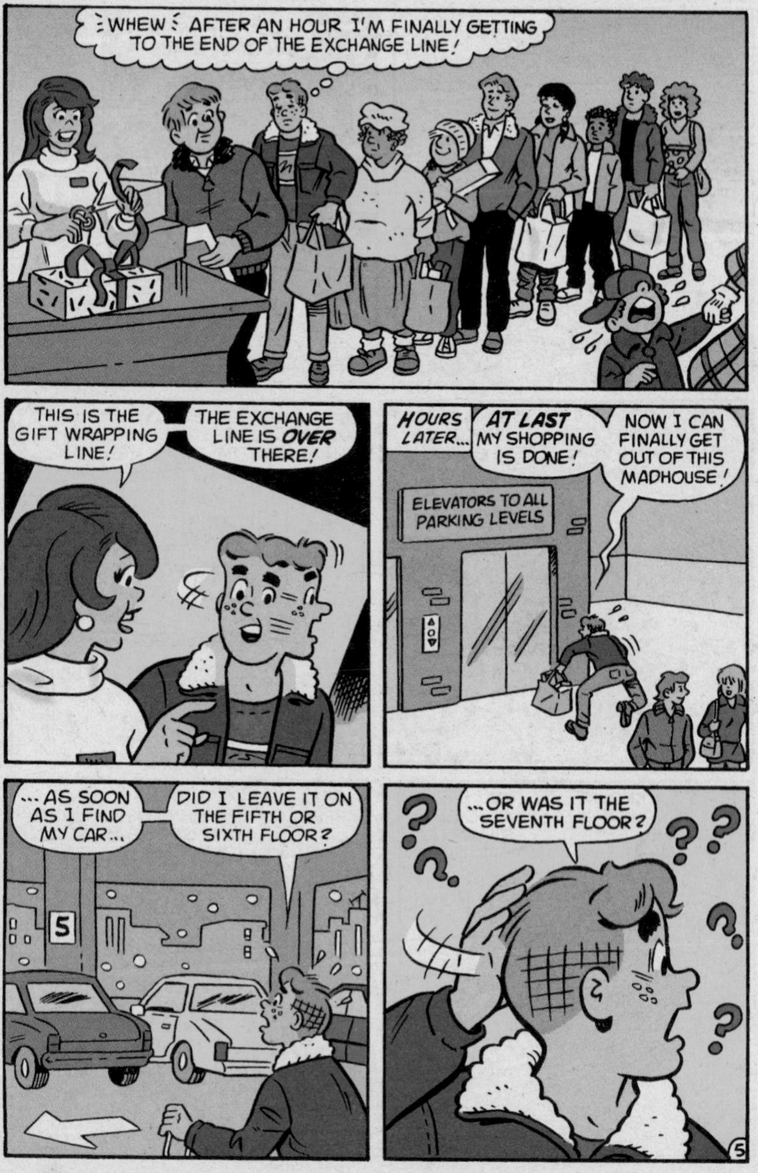

WHEW! AFTER AN HOUR I'M FINALLY GETTING TO THE END OF THE EXCHANGE LINE!
THIS IS THE GIFT WRAPPING LINE!
THE EXCHANGE LINE IS OVER THERE!
HOURS LATER...
AT LAST MY SHOPPING IS DONE!
NOW I CAN FINALLY GET OUT OF THIS MADHOUSE!
ELEVATORS TO ALL PARKING LEVELS
...AS SOON AS I FIND MY CAR...
DID I LEAVE IT ON THE FIFTH OR SIXTH FLOOR?
5
...OR WAS IT THE SEVENTH FLOOR?
5

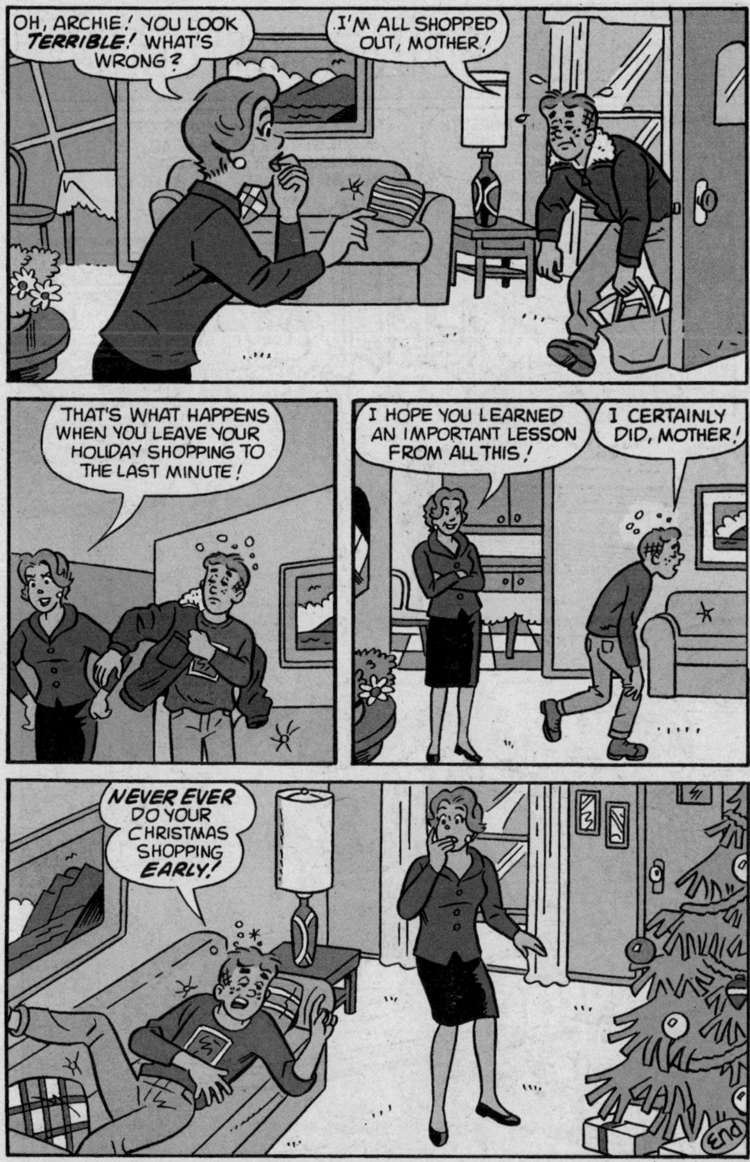
OH, ARCHIE! YOU LOOK TERRIBLE! WHAT'S WRONG?
I'M ALL SHOPPED OUT, MOTHER!
THAT'S WHAT HAPPENS WHEN YOU LEAVE YOUR HOLIDAY SHOPPING TO THE LAST MINUTE!
I HOPE YOU LEARNED AN IMPORTANT LESSON FROM ALL THIS!
I CERTAINLY DID, MOTHER!
NEVER EVER DO YOUR CHRISTMAS SHOPPING EARLY!
END

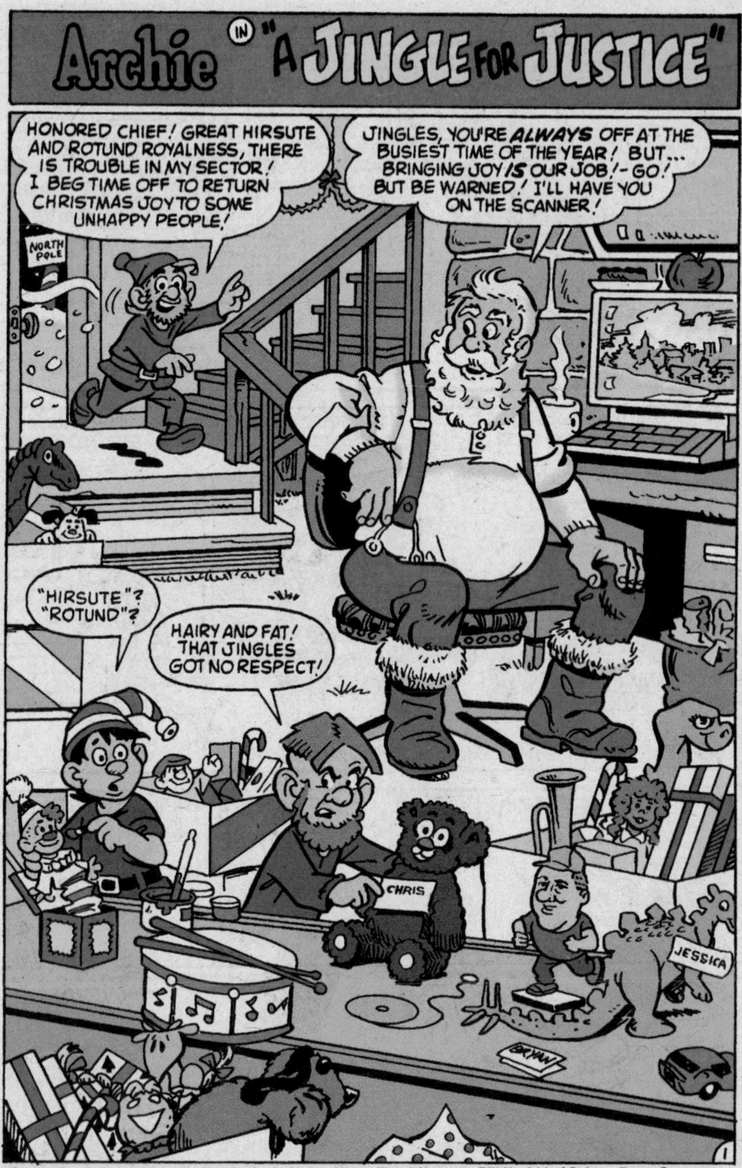
Archie (IN) "A JINGLE FOR JUSTICE"
HONORED CHIEF! GREAT HIRSUTE AND ROTUND ROYALNESS, THERE IS TROUBLE IN MY SECTOR! I BEG TIME OFF TO RETURN CHRISTMAS JOY TO SOME UNHAPPY PEOPLE!
JINGLES, YOU'RE ***ALWAYS*** OFF AT THE BUSIEST TIME OF THE YEAR! BUT... BRINGING JOY ***IS*** OUR JOB!- GO! BUT BE WARNED! I'LL HAVE YOU ON THE SCANNER!
NORTH POLE
"HIRSUTE"? "ROTUND"?
HAIRY AND FAT! THAT JINGLES GOT NO RESPECT!
CHRIS
JESSICA
BRYAN
1

Script: Frank Doyle / Pencils: Dan DeCarlo / Inks: Alison Flood / Letters: Bill Yoshida / Colors: Barry Grossman

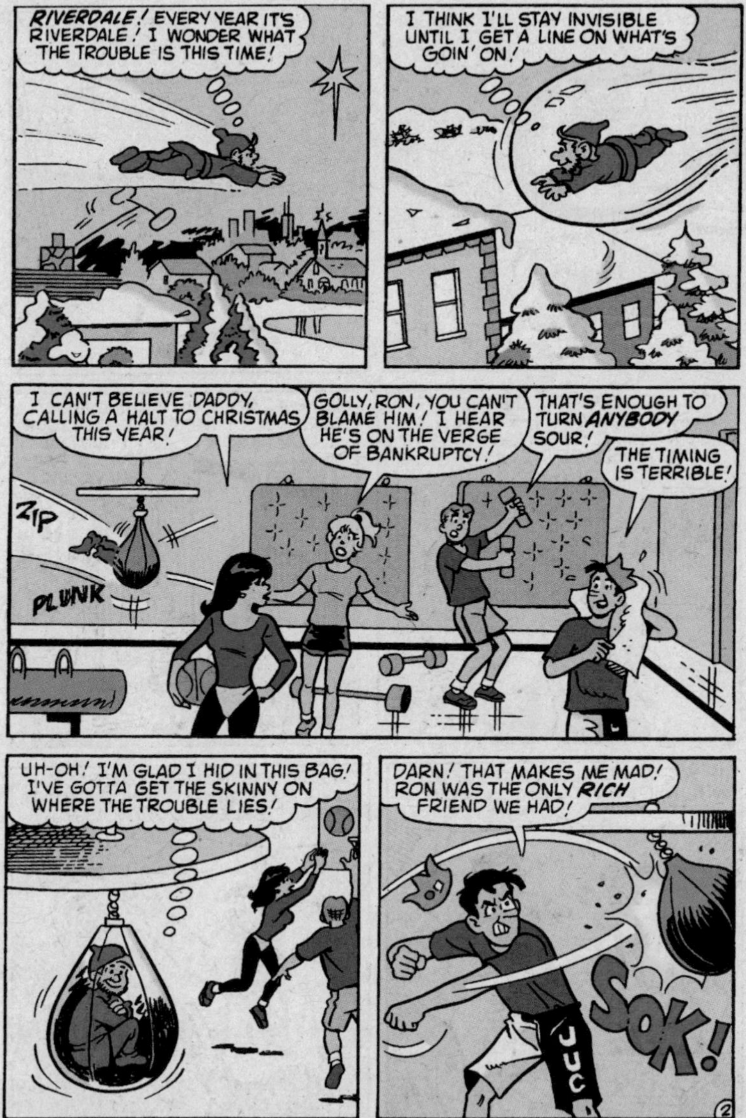
RIVERDALE! EVERY YEAR IT'S RIVERDALE! I WONDER WHAT THE TROUBLE IS THIS TIME!
I THINK I'LL STAY INVISIBLE UNTIL I GET A LINE ON WHAT'S GOIN' ON!
I CAN'T BELIEVE DADDY, CALLING A HALT TO CHRISTMAS THIS YEAR!
GOLLY, RON, YOU CAN'T BLAME HIM! I HEAR HE'S ON THE VERGE OF BANKRUPTCY!
THAT'S ENOUGH TO TURN ANYBODY SOUR!
THE TIMING IS TERRIBLE!
ZIP
PLUNK
UH-OH! I'M GLAD I HID IN THIS BAG! I'VE GOTTA GET THE SKINNY ON WHERE THE TROUBLE LIES!
DARN! THAT MAKES ME MAD! RON WAS THE ONLY RICH FRIEND WE HAD!
SOK!
2

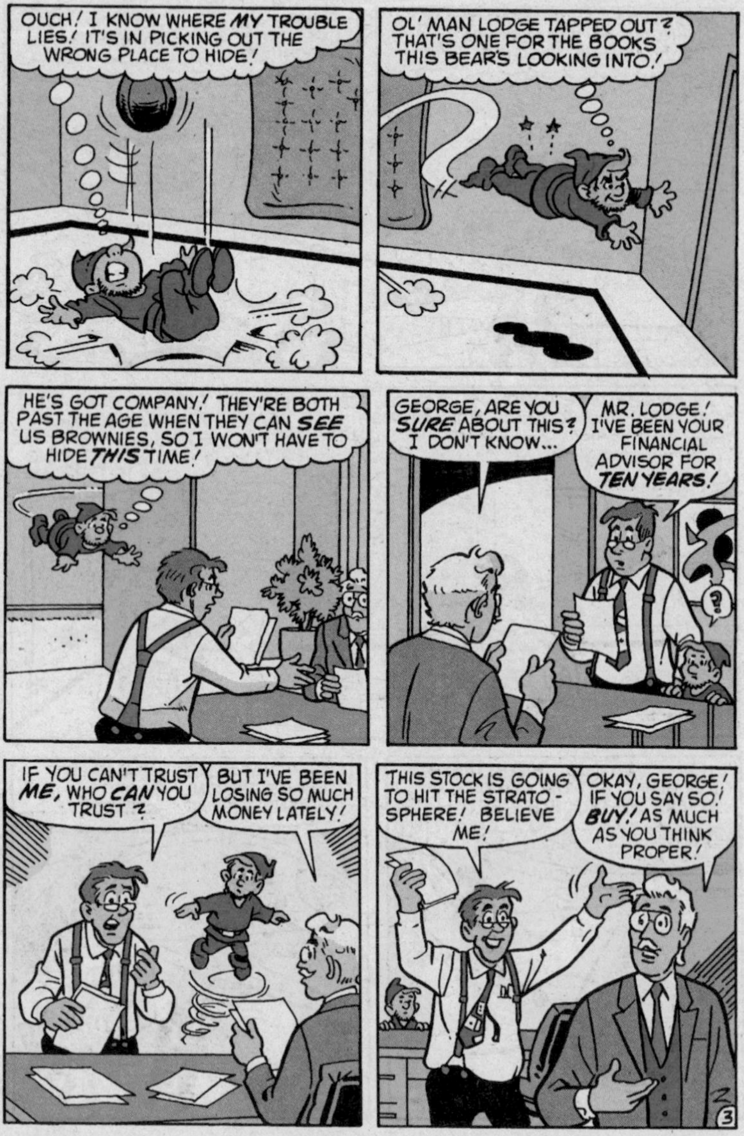
OUCH! I KNOW WHERE MY TROUBLE LIES! IT'S IN PICKING OUT THE WRONG PLACE TO HIDE!
OL' MAN LODGE TAPPED OUT? THAT'S ONE FOR THE BOOKS THIS BEAR'S LOOKING INTO!
HE'S GOT COMPANY! THEY'RE BOTH PAST THE AGE WHEN THEY CAN SEE US BROWNIES, SO I WON'T HAVE TO HIDE THIS TIME!
GEORGE, ARE YOU SURE ABOUT THIS? I DON'T KNOW...
MR. LODGE! I'VE BEEN YOUR FINANCIAL ADVISOR FOR TEN YEARS!
?
IF YOU CAN'T TRUST ME, WHO CAN YOU TRUST?
BUT I'VE BEEN LOSING SO MUCH MONEY LATELY!
THIS STOCK IS GOING TO HIT THE STRATO-SPHERE! BELIEVE ME!
OKAY, GEORGE! IF YOU SAY SO! BUY! AS MUCH AS YOU THINK PROPER!
3

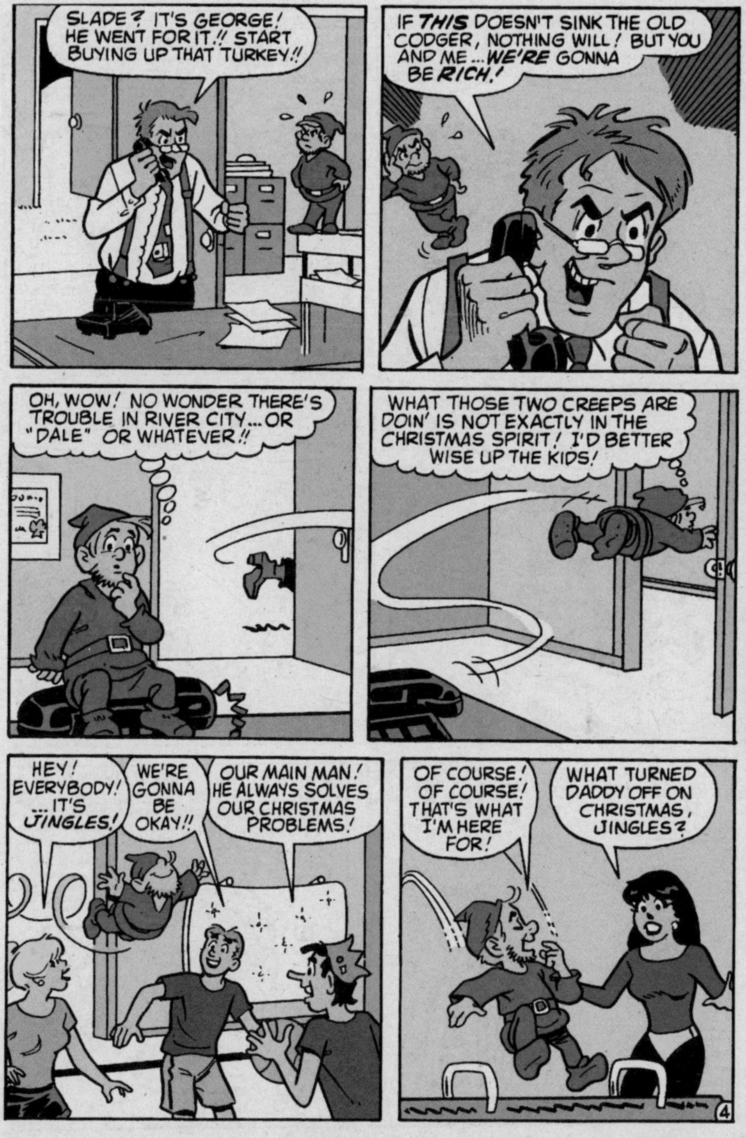
SLADE? IT'S GEORGE! HE WENT FOR IT!! START BUYING UP THAT TURKEY!!
IF THIS DOESN'T SINK THE OLD CODGER, NOTHING WILL! BUT YOU AND ME... WE'RE GONNA BE RICH!
OH, WOW! NO WONDER THERE'S TROUBLE IN RIVER CITY... OR "DALE" OR WHATEVER!!
WHAT THOSE TWO CREEPS ARE DOIN' IS NOT EXACTLY IN THE CHRISTMAS SPIRIT! I'D BETTER WISE UP THE KIDS!
HEY! EVERYBODY! ...IT'S JINGLES!
WE'RE GONNA BE OKAY!!
OUR MAIN MAN! HE ALWAYS SOLVES OUR CHRISTMAS PROBLEMS!
OF COURSE! OF COURSE! THAT'S WHAT I'M HERE FOR!
WHAT TURNED DADDY OFF ON CHRISTMAS, JINGLES?
4

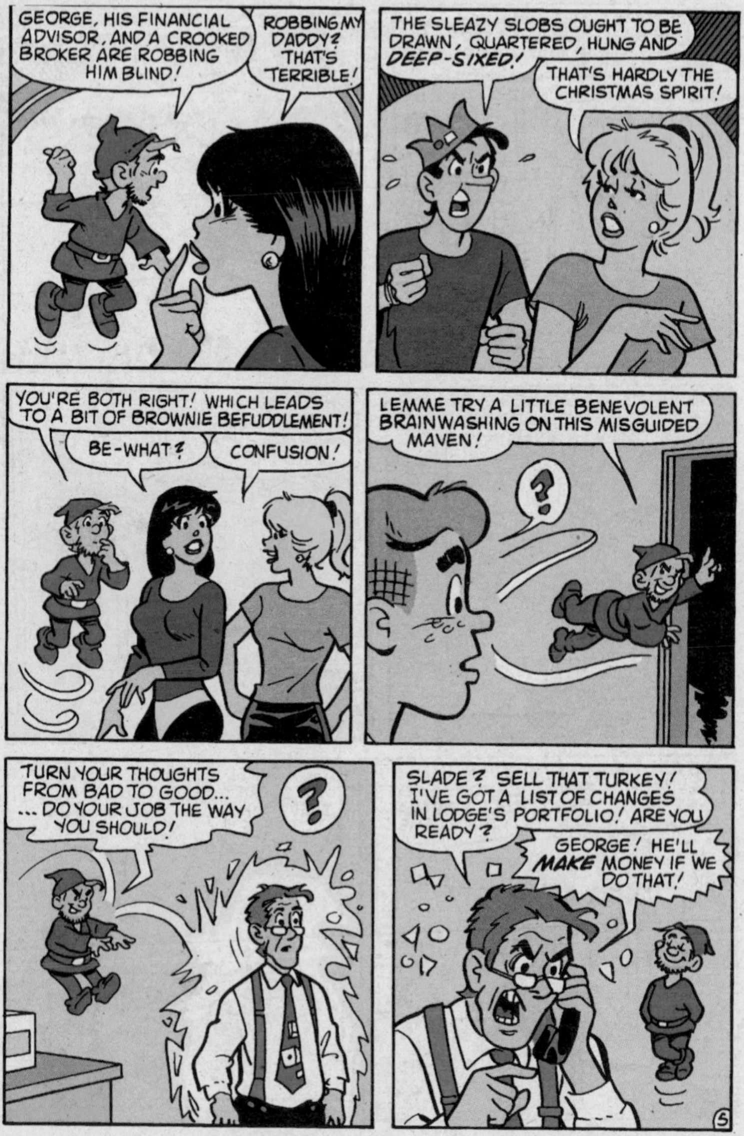
GEORGE, HIS FINANCIAL ADVISOR, AND A CROOKED BROKER ARE ROBBING HIM BLIND!
ROBBING MY DADDY? THAT'S TERRIBLE!
THE SLEAZY SLOBS OUGHT TO BE DRAWN, QUARTERED, HUNG AND DEEP-SIXED!
THAT'S HARDLY THE CHRISTMAS SPIRIT!
YOU'RE BOTH RIGHT! WHICH LEADS TO A BIT OF BROWNIE BEFUDDLEMENT!
BE-WHAT?
CONFUSION!
LEMME TRY A LITTLE BENEVOLENT BRAINWASHING ON THIS MISGUIDED MAVEN!
?
TURN YOUR THOUGHTS FROM BAD TO GOOD... ...DO YOUR JOB THE WAY YOU SHOULD!
?
SLADE? SELL THAT TURKEY! I'VE GOT A LIST OF CHANGES IN LODGE'S PORTFOLIO! ARE YOU READY?
GEORGE! HE'LL MAKE MONEY IF WE DO THAT!
5

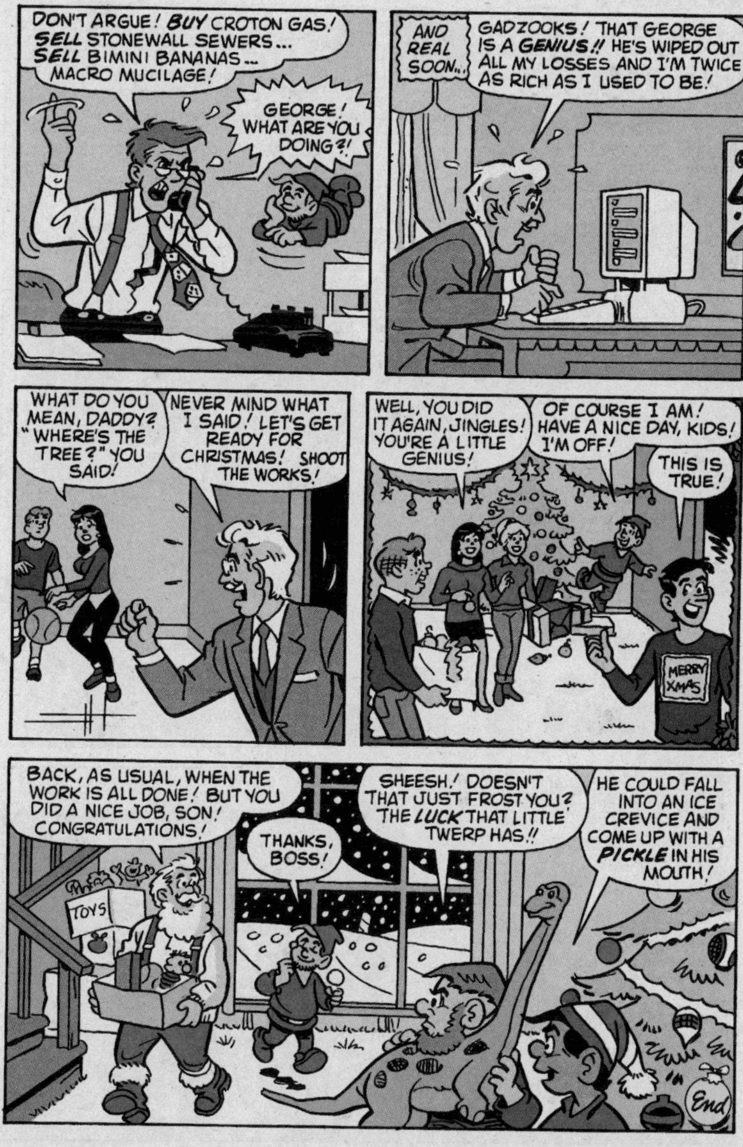

DON'T ARGUE! BUY CROTON GAS! SELL STONEWALL SEWERS... SELL BIMINI BANANAS... MACRO MUCILAGE!
GEORGE! WHAT ARE YOU DOING?!
AND REAL SOON...
GADZOOKS! THAT GEORGE IS A GENIUS!! HE'S WIPED OUT ALL MY LOSSES AND I'M TWICE AS RICH AS I USED TO BE!
WHAT DO YOU MEAN, DADDY? "WHERE'S THE TREE?" YOU SAID!
NEVER MIND WHAT I SAID! LET'S GET READY FOR CHRISTMAS! SHOOT THE WORKS!
WELL, YOU DID IT AGAIN, JINGLES! YOU'RE A LITTLE GENIUS!
OF COURSE I AM! HAVE A NICE DAY, KIDS! I'M OFF!
THIS IS TRUE!
MERRY XMAS
BACK, AS USUAL, WHEN THE WORK IS ALL DONE! BUT YOU DID A NICE JOB, SON! CONGRATULATIONS!
THANKS, BOSS!
SHEESH! DOESN'T THAT JUST FROST YOU? THE LUCK THAT LITTLE TWERP HAS!!
HE COULD FALL INTO AN ICE CREVICE AND COME UP WITH A PICKLE IN HIS MOUTH!
TOYS
End

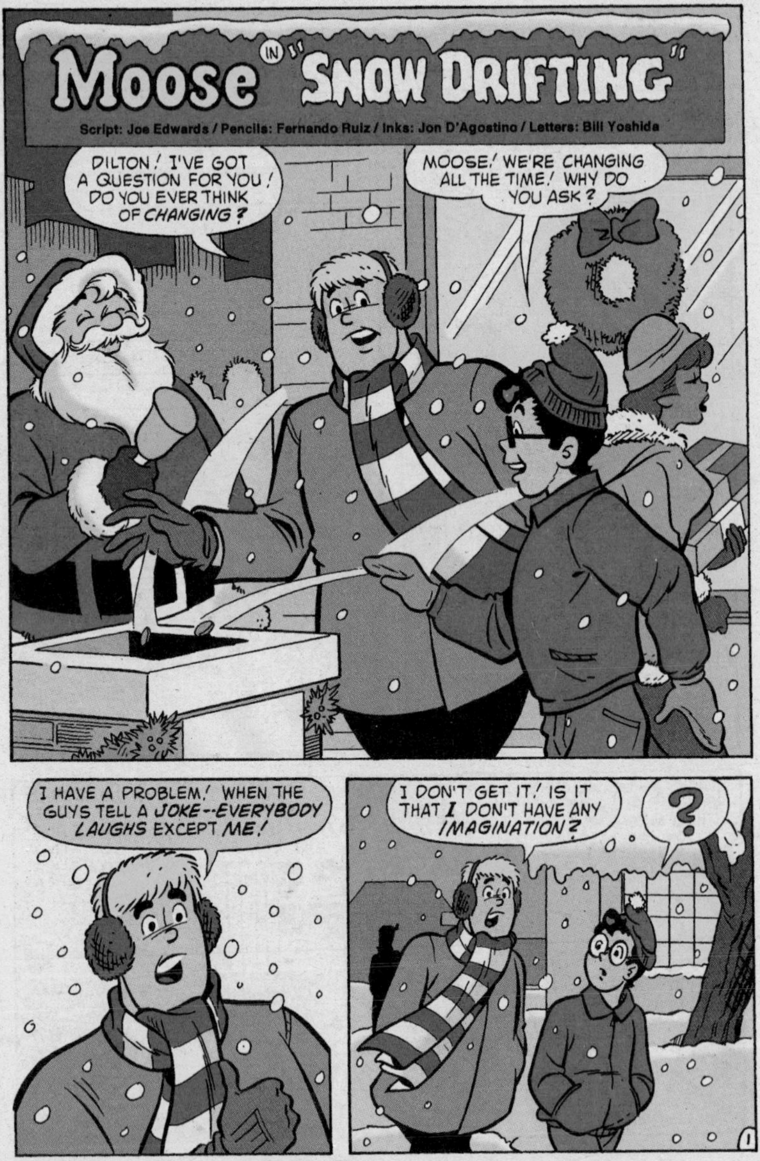

Moose IN "SNOW DRIFTING"
Script: Joe Edwards / Pencils: Fernando Ruiz / Inks: Jon D'Agostino / Letters: Bill Yoshida
DILTON! I'VE GOT A QUESTION FOR YOU! DO YOU EVER THINK OF CHANGING?
MOOSE! WE'RE CHANGING ALL THE TIME! WHY DO YOU ASK?
I HAVE A PROBLEM! WHEN THE GUYS TELL A JOKE--EVERYBODY LAUGHS EXCEPT ME!
I DON'T GET IT! IS IT THAT I DON'T HAVE ANY IMAGINATION?
?

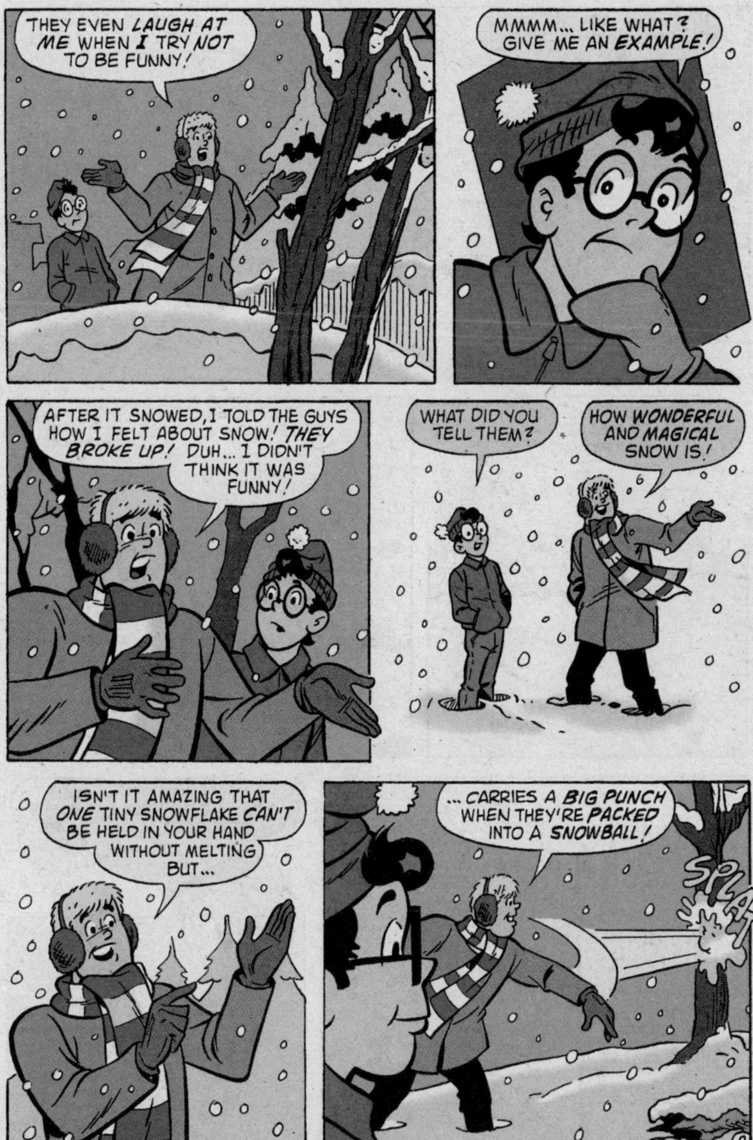
THEY EVEN LAUGH AT ME WHEN I TRY NOT TO BE FUNNY!
MMMM... LIKE WHAT? GIVE ME AN EXAMPLE!
AFTER IT SNOWED, I TOLD THE GUYS HOW I FELT ABOUT SNOW! THEY BROKE UP! DUH... I DIDN'T THINK IT WAS FUNNY!
WHAT DID YOU TELL THEM?
HOW WONDERFUL AND MAGICAL SNOW IS!
ISN'T IT AMAZING THAT ONE TINY SNOWFLAKE CAN'T BE HELD IN YOUR HAND WITHOUT MELTING BUT...
...CARRIES A BIG PUNCH WHEN THEY'RE PACKED INTO A SNOWBALL!
SPLAT
2

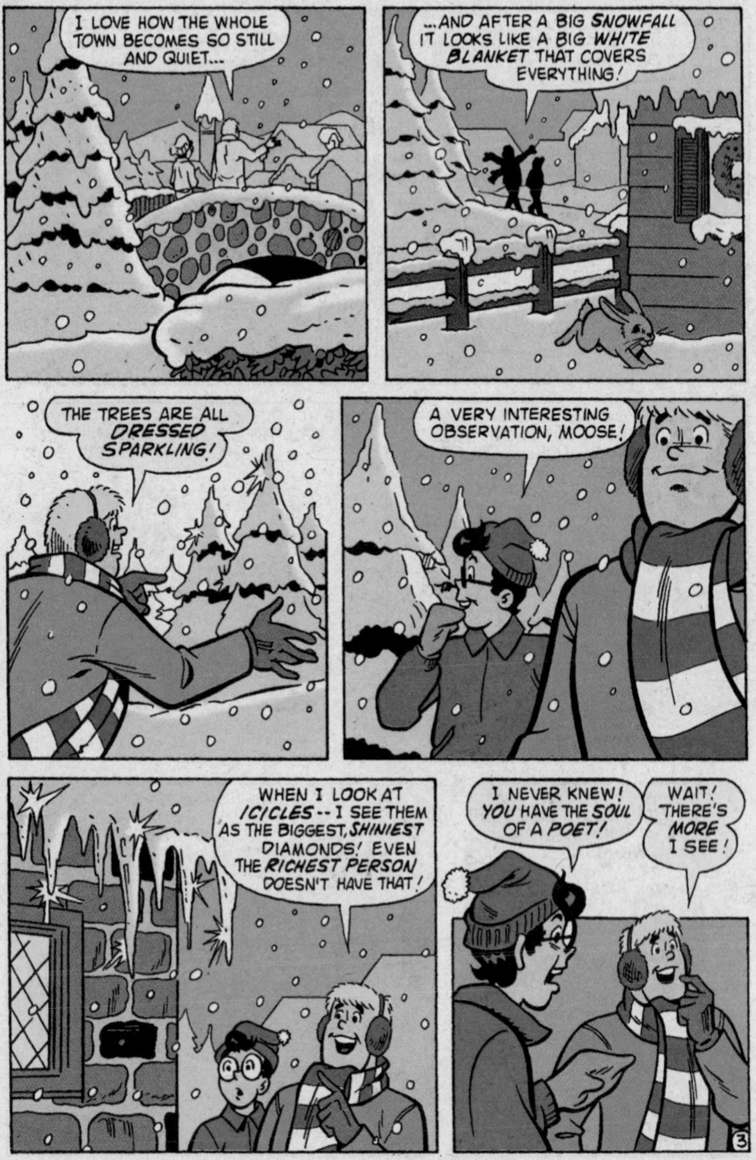
I LOVE HOW THE WHOLE TOWN BECOMES SO STILL AND QUIET...
...AND AFTER A BIG SNOWFALL IT LOOKS LIKE A BIG WHITE BLANKET THAT COVERS EVERYTHING!
THE TREES ARE ALL DRESSED SPARKLING!
A VERY INTERESTING OBSERVATION, MOOSE!
WHEN I LOOK AT ICICLES -- I SEE THEM AS THE BIGGEST, SHINIEST DIAMONDS! EVEN THE RICHEST PERSON DOESN'T HAVE THAT!
I NEVER KNEW! YOU HAVE THE SOUL OF A POET!
WAIT! THERE'S MORE I SEE!
3

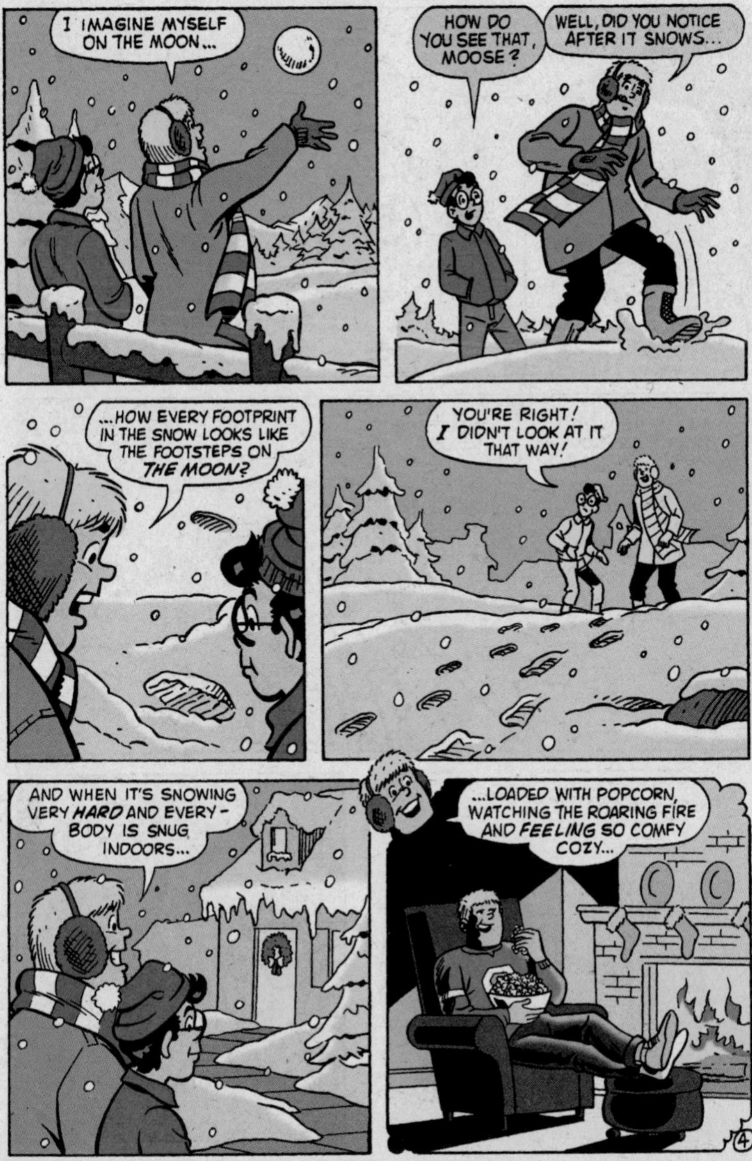
I IMAGINE MYSELF ON THE MOON...
HOW DO YOU SEE THAT, MOOSE?
WELL, DID YOU NOTICE AFTER IT SNOWS...
...HOW EVERY FOOTPRINT IN THE SNOW LOOKS LIKE THE FOOTSTEPS ON THE MOON?
YOU'RE RIGHT! I DIDN'T LOOK AT IT THAT WAY!
AND WHEN IT'S SNOWING VERY HARD AND EVERY-BODY IS SNUG INDOORS...
...LOADED WITH POPCORN, WATCHING THE ROARING FIRE AND FEELING SO COMFY COZY...
4

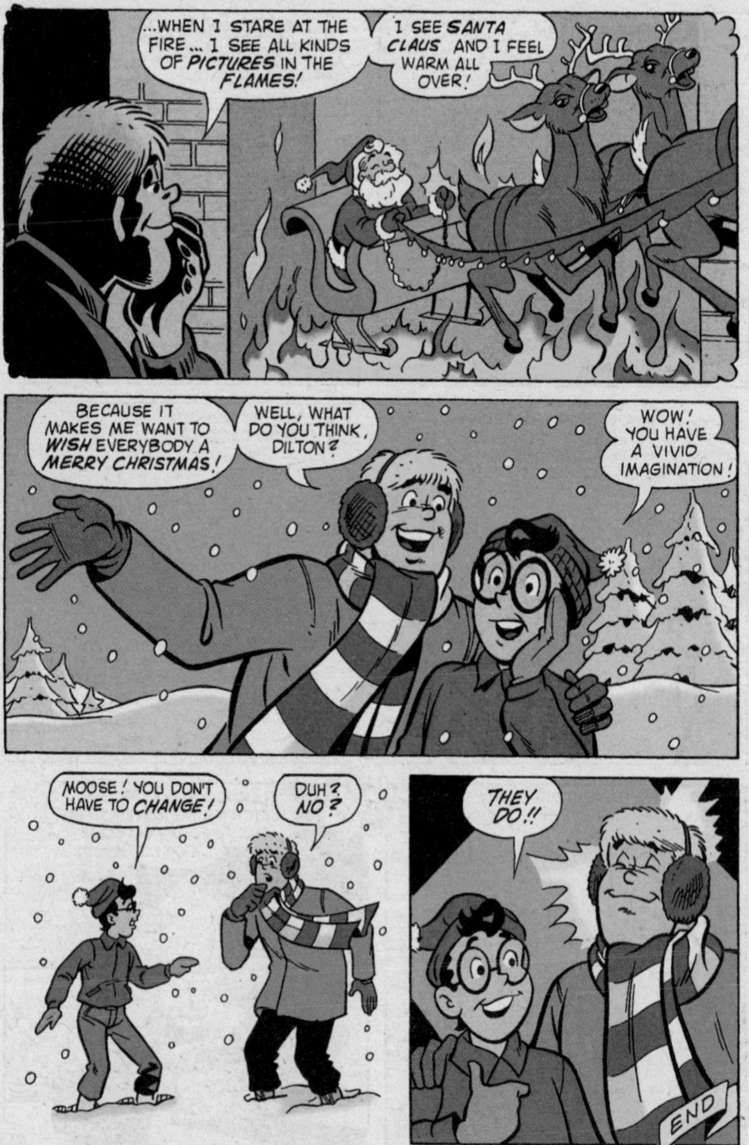

...WHEN I STARE AT THE FIRE ... I SEE ALL KINDS OF PICTURES IN THE FLAMES!
I SEE SANTA CLAUS AND I FEEL WARM ALL OVER!
BECAUSE IT MAKES ME WANT TO WISH EVERYBODY A MERRY CHRISTMAS!
WELL, WHAT DO YOU THINK, DILTON?
WOW! YOU HAVE A VIVID IMAGINATION!
MOOSE! YOU DON'T HAVE TO CHANGE!
DUH? NO?
THEY DO!!
END

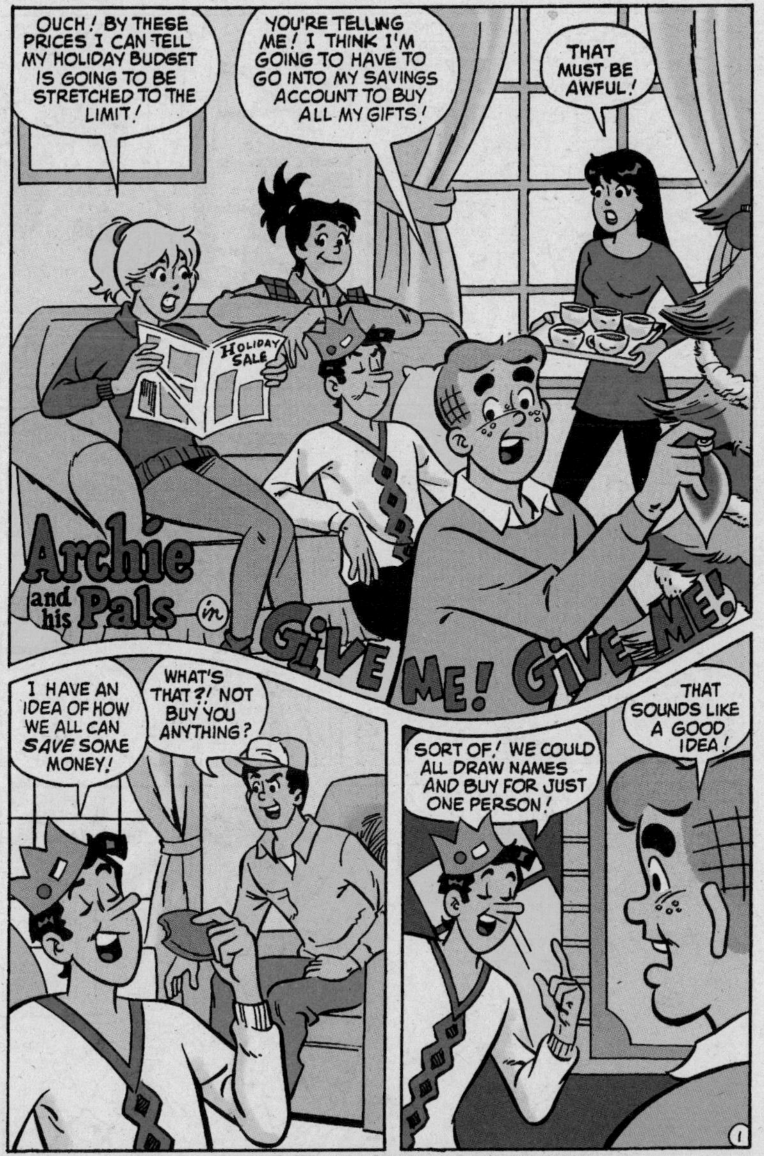
OUCH! BY THESE PRICES I CAN TELL MY HOLIDAY BUDGET IS GOING TO BE STRETCHED TO THE LIMIT!
YOU'RE TELLING ME! I THINK I'M GOING TO HAVE TO GO INTO MY SAVINGS ACCOUNT TO BUY ALL MY GIFTS!
THAT MUST BE AWFUL!
HOLIDAY SALE
Archie and his Pals in
GIVE ME! GIVE ME!
I HAVE AN IDEA OF HOW WE ALL CAN SAVE SOME MONEY!
WHAT'S THAT?! NOT BUY YOU ANYTHING?
SORT OF! WE COULD ALL DRAW NAMES AND BUY FOR JUST ONE PERSON!
THAT SOUNDS LIKE A GOOD IDEA!
1

Script & Pencils: Bill Golliher / Inks: Rudy Lapick / Letters: Bill Yoshida

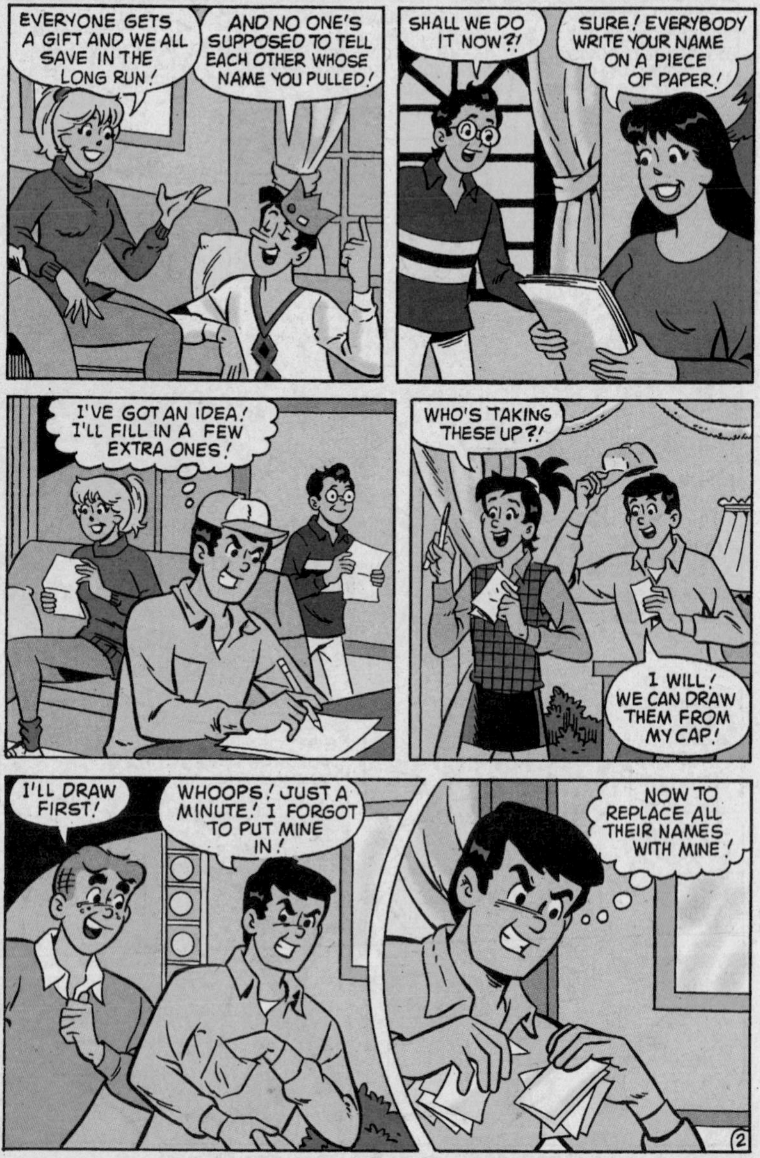
EVERYONE GETS A GIFT AND WE ALL SAVE IN THE LONG RUN!
AND NO ONE'S SUPPOSED TO TELL EACH OTHER WHOSE NAME YOU PULLED!
SHALL WE DO IT NOW?!
SURE! EVERYBODY WRITE YOUR NAME ON A PIECE OF PAPER!
I'VE GOT AN IDEA! I'LL FILL IN A FEW EXTRA ONES!
WHO'S TAKING THESE UP?!
I WILL! WE CAN DRAW THEM FROM MY CAP!
I'LL DRAW FIRST!
WHOOPS! JUST A MINUTE! I FORGOT TO PUT MINE IN!
NOW TO REPLACE ALL THEIR NAMES WITH MINE!
2

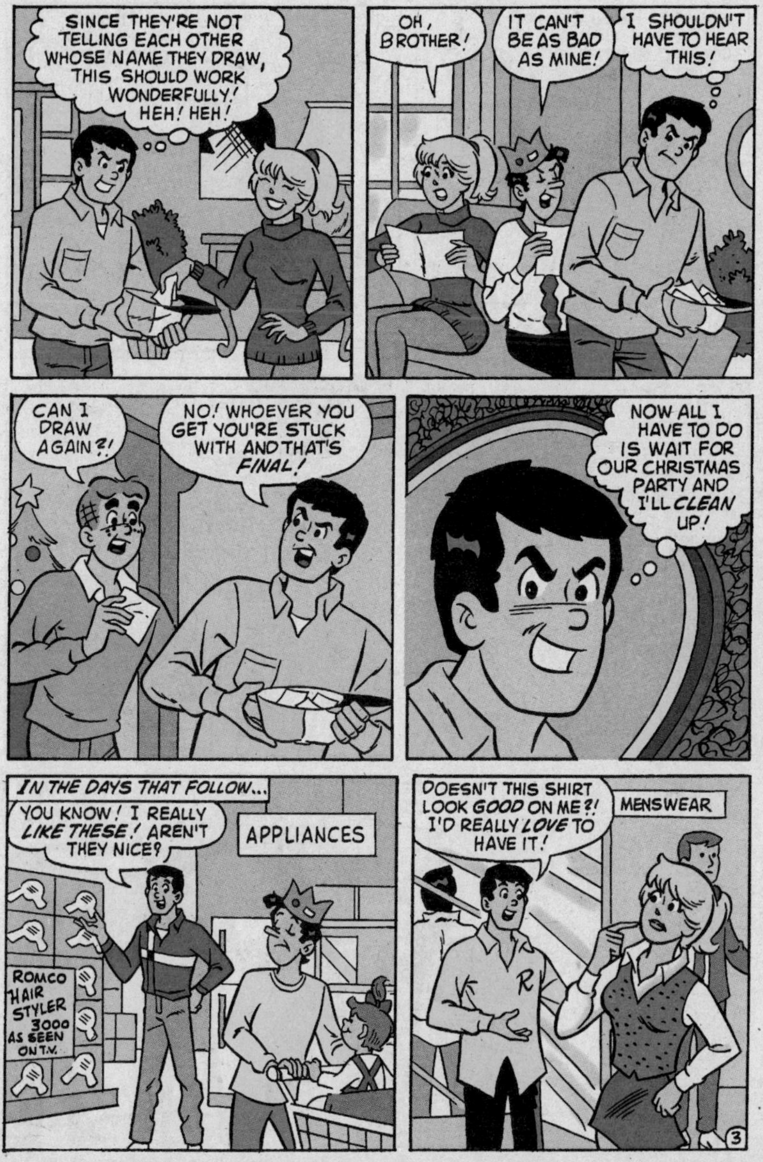
SINCE THEY'RE NOT TELLING EACH OTHER WHOSE NAME THEY DRAW, THIS SHOULD WORK WONDERFULLY! HEH! HEH!
OH, BROTHER!
IT CAN'T BE AS BAD AS MINE!
I SHOULDN'T HAVE TO HEAR THIS!
CAN I DRAW AGAIN?!
NO! WHOEVER YOU GET YOU'RE STUCK WITH AND THAT'S FINAL!
NOW ALL I HAVE TO DO IS WAIT FOR OUR CHRISTMAS PARTY AND I'LL CLEAN UP!
IN THE DAYS THAT FOLLOW...
YOU KNOW! I REALLY LIKE THESE! AREN'T THEY NICE?
APPLIANCES
ROMCO HAIR STYLER 3000 AS SEEN ON T.V.
DOESN'T THIS SHIRT LOOK GOOD ON ME?! I'D REALLY LOVE TO HAVE IT!
MENSWEAR
3

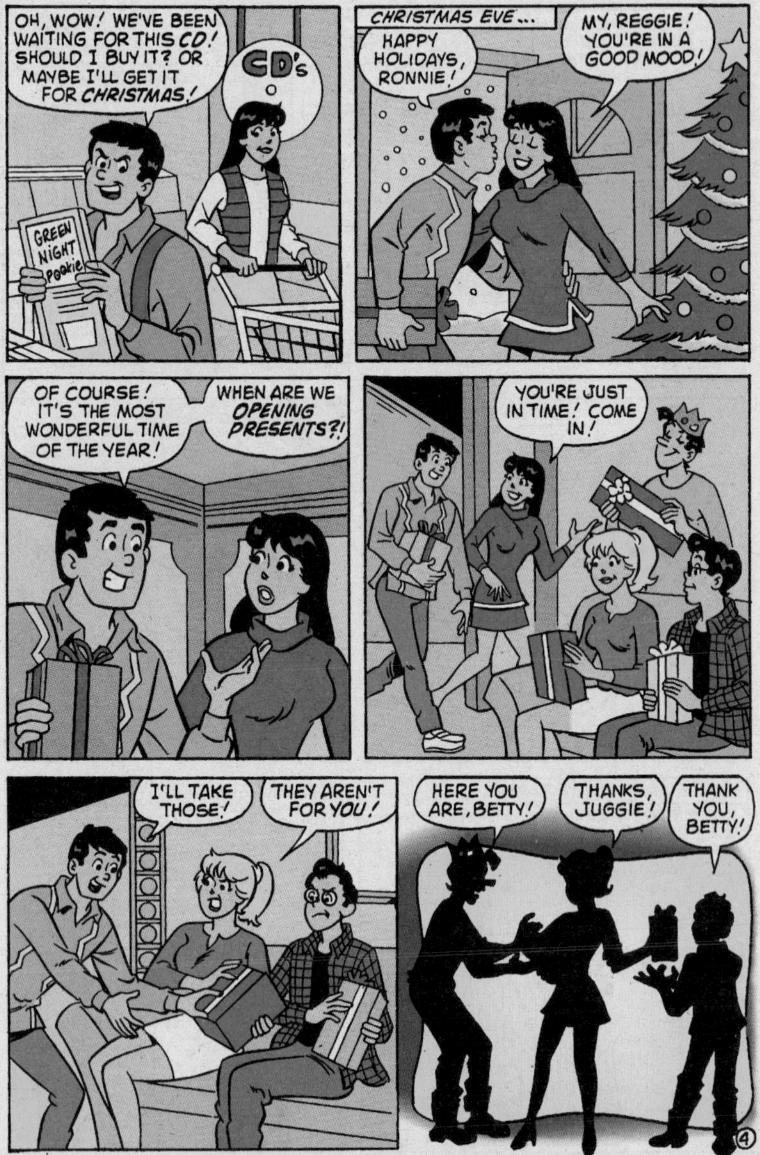

OH, WOW! WE'VE BEEN WAITING FOR THIS CD! SHOULD I BUY IT? OR MAYBE I'LL GET IT FOR CHRISTMAS!
CD's
GREEN NIGHT Pookie
CHRISTMAS EVE...
HAPPY HOLIDAYS, RONNIE!
MY, REGGIE! YOU'RE IN A GOOD MOOD!
OF COURSE! IT'S THE MOST WONDERFUL TIME OF THE YEAR!
WHEN ARE WE OPENING PRESENTS?!
YOU'RE JUST IN TIME! COME IN!
I'LL TAKE THOSE!
THEY AREN'T FOR YOU!
HERE YOU ARE, BETTY!
THANKS, JUGGIE!
THANK YOU, BETTY!
4

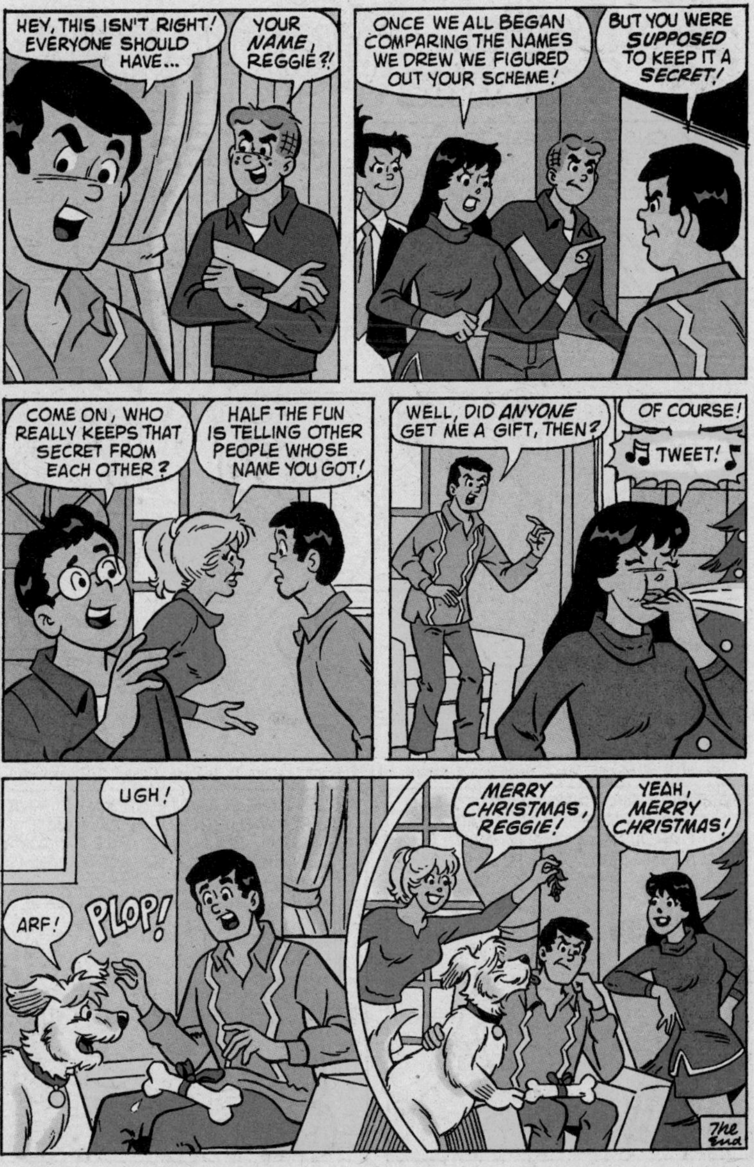
HEY, THIS ISN'T RIGHT! EVERYONE SHOULD HAVE...
YOUR NAME, REGGIE?!
ONCE WE ALL BEGAN COMPARING THE NAMES WE DREW WE FIGURED OUT YOUR SCHEME!
BUT YOU WERE SUPPOSED TO KEEP IT A SECRET!
COME ON, WHO REALLY KEEPS THAT SECRET FROM EACH OTHER?
HALF THE FUN IS TELLING OTHER PEOPLE WHOSE NAME YOU GOT!
WELL, DID ANYONE GET ME A GIFT, THEN?
OF COURSE!
TWEET!
UGH!
ARF!
PLOP!
MERRY CHRISTMAS, REGGIE!
YEAH, MERRY CHRISTMAS!
The End

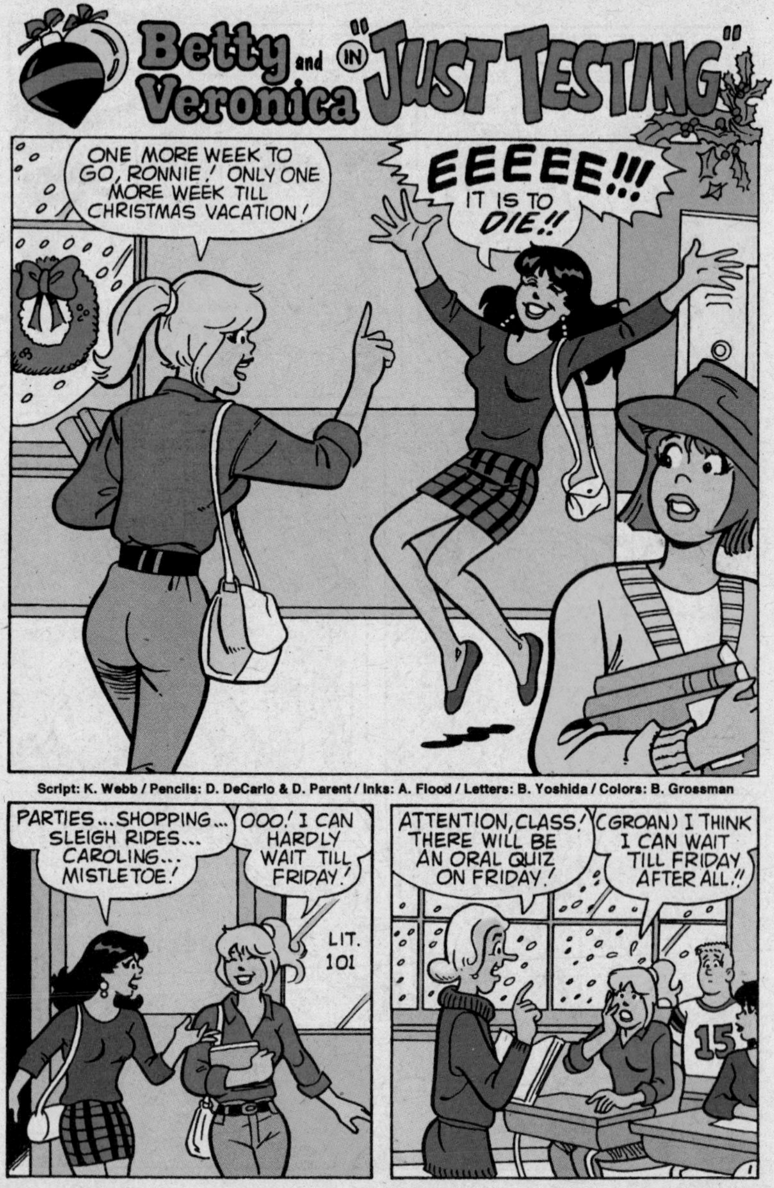
Betty and Veronica in "JUST TESTING"
ONE MORE WEEK TO GO, RONNIE! ONLY ONE MORE WEEK TILL CHRISTMAS VACATION!
EEEEE!!! IT IS TO DIE!!
Script: K. Webb / Pencils: D. DeCarlo & D. Parent / Inks: A. Flood / Letters: B. Yoshida / Colors: B. Grossman
PARTIES...SHOPPING... SLEIGH RIDES... CAROLING... MISTLETOE!
OOO! I CAN HARDLY WAIT TILL FRIDAY!
LIT. 101
ATTENTION, CLASS! THERE WILL BE AN ORAL QUIZ ON FRIDAY!
(GROAN) I THINK I CAN WAIT TILL FRIDAY AFTER ALL!!
15
1

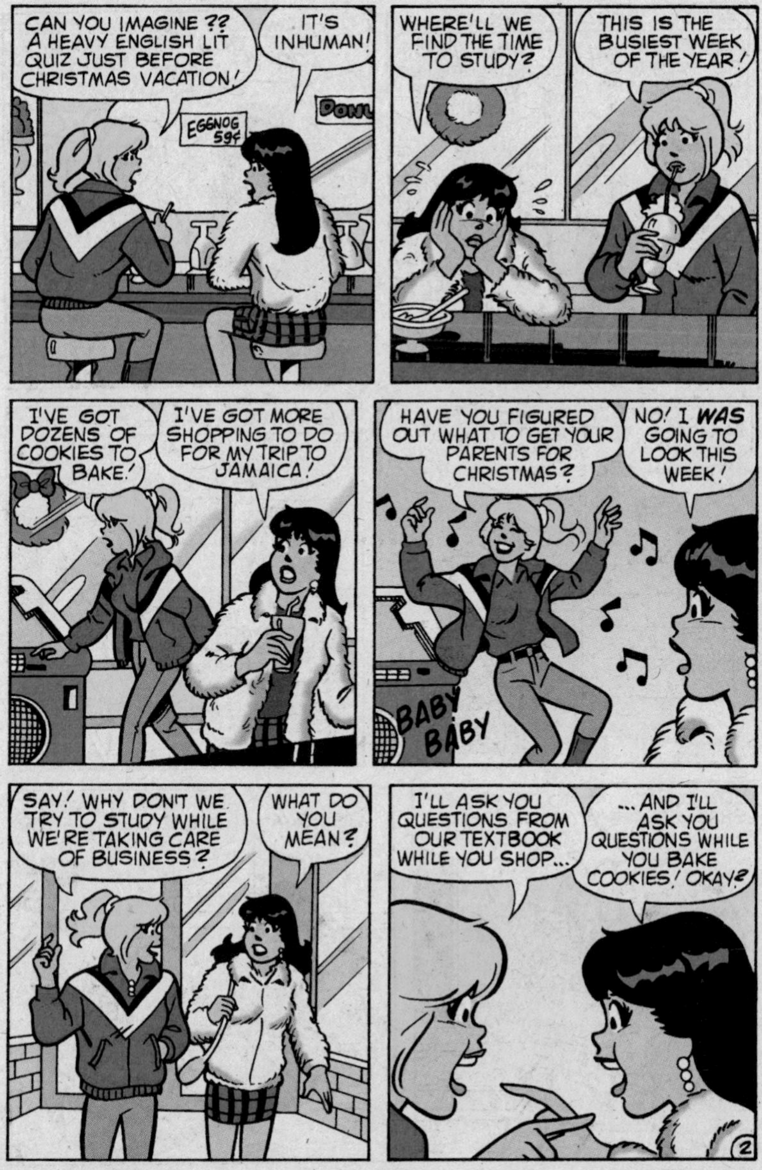

CAN YOU IMAGINE ?? A HEAVY ENGLISH LIT QUIZ JUST BEFORE CHRISTMAS VACATION!
IT'S INHUMAN!
EGGNOG 59¢
DONU
WHERE'LL WE FIND THE TIME TO STUDY?
THIS IS THE BUSIEST WEEK OF THE YEAR!
I'VE GOT DOZENS OF COOKIES TO BAKE!
I'VE GOT MORE SHOPPING TO DO FOR MY TRIP TO JAMAICA!
HAVE YOU FIGURED OUT WHAT TO GET YOUR PARENTS FOR CHRISTMAS?
NO! I **WAS** GOING TO LOOK THIS WEEK!
BABY BABY
SAY! WHY DON'T WE TRY TO STUDY WHILE WE'RE TAKING CARE OF BUSINESS?
WHAT DO YOU MEAN?
I'LL ASK YOU QUESTIONS FROM OUR TEXTBOOK WHILE YOU SHOP...
...AND I'LL ASK YOU QUESTIONS WHILE YOU BAKE COOKIES! OKAY?

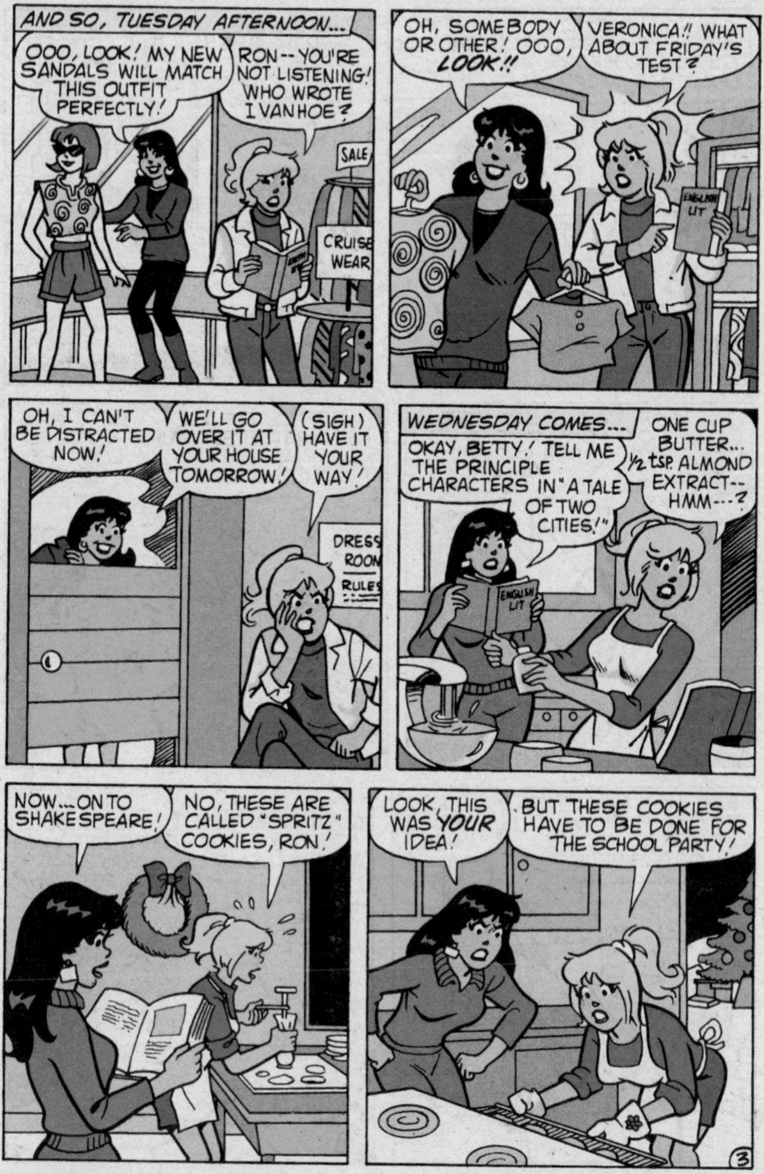
AND SO, TUESDAY AFTERNOON...
OOO, LOOK! MY NEW SANDALS WILL MATCH THIS OUTFIT PERFECTLY!
RON -- YOU'RE NOT LISTENING! WHO WROTE IVANHOE?
SALE
CRUISE WEAR
ENGLISH LIT
OH, SOMEBODY OR OTHER! OOO, LOOK!!
VERONICA!! WHAT ABOUT FRIDAY'S TEST?
ENGLISH LIT
OH, I CAN'T BE DISTRACTED NOW!
WE'LL GO OVER IT AT YOUR HOUSE TOMORROW!
(SIGH) HAVE IT YOUR WAY!
DRESS ROOM RULES
WEDNESDAY COMES...
OKAY, BETTY! TELL ME THE PRINCIPLE CHARACTERS IN "A TALE OF TWO CITIES!"
ONE CUP BUTTER... 1/2 tsp. ALMOND EXTRACT-- HMM---?
ENGLISH LIT
NOW... ON TO SHAKESPEARE!
NO, THESE ARE CALLED "SPRITZ" COOKIES, RON!
LOOK, THIS WAS YOUR IDEA!
BUT THESE COOKIES HAVE TO BE DONE FOR THE SCHOOL PARTY!
3

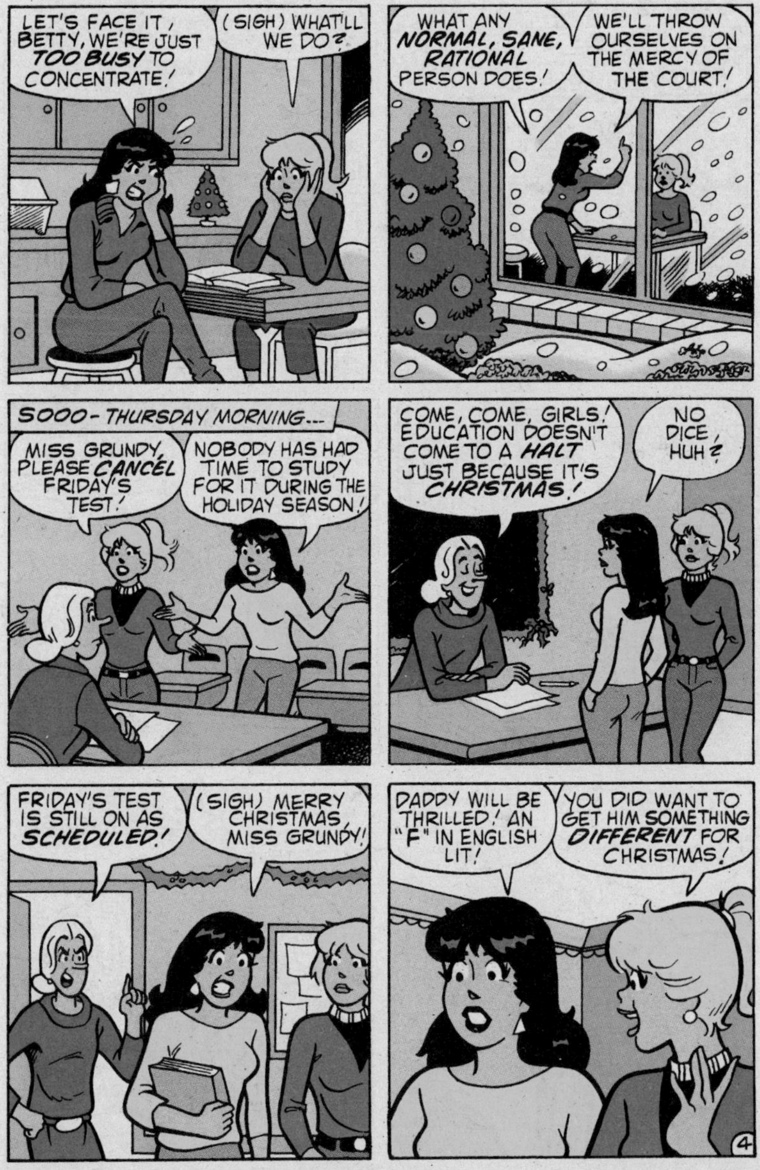
LET'S FACE IT, BETTY, WE'RE JUST TOO BUSY TO CONCENTRATE!
(SIGH) WHAT'LL WE DO?
WHAT ANY NORMAL, SANE, RATIONAL PERSON DOES!
WE'LL THROW OURSELVES ON THE MERCY OF THE COURT!
SOOO- THURSDAY MORNING...
MISS GRUNDY, PLEASE CANCEL FRIDAY'S TEST!
NOBODY HAS HAD TIME TO STUDY FOR IT DURING THE HOLIDAY SEASON!
COME, COME, GIRLS! EDUCATION DOESN'T COME TO A HALT JUST BECAUSE IT'S CHRISTMAS!
NO DICE, HUH?
FRIDAY'S TEST IS STILL ON AS SCHEDULED!
(SIGH) MERRY CHRISTMAS, MISS GRUNDY!
DADDY WILL BE THRILLED! AN "F" IN ENGLISH LIT!
YOU DID WANT TO GET HIM SOMETHING DIFFERENT FOR CHRISTMAS!
4

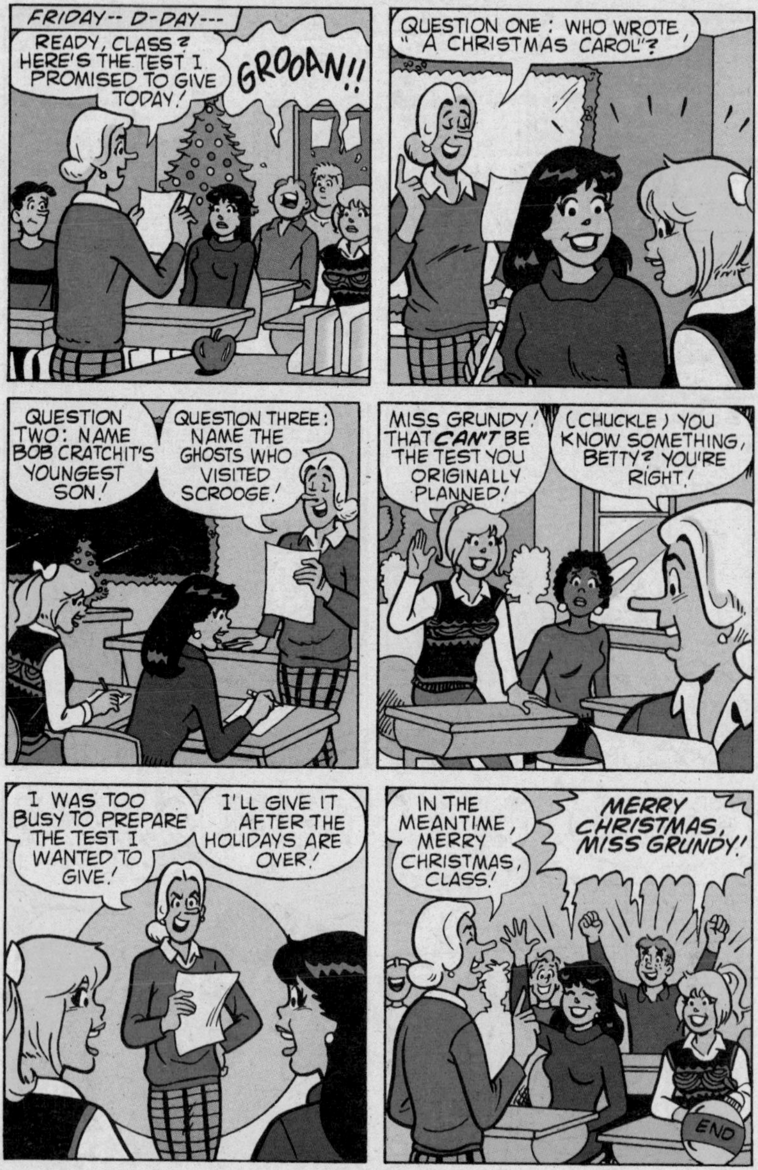
FRIDAY-- D-DAY---
READY, CLASS? HERE'S THE TEST I PROMISED TO GIVE TODAY!
GROOAN!!
QUESTION ONE: WHO WROTE, "A CHRISTMAS CAROL"?
QUESTION TWO: NAME BOB CRATCHIT'S YOUNGEST SON!
QUESTION THREE: NAME THE GHOSTS WHO VISITED SCROOGE!
MISS GRUNDY! THAT CAN'T BE THE TEST YOU ORIGINALLY PLANNED!
(CHUCKLE) YOU KNOW SOMETHING, BETTY? YOU'RE RIGHT!
I WAS TOO BUSY TO PREPARE THE TEST I WANTED TO GIVE!
I'LL GIVE IT AFTER THE HOLIDAYS ARE OVER!
IN THE MEANTIME, MERRY CHRISTMAS, CLASS!
MERRY CHRISTMAS, MISS GRUNDY!
END

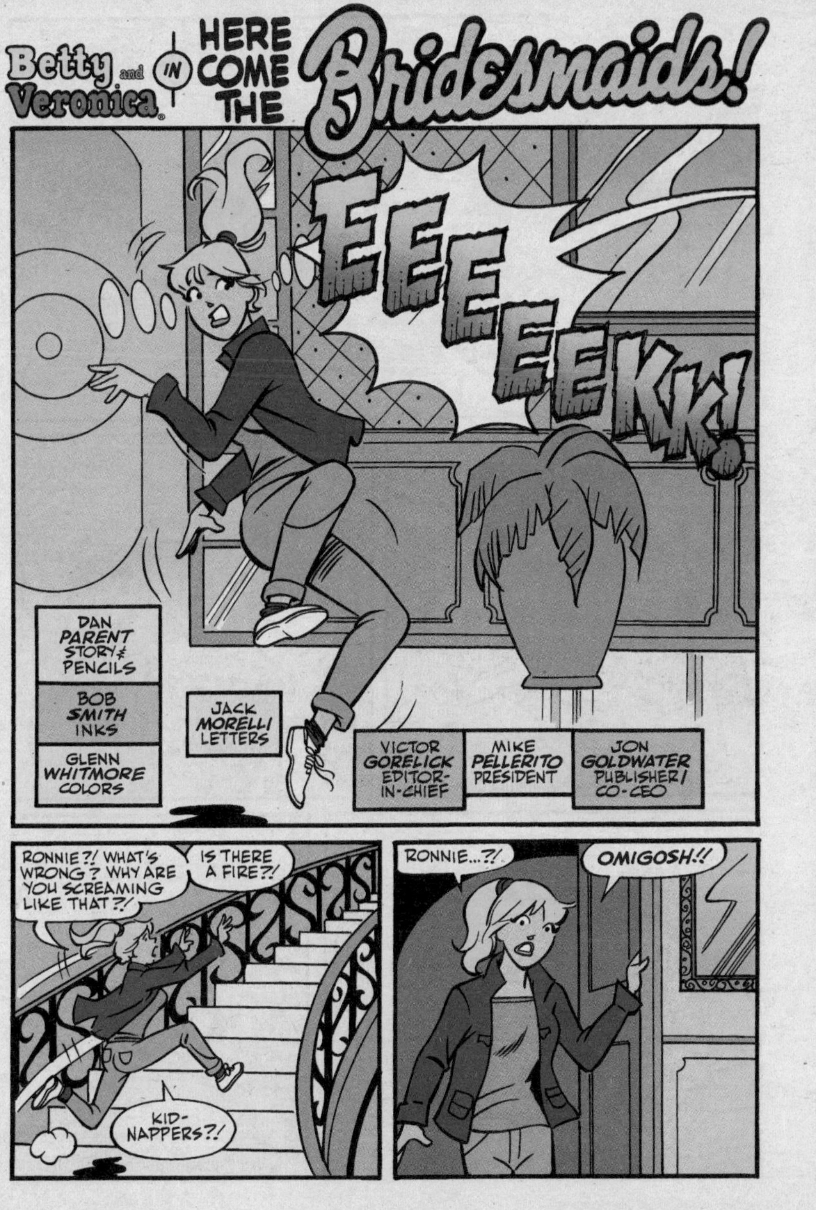
Betty and Veronica IN HERE COME THE Bridesmaids!
EEEEEKK!
DAN PARENT STORY & PENCILS
BOB SMITH INKS
GLENN WHITMORE COLORS
JACK MORELLI LETTERS
VICTOR GORELICK EDITOR-IN-CHIEF
MIKE PELLERITO PRESIDENT
JON GOLDWATER PUBLISHER/ CO-CEO
RONNIE?! WHAT'S WRONG? WHY ARE YOU SCREAMING LIKE THAT?!
IS THERE A FIRE?!
KID-NAPPERS?!
RONNIE...?!
OMIGOSH!!

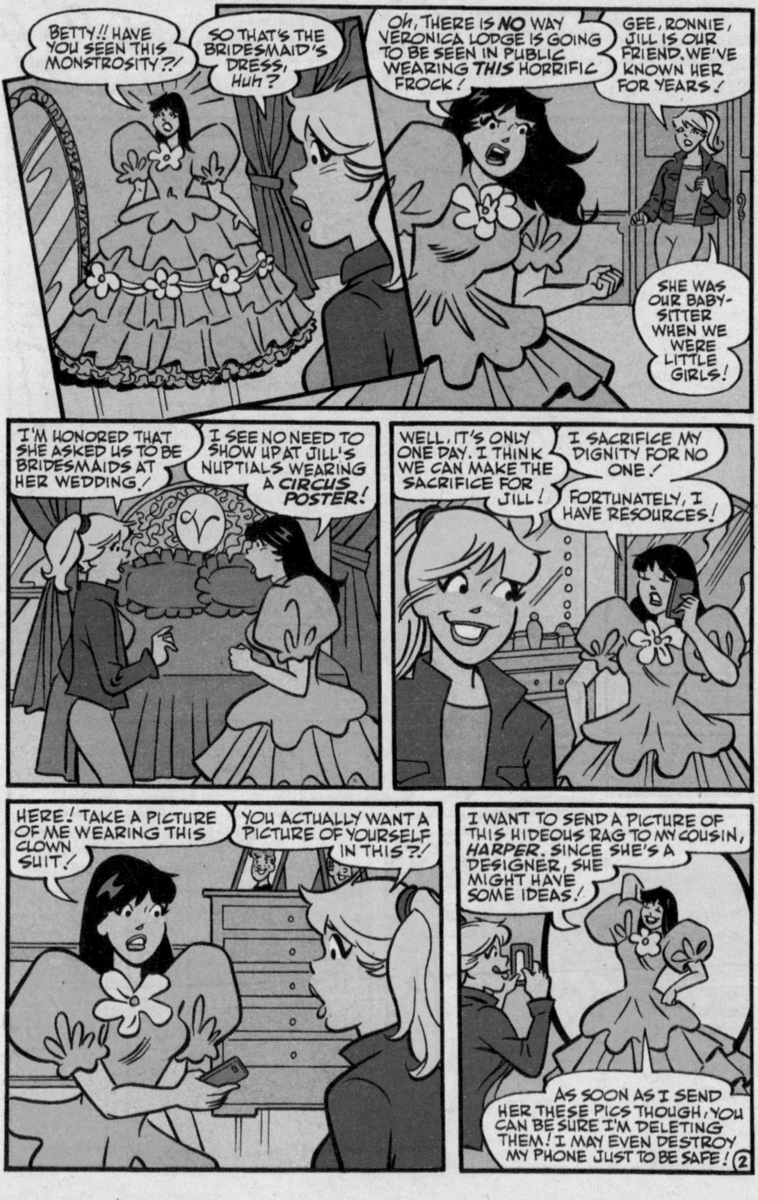
BETTY!! HAVE YOU SEEN THIS MONSTROSITY?!
SO THAT'S THE BRIDESMAID'S DRESS, HUH?
OH, THERE IS NO WAY VERONICA LODGE IS GOING TO BE SEEN IN PUBLIC WEARING THIS HORRIFIC FROCK!
GEE, RONNIE, JILL IS OUR FRIEND. WE'VE KNOWN HER FOR YEARS!
SHE WAS OUR BABY-SITTER WHEN WE WERE LITTLE GIRLS!
I'M HONORED THAT SHE ASKED US TO BE BRIDESMAIDS AT HER WEDDING!
I SEE NO NEED TO SHOW UP AT JILL'S NUPTIALS WEARING A CIRCUS POSTER!
WELL, IT'S ONLY ONE DAY. I THINK WE CAN MAKE THE SACRIFICE FOR JILL!
I SACRIFICE MY DIGNITY FOR NO ONE!
FORTUNATELY, I HAVE RESOURCES!
HERE! TAKE A PICTURE OF ME WEARING THIS CLOWN SUIT!
YOU ACTUALLY WANT A PICTURE OF YOURSELF IN THIS?!
I WANT TO SEND A PICTURE OF THIS HIDEOUS RAG TO MY COUSIN, HARPER. SINCE SHE'S A DESIGNER, SHE MIGHT HAVE SOME IDEAS!
AS SOON AS I SEND HER THESE PICS THOUGH, YOU CAN BE SURE I'M DELETING THEM! I MAY EVEN DESTROY MY PHONE JUST TO BE SAFE!
2

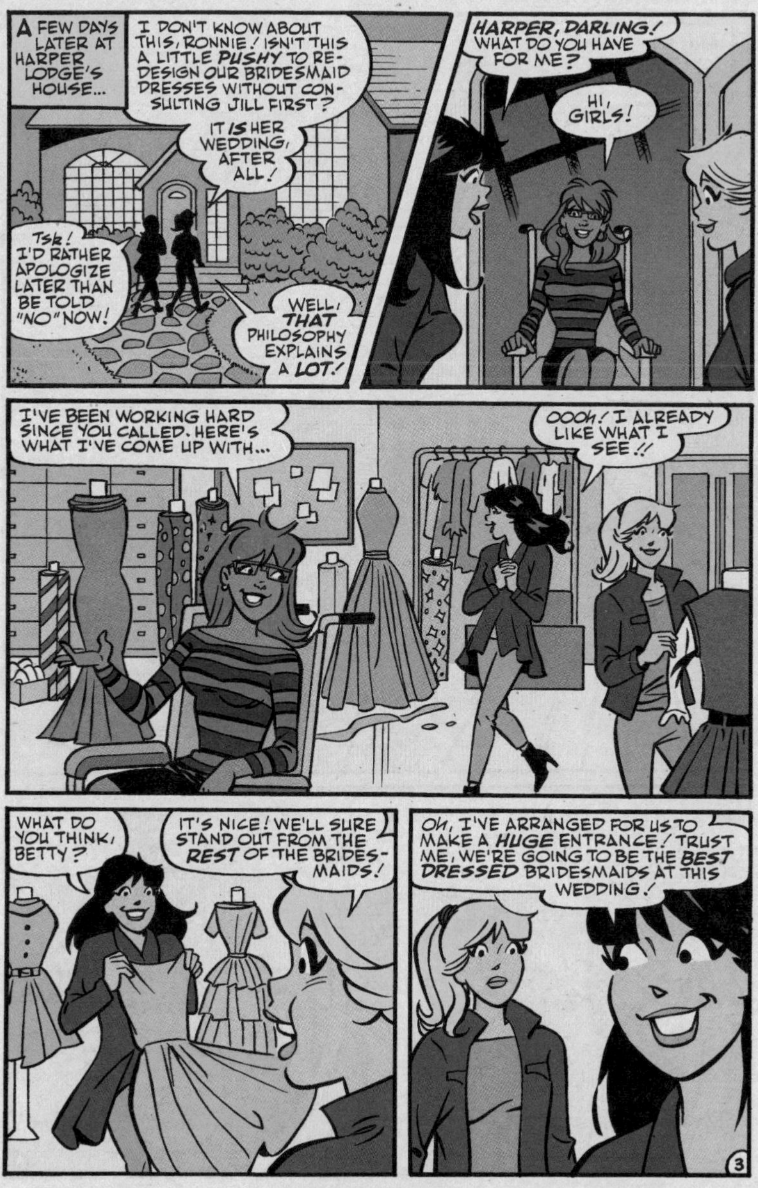
A FEW DAYS LATER AT HARPER LODGE'S HOUSE...
I DON'T KNOW ABOUT THIS, RONNIE! ISN'T THIS A LITTLE PUSHY TO RE-DESIGN OUR BRIDESMAID DRESSES WITHOUT CON-SULTING JILL FIRST?
IT IS HER WEDDING, AFTER ALL!
Tsk! I'D RATHER APOLOGIZE LATER THAN BE TOLD "NO" NOW!
WELL, THAT PHILOSOPHY EXPLAINS A LOT!
HARPER, DARLING! WHAT DO YOU HAVE FOR ME?
HI, GIRLS!
I'VE BEEN WORKING HARD SINCE YOU CALLED. HERE'S WHAT I'VE COME UP WITH...
OOOh! I ALREADY LIKE WHAT I SEE!!
WHAT DO YOU THINK, BETTY?
IT'S NICE! WE'LL SURE STAND OUT FROM THE REST OF THE BRIDES-MAIDS!
Oh, I'VE ARRANGED FOR US TO MAKE A HUGE ENTRANCE! TRUST ME, WE'RE GOING TO BE THE BEST DRESSED BRIDESMAIDS AT THIS WEDDING!
3

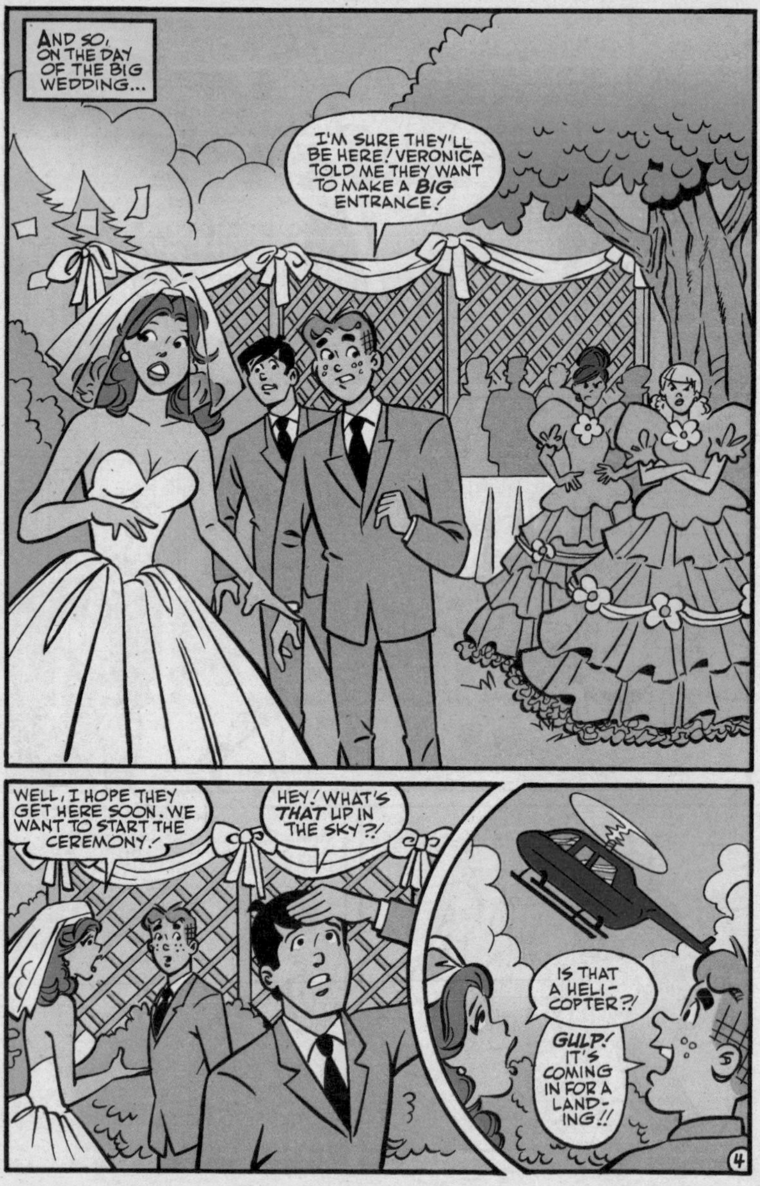
AND SO, ON THE DAY OF THE BIG WEDDING...
I'M SURE THEY'LL BE HERE! VERONICA TOLD ME THEY WANT TO MAKE A BIG ENTRANCE!
WELL, I HOPE THEY GET HERE SOON. WE WANT TO START THE CEREMONY!
HEY! WHAT'S THAT UP IN THE SKY?!
IS THAT A HELI-COPTER?!
GULP! IT'S COMING IN FOR A LAND-ING!!
4

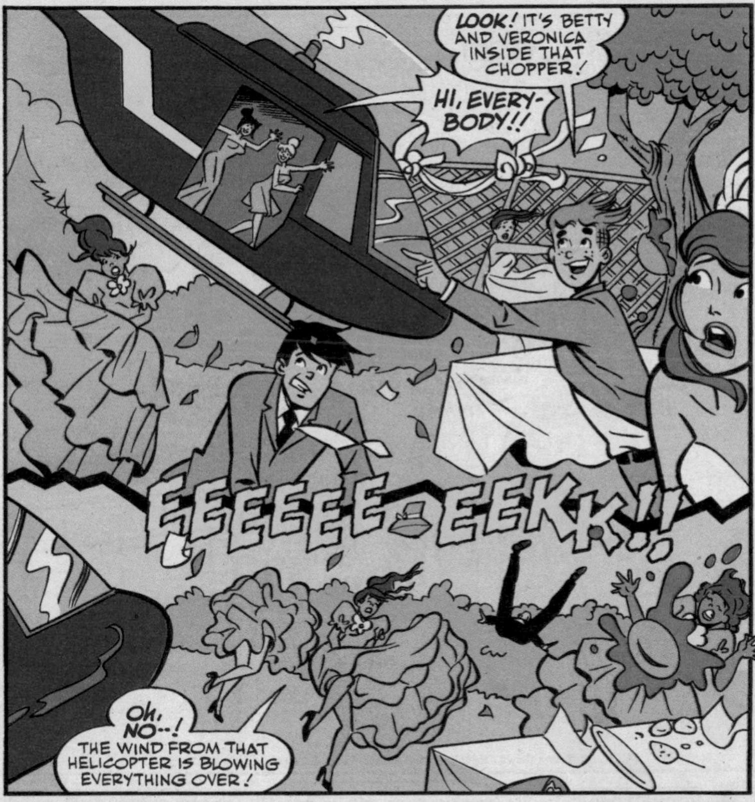
LOOK! IT'S BETTY AND VERONICA INSIDE THAT CHOPPER!
HI, EVERY-BODY!!
EEEEEE-EEKK!!
Oh, NO--! THE WIND FROM THAT HELICOPTER IS BLOWING EVERYTHING OVER!
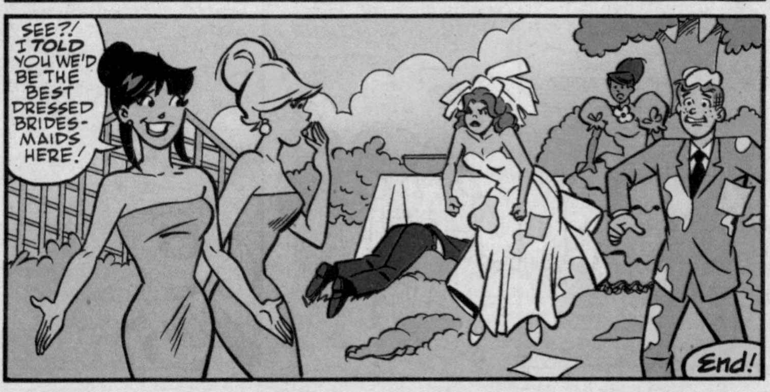
SEE?! I TOLD YOU WE'D BE THE BEST DRESSED BRIDES-MAIDS HERE!
End!

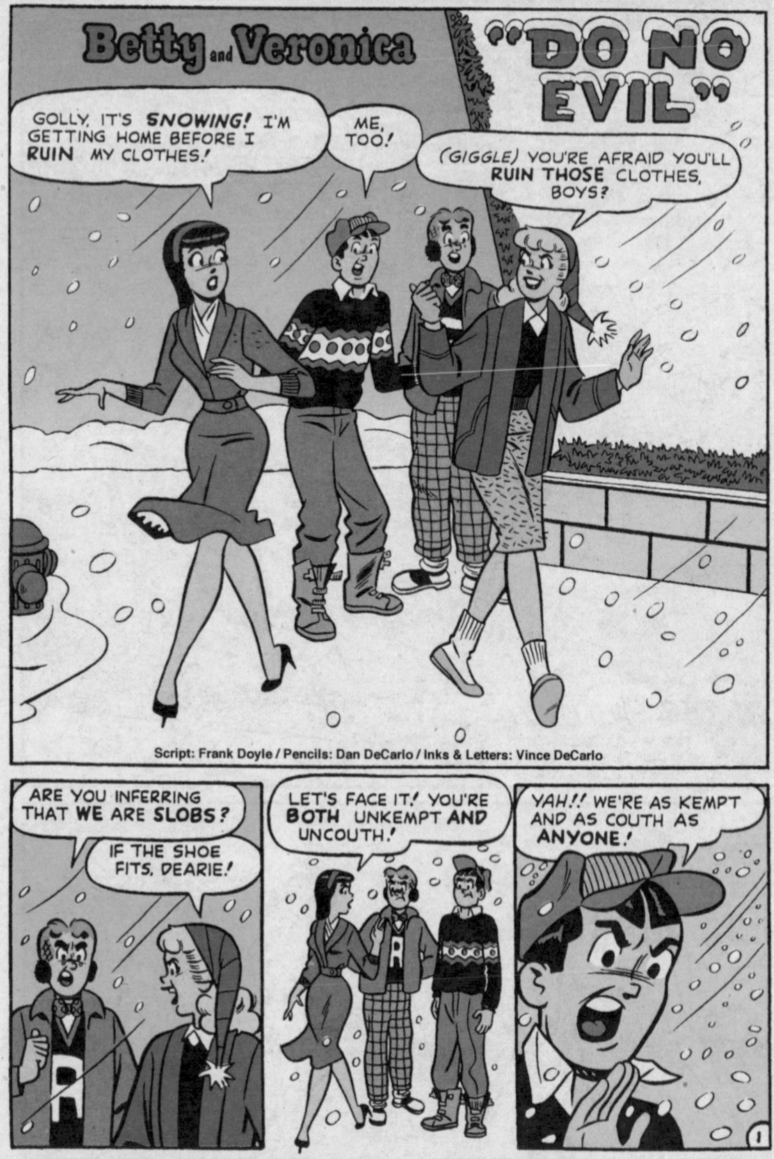
Betty and Veronica
"DO NO EVIL"
GOLLY, IT'S SNOWING! I'M GETTING HOME BEFORE I RUIN MY CLOTHES!
ME, TOO!
(GIGGLE) YOU'RE AFRAID YOU'LL RUIN THOSE CLOTHES, BOYS?
Script: Frank Doyle / Pencils: Dan DeCarlo / Inks & Letters: Vince DeCarlo
ARE YOU INFERRING THAT WE ARE SLOBS?
IF THE SHOE FITS, DEARIE!
LET'S FACE IT! YOU'RE BOTH UNKEMPT AND UNCOUTH!
YAH!! WE'RE AS KEMPT AND AS COUTH AS ANYONE!
1

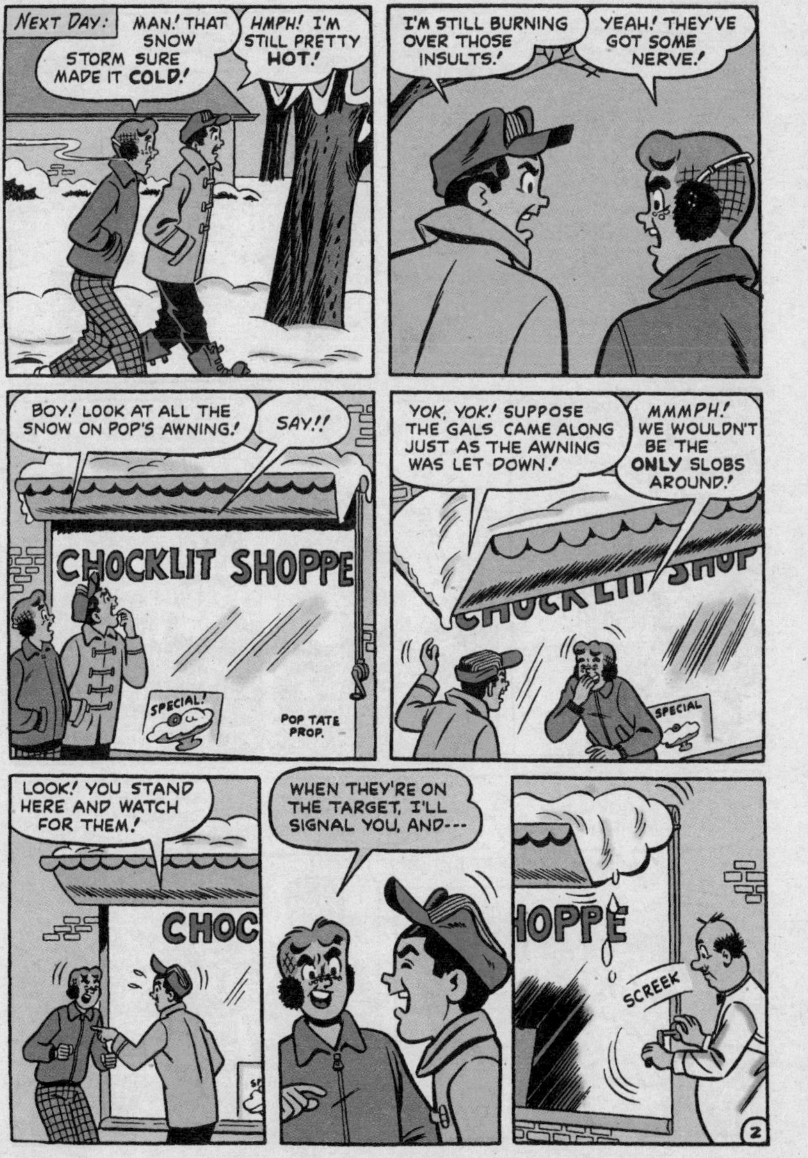
NEXT DAY:
MAN! THAT SNOW STORM SURE MADE IT COLD!
HMPH! I'M STILL PRETTY HOT!
I'M STILL BURNING OVER THOSE INSULTS!
YEAH! THEY'VE GOT SOME NERVE!
BOY! LOOK AT ALL THE SNOW ON POP'S AWNING!
SAY!!
CHOCKLIT SHOPPE
SPECIAL!
POP TATE PROP.
YOK, YOK! SUPPOSE THE GALS CAME ALONG JUST AS THE AWNING WAS LET DOWN!
MMMPH! WE WOULDN'T BE THE ONLY SLOBS AROUND!
SPECIAL
LOOK! YOU STAND HERE AND WATCH FOR THEM!
CHOC
WHEN THEY'RE ON THE TARGET, I'LL SIGNAL YOU, AND---
HOPPE
SCREEK
2

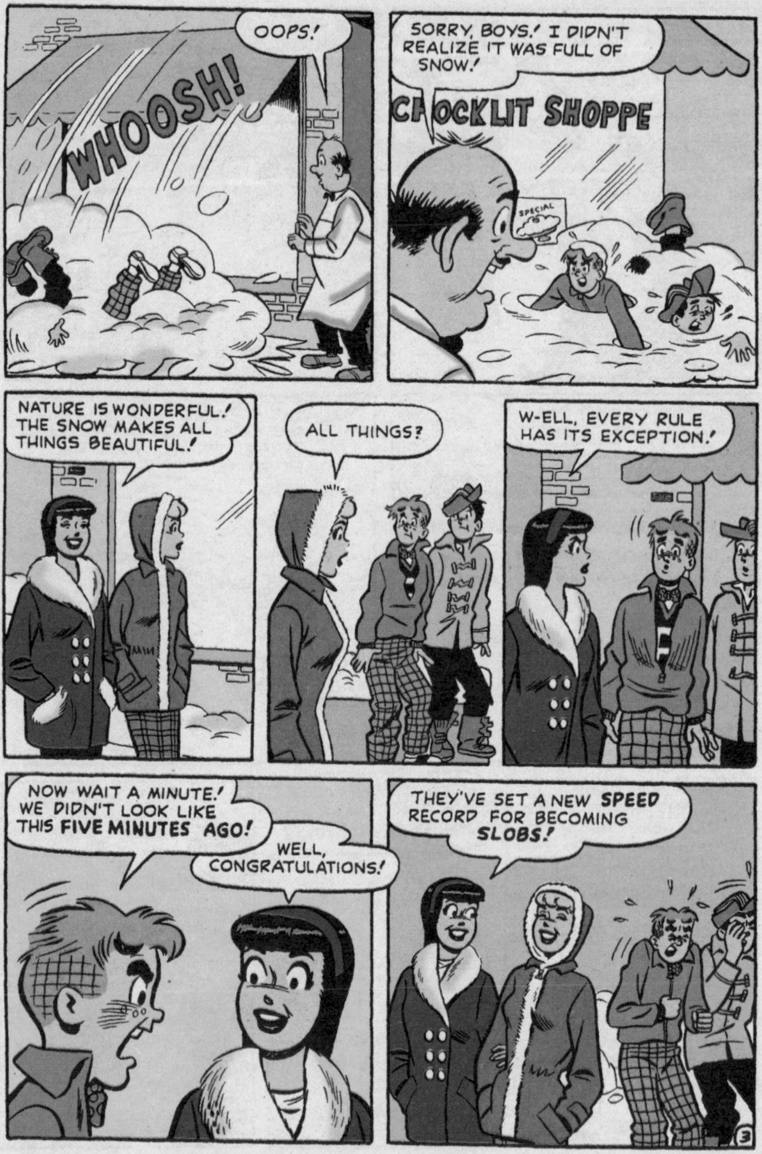

WHOOSH!
OOPS!
SORRY, BOYS.! I DIDN'T REALIZE IT WAS FULL OF SNOW.!
CHOCKLIT SHOPPE
SPECIAL
NATURE IS WONDERFUL.! THE SNOW MAKES ALL THINGS BEAUTIFUL.!
ALL THINGS?
W-ELL, EVERY RULE HAS ITS EXCEPTION.!
NOW WAIT A MINUTE.! WE DIDN'T LOOK LIKE THIS FIVE MINUTES AGO!
WELL, CONGRATULATIONS!
THEY'VE SET A NEW SPEED RECORD FOR BECOMING SLOBS.!
3

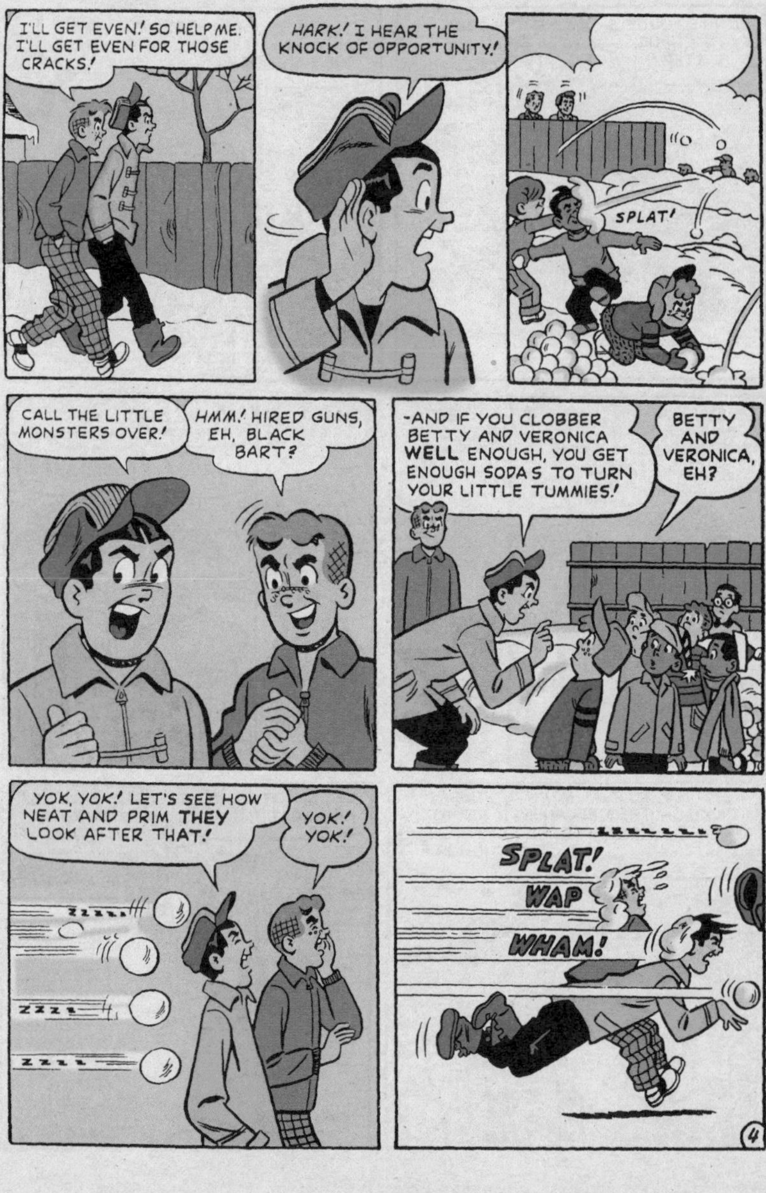

I'LL GET EVEN! SO HELP ME. I'LL GET EVEN FOR THOSE CRACKS!
HARK! I HEAR THE KNOCK OF OPPORTUNITY!
SPLAT!
CALL THE LITTLE MONSTERS OVER!
HMM! HIRED GUNS, EH, BLACK BART?
-AND IF YOU CLOBBER BETTY AND VERONICA WELL ENOUGH, YOU GET ENOUGH SODAS TO TURN YOUR LITTLE TUMMIES!
BETTY AND VERONICA, EH?
YOK, YOK! LET'S SEE HOW NEAT AND PRIM THEY LOOK AFTER THAT!
YOK! YOK!
SPLAT!
WAP
WHAM!
4

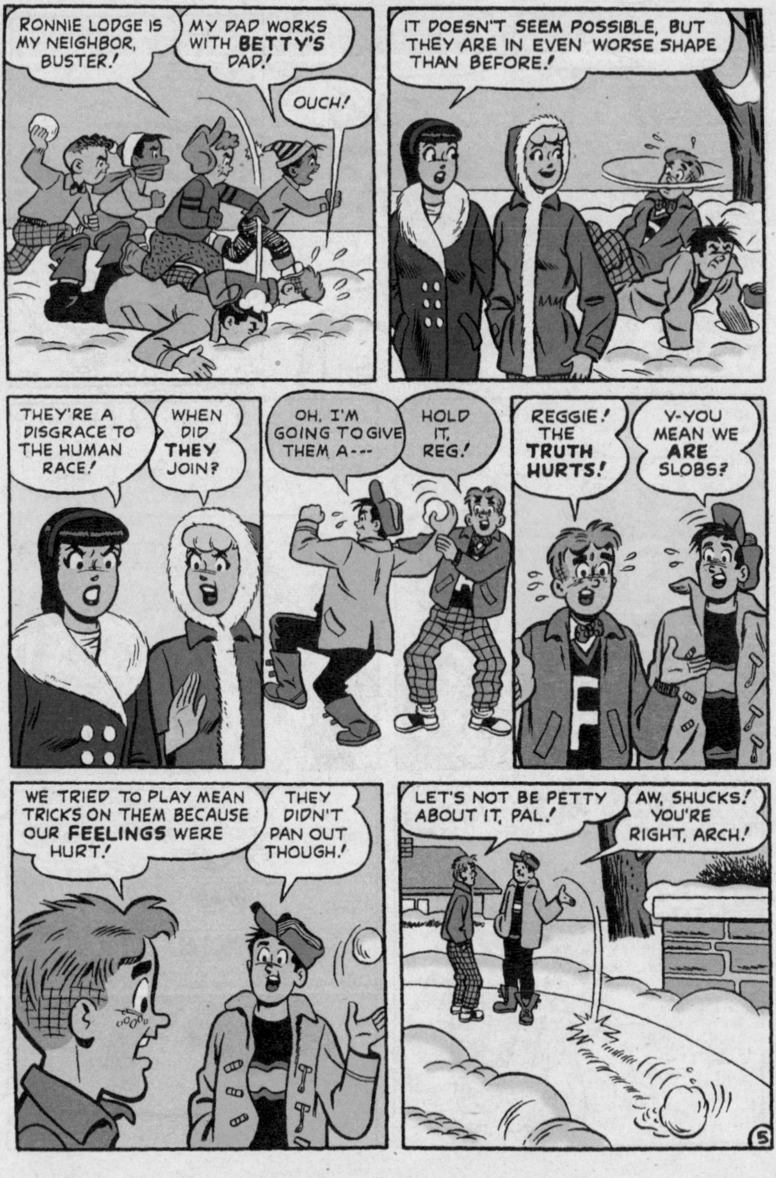
RONNIE LODGE IS MY NEIGHBOR, BUSTER!
MY DAD WORKS WITH BETTY'S DAD!
OUCH!
IT DOESN'T SEEM POSSIBLE, BUT THEY ARE IN EVEN WORSE SHAPE THAN BEFORE!
THEY'RE A DISGRACE TO THE HUMAN RACE!
WHEN DID THEY JOIN?
OH, I'M GOING TO GIVE THEM A---
HOLD IT, REG!
REGGIE! THE TRUTH HURTS!
Y-YOU MEAN WE ARE SLOBS?
WE TRIED TO PLAY MEAN TRICKS ON THEM BECAUSE OUR FEELINGS WERE HURT!
THEY DIDN'T PAN OUT THOUGH!
LET'S NOT BE PETTY ABOUT IT, PAL!
AW, SHUCKS! YOU'RE RIGHT, ARCH!
5

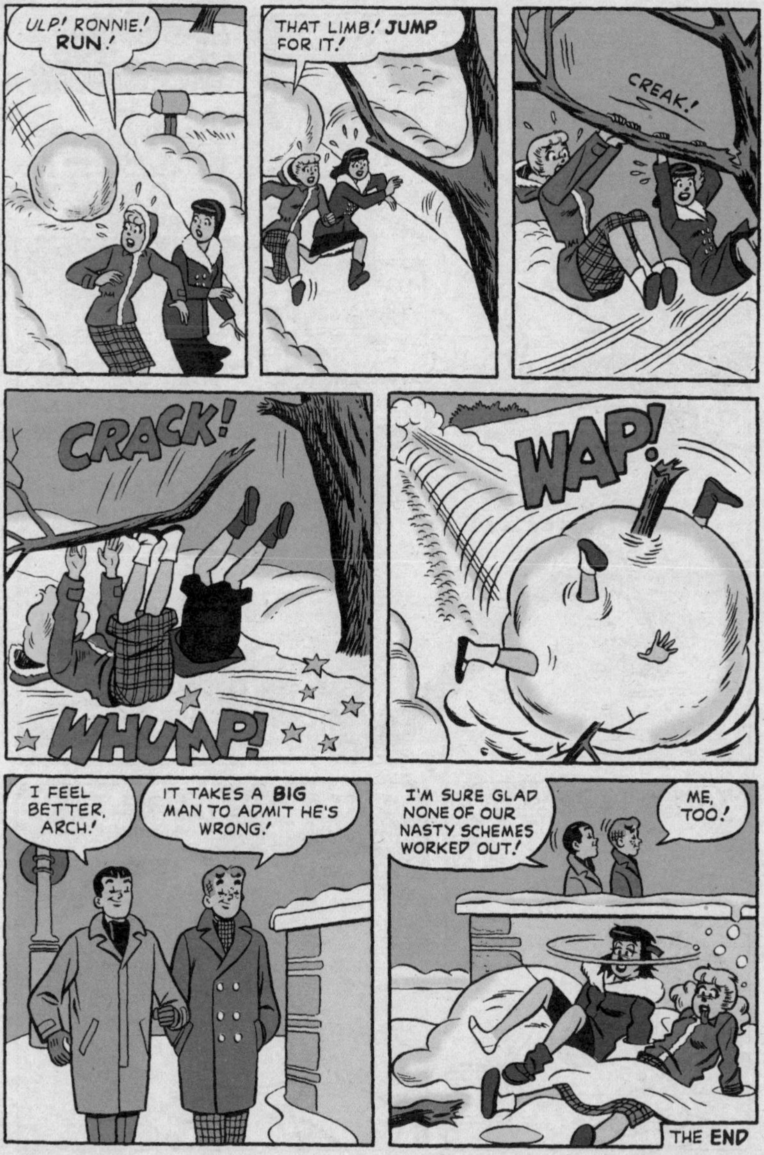
ULP! RONNIE! RUN!
THAT LIMB! JUMP FOR IT!
CREAK!
CRACK!
WHUMP!
WAP!
I FEEL BETTER, ARCH!
IT TAKES A BIG MAN TO ADMIT HE'S WRONG!
I'M SURE GLAD NONE OF OUR NASTY SCHEMES WORKED OUT!
ME, TOO!
THE END

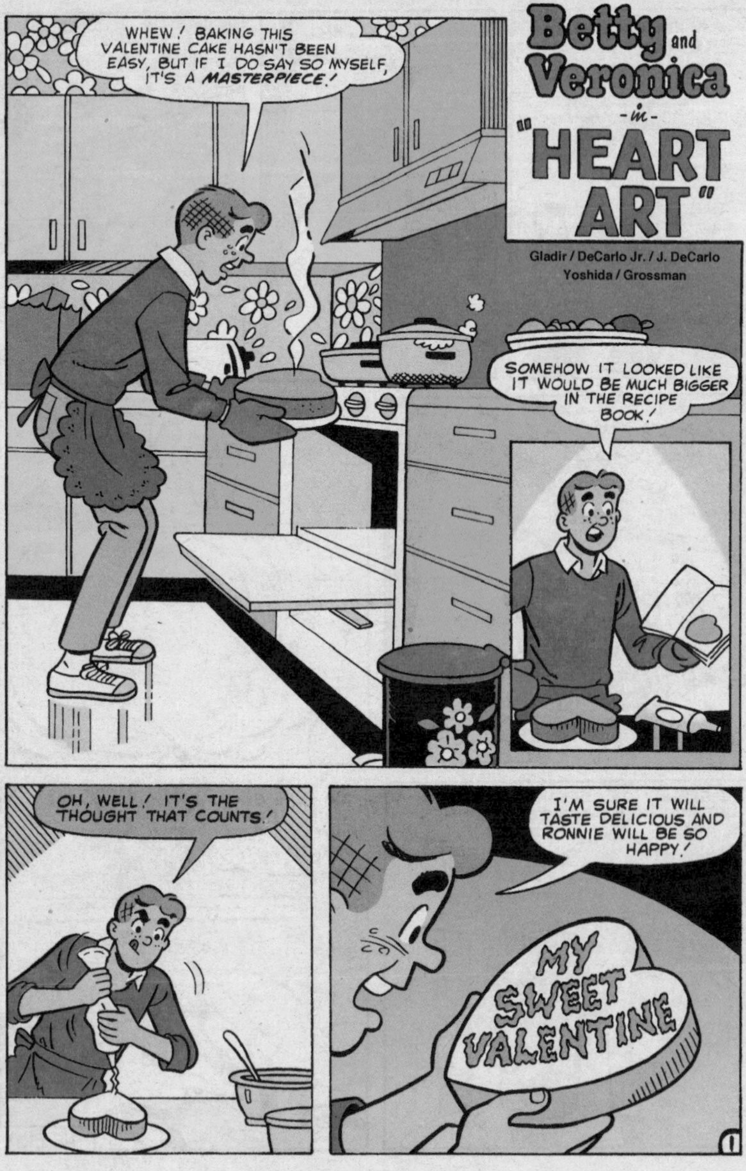
Betty and Veronica
-in-
"HEART ART"
Gladir / DeCarlo Jr. / J. DeCarlo
Yoshida / Grossman
WHEW! BAKING THIS VALENTINE CAKE HASN'T BEEN EASY, BUT IF I DO SAY SO MYSELF, IT'S A MASTERPIECE!
SOMEHOW IT LOOKED LIKE IT WOULD BE MUCH BIGGER IN THE RECIPE BOOK!
OH, WELL! IT'S THE THOUGHT THAT COUNTS!
I'M SURE IT WILL TASTE DELICIOUS AND RONNIE WILL BE SO HAPPY!
MY SWEET VALENTINE
1

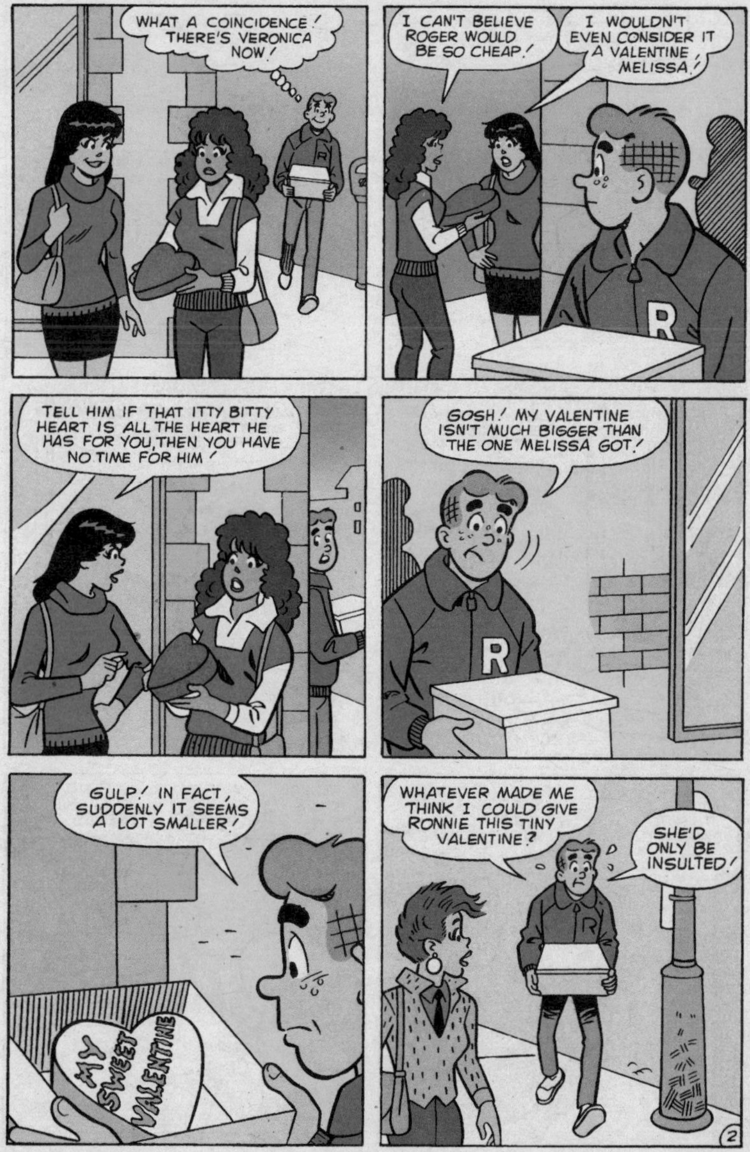
WHAT A COINCIDENCE! THERE'S VERONICA NOW!
I CAN'T BELIEVE ROGER WOULD BE SO CHEAP!
I WOULDN'T EVEN CONSIDER IT A VALENTINE, MELISSA!
TELL HIM IF THAT ITTY BITTY HEART IS ALL THE HEART HE HAS FOR YOU, THEN YOU HAVE NO TIME FOR HIM!
GOSH! MY VALENTINE ISN'T MUCH BIGGER THAN THE ONE MELISSA GOT!
GULP! IN FACT, SUDDENLY IT SEEMS A LOT SMALLER!
MY SWEET VALENTINE
WHATEVER MADE ME THINK I COULD GIVE RONNIE THIS TINY VALENTINE?
SHE'D ONLY BE INSULTED!
2

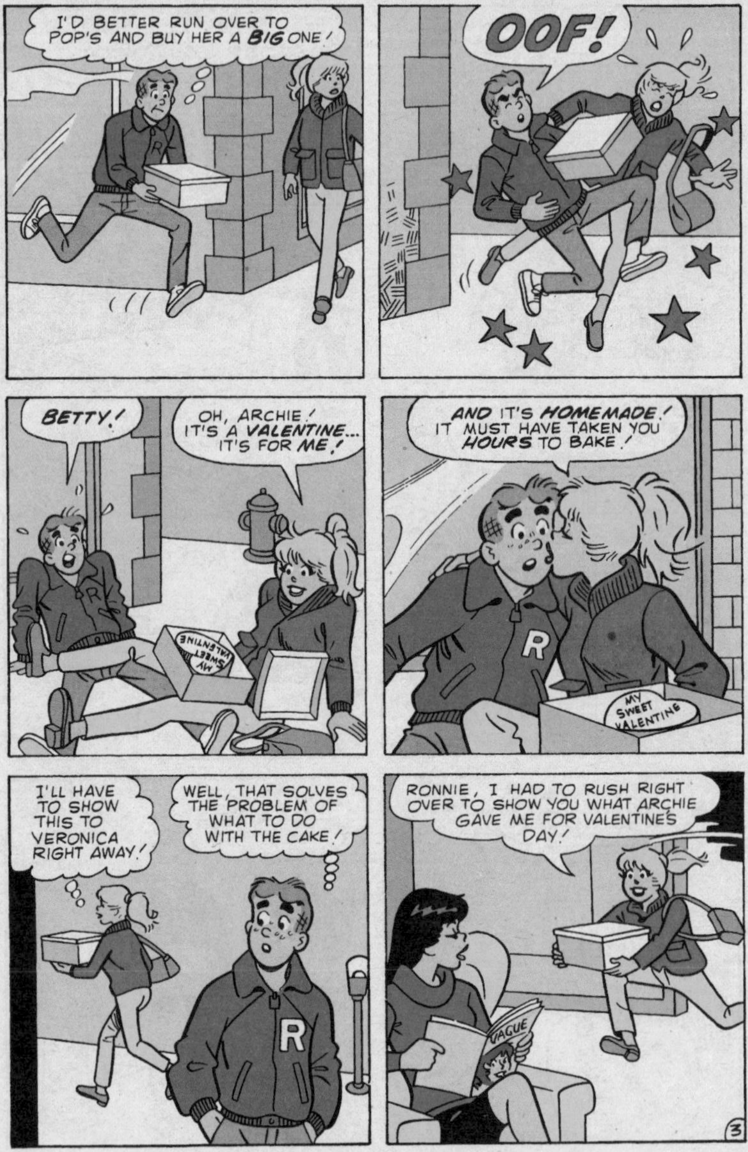

I'D BETTER RUN OVER TO POP'S AND BUY HER A BIG ONE!
OOF!
BETTY!
OH, ARCHIE! IT'S A VALENTINE... IT'S FOR ME!
MY SWEET VALENTINE
AND IT'S HOMEMADE! IT MUST HAVE TAKEN YOU HOURS TO BAKE!
MY SWEET VALENTINE
I'LL HAVE TO SHOW THIS TO VERONICA RIGHT AWAY!
WELL, THAT SOLVES THE PROBLEM OF WHAT TO DO WITH THE CAKE!
RONNIE, I HAD TO RUSH RIGHT OVER TO SHOW YOU WHAT ARCHIE GAVE ME FOR VALENTINE'S DAY!
VAGUE
3

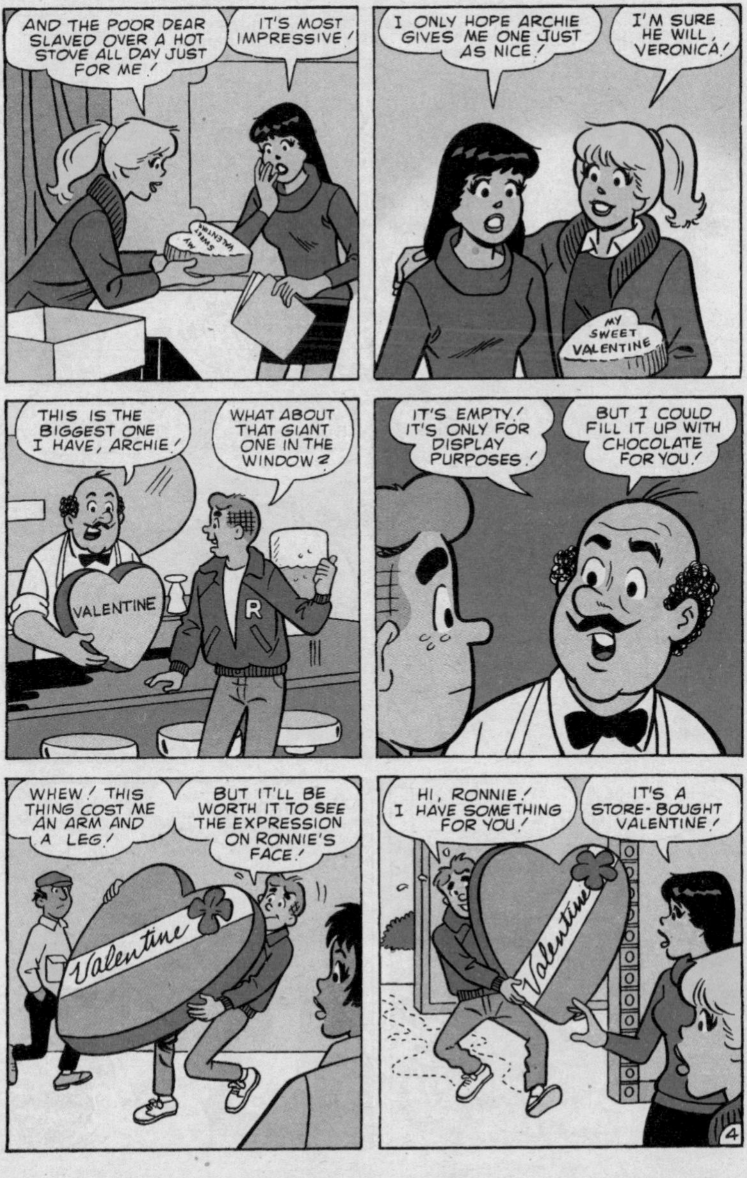
AND THE POOR DEAR SLAVED OVER A HOT STOVE ALL DAY JUST FOR ME!
IT'S MOST IMPRESSIVE!
MY SWEET VALENTINE
I ONLY HOPE ARCHIE GIVES ME ONE JUST AS NICE!
I'M SURE HE WILL, VERONICA!
MY SWEET VALENTINE
THIS IS THE BIGGEST ONE I HAVE, ARCHIE!
WHAT ABOUT THAT GIANT ONE IN THE WINDOW?
VALENTINE
R
IT'S EMPTY! IT'S ONLY FOR DISPLAY PURPOSES!
BUT I COULD FILL IT UP WITH CHOCOLATE FOR YOU!
WHEW! THIS THING COST ME AN ARM AND A LEG!
BUT IT'LL BE WORTH IT TO SEE THE EXPRESSION ON RONNIE'S FACE!
Valentine
HI, RONNIE! I HAVE SOMETHING FOR YOU!
IT'S A STORE-BOUGHT VALENTINE!
Valentine
4

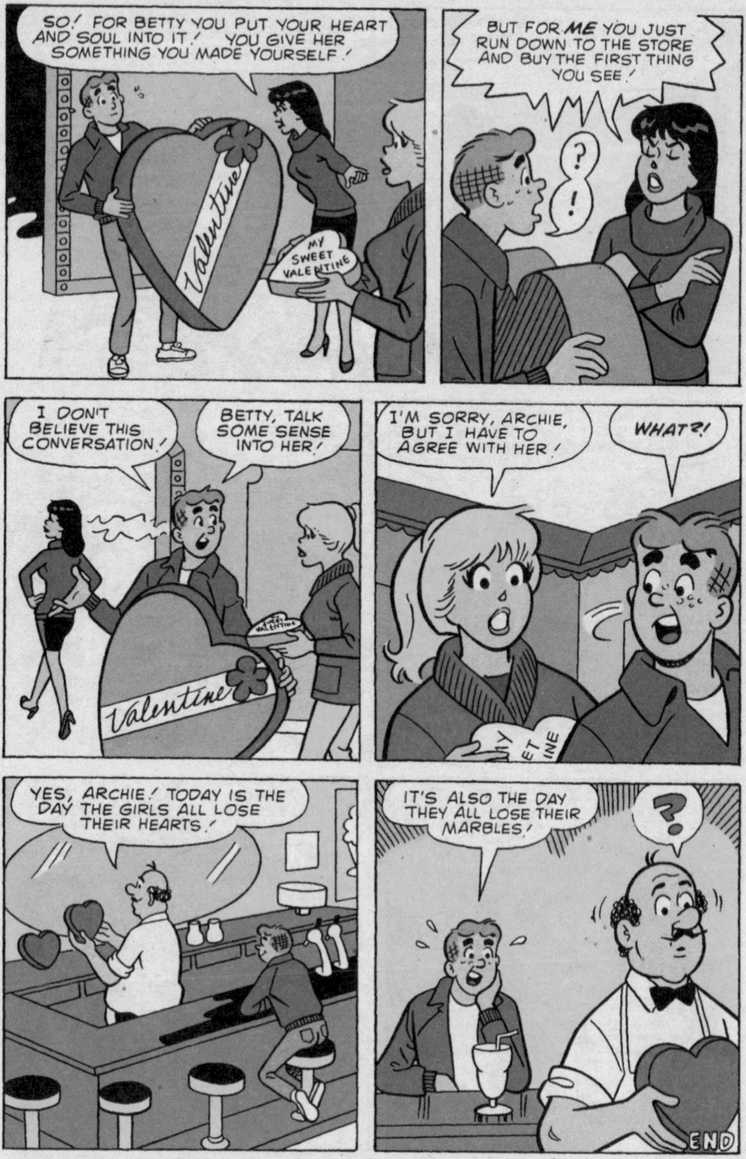
SO! FOR BETTY YOU PUT YOUR HEART AND SOUL INTO IT! YOU GIVE HER SOMETHING YOU MADE YOURSELF!
Valentine
MY SWEET VALENTINE
BUT FOR ME YOU JUST RUN DOWN TO THE STORE AND BUY THE FIRST THING YOU SEE!
?
!
I DON'T BELIEVE THIS CONVERSATION!
BETTY, TALK SOME SENSE INTO HER!
Valentine
I'M SORRY, ARCHIE, BUT I HAVE TO AGREE WITH HER!
WHAT?!
YES, ARCHIE! TODAY IS THE DAY THE GIRLS ALL LOSE THEIR HEARTS!
IT'S ALSO THE DAY THEY ALL LOSE THEIR MARBLES!
?
END

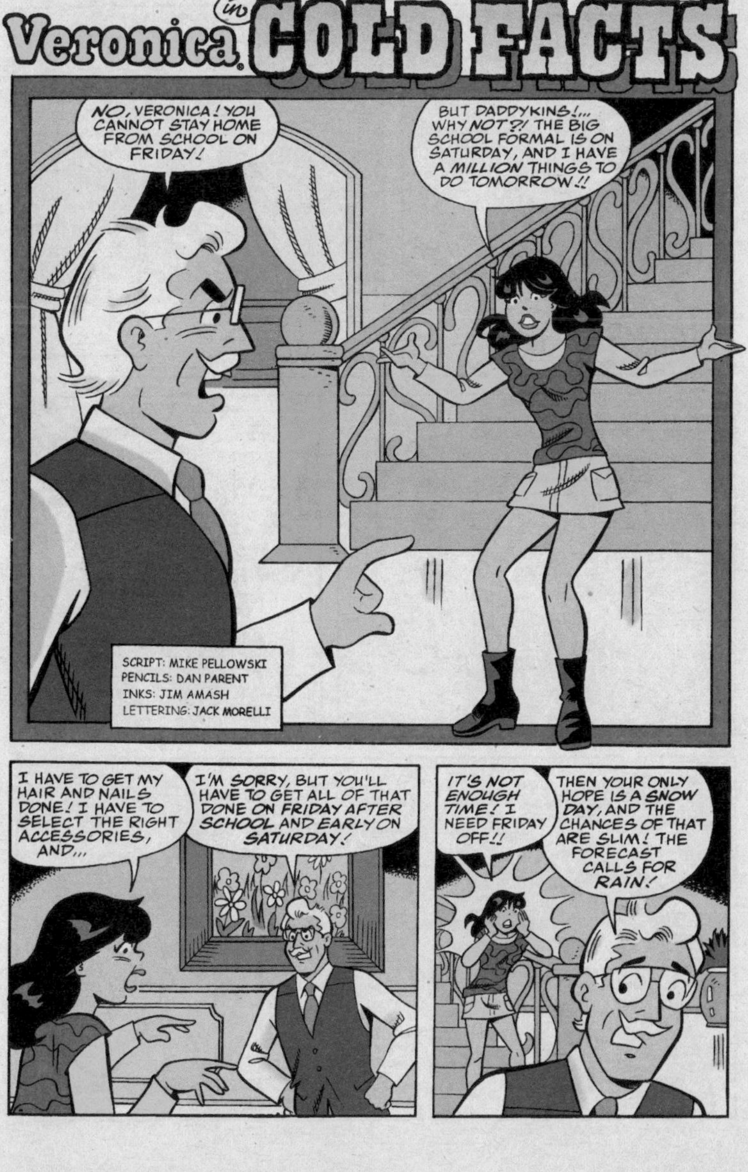
Veronica in COLD FACTS
NO, VERONICA! YOU CANNOT STAY HOME FROM SCHOOL ON FRIDAY!
BUT DADDYKINS!... WHY NOT?! THE BIG SCHOOL FORMAL IS ON SATURDAY, AND I HAVE A MILLION THINGS TO DO TOMORROW!!
SCRIPT: MIKE PELLOWSKI
PENCILS: DAN PARENT
INKS: JIM AMASH
LETTERING: JACK MORELLI
I HAVE TO GET MY HAIR AND NAILS DONE! I HAVE TO SELECT THE RIGHT ACCESSORIES, AND...
I'M SORRY, BUT YOU'LL HAVE TO GET ALL OF THAT DONE ON FRIDAY AFTER SCHOOL AND EARLY ON SATURDAY!
IT'S NOT ENOUGH TIME! I NEED FRIDAY OFF!!
THEN YOUR ONLY HOPE IS A SNOW DAY, AND THE CHANCES OF THAT ARE SLIM! THE FORECAST CALLS FOR RAIN!

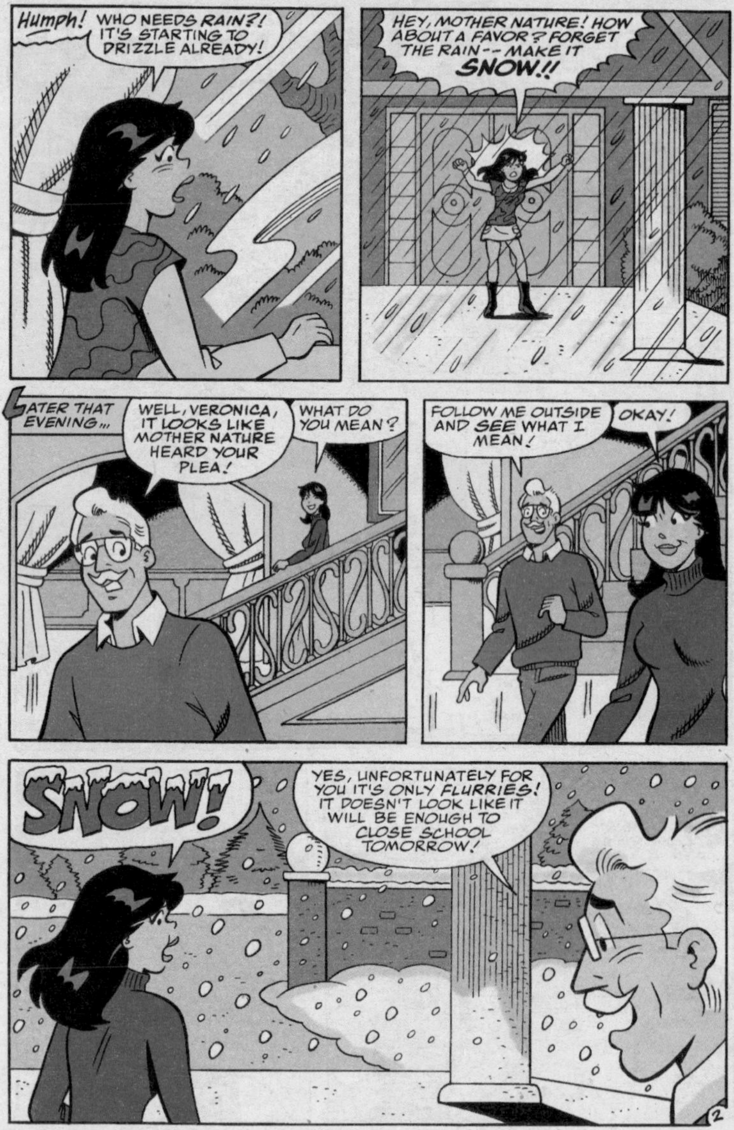
Humph!
WHO NEEDS RAIN?! IT'S STARTING TO DRIZZLE ALREADY!
HEY, MOTHER NATURE! HOW ABOUT A FAVOR? FORGET THE RAIN-- MAKE IT SNOW!!
LATER THAT EVENING...
WELL, VERONICA, IT LOOKS LIKE MOTHER NATURE HEARD YOUR PLEA!
WHAT DO YOU MEAN?
FOLLOW ME OUTSIDE AND SEE WHAT I MEAN!
OKAY!
SNOW!
YES, UNFORTUNATELY FOR YOU IT'S ONLY FLURRIES! IT DOESN'T LOOK LIKE IT WILL BE ENOUGH TO CLOSE SCHOOL TOMORROW!
2

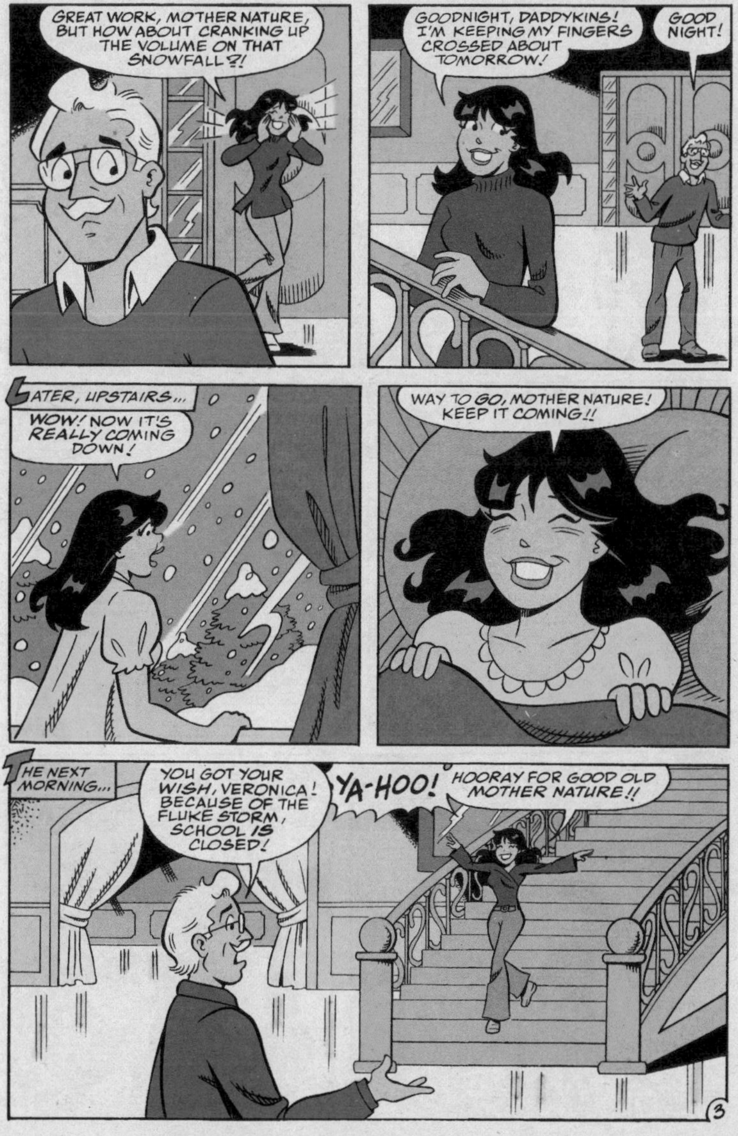
GREAT WORK, MOTHER NATURE, BUT HOW ABOUT CRANKING UP THE VOLUME ON THAT SNOWFALL?!
GOODNIGHT, DADDYKINS! I'M KEEPING MY FINGERS CROSSED ABOUT TOMORROW!
GOOD NIGHT!
LATER, UPSTAIRS...
WOW! NOW IT'S REALLY COMING DOWN!
WAY TO GO, MOTHER NATURE! KEEP IT COMING!!
THE NEXT MORNING...
YOU GOT YOUR WISH, VERONICA! BECAUSE OF THE FLUKE STORM, SCHOOL IS CLOSED!
YA-HOO!
HOORAY FOR GOOD OLD MOTHER NATURE!!
3

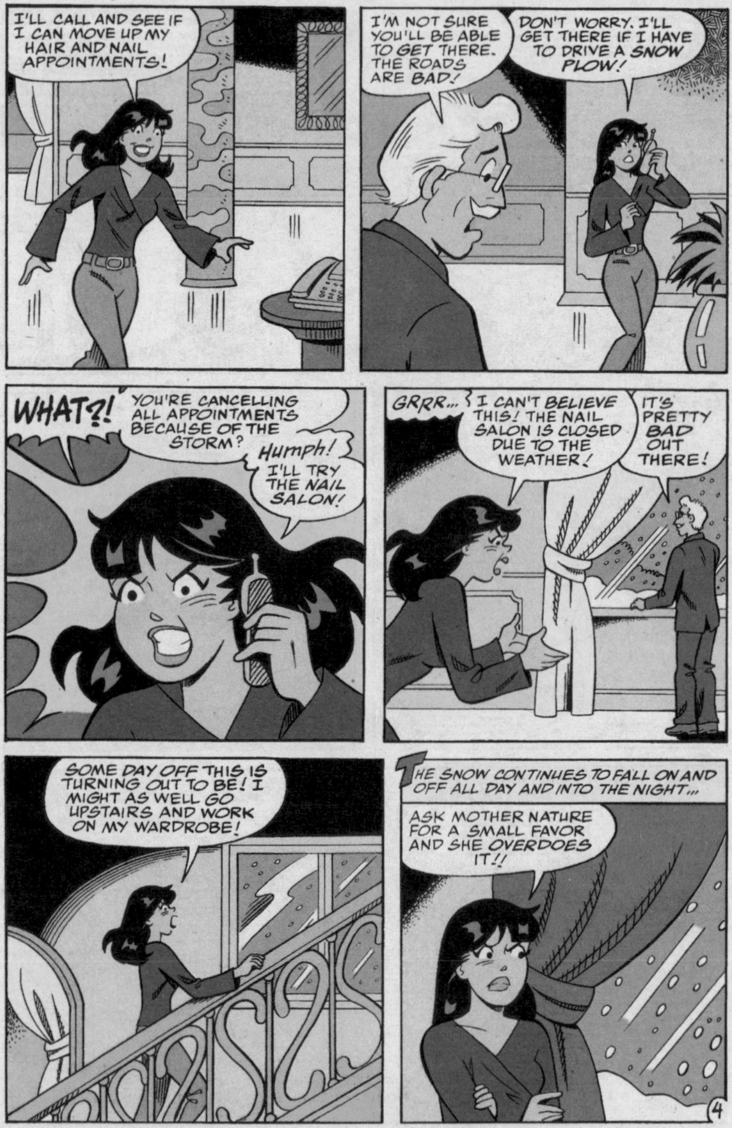
I'LL CALL AND SEE IF I CAN MOVE UP MY HAIR AND NAIL APPOINTMENTS!
I'M NOT SURE YOU'LL BE ABLE TO GET THERE. THE ROADS ARE BAD!
DON'T WORRY. I'LL GET THERE IF I HAVE TO DRIVE A SNOW PLOW!
WHAT?!
YOU'RE CANCELLING ALL APPOINTMENTS BECAUSE OF THE STORM?
Humph! I'LL TRY THE NAIL SALON!
GRRR...
I CAN'T BELIEVE THIS! THE NAIL SALON IS CLOSED DUE TO THE WEATHER!
IT'S PRETTY BAD OUT THERE!
SOME DAY OFF THIS IS TURNING OUT TO BE! I MIGHT AS WELL GO UPSTAIRS AND WORK ON MY WARDROBE!
THE SNOW CONTINUES TO FALL ON AND OFF ALL DAY AND INTO THE NIGHT...
ASK MOTHER NATURE FOR A SMALL FAVOR AND SHE OVERDOES IT!!

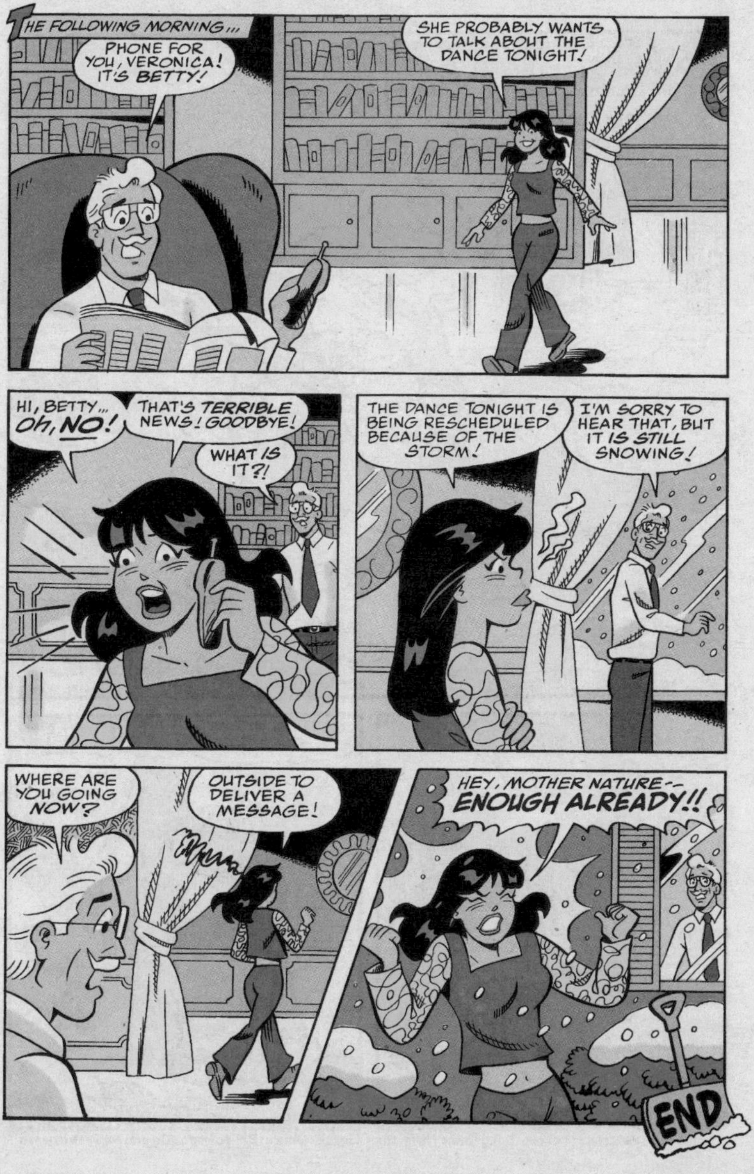
THE FOLLOWING MORNING...
PHONE FOR YOU, VERONICA! IT'S BETTY!
SHE PROBABLY WANTS TO TALK ABOUT THE DANCE TONIGHT!
HI, BETTY... Oh, NO!
THAT'S TERRIBLE NEWS! GOODBYE!
WHAT IS IT?!
THE DANCE TONIGHT IS BEING RESCHEDULED BECAUSE OF THE STORM!
I'M SORRY TO HEAR THAT, BUT IT IS STILL SNOWING!
WHERE ARE YOU GOING NOW?
OUTSIDE TO DELIVER A MESSAGE!
HEY, MOTHER NATURE-- ENOUGH ALREADY!!
END

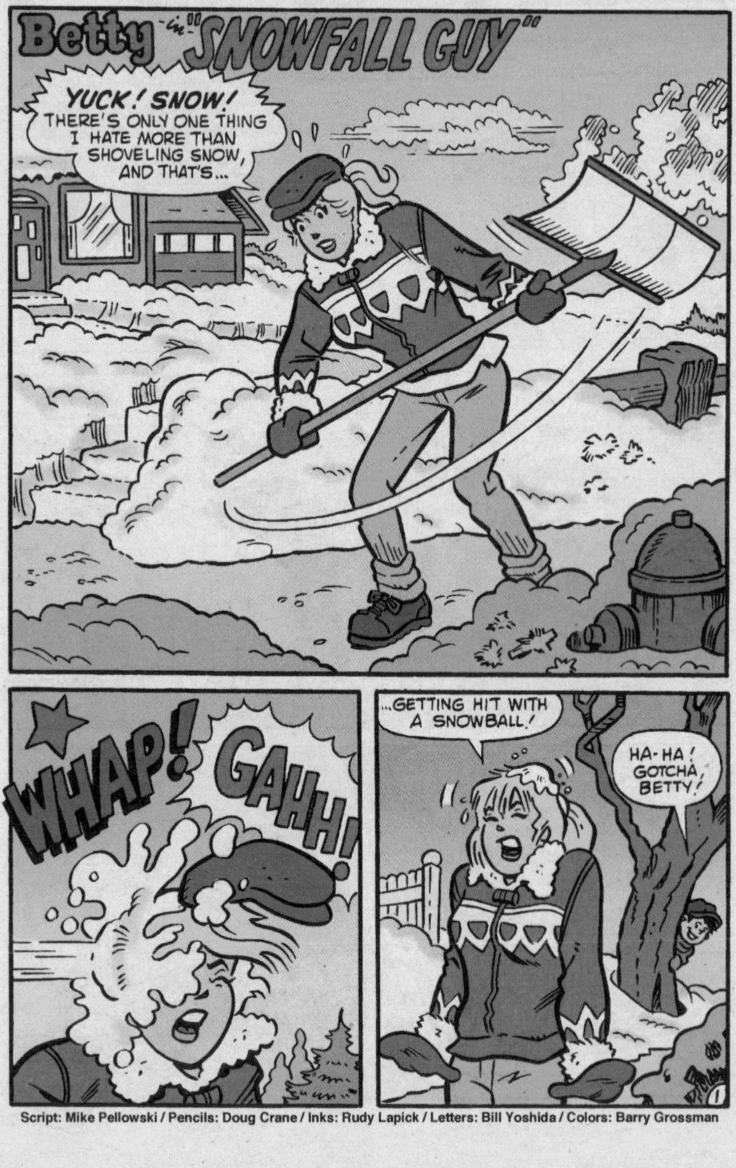
Betty in "SNOWFALL GUY"
YUCK! SNOW! THERE'S ONLY ONE THING I HATE MORE THAN SHOVELING SNOW, AND THAT'S...
WHAP!
GAHH!
...GETTING HIT WITH A SNOWBALL!
HA-HA! GOTCHA, BETTY!

Script: Mike Pellowski / Pencils: Doug Crane / Inks: Rudy Lapick / Letters: Bill Yoshida / Colors: Barry Grossman

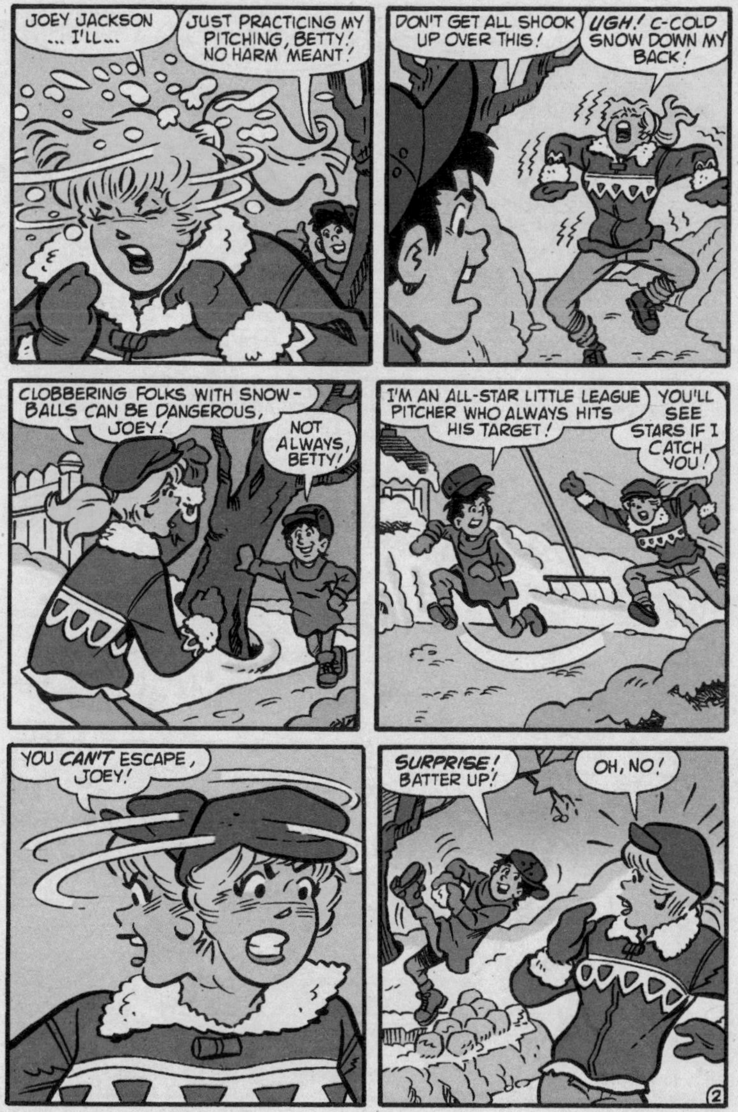
JOEY JACKSON ... I'LL...
JUST PRACTICING MY PITCHING, BETTY! NO HARM MEANT!
DON'T GET ALL SHOOK UP OVER THIS!
UGH! C-COLD SNOW DOWN MY BACK!
CLOBBERING FOLKS WITH SNOW-BALLS CAN BE DANGEROUS, JOEY!
NOT ALWAYS, BETTY!
I'M AN ALL-STAR LITTLE LEAGUE PITCHER WHO ALWAYS HITS HIS TARGET!
YOU'LL SEE STARS IF I CATCH YOU!
YOU CAN'T ESCAPE, JOEY!
SURPRISE! BATTER UP!
OH, NO!
2

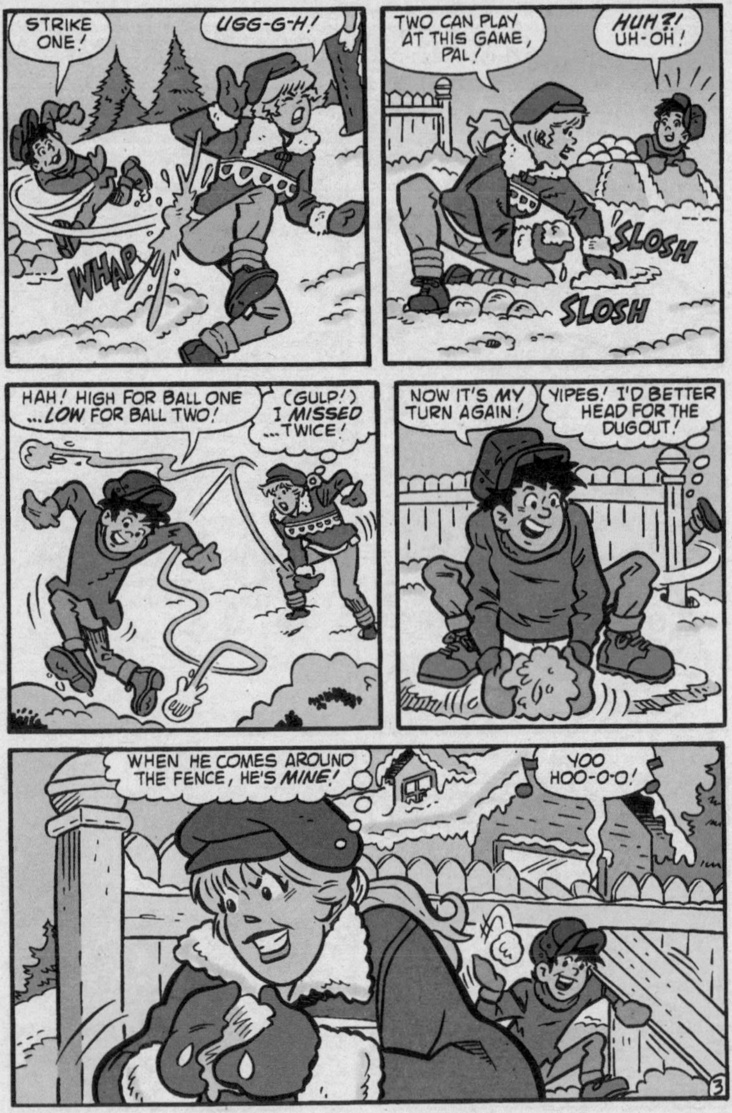
STRIKE ONE!
UGG-G-H!
WHAP
TWO CAN PLAY AT THIS GAME, PAL!
HUH?! UH-OH!
SLOSH
SLOSH
HAH! HIGH FOR BALL ONE ...LOW FOR BALL TWO!
(GULP!) I MISSED ...TWICE!
NOW IT'S MY TURN AGAIN!
YIPES! I'D BETTER HEAD FOR THE DUGOUT!
WHEN HE COMES AROUND THE FENCE, HE'S MINE!
YOO HOO-O-O!
3

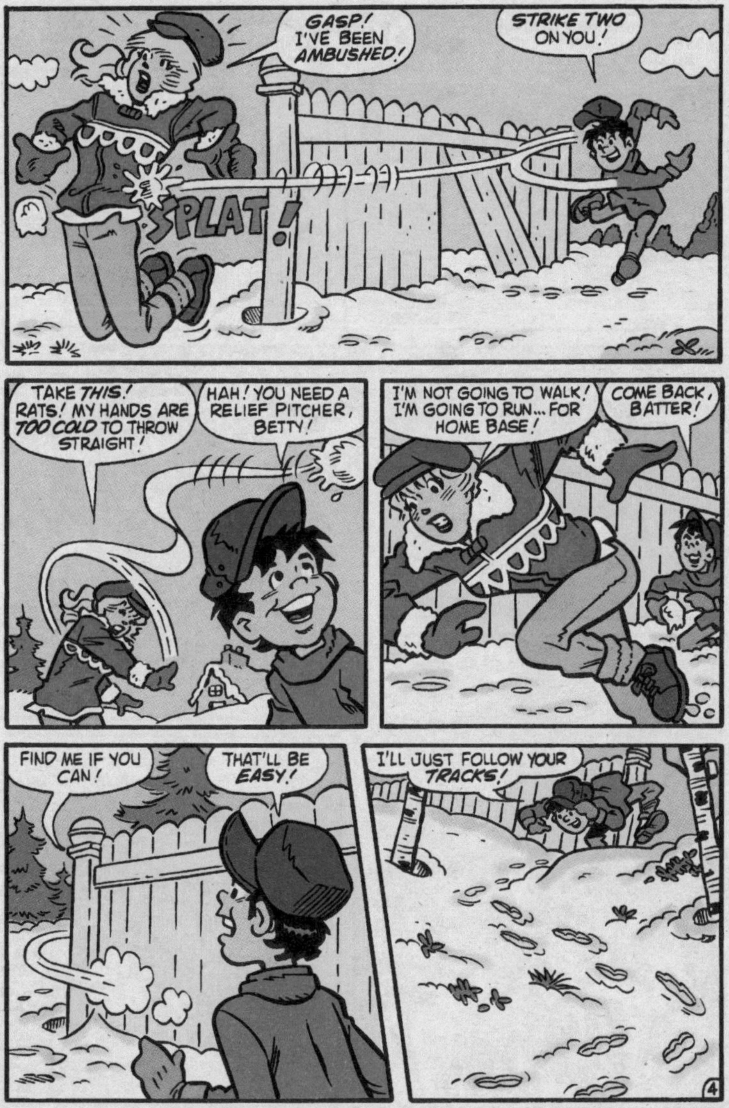
GASP! I'VE BEEN AMBUSHED!
STRIKE TWO ON YOU!
SPLAT!
TAKE THIS! RATS! MY HANDS ARE TOO COLD TO THROW STRAIGHT!
HAH! YOU NEED A RELIEF PITCHER, BETTY!
I'M NOT GOING TO WALK! I'M GOING TO RUN... FOR HOME BASE!
COME BACK, BATTER!
FIND ME IF YOU CAN!
THAT'LL BE EASY!
I'LL JUST FOLLOW YOUR TRACKS!
4

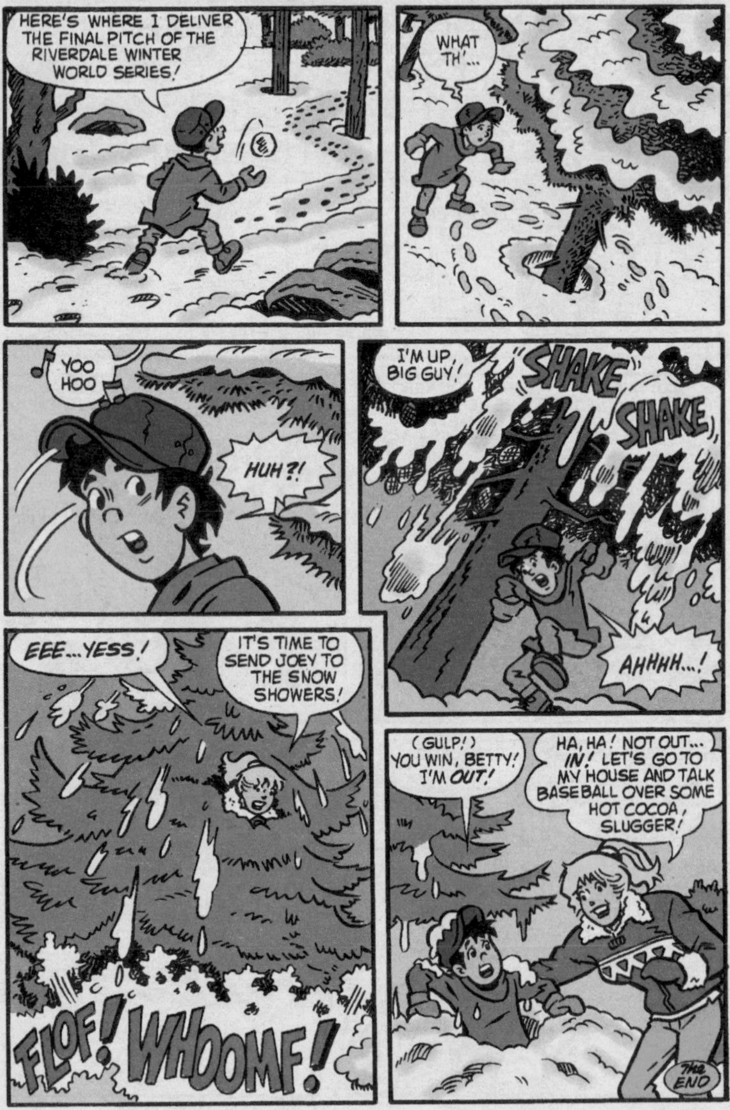
HERE'S WHERE I DELIVER THE FINAL PITCH OF THE RIVERDALE WINTER WORLD SERIES!
WHAT TH'...
YOO HOO
HUH?!
I'M UP, BIG GUY!
SHAKE
SHAKE
AHHHH...!
EEE...YESS!
IT'S TIME TO SEND JOEY TO THE SNOW SHOWERS!
FLOF! WHOOMF!
(GULP!) YOU WIN, BETTY! I'M OUT!
HA, HA! NOT OUT... IN! LET'S GO TO MY HOUSE AND TALK BASEBALL OVER SOME HOT COCOA, SLUGGER!
THE END

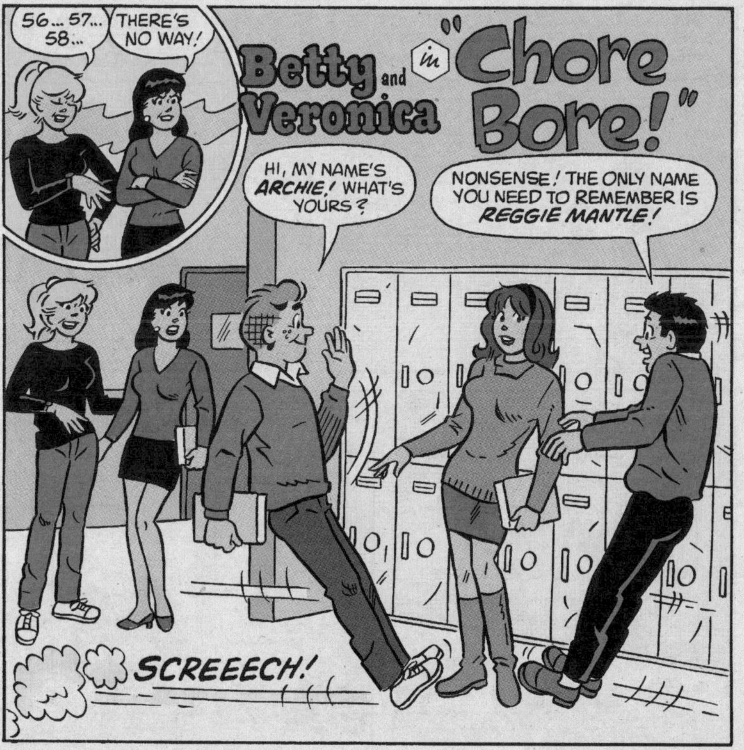
56... 57... 58...
THERE'S NO WAY!
Betty and Veronica in "Chore Bore!"
HI, MY NAME'S ARCHIE! WHAT'S YOURS?
NONSENSE! THE ONLY NAME YOU NEED TO REMEMBER IS REGGIE MANTLE!
SCREEECH!

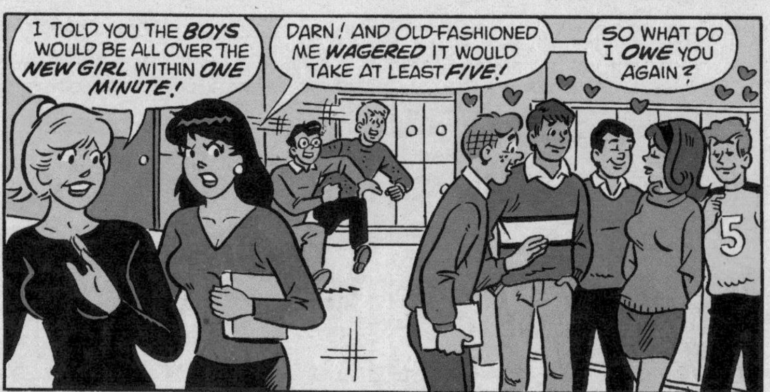
I TOLD YOU THE BOYS WOULD BE ALL OVER THE NEW GIRL WITHIN ONE MINUTE!
DARN! AND OLD-FASHIONED ME WAGERED IT WOULD TAKE AT LEAST FIVE!
SO WHAT DO I OWE YOU AGAIN?
5

Script: George Gladir / Pencils: Jeff Shultz / Inks: Rudy Lapick / Letters: Bill Yoshida

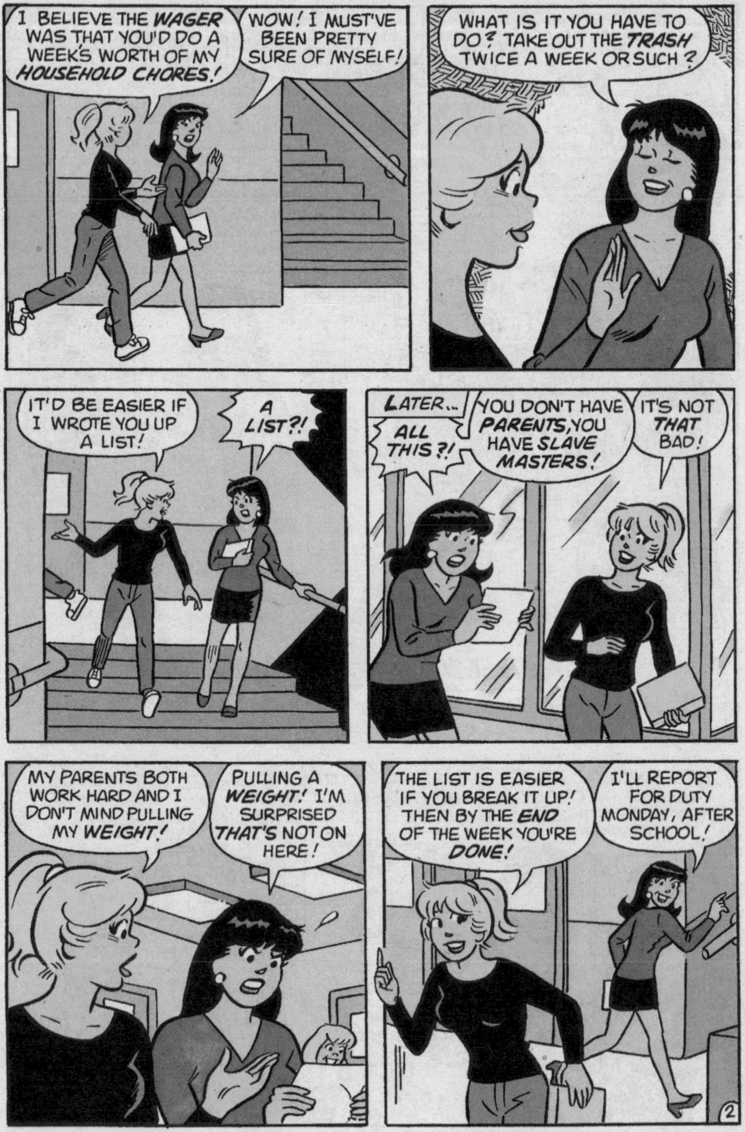
I BELIEVE THE WAGER WAS THAT YOU'D DO A WEEK'S WORTH OF MY HOUSEHOLD CHORES!
WOW! I MUST'VE BEEN PRETTY SURE OF MYSELF!
WHAT IS IT YOU HAVE TO DO? TAKE OUT THE TRASH TWICE A WEEK OR SUCH?
IT'D BE EASIER IF I WROTE YOU UP A LIST!
A LIST?!
LATER...
ALL THIS?!
YOU DON'T HAVE PARENTS, YOU HAVE SLAVE MASTERS!
IT'S NOT THAT BAD!
MY PARENTS BOTH WORK HARD AND I DON'T MIND PULLING MY WEIGHT!
PULLING A WEIGHT! I'M SURPRISED THAT'S NOT ON HERE!
THE LIST IS EASIER IF YOU BREAK IT UP! THEN BY THE END OF THE WEEK YOU'RE DONE!
I'LL REPORT FOR DUTY MONDAY, AFTER SCHOOL!
2

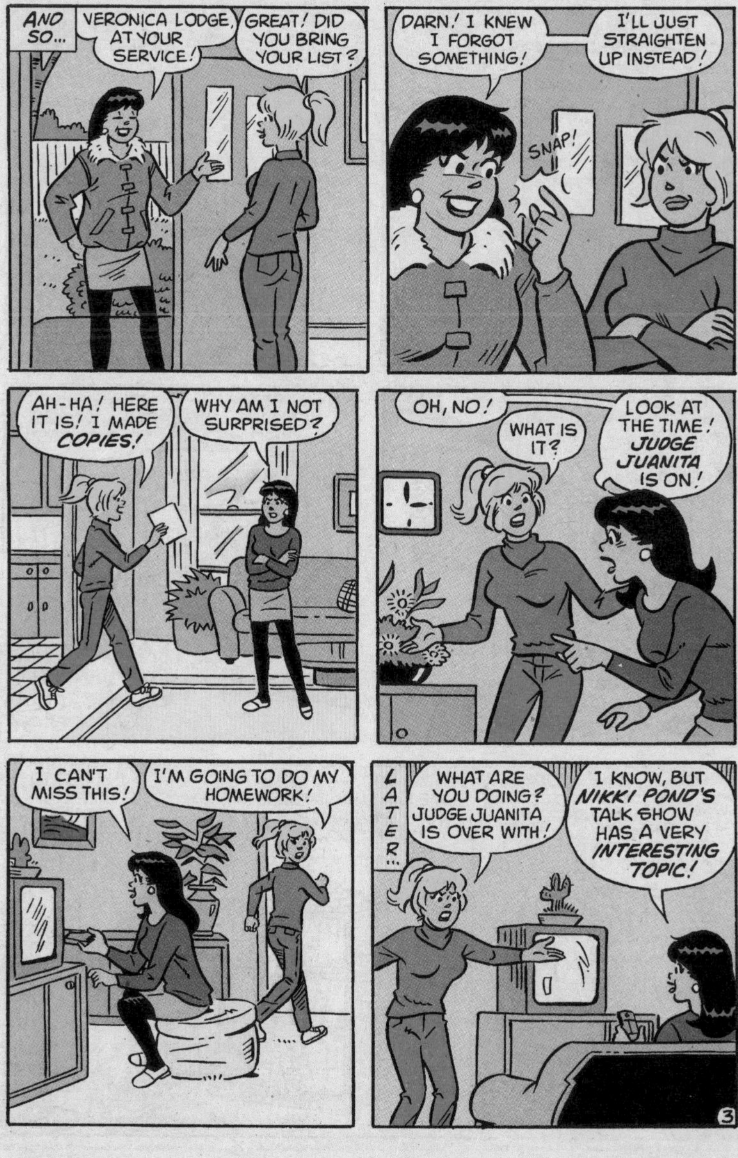
AND SO...
VERONICA LODGE, AT YOUR SERVICE!
GREAT! DID YOU BRING YOUR LIST?
DARN! I KNEW I FORGOT SOMETHING!
I'LL JUST STRAIGHTEN UP INSTEAD!
SNAP!
AH-HA! HERE IT IS! I MADE COPIES!
WHY AM I NOT SURPRISED?
OH, NO!
WHAT IS IT?
LOOK AT THE TIME! JUDGE JUANITA IS ON!
I CAN'T MISS THIS!
I'M GOING TO DO MY HOMEWORK!
LATER...
WHAT ARE YOU DOING? JUDGE JUANITA IS OVER WITH!
I KNOW, BUT NIKKI POND'S TALK SHOW HAS A VERY INTERESTING TOPIC!
3

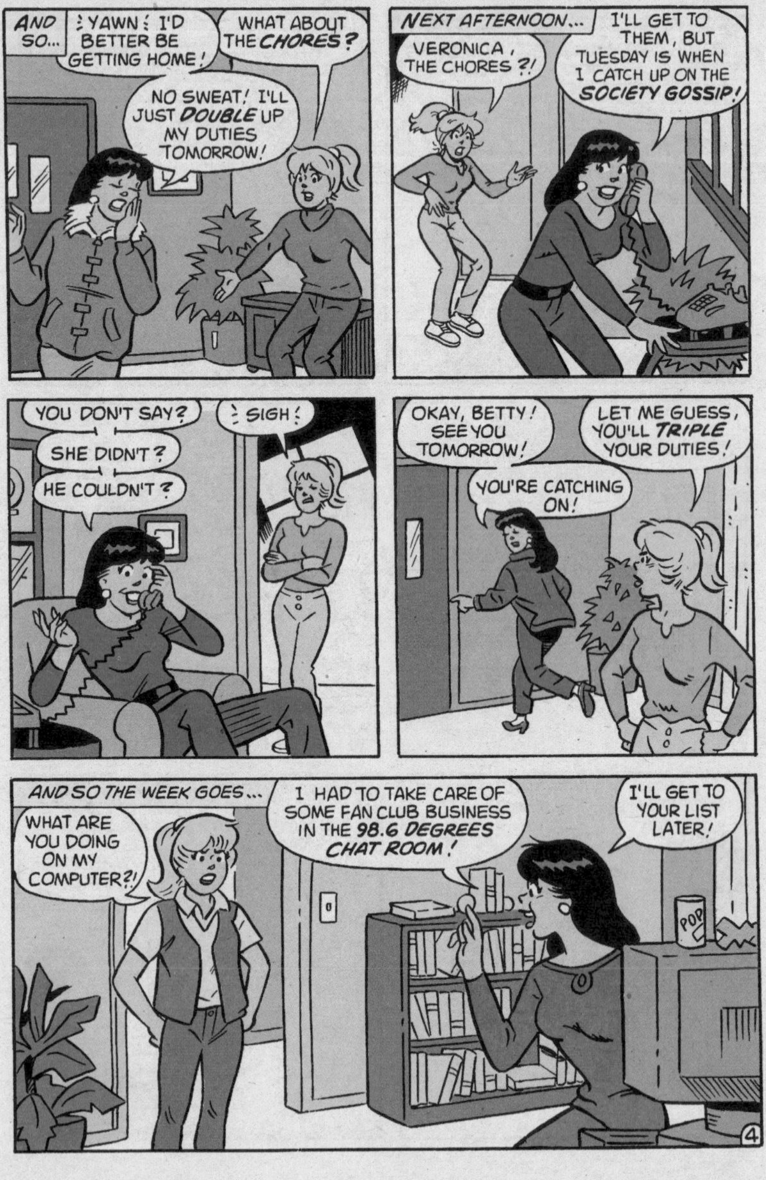

AND SO...
YAWN! I'D BETTER BE GETTING HOME!
WHAT ABOUT THE CHORES?
NO SWEAT! I'LL JUST DOUBLE UP MY DUTIES TOMORROW!
NEXT AFTERNOON...
VERONICA, THE CHORES?!
I'LL GET TO THEM, BUT TUESDAY IS WHEN I CATCH UP ON THE SOCIETY GOSSIP!
YOU DON'T SAY?
SHE DIDN'T?
HE COULDN'T?
SIGH!
OKAY, BETTY! SEE YOU TOMORROW!
LET ME GUESS, YOU'LL TRIPLE YOUR DUTIES!
YOU'RE CATCHING ON!
AND SO THE WEEK GOES...
WHAT ARE YOU DOING ON MY COMPUTER?!
I HAD TO TAKE CARE OF SOME FAN CLUB BUSINESS IN THE 98.6 DEGREES CHAT ROOM!
I'LL GET TO YOUR LIST LATER!
POP
4

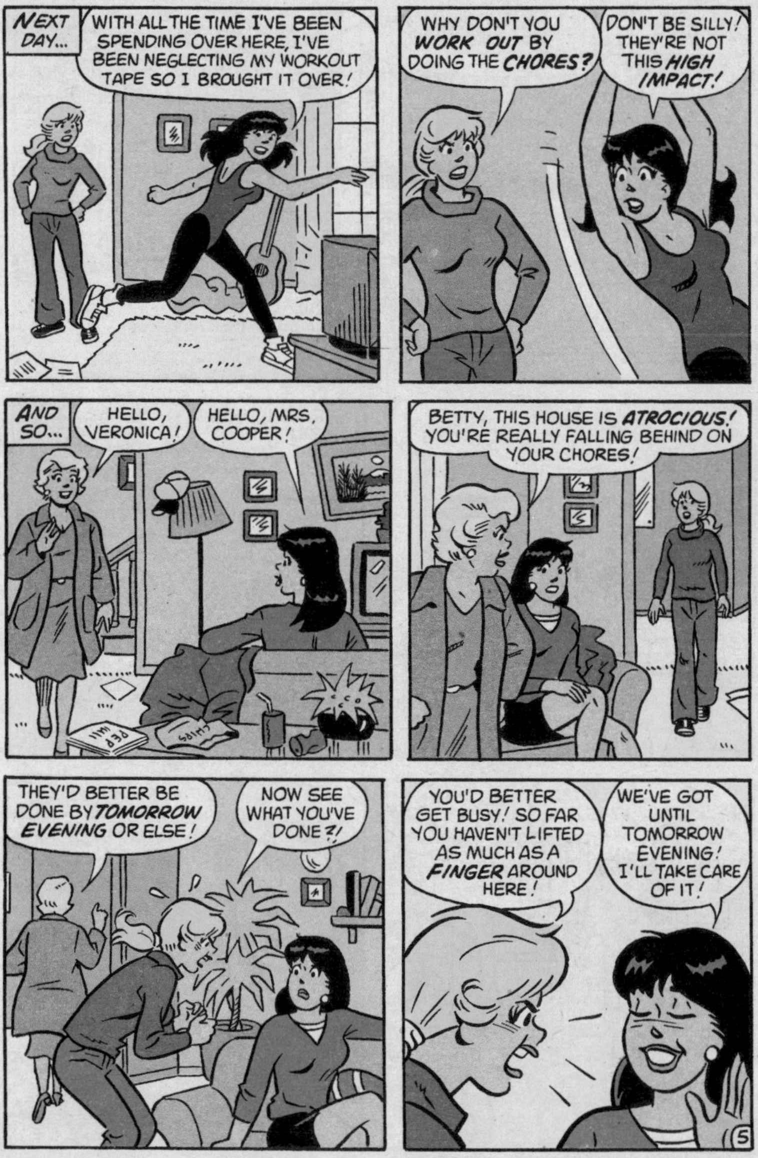
NEXT DAY...
WITH ALL THE TIME I'VE BEEN SPENDING OVER HERE, I'VE BEEN NEGLECTING MY WORKOUT TAPE SO I BROUGHT IT OVER!
WHY DON'T YOU WORK OUT BY DOING THE CHORES?
DON'T BE SILLY! THEY'RE NOT THIS HIGH IMPACT!
AND SO...
HELLO, VERONICA!
HELLO, MRS. COOPER!
BETTY, THIS HOUSE IS ATROCIOUS! YOU'RE REALLY FALLING BEHIND ON YOUR CHORES!
THEY'D BETTER BE DONE BY TOMORROW EVENING OR ELSE!
NOW SEE WHAT YOU'VE DONE?!
YOU'D BETTER GET BUSY! SO FAR YOU HAVEN'T LIFTED AS MUCH AS A FINGER AROUND HERE!
WE'VE GOT UNTIL TOMORROW EVENING! I'LL TAKE CARE OF IT!
5

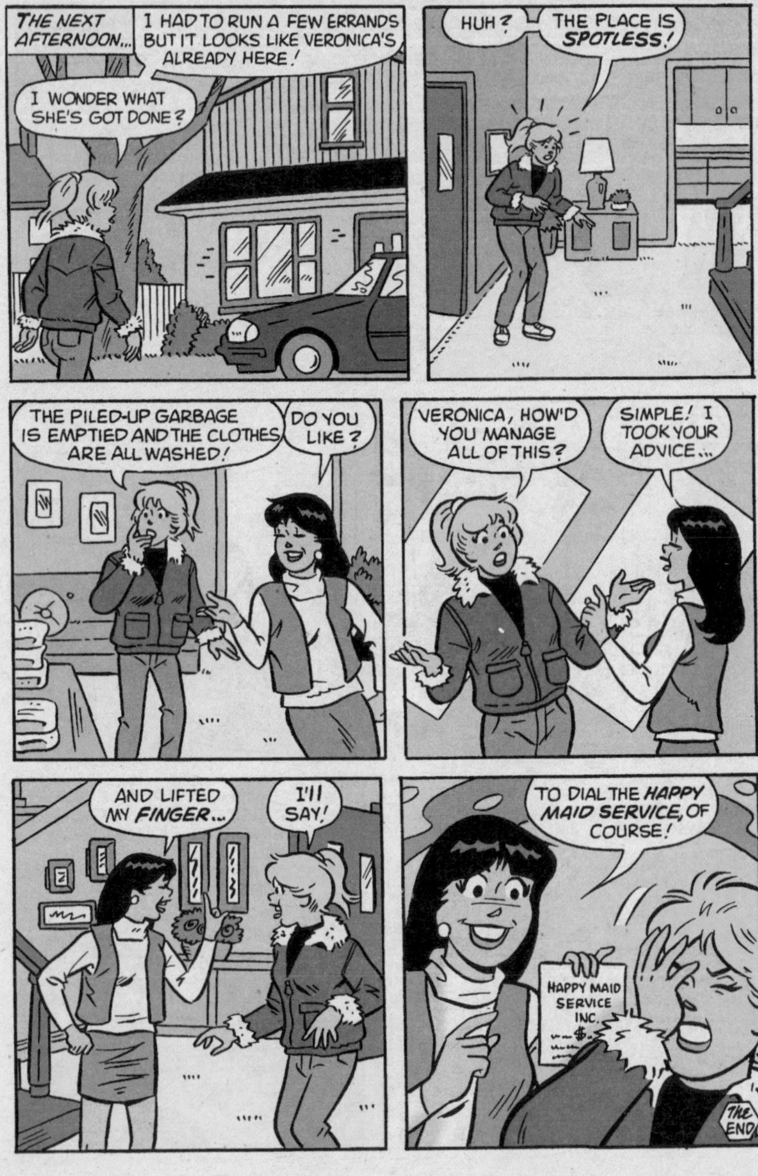
THE NEXT AFTERNOON...
I HAD TO RUN A FEW ERRANDS BUT IT LOOKS LIKE VERONICA'S ALREADY HERE!
I WONDER WHAT SHE'S GOT DONE?
HUH?
THE PLACE IS SPOTLESS!
THE PILED-UP GARBAGE IS EMPTIED AND THE CLOTHES ARE ALL WASHED!
DO YOU LIKE?
VERONICA, HOW'D YOU MANAGE ALL OF THIS?
SIMPLE! I TOOK YOUR ADVICE...
AND LIFTED MY FINGER...
I'll SAY!
TO DIAL THE HAPPY MAID SERVICE, OF COURSE!
HAPPY MAID SERVICE INC.
$
THE END

Jughead and Archie IN OH, BROTHER...OR SISTER

WOW, ARCH! LOOK AT *THAT!*

YOU KNOW IT, JUG!

THERE'S JUST ENOUGH *SNOW* TO CLOSE THE SCHOOLS, BUT NOT SO MUCH THAT WE CAN'T *ENJOY* IT!

IT'S THE PERFECT **SNOW DAY!**

DAN *PARENT* STORY & PENCILS

BOB SMITH INKS

JACK MORELLI LETTERS

GLENN WHITMORE COLORS

VICTOR *GORELICK* EDITOR-IN-CHIEF

MIKE *PELLERITO* PRESIDENT

JON *GOLDWATER* PUBLISHER/ CO-CEO

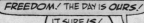

FREEDOM! THE DAY IS *OURS!*

IT SURE *IS!* WHAT ARE WE GONNA *DO* WITH IT?

THE ANSWER IS AN EASY ONE, PAL... *BINGE VIDEO GAMING!*

WHADDAYA WANNA START WITH? *FALL OF DUTY IV* OR *MUTANT DRAGON RAIDERS?!*

1

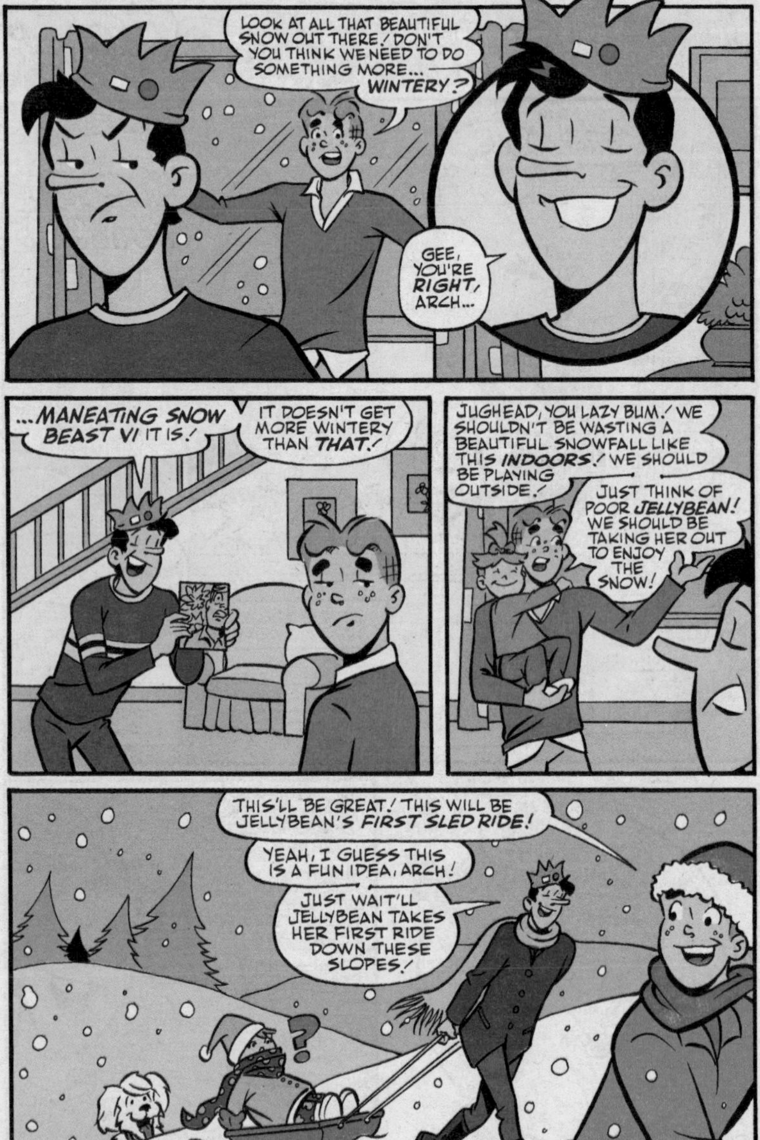
LOOK AT ALL THAT BEAUTIFUL SNOW OUT THERE! DON'T YOU THINK WE NEED TO DO SOMETHING MORE... WINTERY?
GEE, YOU'RE RIGHT, ARCH...
...MANEATING SNOW BEAST VI IT IS!
IT DOESN'T GET MORE WINTERY THAN THAT!
JUGHEAD, YOU LAZY BUM! WE SHOULDN'T BE WASTING A BEAUTIFUL SNOWFALL LIKE THIS INDOORS! WE SHOULD BE PLAYING OUTSIDE!
JUST THINK OF POOR JELLYBEAN! WE SHOULD BE TAKING HER OUT TO ENJOY THE SNOW!
THIS'LL BE GREAT! THIS WILL BE JELLYBEAN'S FIRST SLED RIDE!
YEAH, I GUESS THIS IS A FUN IDEA, ARCH!
JUST WAIT'LL JELLYBEAN TAKES HER FIRST RIDE DOWN THESE SLOPES!
?
2

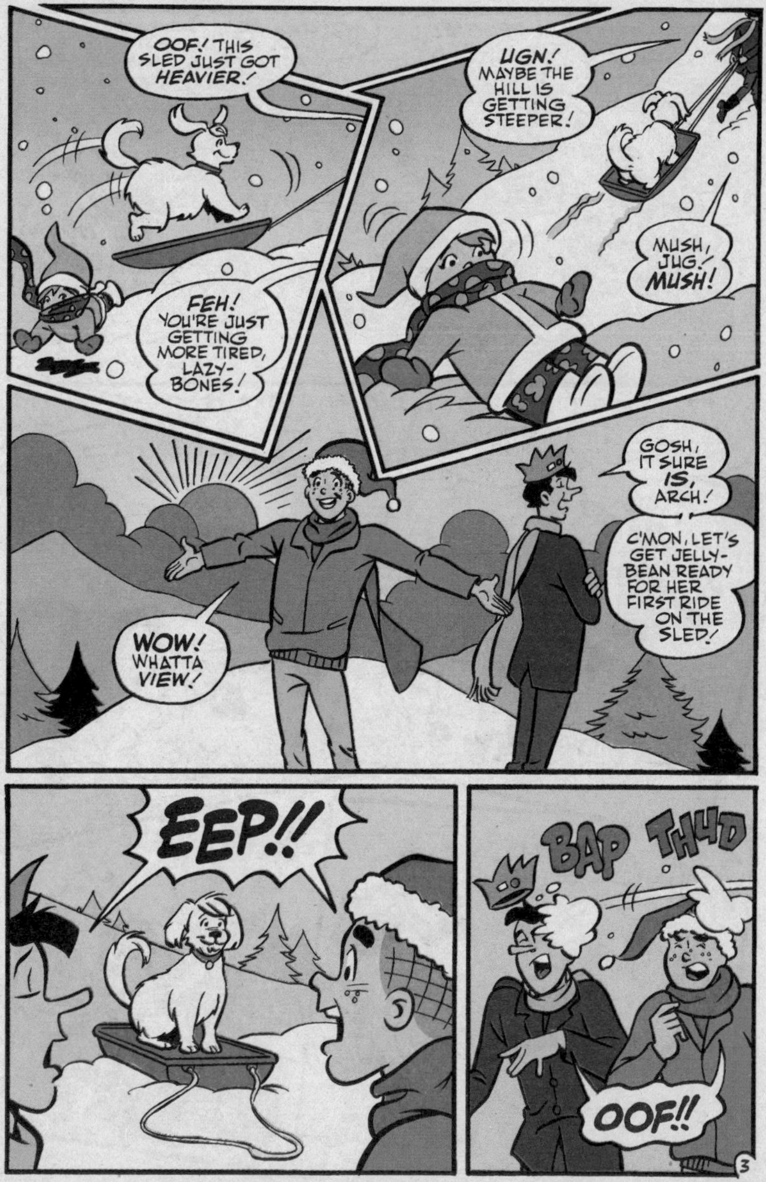

OOF! THIS SLED JUST GOT HEAVIER!
FEH! YOU'RE JUST GETTING MORE TIRED, LAZY-BONES!
UGN! MAYBE THE HILL IS GETTING STEEPER!
MUSH, JUG! MUSH!
WOW! WHATTA VIEW!
GOSH, IT SURE IS, ARCH!
C'MON, LET'S GET JELLY-BEAN READY FOR HER FIRST RIDE ON THE SLED!
EEP!!
BAP
THUD
OOF!!

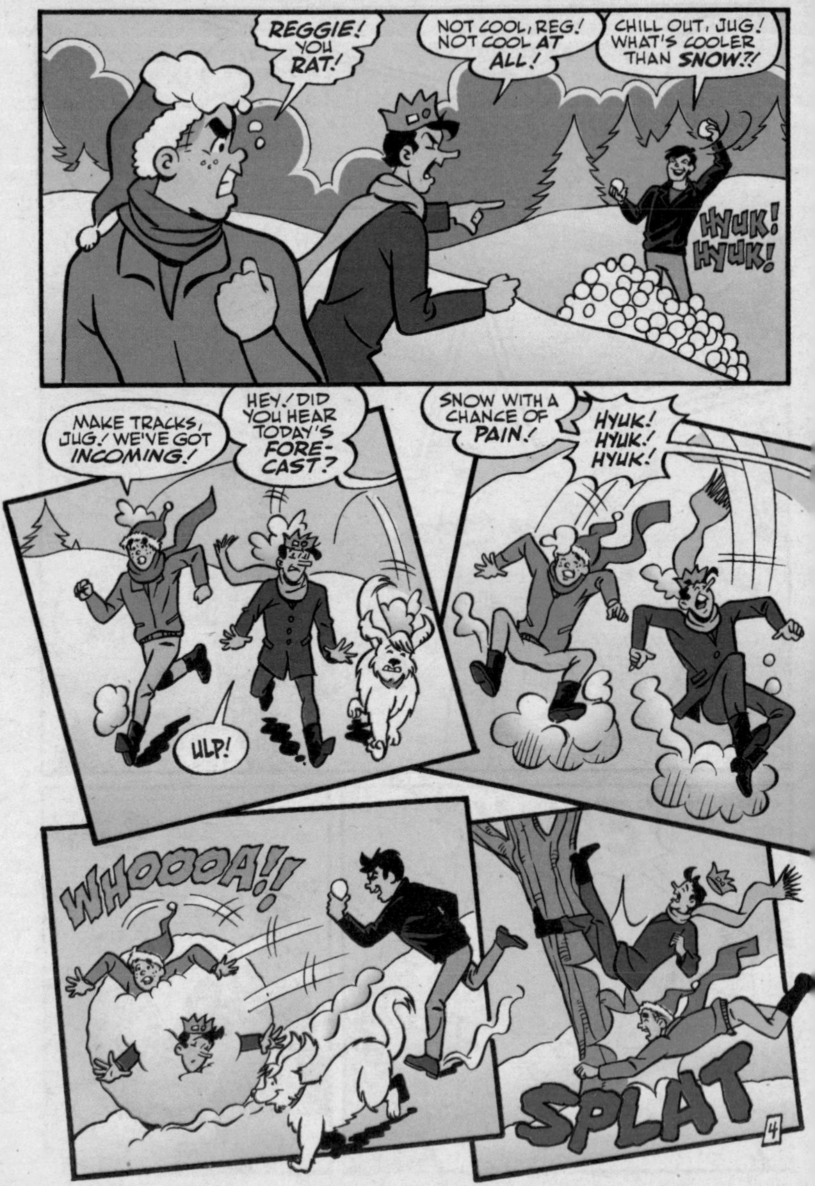
REGGIE! YOU RAT!
NOT COOL, REG! NOT COOL AT ALL!
CHILL OUT, JUG! WHAT'S COOLER THAN SNOW?!
HYUK! HYUK!
MAKE TRACKS, JUG! WE'VE GOT INCOMING!
HEY! DID YOU HEAR TODAY'S FORE-CAST?
ULP!
SNOW WITH A CHANCE OF PAIN!
HYUK! HYUK! HYUK!
WHOOOA!!
SPLAT
4

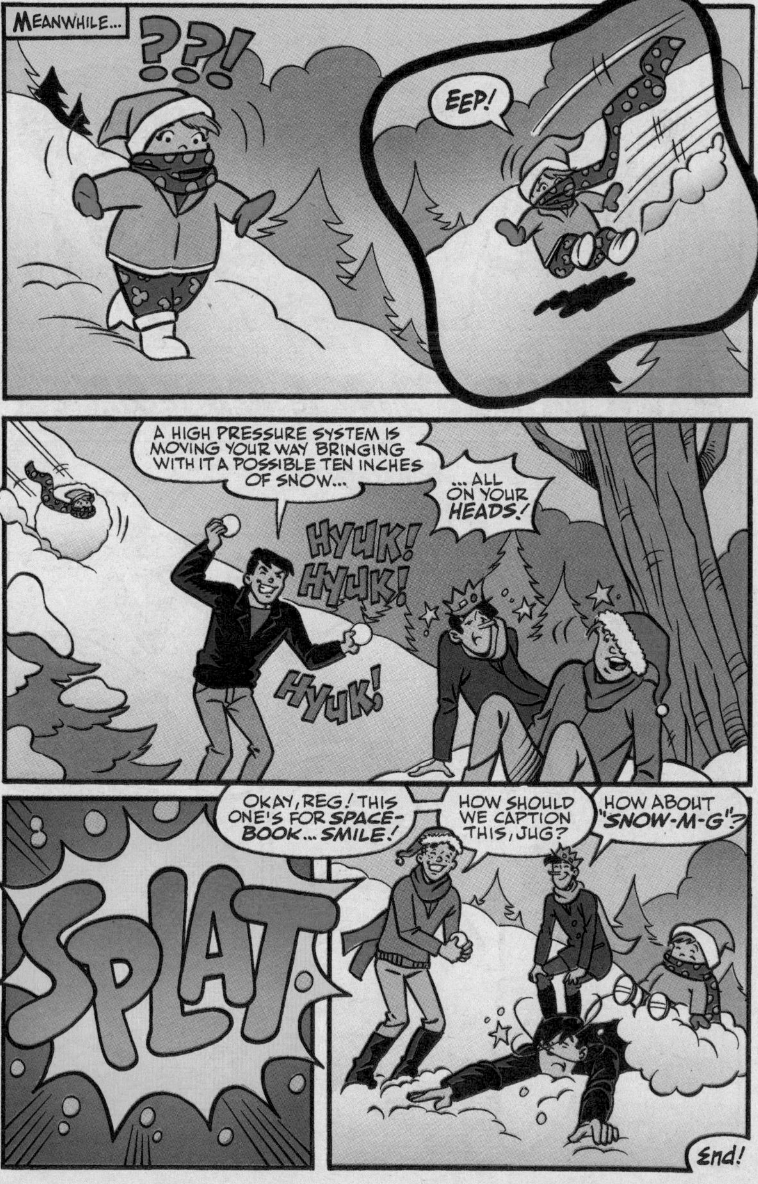
MEANWHILE...
??!
EEP!
A HIGH PRESSURE SYSTEM IS MOVING YOUR WAY BRINGING WITH IT A POSSIBLE TEN INCHES OF SNOW...
... ALL ON YOUR HEADS!
HYUK! HYUK!
HYUK!
SPLAT
OKAY, REG! THIS ONE'S FOR SPACE-BOOK... SMILE!
HOW SHOULD WE CAPTION THIS, JUG?
HOW ABOUT "SNOW-M-G"?
End!

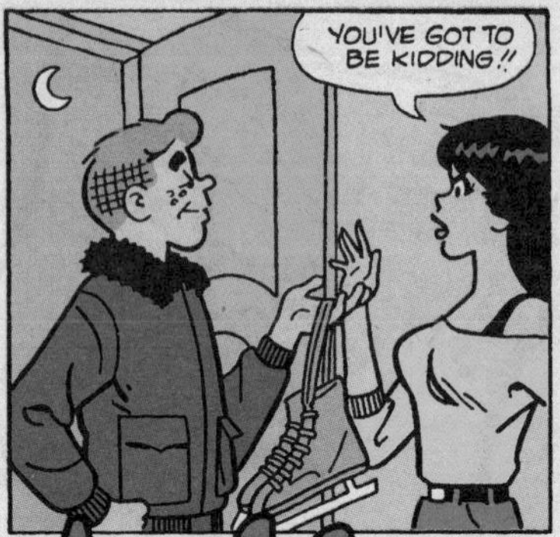
YOU'VE GOT TO BE KIDDING!!

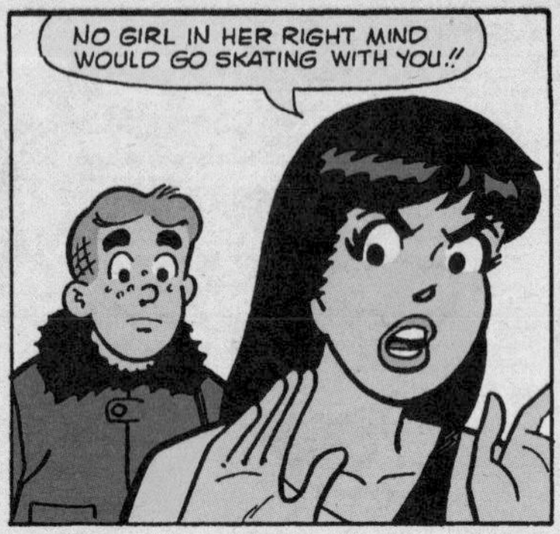
NO GIRL IN HER RIGHT MIND WOULD GO SKATING WITH YOU!!

Archie in "The ICE BREAKER"

Script: Doyle / Pencils: DeCarlo Jr. / Inks: J. DeCarlo / Letters: Yoshida

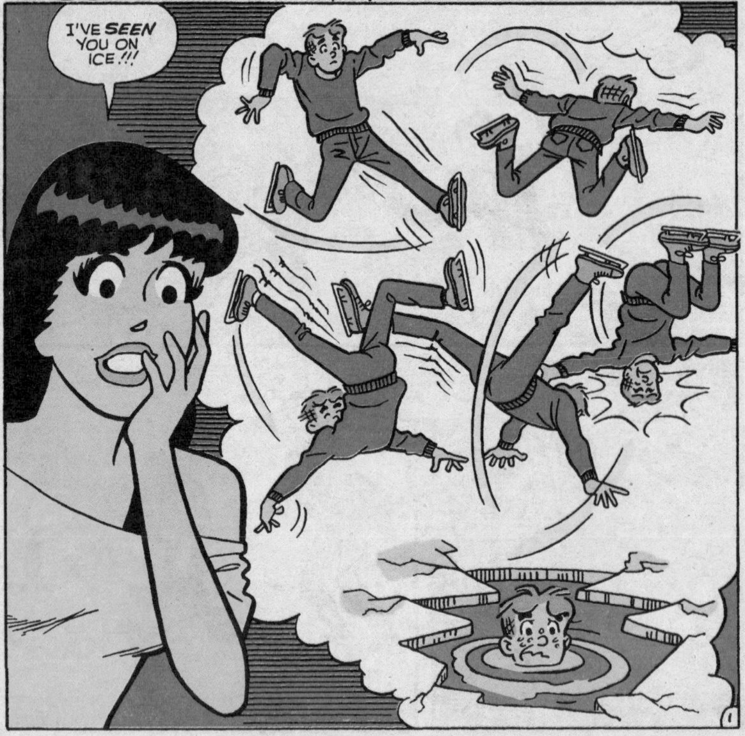
I'VE SEEN YOU ON ICE!!!
1

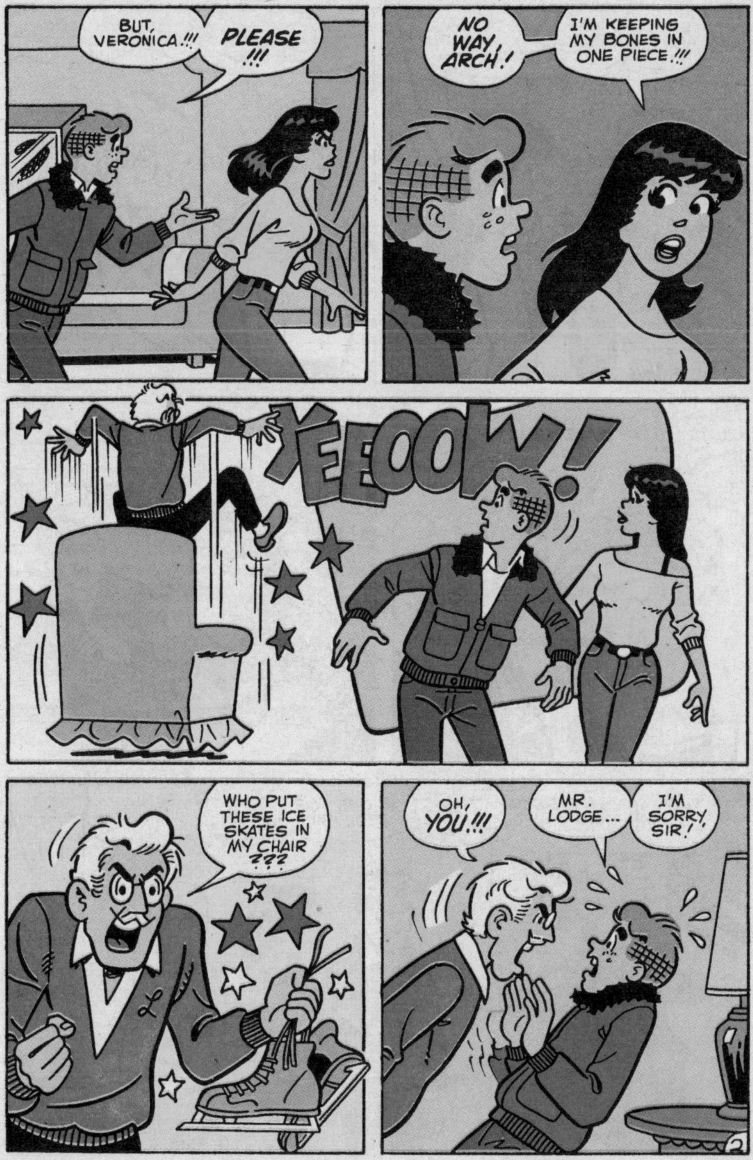

BUT, VERONICA.!!!
PLEASE !!!
NO WAY, ARCH.!
I'M KEEPING MY BONES IN ONE PIECE.!!!
YEEOOW!
WHO PUT THESE ICE SKATES IN MY CHAIR ???
OH, YOU.!!!
MR. LODGE...
I'M SORRY, SIR!
2

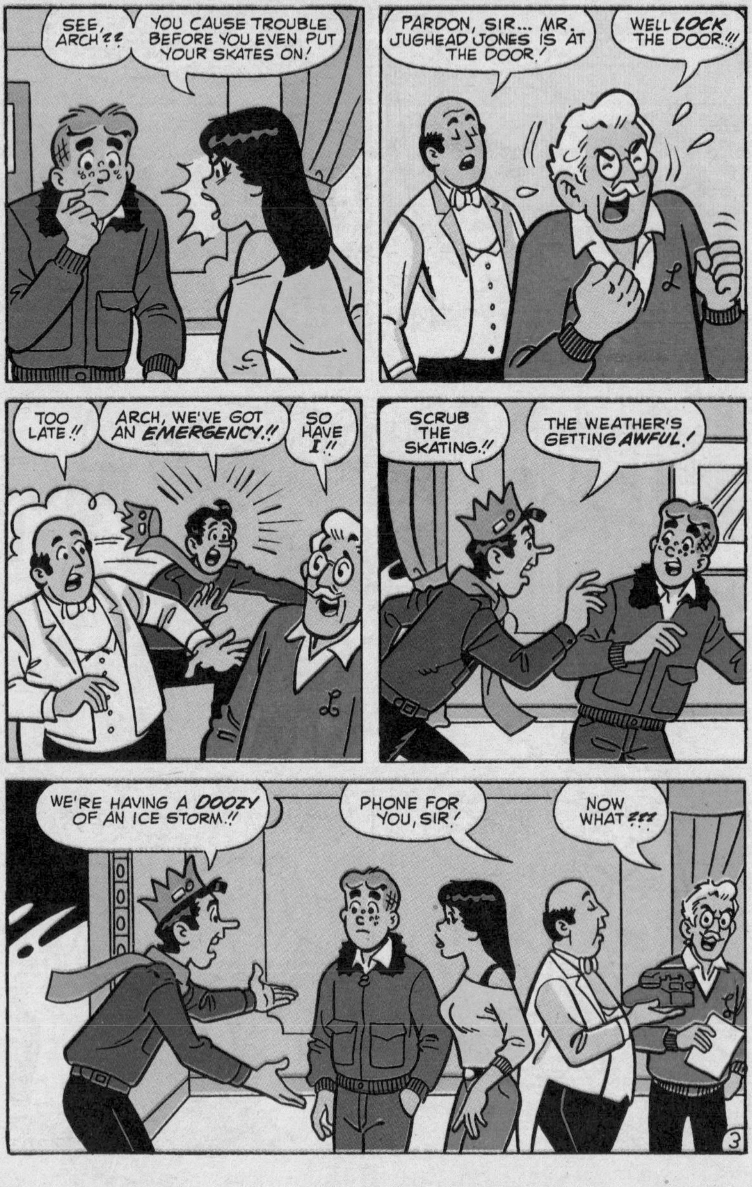
SEE, ARCH???
YOU CAUSE TROUBLE BEFORE YOU EVEN PUT YOUR SKATES ON!
PARDON, SIR... MR. JUGHEAD JONES IS AT THE DOOR!
WELL LOCK THE DOOR!!!
TOO LATE!!
ARCH, WE'VE GOT AN EMERGENCY!!
SO HAVE I!!
SCRUB THE SKATING!!
THE WEATHER'S GETTING AWFUL!
WE'RE HAVING A DOOZY OF AN ICE STORM!!
PHONE FOR YOU, SIR!
NOW WHAT???

WHAT??? IT IS??? YOU CAN'T! OH, NO.!!!

THIS IS *AWFUL!!!*

WHAT IS IT, DADDY?

THE MESSENGER SERVICE CAN'T GET UP THE HILL BECAUSE OF THE ICE STORM!

GASP.!!!

AND I'VE GOT THIS SEALED BID THAT *ABSOLUTELY, POSITIVELY* HAS TO GET TO THE TOWN HALL BY 8:00 TONIGHT!

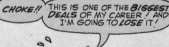

CHOKE!! THIS IS ONE OF THE *BIGGEST DEALS* OF MY CAREER! AND I'M GOING TO *LOSE* IT!

4

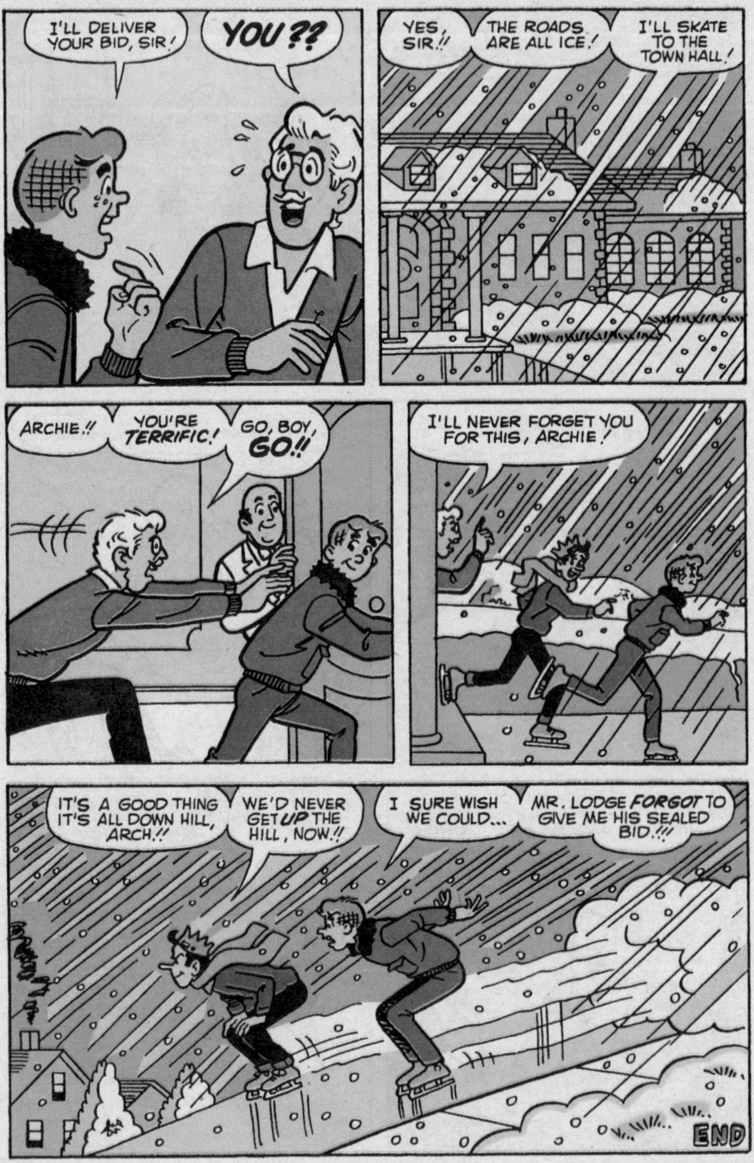

I'LL DELIVER YOUR BID, SIR!
YOU??
YES, SIR!!
THE ROADS ARE ALL ICE!
I'LL SKATE TO THE TOWN HALL!
ARCHIE!!
YOU'RE TERRIFIC!
GO, BOY, GO!!
I'LL NEVER FORGET YOU FOR THIS, ARCHIE!
IT'S A GOOD THING IT'S ALL DOWN HILL, ARCH!!
WE'D NEVER GET UP THE HILL, NOW!!
I SURE WISH WE COULD...
MR. LODGE FORGOT TO GIVE ME HIS SEALED BID!!!
END

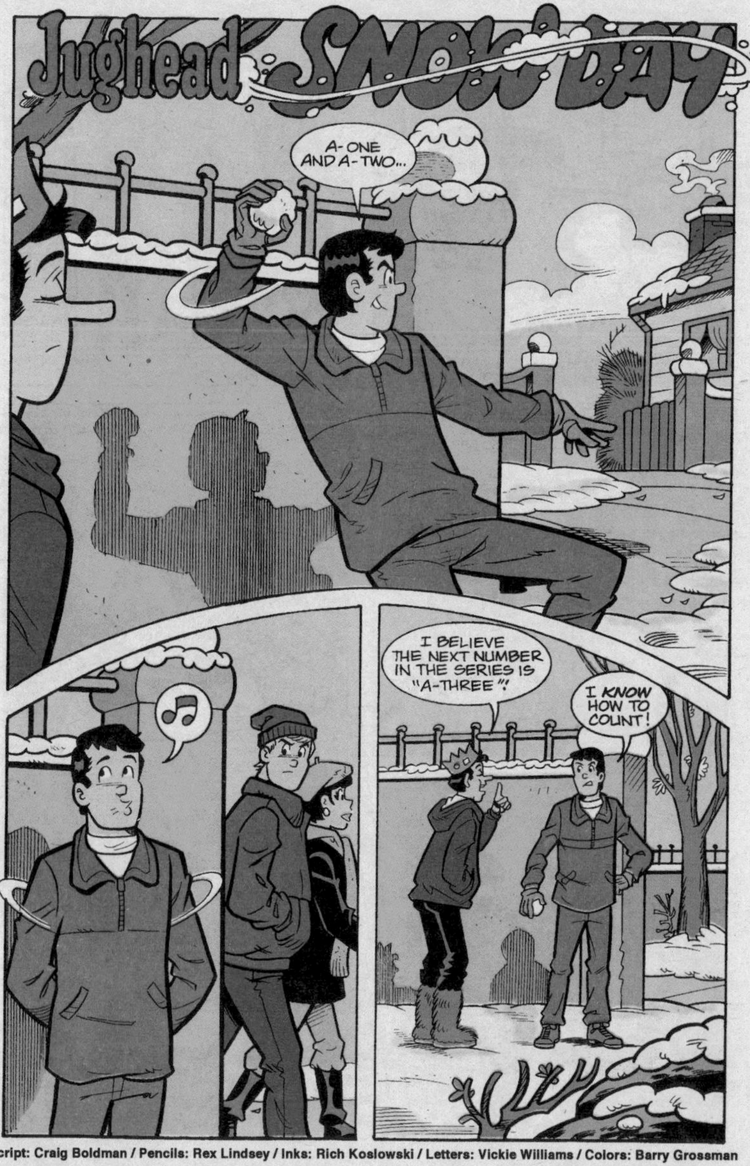
Jughead
SNOW DAY
A-ONE AND A-TWO...
I BELIEVE THE NEXT NUMBER IN THE SERIES IS "A-THREE"!
I KNOW HOW TO COUNT!

Script: Craig Boldman / Pencils: Rex Lindsey / Inks: Rich Koslowski / Letters: Vickie Williams / Colors: Barry Grossman

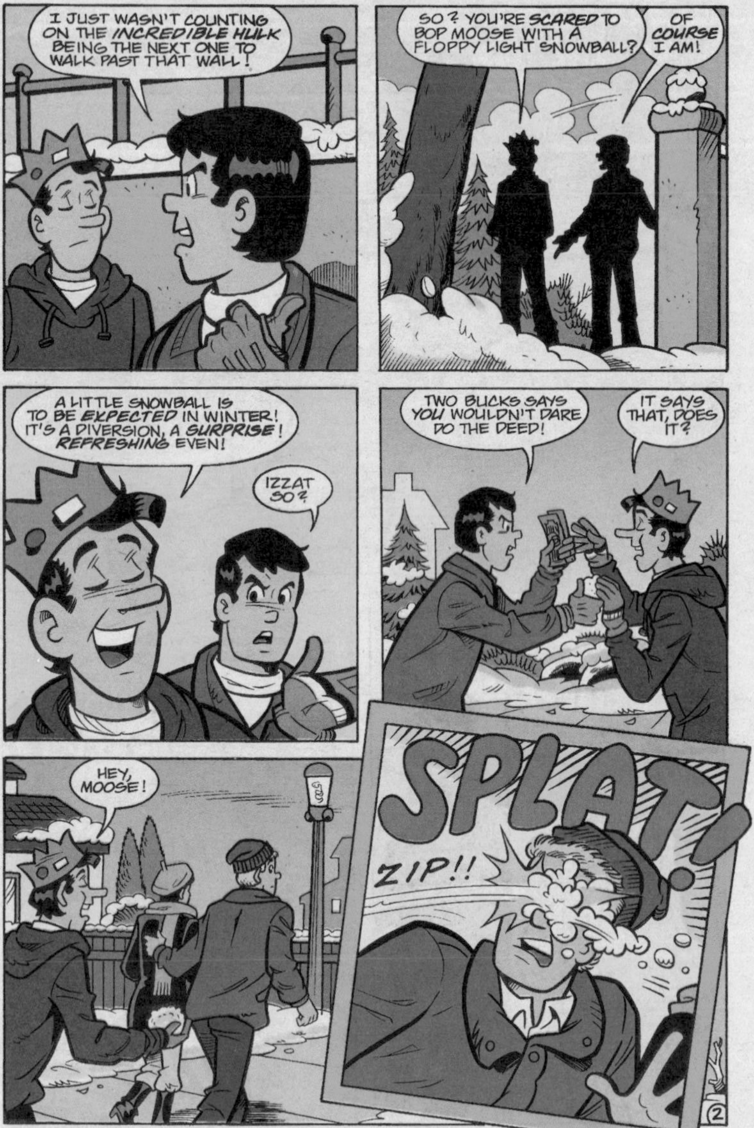

I JUST WASN'T COUNTING ON THE INCREDIBLE HULK BEING THE NEXT ONE TO WALK PAST THAT WALL!
SO? YOU'RE SCARED TO BOP MOOSE WITH A FLOPPY LIGHT SNOWBALL?
OF COURSE I AM!
A LITTLE SNOWBALL IS TO BE EXPECTED IN WINTER! IT'S A DIVERSION, A SURPRISE! REFRESHING EVEN!
IZZAT SO?
TWO BUCKS SAYS YOU WOULDN'T DARE DO THE DEED!
IT SAYS THAT, DOES IT?
HEY, MOOSE!
SPLAT!
ZIP!!
2

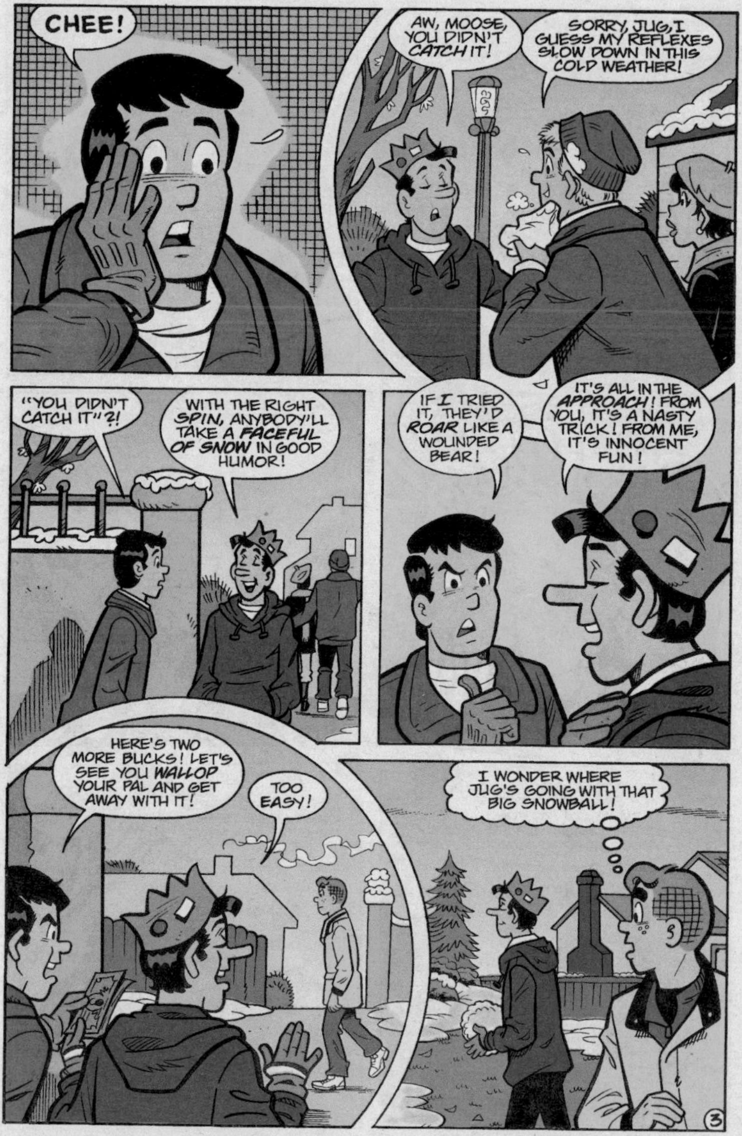

CHEE!
AW, MOOSE, YOU DIDN'T CATCH IT!
SORRY, JUG, I GUESS MY REFLEXES SLOW DOWN IN THIS COLD WEATHER!
"YOU DIDN'T CATCH IT"?!
WITH THE RIGHT SPIN, ANYBODY'LL TAKE A FACEFUL OF SNOW IN GOOD HUMOR!
IF I TRIED IT, THEY'D ROAR LIKE A WOUNDED BEAR!
IT'S ALL IN THE APPROACH! FROM YOU, IT'S A NASTY TRICK! FROM ME, IT'S INNOCENT FUN!
HERE'S TWO MORE BUCKS! LET'S SEE YOU WALLOP YOUR PAL AND GET AWAY WITH IT!
TOO EASY!
I WONDER WHERE JUG'S GOING WITH THAT BIG SNOWBALL!
3

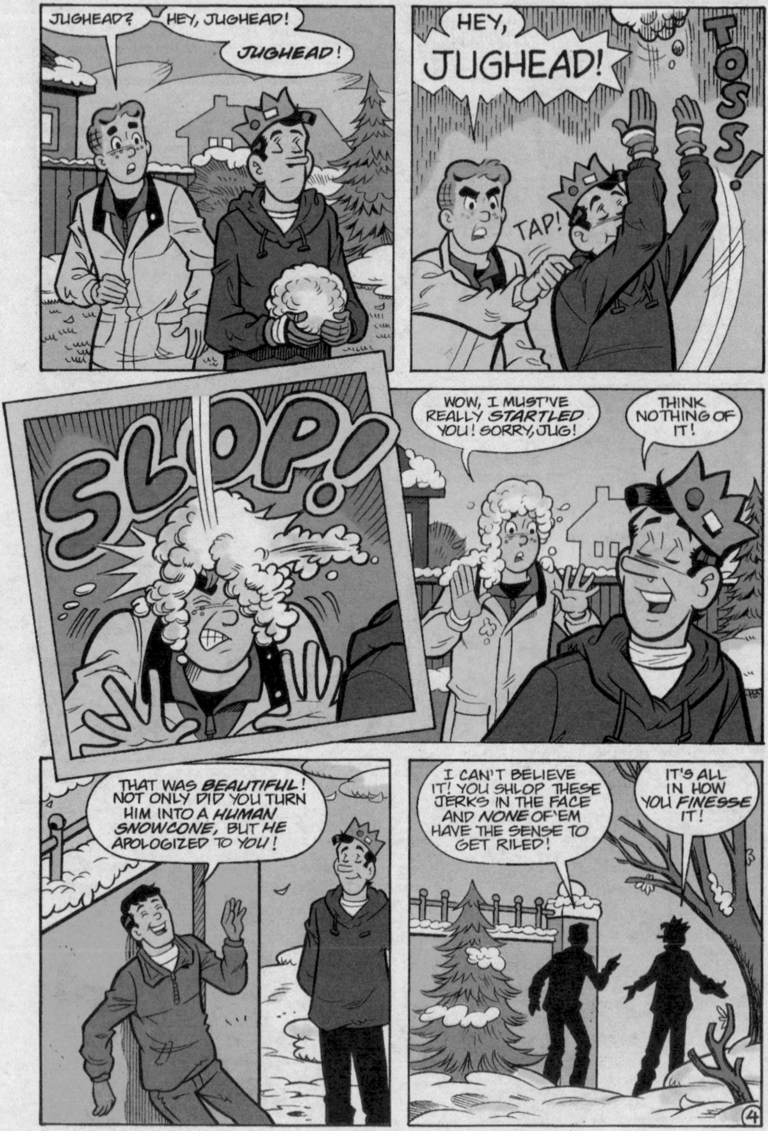
JUGHEAD?
HEY, JUGHEAD!
JUGHEAD!
HEY, JUGHEAD!
TOSS!
TAP!
SLOP!
WOW, I MUST'VE REALLY STARTLED YOU! SORRY, JUG!
THINK NOTHING OF IT!
THAT WAS BEAUTIFUL! NOT ONLY DID YOU TURN HIM INTO A HUMAN SNOWCONE, BUT HE APOLOGIZED TO YOU!
I CAN'T BELIEVE IT! YOU SHLOP THESE JERKS IN THE FACE AND NONE OF 'EM HAVE THE SENSE TO GET RILED!
IT'S ALL IN HOW YOU FINESSE IT!
4

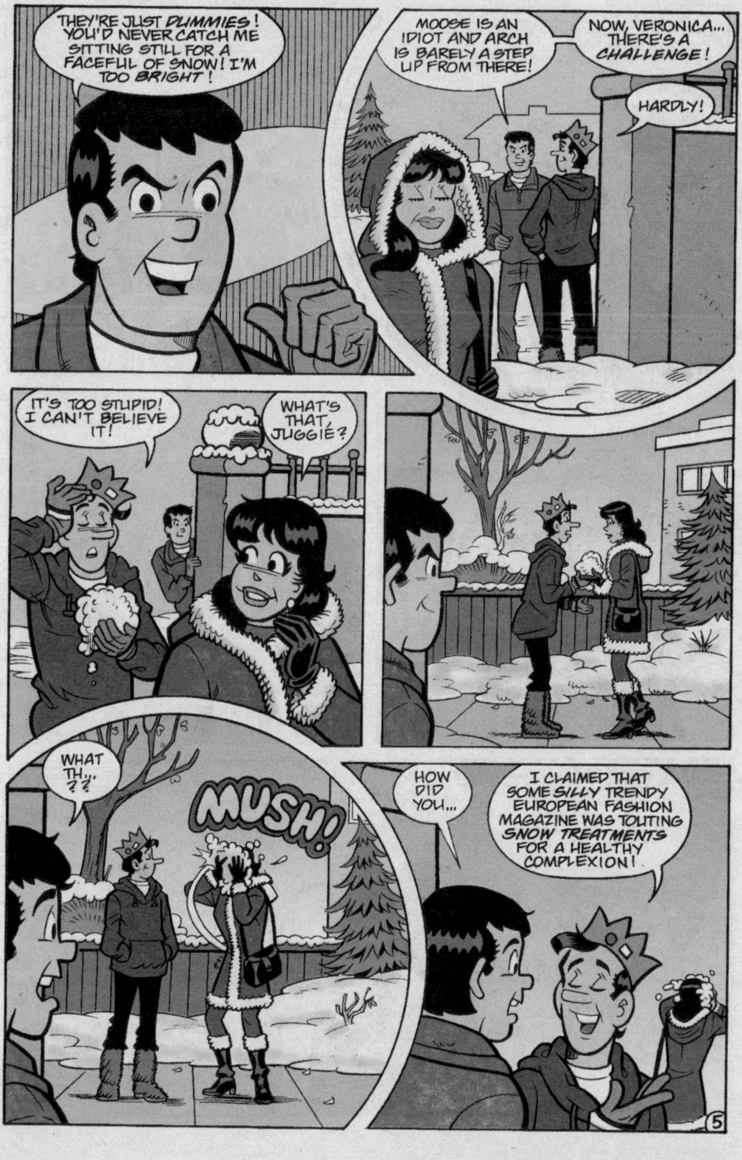
THEY'RE JUST DUMMIES! YOU'D NEVER CATCH ME SITTING STILL FOR A FACEFUL OF SNOW! I'M TOO BRIGHT!
MOOSE IS AN IDIOT AND ARCH IS BARELY A STEP UP FROM THERE!
NOW, VERONICA... THERE'S A CHALLENGE!
HARDLY!
IT'S TOO STUPID! I CAN'T BELIEVE IT!
WHAT'S THAT, JUGGIE?
WHAT TH...??
MUSH!
HOW DID YOU...
I CLAIMED THAT SOME SILLY TRENDY EUROPEAN FASHION MAGAZINE WAS TOUTING SNOW TREATMENTS FOR A HEALTHY COMPLEXION!
5

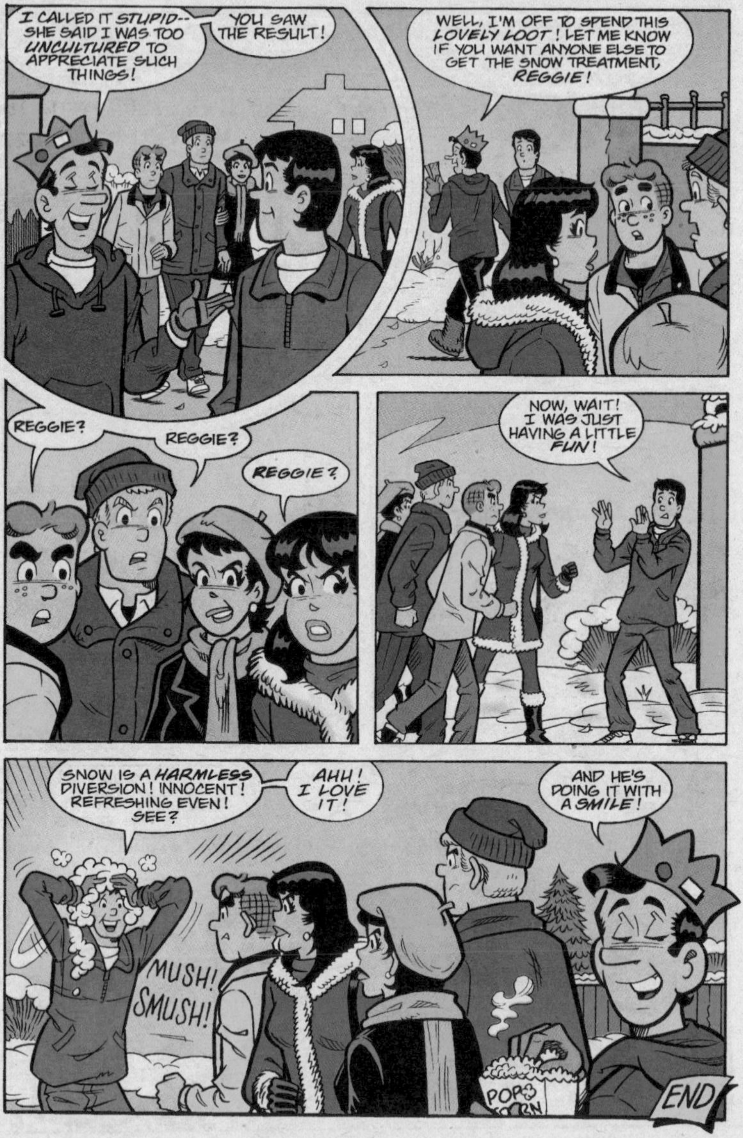
I CALLED IT STUPID-- SHE SAID I WAS TOO UNCULTURED TO APPRECIATE SUCH THINGS!
YOU SAW THE RESULT!
WELL, I'M OFF TO SPEND THIS LOVELY LOOT! LET ME KNOW IF YOU WANT ANYONE ELSE TO GET THE SNOW TREATMENT, REGGIE!
REGGIE?
REGGIE?
REGGIE?
NOW, WAIT! I WAS JUST HAVING A LITTLE FUN!
SNOW IS A HARMLESS DIVERSION! INNOCENT! REFRESHING EVEN! SEE?
AHH! I LOVE IT!
MUSH! SMUSH!
AND HE'S DOING IT WITH A SMILE!
POP CORN
END

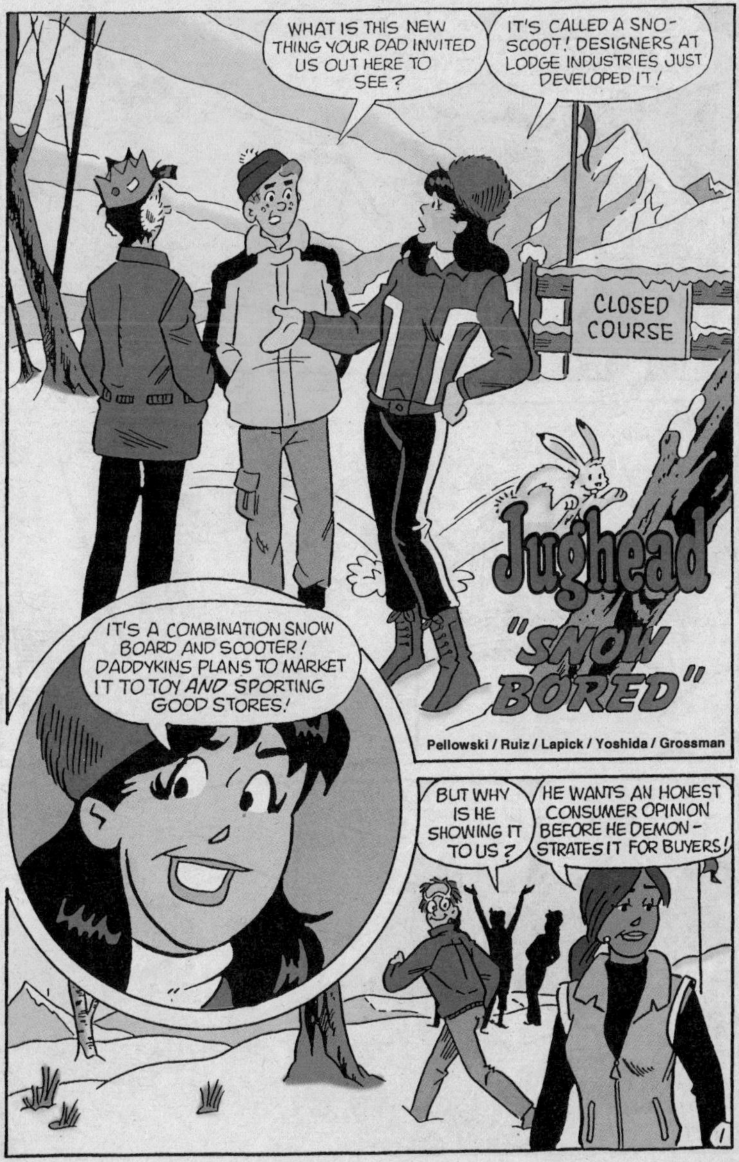
WHAT IS THIS NEW THING YOUR DAD INVITED US OUT HERE TO SEE?
IT'S CALLED A SNO-SCOOT! DESIGNERS AT LODGE INDUSTRIES JUST DEVELOPED IT!
CLOSED COURSE
Jughead
"SNOW BORED"
Pellowski / Ruiz / Lapick / Yoshida / Grossman
IT'S A COMBINATION SNOW BOARD AND SCOOTER! DADDYKINS PLANS TO MARKET IT TO TOY AND SPORTING GOOD STORES!
BUT WHY IS HE SHOWING IT TO US?
HE WANTS AN HONEST CONSUMER OPINION BEFORE HE DEMON-STRATES IT FOR BUYERS!
1

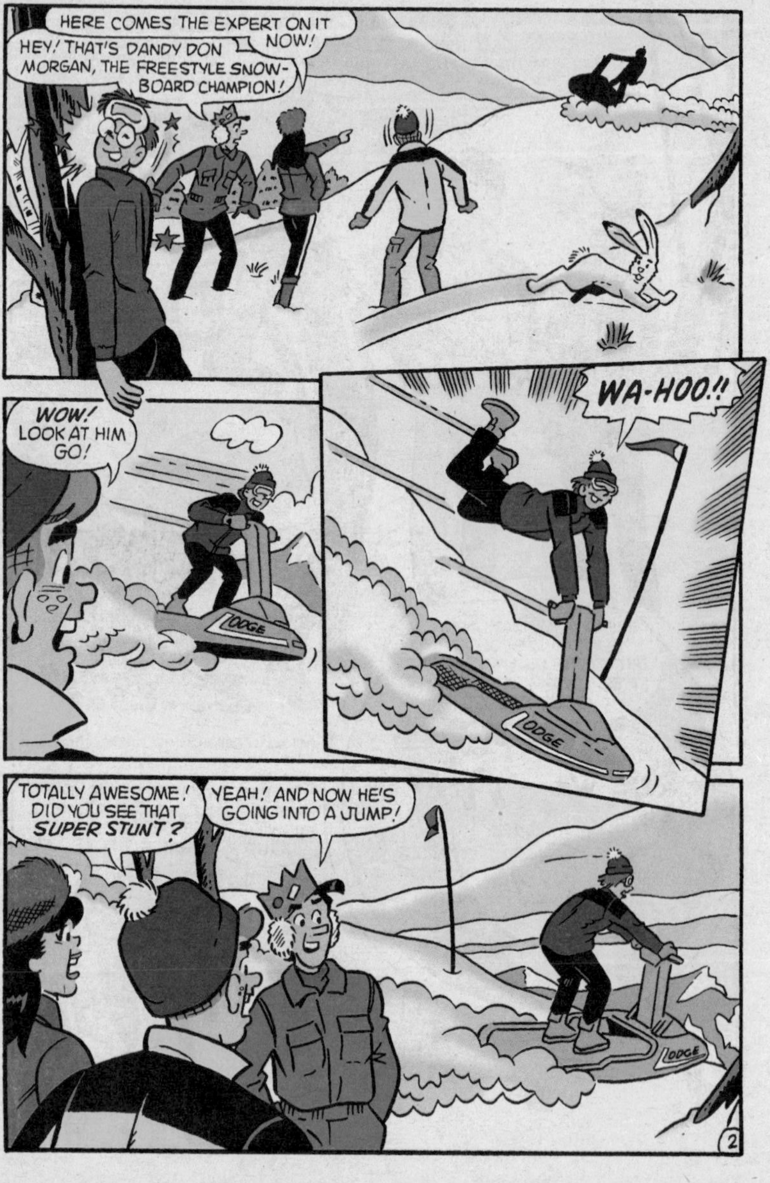
HERE COMES THE EXPERT ON IT NOW!
HEY! THAT'S DANDY DON MORGAN, THE FREESTYLE SNOW-BOARD CHAMPION!
WOW! LOOK AT HIM GO!
WA-HOO!!
LODGE
TOTALLY AWESOME! DID YOU SEE THAT SUPER STUNT?
YEAH! AND NOW HE'S GOING INTO A JUMP!
LODGE
2

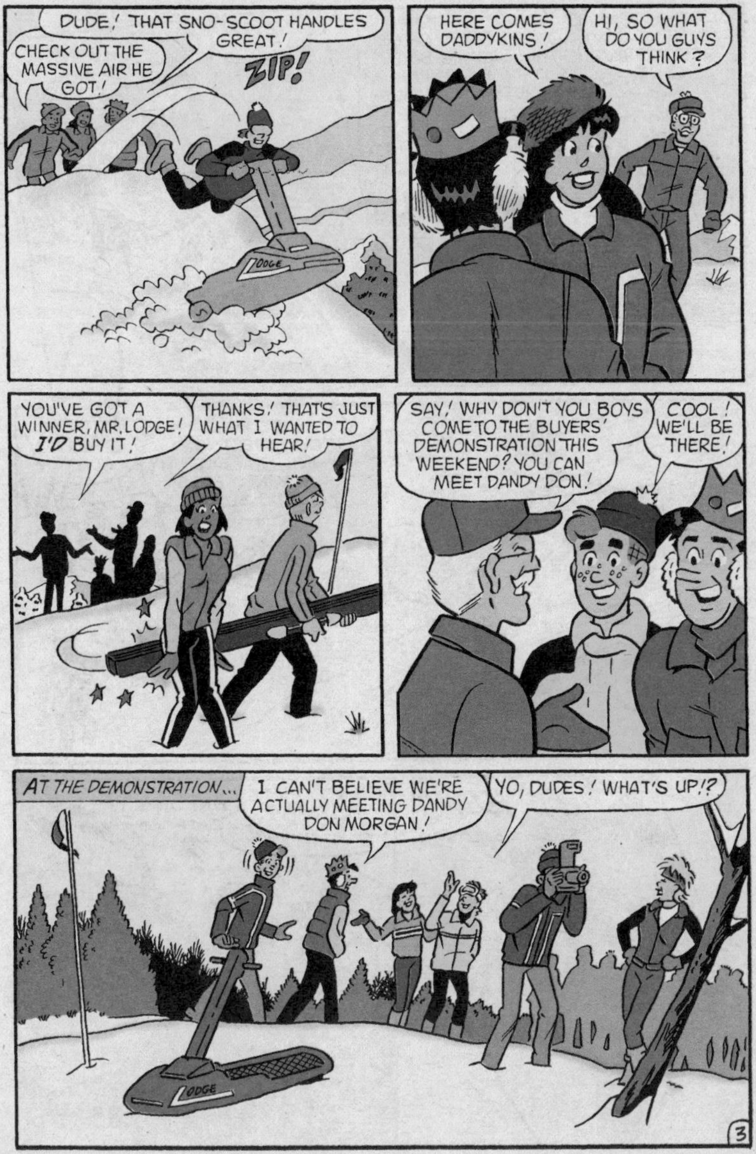
DUDE! THAT SNO-SCOOT HANDLES GREAT!
CHECK OUT THE MASSIVE AIR HE GOT!
ZIP!
LODGE
HERE COMES DADDYKINS!
HI, SO WHAT DO YOU GUYS THINK?
YOU'VE GOT A WINNER, MR. LODGE! I'D BUY IT!
THANKS! THAT'S JUST WHAT I WANTED TO HEAR!
SAY! WHY DON'T YOU BOYS COME TO THE BUYERS' DEMONSTRATION THIS WEEKEND? YOU CAN MEET DANDY DON!
COOL! WE'LL BE THERE!
AT THE DEMONSTRATION...
I CAN'T BELIEVE WE'RE ACTUALLY MEETING DANDY DON MORGAN!
YO, DUDES! WHAT'S UP!?
LODGE
3

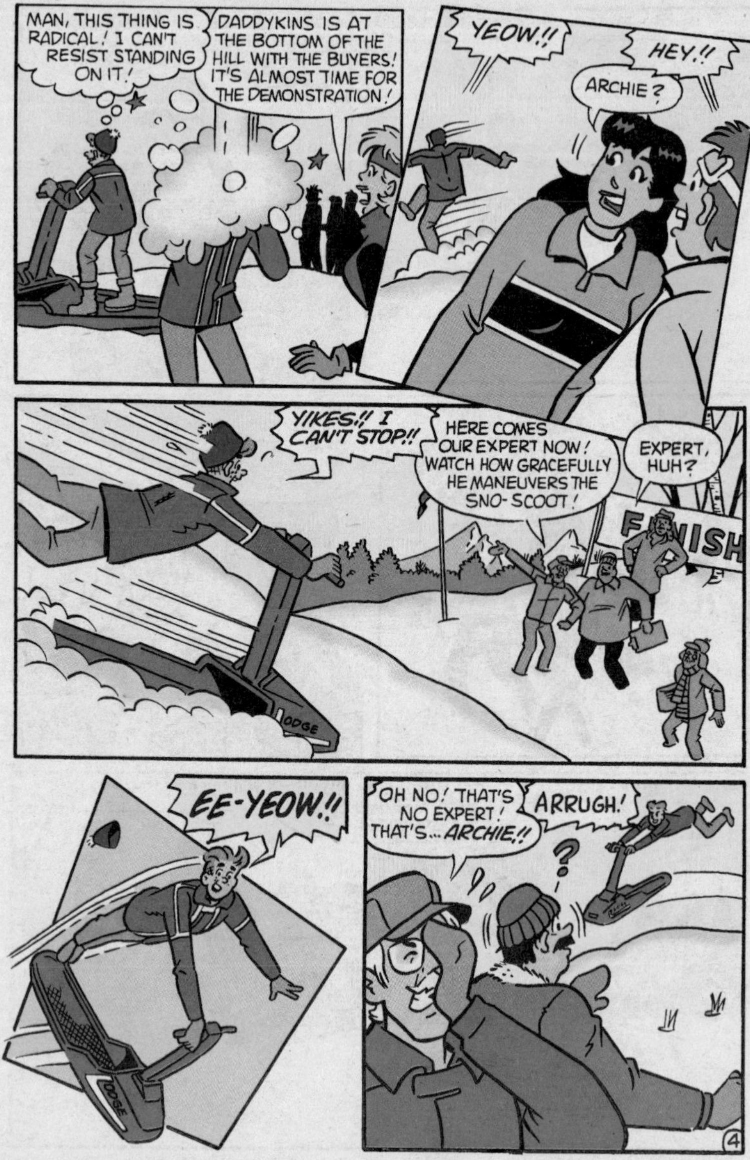

MAN, THIS THING IS RADICAL! I CAN'T RESIST STANDING ON IT!
DADDYKINS IS AT THE BOTTOM OF THE HILL WITH THE BUYERS! IT'S ALMOST TIME FOR THE DEMONSTRATION!
YEOW!!
HEY!!
ARCHIE?
YIKES!! I CAN'T STOP!!
HERE COMES OUR EXPERT NOW! WATCH HOW GRACEFULLY HE MANEUVERS THE SNO-SCOOT!
EXPERT, HUH?
FINISH
ODGE
EE-YEOW!!
DGE
OH NO! THAT'S NO EXPERT! THAT'S... ARCHIE!!
ARRUGH!
4

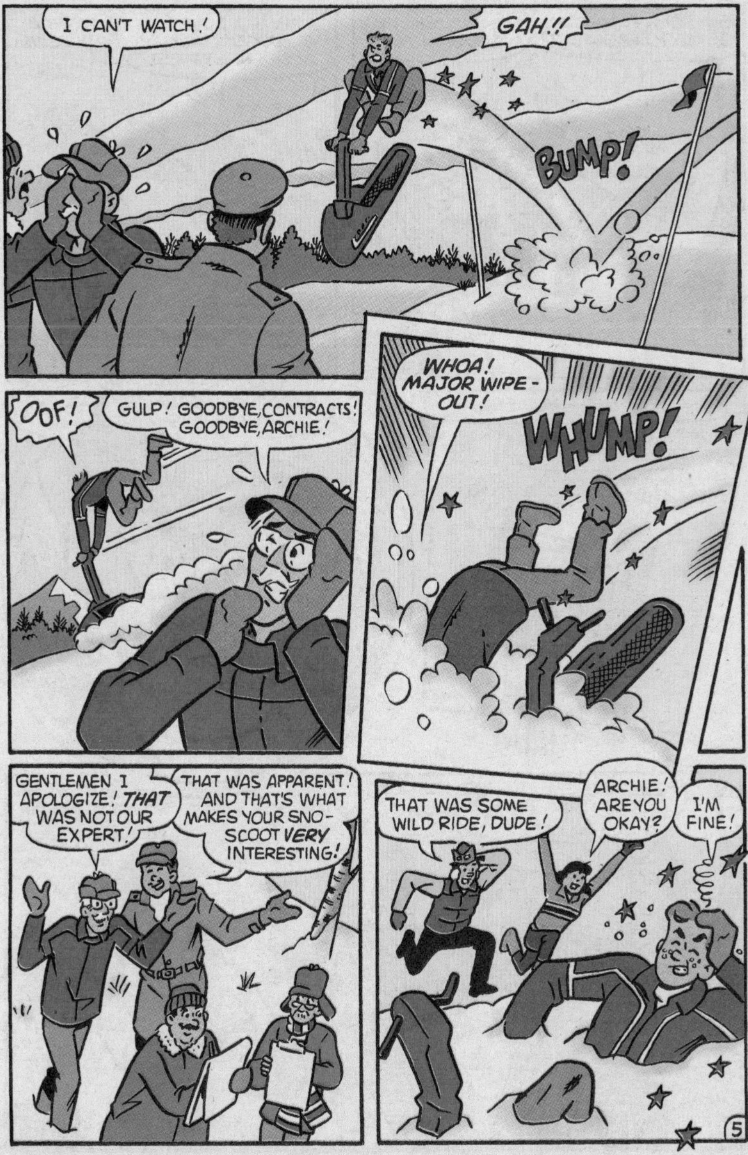
I CAN'T WATCH!
GAH!!
BUMP!
OOF!
GULP! GOODBYE, CONTRACTS! GOODBYE, ARCHIE!
WHOA! MAJOR WIPE-OUT!
WHUMP!
GENTLEMEN I APOLOGIZE! THAT WAS NOT OUR EXPERT!
THAT WAS APPARENT! AND THAT'S WHAT MAKES YOUR SNO-SCOOT VERY INTERESTING!
THAT WAS SOME WILD RIDE, DUDE!
ARCHIE! ARE YOU OKAY?
I'M FINE!
5

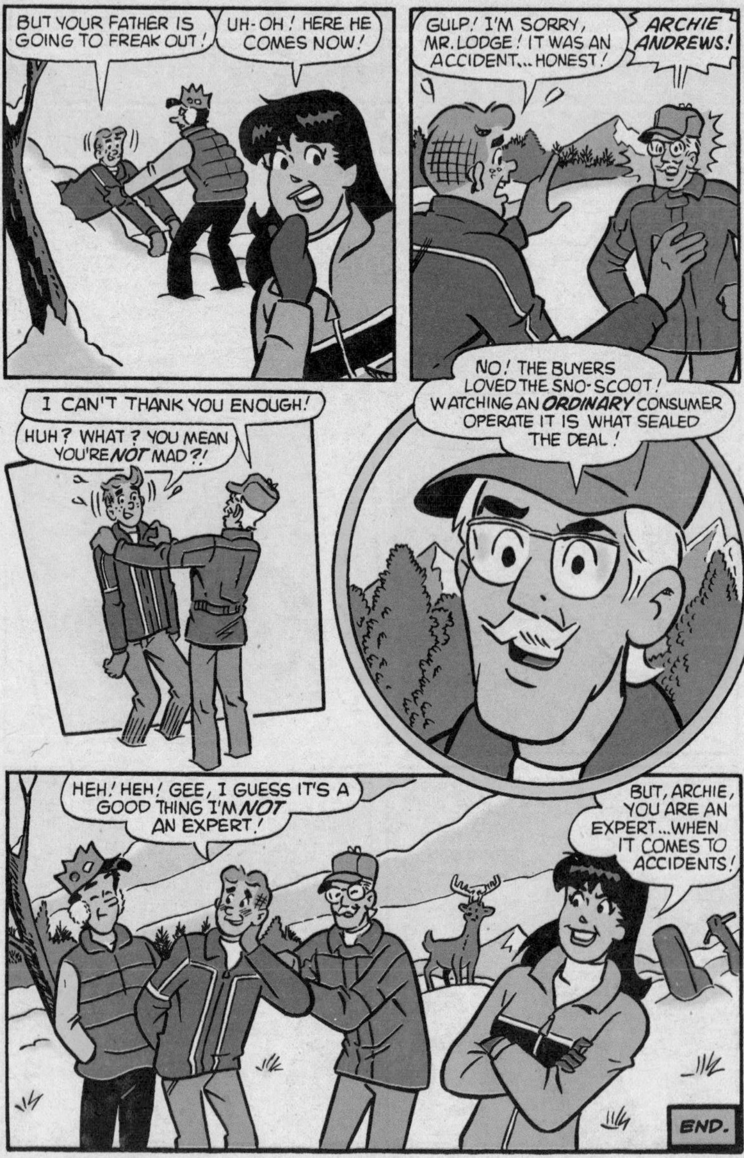
BUT YOUR FATHER IS GOING TO FREAK OUT!
UH-OH! HERE HE COMES NOW!
GULP! I'M SORRY, MR. LODGE! IT WAS AN ACCIDENT... HONEST!
ARCHIE ANDREWS!
I CAN'T THANK YOU ENOUGH!
HUH? WHAT? YOU MEAN YOU'RE NOT MAD?!
NO! THE BUYERS LOVED THE SNO-SCOOT! WATCHING AN ORDINARY CONSUMER OPERATE IT IS WHAT SEALED THE DEAL!
HEH! HEH! GEE, I GUESS IT'S A GOOD THING I'M NOT AN EXPERT!
BUT, ARCHIE, YOU ARE AN EXPERT... WHEN IT COMES TO ACCIDENTS!
END.

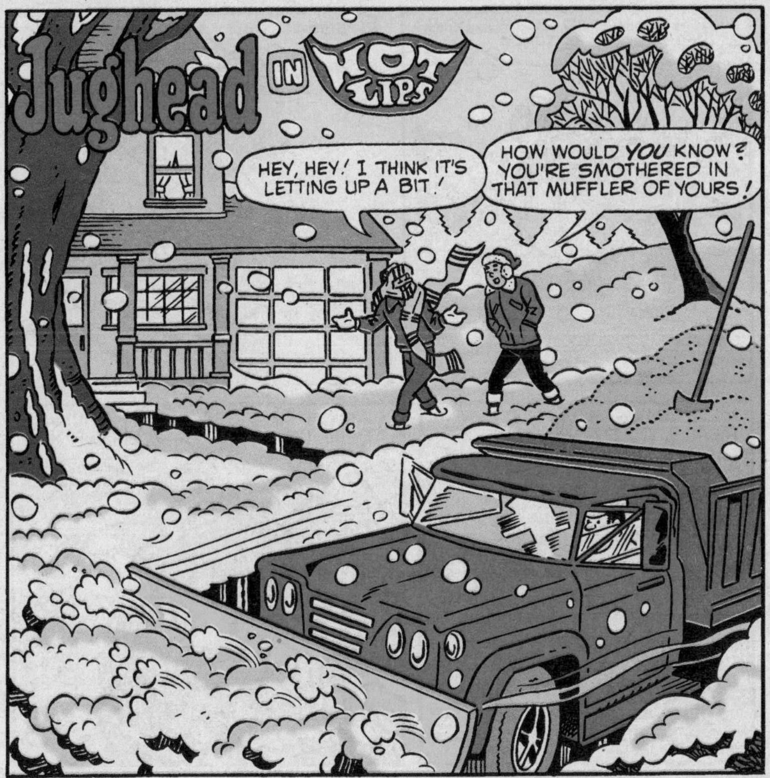
Jughead IN HOT LIPS
HEY, HEY! I THINK IT'S LETTING UP A BIT!
HOW WOULD YOU KNOW? YOU'RE SMOTHERED IN THAT MUFFLER OF YOURS!

Script: Frank Doyle / Pencils: Doug Crane / Inks: Rudy Lapick / Letters: Bill Yoshida / Colors: Barry Grossman

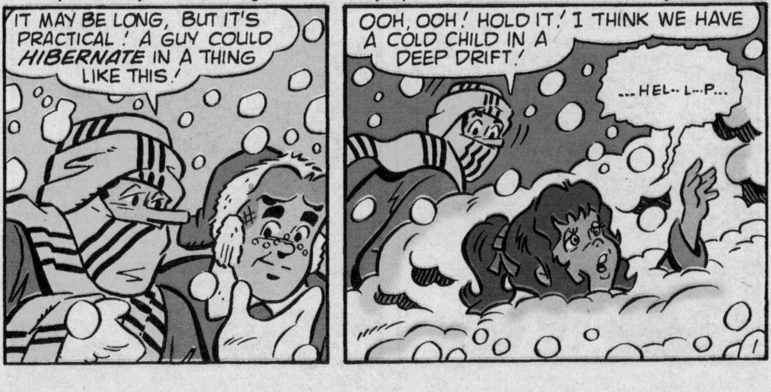
IT MAY BE LONG, BUT IT'S PRACTICAL! A GUY COULD HIBERNATE IN A THING LIKE THIS!
OOH, OOH! HOLD IT! I THINK WE HAVE A COLD CHILD IN A DEEP DRIFT!
...HEL.. L...P...

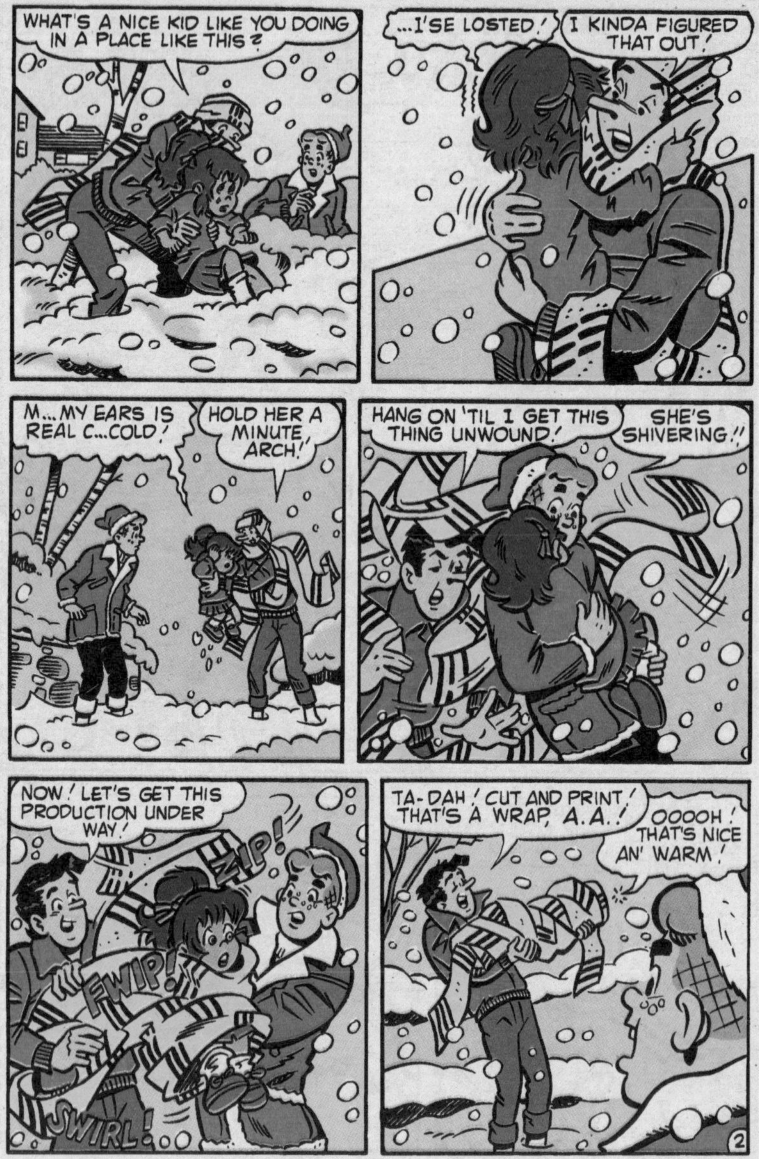

WHAT'S A NICE KID LIKE YOU DOING IN A PLACE LIKE THIS?
...I'SE LOSTED!
I KINDA FIGURED THAT OUT!
M...MY EARS IS REAL C...COLD!
HOLD HER A MINUTE, ARCH!
HANG ON 'TIL I GET THIS THING UNWOUND!
SHE'S SHIVERING!!
NOW! LET'S GET THIS PRODUCTION UNDER WAY!
ZIP!
FWIP!
SWIRL!
TA-DAH! CUT AND PRINT! THAT'S A WRAP, A.A.!
OOOOH! THAT'S NICE AN' WARM!

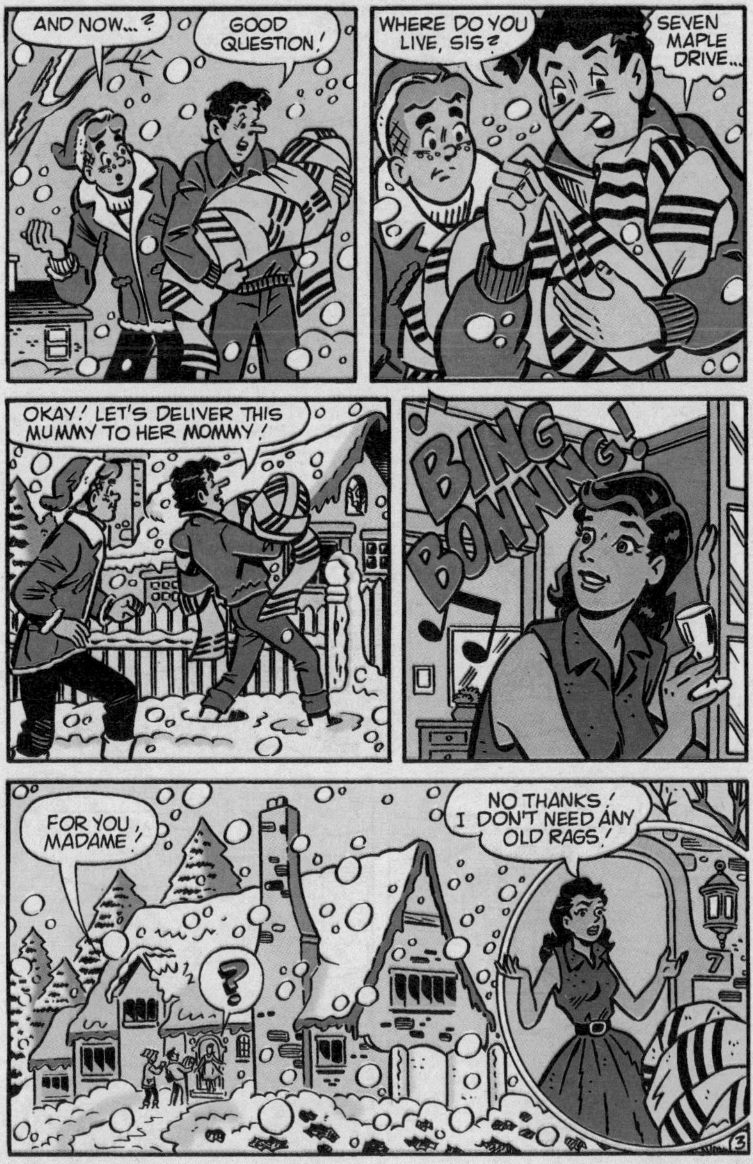
AND NOW...?
GOOD QUESTION!
WHERE DO YOU LIVE, SIS?
SEVEN MAPLE DRIVE...
OKAY! LET'S DELIVER THIS MUMMY TO HER MOMMY!
BING BONNNG!
FOR YOU MADAME!
NO THANKS! I DON'T NEED ANY OLD RAGS!
7
3

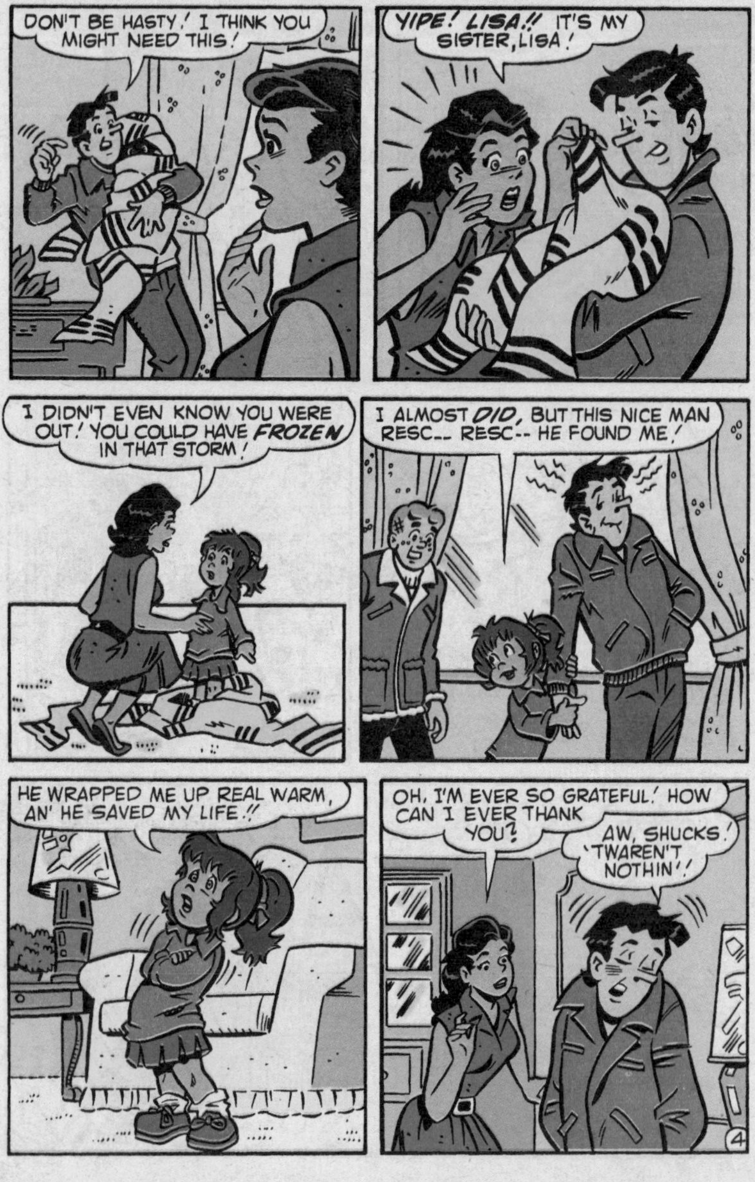
DON'T BE HASTY! I THINK YOU MIGHT NEED THIS!
YIPE! LISA!! IT'S MY SISTER, LISA!
I DIDN'T EVEN KNOW YOU WERE OUT! YOU COULD HAVE FROZEN IN THAT STORM!
I ALMOST DID, BUT THIS NICE MAN RESC-- RESC-- HE FOUND ME!
HE WRAPPED ME UP REAL WARM, AN' HE SAVED MY LIFE!!
OH, I'M EVER SO GRATEFUL! HOW CAN I EVER THANK YOU?
AW, SHUCKS! 'TWAREN'T NOTHIN'!
4

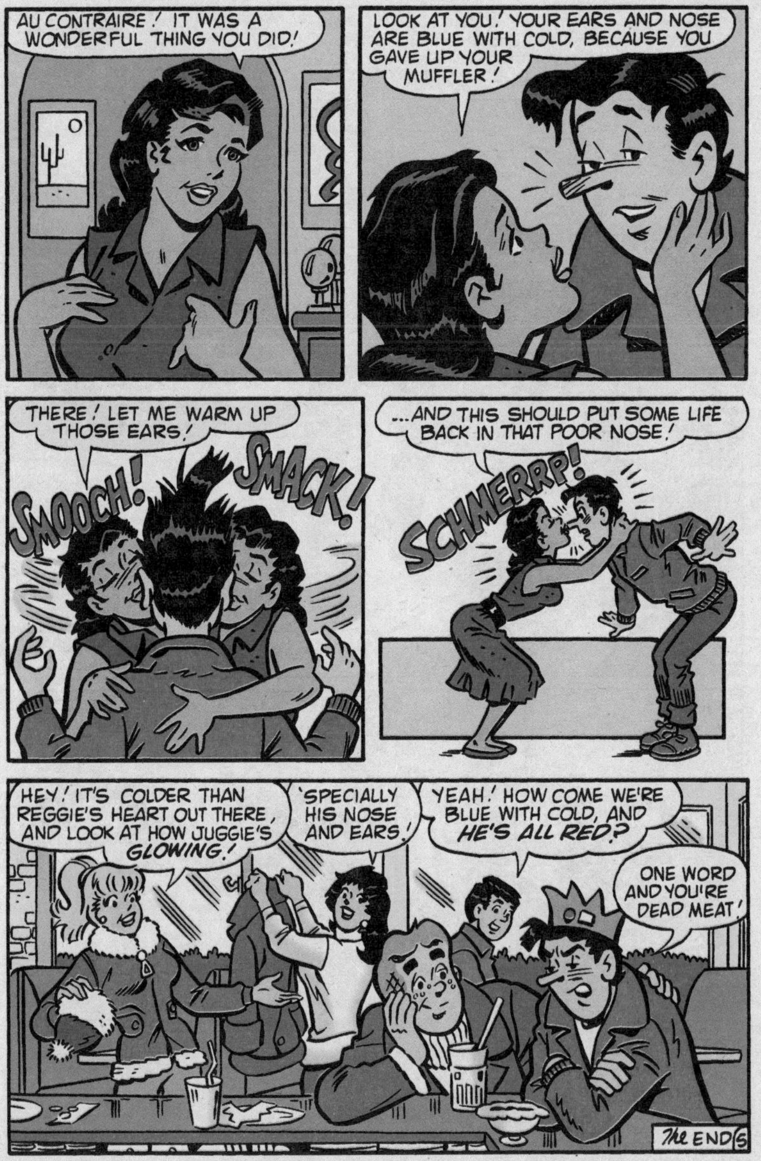
AU CONTRAIRE! IT WAS A WONDERFUL THING YOU DID!
LOOK AT YOU! YOUR EARS AND NOSE ARE BLUE WITH COLD, BECAUSE YOU GAVE UP YOUR MUFFLER!
THERE! LET ME WARM UP THOSE EARS!
SMOOCH!
SMACK!
...AND THIS SHOULD PUT SOME LIFE BACK IN THAT POOR NOSE!
SCHMERRP!
HEY! IT'S COLDER THAN REGGIE'S HEART OUT THERE, AND LOOK AT HOW JUGGIE'S GLOWING!
'SPECIALLY HIS NOSE AND EARS!
YEAH! HOW COME WE'RE BLUE WITH COLD, AND HE'S ALL RED?
ONE WORD AND YOU'RE DEAD MEAT!
The END
5

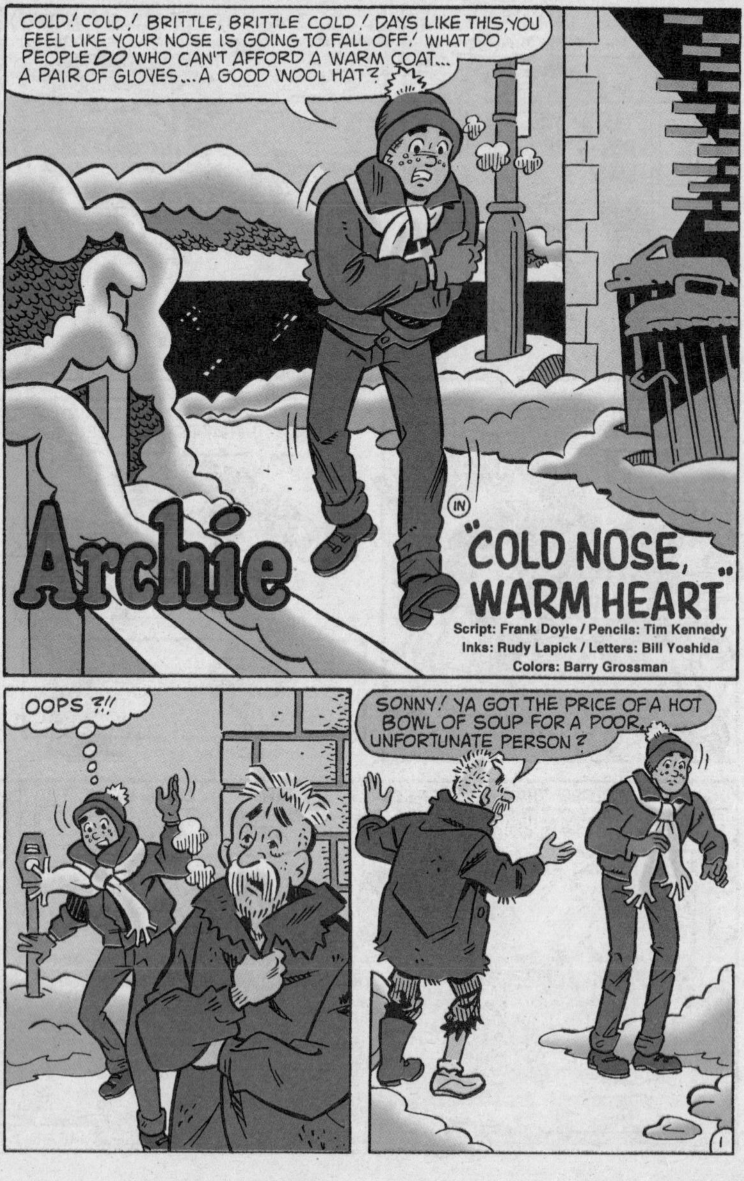
COLD! COLD! BRITTLE, BRITTLE COLD! DAYS LIKE THIS, YOU FEEL LIKE YOUR NOSE IS GOING TO FALL OFF! WHAT DO PEOPLE DO WHO CAN'T AFFORD A WARM COAT... A PAIR OF GLOVES... A GOOD WOOL HAT?
Archie
IN
"COLD NOSE, WARM HEART"
Script: Frank Doyle / Pencils: Tim Kennedy
Inks: Rudy Lapick / Letters: Bill Yoshida
Colors: Barry Grossman
OOPS ?!!
SONNY! YA GOT THE PRICE OF A HOT BOWL OF SOUP FOR A POOR, UNFORTUNATE PERSON?
1

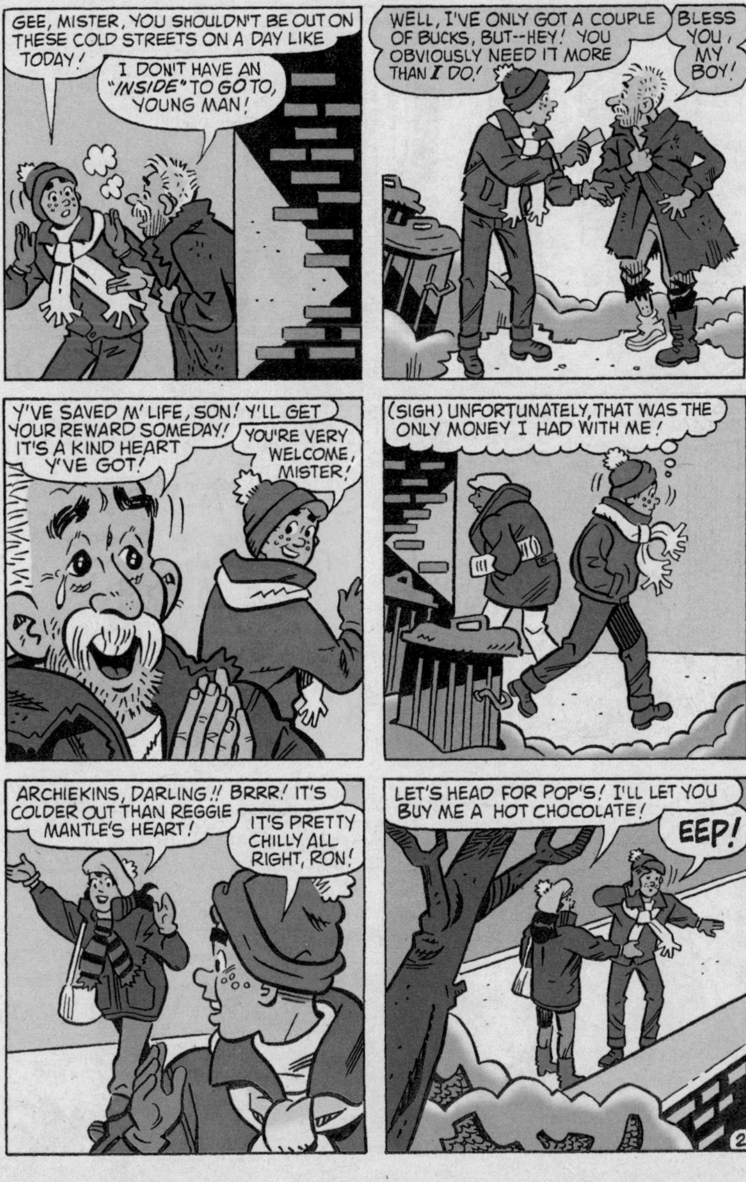

GEE, MISTER, YOU SHOULDN'T BE OUT ON THESE COLD STREETS ON A DAY LIKE TODAY!
I DON'T HAVE AN "INSIDE" TO GO TO, YOUNG MAN!
WELL, I'VE ONLY GOT A COUPLE OF BUCKS, BUT--HEY! YOU OBVIOUSLY NEED IT MORE THAN I DO!
BLESS YOU, MY BOY!
Y'VE SAVED M' LIFE, SON! Y'LL GET YOUR REWARD SOMEDAY! IT'S A KIND HEART Y'VE GOT!
YOU'RE VERY WELCOME, MISTER!
(SIGH) UNFORTUNATELY, THAT WAS THE ONLY MONEY I HAD WITH ME!
ARCHIEKINS, DARLING!! BRRR! IT'S COLDER OUT THAN REGGIE MANTLE'S HEART!
IT'S PRETTY CHILLY ALL RIGHT, RON!
LET'S HEAD FOR POP'S! I'LL LET YOU BUY ME A HOT CHOCOLATE!
EEP!

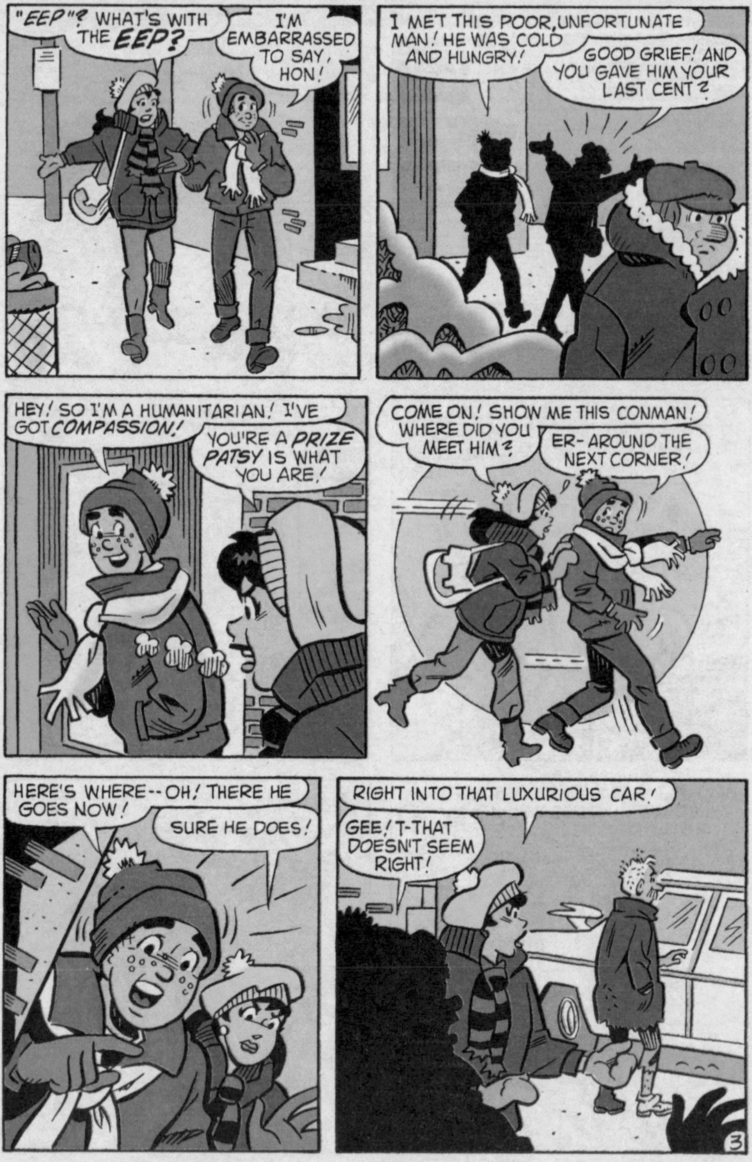
"EEP"? WHAT'S WITH THE EEP?
I'M EMBARRASSED TO SAY, HON!
I MET THIS POOR, UNFORTUNATE MAN! HE WAS COLD AND HUNGRY!
GOOD GRIEF! AND YOU GAVE HIM YOUR LAST CENT?
HEY! SO I'M A HUMANITARIAN! I'VE GOT COMPASSION!
YOU'RE A PRIZE PATSY IS WHAT YOU ARE!
COME ON! SHOW ME THIS CONMAN! WHERE DID YOU MEET HIM?
ER- AROUND THE NEXT CORNER!
HERE'S WHERE--OH! THERE HE GOES NOW!
SURE HE DOES!
RIGHT INTO THAT LUXURIOUS CAR!
GEE! T-THAT DOESN'T SEEM RIGHT!
3

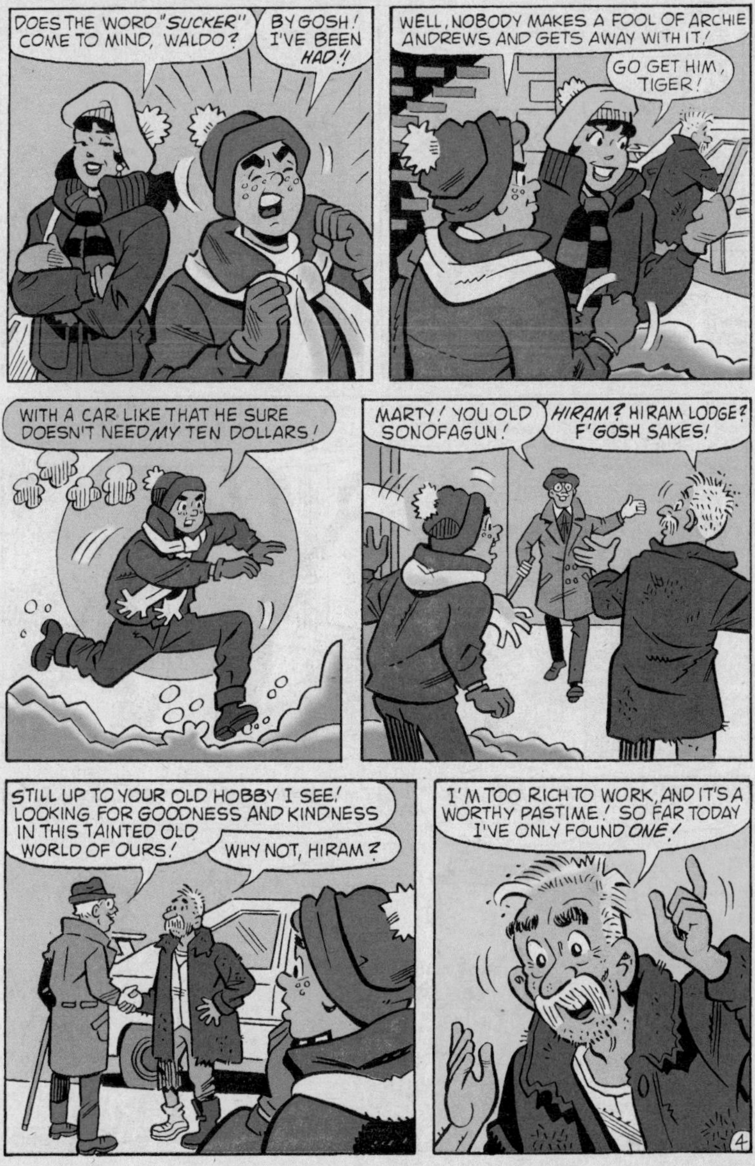
DOES THE WORD "SUCKER" COME TO MIND, WALDO?
BY GOSH! I'VE BEEN HAD!!
WELL, NOBODY MAKES A FOOL OF ARCHIE ANDREWS AND GETS AWAY WITH IT!
GO GET HIM, TIGER!
WITH A CAR LIKE THAT HE SURE DOESN'T NEED MY TEN DOLLARS!
MARTY! YOU OLD SONOFAGUN!
HIRAM? HIRAM LODGE? F'GOSH SAKES!
STILL UP TO YOUR OLD HOBBY I SEE! LOOKING FOR GOODNESS AND KINDNESS IN THIS TAINTED OLD WORLD OF OURS!
WHY NOT, HIRAM?
I'M TOO RICH TO WORK, AND IT'S A WORTHY PASTIME! SO FAR TODAY I'VE ONLY FOUND ONE!
4

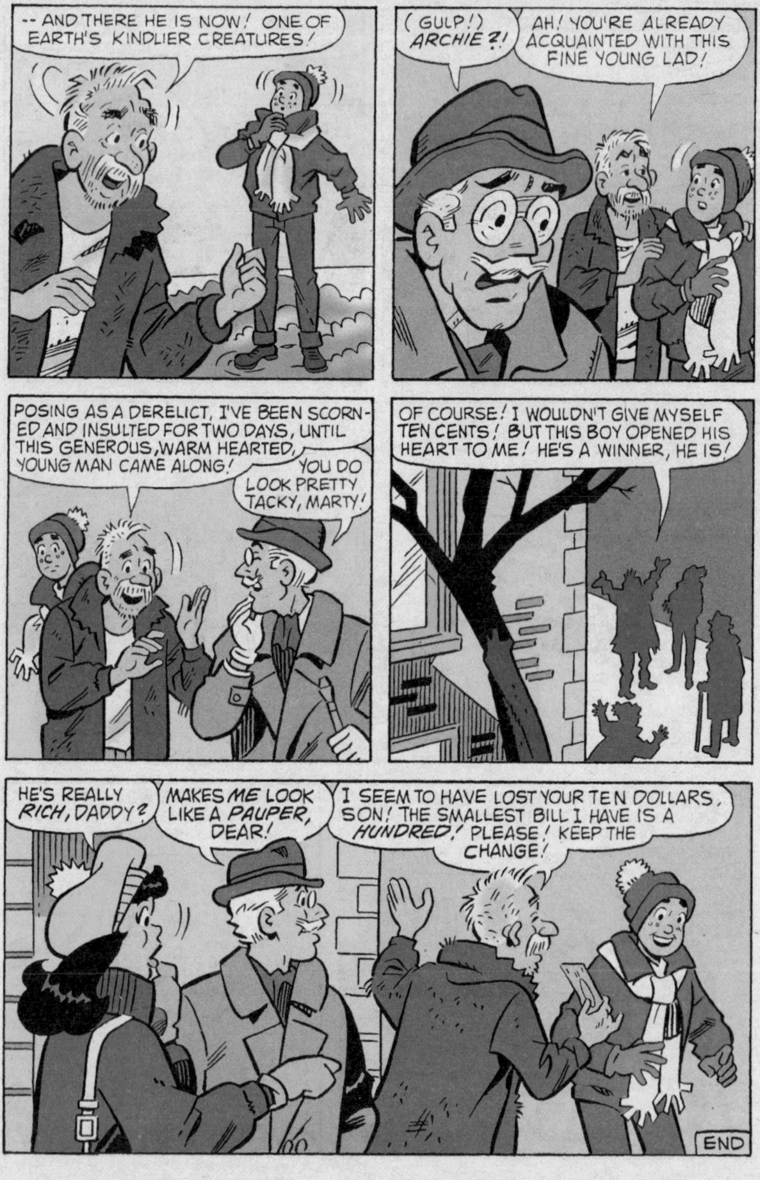
-- AND THERE HE IS NOW! ONE OF EARTH'S KINDLIER CREATURES!
(GULP!) ARCHIE ?!
AH! YOU'RE ALREADY ACQUAINTED WITH THIS FINE YOUNG LAD!
POSING AS A DERELICT, I'VE BEEN SCORNED AND INSULTED FOR TWO DAYS, UNTIL THIS GENEROUS, WARM HEARTED, YOUNG MAN CAME ALONG!
YOU DO LOOK PRETTY TACKY, MARTY!
OF COURSE! I WOULDN'T GIVE MYSELF TEN CENTS! BUT THIS BOY OPENED HIS HEART TO ME! HE'S A WINNER, HE IS!
HE'S REALLY RICH, DADDY?
MAKES ME LOOK LIKE A PAUPER, DEAR!
I SEEM TO HAVE LOST YOUR TEN DOLLARS, SON! THE SMALLEST BILL I HAVE IS A HUNDRED! PLEASE! KEEP THE CHANGE!
END

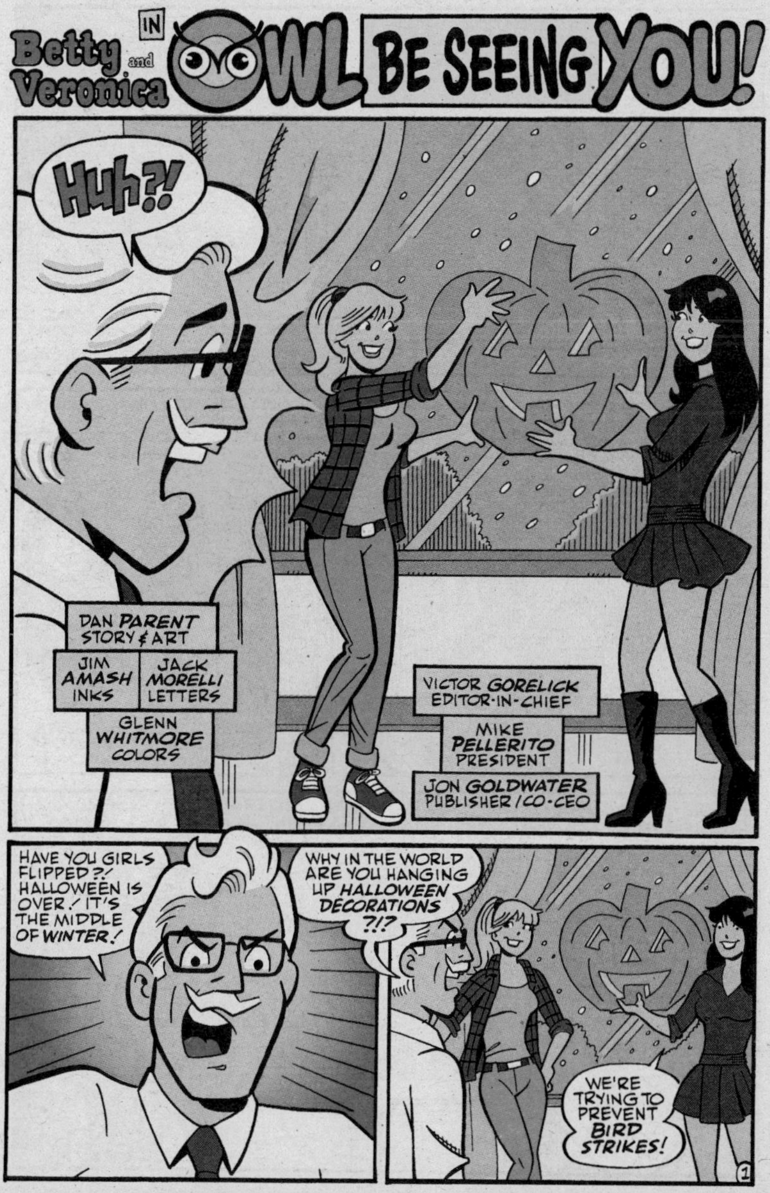

Betty and Veronica IN OWL BE SEEING YOU!
Huh?!
DAN PARENT STORY & ART
JIM AMASH INKS
JACK MORELLI LETTERS
GLENN WHITMORE COLORS
VICTOR GORELICK EDITOR-IN-CHIEF
MIKE PELLERITO PRESIDENT
JON GOLDWATER PUBLISHER / CO-CEO
HAVE YOU GIRLS FLIPPED?! HALLOWEEN IS OVER! IT'S THE MIDDLE OF WINTER!
WHY IN THE WORLD ARE YOU HANGING UP HALLOWEEN DECORATIONS ?!?
WE'RE TRYING TO PREVENT BIRD STRIKES!
1

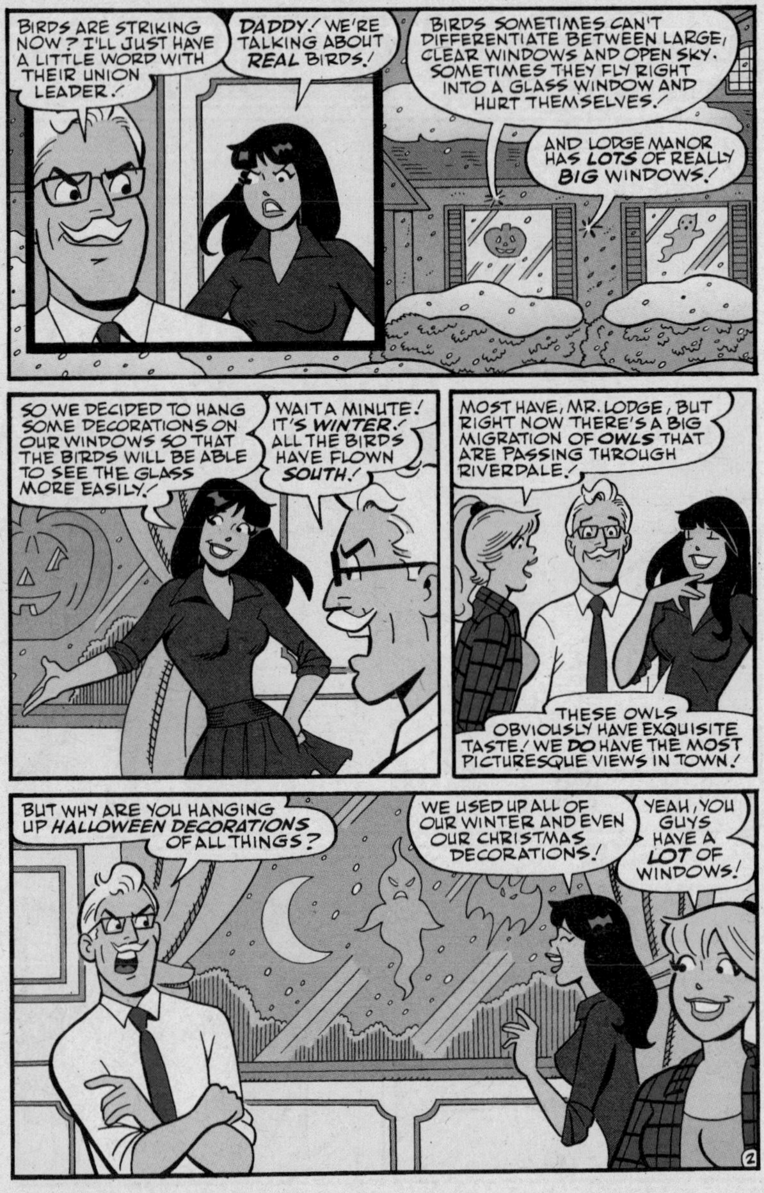

BIRDS ARE STRIKING NOW? I'LL JUST HAVE A LITTLE WORD WITH THEIR UNION LEADER!
DADDY! WE'RE TALKING ABOUT REAL BIRDS!
BIRDS SOMETIMES CAN'T DIFFERENTIATE BETWEEN LARGE, CLEAR WINDOWS AND OPEN SKY. SOMETIMES THEY FLY RIGHT INTO A GLASS WINDOW AND HURT THEMSELVES!
AND LODGE MANOR HAS LOTS OF REALLY BIG WINDOWS!
SO WE DECIDED TO HANG SOME DECORATIONS ON OUR WINDOWS SO THAT THE BIRDS WILL BE ABLE TO SEE THE GLASS MORE EASILY!
WAIT A MINUTE! IT'S WINTER! ALL THE BIRDS HAVE FLOWN SOUTH!
MOST HAVE, MR. LODGE, BUT RIGHT NOW THERE'S A BIG MIGRATION OF OWLS THAT ARE PASSING THROUGH RIVERDALE!
THESE OWLS OBVIOUSLY HAVE EXQUISITE TASTE! WE DO HAVE THE MOST PICTURESQUE VIEWS IN TOWN!
BUT WHY ARE YOU HANGING UP HALLOWEEN DECORATIONS OF ALL THINGS?
WE USED UP ALL OF OUR WINTER AND EVEN OUR CHRISTMAS DECORATIONS!
YEAH, YOU GUYS HAVE A LOT OF WINDOWS!
2

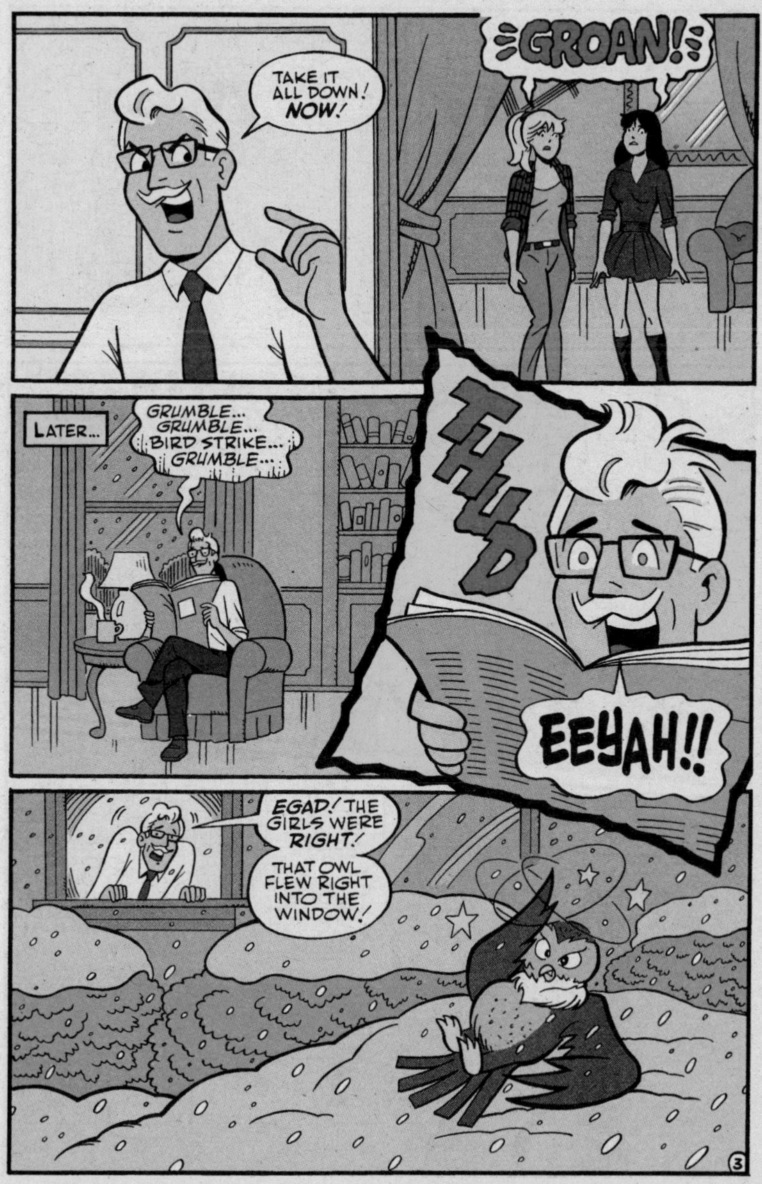
TAKE IT ALL DOWN! NOW!
GROAN!
LATER...
GRUMBLE... GRUMBLE... BIRD STRIKE... GRUMBLE...
THUD
EEYAH!!
EGAD! THE GIRLS WERE RIGHT!
THAT OWL FLEW RIGHT INTO THE WINDOW!
3

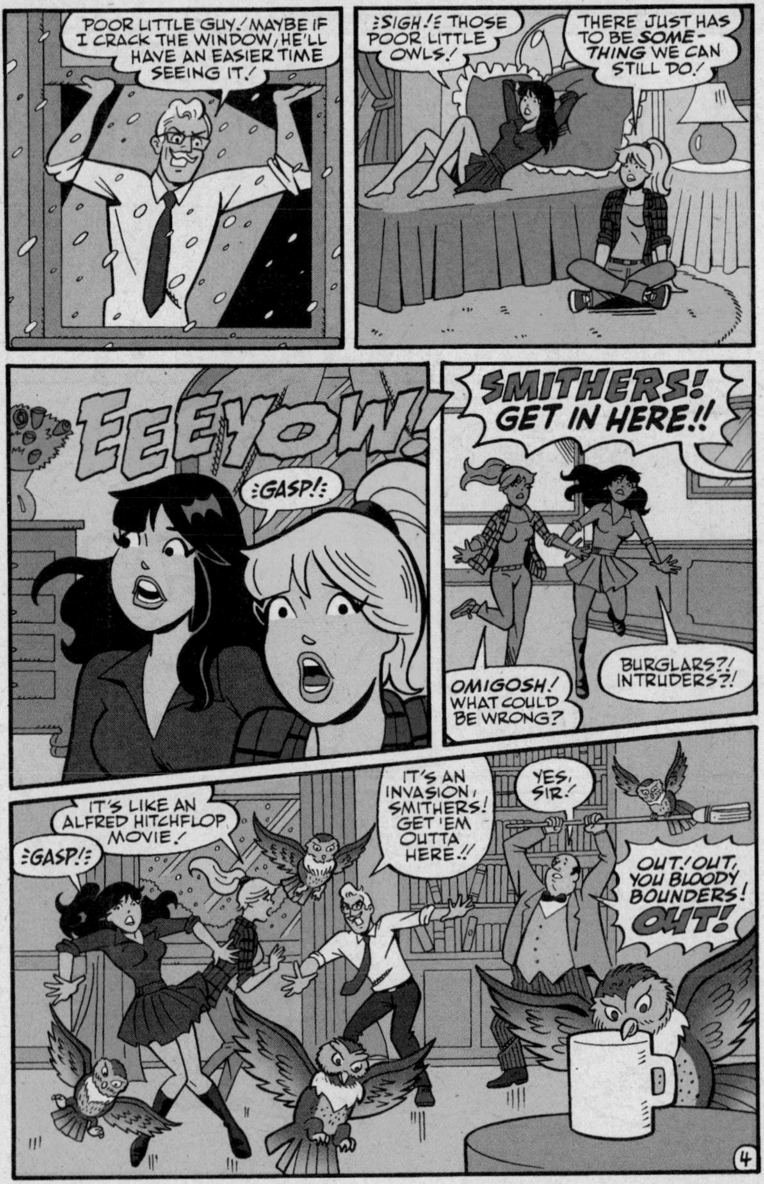

POOR LITTLE GUY! MAYBE IF I CRACK THE WINDOW, HE'LL HAVE AN EASIER TIME SEEING IT!
SIGH! THOSE POOR LITTLE OWLS!
THERE JUST HAS TO BE SOMETHING WE CAN STILL DO!
EEEYOW!
GASP!
SMITHERS! GET IN HERE!!
OMIGOSH! WHAT COULD BE WRONG?
BURGLARS?! INTRUDERS?!
GASP!
IT'S LIKE AN ALFRED HITCHFLOP MOVIE!
IT'S AN INVASION, SMITHERS! GET 'EM OUTTA HERE!!
YES, SIR!
OUT! OUT, YOU BLOODY BOUNDERS! OUT!

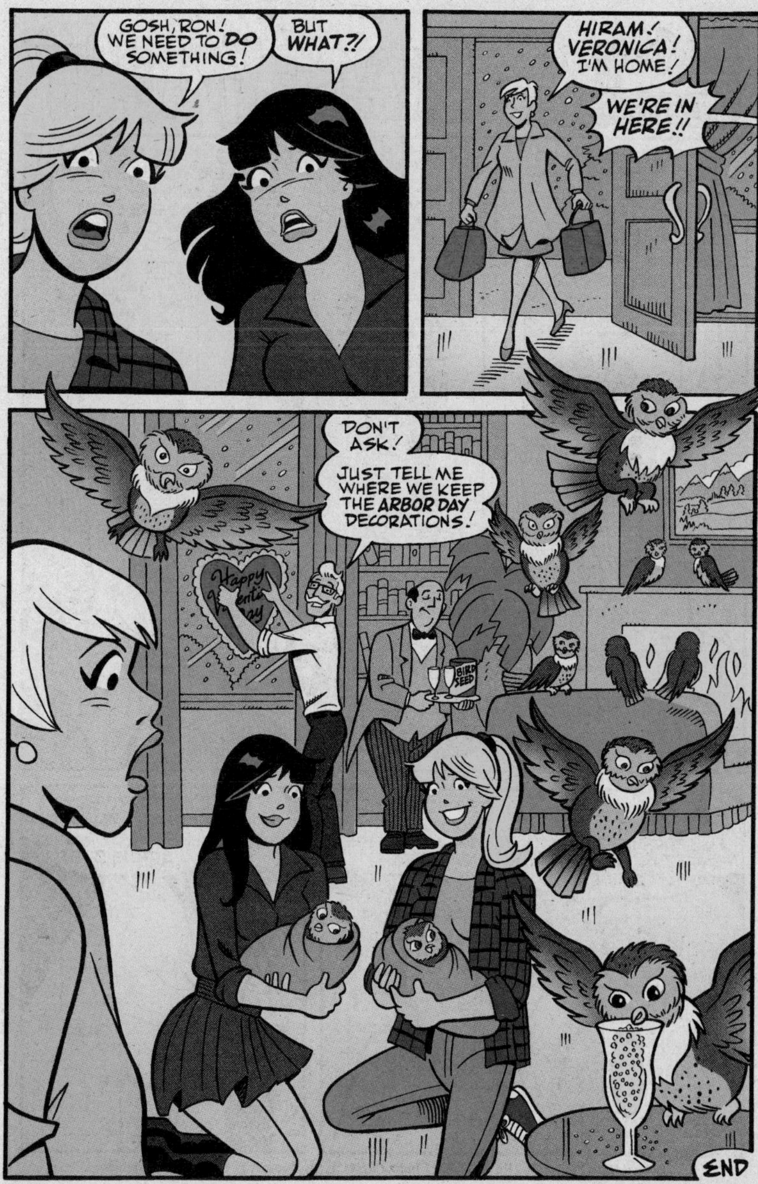
GOSH, RON! WE NEED TO DO SOMETHING!
BUT WHAT?!
HIRAM! VERONICA! I'M HOME!
WE'RE IN HERE!!
DON'T ASK!
JUST TELL ME WHERE WE KEEP THE ARBOR DAY DECORATIONS!
BIRD SEED
END

Betty and Veronica in "Stage Fright"

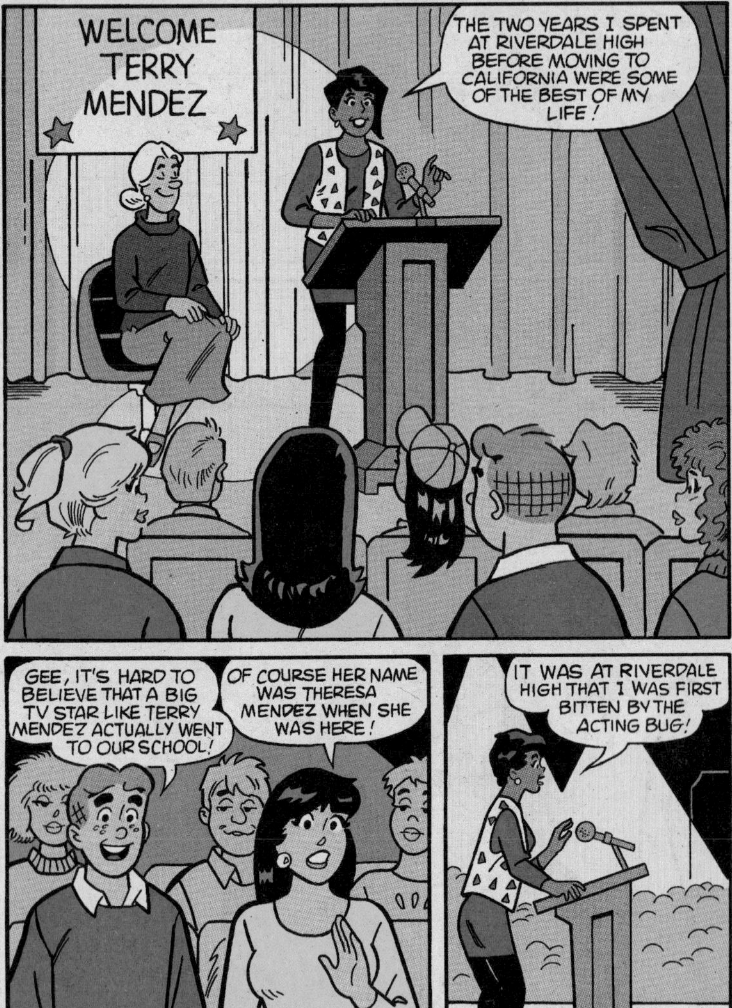

WELCOME TERRY MENDEZ
THE TWO YEARS I SPENT AT RIVERDALE HIGH BEFORE MOVING TO CALIFORNIA WERE SOME OF THE BEST OF MY LIFE!
GEE, IT'S HARD TO BELIEVE THAT A BIG TV STAR LIKE TERRY MENDEZ ACTUALLY WENT TO OUR SCHOOL!
OF COURSE HER NAME WAS THERESA MENDEZ WHEN SHE WAS HERE!
IT WAS AT RIVERDALE HIGH THAT I WAS FIRST BITTEN BY THE ACTING BUG!

Script: Mike Pellowski / Pencils: Jeff Shultz / Inks: Henry Scarpelli / Letters: Bill Yoshida

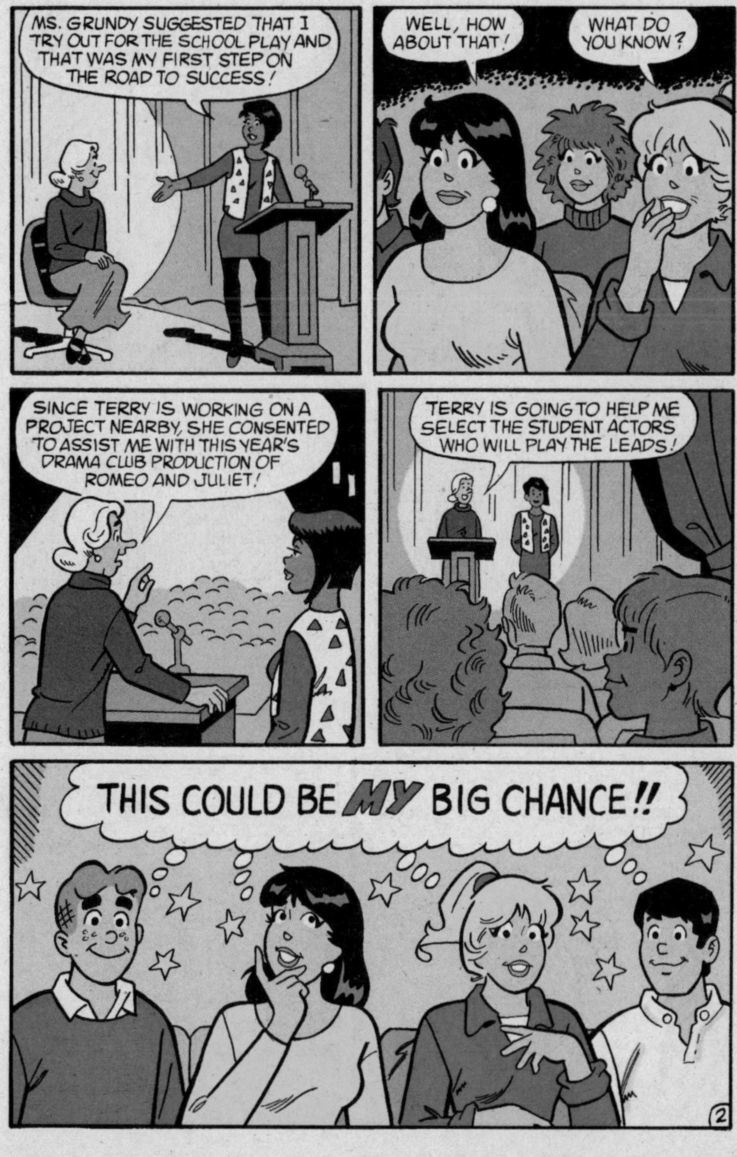
MS. GRUNDY SUGGESTED THAT I TRY OUT FOR THE SCHOOL PLAY AND THAT WAS MY FIRST STEP ON THE ROAD TO SUCCESS!
WELL, HOW ABOUT THAT!
WHAT DO YOU KNOW?
SINCE TERRY IS WORKING ON A PROJECT NEARBY, SHE CONSENTED TO ASSIST ME WITH THIS YEAR'S DRAMA CLUB PRODUCTION OF ROMEO AND JULIET!
TERRY IS GOING TO HELP ME SELECT THE STUDENT ACTORS WHO WILL PLAY THE LEADS!
THIS COULD BE MY BIG CHANCE!!
2

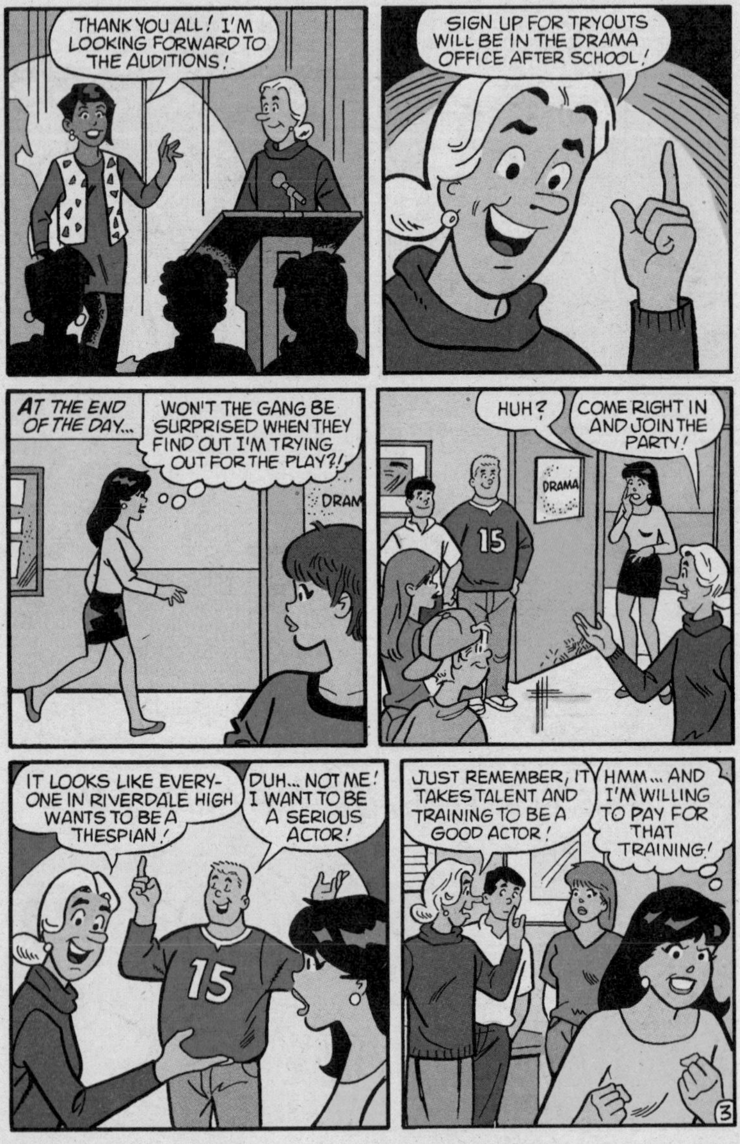
THANK YOU ALL! I'M LOOKING FORWARD TO THE AUDITIONS!
SIGN UP FOR TRYOUTS WILL BE IN THE DRAMA OFFICE AFTER SCHOOL!
AT THE END OF THE DAY...
WON'T THE GANG BE SURPRISED WHEN THEY FIND OUT I'M TRYING OUT FOR THE PLAY?!
DRAM
HUH?
COME RIGHT IN AND JOIN THE PARTY!
DRAMA
15
IT LOOKS LIKE EVERY-ONE IN RIVERDALE HIGH WANTS TO BE A THESPIAN!
DUH... NOT ME! I WANT TO BE A SERIOUS ACTOR!
15
JUST REMEMBER, IT TAKES TALENT AND TRAINING TO BE A GOOD ACTOR!
HMM... AND I'M WILLING TO PAY FOR THAT TRAINING!
3

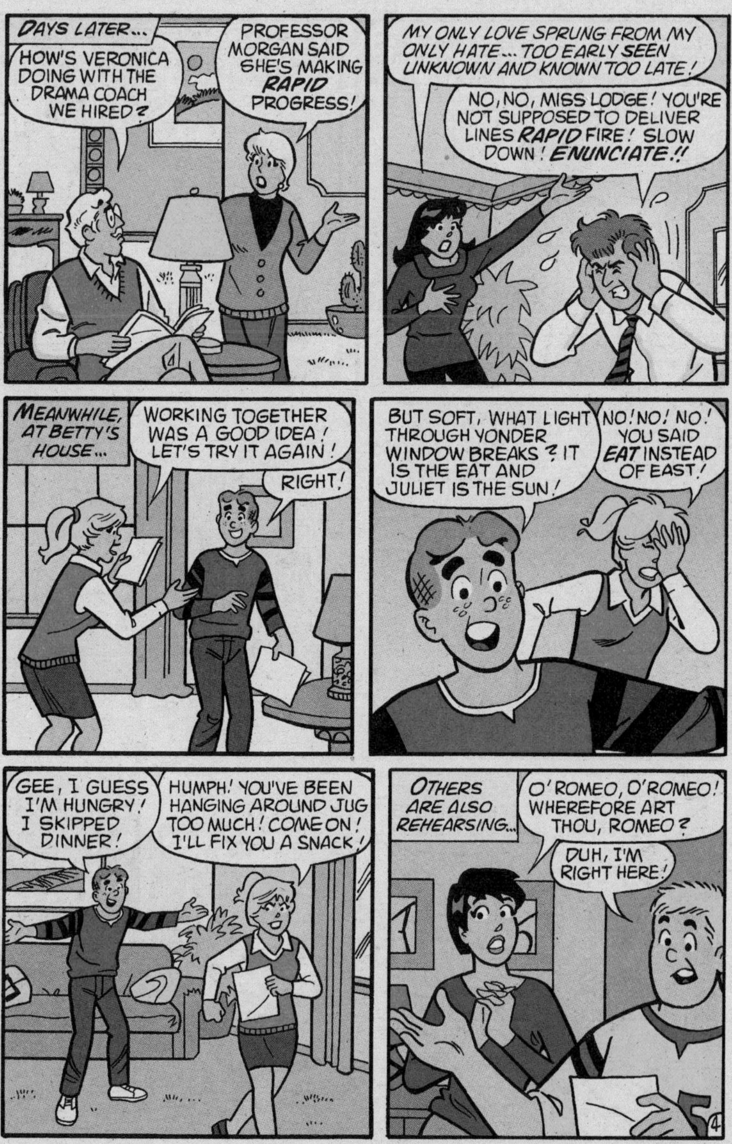
DAYS LATER...
HOW'S VERONICA DOING WITH THE DRAMA COACH WE HIRED?
PROFESSOR MORGAN SAID SHE'S MAKING RAPID PROGRESS!
MY ONLY LOVE SPRUNG FROM MY ONLY HATE... TOO EARLY SEEN UNKNOWN AND KNOWN TOO LATE!
NO, NO, MISS LODGE! YOU'RE NOT SUPPOSED TO DELIVER LINES RAPID FIRE! SLOW DOWN! ENUNCIATE!!
MEANWHILE, AT BETTY'S HOUSE...
WORKING TOGETHER WAS A GOOD IDEA! LET'S TRY IT AGAIN!
RIGHT!
BUT SOFT, WHAT LIGHT THROUGH YONDER WINDOW BREAKS? IT IS THE EAT AND JULIET IS THE SUN!
NO! NO! NO! YOU SAID EAT INSTEAD OF EAST!
GEE, I GUESS I'M HUNGRY! I SKIPPED DINNER!
HUMPH! YOU'VE BEEN HANGING AROUND JUG TOO MUCH! COME ON! I'LL FIX YOU A SNACK!
OTHERS ARE ALSO REHEARSING...
O' ROMEO, O' ROMEO! WHEREFORE ART THOU, ROMEO?
DUH, I'M RIGHT HERE!
4

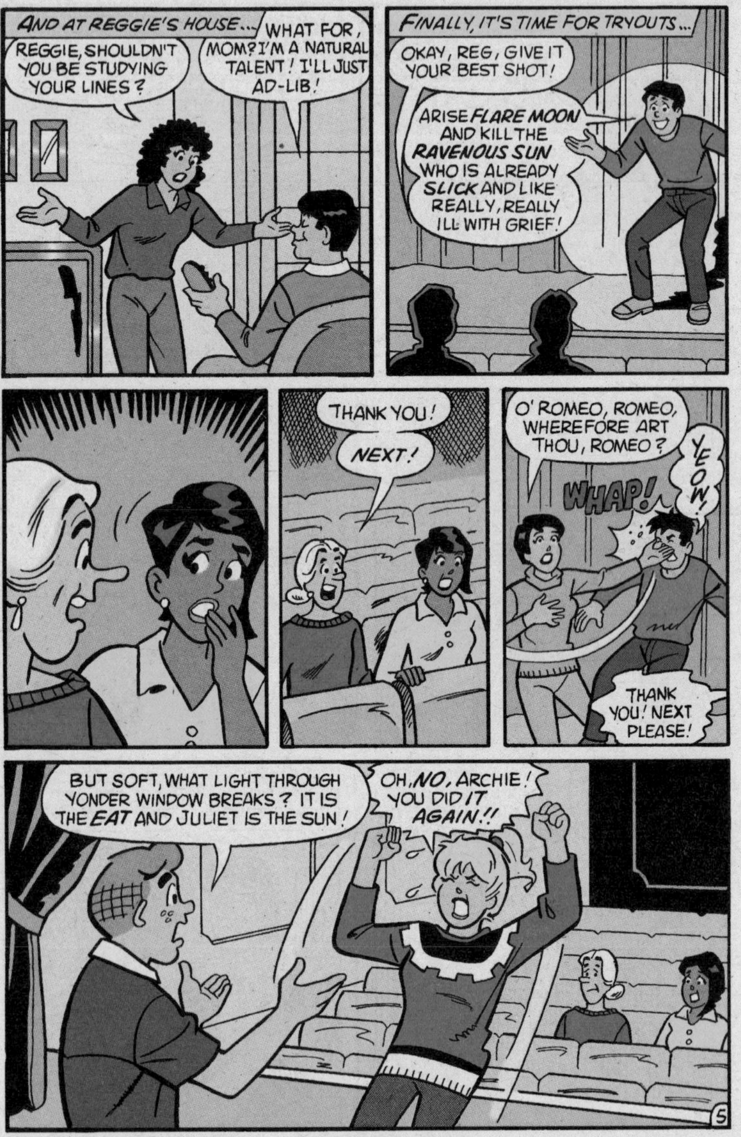
AND AT REGGIE'S HOUSE...
REGGIE, SHOULDN'T YOU BE STUDYING YOUR LINES?
WHAT FOR, MOM? I'M A NATURAL TALENT! I'LL JUST AD-LIB!
FINALLY, IT'S TIME FOR TRYOUTS...
OKAY, REG, GIVE IT YOUR BEST SHOT!
ARISE FLARE MOON AND KILL THE RAVENOUS SUN WHO IS ALREADY SLICK AND LIKE REALLY, REALLY ILL WITH GRIEF!
THANK YOU!
NEXT!
O' ROMEO, ROMEO, WHEREFORE ART THOU, ROMEO?
WHAP!
YEOW!
THANK YOU! NEXT PLEASE!
BUT SOFT, WHAT LIGHT THROUGH YONDER WINDOW BREAKS? IT IS THE EAT AND JULIET IS THE SUN!
OH, NO, ARCHIE! YOU DID IT AGAIN!!
5

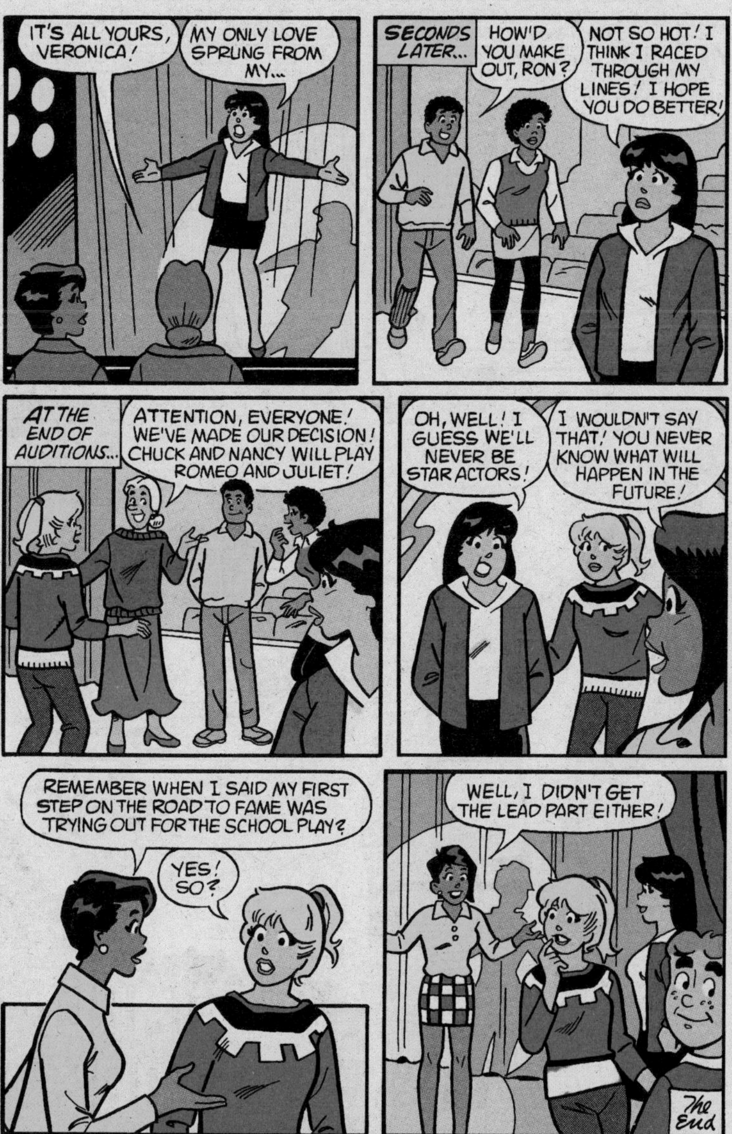
IT'S ALL YOURS, VERONICA!
MY ONLY LOVE SPRUNG FROM MY...
SECONDS LATER...
HOW'D YOU MAKE OUT, RON?
NOT SO HOT! I THINK I RACED THROUGH MY LINES! I HOPE YOU DO BETTER!
AT THE END OF AUDITIONS...
ATTENTION, EVERYONE! WE'VE MADE OUR DECISION! CHUCK AND NANCY WILL PLAY ROMEO AND JULIET!
OH, WELL! I GUESS WE'LL NEVER BE STAR ACTORS!
I WOULDN'T SAY THAT! YOU NEVER KNOW WHAT WILL HAPPEN IN THE FUTURE!
REMEMBER WHEN I SAID MY FIRST STEP ON THE ROAD TO FAME WAS TRYING OUT FOR THE SCHOOL PLAY?
YES! SO?
WELL, I DIDN'T GET THE LEAD PART EITHER!
The End

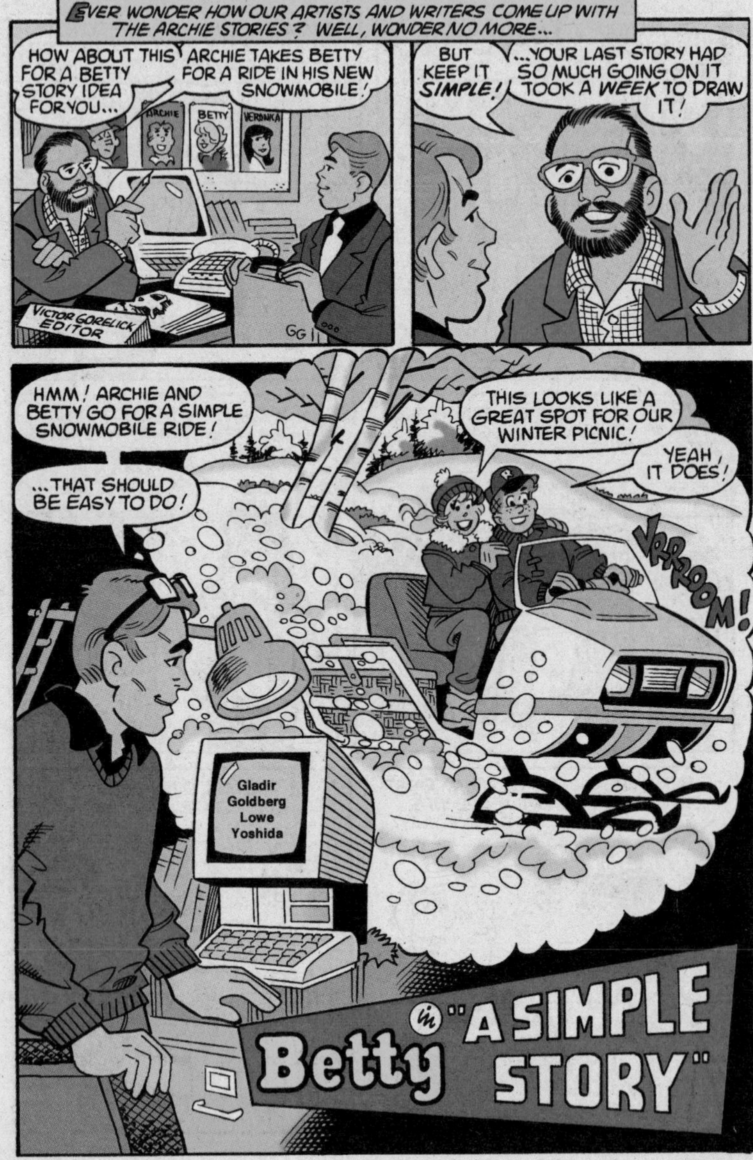

EVER WONDER HOW OUR ARTISTS AND WRITERS COME UP WITH THE ARCHIE STORIES? WELL, WONDER NO MORE...
HOW ABOUT THIS FOR A BETTY STORY IDEA FOR YOU...
ARCHIE TAKES BETTY FOR A RIDE IN HIS NEW SNOWMOBILE!
ARCHIE
BETTY
VERONICA
VICTOR GORELICK EDITOR
GG
BUT KEEP IT SIMPLE!
...YOUR LAST STORY HAD SO MUCH GOING ON IT TOOK A WEEK TO DRAW IT!
HMM! ARCHIE AND BETTY GO FOR A SIMPLE SNOWMOBILE RIDE!
...THAT SHOULD BE EASY TO DO!
THIS LOOKS LIKE A GREAT SPOT FOR OUR WINTER PICNIC!
YEAH, IT DOES!
VRRROOOM!
Gladir
Goldberg
Lowe
Yoshida
Betty in "A SIMPLE STORY"

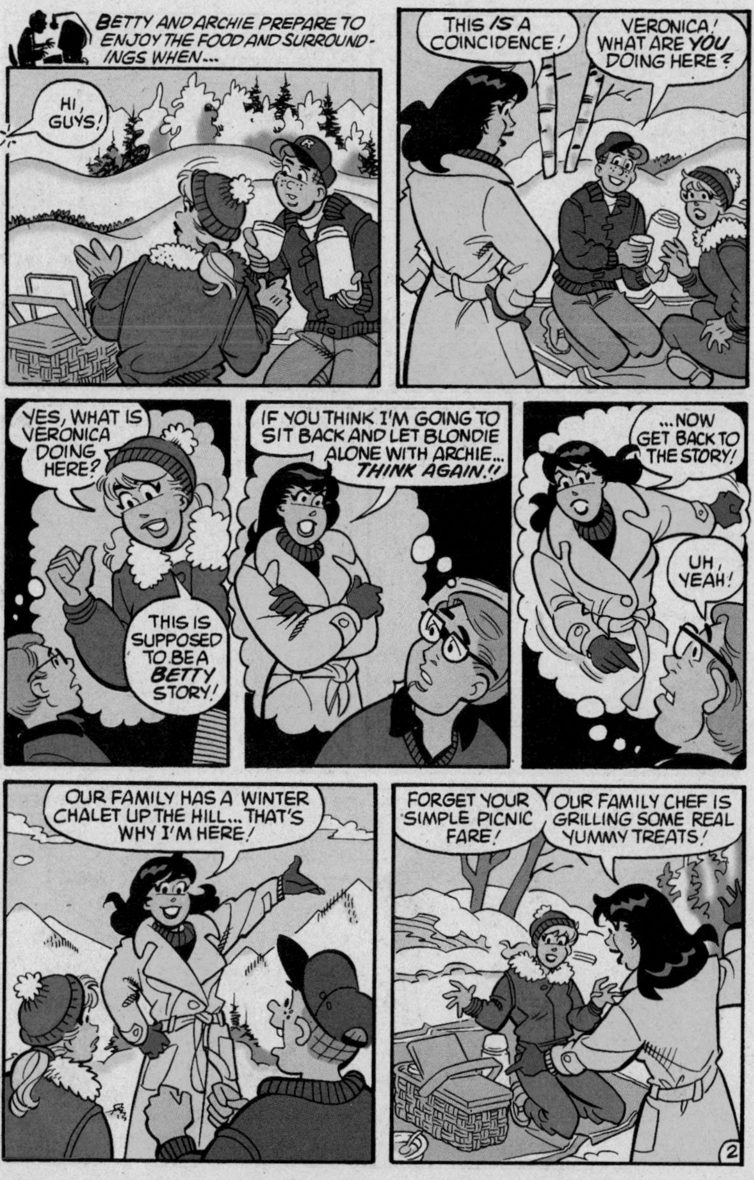

BETTY AND ARCHIE PREPARE TO ENJOY THE FOOD AND SURROUNDINGS WHEN...
HI, GUYS!
THIS IS A COINCIDENCE!
VERONICA! WHAT ARE YOU DOING HERE?
YES, WHAT IS VERONICA DOING HERE?
THIS IS SUPPOSED TO BE A BETTY STORY!
IF YOU THINK I'M GOING TO SIT BACK AND LET BLONDIE ALONE WITH ARCHIE... THINK AGAIN!!
...NOW GET BACK TO THE STORY!
UH, YEAH!
OUR FAMILY HAS A WINTER CHALET UP THE HILL... THAT'S WHY I'M HERE!
FORGET YOUR SIMPLE PICNIC FARE!
OUR FAMILY CHEF IS GRILLING SOME REAL YUMMY TREATS!
2

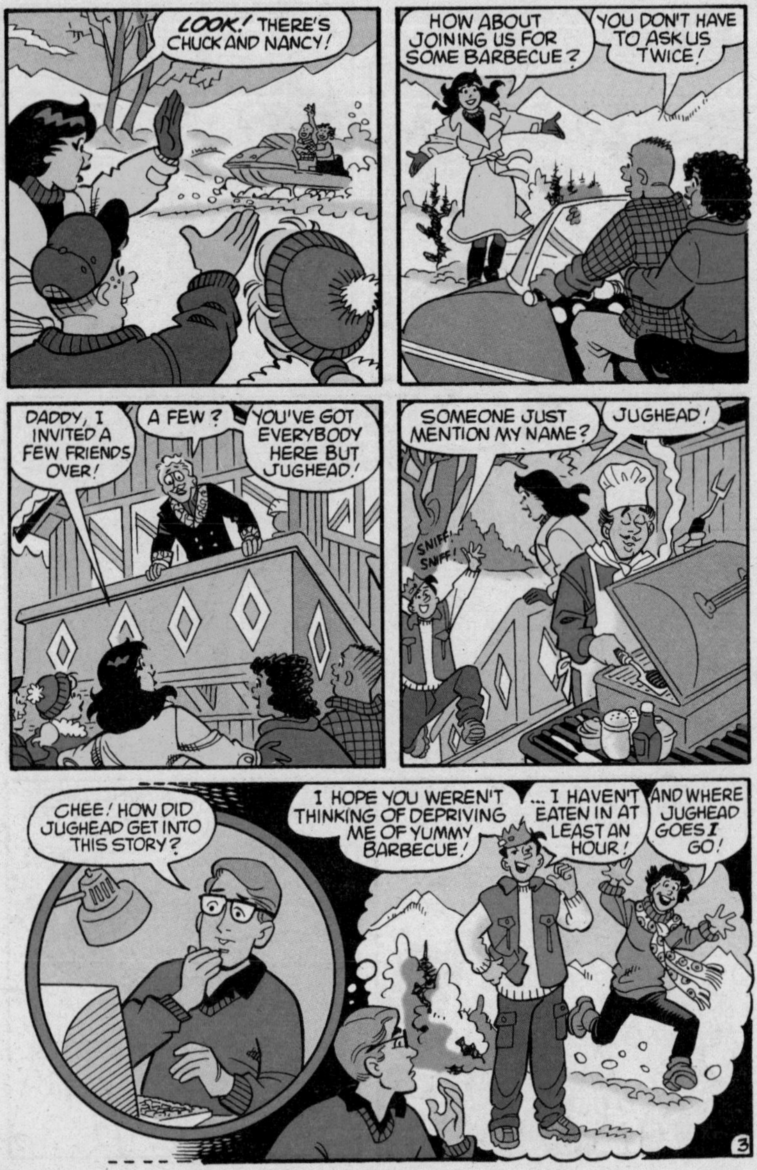
LOOK! THERE'S CHUCK AND NANCY!
HOW ABOUT JOINING US FOR SOME BARBECUE?
YOU DON'T HAVE TO ASK US TWICE!
DADDY, I INVITED A FEW FRIENDS OVER!
A FEW?
YOU'VE GOT EVERYBODY HERE BUT JUGHEAD!
SOMEONE JUST MENTION MY NAME?
JUGHEAD!
SNIFF! SNIFF!
CHEE! HOW DID JUGHEAD GET INTO THIS STORY?
I HOPE YOU WEREN'T THINKING OF DEPRIVING ME OF YUMMY BARBECUE!
... I HAVEN'T EATEN IN AT LEAST AN HOUR!
AND WHERE JUGHEAD GOES I GO!
3

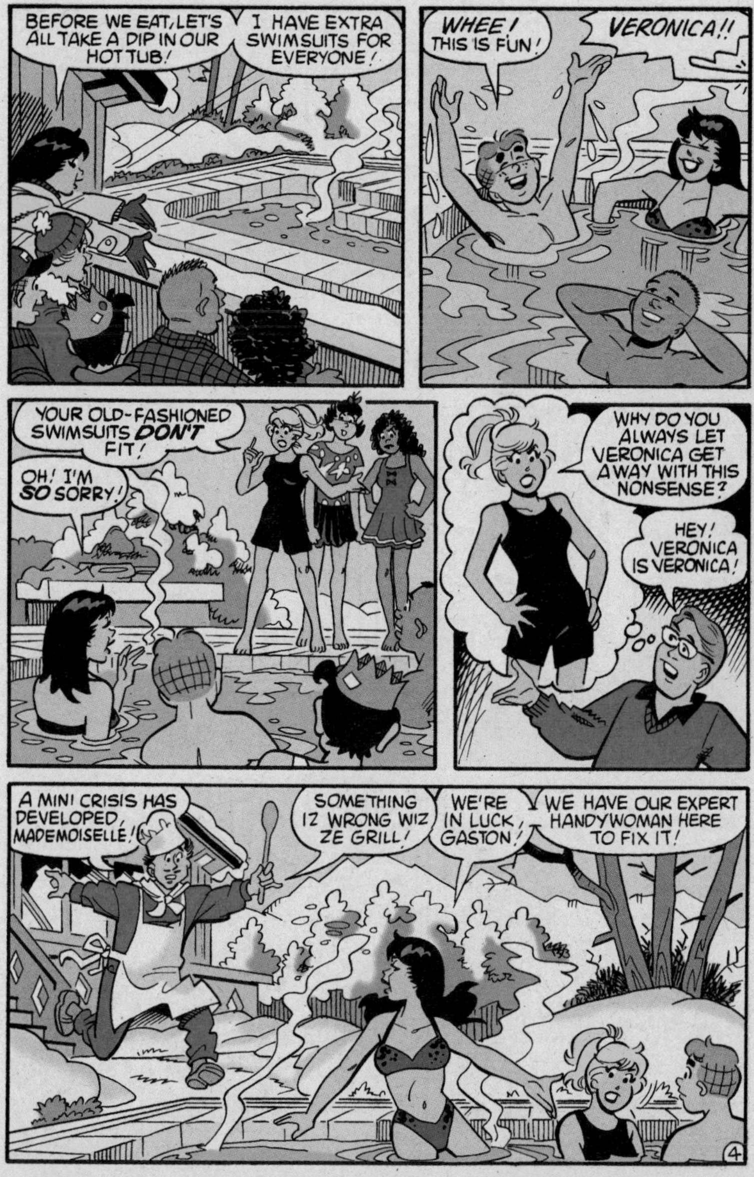

BEFORE WE EAT, LET'S ALL TAKE A DIP IN OUR HOT TUB!
I HAVE EXTRA SWIMSUITS FOR EVERYONE!
WHEE! THIS IS FUN!
VERONICA!!
YOUR OLD-FASHIONED SWIMSUITS DON'T FIT!
OH! I'M SO SORRY!
WHY DO YOU ALWAYS LET VERONICA GET AWAY WITH THIS NONSENSE?
HEY! VERONICA IS VERONICA!
A MINI CRISIS HAS DEVELOPED, MADEMOISELLE!
SOMETHING IZ WRONG WIZ ZE GRILL!
WE'RE IN LUCK, GASTON!
WE HAVE OUR EXPERT HANDYWOMAN HERE TO FIX IT!
4

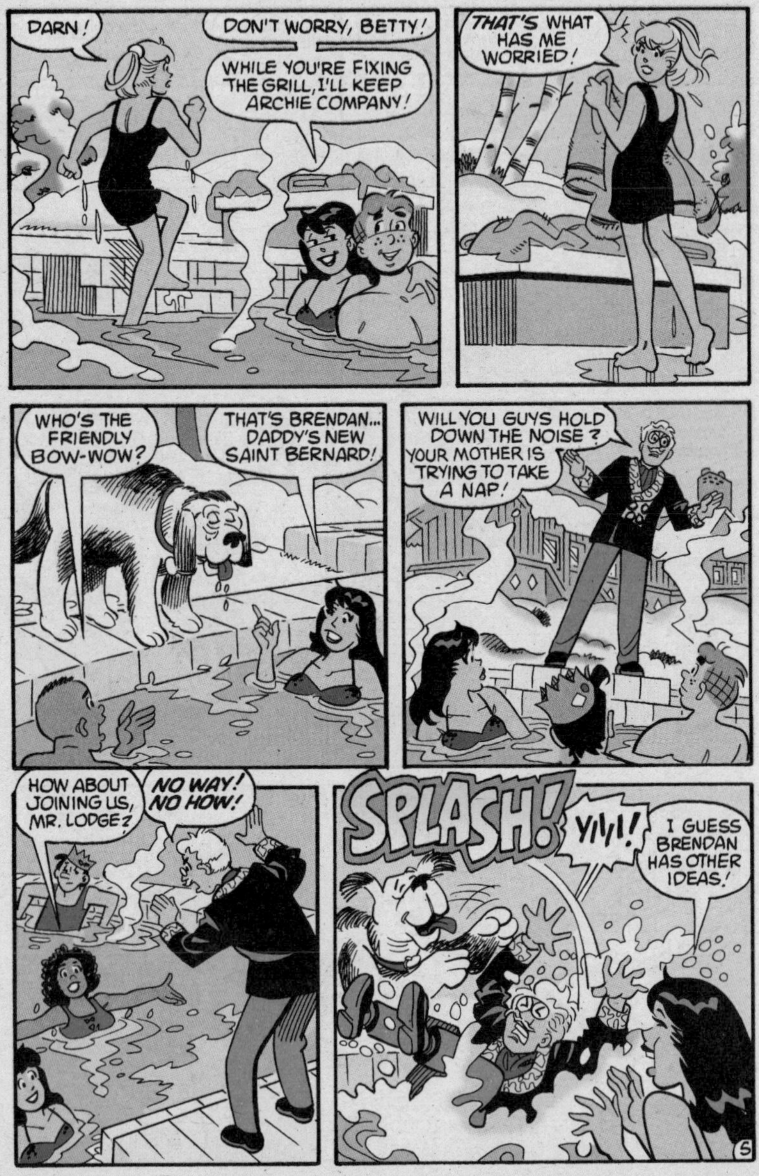
DARN!
DON'T WORRY, BETTY!
WHILE YOU'RE FIXING THE GRILL, I'LL KEEP ARCHIE COMPANY!
THAT'S WHAT HAS ME WORRIED!
WHO'S THE FRIENDLY BOW-WOW?
THAT'S BRENDAN... DADDY'S NEW SAINT BERNARD!
WILL YOU GUYS HOLD DOWN THE NOISE? YOUR MOTHER IS TRYING TO TAKE A NAP!
HOW ABOUT JOINING US, MR. LODGE?
NO WAY! NO HOW!
SPLASH!
YIVI!
I GUESS BRENDAN HAS OTHER IDEAS!
5

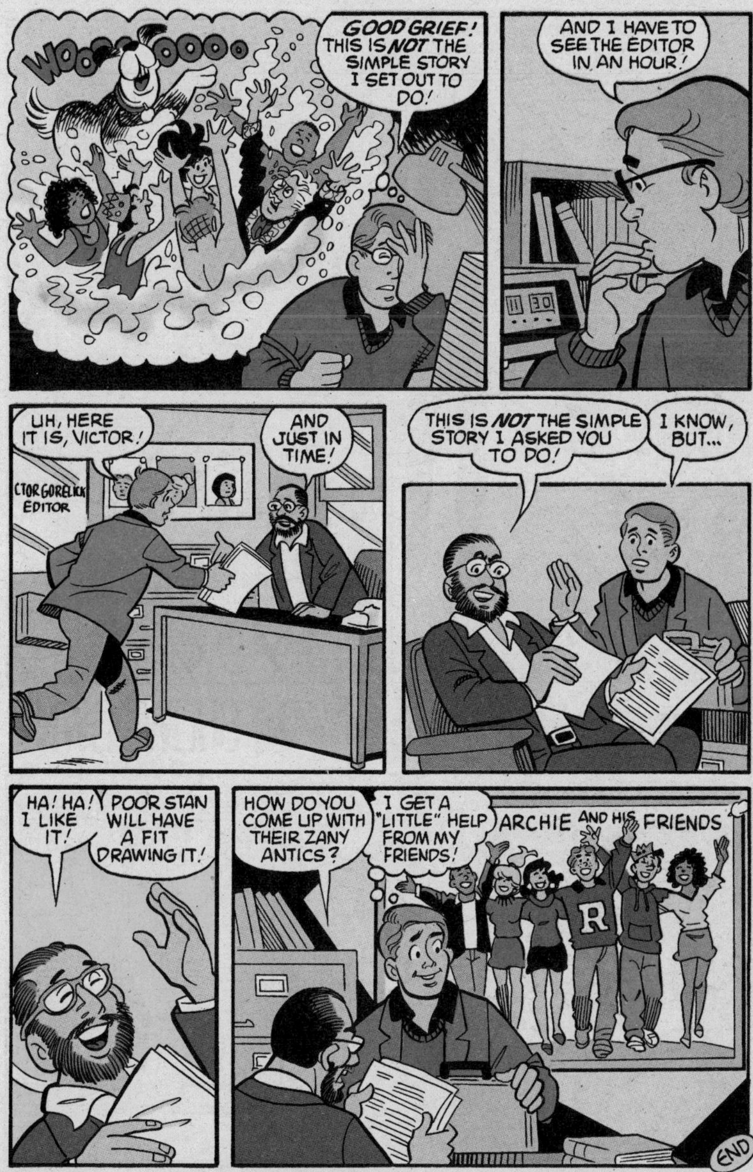
WOOOOOOOO
GOOD GRIEF! THIS IS NOT THE SIMPLE STORY I SET OUT TO DO!
AND I HAVE TO SEE THE EDITOR IN AN HOUR!
UH, HERE IT IS, VICTOR!
CTOR GORELICK EDITOR
AND JUST IN TIME!
THIS IS NOT THE SIMPLE STORY I ASKED YOU TO DO!
I KNOW, BUT...
HA! HA! I LIKE IT!
POOR STAN WILL HAVE A FIT DRAWING IT!
HOW DO YOU COME UP WITH THEIR ZANY ANTICS?
I GET A "LITTLE" HELP FROM MY FRIENDS!
ARCHIE AND HIS FRIENDS
R
END

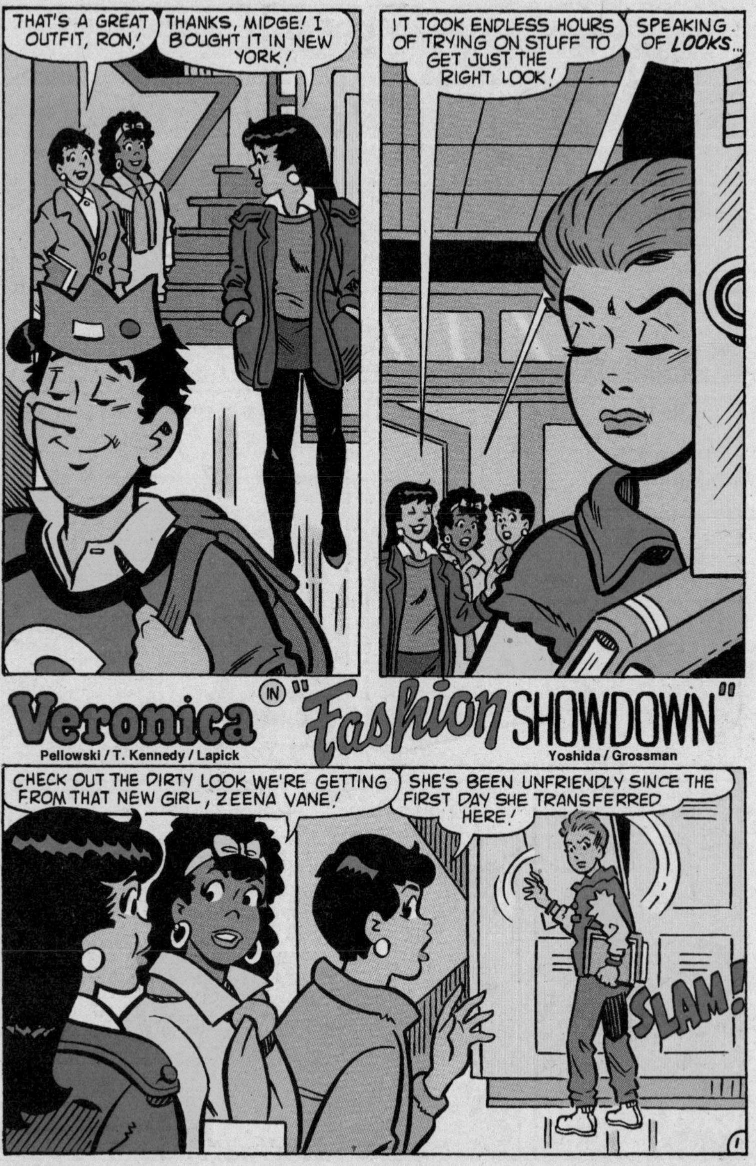
THAT'S A GREAT OUTFIT, RON!
THANKS, MIDGE! I BOUGHT IT IN NEW YORK!
IT TOOK ENDLESS HOURS OF TRYING ON STUFF TO GET JUST THE RIGHT LOOK!
SPEAKING OF LOOKS...
Veronica IN "Fashion SHOWDOWN"
Pellowski / T. Kennedy / Lapick
Yoshida / Grossman
CHECK OUT THE DIRTY LOOK WE'RE GETTING FROM THAT NEW GIRL, ZEENA VANE!
SHE'S BEEN UNFRIENDLY SINCE THE FIRST DAY SHE TRANSFERRED HERE!
SLAM!
1

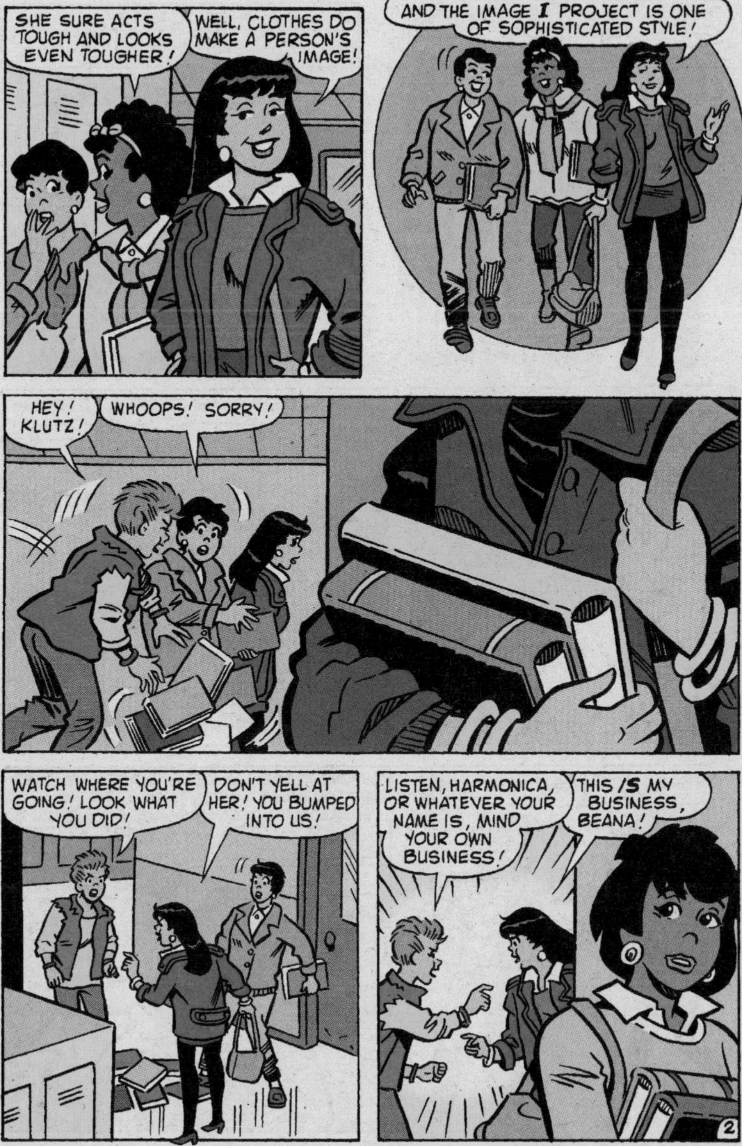

SHE SURE ACTS TOUGH AND LOOKS EVEN TOUGHER!
WELL, CLOTHES DO MAKE A PERSON'S IMAGE!
AND THE IMAGE I PROJECT IS ONE OF SOPHISTICATED STYLE!
HEY! KLUTZ!
WHOOPS! SORRY!
WATCH WHERE YOU'RE GOING! LOOK WHAT YOU DID!
DON'T YELL AT HER! YOU BUMPED INTO US!
LISTEN, HARMONICA, OR WHATEVER YOUR NAME IS, MIND YOUR OWN BUSINESS!
THIS IS MY BUSINESS, BEANA!
2

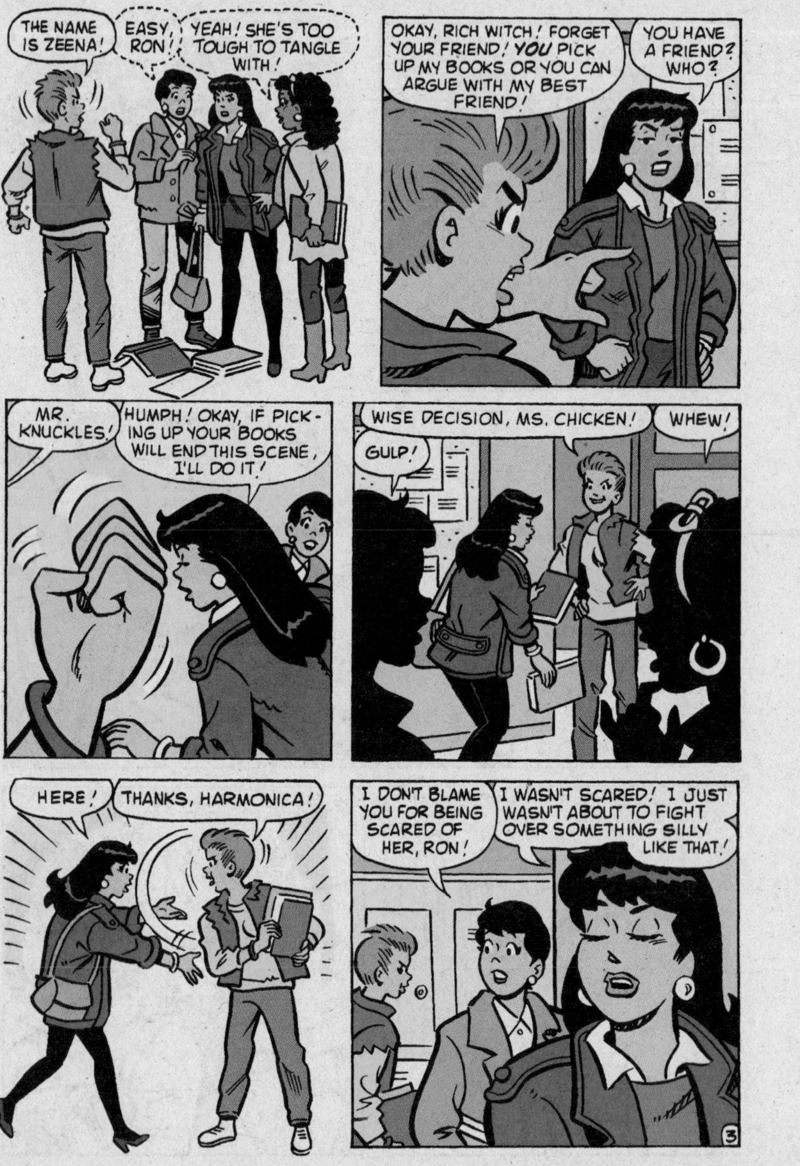
THE NAME IS ZEENA!
EASY, RON!
YEAH! SHE'S TOO TOUGH TO TANGLE WITH!
OKAY, RICH WITCH! FORGET YOUR FRIEND! YOU PICK UP MY BOOKS OR YOU CAN ARGUE WITH MY BEST FRIEND!
YOU HAVE A FRIEND? WHO?
MR. KNUCKLES!
HUMPH! OKAY, IF PICKING UP YOUR BOOKS WILL END THIS SCENE, I'LL DO IT!
WISE DECISION, MS. CHICKEN!
WHEW!
GULP!
HERE!
THANKS, HARMONICA!
I DON'T BLAME YOU FOR BEING SCARED OF HER, RON!
I WASN'T SCARED! I JUST WASN'T ABOUT TO FIGHT OVER SOMETHING SILLY LIKE THAT!
3

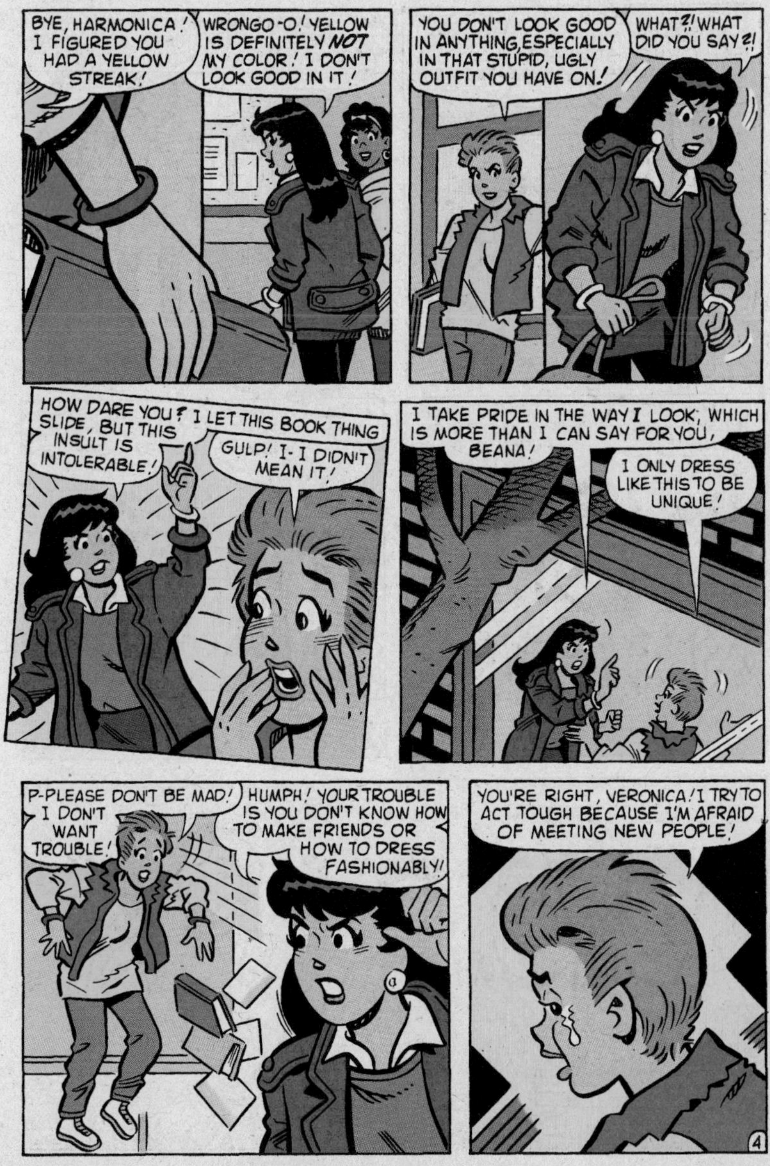
BYE, HARMONICA! I FIGURED YOU HAD A YELLOW STREAK!
WRONGO-O! YELLOW IS DEFINITELY *NOT* MY COLOR! I DON'T LOOK GOOD IN IT!
YOU DON'T LOOK GOOD IN ANYTHING, ESPECIALLY IN THAT STUPID, UGLY OUTFIT YOU HAVE ON!
WHAT?! WHAT DID YOU SAY?!
HOW DARE YOU? I LET THIS BOOK THING SLIDE, BUT THIS INSULT IS INTOLERABLE!
GULP! I- I DIDN'T MEAN IT!
I TAKE PRIDE IN THE WAY I LOOK, WHICH IS MORE THAN I CAN SAY FOR YOU, BEANA!
I ONLY DRESS LIKE THIS TO BE UNIQUE!
P-PLEASE DON'T BE MAD! I DON'T WANT TROUBLE!
HUMPH! YOUR TROUBLE IS YOU DON'T KNOW HOW TO MAKE FRIENDS OR HOW TO DRESS FASHIONABLY!
YOU'RE RIGHT, VERONICA! I TRY TO ACT TOUGH BECAUSE I'M AFRAID OF MEETING NEW PEOPLE!
4

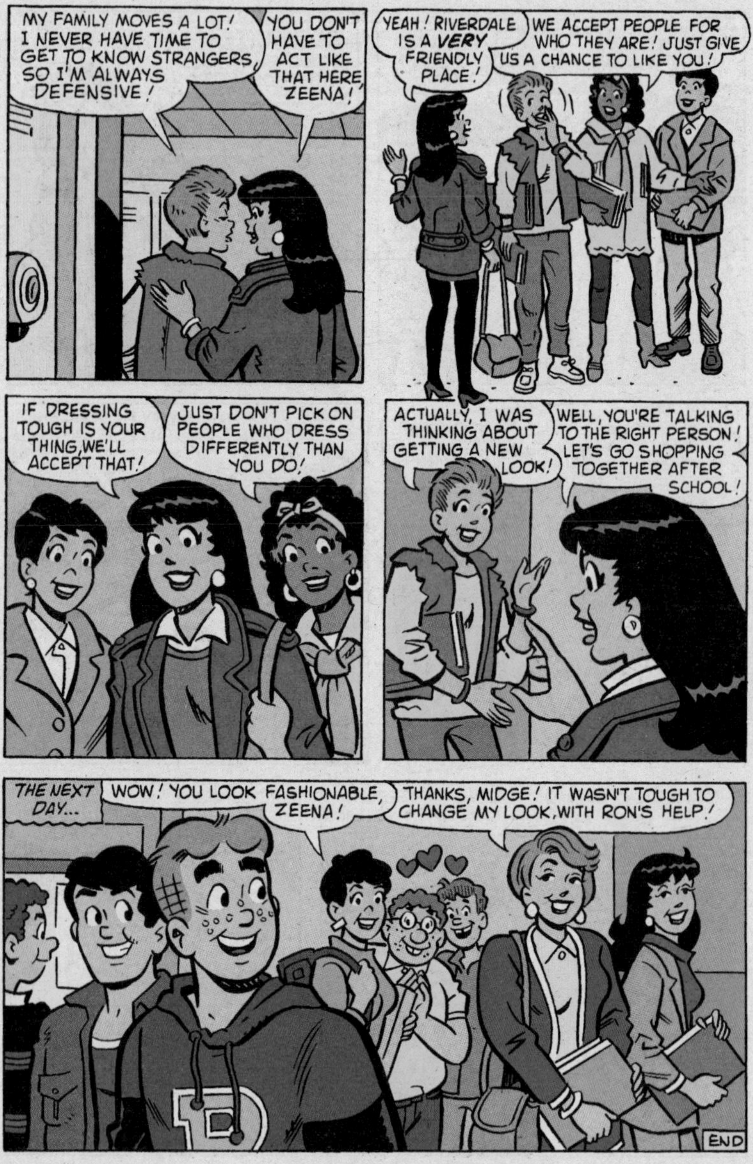
MY FAMILY MOVES A LOT! I NEVER HAVE TIME TO GET TO KNOW STRANGERS, SO I'M ALWAYS DEFENSIVE!
YOU DON'T HAVE TO ACT LIKE THAT HERE, ZEENA!
YEAH! RIVERDALE IS A VERY FRIENDLY PLACE!
WE ACCEPT PEOPLE FOR WHO THEY ARE! JUST GIVE US A CHANCE TO LIKE YOU!
IF DRESSING TOUGH IS YOUR THING, WE'LL ACCEPT THAT!
JUST DON'T PICK ON PEOPLE WHO DRESS DIFFERENTLY THAN YOU DO!
ACTUALLY, I WAS THINKING ABOUT GETTING A NEW LOOK!
WELL, YOU'RE TALKING TO THE RIGHT PERSON! LET'S GO SHOPPING TOGETHER AFTER SCHOOL!
THE NEXT DAY...
WOW! YOU LOOK FASHIONABLE, ZEENA!
THANKS, MIDGE! IT WASN'T TOUGH TO CHANGE MY LOOK, WITH RON'S HELP!
END

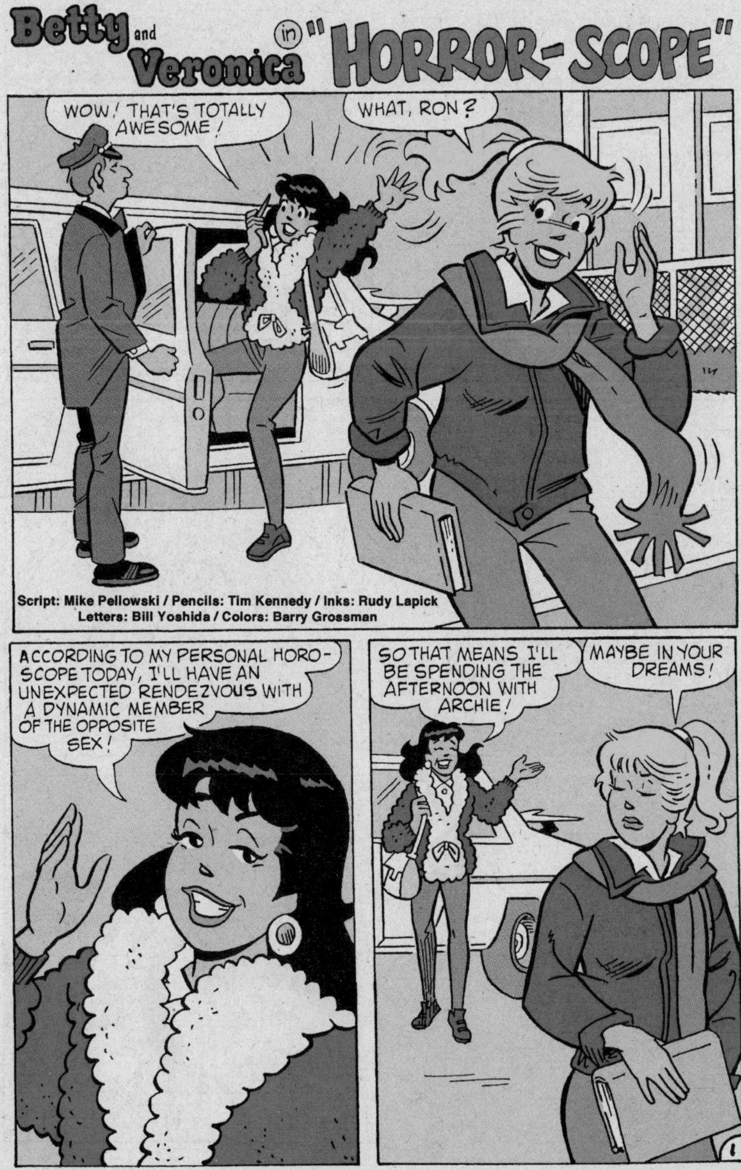
Betty and Veronica in "HORROR-SCOPE"
WOW! THAT'S TOTALLY AWESOME!
WHAT, RON?
Script: Mike Pellowski / Pencils: Tim Kennedy / Inks: Rudy Lapick
Letters: Bill Yoshida / Colors: Barry Grossman
ACCORDING TO MY PERSONAL HORO-SCOPE TODAY, I'LL HAVE AN UNEXPECTED RENDEZVOUS WITH A DYNAMIC MEMBER OF THE OPPOSITE SEX!
SO THAT MEANS I'LL BE SPENDING THE AFTERNOON WITH ARCHIE!
MAYBE IN YOUR DREAMS!
1

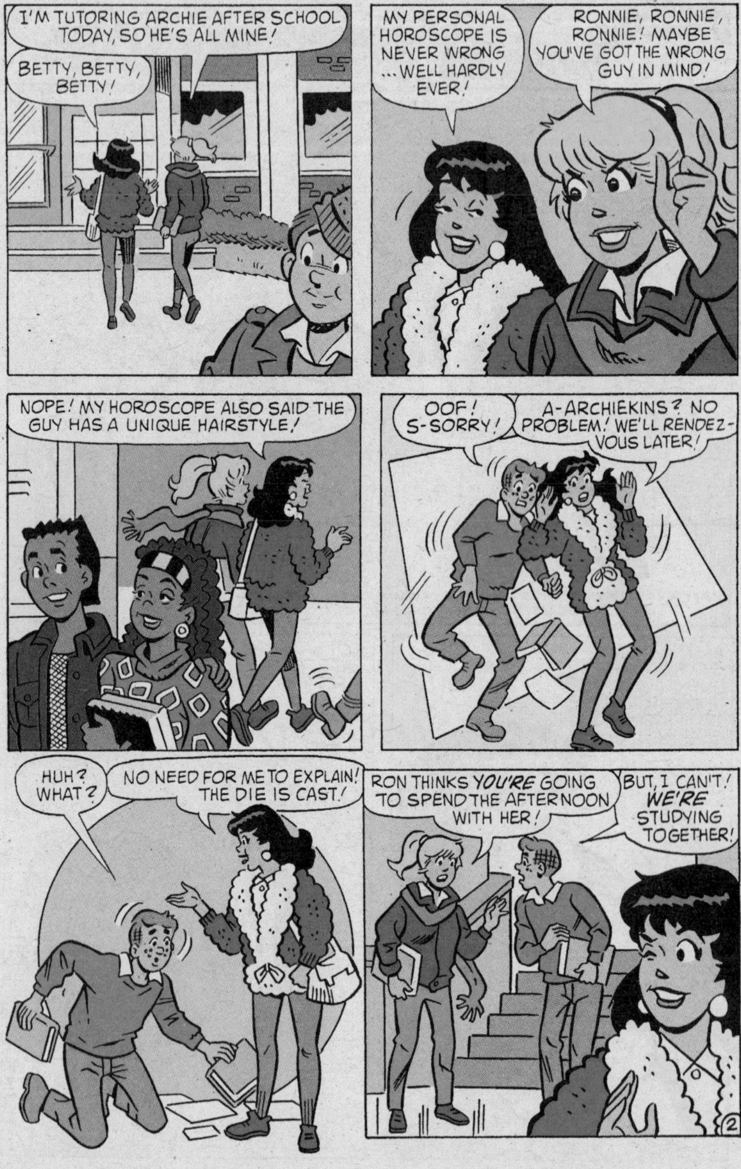

I'M TUTORING ARCHIE AFTER SCHOOL TODAY, SO HE'S ALL MINE!
BETTY, BETTY, BETTY!
MY PERSONAL HOROSCOPE IS NEVER WRONG ...WELL HARDLY EVER!
RONNIE, RONNIE, RONNIE! MAYBE YOU'VE GOT THE WRONG GUY IN MIND!
NOPE! MY HOROSCOPE ALSO SAID THE GUY HAS A UNIQUE HAIRSTYLE!
OOF! S-SORRY!
A-ARCHIEKINS? NO PROBLEM! WE'LL RENDEZ-VOUS LATER!
HUH? WHAT?
NO NEED FOR ME TO EXPLAIN! THE DIE IS CAST!
RON THINKS *YOU'RE* GOING TO SPEND THE AFTERNOON WITH HER!
BUT, I CAN'T! *WE'RE* STUDYING TOGETHER!

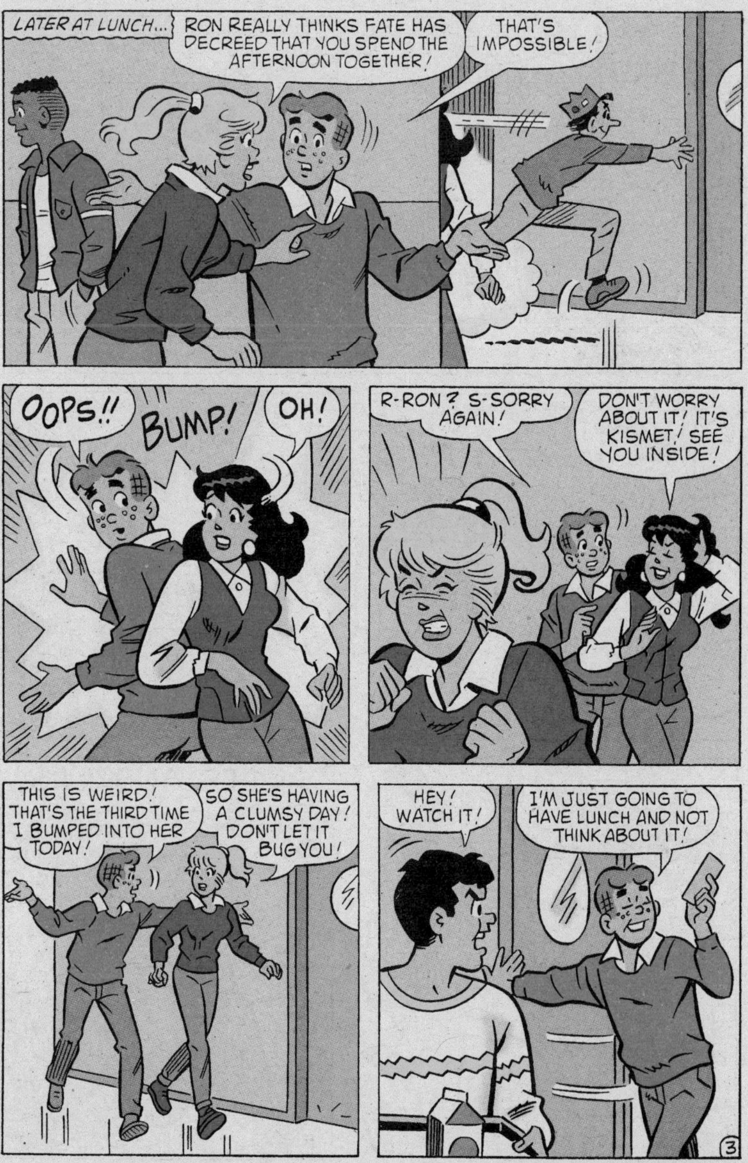
LATER AT LUNCH...
RON REALLY THINKS FATE HAS DECREED THAT YOU SPEND THE AFTERNOON TOGETHER!
THAT'S IMPOSSIBLE!
OOPS!!
BUMP!
OH!
R-RON? S-SORRY AGAIN!
DON'T WORRY ABOUT IT! IT'S KISMET! SEE YOU INSIDE!
THIS IS WEIRD! THAT'S THE THIRD TIME I BUMPED INTO HER TODAY!
SO SHE'S HAVING A CLUMSY DAY! DON'T LET IT BUG YOU!
HEY! WATCH IT!
I'M JUST GOING TO HAVE LUNCH AND NOT THINK ABOUT IT!
3

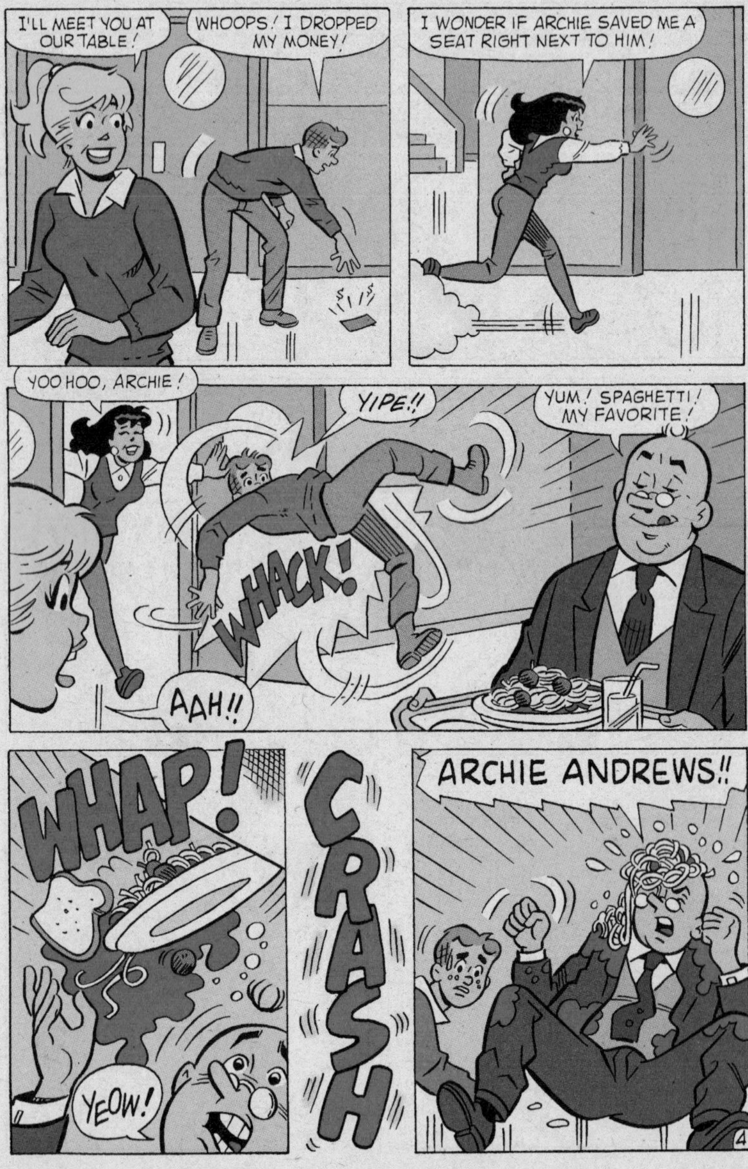
I'LL MEET YOU AT OUR TABLE!
WHOOPS! I DROPPED MY MONEY!
I WONDER IF ARCHIE SAVED ME A SEAT RIGHT NEXT TO HIM!
YOO HOO, ARCHIE!
YIPE!!
YUM! SPAGHETTI! MY FAVORITE!
WHACK!
AAH!!
WHAP!
YEOW!
CRASH
ARCHIE ANDREWS!!
4

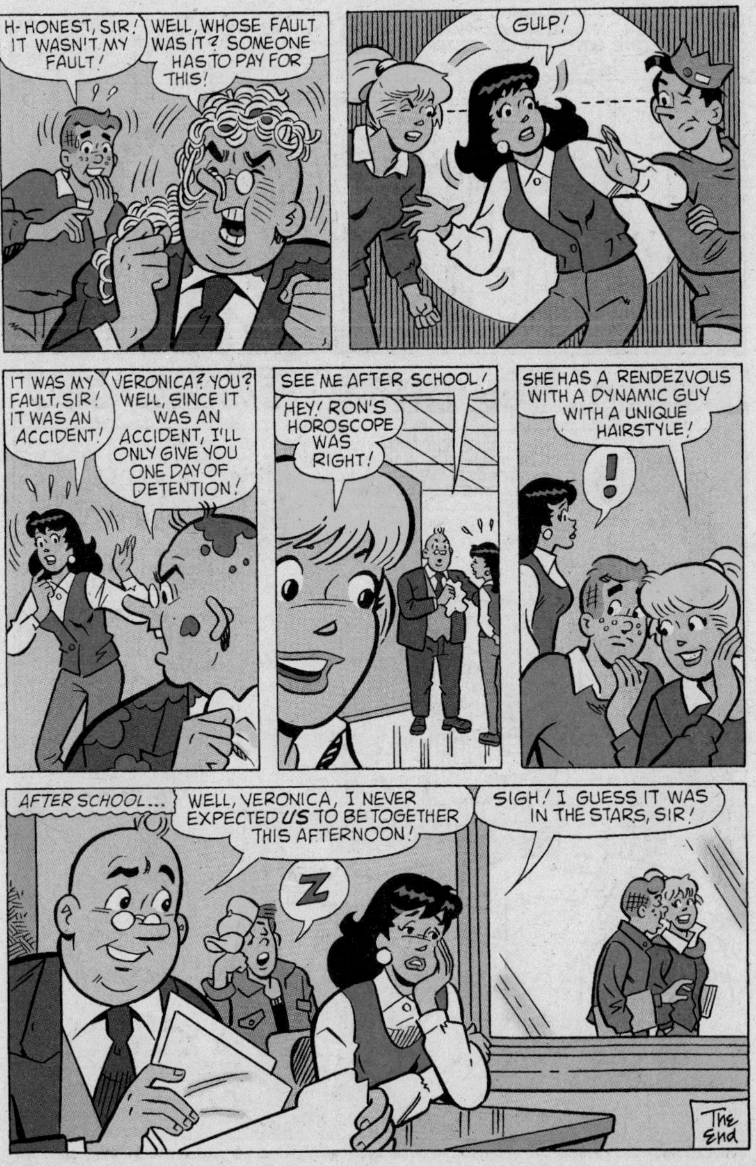
H-HONEST, SIR! IT WASN'T MY FAULT!
WELL, WHOSE FAULT WAS IT? SOMEONE HAS TO PAY FOR THIS!
GULP!
IT WAS MY FAULT, SIR! IT WAS AN ACCIDENT!
VERONICA? YOU? WELL, SINCE IT WAS AN ACCIDENT, I'LL ONLY GIVE YOU ONE DAY OF DETENTION!
SEE ME AFTER SCHOOL!
HEY! RON'S HOROSCOPE WAS RIGHT!
SHE HAS A RENDEZVOUS WITH A DYNAMIC GUY WITH A UNIQUE HAIRSTYLE!
!
AFTER SCHOOL...
WELL, VERONICA, I NEVER EXPECTED US TO BE TOGETHER THIS AFTERNOON!
Z
SIGH! I GUESS IT WAS IN THE STARS, SIR!
The End

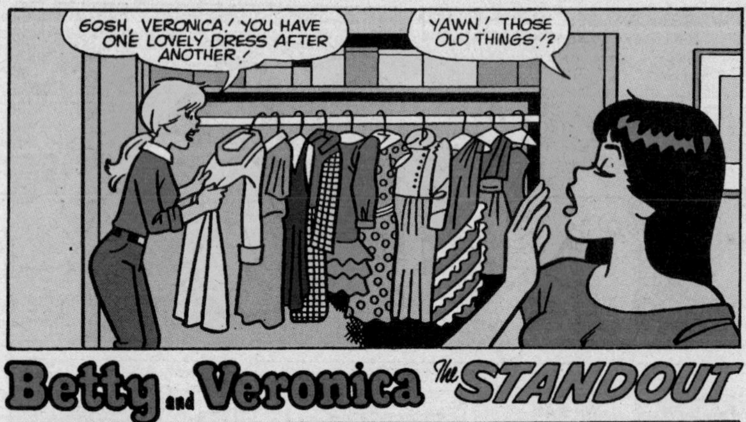

GOSH, VERONICA! YOU HAVE ONE LOVELY DRESS AFTER ANOTHER!
YAWN! THOSE OLD THINGS!?

Betty and Veronica — The STANDOUT

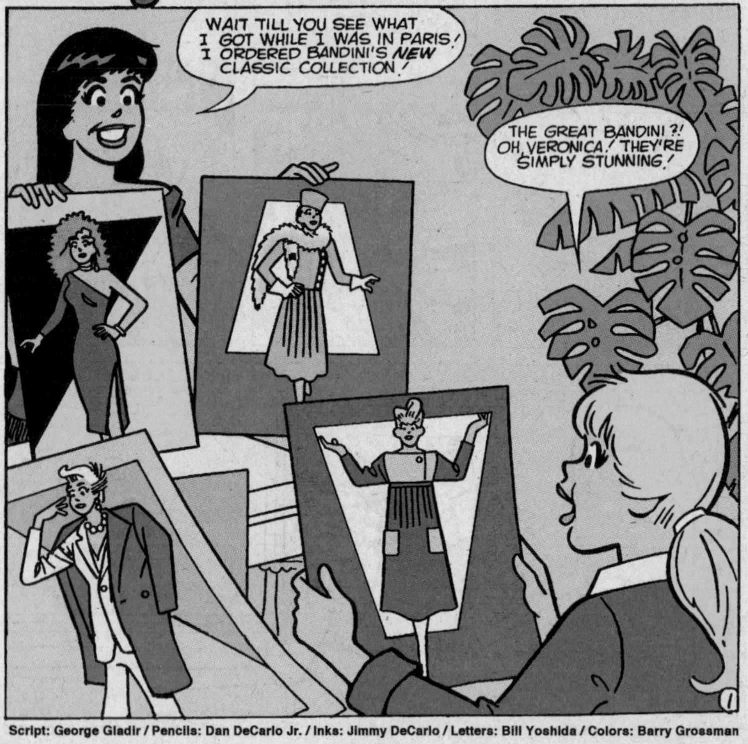

WAIT TILL YOU SEE WHAT I GOT WHILE I WAS IN PARIS! I ORDERED BANDINI'S *NEW* CLASSIC COLLECTION!
THE GREAT BANDINI?! OH, VERONICA! THEY'RE SIMPLY STUNNING!
1

Script: George Gladir / Pencils: Dan DeCarlo Jr. / Inks: Jimmy DeCarlo / Letters: Bill Yoshida / Colors: Barry Grossman

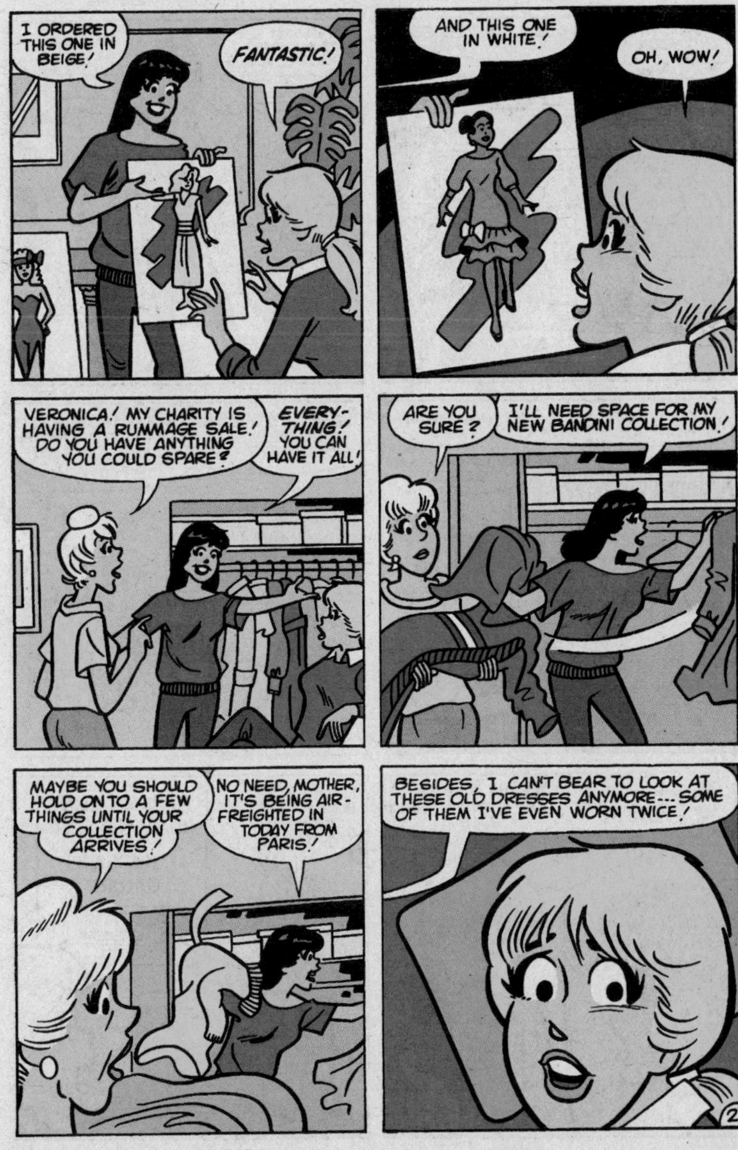
I ORDERED THIS ONE IN BEIGE!
FANTASTIC!
AND THIS ONE IN WHITE!
OH, WOW!
VERONICA! MY CHARITY IS HAVING A RUMMAGE SALE! DO YOU HAVE ANYTHING YOU COULD SPARE?
EVERY-THING! YOU CAN HAVE IT ALL!
ARE YOU SURE?
I'LL NEED SPACE FOR MY NEW BANDINI COLLECTION!
MAYBE YOU SHOULD HOLD ON TO A FEW THINGS UNTIL YOUR COLLECTION ARRIVES!
NO NEED, MOTHER, IT'S BEING AIR-FREIGHTED IN TODAY FROM PARIS!
BESIDES, I CAN'T BEAR TO LOOK AT THESE OLD DRESSES ANYMORE--- SOME OF THEM I'VE EVEN WORN TWICE!
2

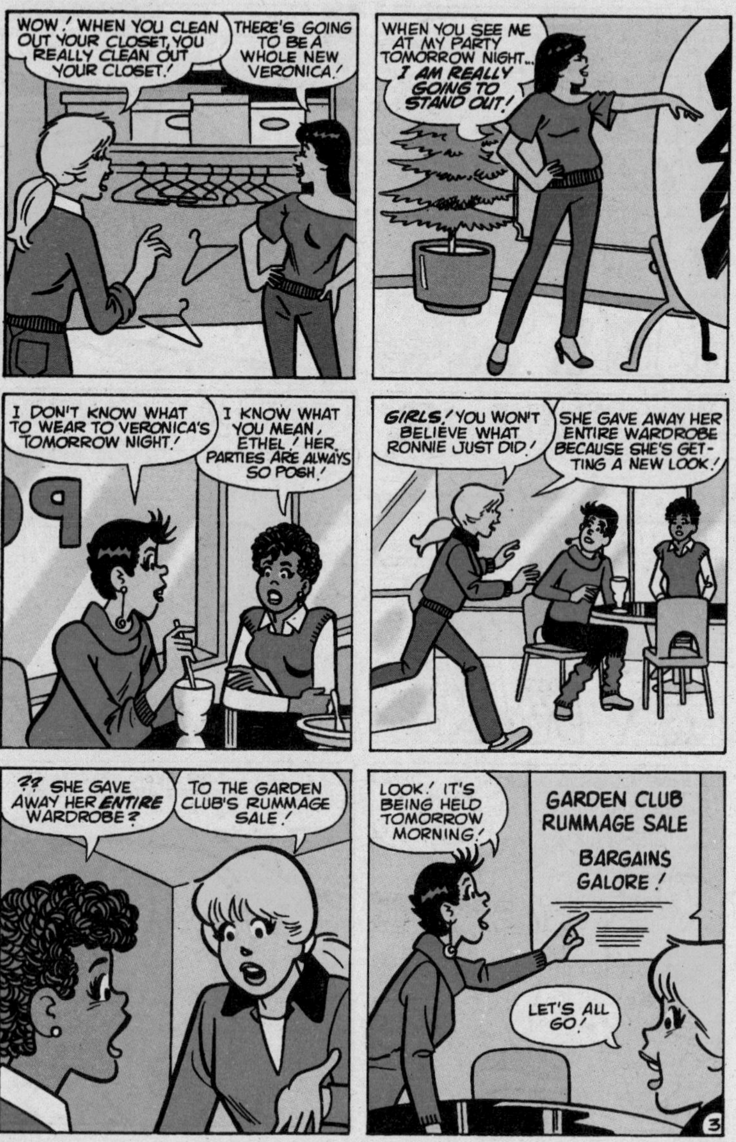
WOW! WHEN YOU CLEAN OUT YOUR CLOSET, YOU REALLY CLEAN OUT YOUR CLOSET!
THERE'S GOING TO BE A WHOLE NEW VERONICA!
WHEN YOU SEE ME AT MY PARTY TOMORROW NIGHT... I AM REALLY GOING TO STAND OUT!
I DON'T KNOW WHAT TO WEAR TO VERONICA'S TOMORROW NIGHT!
I KNOW WHAT YOU MEAN, ETHEL! HER PARTIES ARE ALWAYS SO POSH!
GIRLS! YOU WON'T BELIEVE WHAT RONNIE JUST DID!
SHE GAVE AWAY HER ENTIRE WARDROBE BECAUSE SHE'S GETTING A NEW LOOK!
?? SHE GAVE AWAY HER ENTIRE WARDROBE?
TO THE GARDEN CLUB'S RUMMAGE SALE!
LOOK! IT'S BEING HELD TOMORROW MORNING!
GARDEN CLUB RUMMAGE SALE
BARGAINS GALORE!
LET'S ALL GO!
3

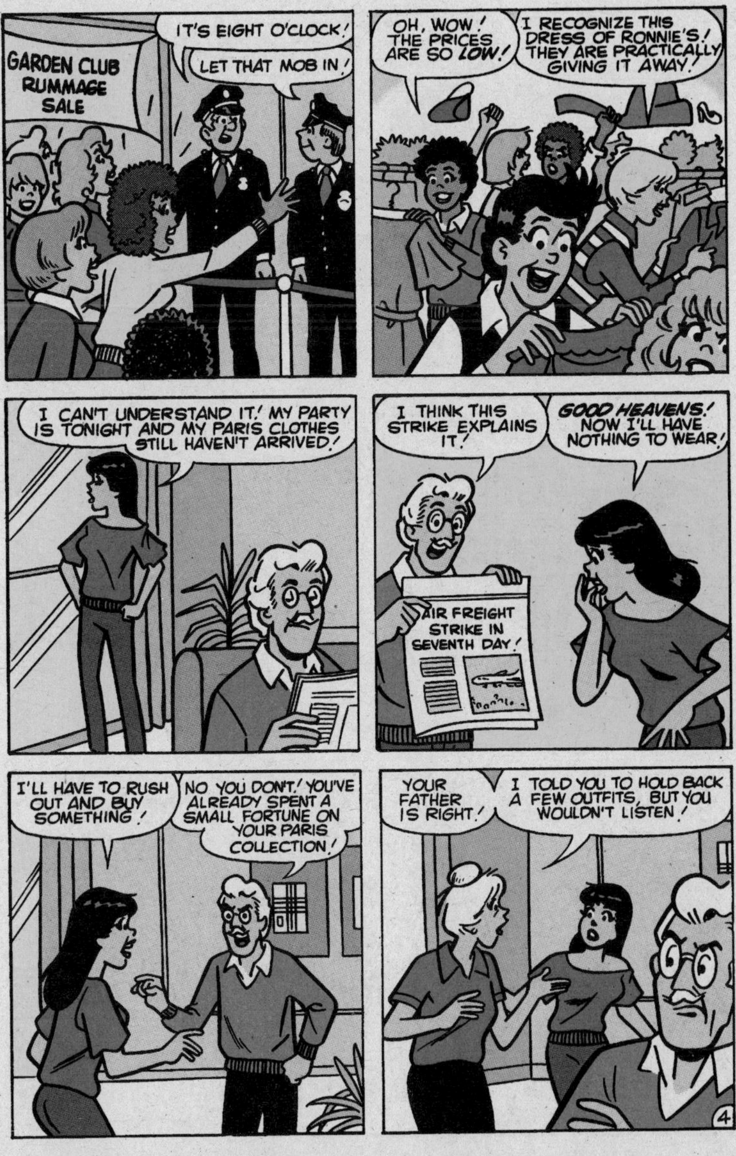
GARDEN CLUB RUMMAGE SALE
IT'S EIGHT O'CLOCK!
LET THAT MOB IN!
OH, WOW! THE PRICES ARE SO *LOW*!
I RECOGNIZE THIS DRESS OF RONNIE'S! THEY ARE PRACTICALLY GIVING IT AWAY!
I CAN'T UNDERSTAND IT! MY PARTY IS TONIGHT AND MY PARIS CLOTHES STILL HAVEN'T ARRIVED!
I THINK THIS STRIKE EXPLAINS IT!
AIR FREIGHT STRIKE IN SEVENTH DAY!
GOOD HEAVENS! NOW I'LL HAVE NOTHING TO WEAR!
I'LL HAVE TO RUSH OUT AND BUY SOMETHING!
NO YOU DON'T! YOU'VE ALREADY SPENT A SMALL FORTUNE ON YOUR PARIS COLLECTION!
YOUR FATHER IS RIGHT!
I TOLD YOU TO HOLD BACK A FEW OUTFITS, BUT YOU WOULDN'T LISTEN!
4

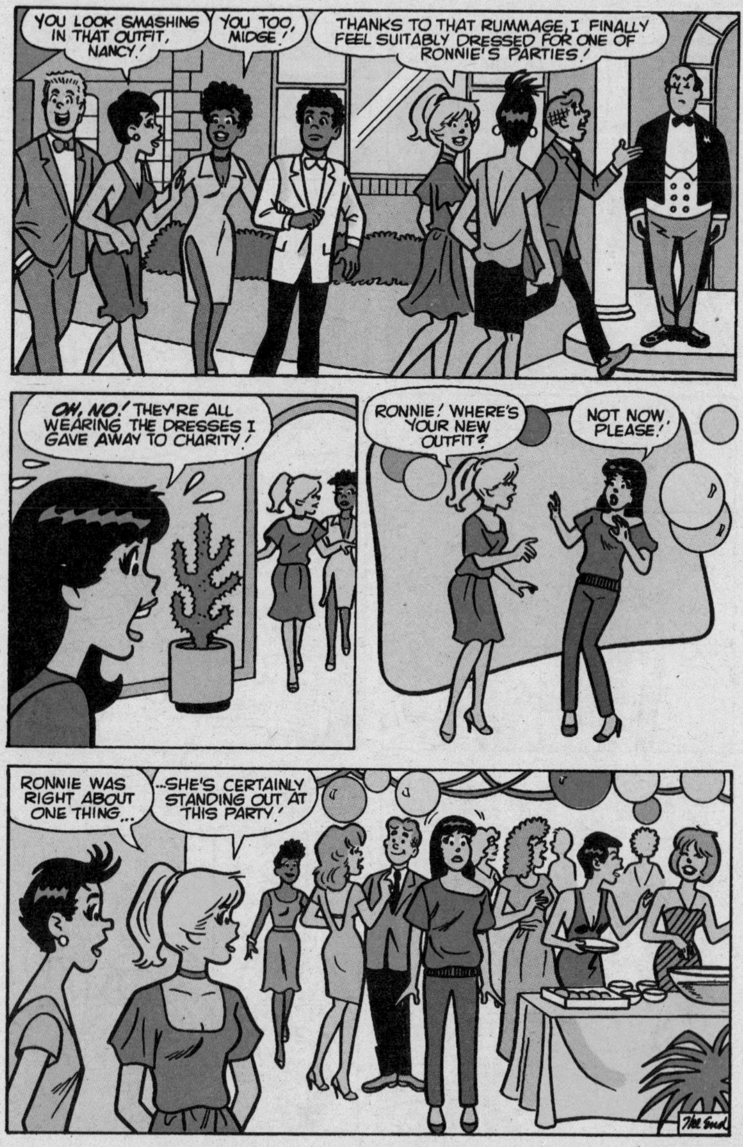
YOU LOOK SMASHING IN THAT OUTFIT, NANCY!
YOU TOO, MIDGE!
THANKS TO THAT RUMMAGE, I FINALLY FEEL SUITABLY DRESSED FOR ONE OF RONNIE'S PARTIES!
OH, NO! THEY'RE ALL WEARING THE DRESSES I GAVE AWAY TO CHARITY!
RONNIE! WHERE'S YOUR NEW OUTFIT?
NOT NOW, PLEASE!
RONNIE WAS RIGHT ABOUT ONE THING...
...SHE'S CERTAINLY STANDING OUT AT THIS PARTY!
The End

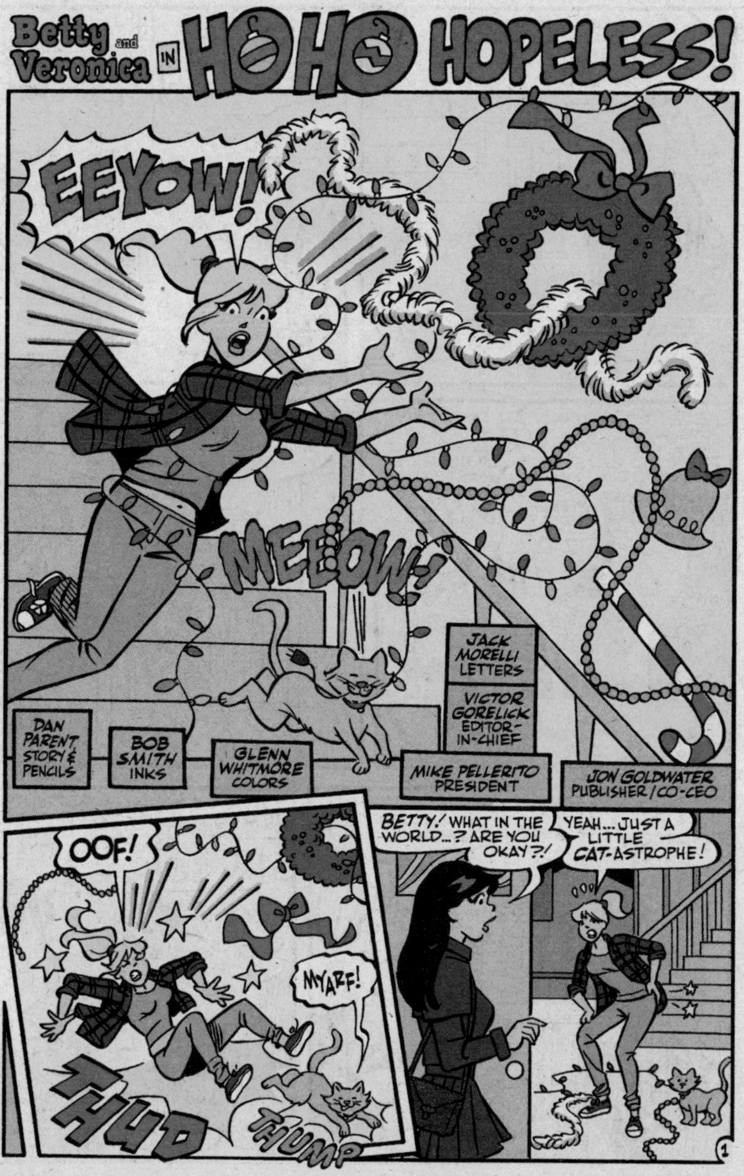

Betty and Veronica IN HO HO HOPELESS!
EEYOW!
MEEOW!
JACK MORELLI LETTERS
VICTOR GORELICK EDITOR-IN-CHIEF
DAN PARENT STORY & PENCILS
BOB SMITH INKS
GLENN WHITMORE COLORS
MIKE PELLERITO PRESIDENT
JON GOLDWATER PUBLISHER / CO-CEO
OOF!
MYARF!
THUD
THUMP
BETTY! WHAT IN THE WORLD...? ARE YOU OKAY?!
YEAH... JUST A LITTLE CAT-ASTROPHE!

I WAS BRINGING DOWN OUR CHRISTMAS DECORATIONS WHEN CARAMEL GRABBED THE END OF A STRAND OF LIGHTS AND HELPED ME BRING THEM DOWN EVEN *FASTER!*

GIMME THAT!

MEEOW!

WELL, PUT THAT JUNK DOWN AND LET'S GO CHRISTMAS SHOPPING! I HAVE A LONG LIST OF PEOPLE TO BUY THINGS FOR... ME, MYSELF AND I!

I CAN'T, RONNIE! I PROMISED MY FOLKS I'D PUT UP THE CHRISTMAS DECORATIONS TODAY!

AREN'T YOU DECORATING *YOUR* HOUSE?

OF COURSE I AM, BETTY DEAR! I JUST ORDERED MY STAFF TO SHOOT THE WORKS. LIGHTS, WREATHS, *EVERYTHING!*

THE CHRISTMAS SEASON IS ALL ABOUT GIVING... SO I THOUGHT I'D GIVE MY STAFF *LOTS OF OVERTIME!*

YOU'RE TOO GOOD TO THEM, MISS SCROOGE!

Oh, BETTY!

GROAN HI, HOLLY...!

Y'KNOW, BETTY, IT'S TIME YOU DECORATED YOUR LITTLE HOME FOR THE HOLIDAYS! THE NEIGHBORHOOD WAS STARTING TO TALK!

UGH! HOLLY HOSSENFUSS! AND THEY CALL *ME* A SNOB!

2

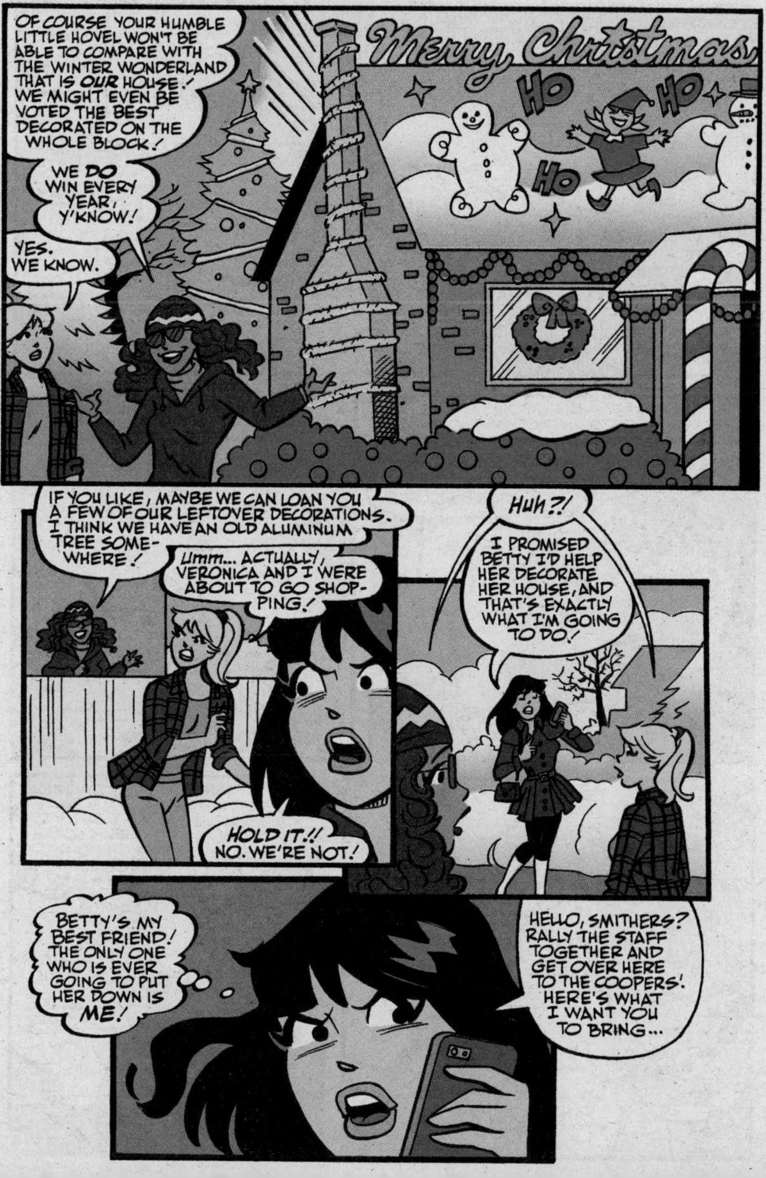

OF COURSE YOUR HUMBLE LITTLE HOVEL WON'T BE ABLE TO COMPARE WITH THE WINTER WONDERLAND THAT IS OUR HOUSE! WE MIGHT EVEN BE VOTED THE BEST DECORATED ON THE WHOLE BLOCK!
WE DO WIN EVERY YEAR, Y'KNOW!
YES. WE KNOW.
Merry Christmas
HO
HO
HO
IF YOU LIKE, MAYBE WE CAN LOAN YOU A FEW OF OUR LEFTOVER DECORATIONS. I THINK WE HAVE AN OLD ALUMINUM TREE SOMEWHERE!
Umm... ACTUALLY, VERONICA AND I WERE ABOUT TO GO SHOPPING!
HOLD IT!! NO. WE'RE NOT!
Huh?!
I PROMISED BETTY I'D HELP HER DECORATE HER HOUSE, AND THAT'S EXACTLY WHAT I'M GOING TO DO!
BETTY'S MY BEST FRIEND! THE ONLY ONE WHO IS EVER GOING TO PUT HER DOWN IS ME!
HELLO, SMITHERS? RALLY THE STAFF TOGETHER AND GET OVER HERE TO THE COOPERS'. HERE'S WHAT I WANT YOU TO BRING...

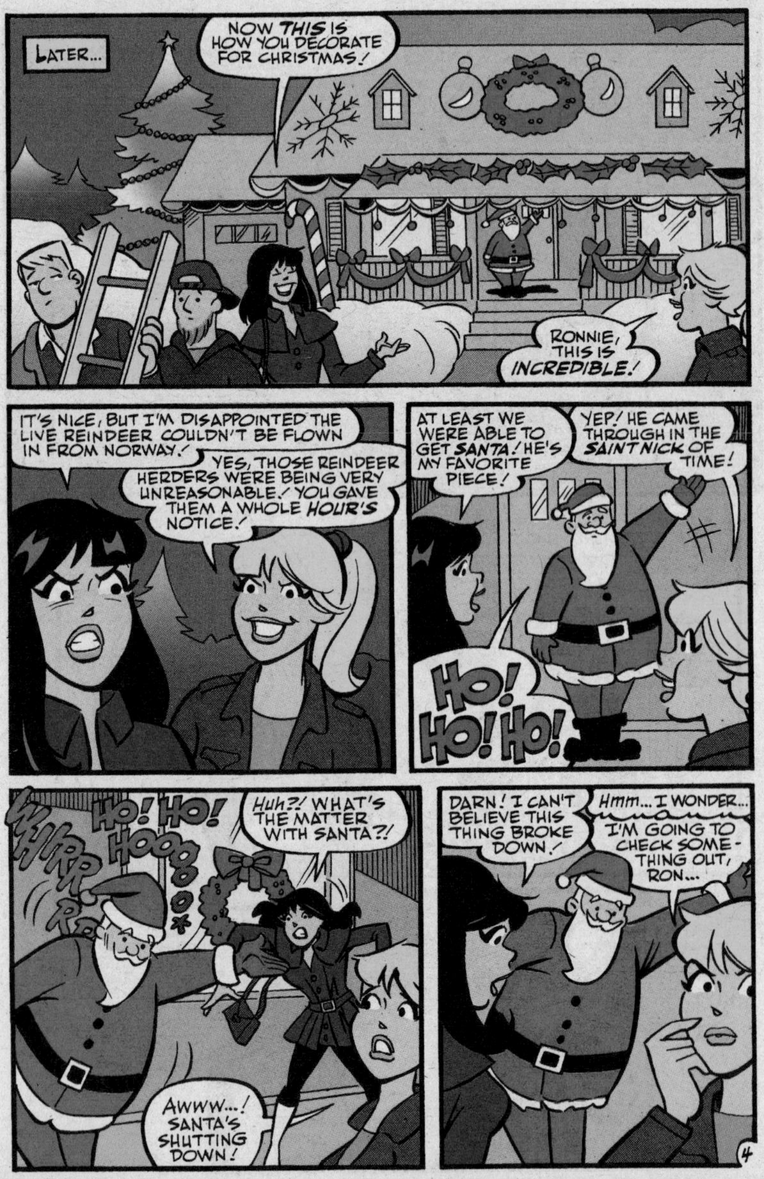

LATER...
NOW THIS IS HOW YOU DECORATE FOR CHRISTMAS!
RONNIE, THIS IS INCREDIBLE!
IT'S NICE, BUT I'M DISAPPOINTED THE LIVE REINDEER COULDN'T BE FLOWN IN FROM NORWAY!
YES, THOSE REINDEER HERDERS WERE BEING VERY UNREASONABLE! YOU GAVE THEM A WHOLE HOUR'S NOTICE!
AT LEAST WE WERE ABLE TO GET SANTA! HE'S MY FAVORITE PIECE!
YEP! HE CAME THROUGH IN THE SAINT NICK OF TIME!
HO! HO! HO!
WHIRR
HO! HO! HOOOooo
Huh?! WHAT'S THE MATTER WITH SANTA?!
AWWW...! SANTA'S SHUTTING DOWN!
DARN! I CAN'T BELIEVE THIS THING BROKE DOWN!
Hmm... I WONDER...
I'M GOING TO CHECK SOMETHING OUT, RON...

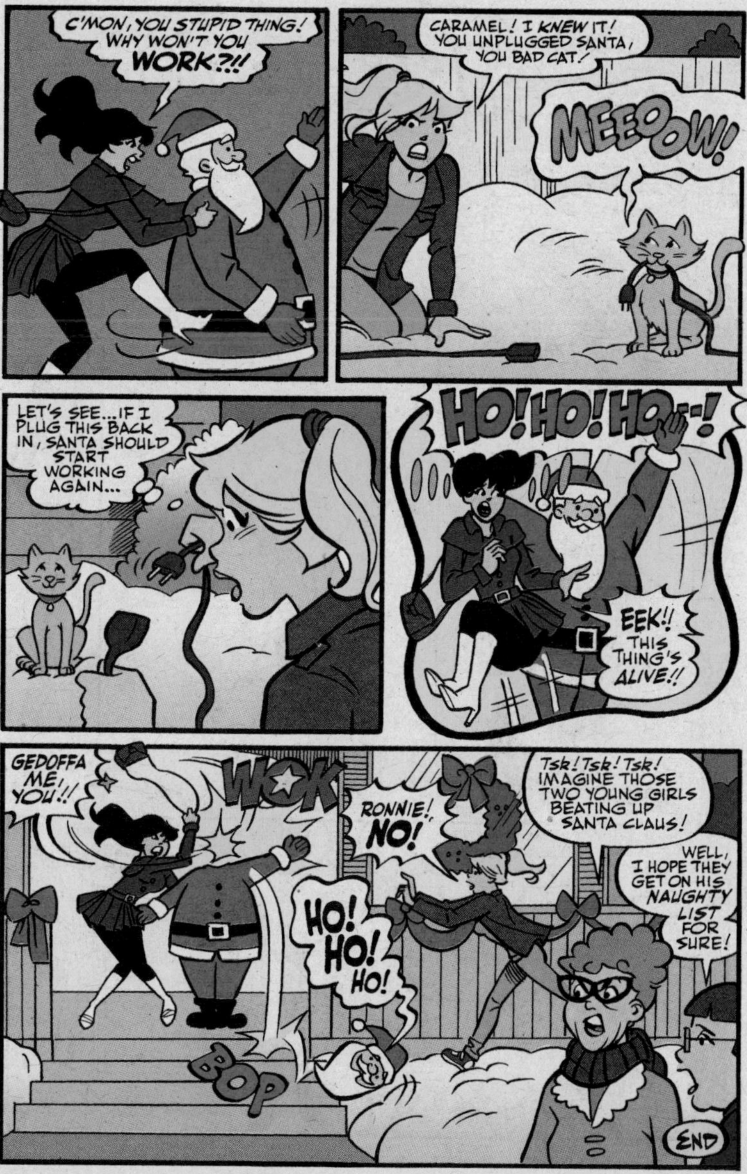
C'MON, YOU STUPID THING! WHY WON'T YOU WORK?!!
CARAMEL! I KNEW IT! YOU UNPLUGGED SANTA, YOU BAD CAT!
MEEOOOW!
LET'S SEE...IF I PLUG THIS BACK IN, SANTA SHOULD START WORKING AGAIN...
HO! HO! HO--!
EEK!! THIS THING'S ALIVE!!
GEDOFFA ME, YOU!!
WOK
RONNIE! NO!
Tsk! Tsk! Tsk! IMAGINE THOSE TWO YOUNG GIRLS BEATING UP SANTA CLAUS!
WELL, I HOPE THEY GET ON HIS NAUGHTY LIST FOR SURE!
HO! HO! HO!
BOP
END

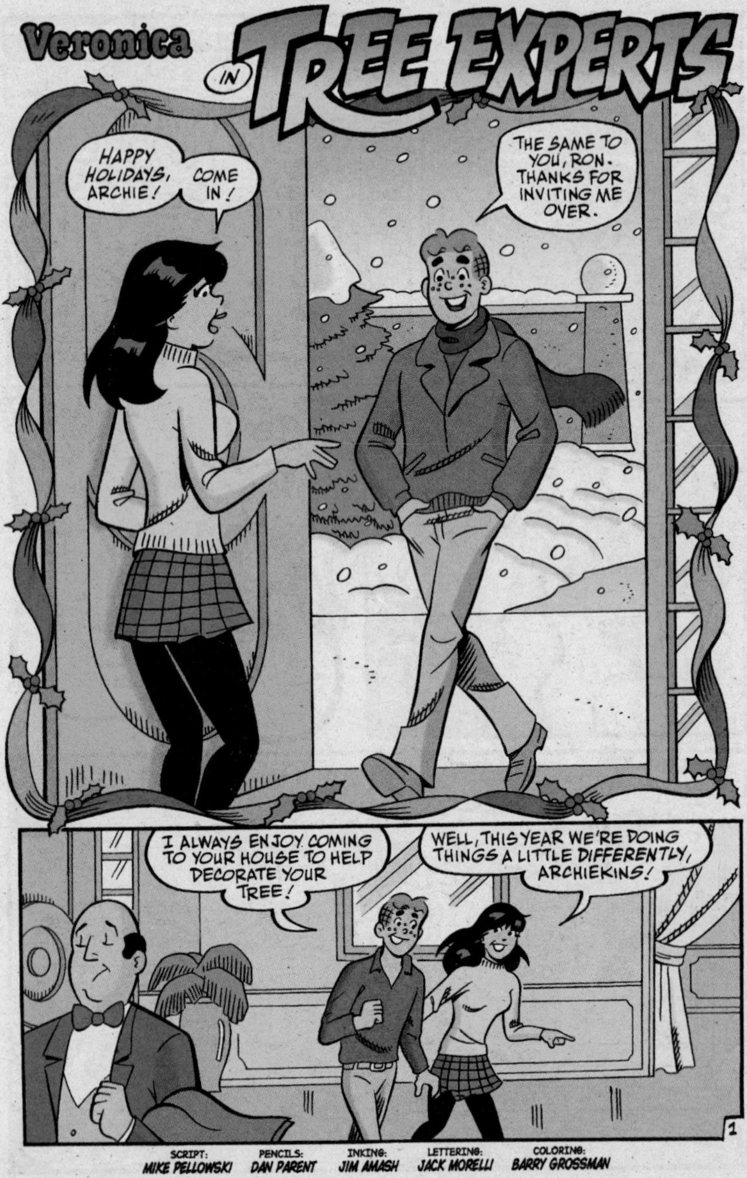
Veronica
IN
TREE EXPERTS
HAPPY HOLIDAYS, ARCHIE!
COME IN!
THE SAME TO YOU, RON. THANKS FOR INVITING ME OVER.
I ALWAYS ENJOY COMING TO YOUR HOUSE TO HELP DECORATE YOUR TREE!
WELL, THIS YEAR WE'RE DOING THINGS A LITTLE DIFFERENTLY, ARCHIEKINS!
1

SCRIPT: MIKE PELLOWSKI PENCILS: DAN PARENT INKING: JIM AMASH LETTERING: JACK MORELLI COLORING: BARRY GROSSMAN

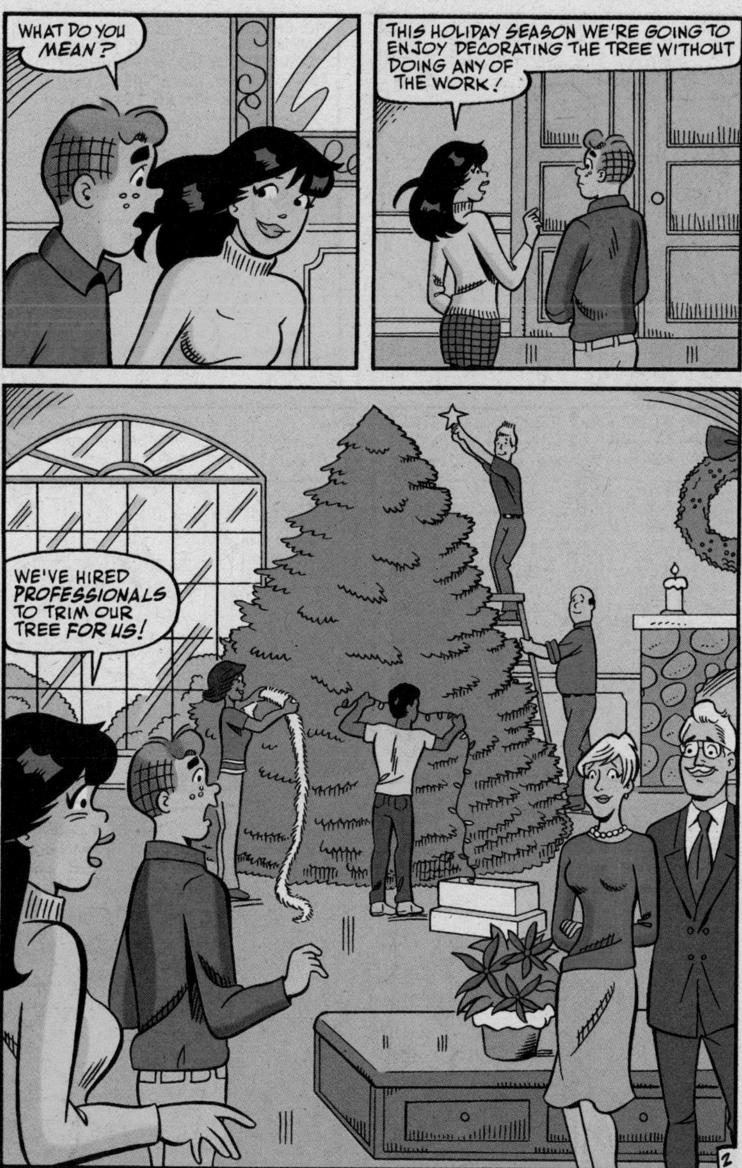
WHAT DO YOU MEAN?
THIS HOLIDAY SEASON WE'RE GOING TO ENJOY DECORATING THE TREE WITHOUT DOING ANY OF THE WORK!
WE'VE HIRED PROFESSIONALS TO TRIM OUR TREE FOR US!
2

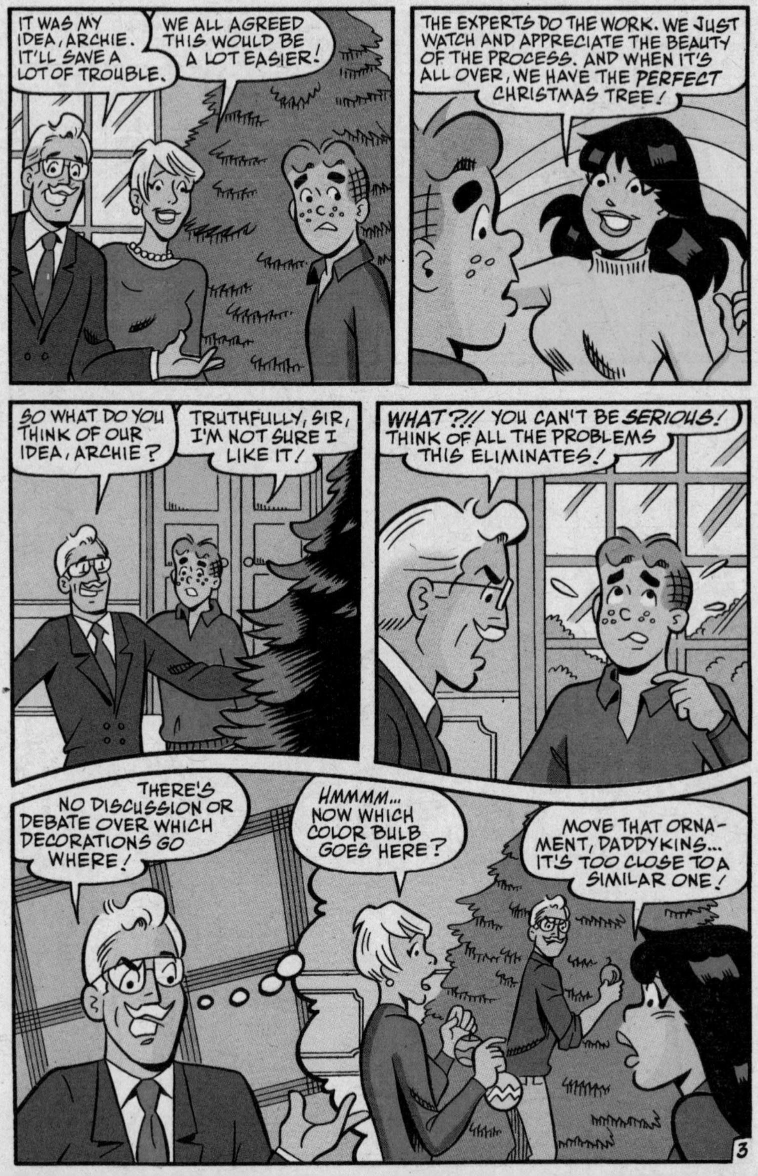
IT WAS MY IDEA, ARCHIE. IT'LL SAVE A LOT OF TROUBLE.
WE ALL AGREED THIS WOULD BE A LOT EASIER!
THE EXPERTS DO THE WORK. WE JUST WATCH AND APPRECIATE THE BEAUTY OF THE PROCESS. AND WHEN IT'S ALL OVER, WE HAVE THE PERFECT CHRISTMAS TREE!
SO WHAT DO YOU THINK OF OUR IDEA, ARCHIE?
TRUTHFULLY, SIR, I'M NOT SURE I LIKE IT!
WHAT?!! YOU CAN'T BE SERIOUS! THINK OF ALL THE PROBLEMS THIS ELIMINATES!
THERE'S NO DISCUSSION OR DEBATE OVER WHICH DECORATIONS GO WHERE!
HMMMM... NOW WHICH COLOR BULB GOES HERE?
MOVE THAT ORNAMENT, DADDYKINS... IT'S TOO CLOSE TO A SIMILAR ONE!
3

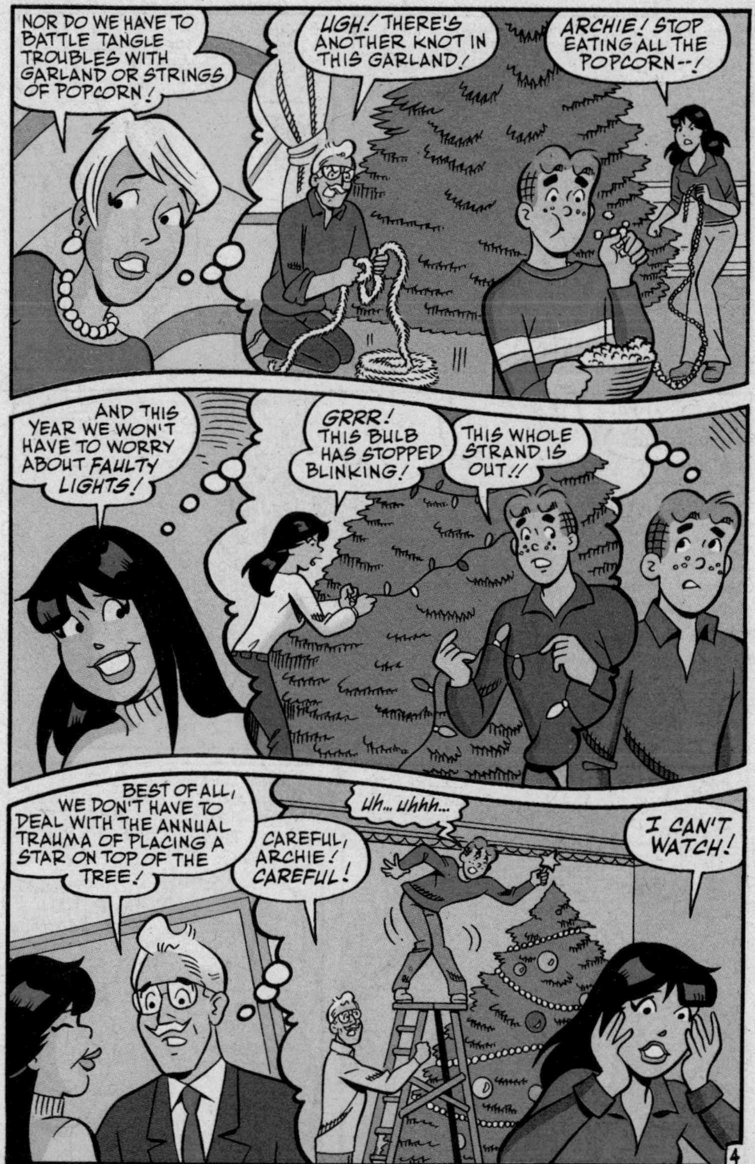

NOR DO WE HAVE TO BATTLE TANGLE TROUBLES WITH GARLAND OR STRINGS OF POPCORN!
UGH! THERE'S ANOTHER KNOT IN THIS GARLAND!
ARCHIE! STOP EATING ALL THE POPCORN--!
AND THIS YEAR WE WON'T HAVE TO WORRY ABOUT FAULTY LIGHTS!
GRRR! THIS BULB HAS STOPPED BLINKING!
THIS WHOLE STRAND IS OUT!!
BEST OF ALL, WE DON'T HAVE TO DEAL WITH THE ANNUAL TRAUMA OF PLACING A STAR ON TOP OF THE TREE!
CAREFUL, ARCHIE! CAREFUL!
UH... UHHH...
I CAN'T WATCH!

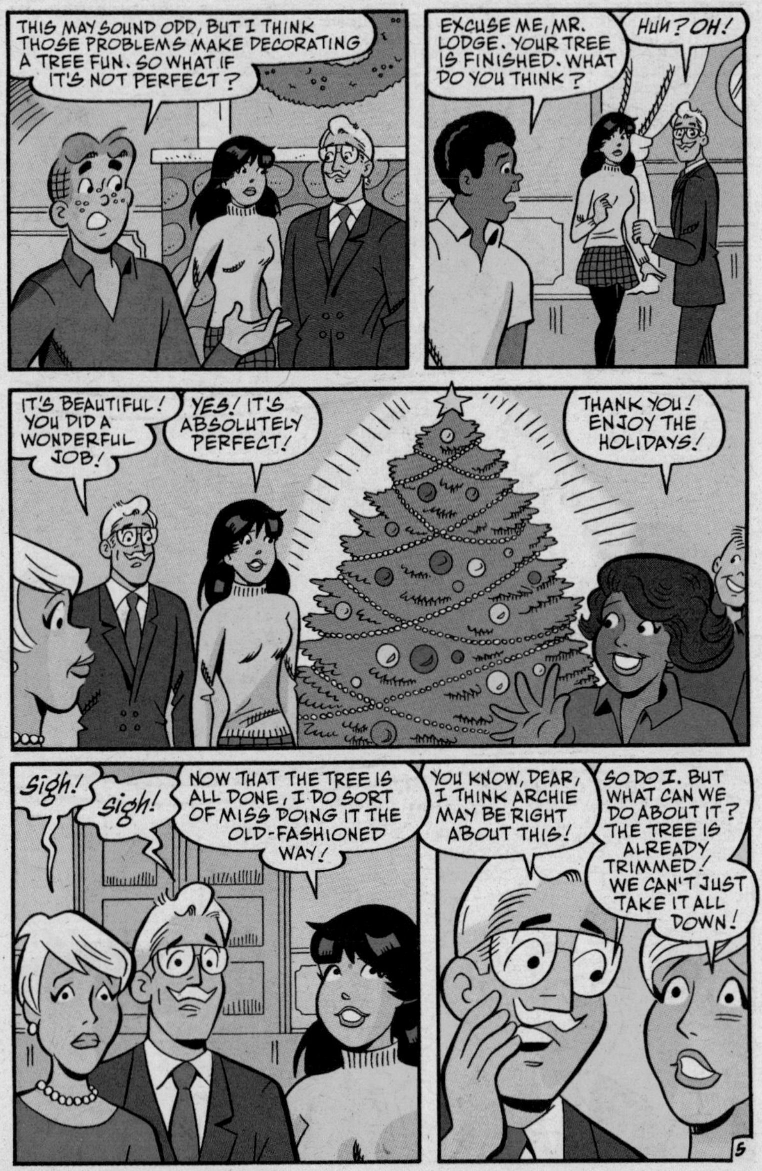
THIS MAY SOUND ODD, BUT I THINK THOSE PROBLEMS MAKE DECORATING A TREE FUN. SO WHAT IF IT'S NOT PERFECT?
EXCUSE ME, MR. LODGE. YOUR TREE IS FINISHED. WHAT DO YOU THINK?
HUH? OH!
IT'S BEAUTIFUL! YOU DID A WONDERFUL JOB!
YES! IT'S ABSOLUTELY PERFECT!
THANK YOU! ENJOY THE HOLIDAYS!
Sigh!
sigh!
NOW THAT THE TREE IS ALL DONE, I DO SORT OF MISS DOING IT THE OLD-FASHIONED WAY!
YOU KNOW, DEAR, I THINK ARCHIE MAY BE RIGHT ABOUT THIS!
SO DO I. BUT WHAT CAN WE DO ABOUT IT? THE TREE IS ALREADY TRIMMED! WE CAN'T JUST TAKE IT ALL DOWN!
5

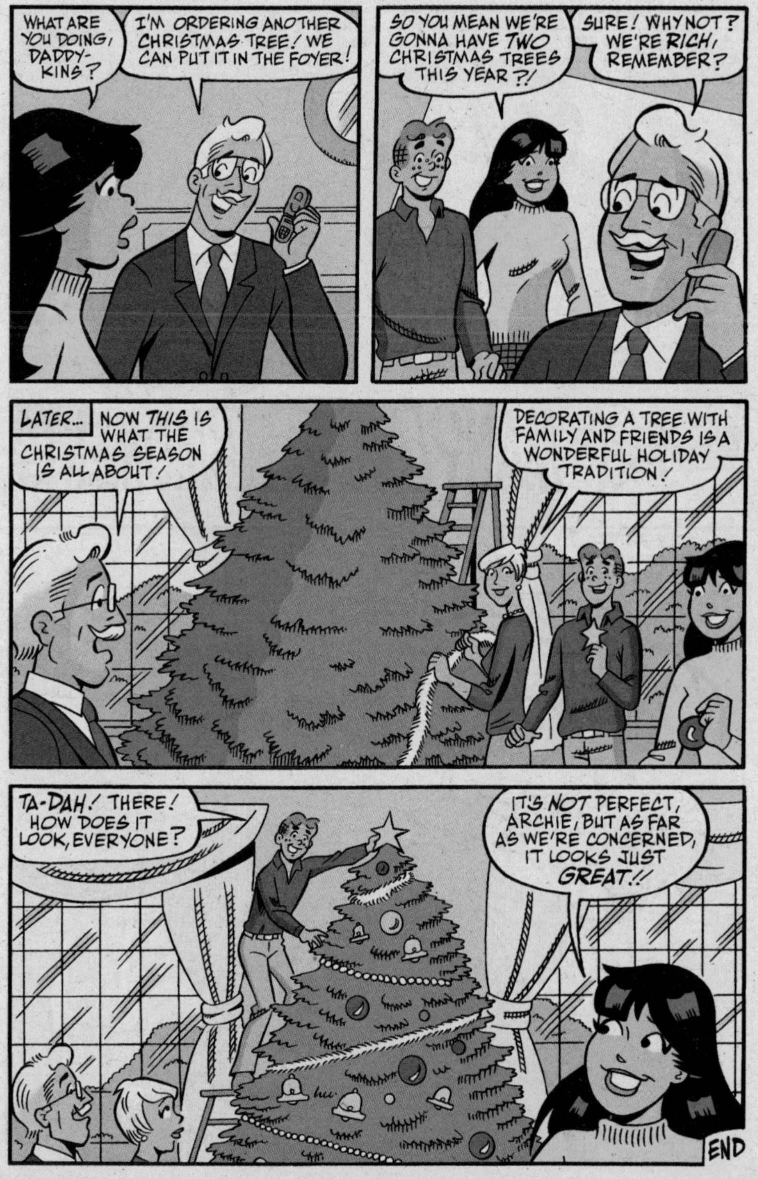
WHAT ARE YOU DOING, DADDY-KINS?
I'M ORDERING ANOTHER CHRISTMAS TREE! WE CAN PUT IT IN THE FOYER!
SO YOU MEAN WE'RE GONNA HAVE TWO CHRISTMAS TREES THIS YEAR?!
SURE! WHY NOT? WE'RE RICH, REMEMBER?
LATER...
NOW THIS IS WHAT THE CHRISTMAS SEASON IS ALL ABOUT!
DECORATING A TREE WITH FAMILY AND FRIENDS IS A WONDERFUL HOLIDAY TRADITION!
TA-DAH! THERE! HOW DOES IT LOOK, EVERYONE?
IT'S NOT PERFECT, ARCHIE, BUT AS FAR AS WE'RE CONCERNED, IT LOOKS JUST GREAT!!
END

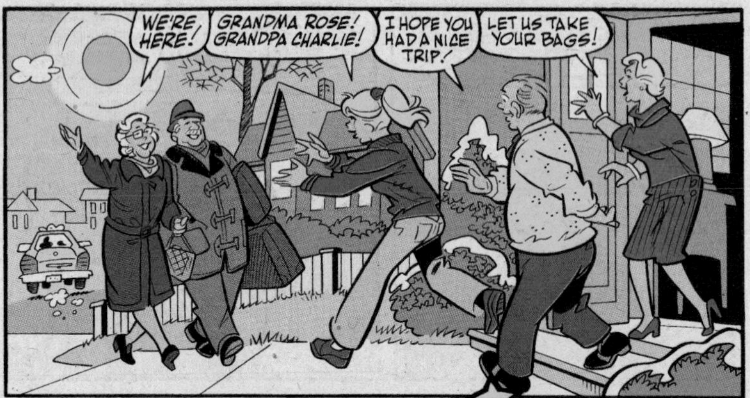
WE'RE HERE!
GRANDMA ROSE! GRANDPA CHARLIE!
I HOPE YOU HAD A NICE TRIP!
LET US TAKE YOUR BAGS!

Betty® IN MANY MAGIC MOMENTS

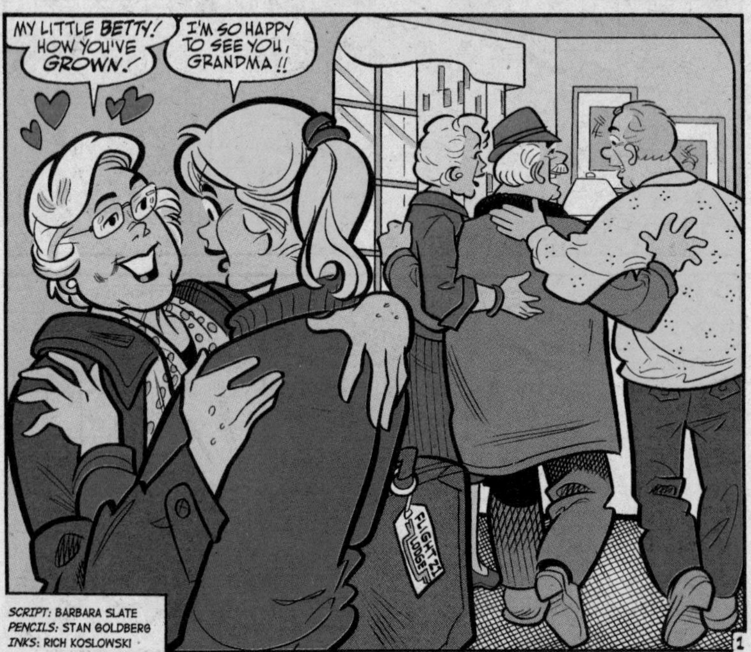
MY LITTLE BETTY! HOW YOU'VE GROWN!
I'M SO HAPPY TO SEE YOU, GRANDMA!!
FLIGHT 21 LODGE

SCRIPT: BARBARA SLATE
PENCILS: STAN GOLDBERG
INKS: RICH KOSLOWSKI

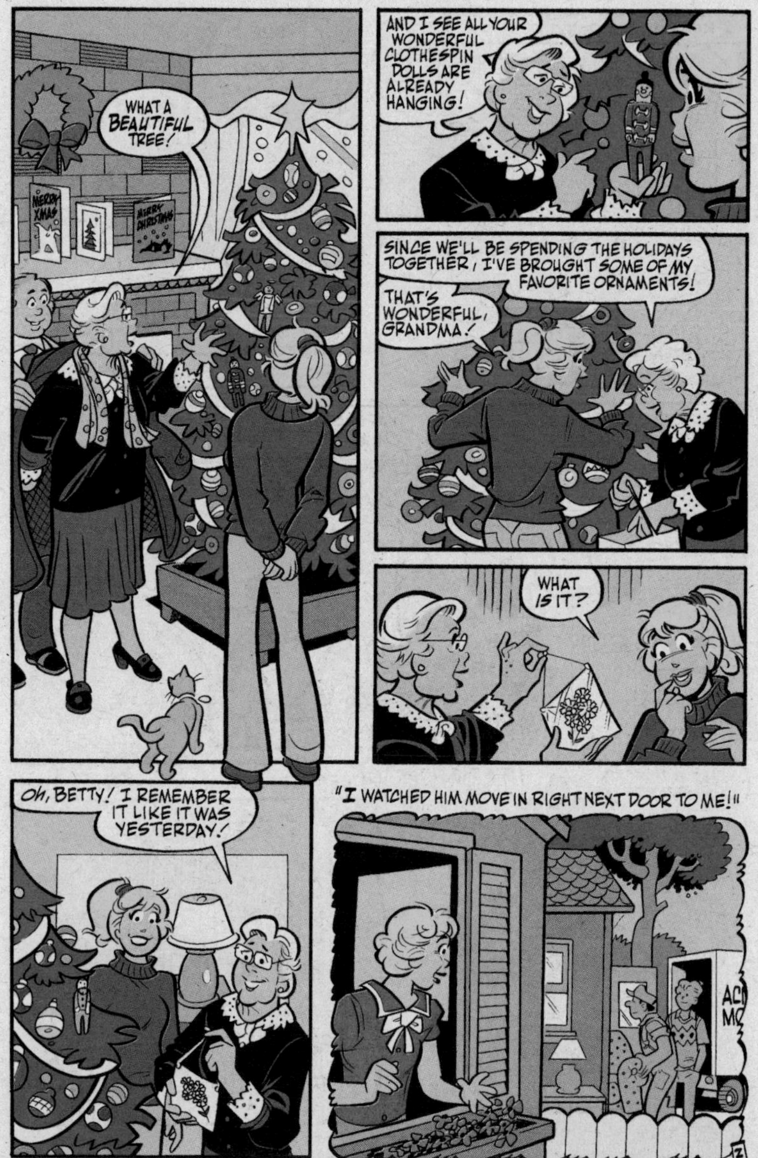
WHAT A BEAUTIFUL TREE!
MERRY XMAS
MERRY CHRISTMAS
AND I SEE ALL YOUR WONDERFUL CLOTHESPIN DOLLS ARE ALREADY HANGING!
SINCE WE'LL BE SPENDING THE HOLIDAYS TOGETHER, I'VE BROUGHT SOME OF MY FAVORITE ORNAMENTS!
THAT'S WONDERFUL, GRANDMA!
WHAT IS IT?
Oh, BETTY! I REMEMBER IT LIKE IT WAS YESTERDAY!
"I WATCHED HIM MOVE IN RIGHT NEXT DOOR TO ME!"

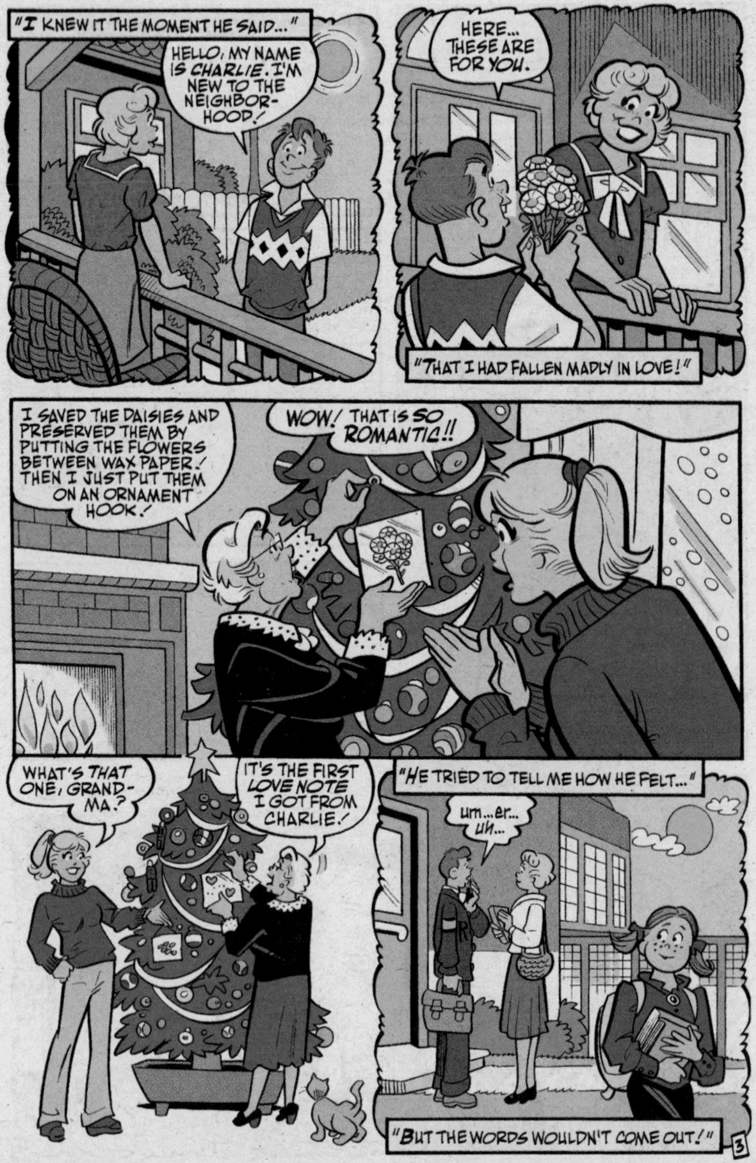
"I KNEW IT THE MOMENT HE SAID..."
HELLO, MY NAME IS CHARLIE. I'M NEW TO THE NEIGHBOR-HOOD!
HERE... THESE ARE FOR YOU.
"THAT I HAD FALLEN MADLY IN LOVE!"
I SAVED THE DAISIES AND PRESERVED THEM BY PUTTING THE FLOWERS BETWEEN WAX PAPER! THEN I JUST PUT THEM ON AN ORNAMENT HOOK!
WOW! THAT IS SO ROMANTIC!!
WHAT'S THAT ONE, GRAND-MA?
IT'S THE FIRST LOVE NOTE I GOT FROM CHARLIE!
"HE TRIED TO TELL ME HOW HE FELT..."
um...er... uh...
"BUT THE WORDS WOULDN'T COME OUT!"
3

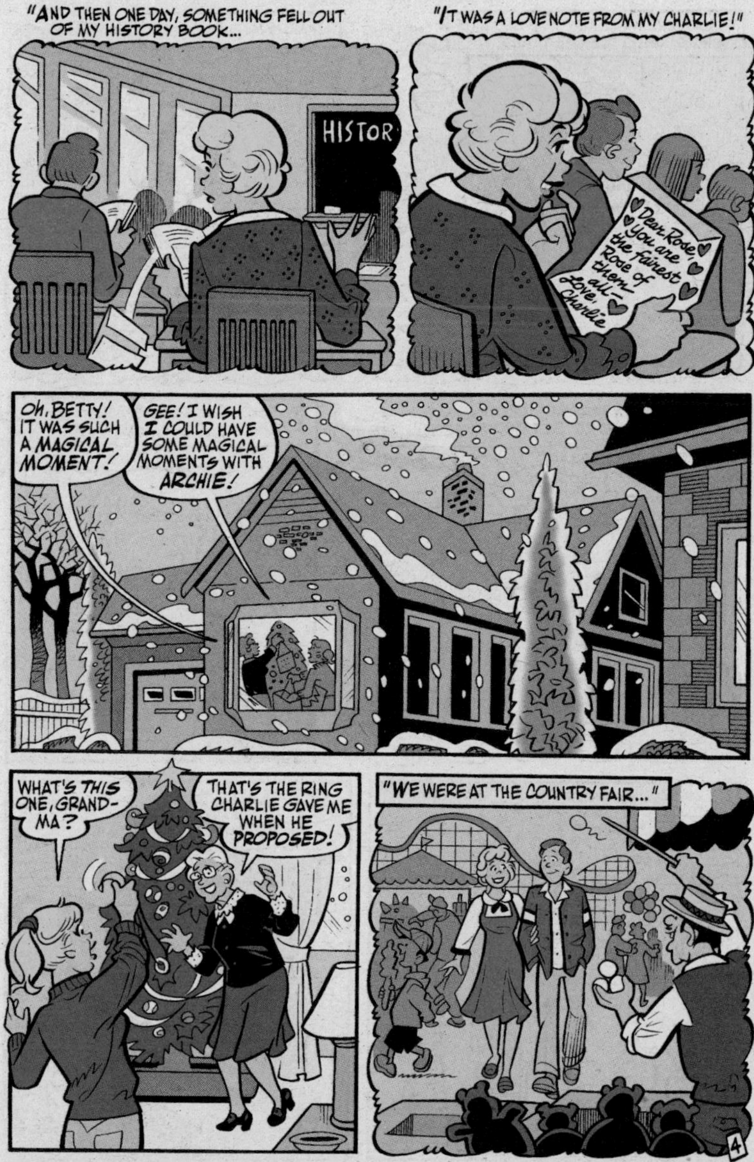
"AND THEN ONE DAY, SOMETHING FELL OUT OF MY HISTORY BOOK...
HISTOR
"IT WAS A LOVE NOTE FROM MY CHARLIE!"
Dear Rose, You are the fairest Rose of them all— Love, Charlie
OH, BETTY! IT WAS SUCH A MAGICAL MOMENT!
GEE! I WISH I COULD HAVE SOME MAGICAL MOMENTS WITH ARCHIE!
WHAT'S THIS ONE, GRANDMA?
THAT'S THE RING CHARLIE GAVE ME WHEN HE PROPOSED!
"WE WERE AT THE COUNTRY FAIR..."
4

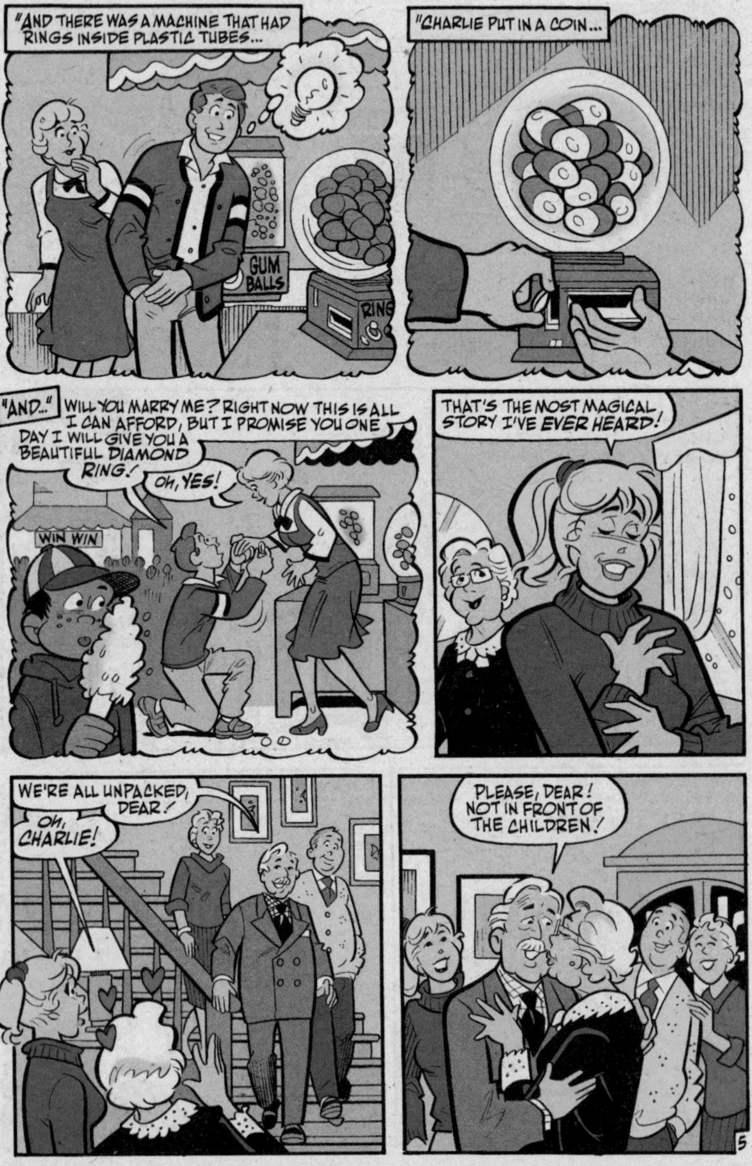
"AND THERE WAS A MACHINE THAT HAD RINGS INSIDE PLASTIC TUBES...
GUM BALLS
RING
"CHARLIE PUT IN A COIN...
"AND..."
WILL YOU MARRY ME? RIGHT NOW THIS IS ALL I CAN AFFORD, BUT I PROMISE YOU ONE DAY I WILL GIVE YOU A BEAUTIFUL DIAMOND RING!
OH, YES!
WIN WIN
THAT'S THE MOST MAGICAL STORY I'VE EVER HEARD!
WE'RE ALL UNPACKED, DEAR!
OH, CHARLIE!
PLEASE, DEAR! NOT IN FRONT OF THE CHILDREN!

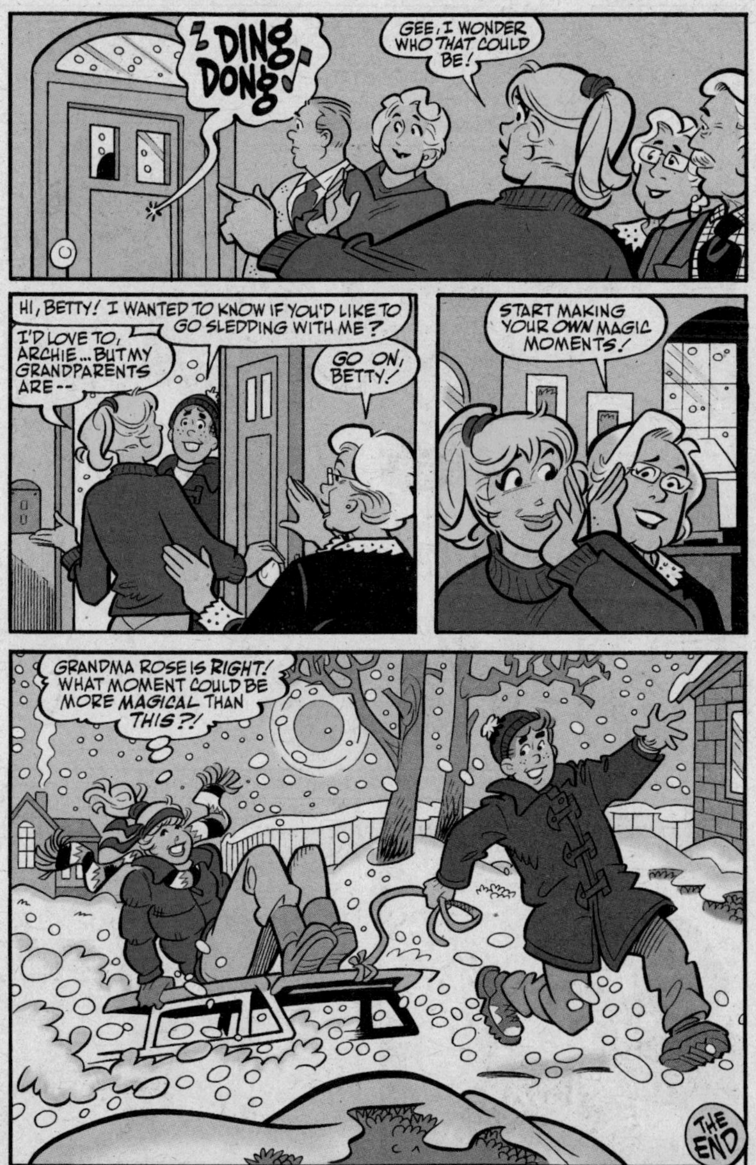
DING DONG
GEE, I WONDER WHO THAT COULD BE!
HI, BETTY! I WANTED TO KNOW IF YOU'D LIKE TO GO SLEDDING WITH ME?
I'D LOVE TO, ARCHIE... BUT MY GRANDPARENTS ARE --
GO ON, BETTY!
START MAKING YOUR OWN MAGIC MOMENTS!
GRANDMA ROSE IS RIGHT! WHAT MOMENT COULD BE MORE MAGICAL THAN THIS?!
THE END

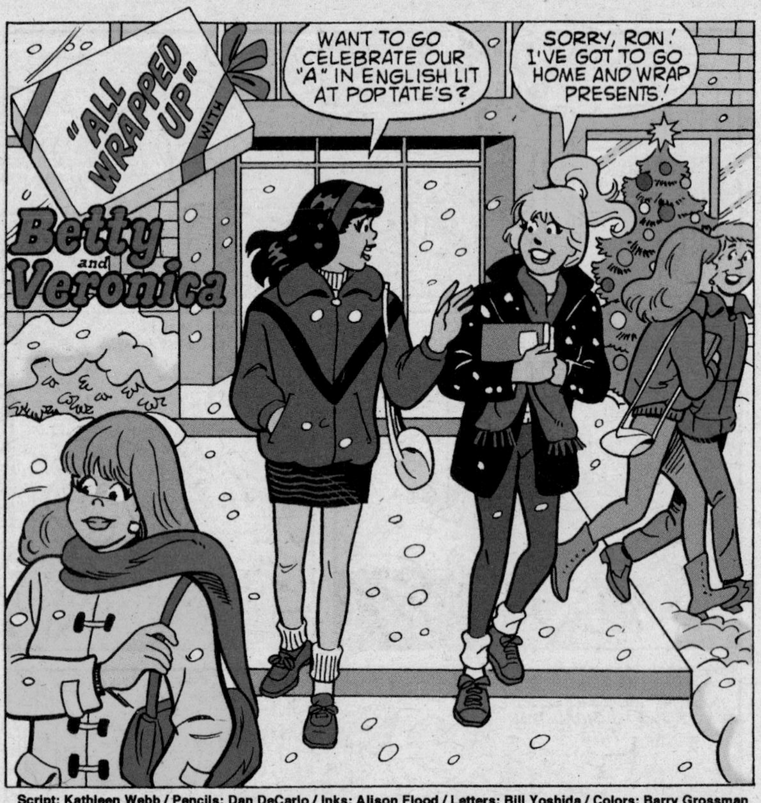
"ALL WRAPPED UP" WITH
Betty and Veronica
WANT TO GO CELEBRATE OUR "A" IN ENGLISH LIT AT POP TATE'S?
SORRY, RON! I'VE GOT TO GO HOME AND WRAP PRESENTS!

Script: Kathleen Webb / Pencils: Dan DeCarlo / Inks: Alison Flood / Letters: Bill Yoshida / Colors: Barry Grossman

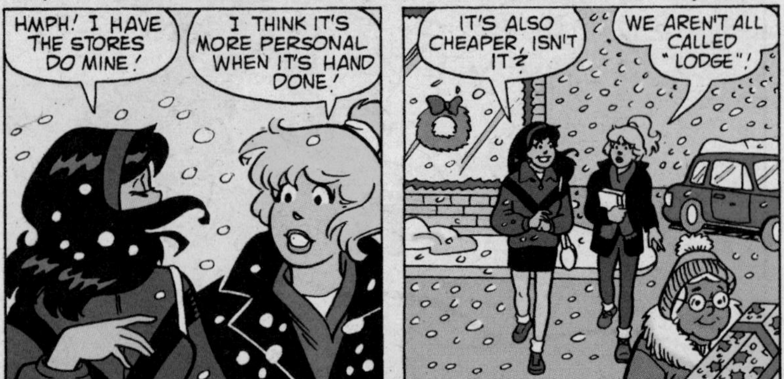
HMPH! I HAVE THE STORES DO MINE!
I THINK IT'S MORE PERSONAL WHEN IT'S HAND DONE!
IT'S ALSO CHEAPER, ISN'T IT?
WE AREN'T ALL CALLED "LODGE"!

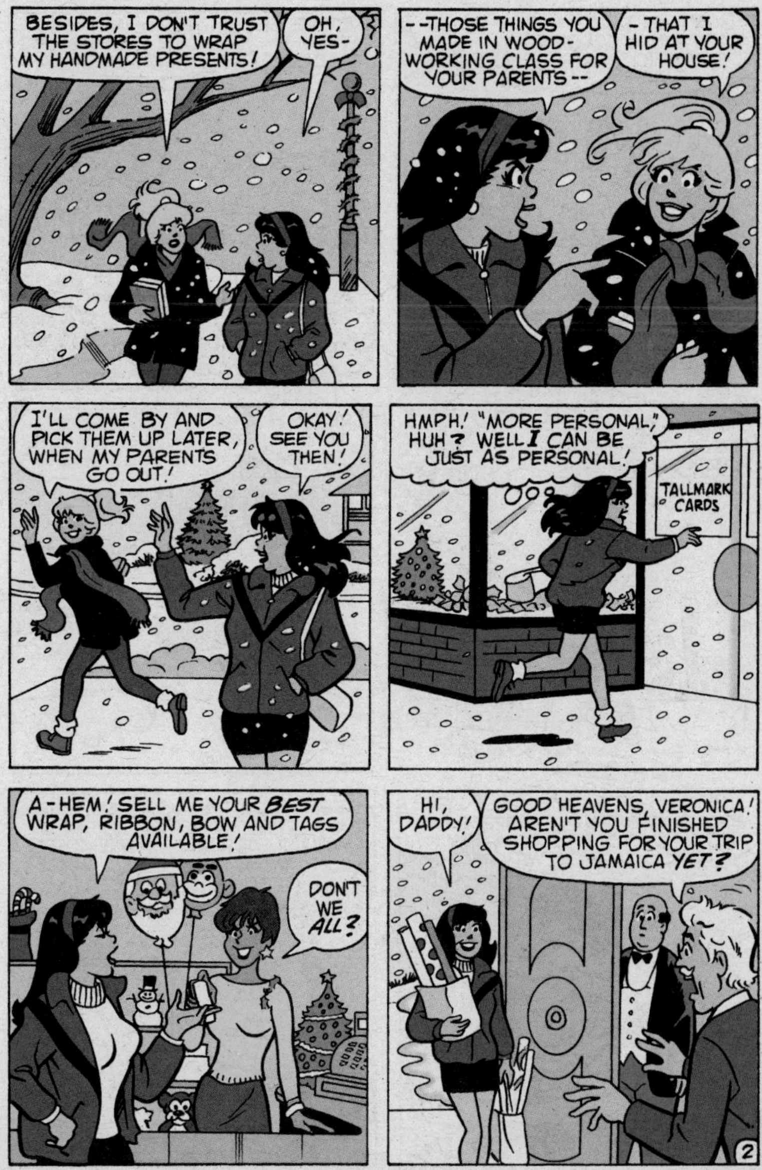

BESIDES, I DON'T TRUST THE STORES TO WRAP MY HANDMADE PRESENTS!
OH, YES-
--THOSE THINGS YOU MADE IN WOOD-WORKING CLASS FOR YOUR PARENTS--
-THAT I HID AT YOUR HOUSE!
I'LL COME BY AND PICK THEM UP LATER, WHEN MY PARENTS GO OUT!
OKAY! SEE YOU THEN!
HMPH! "MORE PERSONAL," HUH? WELL I CAN BE JUST AS PERSONAL!
TALLMARK CARDS
A-HEM! SELL ME YOUR BEST WRAP, RIBBON, BOW AND TAGS AVAILABLE!
DON'T WE ALL?
HI, DADDY!
GOOD HEAVENS, VERONICA! AREN'T YOU FINISHED SHOPPING FOR YOUR TRIP TO JAMAICA YET?
2

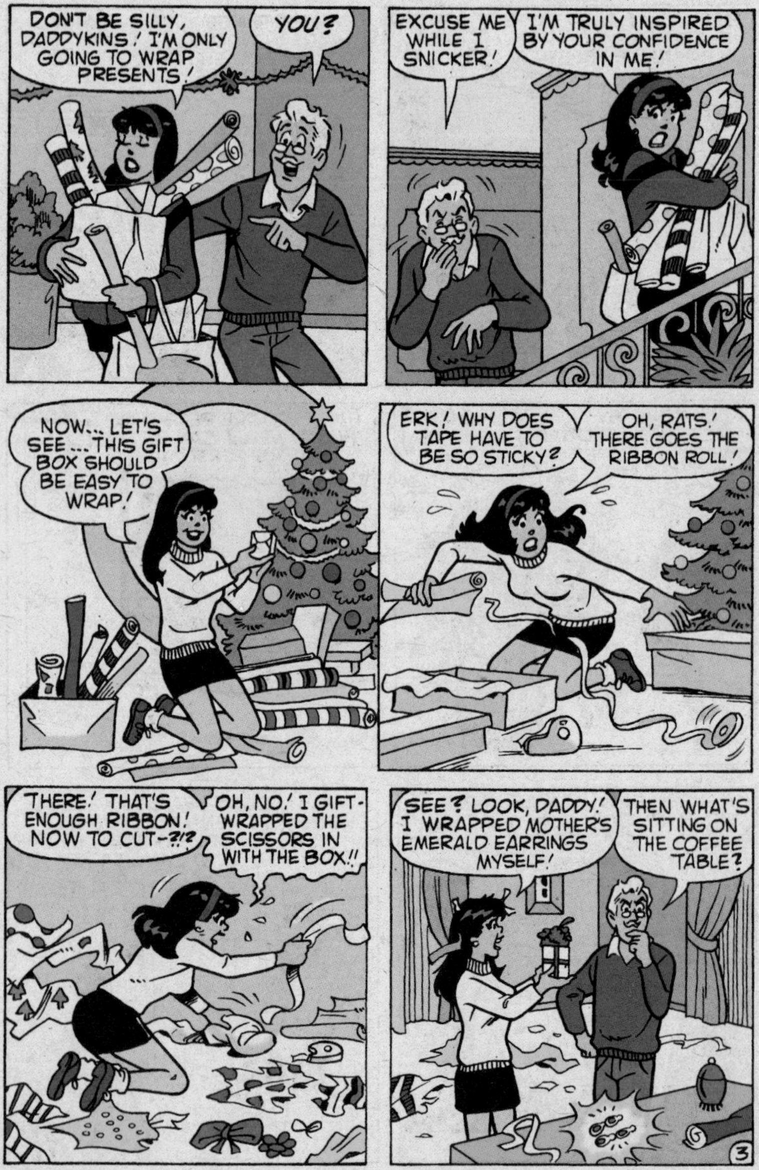
DON'T BE SILLY, DADDYKINS! I'M ONLY GOING TO WRAP PRESENTS!
YOU?
EXCUSE ME WHILE I SNICKER!
I'M TRULY INSPIRED BY YOUR CONFIDENCE IN ME!
NOW... LET'S SEE... THIS GIFT BOX SHOULD BE EASY TO WRAP!
ERK! WHY DOES TAPE HAVE TO BE SO STICKY?
OH, RATS! THERE GOES THE RIBBON ROLL!
THERE! THAT'S ENOUGH RIBBON! NOW TO CUT-?!?
OH, NO! I GIFT-WRAPPED THE SCISSORS IN WITH THE BOX!!
SEE? LOOK, DADDY! I WRAPPED MOTHER'S EMERALD EARRINGS MYSELF!
THEN WHAT'S SITTING ON THE COFFEE TABLE?
3

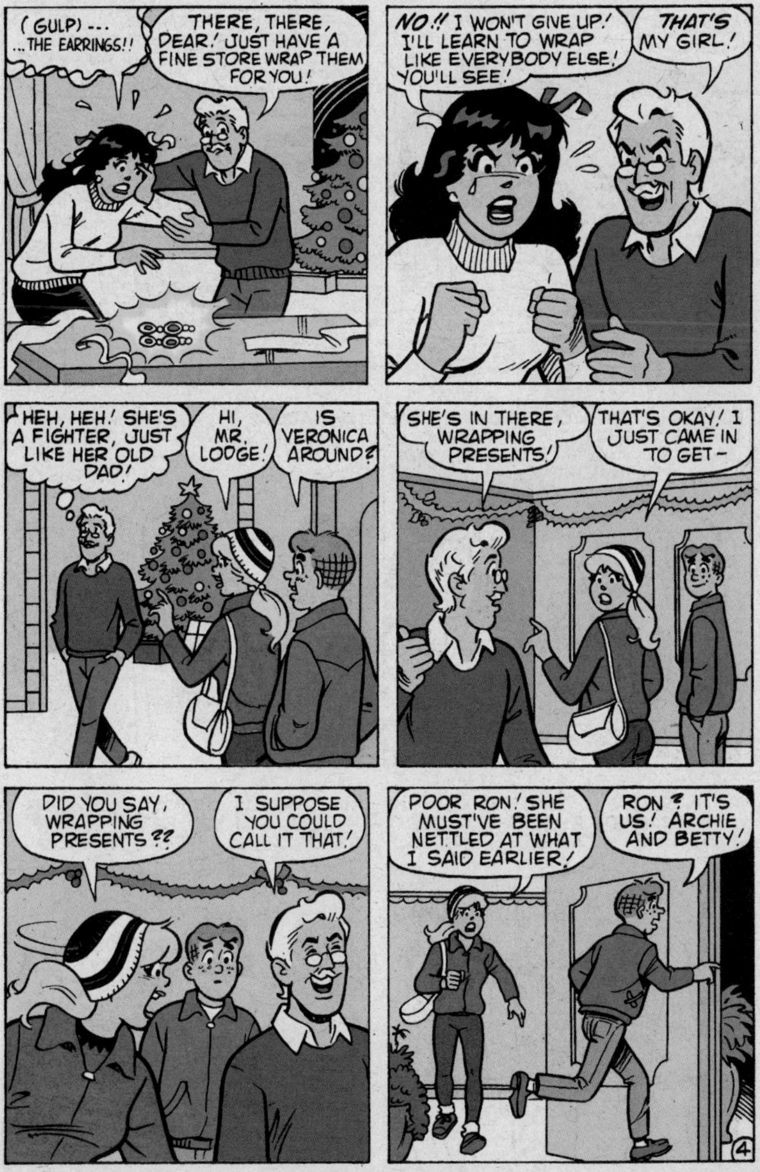
(GULP) ... ...THE EARRINGS!!
THERE, THERE, DEAR! JUST HAVE A FINE STORE WRAP THEM FOR YOU!
NO!! I WON'T GIVE UP! I'LL LEARN TO WRAP LIKE EVERYBODY ELSE! YOU'LL SEE!
THAT'S MY GIRL!
HEH, HEH! SHE'S A FIGHTER, JUST LIKE HER OLD DAD!
HI, MR. LODGE!
IS VERONICA AROUND?
SHE'S IN THERE, WRAPPING PRESENTS!
THAT'S OKAY! I JUST CAME IN TO GET -
DID YOU SAY, WRAPPING PRESENTS??
I SUPPOSE YOU COULD CALL IT THAT!
POOR RON! SHE MUST'VE BEEN NETTLED AT WHAT I SAID EARLIER!
RON? IT'S US! ARCHIE AND BETTY!
4

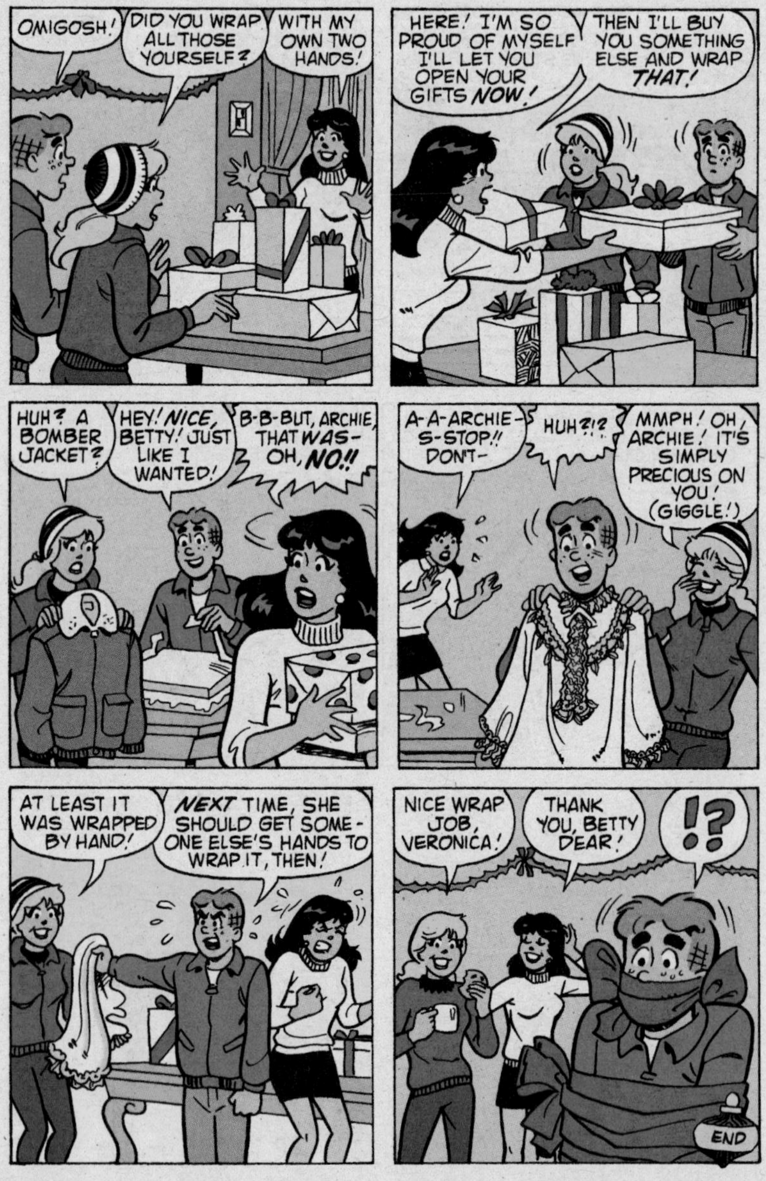

OMIGOSH!
DID YOU WRAP ALL THOSE YOURSELF?
WITH MY OWN TWO HANDS!
HERE! I'M SO PROUD OF MYSELF I'LL LET YOU OPEN YOUR GIFTS NOW!
THEN I'LL BUY YOU SOMETHING ELSE AND WRAP THAT!
HUH? A BOMBER JACKET?
HEY! NICE, BETTY! JUST LIKE I WANTED!
B-B-BUT, ARCHIE, THAT WAS- OH, NO!!
A-A-ARCHIE- S-STOP!! DON'T-
HUH?!?
MMPH! OH, ARCHIE! IT'S SIMPLY PRECIOUS ON YOU! (GIGGLE!)
AT LEAST IT WAS WRAPPED BY HAND!
NEXT TIME, SHE SHOULD GET SOME-ONE ELSE'S HANDS TO WRAP IT, THEN!
NICE WRAP JOB, VERONICA!
THANK YOU, BETTY DEAR!
!?
END

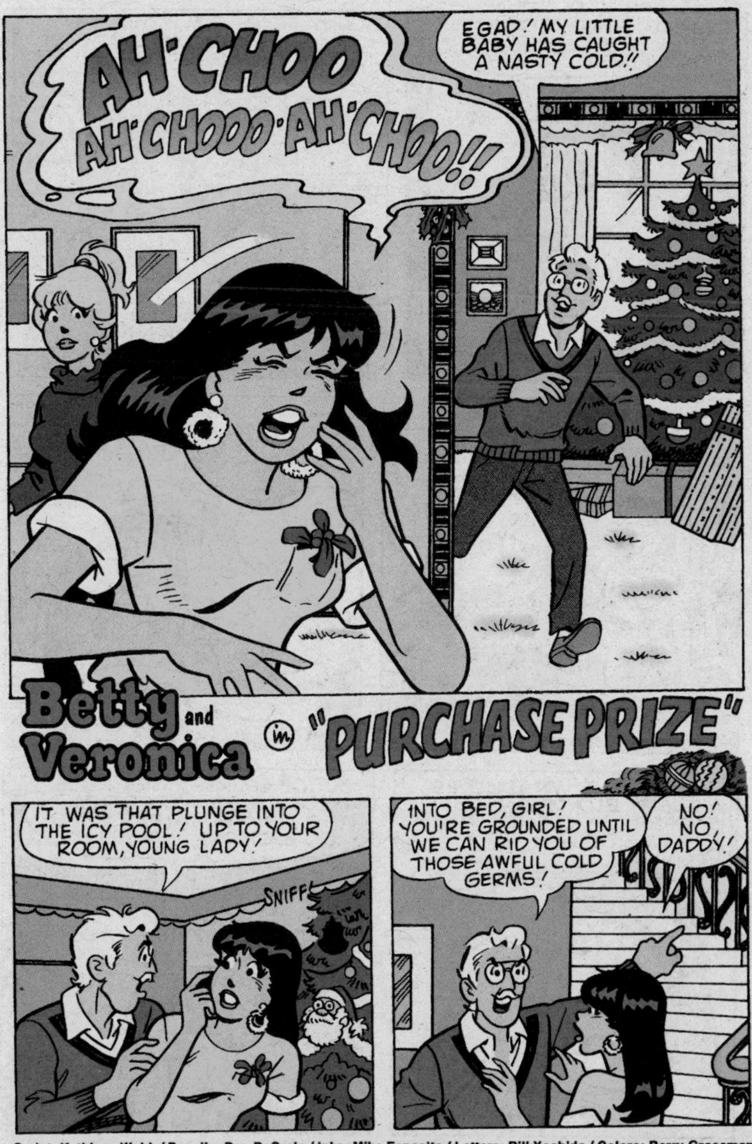
AH-CHOO AH-CHOOO-AH-CHOO!!
EGAD! MY LITTLE BABY HAS CAUGHT A NASTY COLD!!
Betty and Veronica in "PURCHASE PRIZE"
IT WAS THAT PLUNGE INTO THE ICY POOL! UP TO YOUR ROOM, YOUNG LADY!
SNIFF
INTO BED, GIRL! YOU'RE GROUNDED UNTIL WE CAN RID YOU OF THOSE AWFUL COLD GERMS!
NO! NO, DADDY!

Script: Kathleen Webb / Pencils: Dan DeCarlo / Inks: Mike Esposito / Letters: Bill Yoshida / Colors: Barry Grossman

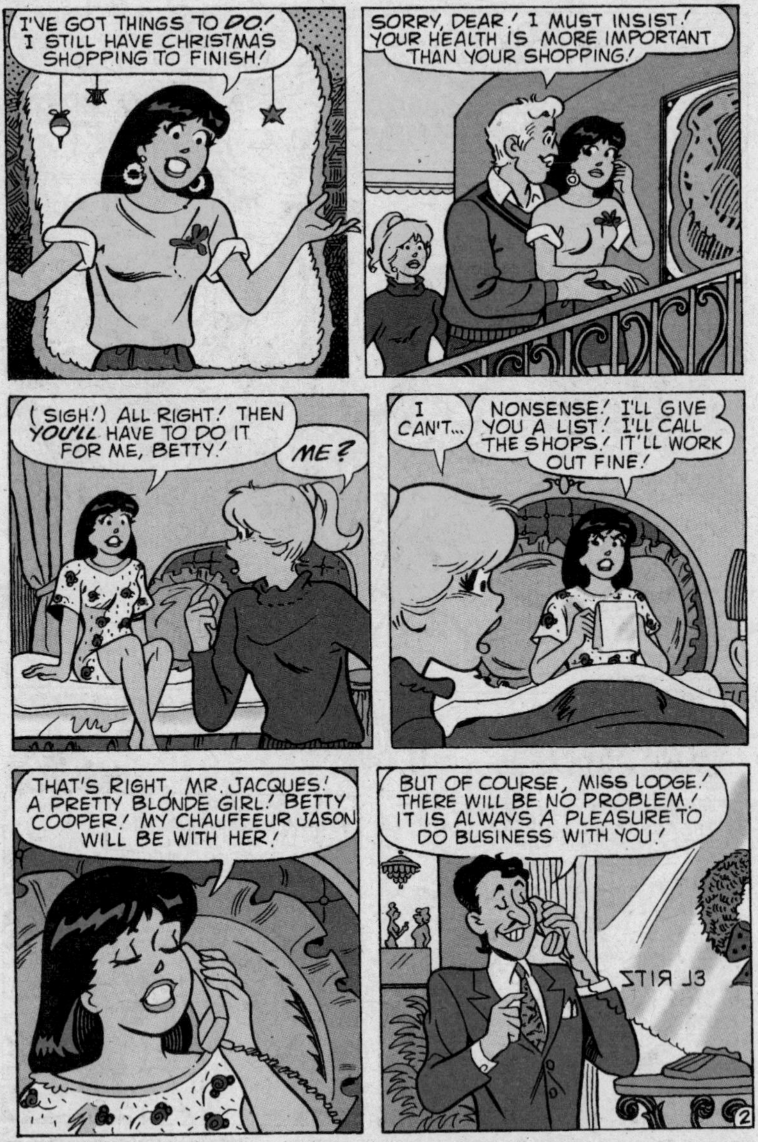

I'VE GOT THINGS TO *DO!* I STILL HAVE CHRISTMAS SHOPPING TO FINISH!
SORRY, DEAR! I MUST INSIST! YOUR HEALTH IS MORE IMPORTANT THAN YOUR SHOPPING!
(SIGH!) ALL RIGHT! THEN *YOU'LL* HAVE TO DO IT FOR ME, BETTY!
ME?
I CAN'T...
NONSENSE! I'LL GIVE YOU A LIST! I'LL CALL THE SHOPS! IT'LL WORK OUT FINE!
THAT'S RIGHT, MR. JACQUES! A PRETTY BLONDE GIRL! BETTY COOPER! MY CHAUFFEUR JASON WILL BE WITH HER!
BUT OF COURSE, MISS LODGE! THERE WILL BE NO PROBLEM! IT IS ALWAYS A PLEASURE TO DO BUSINESS WITH YOU!
EL RITZ
2

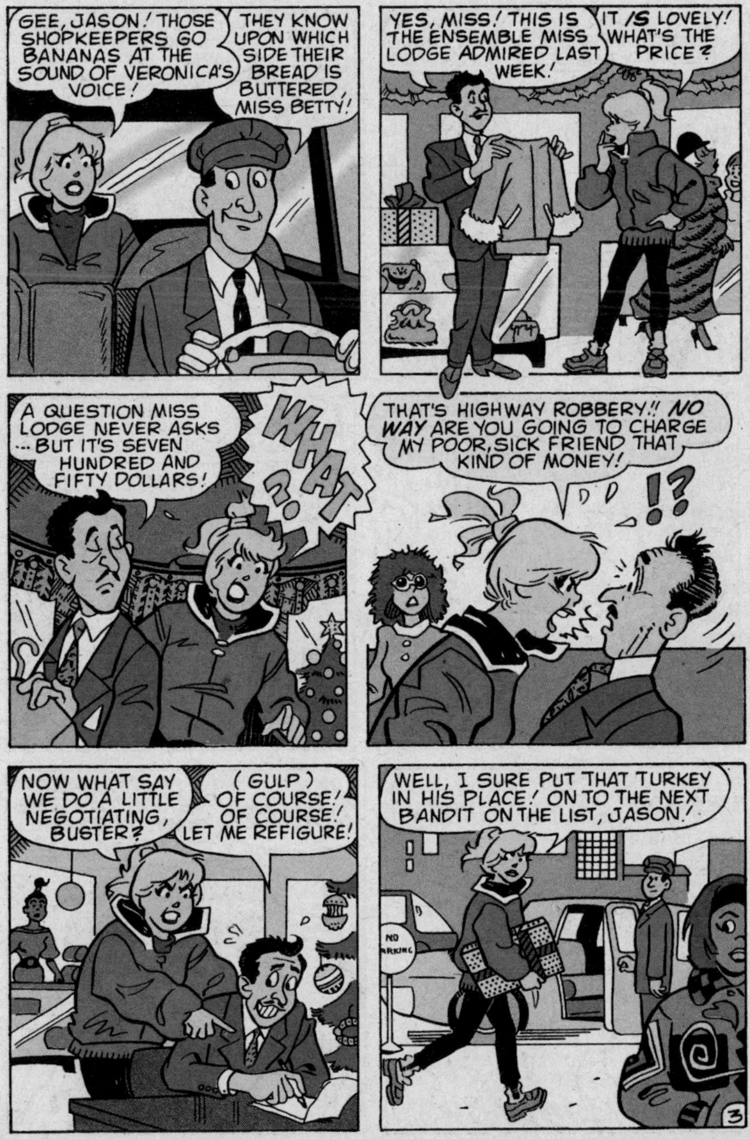

GEE, JASON! THOSE SHOPKEEPERS GO BANANAS AT THE SOUND OF VERONICA'S VOICE!
THEY KNOW UPON WHICH SIDE THEIR BREAD IS BUTTERED, MISS BETTY!
YES, MISS! THIS IS THE ENSEMBLE MISS LODGE ADMIRED LAST WEEK!
IT IS LOVELY! WHAT'S THE PRICE?
A QUESTION MISS LODGE NEVER ASKS ... BUT IT'S SEVEN HUNDRED AND FIFTY DOLLARS!
WHAT?!
THAT'S HIGHWAY ROBBERY!! NO WAY ARE YOU GOING TO CHARGE MY POOR, SICK FRIEND THAT KIND OF MONEY!
!?
NOW WHAT SAY WE DO A LITTLE NEGOTIATING, BUSTER?
(GULP) OF COURSE! OF COURSE! LET ME REFIGURE!
WELL, I SURE PUT THAT TURKEY IN HIS PLACE! ON TO THE NEXT BANDIT ON THE LIST, JASON!
NO PARKING
3

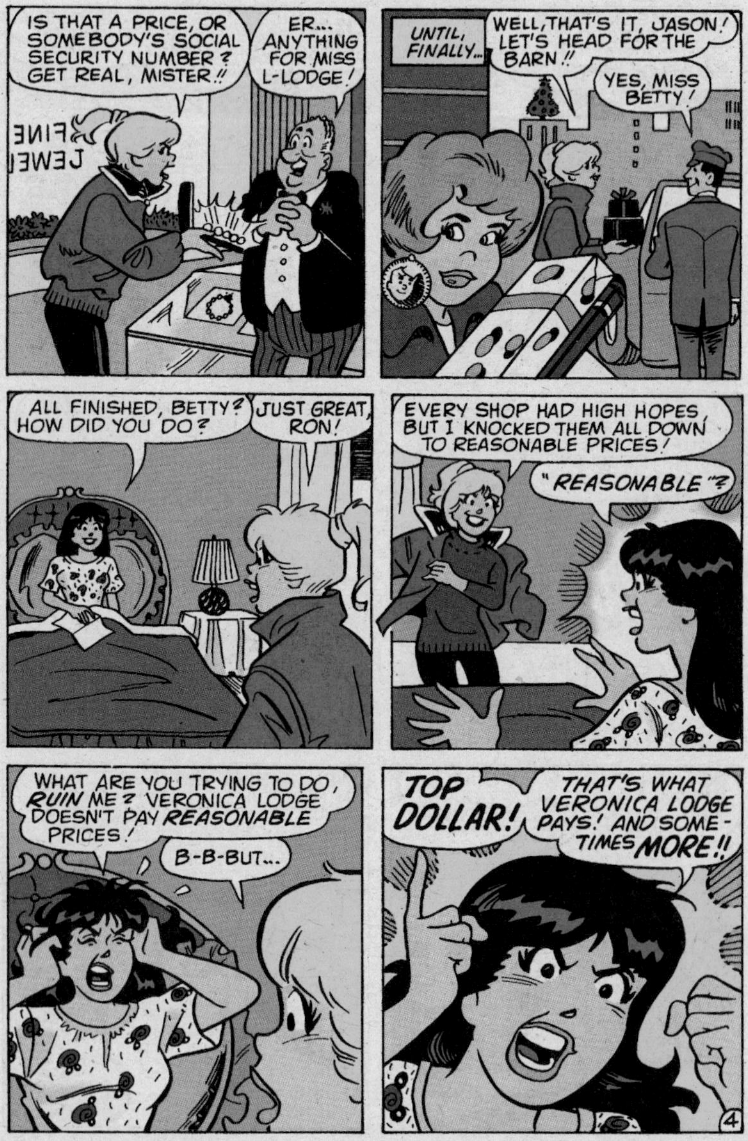
IS THAT A PRICE, OR SOMEBODY'S SOCIAL SECURITY NUMBER? GET REAL, MISTER!!
ER... ANYTHING FOR MISS L-LODGE!
UNTIL, FINALLY...
WELL, THAT'S IT, JASON! LET'S HEAD FOR THE BARN!!
YES, MISS BETTY!
ALL FINISHED, BETTY? HOW DID YOU DO?
JUST GREAT, RON!
EVERY SHOP HAD HIGH HOPES, BUT I KNOCKED THEM ALL DOWN TO REASONABLE PRICES!
"REASONABLE"?
WHAT ARE YOU TRYING TO DO, RUIN ME? VERONICA LODGE DOESN'T PAY REASONABLE PRICES!
B-B-BUT...
TOP DOLLAR!
THAT'S WHAT VERONICA LODGE PAYS! AND SOMETIMES MORE!!
4

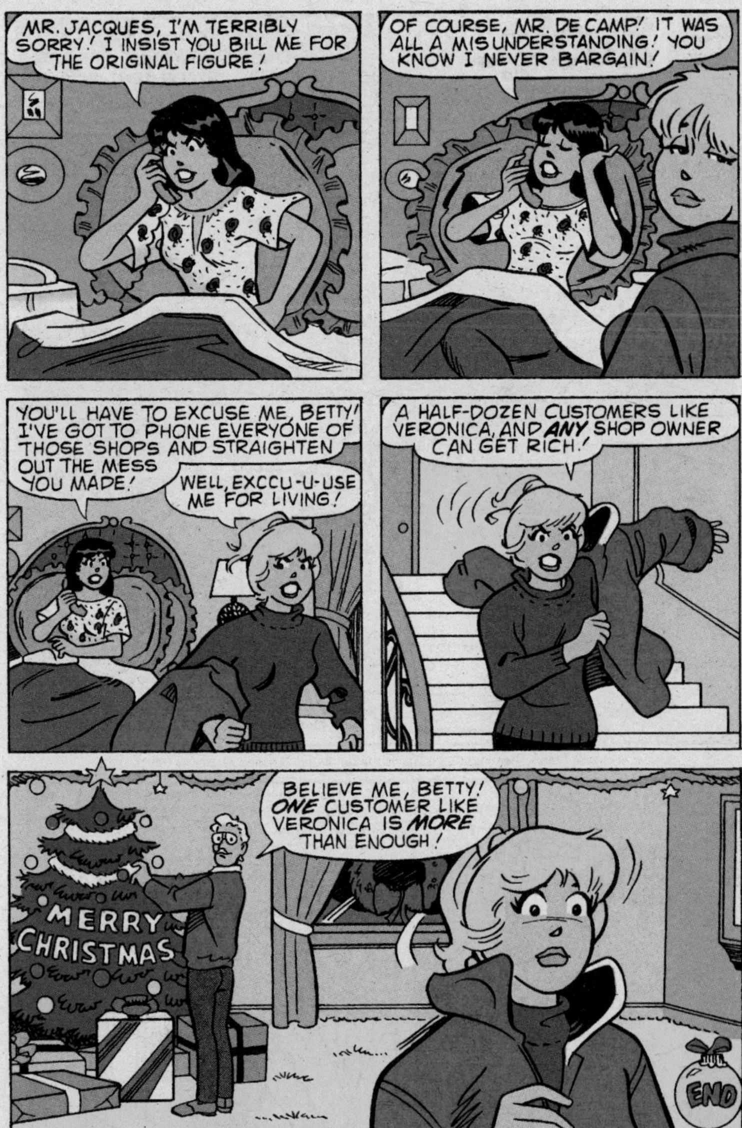
MR. JACQUES, I'M TERRIBLY SORRY! I INSIST YOU BILL ME FOR THE ORIGINAL FIGURE!
OF COURSE, MR. DE CAMP! IT WAS ALL A MISUNDERSTANDING! YOU KNOW I NEVER BARGAIN!
YOU'LL HAVE TO EXCUSE ME, BETTY! I'VE GOT TO PHONE EVERYONE OF THOSE SHOPS AND STRAIGHTEN OUT THE MESS YOU MADE!
WELL, EXCCU-U-USE ME FOR LIVING!
A HALF-DOZEN CUSTOMERS LIKE VERONICA, AND ANY SHOP OWNER CAN GET RICH!
BELIEVE ME, BETTY! ONE CUSTOMER LIKE VERONICA IS MORE THAN ENOUGH!
MERRY CHRISTMAS
END

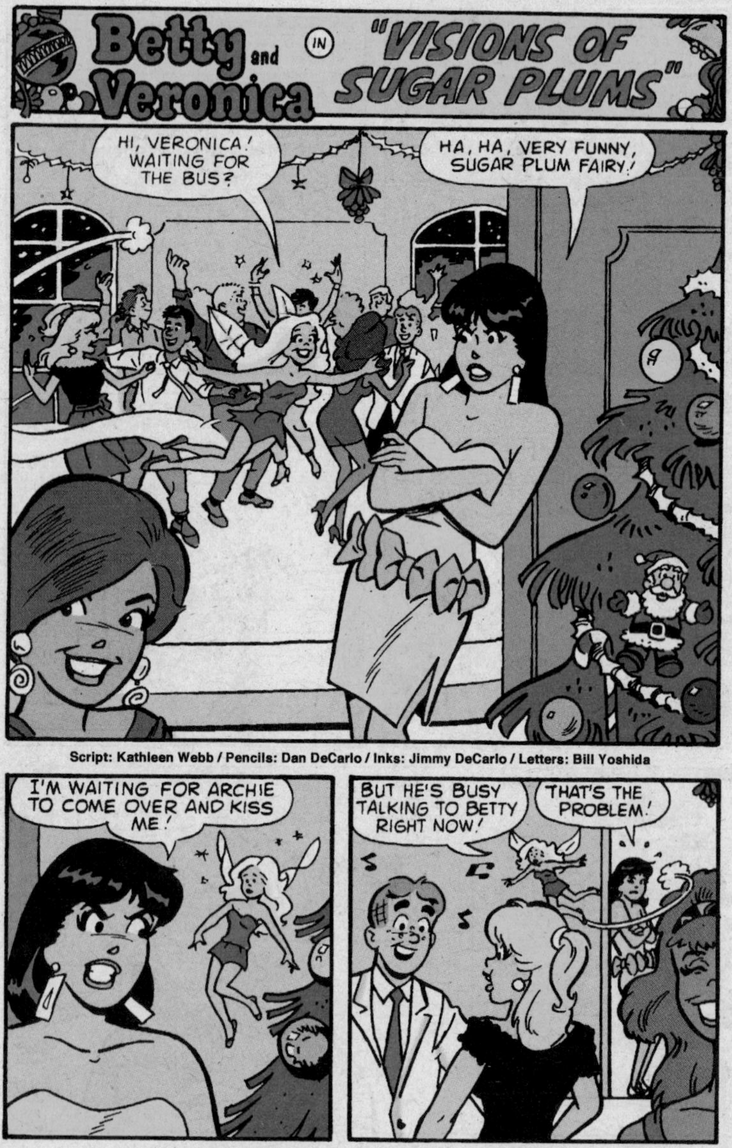
Betty and Veronica
IN
"VISIONS OF SUGAR PLUMS"
HI, VERONICA! WAITING FOR THE BUS?
HA, HA, VERY FUNNY, SUGAR PLUM FAIRY!
I'M WAITING FOR ARCHIE TO COME OVER AND KISS ME!
BUT HE'S BUSY TALKING TO BETTY RIGHT NOW!
THAT'S THE PROBLEM!

Script: Kathleen Webb / Pencils: Dan DeCarlo / Inks: Jimmy DeCarlo / Letters: Bill Yoshida

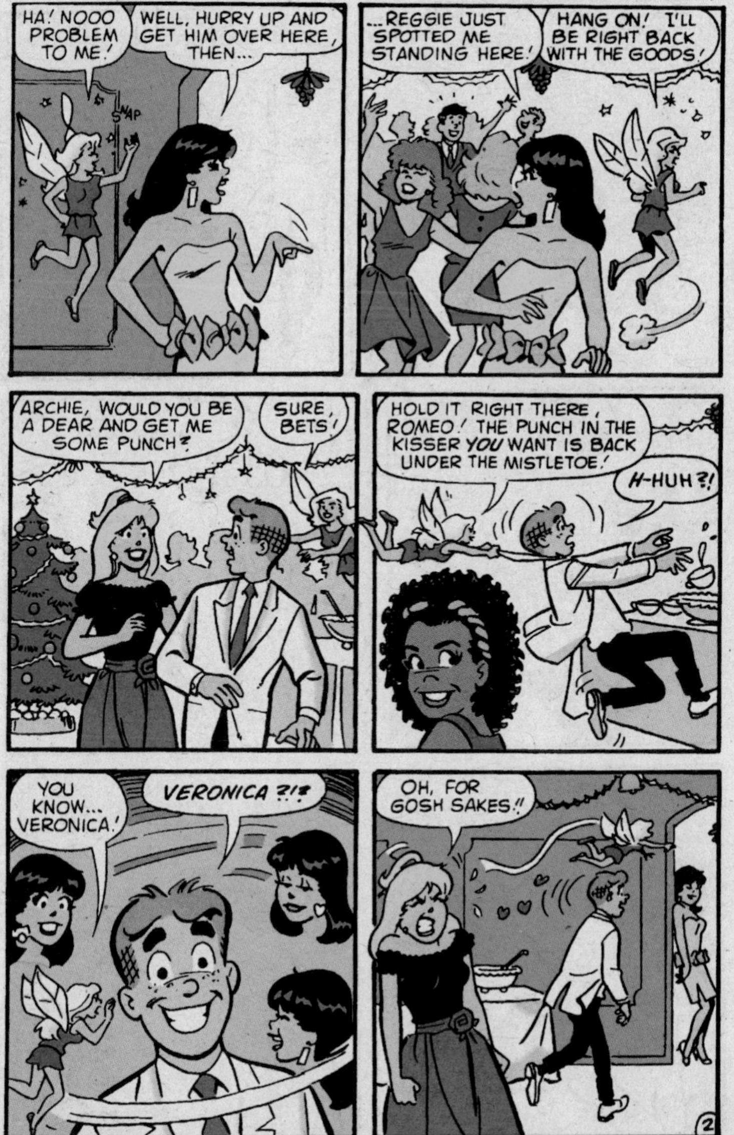
HA! NOOO PROBLEM TO ME!
WELL, HURRY UP AND GET HIM OVER HERE, THEN...
SNAP
...REGGIE JUST SPOTTED ME STANDING HERE!
HANG ON! I'LL BE RIGHT BACK WITH THE GOODS!
ARCHIE, WOULD YOU BE A DEAR AND GET ME SOME PUNCH?
SURE, BETS!
HOLD IT RIGHT THERE, ROMEO! THE PUNCH IN THE KISSER YOU WANT IS BACK UNDER THE MISTLETOE!
H-HUH?!
YOU KNOW... VERONICA!
VERONICA?!?
OH, FOR GOSH SAKES!!
2

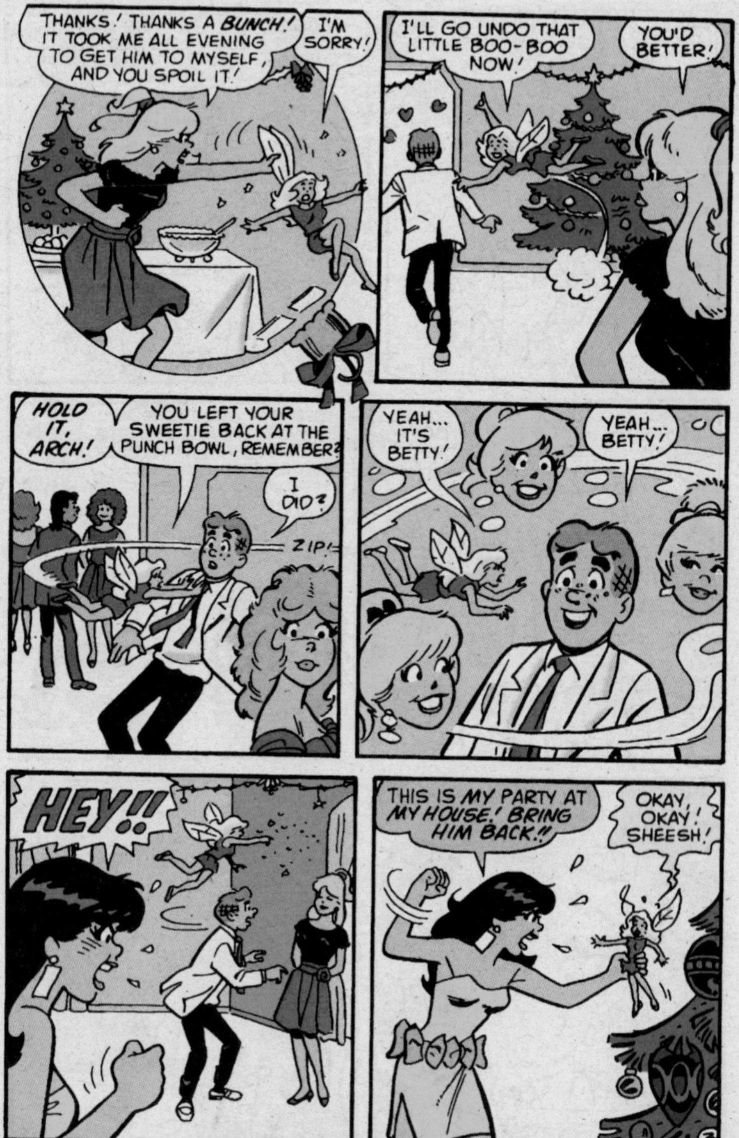

THANKS! THANKS A BUNCH! IT TOOK ME ALL EVENING TO GET HIM TO MYSELF, AND YOU SPOIL IT!
I'M SORRY!
I'LL GO UNDO THAT LITTLE BOO-BOO NOW!
YOU'D BETTER!
HOLD IT, ARCH!
YOU LEFT YOUR SWEETIE BACK AT THE PUNCH BOWL, REMEMBER?
I DID?
ZIP!
YEAH... IT'S BETTY!
YEAH... BETTY!
HEY!!
THIS IS MY PARTY AT MY HOUSE! BRING HIM BACK!!
OKAY, OKAY! SHEESH!
3

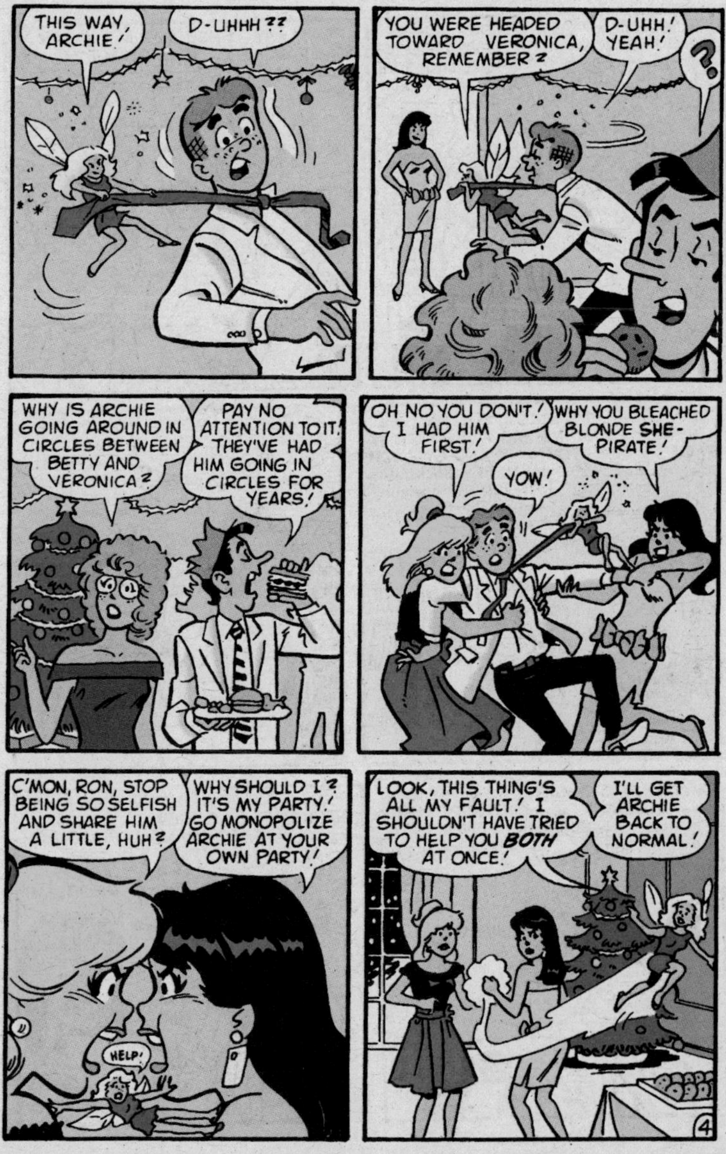
THIS WAY, ARCHIE!
D-UHHH??
YOU WERE HEADED TOWARD VERONICA, REMEMBER?
D-UHH! YEAH!
?
WHY IS ARCHIE GOING AROUND IN CIRCLES BETWEEN BETTY AND VERONICA?
PAY NO ATTENTION TO IT! THEY'VE HAD HIM GOING IN CIRCLES FOR YEARS!
OH NO YOU DON'T! I HAD HIM FIRST!
YOW!
WHY YOU BLEACHED BLONDE SHE-PIRATE!
C'MON, RON, STOP BEING SO SELFISH AND SHARE HIM A LITTLE, HUH?
WHY SHOULD I? IT'S MY PARTY! GO MONOPOLIZE ARCHIE AT YOUR OWN PARTY!
HELP!
LOOK, THIS THING'S ALL MY FAULT! I SHOULDN'T HAVE TRIED TO HELP YOU BOTH AT ONCE!
I'LL GET ARCHIE BACK TO NORMAL!
4

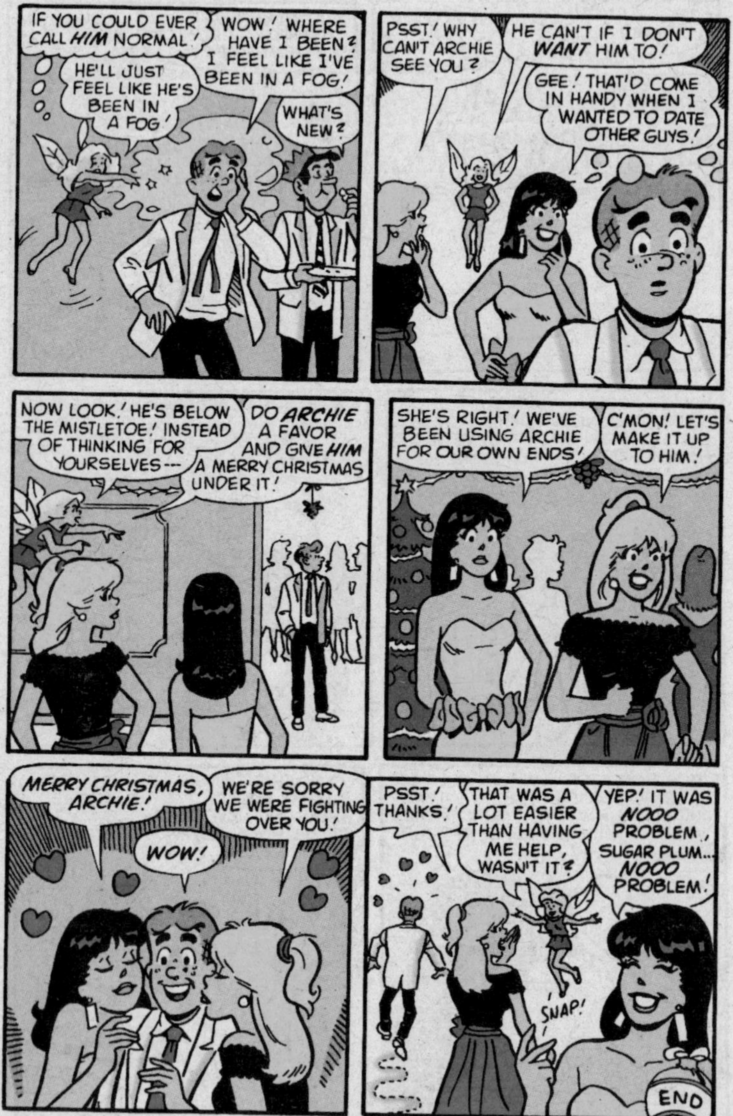
IF YOU COULD EVER CALL HIM NORMAL!
WOW! WHERE HAVE I BEEN? I FEEL LIKE I'VE BEEN IN A FOG!
HE'LL JUST FEEL LIKE HE'S BEEN IN A FOG!
WHAT'S NEW?
PSST! WHY CAN'T ARCHIE SEE YOU?
HE CAN'T IF I DON'T WANT HIM TO!
GEE! THAT'D COME IN HANDY WHEN I WANTED TO DATE OTHER GUYS!
NOW LOOK! HE'S BELOW THE MISTLETOE! INSTEAD OF THINKING FOR YOURSELVES---
DO ARCHIE A FAVOR AND GIVE HIM A MERRY CHRISTMAS UNDER IT!
SHE'S RIGHT! WE'VE BEEN USING ARCHIE FOR OUR OWN ENDS!
C'MON! LET'S MAKE IT UP TO HIM!
MERRY CHRISTMAS, ARCHIE!
WE'RE SORRY WE WERE FIGHTING OVER YOU!
WOW!
PSST! THANKS!
THAT WAS A LOT EASIER THAN HAVING ME HELP, WASN'T IT?
YEP! IT WAS NOOO PROBLEM, SUGAR PLUM... NOOO PROBLEM!
SNAP!
END

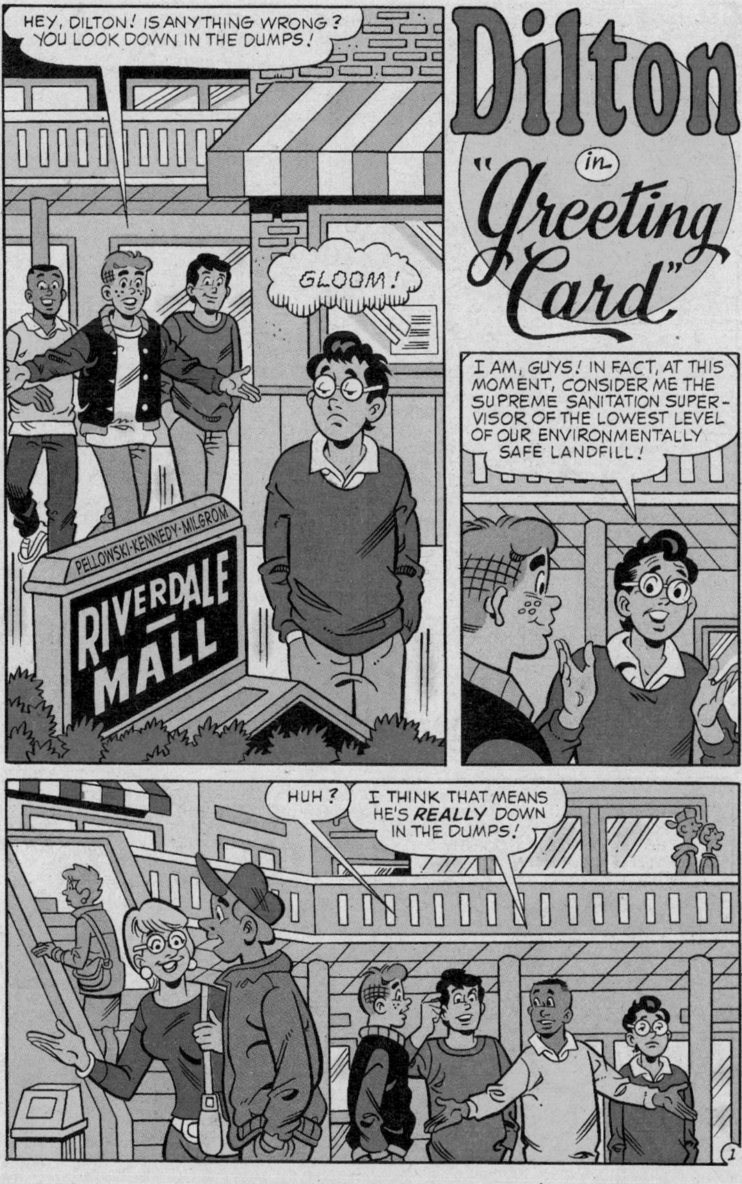
Dilton
in
"Greeting Card"
HEY, DILTON! IS ANYTHING WRONG? YOU LOOK DOWN IN THE DUMPS!
GLOOM!
PELLOWSKI-KENNEDY-MILGROM
RIVERDALE MALL
I AM, GUYS! IN FACT, AT THIS MOMENT, CONSIDER ME THE SUPREME SANITATION SUPER-VISOR OF THE LOWEST LEVEL OF OUR ENVIRONMENTALLY SAFE LANDFILL!
HUH?
I THINK THAT MEANS HE'S REALLY DOWN IN THE DUMPS!
1

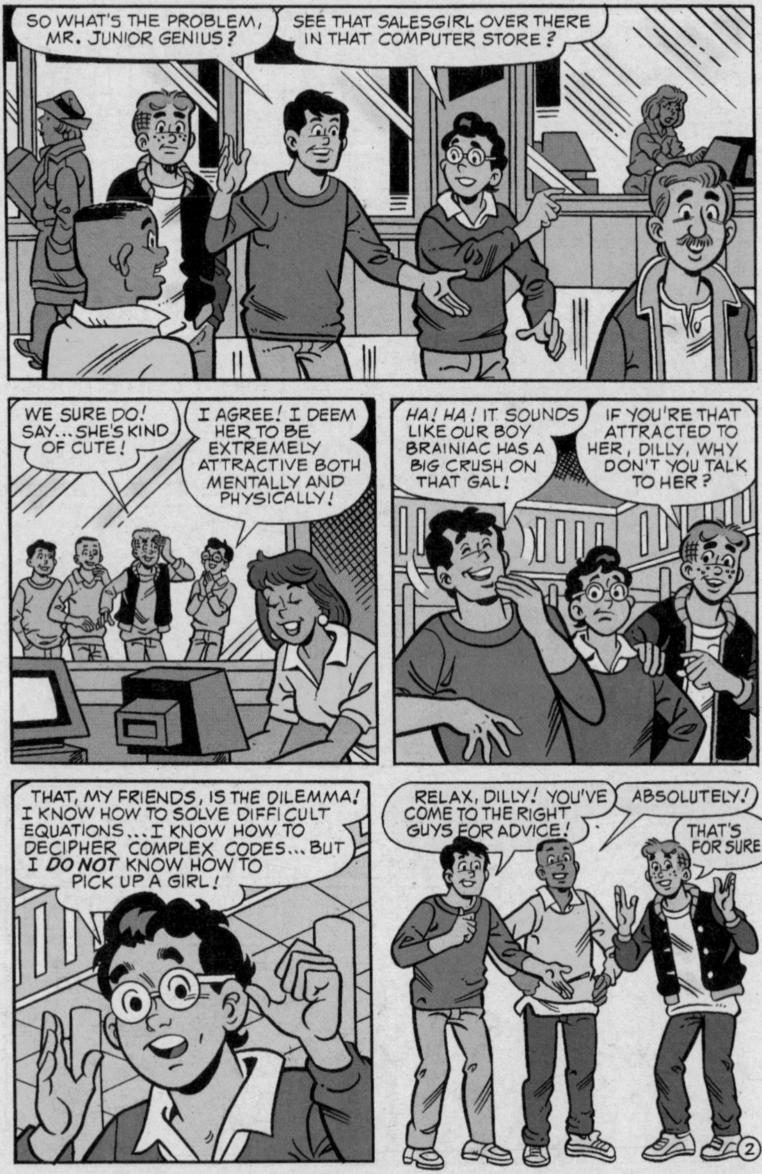
SO WHAT'S THE PROBLEM, MR. JUNIOR GENIUS?
SEE THAT SALESGIRL OVER THERE IN THAT COMPUTER STORE?
WE SURE DO! SAY...SHE'S KIND OF CUTE!
I AGREE! I DEEM HER TO BE EXTREMELY ATTRACTIVE BOTH MENTALLY AND PHYSICALLY!
HA! HA! IT SOUNDS LIKE OUR BOY BRAINIAC HAS A BIG CRUSH ON THAT GAL!
IF YOU'RE THAT ATTRACTED TO HER, DILLY, WHY DON'T YOU TALK TO HER?
THAT, MY FRIENDS, IS THE DILEMMA! I KNOW HOW TO SOLVE DIFFICULT EQUATIONS...I KNOW HOW TO DECIPHER COMPLEX CODES...BUT I DO NOT KNOW HOW TO PICK UP A GIRL!
RELAX, DILLY! YOU'VE COME TO THE RIGHT GUYS FOR ADVICE!
ABSOLUTELY!
THAT'S FOR SURE!
2

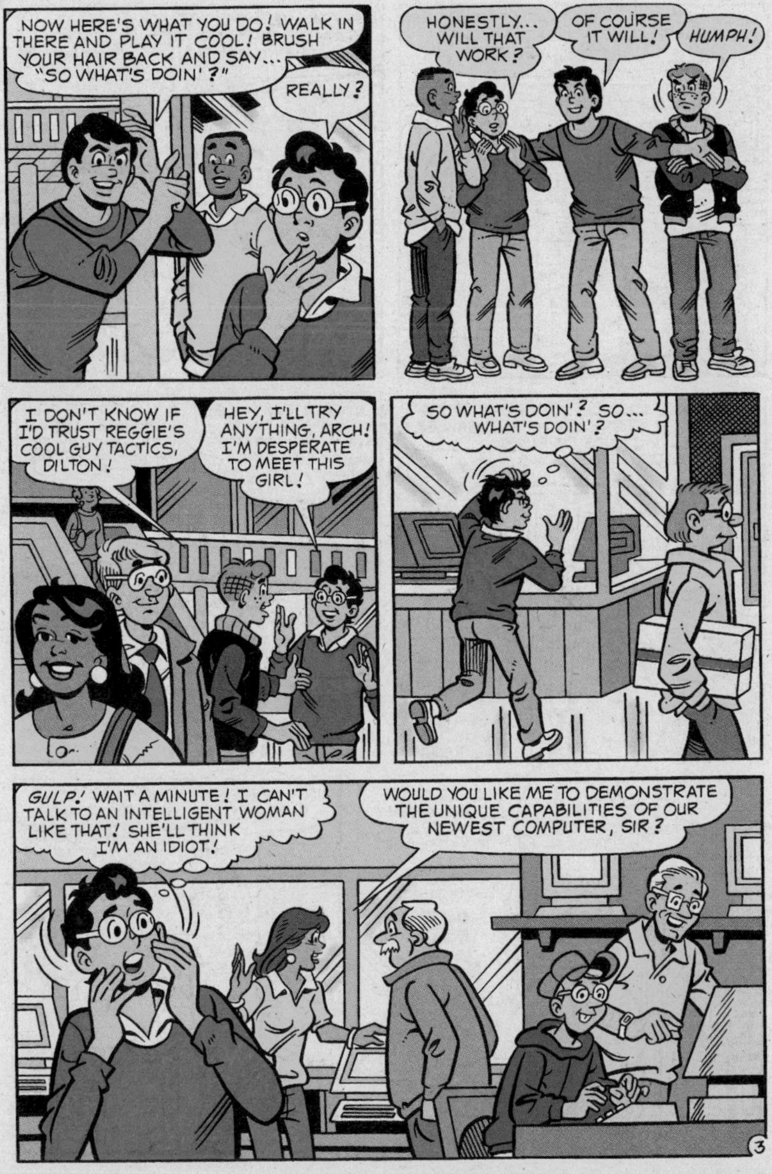
NOW HERE'S WHAT YOU DO! WALK IN THERE AND PLAY IT COOL! BRUSH YOUR HAIR BACK AND SAY... "SO WHAT'S DOIN'?"
REALLY?
HONESTLY... WILL THAT WORK?
OF COURSE IT WILL!
HUMPH!
I DON'T KNOW IF I'D TRUST REGGIE'S COOL GUY TACTICS, DILTON!
HEY, I'LL TRY ANYTHING, ARCH! I'M DESPERATE TO MEET THIS GIRL!
SO WHAT'S DOIN'? SO... WHAT'S DOIN'?
GULP! WAIT A MINUTE! I CAN'T TALK TO AN INTELLIGENT WOMAN LIKE THAT! SHE'LL THINK I'M AN IDIOT!
WOULD YOU LIKE ME TO DEMONSTRATE THE UNIQUE CAPABILITIES OF OUR NEWEST COMPUTER, SIR?
3

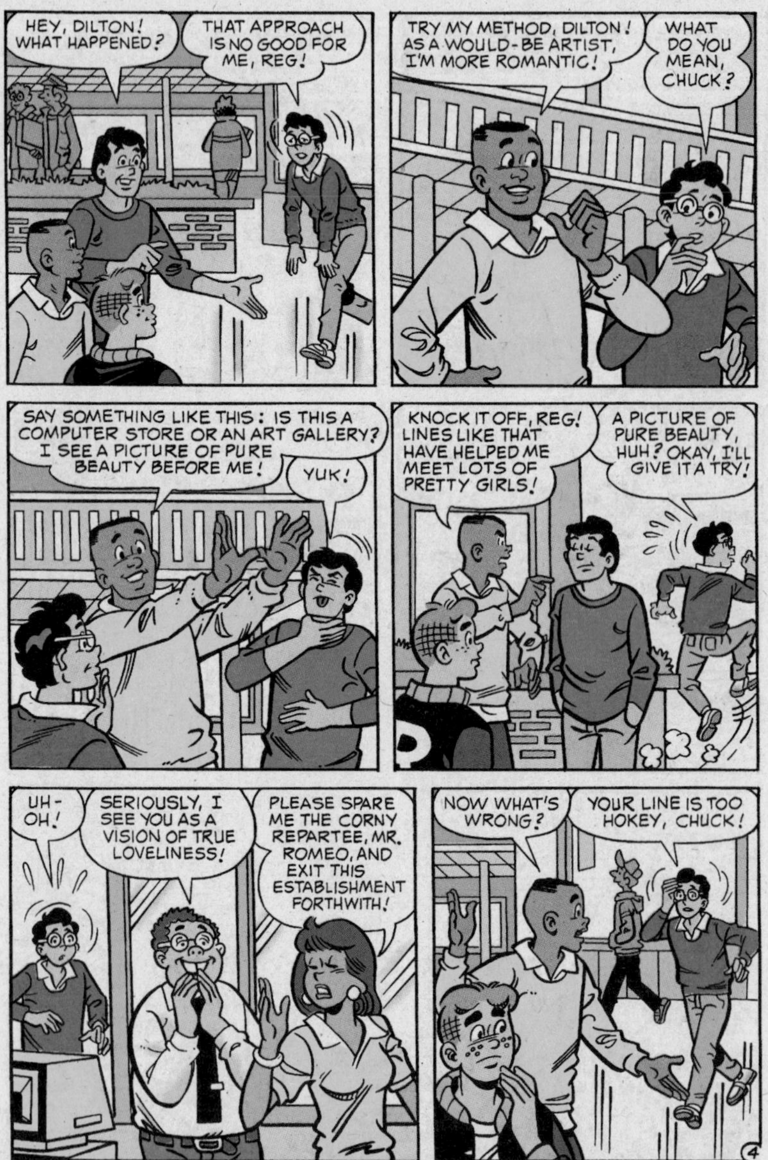
HEY, DILTON! WHAT HAPPENED?
THAT APPROACH IS NO GOOD FOR ME, REG!
TRY MY METHOD, DILTON! AS A WOULD-BE ARTIST, I'M MORE ROMANTIC!
WHAT DO YOU MEAN, CHUCK?
SAY SOMETHING LIKE THIS: IS THIS A COMPUTER STORE OR AN ART GALLERY? I SEE A PICTURE OF PURE BEAUTY BEFORE ME!
YUK!
KNOCK IT OFF, REG! LINES LIKE THAT HAVE HELPED ME MEET LOTS OF PRETTY GIRLS!
A PICTURE OF PURE BEAUTY, HUH? OKAY, I'LL GIVE IT A TRY!
UH-OH!
SERIOUSLY, I SEE YOU AS A VISION OF TRUE LOVELINESS!
PLEASE SPARE ME THE CORNY REPARTEE, MR. ROMEO, AND EXIT THIS ESTABLISHMENT FORTHWITH!
NOW WHAT'S WRONG?
YOUR LINE IS TOO HOKEY, CHUCK!
4

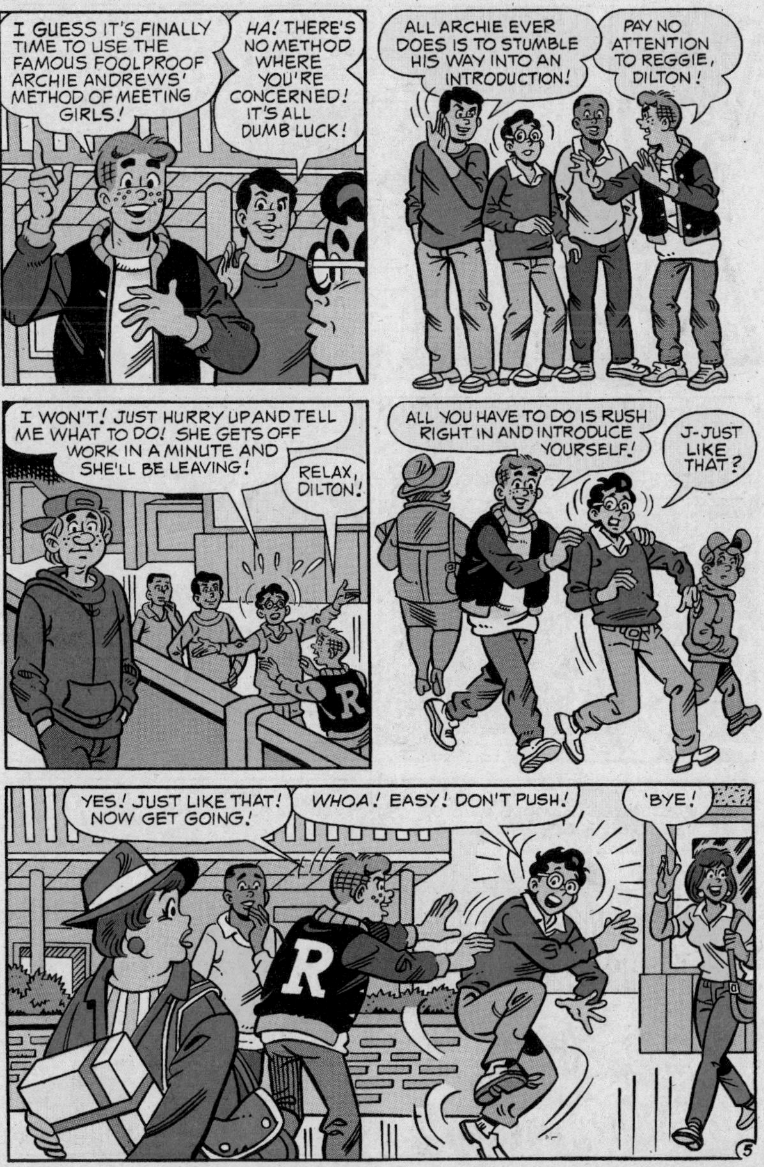
I GUESS IT'S FINALLY TIME TO USE THE FAMOUS FOOLPROOF ARCHIE ANDREWS' METHOD OF MEETING GIRLS!
HA! THERE'S NO METHOD WHERE YOU'RE CONCERNED! IT'S ALL DUMB LUCK!
ALL ARCHIE EVER DOES IS TO STUMBLE HIS WAY INTO AN INTRODUCTION!
PAY NO ATTENTION TO REGGIE, DILTON!
I WON'T! JUST HURRY UP AND TELL ME WHAT TO DO! SHE GETS OFF WORK IN A MINUTE AND SHE'LL BE LEAVING!
RELAX, DILTON!
ALL YOU HAVE TO DO IS RUSH RIGHT IN AND INTRODUCE YOURSELF!
J-JUST LIKE THAT?
YES! JUST LIKE THAT! NOW GET GOING!
WHOA! EASY! DON'T PUSH!
'BYE!
5

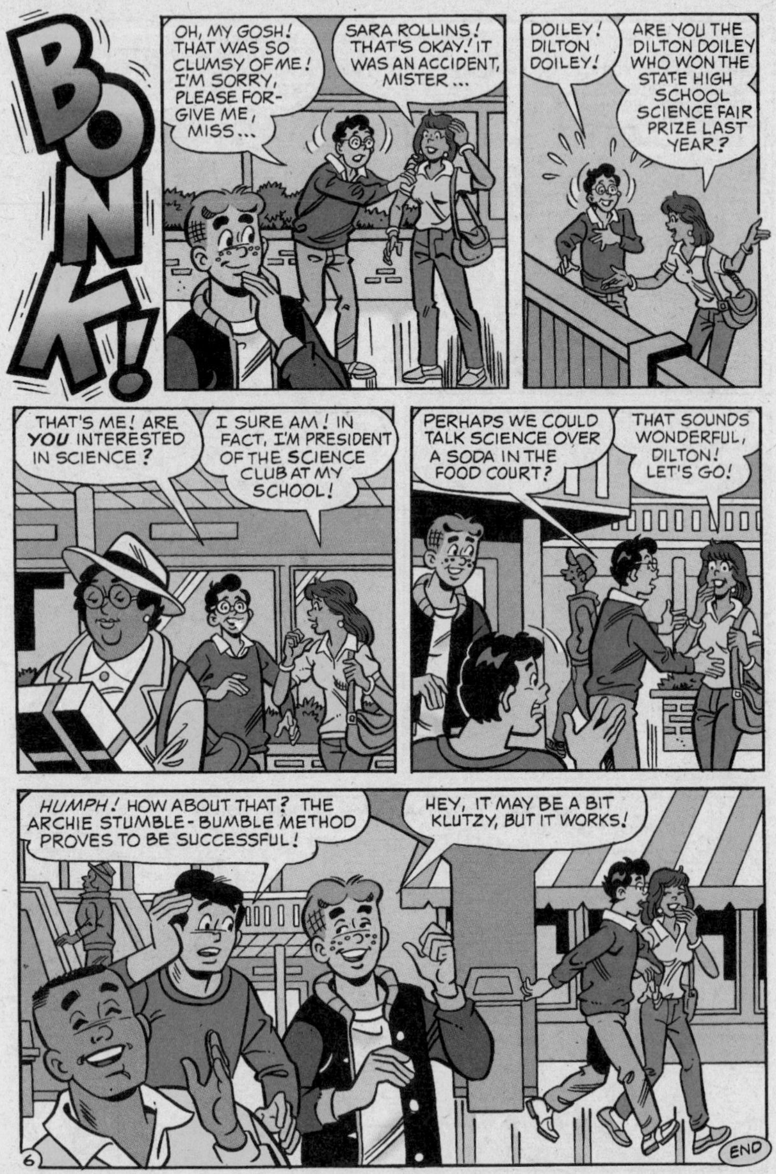
BONK!
OH, MY GOSH! THAT WAS SO CLUMSY OF ME! I'M SORRY, PLEASE FOR-GIVE ME, MISS...
SARA ROLLINS! THAT'S OKAY! IT WAS AN ACCIDENT, MISTER...
DOILEY! DILTON DOILEY!
ARE YOU THE DILTON DOILEY WHO WON THE STATE HIGH SCHOOL SCIENCE FAIR PRIZE LAST YEAR?
THAT'S ME! ARE YOU INTERESTED IN SCIENCE?
I SURE AM! IN FACT, I'M PRESIDENT OF THE SCIENCE CLUB AT MY SCHOOL!
PERHAPS WE COULD TALK SCIENCE OVER A SODA IN THE FOOD COURT?
THAT SOUNDS WONDERFUL, DILTON! LET'S GO!
HUMPH! HOW ABOUT THAT? THE ARCHIE STUMBLE-BUMBLE METHOD PROVES TO BE SUCCESSFUL!
HEY, IT MAY BE A BIT KLUTZY, BUT IT WORKS!
6
END

Archie & Friends' Fables #1

" THE PRINCESS AND THE PARTY POOPER "

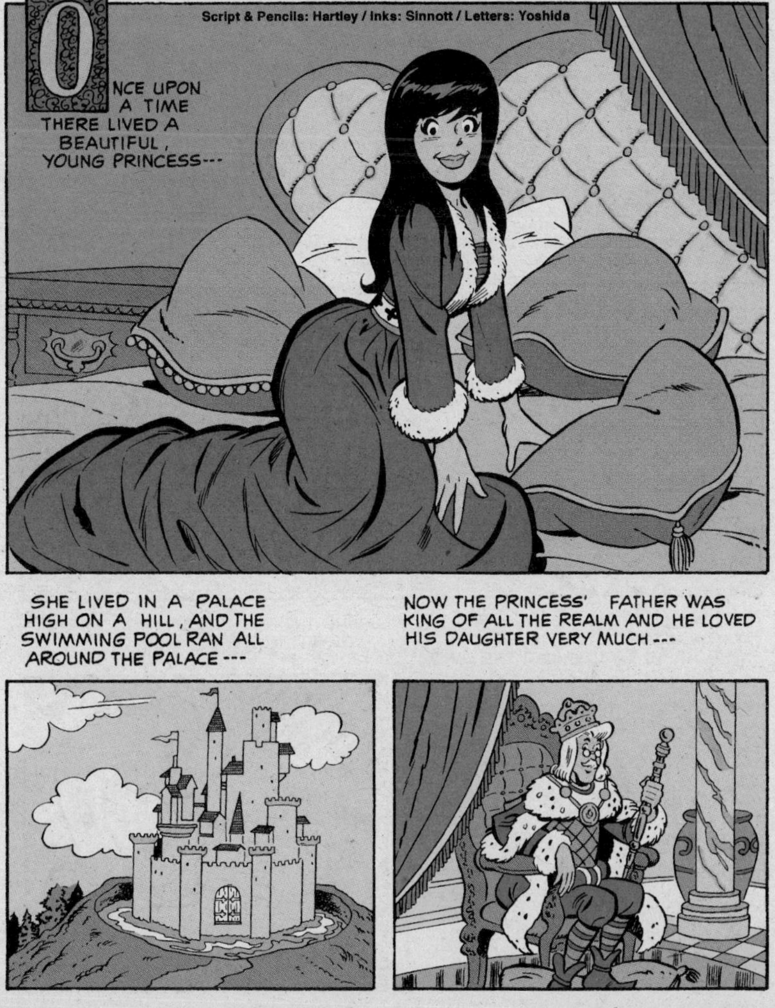

Script & Pencils: Hartley / Inks: Sinnott / Letters: Yoshida
ONCE UPON A TIME THERE LIVED A BEAUTIFUL, YOUNG PRINCESS---
SHE LIVED IN A PALACE HIGH ON A HILL, AND THE SWIMMING POOL RAN ALL AROUND THE PALACE ---
NOW THE PRINCESS' FATHER WAS KING OF ALL THE REALM AND HE LOVED HIS DAUGHTER VERY MUCH ---

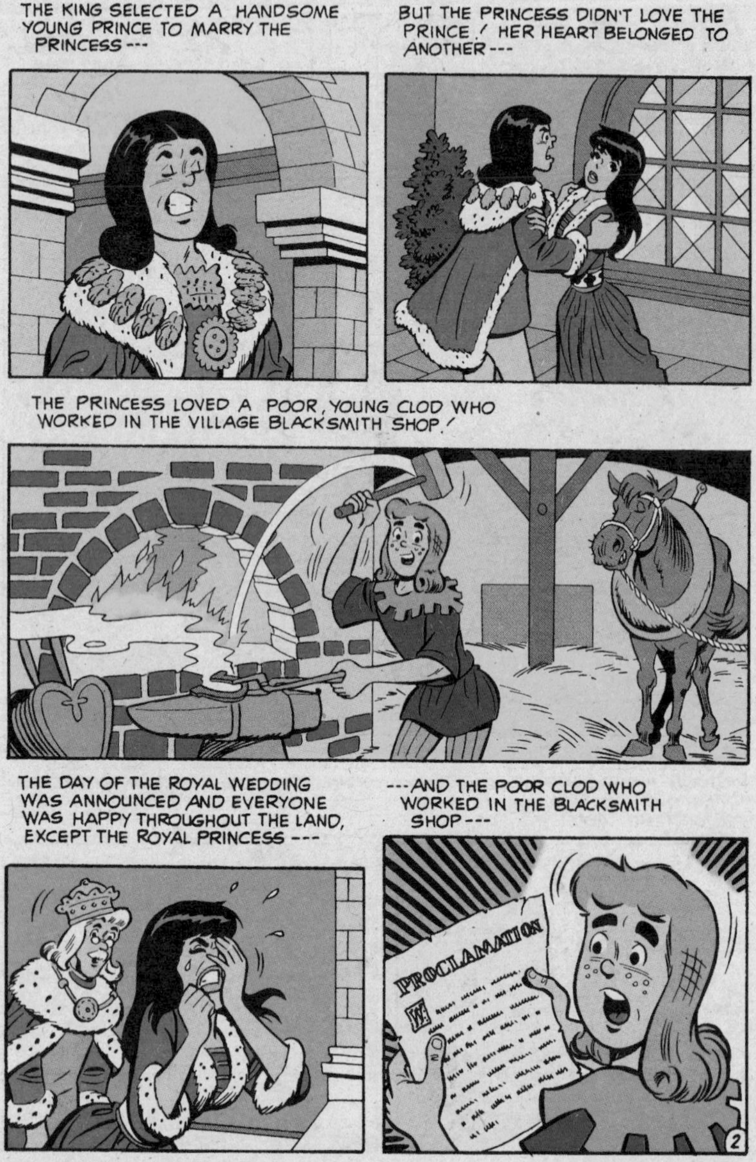
THE KING SELECTED A HANDSOME YOUNG PRINCE TO MARRY THE PRINCESS---
BUT THE PRINCESS DIDN'T LOVE THE PRINCE! HER HEART BELONGED TO ANOTHER---
THE PRINCESS LOVED A POOR, YOUNG CLOD WHO WORKED IN THE VILLAGE BLACKSMITH SHOP!
THE DAY OF THE ROYAL WEDDING WAS ANNOUNCED AND EVERYONE WAS HAPPY THROUGHOUT THE LAND, EXCEPT THE ROYAL PRINCESS---
---AND THE POOR CLOD WHO WORKED IN THE BLACKSMITH SHOP---
PROCLAMATION
2

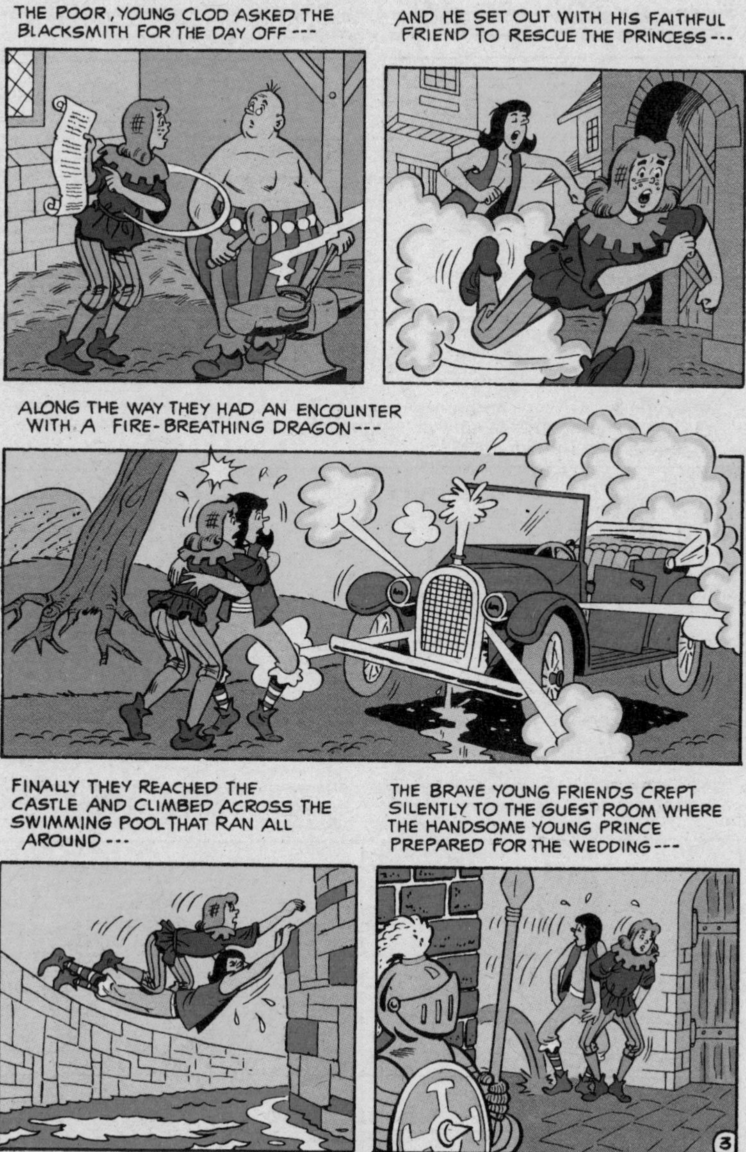
THE POOR, YOUNG CLOD ASKED THE BLACKSMITH FOR THE DAY OFF ---
AND HE SET OUT WITH HIS FAITHFUL FRIEND TO RESCUE THE PRINCESS ---
ALONG THE WAY THEY HAD AN ENCOUNTER WITH A FIRE-BREATHING DRAGON ---
FINALLY THEY REACHED THE CASTLE AND CLIMBED ACROSS THE SWIMMING POOL THAT RAN ALL AROUND ---
THE BRAVE YOUNG FRIENDS CREPT SILENTLY TO THE GUEST ROOM WHERE THE HANDSOME YOUNG PRINCE PREPARED FOR THE WEDDING ---
3

THE BRAVE YOUNG FRIENDS QUICKLY OVERCAME THE PRINCE---

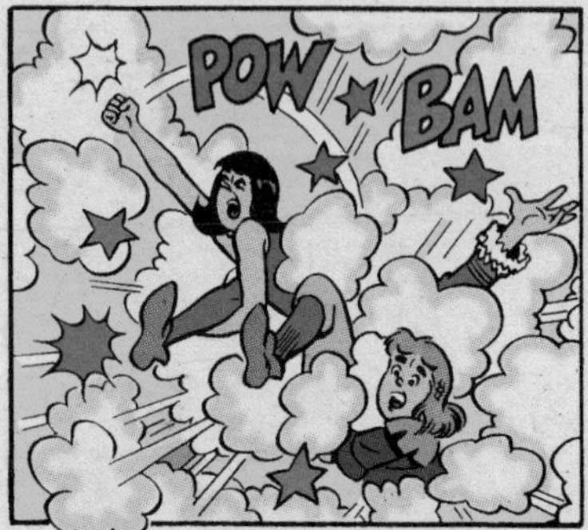
POW
BAM

AND THE POOR YOUNG CLOD PUT ON THE PRINCE'S UNIFORM---

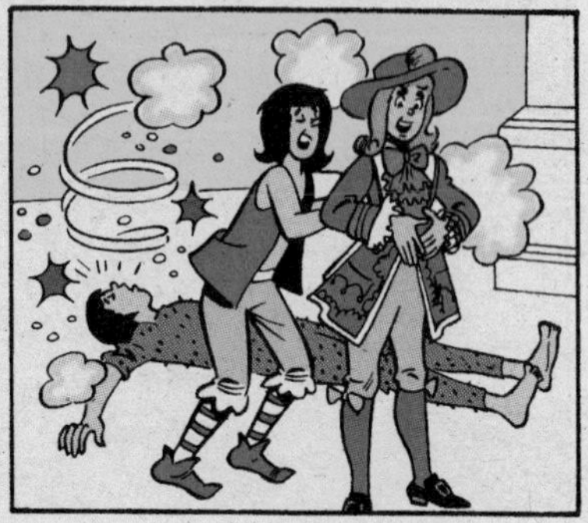

MEAN WHILE, ALL THE LADIES-IN-WAITING WERE PREPARING THE BEAUTIFUL, YOUNG PRINCESS FOR THE WEDDING---

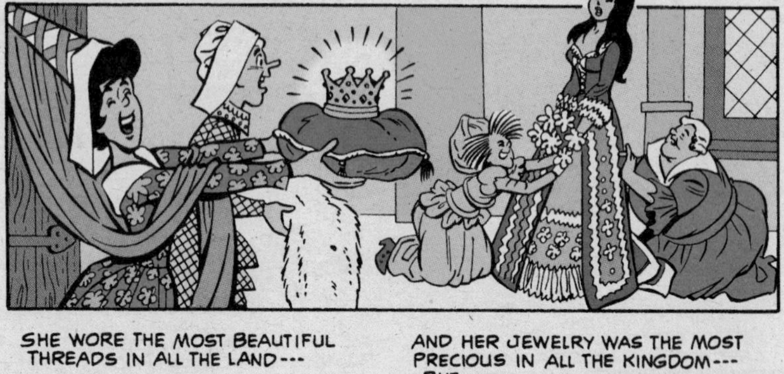

SHE WORE THE MOST BEAUTIFUL THREADS IN ALL THE LAND---

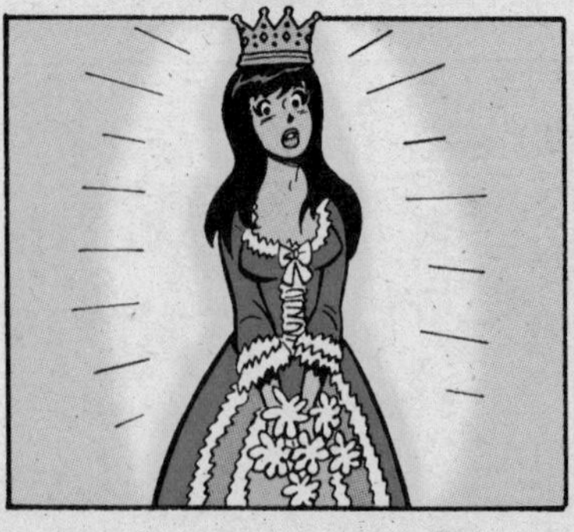

AND HER JEWELRY WAS THE MOST PRECIOUS IN ALL THE KINGDOM--- BUT---

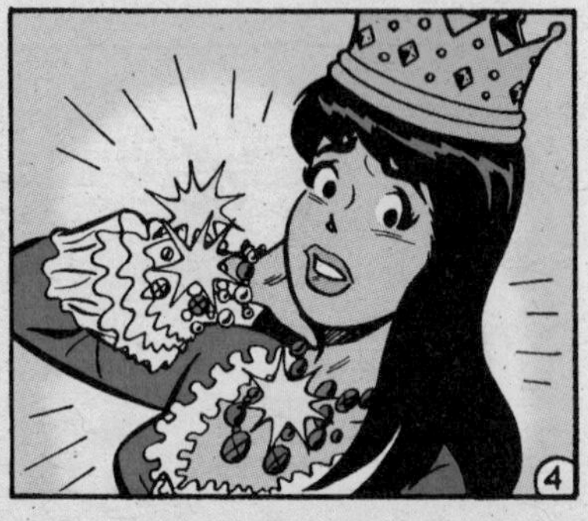

THE PRINCESS WAS VERY SAD AS SHE WALKED DOWN THE AISLE---

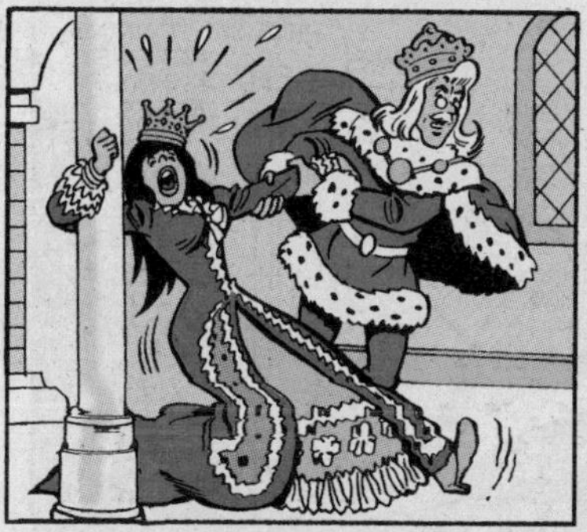

HOW WAS SHE TO KNOW THAT HER TRUE LOVER HAD SO CLEVERLY SAVED THE DAY---

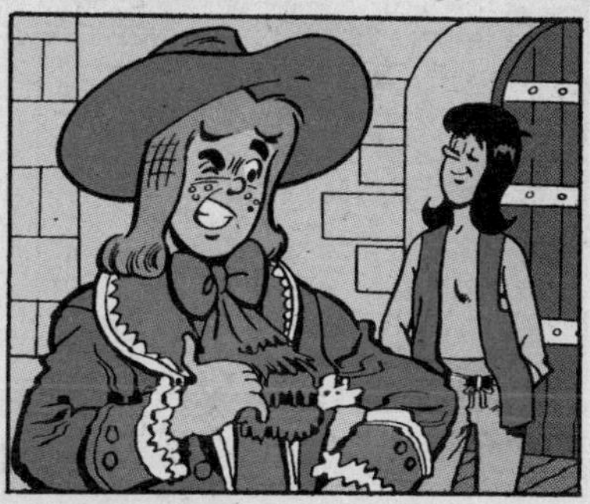

BUT AS THE POOR, YOUNG CLOD STEPPED FORWARD, HE TRIPPED ON THE ROYAL STAIRS AND FLIPPED HIS ROYAL MASQUERADE AND BLEW THE WHOLE BIT---

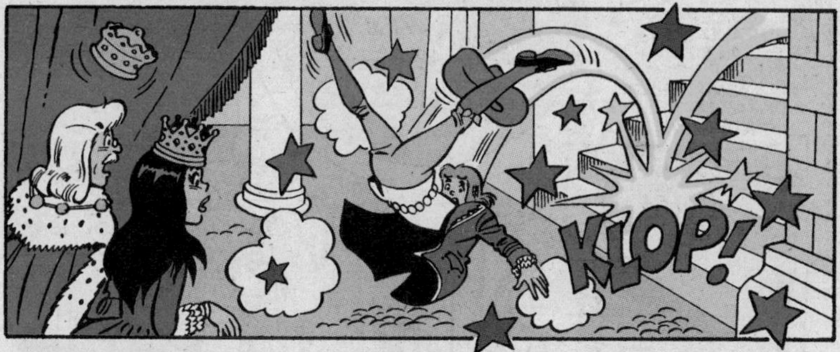
KLOP!

WHICH ONLY GOES TO PROVE THAT PEOPLE HAVE CHANGED ON THE OUTSIDE OVER THE YEARS, BUT THEY'RE STILL THE SAME ON THE INSIDE!

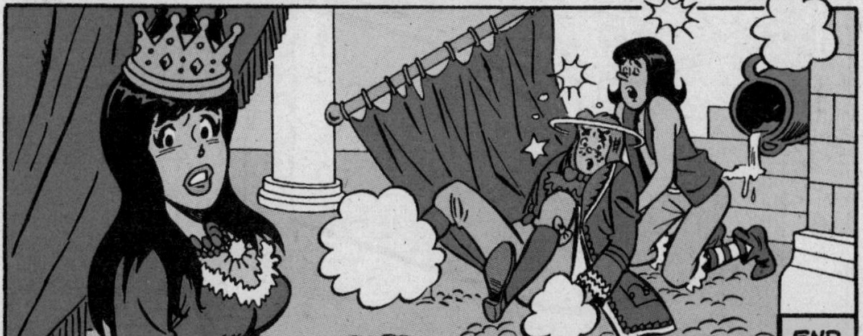
END.

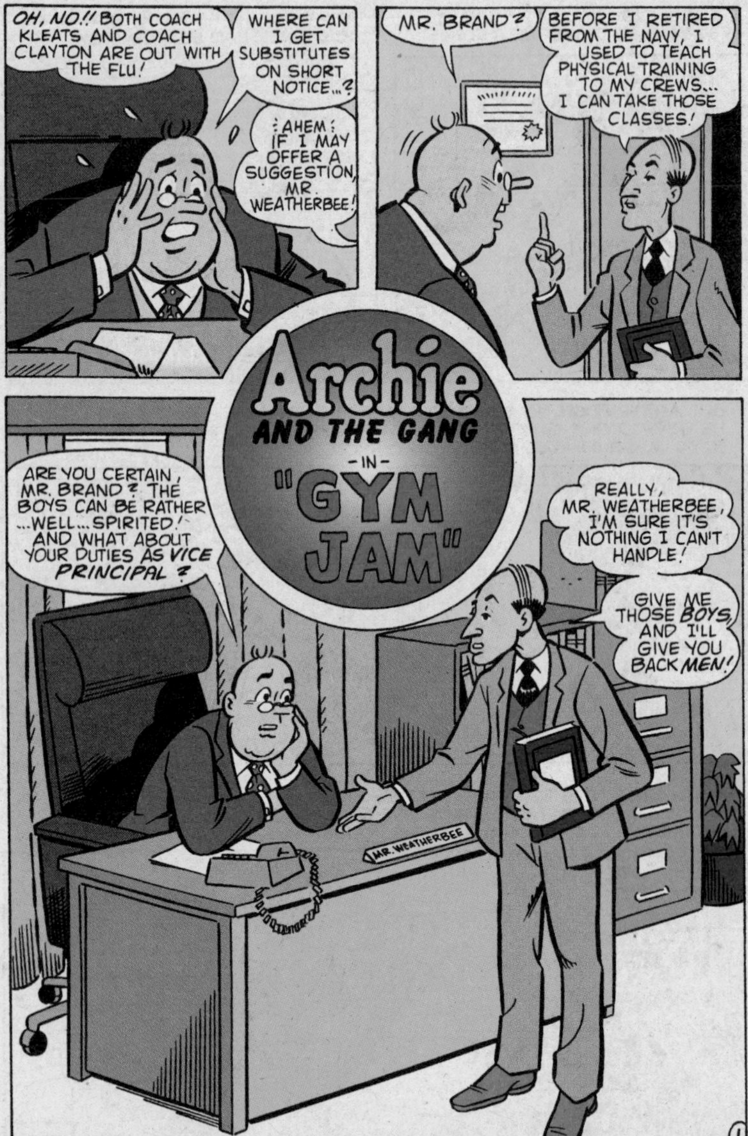

OH, NO!! BOTH COACH KLEATS AND COACH CLAYTON ARE OUT WITH THE FLU!
WHERE CAN I GET SUBSTITUTES ON SHORT NOTICE...?
:AHEM: IF I MAY OFFER A SUGGESTION, MR. WEATHERBEE!
MR. BRAND?
BEFORE I RETIRED FROM THE NAVY, I USED TO TEACH PHYSICAL TRAINING TO MY CREWS... I CAN TAKE THOSE CLASSES!
Archie
AND THE GANG
-IN-
"GYM JAM"
ARE YOU CERTAIN, MR. BRAND? THE BOYS CAN BE RATHER ...WELL...SPIRITED! AND WHAT ABOUT YOUR DUTIES AS VICE PRINCIPAL?
REALLY, MR. WEATHERBEE, I'M SURE IT'S NOTHING I CAN'T HANDLE!
GIVE ME THOSE BOYS, AND I'LL GIVE YOU BACK MEN!
MR. WEATHERBEE
1

Script: Rich Margopoulos / Pencils: Chris Allan / Inks: Rudy Lapick / Letters: Bill Yoshida / Colors: Barry Grossman

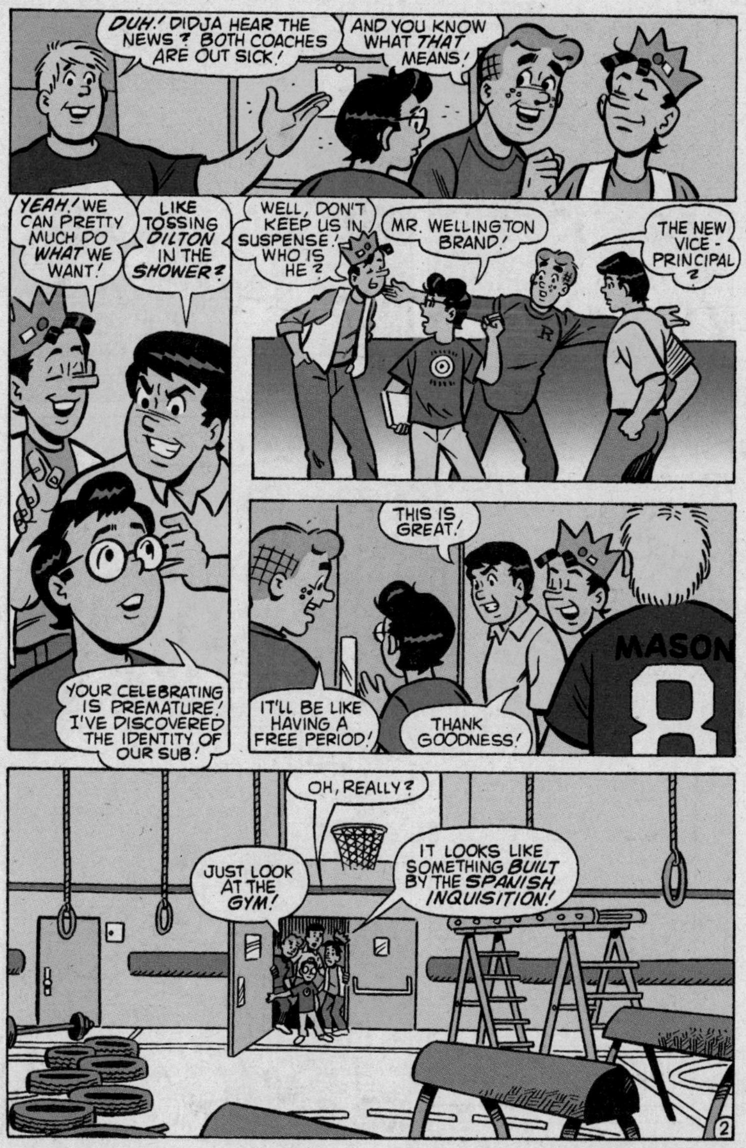
DUH! DIDJA HEAR THE NEWS? BOTH COACHES ARE OUT SICK!
AND YOU KNOW WHAT THAT MEANS!
YEAH! WE CAN PRETTY MUCH DO WHAT WE WANT!
LIKE TOSSING DILTON IN THE SHOWER?
YOUR CELEBRATING IS PREMATURE! I'VE DISCOVERED THE IDENTITY OF OUR SUB!
WELL, DON'T KEEP US IN SUSPENSE! WHO IS HE?
MR. WELLINGTON BRAND!
THE NEW VICE-PRINCIPAL?
THIS IS GREAT!
MASON
8
IT'LL BE LIKE HAVING A FREE PERIOD!
THANK GOODNESS!
OH, REALLY?
JUST LOOK AT THE GYM!
IT LOOKS LIKE SOMETHING BUILT BY THE SPANISH INQUISITION!

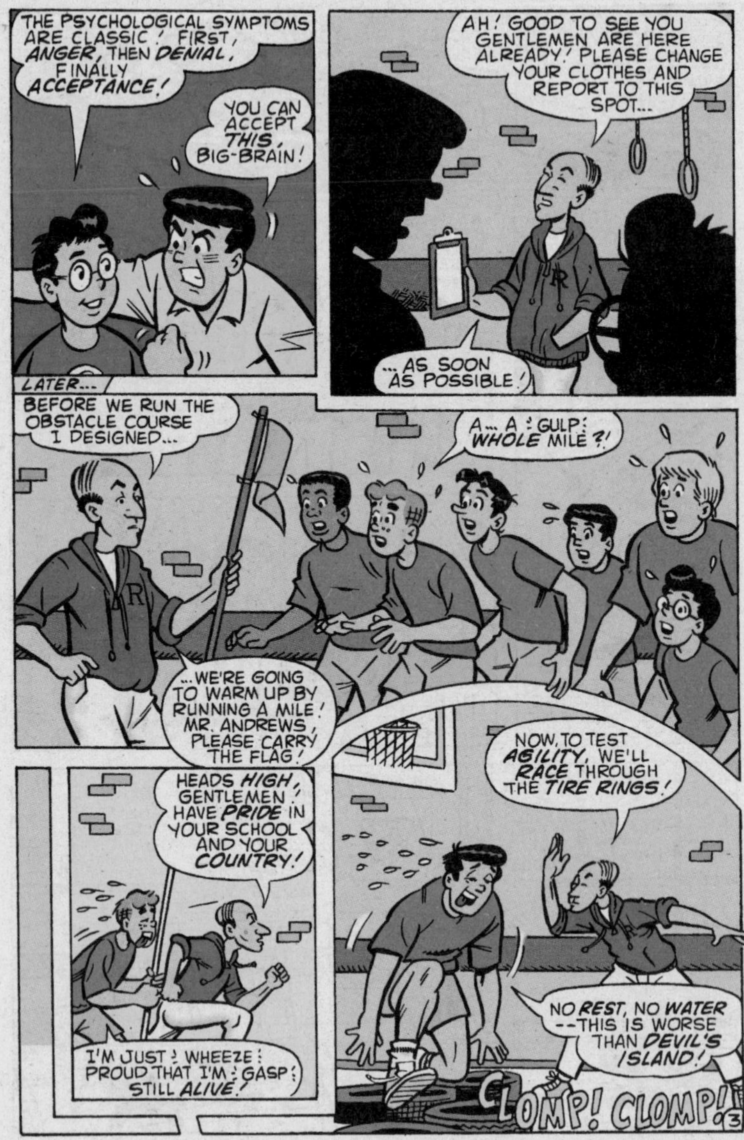
THE PSYCHOLOGICAL SYMPTOMS ARE CLASSIC! FIRST, ANGER, THEN DENIAL, FINALLY ACCEPTANCE!
YOU CAN ACCEPT THIS, BIG-BRAIN!
AH! GOOD TO SEE YOU GENTLEMEN ARE HERE ALREADY! PLEASE CHANGE YOUR CLOTHES AND REPORT TO THIS SPOT...
...AS SOON AS POSSIBLE!
LATER...
BEFORE WE RUN THE OBSTACLE COURSE I DESIGNED...
...WE'RE GOING TO WARM UP BY RUNNING A MILE! MR. ANDREWS, PLEASE CARRY THE FLAG!
A... A :GULP: WHOLE MILE ?!
HEADS HIGH, GENTLEMEN! HAVE PRIDE IN YOUR SCHOOL AND YOUR COUNTRY!
I'M JUST :WHEEZE: PROUD THAT I'M :GASP: STILL ALIVE!
NOW, TO TEST AGILITY, WE'LL RACE THROUGH THE TIRE RINGS!
NO REST, NO WATER --THIS IS WORSE THAN DEVIL'S ISLAND!
CLOMP! CLOMP!

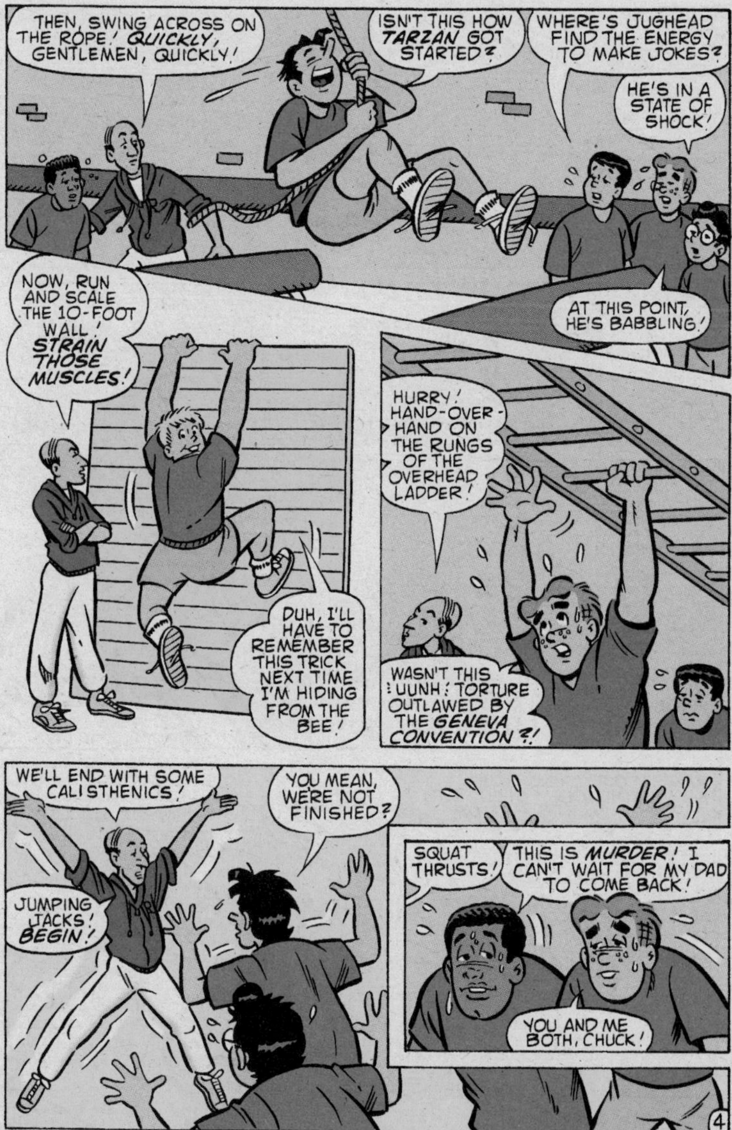
THEN, SWING ACROSS ON THE ROPE! QUICKLY, GENTLEMEN, QUICKLY!
ISN'T THIS HOW TARZAN GOT STARTED?
WHERE'S JUGHEAD FIND THE ENERGY TO MAKE JOKES?
HE'S IN A STATE OF SHOCK!
AT THIS POINT, HE'S BABBLING!
NOW, RUN AND SCALE THE 10-FOOT WALL! STRAIN THOSE MUSCLES!
DUH, I'LL HAVE TO REMEMBER THIS TRICK NEXT TIME I'M HIDING FROM THE BEE!
HURRY! HAND-OVER-HAND ON THE RUNGS OF THE OVERHEAD LADDER!
WASN'T THIS :UUNH: TORTURE OUTLAWED BY THE GENEVA CONVENTION?!
WE'LL END WITH SOME CALISTHENICS!
YOU MEAN, WE'RE NOT FINISHED?
JUMPING JACKS! BEGIN!
SQUAT THRUSTS!
THIS IS MURDER! I CAN'T WAIT FOR MY DAD TO COME BACK!
YOU AND ME BOTH, CHUCK!
4

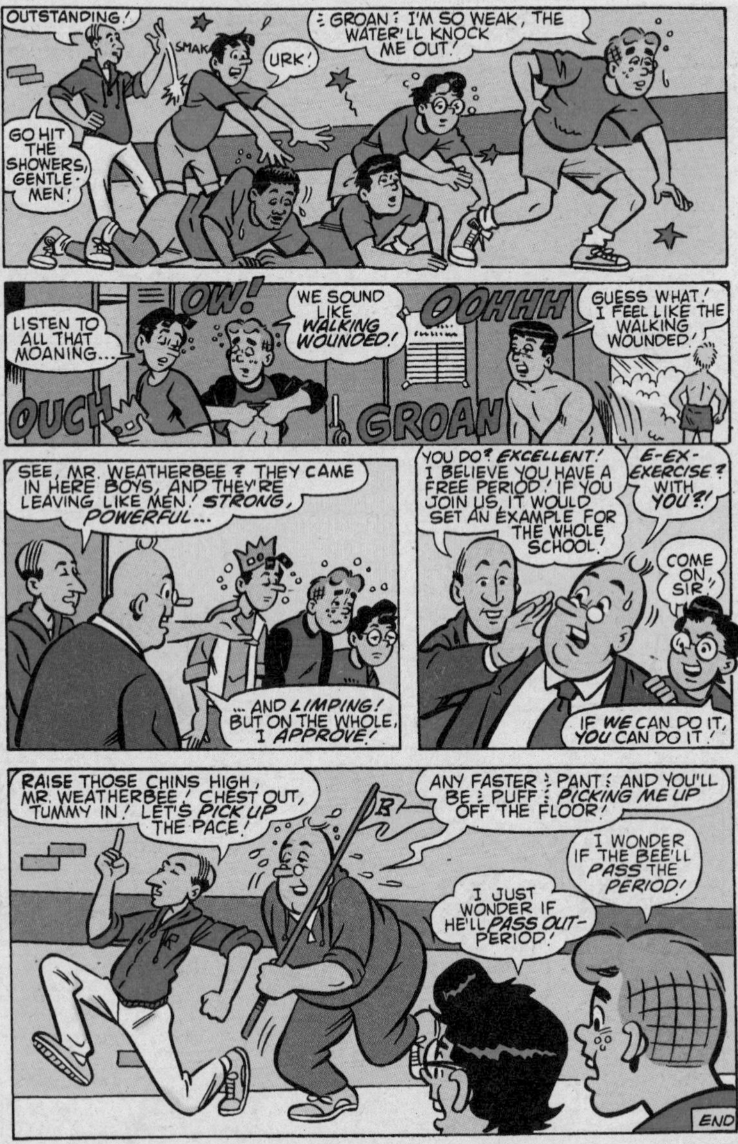
OUTSTANDING!
SMAK
URK!
GROAN! I'M SO WEAK, THE WATER'LL KNOCK ME OUT!
GO HIT THE SHOWERS, GENTLE-MEN!
OW!
LISTEN TO ALL THAT MOANING...
WE SOUND LIKE WALKING WOUNDED!
OOHHH
GUESS WHAT! I FEEL LIKE THE WALKING WOUNDED!
OUCH
GROAN
SEE, MR. WEATHERBEE? THEY CAME IN HERE BOYS, AND THEY'RE LEAVING LIKE MEN! STRONG, POWERFUL...
... AND LIMPING! BUT ON THE WHOLE, I APPROVE!
YOU DO? EXCELLENT! I BELIEVE YOU HAVE A FREE PERIOD! IF YOU JOIN US, IT WOULD SET AN EXAMPLE FOR THE WHOLE SCHOOL!
E-EX-EXERCISE? WITH YOU?!
COME ON, SIR!
IF WE CAN DO IT, YOU CAN DO IT!
RAISE THOSE CHINS HIGH, MR. WEATHERBEE! CHEST OUT, TUMMY IN! LET'S PICK UP THE PACE!
ANY FASTER ! PANT ! AND YOU'LL BE ! PUFF ! PICKING ME UP OFF THE FLOOR!
I WONDER IF THE BEE'LL PASS THE PERIOD!
I JUST WONDER IF HE'LL PASS OUT-PERIOD!
END

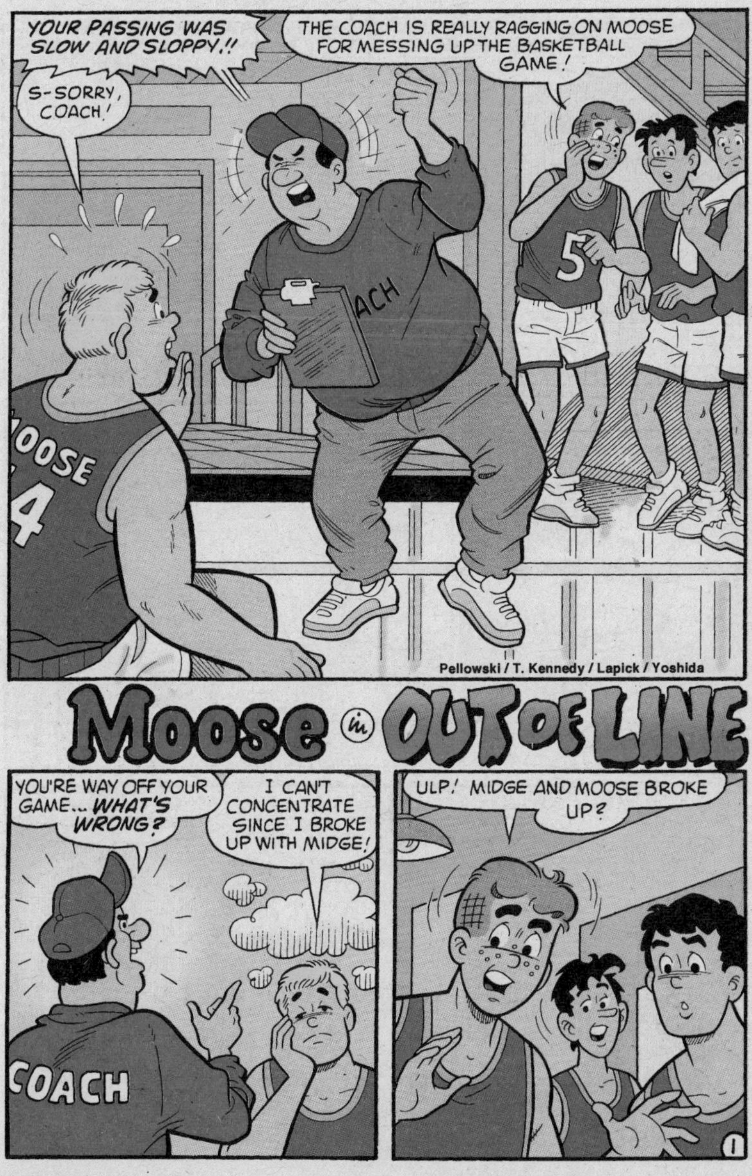

YOUR PASSING WAS SLOW AND SLOPPY!!
S-SORRY, COACH!
THE COACH IS REALLY RAGGING ON MOOSE FOR MESSING UP THE BASKETBALL GAME!
Pellowski / T. Kennedy / Lapick / Yoshida
Moose in OUT OF LINE
YOU'RE WAY OFF YOUR GAME... WHAT'S WRONG?
I CAN'T CONCENTRATE SINCE I BROKE UP WITH MIDGE!
ULP! MIDGE AND MOOSE BROKE UP?
1

UH-OH, ARCH! THE BIG GUY'S PROBLEM IS *BIG TROUBLE* FOR ME!

HOW DO YOU FIGURE THAT, REGGIE?

WHEN MOOSE IS NOT DOING *WELL,* OUR TEAM DOESN'T DO WELL!

...THAT MEANS I DON'T DO WELL WITH ADMIRING *FEMALE* SPORT FANS!

WHAT HAPPENED THAT YOU AND MIDGE SPLIT?

IT WAS MY *BIG MOUTH...*

BIG MOUTH ?!

YEAH...SHE SAYS I'M *BORING.!!*

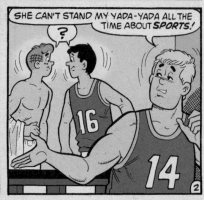

SHE CAN'T STAND MY YADA-YADA ALL THE TIME ABOUT *SPORTS!*

?

2

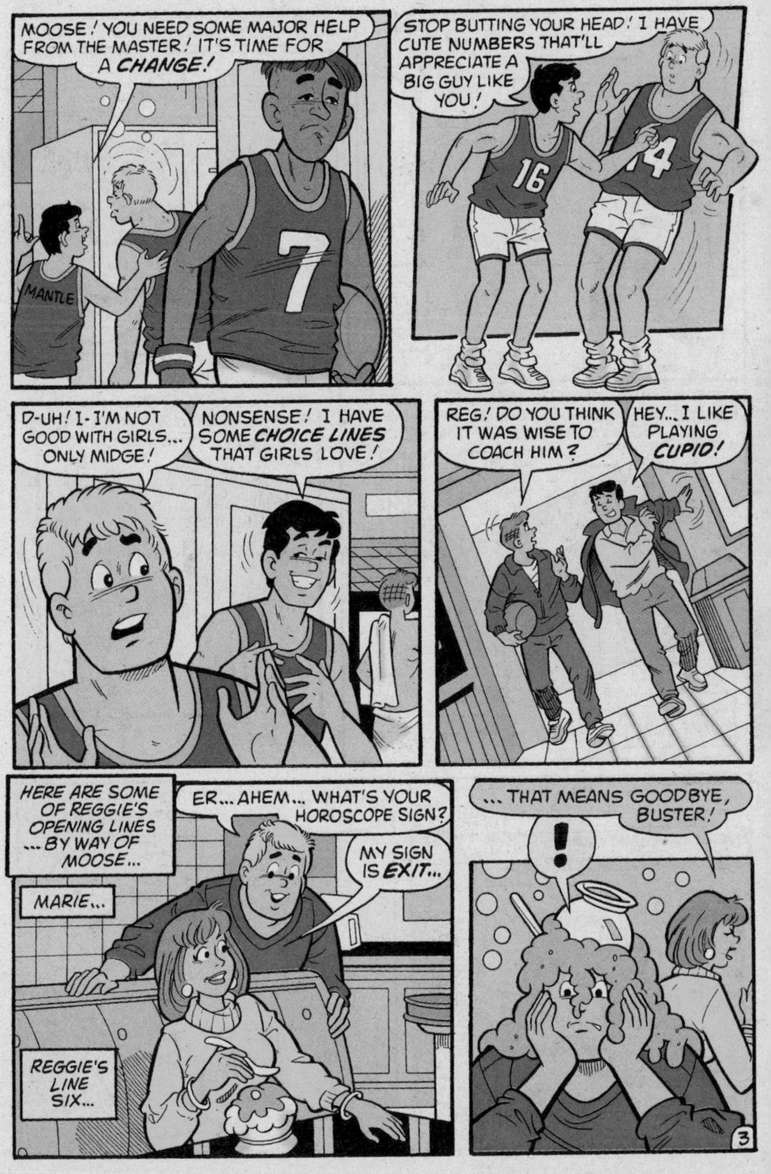

MOOSE! YOU NEED SOME MAJOR HELP FROM THE MASTER! IT'S TIME FOR A CHANGE!
MANTLE
7
STOP BUTTING YOUR HEAD! I HAVE CUTE NUMBERS THAT'LL APPRECIATE A BIG GUY LIKE YOU!
16
14
D-UH! I-I'M NOT GOOD WITH GIRLS... ONLY MIDGE!
NONSENSE! I HAVE SOME CHOICE LINES THAT GIRLS LOVE!
REG! DO YOU THINK IT WAS WISE TO COACH HIM?
HEY... I LIKE PLAYING CUPID!
HERE ARE SOME OF REGGIE'S OPENING LINES ... BY WAY OF MOOSE...
MARIE...
ER... AHEM... WHAT'S YOUR HOROSCOPE SIGN?
MY SIGN IS EXIT...
REGGIE'S LINE SIX...
... THAT MEANS GOODBYE, BUSTER!
!
3

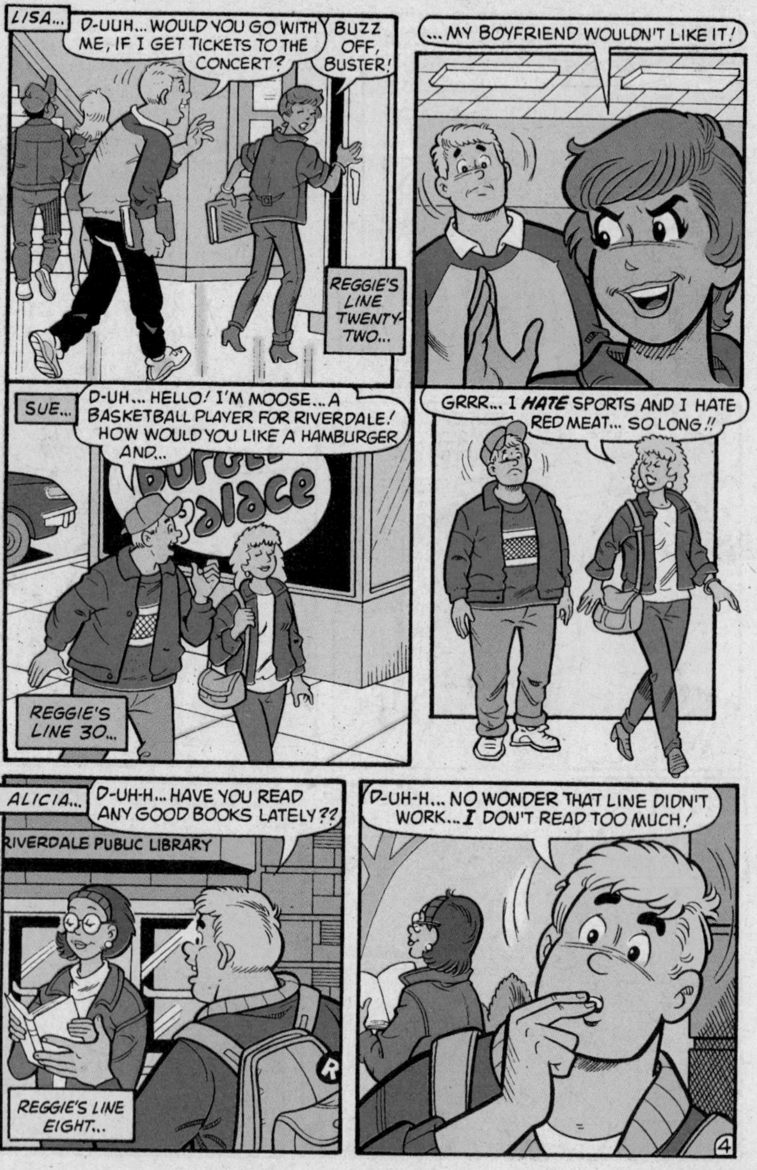

LISA...
D-UUH... WOULD YOU GO WITH ME, IF I GET TICKETS TO THE CONCERT?
BUZZ OFF, BUSTER!
REGGIE'S LINE TWENTY-TWO...
... MY BOYFRIEND WOULDN'T LIKE IT!
SUE...
D-UH... HELLO! I'M MOOSE... A BASKETBALL PLAYER FOR RIVERDALE! HOW WOULD YOU LIKE A HAMBURGER AND...
REGGIE'S LINE 30...
GRRR... I HATE SPORTS AND I HATE RED MEAT... SO LONG!!
ALICIA...
D-UH-H... HAVE YOU READ ANY GOOD BOOKS LATELY??
RIVERDALE PUBLIC LIBRARY
REGGIE'S LINE EIGHT...
D-UH-H... NO WONDER THAT LINE DIDN'T WORK... I DON'T READ TOO MUCH!

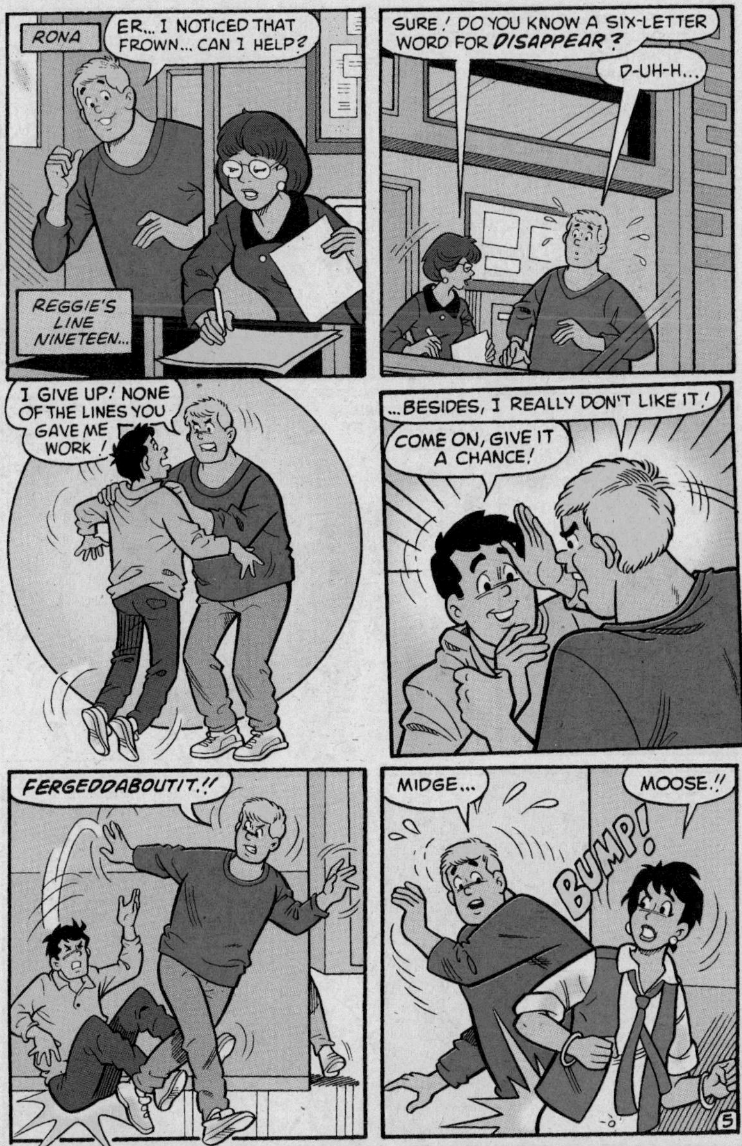

RONA
ER... I NOTICED THAT FROWN... CAN I HELP?
REGGIE'S LINE NINETEEN...
SURE! DO YOU KNOW A SIX-LETTER WORD FOR DISAPPEAR?
D-UH-H...
I GIVE UP! NONE OF THE LINES YOU GAVE ME WORK!
...BESIDES, I REALLY DON'T LIKE IT!
COME ON, GIVE IT A CHANCE!
FERGEDDABOUTIT!!
MIDGE...
MOOSE!!
BUMP!
5

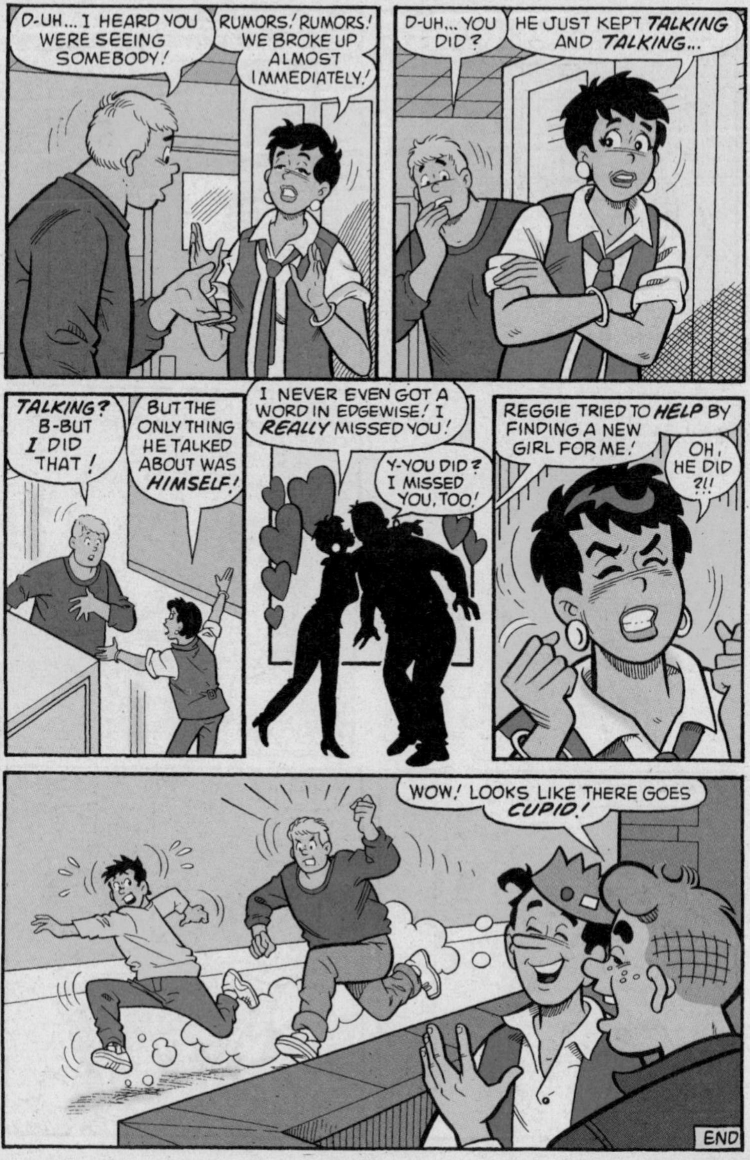
D-UH... I HEARD YOU WERE SEEING SOMEBODY!
RUMORS! RUMORS! WE BROKE UP ALMOST IMMEDIATELY!
D-UH... YOU DID?
HE JUST KEPT TALKING AND TALKING...
TALKING? B-BUT I DID THAT!
BUT THE ONLY THING HE TALKED ABOUT WAS HIMSELF!
I NEVER EVEN GOT A WORD IN EDGEWISE! I REALLY MISSED YOU!
Y-YOU DID? I MISSED YOU, TOO!
REGGIE TRIED TO HELP BY FINDING A NEW GIRL FOR ME!
OH, HE DID ?!!
WOW! LOOKS LIKE THERE GOES CUPID!
END

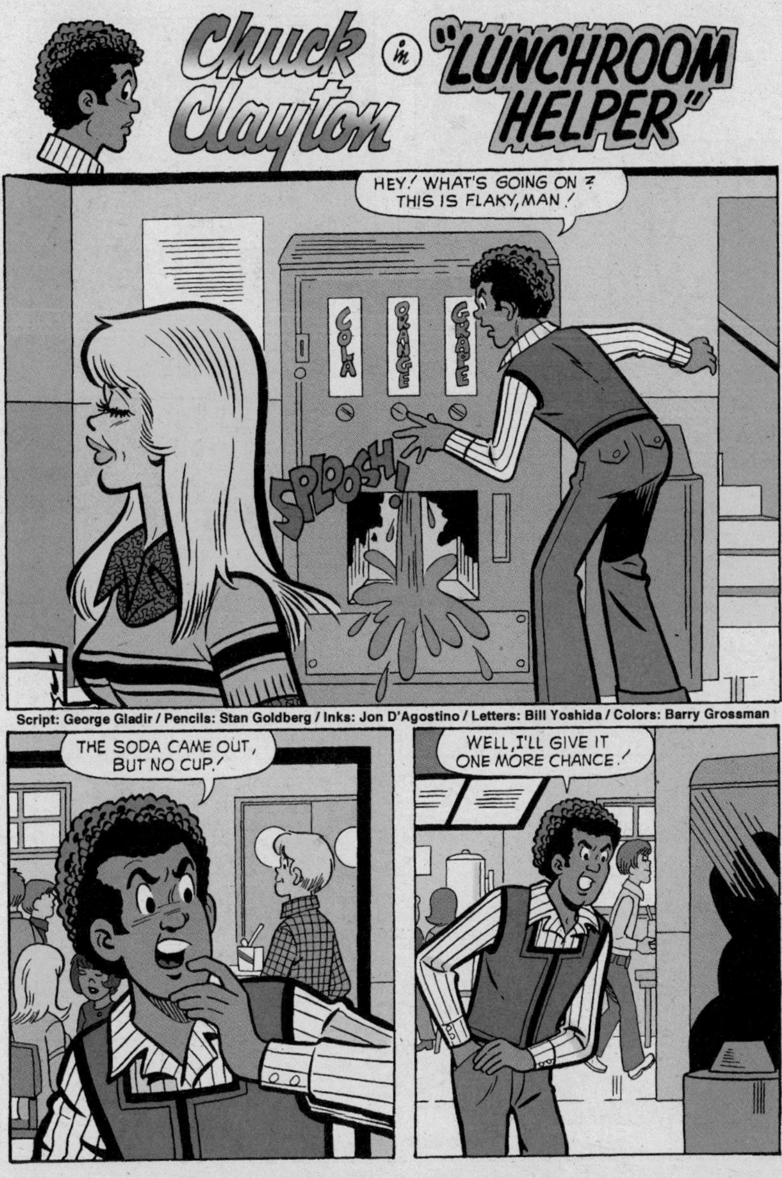
Chuck Clayton in "LUNCHROOM HELPER"
HEY! WHAT'S GOING ON ? THIS IS FLAKY, MAN!
COLA
ORANGE
GRAPE
SPLOOSH!
THE SODA CAME OUT, BUT NO CUP!
WELL, I'LL GIVE IT ONE MORE CHANCE!

Script: George Gladir / Pencils: Stan Goldberg / Inks: Jon D'Agostino / Letters: Bill Yoshida / Colors: Barry Grossman

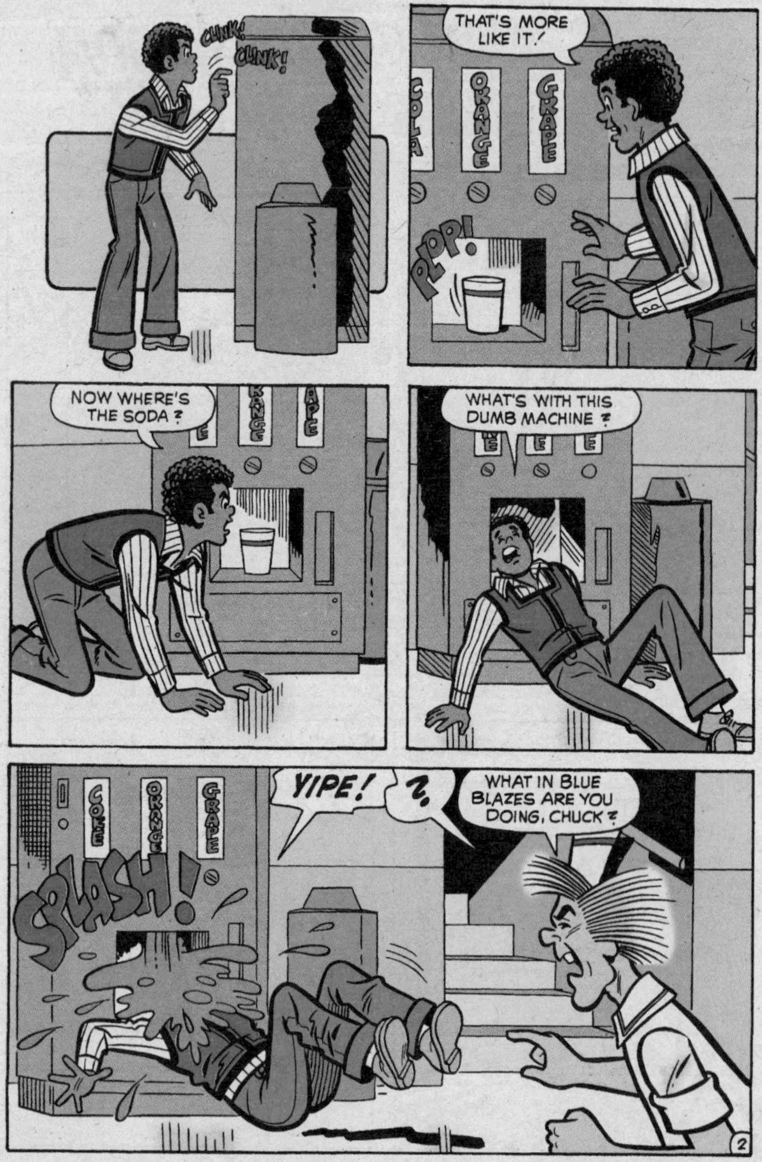

CLUNK!
CLUNK!
THAT'S MORE LIKE IT!
COLA
ORANGE
GRAPE
PLOP!
NOW WHERE'S THE SODA?
WHAT'S WITH THIS DUMB MACHINE?
COKE
ORANGE
GRAPE
SPLASH!
YIPE!
?
WHAT IN BLUE BLAZES ARE YOU DOING, CHUCK?
2

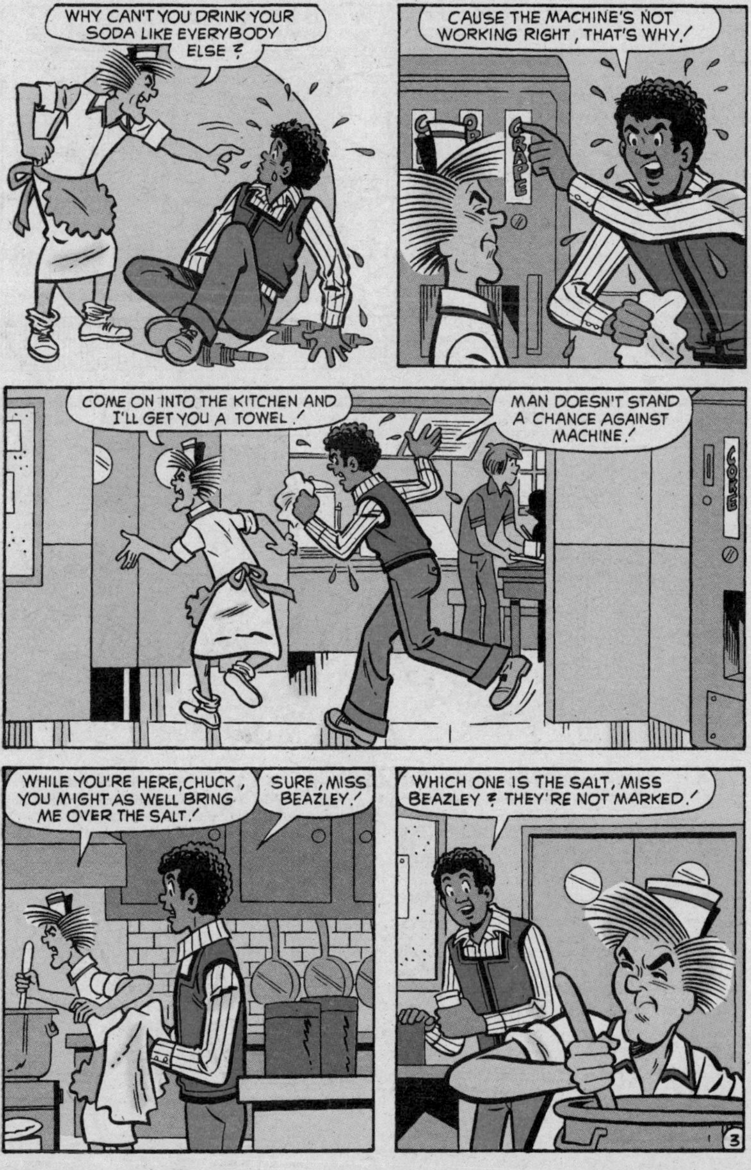

WHY CAN'T YOU DRINK YOUR SODA LIKE EVERYBODY ELSE ?
CAUSE THE MACHINE'S NOT WORKING RIGHT, THAT'S WHY!
GRAPE
COME ON INTO THE KITCHEN AND I'LL GET YOU A TOWEL!
MAN DOESN'T STAND A CHANCE AGAINST MACHINE!
COKE
WHILE YOU'RE HERE, CHUCK, YOU MIGHT AS WELL BRING ME OVER THE SALT!
SURE, MISS BEAZLEY!
WHICH ONE IS THE SALT, MISS BEAZLEY ? THEY'RE NOT MARKED!
3

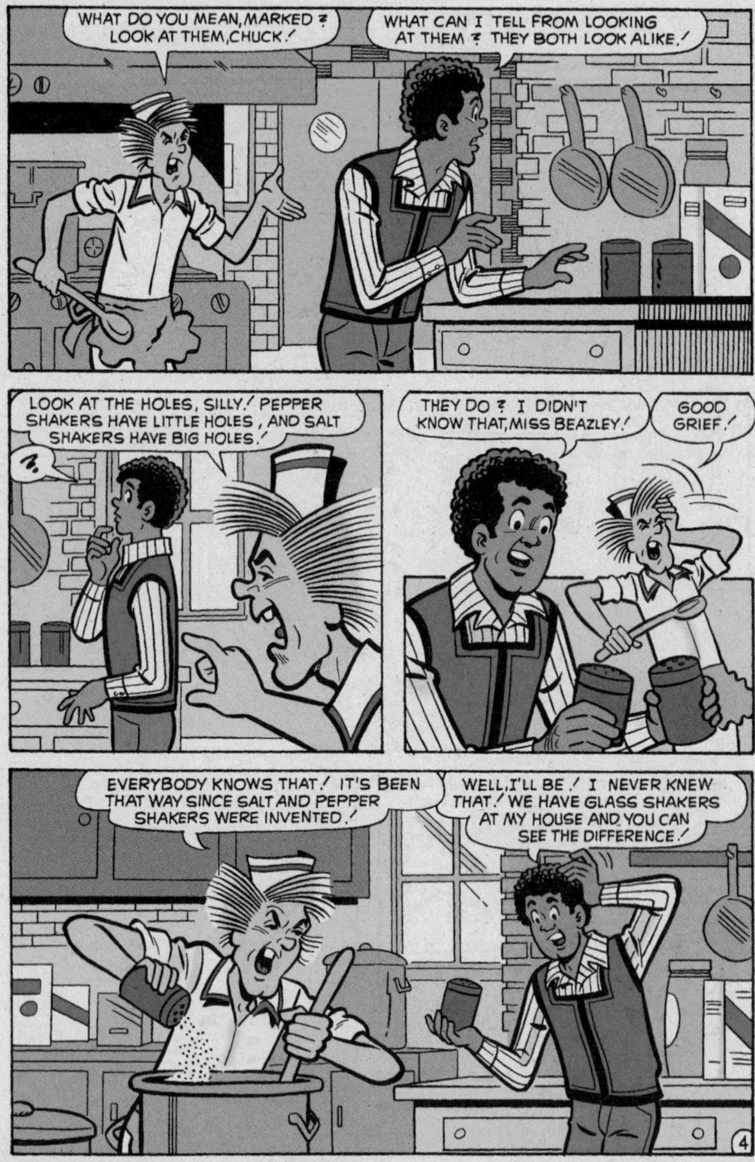
WHAT DO YOU MEAN, MARKED? LOOK AT THEM, CHUCK!
WHAT CAN I TELL FROM LOOKING AT THEM? THEY BOTH LOOK ALIKE!
LOOK AT THE HOLES, SILLY! PEPPER SHAKERS HAVE LITTLE HOLES, AND SALT SHAKERS HAVE BIG HOLES!
?
THEY DO? I DIDN'T KNOW THAT, MISS BEAZLEY!
GOOD GRIEF!
EVERYBODY KNOWS THAT! IT'S BEEN THAT WAY SINCE SALT AND PEPPER SHAKERS WERE INVENTED!
WELL, I'LL BE! I NEVER KNEW THAT! WE HAVE GLASS SHAKERS AT MY HOUSE AND YOU CAN SEE THE DIFFERENCE!
4

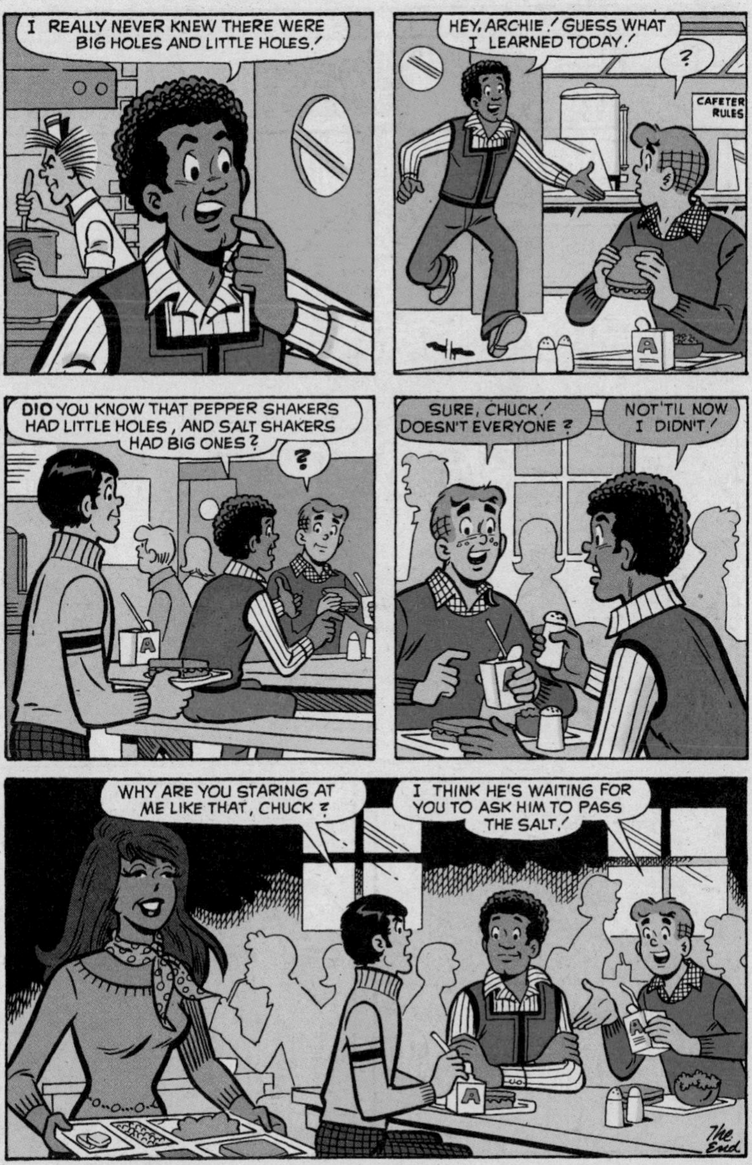

I REALLY NEVER KNEW THERE WERE BIG HOLES AND LITTLE HOLES!
HEY, ARCHIE! GUESS WHAT I LEARNED TODAY!
?
CAFETER RULES
DID YOU KNOW THAT PEPPER SHAKERS HAD LITTLE HOLES, AND SALT SHAKERS HAD BIG ONES?
?
SURE, CHUCK! DOESN'T EVERYONE?
NOT 'TIL NOW I DIDN'T!
WHY ARE YOU STARING AT ME LIKE THAT, CHUCK?
I THINK HE'S WAITING FOR YOU TO ASK HIM TO PASS THE SALT!
The End

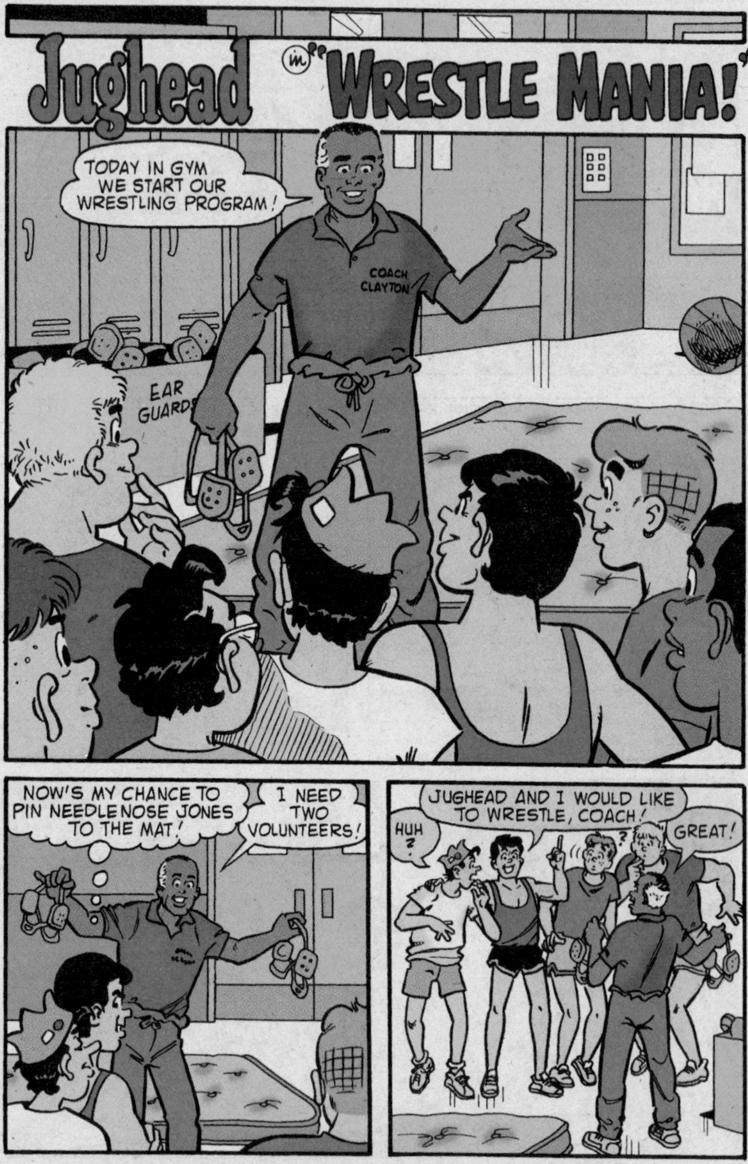
Jughead in "WRESTLE MANIA!"
TODAY IN GYM WE START OUR WRESTLING PROGRAM!
COACH CLAYTON
EAR GUARDS
NOW'S MY CHANCE TO PIN NEEDLENOSE JONES TO THE MAT!
I NEED TWO VOLUNTEERS!
JUGHEAD AND I WOULD LIKE TO WRESTLE, COACH!
HUH ?
?
GREAT!

Script: George Gladir / Pencils: Stan Goldberg / Inks: Rudy Lapick / Letters: Bill Yoshida

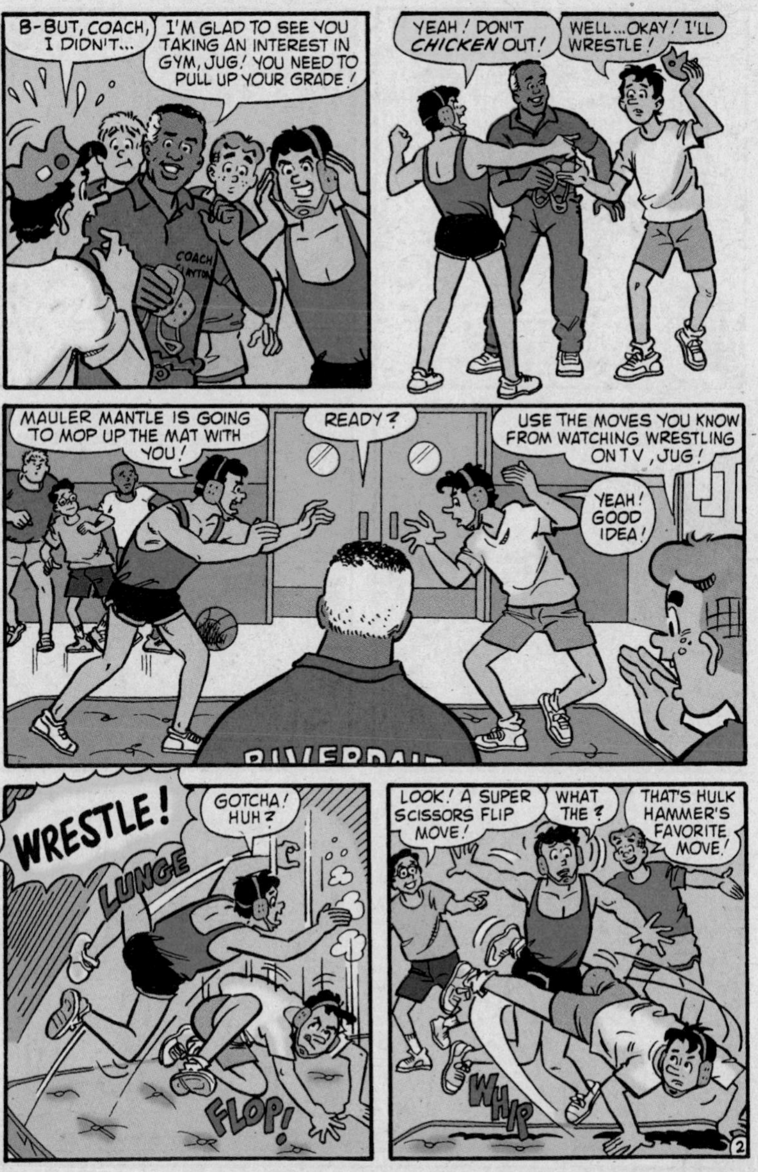
B-BUT, COACH, I DIDN'T...
I'M GLAD TO SEE YOU TAKING AN INTEREST IN GYM, JUG! YOU NEED TO PULL UP YOUR GRADE!
COACH CLAYTON
YEAH! DON'T CHICKEN OUT!
WELL...OKAY! I'LL WRESTLE!
MAULER MANTLE IS GOING TO MOP UP THE MAT WITH YOU!
READY?
USE THE MOVES YOU KNOW FROM WATCHING WRESTLING ON TV, JUG!
YEAH! GOOD IDEA!
WRESTLE!
GOTCHA! HUH?
LUNGE
FLOP!
LOOK! A SUPER SCISSORS FLIP MOVE!
WHAT THE?
THAT'S HULK HAMMER'S FAVORITE MOVE!
WHIP

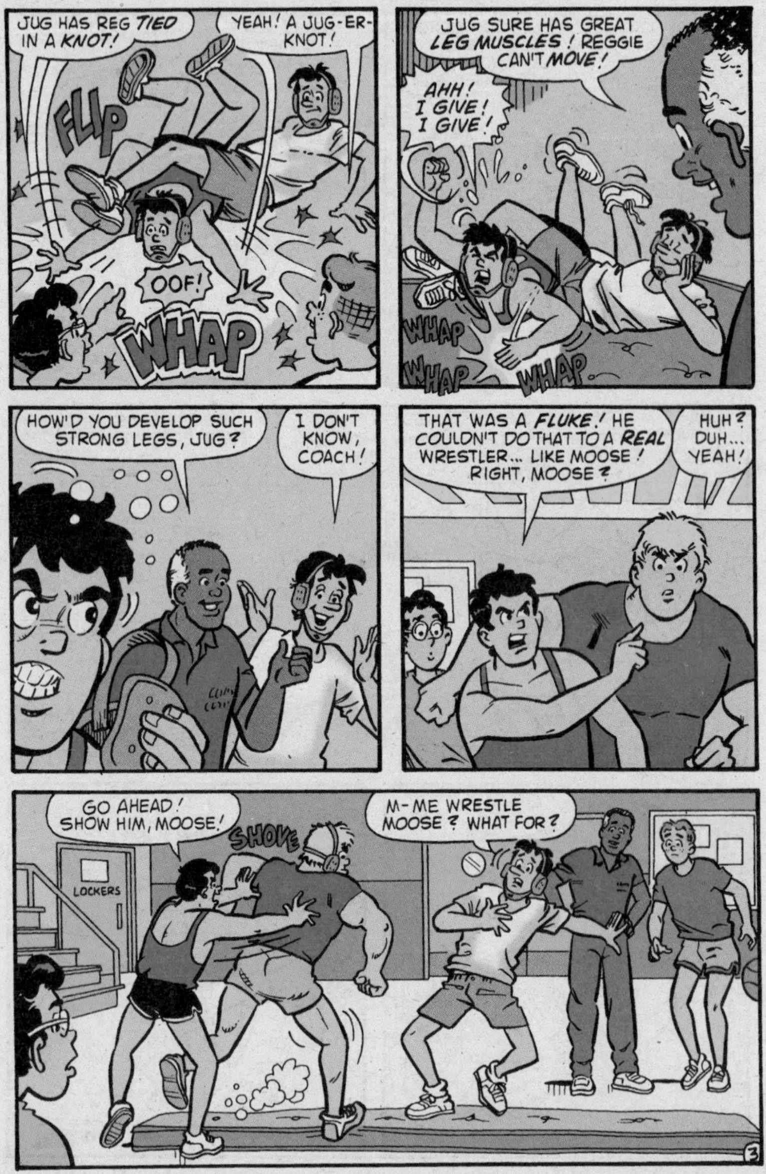
JUG HAS REG TIED IN A KNOT!
YEAH! A JUG-ER-KNOT!
FLIP
OOF!
WHAP
JUG SURE HAS GREAT LEG MUSCLES! REGGIE CAN'T MOVE!
AHH! I GIVE! I GIVE!
WHAP
WHAP
WHAP
HOW'D YOU DEVELOP SUCH STRONG LEGS, JUG?
I DON'T KNOW, COACH!
THAT WAS A FLUKE! HE COULDN'T DO THAT TO A REAL WRESTLER... LIKE MOOSE! RIGHT, MOOSE?
HUH? DUH... YEAH!
GO AHEAD! SHOW HIM, MOOSE!
SHOVE
LOCKERS
M-ME WRESTLE MOOSE? WHAT FOR?
3

SEE, HE THINKS HE CAN BEAT YOU, MOOSE!

WHAT?

NO! REALLY I DON'T...

YOU DON'T HAVE ANY *RESPECT* FOR MOOSE AS A *WRESTLER*?

GRRR... CHARGE!

NO, MOOSE! NO! THAT'S NOT WHAT I *MEANT*!

HE USED THE SAME MOVE AGAIN!

WHOOPS!!

FLIP

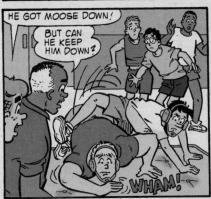

HE GOT MOOSE DOWN!

BUT CAN HE KEEP HIM DOWN?

WHAM!

I WISH I KNEW HOW JUG DEVELOPED ALL THAT STRENGTH IN HIS LEGS!

HE NEVER WORKS OUT OR ANYTHING!

4

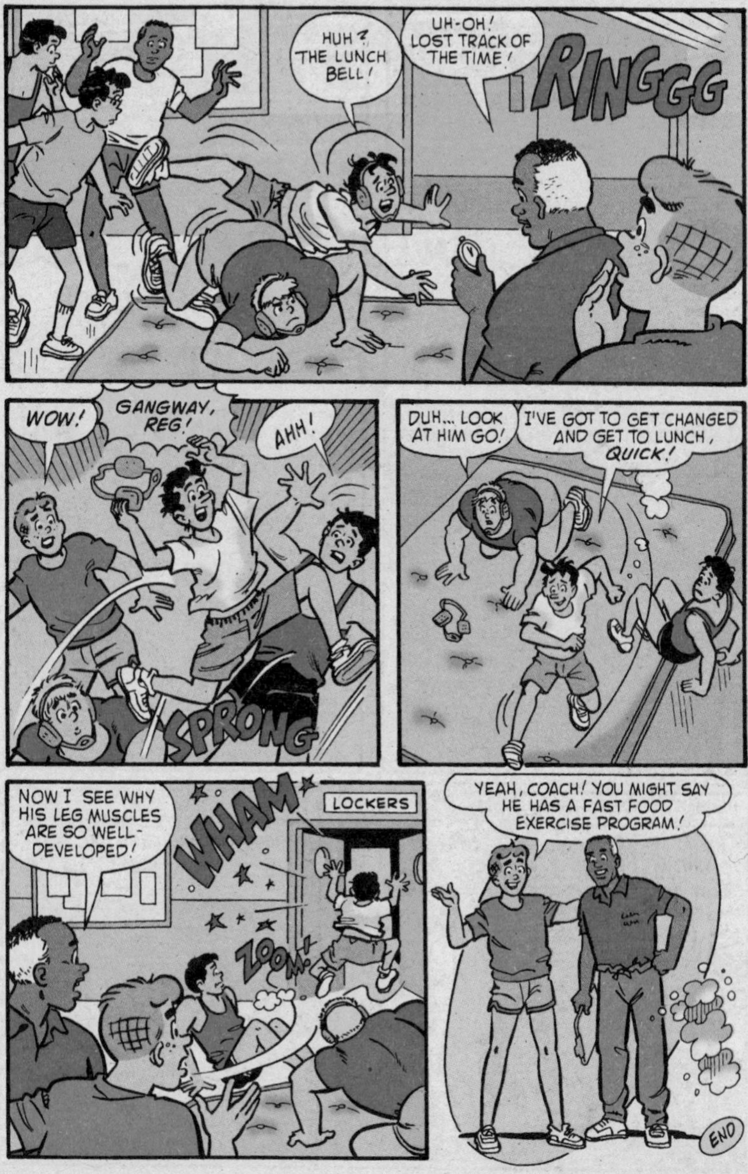
HUH? THE LUNCH BELL!
UH-OH! LOST TRACK OF THE TIME!
RINGGG
WOW!
GANGWAY, REG!
AHH!
SPRONG
DUH... LOOK AT HIM GO!
I'VE GOT TO GET CHANGED AND GET TO LUNCH, QUICK!
NOW I SEE WHY HIS LEG MUSCLES ARE SO WELL-DEVELOPED!
WHAM
LOCKERS
ZOOM!
YEAH, COACH! YOU MIGHT SAY HE HAS A FAST FOOD EXERCISE PROGRAM!
END

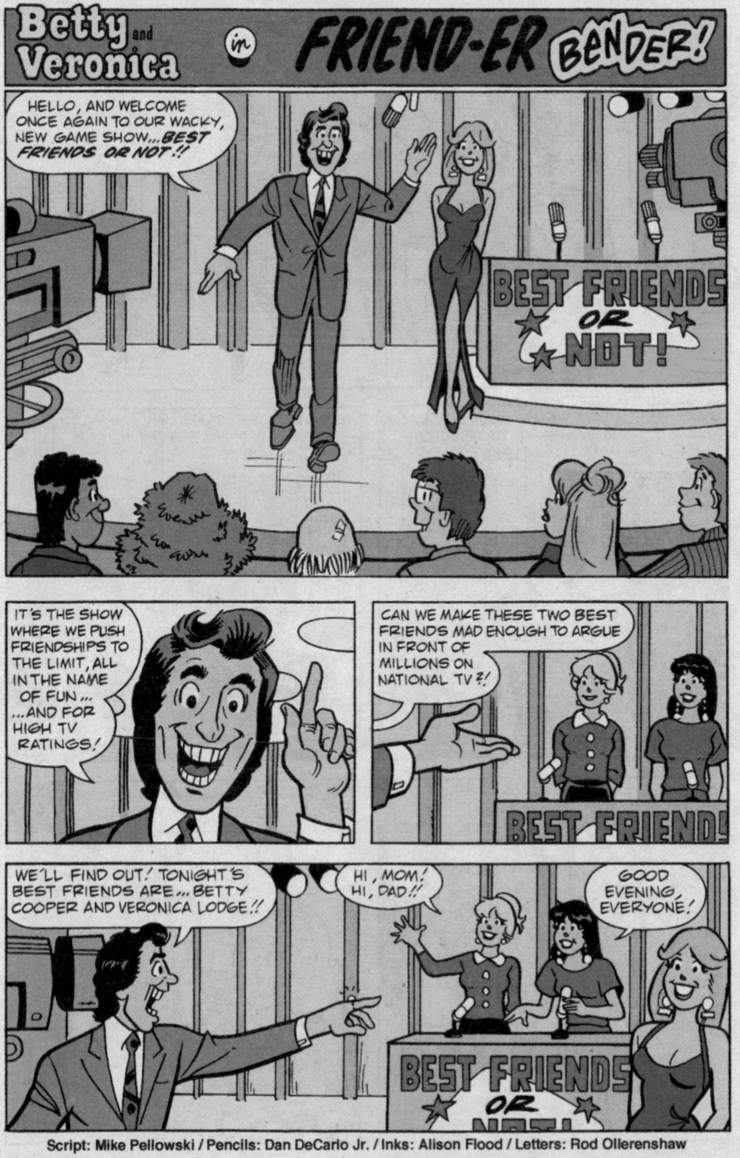
Betty and Veronica in FRIEND-ER BENDER!
HELLO, AND WELCOME ONCE AGAIN TO OUR WACKY, NEW GAME SHOW... BEST FRIENDS OR NOT!!
BEST FRIENDS OR NOT!
IT'S THE SHOW WHERE WE PUSH FRIENDSHIPS TO THE LIMIT, ALL IN THE NAME OF FUN...
...AND FOR HIGH TV RATINGS!
CAN WE MAKE THESE TWO BEST FRIENDS MAD ENOUGH TO ARGUE IN FRONT OF MILLIONS ON NATIONAL TV?!
BEST FRIENDS
WE'LL FIND OUT! TONIGHT'S BEST FRIENDS ARE... BETTY COOPER AND VERONICA LODGE!!
HI, MOM! HI, DAD!!
GOOD EVENING, EVERYONE!
BEST FRIENDS OR

Script: Mike Pellowski / Pencils: Dan DeCarlo Jr. / Inks: Alison Flood / Letters: Rod Ollerenshaw

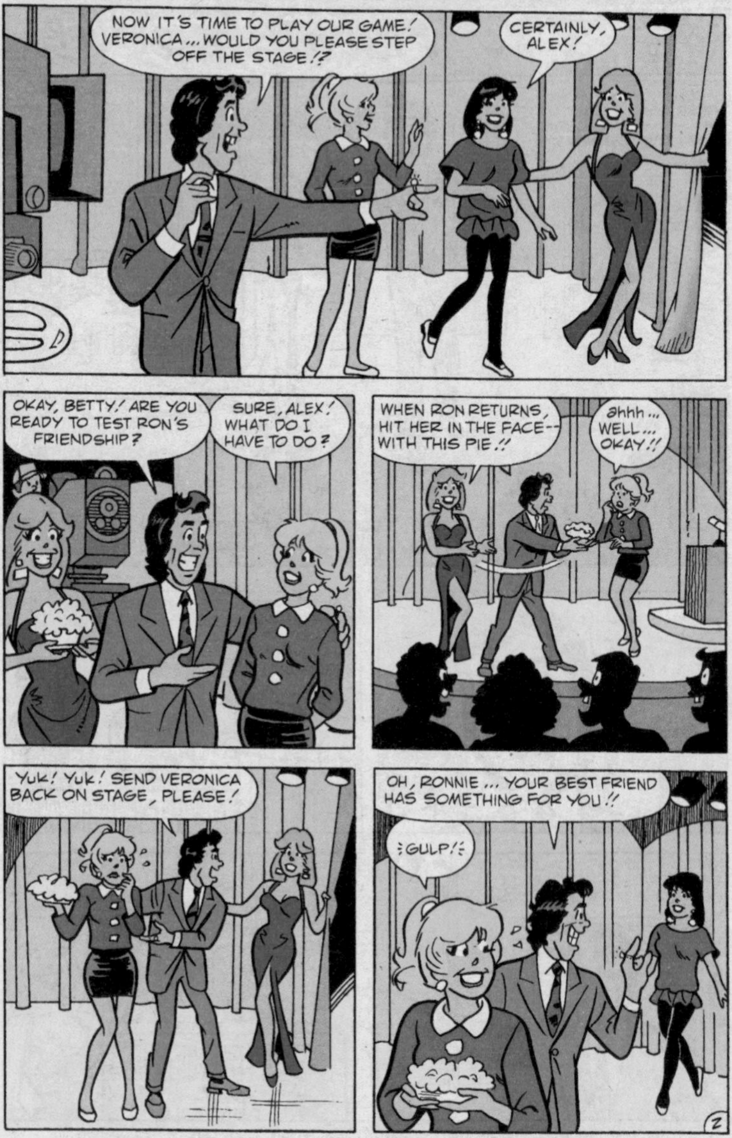
NOW IT'S TIME TO PLAY OUR GAME! VERONICA ... WOULD YOU PLEASE STEP OFF THE STAGE!?
CERTAINLY, ALEX!
OKAY, BETTY! ARE YOU READY TO TEST RON'S FRIENDSHIP?
SURE, ALEX! WHAT DO I HAVE TO DO?
WHEN RON RETURNS, HIT HER IN THE FACE-- WITH THIS PIE!!
ahhh ... WELL ... OKAY!!
YUK! YUK! SEND VERONICA BACK ON STAGE, PLEASE!
OH, RONNIE ... YOUR BEST FRIEND HAS SOMETHING FOR YOU!!
GULP!
2

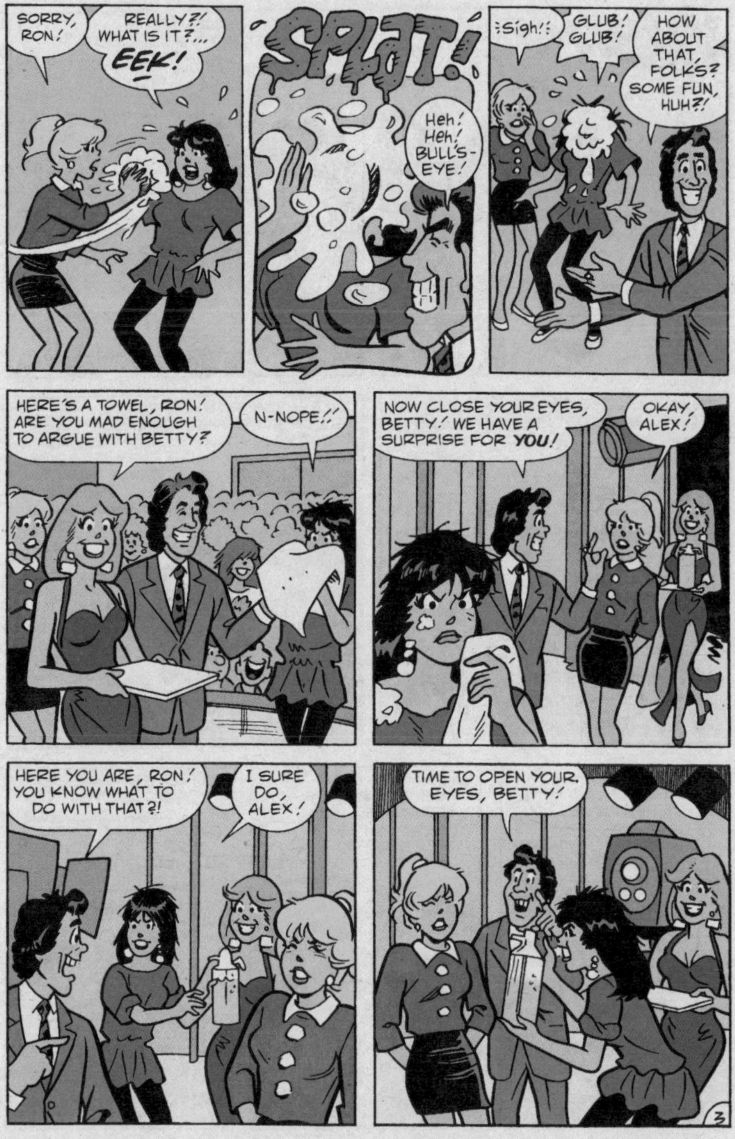

SORRY, RON!
REALLY?! WHAT IS IT?... EEK!
SPLAT!
Heh! Heh! BULL'S-EYE!
Sigh!
GLUB! GLUB!
HOW ABOUT THAT, FOLKS? SOME FUN, HUH?!
HERE'S A TOWEL, RON! ARE YOU MAD ENOUGH TO ARGUE WITH BETTY?
N-NOPE!!
NOW CLOSE YOUR EYES, BETTY! WE HAVE A SURPRISE FOR YOU!
OKAY, ALEX!
HERE YOU ARE, RON! YOU KNOW WHAT TO DO WITH THAT?!
I SURE DO, ALEX!
TIME TO OPEN YOUR EYES, BETTY!
3

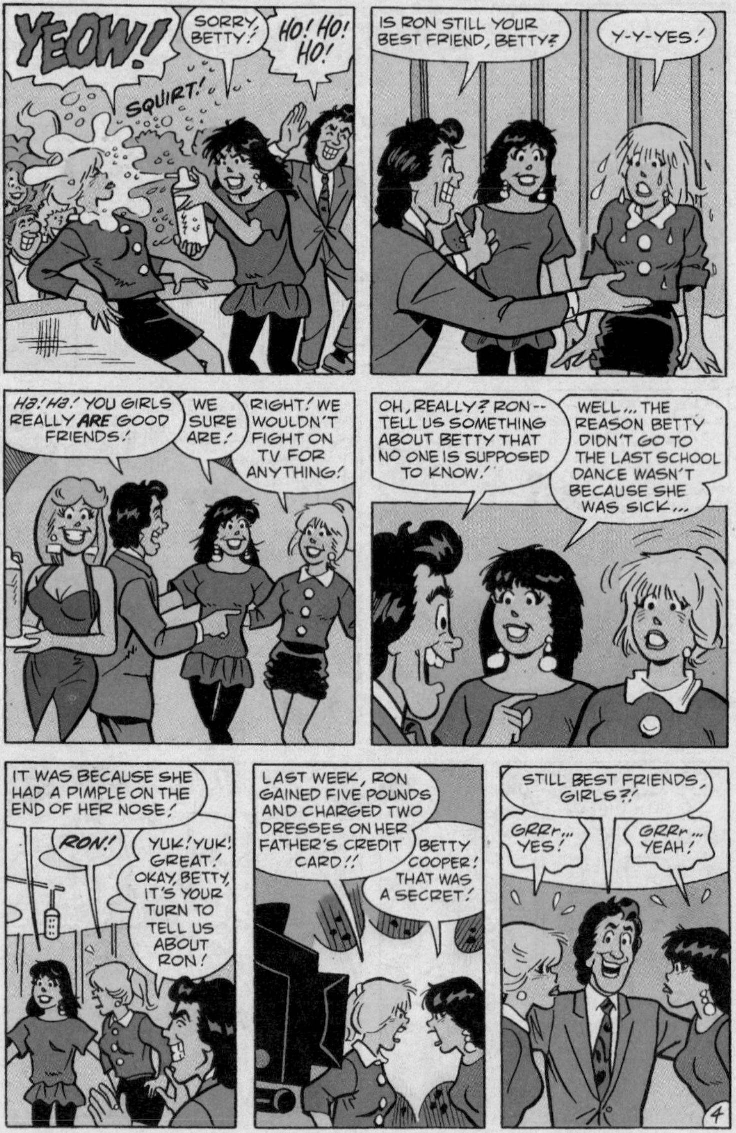

YEOW!
SORRY, BETTY!
HO! HO! HO!
SQUIRT!
IS RON STILL YOUR BEST FRIEND, BETTY?
Y-Y-YES!
HA! HA! YOU GIRLS REALLY ARE GOOD FRIENDS!
WE SURE ARE!
RIGHT! WE WOULDN'T FIGHT ON TV FOR ANYTHING!
OH, REALLY? RON -- TELL US SOMETHING ABOUT BETTY THAT NO ONE IS SUPPOSED TO KNOW!
WELL... THE REASON BETTY DIDN'T GO TO THE LAST SCHOOL DANCE WASN'T BECAUSE SHE WAS SICK...
IT WAS BECAUSE SHE HAD A PIMPLE ON THE END OF HER NOSE!
RON!
YUK! YUK! GREAT! OKAY, BETTY, IT'S YOUR TURN TO TELL US ABOUT RON!
LAST WEEK, RON GAINED FIVE POUNDS AND CHARGED TWO DRESSES ON HER FATHER'S CREDIT CARD!!
BETTY COOPER! THAT WAS A SECRET!
STILL BEST FRIENDS, GIRLS?!
GRRr... YES!
GRRr... YEAH!
4

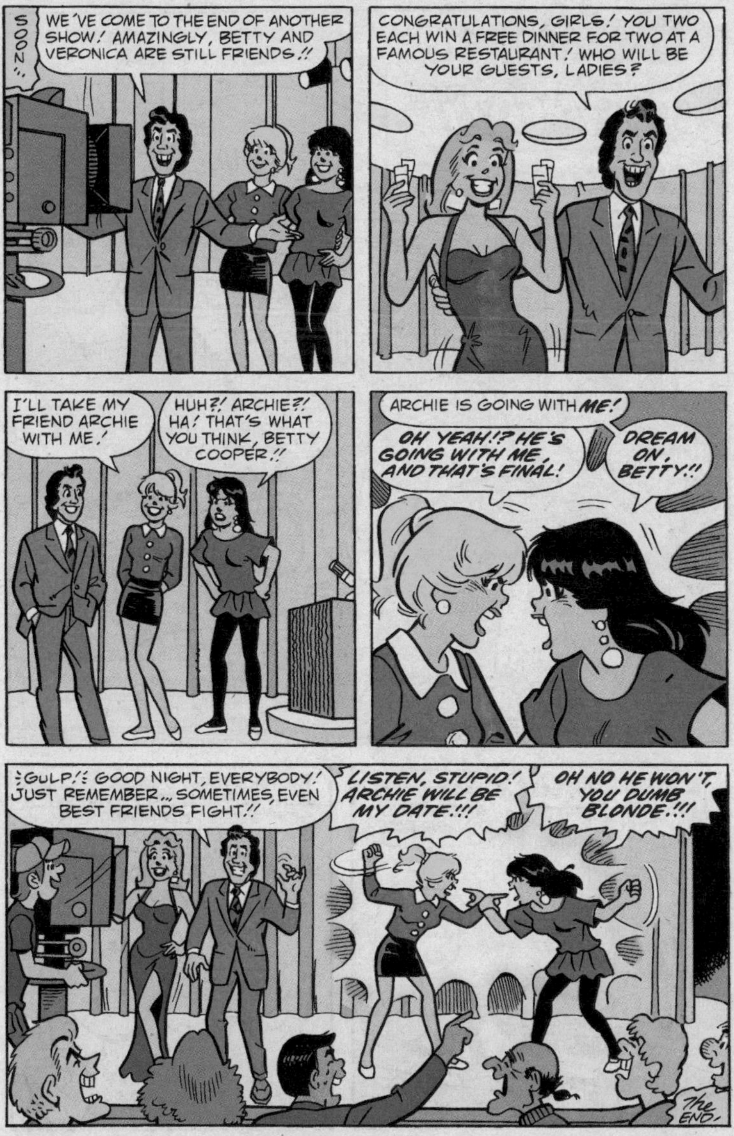
SOON...
WE'VE COME TO THE END OF ANOTHER SHOW! AMAZINGLY, BETTY AND VERONICA ARE STILL FRIENDS!!
CONGRATULATIONS, GIRLS! YOU TWO EACH WIN A FREE DINNER FOR TWO AT A FAMOUS RESTAURANT! WHO WILL BE YOUR GUESTS, LADIES?
I'LL TAKE MY FRIEND ARCHIE WITH ME!
HUH?! ARCHIE?! HA! THAT'S WHAT YOU THINK, BETTY COOPER!!
ARCHIE IS GOING WITH ME!
OH YEAH!? HE'S GOING WITH ME, AND THAT'S FINAL!
DREAM ON, BETTY!!
GULP! GOOD NIGHT, EVERYBODY! JUST REMEMBER... SOMETIMES, EVEN BEST FRIENDS FIGHT!!
LISTEN, STUPID! ARCHIE WILL BE MY DATE!!!
OH NO HE WON'T, YOU DUMB BLONDE!!!
The END.

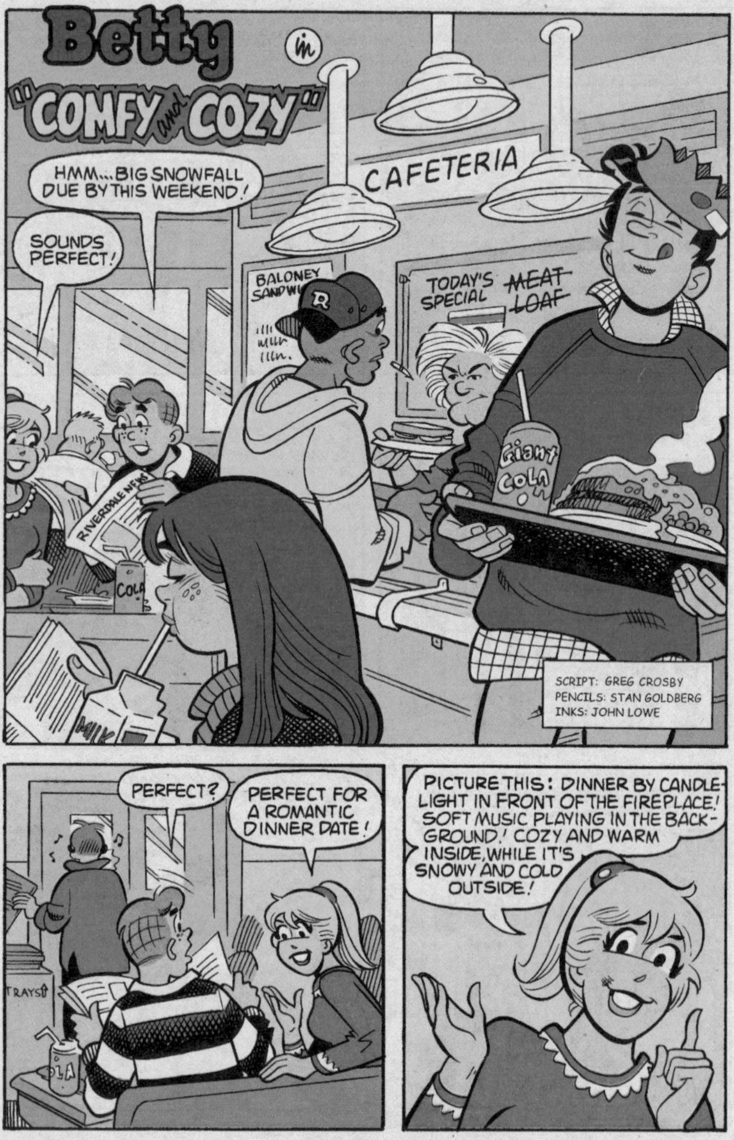

Betty in
"COMFY and COZY"
HMM... BIG SNOWFALL DUE BY THIS WEEKEND!
SOUNDS PERFECT!
CAFETERIA
BALONEY SANDWI
TODAY'S SPECIAL MEAT LOAF
RIVERDALE NEWS
COLA
Giant COLA
MILK
SCRIPT: GREG CROSBY
PENCILS: STAN GOLDBERG
INKS: JOHN LOWE
PERFECT?
PERFECT FOR A ROMANTIC DINNER DATE!
TRAYS
PICTURE THIS: DINNER BY CANDLE-LIGHT IN FRONT OF THE FIREPLACE! SOFT MUSIC PLAYING IN THE BACK-GROUND! COZY AND WARM INSIDE, WHILE IT'S SNOWY AND COLD OUTSIDE!

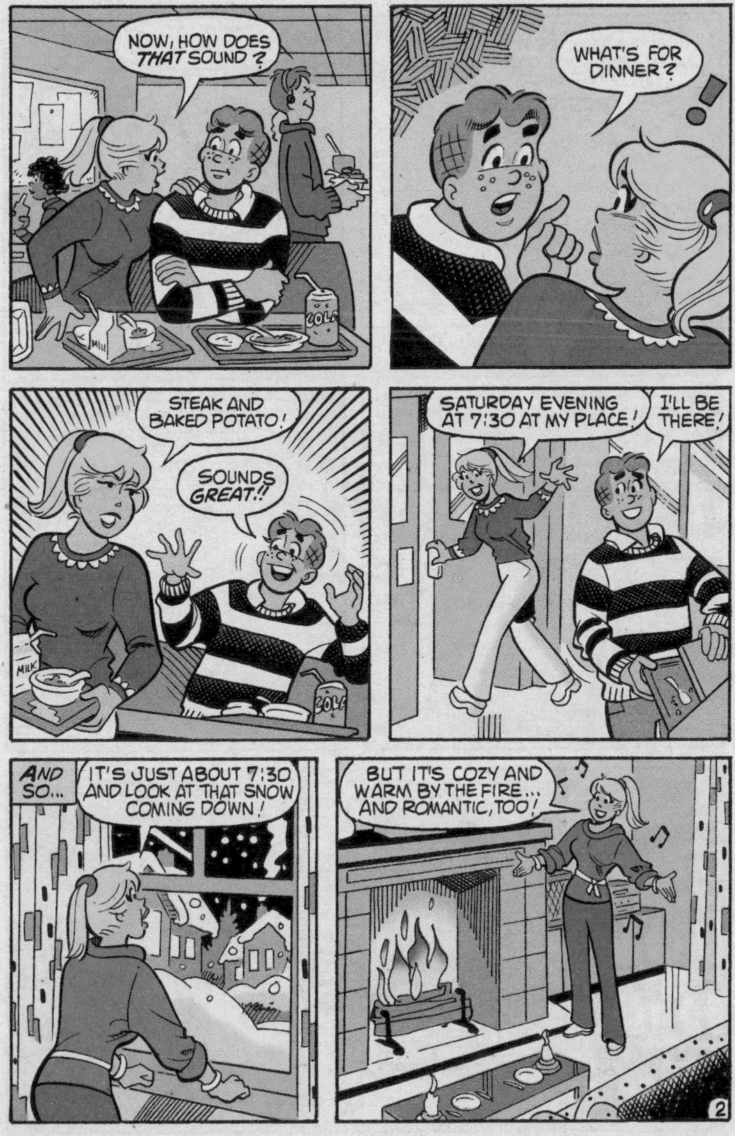
NOW, HOW DOES THAT SOUND ?
WHAT'S FOR DINNER ?
!
STEAK AND BAKED POTATO !
SOUNDS GREAT !!
SATURDAY EVENING AT 7:30 AT MY PLACE !
I'LL BE THERE !
AND SO...
IT'S JUST ABOUT 7:30 AND LOOK AT THAT SNOW COMING DOWN !
BUT IT'S COZY AND WARM BY THE FIRE... AND ROMANTIC, TOO !

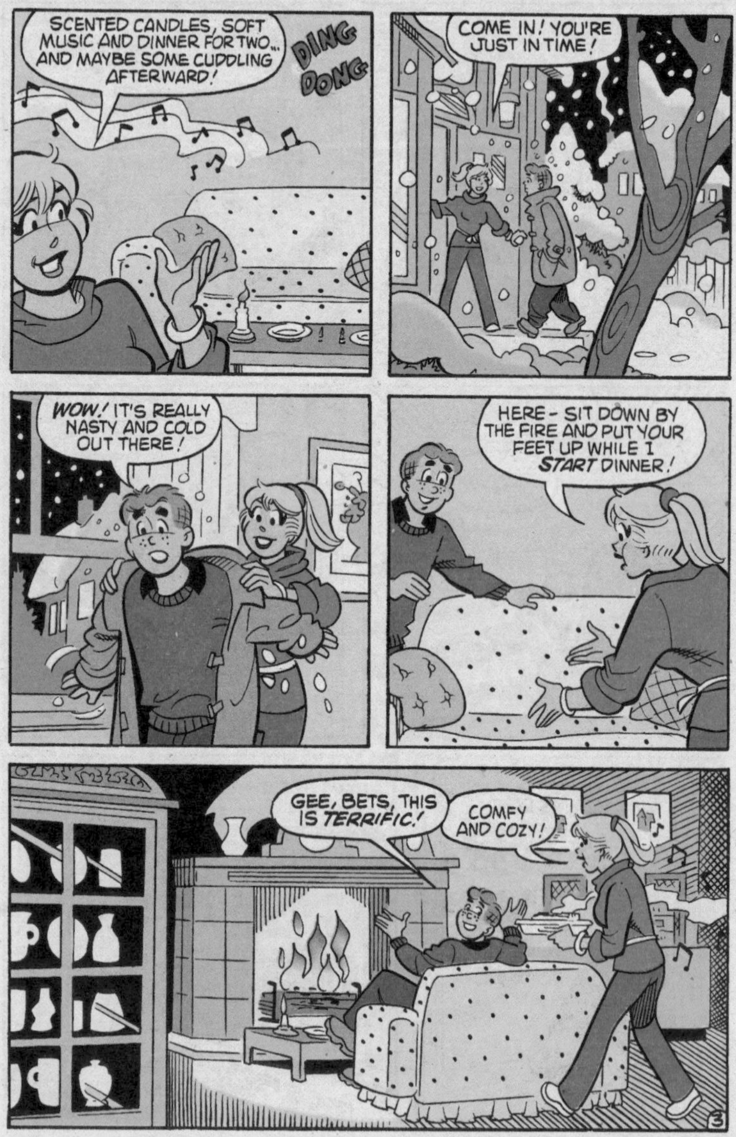
SCENTED CANDLES, SOFT MUSIC AND DINNER FOR TWO... AND MAYBE SOME CUDDLING AFTERWARD!
DING DONG
COME IN! YOU'RE JUST IN TIME!
WOW! IT'S REALLY NASTY AND COLD OUT THERE!
HERE - SIT DOWN BY THE FIRE AND PUT YOUR FEET UP WHILE I START DINNER!
GEE, BETS, THIS IS TERRIFIC!
COMFY AND COZY!
3

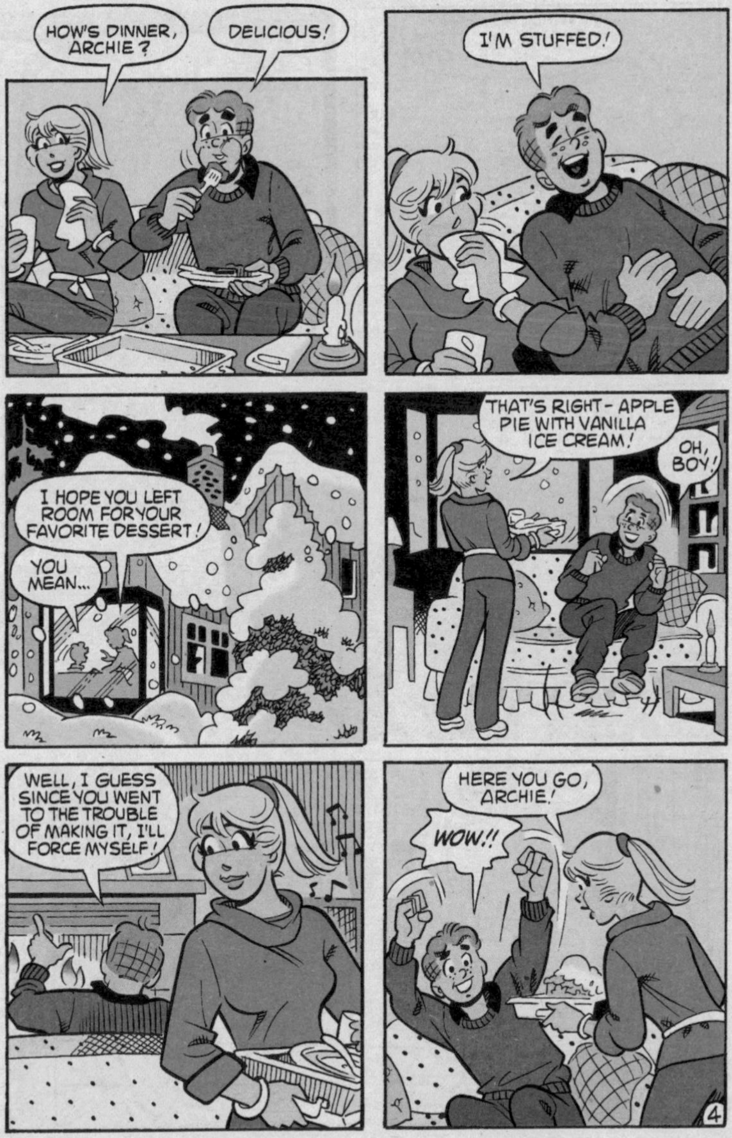
HOW'S DINNER, ARCHIE?
DELICIOUS!
I'M STUFFED!
I HOPE YOU LEFT ROOM FOR YOUR FAVORITE DESSERT!
YOU MEAN...
THAT'S RIGHT - APPLE PIE WITH VANILLA ICE CREAM!
OH, BOY!
WELL, I GUESS SINCE YOU WENT TO THE TROUBLE OF MAKING IT, I'LL FORCE MYSELF!
HERE YOU GO, ARCHIE!
WOW!!
4

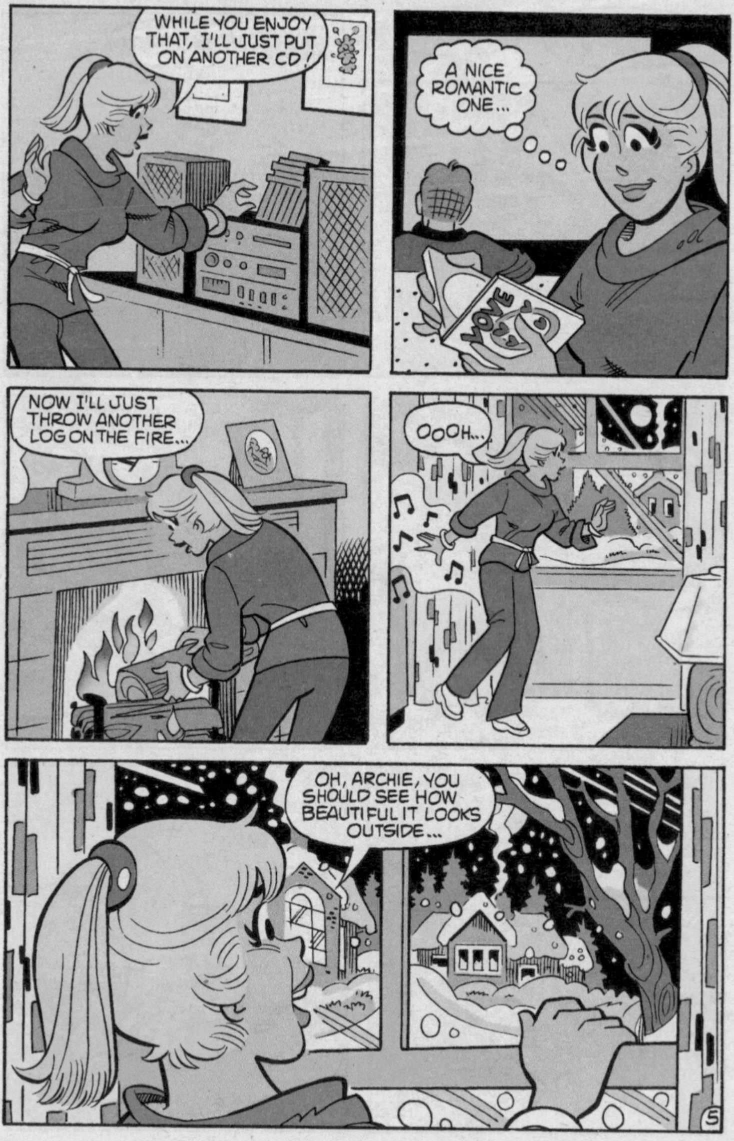
WHILE YOU ENJOY THAT, I'LL JUST PUT ON ANOTHER CD!
A NICE ROMANTIC ONE...
LOVE
NOW I'LL JUST THROW ANOTHER LOG ON THE FIRE...
OOOH...
OH, ARCHIE, YOU SHOULD SEE HOW BEAUTIFUL IT LOOKS OUTSIDE...
5

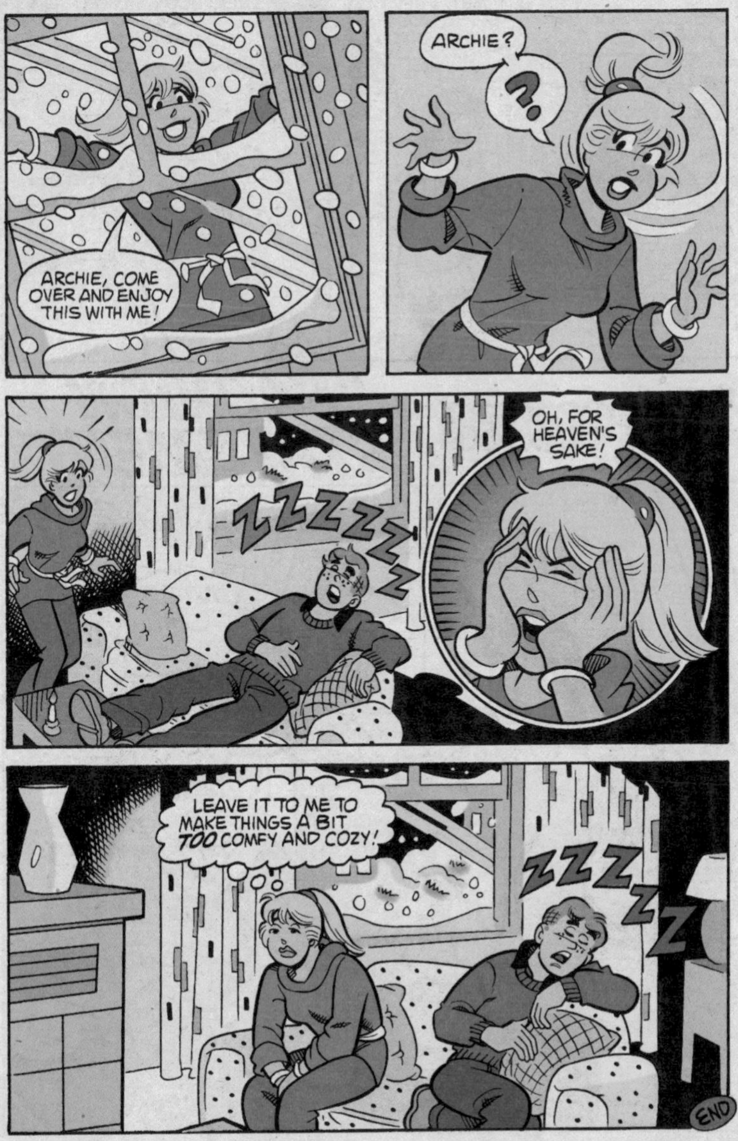
ARCHIE, COME OVER AND ENJOY THIS WITH ME!
ARCHIE?
?
OH, FOR HEAVEN'S SAKE!
ZZZZZZZ
LEAVE IT TO ME TO MAKE THINGS A BIT TOO COMFY AND COZY!
ZZZZZ
END

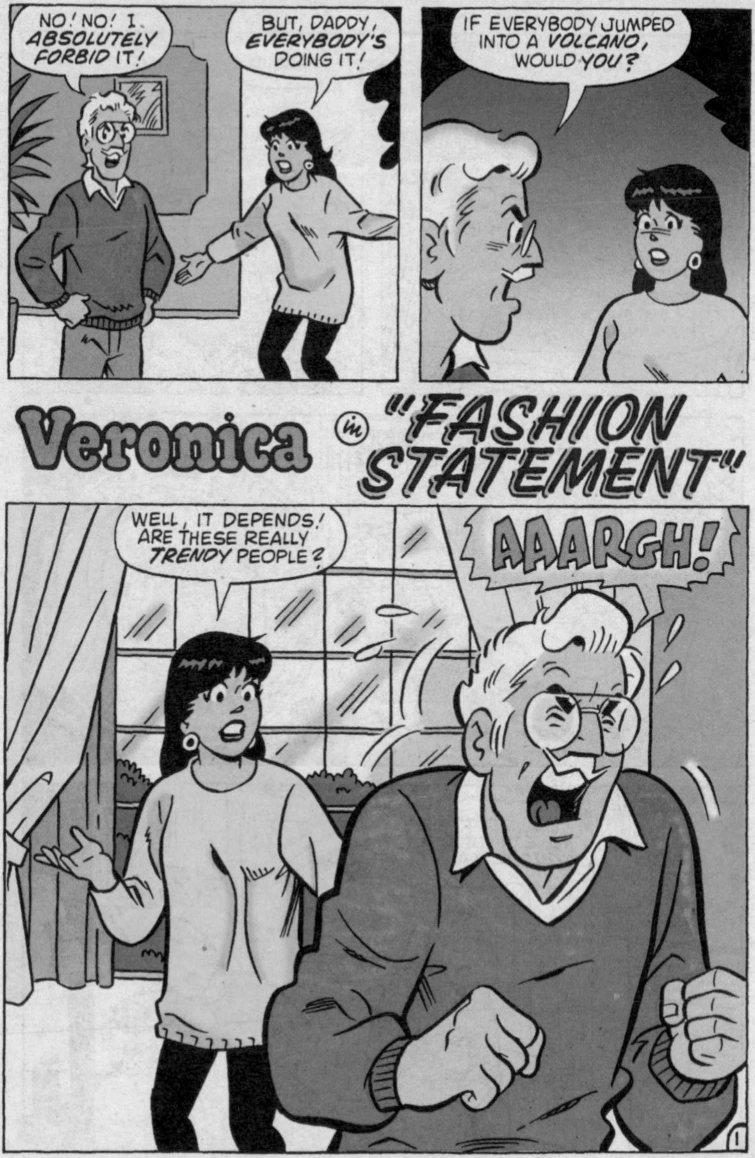
NO! NO! I ABSOLUTELY FORBID IT!
BUT, DADDY, EVERYBODY'S DOING IT!
IF EVERYBODY JUMPED INTO A VOLCANO, WOULD YOU?
Veronica in "FASHION STATEMENT"
WELL, IT DEPENDS! ARE THESE REALLY TRENDY PEOPLE?
AAARGH!
1

Script: Hal Smith / Pencils: Jeff Shultz / Inks: Rudy Lapick / Letters: Bill Yoshida / Colors: Barry Grossman

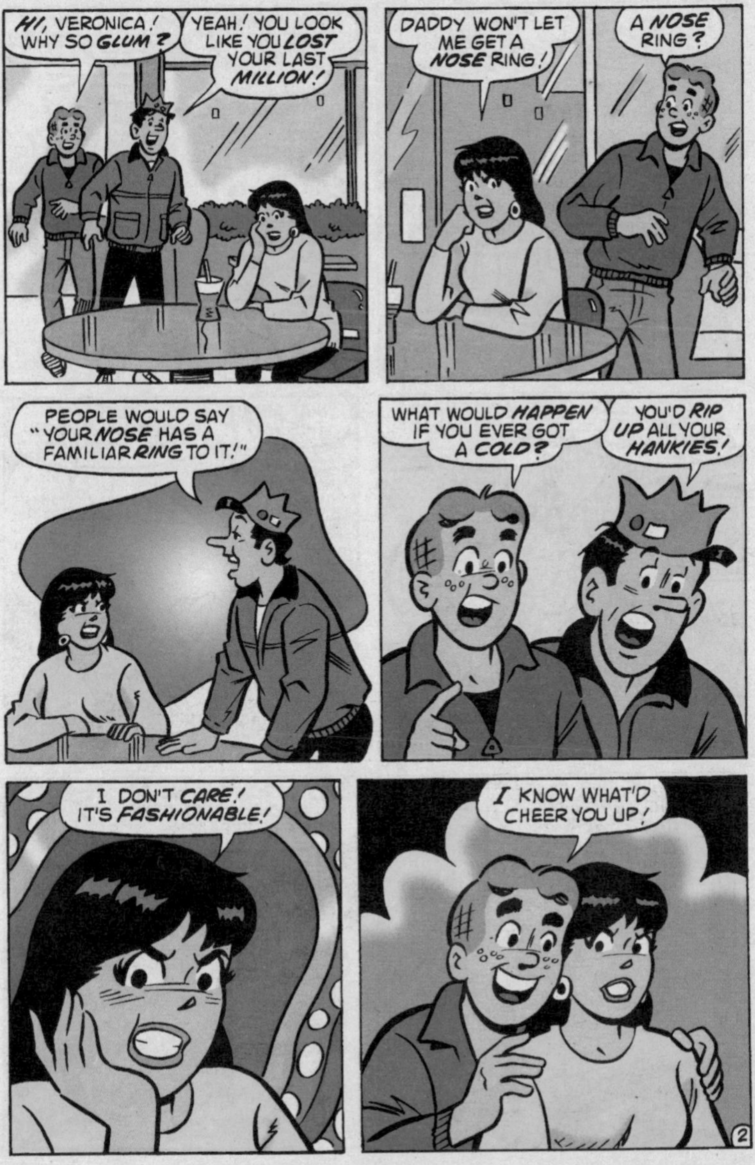
HI, VERONICA! WHY SO GLUM?
YEAH! YOU LOOK LIKE YOU LOST YOUR LAST MILLION!
DADDY WON'T LET ME GET A NOSE RING!
A NOSE RING?
PEOPLE WOULD SAY "YOUR NOSE HAS A FAMILIAR RING TO IT!"
WHAT WOULD HAPPEN IF YOU EVER GOT A COLD?
YOU'D RIP UP ALL YOUR HANKIES!
I DON'T CARE! IT'S FASHIONABLE!
I KNOW WHAT'D CHEER YOU UP!
2

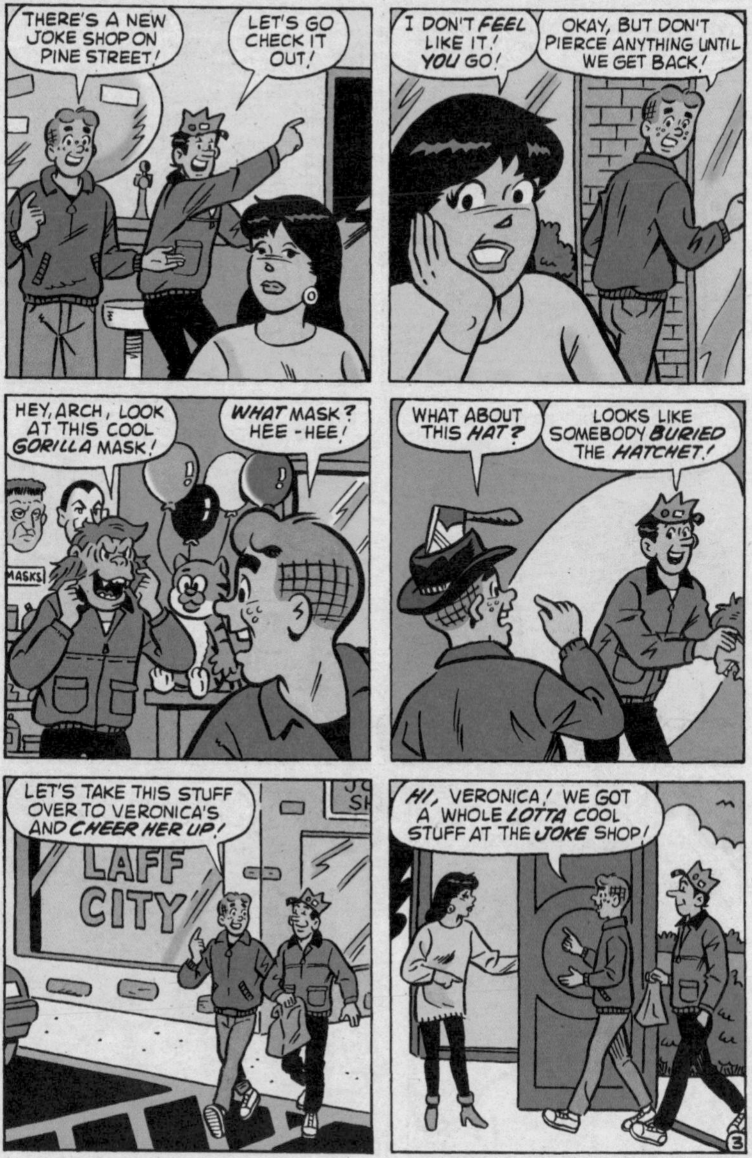

THERE'S A NEW JOKE SHOP ON PINE STREET!
LET'S GO CHECK IT OUT!
I DON'T FEEL LIKE IT! YOU GO!
OKAY, BUT DON'T PIERCE ANYTHING UNTIL WE GET BACK!
HEY, ARCH, LOOK AT THIS COOL GORILLA MASK!
WHAT MASK? HEE-HEE!
MASKS
WHAT ABOUT THIS HAT?
LOOKS LIKE SOMEBODY BURIED THE HATCHET!
LET'S TAKE THIS STUFF OVER TO VERONICA'S AND CHEER HER UP!
LAFF CITY
HI, VERONICA! WE GOT A WHOLE LOTTA COOL STUFF AT THE JOKE SHOP!
3

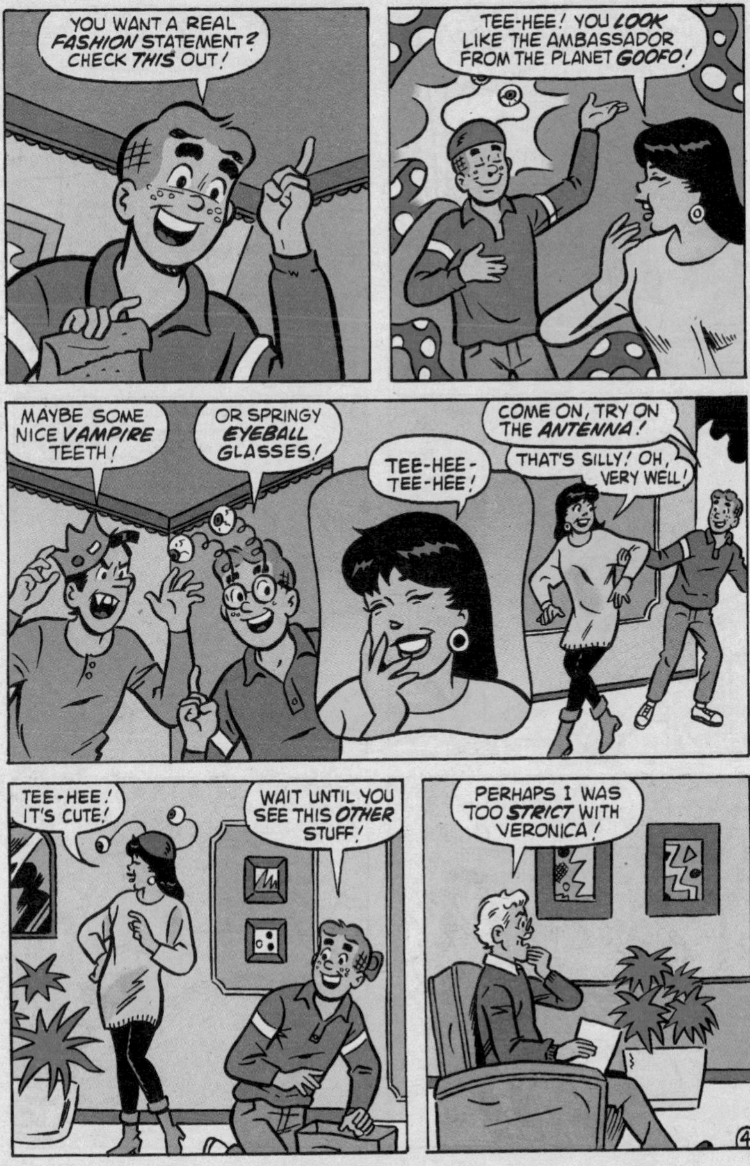

YOU WANT A REAL FASHION STATEMENT? CHECK THIS OUT!
TEE-HEE! YOU LOOK LIKE THE AMBASSADOR FROM THE PLANET GOOFO!
MAYBE SOME NICE VAMPIRE TEETH!
OR SPRINGY EYEBALL GLASSES!
TEE-HEE-TEE-HEE!
COME ON, TRY ON THE ANTENNA!
THAT'S SILLY! OH, VERY WELL!
TEE-HEE! IT'S CUTE!
WAIT UNTIL YOU SEE THIS OTHER STUFF!
PERHAPS I WAS TOO STRICT WITH VERONICA!
4

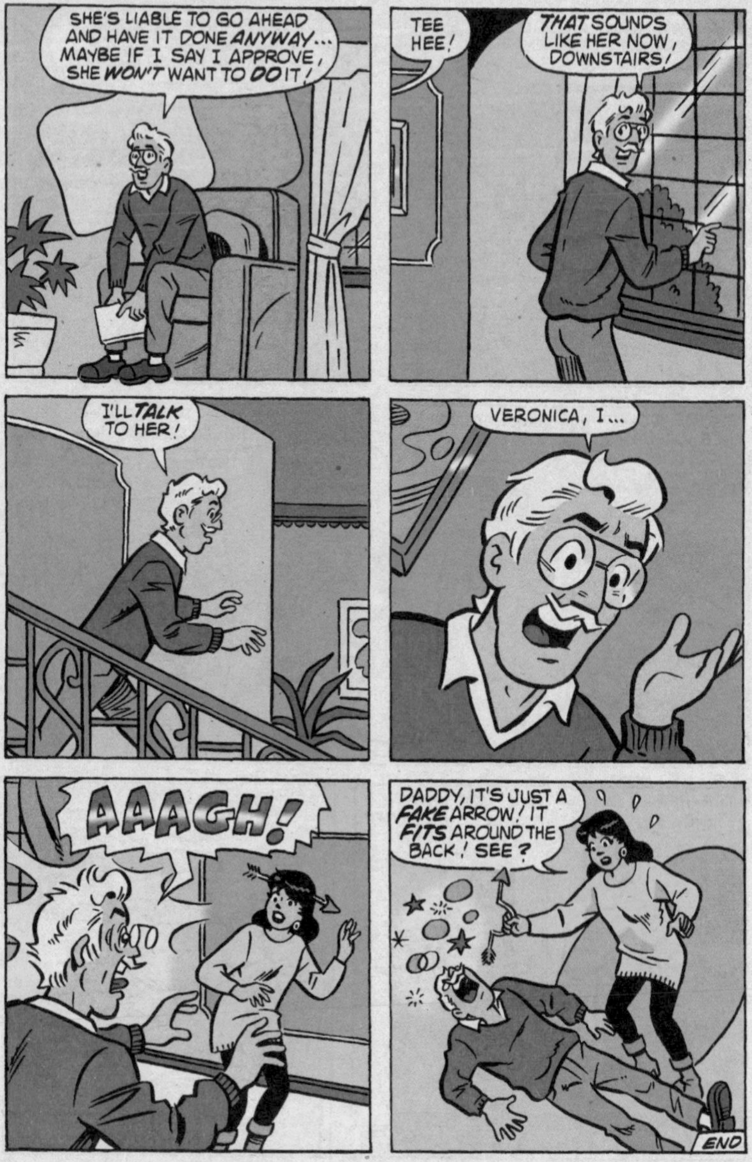
SHE'S LIABLE TO GO AHEAD AND HAVE IT DONE ANYWAY... MAYBE IF I SAY I APPROVE, SHE WON'T WANT TO DO IT!
TEE HEE!
THAT SOUNDS LIKE HER NOW, DOWNSTAIRS!
I'LL TALK TO HER!
VERONICA, I...
AAAGH!
DADDY, IT'S JUST A FAKE ARROW! IT FITS AROUND THE BACK! SEE?
END

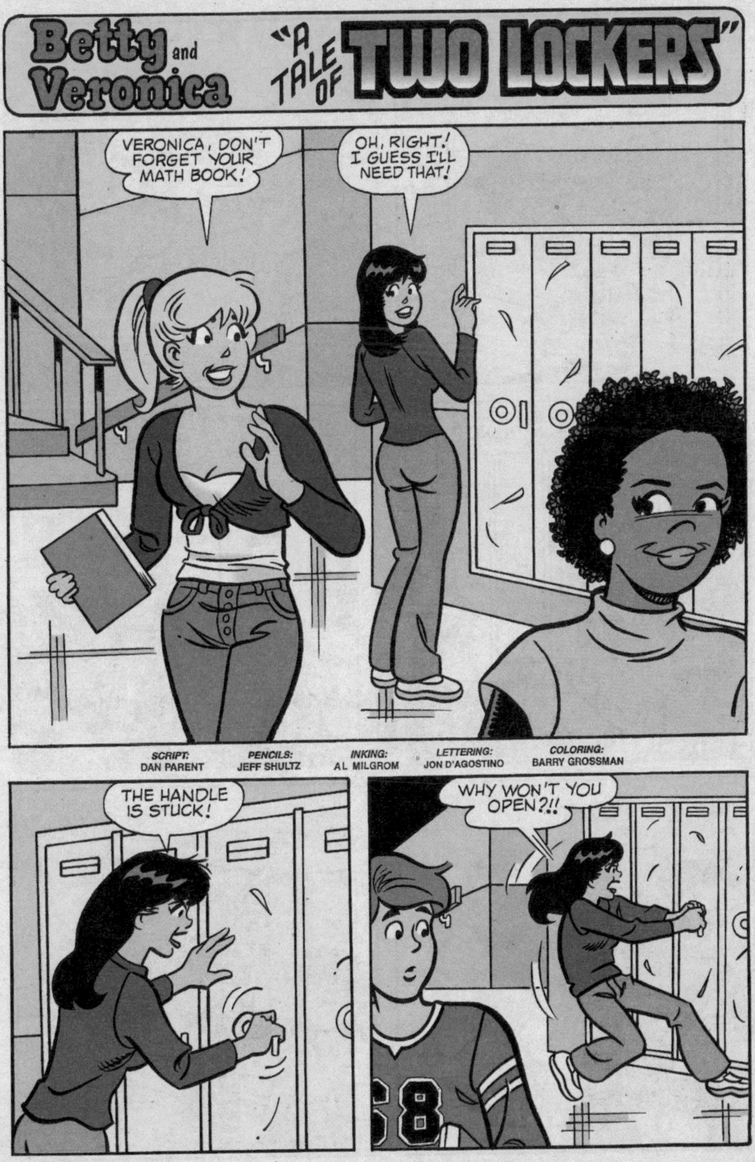
Betty and Veronica
"A TALE OF TWO LOCKERS"
VERONICA, DON'T FORGET YOUR MATH BOOK!
OH, RIGHT! I GUESS I'LL NEED THAT!
SCRIPT: DAN PARENT
PENCILS: JEFF SHULTZ
INKING: AL MILGROM
LETTERING: JON D'AGOSTINO
COLORING: BARRY GROSSMAN
THE HANDLE IS STUCK!
WHY WON'T YOU OPEN?!!

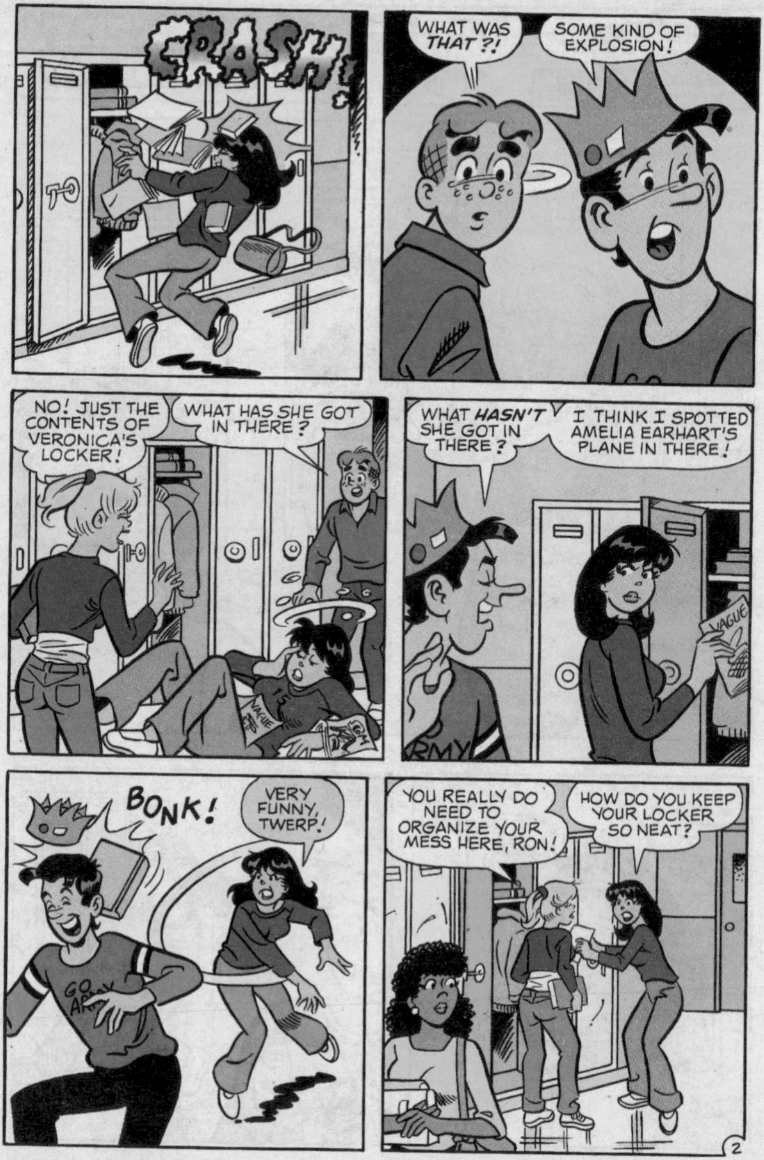
CRASH!
WHAT WAS THAT ?!
SOME KIND OF EXPLOSION!
NO! JUST THE CONTENTS OF VERONICA'S LOCKER!
WHAT HAS SHE GOT IN THERE ?
VAGUE
WHAT HASN'T SHE GOT IN THERE ?
I THINK I SPOTTED AMELIA EARHART'S PLANE IN THERE!
VAGUE
BONK!
VERY FUNNY, TWERP!
YOU REALLY DO NEED TO ORGANIZE YOUR MESS HERE, RON!
HOW DO YOU KEEP YOUR LOCKER SO NEAT?

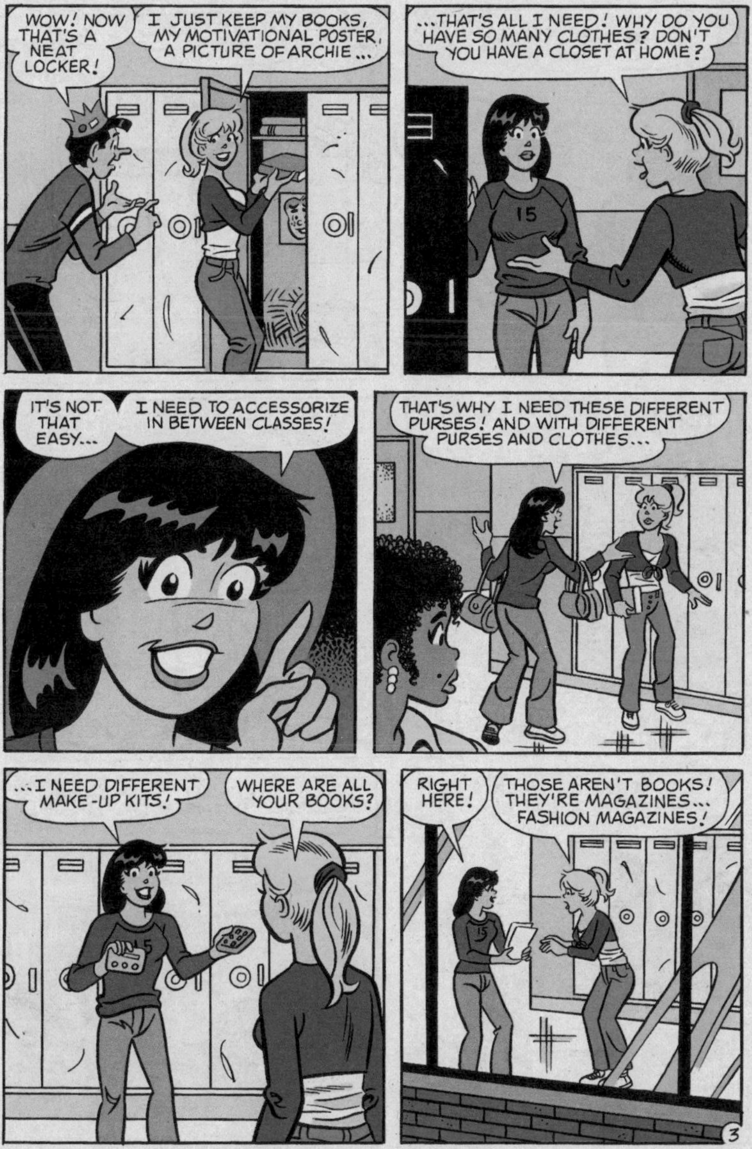
WOW! NOW THAT'S A NEAT LOCKER!
I JUST KEEP MY BOOKS, MY MOTIVATIONAL POSTER, A PICTURE OF ARCHIE...
...THAT'S ALL I NEED! WHY DO YOU HAVE SO MANY CLOTHES? DON'T YOU HAVE A CLOSET AT HOME?
15
IT'S NOT THAT EASY...
I NEED TO ACCESSORIZE IN BETWEEN CLASSES!
THAT'S WHY I NEED THESE DIFFERENT PURSES! AND WITH DIFFERENT PURSES AND CLOTHES...
...I NEED DIFFERENT MAKE-UP KITS!
WHERE ARE ALL YOUR BOOKS?
RIGHT HERE!
THOSE AREN'T BOOKS! THEY'RE MAGAZINES... FASHION MAGAZINES!

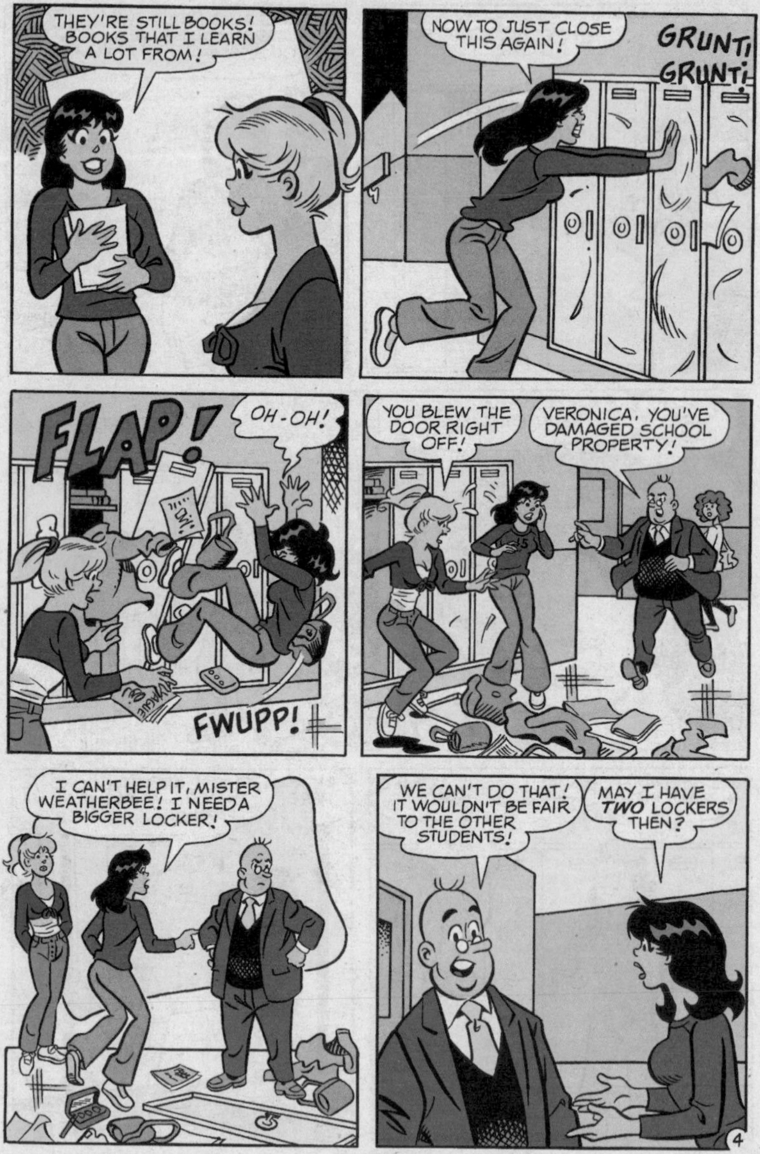

THEY'RE STILL BOOKS! BOOKS THAT I LEARN A LOT FROM!
NOW TO JUST CLOSE THIS AGAIN!
GRUNT! GRUNT!
FLAP!
OH-OH!
FWUPP!
YOU BLEW THE DOOR RIGHT OFF!
VERONICA, YOU'VE DAMAGED SCHOOL PROPERTY!
I CAN'T HELP IT, MISTER WEATHERBEE! I NEED A BIGGER LOCKER!
WE CAN'T DO THAT! IT WOULDN'T BE FAIR TO THE OTHER STUDENTS!
MAY I HAVE TWO LOCKERS THEN?

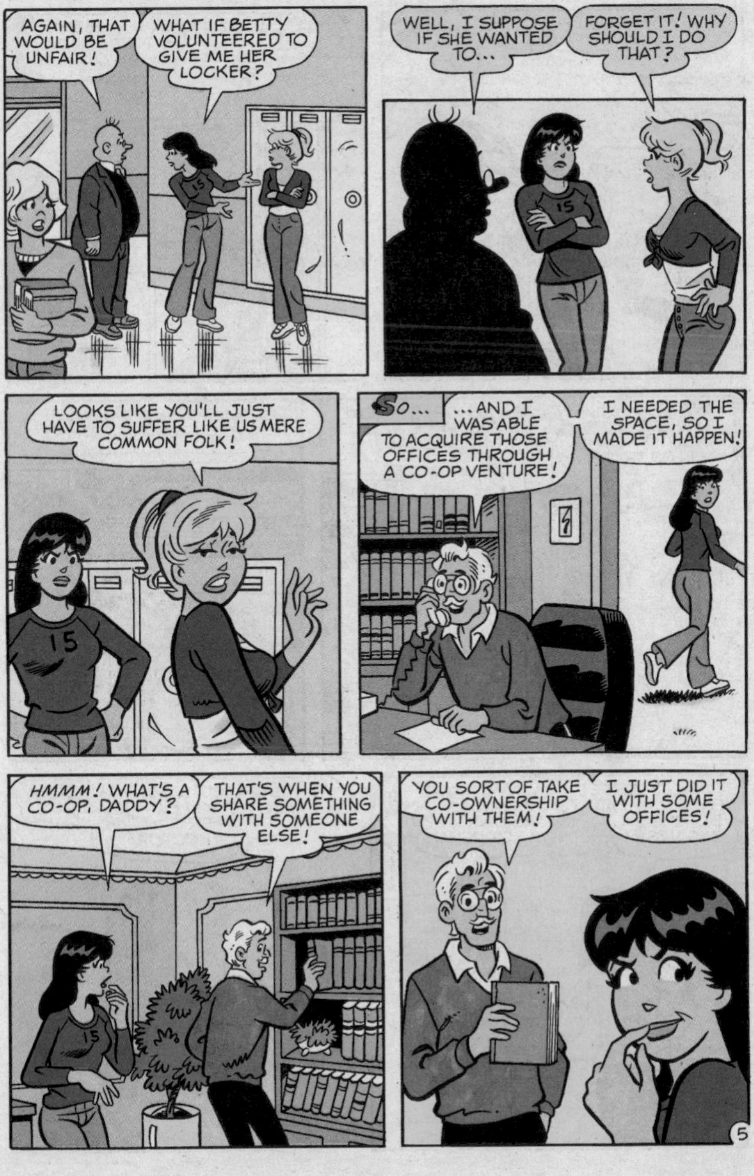
AGAIN, THAT WOULD BE UNFAIR!
WHAT IF BETTY VOLUNTEERED TO GIVE ME HER LOCKER?
WELL, I SUPPOSE IF SHE WANTED TO...
FORGET IT! WHY SHOULD I DO THAT?
LOOKS LIKE YOU'LL JUST HAVE TO SUFFER LIKE US MERE COMMON FOLK!
SO...
...AND I WAS ABLE TO ACQUIRE THOSE OFFICES THROUGH A CO-OP VENTURE!
I NEEDED THE SPACE, SO I MADE IT HAPPEN!
HMMM! WHAT'S A CO-OP, DADDY?
THAT'S WHEN YOU SHARE SOMETHING WITH SOMEONE ELSE!
YOU SORT OF TAKE CO-OWNERSHIP WITH THEM!
I JUST DID IT WITH SOME OFFICES!
5

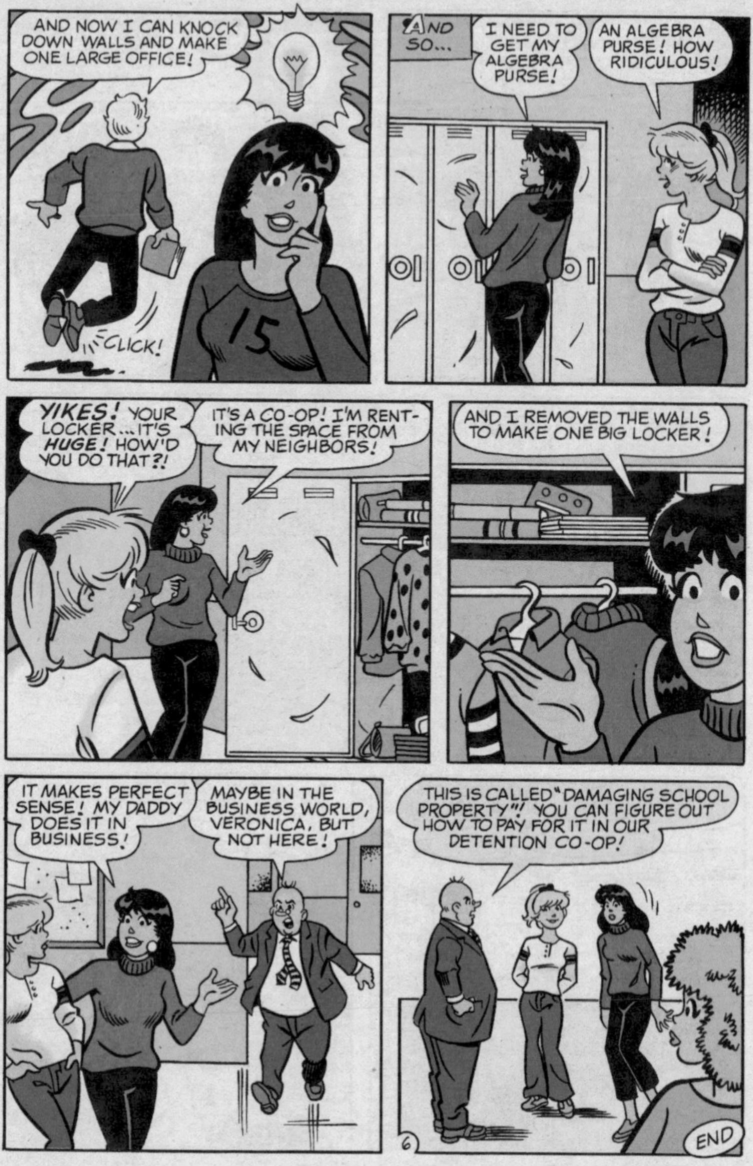

AND NOW I CAN KNOCK DOWN WALLS AND MAKE ONE LARGE OFFICE!
CLICK!
AND SO...
I NEED TO GET MY ALGEBRA PURSE!
AN ALGEBRA PURSE! HOW RIDICULOUS!
YIKES! YOUR LOCKER...IT'S HUGE! HOW'D YOU DO THAT?!
IT'S A CO-OP! I'M RENTING THE SPACE FROM MY NEIGHBORS!
AND I REMOVED THE WALLS TO MAKE ONE BIG LOCKER!
IT MAKES PERFECT SENSE! MY DADDY DOES IT IN BUSINESS!
MAYBE IN THE BUSINESS WORLD, VERONICA, BUT NOT HERE!
THIS IS CALLED "DAMAGING SCHOOL PROPERTY"! YOU CAN FIGURE OUT HOW TO PAY FOR IT IN OUR DETENTION CO-OP!
6
END

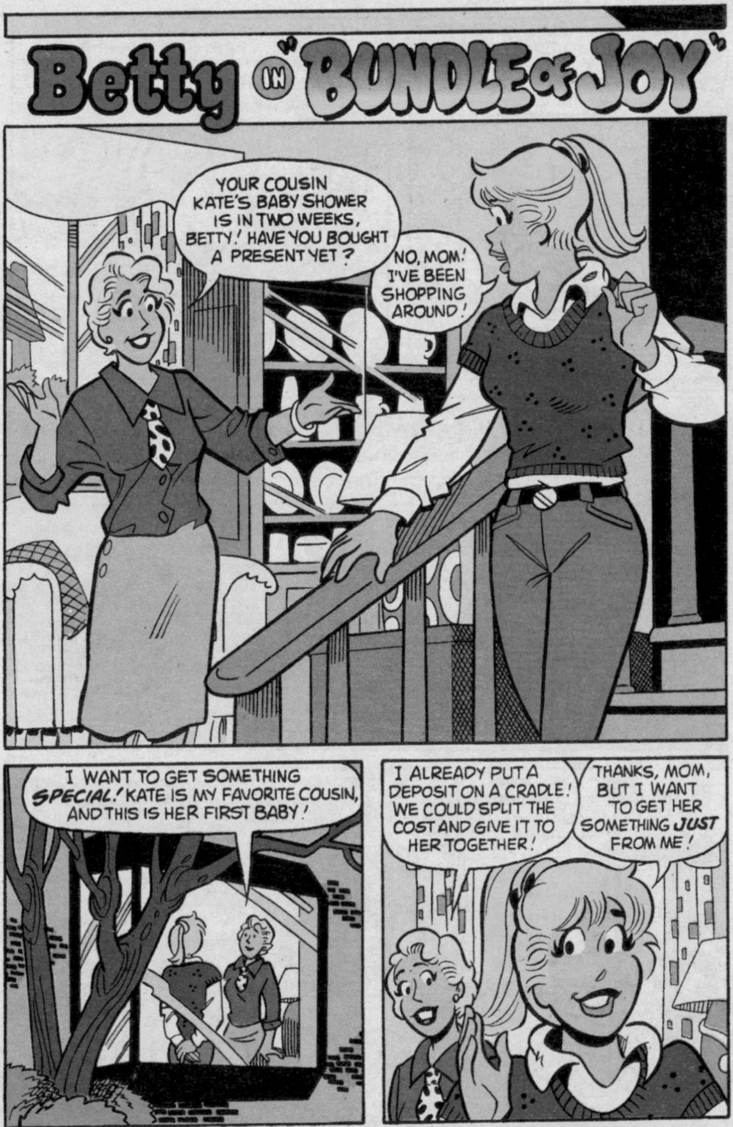

Betty IN "BUNDLE of JOY"
YOUR COUSIN KATE'S BABY SHOWER IS IN TWO WEEKS, BETTY! HAVE YOU BOUGHT A PRESENT YET?
NO, MOM! I'VE BEEN SHOPPING AROUND!
I WANT TO GET SOMETHING SPECIAL! KATE IS MY FAVORITE COUSIN, AND THIS IS HER FIRST BABY!
I ALREADY PUT A DEPOSIT ON A CRADLE! WE COULD SPLIT THE COST AND GIVE IT TO HER TOGETHER!
THANKS, MOM, BUT I WANT TO GET HER SOMETHING JUST FROM ME!

Script: Mike Pellowski / Pencils: Stan Goldberg / Inks: John Lowe / Letters: Bill Yoshida

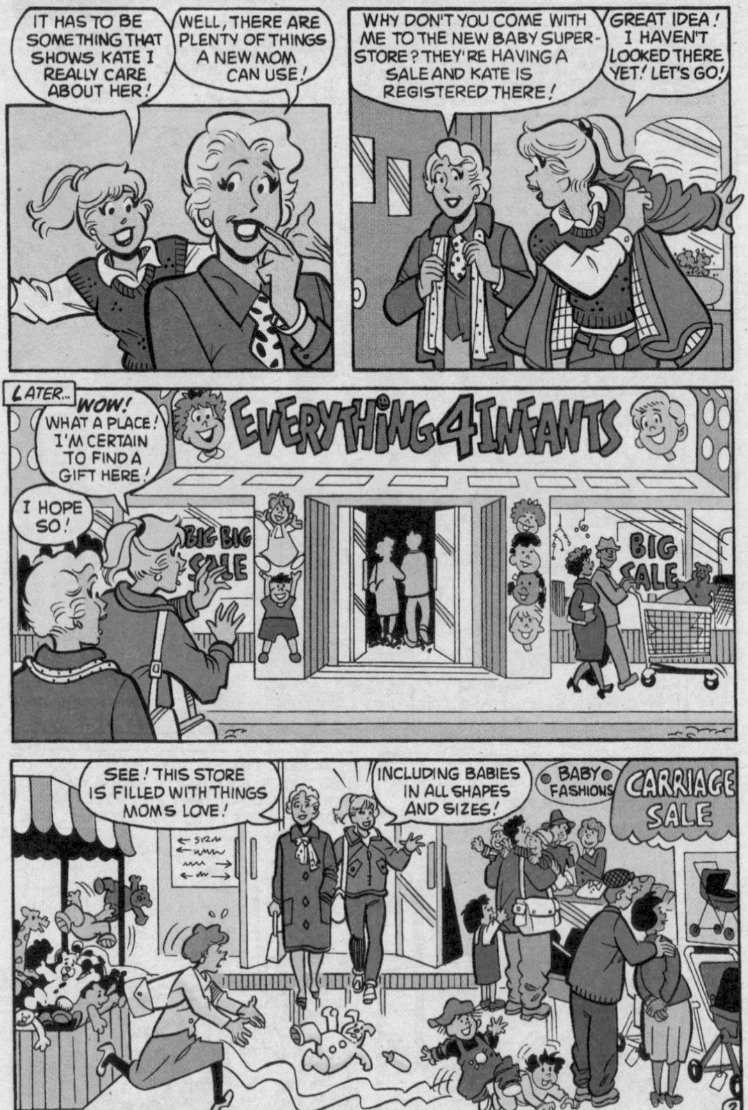

IT HAS TO BE SOMETHING THAT SHOWS KATE I REALLY CARE ABOUT HER!
WELL, THERE ARE PLENTY OF THINGS A NEW MOM CAN USE!
WHY DON'T YOU COME WITH ME TO THE NEW BABY SUPER-STORE? THEY'RE HAVING A SALE AND KATE IS REGISTERED THERE!
GREAT IDEA! I HAVEN'T LOOKED THERE YET! LET'S GO!
LATER...
EVERYTHING 4 INFANTS
WOW! WHAT A PLACE! I'M CERTAIN TO FIND A GIFT HERE!
I HOPE SO!
BIG BIG SALE
BIG SALE
SEE! THIS STORE IS FILLED WITH THINGS MOMS LOVE!
INCLUDING BABIES IN ALL SHAPES AND SIZES!
BABY FASHIONS
CARRIAGE SALE
2

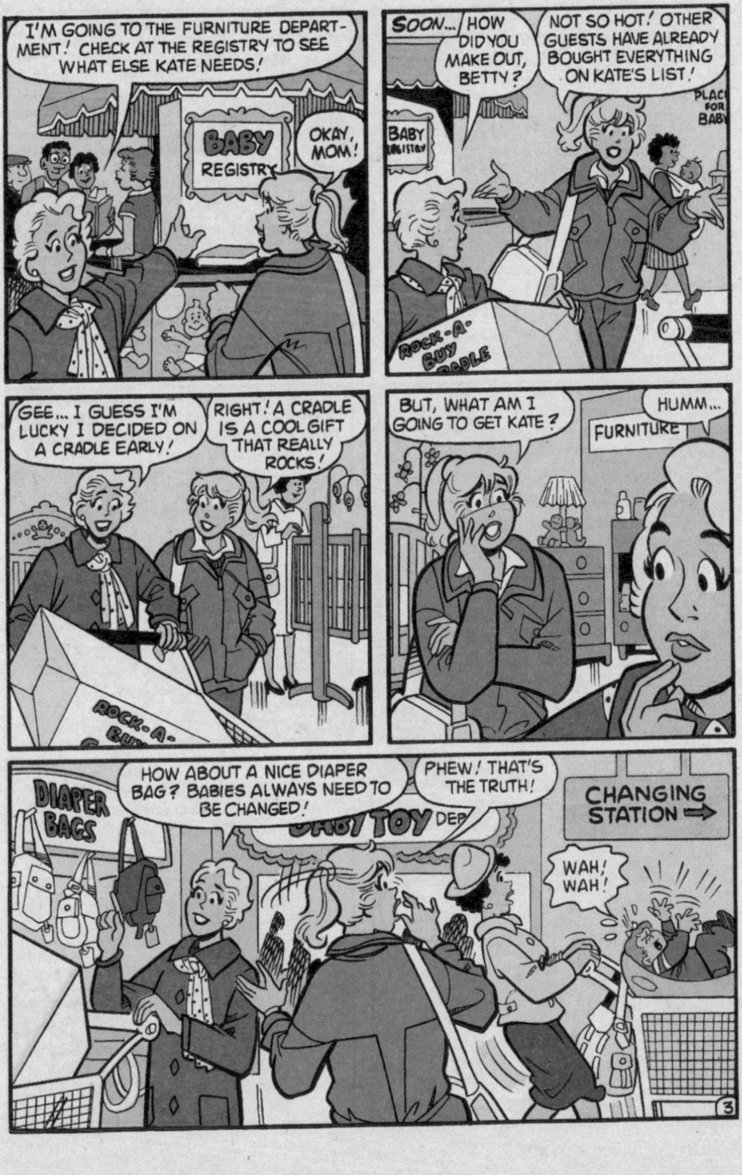

I'M GOING TO THE FURNITURE DEPARTMENT! CHECK AT THE REGISTRY TO SEE WHAT ELSE KATE NEEDS!
BABY REGISTRY
OKAY, MOM!
SOON...
HOW DID YOU MAKE OUT, BETTY?
NOT SO HOT! OTHER GUESTS HAVE ALREADY BOUGHT EVERYTHING ON KATE'S LIST!
BABY REGISTRY
GEE... I GUESS I'M LUCKY I DECIDED ON A CRADLE EARLY!
RIGHT! A CRADLE IS A COOL GIFT THAT REALLY ROCKS!
BUT, WHAT AM I GOING TO GET KATE?
HUMM...
FURNITURE
HOW ABOUT A NICE DIAPER BAG? BABIES ALWAYS NEED TO BE CHANGED!
PHEW! THAT'S THE TRUTH!
DIAPER BAGS
CHANGING STATION
WAH! WAH!

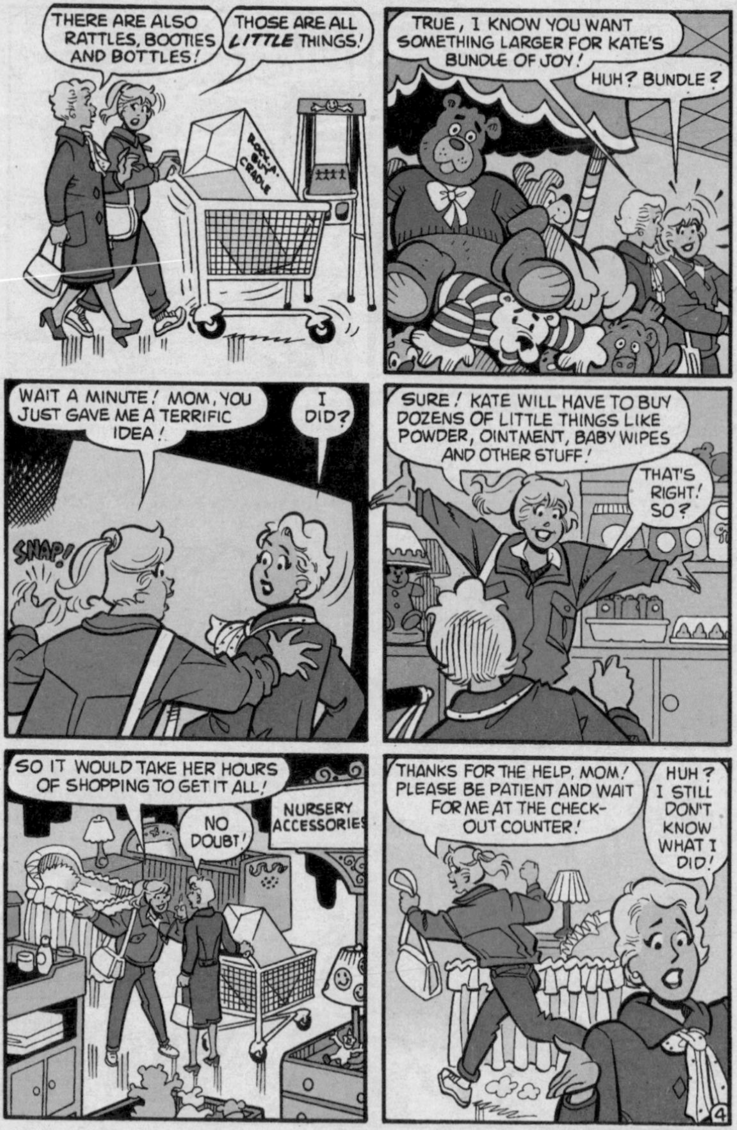
THERE ARE ALSO RATTLES, BOOTIES AND BOTTLES!
THOSE ARE ALL LITTLE THINGS!
ROCK-A-BYE CRADLE
TRUE, I KNOW YOU WANT SOMETHING LARGER FOR KATE'S BUNDLE OF JOY!
HUH? BUNDLE?
WAIT A MINUTE! MOM, YOU JUST GAVE ME A TERRIFIC IDEA!
I DID?
SNAP!
SURE! KATE WILL HAVE TO BUY DOZENS OF LITTLE THINGS LIKE POWDER, OINTMENT, BABY WIPES AND OTHER STUFF!
THAT'S RIGHT! SO?
SO IT WOULD TAKE HER HOURS OF SHOPPING TO GET IT ALL!
NO DOUBT!
NURSERY ACCESSORIES
THANKS FOR THE HELP, MOM! PLEASE BE PATIENT AND WAIT FOR ME AT THE CHECK-OUT COUNTER!
HUH? I STILL DON'T KNOW WHAT I DID!
4

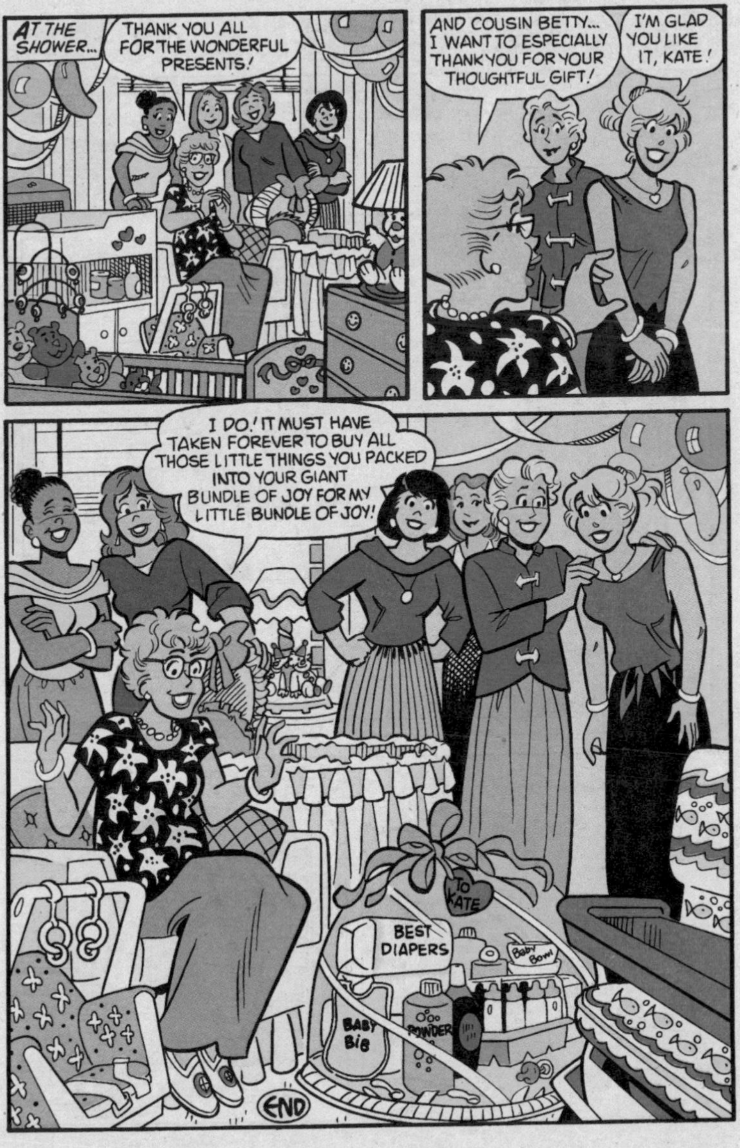
AT THE SHOWER...
THANK YOU ALL FOR THE WONDERFUL PRESENTS!
AND COUSIN BETTY... I WANT TO ESPECIALLY THANK YOU FOR YOUR THOUGHTFUL GIFT!
I'M GLAD YOU LIKE IT, KATE!
I DO! IT MUST HAVE TAKEN FOREVER TO BUY ALL THOSE LITTLE THINGS YOU PACKED INTO YOUR GIANT BUNDLE OF JOY FOR MY LITTLE BUNDLE OF JOY!
TO KATE
BEST DIAPERS
BABY BOWL
BABY BIB
POWDER
END

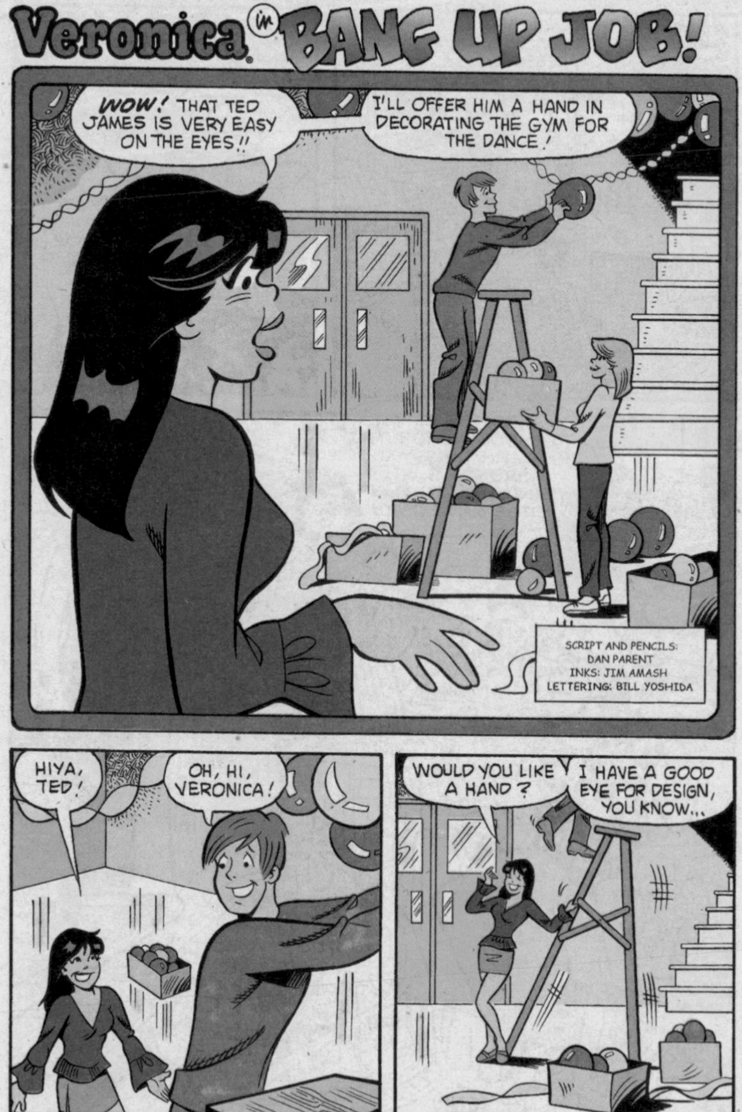
Veronica in BANG UP JOB!
WOW! THAT TED JAMES IS VERY EASY ON THE EYES!!
I'LL OFFER HIM A HAND IN DECORATING THE GYM FOR THE DANCE!
SCRIPT AND PENCILS: DAN PARENT
INKS: JIM AMASH
LETTERING: BILL YOSHIDA
HIYA, TED!
OH, HI, VERONICA!
WOULD YOU LIKE A HAND?
I HAVE A GOOD EYE FOR DESIGN, YOU KNOW...

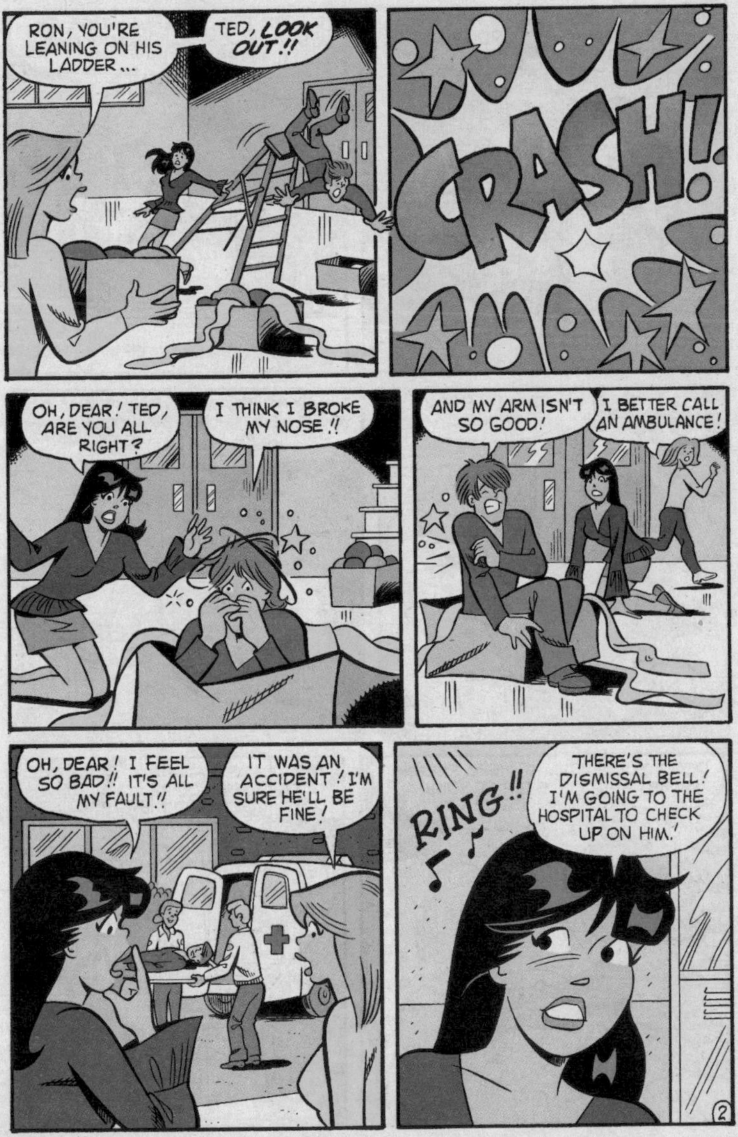

RON, YOU'RE LEANING ON HIS LADDER...
TED, LOOK OUT.!!
CRASH!
OH, DEAR! TED, ARE YOU ALL RIGHT?
I THINK I BROKE MY NOSE!!
AND MY ARM ISN'T SO GOOD!
I BETTER CALL AN AMBULANCE!
OH, DEAR! I FEEL SO BAD!! IT'S ALL MY FAULT!!
IT WAS AN ACCIDENT! I'M SURE HE'LL BE FINE!
RING!!
THERE'S THE DISMISSAL BELL! I'M GOING TO THE HOSPITAL TO CHECK UP ON HIM.
2

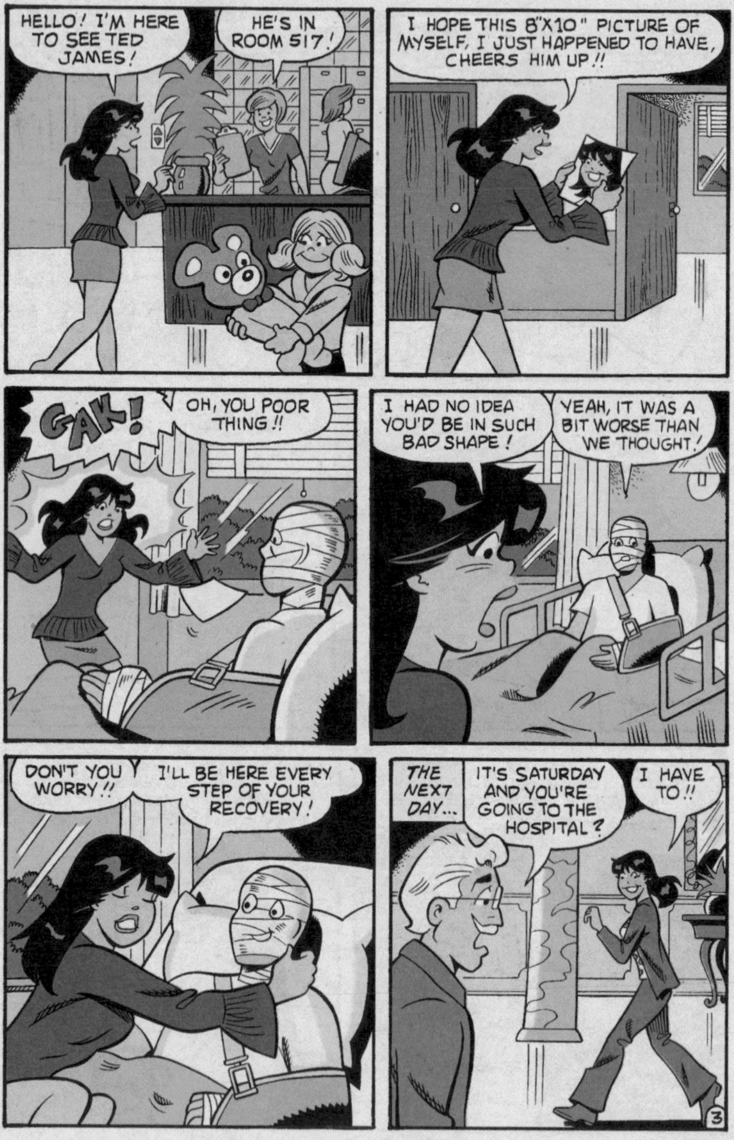
HELLO! I'M HERE TO SEE TED JAMES!
HE'S IN ROOM 517!
I HOPE THIS 8"X10" PICTURE OF MYSELF, I JUST HAPPENED TO HAVE, CHEERS HIM UP!!
GAK!
OH, YOU POOR THING!!
I HAD NO IDEA YOU'D BE IN SUCH BAD SHAPE!
YEAH, IT WAS A BIT WORSE THAN WE THOUGHT!
DON'T YOU WORRY!!
I'LL BE HERE EVERY STEP OF YOUR RECOVERY!
THE NEXT DAY...
IT'S SATURDAY AND YOU'RE GOING TO THE HOSPITAL?
I HAVE TO!!
3

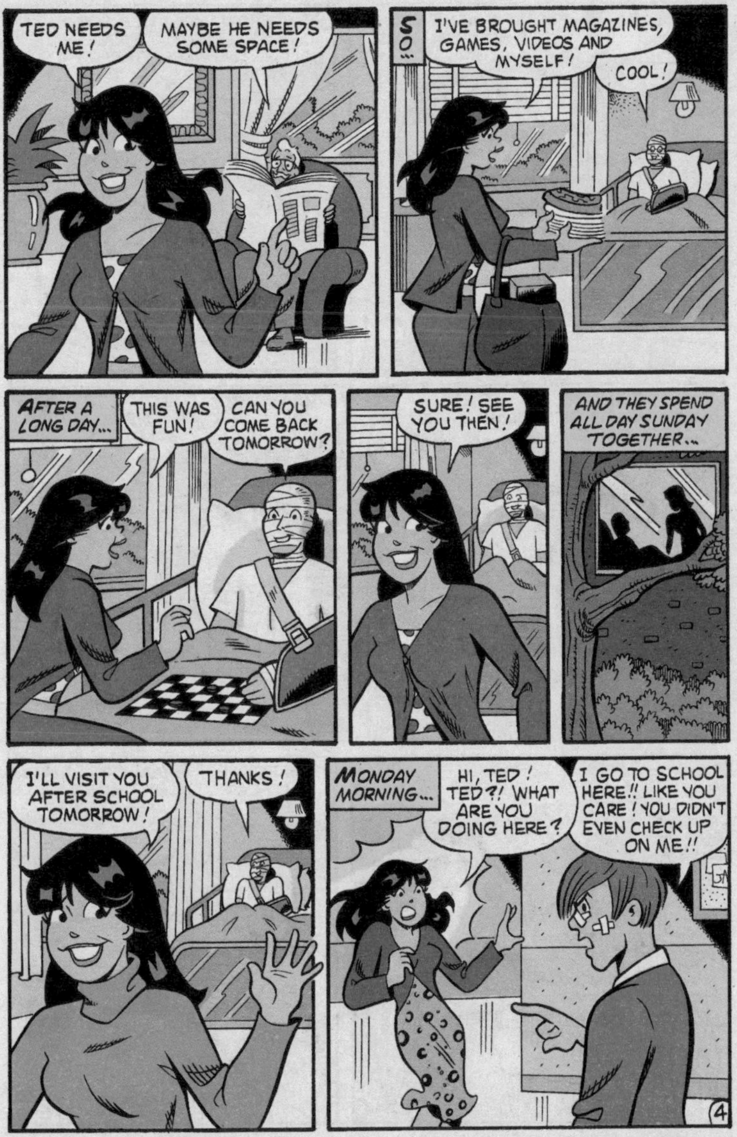
TED NEEDS ME!
MAYBE HE NEEDS SOME SPACE!
SO...
I'VE BROUGHT MAGAZINES, GAMES, VIDEOS AND MYSELF!
COOL!
AFTER A LONG DAY...
THIS WAS FUN!
CAN YOU COME BACK TOMORROW?
SURE! SEE YOU THEN!
AND THEY SPEND ALL DAY SUNDAY TOGETHER...
I'LL VISIT YOU AFTER SCHOOL TOMORROW!
THANKS!
MONDAY MORNING...
HI, TED! TED?! WHAT ARE YOU DOING HERE?
I GO TO SCHOOL HERE!! LIKE YOU CARE! YOU DIDN'T EVEN CHECK UP ON ME!!
4

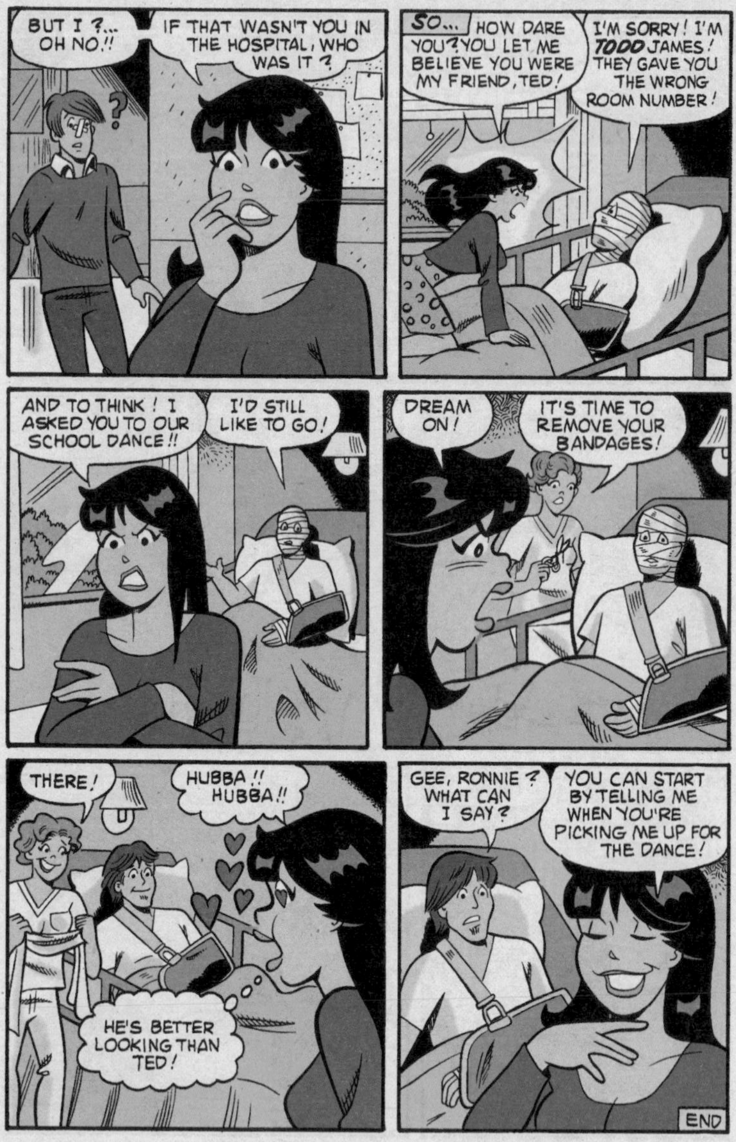
BUT I ?... OH NO.!!
IF THAT WASN'T YOU IN THE HOSPITAL, WHO WAS IT ?
SO...
HOW DARE YOU? YOU LET ME BELIEVE YOU WERE MY FRIEND, TED!
I'M SORRY! I'M TODD JAMES! THEY GAVE YOU THE WRONG ROOM NUMBER!
AND TO THINK! I ASKED YOU TO OUR SCHOOL DANCE!!
I'D STILL LIKE TO GO!
DREAM ON!
IT'S TIME TO REMOVE YOUR BANDAGES!
THERE!
HUBBA!! HUBBA!!
HE'S BETTER LOOKING THAN TED!
GEE, RONNIE? WHAT CAN I SAY?
YOU CAN START BY TELLING ME WHEN YOU'RE PICKING ME UP FOR THE DANCE!
END

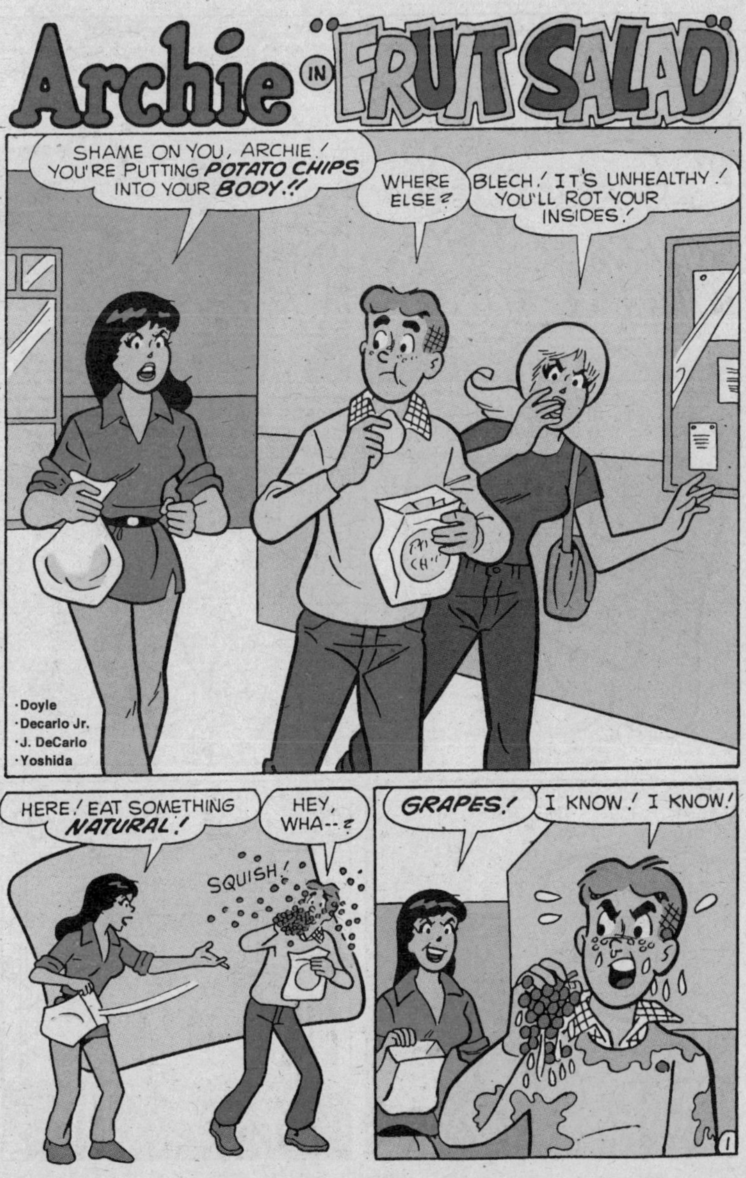
Archie IN "FRUIT SALAD"
SHAME ON YOU, ARCHIE! YOU'RE PUTTING POTATO CHIPS INTO YOUR BODY!!
WHERE ELSE?
BLECH! IT'S UNHEALTHY! YOU'LL ROT YOUR INSIDES!
·Doyle
·Decarlo Jr.
·J. DeCarlo
·Yoshida
HERE! EAT SOMETHING NATURAL!
HEY, WHA--?
SQUISH!
GRAPES!
I KNOW! I KNOW!
1

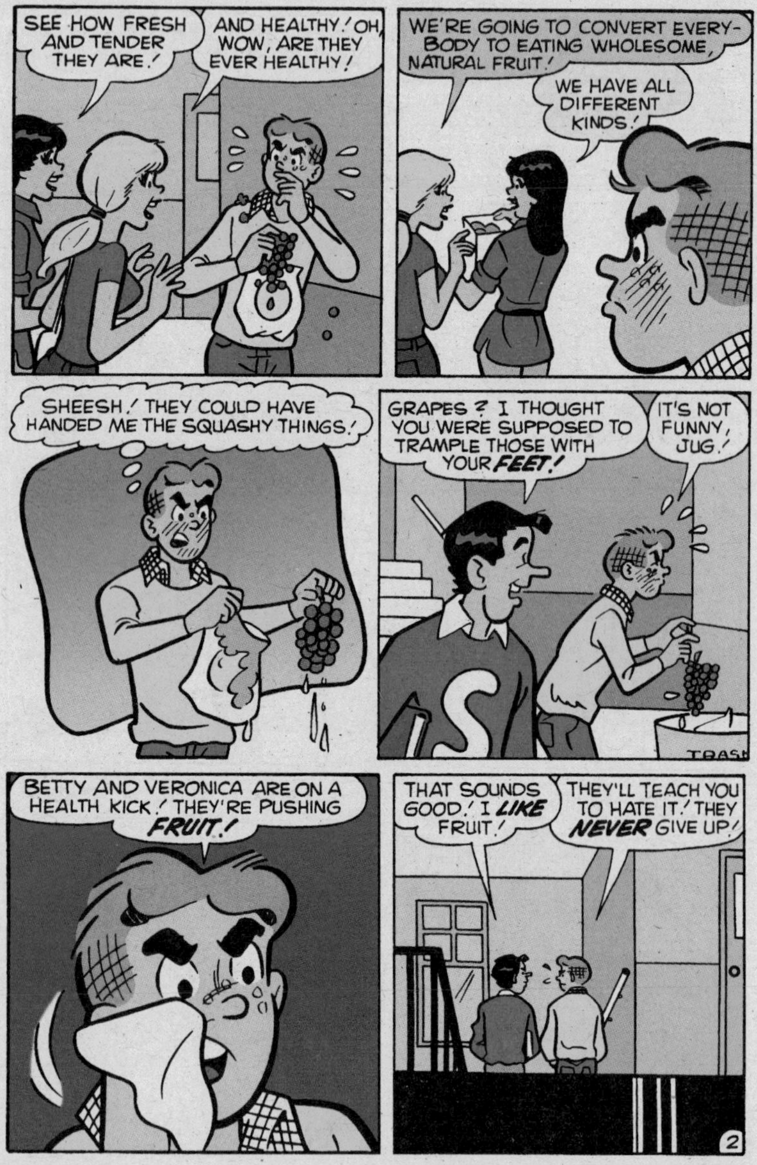
SEE HOW FRESH AND TENDER THEY ARE!
AND HEALTHY! OH, WOW, ARE THEY EVER HEALTHY!
WE'RE GOING TO CONVERT EVERY-BODY TO EATING WHOLESOME, NATURAL FRUIT!
WE HAVE ALL DIFFERENT KINDS!
SHEESH! THEY COULD HAVE HANDED ME THE SQUASHY THINGS!
GRAPES? I THOUGHT YOU WERE SUPPOSED TO TRAMPLE THOSE WITH YOUR FEET!
IT'S NOT FUNNY, JUG!
BETTY AND VERONICA ARE ON A HEALTH KICK! THEY'RE PUSHING FRUIT!
THAT SOUNDS GOOD! I LIKE FRUIT!
THEY'LL TEACH YOU TO HATE IT! THEY NEVER GIVE UP!
2

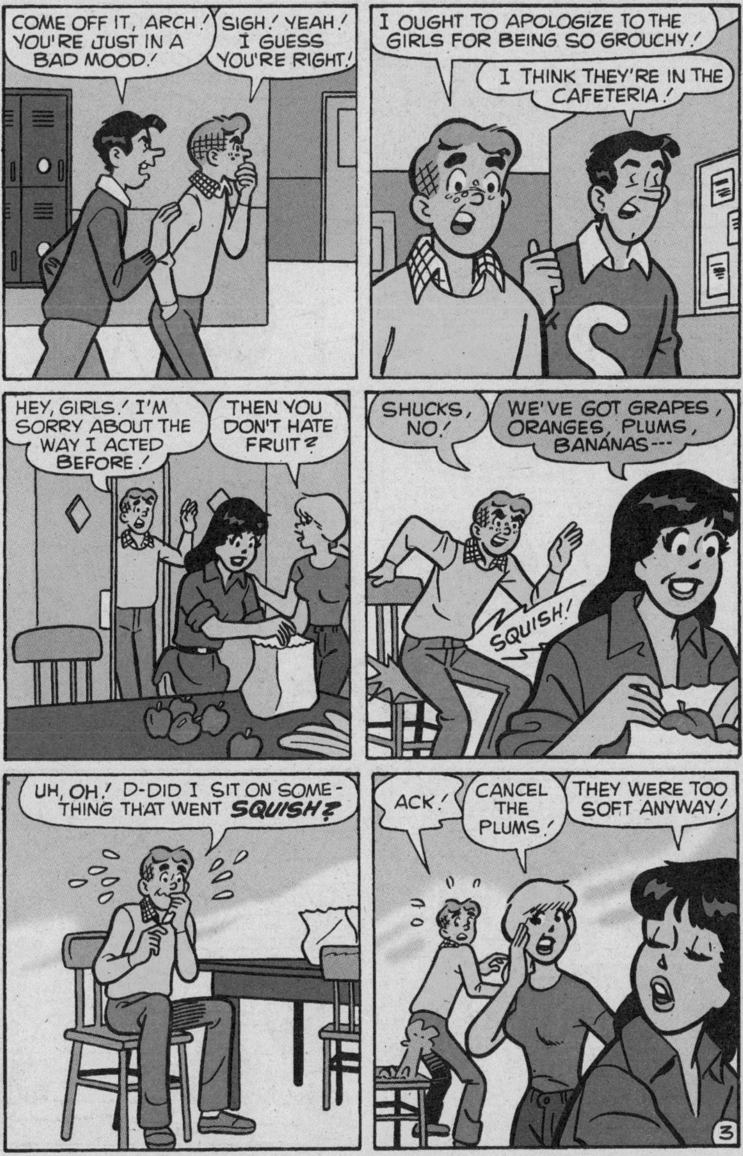
COME OFF IT, ARCH! YOU'RE JUST IN A BAD MOOD!
SIGH! YEAH! I GUESS YOU'RE RIGHT!
I OUGHT TO APOLOGIZE TO THE GIRLS FOR BEING SO GROUCHY!
I THINK THEY'RE IN THE CAFETERIA!
HEY, GIRLS! I'M SORRY ABOUT THE WAY I ACTED BEFORE!
THEN YOU DON'T HATE FRUIT?
SHUCKS, NO!
WE'VE GOT GRAPES, ORANGES, PLUMS, BANANAS---
SQUISH!
UH, OH! D-DID I SIT ON SOME-THING THAT WENT SQUISH?
ACK!
CANCEL THE PLUMS!
THEY WERE TOO SOFT ANYWAY!
3

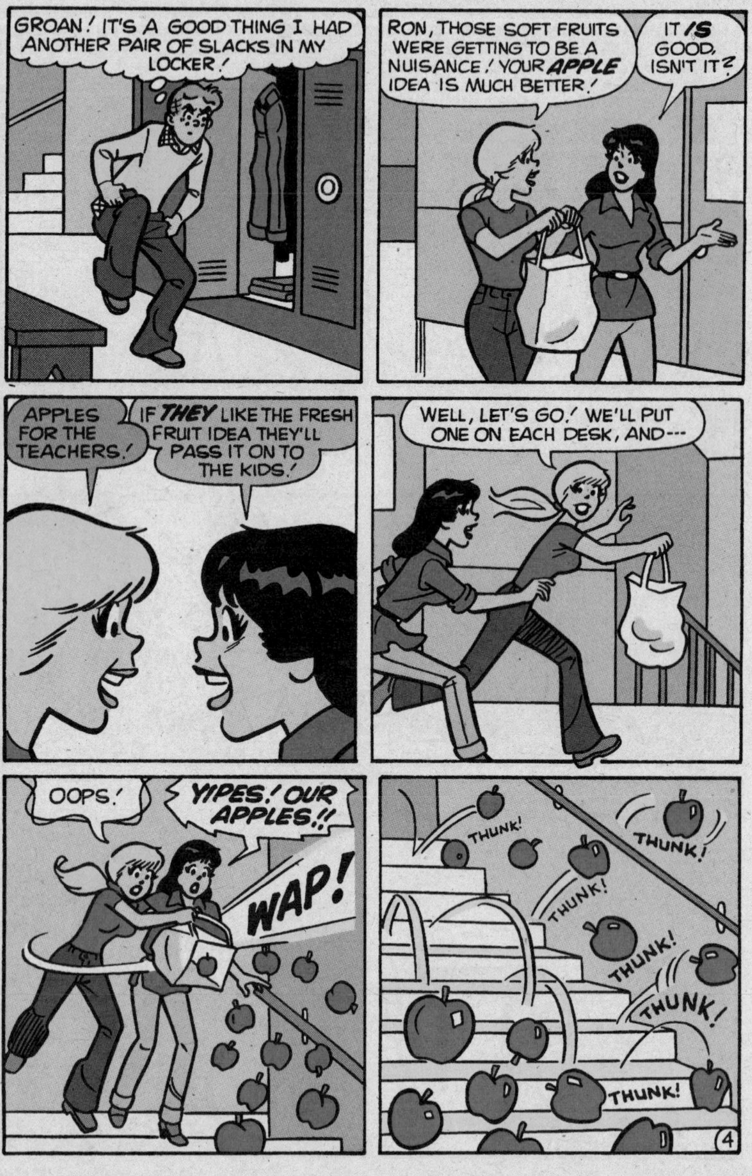
GROAN! IT'S A GOOD THING I HAD ANOTHER PAIR OF SLACKS IN MY LOCKER!
RON, THOSE SOFT FRUITS WERE GETTING TO BE A NUISANCE! YOUR APPLE IDEA IS MUCH BETTER!
IT IS GOOD, ISN'T IT?
APPLES FOR THE TEACHERS!
IF THEY LIKE THE FRESH FRUIT IDEA THEY'LL PASS IT ON TO THE KIDS!
WELL, LET'S GO! WE'LL PUT ONE ON EACH DESK, AND---
OOPS!
YIPES! OUR APPLES!!
WAP!
THUNK!
THUNK!
THUNK!
THUNK!
THUNK!
THUNK!
4

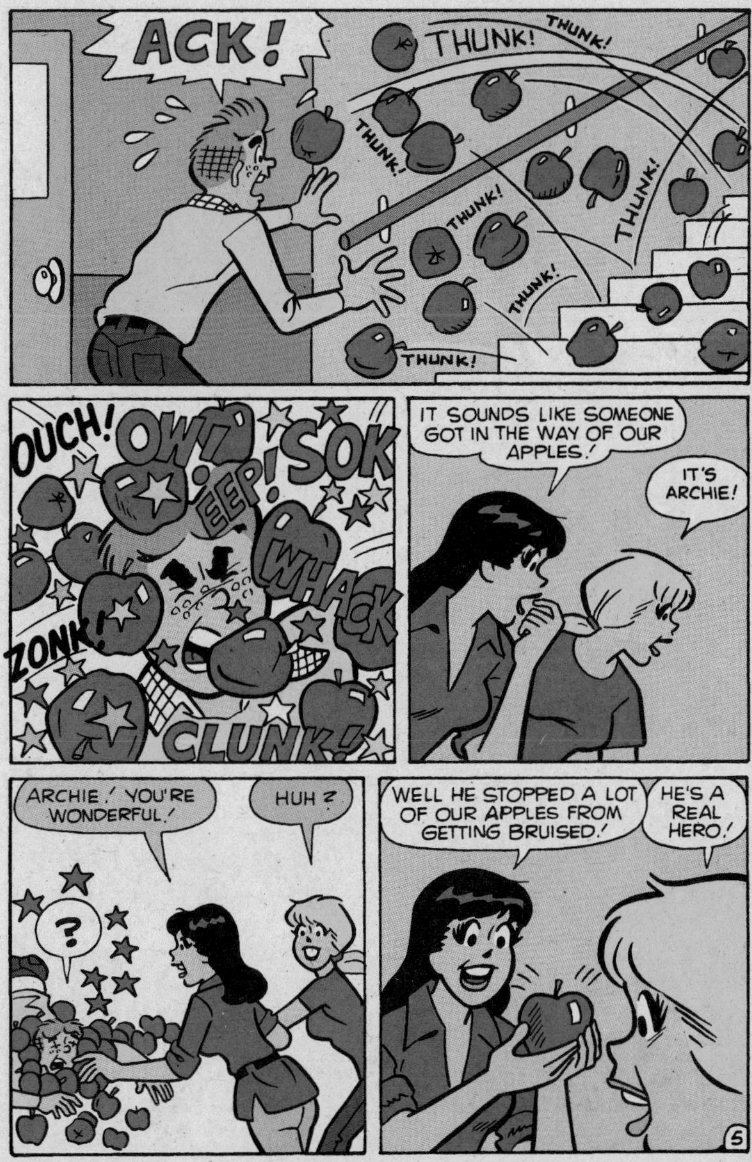

ACK!
THUNK!
THUNK!
THUNK!
THUNK!
THUNK!
THUNK!
THUNK!
OUCH!
OW!
SOK
EEP!
WHACK
ZONK!
CLUNK!
IT SOUNDS LIKE SOMEONE GOT IN THE WAY OF OUR APPLES!
IT'S ARCHIE!
ARCHIE! YOU'RE WONDERFUL!
HUH?
?
WELL HE STOPPED A LOT OF OUR APPLES FROM GETTING BRUISED!
HE'S A REAL HERO!
5

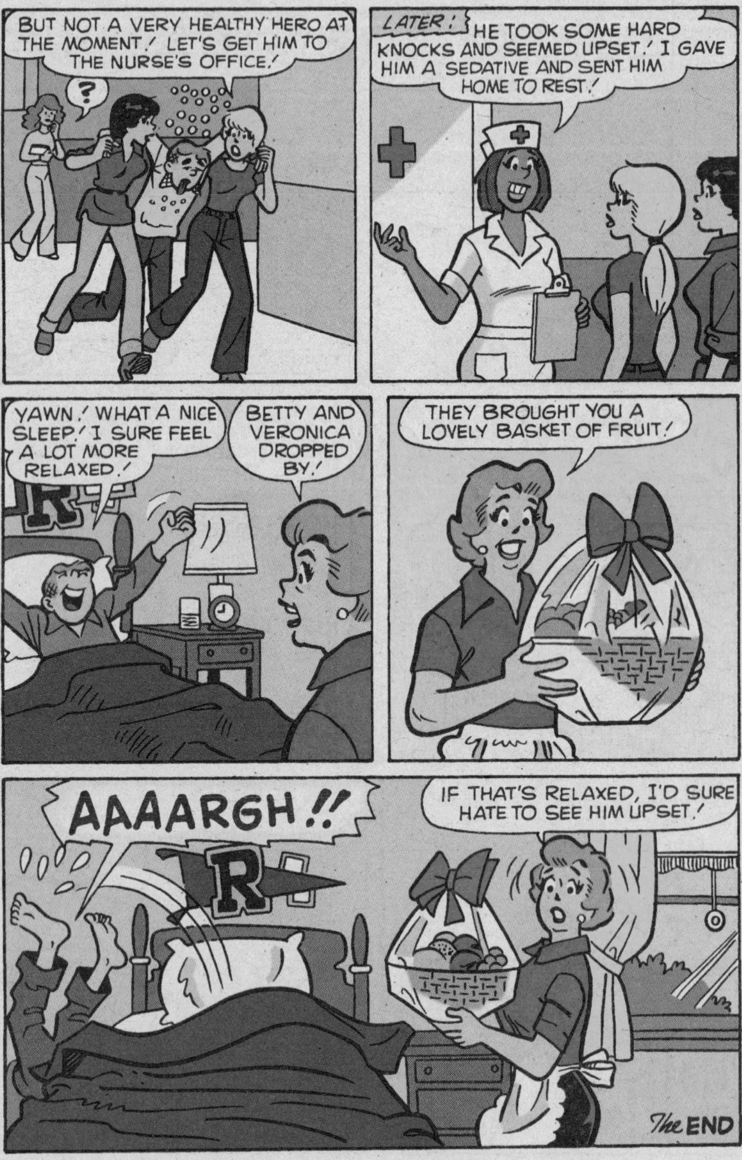

BUT NOT A VERY HEALTHY HERO AT THE MOMENT! LET'S GET HIM TO THE NURSE'S OFFICE!
?
LATER!
HE TOOK SOME HARD KNOCKS AND SEEMED UPSET! I GAVE HIM A SEDATIVE AND SENT HIM HOME TO REST!
YAWN! WHAT A NICE SLEEP! I SURE FEEL A LOT MORE RELAXED!
BETTY AND VERONICA DROPPED BY!
THEY BROUGHT YOU A LOVELY BASKET OF FRUIT!
AAAARGH!!
IF THAT'S RELAXED, I'D SURE HATE TO SEE HIM UPSET!
The END

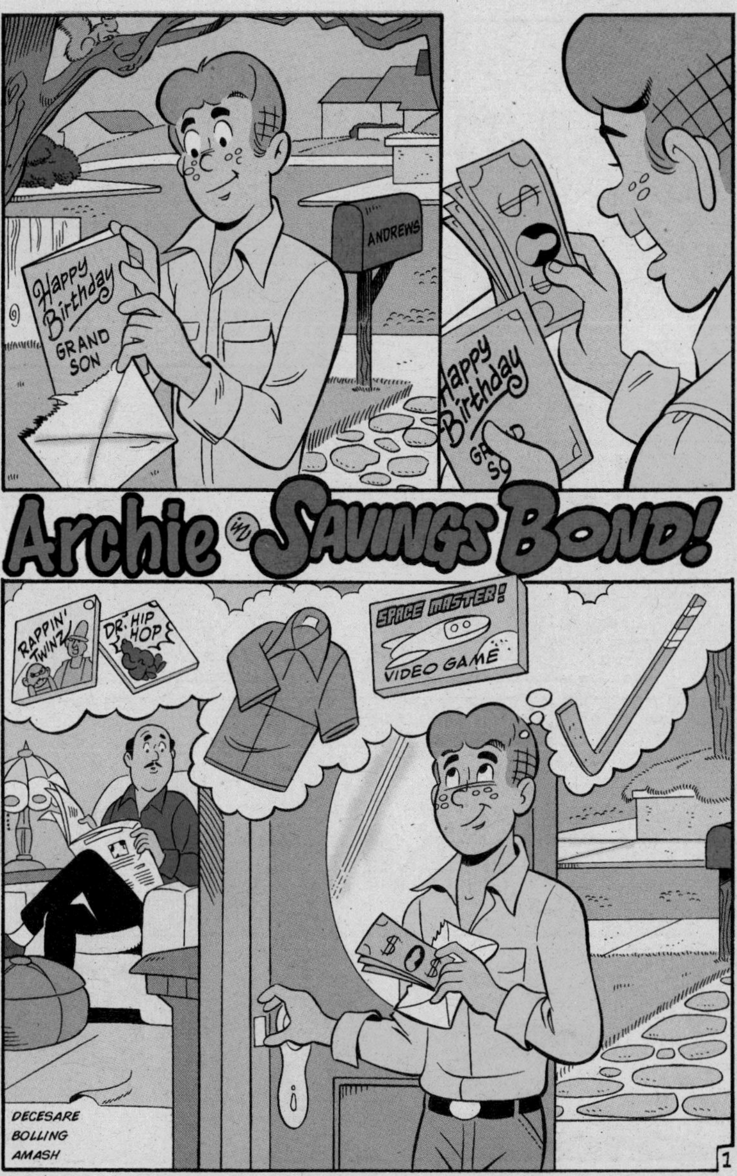

ANDREWS
Happy Birthday GRAND SON
Archie in SAVINGS BOND!
RAPPIN' TWINZ
DR. HIP HOP
SPACE MASTER!
VIDEO GAME
DECESARE
BOLLING
AMASH

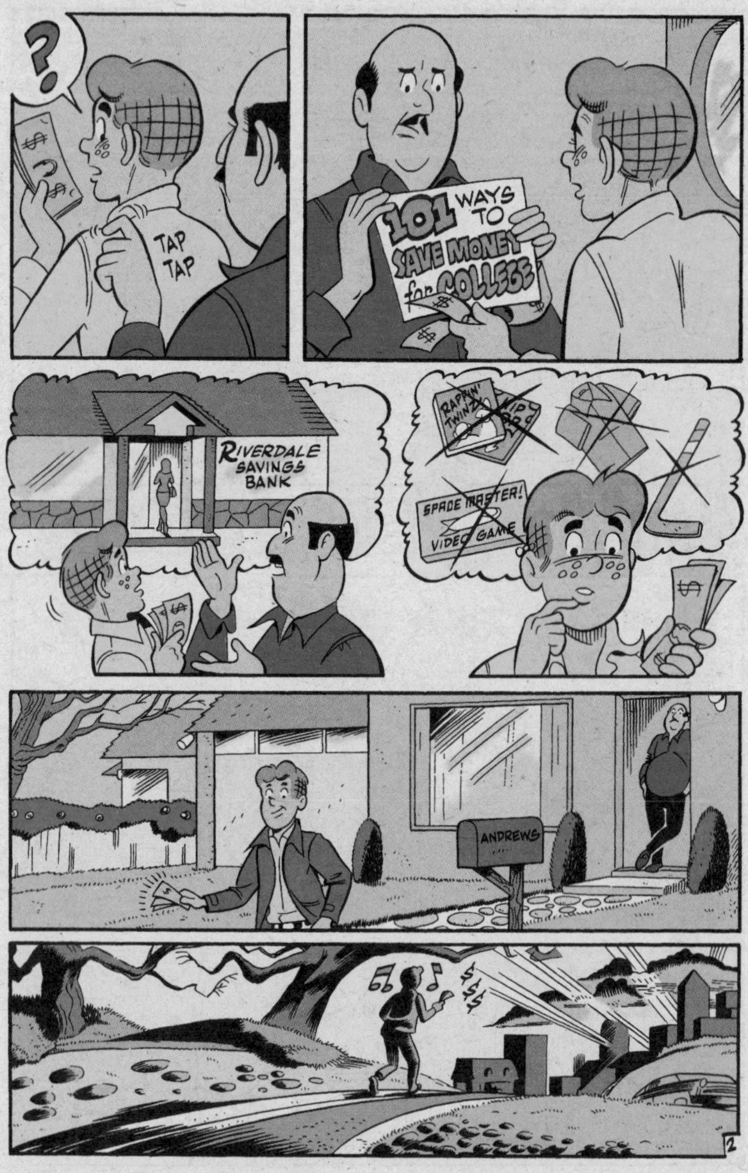
?
TAP TAP
101 WAYS TO SAVE MONEY for COLLEGE
RIVERDALE SAVINGS BANK
RAPPIN' TWINZ
SPACE MASTER! VIDEO GAME
ANDREWS
$$$
2

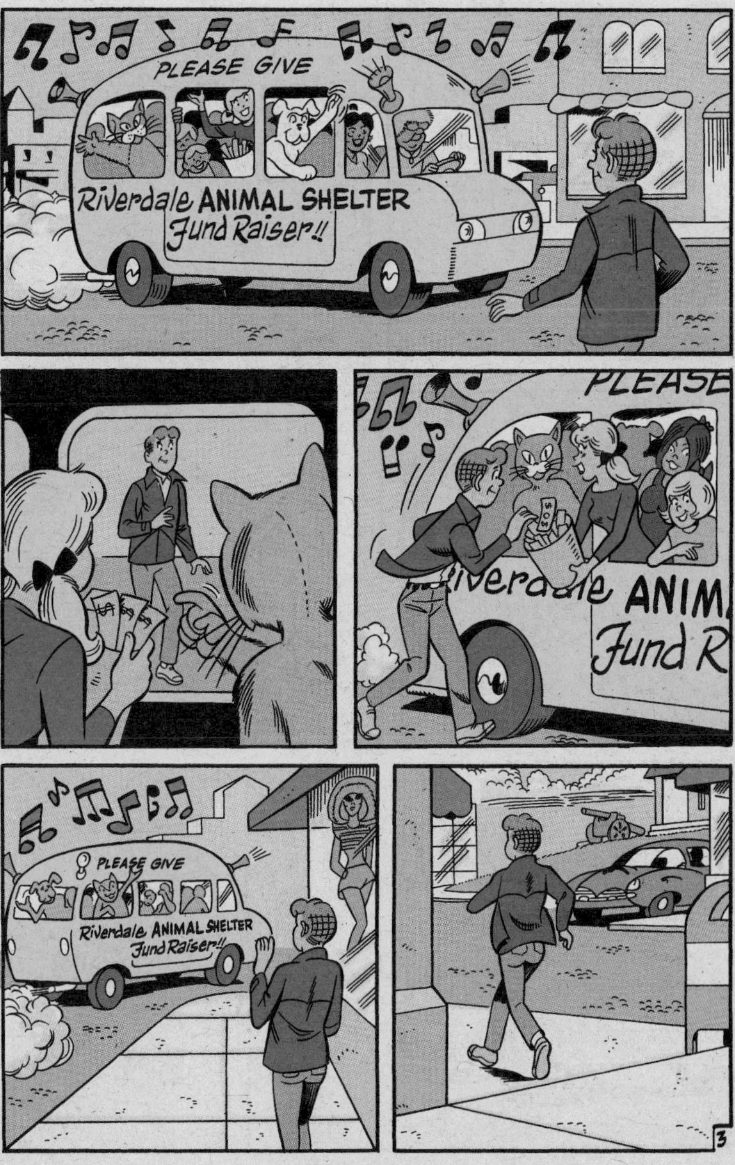
PLEASE GIVE
Riverdale ANIMAL SHELTER
Fund Raiser!!
PLEASE
Riverdale ANIM
Fund R
PLEASE GIVE
Riverdale ANIMAL SHELTER
Fund Raiser!!

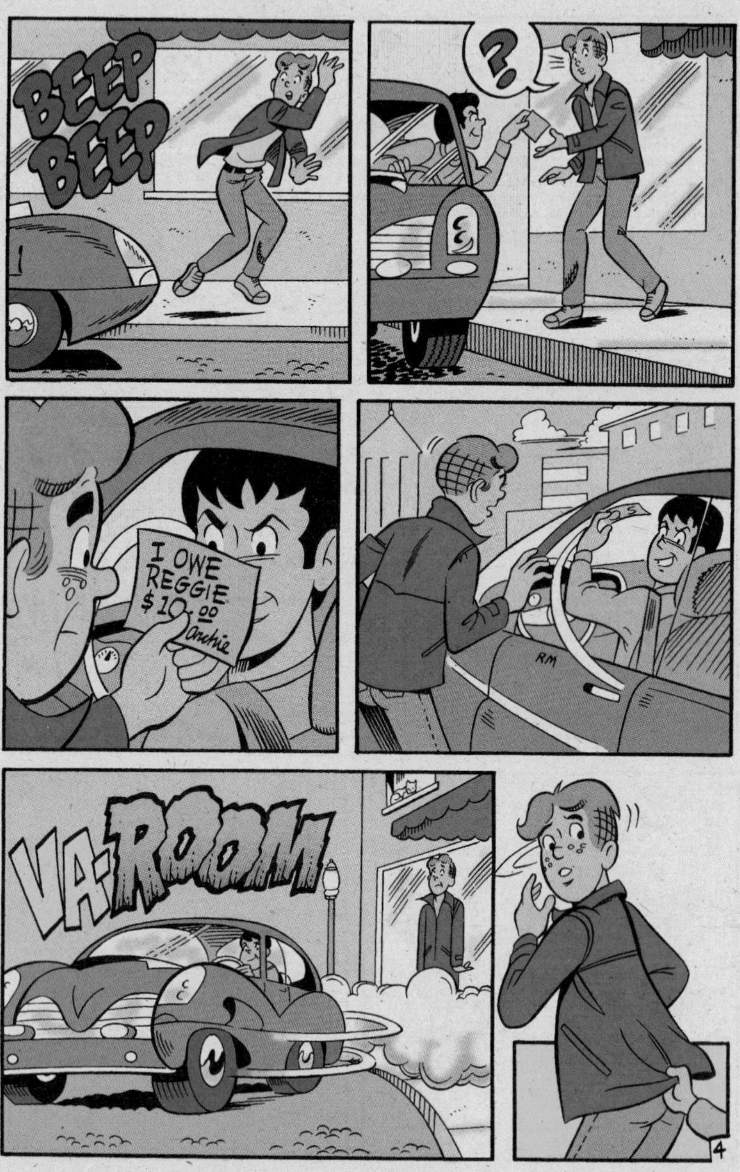
BEEP BEEP
?
I OWE REGGIE $10.00 Archie
VA-ROOM
4

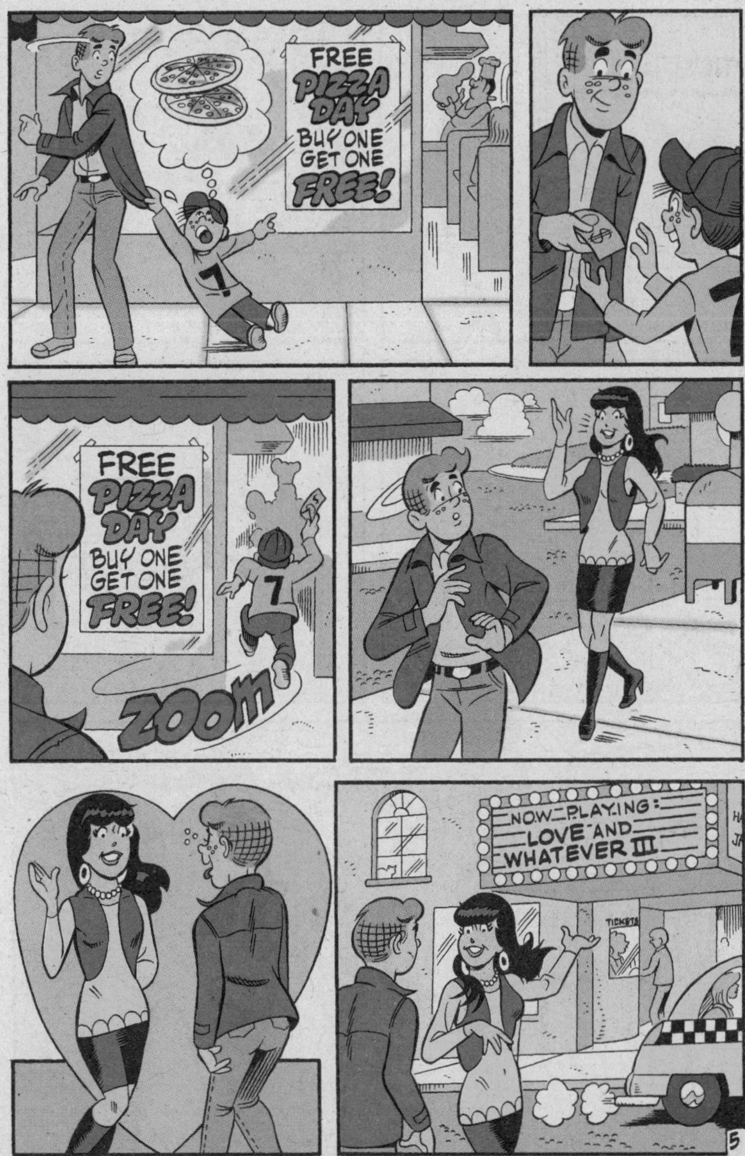
FREE
PIZZA DAY
BUY ONE GET ONE
FREE!
FREE
PIZZA DAY
BUY ONE GET ONE
FREE!
ZOOM
NOW PLAYING:
LOVE AND WHATEVER III
TICKETS

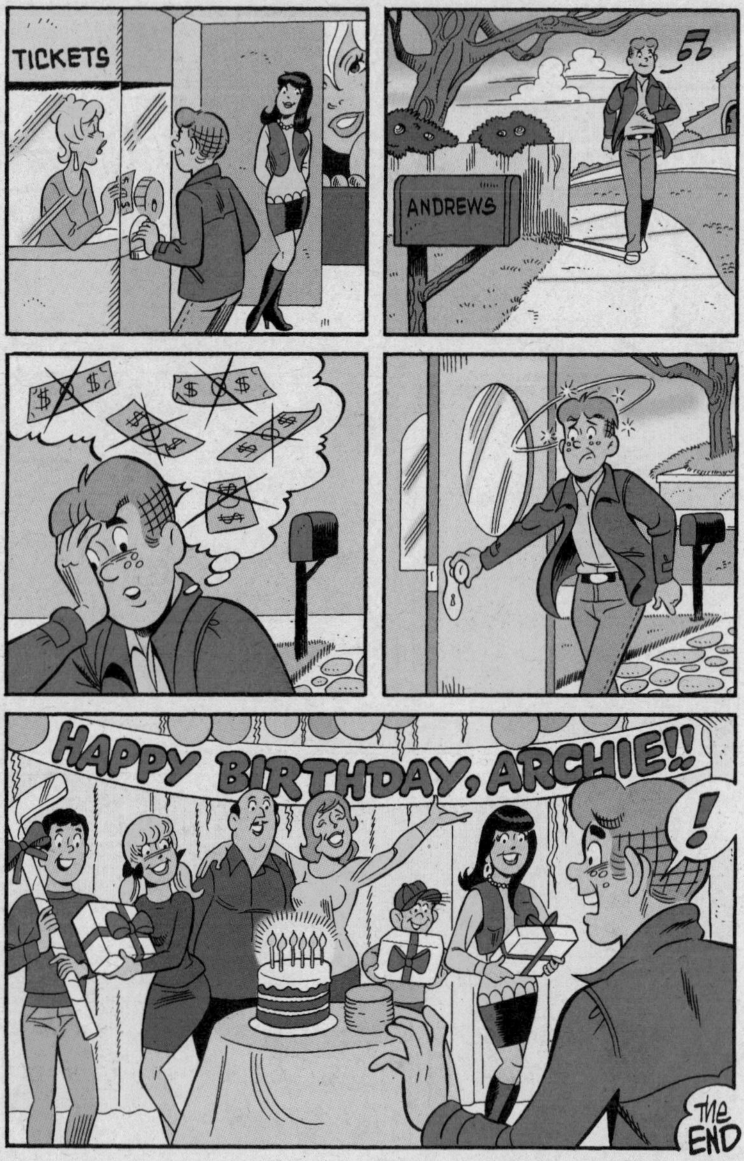
TICKETS
ANDREWS
HAPPY BIRTHDAY, ARCHIE!!
!
THE END

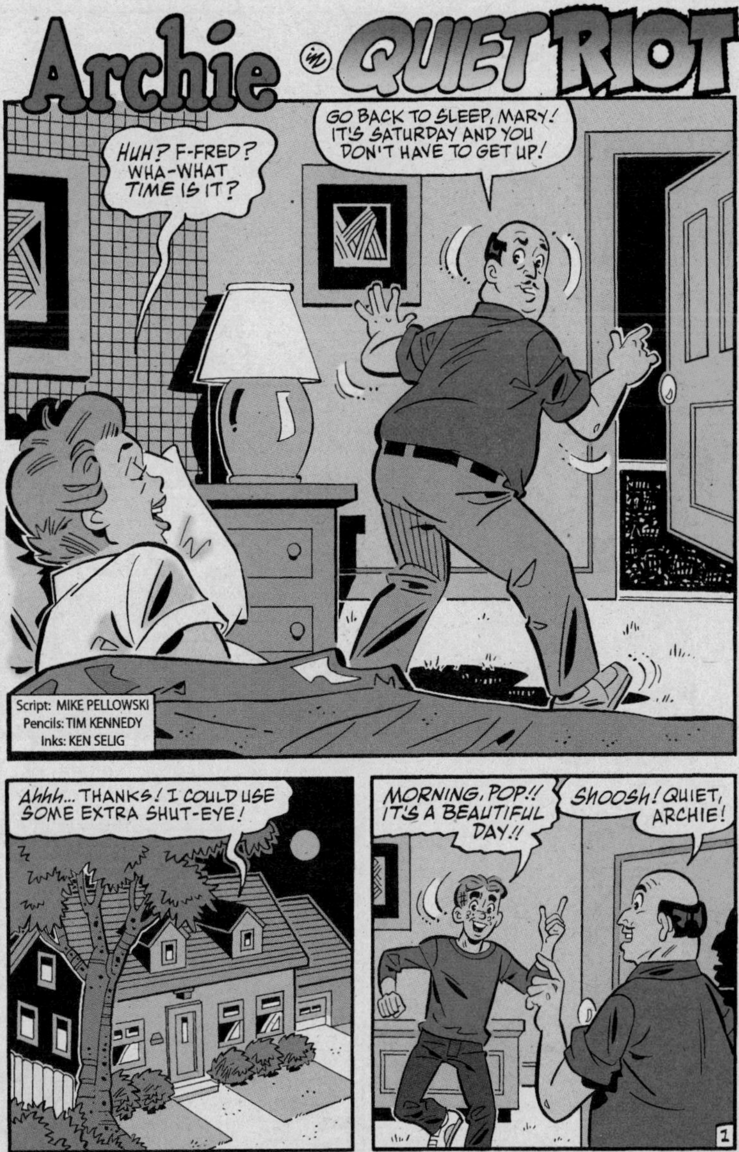
Archie in QUIET RIOT
HUH? F-FRED? WHA-WHAT TIME IS IT?
GO BACK TO SLEEP, MARY! IT'S SATURDAY AND YOU DON'T HAVE TO GET UP!
Script: MIKE PELLOWSKI
Pencils: TIM KENNEDY
Inks: KEN SELIG
Ahhh... THANKS! I COULD USE SOME EXTRA SHUT-EYE!
MORNING, POP!! IT'S A BEAUTIFUL DAY!!
Shoosh! QUIET, ARCHIE!
1

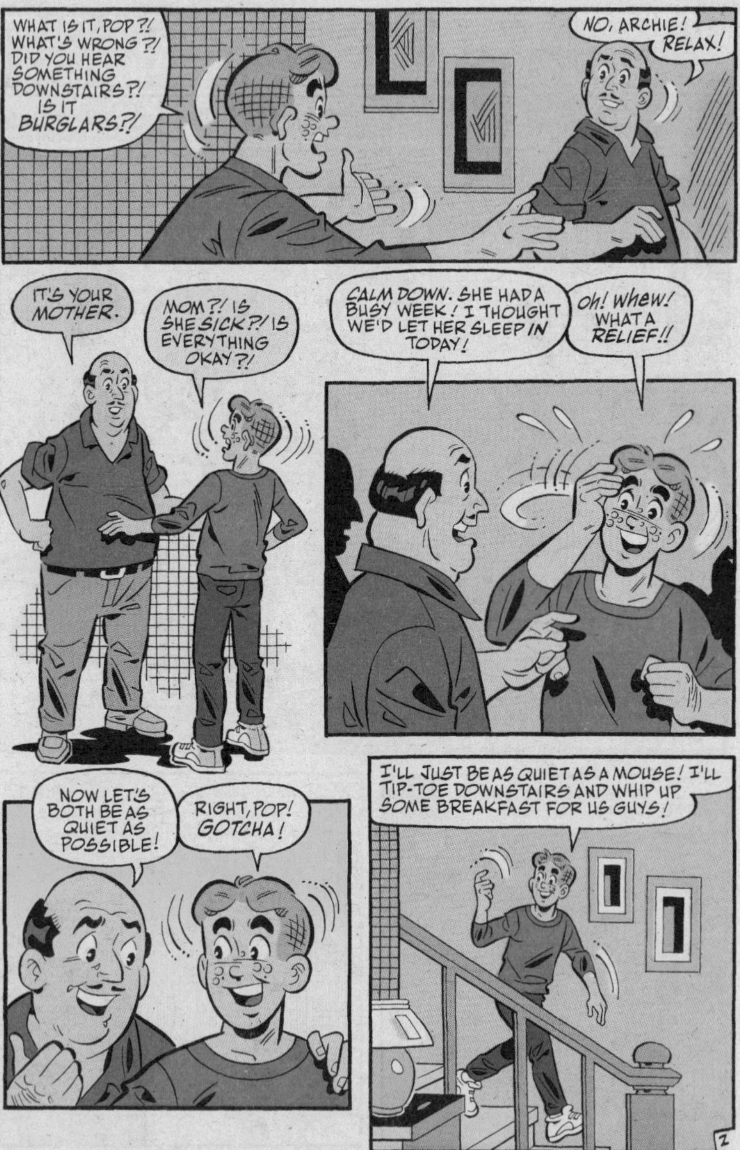
WHAT IS IT, POP?! WHAT'S WRONG?! DID YOU HEAR SOMETHING DOWNSTAIRS?! IS IT BURGLARS?!
NO, ARCHIE! RELAX!
IT'S YOUR MOTHER.
MOM?! IS SHE SICK?! IS EVERYTHING OKAY?!
CALM DOWN. SHE HAD A BUSY WEEK! I THOUGHT WE'D LET HER SLEEP IN TODAY!
Oh! whew! WHAT A RELIEF!!
NOW LET'S BOTH BE AS QUIET AS POSSIBLE!
RIGHT, POP! GOTCHA!
I'LL JUST BE AS QUIET AS A MOUSE! I'LL TIP-TOE DOWNSTAIRS AND WHIP UP SOME BREAKFAST FOR US GUYS!
2

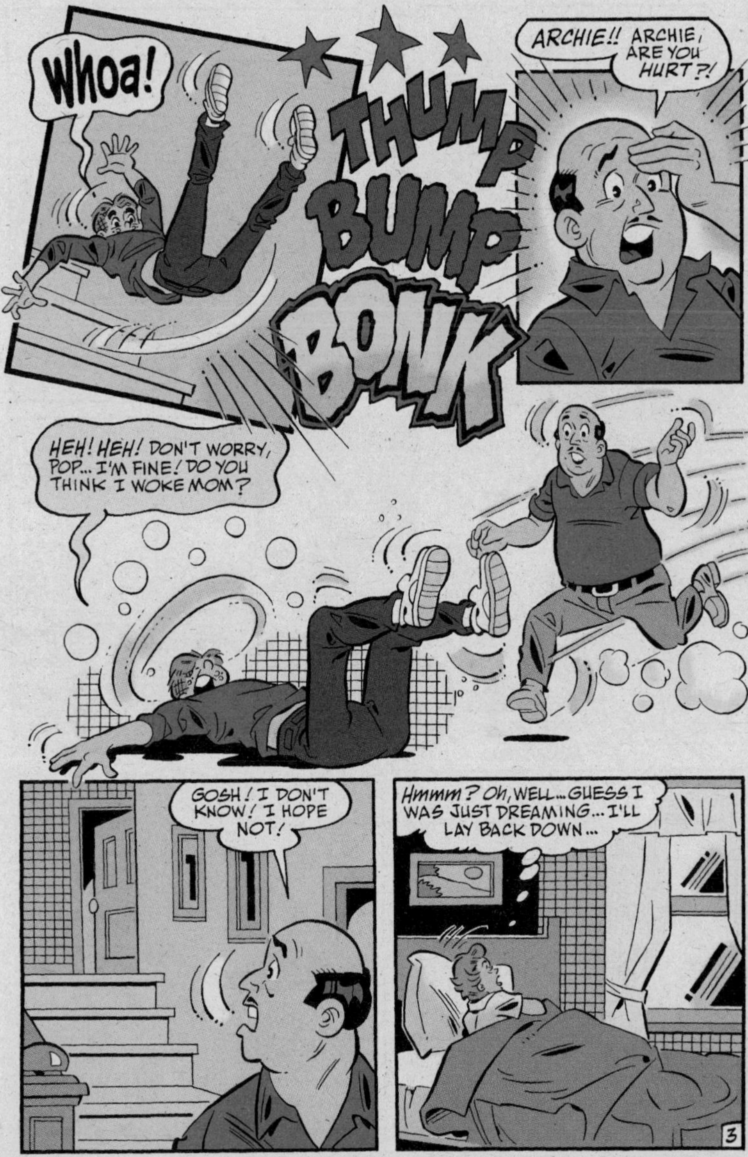
Whoa!
THUMP
BUMP
BONK
ARCHIE!! ARCHIE, ARE YOU HURT?!
HEH! HEH! DON'T WORRY, POP... I'M FINE! DO YOU THINK I WOKE MOM?
GOSH! I DON'T KNOW! I HOPE NOT!
Hmmm? Oh, WELL... GUESS I WAS JUST DREAMING... I'LL LAY BACK DOWN...
3

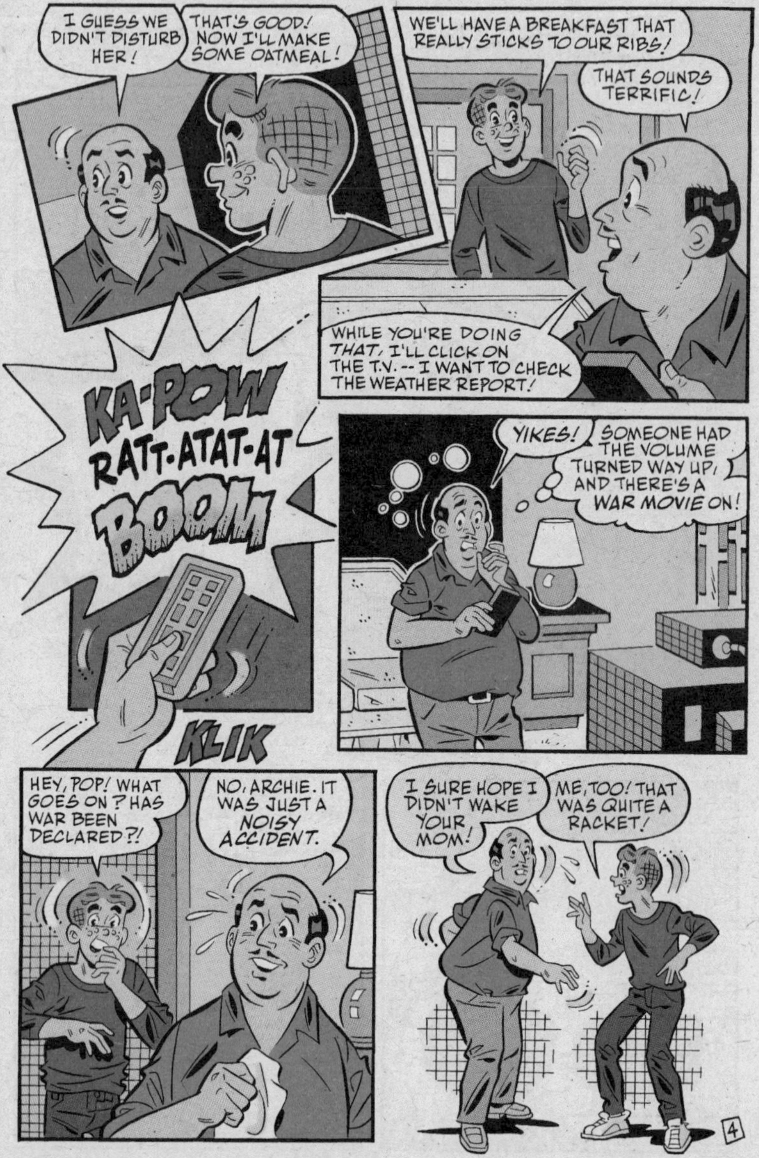
I GUESS WE DIDN'T DISTURB HER!
THAT'S GOOD! NOW I'LL MAKE SOME OATMEAL!
WE'LL HAVE A BREAKFAST THAT REALLY STICKS TO OUR RIBS!
THAT SOUNDS TERRIFIC!
WHILE YOU'RE DOING THAT, I'LL CLICK ON THE T.V. -- I WANT TO CHECK THE WEATHER REPORT!
KA-POW
RATT-ATAT-AT
BOOM
KLIK
YIKES!
SOMEONE HAD THE VOLUME TURNED WAY UP, AND THERE'S A WAR MOVIE ON!
HEY, POP! WHAT GOES ON? HAS WAR BEEN DECLARED?!
NO, ARCHIE. IT WAS JUST A NOISY ACCIDENT.
I SURE HOPE I DIDN'T WAKE YOUR MOM!
ME, TOO! THAT WAS QUITE A RACKET!
4

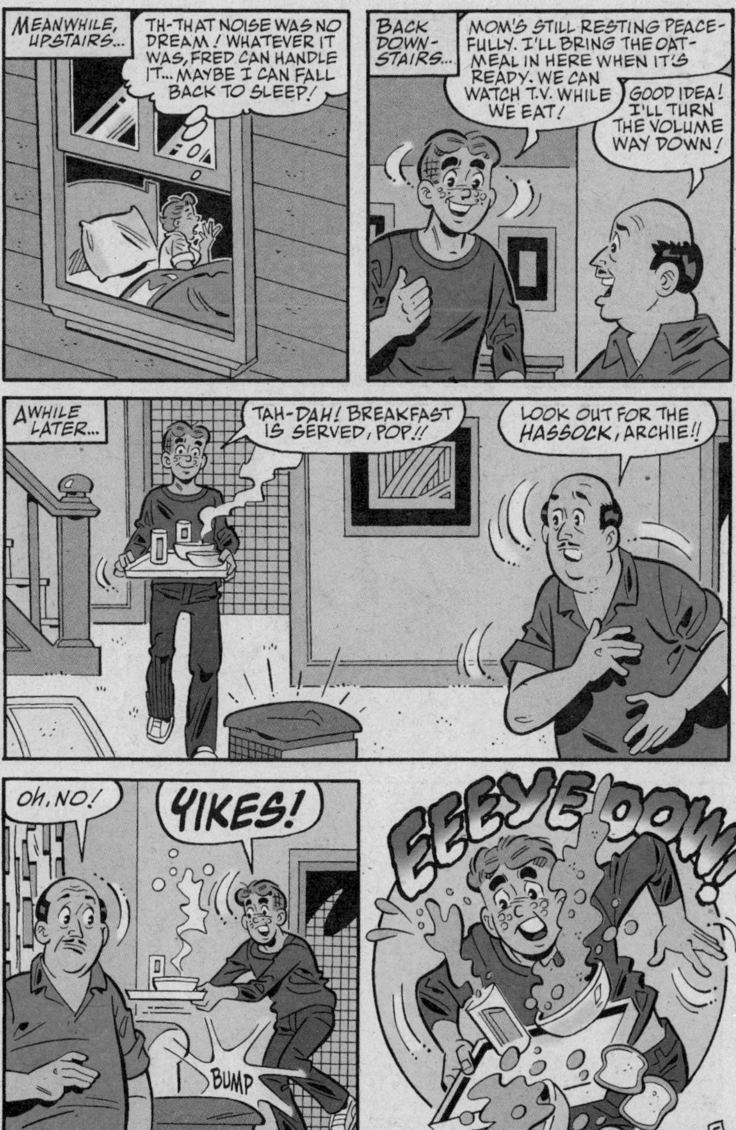

MEANWHILE, UPSTAIRS...
TH-THAT NOISE WAS NO DREAM! WHATEVER IT WAS, FRED CAN HANDLE IT... MAYBE I CAN FALL BACK TO SLEEP!
BACK DOWN-STAIRS...
MOM'S STILL RESTING PEACE-FULLY. I'LL BRING THE OAT-MEAL IN HERE WHEN IT'S READY. WE CAN WATCH T.V. WHILE WE EAT!
GOOD IDEA! I'LL TURN THE VOLUME WAY DOWN!
AWHILE LATER...
TAH-DAH! BREAKFAST IS SERVED, POP!!
LOOK OUT FOR THE HASSOCK, ARCHIE!!
Oh, NO!
YIKES!
BUMP
EEEYEOOOW!!
5

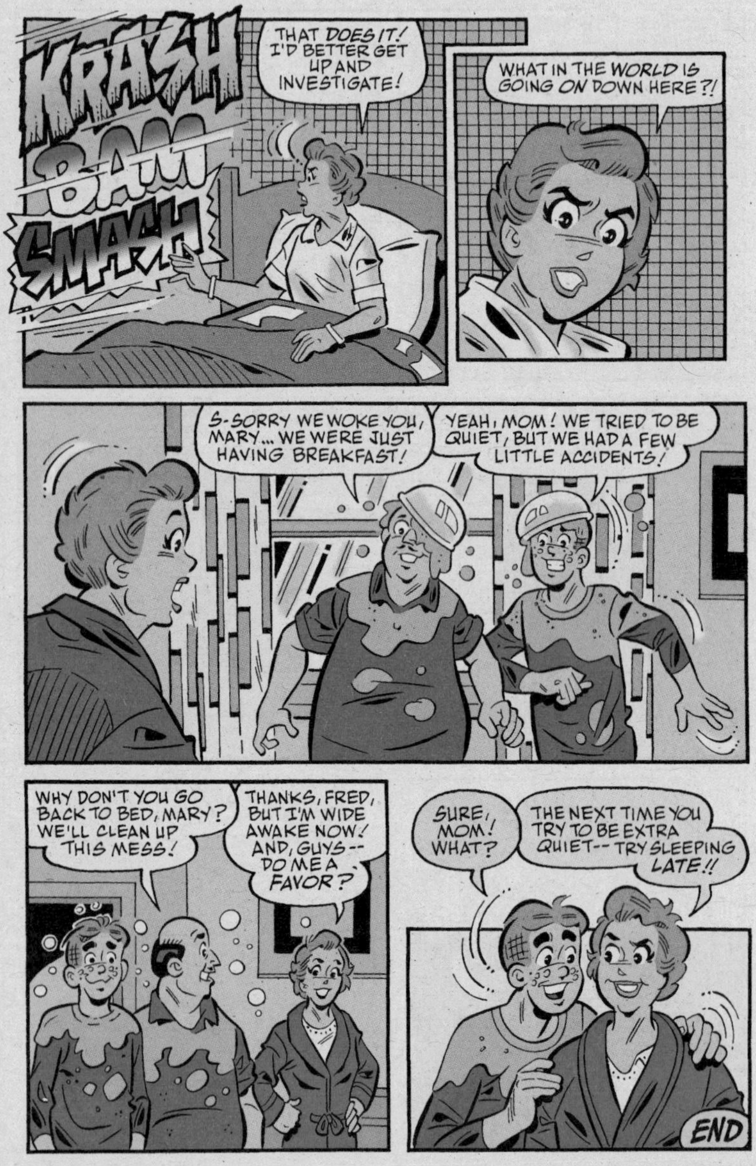
KRASH
BAM
SMASH
THAT DOES IT! I'D BETTER GET UP AND INVESTIGATE!
WHAT IN THE WORLD IS GOING ON DOWN HERE?!
S-SORRY WE WOKE YOU, MARY... WE WERE JUST HAVING BREAKFAST!
YEAH, MOM! WE TRIED TO BE QUIET, BUT WE HAD A FEW LITTLE ACCIDENTS!
WHY DON'T YOU GO BACK TO BED, MARY? WE'LL CLEAN UP THIS MESS!
THANKS, FRED, BUT I'M WIDE AWAKE NOW! AND, GUYS -- DO ME A FAVOR?
SURE, MOM! WHAT?
THE NEXT TIME YOU TRY TO BE EXTRA QUIET -- TRY SLEEPING LATE!!
END

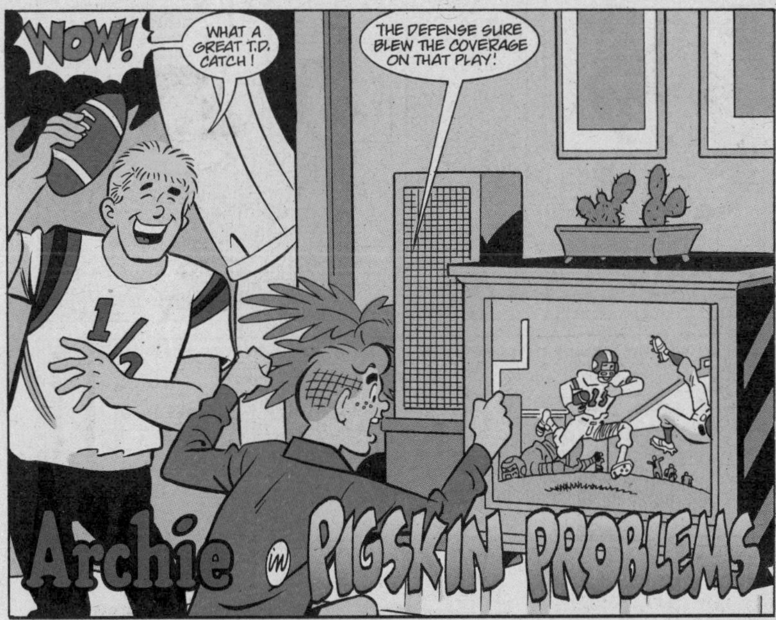
WOW!
WHAT A GREAT T.D. CATCH!
THE DEFENSE SURE BLEW THE COVERAGE ON THAT PLAY!
Archie in PIGSKIN PROBLEMS

SCRIPT: MIKE PELLOWSKI PENCILS: PAT KENNEDY INKS: BOB SMITH
COLORS: BARRY GROSSMAN LETTERS: VICKIE WILLIAMS

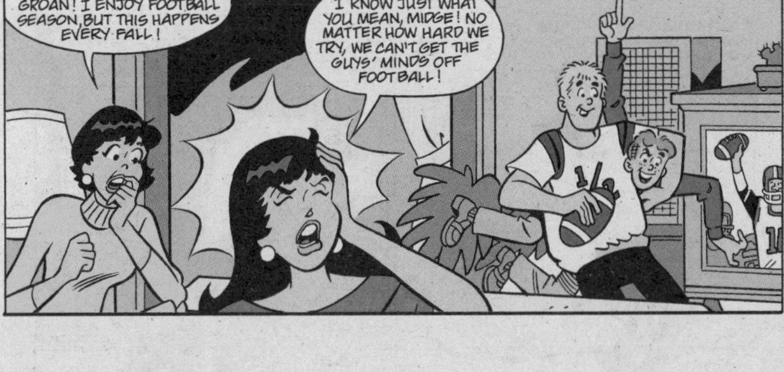
GROAN! I ENJOY FOOTBALL SEASON, BUT THIS HAPPENS EVERY FALL!
I KNOW JUST WHAT YOU MEAN, MIDGE! NO MATTER HOW HARD WE TRY, WE CAN'T GET THE GUYS' MINDS OFF FOOTBALL!

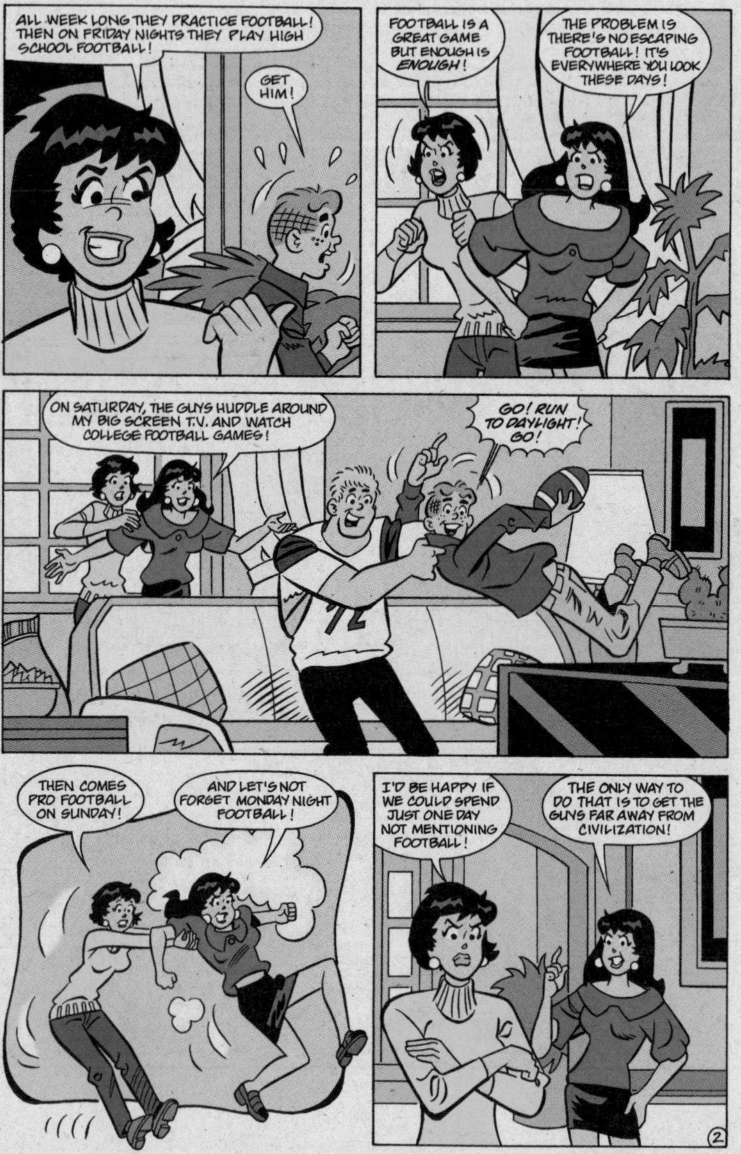

ALL WEEK LONG THEY PRACTICE FOOTBALL! THEN ON FRIDAY NIGHTS THEY PLAY HIGH SCHOOL FOOTBALL!
GET HIM!
FOOTBALL IS A GREAT GAME BUT ENOUGH IS ENOUGH!
THE PROBLEM IS THERE'S NO ESCAPING FOOTBALL! IT'S EVERYWHERE YOU LOOK THESE DAYS!
ON SATURDAY, THE GUYS HUDDLE AROUND MY BIG SCREEN T.V. AND WATCH COLLEGE FOOTBALL GAMES!
GO! RUN TO DAYLIGHT! GO!
THEN COMES PRO FOOTBALL ON SUNDAY!
AND LET'S NOT FORGET MONDAY NIGHT FOOTBALL!
I'D BE HAPPY IF WE COULD SPEND JUST ONE DAY NOT MENTIONING FOOTBALL!
THE ONLY WAY TO DO THAT IS TO GET THE GUYS FAR AWAY FROM CIVILIZATION!
2

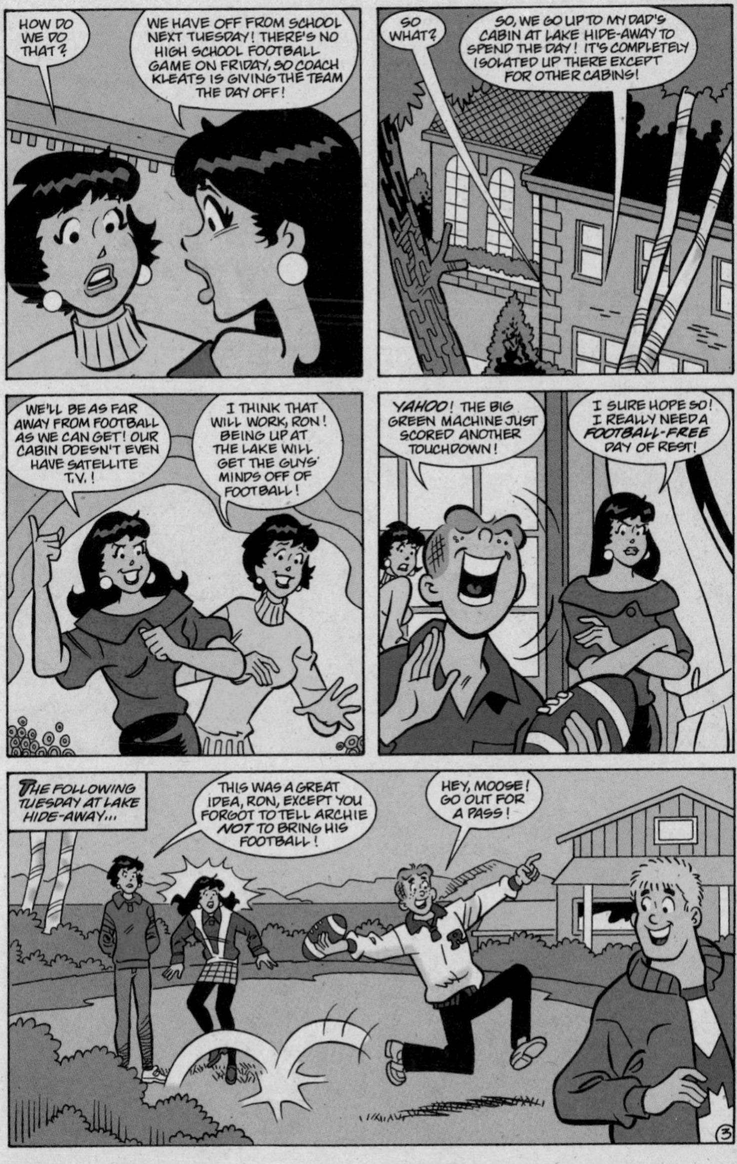

HOW DO WE DO THAT?
WE HAVE OFF FROM SCHOOL NEXT TUESDAY! THERE'S NO HIGH SCHOOL FOOTBALL GAME ON FRIDAY, SO COACH KLEATS IS GIVING THE TEAM THE DAY OFF!
SO WHAT?
SO, WE GO UP TO MY DAD'S CABIN AT LAKE HIDE-AWAY TO SPEND THE DAY! IT'S COMPLETELY ISOLATED UP THERE EXCEPT FOR OTHER CABINS!
WE'LL BE AS FAR AWAY FROM FOOTBALL AS WE CAN GET! OUR CABIN DOESN'T EVEN HAVE SATELLITE T.V.!
I THINK THAT WILL WORK, RON! BEING UP AT THE LAKE WILL GET THE GUYS' MINDS OFF OF FOOTBALL!
YAHOO! THE BIG GREEN MACHINE JUST SCORED ANOTHER TOUCHDOWN!
I SURE HOPE SO! I REALLY NEED A FOOTBALL-FREE DAY OF REST!
THE FOLLOWING TUESDAY AT LAKE HIDE-AWAY...
THIS WAS A GREAT IDEA, RON, EXCEPT YOU FORGOT TO TELL ARCHIE NOT TO BRING HIS FOOTBALL!
HEY, MOOSE! GO OUT FOR A PASS!
3

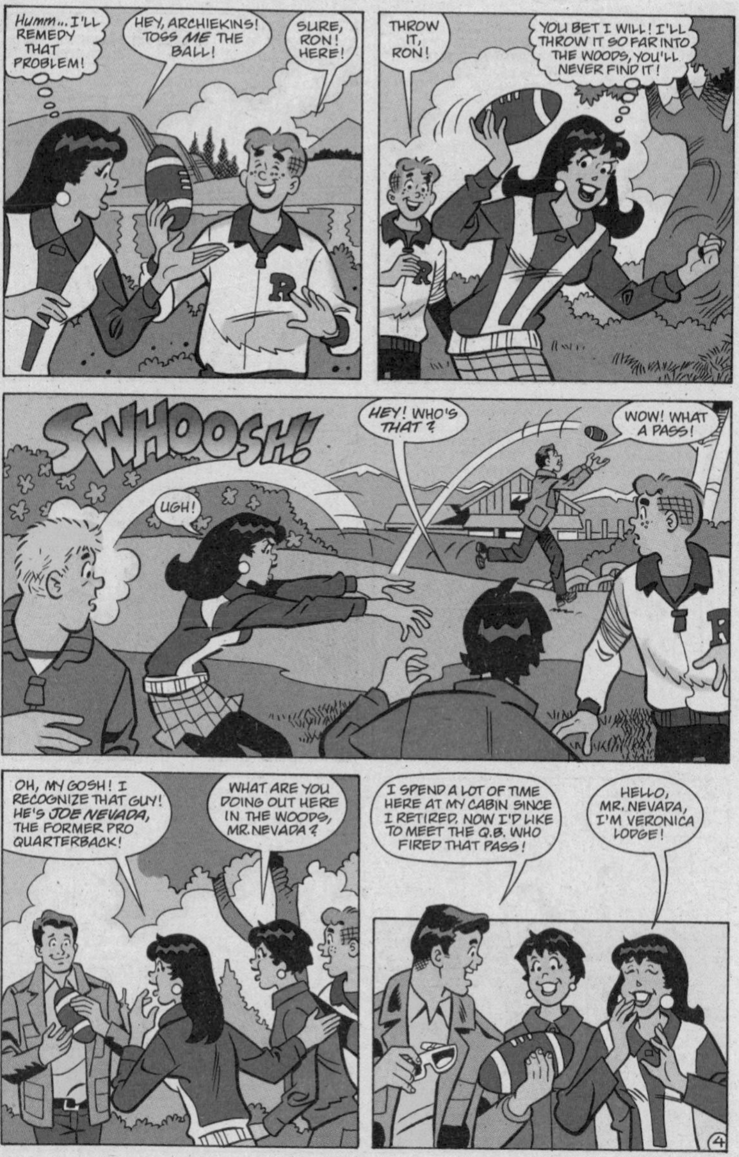
Humm... I'LL REMEDY THAT PROBLEM!
HEY, ARCHIEKINS! TOSS ME THE BALL!
SURE, RON! HERE!
THROW IT, RON!
YOU BET I WILL! I'LL THROW IT SO FAR INTO THE WOODS, YOU'LL NEVER FIND IT!
SWHOOSH!
HEY! WHO'S THAT?
WOW! WHAT A PASS!
UGH!
OH, MY GOSH! I RECOGNIZE THAT GUY! HE'S JOE NEVADA, THE FORMER PRO QUARTERBACK!
WHAT ARE YOU DOING OUT HERE IN THE WOODS, MR. NEVADA?
I SPEND A LOT OF TIME HERE AT MY CABIN SINCE I RETIRED. NOW I'D LIKE TO MEET THE Q.B. WHO FIRED THAT PASS!
HELLO, MR. NEVADA, I'M VERONICA LODGE!
4

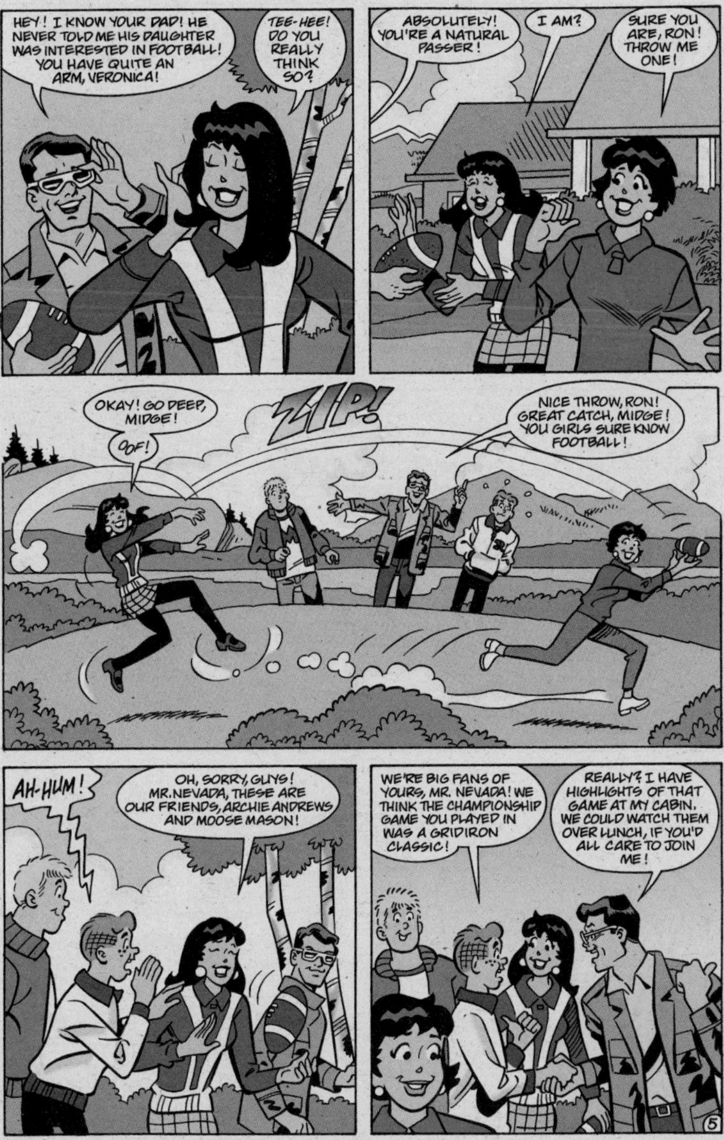
HEY! I KNOW YOUR DAD! HE NEVER TOLD ME HIS DAUGHTER WAS INTERESTED IN FOOTBALL! YOU HAVE QUITE AN ARM, VERONICA!
TEE-HEE! DO YOU REALLY THINK SO?
ABSOLUTELY! YOU'RE A NATURAL PASSER!
I AM?
SURE YOU ARE, RON! THROW ME ONE!
OKAY! GO DEEP, MIDGE!
ZIP!
OOF!
NICE THROW, RON! GREAT CATCH, MIDGE! YOU GIRLS SURE KNOW FOOTBALL!
AH-HUM!
OH, SORRY, GUYS! MR. NEVADA, THESE ARE OUR FRIENDS, ARCHIE ANDREWS AND MOOSE MASON!
WE'RE BIG FANS OF YOURS, MR. NEVADA! WE THINK THE CHAMPIONSHIP GAME YOU PLAYED IN WAS A GRIDIRON CLASSIC!
REALLY? I HAVE HIGHLIGHTS OF THAT GAME AT MY CABIN. WE COULD WATCH THEM OVER LUNCH, IF YOU'D ALL CARE TO JOIN ME!
5

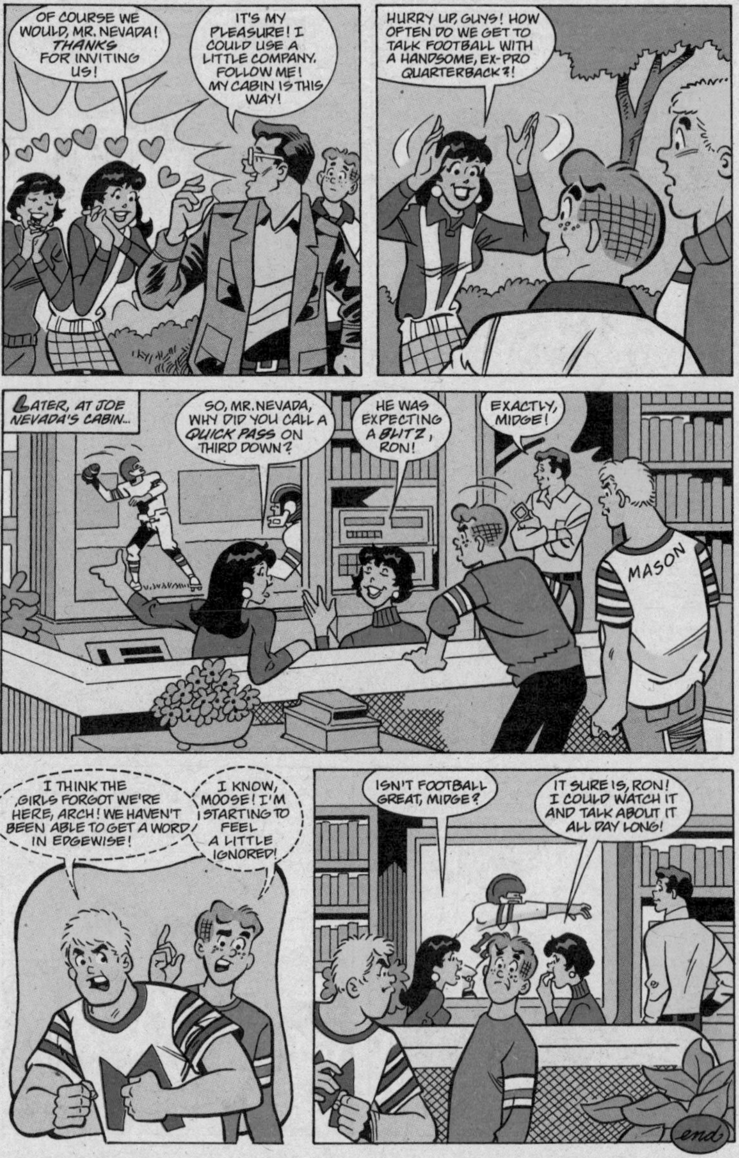
OF COURSE WE WOULD, MR. NEVADA! THANKS FOR INVITING US!
IT'S MY PLEASURE! I COULD USE A LITTLE COMPANY. FOLLOW ME! MY CABIN IS THIS WAY!
HURRY UP, GUYS! HOW OFTEN DO WE GET TO TALK FOOTBALL WITH A HANDSOME, EX-PRO QUARTERBACK?!
LATER, AT JOE NEVADA'S CABIN...
SO, MR. NEVADA, WHY DID YOU CALL A QUICK PASS ON THIRD DOWN?
HE WAS EXPECTING A BLITZ, RON!
EXACTLY, MIDGE!
MASON
I THINK THE GIRLS FORGOT WE'RE HERE, ARCH! WE HAVEN'T BEEN ABLE TO GET A WORD IN EDGEWISE!
I KNOW, MOOSE! I'M STARTING TO FEEL A LITTLE IGNORED!
ISN'T FOOTBALL GREAT, MIDGE?
IT SURE IS, RON! I COULD WATCH IT AND TALK ABOUT IT ALL DAY LONG!
end

Archie in "Video Deja Vu"

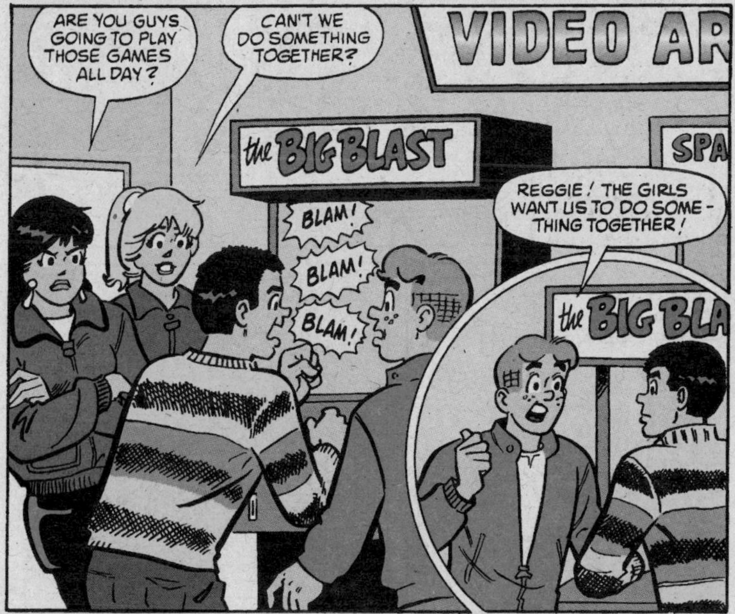

ARE YOU GUYS GOING TO PLAY THOSE GAMES ALL DAY?
CAN'T WE DO SOMETHING TOGETHER?
VIDEO AR
the BIG BLAST
SPA
BLAM!
BLAM!
BLAM!
REGGIE! THE GIRLS WANT US TO DO SOME-THING TOGETHER!
the BIG BLA

Script: George Gladir / Pencils: Dan DeCarlo / Inks: Mike Esposito / Letters: Bill Yoshida / Colors: Barry Grossman

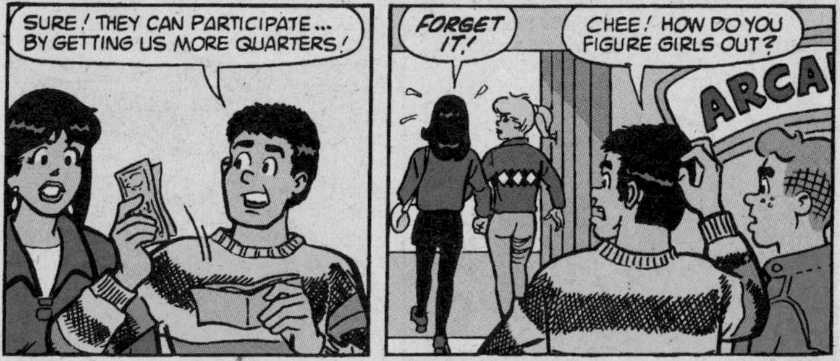

SURE! THEY CAN PARTICIPATE... BY GETTING US MORE QUARTERS!
FORGET IT!
CHEE! HOW DO YOU FIGURE GIRLS OUT?
ARCA

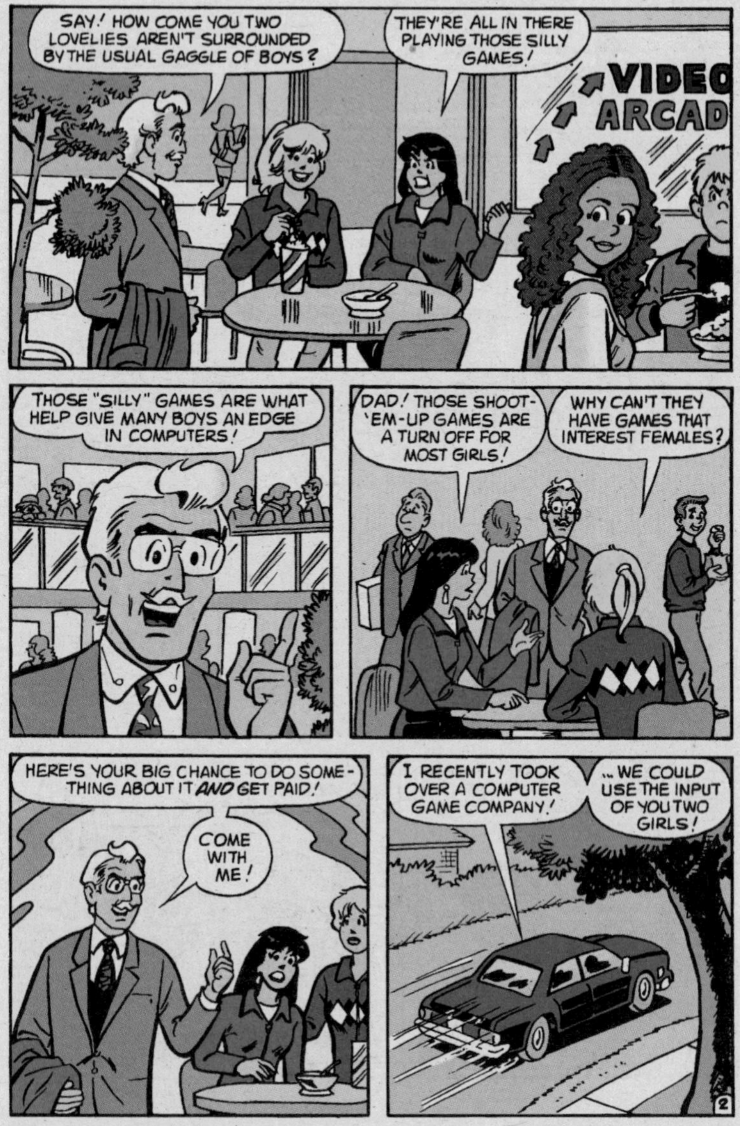
SAY! HOW COME YOU TWO LOVELIES AREN'T SURROUNDED BY THE USUAL GAGGLE OF BOYS?
THEY'RE ALL IN THERE PLAYING THOSE SILLY GAMES!
VIDEO ARCAD
THOSE "SILLY" GAMES ARE WHAT HELP GIVE MANY BOYS AN EDGE IN COMPUTERS!
DAD! THOSE SHOOT-'EM-UP GAMES ARE A TURN OFF FOR MOST GIRLS!
WHY CAN'T THEY HAVE GAMES THAT INTEREST FEMALES?
HERE'S YOUR BIG CHANCE TO DO SOME-THING ABOUT IT AND GET PAID!
COME WITH ME!
I RECENTLY TOOK OVER A COMPUTER GAME COMPANY!
...WE COULD USE THE INPUT OF YOU TWO GIRLS!
2

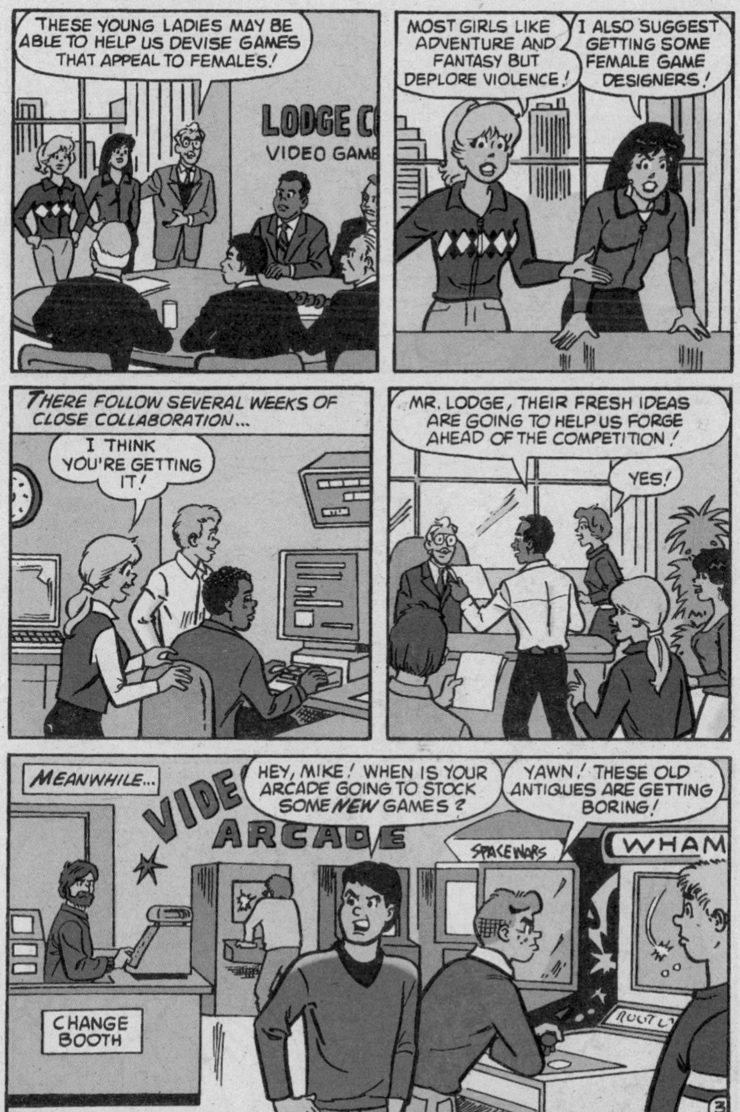
THESE YOUNG LADIES MAY BE ABLE TO HELP US DEVISE GAMES THAT APPEAL TO FEMALES!
LODGE C
VIDEO GAME
MOST GIRLS LIKE ADVENTURE AND FANTASY BUT DEPLORE VIOLENCE!
I ALSO SUGGEST GETTING SOME FEMALE GAME DESIGNERS!
THERE FOLLOW SEVERAL WEEKS OF CLOSE COLLABORATION...
I THINK YOU'RE GETTING IT!
MR. LODGE, THEIR FRESH IDEAS ARE GOING TO HELP US FORGE AHEAD OF THE COMPETITION!
YES!
MEANWHILE...
VIDE
ARCADE
HEY, MIKE! WHEN IS YOUR ARCADE GOING TO STOCK SOME NEW GAMES?
YAWN! THESE OLD ANTIQUES ARE GETTING BORING!
SPACE WARS
WHAM
CHANGE BOOTH
3

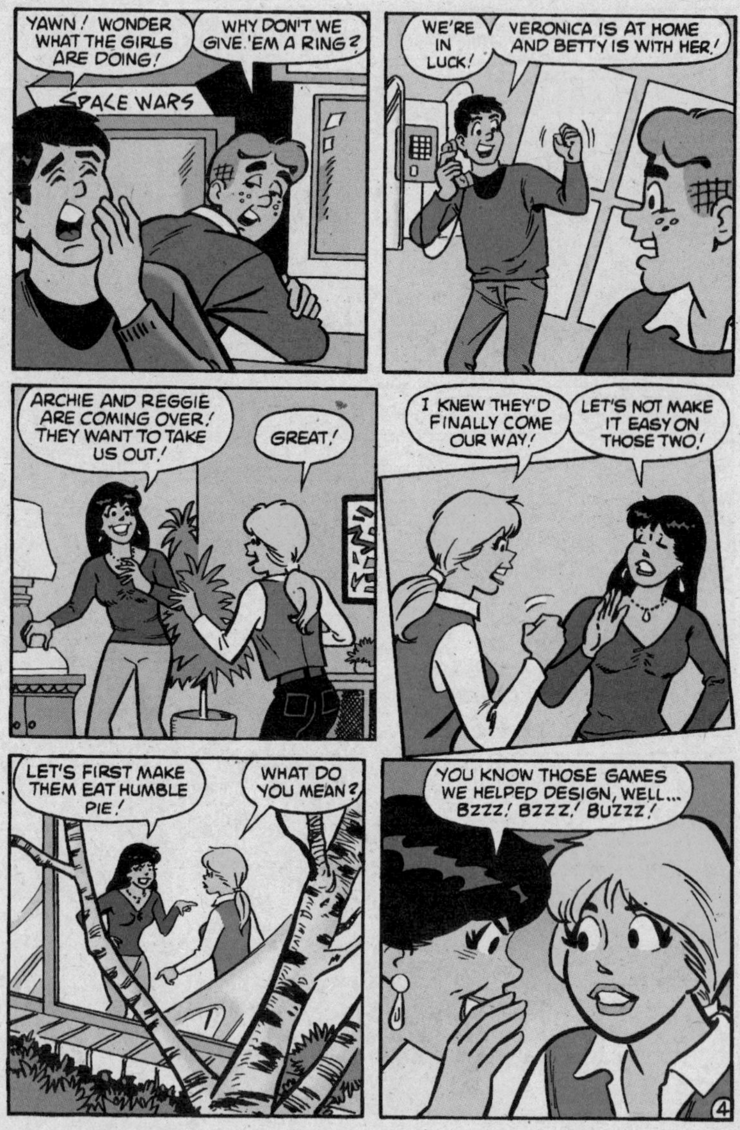
YAWN! WONDER WHAT THE GIRLS ARE DOING!
WHY DON'T WE GIVE 'EM A RING?
SPACE WARS
WE'RE IN LUCK!
VERONICA IS AT HOME AND BETTY IS WITH HER!
ARCHIE AND REGGIE ARE COMING OVER! THEY WANT TO TAKE US OUT!
GREAT!
I KNEW THEY'D FINALLY COME OUR WAY!
LET'S NOT MAKE IT EASY ON THOSE TWO!
LET'S FIRST MAKE THEM EAT HUMBLE PIE!
WHAT DO YOU MEAN?
YOU KNOW THOSE GAMES WE HELPED DESIGN, WELL... BZZZ! BZZZ! BUZZZ!
4

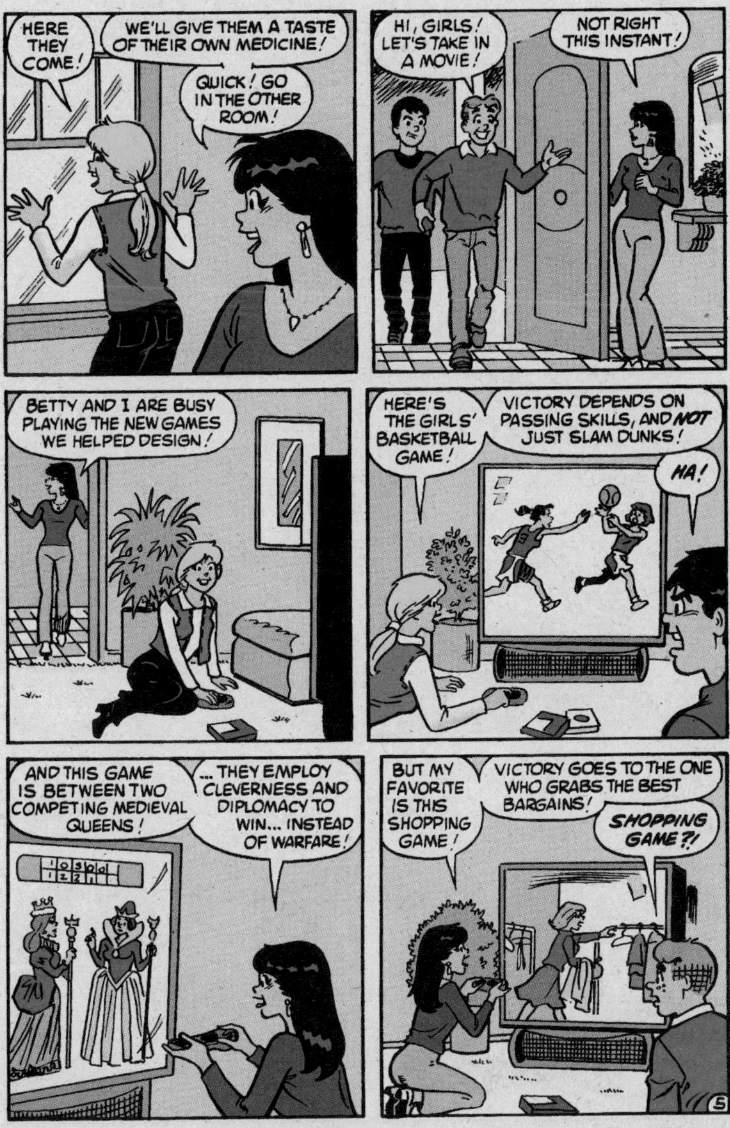
HERE THEY COME!
WE'LL GIVE THEM A TASTE OF THEIR OWN MEDICINE!
QUICK! GO IN THE OTHER ROOM!
HI, GIRLS! LET'S TAKE IN A MOVIE!
NOT RIGHT THIS INSTANT!
BETTY AND I ARE BUSY PLAYING THE NEW GAMES WE HELPED DESIGN!
HERE'S THE GIRLS' BASKETBALL GAME!
VICTORY DEPENDS ON PASSING SKILLS, AND NOT JUST SLAM DUNKS!
HA!
AND THIS GAME IS BETWEEN TWO COMPETING MEDIEVAL QUEENS!
... THEY EMPLOY CLEVERNESS AND DIPLOMACY TO WIN... INSTEAD OF WARFARE!
BUT MY FAVORITE IS THIS SHOPPING GAME!
VICTORY GOES TO THE ONE WHO GRABS THE BEST BARGAINS!
SHOPPING GAME?!
5

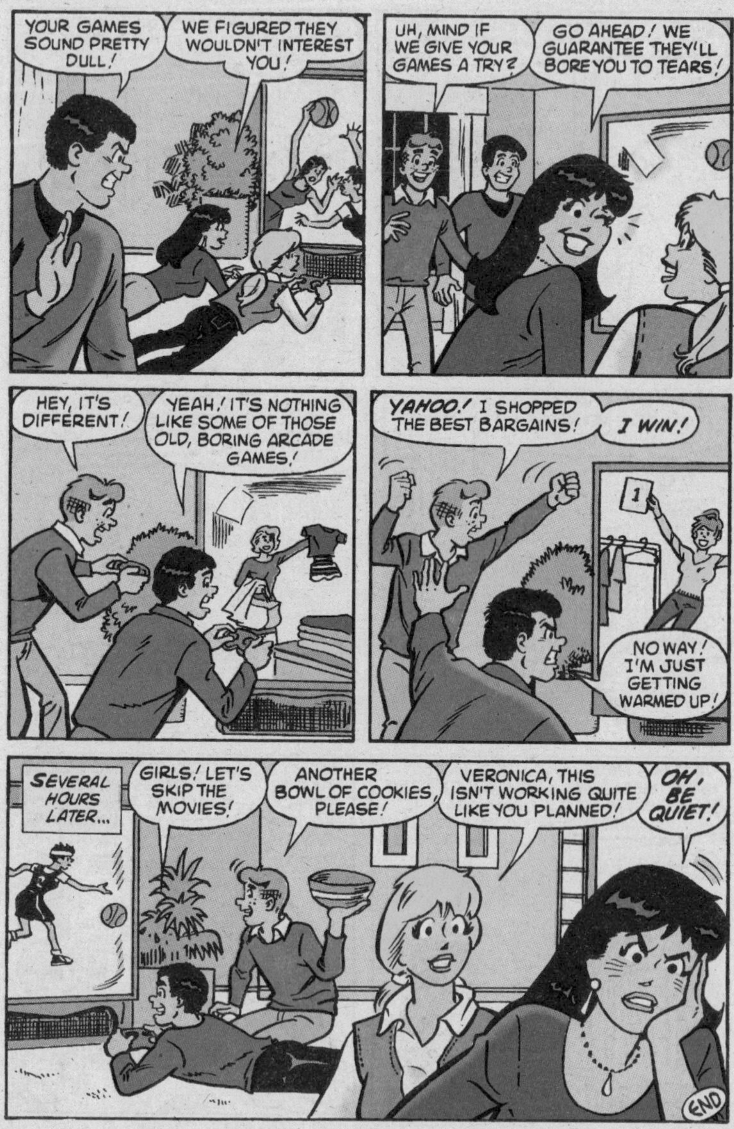
YOUR GAMES SOUND PRETTY DULL!
WE FIGURED THEY WOULDN'T INTEREST YOU!
UH, MIND IF WE GIVE YOUR GAMES A TRY?
GO AHEAD! WE GUARANTEE THEY'LL BORE YOU TO TEARS!
HEY, IT'S DIFFERENT!
YEAH! IT'S NOTHING LIKE SOME OF THOSE OLD, BORING ARCADE GAMES!
YAHOO! I SHOPPED THE BEST BARGAINS!
I WIN!
1
NO WAY! I'M JUST GETTING WARMED UP!
SEVERAL HOURS LATER...
GIRLS! LET'S SKIP THE MOVIES!
ANOTHER BOWL OF COOKIES, PLEASE!
VERONICA, THIS ISN'T WORKING QUITE LIKE YOU PLANNED!
OH, BE QUIET!
END

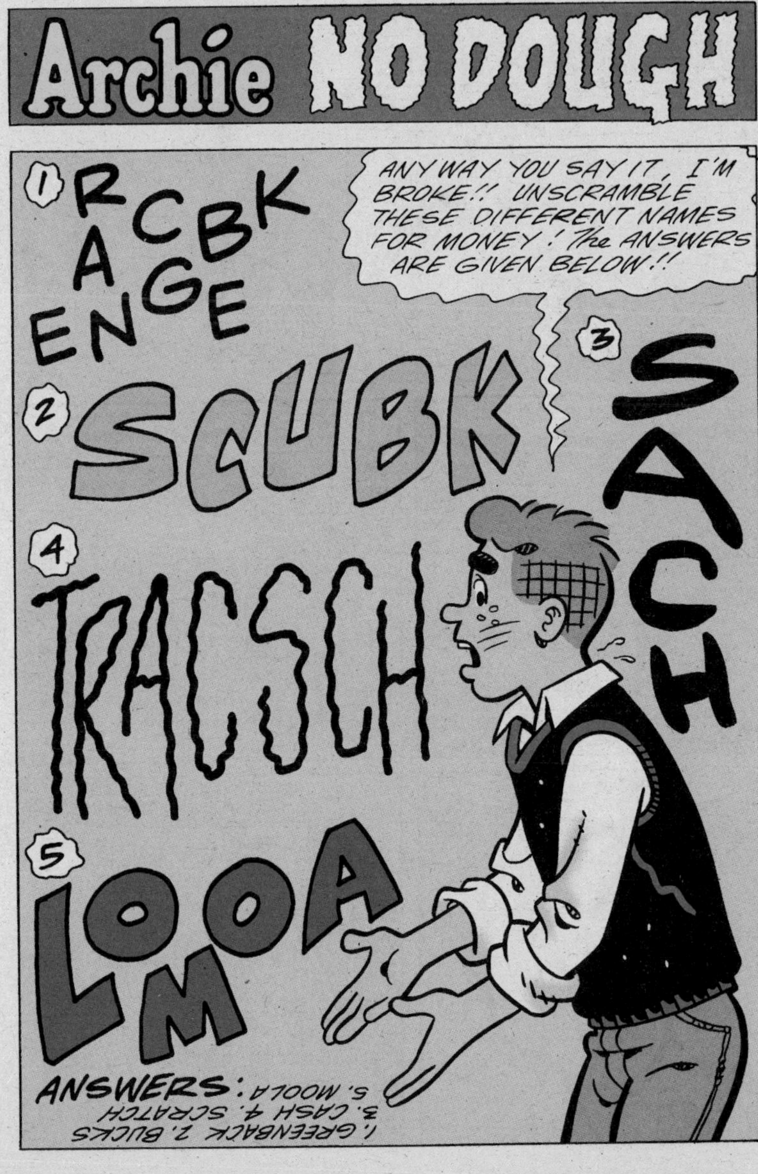

Archie NO DOUGH
1
R CBK
A
ENGE
ANY WAY YOU SAY IT, I'M BROKE!! UNSCRAMBLE THESE DIFFERENT NAMES FOR MONEY! The ANSWERS ARE GIVEN BELOW!!
2
SCUBK
3
SACH
4
TRACSCH
5
LOOA
M
ANSWERS:
1. GREENBACK 2. BUCKS
3. CASH 4. SCRATCH
5. MOOLA

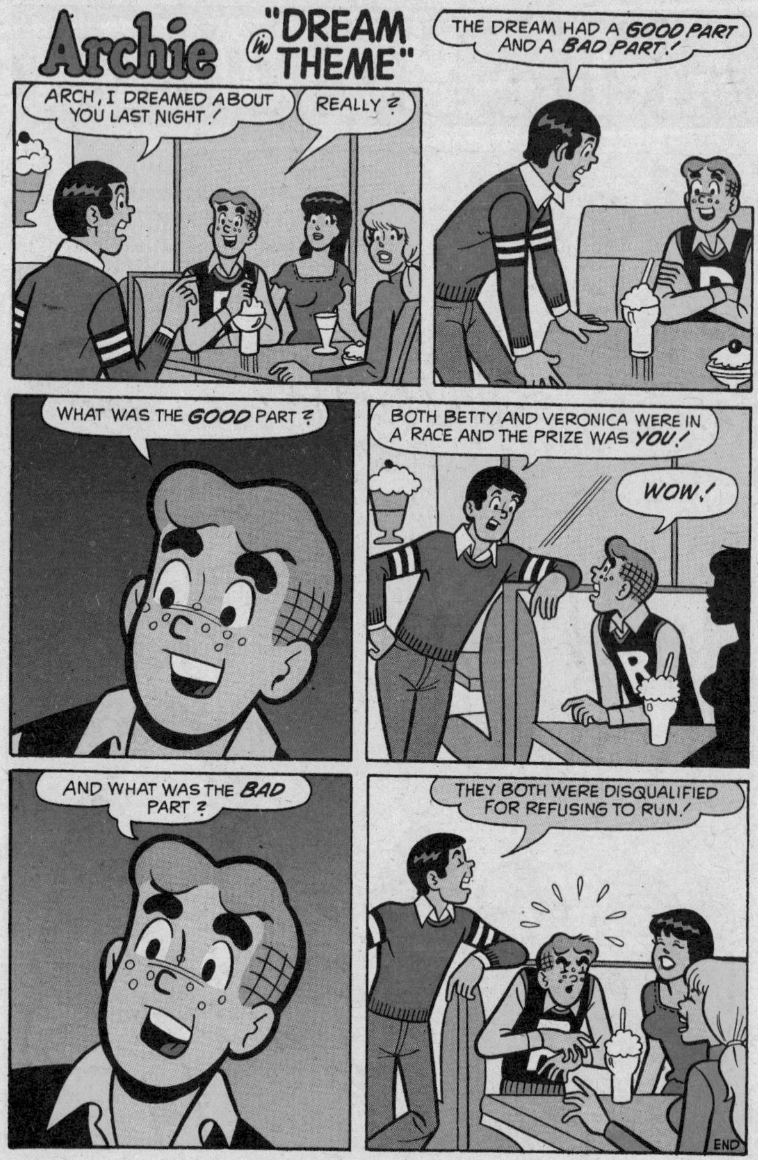

Archie in "DREAM THEME"
ARCH, I DREAMED ABOUT YOU LAST NIGHT!
REALLY?
THE DREAM HAD A GOOD PART AND A BAD PART!
WHAT WAS THE GOOD PART?
BOTH BETTY AND VERONICA WERE IN A RACE AND THE PRIZE WAS YOU!
WOW!
AND WHAT WAS THE BAD PART?
THEY BOTH WERE DISQUALIFIED FOR REFUSING TO RUN!
END

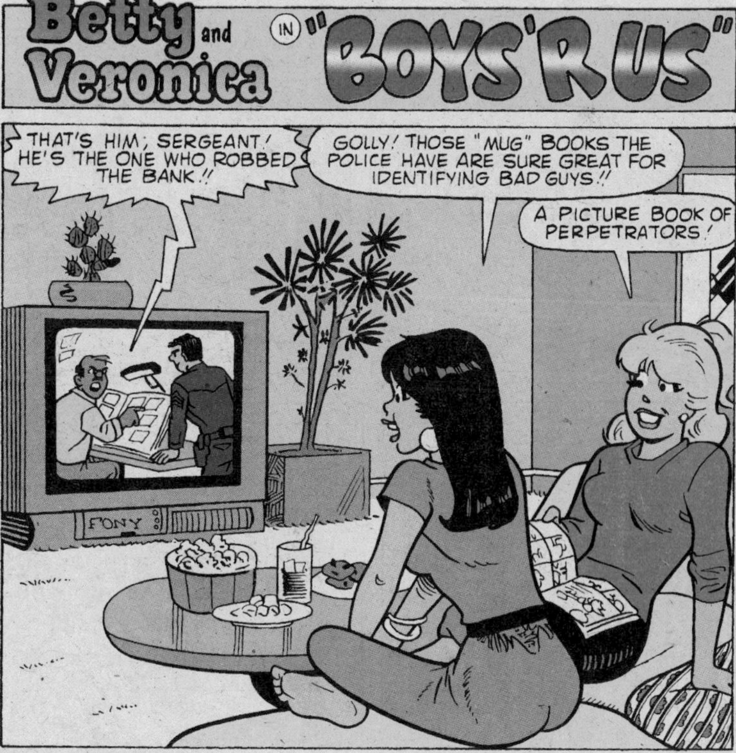
Betty and Veronica
IN "BOYS'R US"
THAT'S HIM, SERGEANT! HE'S THE ONE WHO ROBBED THE BANK!!
GOLLY! THOSE "MUG" BOOKS THE POLICE HAVE ARE SURE GREAT FOR IDENTIFYING BAD GUYS!!
A PICTURE BOOK OF PERPETRATORS!
FONY

Script: Mike Pellowski / Art: Jeff Shultz / Letters: Bill Yoshida / Colors: Barry Grossman

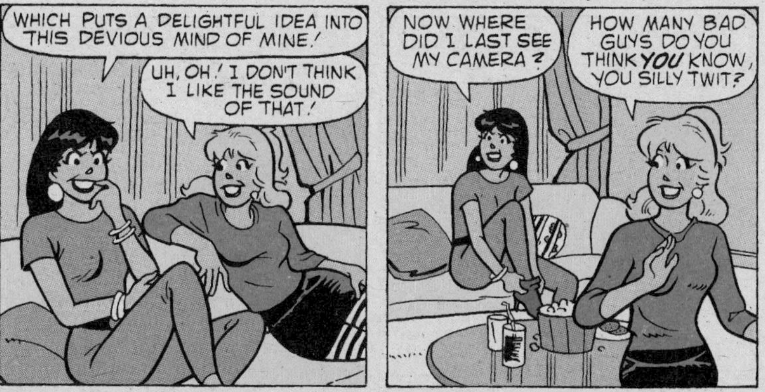
WHICH PUTS A DELIGHTFUL IDEA INTO THIS DEVIOUS MIND OF MINE!
UH, OH! I DON'T THINK I LIKE THE SOUND OF THAT!
NOW WHERE DID I LAST SEE MY CAMERA?
HOW MANY BAD GUYS DO YOU THINK YOU KNOW, YOU SILLY TWIT?

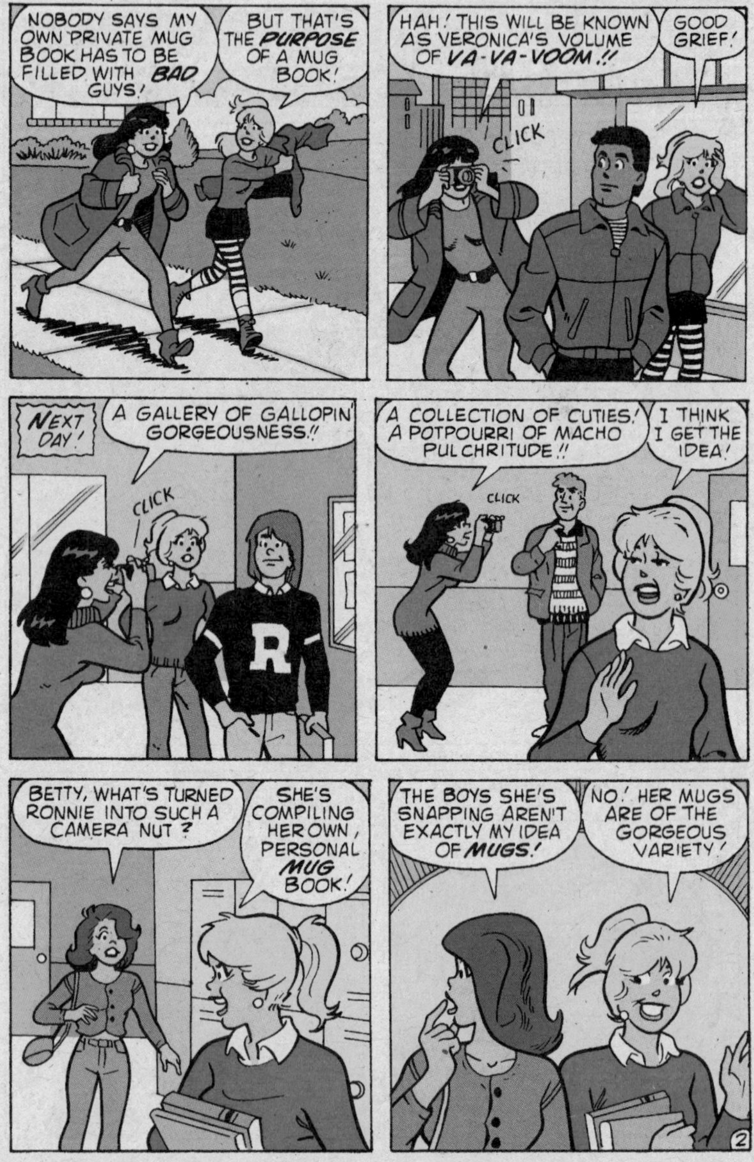
NOBODY SAYS MY OWN PRIVATE MUG BOOK HAS TO BE FILLED WITH BAD GUYS!
BUT THAT'S THE PURPOSE OF A MUG BOOK!
HAH! THIS WILL BE KNOWN AS VERONICA'S VOLUME OF VA-VA-VOOM!!
CLICK
GOOD GRIEF!
NEXT DAY!
A GALLERY OF GALLOPIN' GORGEOUSNESS!!
CLICK
R
A COLLECTION OF CUTIES! A POTPOURRI OF MACHO PULCHRITUDE!!
CLICK
I THINK I GET THE IDEA!
BETTY, WHAT'S TURNED RONNIE INTO SUCH A CAMERA NUT?
SHE'S COMPILING HER OWN, PERSONAL MUG BOOK!
THE BOYS SHE'S SNAPPING AREN'T EXACTLY MY IDEA OF MUGS!
NO! HER MUGS ARE OF THE GORGEOUS VARIETY!
2

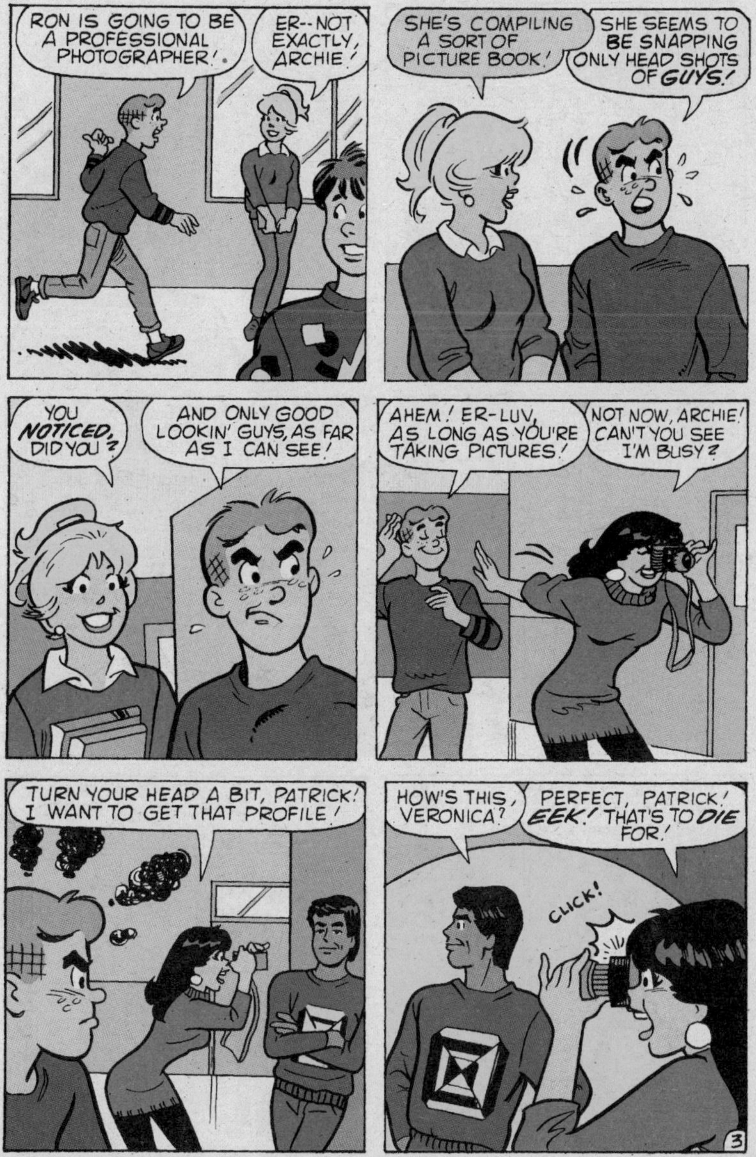
RON IS GOING TO BE A PROFESSIONAL PHOTOGRAPHER!
ER--NOT EXACTLY, ARCHIE!
SHE'S COMPILING A SORT OF PICTURE BOOK!
SHE SEEMS TO BE SNAPPING ONLY HEAD SHOTS OF GUYS!
YOU NOTICED, DID YOU?
AND ONLY GOOD LOOKIN' GUYS, AS FAR AS I CAN SEE!
AHEM! ER-LUV, AS LONG AS YOU'RE TAKING PICTURES!
NOT NOW, ARCHIE! CAN'T YOU SEE I'M BUSY?
TURN YOUR HEAD A BIT, PATRICK! I WANT TO GET THAT PROFILE!
HOW'S THIS, VERONICA?
PERFECT, PATRICK! EEK! THAT'S TO DIE FOR!
CLICK!
3

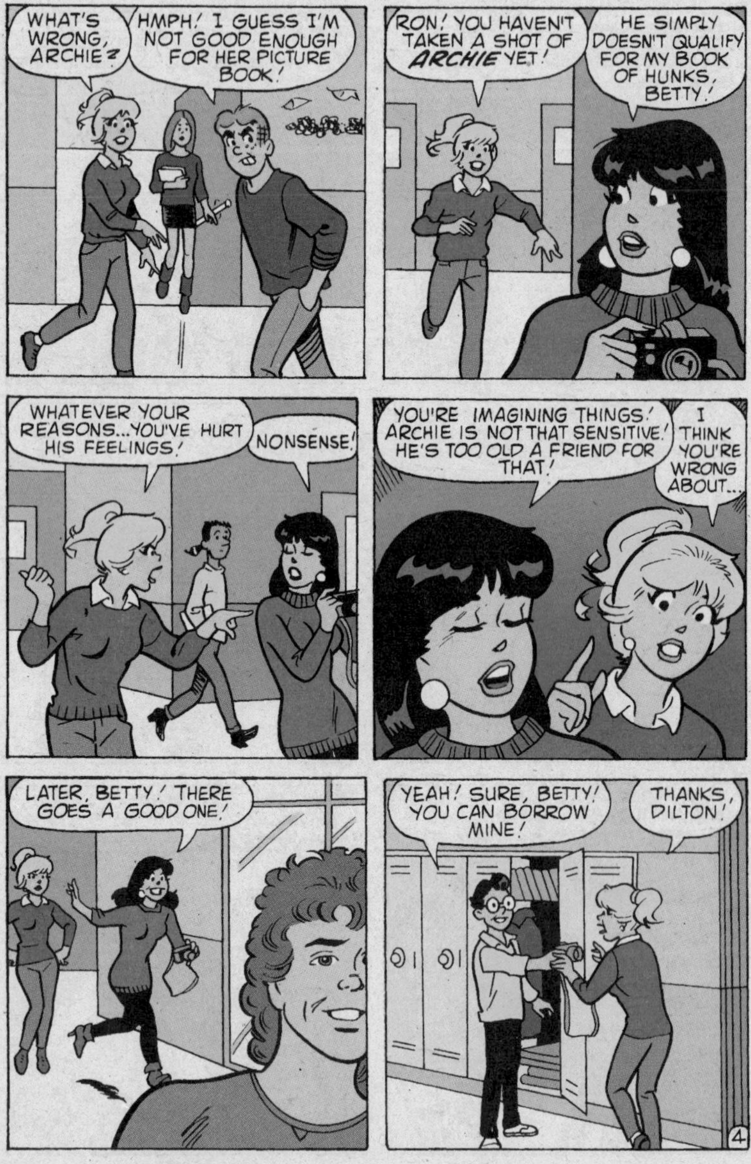
WHAT'S WRONG, ARCHIE?
HMPH! I GUESS I'M NOT GOOD ENOUGH FOR HER PICTURE BOOK!
RON! YOU HAVEN'T TAKEN A SHOT OF ARCHIE YET!
HE SIMPLY DOESN'T QUALIFY FOR MY BOOK OF HUNKS, BETTY!
WHATEVER YOUR REASONS...YOU'VE HURT HIS FEELINGS!
NONSENSE!
YOU'RE IMAGINING THINGS! ARCHIE IS NOT THAT SENSITIVE! HE'S TOO OLD A FRIEND FOR THAT!
I THINK YOU'RE WRONG ABOUT...
LATER, BETTY! THERE GOES A GOOD ONE!
YEAH! SURE, BETTY! YOU CAN BORROW MINE!
THANKS, DILTON!
4

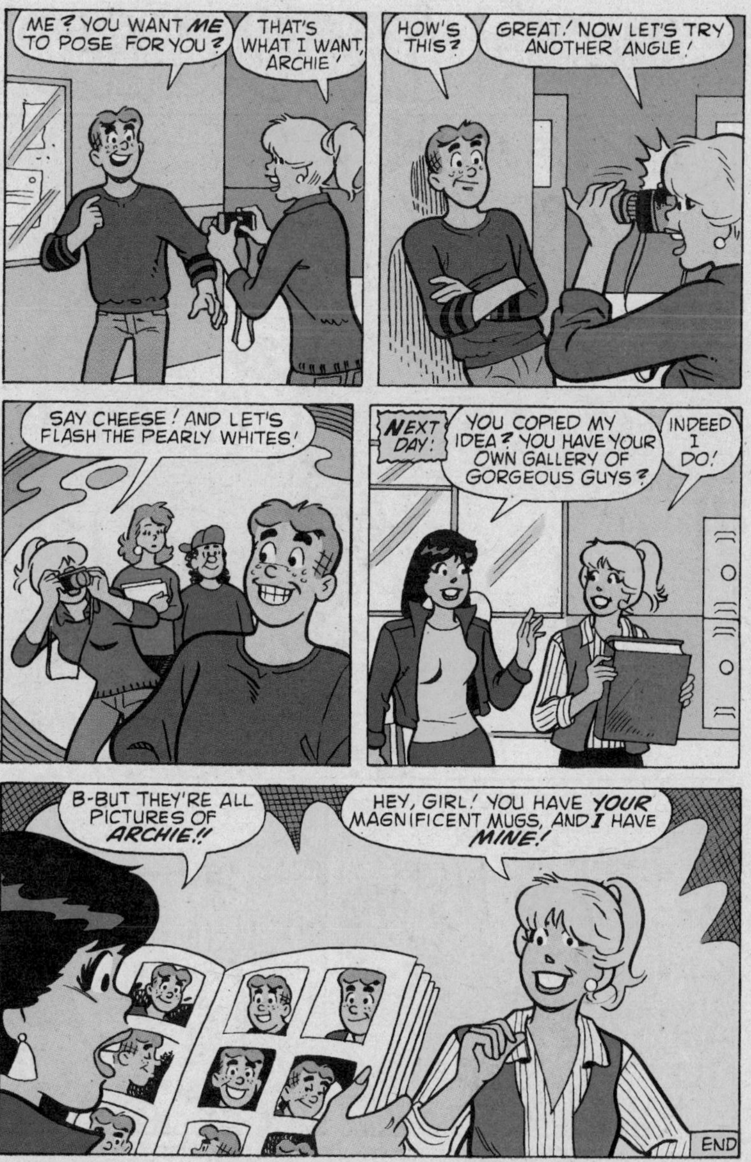
ME? YOU WANT ME TO POSE FOR YOU?
THAT'S WHAT I WANT, ARCHIE!
HOW'S THIS?
GREAT! NOW LET'S TRY ANOTHER ANGLE!
SAY CHEESE! AND LET'S FLASH THE PEARLY WHITES!
NEXT DAY!
YOU COPIED MY IDEA? YOU HAVE YOUR OWN GALLERY OF GORGEOUS GUYS?
INDEED I DO!
B-BUT THEY'RE ALL PICTURES OF ARCHIE!!
HEY, GIRL! YOU HAVE YOUR MAGNIFICENT MUGS, AND I HAVE MINE!
END

Betty in "MINDGRIND"

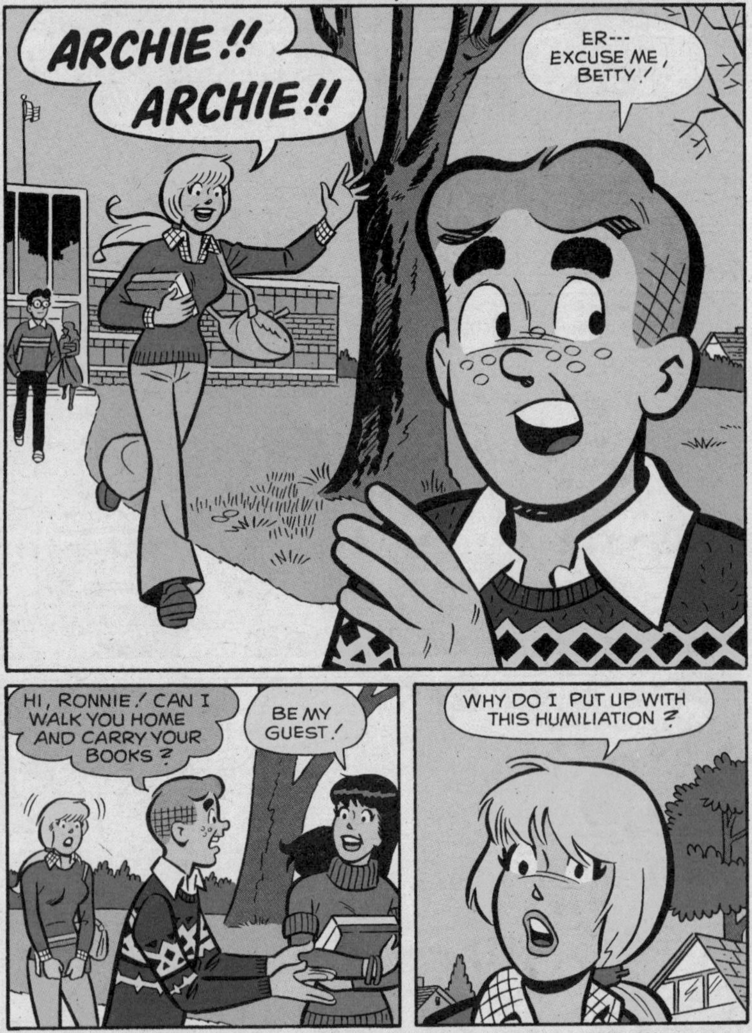

ARCHIE!! ARCHIE!!
ER--- EXCUSE ME, BETTY!
HI, RONNIE! CAN I WALK YOU HOME AND CARRY YOUR BOOKS?
BE MY GUEST!
WHY DO I PUT UP WITH THIS HUMILIATION?

Script: George Gladir / Pencils: Dan DeCarlo Jr. / Inks: Rudy Lapick / Letters: Bill Yoshida

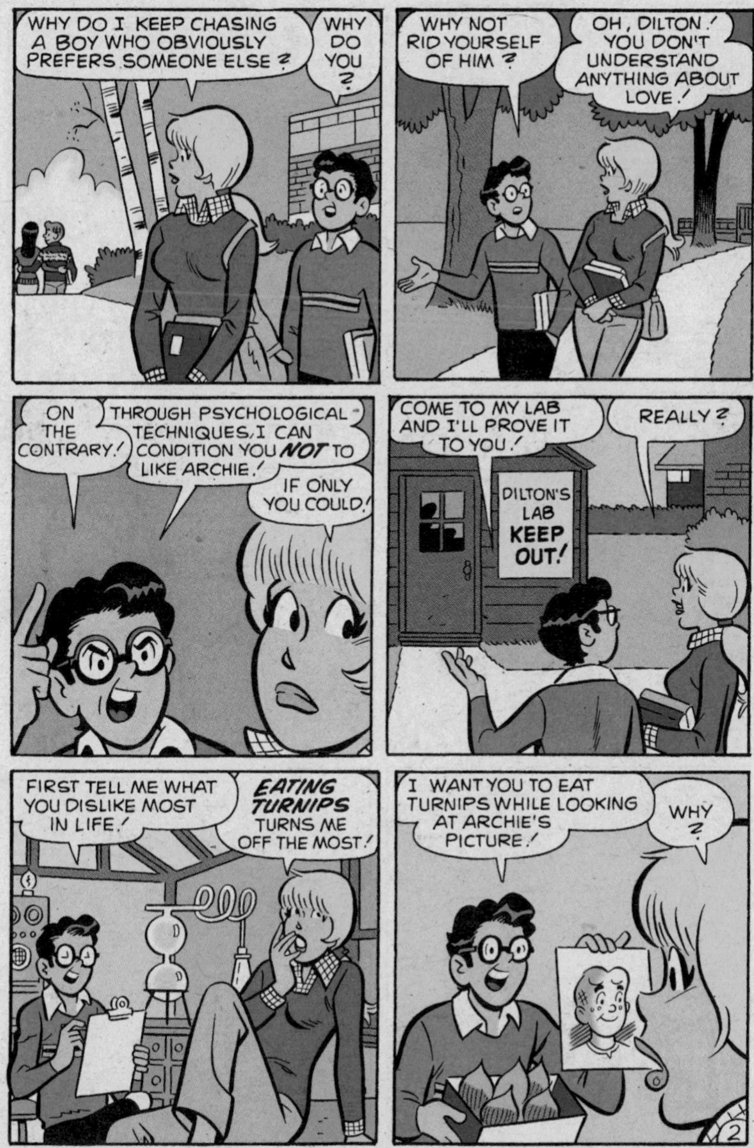
WHY DO I KEEP CHASING A BOY WHO OBVIOUSLY PREFERS SOMEONE ELSE?
WHY DO YOU?
WHY NOT RID YOURSELF OF HIM?
OH, DILTON! YOU DON'T UNDERSTAND ANYTHING ABOUT LOVE!
ON THE CONTRARY!
THROUGH PSYCHOLOGICAL TECHNIQUES, I CAN CONDITION YOU NOT TO LIKE ARCHIE!
IF ONLY YOU COULD!
COME TO MY LAB AND I'LL PROVE IT TO YOU!
REALLY?
DILTON'S LAB KEEP OUT!
FIRST TELL ME WHAT YOU DISLIKE MOST IN LIFE!
EATING TURNIPS TURNS ME OFF THE MOST!
I WANT YOU TO EAT TURNIPS WHILE LOOKING AT ARCHIE'S PICTURE!
WHY?
2

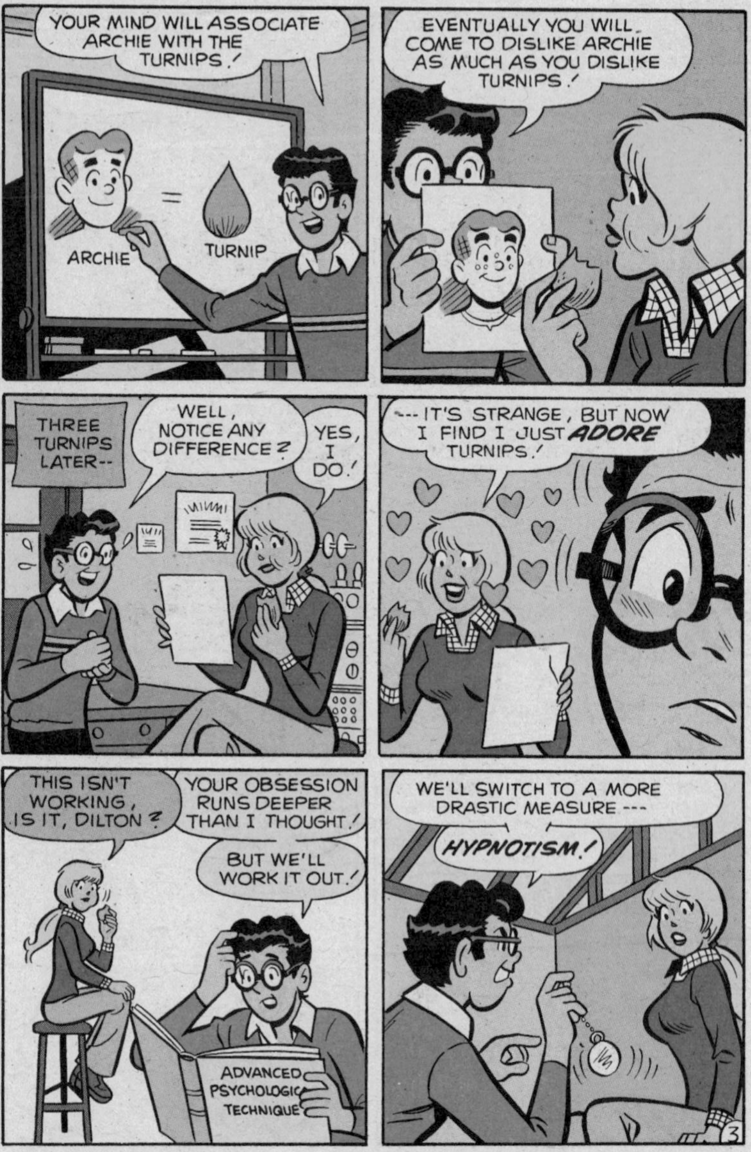

YOUR MIND WILL ASSOCIATE ARCHIE WITH THE TURNIPS!
ARCHIE
TURNIP
EVENTUALLY YOU WILL COME TO DISLIKE ARCHIE AS MUCH AS YOU DISLIKE TURNIPS!
THREE TURNIPS LATER--
WELL, NOTICE ANY DIFFERENCE?
YES, I DO!
---IT'S STRANGE, BUT NOW I FIND I JUST ADORE TURNIPS!
THIS ISN'T WORKING, IS IT, DILTON?
YOUR OBSESSION RUNS DEEPER THAN I THOUGHT!
BUT WE'LL WORK IT OUT!
ADVANCED PSYCHOLOGIC TECHNIQUE
WE'LL SWITCH TO A MORE DRASTIC MEASURE ---
HYPNOTISM!
3

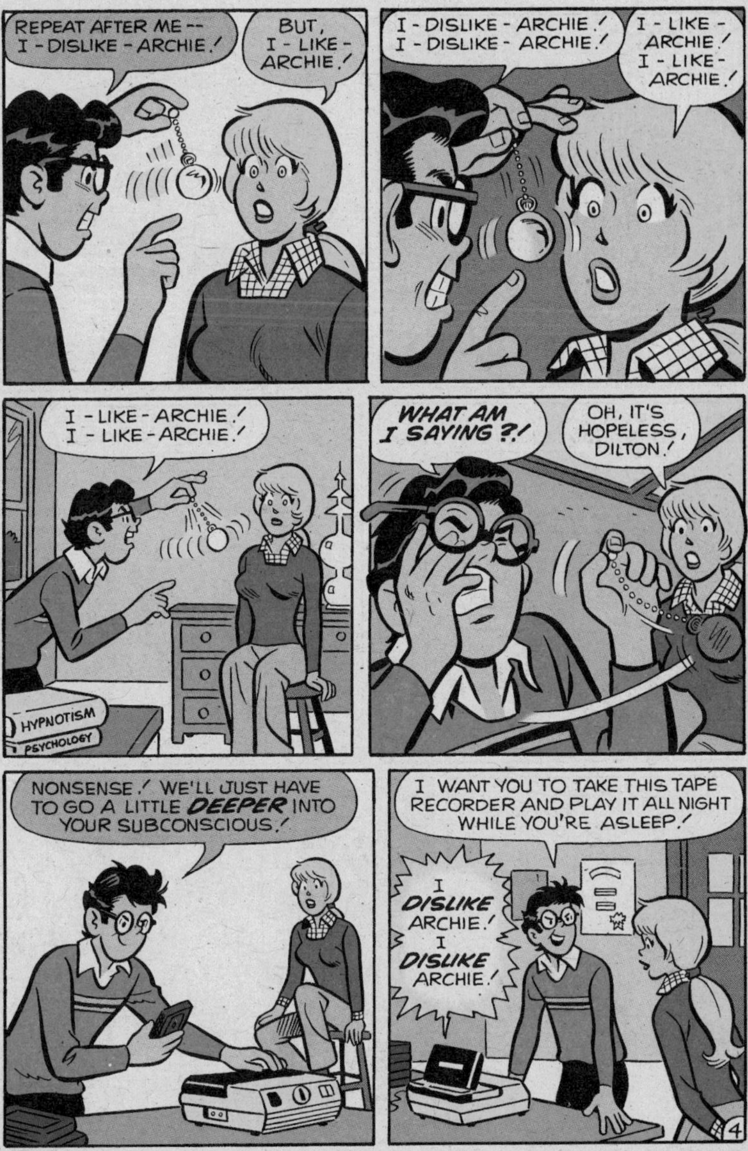
REPEAT AFTER ME -- I - DISLIKE - ARCHIE.!
BUT, I - LIKE - ARCHIE.!
I - DISLIKE - ARCHIE.! I - DISLIKE - ARCHIE.!
I - LIKE - ARCHIE.! I - LIKE - ARCHIE.!
I - LIKE - ARCHIE.! I - LIKE - ARCHIE.!
HYPNOTISM
PSYCHOLOGY
WHAT AM I SAYING ?!
OH, IT'S HOPELESS, DILTON.!
NONSENSE.! WE'LL JUST HAVE TO GO A LITTLE DEEPER INTO YOUR SUBCONSCIOUS.!
I WANT YOU TO TAKE THIS TAPE RECORDER AND PLAY IT ALL NIGHT WHILE YOU'RE ASLEEP.!
I DISLIKE ARCHIE.! I DISLIKE ARCHIE.!
4

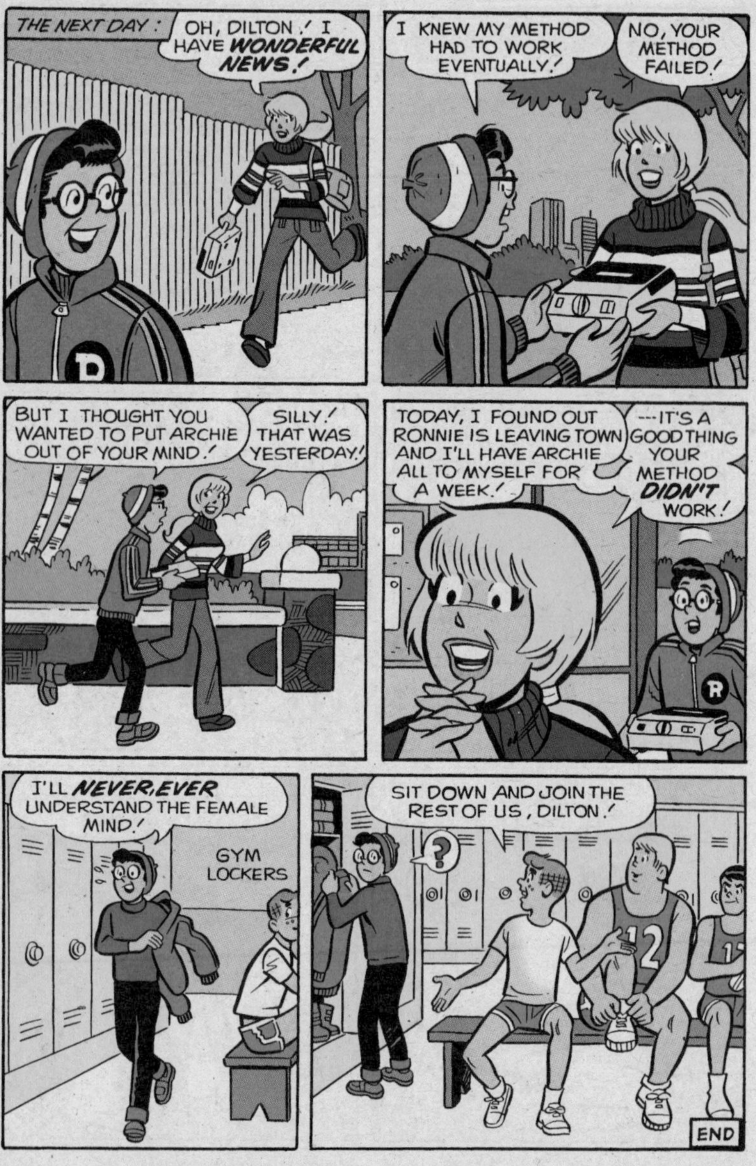
THE NEXT DAY :
OH, DILTON ! I HAVE WONDERFUL NEWS !
I KNEW MY METHOD HAD TO WORK EVENTUALLY !
NO, YOUR METHOD FAILED !
BUT I THOUGHT YOU WANTED TO PUT ARCHIE OUT OF YOUR MIND !
SILLY ! THAT WAS YESTERDAY !
TODAY, I FOUND OUT RONNIE IS LEAVING TOWN AND I'LL HAVE ARCHIE ALL TO MYSELF FOR A WEEK !
---IT'S A GOOD THING YOUR METHOD DIDN'T WORK !
I'LL NEVER, EVER UNDERSTAND THE FEMALE MIND !
GYM LOCKERS
?
SIT DOWN AND JOIN THE REST OF US , DILTON !
END

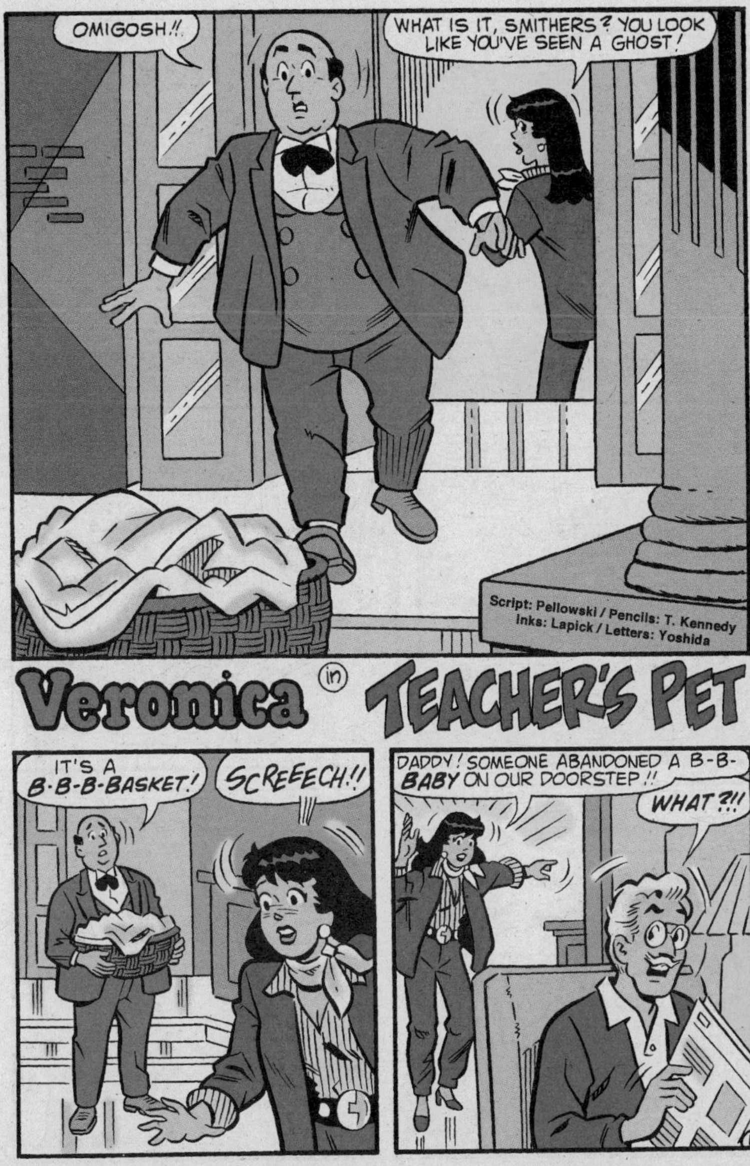
OMIGOSH!!
WHAT IS IT, SMITHERS? YOU LOOK LIKE YOU'VE SEEN A GHOST!
Script: Pellowski / Pencils: T. Kennedy
Inks: Lapick / Letters: Yoshida
Veronica in TEACHER'S PET
IT'S A B-B-B-BASKET!
SCREEECH!!
DADDY! SOMEONE ABANDONED A B-B-BABY ON OUR DOORSTEP!!
WHAT?!!

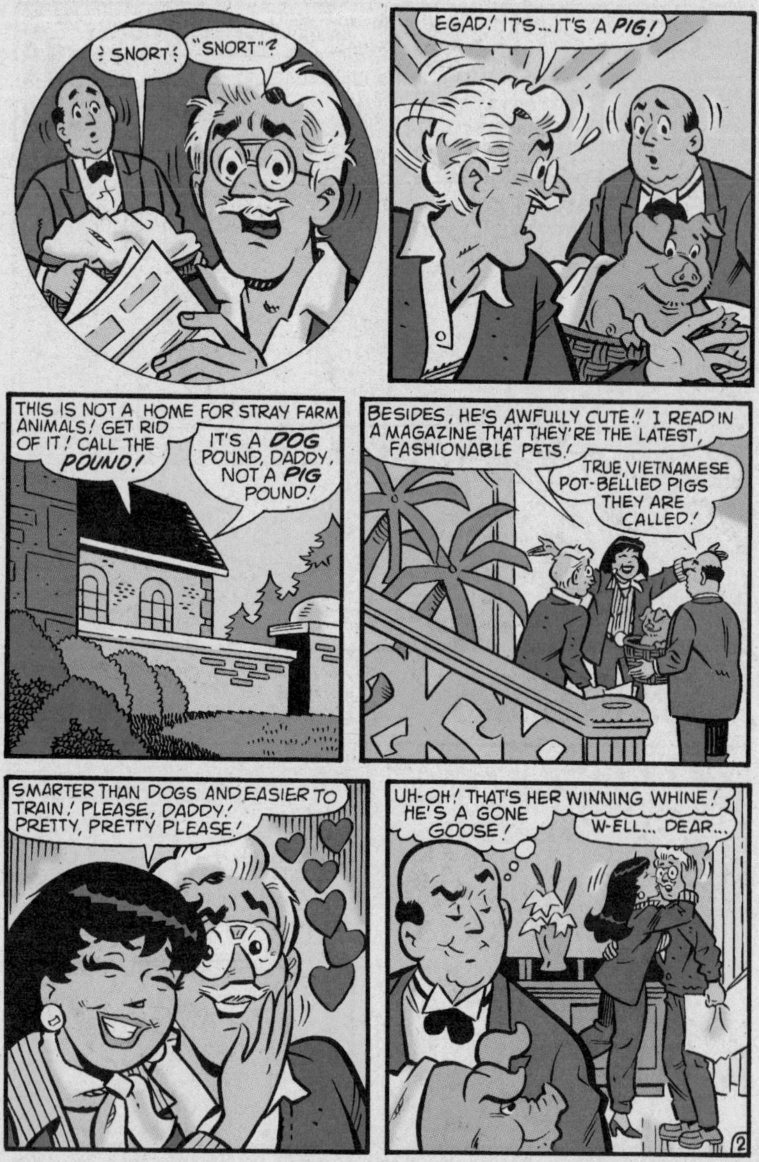

SNORT
"SNORT"?
EGAD! IT'S...IT'S A PIG!
THIS IS NOT A HOME FOR STRAY FARM ANIMALS! GET RID OF IT! CALL THE POUND!
IT'S A DOG POUND, DADDY, NOT A PIG POUND!
BESIDES, HE'S AWFULLY CUTE!! I READ IN A MAGAZINE THAT THEY'RE THE LATEST, FASHIONABLE PETS!
TRUE, VIETNAMESE POT-BELLIED PIGS THEY ARE CALLED!
SMARTER THAN DOGS AND EASIER TO TRAIN! PLEASE, DADDY! PRETTY, PRETTY PLEASE!
UH-OH! THAT'S HER WINNING WHINE! HE'S A GONE GOOSE!
W-ELL... DEAR...
2

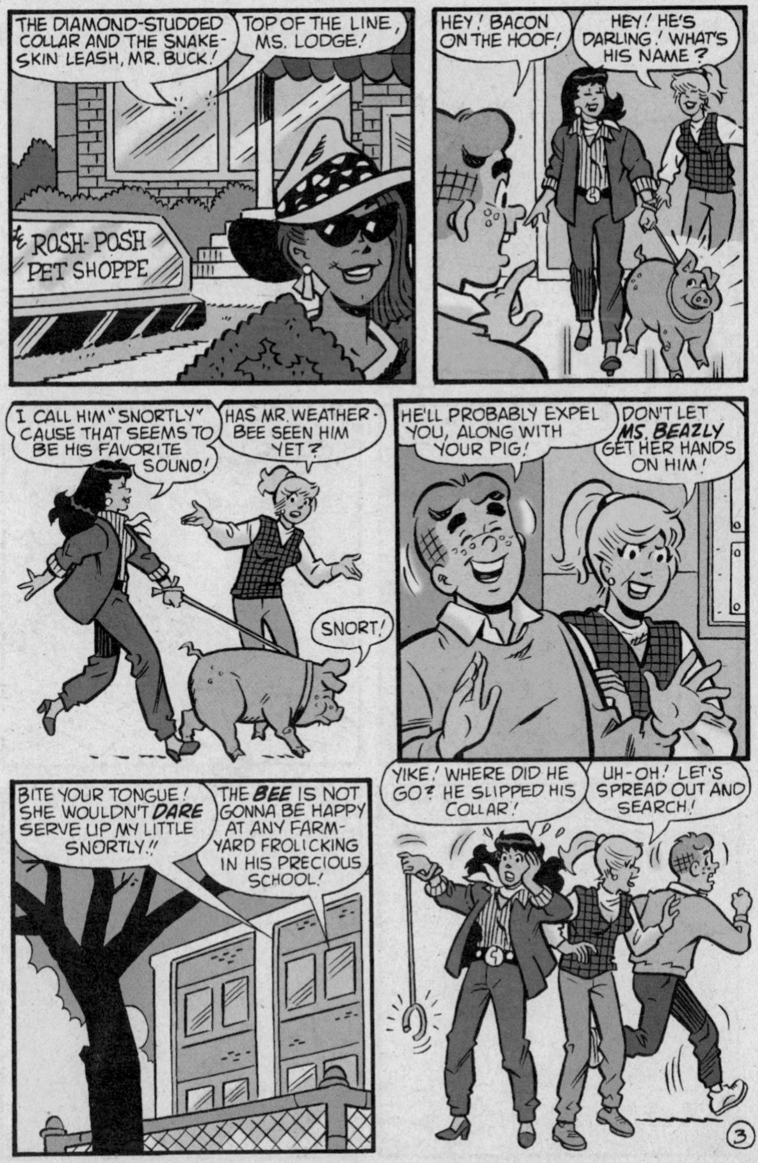
THE DIAMOND-STUDDED COLLAR AND THE SNAKE-SKIN LEASH, MR. BUCK!
TOP OF THE LINE, MS. LODGE!
ROSH-POSH PET SHOPPE
HEY! BACON ON THE HOOF!
HEY! HE'S DARLING! WHAT'S HIS NAME?
I CALL HIM "SNORTLY" 'CAUSE THAT SEEMS TO BE HIS FAVORITE SOUND!
HAS MR. WEATHERBEE SEEN HIM YET?
SNORT!
HE'LL PROBABLY EXPEL YOU, ALONG WITH YOUR PIG!
DON'T LET MS. BEAZLY GET HER HANDS ON HIM!
BITE YOUR TONGUE! SHE WOULDN'T DARE SERVE UP MY LITTLE SNORTLY!!
THE BEE IS NOT GONNA BE HAPPY AT ANY FARMYARD FROLICKING IN HIS PRECIOUS SCHOOL!
YIKE! WHERE DID HE GO? HE SLIPPED HIS COLLAR!
UH-OH! LET'S SPREAD OUT AND SEARCH!

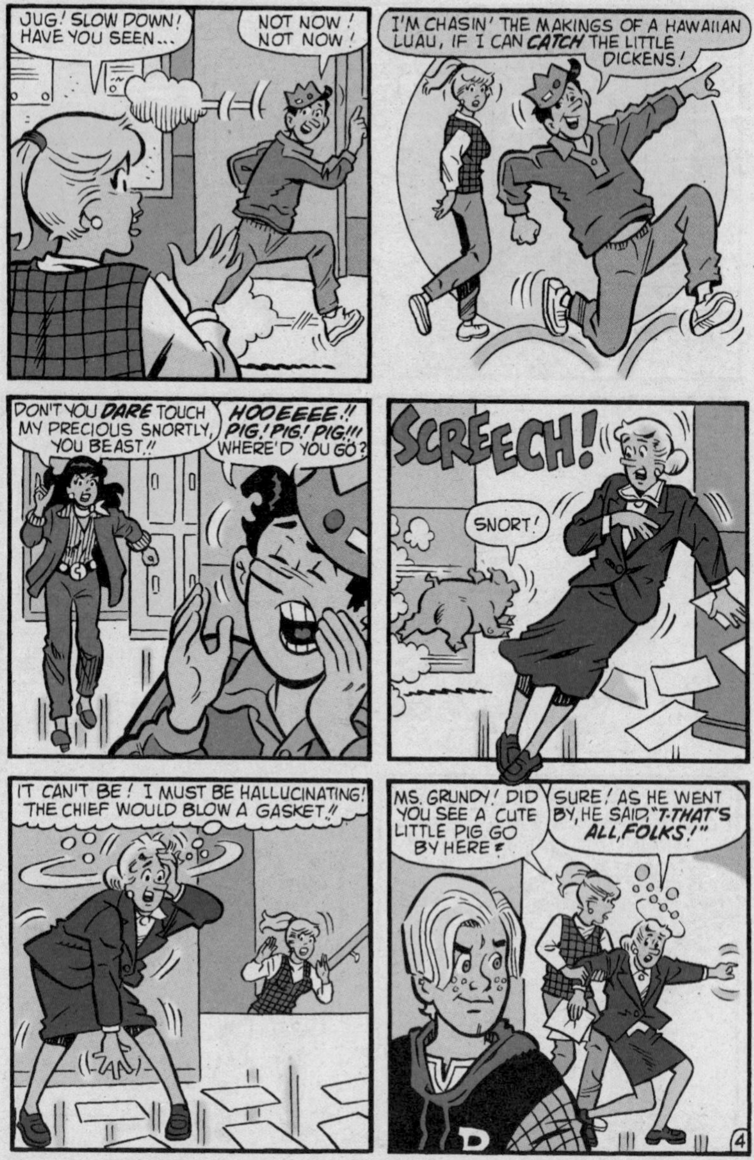
JUG! SLOW DOWN! HAVE YOU SEEN...
NOT NOW! NOT NOW!
I'M CHASIN' THE MAKINGS OF A HAWAIIAN LUAU, IF I CAN CATCH THE LITTLE DICKENS!
DON'T YOU DARE TOUCH MY PRECIOUS SNORTLY, YOU BEAST!!
HOOEEEE!! PIG! PIG! PIG!!! WHERE'D YOU GO?
SCREECH!
SNORT!
IT CAN'T BE! I MUST BE HALLUCINATING! THE CHIEF WOULD BLOW A GASKET!!
MS. GRUNDY! DID YOU SEE A CUTE LITTLE PIG GO BY HERE?
SURE! AS HE WENT BY, HE SAID, "T-THAT'S ALL, FOLKS!"
4

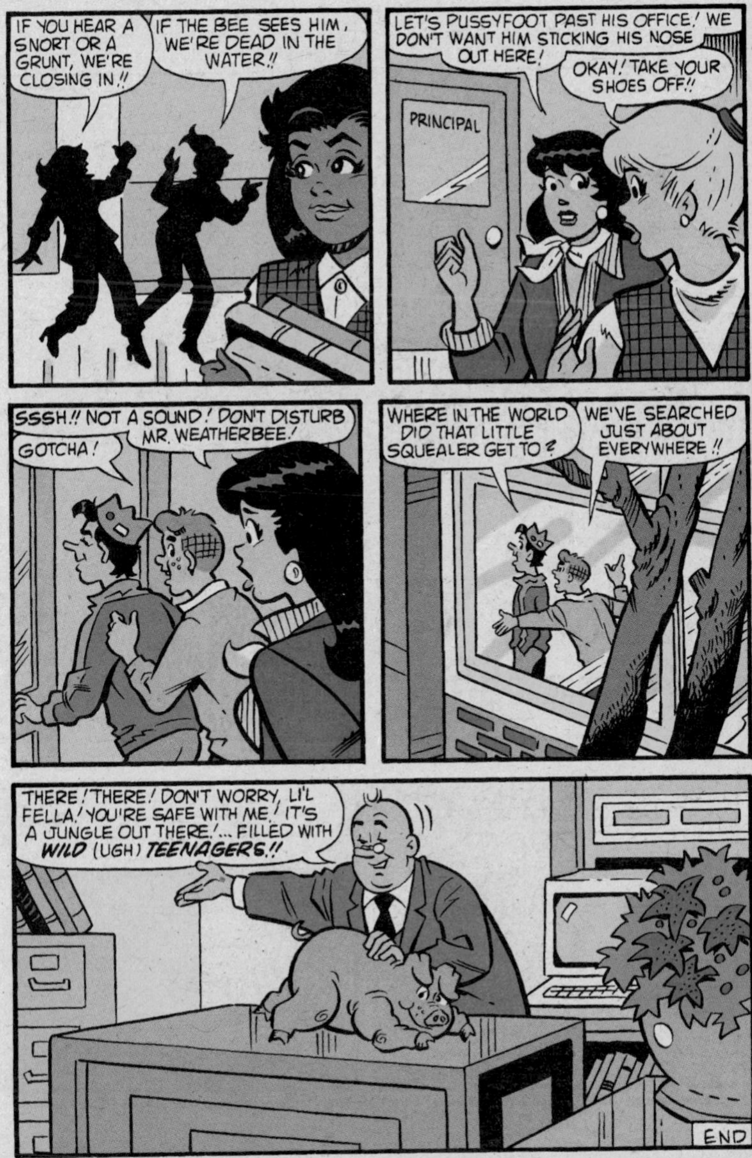
IF YOU HEAR A SNORT OR A GRUNT, WE'RE CLOSING IN!!
IF THE BEE SEES HIM, WE'RE DEAD IN THE WATER!!
LET'S PUSSYFOOT PAST HIS OFFICE! WE DON'T WANT HIM STICKING HIS NOSE OUT HERE!
OKAY! TAKE YOUR SHOES OFF!!
PRINCIPAL
SSSH!! NOT A SOUND! DON'T DISTURB MR. WEATHERBEE!
GOTCHA!
WHERE IN THE WORLD DID THAT LITTLE SQUEALER GET TO?
WE'VE SEARCHED JUST ABOUT EVERYWHERE!!
THERE! THERE! DON'T WORRY, LI'L FELLA! YOU'RE SAFE WITH ME! IT'S A JUNGLE OUT THERE!... FILLED WITH WILD (UGH) TEENAGERS!!
END

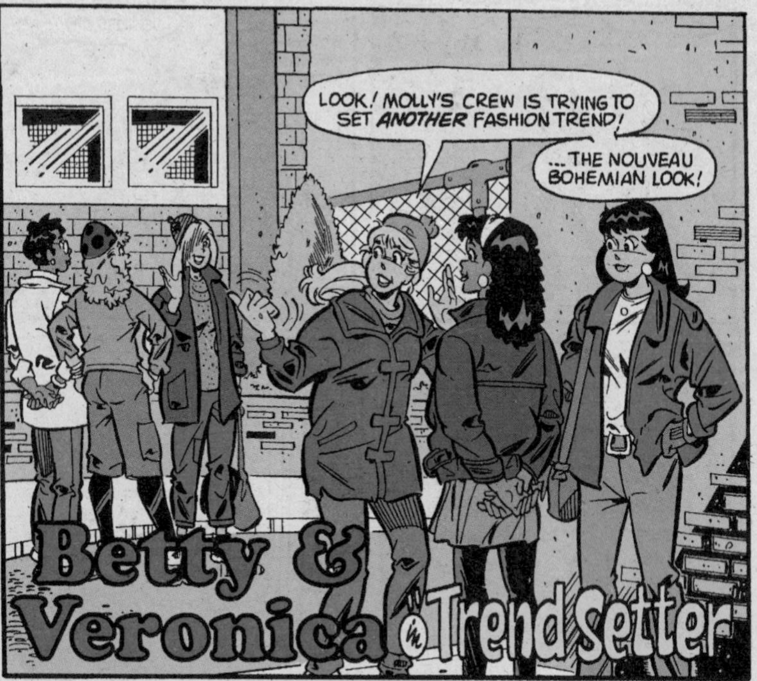
LOOK! MOLLY'S CREW IS TRYING TO SET ANOTHER FASHION TREND!
...THE NOUVEAU BOHEMIAN LOOK!
Betty & Veronica in Trend Setter

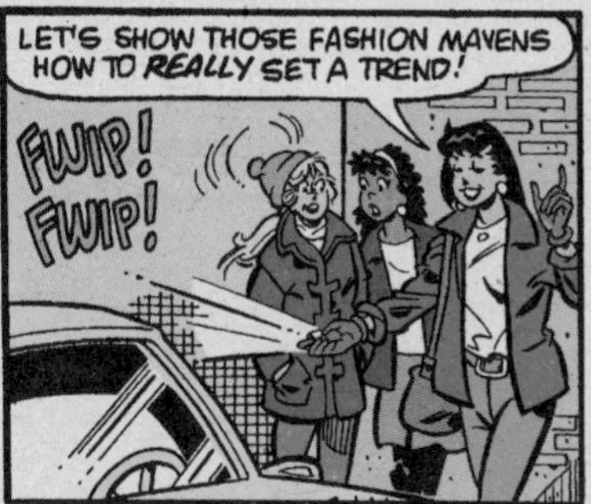
LET'S SHOW THOSE FASHION MAVENS HOW TO REALLY SET A TREND!
FWIP! FWIP!

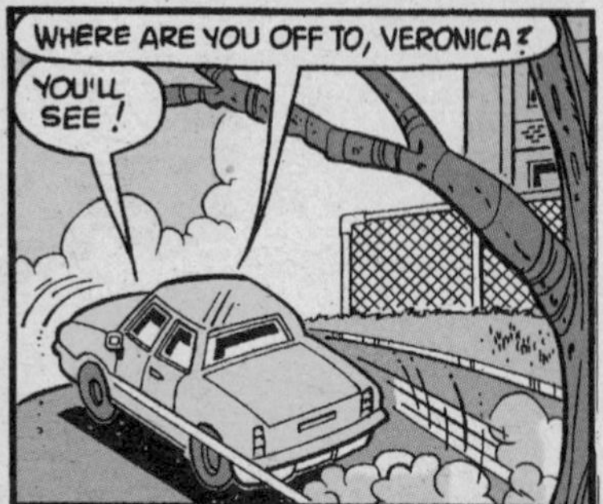
WHERE ARE YOU OFF TO, VERONICA?
YOU'LL SEE!

Script: George Gladir / Pencils: Tim Kennedy / Inks: Ken Selig / Letters: Bill Yoshida / Colors: Frank Gagliardo

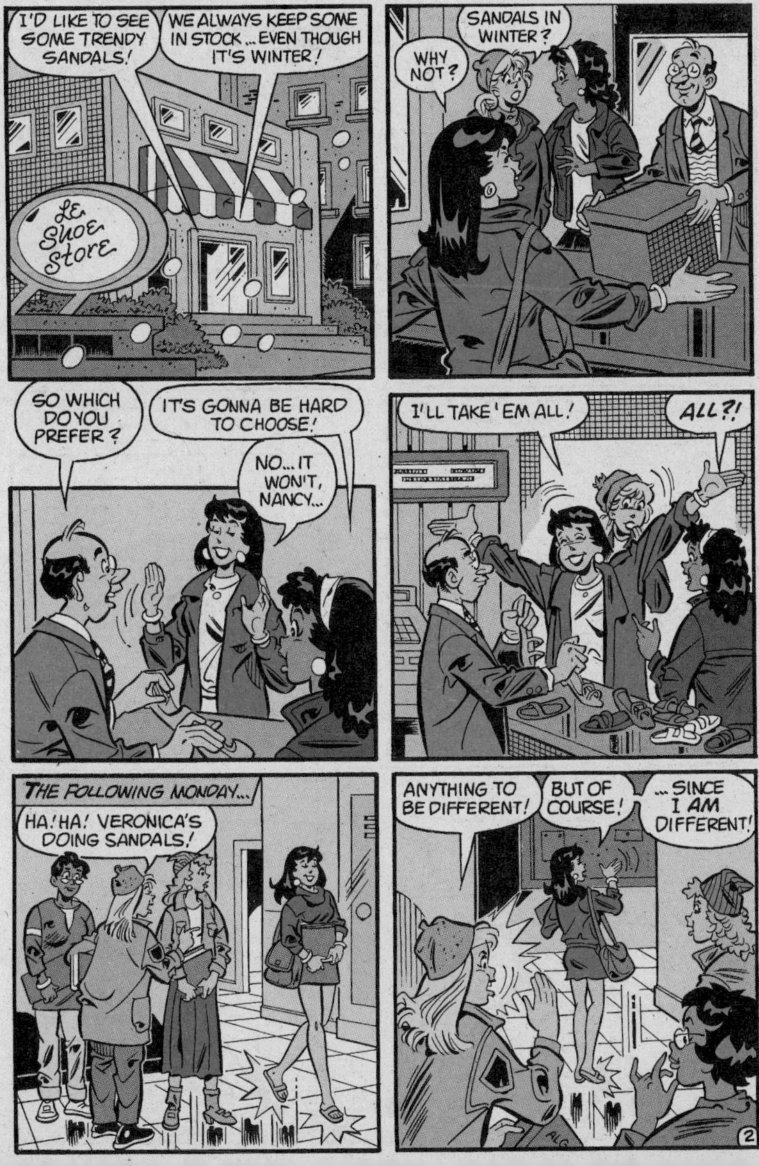

I'D LIKE TO SEE SOME TRENDY SANDALS!
WE ALWAYS KEEP SOME IN STOCK... EVEN THOUGH IT'S WINTER!
Le Shoe Store
SANDALS IN WINTER?
WHY NOT?
SO WHICH DO YOU PREFER?
IT'S GONNA BE HARD TO CHOOSE!
NO... IT WON'T, NANCY...
I'LL TAKE 'EM ALL!
ALL?!
THE FOLLOWING MONDAY...
HA! HA! VERONICA'S DOING SANDALS!
ANYTHING TO BE DIFFERENT!
BUT OF COURSE!
... SINCE I AM DIFFERENT!
2

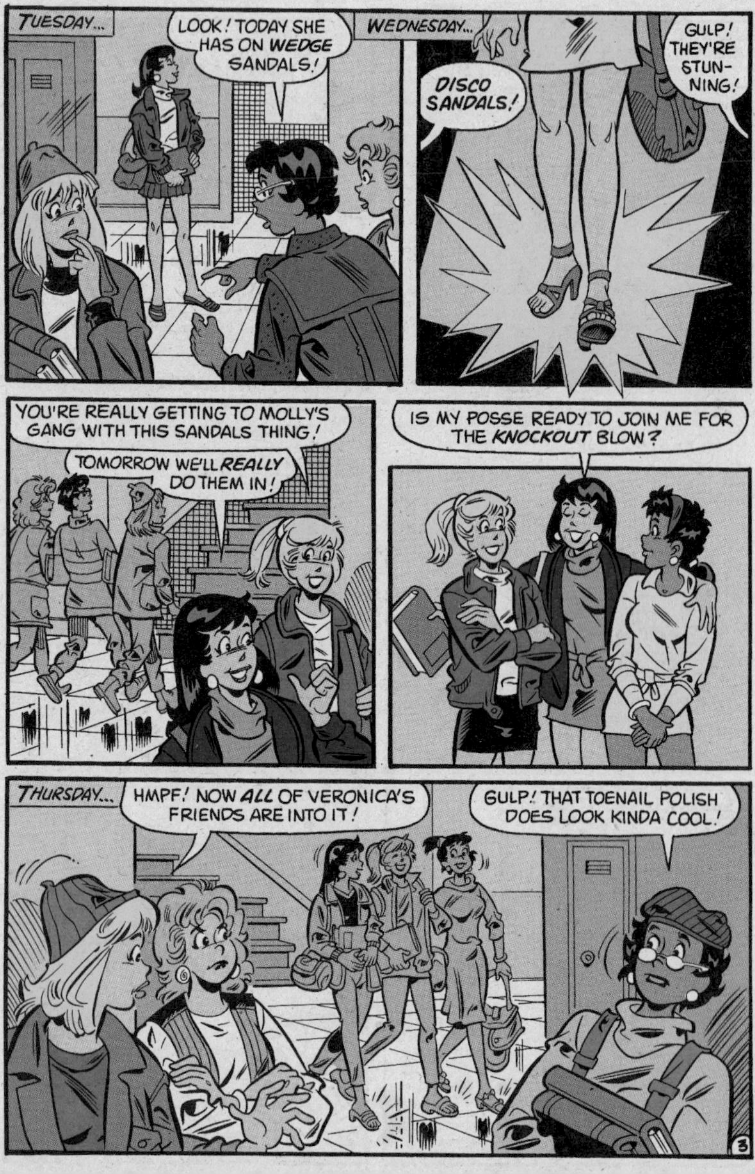
TUESDAY...
LOOK! TODAY SHE HAS ON WEDGE SANDALS!
WEDNESDAY...
DISCO SANDALS!
GULP! THEY'RE STUN-NING!
YOU'RE REALLY GETTING TO MOLLY'S GANG WITH THIS SANDALS THING!
TOMORROW WE'LL REALLY DO THEM IN!
IS MY POSSE READY TO JOIN ME FOR THE KNOCKOUT BLOW?
THURSDAY...
HMPF! NOW ALL OF VERONICA'S FRIENDS ARE INTO IT!
GULP! THAT TOENAIL POLISH DOES LOOK KINDA COOL!
3

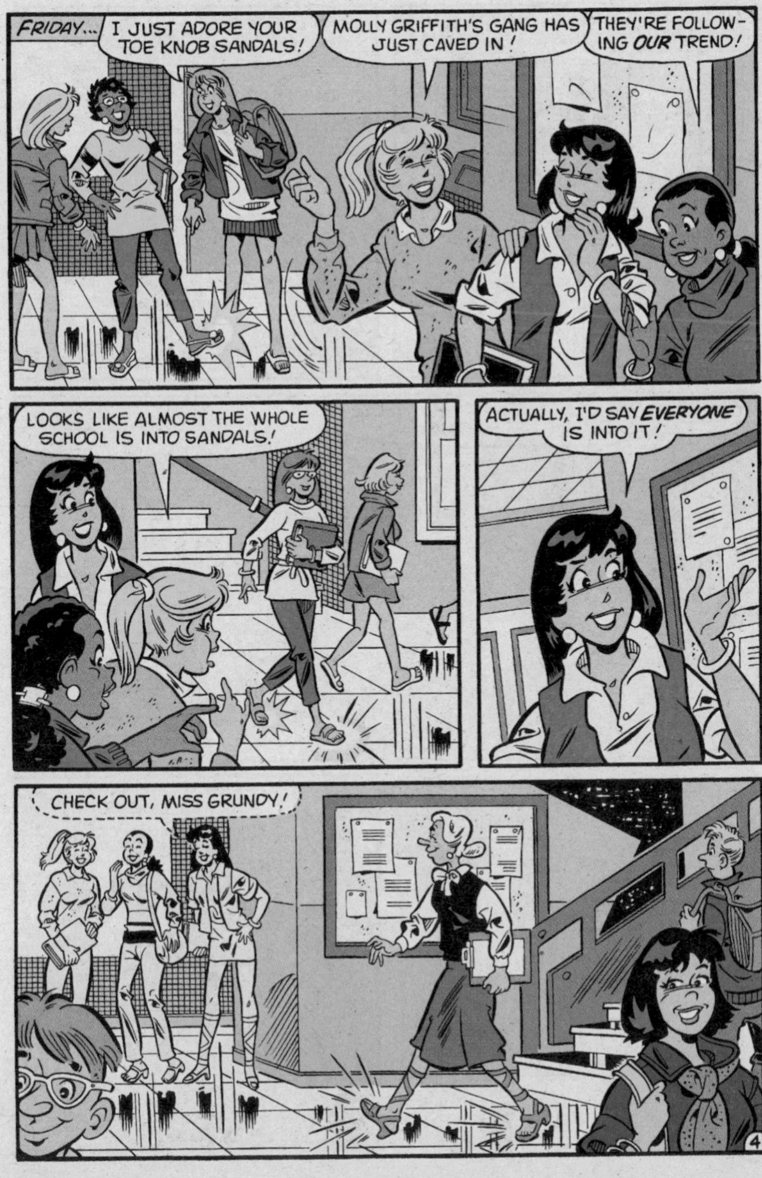
FRIDAY...
I JUST ADORE YOUR TOE KNOB SANDALS!
MOLLY GRIFFITH'S GANG HAS JUST CAVED IN!
THEY'RE FOLLOWING OUR TREND!
LOOKS LIKE ALMOST THE WHOLE SCHOOL IS INTO SANDALS!
ACTUALLY, I'D SAY EVERYONE IS INTO IT!
CHECK OUT, MISS GRUNDY!
4

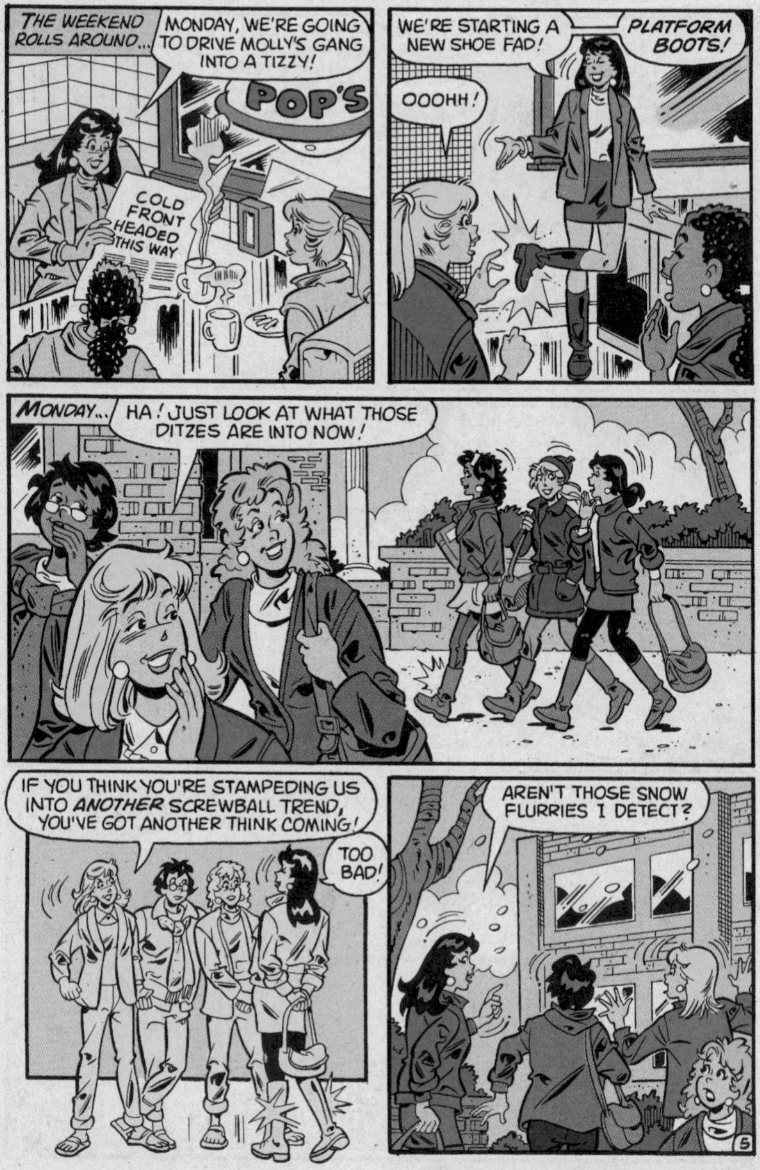
THE WEEKEND ROLLS AROUND...
MONDAY, WE'RE GOING TO DRIVE MOLLY'S GANG INTO A TIZZY!
POP'S
COLD FRONT HEADED THIS WAY
WE'RE STARTING A NEW SHOE FAD!
PLATFORM BOOTS!
OOOHH!
MONDAY...
HA! JUST LOOK AT WHAT THOSE DITZES ARE INTO NOW!
IF YOU THINK YOU'RE STAMPEDING US INTO ANOTHER SCREWBALL TREND, YOU'VE GOT ANOTHER THINK COMING!
TOO BAD!
AREN'T THOSE SNOW FLURRIES I DETECT?
5

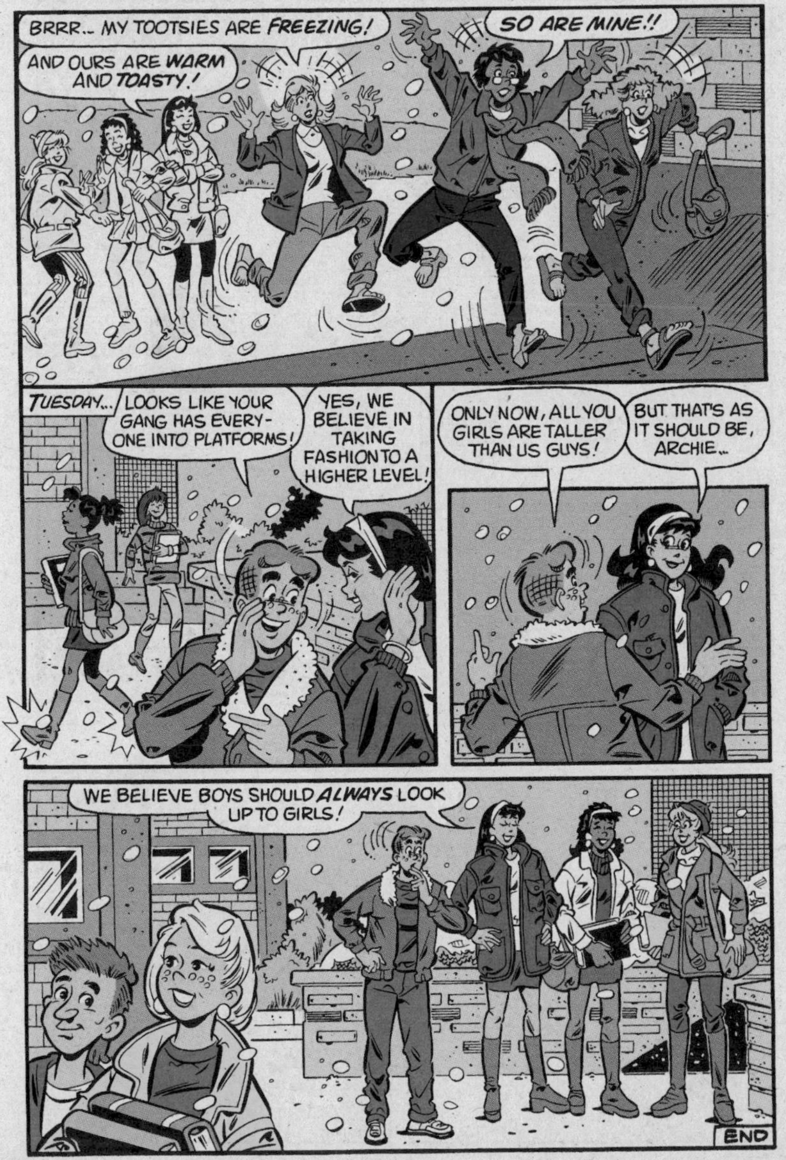
BRRR.. MY TOOTSIES ARE FREEZING!
AND OURS ARE WARM AND TOASTY!
SO ARE MINE!!
TUESDAY...
LOOKS LIKE YOUR GANG HAS EVERY-ONE INTO PLATFORMS!
YES, WE BELIEVE IN TAKING FASHION TO A HIGHER LEVEL!
ONLY NOW, ALL YOU GIRLS ARE TALLER THAN US GUYS!
BUT THAT'S AS IT SHOULD BE, ARCHIE...
WE BELIEVE BOYS SHOULD ALWAYS LOOK UP TO GIRLS!
END

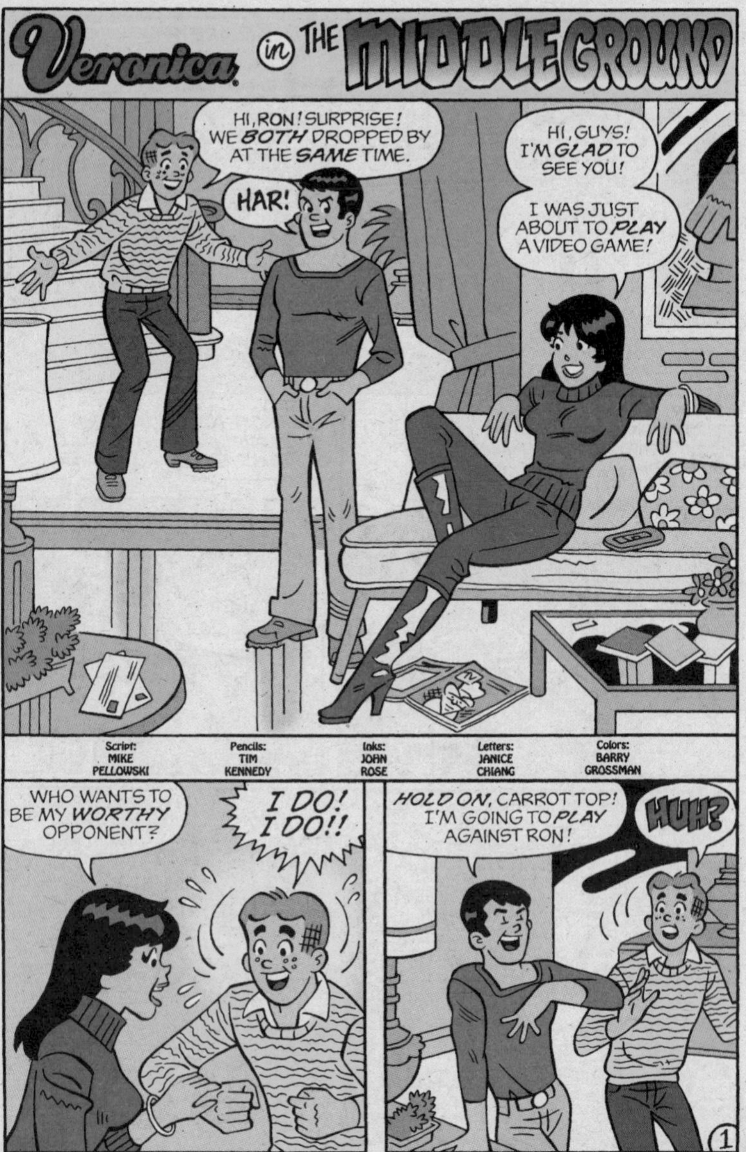

Veronica in THE MIDDLE GROUND
HI, RON! SURPRISE! WE BOTH DROPPED BY AT THE SAME TIME.
HAR!
HI, GUYS! I'M GLAD TO SEE YOU!
I WAS JUST ABOUT TO PLAY A VIDEO GAME!
Script: MIKE PELLOWSKI
Pencils: TIM KENNEDY
Inks: JOHN ROSE
Letters: JANICE CHIANG
Colors: BARRY GROSSMAN
WHO WANTS TO BE MY WORTHY OPPONENT?
I DO! I DO!!
HOLD ON, CARROT TOP! I'M GOING TO PLAY AGAINST RON!
HUH?
1

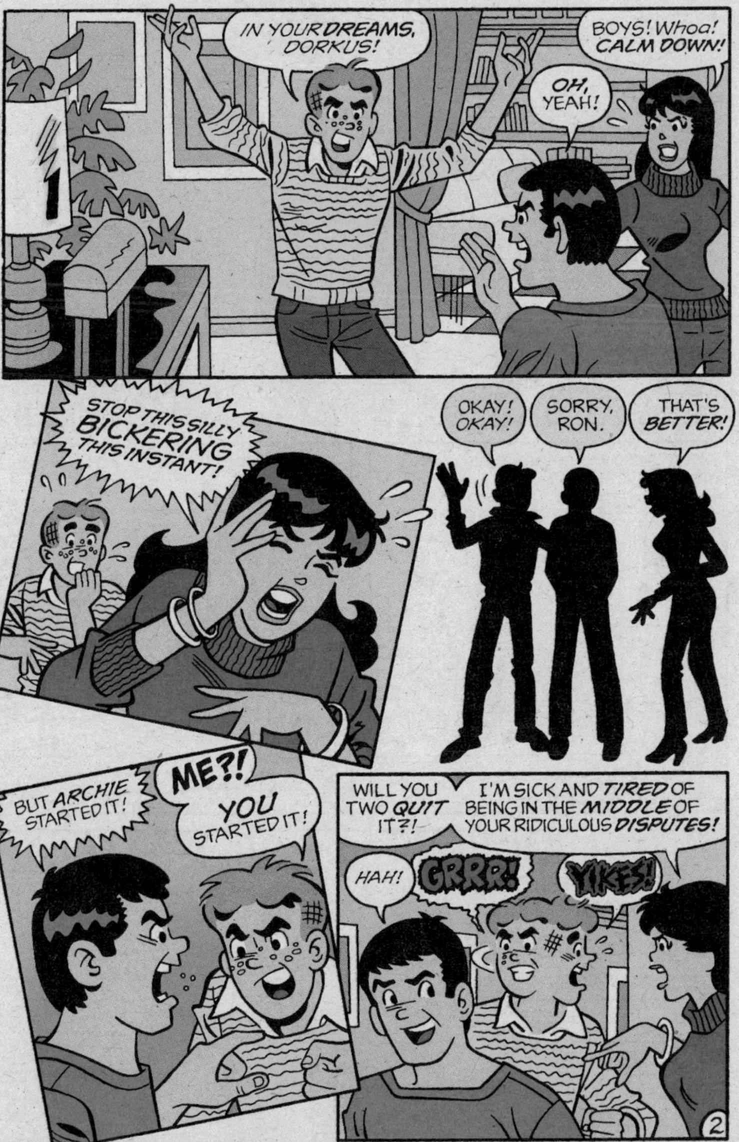

IN YOUR DREAMS, DORKUS!
OH, YEAH!
BOYS! Whoa! CALM DOWN!
STOP THIS SILLY BICKERING THIS INSTANT!
OKAY! OKAY!
SORRY, RON.
THAT'S BETTER!
BUT ARCHIE STARTED IT!
ME?!
YOU STARTED IT!
WILL YOU TWO QUIT IT?!
I'M SICK AND TIRED OF BEING IN THE MIDDLE OF YOUR RIDICULOUS DISPUTES!
HAH!
GRRR!
YIKES!
2

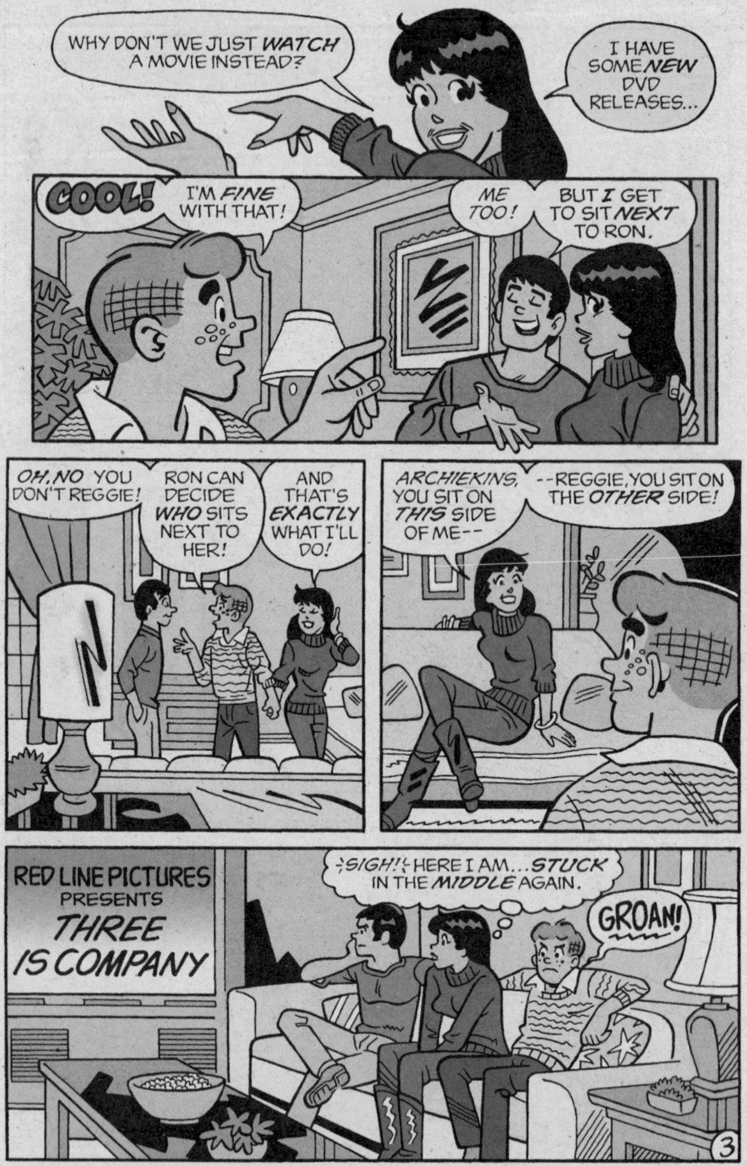

WHY DON'T WE JUST WATCH A MOVIE INSTEAD?
I HAVE SOME NEW DVD RELEASES...
COOL!
I'M FINE WITH THAT!
ME TOO!
BUT I GET TO SIT NEXT TO RON.
OH, NO YOU DON'T REGGIE!
RON CAN DECIDE WHO SITS NEXT TO HER!
AND THAT'S EXACTLY WHAT I'LL DO!
ARCHIEKINS, YOU SIT ON THIS SIDE OF ME--
--REGGIE, YOU SIT ON THE OTHER SIDE!
RED LINE PICTURES PRESENTS THREE IS COMPANY
SIGH! HERE I AM... STUCK IN THE MIDDLE AGAIN.
GROAN!

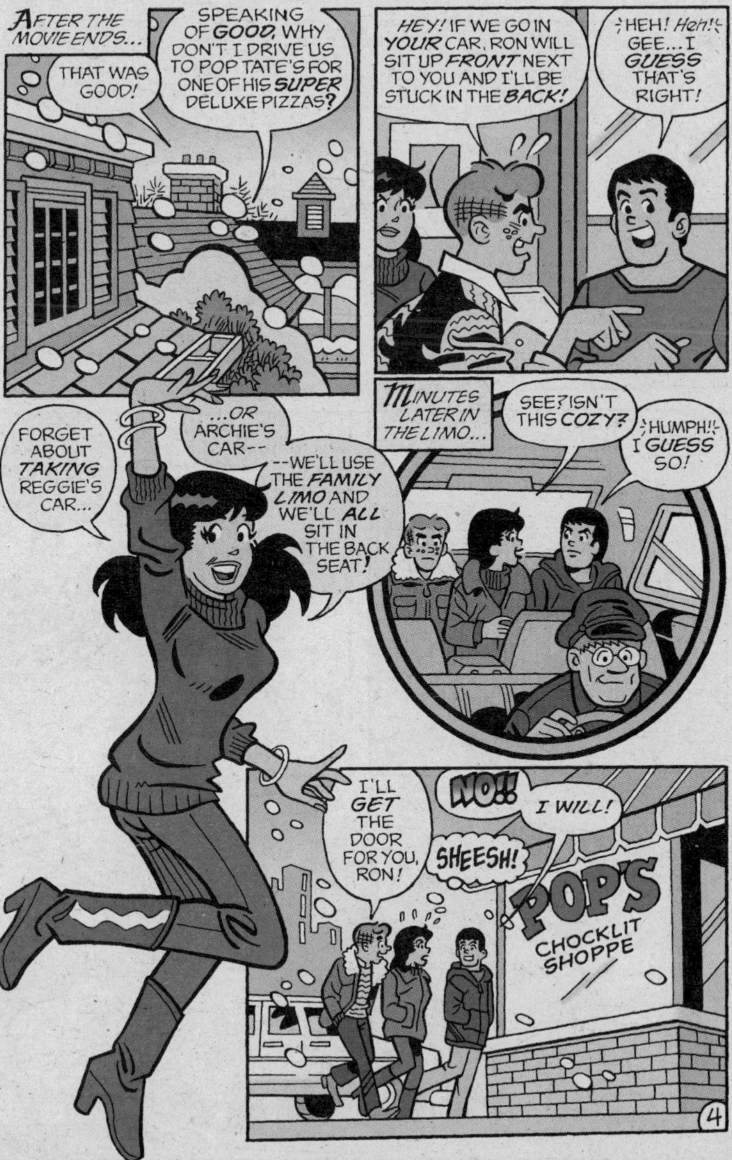

AFTER THE MOVIE ENDS...
THAT WAS GOOD!
SPEAKING OF GOOD, WHY DON'T I DRIVE US TO POP TATE'S FOR ONE OF HIS SUPER DELUXE PIZZAS?
HEY! IF WE GO IN YOUR CAR, RON WILL SIT UP FRONT NEXT TO YOU AND I'LL BE STUCK IN THE BACK!
HEH! Heh! GEE... I GUESS THAT'S RIGHT!
FORGET ABOUT TAKING REGGIE'S CAR...
...OR ARCHIE'S CAR--
--WE'LL USE THE FAMILY LIMO AND WE'LL ALL SIT IN THE BACK SEAT!
MINUTES LATER IN THE LIMO...
SEE? ISN'T THIS COZY?
HUMPH! I GUESS SO!
I'LL GET THE DOOR FOR YOU, RON!
NO!!
I WILL!
SHEESH!
POP'S
CHOCKLIT SHOPPE
4

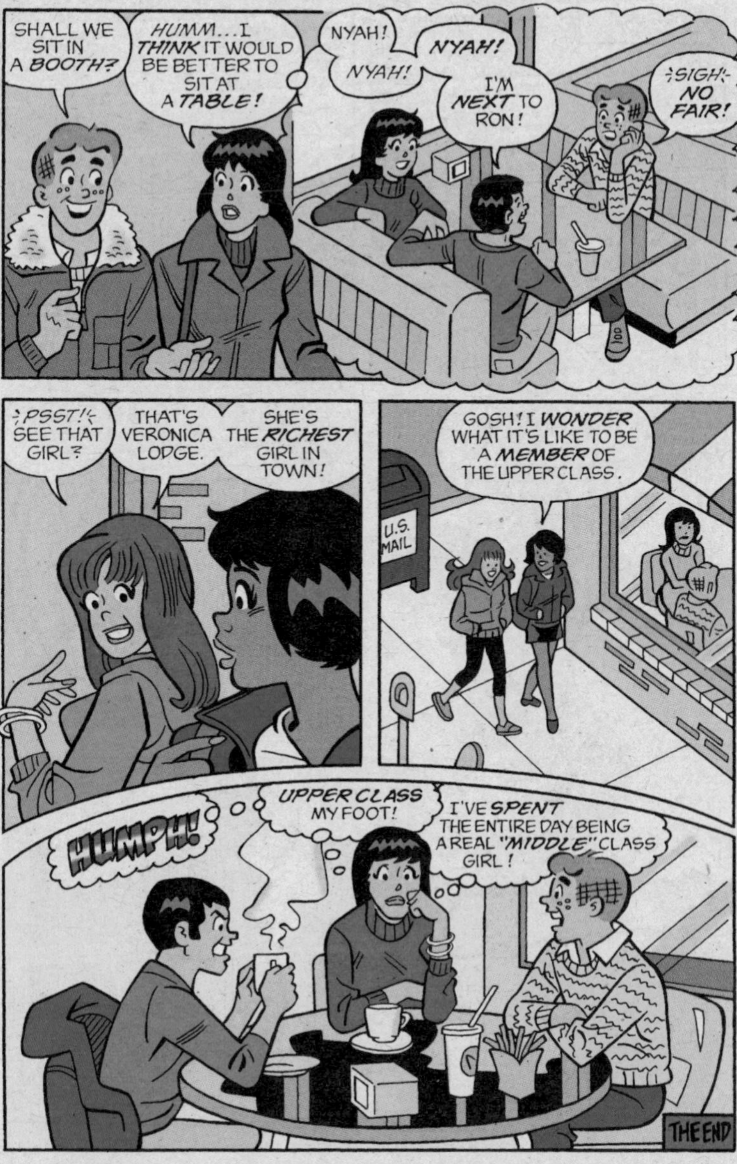
SHALL WE SIT IN A BOOTH?
HUMM...I THINK IT WOULD BE BETTER TO SIT AT A TABLE!
NYAH!
NYAH!
NYAH!
I'M NEXT TO RON!
-SIGH- NO FAIR!
-PSST!- SEE THAT GIRL?
THAT'S VERONICA LODGE.
SHE'S THE RICHEST GIRL IN TOWN!
GOSH! I WONDER WHAT IT'S LIKE TO BE A MEMBER OF THE UPPER CLASS.
U.S. MAIL
HUMPH!
UPPER CLASS MY FOOT!
I'VE SPENT THE ENTIRE DAY BEING A REAL "MIDDLE" CLASS GIRL!
THE END

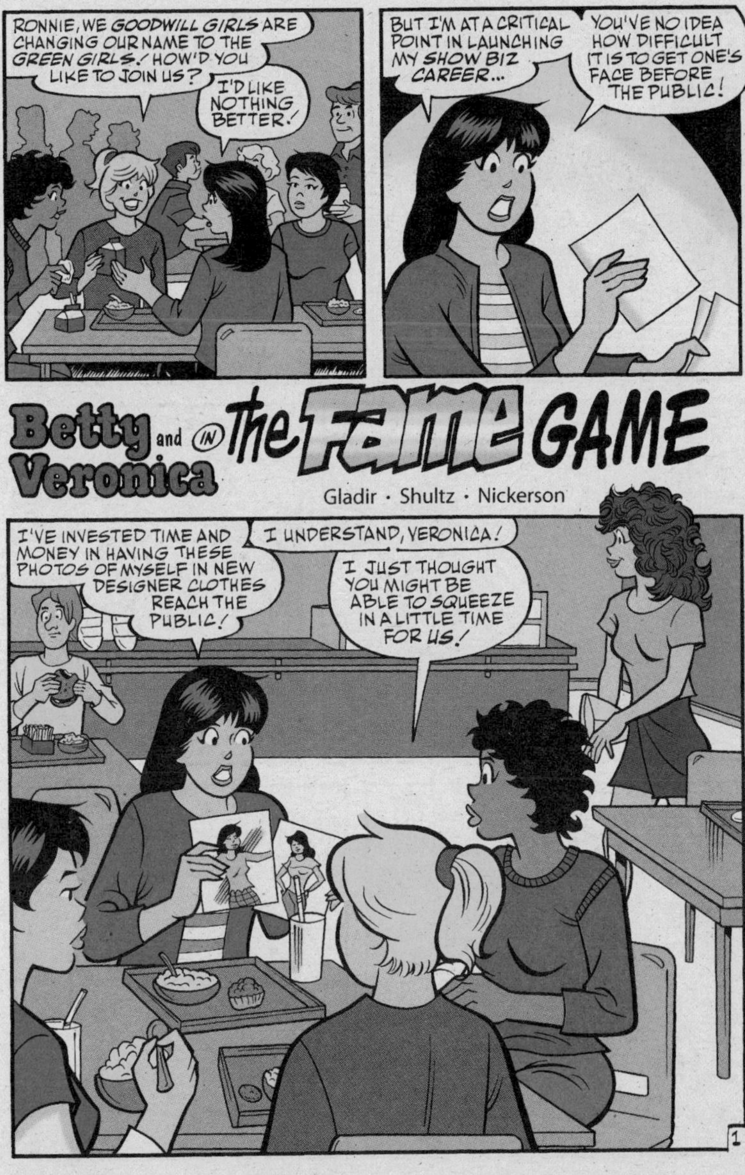
RONNIE, WE GOODWILL GIRLS ARE CHANGING OUR NAME TO THE GREEN GIRLS! HOW'D YOU LIKE TO JOIN US?
I'D LIKE NOTHING BETTER!
BUT I'M AT A CRITICAL POINT IN LAUNCHING MY SHOW BIZ CAREER...
YOU'VE NO IDEA HOW DIFFICULT IT IS TO GET ONE'S FACE BEFORE THE PUBLIC!
Betty and Veronica in The Fame Game
Gladir · Shultz · Nickerson
I'VE INVESTED TIME AND MONEY IN HAVING THESE PHOTOS OF MYSELF IN NEW DESIGNER CLOTHES REACH THE PUBLIC!
I UNDERSTAND, VERONICA!
I JUST THOUGHT YOU MIGHT BE ABLE TO SQUEEZE IN A LITTLE TIME FOR US!
1

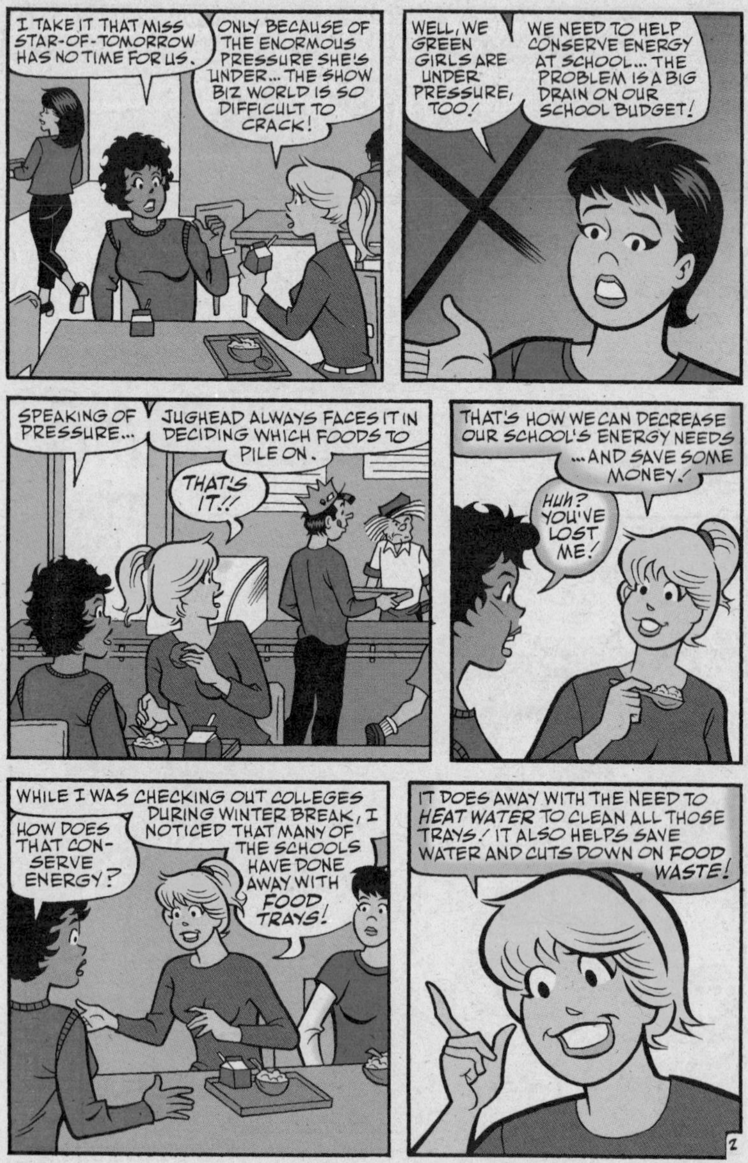

I TAKE IT THAT MISS STAR-OF-TOMORROW HAS NO TIME FOR US.
ONLY BECAUSE OF THE ENORMOUS PRESSURE SHE'S UNDER... THE SHOW BIZ WORLD IS SO DIFFICULT TO CRACK!
WELL, WE GREEN GIRLS ARE UNDER PRESSURE, TOO!
WE NEED TO HELP CONSERVE ENERGY AT SCHOOL... THE PROBLEM IS A BIG DRAIN ON OUR SCHOOL BUDGET!
SPEAKING OF PRESSURE...
JUGHEAD ALWAYS FACES IT IN DECIDING WHICH FOODS TO PILE ON.
THAT'S IT!!
THAT'S HOW WE CAN DECREASE OUR SCHOOL'S ENERGY NEEDS ...AND SAVE SOME MONEY!
HUH? YOU'VE LOST ME!
WHILE I WAS CHECKING OUT COLLEGES DURING WINTER BREAK, I NOTICED THAT MANY OF THE SCHOOLS HAVE DONE AWAY WITH FOOD TRAYS!
HOW DOES THAT CON-SERVE ENERGY?
IT DOES AWAY WITH THE NEED TO HEAT WATER TO CLEAN ALL THOSE TRAYS! IT ALSO HELPS SAVE WATER AND CUTS DOWN ON FOOD WASTE!
2

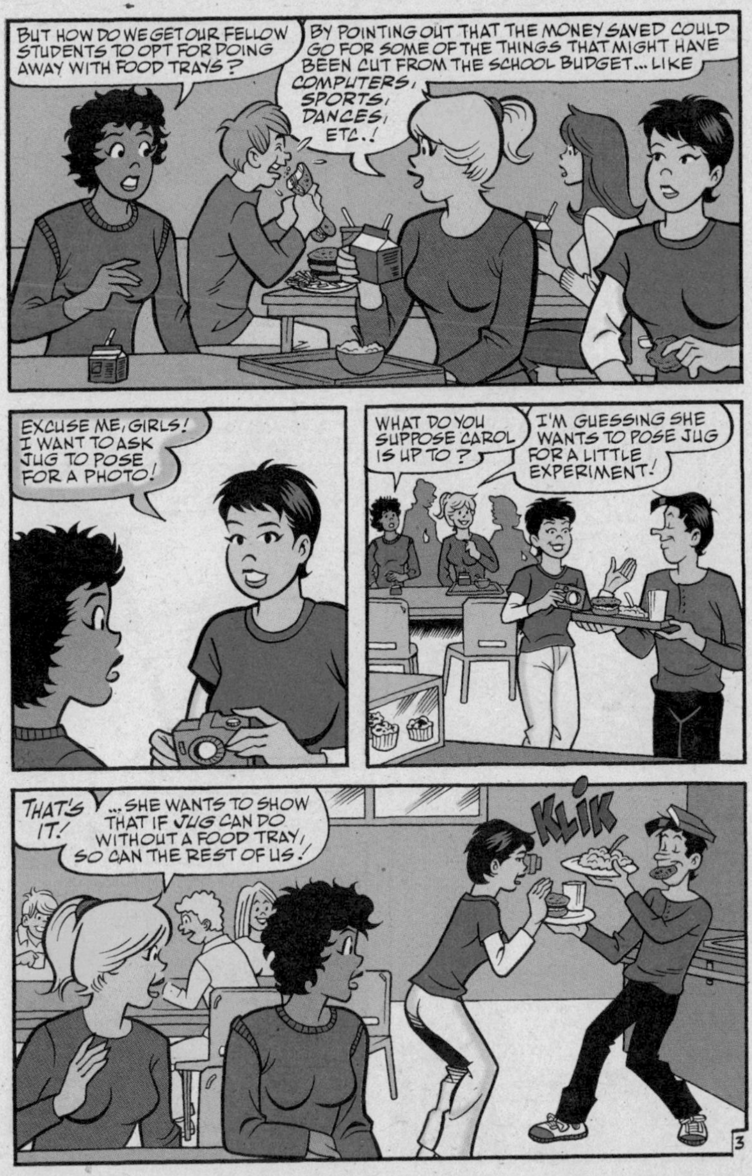

BUT HOW DO WE GET OUR FELLOW STUDENTS TO OPT FOR DOING AWAY WITH FOOD TRAYS?
BY POINTING OUT THAT THE MONEY SAVED COULD GO FOR SOME OF THE THINGS THAT MIGHT HAVE BEEN CUT FROM THE SCHOOL BUDGET... LIKE COMPUTERS, SPORTS, DANCES, ETC.!
EXCUSE ME, GIRLS! I WANT TO ASK JUG TO POSE FOR A PHOTO!
WHAT DO YOU SUPPOSE CAROL IS UP TO?
I'M GUESSING SHE WANTS TO POSE JUG FOR A LITTLE EXPERIMENT!
THAT'S IT!
...SHE WANTS TO SHOW THAT IF JUG CAN DO WITHOUT A FOOD TRAY, SO CAN THE REST OF US!
KLIK

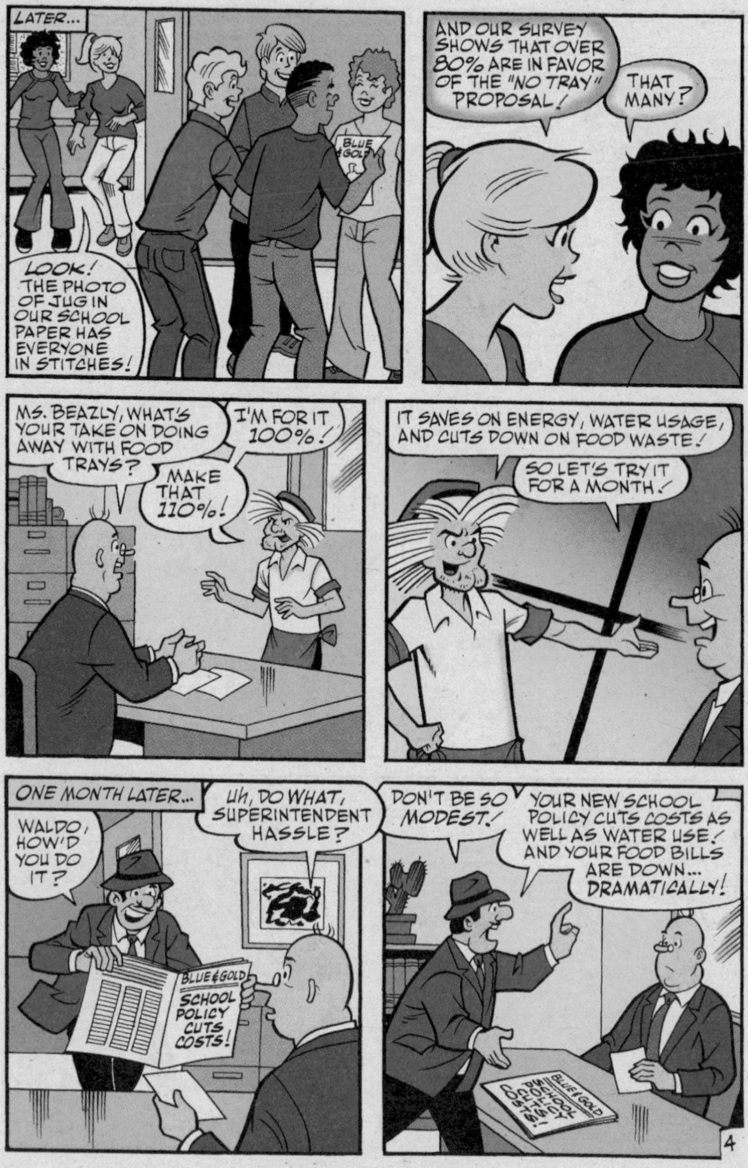
LATER...
LOOK! THE PHOTO OF JUG IN OUR SCHOOL PAPER HAS EVERYONE IN STITCHES!
BLUE & GOLD
AND OUR SURVEY SHOWS THAT OVER 80% ARE IN FAVOR OF THE "NO TRAY" PROPOSAL!
THAT MANY?
MS. BEAZLY, WHAT'S YOUR TAKE ON DOING AWAY WITH FOOD TRAYS?
I'M FOR IT 100%!
MAKE THAT 110%!
IT SAVES ON ENERGY, WATER USAGE, AND CUTS DOWN ON FOOD WASTE!
SO LET'S TRY IT FOR A MONTH!
ONE MONTH LATER...
WALDO, HOW'D YOU DO IT?
UH, DO WHAT, SUPERINTENDENT HASSLE?
BLUE & GOLD
SCHOOL POLICY CUTS COSTS!
DON'T BE SO MODEST!
YOUR NEW SCHOOL POLICY CUTS COSTS AS WELL AS WATER USE! AND YOUR FOOD BILLS ARE DOWN... DRAMATICALLY!
BLUE & GOLD
SCHOOL POLICY CUTS COSTS!

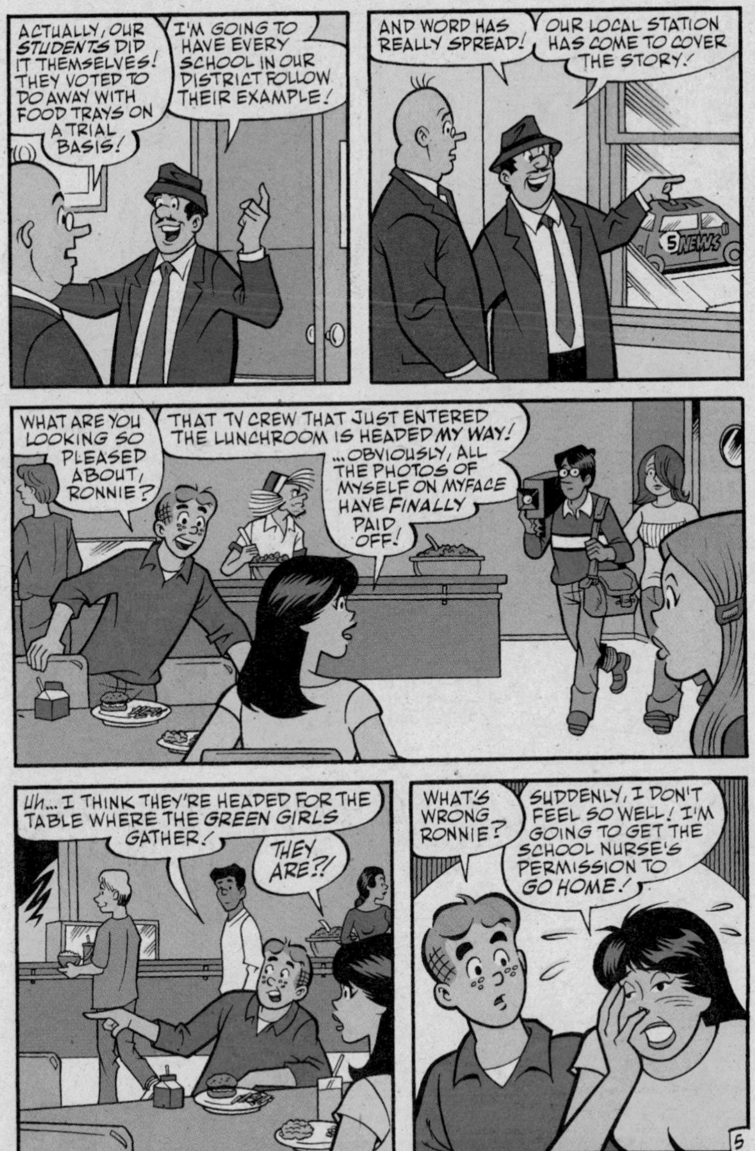
ACTUALLY, OUR STUDENTS DID IT THEMSELVES! THEY VOTED TO DO AWAY WITH FOOD TRAYS ON A TRIAL BASIS!
I'M GOING TO HAVE EVERY SCHOOL IN OUR DISTRICT FOLLOW THEIR EXAMPLE!
AND WORD HAS REALLY SPREAD!
OUR LOCAL STATION HAS COME TO COVER THE STORY!
5 NEWS
WHAT ARE YOU LOOKING SO PLEASED ABOUT, RONNIE?
THAT TV CREW THAT JUST ENTERED THE LUNCHROOM IS HEADED MY WAY!
...OBVIOUSLY, ALL THE PHOTOS OF MYSELF ON MYFACE HAVE FINALLY PAID OFF!
Uh... I THINK THEY'RE HEADED FOR THE TABLE WHERE THE GREEN GIRLS GATHER!
THEY ARE?!
WHAT'S WRONG RONNIE?
SUDDENLY, I DON'T FEEL SO WELL! I'M GOING TO GET THE SCHOOL NURSE'S PERMISSION TO GO HOME!
5

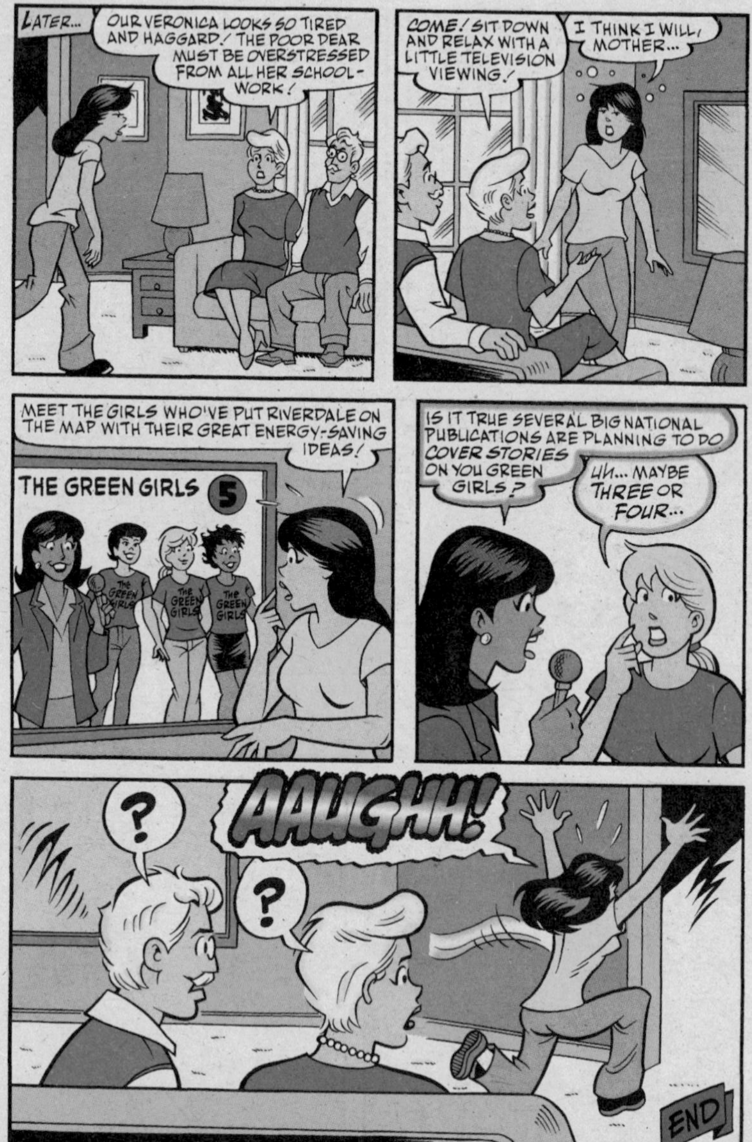

LATER...
OUR VERONICA LOOKS SO TIRED AND HAGGARD! THE POOR DEAR MUST BE OVERSTRESSED FROM ALL HER SCHOOL-WORK!
COME! SIT DOWN AND RELAX WITH A LITTLE TELEVISION VIEWING!
I THINK I WILL, MOTHER...
MEET THE GIRLS WHO'VE PUT RIVERDALE ON THE MAP WITH THEIR GREAT ENERGY-SAVING IDEAS!
THE GREEN GIRLS
5
THE GREEN GIRLS
THE GREEN GIRLS
THE GREEN GIRLS
IS IT TRUE SEVERAL BIG NATIONAL PUBLICATIONS ARE PLANNING TO DO COVER STORIES ON YOU GREEN GIRLS?
UH... MAYBE THREE OR FOUR...
?
AAUGHH!
?
END

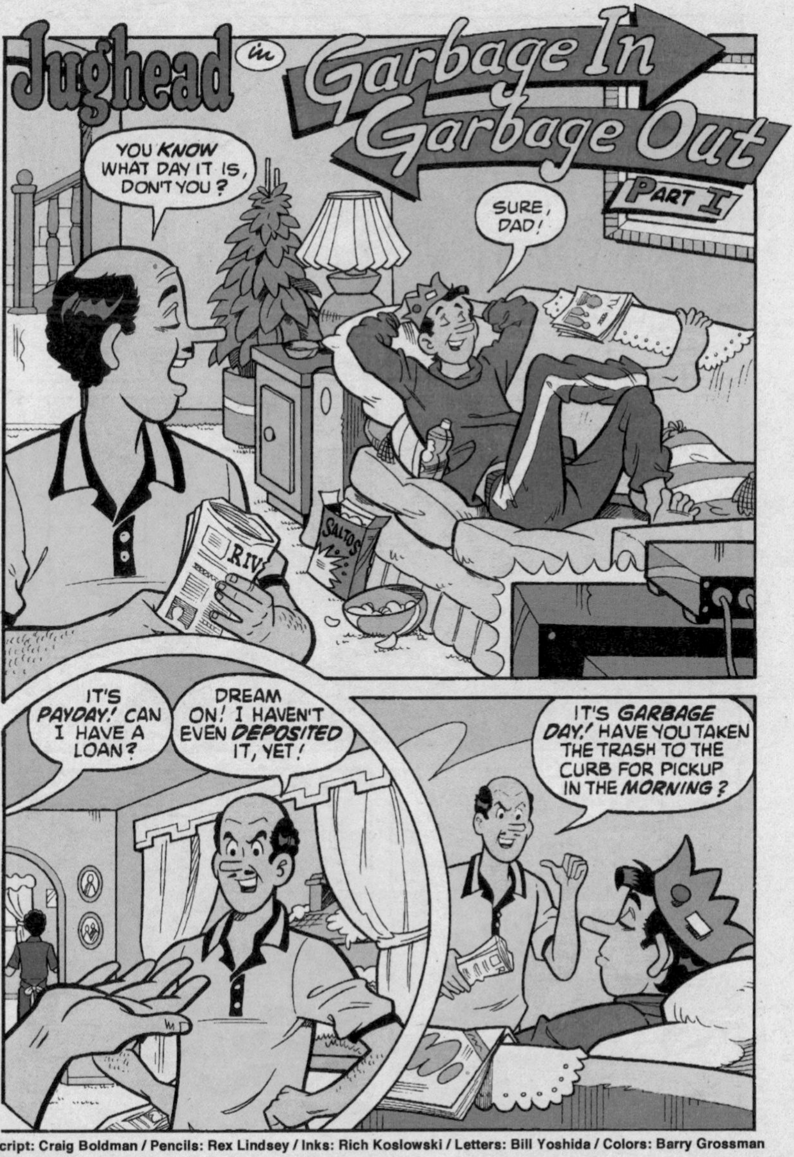
Jughead in
Garbage In Garbage Out
PART I
YOU KNOW WHAT DAY IT IS, DON'T YOU?
SURE, DAD!
IT'S PAYDAY! CAN I HAVE A LOAN?
DREAM ON! I HAVEN'T EVEN DEPOSITED IT, YET!
IT'S GARBAGE DAY! HAVE YOU TAKEN THE TRASH TO THE CURB FOR PICKUP IN THE MORNING?

Script: Craig Boldman / Pencils: Rex Lindsey / Inks: Rich Koslowski / Letters: Bill Yoshida / Colors: Barry Grossman

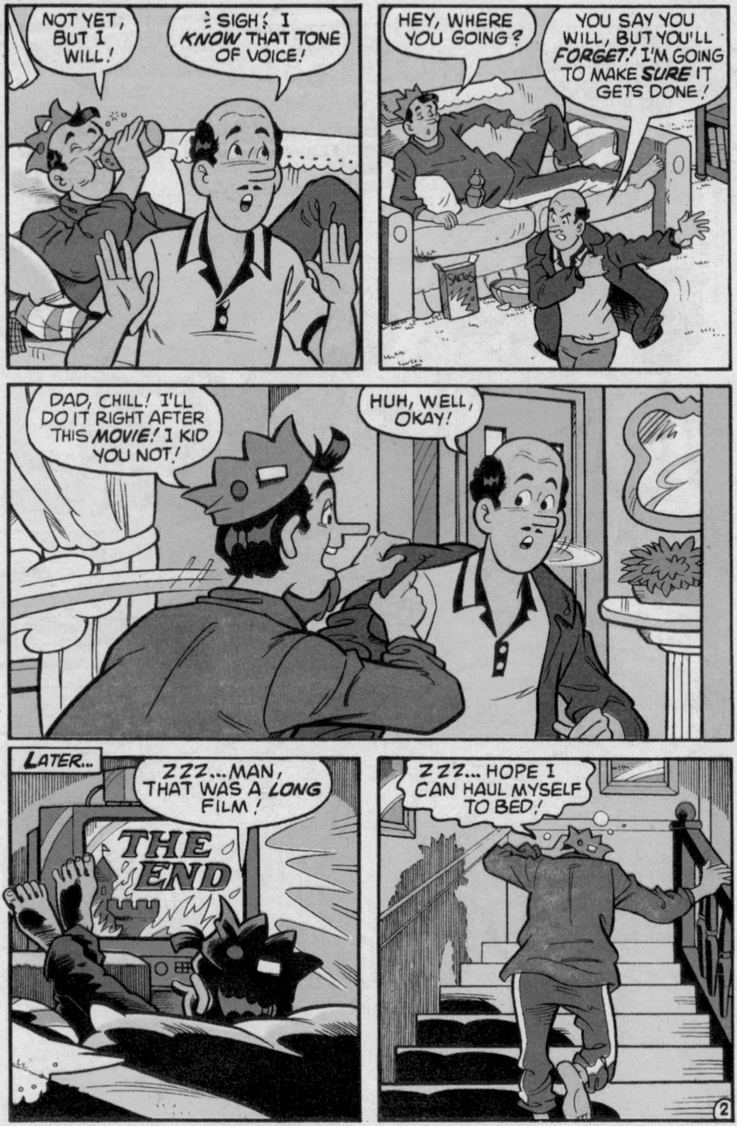
NOT YET, BUT I WILL!
SIGH! I KNOW THAT TONE OF VOICE!
HEY, WHERE YOU GOING?
YOU SAY YOU WILL, BUT YOU'LL FORGET! I'M GOING TO MAKE SURE IT GETS DONE!
SALTOS
DAD, CHILL! I'LL DO IT RIGHT AFTER THIS MOVIE! I KID YOU NOT!
HUH, WELL, OKAY!
LATER...
ZZZ...MAN, THAT WAS A LONG FILM!
THE END
ZZZ... HOPE I CAN HAUL MYSELF TO BED!
2

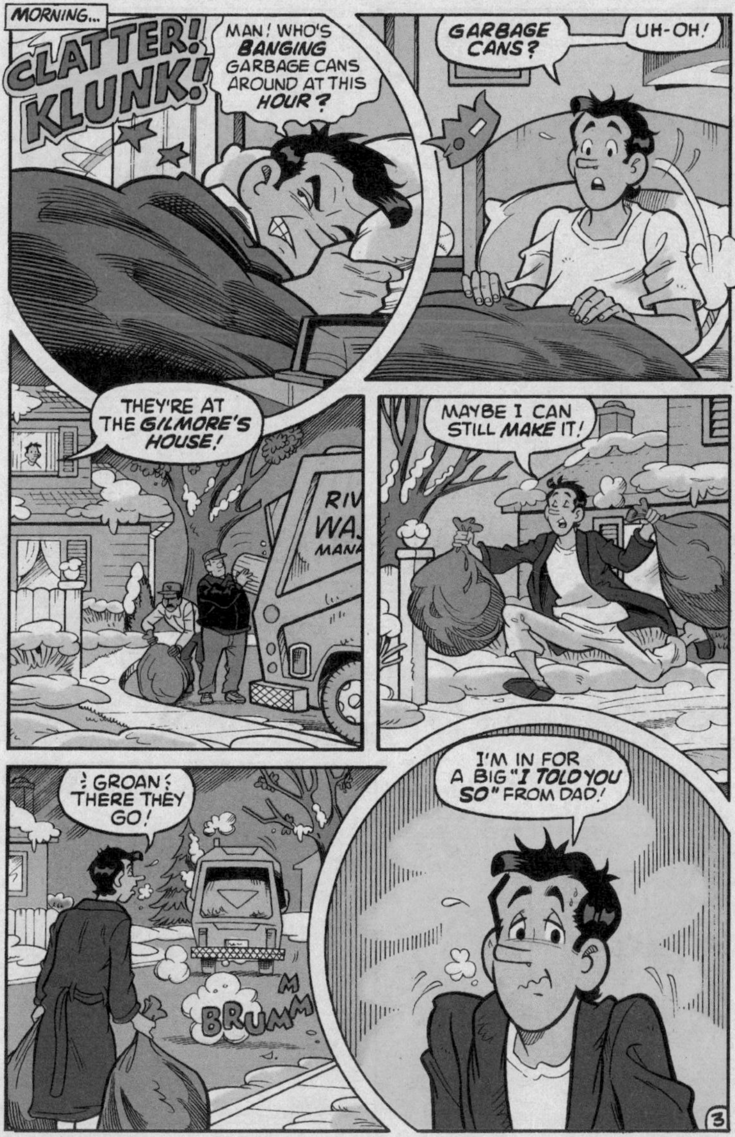
MORNING...
CLATTER! KLUNK!
MAN! WHO'S BANGING GARBAGE CANS AROUND AT THIS HOUR?
GARBAGE CANS?
UH-OH!
THEY'RE AT THE GILMORE'S HOUSE!
RIV WAS MANA
MAYBE I CAN STILL MAKE IT!
GROAN THERE THEY GO!
BRUMMM
I'M IN FOR A BIG "I TOLD YOU SO" FROM DAD!
3

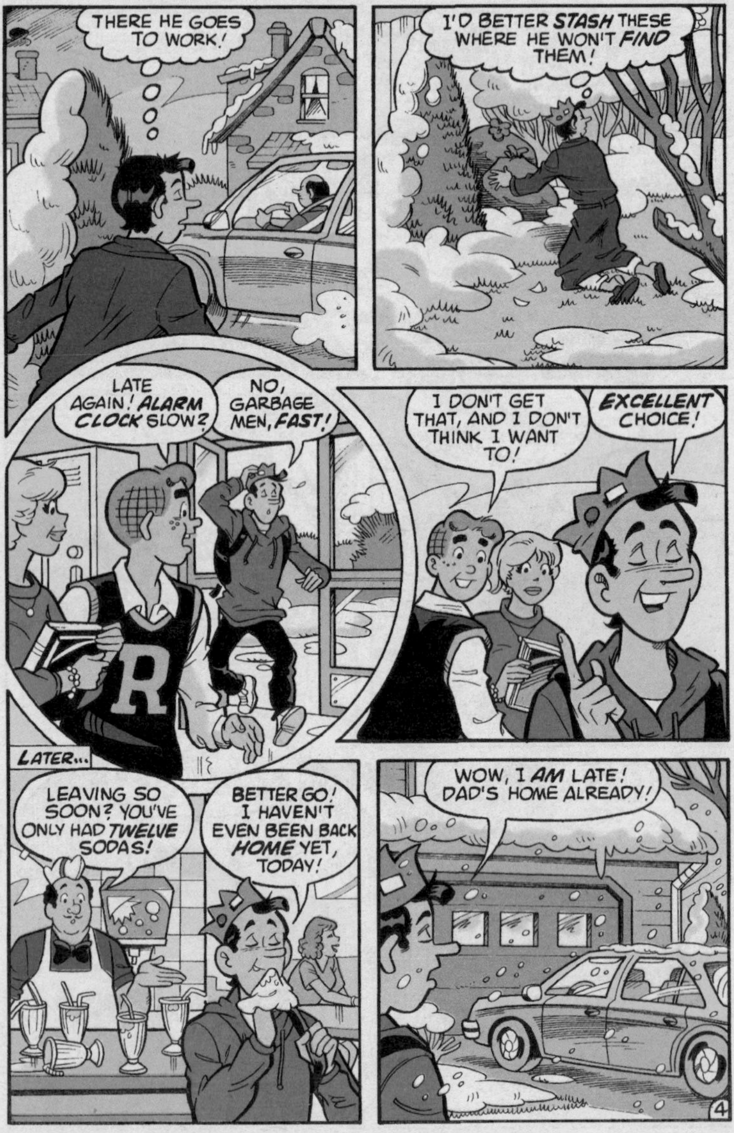
THERE HE GOES TO WORK!
I'D BETTER STASH THESE WHERE HE WON'T FIND THEM!
LATE AGAIN! ALARM CLOCK SLOW?
NO, GARBAGE MEN, FAST!
I DON'T GET THAT, AND I DON'T THINK I WANT TO!
EXCELLENT CHOICE!
LATER...
LEAVING SO SOON? YOU'VE ONLY HAD TWELVE SODAS!
BETTER GO! I HAVEN'T EVEN BEEN BACK HOME YET, TODAY!
WOW, I AM LATE! DAD'S HOME ALREADY!
4

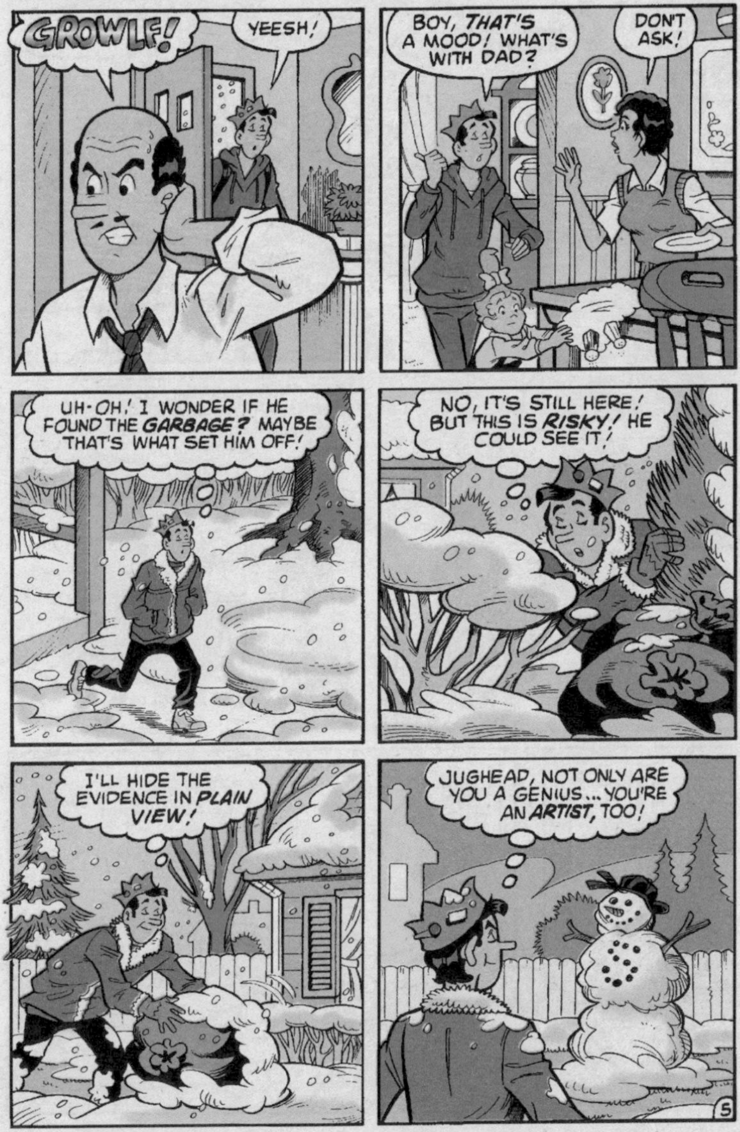
GROWLF!
YEESH!
BOY, THAT'S A MOOD! WHAT'S WITH DAD?
DON'T ASK!
UH-OH! I WONDER IF HE FOUND THE GARBAGE? MAYBE THAT'S WHAT SET HIM OFF!
NO, IT'S STILL HERE! BUT THIS IS RISKY! HE COULD SEE IT!
I'LL HIDE THE EVIDENCE IN PLAIN VIEW!
JUGHEAD, NOT ONLY ARE YOU A GENIUS... YOU'RE AN ARTIST, TOO!
5

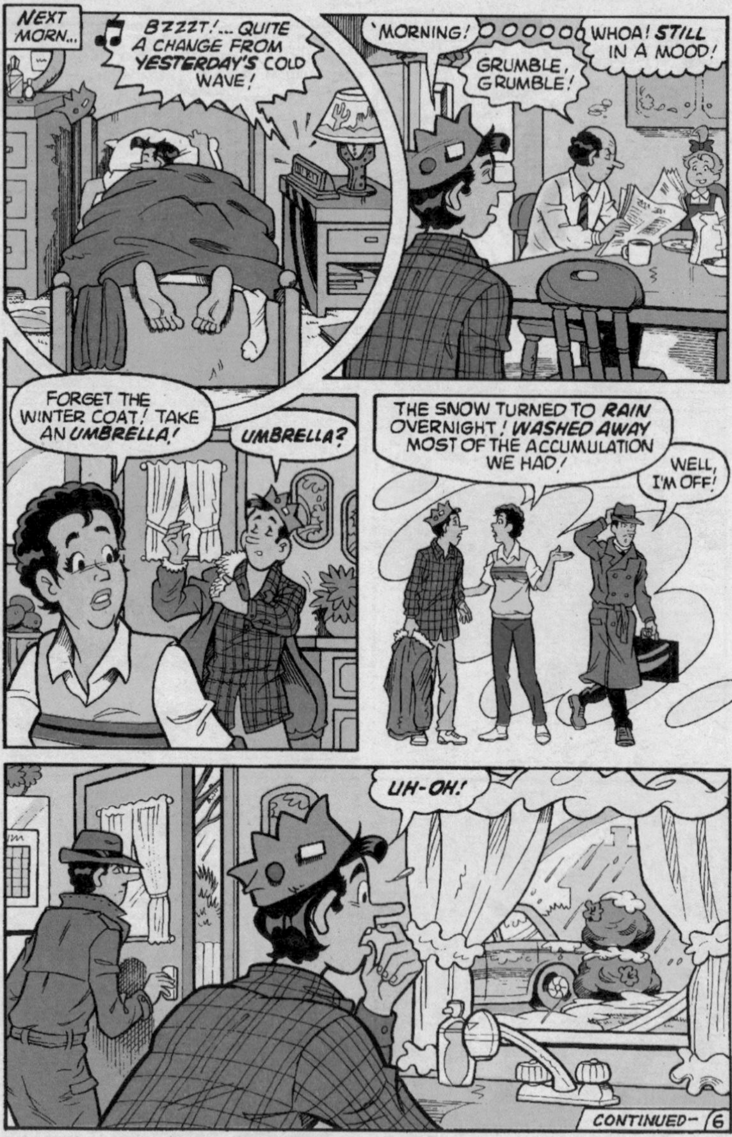
NEXT MORN...
BZZZT!... QUITE A CHANGE FROM YESTERDAY'S COLD WAVE!
'MORNING!
OOOOOO
GRUMBLE, GRUMBLE!
WHOA! STILL IN A MOOD!
FORGET THE WINTER COAT! TAKE AN UMBRELLA!
UMBRELLA?
THE SNOW TURNED TO RAIN OVERNIGHT! WASHED AWAY MOST OF THE ACCUMULATION WE HAD!
WELL, I'M OFF!
UH-OH!
CONTINUED-

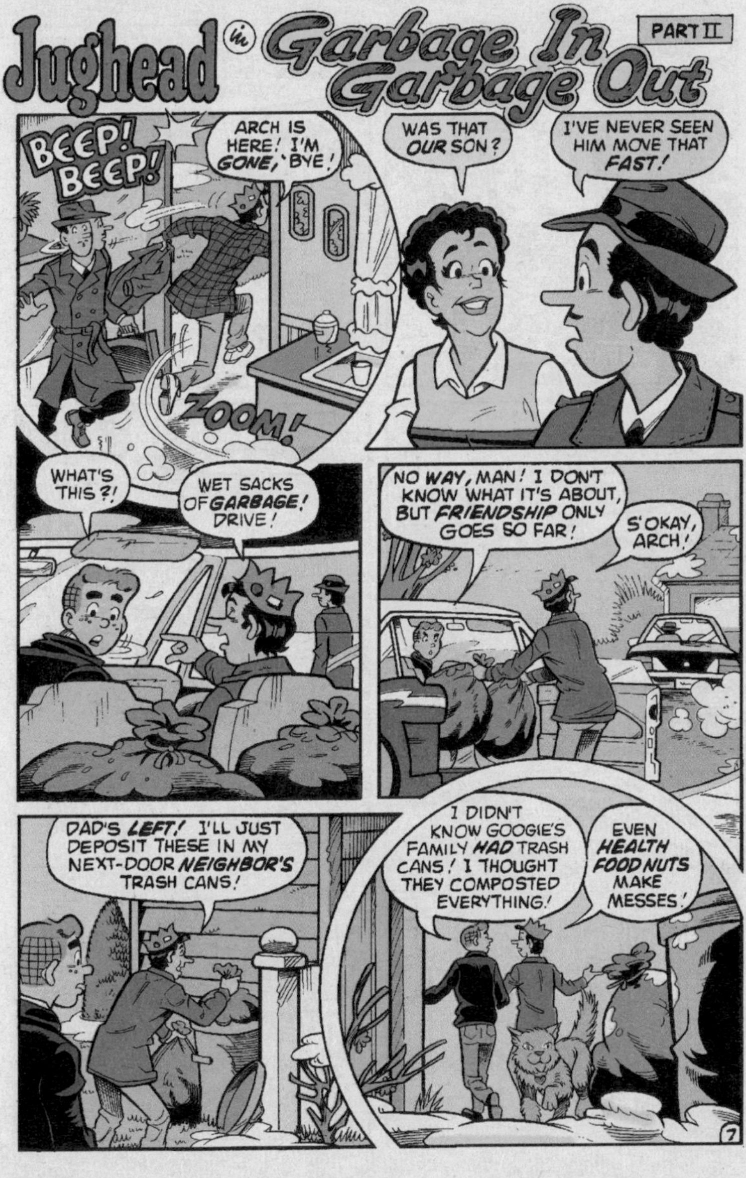
Jughead in Garbage In Garbage Out
PART II
BEEP! BEEP!
ARCH IS HERE! I'M GONE, 'BYE!
ZOOM!
WAS THAT OUR SON?
I'VE NEVER SEEN HIM MOVE THAT FAST!
WHAT'S THIS ?!
WET SACKS OF GARBAGE! DRIVE!
NO WAY, MAN! I DON'T KNOW WHAT IT'S ABOUT, BUT FRIENDSHIP ONLY GOES SO FAR!
S'OKAY, ARCH!
DAD'S LEFT! I'LL JUST DEPOSIT THESE IN MY NEXT-DOOR NEIGHBOR'S TRASH CANS!
I DIDN'T KNOW GOOGIE'S FAMILY HAD TRASH CANS! I THOUGHT THEY COMPOSTED EVERYTHING!
EVEN HEALTH FOOD NUTS MAKE MESSES!
7

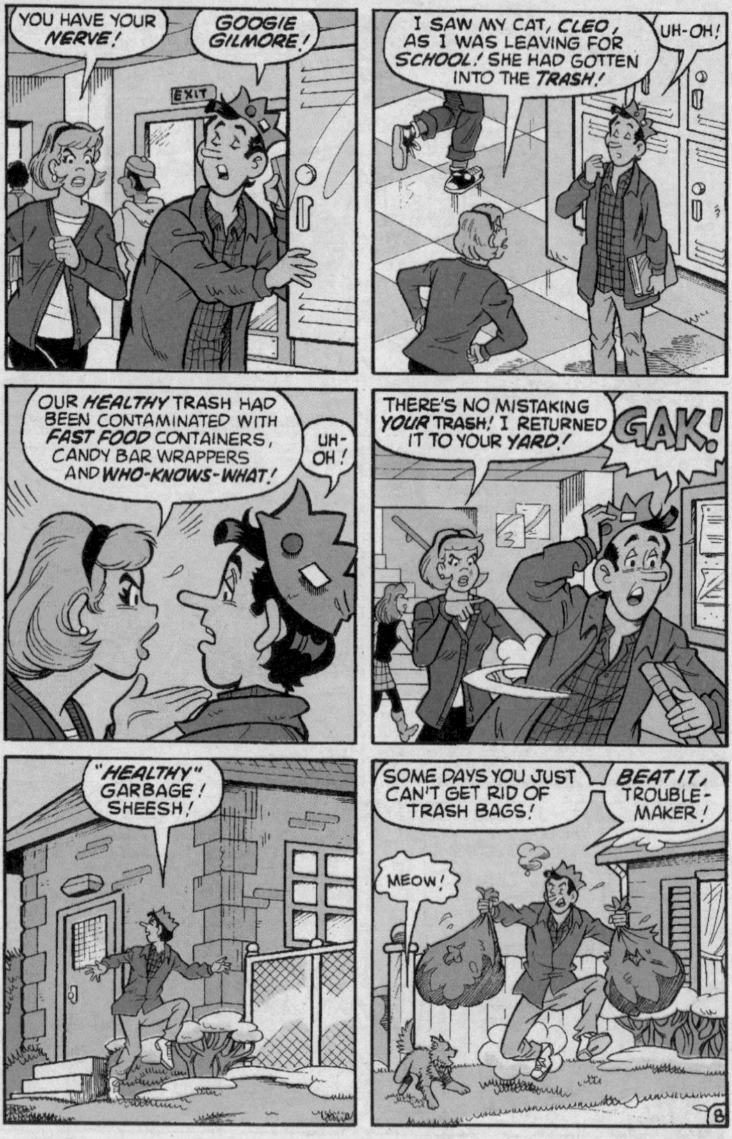

YOU HAVE YOUR NERVE!
GOOGIE GILMORE!
I SAW MY CAT, CLEO, AS I WAS LEAVING FOR SCHOOL! SHE HAD GOTTEN INTO THE TRASH!
UH-OH!
OUR HEALTHY TRASH HAD BEEN CONTAMINATED WITH FAST FOOD CONTAINERS, CANDY BAR WRAPPERS AND WHO-KNOWS-WHAT!
UH-OH!
THERE'S NO MISTAKING YOUR TRASH! I RETURNED IT TO YOUR YARD!
GAK!
"HEALTHY" GARBAGE! SHEESH!
SOME DAYS YOU JUST CAN'T GET RID OF TRASH BAGS!
BEAT IT, TROUBLE-MAKER!
MEOW!
8

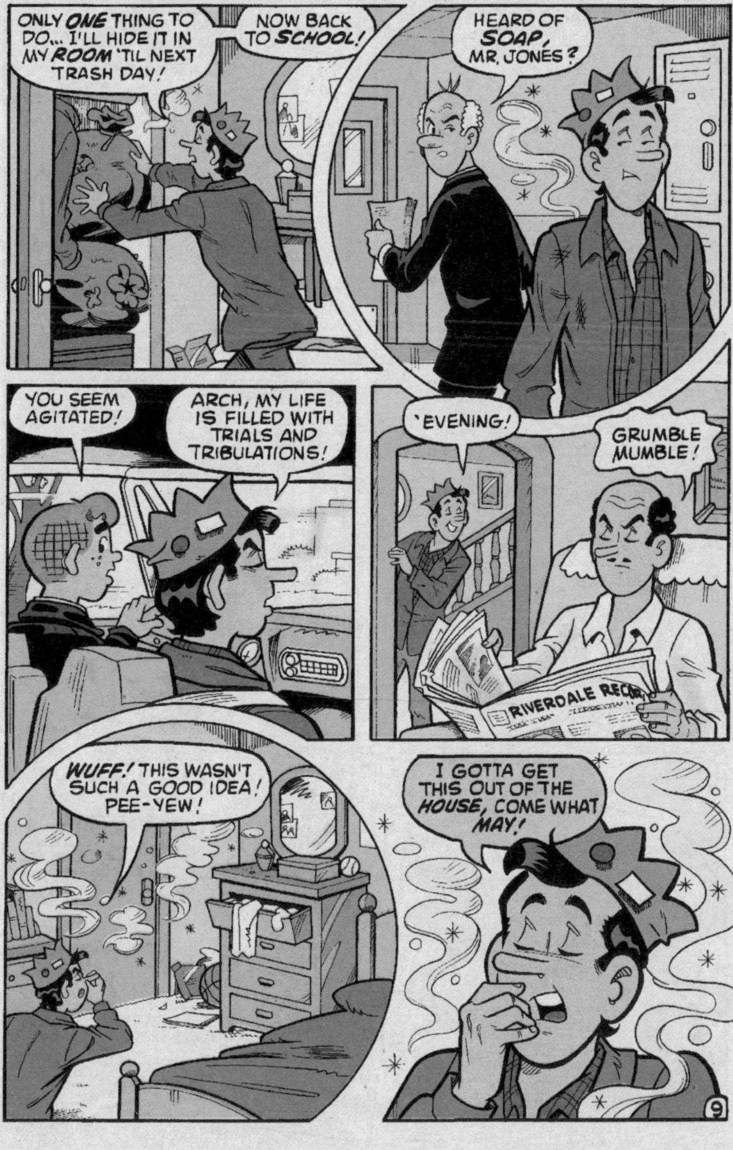
ONLY ONE THING TO DO... I'LL HIDE IT IN MY ROOM 'TIL NEXT TRASH DAY!
NOW BACK TO SCHOOL!
HEARD OF SOAP, MR. JONES?
YOU SEEM AGITATED!
ARCH, MY LIFE IS FILLED WITH TRIALS AND TRIBULATIONS!
'EVENING!
GRUMBLE MUMBLE!
RIVERDALE RECOR
WUFF! THIS WASN'T SUCH A GOOD IDEA! PEE-YEW!
I GOTTA GET THIS OUT OF THE HOUSE, COME WHAT MAY!
9

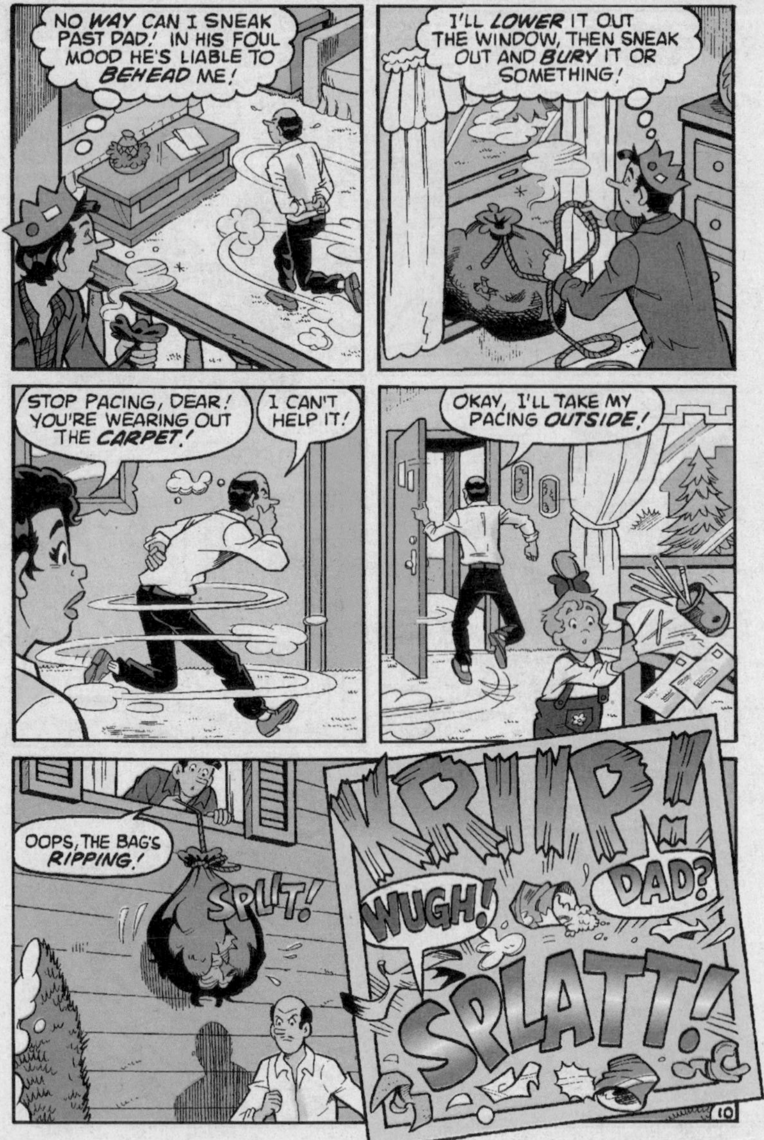
NO *WAY* CAN I SNEAK PAST DAD! IN HIS FOUL MOOD HE'S LIABLE TO *BEHEAD* ME!
I'LL *LOWER* IT OUT THE WINDOW, THEN SNEAK OUT AND *BURY* IT OR SOMETHING!
STOP PACING, DEAR! YOU'RE WEARING OUT THE *CARPET*!
I CAN'T HELP IT!
OKAY, I'LL TAKE MY PACING *OUTSIDE*!
OOPS, THE BAG'S *RIPPING*!
SPLIT!
KRIP!!
WUGH!
DAD?
SPLATT!

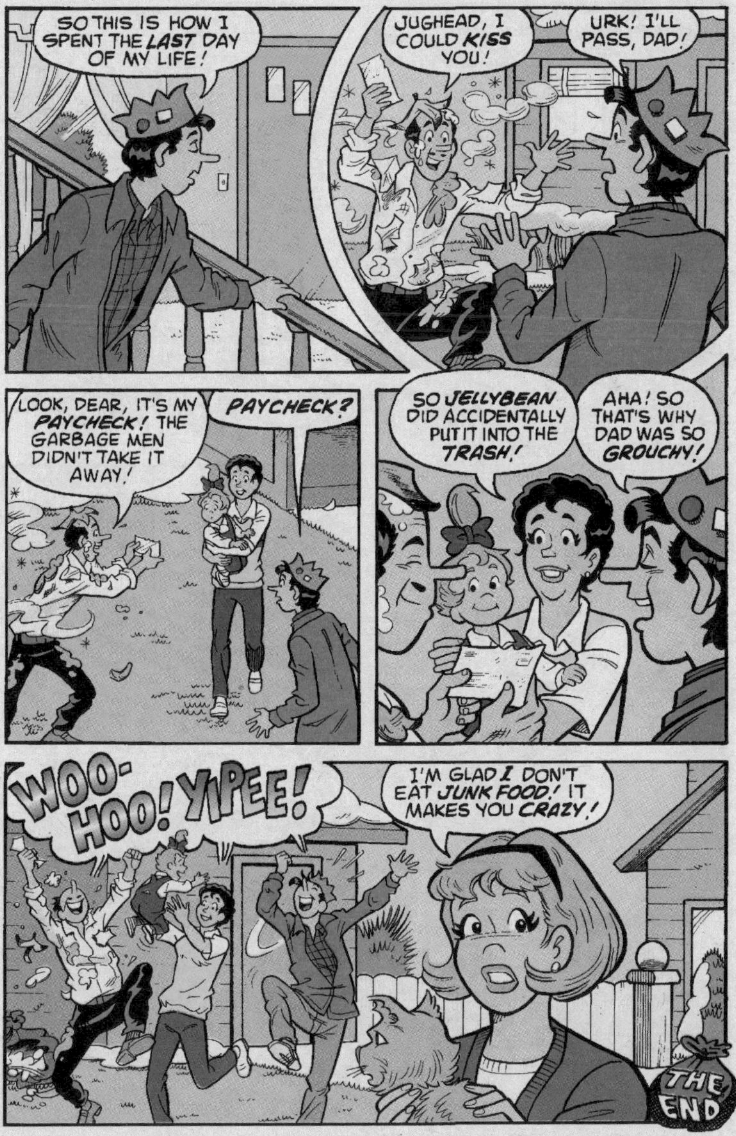
SO THIS IS HOW I SPENT THE LAST DAY OF MY LIFE!
JUGHEAD, I COULD KISS YOU!
URK! I'LL PASS, DAD!
LOOK, DEAR, IT'S MY PAYCHECK! THE GARBAGE MEN DIDN'T TAKE IT AWAY!
PAYCHECK?
SO JELLYBEAN DID ACCIDENTALLY PUT IT INTO THE TRASH!
AHA! SO THAT'S WHY DAD WAS SO GROUCHY!
WOO-HOO! YIPEE!
I'M GLAD I DON'T EAT JUNK FOOD! IT MAKES YOU CRAZY!
THE END

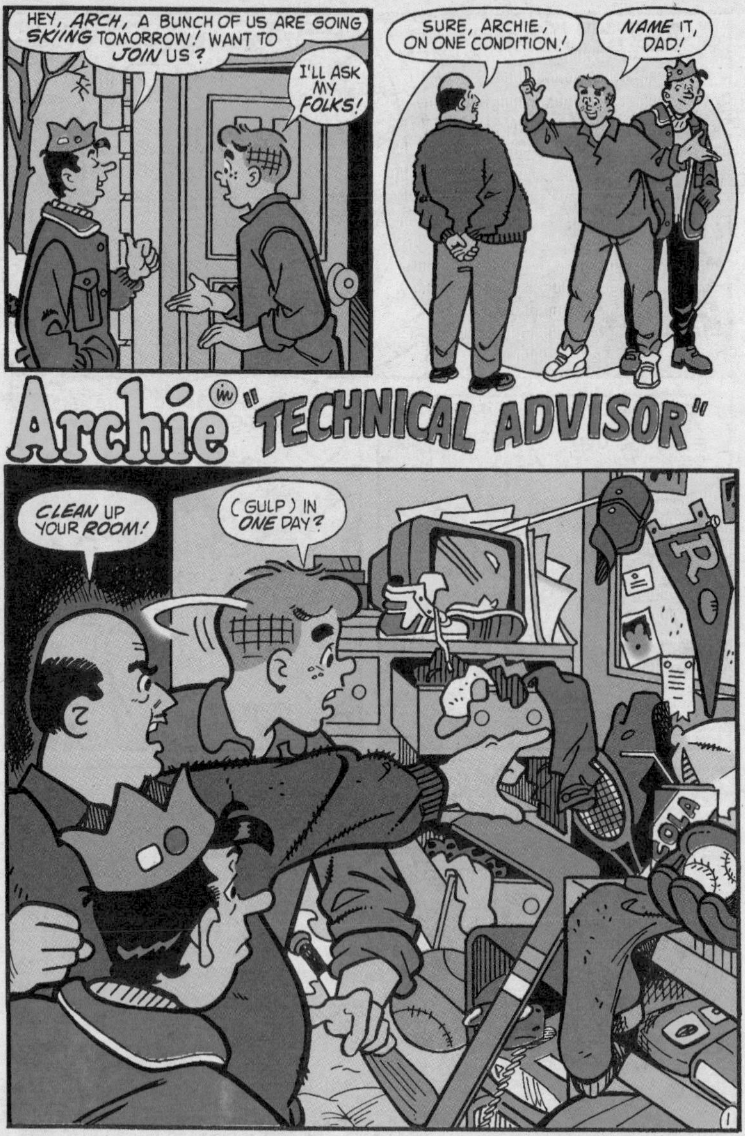
HEY, ARCH, A BUNCH OF US ARE GOING SKIING TOMORROW! WANT TO JOIN US?
I'LL ASK MY FOLKS!
SURE, ARCHIE, ON ONE CONDITION!
NAME IT, DAD!
Archie in "TECHNICAL ADVISOR"
CLEAN UP YOUR ROOM!
(GULP) IN ONE DAY?
1

Script: Hal Smith / Pencils: Stan Goldberg / Inks: Henry Scarpelli / Letters: Bill Yoshida / Colors: Barry Grossman

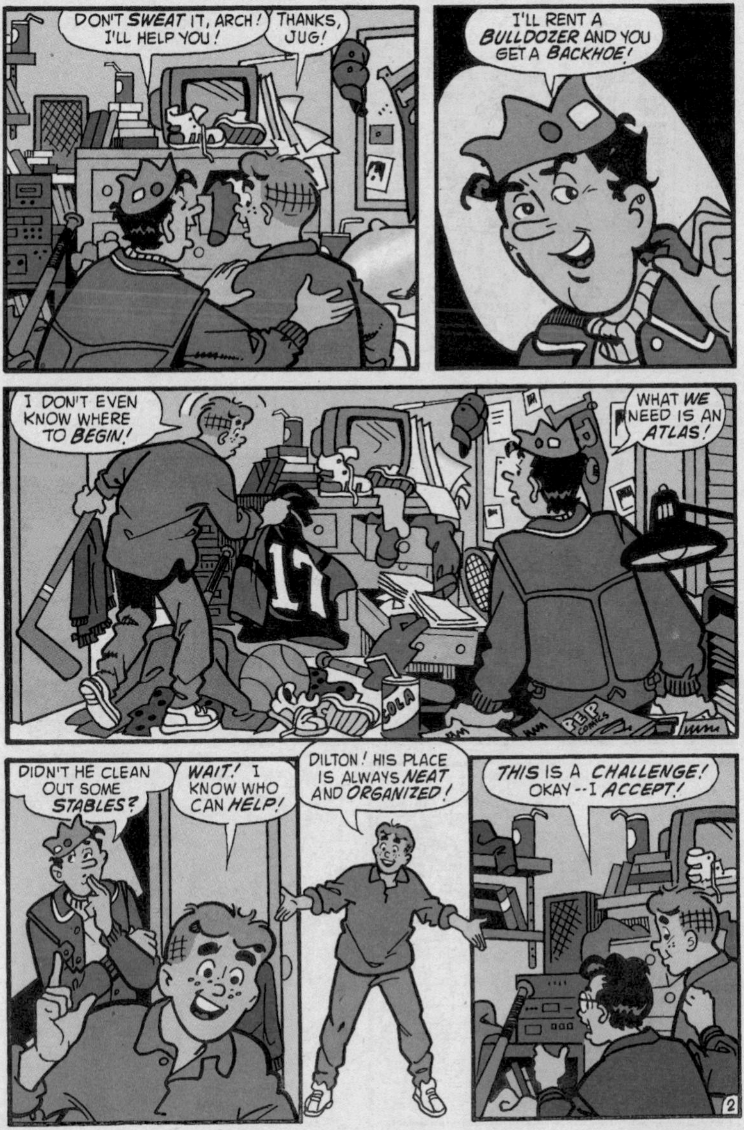

DON'T SWEAT IT, ARCH! I'LL HELP YOU!
THANKS, JUG!
I'LL RENT A BULLDOZER AND YOU GET A BACKHOE!
I DON'T EVEN KNOW WHERE TO BEGIN!
WHAT WE NEED IS AN ATLAS!
17
COLA
PEP COMICS
DIDN'T HE CLEAN OUT SOME STABLES?
WAIT! I KNOW WHO CAN HELP!
DILTON! HIS PLACE IS ALWAYS NEAT AND ORGANIZED!
THIS IS A CHALLENGE! OKAY -- I ACCEPT!

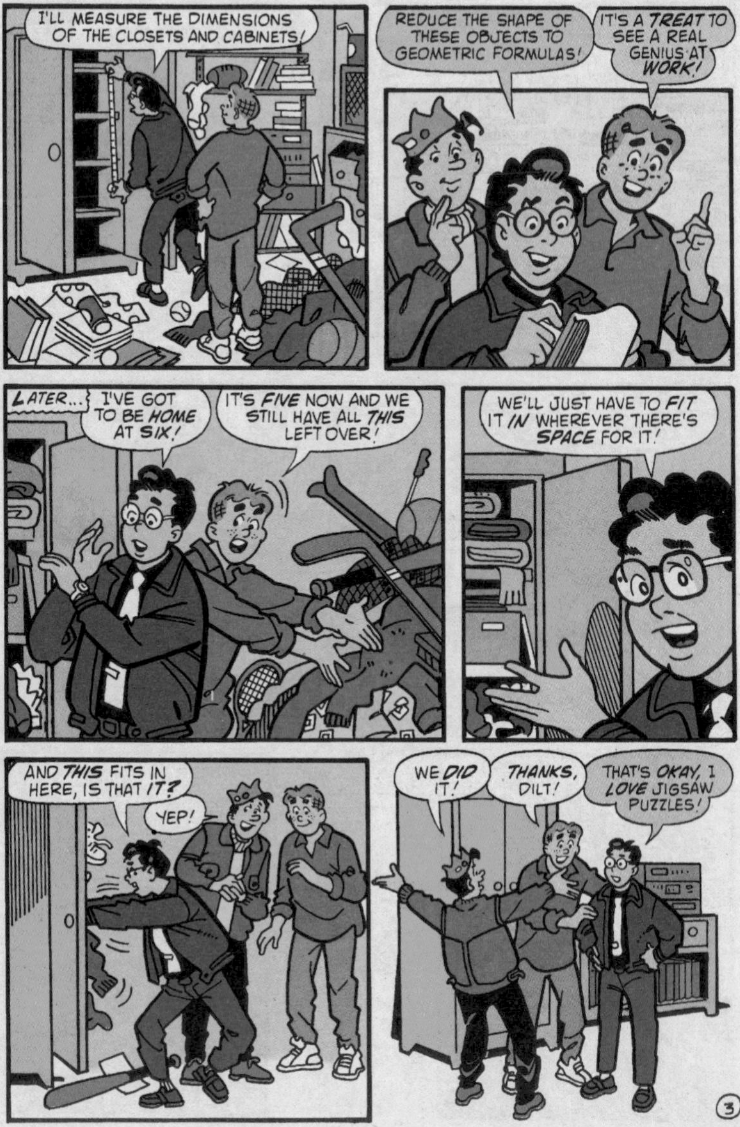

I'LL MEASURE THE DIMENSIONS OF THE CLOSETS AND CABINETS!
REDUCE THE SHAPE OF THESE OBJECTS TO GEOMETRIC FORMULAS!
IT'S A TREAT TO SEE A REAL GENIUS AT WORK!
LATER...
I'VE GOT TO BE HOME AT SIX!
IT'S FIVE NOW AND WE STILL HAVE ALL THIS LEFT OVER!
WE'LL JUST HAVE TO FIT IT IN WHEREVER THERE'S SPACE FOR IT!
AND THIS FITS IN HERE, IS THAT IT?
YEP!
WE DID IT!
THANKS, DILT!
THAT'S OKAY, I LOVE JIGSAW PUZZLES!

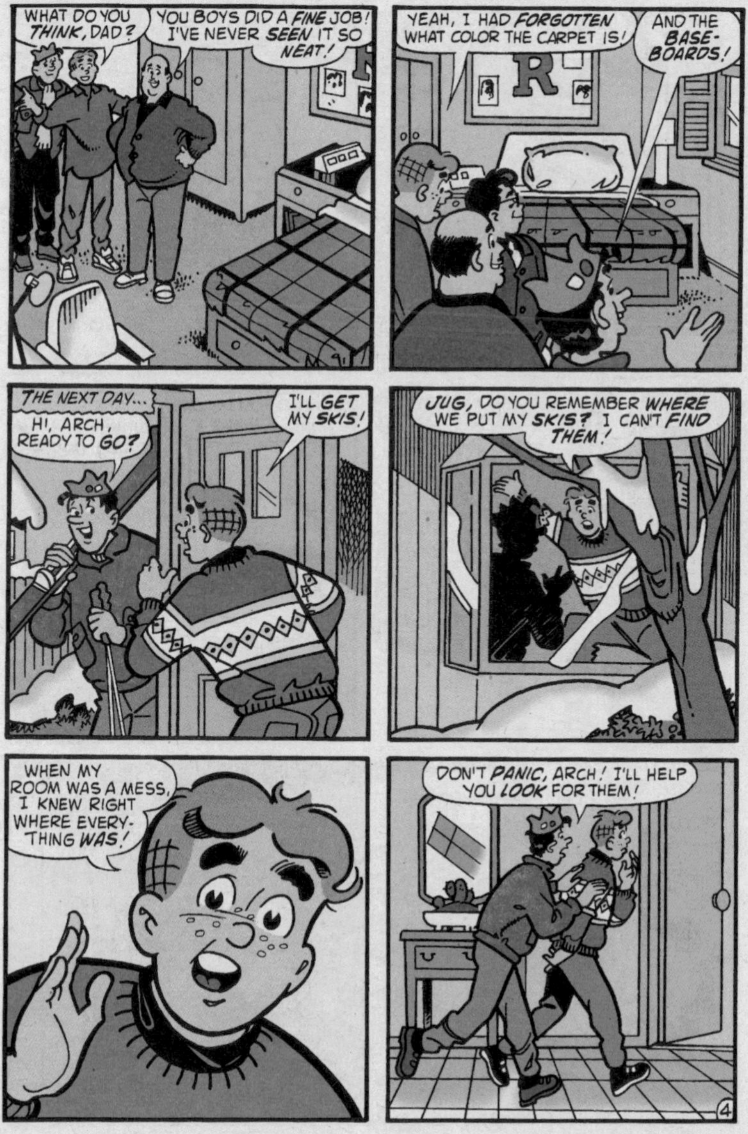
WHAT DO YOU THINK, DAD?
YOU BOYS DID A FINE JOB! I'VE NEVER SEEN IT SO NEAT!
YEAH, I HAD FORGOTTEN WHAT COLOR THE CARPET IS!
AND THE BASE-BOARDS!
THE NEXT DAY...
HI, ARCH, READY TO GO?
I'LL GET MY SKIS!
JUG, DO YOU REMEMBER WHERE WE PUT MY SKIS? I CAN'T FIND THEM!
WHEN MY ROOM WAS A MESS, I KNEW RIGHT WHERE EVERY-THING WAS!
DON'T PANIC, ARCH! I'LL HELP YOU LOOK FOR THEM!
4

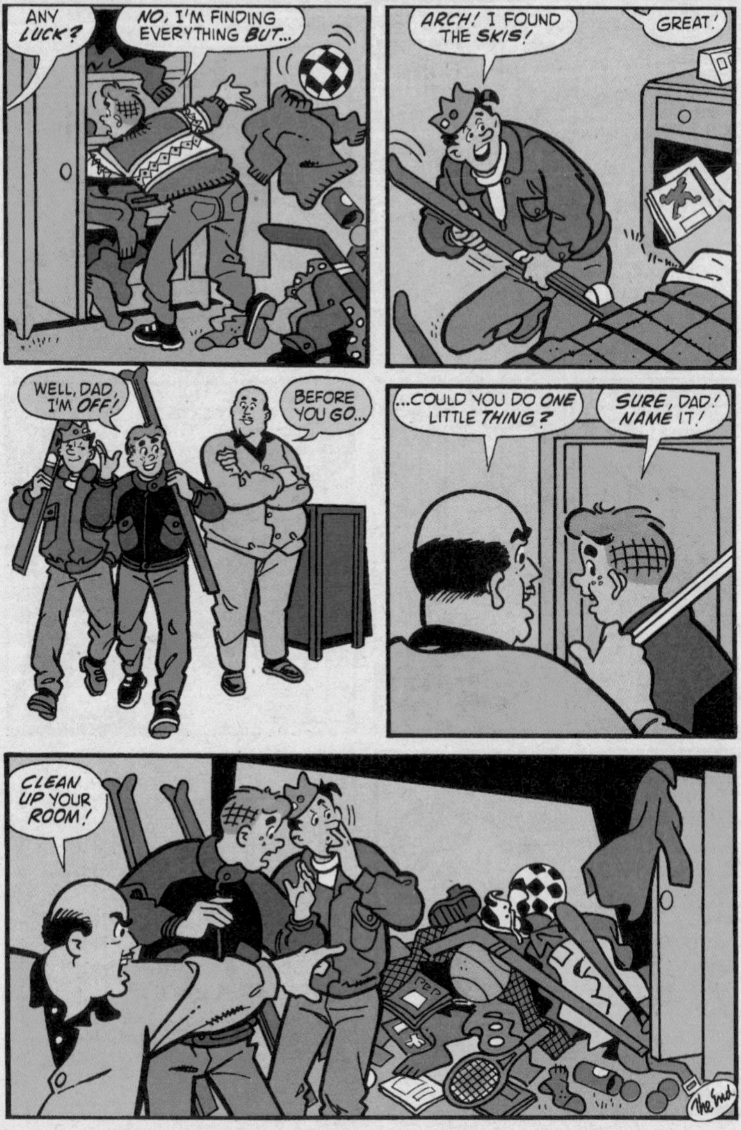
ANY LUCK?
NO, I'M FINDING EVERYTHING BUT...
ARCH! I FOUND THE SKIS!
GREAT!
WELL, DAD, I'M OFF!
BEFORE YOU GO...
...COULD YOU DO ONE LITTLE THING?
SURE, DAD! NAME IT!
CLEAN UP YOUR ROOM!
PEP
The End

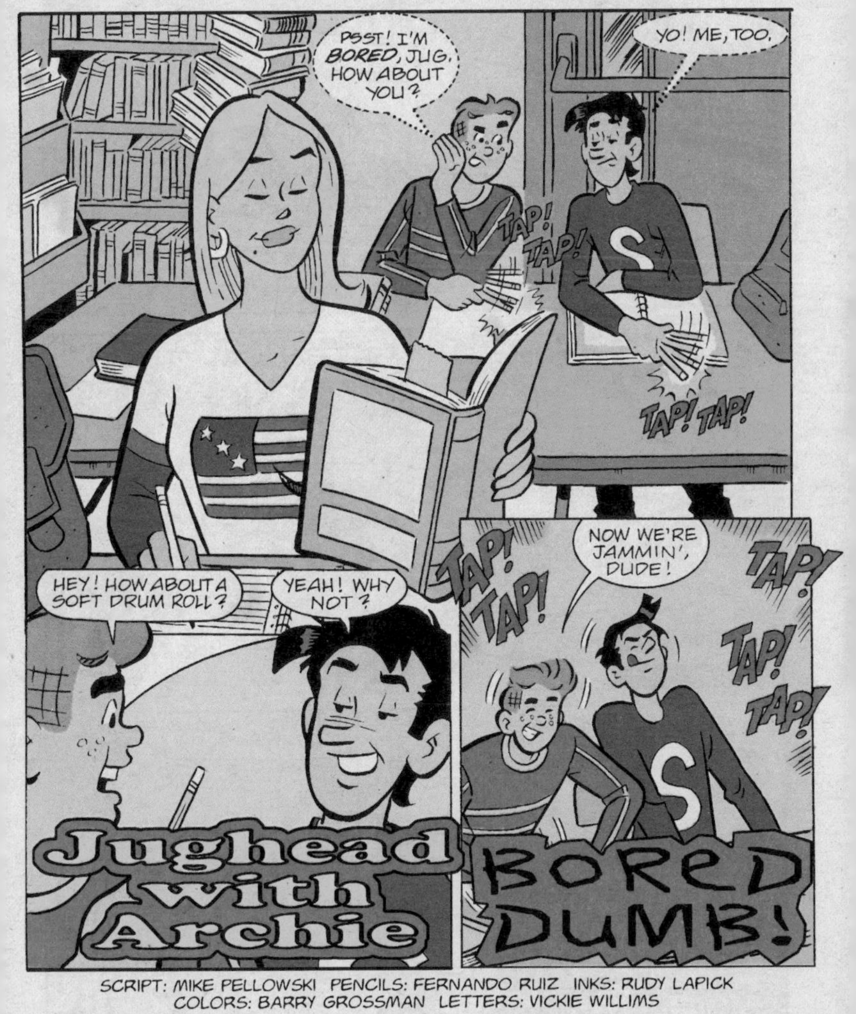
PSST! I'M BORED, JUG. HOW ABOUT YOU?
YO! ME, TOO.
TAP! TAP!
TAP! TAP!
HEY! HOW ABOUT A SOFT DRUM ROLL?
YEAH! WHY NOT?
TAP! TAP!
NOW WE'RE JAMMIN', DUDE!
TAP! TAP! TAP!
Jughead with Archie
BORED DUMB!

SCRIPT: MIKE PELLOWSKI PENCILS: FERNANDO RUIZ INKS: RUDY LAPICK
COLORS: BARRY GROSSMAN LETTERS: VICKIE WILLIMS

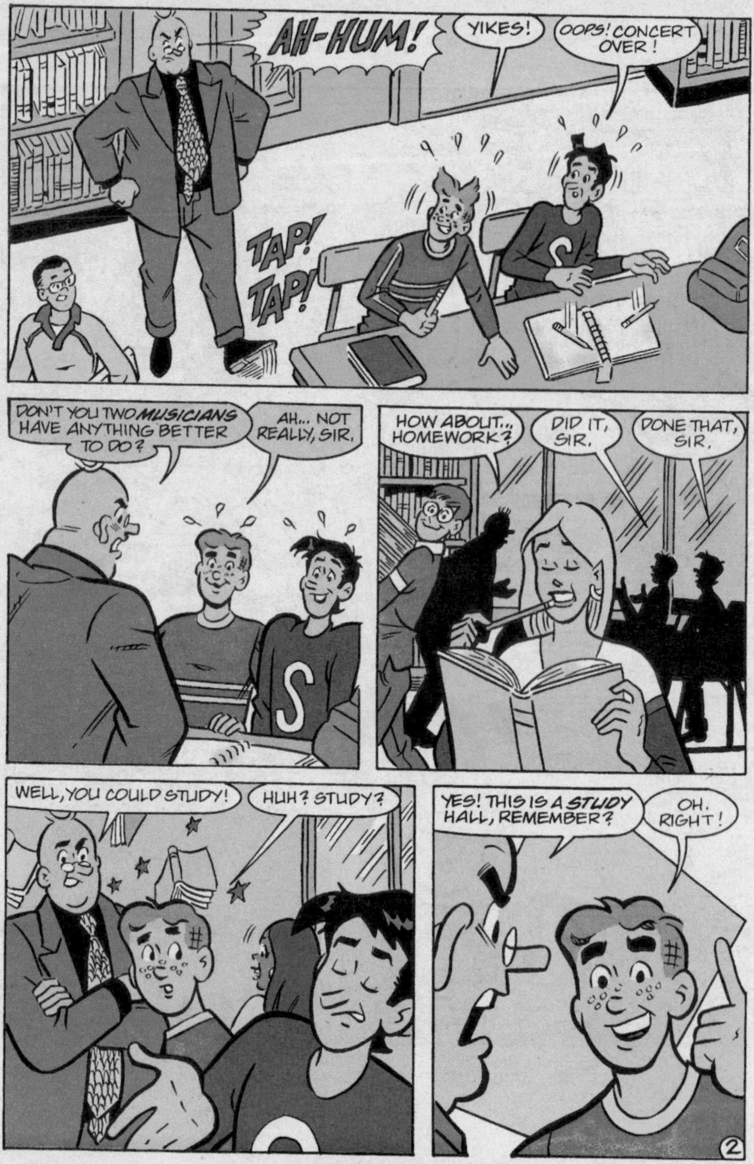
AH-HUM!
YIKES!
OOPS! CONCERT OVER!
TAP! TAP!
DON'T YOU TWO MUSICIANS HAVE ANYTHING BETTER TO DO?
AH... NOT REALLY, SIR.
HOW ABOUT... HOMEWORK?
DID IT, SIR.
DONE THAT, SIR.
WELL, YOU COULD STUDY!
HUH? STUDY?
YES! THIS IS A STUDY HALL, REMEMBER?
OH. RIGHT!
2

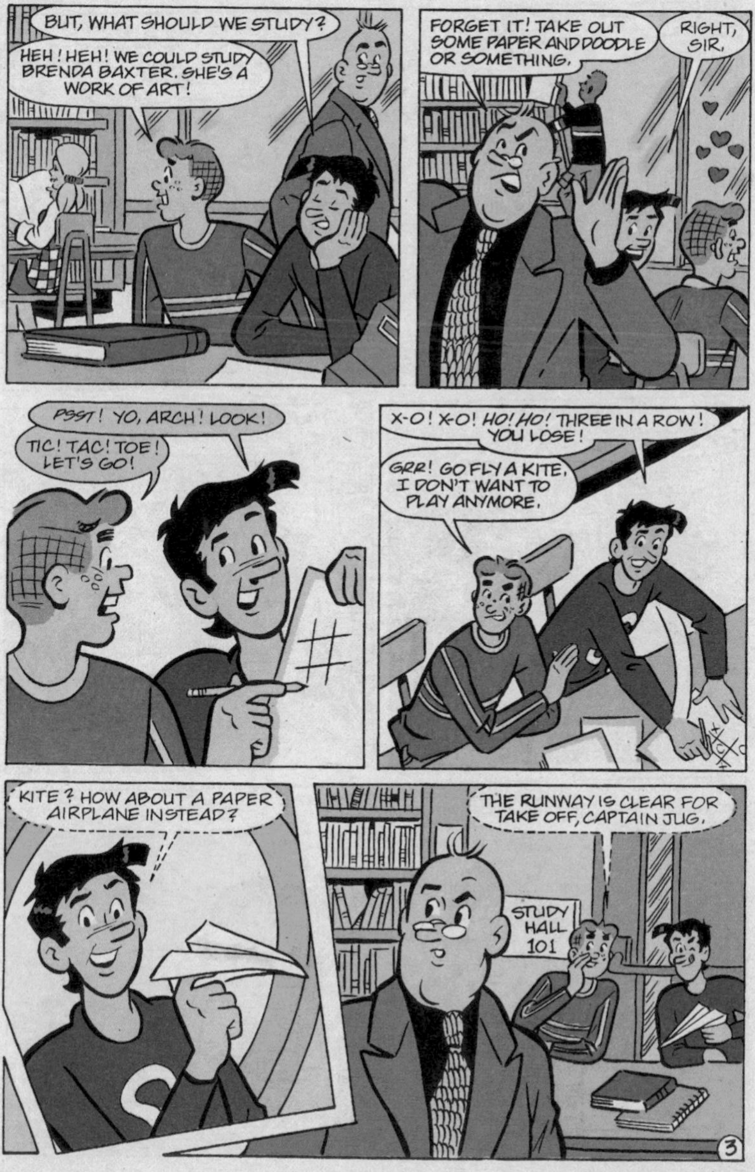
BUT, WHAT SHOULD WE STUDY?
HEH! HEH! WE COULD STUDY BRENDA BAXTER. SHE'S A WORK OF ART!
FORGET IT! TAKE OUT SOME PAPER AND DOODLE OR SOMETHING.
RIGHT, SIR.
PSST! YO, ARCH! LOOK!
TIC! TAC! TOE! LET'S GO!
X-O! X-O! HO! HO! THREE IN A ROW! YOU LOSE!
GRR! GO FLY A KITE. I DON'T WANT TO PLAY ANYMORE.
KITE? HOW ABOUT A PAPER AIRPLANE INSTEAD?
THE RUNWAY IS CLEAR FOR TAKE OFF, CAPTAIN JUG.
STUDY HALL 101
3

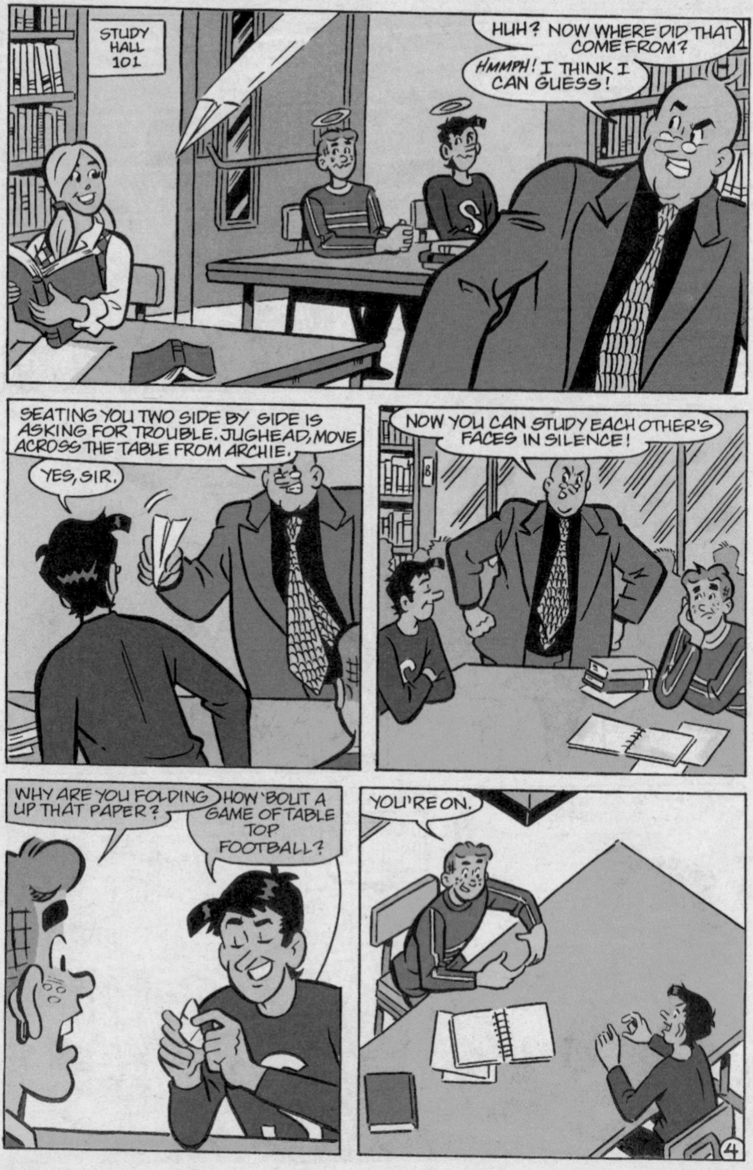
STUDY HALL 101
HUH? NOW WHERE DID THAT COME FROM?
HMMPH! I THINK I CAN GUESS!
SEATING YOU TWO SIDE BY SIDE IS ASKING FOR TROUBLE. JUGHEAD, MOVE ACROSS THE TABLE FROM ARCHIE.
YES, SIR.
NOW YOU CAN STUDY EACH OTHER'S FACES IN SILENCE!
WHY ARE YOU FOLDING UP THAT PAPER?
HOW 'BOUT A GAME OF TABLE TOP FOOTBALL?
YOU'RE ON.
4

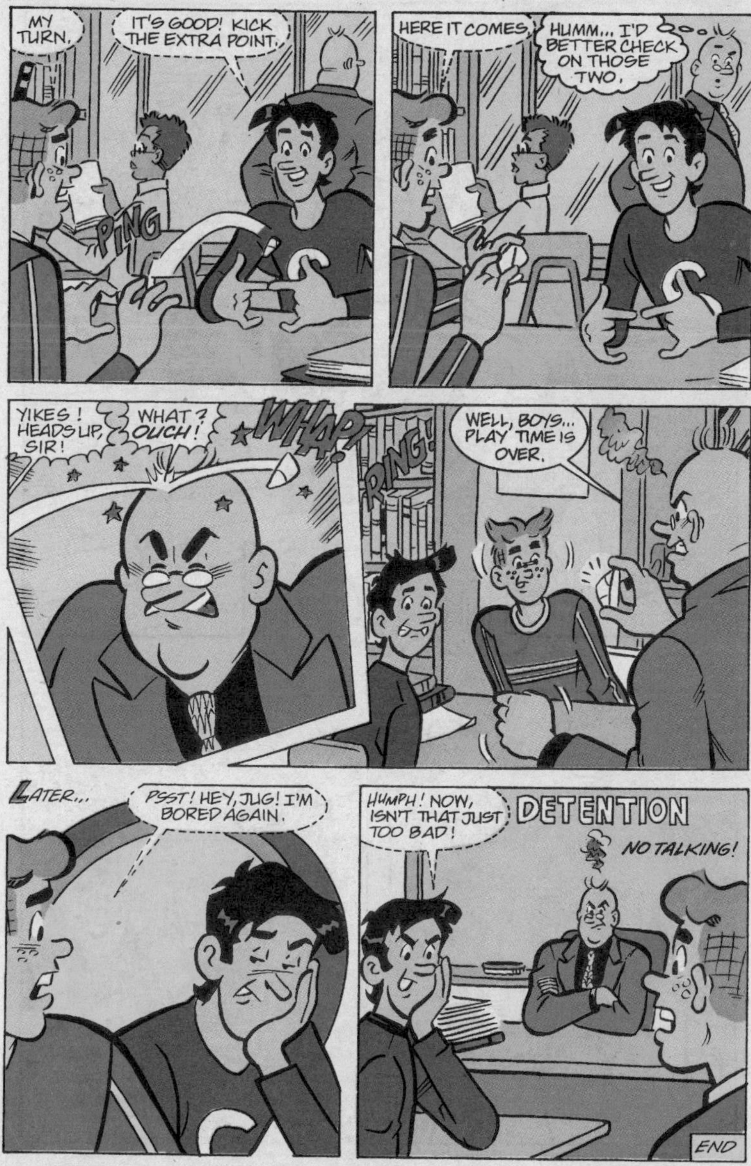

MY TURN.
IT'S GOOD! KICK THE EXTRA POINT.
PING
HERE IT COMES.
HUMM... I'D BETTER CHECK ON THOSE TWO.
YIKES! HEADS UP, SIR!
WHAT? OUCH!
WHAP!
WELL, BOYS... PLAY TIME IS OVER.
RING!
LATER...
PSST! HEY, JUG! I'M BORED AGAIN.
HUMPH! NOW, ISN'T THAT JUST TOO BAD!
DETENTION
NO TALKING!
END

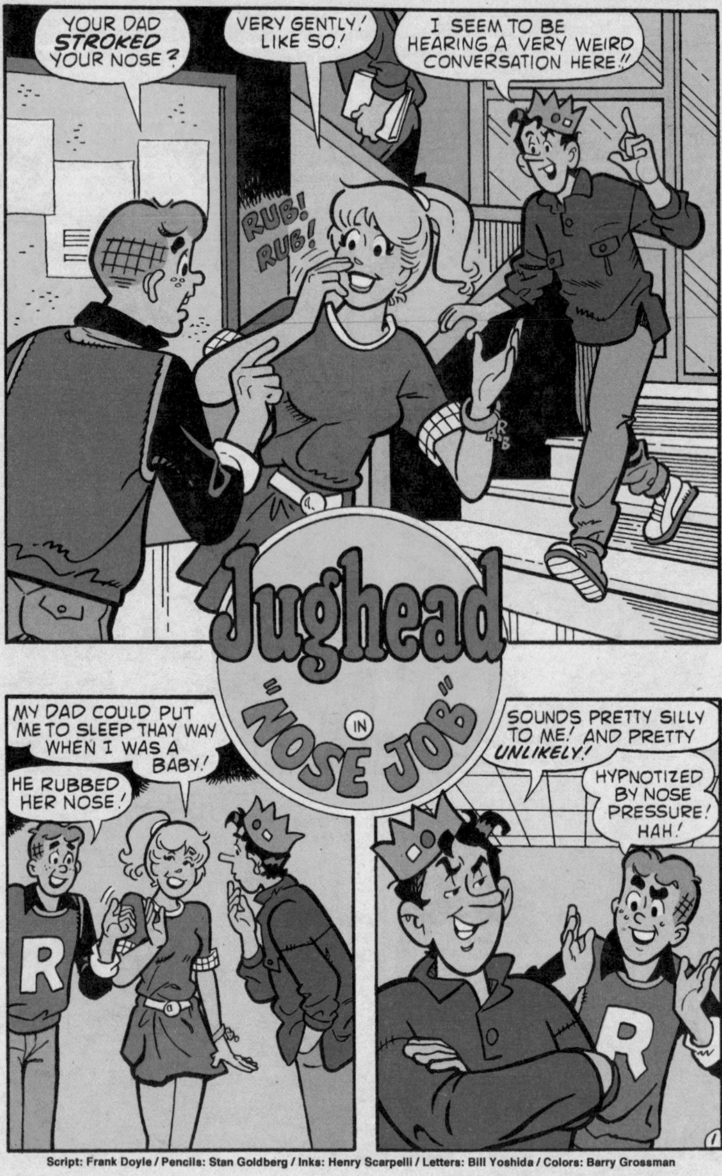
YOUR DAD STROKED YOUR NOSE?
VERY GENTLY! LIKE SO!
I SEEM TO BE HEARING A VERY WEIRD CONVERSATION HERE!!
RUB! RUB!
Jughead
IN
"NOSE JOB"
MY DAD COULD PUT ME TO SLEEP THAY WAY WHEN I WAS A BABY!
HE RUBBED HER NOSE!
SOUNDS PRETTY SILLY TO ME! AND PRETTY UNLIKELY!
HYPNOTIZED BY NOSE PRESSURE! HAH!
1

Script: Frank Doyle / Pencils: Stan Goldberg / Inks: Henry Scarpelli / Letters: Bill Yoshida / Colors: Barry Grossman

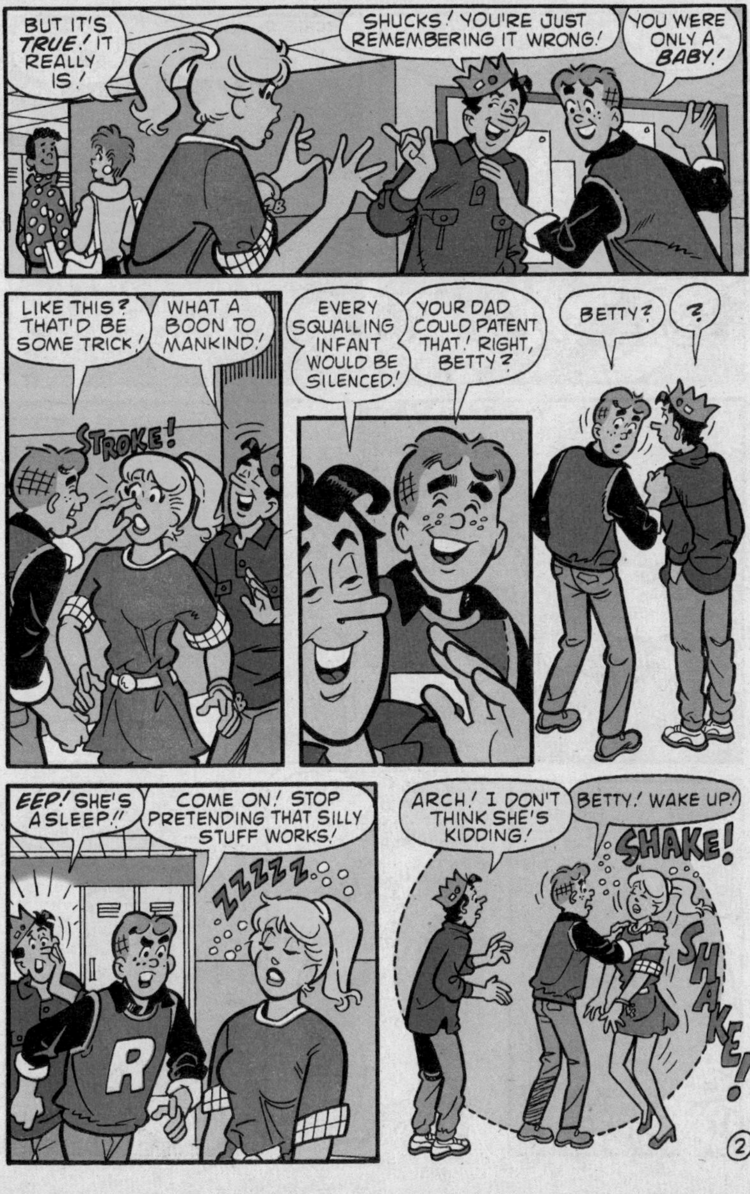
BUT IT'S TRUE! IT REALLY IS!
SHUCKS! YOU'RE JUST REMEMBERING IT WRONG!
YOU WERE ONLY A BABY!
LIKE THIS? THAT'D BE SOME TRICK!
WHAT A BOON TO MANKIND!
STROKE!
EVERY SQUALLING INFANT WOULD BE SILENCED!
YOUR DAD COULD PATENT THAT! RIGHT, BETTY?
BETTY?
?
EEP! SHE'S ASLEEP!!
COME ON! STOP PRETENDING THAT SILLY STUFF WORKS!
ZZZZZ
ARCH! I DON'T THINK SHE'S KIDDING!
BETTY! WAKE UP!
SHAKE!
SHAKE!
2

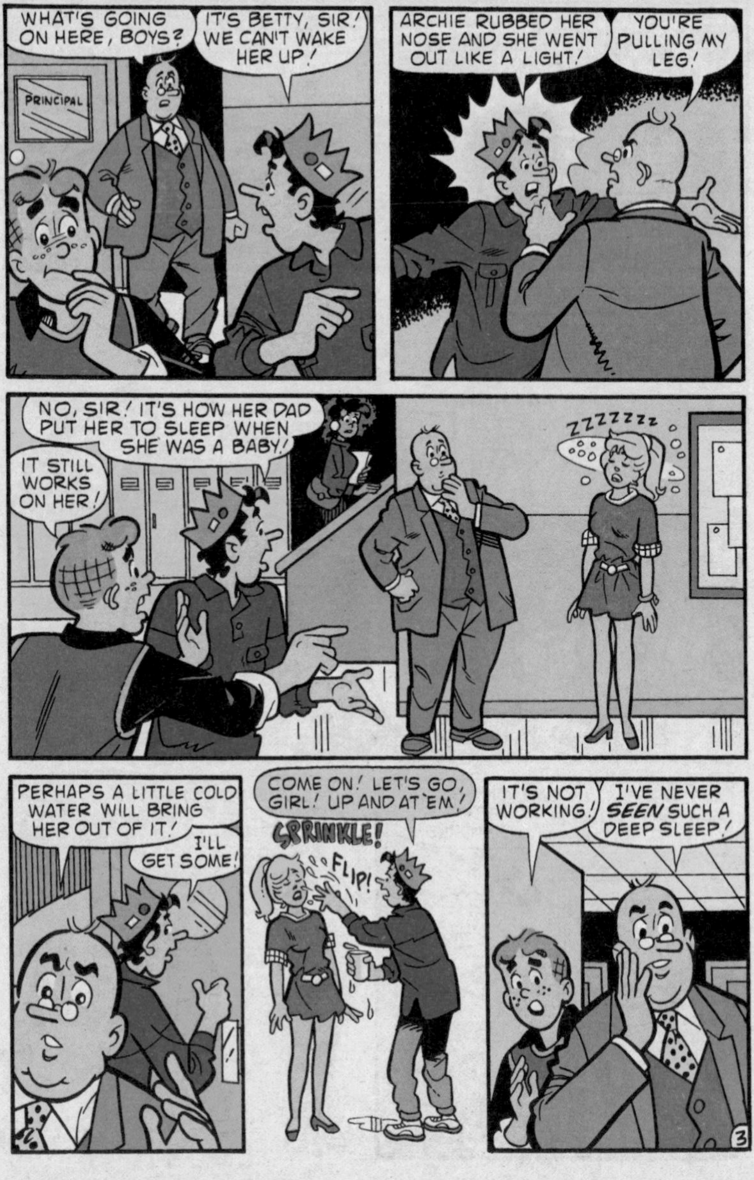
WHAT'S GOING ON HERE, BOYS?
IT'S BETTY, SIR! WE CAN'T WAKE HER UP!
PRINCIPAL
ARCHIE RUBBED HER NOSE AND SHE WENT OUT LIKE A LIGHT!
YOU'RE PULLING MY LEG!
NO, SIR! IT'S HOW HER DAD PUT HER TO SLEEP WHEN SHE WAS A BABY!
IT STILL WORKS ON HER!
ZZZZZZZ
PERHAPS A LITTLE COLD WATER WILL BRING HER OUT OF IT!
I'LL GET SOME!
COME ON! LET'S GO, GIRL! UP AND AT 'EM!
SPRINKLE!
FLIP!
IT'S NOT WORKING!
I'VE NEVER SEEN SUCH A DEEP SLEEP!
3

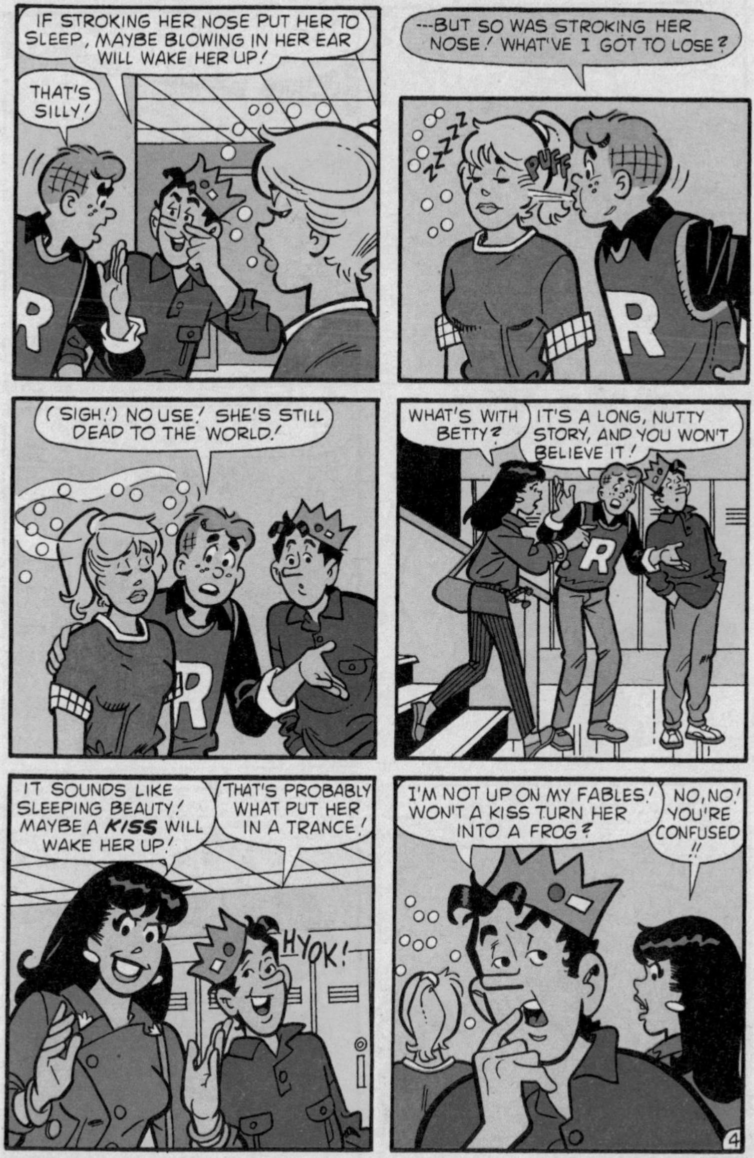
IF STROKING HER NOSE PUT HER TO SLEEP, MAYBE BLOWING IN HER EAR WILL WAKE HER UP!
THAT'S SILLY!
---BUT SO WAS STROKING HER NOSE! WHAT'VE I GOT TO LOSE?
ZZZZ
PUFF
(SIGH!) NO USE! SHE'S STILL DEAD TO THE WORLD!
WHAT'S WITH BETTY?
IT'S A LONG, NUTTY STORY, AND YOU WON'T BELIEVE IT!
IT SOUNDS LIKE SLEEPING BEAUTY! MAYBE A KISS WILL WAKE HER UP!
THAT'S PROBABLY WHAT PUT HER IN A TRANCE!
HYOK!
I'M NOT UP ON MY FABLES! WON'T A KISS TURN HER INTO A FROG?
NO, NO! YOU'RE CONFUSED!!
4

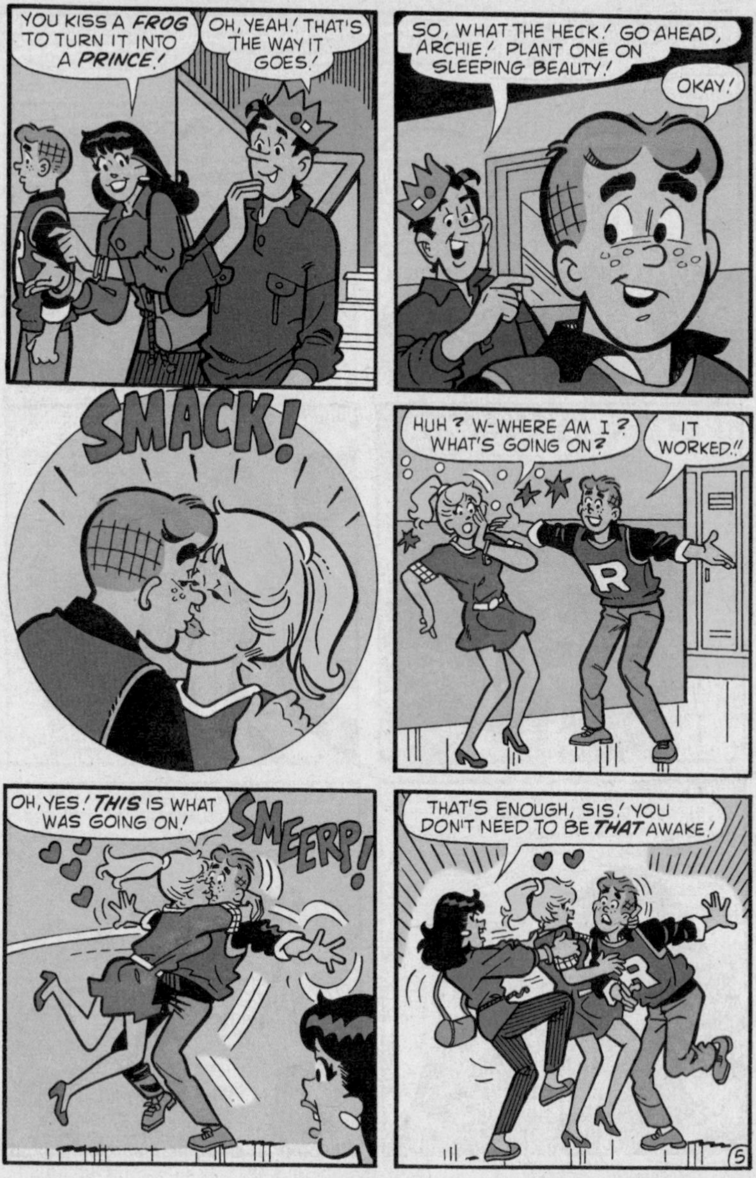
YOU KISS A *FROG* TO TURN IT INTO A *PRINCE*!
OH, YEAH! THAT'S THE WAY IT GOES!
SO, WHAT THE HECK! GO AHEAD, ARCHIE! PLANT ONE ON SLEEPING BEAUTY!
OKAY!
SMACK!
HUH? W-WHERE AM I? WHAT'S GOING ON?
IT WORKED!!
OH, YES! *THIS* IS WHAT WAS GOING ON!
SMEERP!
THAT'S ENOUGH, SIS! YOU DON'T NEED TO BE *THAT* AWAKE!
5

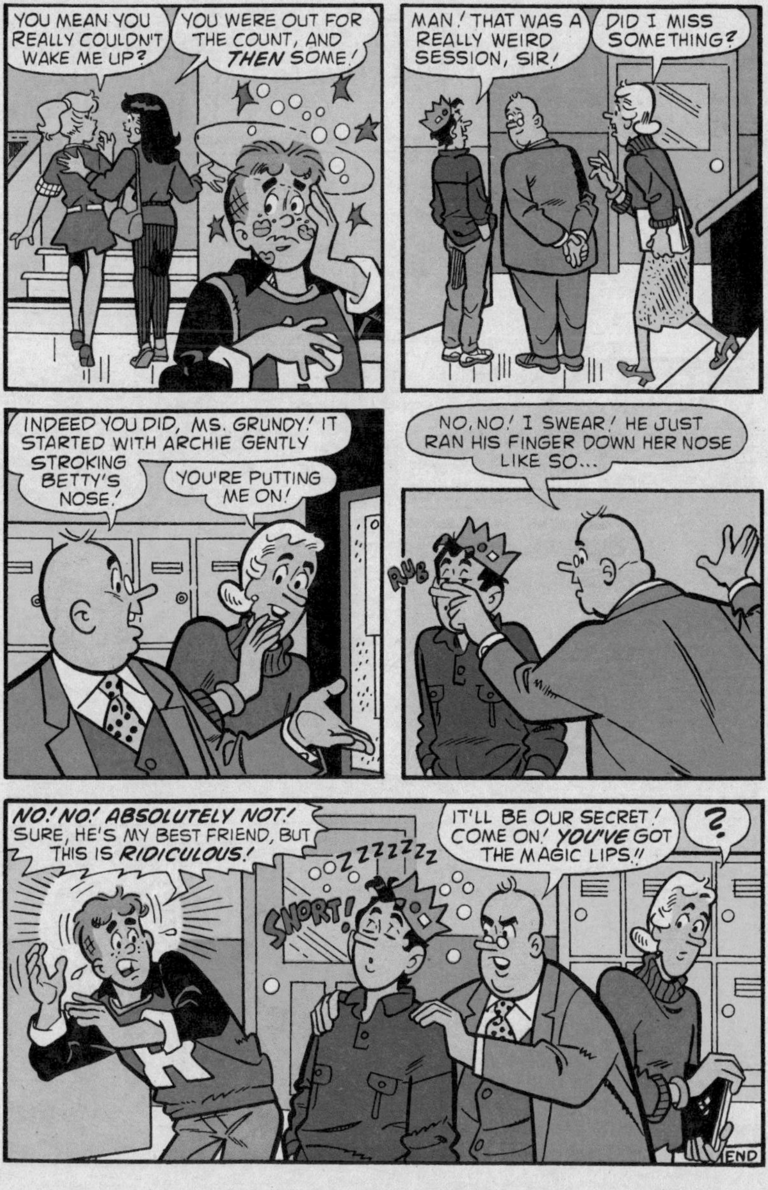
YOU MEAN YOU REALLY COULDN'T WAKE ME UP?
YOU WERE OUT FOR THE COUNT, AND THEN SOME!
MAN! THAT WAS A REALLY WEIRD SESSION, SIR!
DID I MISS SOMETHING?
INDEED YOU DID, MS. GRUNDY! IT STARTED WITH ARCHIE GENTLY STROKING BETTY'S NOSE!
YOU'RE PUTTING ME ON!
NO, NO! I SWEAR! HE JUST RAN HIS FINGER DOWN HER NOSE LIKE SO...
RUB
NO! NO! ABSOLUTELY NOT! SURE, HE'S MY BEST FRIEND, BUT THIS IS RIDICULOUS!
ZZZZZZZ
SNORT!
IT'LL BE OUR SECRET! COME ON! YOU'VE GOT THE MAGIC LIPS!!
?
END

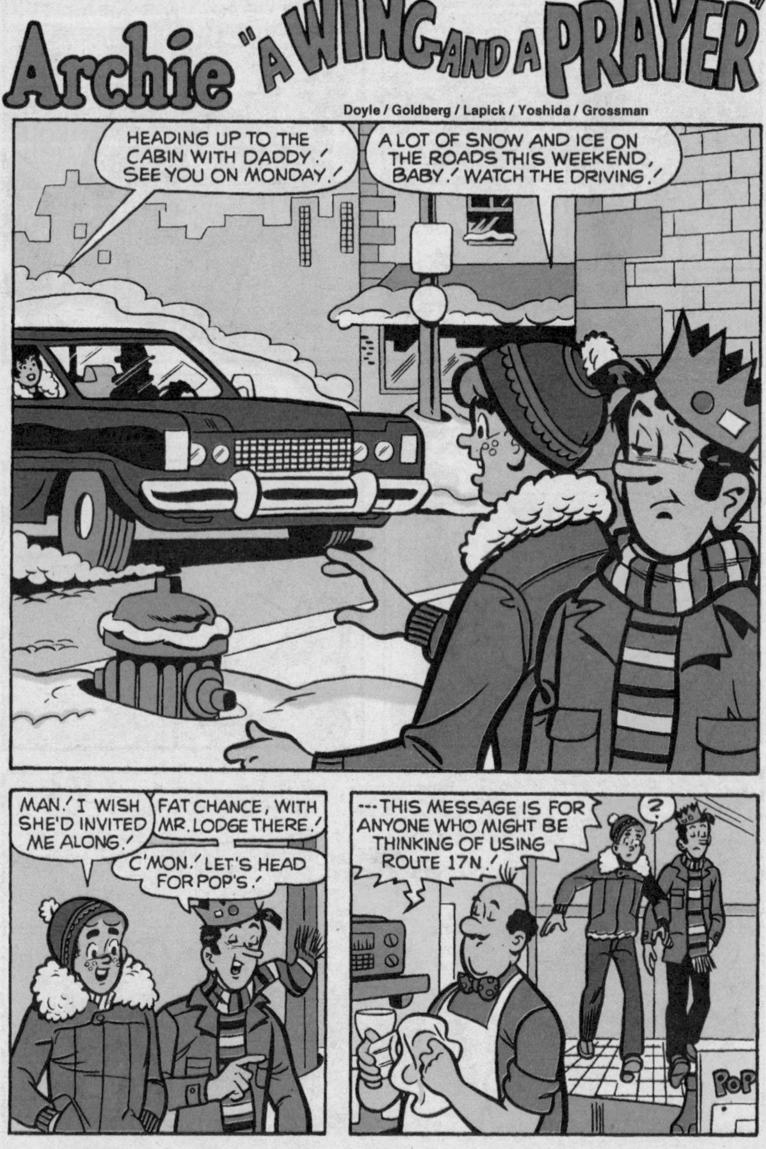

Archie "A WING AND A PRAYER"
Doyle / Goldberg / Lapick / Yoshida / Grossman
HEADING UP TO THE CABIN WITH DADDY! SEE YOU ON MONDAY!
A LOT OF SNOW AND ICE ON THE ROADS THIS WEEKEND, BABY! WATCH THE DRIVING!
MAN! I WISH SHE'D INVITED ME ALONG!
FAT CHANCE, WITH MR. LODGE THERE!
C'MON! LET'S HEAD FOR POP'S!
---THIS MESSAGE IS FOR ANYONE WHO MIGHT BE THINKING OF USING ROUTE 17N!
?
POP

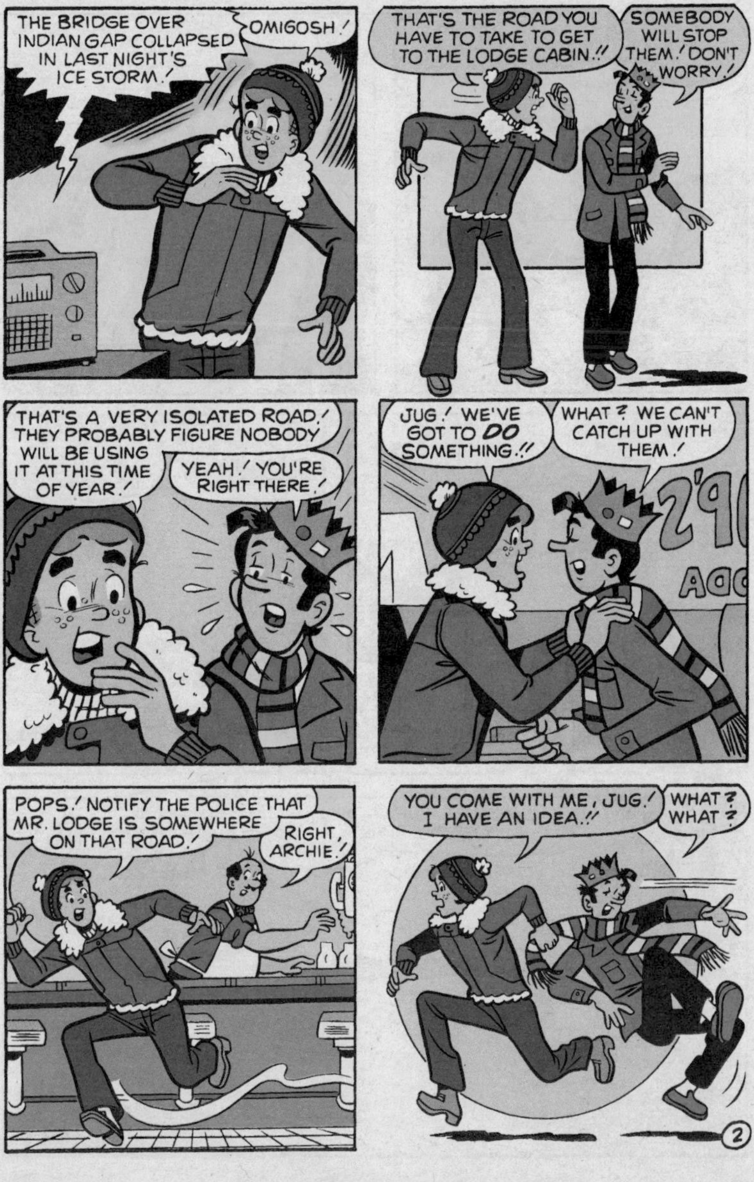
THE BRIDGE OVER INDIAN GAP COLLAPSED IN LAST NIGHT'S ICE STORM!
OMIGOSH!
THAT'S THE ROAD YOU HAVE TO TAKE TO GET TO THE LODGE CABIN!!
SOMEBODY WILL STOP THEM! DON'T WORRY!
THAT'S A VERY ISOLATED ROAD! THEY PROBABLY FIGURE NOBODY WILL BE USING IT AT THIS TIME OF YEAR!
YEAH! YOU'RE RIGHT THERE!
JUG! WE'VE GOT TO DO SOMETHING!!
WHAT? WE CAN'T CATCH UP WITH THEM!
POPS! NOTIFY THE POLICE THAT MR. LODGE IS SOMEWHERE ON THAT ROAD!
RIGHT ARCHIE!
YOU COME WITH ME, JUG! I HAVE AN IDEA!!
WHAT? WHAT?
2

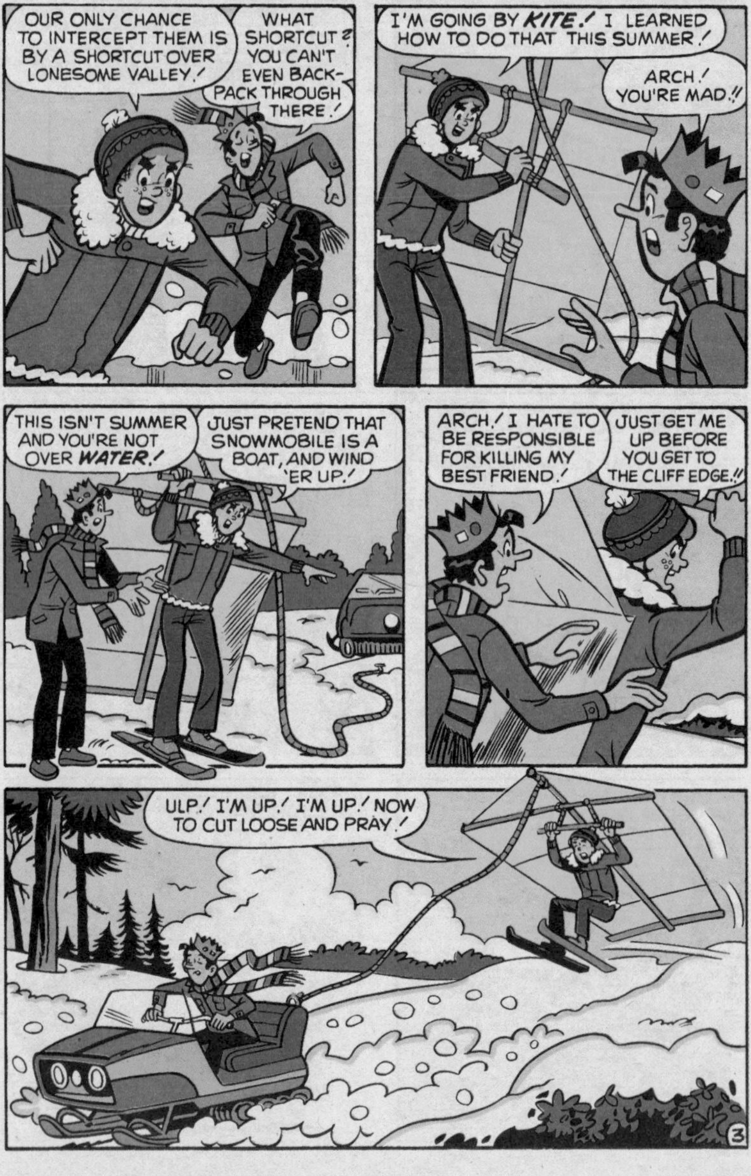
OUR ONLY CHANCE TO INTERCEPT THEM IS BY A SHORTCUT OVER LONESOME VALLEY!
WHAT SHORTCUT? YOU CAN'T EVEN BACK-PACK THROUGH THERE!
I'M GOING BY KITE! I LEARNED HOW TO DO THAT THIS SUMMER!
ARCH! YOU'RE MAD!!
THIS ISN'T SUMMER AND YOU'RE NOT OVER WATER!
JUST PRETEND THAT SNOWMOBILE IS A BOAT, AND WIND 'ER UP!
ARCH! I HATE TO BE RESPONSIBLE FOR KILLING MY BEST FRIEND!
JUST GET ME UP BEFORE YOU GET TO THE CLIFF EDGE!!
ULP! I'M UP! I'M UP! NOW TO CUT LOOSE AND PRAY!
3

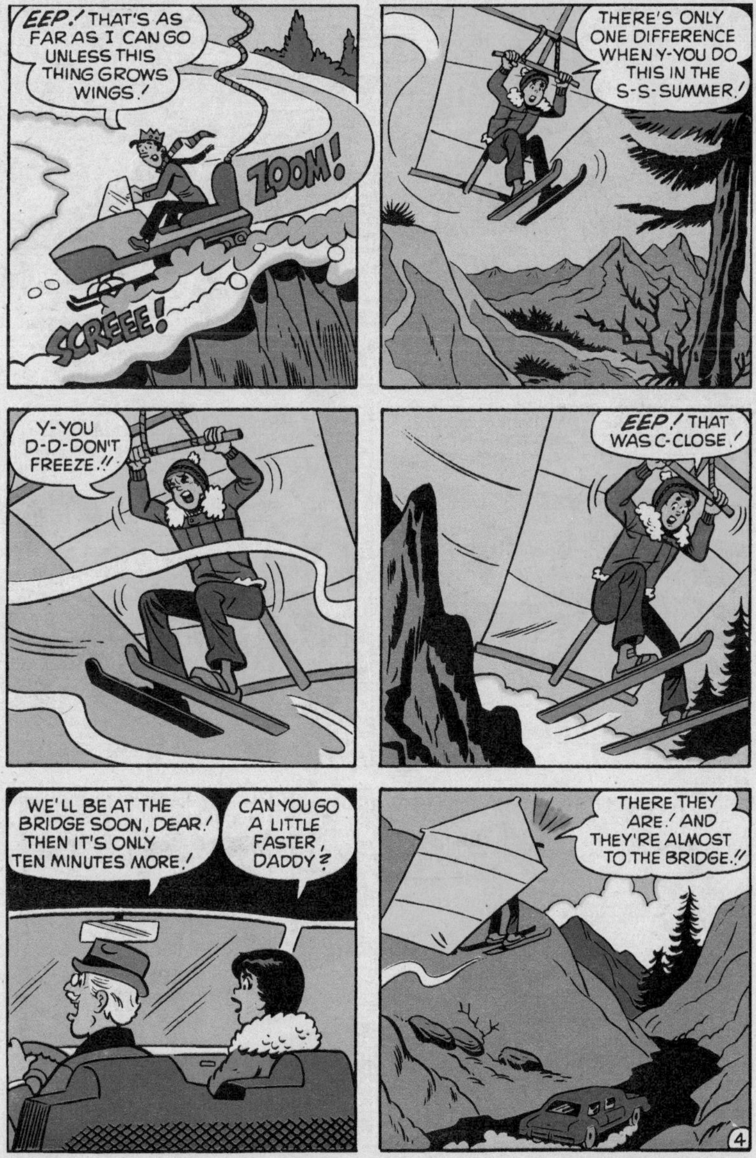
EEP! THAT'S AS FAR AS I CAN GO UNLESS THIS THING GROWS WINGS!
ZOOM!
SCREEEE!
THERE'S ONLY ONE DIFFERENCE WHEN Y-YOU DO THIS IN THE S-S-SUMMER!
Y-YOU D-D-DON'T FREEZE!!
EEP! THAT WAS C-CLOSE!
WE'LL BE AT THE BRIDGE SOON, DEAR! THEN IT'S ONLY TEN MINUTES MORE!
CAN YOU GO A LITTLE FASTER, DADDY?
THERE THEY ARE! AND THEY'RE ALMOST TO THE BRIDGE!!
4

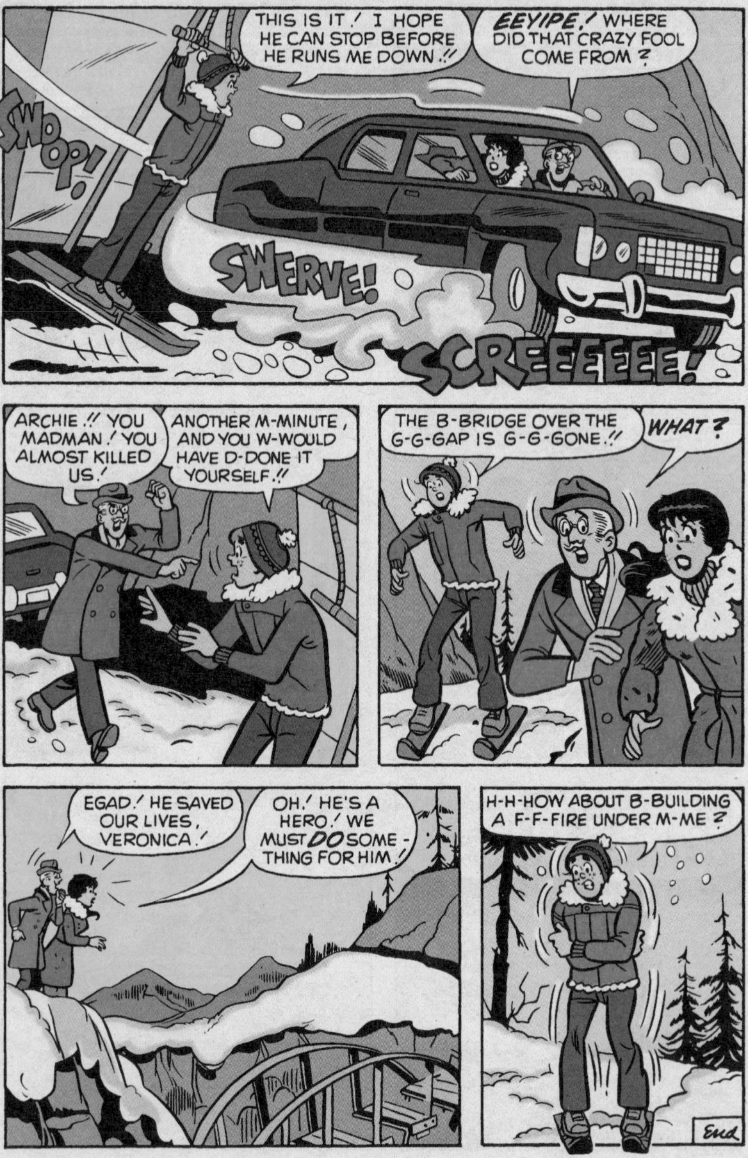
THIS IS IT ! I HOPE HE CAN STOP BEFORE HE RUNS ME DOWN !!
EEYIPE ! WHERE DID THAT CRAZY FOOL COME FROM ?
SWOOP!
SWERVE!
SCREEEEEEE!
ARCHIE !! YOU MADMAN ! YOU ALMOST KILLED US !
ANOTHER M-MINUTE, AND YOU W-WOULD HAVE D-DONE IT YOURSELF !!
THE B-BRIDGE OVER THE G-G-GAP IS G-G-GONE !!
WHAT ?
EGAD ! HE SAVED OUR LIVES, VERONICA !
OH ! HE'S A HERO ! WE MUST DO SOME-THING FOR HIM !
H-H-HOW ABOUT B-BUILDING A F-F-FIRE UNDER M-ME ?
End

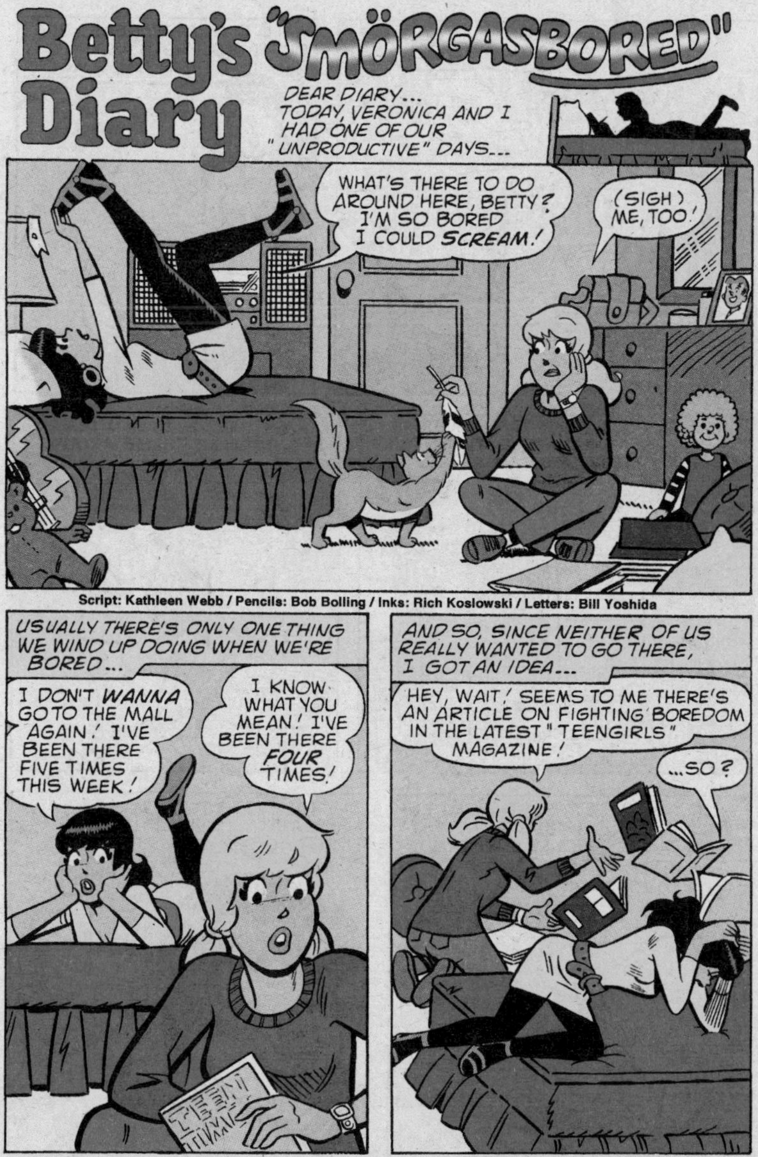
Betty's Diary
"SMÖRGASBORED"
DEAR DIARY... TODAY, VERONICA AND I HAD ONE OF OUR "UNPRODUCTIVE" DAYS...
WHAT'S THERE TO DO AROUND HERE, BETTY? I'M SO BORED I COULD SCREAM!
(SIGH) ME, TOO!
Script: Kathleen Webb / Pencils: Bob Bolling / Inks: Rich Koslowski / Letters: Bill Yoshida
USUALLY THERE'S ONLY ONE THING WE WIND UP DOING WHEN WE'RE BORED...
I DON'T WANNA GO TO THE MALL AGAIN! I'VE BEEN THERE FIVE TIMES THIS WEEK!
I KNOW WHAT YOU MEAN! I'VE BEEN THERE FOUR TIMES!
AND SO, SINCE NEITHER OF US REALLY WANTED TO GO THERE, I GOT AN IDEA...
HEY, WAIT! SEEMS TO ME THERE'S AN ARTICLE ON FIGHTING BOREDOM IN THE LATEST "TEENGIRLS" MAGAZINE!
...SO?

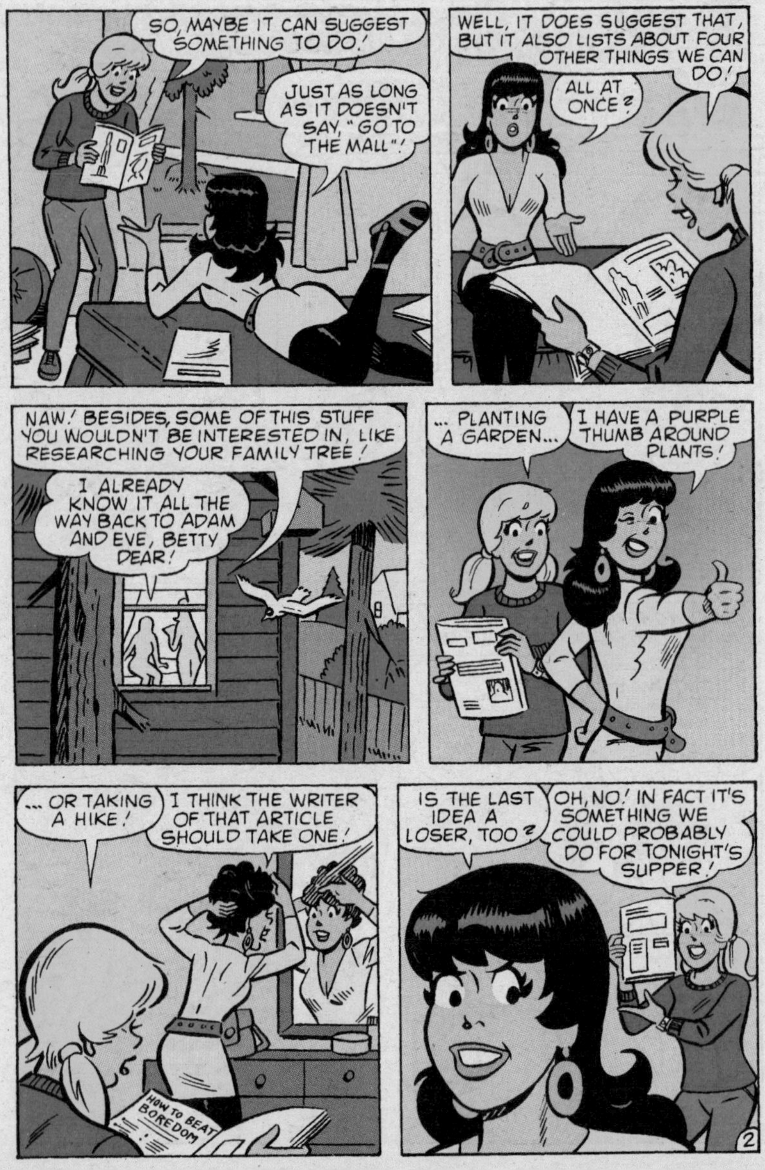
SO, MAYBE IT CAN SUGGEST SOMETHING TO DO!
JUST AS LONG AS IT DOESN'T SAY, "GO TO THE MALL"!
WELL, IT DOES SUGGEST THAT, BUT IT ALSO LISTS ABOUT FOUR OTHER THINGS WE CAN DO!
ALL AT ONCE?
NAW! BESIDES, SOME OF THIS STUFF YOU WOULDN'T BE INTERESTED IN, LIKE RESEARCHING YOUR FAMILY TREE!
I ALREADY KNOW IT ALL THE WAY BACK TO ADAM AND EVE, BETTY DEAR!
... PLANTING A GARDEN...
I HAVE A PURPLE THUMB AROUND PLANTS!
... OR TAKING A HIKE!
I THINK THE WRITER OF THAT ARTICLE SHOULD TAKE ONE!
HOW TO BEAT BOREDOM
IS THE LAST IDEA A LOSER, TOO?
OH, NO! IN FACT IT'S SOMETHING WE COULD PROBABLY DO FOR TONIGHT'S SUPPER!
2

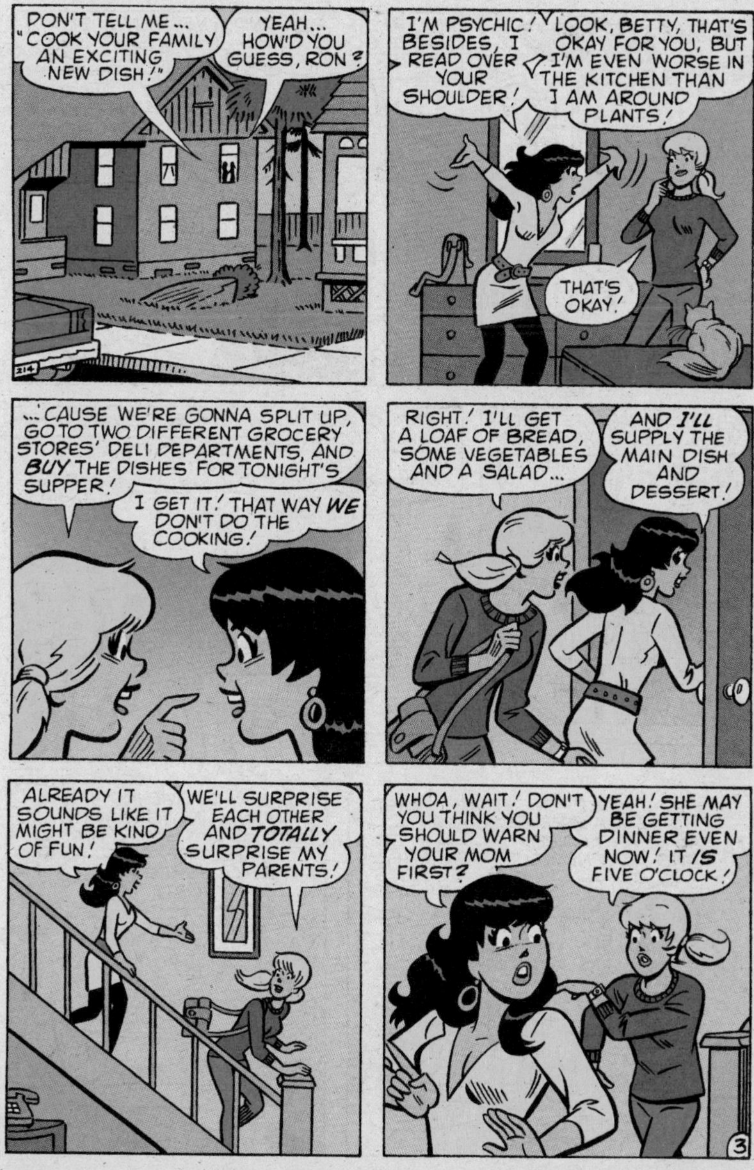
DON'T TELL ME... "COOK YOUR FAMILY AN EXCITING NEW DISH!"
YEAH... HOW'D YOU GUESS, RON?
214
I'M PSYCHIC! BESIDES, I READ OVER YOUR SHOULDER!
LOOK, BETTY, THAT'S OKAY FOR YOU, BUT I'M EVEN WORSE IN THE KITCHEN THAN I AM AROUND PLANTS!
THAT'S OKAY!
...'CAUSE WE'RE GONNA SPLIT UP, GO TO TWO DIFFERENT GROCERY STORES' DELI DEPARTMENTS, AND BUY THE DISHES FOR TONIGHT'S SUPPER!
I GET IT! THAT WAY WE DON'T DO THE COOKING!
RIGHT! I'LL GET A LOAF OF BREAD, SOME VEGETABLES AND A SALAD...
AND I'LL SUPPLY THE MAIN DISH AND DESSERT!
ALREADY IT SOUNDS LIKE IT MIGHT BE KIND OF FUN!
WE'LL SURPRISE EACH OTHER AND TOTALLY SURPRISE MY PARENTS!
WHOA, WAIT! DON'T YOU THINK YOU SHOULD WARN YOUR MOM FIRST?
YEAH! SHE MAY BE GETTING DINNER EVEN NOW! IT IS FIVE O'CLOCK!
3

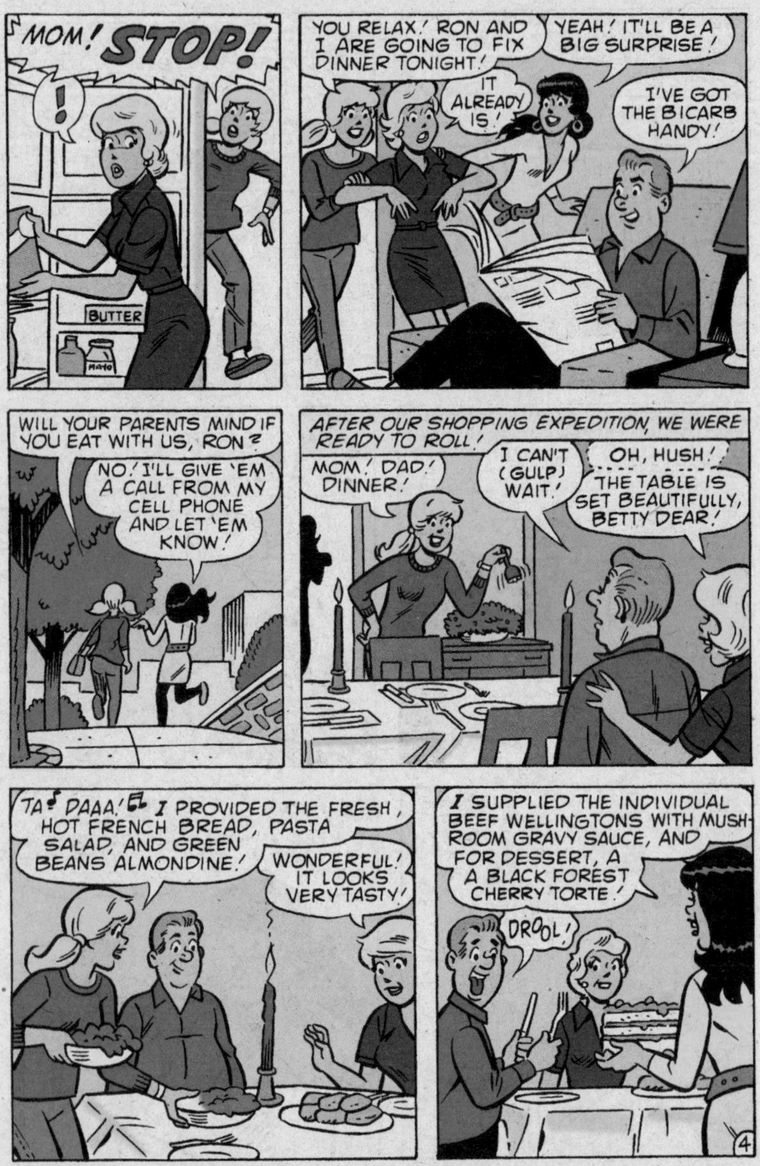
MOM! STOP!
!
YOU RELAX! RON AND I ARE GOING TO FIX DINNER TONIGHT!
YEAH! IT'LL BE A BIG SURPRISE!
IT ALREADY IS!
I'VE GOT THE BICARB HANDY!
BUTTER
MAYO
WILL YOUR PARENTS MIND IF YOU EAT WITH US, RON?
NO! I'LL GIVE 'EM A CALL FROM MY CELL PHONE AND LET 'EM KNOW!
AFTER OUR SHOPPING EXPEDITION, WE WERE READY TO ROLL!
MOM! DAD! DINNER!
I CAN'T (GULP) WAIT!
OH, HUSH!
THE TABLE IS SET BEAUTIFULLY, BETTY DEAR!
TA DAAA! I PROVIDED THE FRESH, HOT FRENCH BREAD, PASTA SALAD, AND GREEN BEANS ALMONDINE!
WONDERFUL! IT LOOKS VERY TASTY!
I SUPPLIED THE INDIVIDUAL BEEF WELLINGTONS WITH MUSH-ROOM GRAVY SAUCE, AND FOR DESSERT, A A BLACK FOREST CHERRY TORTE!
DROOL!
4

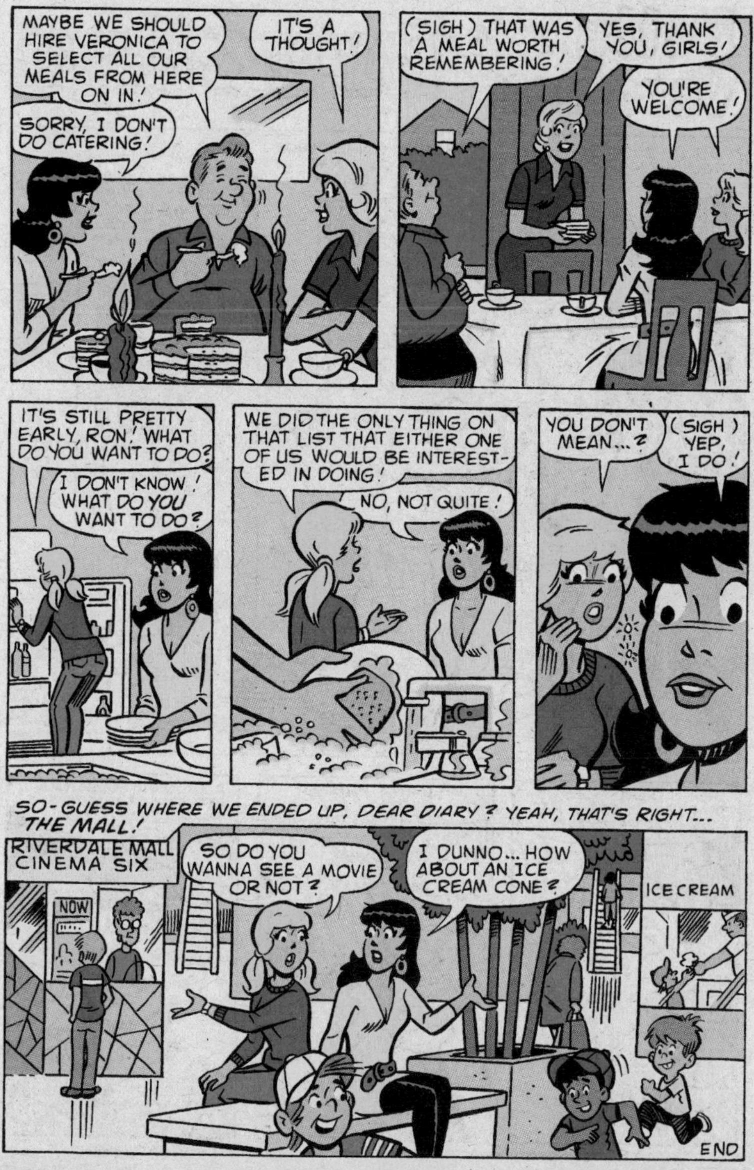

MAYBE WE SHOULD HIRE VERONICA TO SELECT ALL OUR MEALS FROM HERE ON IN!
IT'S A THOUGHT!
SORRY, I DON'T DO CATERING!
(SIGH) THAT WAS A MEAL WORTH REMEMBERING!
YES, THANK YOU, GIRLS!
YOU'RE WELCOME!
IT'S STILL PRETTY EARLY, RON! WHAT DO YOU WANT TO DO?
I DON'T KNOW! WHAT DO YOU WANT TO DO?
WE DID THE ONLY THING ON THAT LIST THAT EITHER ONE OF US WOULD BE INTERESTED IN DOING!
NO, NOT QUITE!
YOU DON'T MEAN...?
(SIGH) YEP, I DO!
SO-GUESS WHERE WE ENDED UP, DEAR DIARY? YEAH, THAT'S RIGHT... THE MALL!
RIVERDALE MALL CINEMA SIX
NOW
SO DO YOU WANNA SEE A MOVIE OR NOT?
I DUNNO... HOW ABOUT AN ICE CREAM CONE?
ICE CREAM
END

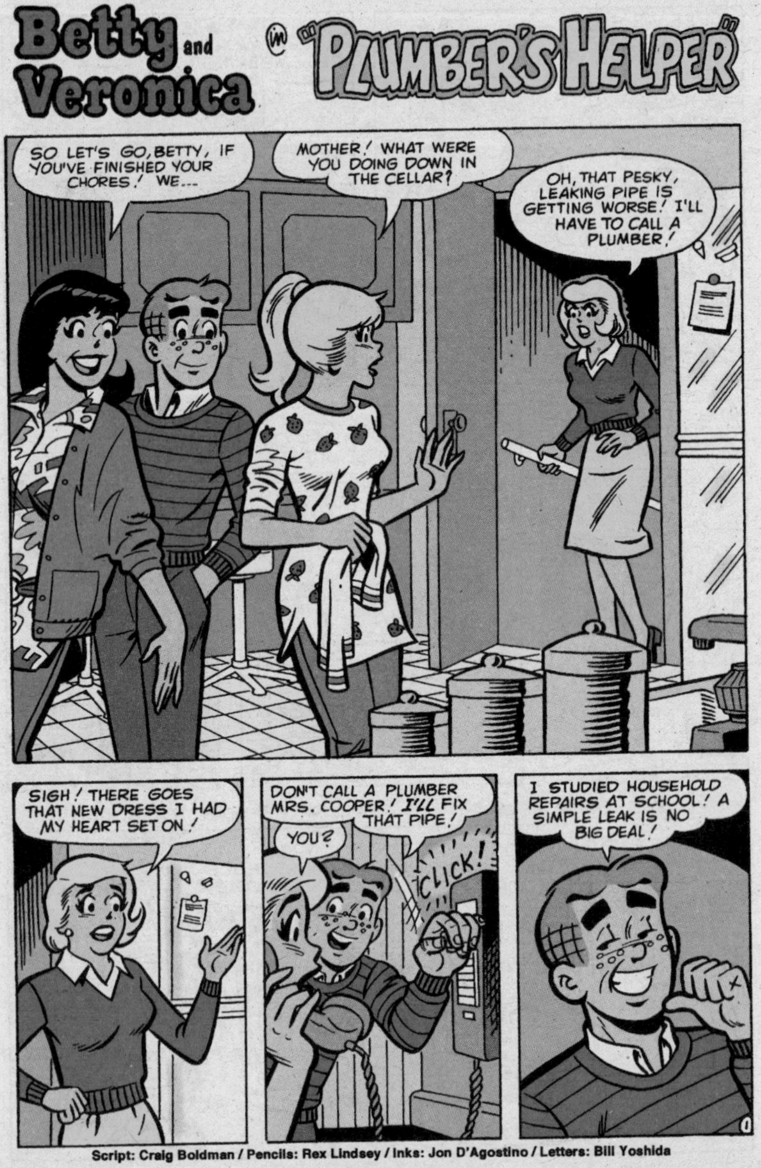
Betty and Veronica
in "PLUMBER'S HELPER"
SO LET'S GO, BETTY, IF YOU'VE FINISHED YOUR CHORES! WE...
MOTHER! WHAT WERE YOU DOING DOWN IN THE CELLAR?
OH, THAT PESKY, LEAKING PIPE IS GETTING WORSE! I'LL HAVE TO CALL A PLUMBER!
SIGH! THERE GOES THAT NEW DRESS I HAD MY HEART SET ON!
DON'T CALL A PLUMBER MRS. COOPER! I'LL FIX THAT PIPE!
YOU?
CLICK!
I STUDIED HOUSEHOLD REPAIRS AT SCHOOL! A SIMPLE LEAK IS NO BIG DEAL!
1

Script: Craig Boldman / Pencils: Rex Lindsey / Inks: Jon D'Agostino / Letters: Bill Yoshida

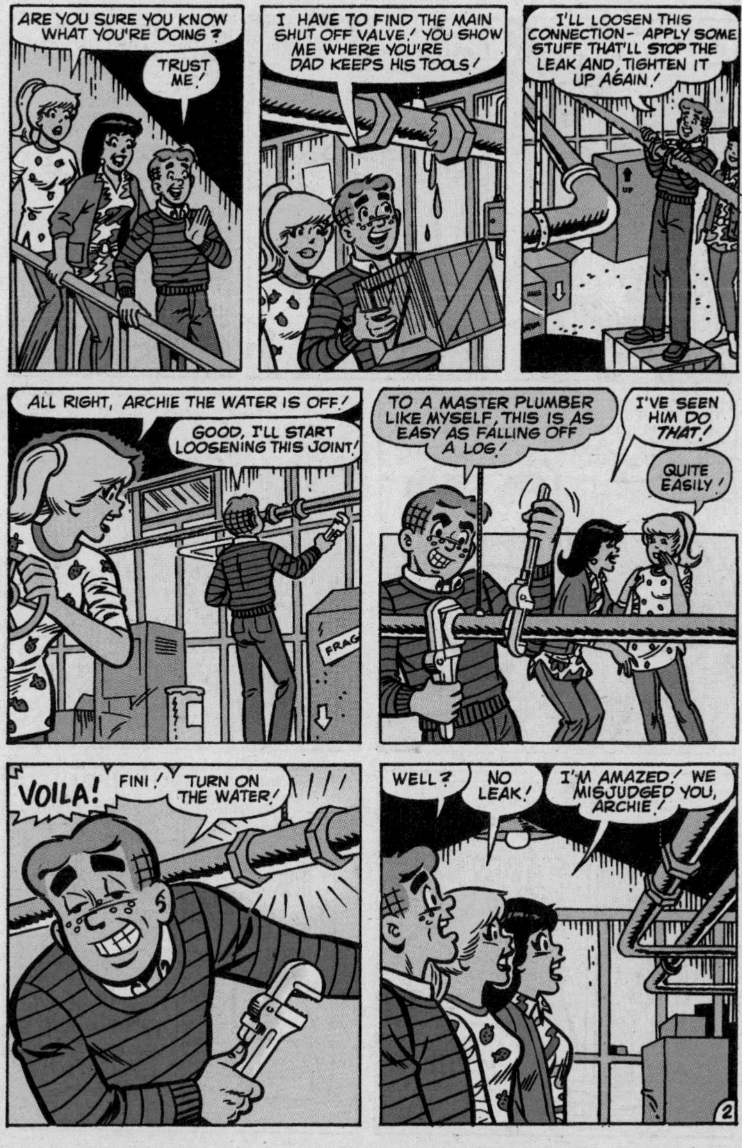
ARE YOU SURE YOU KNOW WHAT YOU'RE DOING?
TRUST ME!
I HAVE TO FIND THE MAIN SHUT OFF VALVE! YOU SHOW ME WHERE YOU'RE DAD KEEPS HIS TOOLS!
I'LL LOOSEN THIS CONNECTION- APPLY SOME STUFF THAT'LL STOP THE LEAK AND, TIGHTEN IT UP AGAIN!
UP
ALL RIGHT, ARCHIE THE WATER IS OFF!
GOOD, I'LL START LOOSENING THIS JOINT!
FRAG
TO A MASTER PLUMBER LIKE MYSELF, THIS IS AS EASY AS FALLING OFF A LOG!
I'VE SEEN HIM DO THAT!
QUITE EASILY!
VOILA!
FINI!
TURN ON THE WATER!
WELL?
NO LEAK!
I'M AMAZED! WE MISJUDGED YOU, ARCHIE!
2

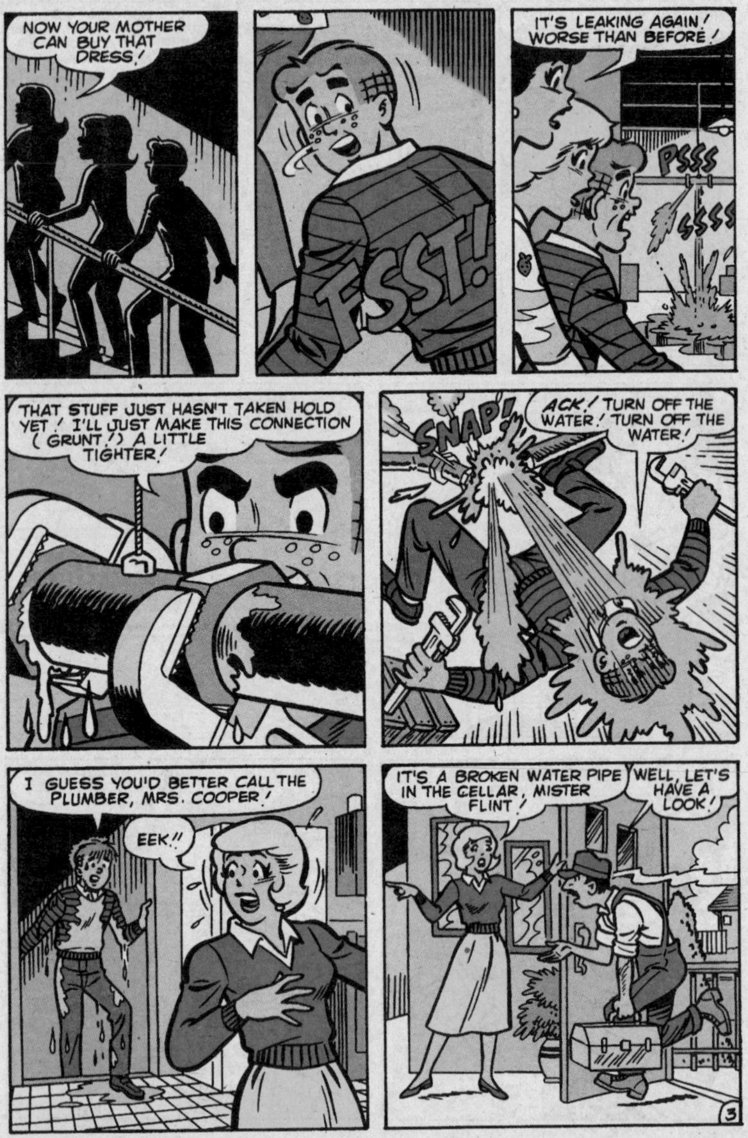
NOW YOUR MOTHER CAN BUY THAT DRESS!
FSST!
IT'S LEAKING AGAIN! WORSE THAN BEFORE!
PSSS
SSSS
THAT STUFF JUST HASN'T TAKEN HOLD YET! I'LL JUST MAKE THIS CONNECTION (GRUNT!) A LITTLE TIGHTER!
SNAP!
ACK! TURN OFF THE WATER! TURN OFF THE WATER!
I GUESS YOU'D BETTER CALL THE PLUMBER, MRS. COOPER!
EEK!!
IT'S A BROKEN WATER PIPE IN THE CELLAR, MISTER FLINT!
WELL, LET'S HAVE A LOOK!
3

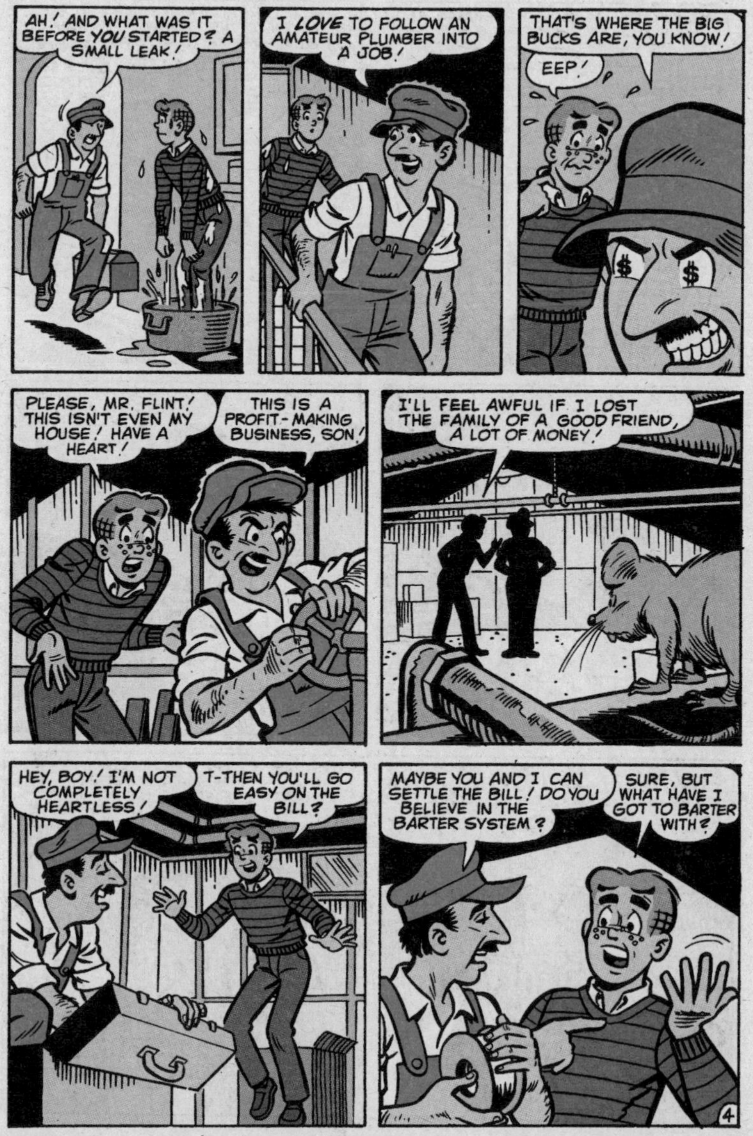
AH! AND WHAT WAS IT BEFORE YOU STARTED? A SMALL LEAK!
I LOVE TO FOLLOW AN AMATEUR PLUMBER INTO A JOB!
THAT'S WHERE THE BIG BUCKS ARE, YOU KNOW!
EEP!
$
$
PLEASE, MR. FLINT! THIS ISN'T EVEN MY HOUSE! HAVE A HEART!
THIS IS A PROFIT-MAKING BUSINESS, SON!
I'LL FEEL AWFUL IF I LOST THE FAMILY OF A GOOD FRIEND, A LOT OF MONEY!
HEY, BOY! I'M NOT COMPLETELY HEARTLESS!
T-THEN YOU'LL GO EASY ON THE BILL?
MAYBE YOU AND I CAN SETTLE THE BILL! DO YOU BELIEVE IN THE BARTER SYSTEM?
SURE, BUT WHAT HAVE I GOT TO BARTER WITH?
4

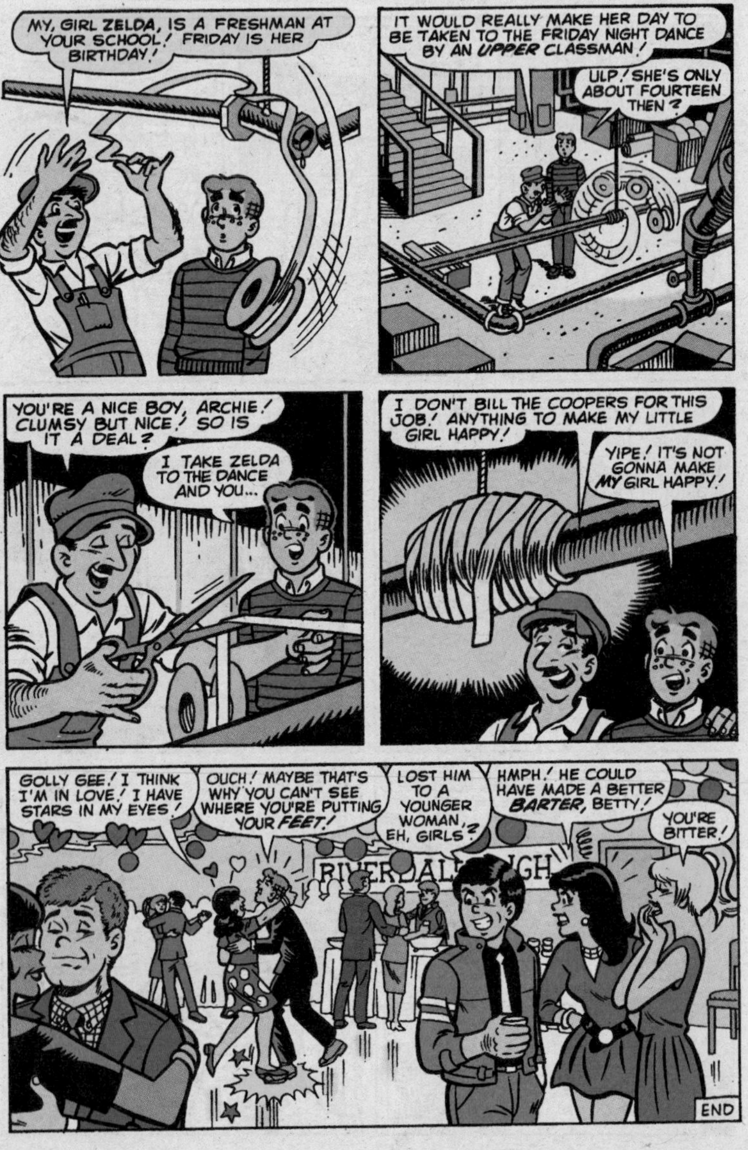
MY, GIRL ZELDA, IS A FRESHMAN AT YOUR SCHOOL! FRIDAY IS HER BIRTHDAY!
IT WOULD REALLY MAKE HER DAY TO BE TAKEN TO THE FRIDAY NIGHT DANCE BY AN UPPER CLASSMAN!
ULP! SHE'S ONLY ABOUT FOURTEEN THEN?
YOU'RE A NICE BOY, ARCHIE! CLUMSY BUT NICE! SO IS IT A DEAL?
I TAKE ZELDA TO THE DANCE AND YOU...
I DON'T BILL THE COOPERS FOR THIS JOB! ANYTHING TO MAKE MY LITTLE GIRL HAPPY!
YIPE! IT'S NOT GONNA MAKE MY GIRL HAPPY!
GOLLY GEE! I THINK I'M IN LOVE! I HAVE STARS IN MY EYES!
OUCH! MAYBE THAT'S WHY YOU CAN'T SEE WHERE YOU'RE PUTTING YOUR FEET!
LOST HIM TO A YOUNGER WOMAN, EH, GIRLS?
HMPH! HE COULD HAVE MADE A BETTER BARTER, BETTY!
YOU'RE BITTER!
RIVERDALE HIGH
END

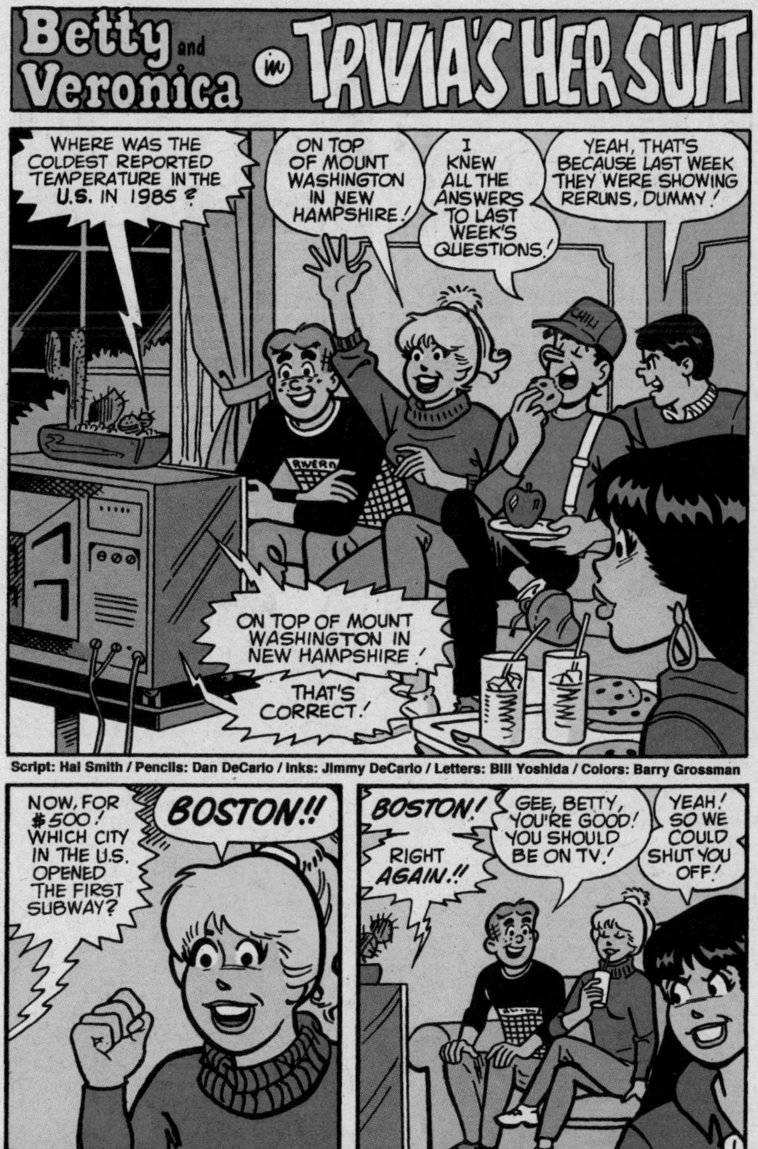
Betty and Veronica in TRIVIA'S HER SUIT
WHERE WAS THE COLDEST REPORTED TEMPERATURE IN THE U.S. IN 1985?
ON TOP OF MOUNT WASHINGTON IN NEW HAMPSHIRE!
I KNEW ALL THE ANSWERS TO LAST WEEK'S QUESTIONS!
YEAH, THAT'S BECAUSE LAST WEEK THEY WERE SHOWING RERUNS, DUMMY!
CHILI
ON TOP OF MOUNT WASHINGTON IN NEW HAMPSHIRE!
THAT'S CORRECT!
Script: Hal Smith / Pencils: Dan DeCarlo / Inks: Jimmy DeCarlo / Letters: Bill Yoshida / Colors: Barry Grossman
NOW, FOR $500! WHICH CITY IN THE U.S. OPENED THE FIRST SUBWAY?
BOSTON!!
BOSTON!
RIGHT AGAIN!!
GEE, BETTY, YOU'RE GOOD! YOU SHOULD BE ON TV!
YEAH! SO WE COULD SHUT YOU OFF!
1

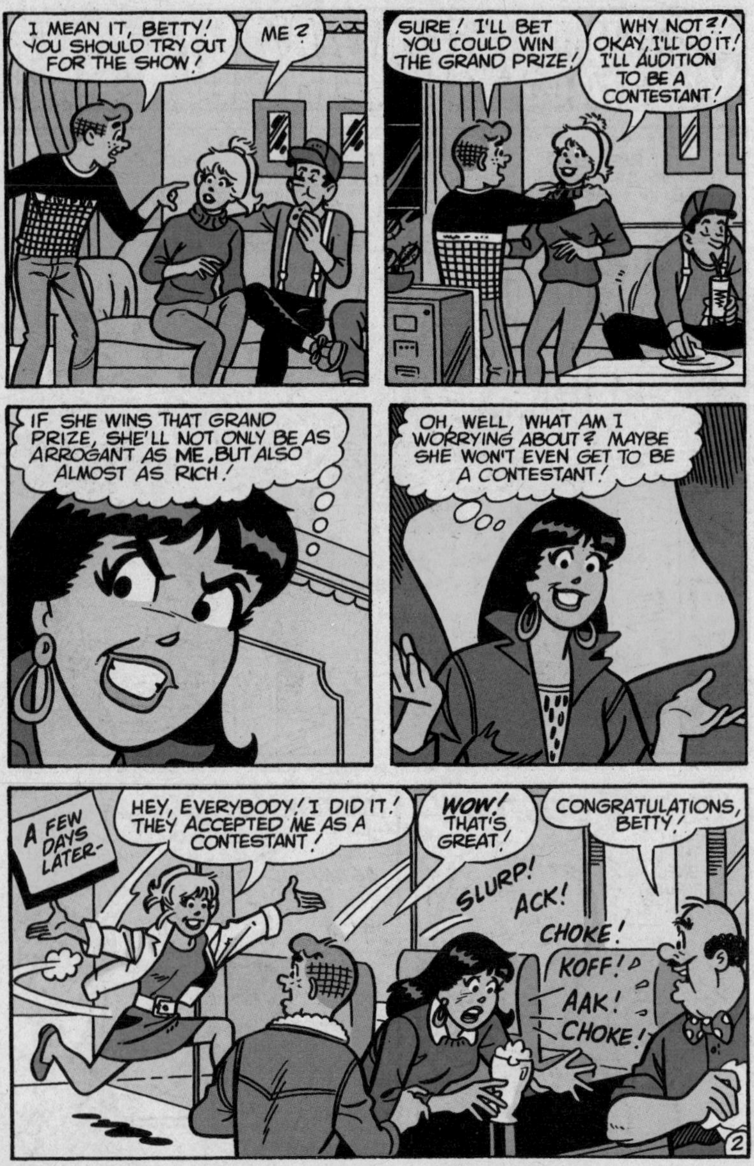
I MEAN IT, BETTY! YOU SHOULD TRY OUT FOR THE SHOW!
ME?
SURE! I'LL BET YOU COULD WIN THE GRAND PRIZE!
WHY NOT?! OKAY, I'LL DO IT! I'LL AUDITION TO BE A CONTESTANT!
IF SHE WINS THAT GRAND PRIZE, SHE'LL NOT ONLY BE AS ARROGANT AS ME, BUT ALSO ALMOST AS RICH!
OH, WELL, WHAT AM I WORRYING ABOUT? MAYBE SHE WON'T EVEN GET TO BE A CONTESTANT!
A FEW DAYS LATER-
HEY, EVERYBODY! I DID IT! THEY ACCEPTED ME AS A CONTESTANT!
WOW! THAT'S GREAT!
CONGRATULATIONS, BETTY!
SLURP!
ACK!
CHOKE!
KOFF!
AAK!
CHOKE!
2

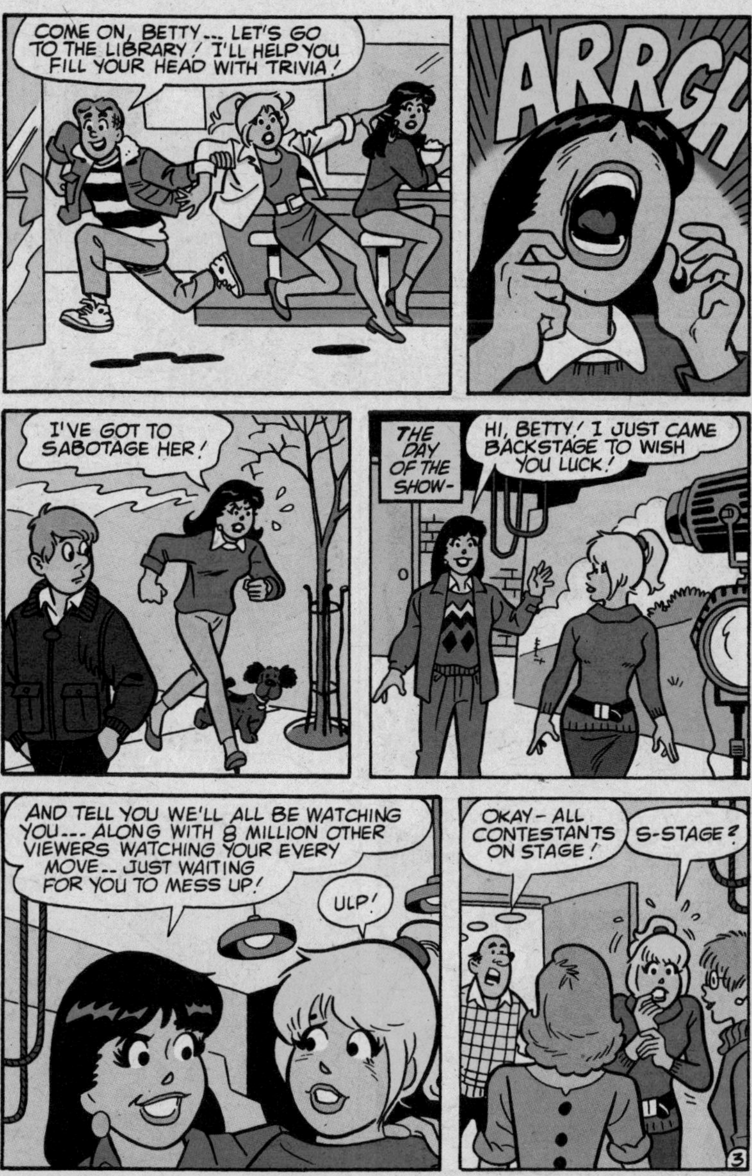
COME ON, BETTY... LET'S GO TO THE LIBRARY! I'LL HELP YOU FILL YOUR HEAD WITH TRIVIA!
ARRGH
I'VE GOT TO SABOTAGE HER!
THE DAY OF THE SHOW-
HI, BETTY! I JUST CAME BACKSTAGE TO WISH YOU LUCK!
AND TELL YOU WE'LL ALL BE WATCHING YOU... ALONG WITH 8 MILLION OTHER VIEWERS WATCHING YOUR EVERY MOVE.. JUST WAITING FOR YOU TO MESS UP!
ULP!
OKAY - ALL CONTESTANTS ON STAGE!
S-STAGE?
3

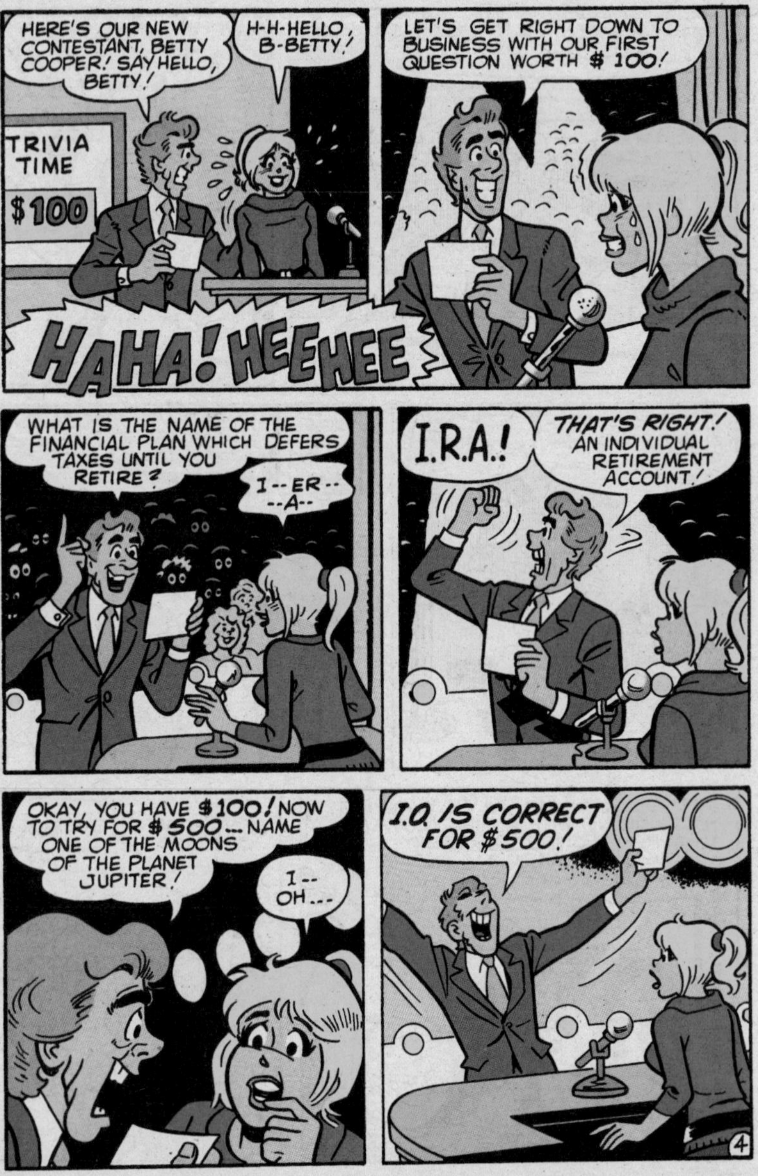
HERE'S OUR NEW CONTESTANT, BETTY COOPER! SAY HELLO, BETTY!
H-H-HELLO, B-BETTY!
TRIVIA TIME
$100
HAHA! HEEHEE
LET'S GET RIGHT DOWN TO BUSINESS WITH OUR FIRST QUESTION WORTH $ 100!
WHAT IS THE NAME OF THE FINANCIAL PLAN WHICH DEFERS TAXES UNTIL YOU RETIRE?
I -- ER -- --A--
I.R.A.!
THAT'S RIGHT! AN INDIVIDUAL RETIREMENT ACCOUNT!
OKAY, YOU HAVE $100! NOW TO TRY FOR $500... NAME ONE OF THE MOONS OF THE PLANET JUPITER!
I -- OH ...
I.Q. IS CORRECT FOR $500!
4

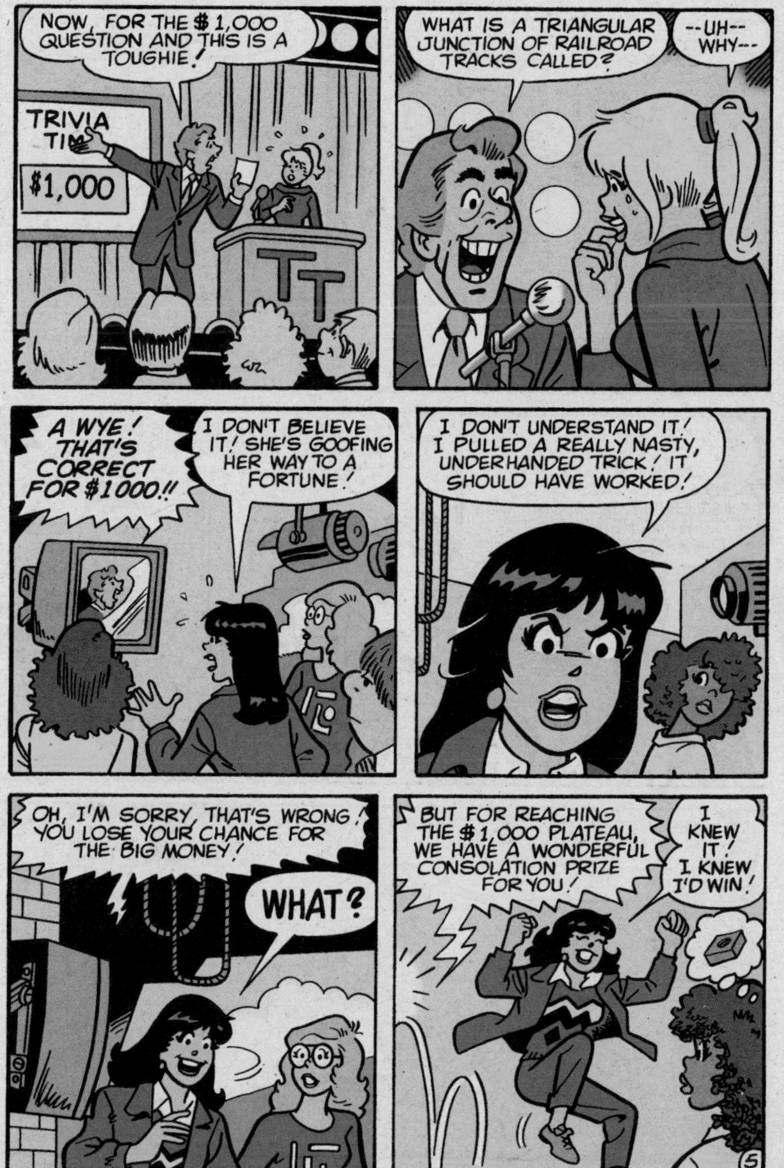
NOW, FOR THE $ 1,000 QUESTION AND THIS IS A TOUGHIE!
TRIVIA TIM
$1,000
WHAT IS A TRIANGULAR JUNCTION OF RAILROAD TRACKS CALLED?
--UH-- WHY---
A WYE! THAT'S CORRECT FOR $1000!!
I DON'T BELIEVE IT! SHE'S GOOFING HER WAY TO A FORTUNE!
I DON'T UNDERSTAND IT! I PULLED A REALLY NASTY, UNDERHANDED TRICK! IT SHOULD HAVE WORKED!
OH, I'M SORRY, THAT'S WRONG! YOU LOSE YOUR CHANCE FOR THE BIG MONEY!
WHAT?
BUT FOR REACHING THE $ 1,000 PLATEAU, WE HAVE A WONDERFUL CONSOLATION PRIZE FOR YOU!
I KNEW IT! I KNEW I'D WIN!
5

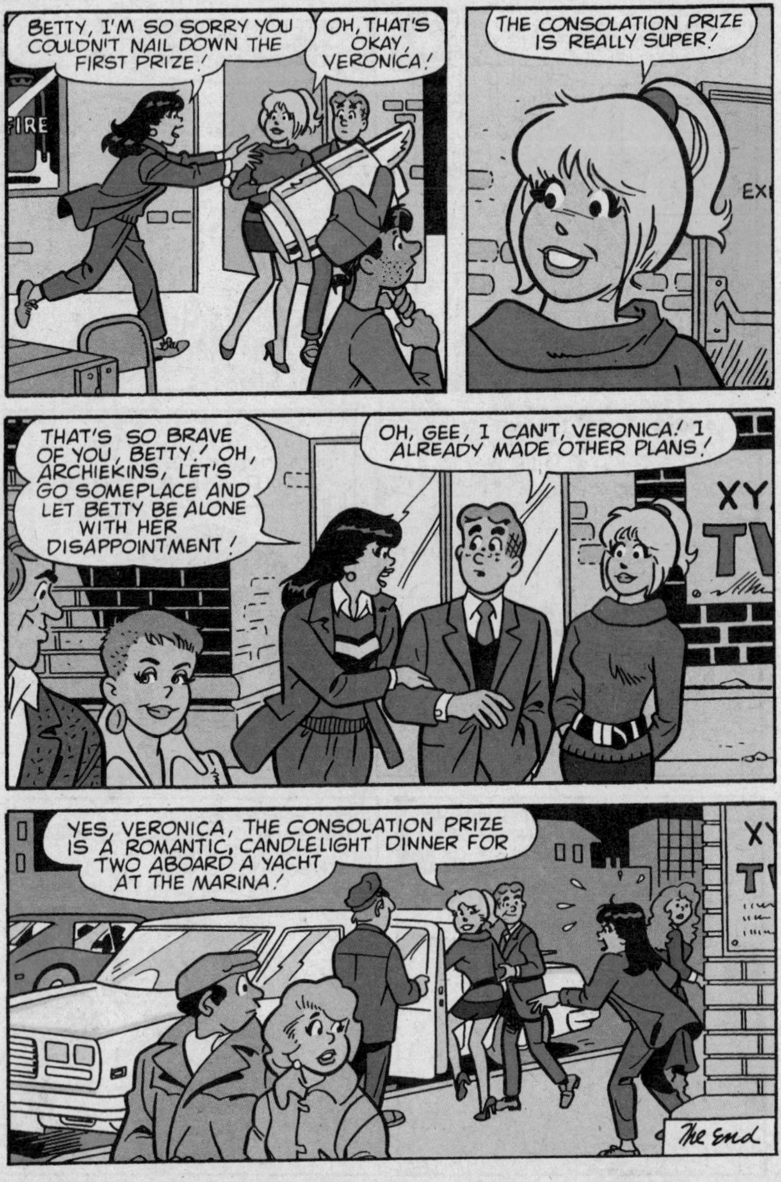
BETTY, I'M SO SORRY YOU COULDN'T NAIL DOWN THE FIRST PRIZE!
OH, THAT'S OKAY, VERONICA!
FIRE
THE CONSOLATION PRIZE IS REALLY SUPER!
THAT'S SO BRAVE OF YOU, BETTY! OH, ARCHIEKINS, LET'S GO SOMEPLACE AND LET BETTY BE ALONE WITH HER DISAPPOINTMENT!
OH, GEE, I CAN'T, VERONICA! I ALREADY MADE OTHER PLANS!
YES, VERONICA, THE CONSOLATION PRIZE IS A ROMANTIC, CANDLELIGHT DINNER FOR TWO ABOARD A YACHT AT THE MARINA!
The End

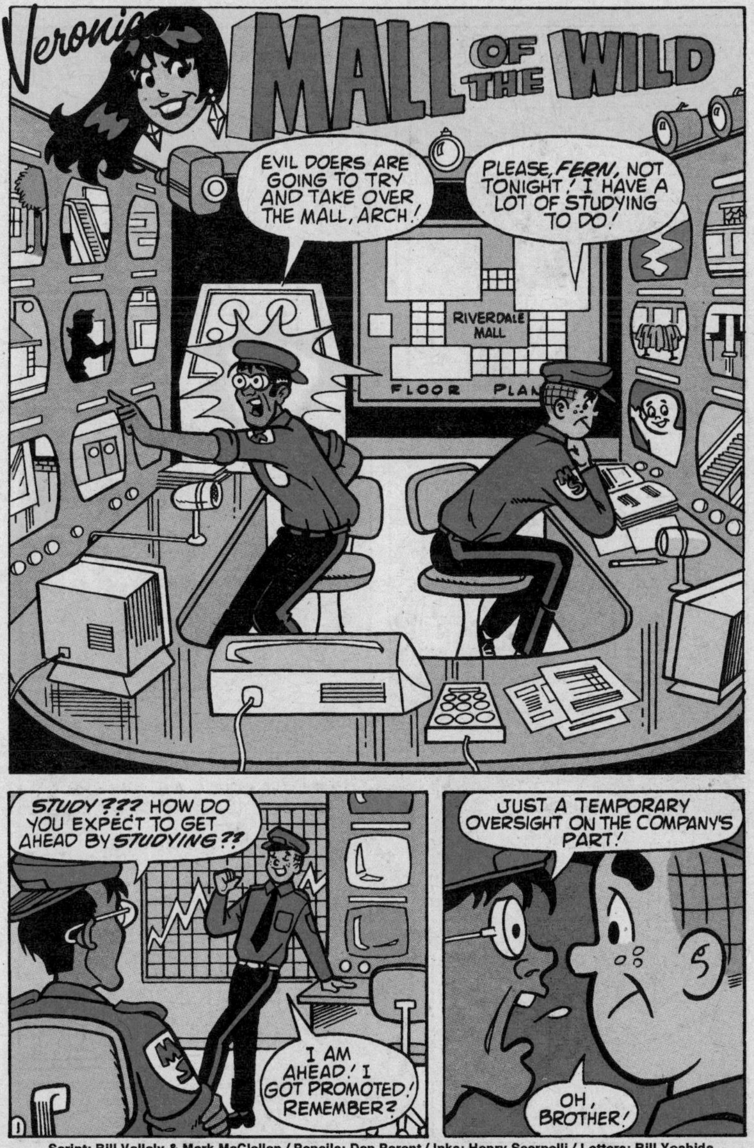
Veronica
MALL OF THE WILD
EVIL DOERS ARE GOING TO TRY AND TAKE OVER THE MALL, ARCH!
PLEASE, FERN, NOT TONIGHT! I HAVE A LOT OF STUDYING TO DO!
RIVERDALE MALL
FLOOR PLAN
STUDY??? HOW DO YOU EXPECT TO GET AHEAD BY STUDYING??
I AM AHEAD! I GOT PROMOTED! REMEMBER?
JUST A TEMPORARY OVERSIGHT ON THE COMPANY'S PART!
OH, BROTHER!

Script: Bill Vallely & Mark McClellan / Pencils: Dan Parent / Inks: Henry Scarpelli / Letters: Bill Yoshida

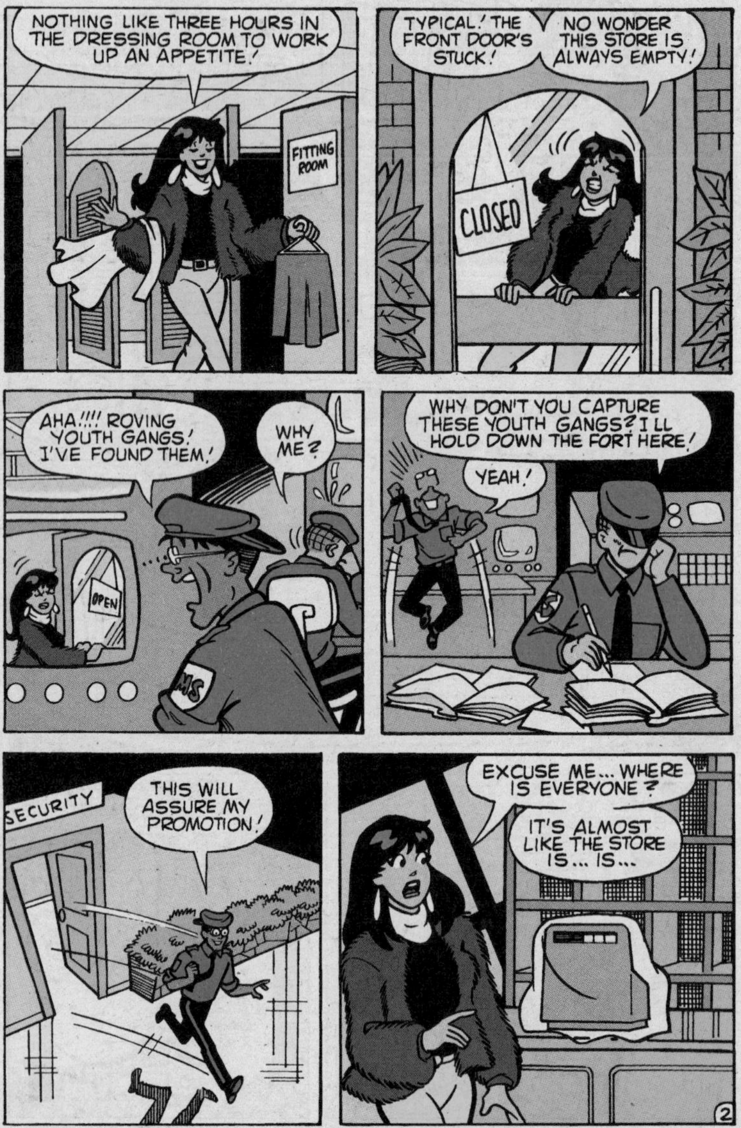
NOTHING LIKE THREE HOURS IN THE DRESSING ROOM TO WORK UP AN APPETITE!
FITTING ROOM
TYPICAL! THE FRONT DOOR'S STUCK!
NO WONDER THIS STORE IS ALWAYS EMPTY!
CLOSED
AHA!!!! ROVING YOUTH GANGS! I'VE FOUND THEM!
WHY ME?
OPEN
WHY DON'T YOU CAPTURE THESE YOUTH GANGS? I'LL HOLD DOWN THE FORT HERE!
YEAH!
SECURITY
THIS WILL ASSURE MY PROMOTION!
EXCUSE ME... WHERE IS EVERYONE?
IT'S ALMOST LIKE THE STORE IS... IS...
2

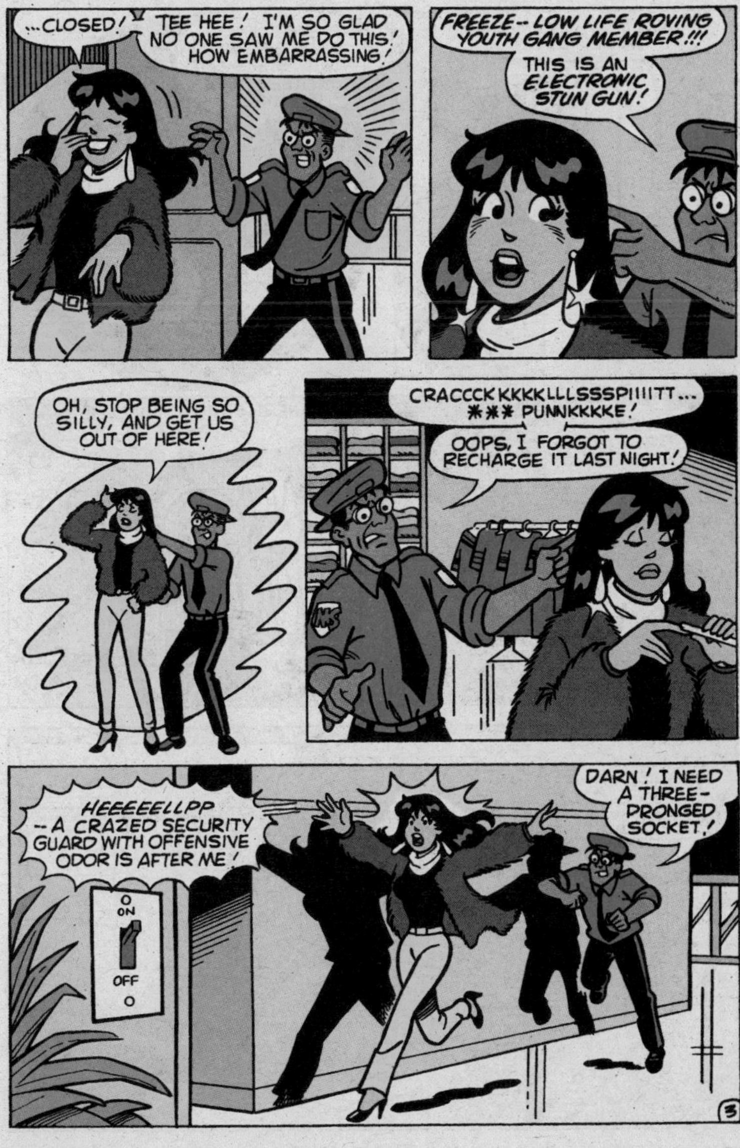
...CLOSED!
TEE HEE! I'M SO GLAD NO ONE SAW ME DO THIS! HOW EMBARRASSING!
FREEZE-- LOW LIFE ROVING YOUTH GANG MEMBER!!!
THIS IS AN ELECTRONIC STUN GUN!
OH, STOP BEING SO SILLY, AND GET US OUT OF HERE!
CRACCCK KKKKLLLSSSPIIIITT... *** PUNNKKKKE!
OOPS, I FORGOT TO RECHARGE IT LAST NIGHT!
HEEEEELLPP --A CRAZED SECURITY GUARD WITH OFFENSIVE ODOR IS AFTER ME!
DARN! I NEED A THREE-PRONGED SOCKET!
ON
OFF
3

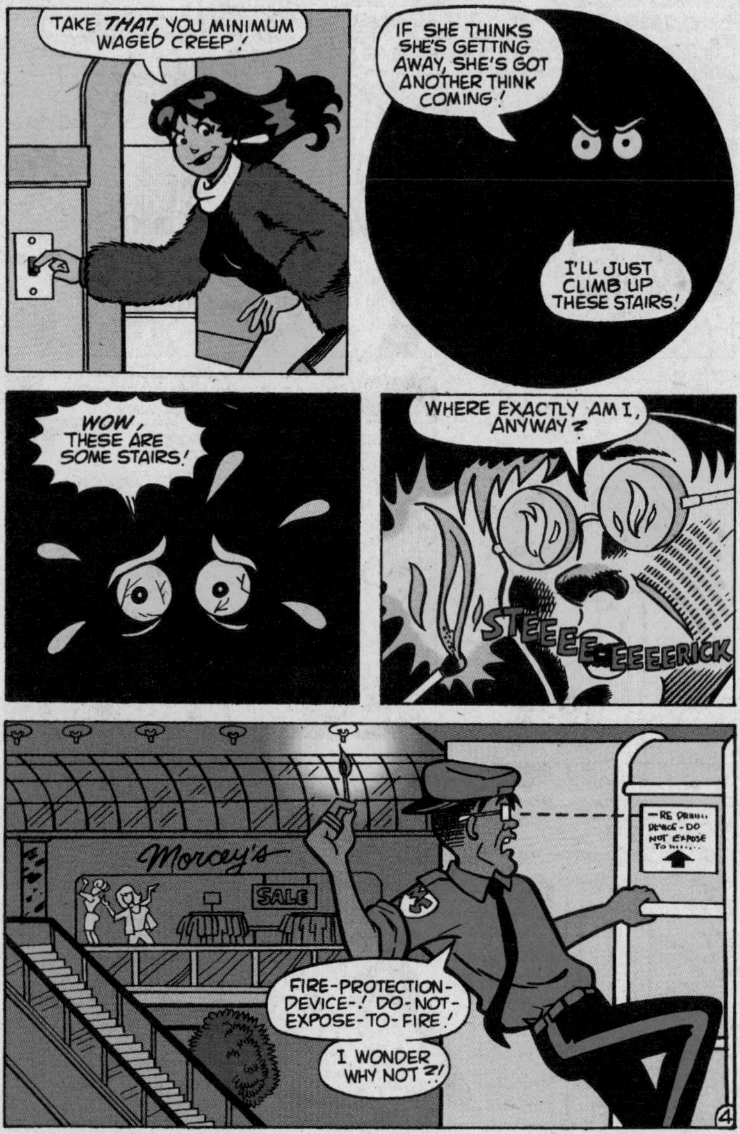

TAKE *THAT*, YOU MINIMUM WAGED CREEP!
IF SHE THINKS SHE'S GETTING AWAY, SHE'S GOT ANOTHER THINK COMING!
I'LL JUST CLIMB UP THESE STAIRS!
WOW, THESE ARE SOME STAIRS!
WHERE EXACTLY AM I, ANYWAY?
STEEEEE-EEEERICK
Moray's
SALE
FIRE-PROTECTION-DEVICE-! DO-NOT-EXPOSE-TO-FIRE!
I WONDER WHY NOT?!
4

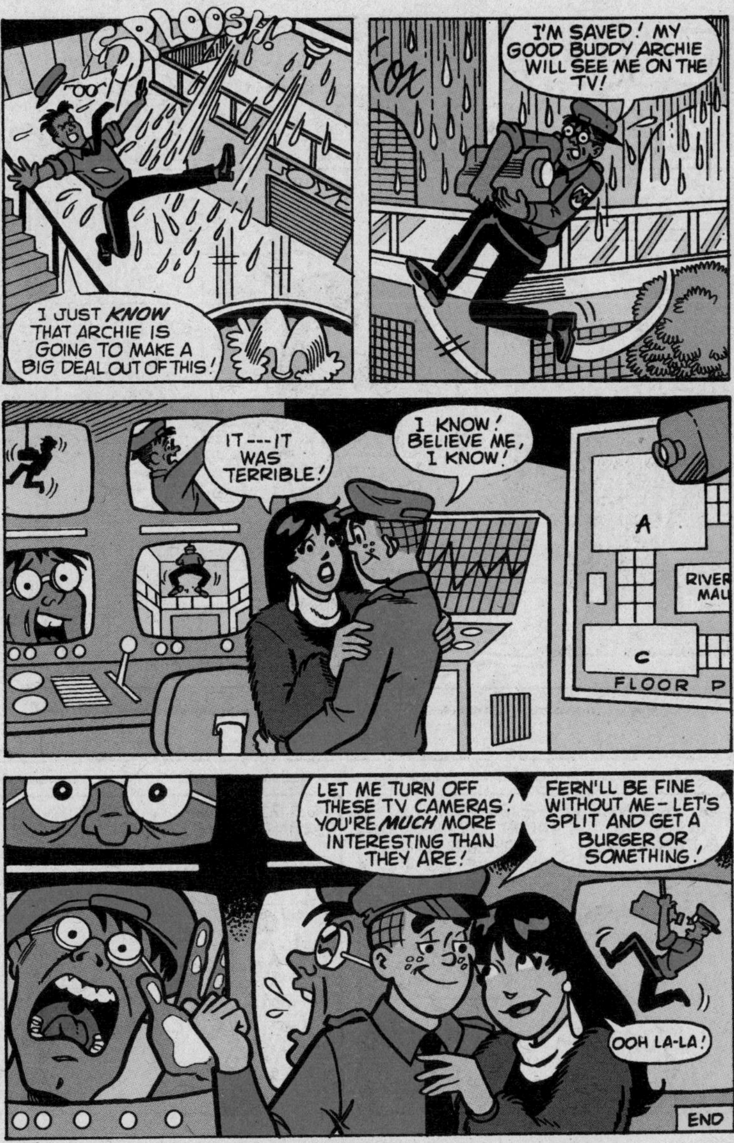
SPLOOSH!
I JUST KNOW THAT ARCHIE IS GOING TO MAKE A BIG DEAL OUT OF THIS!
I'M SAVED! MY GOOD BUDDY ARCHIE WILL SEE ME ON THE TV!
IT---IT WAS TERRIBLE!
I KNOW! BELIEVE ME, I KNOW!
A
RIVER MAL
C
FLOOR P
LET ME TURN OFF THESE TV CAMERAS! YOU'RE MUCH MORE INTERESTING THAN THEY ARE!
FERN'LL BE FINE WITHOUT ME - LET'S SPLIT AND GET A BURGER OR SOMETHING!
OOH LA-LA!
END

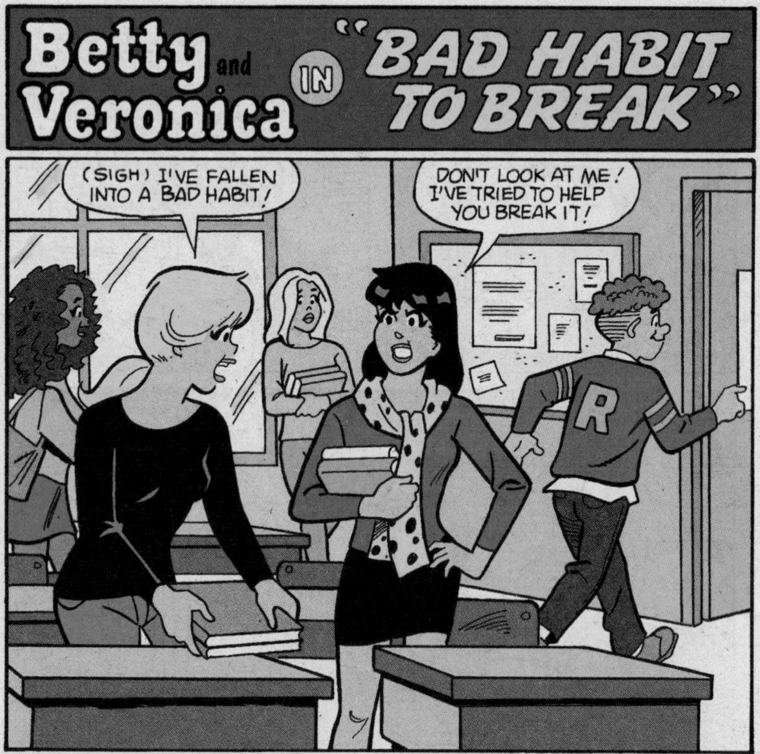
Betty and Veronica IN "BAD HABIT TO BREAK"
(SIGH) I'VE FALLEN INTO A BAD HABIT!
DON'T LOOK AT ME! I'VE TRIED TO HELP YOU BREAK IT!

Script: Kathleen Webb / Pencils: Jeff Shultz / Inks: Henry Scarpelli / Letters: Bill Yoshida / Colors: Barry Grossman

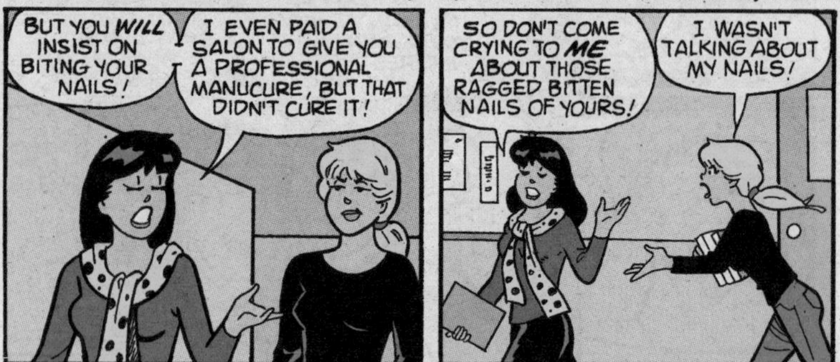
BUT YOU *WILL* INSIST ON BITING YOUR NAILS!
I EVEN PAID A SALON TO GIVE YOU A PROFESSIONAL MANUCURE, BUT THAT DIDN'T CURE IT!
SO DON'T COME CRYING TO *ME* ABOUT THOSE RAGGED BITTEN NAILS OF YOURS!
I WASN'T TALKING ABOUT MY NAILS!

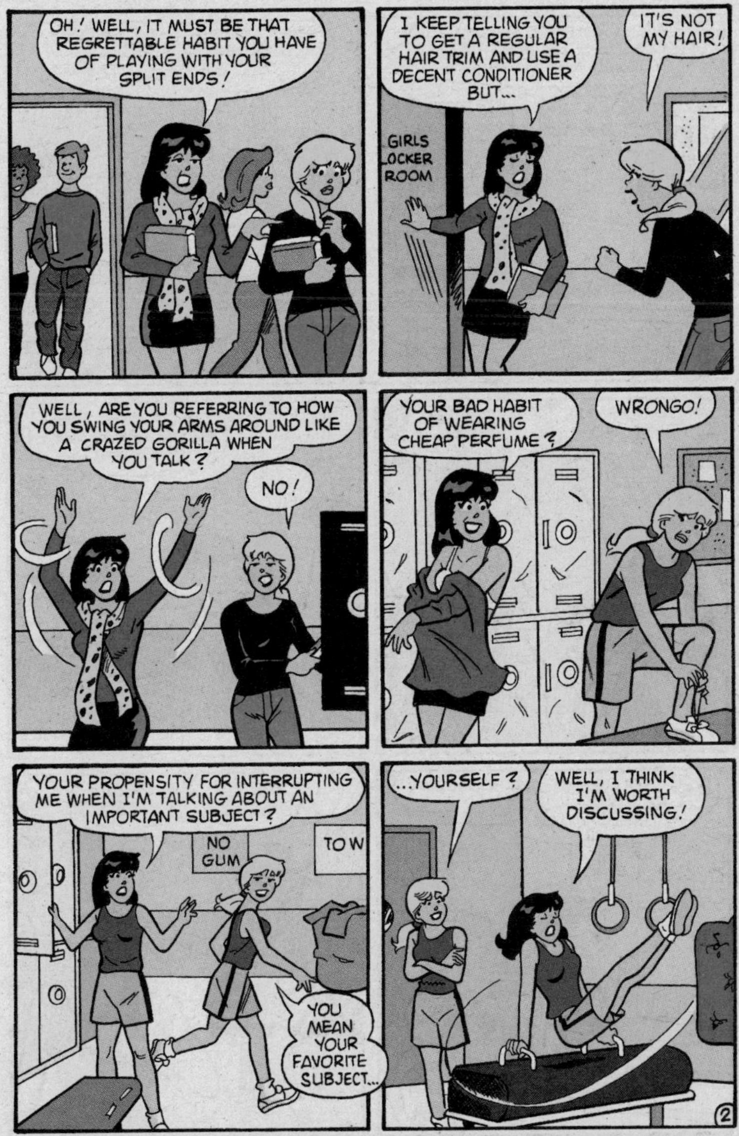
OH! WELL, IT MUST BE THAT REGRETTABLE HABIT YOU HAVE OF PLAYING WITH YOUR SPLIT ENDS!
I KEEP TELLING YOU TO GET A REGULAR HAIR TRIM AND USE A DECENT CONDITIONER BUT...
IT'S NOT MY HAIR!
GIRLS LOCKER ROOM
WELL, ARE YOU REFERRING TO HOW YOU SWING YOUR ARMS AROUND LIKE A CRAZED GORILLA WHEN YOU TALK?
NO!
YOUR BAD HABIT OF WEARING CHEAP PERFUME?
WRONGO!
YOUR PROPENSITY FOR INTERRUPTING ME WHEN I'M TALKING ABOUT AN IMPORTANT SUBJECT?
NO GUM
TOW
YOU MEAN YOUR FAVORITE SUBJECT...
...YOURSELF?
WELL, I THINK I'M WORTH DISCUSSING!
2

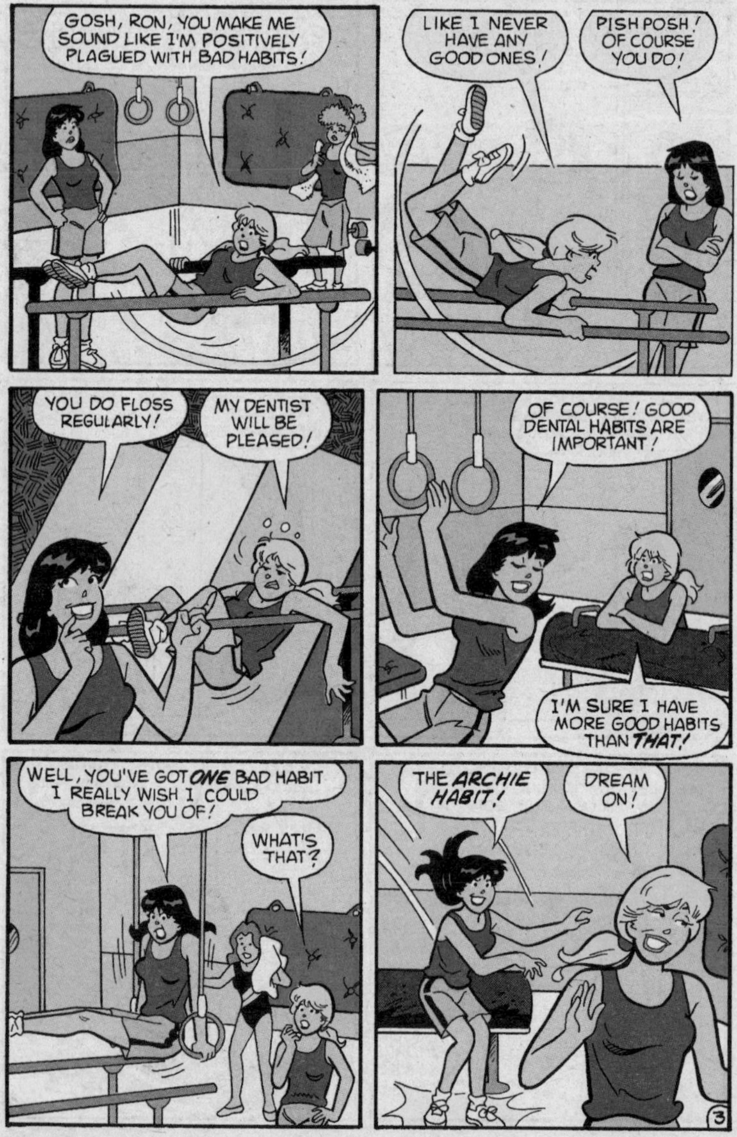
GOSH, RON, YOU MAKE ME SOUND LIKE I'M POSITIVELY PLAGUED WITH BAD HABITS!
LIKE I NEVER HAVE ANY GOOD ONES!
PISH POSH! OF COURSE YOU DO!
YOU DO FLOSS REGULARLY!
MY DENTIST WILL BE PLEASED!
OF COURSE! GOOD DENTAL HABITS ARE IMPORTANT!
I'M SURE I HAVE MORE GOOD HABITS THAN THAT!
WELL, YOU'VE GOT ONE BAD HABIT I REALLY WISH I COULD BREAK YOU OF!
WHAT'S THAT?
THE ARCHIE HABIT!
DREAM ON!
3

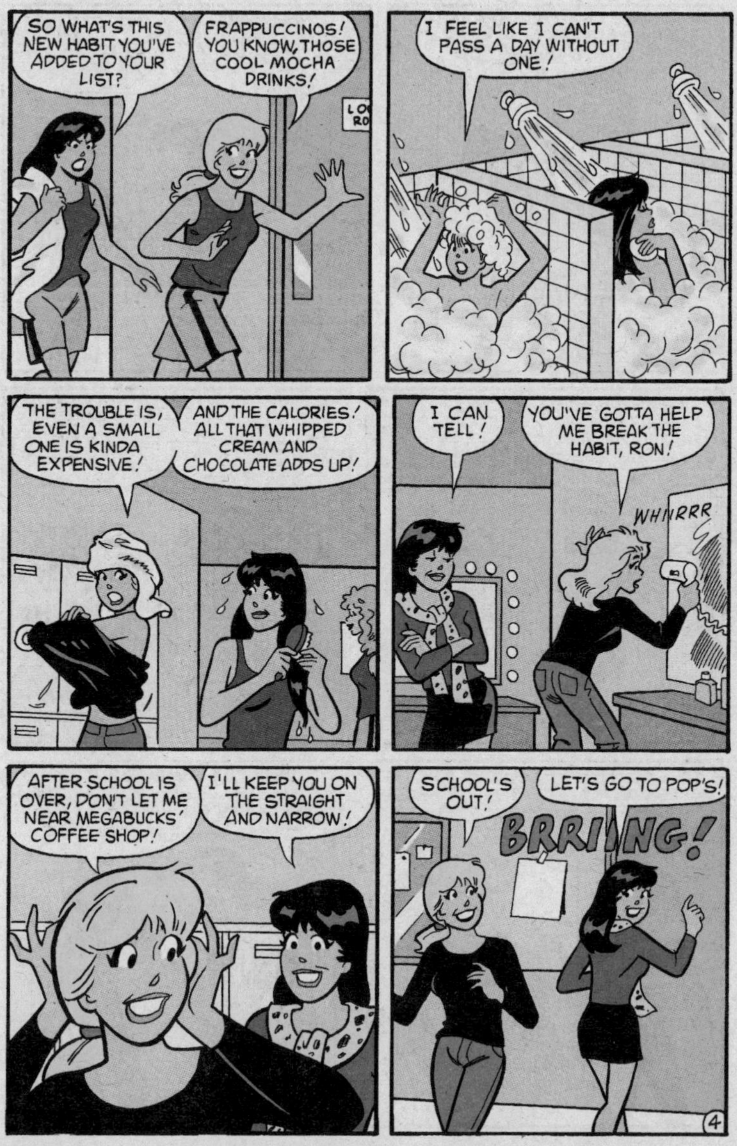
SO WHAT'S THIS NEW HABIT YOU'VE ADDED TO YOUR LIST?
FRAPPUCCINOS! YOU KNOW, THOSE COOL MOCHA DRINKS!
I FEEL LIKE I CAN'T PASS A DAY WITHOUT ONE!
THE TROUBLE IS, EVEN A SMALL ONE IS KINDA EXPENSIVE!
AND THE CALORIES! ALL THAT WHIPPED CREAM AND CHOCOLATE ADDS UP!
I CAN TELL!
YOU'VE GOTTA HELP ME BREAK THE HABIT, RON!
WHIRRR
AFTER SCHOOL IS OVER, DON'T LET ME NEAR MEGABUCKS' COFFEE SHOP!
I'LL KEEP YOU ON THE STRAIGHT AND NARROW!
SCHOOL'S OUT!
LET'S GO TO POP'S!
BRRIING!
4

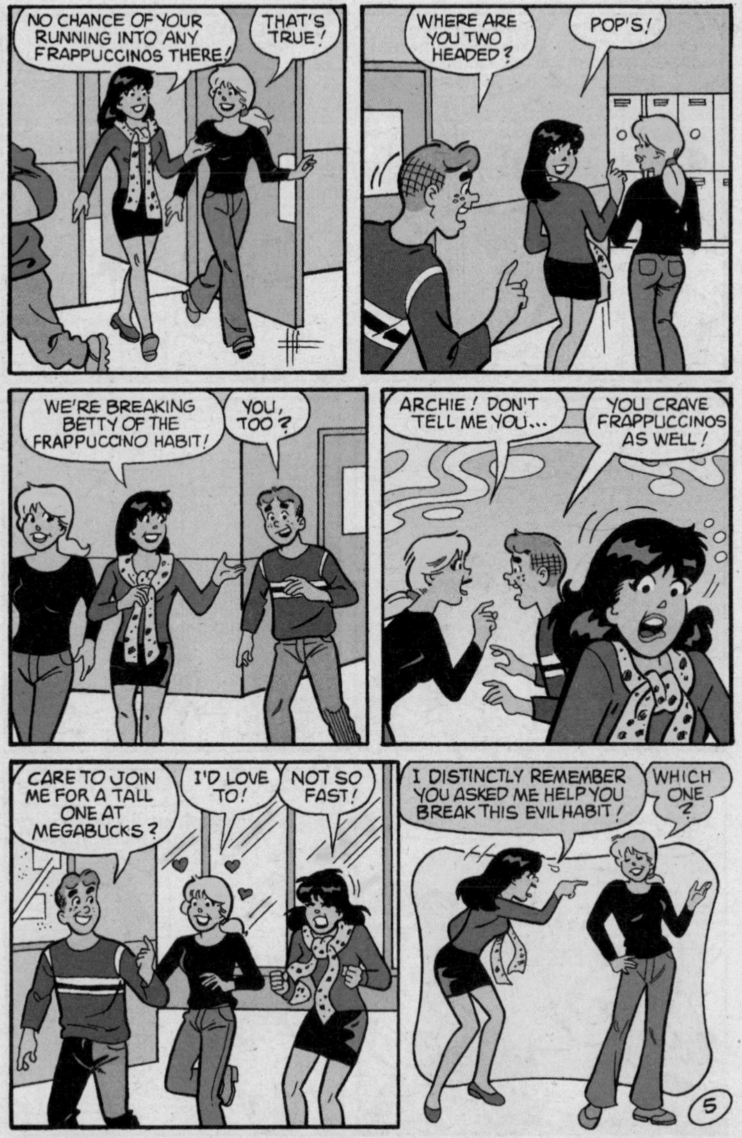
NO CHANCE OF YOUR RUNNING INTO ANY FRAPPUCCINOS THERE!
THAT'S TRUE!
WHERE ARE YOU TWO HEADED?
POP'S!
WE'RE BREAKING BETTY OF THE FRAPPUCCINO HABIT!
YOU, TOO?
ARCHIE! DON'T TELL ME YOU...
YOU CRAVE FRAPPUCCINOS AS WELL!
CARE TO JOIN ME FOR A TALL ONE AT MEGABUCKS?
I'D LOVE TO!
NOT SO FAST!
I DISTINCTLY REMEMBER YOU ASKED ME HELP YOU BREAK THIS EVIL HABIT!
WHICH ONE?

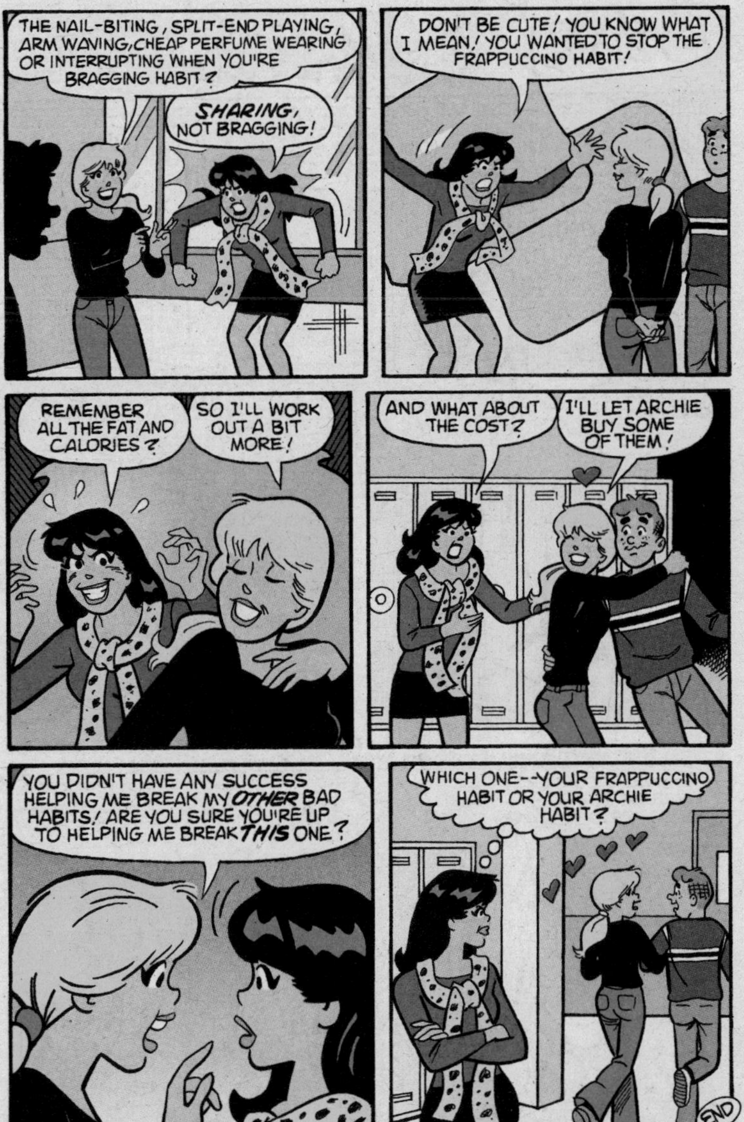
THE NAIL-BITING, SPLIT-END PLAYING, ARM WAVING, CHEAP PERFUME WEARING OR INTERRUPTING WHEN YOU'RE BRAGGING HABIT?
SHARING, NOT BRAGGING!
DON'T BE CUTE! YOU KNOW WHAT I MEAN! YOU WANTED TO STOP THE FRAPPUCCINO HABIT!
REMEMBER ALL THE FAT AND CALORIES?
SO I'LL WORK OUT A BIT MORE!
AND WHAT ABOUT THE COST?
I'LL LET ARCHIE BUY SOME OF THEM!
YOU DIDN'T HAVE ANY SUCCESS HELPING ME BREAK MY OTHER BAD HABITS! ARE YOU SURE YOU'RE UP TO HELPING ME BREAK THIS ONE?
WHICH ONE--YOUR FRAPPUCCINO HABIT OR YOUR ARCHIE HABIT?
END

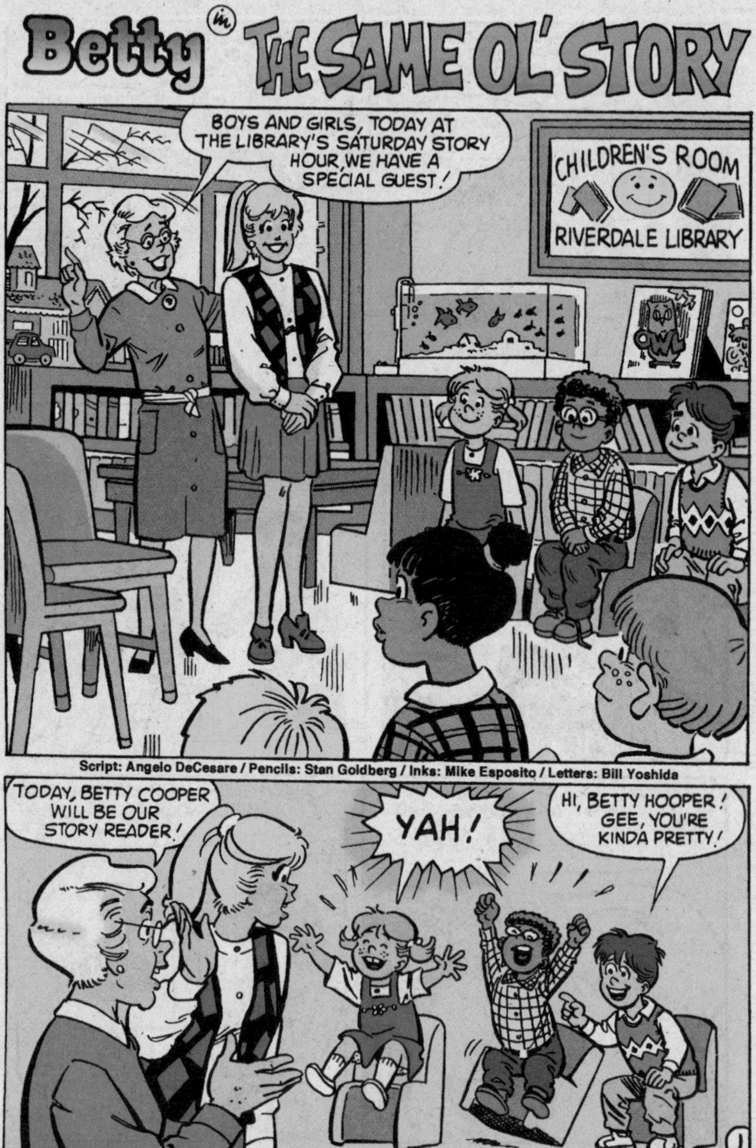
Betty in
THE SAME OL' STORY
BOYS AND GIRLS, TODAY AT THE LIBRARY'S SATURDAY STORY HOUR, WE HAVE A SPECIAL GUEST!
CHILDREN'S ROOM
RIVERDALE LIBRARY
Script: Angelo DeCesare / Pencils: Stan Goldberg / Inks: Mike Esposito / Letters: Bill Yoshida
TODAY, BETTY COOPER WILL BE OUR STORY READER!
YAH!
HI, BETTY HOOPER! GEE, YOU'RE KINDA PRETTY!
1

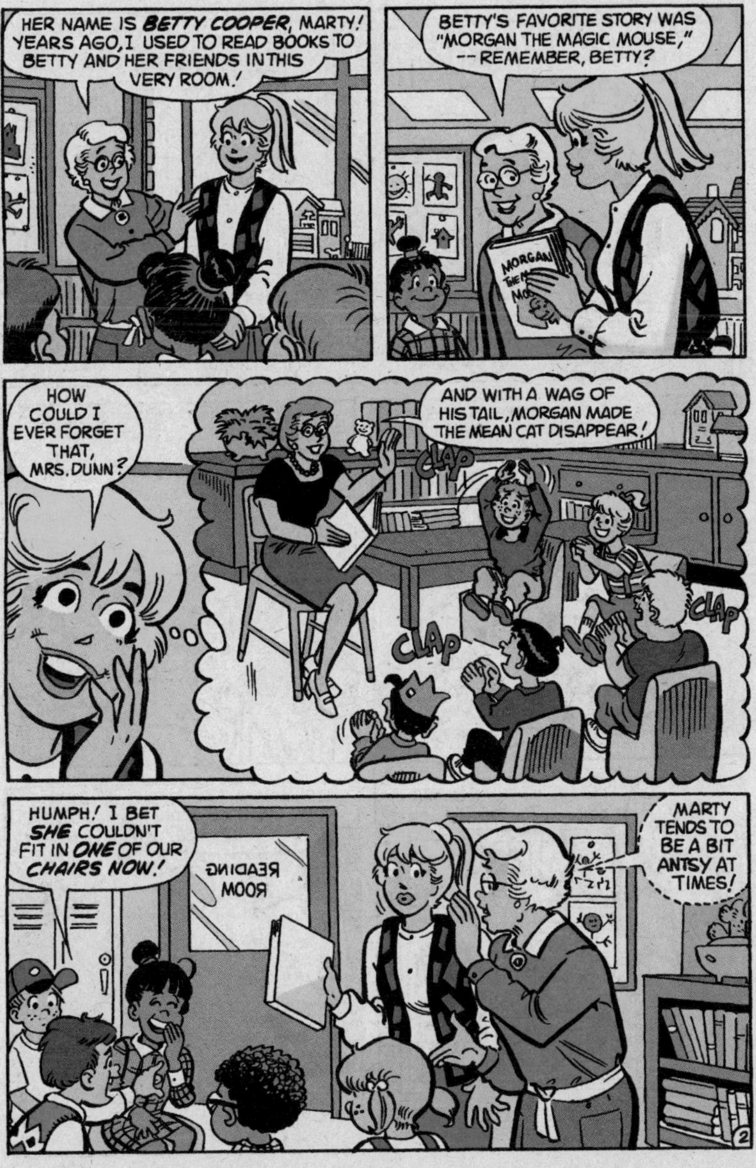

HER NAME IS BETTY COOPER, MARTY! YEARS AGO, I USED TO READ BOOKS TO BETTY AND HER FRIENDS IN THIS VERY ROOM!
BETTY'S FAVORITE STORY WAS "MORGAN THE MAGIC MOUSE," -- REMEMBER, BETTY?
MORGAN
HOW COULD I EVER FORGET THAT, MRS. DUNN?
AND WITH A WAG OF HIS TAIL, MORGAN MADE THE MEAN CAT DISAPPEAR!
CLAP
CLAP
CLAP
HUMPH! I BET SHE COULDN'T FIT IN ONE OF OUR CHAIRS NOW!
READING ROOM
MARTY TENDS TO BE A BIT ANTSY AT TIMES!
2

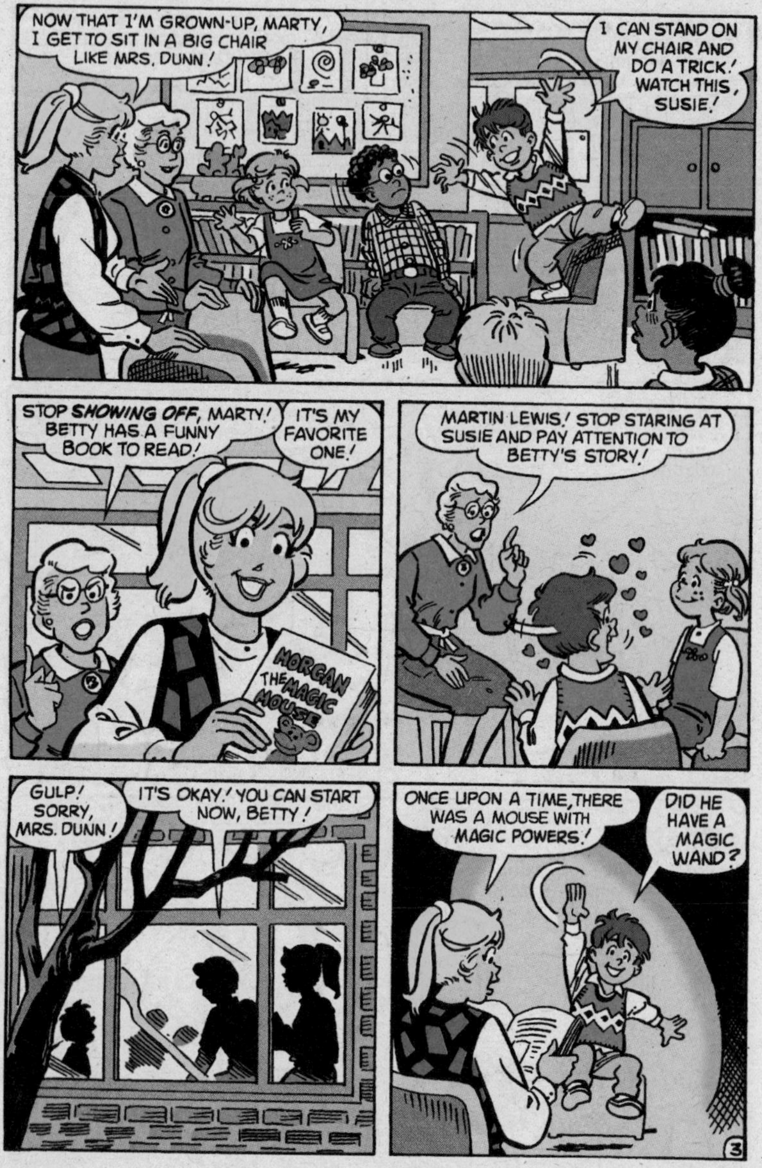
NOW THAT I'M GROWN-UP, MARTY, I GET TO SIT IN A BIG CHAIR LIKE MRS. DUNN!
I CAN STAND ON MY CHAIR AND DO A TRICK! WATCH THIS, SUSIE!
STOP SHOWING OFF, MARTY! BETTY HAS A FUNNY BOOK TO READ!
IT'S MY FAVORITE ONE!
MORGAN THE MAGIC MOUSE
MARTIN LEWIS! STOP STARING AT SUSIE AND PAY ATTENTION TO BETTY'S STORY!
GULP! SORRY, MRS. DUNN!
IT'S OKAY! YOU CAN START NOW, BETTY!
ONCE UPON A TIME, THERE WAS A MOUSE WITH MAGIC POWERS!
DID HE HAVE A MAGIC WAND?
3

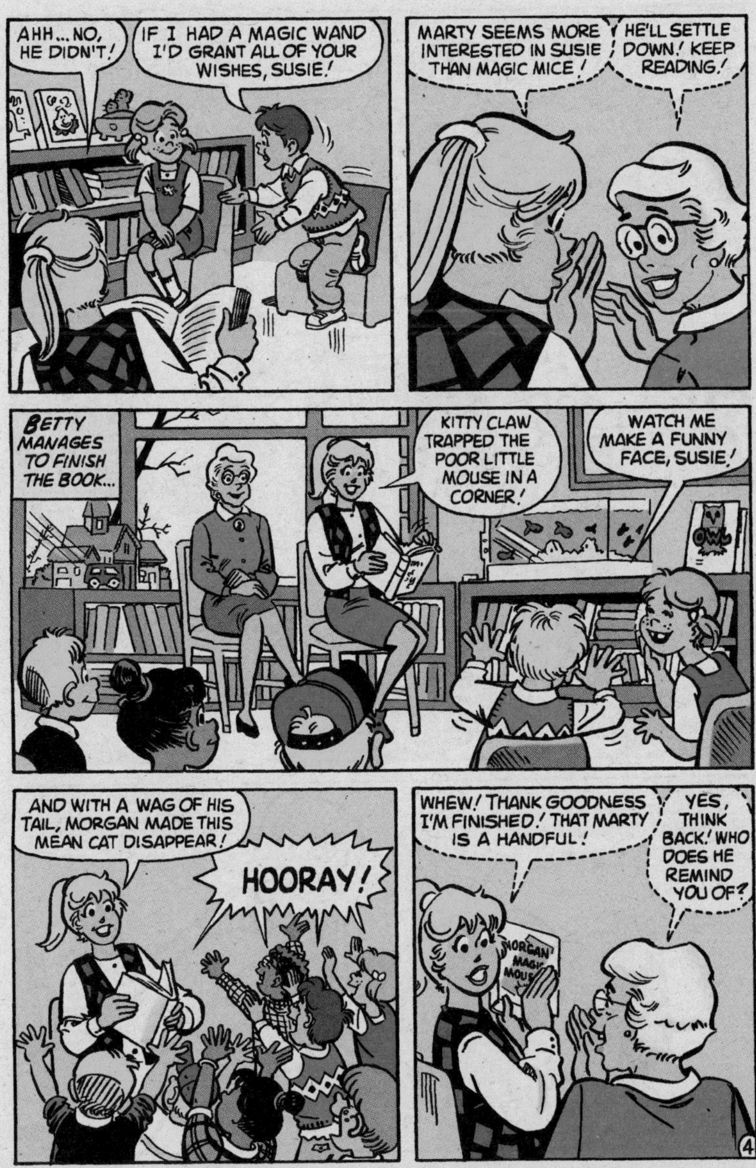
AHH... NO, HE DIDN'T!
IF I HAD A MAGIC WAND I'D GRANT ALL OF YOUR WISHES, SUSIE!
MARTY SEEMS MORE INTERESTED IN SUSIE THAN MAGIC MICE!
HE'LL SETTLE DOWN! KEEP READING!
BETTY MANAGES TO FINISH THE BOOK...
KITTY CLAW TRAPPED THE POOR LITTLE MOUSE IN A CORNER!
WATCH ME MAKE A FUNNY FACE, SUSIE!
OWL
AND WITH A WAG OF HIS TAIL, MORGAN MADE THIS MEAN CAT DISAPPEAR!
HOORAY!
WHEW! THANK GOODNESS I'M FINISHED! THAT MARTY IS A HANDFUL!
YES, THINK BACK! WHO DOES HE REMIND YOU OF?
4

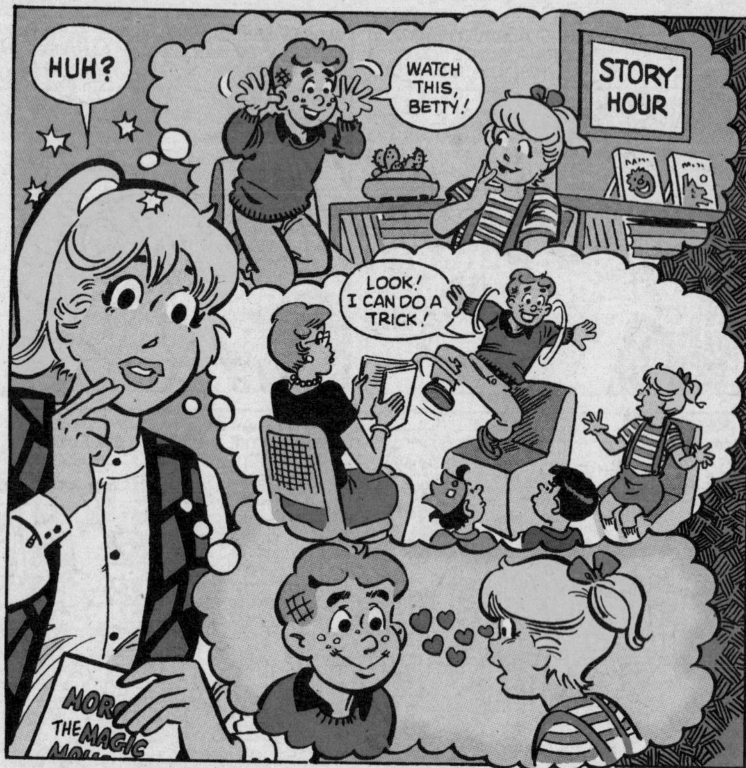
HUH?
WATCH THIS, BETTY!
STORY HOUR
LOOK! I CAN DO A TRICK!
MORG
THE MAGIC

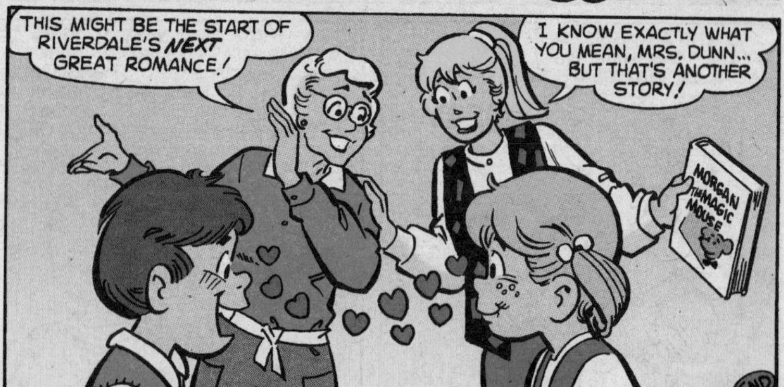
THIS MIGHT BE THE START OF RIVERDALE'S NEXT GREAT ROMANCE!
I KNOW EXACTLY WHAT YOU MEAN, MRS. DUNN... BUT THAT'S ANOTHER STORY!
MORGAN THE MAGIC MOUSE
END

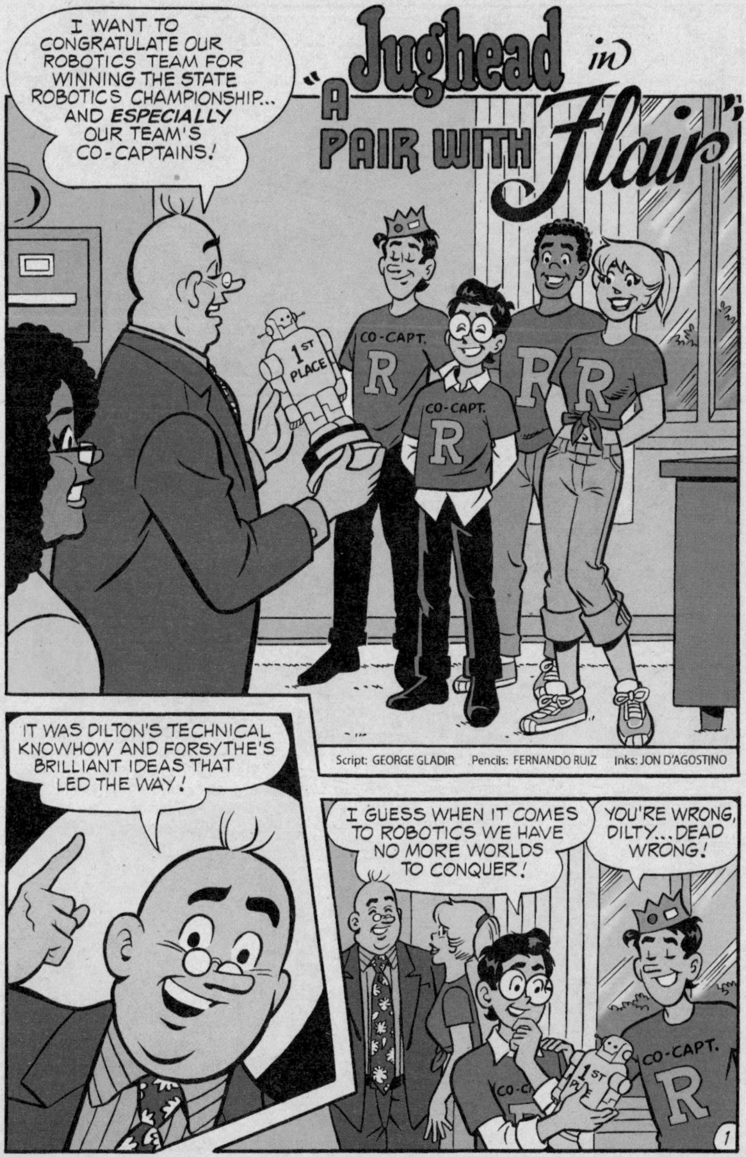

I WANT TO CONGRATULATE OUR ROBOTICS TEAM FOR WINNING THE STATE ROBOTICS CHAMPIONSHIP... AND ESPECIALLY OUR TEAM'S CO-CAPTAINS!
Jughead in "A PAIR WITH Flair"
1ST PLACE
CO-CAPT.
Script: GEORGE GLADIR Pencils: FERNANDO RUIZ Inks: JON D'AGOSTINO
IT WAS DILTON'S TECHNICAL KNOWHOW AND FORSYTHE'S BRILLIANT IDEAS THAT LED THE WAY!
I GUESS WHEN IT COMES TO ROBOTICS WE HAVE NO MORE WORLDS TO CONQUER!
YOU'RE WRONG, DILTY... DEAD WRONG!
1

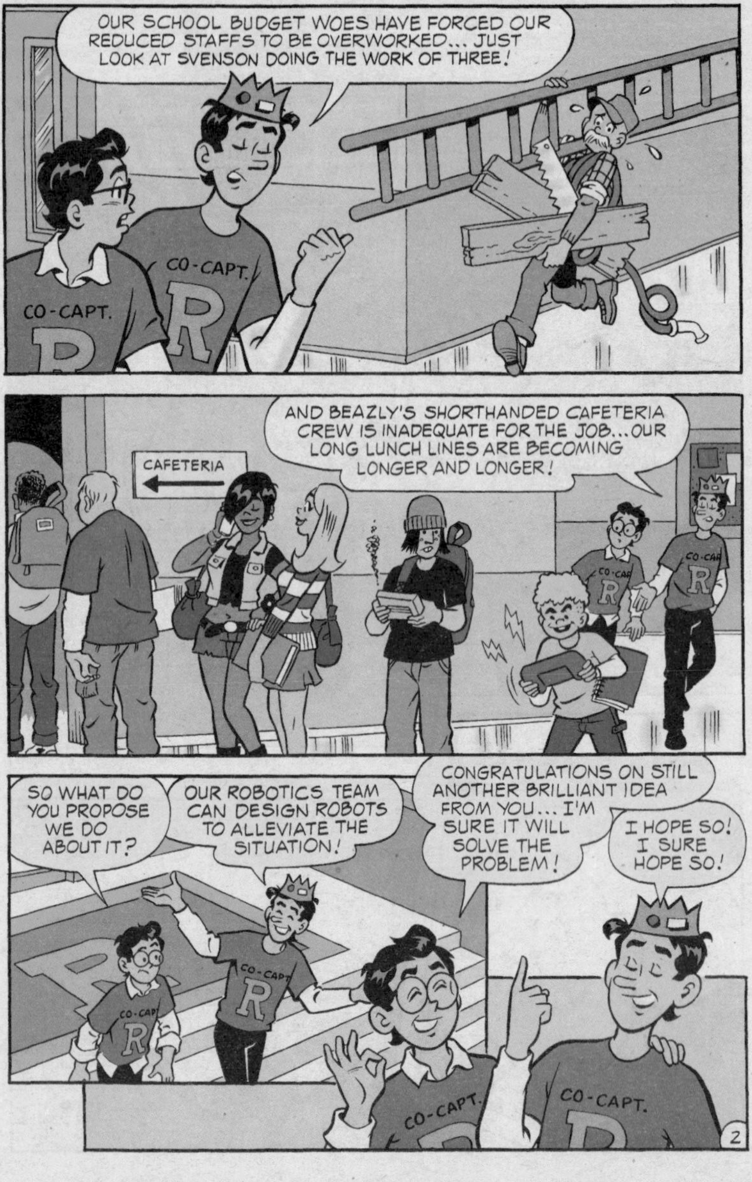

OUR SCHOOL BUDGET WOES HAVE FORCED OUR REDUCED STAFFS TO BE OVERWORKED... JUST LOOK AT SVENSON DOING THE WORK OF THREE!
CO-CAPT.
CO-CAPT.
AND BEAZLY'S SHORTHANDED CAFETERIA CREW IS INADEQUATE FOR THE JOB...OUR LONG LUNCH LINES ARE BECOMING LONGER AND LONGER!
CAFETERIA
SO WHAT DO YOU PROPOSE WE DO ABOUT IT?
OUR ROBOTICS TEAM CAN DESIGN ROBOTS TO ALLEVIATE THE SITUATION!
CONGRATULATIONS ON STILL ANOTHER BRILLIANT IDEA FROM YOU... I'M SURE IT WILL SOLVE THE PROBLEM!
I HOPE SO! I SURE HOPE SO!
CO-CAPT.
CO-CAPT.

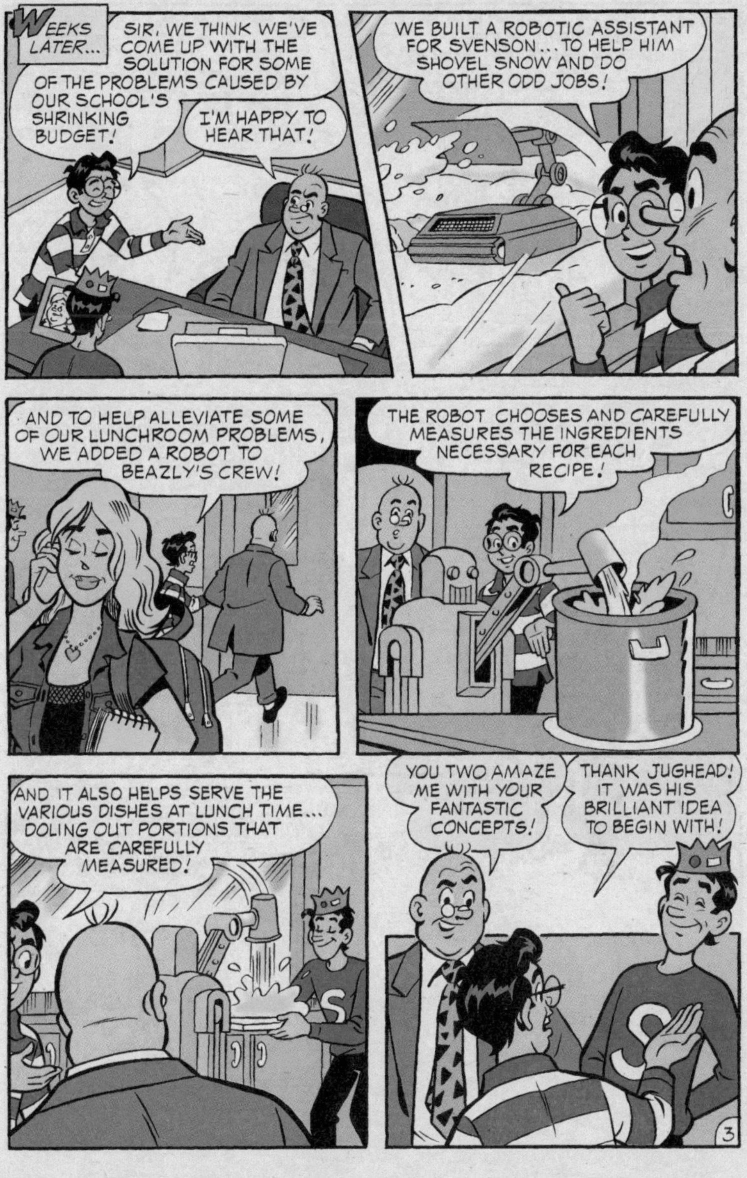
WEEKS LATER...
SIR, WE THINK WE'VE COME UP WITH THE SOLUTION FOR SOME OF THE PROBLEMS CAUSED BY OUR SCHOOL'S SHRINKING BUDGET!
I'M HAPPY TO HEAR THAT!
WE BUILT A ROBOTIC ASSISTANT FOR SVENSON... TO HELP HIM SHOVEL SNOW AND DO OTHER ODD JOBS!
AND TO HELP ALLEVIATE SOME OF OUR LUNCHROOM PROBLEMS, WE ADDED A ROBOT TO BEAZLY'S CREW!
THE ROBOT CHOOSES AND CAREFULLY MEASURES THE INGREDIENTS NECESSARY FOR EACH RECIPE!
AND IT ALSO HELPS SERVE THE VARIOUS DISHES AT LUNCH TIME... DOLING OUT PORTIONS THAT ARE CAREFULLY MEASURED!
YOU TWO AMAZE ME WITH YOUR FANTASTIC CONCEPTS!
THANK JUGHEAD! IT WAS HIS BRILLIANT IDEA TO BEGIN WITH!
3

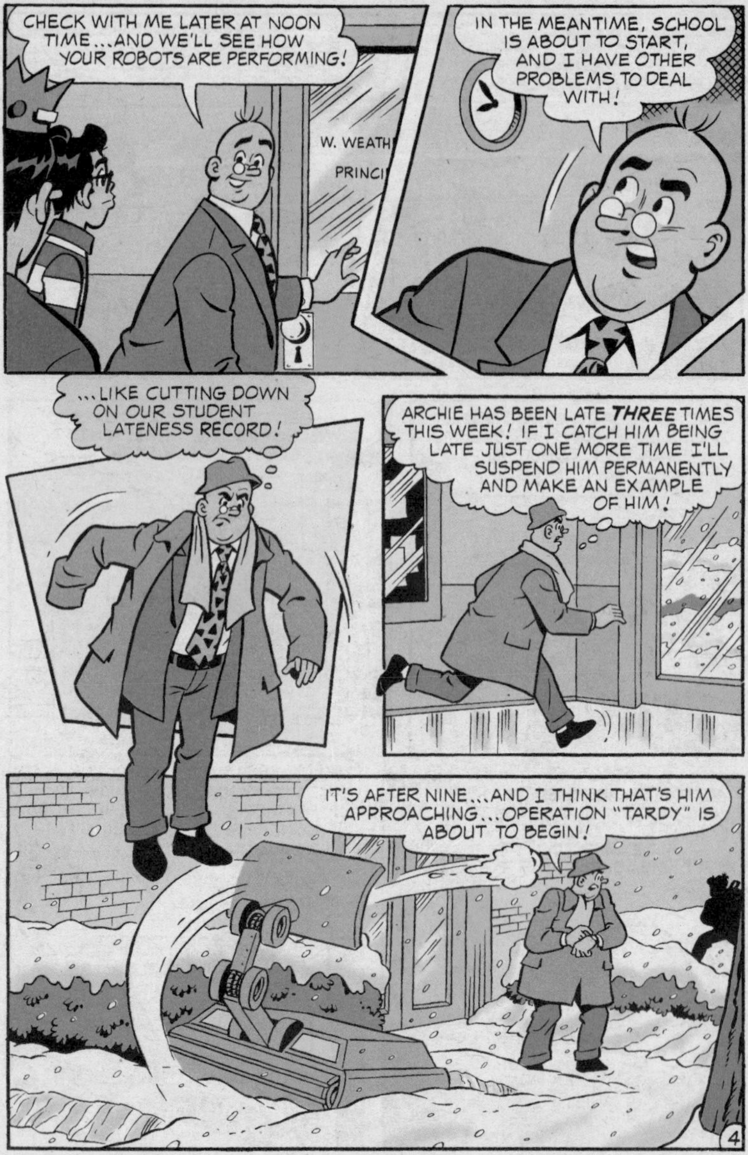
CHECK WITH ME LATER AT NOON TIME...AND WE'LL SEE HOW YOUR ROBOTS ARE PERFORMING!
W. WEATH
PRINCI
IN THE MEANTIME, SCHOOL IS ABOUT TO START, AND I HAVE OTHER PROBLEMS TO DEAL WITH!
...LIKE CUTTING DOWN ON OUR STUDENT LATENESS RECORD!
ARCHIE HAS BEEN LATE THREE TIMES THIS WEEK! IF I CATCH HIM BEING LATE JUST ONE MORE TIME I'LL SUSPEND HIM PERMANENTLY AND MAKE AN EXAMPLE OF HIM!
IT'S AFTER NINE...AND I THINK THAT'S HIM APPROACHING...OPERATION "TARDY" IS ABOUT TO BEGIN!
4

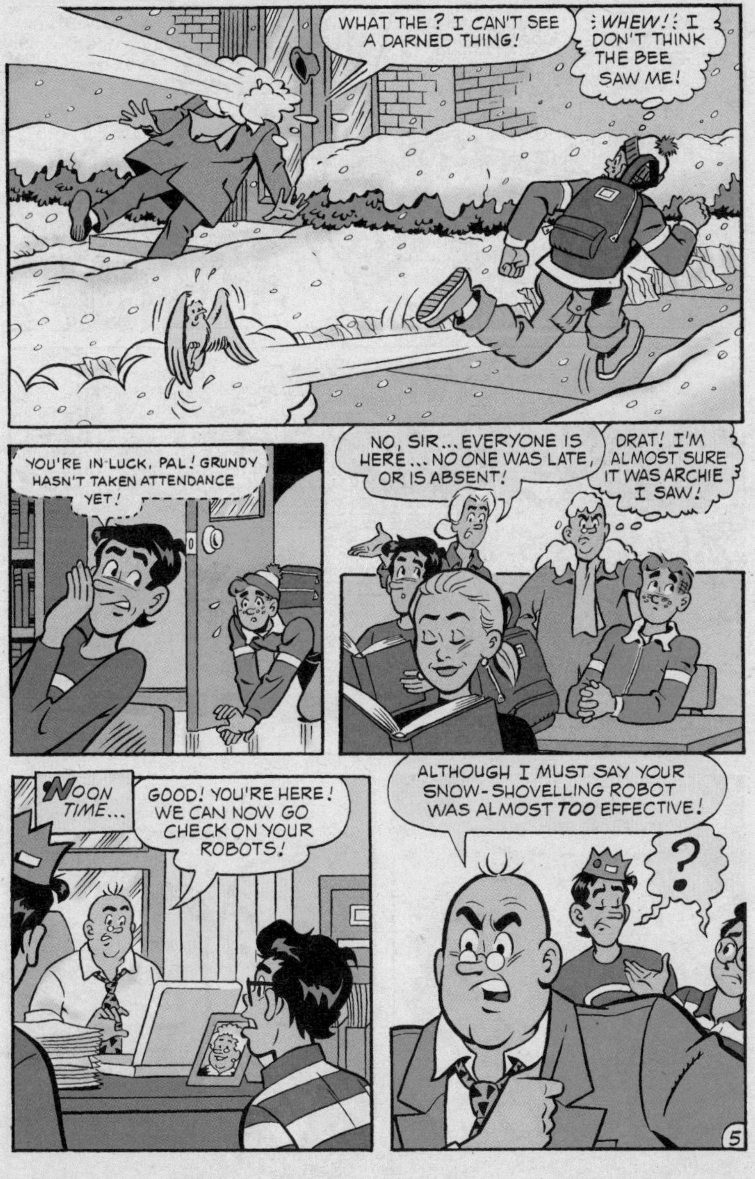
WHAT THE ? I CAN'T SEE A DARNED THING!
WHEW! I DON'T THINK THE BEE SAW ME!
YOU'RE IN LUCK, PAL! GRUNDY HASN'T TAKEN ATTENDANCE YET!
NO, SIR... EVERYONE IS HERE... NO ONE WAS LATE, OR IS ABSENT!
DRAT! I'M ALMOST SURE IT WAS ARCHIE I SAW!
NOON TIME...
GOOD! YOU'RE HERE! WE CAN NOW GO CHECK ON YOUR ROBOTS!
ALTHOUGH I MUST SAY YOUR SNOW-SHOVELLING ROBOT WAS ALMOST TOO EFFECTIVE!
?
5

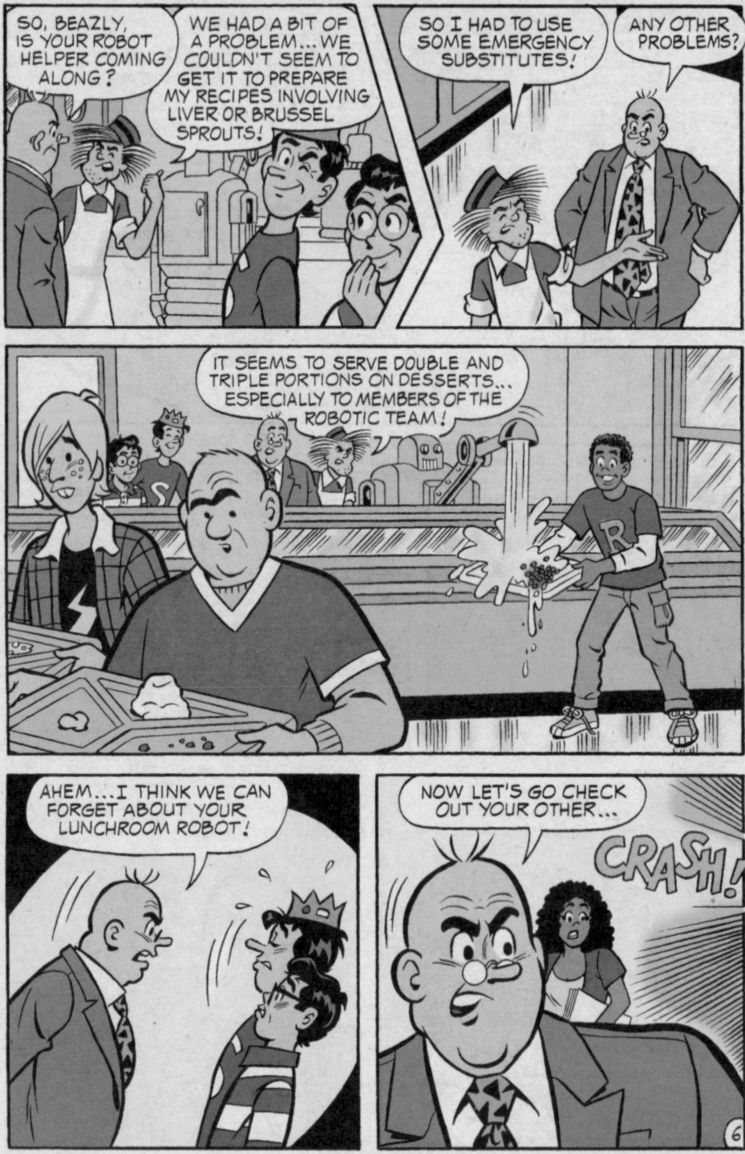
SO, BEAZLY, IS YOUR ROBOT HELPER COMING ALONG?
WE HAD A BIT OF A PROBLEM... WE COULDN'T SEEM TO GET IT TO PREPARE MY RECIPES INVOLVING LIVER OR BRUSSEL SPROUTS!
SO I HAD TO USE SOME EMERGENCY SUBSTITUTES!
ANY OTHER PROBLEMS?
IT SEEMS TO SERVE DOUBLE AND TRIPLE PORTIONS ON DESSERTS... ESPECIALLY TO MEMBERS OF THE ROBOTIC TEAM!
R
AHEM...I THINK WE CAN FORGET ABOUT YOUR LUNCHROOM ROBOT!
NOW LET'S GO CHECK OUT YOUR OTHER...
CRASH!
6

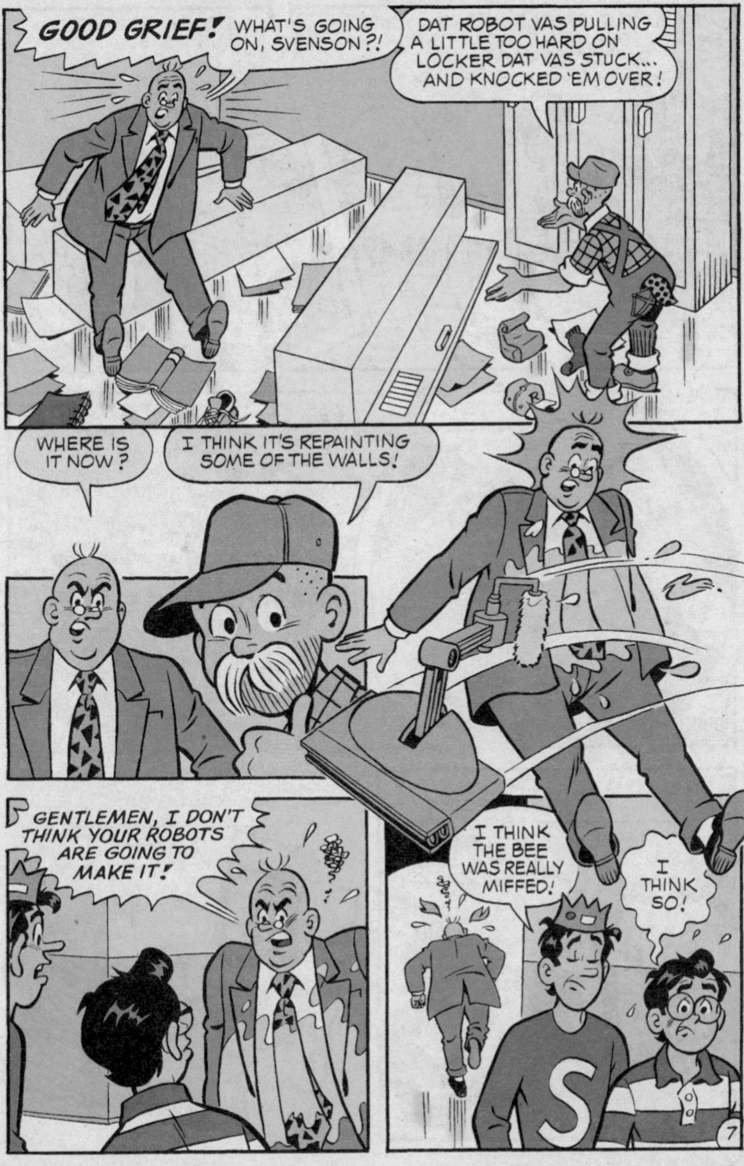
GOOD GRIEF! WHAT'S GOING ON, SVENSON?!
DAT ROBOT VAS PULLING A LITTLE TOO HARD ON LOCKER DAT VAS STUCK... AND KNOCKED 'EM OVER!
WHERE IS IT NOW?
I THINK IT'S REPAINTING SOME OF THE WALLS!
GENTLEMEN, I DON'T THINK YOUR ROBOTS ARE GOING TO MAKE IT!
I THINK THE BEE WAS REALLY MIFFED!
I THINK SO!
7

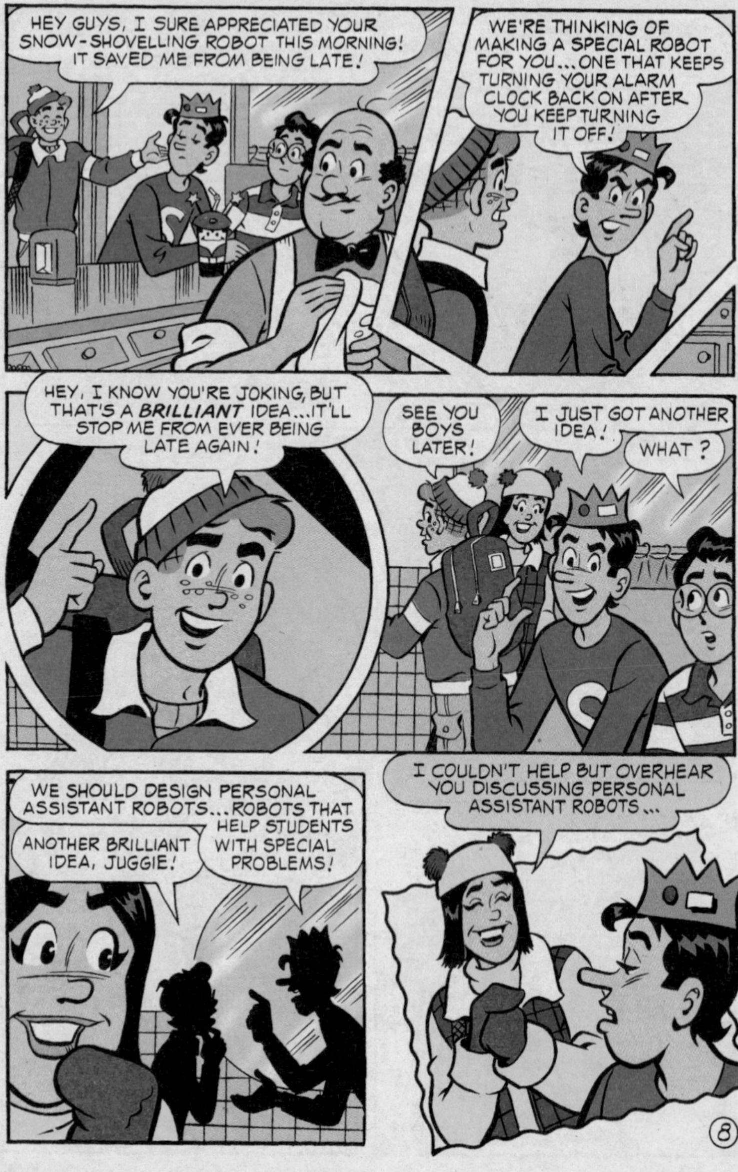
HEY GUYS, I SURE APPRECIATED YOUR SNOW-SHOVELLING ROBOT THIS MORNING! IT SAVED ME FROM BEING LATE!
WE'RE THINKING OF MAKING A SPECIAL ROBOT FOR YOU... ONE THAT KEEPS TURNING YOUR ALARM CLOCK BACK ON AFTER YOU KEEP TURNING IT OFF!
HEY, I KNOW YOU'RE JOKING, BUT THAT'S A BRILLIANT IDEA... IT'LL STOP ME FROM EVER BEING LATE AGAIN!
SEE YOU BOYS LATER!
I JUST GOT ANOTHER IDEA!
WHAT?
WE SHOULD DESIGN PERSONAL ASSISTANT ROBOTS... ROBOTS THAT HELP STUDENTS WITH SPECIAL PROBLEMS!
ANOTHER BRILLIANT IDEA, JUGGIE!
I COULDN'T HELP BUT OVERHEAR YOU DISCUSSING PERSONAL ASSISTANT ROBOTS...
8

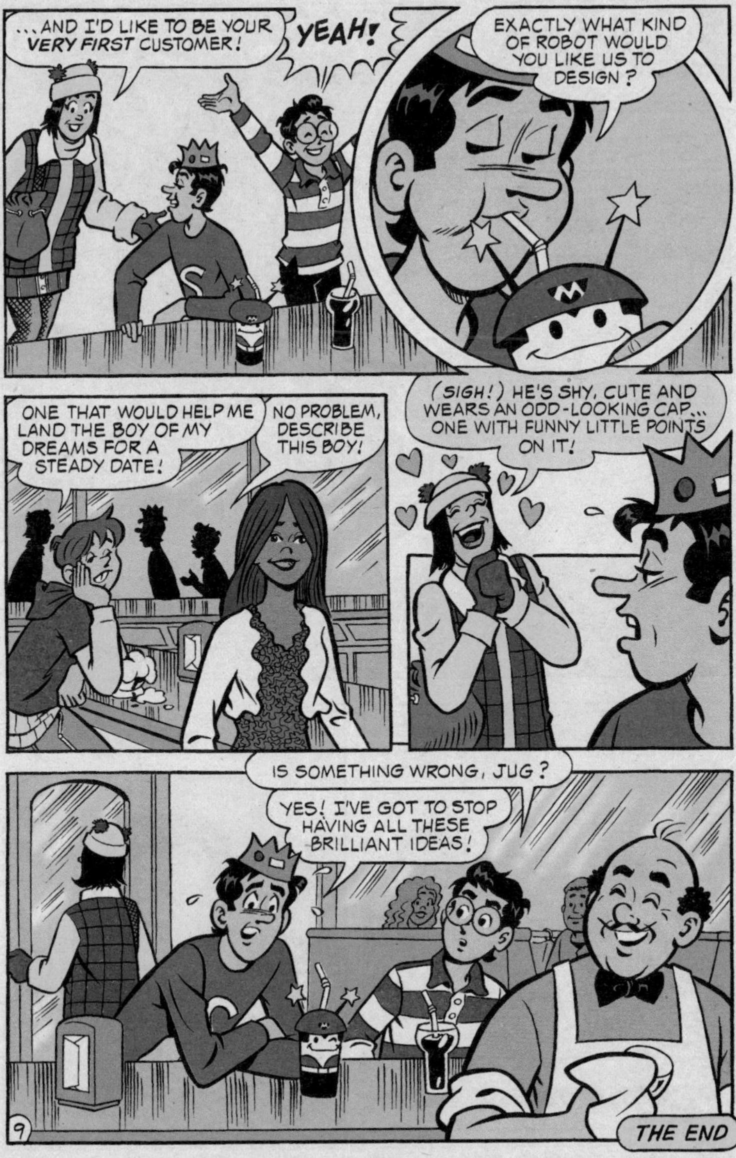
...AND I'D LIKE TO BE YOUR VERY FIRST CUSTOMER!
YEAH!
EXACTLY WHAT KIND OF ROBOT WOULD YOU LIKE US TO DESIGN?
ONE THAT WOULD HELP ME LAND THE BOY OF MY DREAMS FOR A STEADY DATE!
NO PROBLEM, DESCRIBE THIS BOY!
(SIGH!) HE'S SHY, CUTE AND WEARS AN ODD-LOOKING CAP... ONE WITH FUNNY LITTLE POINTS ON IT!
IS SOMETHING WRONG, JUG?
YES! I'VE GOT TO STOP HAVING ALL THESE BRILLIANT IDEAS!
9
THE END

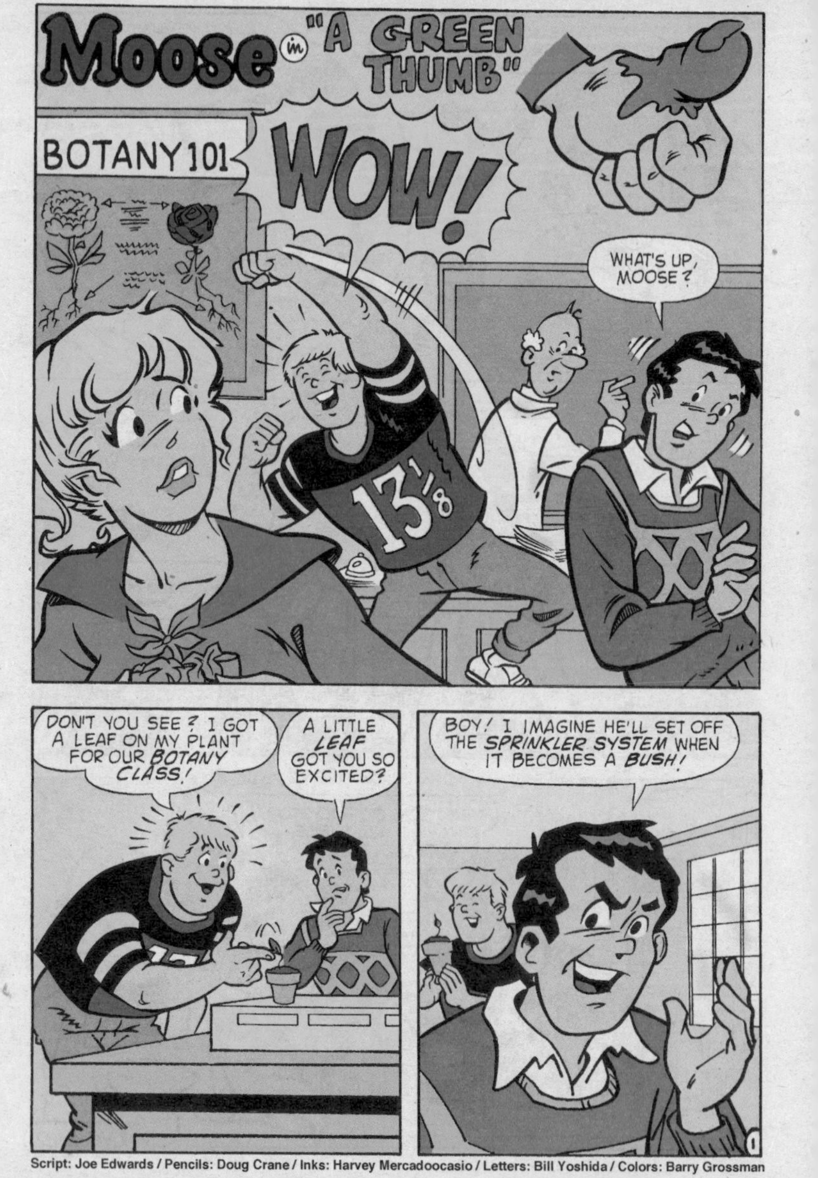
Moose in "A GREEN THUMB"
BOTANY 101
WOW!
WHAT'S UP, MOOSE?
13 1/8
DON'T YOU SEE? I GOT A LEAF ON MY PLANT FOR OUR BOTANY CLASS!
A LITTLE LEAF GOT YOU SO EXCITED?
BOY! I IMAGINE HE'LL SET OFF THE SPRINKLER SYSTEM WHEN IT BECOMES A BUSH!
1

Script: Joe Edwards / Pencils: Doug Crane / Inks: Harvey Mercadoocasio / Letters: Bill Yoshida / Colors: Barry Grossman

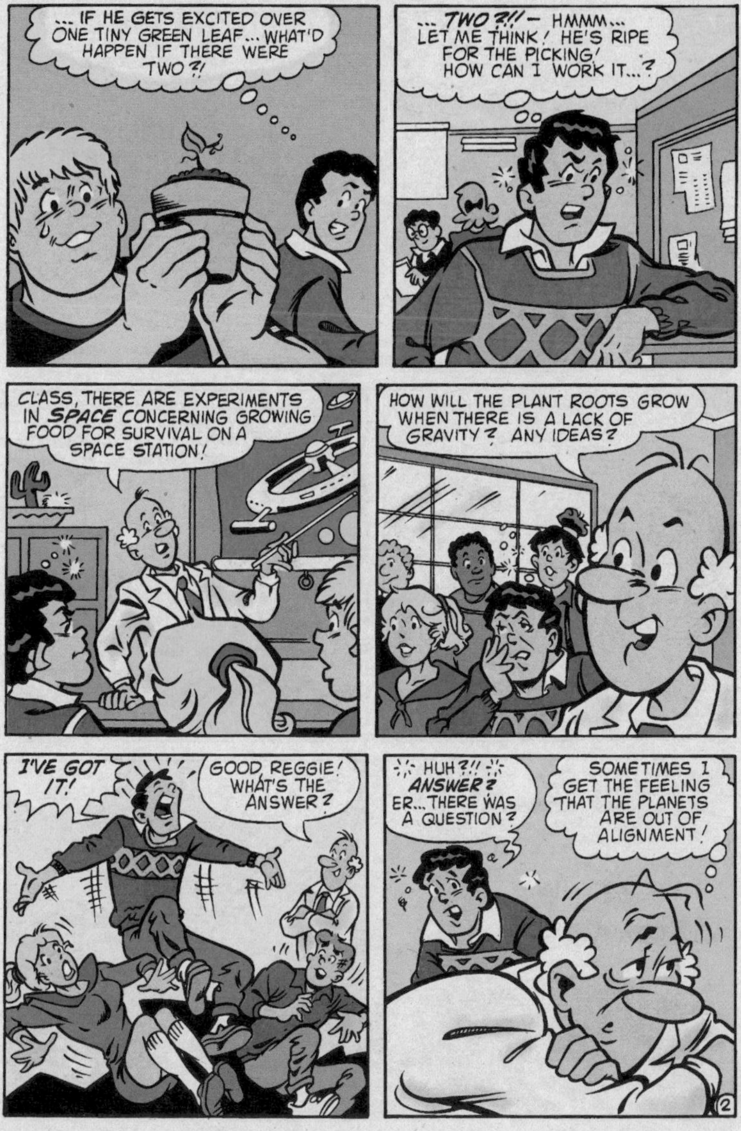
... IF HE GETS EXCITED OVER ONE TINY GREEN LEAF... WHAT'D HAPPEN IF THERE WERE TWO ?!
... TWO ?!! – HMMM... LET ME THINK! HE'S RIPE FOR THE PICKING! HOW CAN I WORK IT...?
CLASS, THERE ARE EXPERIMENTS IN SPACE CONCERNING GROWING FOOD FOR SURVIVAL ON A SPACE STATION!
HOW WILL THE PLANT ROOTS GROW WHEN THERE IS A LACK OF GRAVITY? ANY IDEAS?
I'VE GOT IT!
GOOD, REGGIE! WHAT'S THE ANSWER?
HUH ?!! ANSWER? ER... THERE WAS A QUESTION?
SOMETIMES I GET THE FEELING THAT THE PLANETS ARE OUT OF ALIGNMENT!
2

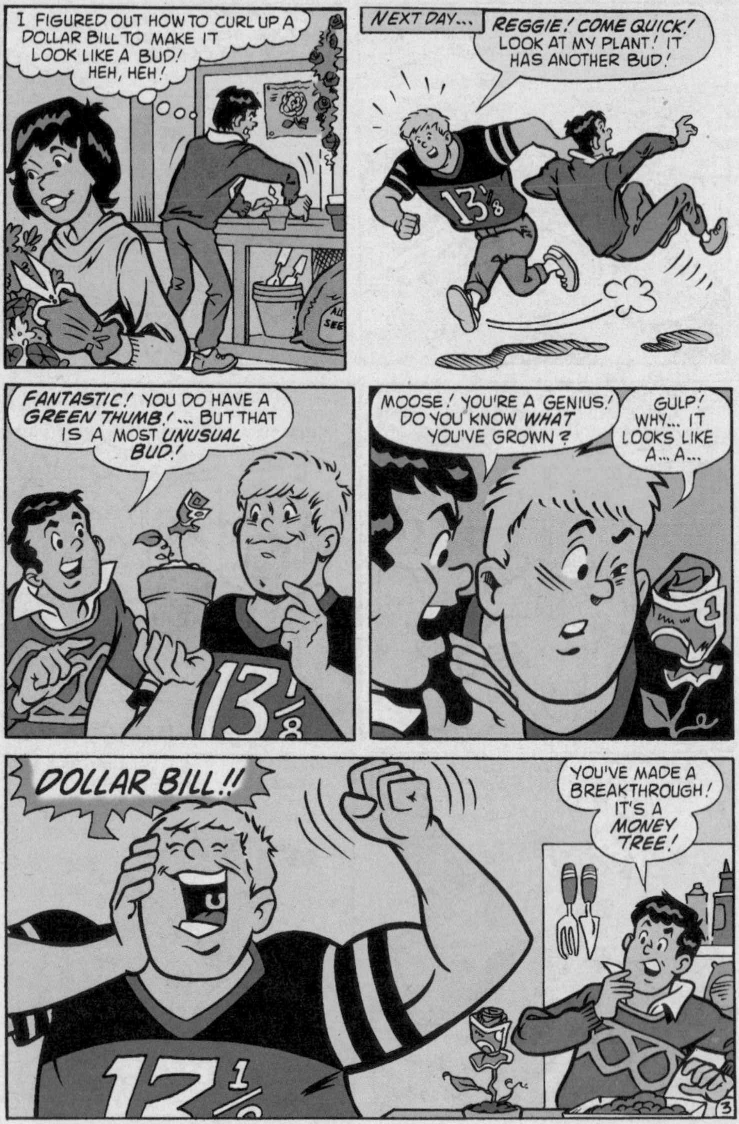
I FIGURED OUT HOW TO CURL UP A DOLLAR BILL TO MAKE IT LOOK LIKE A BUD! HEH, HEH!
NEXT DAY...
REGGIE! COME QUICK! LOOK AT MY PLANT! IT HAS ANOTHER BUD!
FANTASTIC! YOU DO HAVE A GREEN THUMB! ... BUT THAT IS A MOST UNUSUAL BUD!
MOOSE! YOU'RE A GENIUS! DO YOU KNOW WHAT YOU'VE GROWN?
GULP! WHY... IT LOOKS LIKE A... A...
DOLLAR BILL!!
YOU'VE MADE A BREAKTHROUGH! IT'S A MONEY TREE!

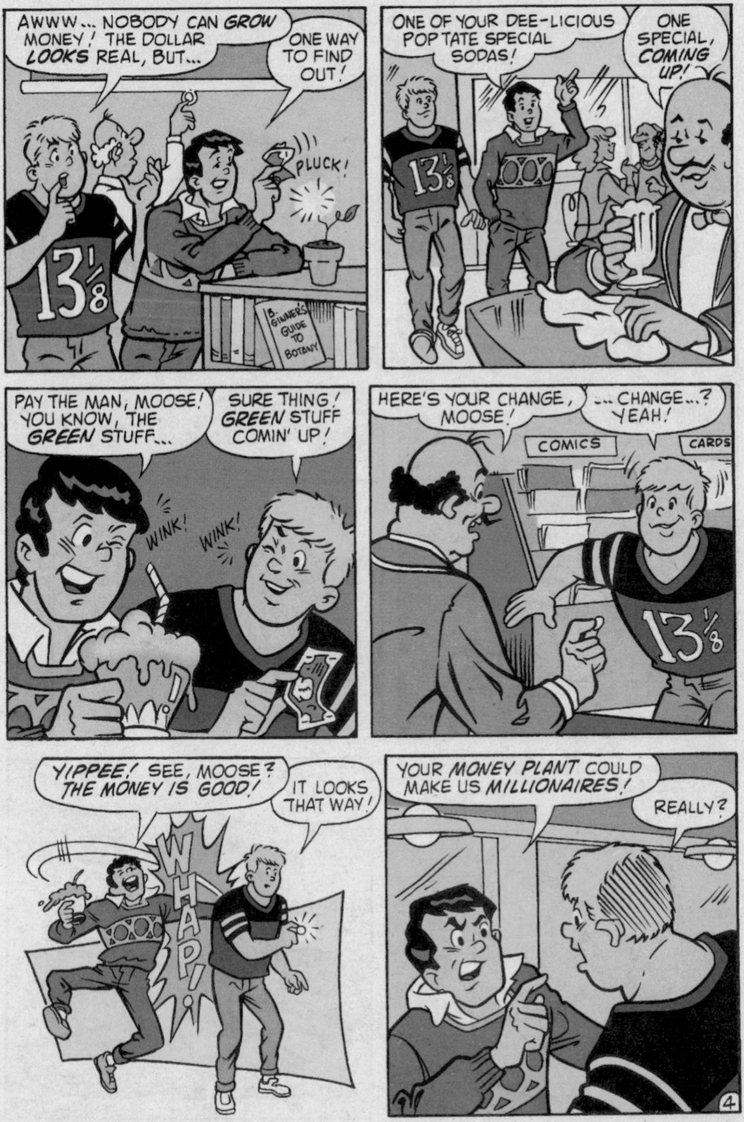
AWWW... NOBODY CAN GROW MONEY! THE DOLLAR LOOKS REAL, BUT...
ONE WAY TO FIND OUT!
PLUCK!
B. GINNER'S GUIDE TO BOTANY
ONE OF YOUR DEE-LICIOUS POP TATE SPECIAL SODAS!
ONE SPECIAL, COMING UP!
PAY THE MAN, MOOSE! YOU KNOW, THE GREEN STUFF...
SURE THING! GREEN STUFF COMIN' UP!
WINK!
WINK!
HERE'S YOUR CHANGE, MOOSE!
...CHANGE...? YEAH!
COMICS
CARDS
YIPPEE! SEE, MOOSE? THE MONEY IS GOOD!
IT LOOKS THAT WAY!
WHAP!
YOUR MONEY PLANT COULD MAKE US MILLIONAIRES!
REALLY?
4

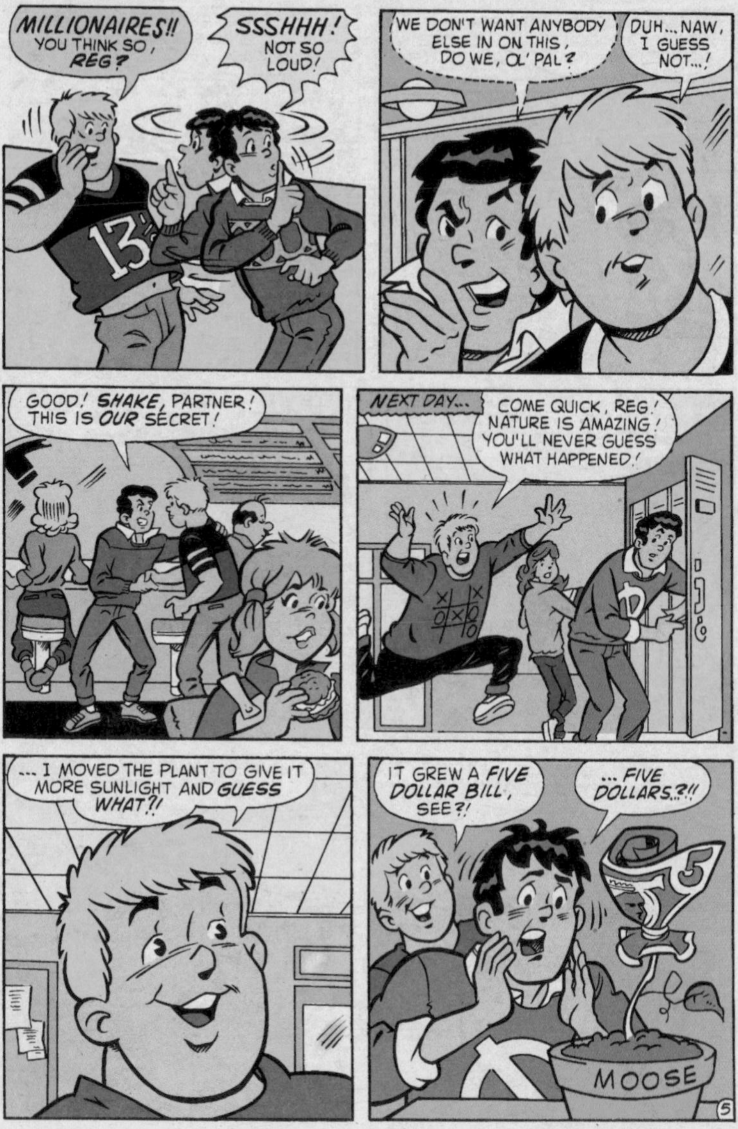
MILLIONAIRES!! YOU THINK SO, REG?
SSSHHH! NOT SO LOUD!
WE DON'T WANT ANYBODY ELSE IN ON THIS, DO WE, OL' PAL?
DUH... NAW, I GUESS NOT...!
GOOD! SHAKE, PARTNER! THIS IS OUR SECRET!
NEXT DAY...
COME QUICK, REG! NATURE IS AMAZING! YOU'LL NEVER GUESS WHAT HAPPENED!
... I MOVED THE PLANT TO GIVE IT MORE SUNLIGHT AND GUESS WHAT?!!
IT GREW A FIVE DOLLAR BILL, SEE?!
... FIVE DOLLARS..?!!
MOOSE
5

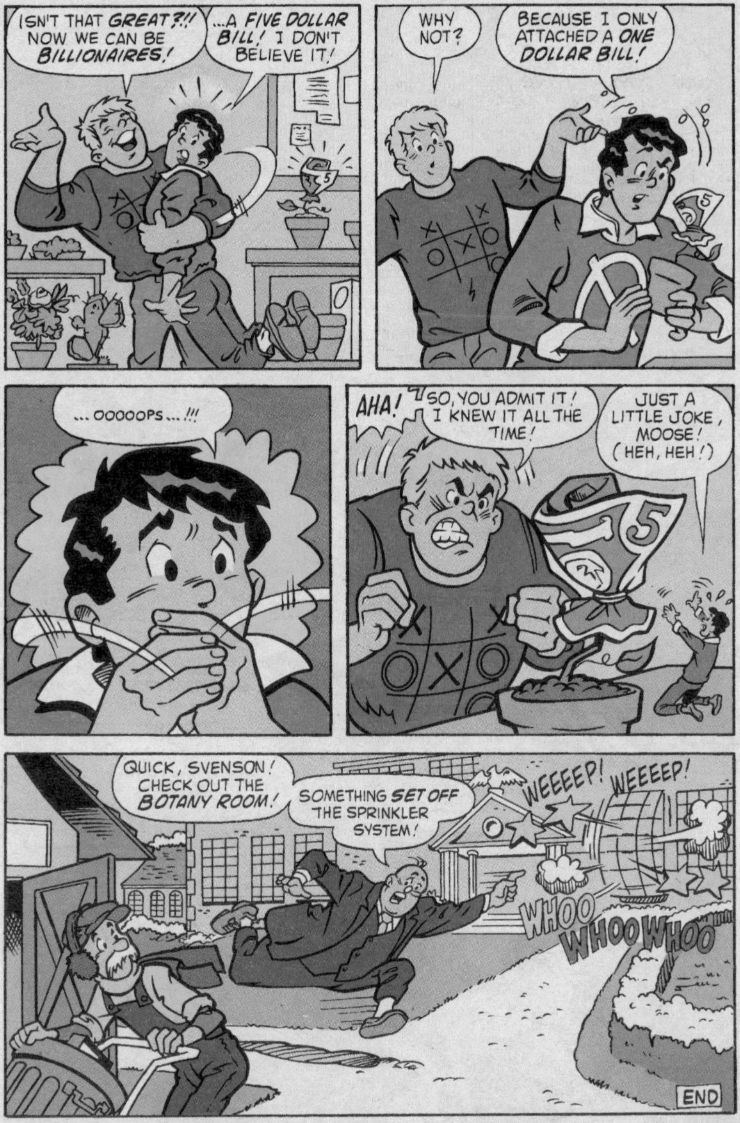
ISN'T THAT GREAT?!! NOW WE CAN BE BILLIONAIRES!
...A FIVE DOLLAR BILL! I DON'T BELIEVE IT!
WHY NOT?
BECAUSE I ONLY ATTACHED A ONE DOLLAR BILL!
... OOOOOPS ... !!!
AHA!
SO, YOU ADMIT IT! I KNEW IT ALL THE TIME!
JUST A LITTLE JOKE, MOOSE! (HEH, HEH!)
QUICK, SVENSON! CHECK OUT THE BOTANY ROOM!
SOMETHING SET OFF THE SPRINKLER SYSTEM!
WEEEEP! WEEEEP!
WHOO WHOO WHOO
END

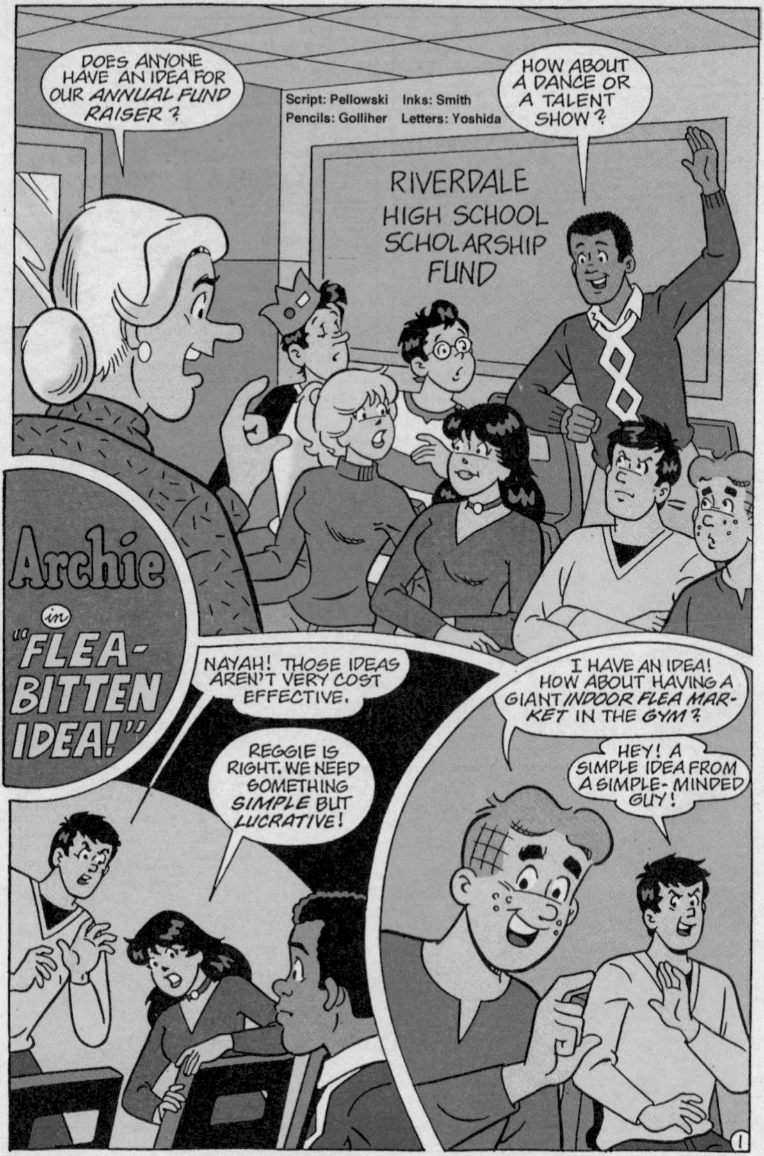
DOES ANYONE HAVE AN IDEA FOR OUR ANNUAL FUND RAISER?
Script: Pellowski Inks: Smith
Pencils: Golliher Letters: Yoshida
HOW ABOUT A DANCE OR A TALENT SHOW?
RIVERDALE HIGH SCHOOL SCHOLARSHIP FUND
Archie in "FLEA-BITTEN IDEA!"
NAYAH! THOSE IDEAS AREN'T VERY COST EFFECTIVE.
REGGIE IS RIGHT. WE NEED SOMETHING SIMPLE BUT LUCRATIVE!
I HAVE AN IDEA! HOW ABOUT HAVING A GIANT INDOOR FLEA MARKET IN THE GYM?
HEY! A SIMPLE IDEA FROM A SIMPLE-MINDED GUY!
1

WE COULD MAKE MONEY RENTING SPACE TO VENDORS *AND* RUN BOOTHS STOCKED WITH *SPECIAL* DONATIONS. WE'LL *DOUBLE* OUR PROFITS!

ACTUALLY, THAT IS A *VERY GOOD* IDEA!

MS. GRUNDY CAN HANDLE THE RENTALS. THE REST OF US CAN PAIR UP AND OPERATE BOOTHS!

I STILL THINK THIS IS A HALF-BAKED *SCHEME*!

THAT GIVES ME ANOTHER *IDEA*! RON AND I WILL RUN A *BAKE-SALE* BOOTH!

WHAT ARE YOU TWO GOING TO SELL?

AH... I'M NOT SURE! BUT I'M *TOYING* WITH A FEW *INTERESTING* CONCEPTS.

HEY, THAT'S *IT*! TOYS!

RIVERDALE HIGH SCHOOL SCHOLARSHIP FUND

LET'S RUN A *USED-TOY* BOOTH! WE BOTH HAVE THINGS WE CAN DONATE!

SOUNDS GOOD TO ME!

PEOPLE ALWAYS BRING THEIR KIDS TO FLEA MARKETS. I BET WE MAKE A *BUNDLE*, JUG!

THEN, IT'S SETTLED, A *FLEA MARKET* IT IS!

②

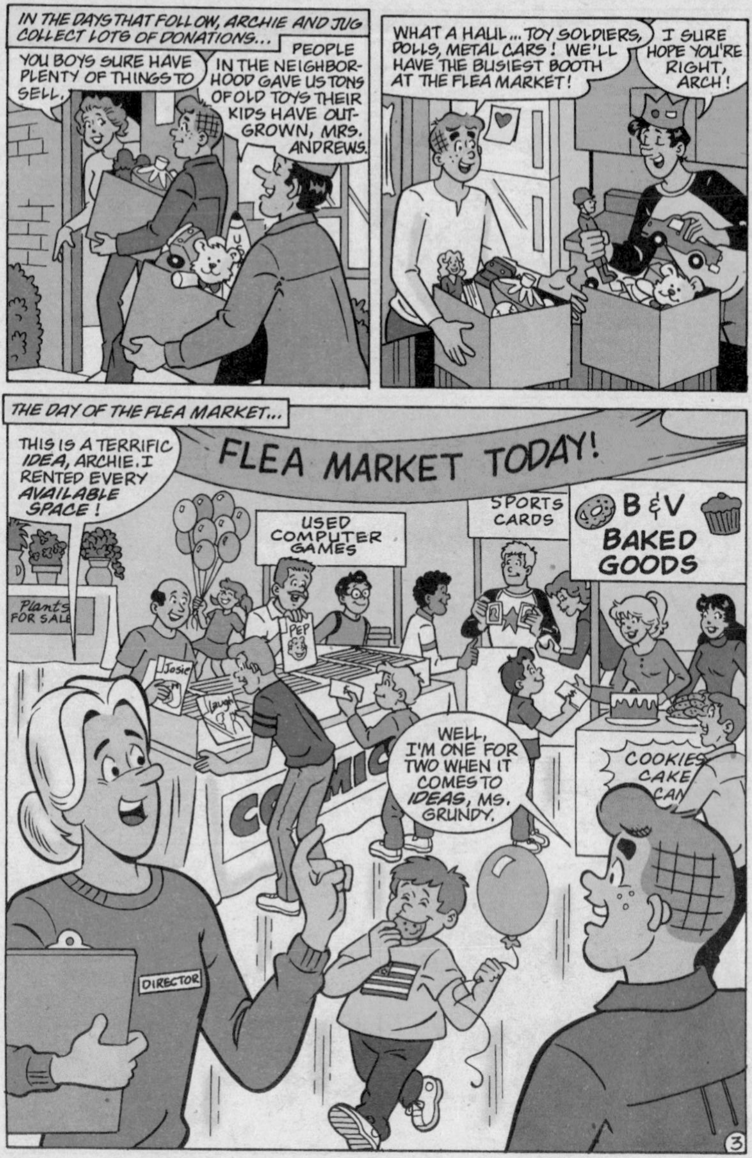
IN THE DAYS THAT FOLLOW, ARCHIE AND JUG COLLECT LOTS OF DONATIONS...
YOU BOYS SURE HAVE PLENTY OF THINGS TO SELL.
PEOPLE IN THE NEIGHBORHOOD GAVE US TONS OF OLD TOYS THEIR KIDS HAVE OUTGROWN, MRS. ANDREWS.
WHAT A HAUL... TOY SOLDIERS, DOLLS, METAL CARS! WE'LL HAVE THE BUSIEST BOOTH AT THE FLEA MARKET!
I SURE HOPE YOU'RE RIGHT, ARCH!
THE DAY OF THE FLEA MARKET...
THIS IS A TERRIFIC IDEA, ARCHIE. I RENTED EVERY AVAILABLE SPACE!
FLEA MARKET TODAY!
USED COMPUTER GAMES
SPORTS CARDS
B & V BAKED GOODS
Plants FOR SALE
PEP
Josie
Laugh
WELL, I'M ONE FOR TWO WHEN IT COMES TO IDEAS, MS. GRUNDY.
COOKIES CAKE
DIRECTOR

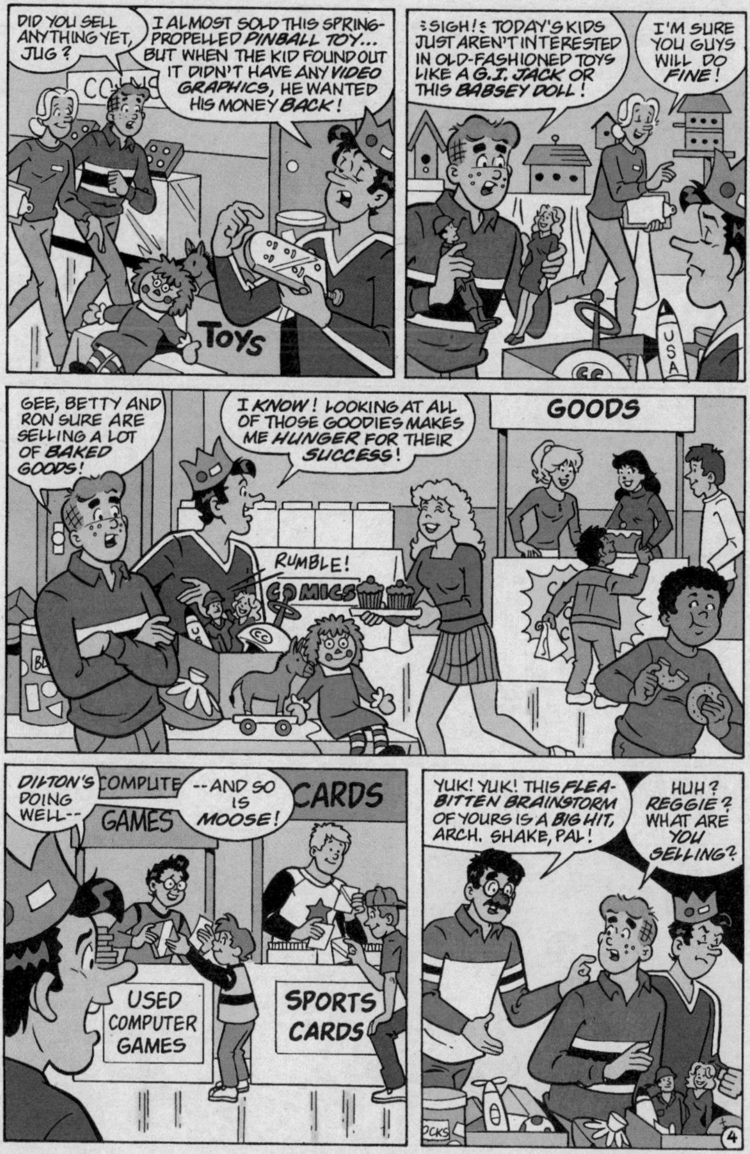
DID YOU SELL ANYTHING YET, JUG?
I ALMOST SOLD THIS SPRING-PROPELLED PINBALL TOY... BUT WHEN THE KID FOUND OUT IT DIDN'T HAVE ANY VIDEO GRAPHICS, HE WANTED HIS MONEY BACK!
TOYS
=SIGH!= TODAY'S KIDS JUST AREN'T INTERESTED IN OLD-FASHIONED TOYS LIKE A G.I. JACK OR THIS BABSEY DOLL!
I'M SURE YOU GUYS WILL DO FINE!
USA
GEE, BETTY AND RON SURE ARE SELLING A LOT OF BAKED GOODS!
I KNOW! LOOKING AT ALL OF THOSE GOODIES MAKES ME HUNGER FOR THEIR SUCCESS!
GOODS
RUMBLE!
COMICS
DILTON'S DOING WELL--
--AND SO IS MOOSE!
COMPUTE
GAMES
CARDS
USED COMPUTER GAMES
SPORTS CARDS
YUK! YUK! THIS FLEA-BITTEN BRAINSTORM OF YOURS IS A BIG HIT, ARCH. SHAKE, PAL!
HUH? REGGIE? WHAT ARE YOU SELLING?
4

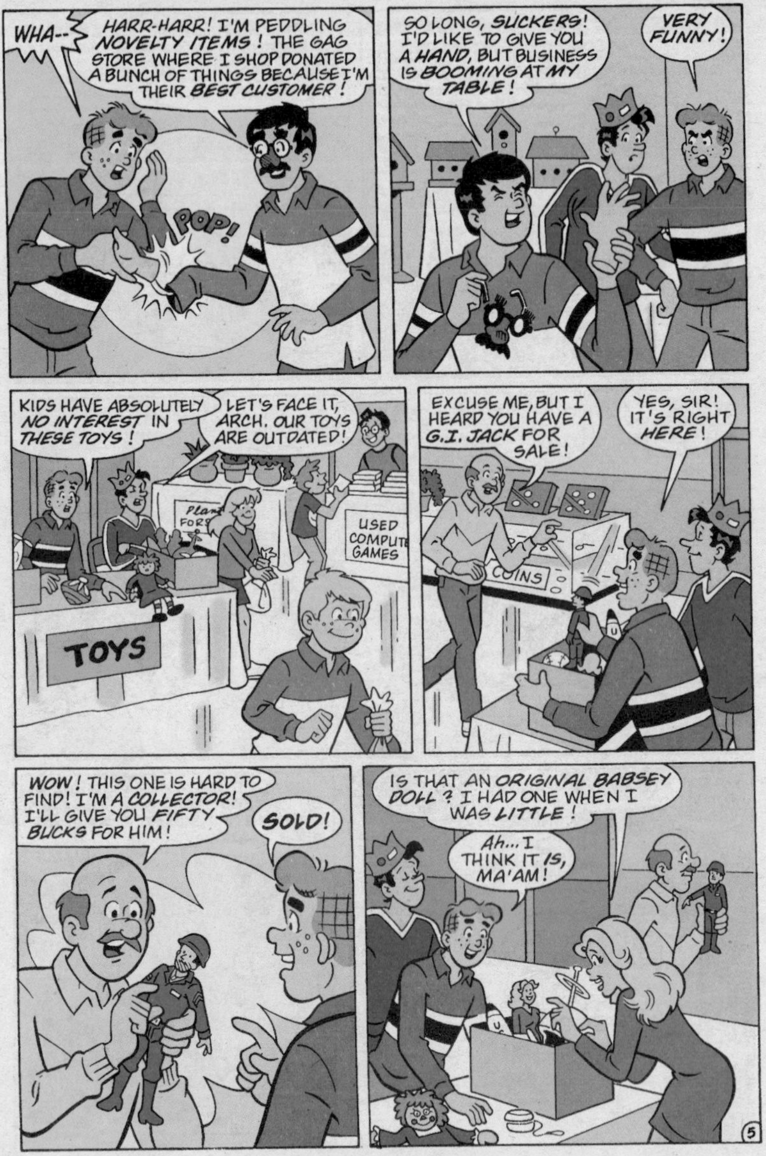
WHA--
HARR-HARR! I'M PEDDLING NOVELTY ITEMS! THE GAG STORE WHERE I SHOP DONATED A BUNCH OF THINGS BECAUSE I'M THEIR BEST CUSTOMER!
POP!
SO LONG, SUCKERS! I'D LIKE TO GIVE YOU A HAND, BUT BUSINESS IS BOOMING AT MY TABLE!
VERY FUNNY!
KIDS HAVE ABSOLUTELY NO INTEREST IN THESE TOYS!
LET'S FACE IT, ARCH. OUR TOYS ARE OUTDATED!
USED COMPUTE GAMES
TOYS
EXCUSE ME, BUT I HEARD YOU HAVE A G.I. JACK FOR SALE!
YES, SIR! IT'S RIGHT HERE!
COINS
WOW! THIS ONE IS HARD TO FIND! I'M A COLLECTOR! I'LL GIVE YOU FIFTY BUCKS FOR HIM!
SOLD!
IS THAT AN ORIGINAL BABSEY DOLL? I HAD ONE WHEN I WAS LITTLE!
Ah... I THINK IT IS, MA'AM!

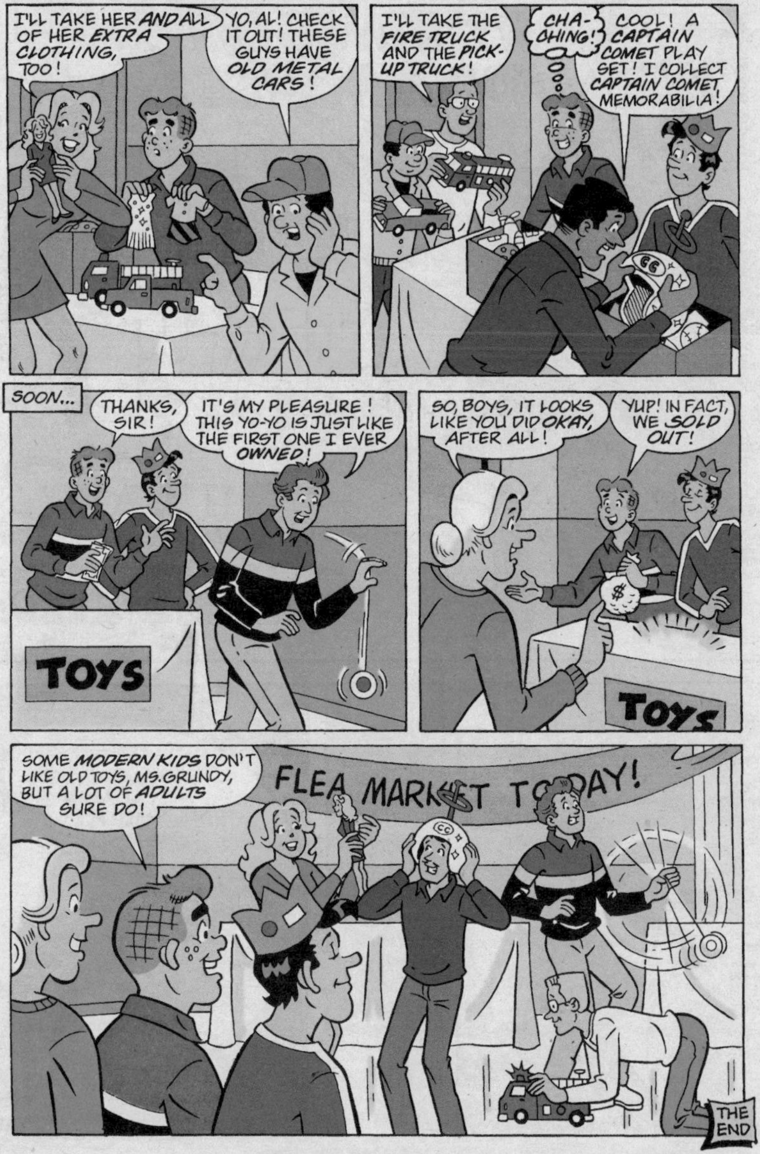

I'LL TAKE HER AND ALL OF HER EXTRA CLOTHING, TOO!
YO, AL! CHECK IT OUT! THESE GUYS HAVE OLD METAL CARS!
I'LL TAKE THE FIRE TRUCK AND THE PICK-UP TRUCK!
CHA-CHING!
COOL! A CAPTAIN COMET PLAY SET! I COLLECT CAPTAIN COMET MEMORABILIA!
SOON...
THANKS, SIR!
IT'S MY PLEASURE! THIS YO-YO IS JUST LIKE THE FIRST ONE I EVER OWNED!
TOYS
SO, BOYS, IT LOOKS LIKE YOU DID OKAY, AFTER ALL!
YUP! IN FACT, WE SOLD OUT!
TOYS
SOME MODERN KIDS DON'T LIKE OLD TOYS, MS.GRUNDY, BUT A LOT OF ADULTS SURE DO!
FLEA MARKET TODAY!
THE END

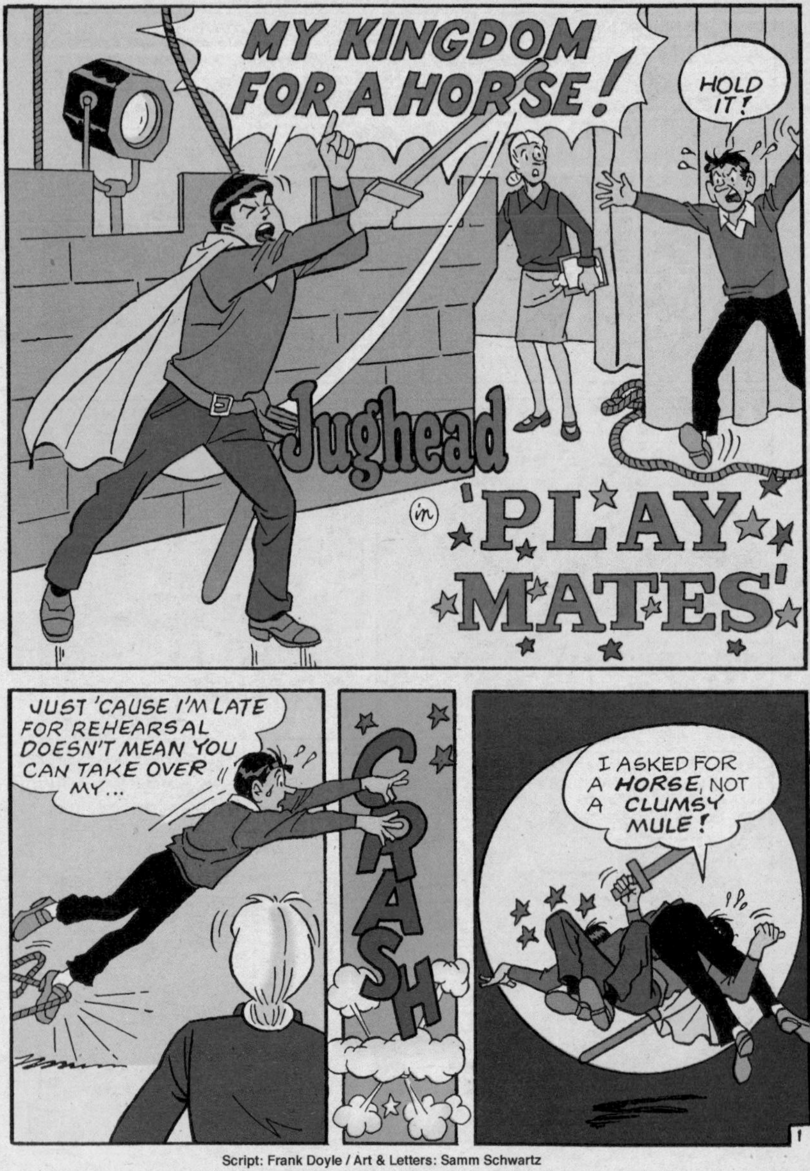
MY KINGDOM FOR A HORSE!
HOLD IT!
Jughead
in 'PLAY MATES'
JUST 'CAUSE I'M LATE FOR REHEARSAL DOESN'T MEAN YOU CAN TAKE OVER MY...
CRASH
I ASKED FOR A HORSE, NOT A CLUMSY MULE!
1

Script: Frank Doyle / Art & Letters: Samm Schwartz

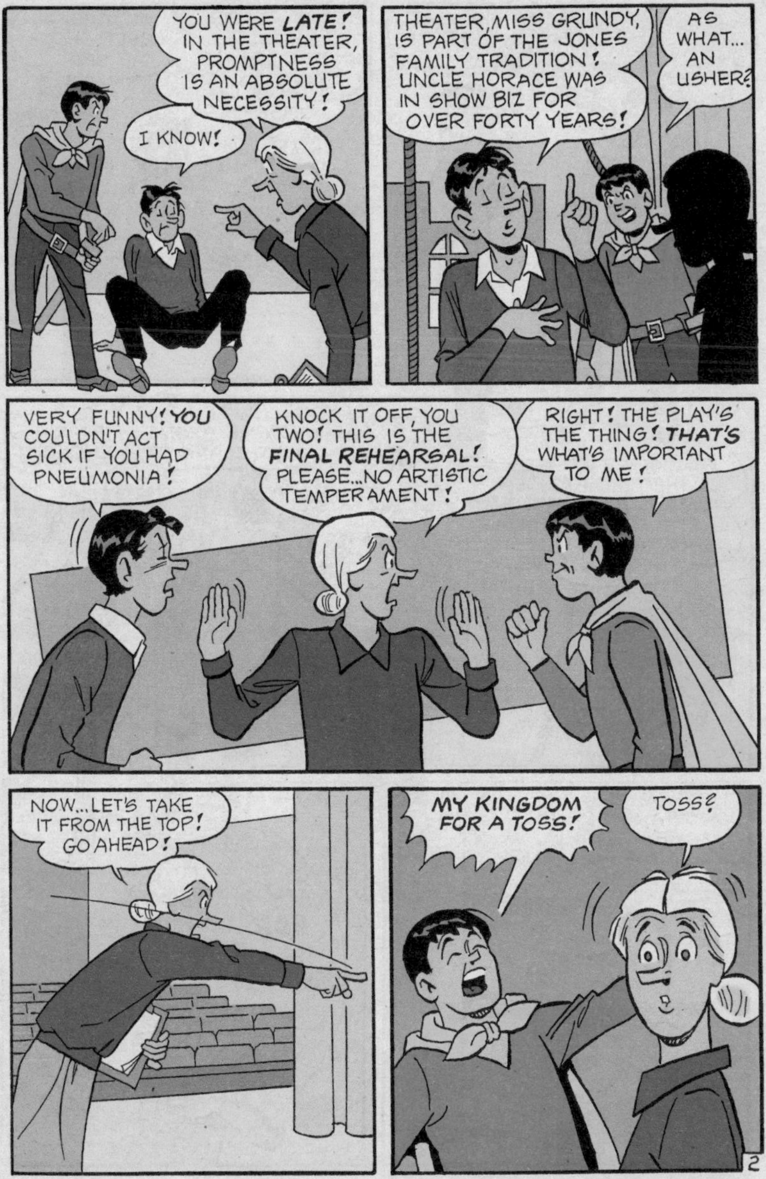
YOU WERE LATE! IN THE THEATER, PROMPTNESS IS AN ABSOLUTE NECESSITY!
I KNOW!
THEATER, MISS GRUNDY, IS PART OF THE JONES FAMILY TRADITION! UNCLE HORACE WAS IN SHOW BIZ FOR OVER FORTY YEARS!
AS WHAT... AN USHER?
VERY FUNNY! YOU COULDN'T ACT SICK IF YOU HAD PNEUMONIA!
KNOCK IT OFF, YOU TWO! THIS IS THE FINAL REHEARSAL! PLEASE...NO ARTISTIC TEMPERAMENT!
RIGHT! THE PLAY'S THE THING! THAT'S WHAT'S IMPORTANT TO ME!
NOW...LET'S TAKE IT FROM THE TOP! GO AHEAD!
MY KINGDOM FOR A TOSS!
TOSS?
2

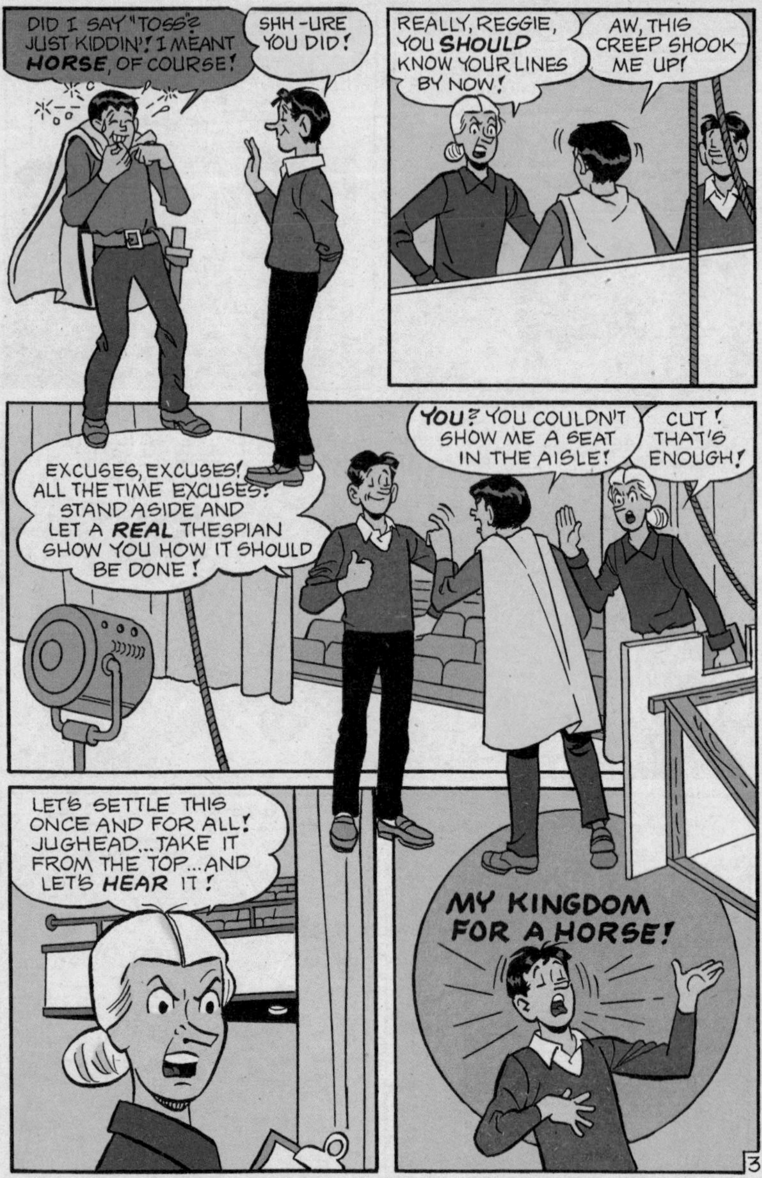
DID I SAY "TOSS"? JUST KIDDIN'! I MEANT **HORSE**, OF COURSE!
SHH-URE YOU DID!
REALLY, REGGIE, YOU **SHOULD** KNOW YOUR LINES BY NOW!
AW, THIS CREEP SHOOK ME UP!
EXCUSES, EXCUSES! ALL THE TIME EXCUSES! STAND ASIDE AND LET A **REAL** THESPIAN SHOW YOU HOW IT SHOULD BE DONE!
YOU? YOU COULDN'T SHOW ME A SEAT IN THE AISLE!
CUT! THAT'S ENOUGH!
LET'S SETTLE THIS ONCE AND FOR ALL! JUGHEAD...TAKE IT FROM THE TOP...AND LET'S **HEAR** IT!
MY KINGDOM FOR A HORSE!
3

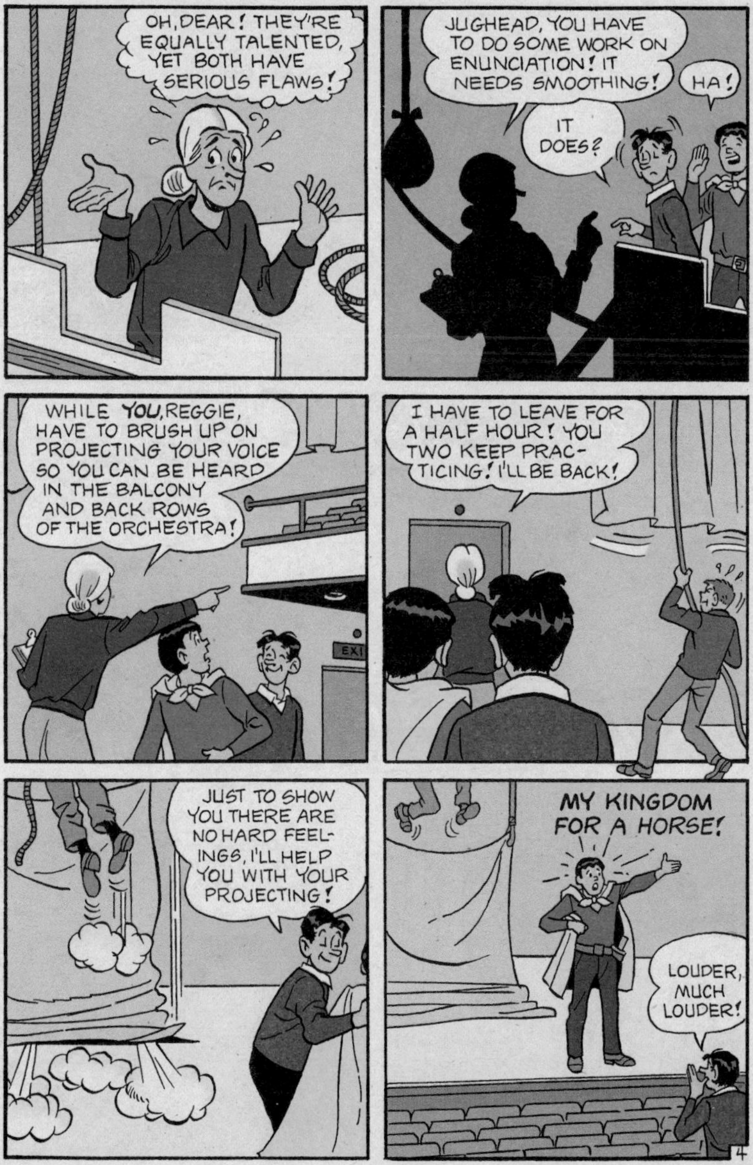
OH, DEAR! THEY'RE EQUALLY TALENTED, YET BOTH HAVE SERIOUS FLAWS!
JUGHEAD, YOU HAVE TO DO SOME WORK ON ENUNCIATION! IT NEEDS SMOOTHING!
HA!
IT DOES?
WHILE YOU, REGGIE, HAVE TO BRUSH UP ON PROJECTING YOUR VOICE SO YOU CAN BE HEARD IN THE BALCONY AND BACK ROWS OF THE ORCHESTRA!
EXI
I HAVE TO LEAVE FOR A HALF HOUR! YOU TWO KEEP PRAC-TICING! I'LL BE BACK!
JUST TO SHOW YOU THERE ARE NO HARD FEEL-INGS, I'LL HELP YOU WITH YOUR PROJECTING!
MY KINGDOM FOR A HORSE!
LOUDER, MUCH LOUDER!
4

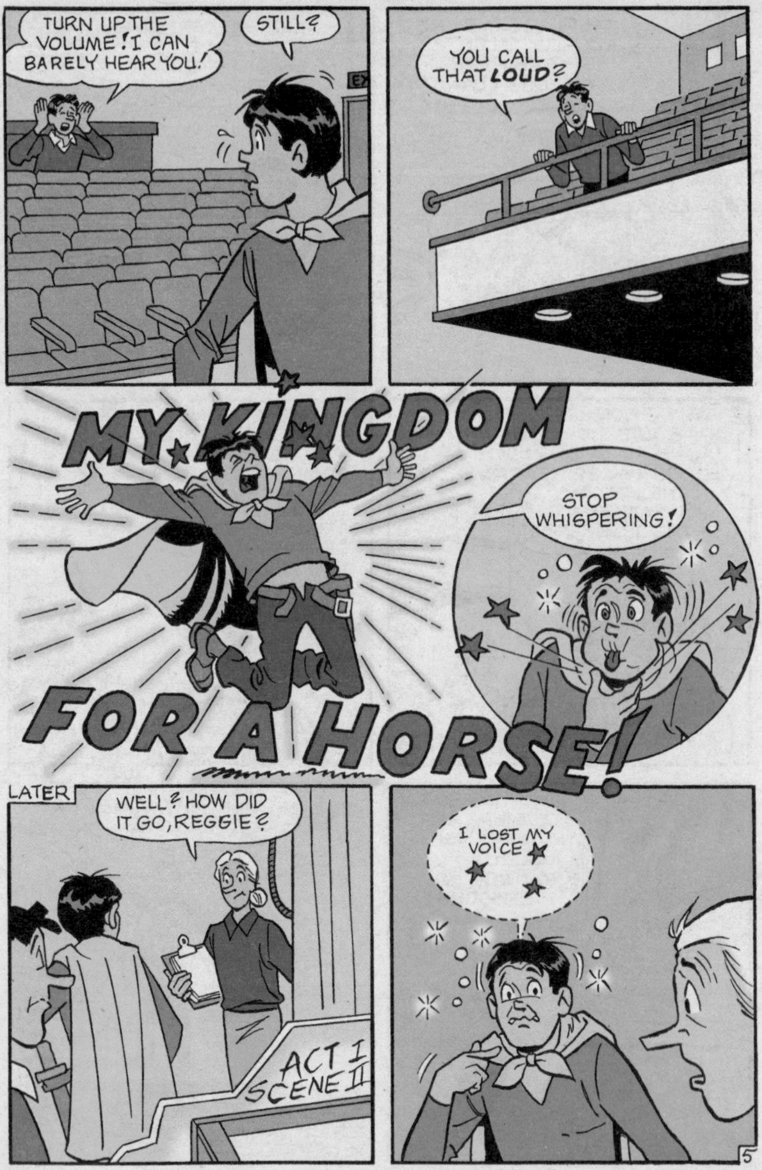
TURN UP THE VOLUME! I CAN BARELY HEAR YOU!
STILL?
YOU CALL THAT **LOUD**?
MY KINGDOM FOR A HORSE!
STOP WHISPERING!
LATER
WELL? HOW DID IT GO, REGGIE?
ACT I SCENE II
I LOST MY VOICE

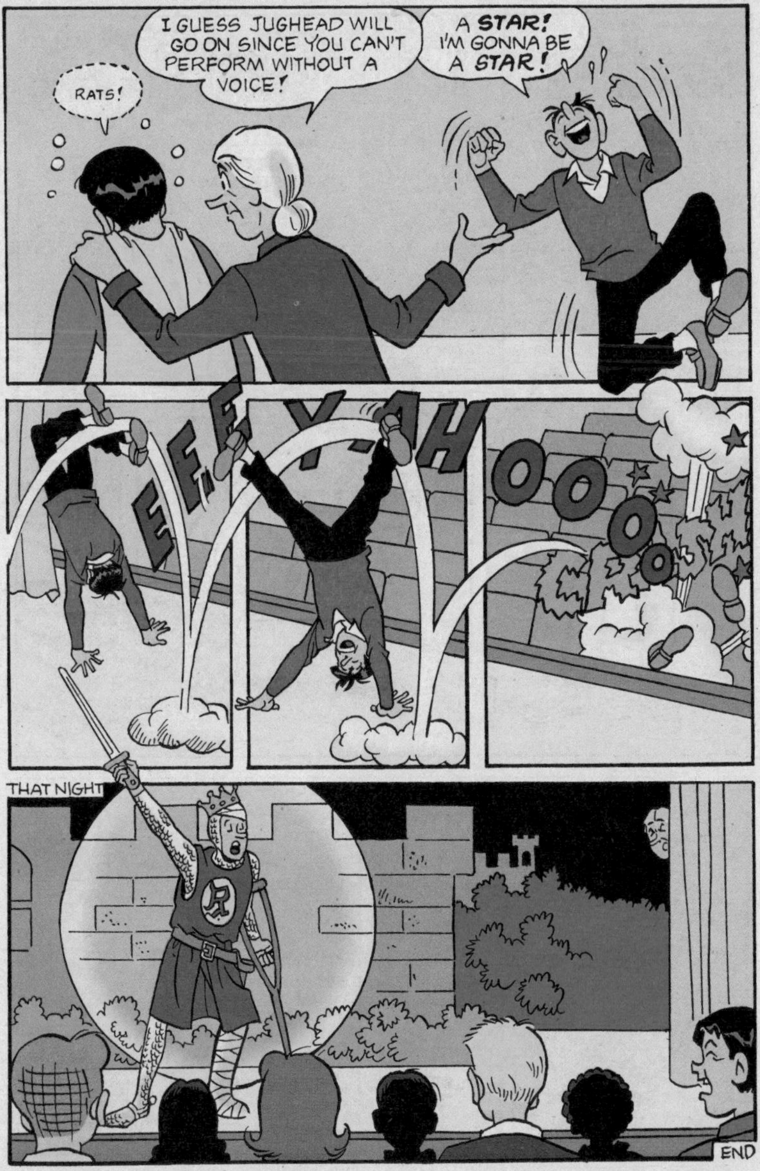
RATS!
I GUESS JUGHEAD WILL GO ON SINCE YOU CAN'T PERFORM WITHOUT A VOICE!
A STAR! I'M GONNA BE A STAR!
EEEY-AHOOOOO
CRASH
THAT NIGHT
END

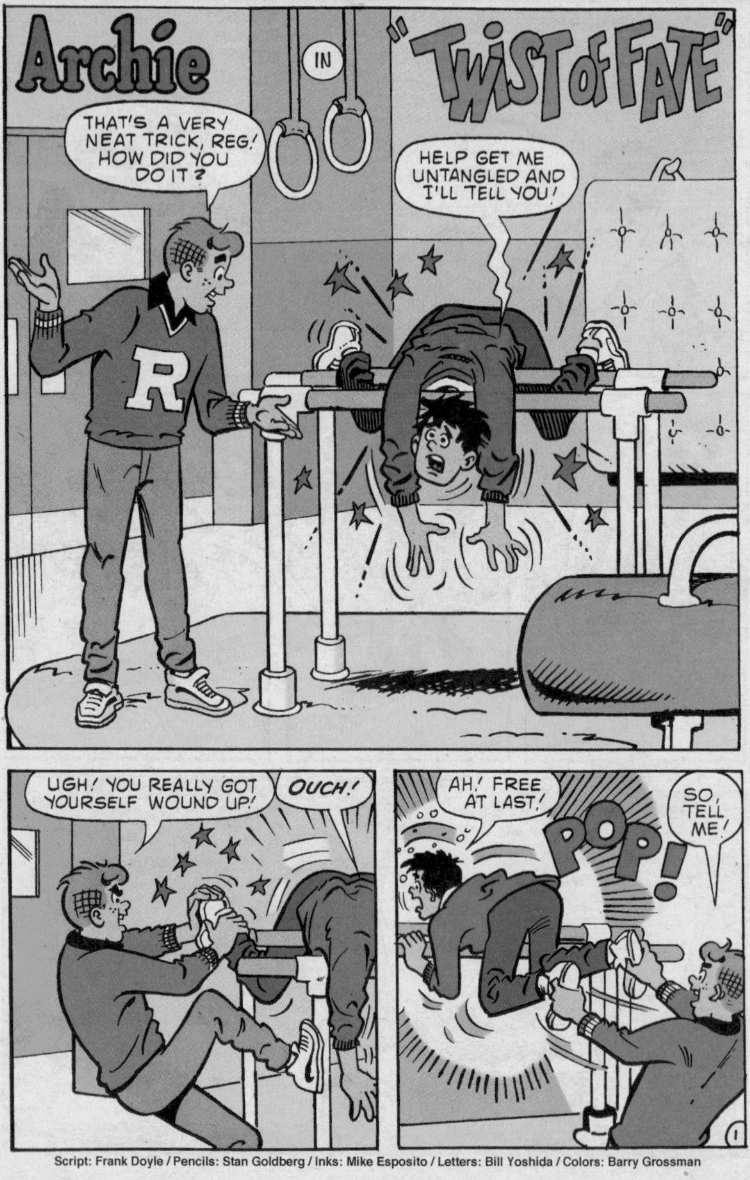
Archie IN "TWIST OF FATE"
THAT'S A VERY NEAT TRICK, REG! HOW DID YOU DO IT?
HELP GET ME UNTANGLED AND I'LL TELL YOU!
UGH! YOU REALLY GOT YOURSELF WOUND UP!
OUCH!
AH! FREE AT LAST!
POP!
SO, TELL ME!
1

Script: Frank Doyle / Pencils: Stan Goldberg / Inks: Mike Esposito / Letters: Bill Yoshida / Colors: Barry Grossman

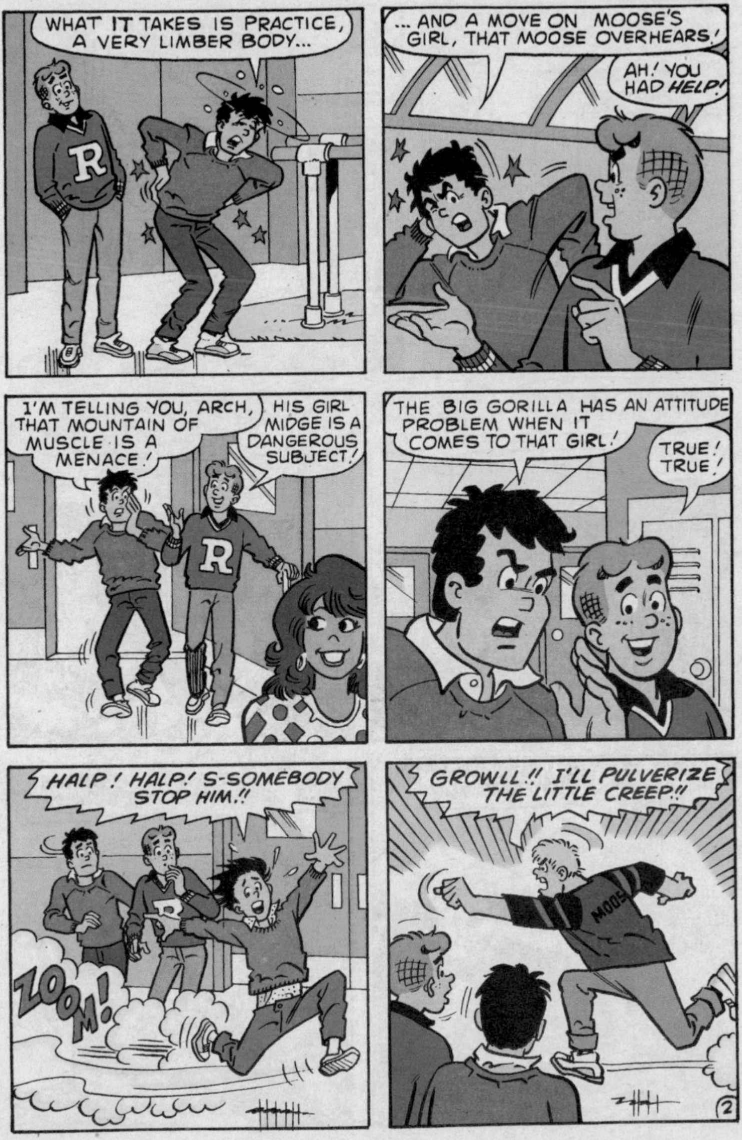
WHAT IT TAKES IS PRACTICE, A VERY LIMBER BODY...
... AND A MOVE ON MOOSE'S GIRL, THAT MOOSE OVERHEARS!
AH! YOU HAD HELP!
I'M TELLING YOU, ARCH, THAT MOUNTAIN OF MUSCLE IS A MENACE!
HIS GIRL MIDGE IS A DANGEROUS SUBJECT!
THE BIG GORILLA HAS AN ATTITUDE PROBLEM WHEN IT COMES TO THAT GIRL!
TRUE! TRUE!
HALP! HALP! S-SOMEBODY STOP HIM!!
ZOOM!
GROWLL!! I'LL PULVERIZE THE LITTLE CREEP!!
MOOSE
2

MY, IT'S BEEN A PEACEFUL MORNING! PROBABLY THE CALM BEFORE THE...

MR. WEATHERBE

... STORM!

SANCTUARY! SANCTUARY!

SLAM!

WHAT DO YOU NEED SANCTUARY FROM?

M-MOOSE! HE'S GONNA *KILL* ME!

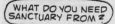

D-UH! I SEEN WHERE YUH WENT, YUH WIMP! COME ON OUTTA THERE!!

SCREECH

WHAT'S IT ALL ABOUT, MOOSE?

HE WUZ TALKIN' TUH MY GURL MIDGE!!

17

SON! I WANT YOU TO CEASE AND DESIST!! *RIGHT NOW!*

"DE-WHUT"?

3

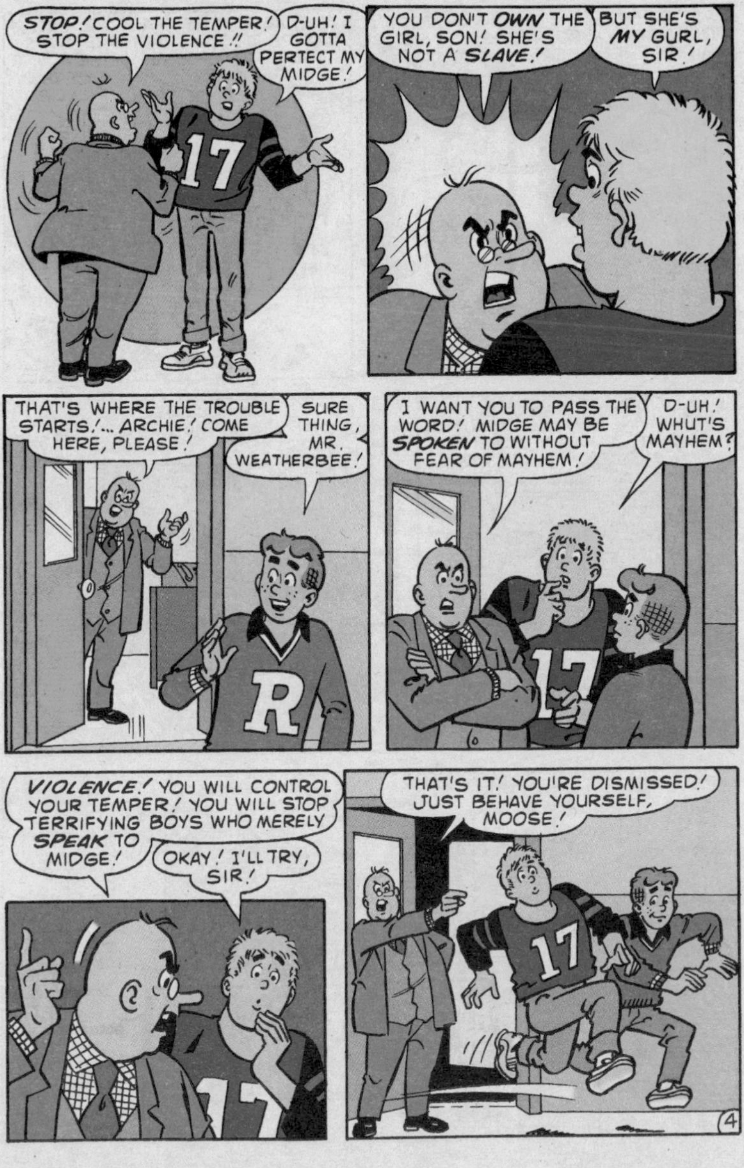
STOP! COOL THE TEMPER! STOP THE VIOLENCE!!
D-UH! I GOTTA PERTECT MY MIDGE!
YOU DON'T OWN THE GIRL, SON! SHE'S NOT A SLAVE!
BUT SHE'S MY GURL, SIR!
THAT'S WHERE THE TROUBLE STARTS!... ARCHIE! COME HERE, PLEASE!
SURE THING, MR. WEATHERBEE!
I WANT YOU TO PASS THE WORD! MIDGE MAY BE SPOKEN TO WITHOUT FEAR OF MAYHEM!
D-UH! WHUT'S MAYHEM?
VIOLENCE! YOU WILL CONTROL YOUR TEMPER! YOU WILL STOP TERRIFYING BOYS WHO MERELY SPEAK TO MIDGE!
OKAY! I'LL TRY, SIR!
THAT'S IT! YOU'RE DISMISSED! JUST BEHAVE YOURSELF, MOOSE!
4

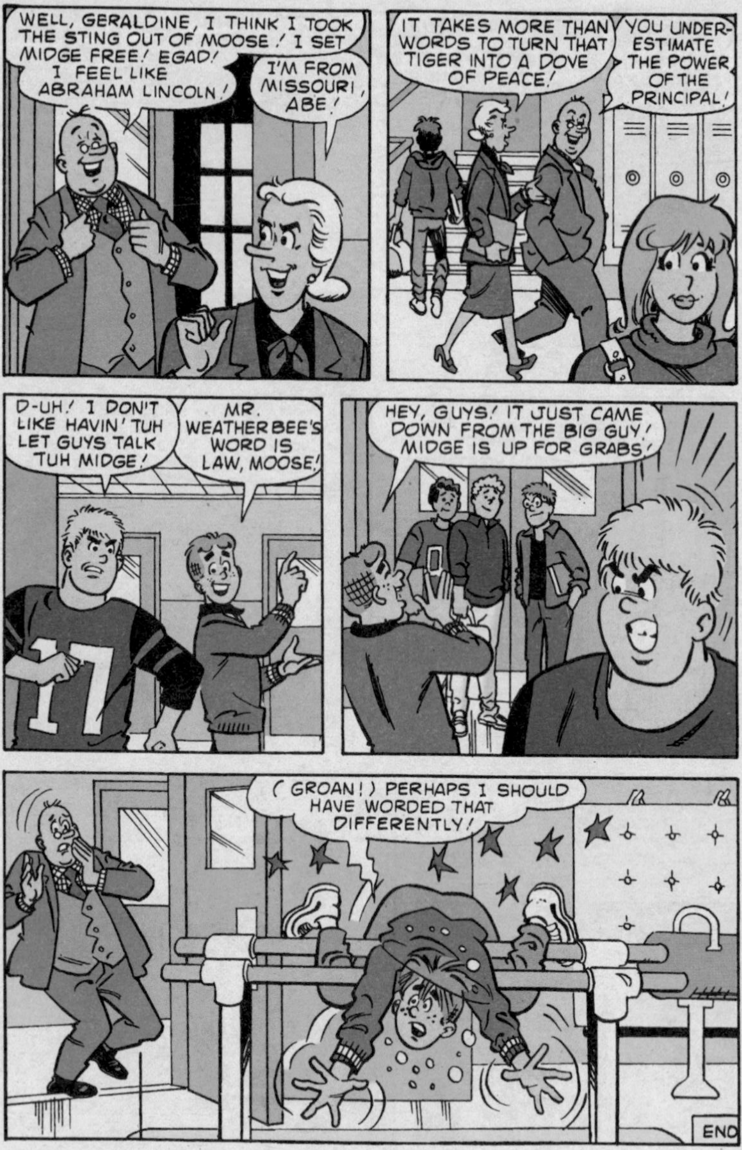
WELL, GERALDINE, I THINK I TOOK THE STING OUT OF MOOSE! I SET MIDGE FREE! EGAD! I FEEL LIKE ABRAHAM LINCOLN!
I'M FROM MISSOURI, ABE!
IT TAKES MORE THAN WORDS TO TURN THAT TIGER INTO A DOVE OF PEACE!
YOU UNDER-ESTIMATE THE POWER OF THE PRINCIPAL!
D-UH! I DON'T LIKE HAVIN' TUH LET GUYS TALK TUH MIDGE!
MR. WEATHERBEE'S WORD IS LAW, MOOSE!
HEY, GUYS! IT JUST CAME DOWN FROM THE BIG GUY! MIDGE IS UP FOR GRABS!
(GROAN!) PERHAPS I SHOULD HAVE WORDED THAT DIFFERENTLY!
END

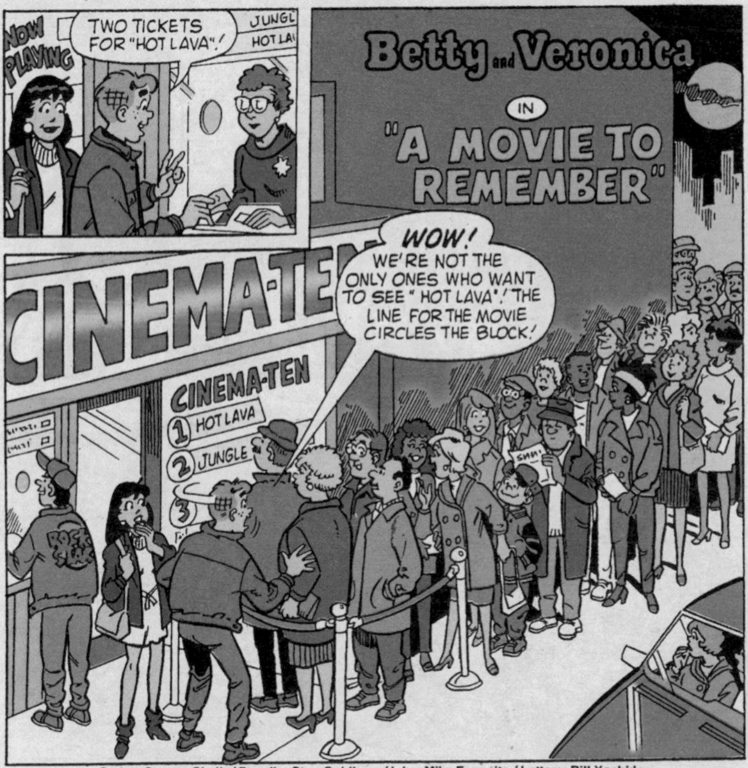

NOW PLAYING
TWO TICKETS FOR "HOT LAVA"!
JUNGL
HOT LA
Betty and Veronica
IN
"A MOVIE TO REMEMBER"
CINEMA-TEN
WOW! WE'RE NOT THE ONLY ONES WHO WANT TO SEE "HOT LAVA"! THE LINE FOR THE MOVIE CIRCLES THE BLOCK!
CINEMA-TEN
1 HOT LAVA
2 JUNGLE
3

Script: George Gladir / Pencils: Stan Goldberg / Inks: Mike Esposito / Letters: Bill Yoshida

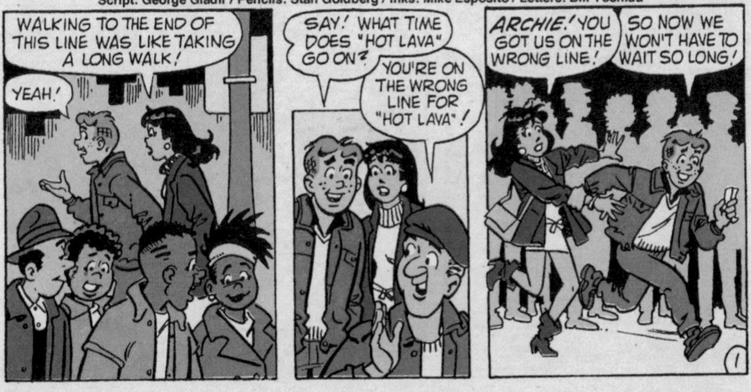

WALKING TO THE END OF THIS LINE WAS LIKE TAKING A LONG WALK!
YEAH!
SAY! WHAT TIME DOES "HOT LAVA" GO ON?
YOU'RE ON THE WRONG LINE FOR "HOT LAVA"!
ARCHIE! YOU GOT US ON THE WRONG LINE!
SO NOW WE WON'T HAVE TO WAIT SO LONG!
1

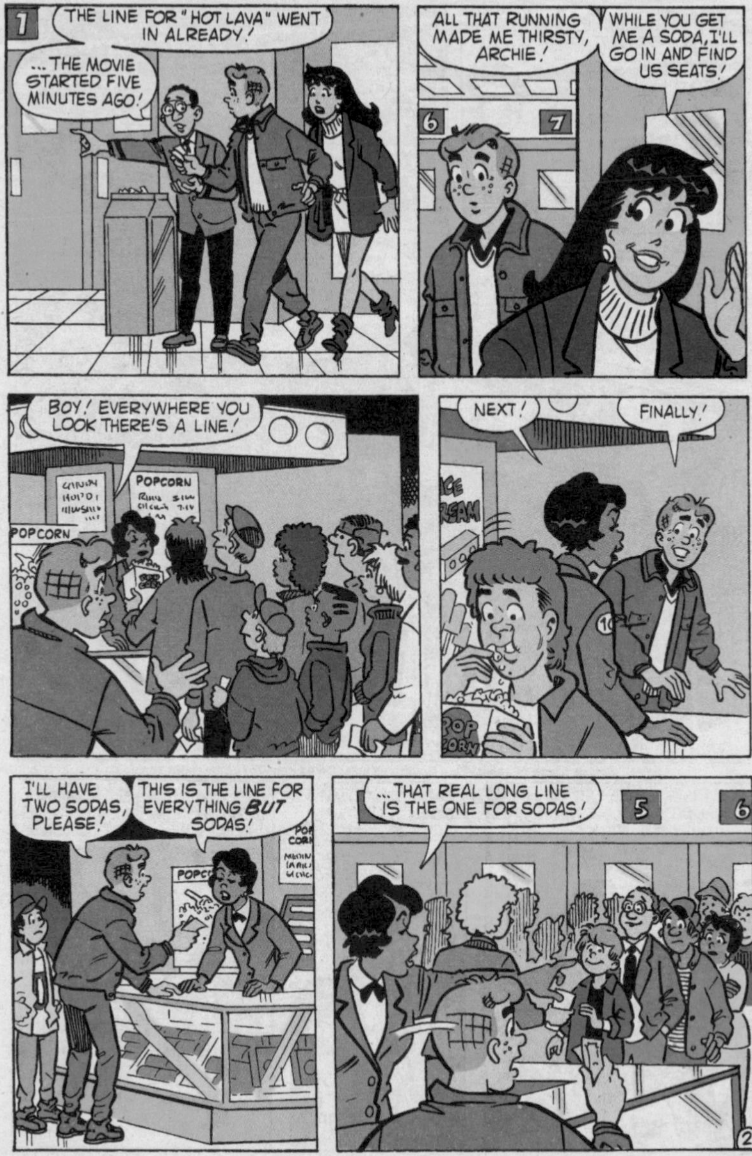
THE LINE FOR "HOT LAVA" WENT IN ALREADY!
...THE MOVIE STARTED FIVE MINUTES AGO!
7
ALL THAT RUNNING MADE ME THIRSTY, ARCHIE!
WHILE YOU GET ME A SODA, I'LL GO IN AND FIND US SEATS!
6
7
BOY! EVERYWHERE YOU LOOK THERE'S A LINE!
POPCORN
POPCORN
NEXT!
FINALLY!
I'LL HAVE TWO SODAS, PLEASE!
THIS IS THE LINE FOR EVERYTHING *BUT* SODAS!
...THAT REAL LONG LINE IS THE ONE FOR SODAS!
5
6
2

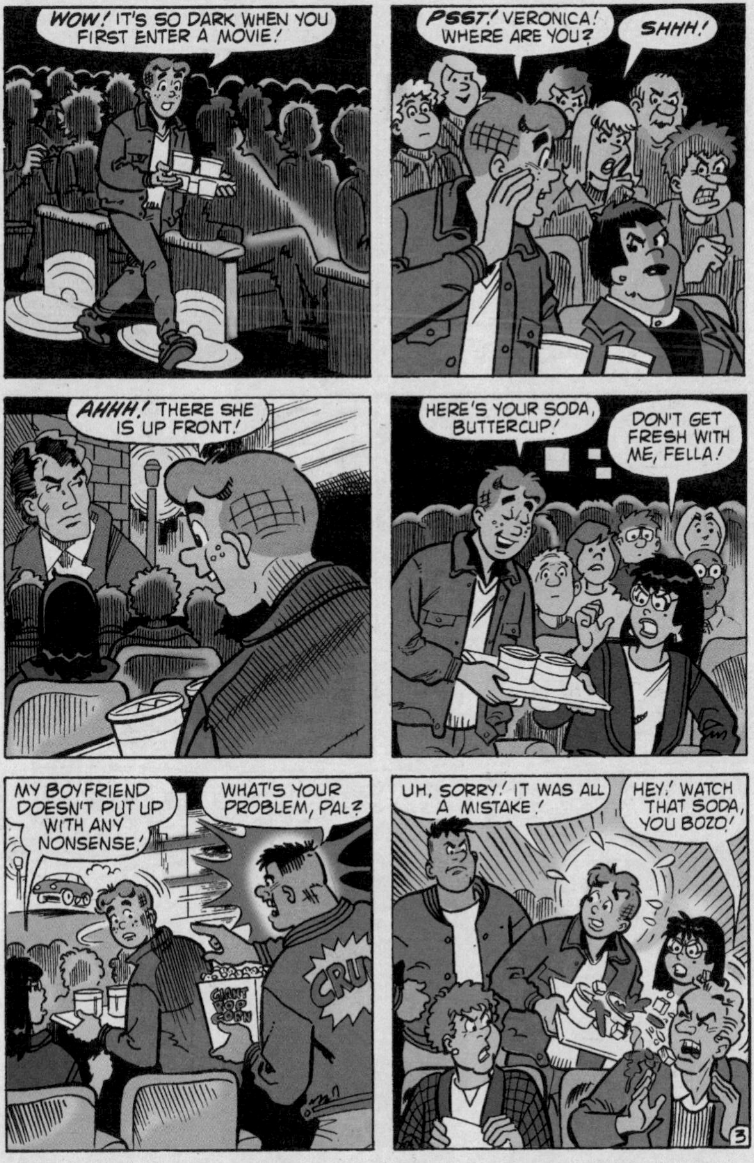
WOW! IT'S SO DARK WHEN YOU FIRST ENTER A MOVIE!
PSST! VERONICA! WHERE ARE YOU?
SHHH!
AHHH! THERE SHE IS UP FRONT!
HERE'S YOUR SODA, BUTTERCUP!
DON'T GET FRESH WITH ME, FELLA!
MY BOYFRIEND DOESN'T PUT UP WITH ANY NONSENSE!
WHAT'S YOUR PROBLEM, PAL?
GIANT POP CORN
UH, SORRY! IT WAS ALL A MISTAKE!
HEY! WATCH THAT SODA, YOU BOZO!
3

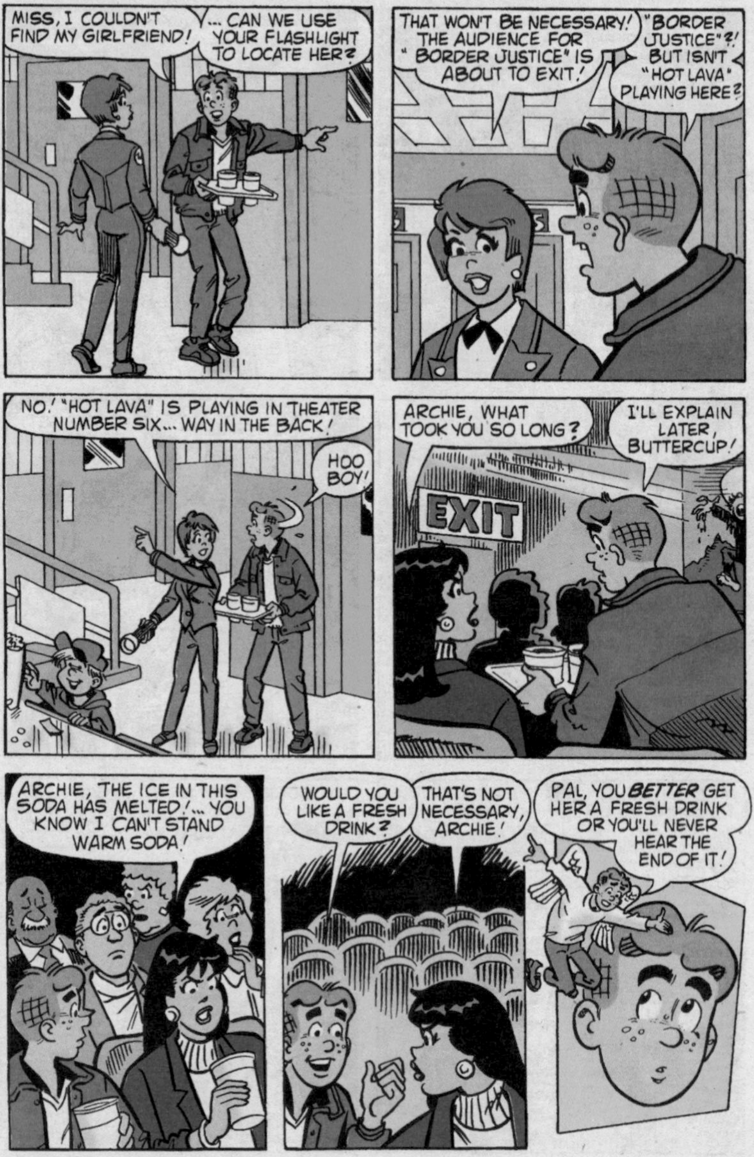
MISS, I COULDN'T FIND MY GIRLFRIEND!
... CAN WE USE YOUR FLASHLIGHT TO LOCATE HER?
THAT WON'T BE NECESSARY! THE AUDIENCE FOR "BORDER JUSTICE" IS ABOUT TO EXIT!
"BORDER JUSTICE"?! BUT ISN'T "HOT LAVA" PLAYING HERE?
NO! "HOT LAVA" IS PLAYING IN THEATER NUMBER SIX... WAY IN THE BACK!
HOO BOY!
ARCHIE, WHAT TOOK YOU SO LONG?
I'LL EXPLAIN LATER, BUTTERCUP!
EXIT
ARCHIE, THE ICE IN THIS SODA HAS MELTED!... YOU KNOW I CAN'T STAND WARM SODA!
WOULD YOU LIKE A FRESH DRINK?
THAT'S NOT NECESSARY, ARCHIE!
PAL, YOU BETTER GET HER A FRESH DRINK OR YOU'LL NEVER HEAR THE END OF IT!

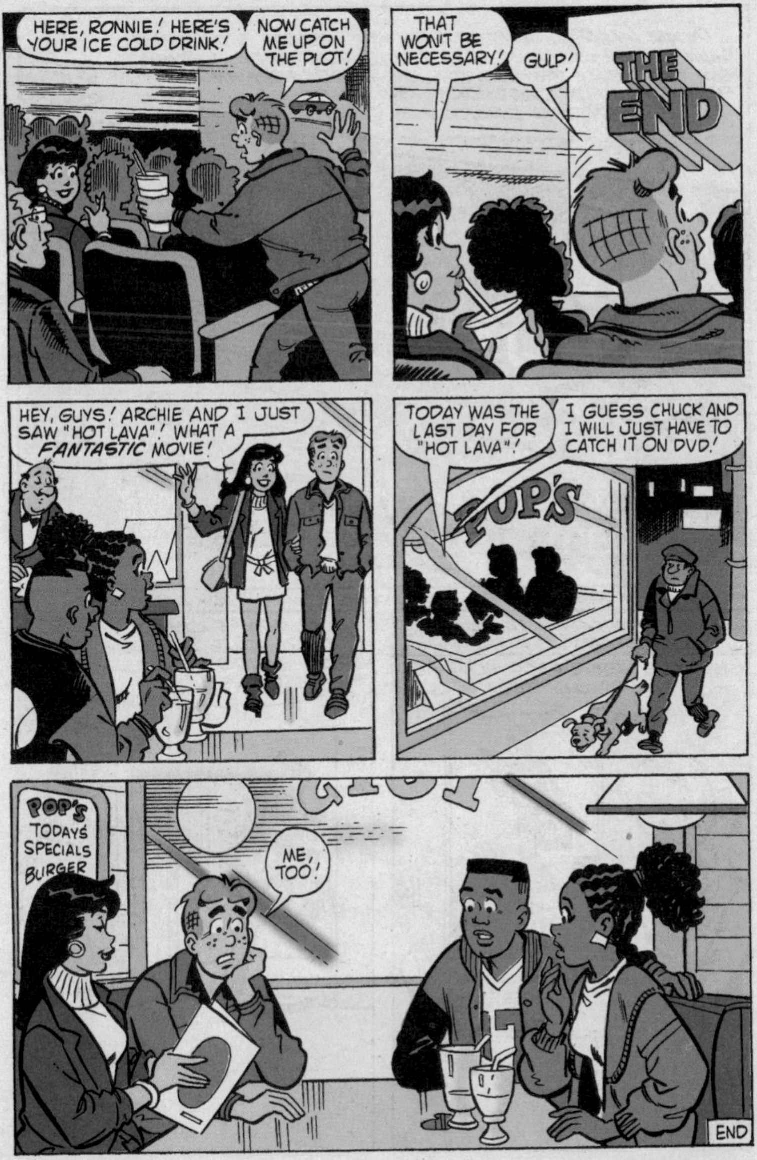
HERE, RONNIE! HERE'S YOUR ICE COLD DRINK!
NOW CATCH ME UP ON THE PLOT!
THAT WON'T BE NECESSARY!
GULP!
THE END
HEY, GUYS! ARCHIE AND I JUST SAW "HOT LAVA"! WHAT A FANTASTIC MOVIE!
TODAY WAS THE LAST DAY FOR "HOT LAVA"!
I GUESS CHUCK AND I WILL JUST HAVE TO CATCH IT ON DVD!
POP'S
POP'S TODAYS SPECIALS BURGER
ME, TOO!
END

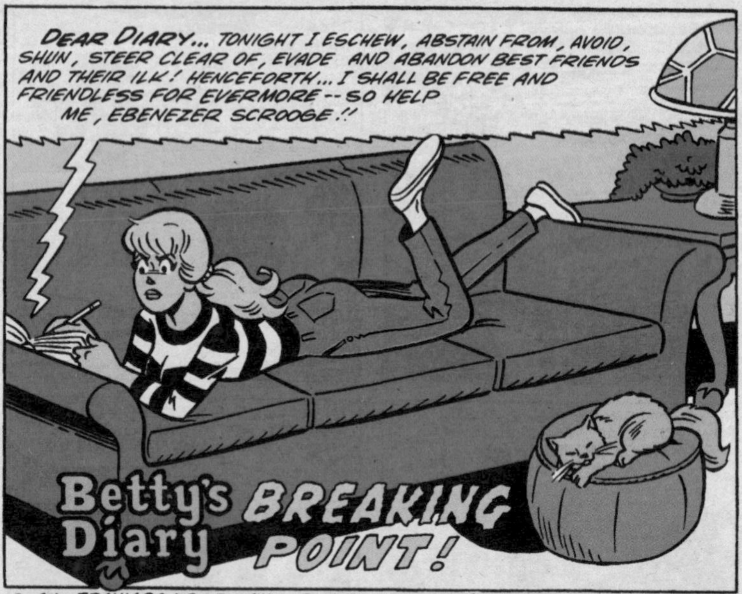
DEAR DIARY... TONIGHT I ESCHEW, ABSTAIN FROM, AVOID, SHUN, STEER CLEAR OF, EVADE AND ABANDON BEST FRIENDS AND THEIR ILK! HENCEFORTH... I SHALL BE FREE AND FRIENDLESS FOR EVERMORE -- SO HELP ME, EBENEZER SCROOGE!!
Betty's Diary
BREAKING POINT!

Script: FRANK DOYLE * Pencilling: BOB BOLLING * Inking: RUDY LAPICK

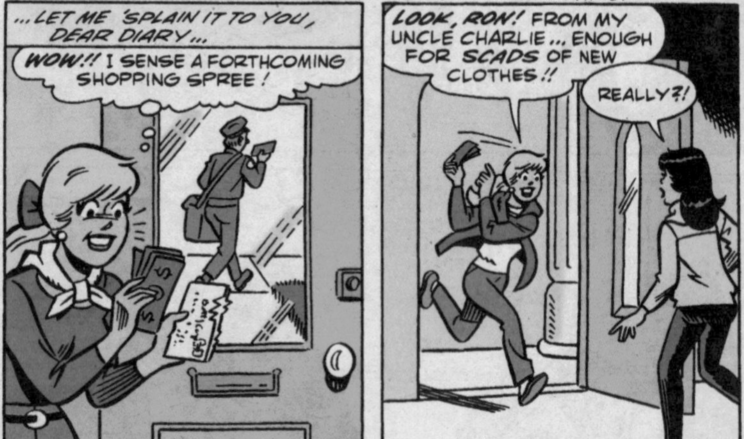
...LET ME 'SPLAIN IT TO YOU, DEAR DIARY...
WOW!! I SENSE A FORTHCOMING SHOPPING SPREE!
LOOK, RON! FROM MY UNCLE CHARLIE... ENOUGH FOR SCADS OF NEW CLOTHES!!
REALLY?!

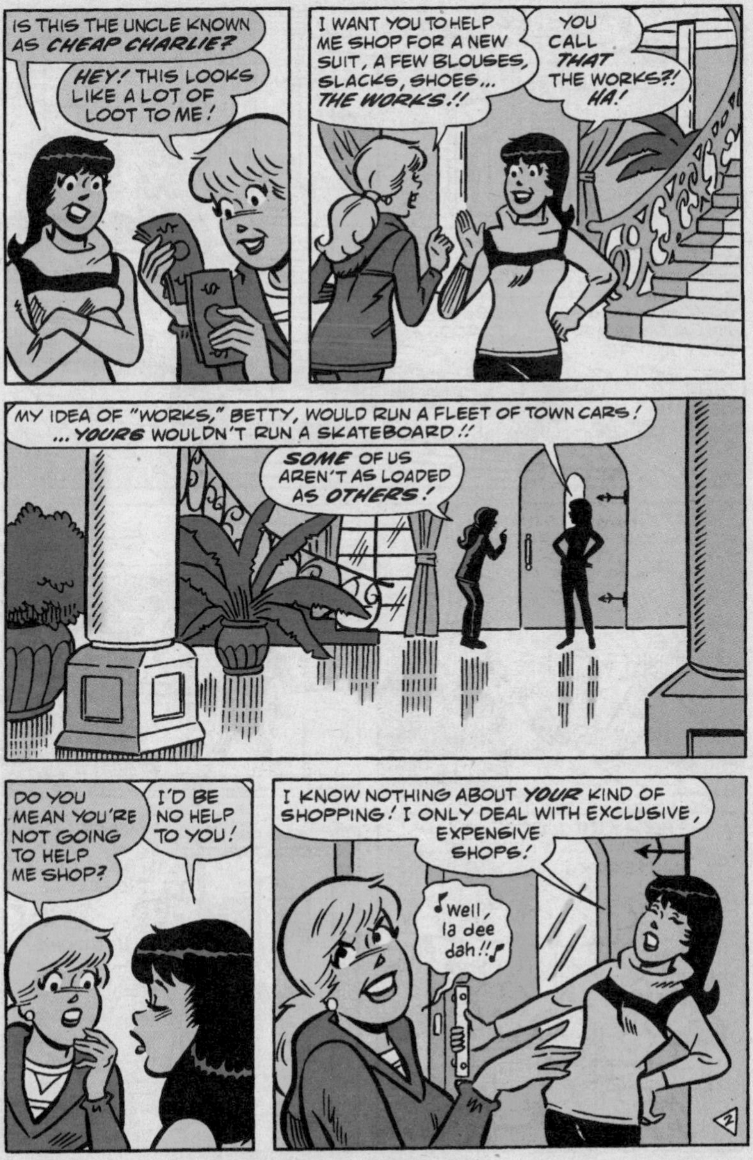
IS THIS THE UNCLE KNOWN AS CHEAP CHARLIE?
HEY! THIS LOOKS LIKE A LOT OF LOOT TO ME!
I WANT YOU TO HELP ME SHOP FOR A NEW SUIT, A FEW BLOUSES, SLACKS, SHOES... THE WORKS!!
YOU CALL THAT THE WORKS?! HA!
MY IDEA OF "WORKS," BETTY, WOULD RUN A FLEET OF TOWN CARS! ...YOURS WOULDN'T RUN A SKATEBOARD!!
SOME OF US AREN'T AS LOADED AS OTHERS!
DO YOU MEAN YOU'RE NOT GOING TO HELP ME SHOP?
I'D BE NO HELP TO YOU!
I KNOW NOTHING ABOUT YOUR KIND OF SHOPPING! I ONLY DEAL WITH EXCLUSIVE, EXPENSIVE SHOPS!
Well, la dee dah!!
2

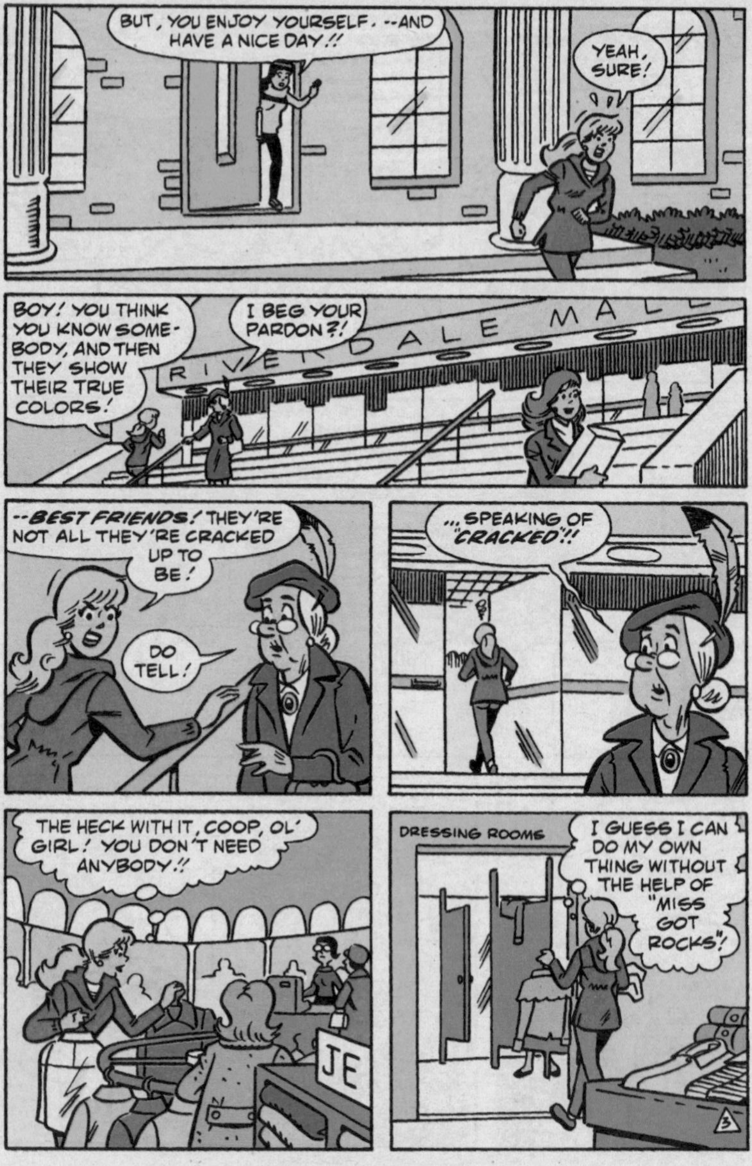

BUT, YOU ENJOY YOURSELF. --AND HAVE A NICE DAY!!
YEAH, SURE!
BOY! YOU THINK YOU KNOW SOME-BODY, AND THEN THEY SHOW THEIR TRUE COLORS!
I BEG YOUR PARDON?!
RIVERDALE MALL
--BEST FRIENDS! THEY'RE NOT ALL THEY'RE CRACKED UP TO BE!
DO TELL!
...SPEAKING OF "CRACKED"!!
THE HECK WITH IT, COOP, OL' GIRL! YOU DON'T NEED ANYBODY!!
JE
DRESSING ROOMS
I GUESS I CAN DO MY OWN THING WITHOUT THE HELP OF "MISS GOT ROCKS"!
3

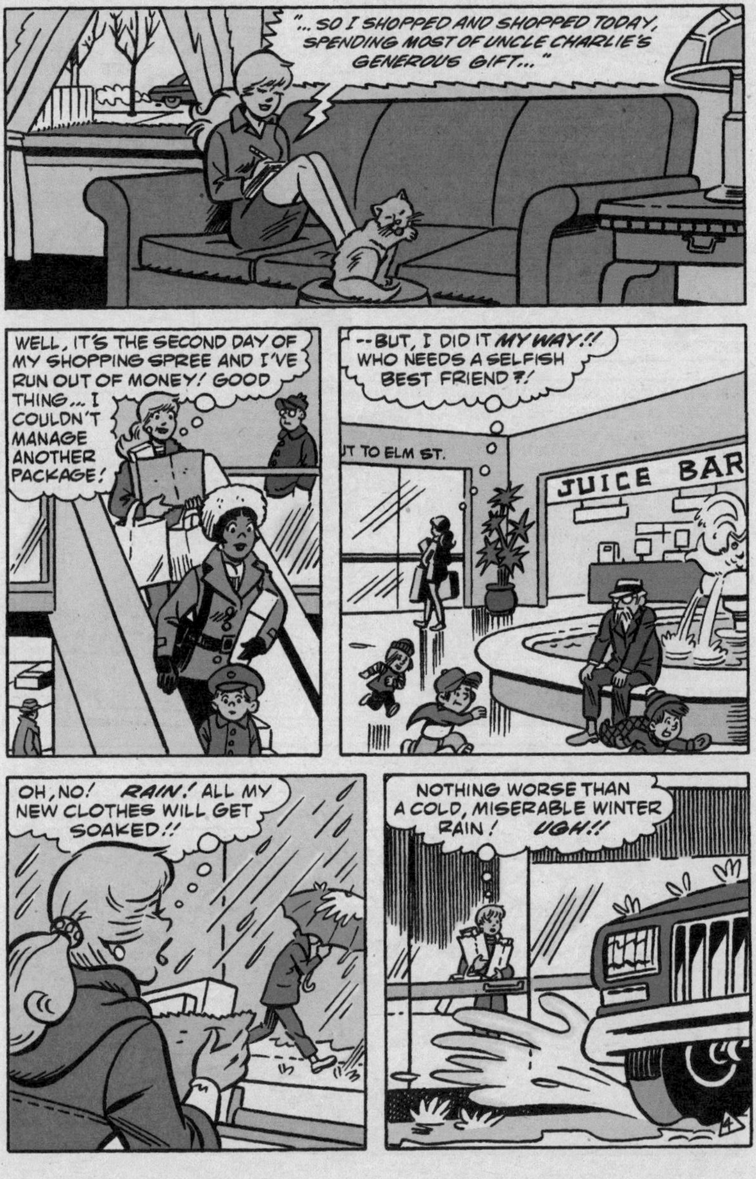
"... SO I SHOPPED AND SHOPPED TODAY, SPENDING MOST OF UNCLE CHARLIE'S GENEROUS GIFT..."
WELL, IT'S THE SECOND DAY OF MY SHOPPING SPREE AND I'VE RUN OUT OF MONEY! GOOD THING... I COULDN'T MANAGE ANOTHER PACKAGE!
--BUT, I DID IT MY WAY!! WHO NEEDS A SELFISH BEST FRIEND?!
T TO ELM ST.
JUICE BAR
OH, NO! RAIN! ALL MY NEW CLOTHES WILL GET SOAKED!!
NOTHING WORSE THAN A COLD, MISERABLE WINTER RAIN! UGH!!
4

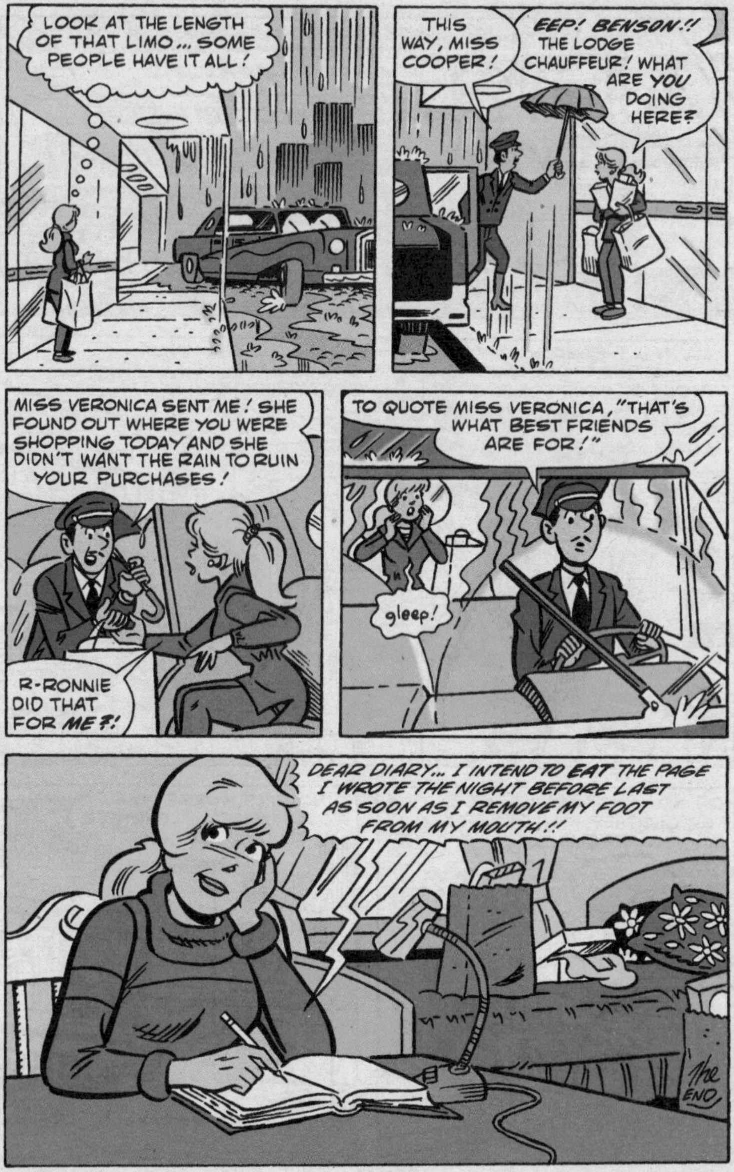
LOOK AT THE LENGTH OF THAT LIMO... SOME PEOPLE HAVE IT ALL!
THIS WAY, MISS COOPER!
EEP! BENSON!! THE LODGE CHAUFFEUR! WHAT ARE YOU DOING HERE?
MISS VERONICA SENT ME! SHE FOUND OUT WHERE YOU WERE SHOPPING TODAY AND SHE DIDN'T WANT THE RAIN TO RUIN YOUR PURCHASES!
R-RONNIE DID THAT FOR ME?!
TO QUOTE MISS VERONICA, "THAT'S WHAT BEST FRIENDS ARE FOR!"
gleep!
DEAR DIARY... I INTEND TO EAT THE PAGE I WROTE THE NIGHT BEFORE LAST AS SOON AS I REMOVE MY FOOT FROM MY MOUTH!!
The END

Veronica in CUSTOMER SERVICE

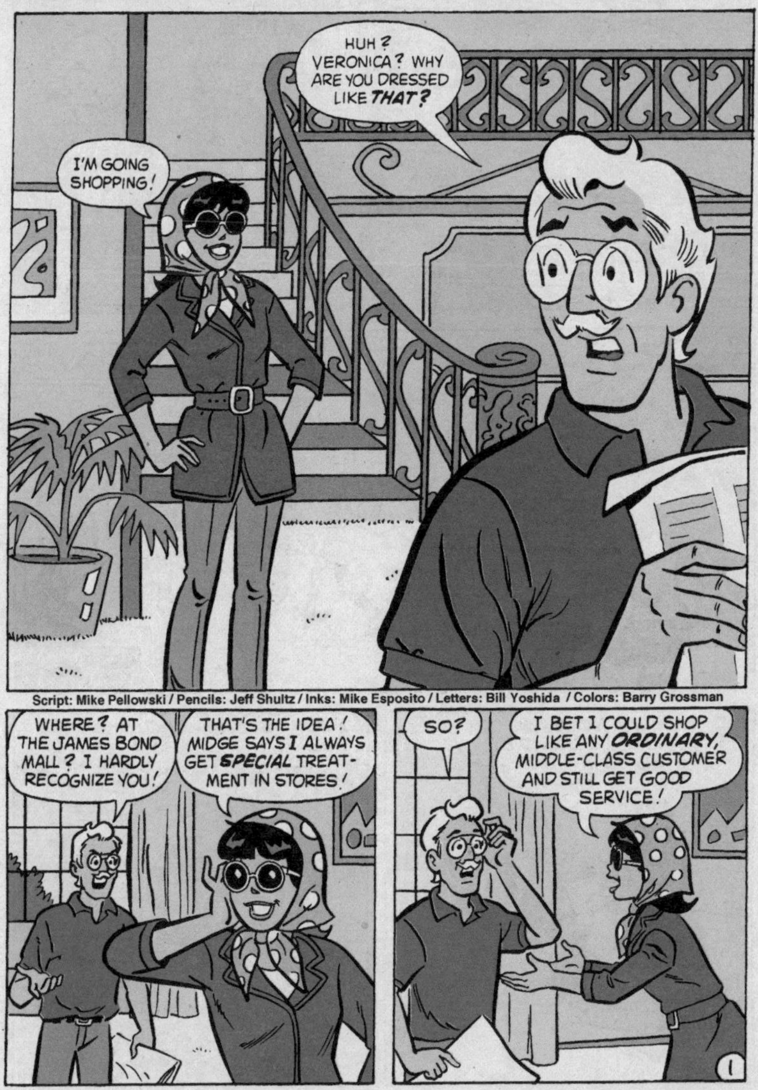
HUH? VERONICA? WHY ARE YOU DRESSED LIKE THAT?
I'M GOING SHOPPING!
Script: Mike Pellowski / Pencils: Jeff Shultz / Inks: Mike Esposito / Letters: Bill Yoshida / Colors: Barry Grossman
WHERE? AT THE JAMES BOND MALL? I HARDLY RECOGNIZE YOU!
THAT'S THE IDEA! MIDGE SAYS I ALWAYS GET SPECIAL TREATMENT IN STORES!
SO?
I BET I COULD SHOP LIKE ANY ORDINARY, MIDDLE-CLASS CUSTOMER AND STILL GET GOOD SERVICE!
1

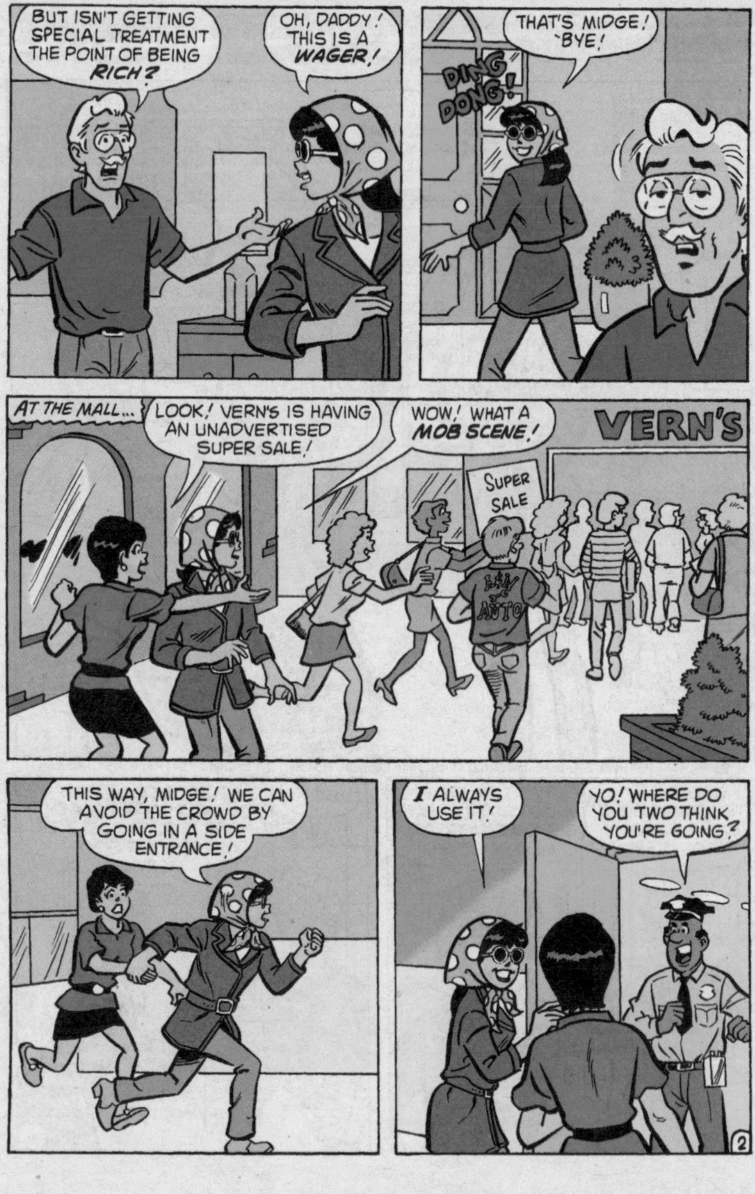
BUT ISN'T GETTING SPECIAL TREATMENT THE POINT OF BEING RICH?
OH, DADDY! THIS IS A WAGER!
DING DONG!
THAT'S MIDGE! 'BYE!
AT THE MALL...
LOOK! VERN'S IS HAVING AN UNADVERTISED SUPER SALE!
WOW! WHAT A MOB SCENE!
VERN'S
SUPER SALE
THIS WAY, MIDGE! WE CAN AVOID THE CROWD BY GOING IN A SIDE ENTRANCE!
I ALWAYS USE IT!
YO! WHERE DO YOU TWO THINK YOU'RE GOING?
2

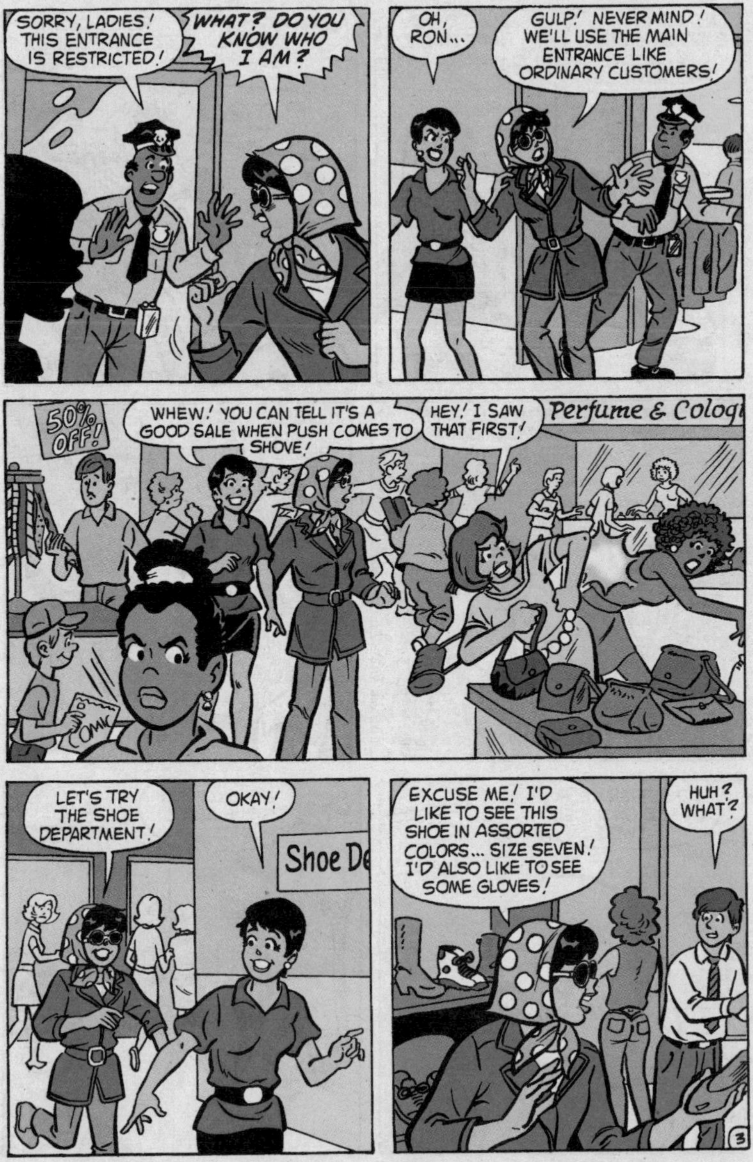
SORRY, LADIES! THIS ENTRANCE IS RESTRICTED!
WHAT? DO YOU KNOW WHO I AM?
OH, RON...
GULP! NEVER MIND! WE'LL USE THE MAIN ENTRANCE LIKE ORDINARY CUSTOMERS!
50% OFF!
WHEW! YOU CAN TELL IT'S A GOOD SALE WHEN PUSH COMES TO SHOVE!
HEY! I SAW THAT FIRST!
Perfume & Cologi
COMIC
LET'S TRY THE SHOE DEPARTMENT!
OKAY!
Shoe De
EXCUSE ME! I'D LIKE TO SEE THIS SHOE IN ASSORTED COLORS... SIZE SEVEN! I'D ALSO LIKE TO SEE SOME GLOVES!
HUH? WHAT?
3

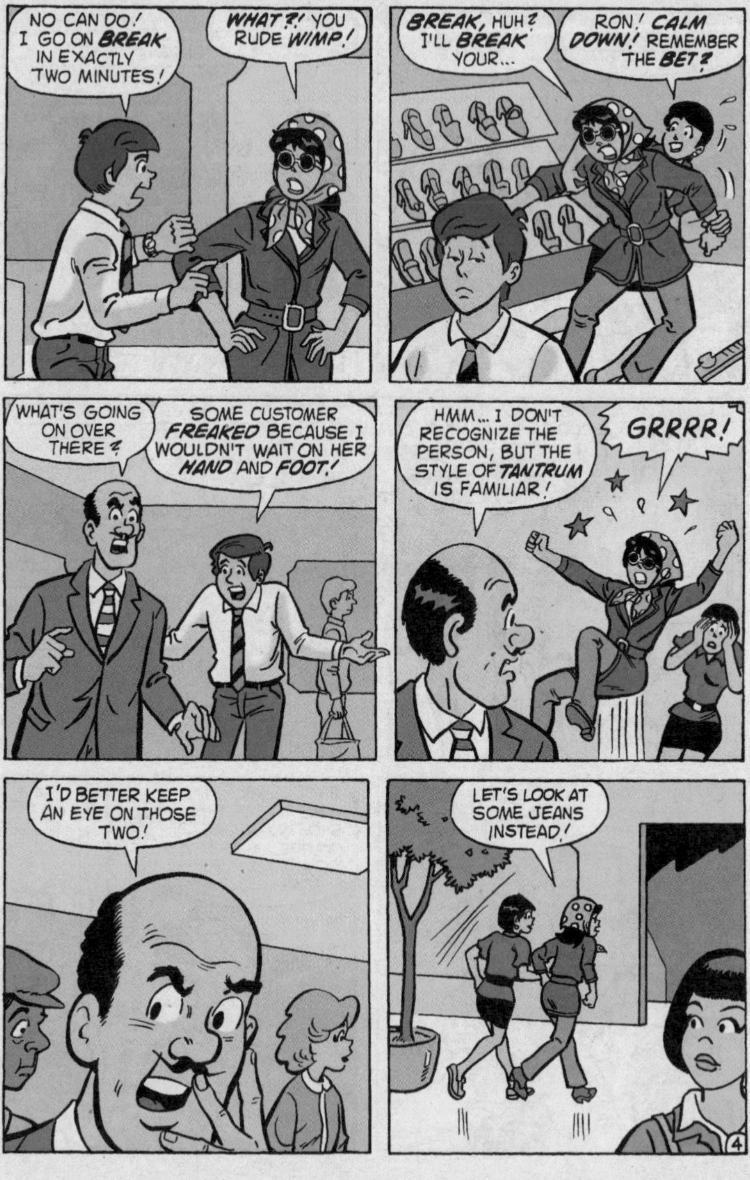
NO CAN DO! I GO ON BREAK IN EXACTLY TWO MINUTES!
WHAT?! YOU RUDE WIMP!
BREAK, HUH? I'LL BREAK YOUR...
RON! CALM DOWN! REMEMBER THE BET?
WHAT'S GOING ON OVER THERE?
SOME CUSTOMER FREAKED BECAUSE I WOULDN'T WAIT ON HER HAND AND FOOT!
HMM... I DON'T RECOGNIZE THE PERSON, BUT THE STYLE OF TANTRUM IS FAMILIAR!
GRRRR!
I'D BETTER KEEP AN EYE ON THOSE TWO!
LET'S LOOK AT SOME JEANS INSTEAD!
4

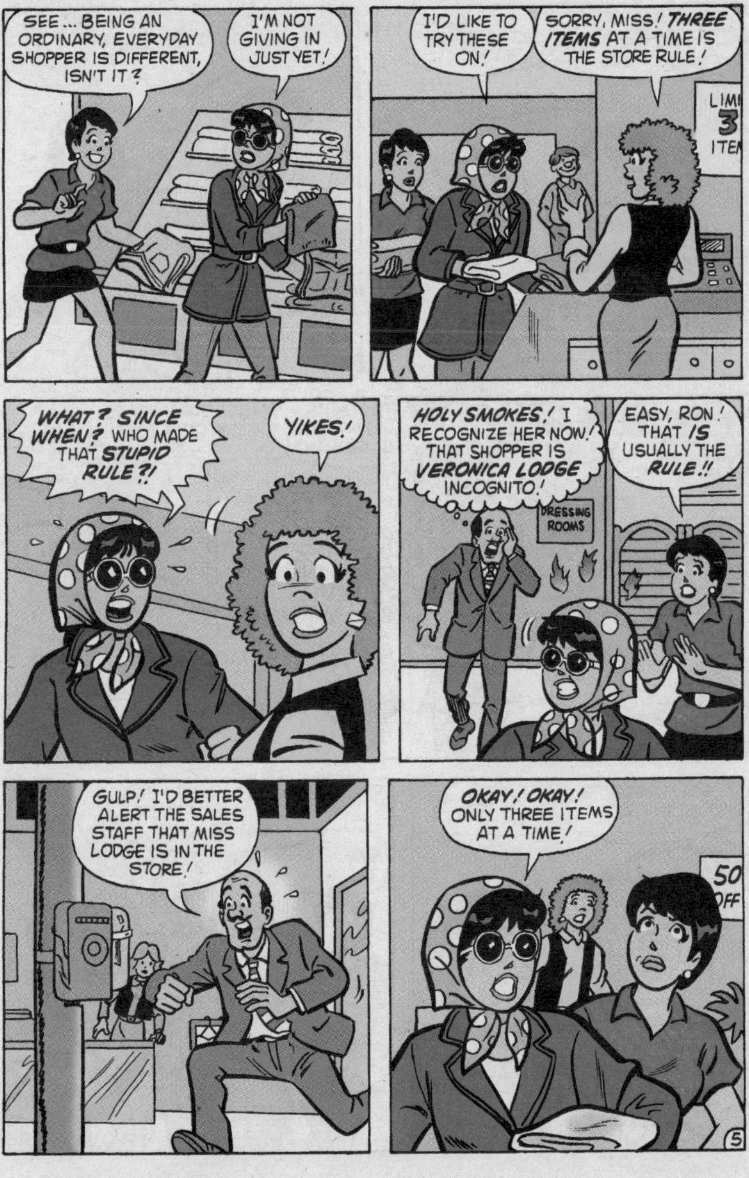
SEE... BEING AN ORDINARY, EVERYDAY SHOPPER IS DIFFERENT, ISN'T IT?
I'M NOT GIVING IN JUST YET!
I'D LIKE TO TRY THESE ON!
SORRY, MISS! THREE ITEMS AT A TIME IS THE STORE RULE!
WHAT? SINCE WHEN? WHO MADE THAT STUPID RULE?!
YIKES!
HOLY SMOKES! I RECOGNIZE HER NOW! THAT SHOPPER IS VERONICA LODGE INCOGNITO!
DRESSING ROOMS
EASY, RON! THAT IS USUALLY THE RULE!!
GULP! I'D BETTER ALERT THE SALES STAFF THAT MISS LODGE IS IN THE STORE!
OKAY! OKAY! ONLY THREE ITEMS AT A TIME!
5

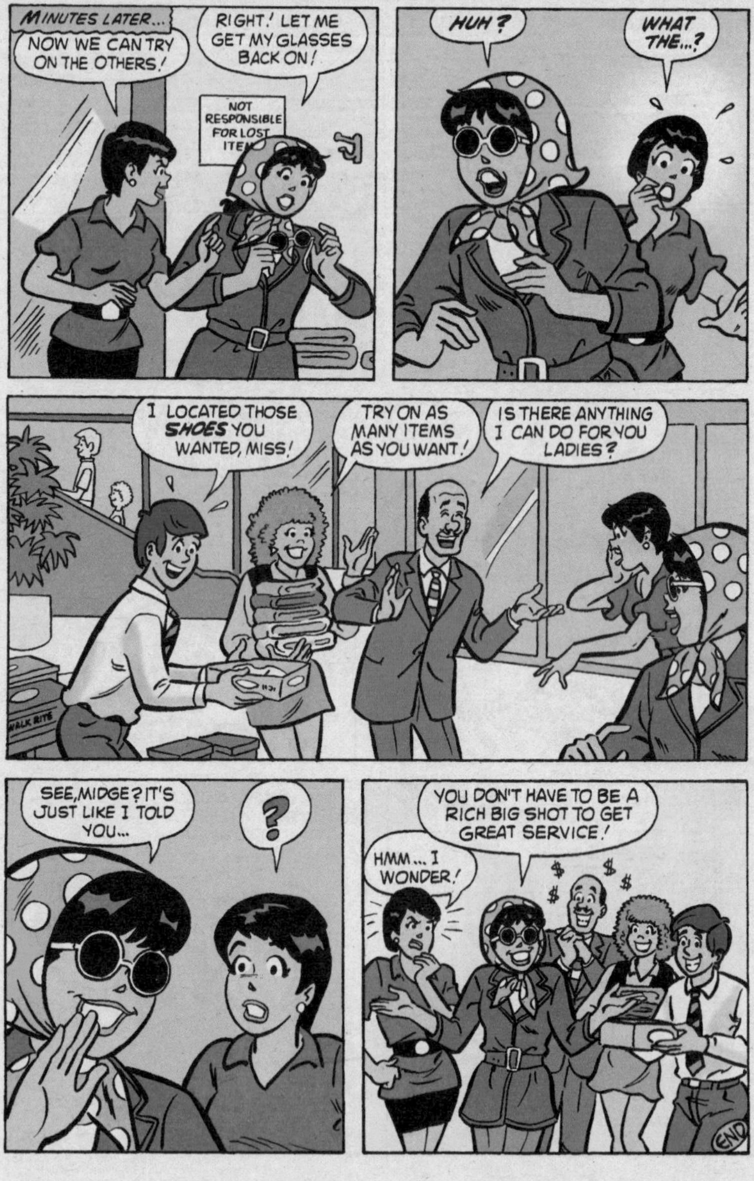

MINUTES LATER...
NOW WE CAN TRY ON THE OTHERS!
RIGHT! LET ME GET MY GLASSES BACK ON!
NOT RESPONSIBLE FOR LOST ITE
HUH?
WHAT THE...?
I LOCATED THOSE SHOES YOU WANTED, MISS!
TRY ON AS MANY ITEMS AS YOU WANT!
IS THERE ANYTHING I CAN DO FOR YOU LADIES?
WALK RITE
SEE, MIDGE? IT'S JUST LIKE I TOLD YOU...
?
YOU DON'T HAVE TO BE A RICH BIG SHOT TO GET GREAT SERVICE!
HMM... I WONDER!
$
$
$
$
END

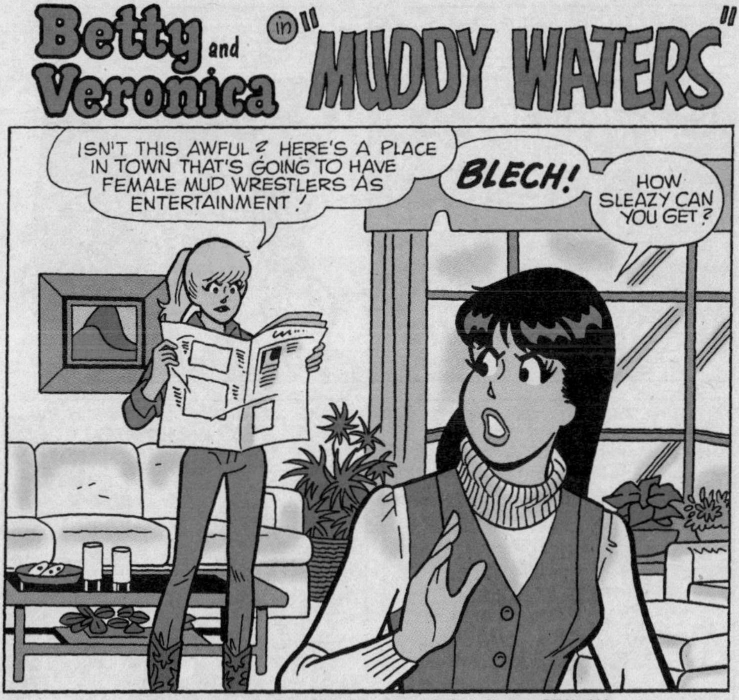

Betty and Veronica in "MUDDY WATERS"
ISN'T THIS AWFUL ? HERE'S A PLACE IN TOWN THAT'S GOING TO HAVE FEMALE MUD WRESTLERS AS ENTERTAINMENT !
BLECH!
HOW SLEAZY CAN YOU GET ?

Script: Frank Doyle / Pencils: Dan DeCarlo / Inks: Jimmy DeCarlo / Letters: Bill Yoshida

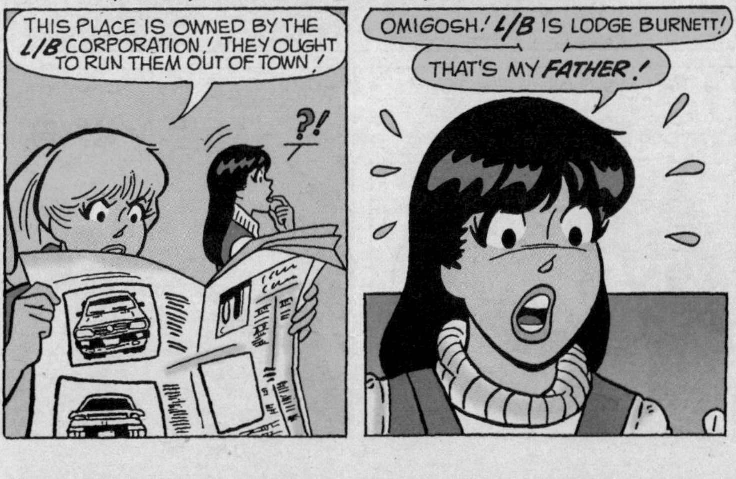

THIS PLACE IS OWNED BY THE L/B CORPORATION ! THEY OUGHT TO RUN THEM OUT OF TOWN !
?!
OMIGOSH ! L/B IS LODGE BURNETT !
THAT'S MY FATHER !
1

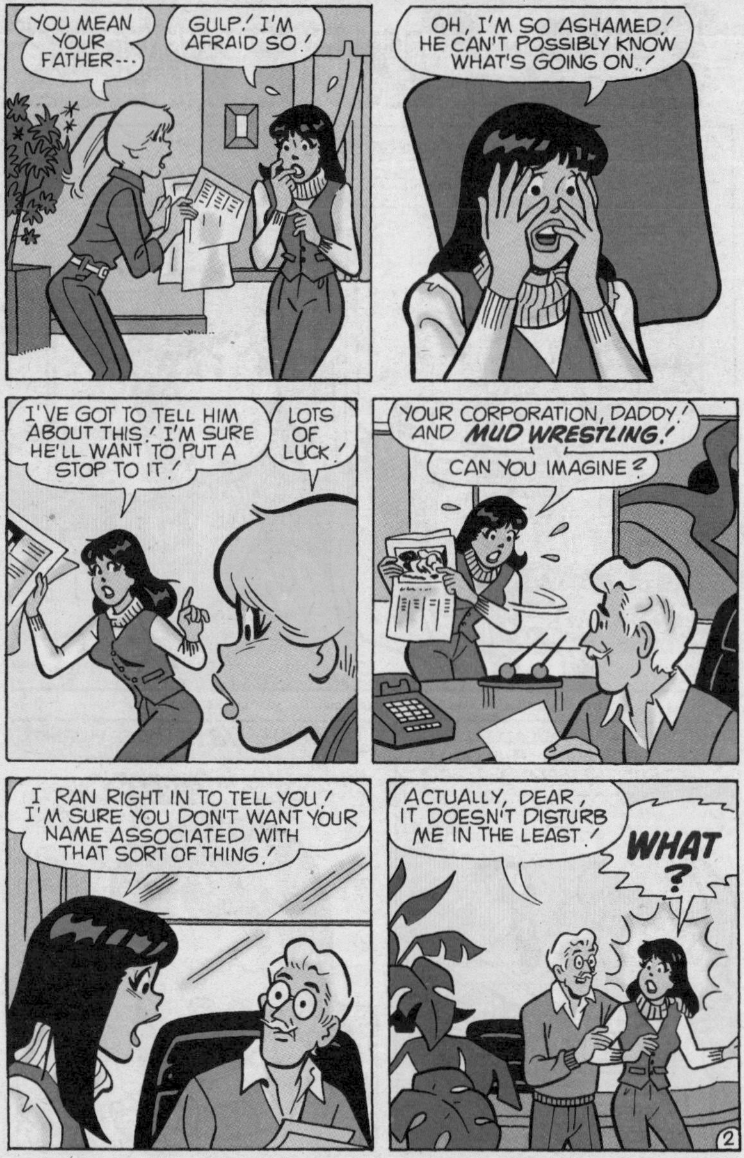
YOU MEAN YOUR FATHER---
GULP! I'M AFRAID SO!
OH, I'M SO ASHAMED! HE CAN'T POSSIBLY KNOW WHAT'S GOING ON..!
I'VE GOT TO TELL HIM ABOUT THIS! I'M SURE HE'LL WANT TO PUT A STOP TO IT!
LOTS OF LUCK!
YOUR CORPORATION, DADDY! AND MUD WRESTLING!
CAN YOU IMAGINE?
I RAN RIGHT IN TO TELL YOU! I'M SURE YOU DON'T WANT YOUR NAME ASSOCIATED WITH THAT SORT OF THING!
ACTUALLY, DEAR, IT DOESN'T DISTURB ME IN THE LEAST!
WHAT?
2

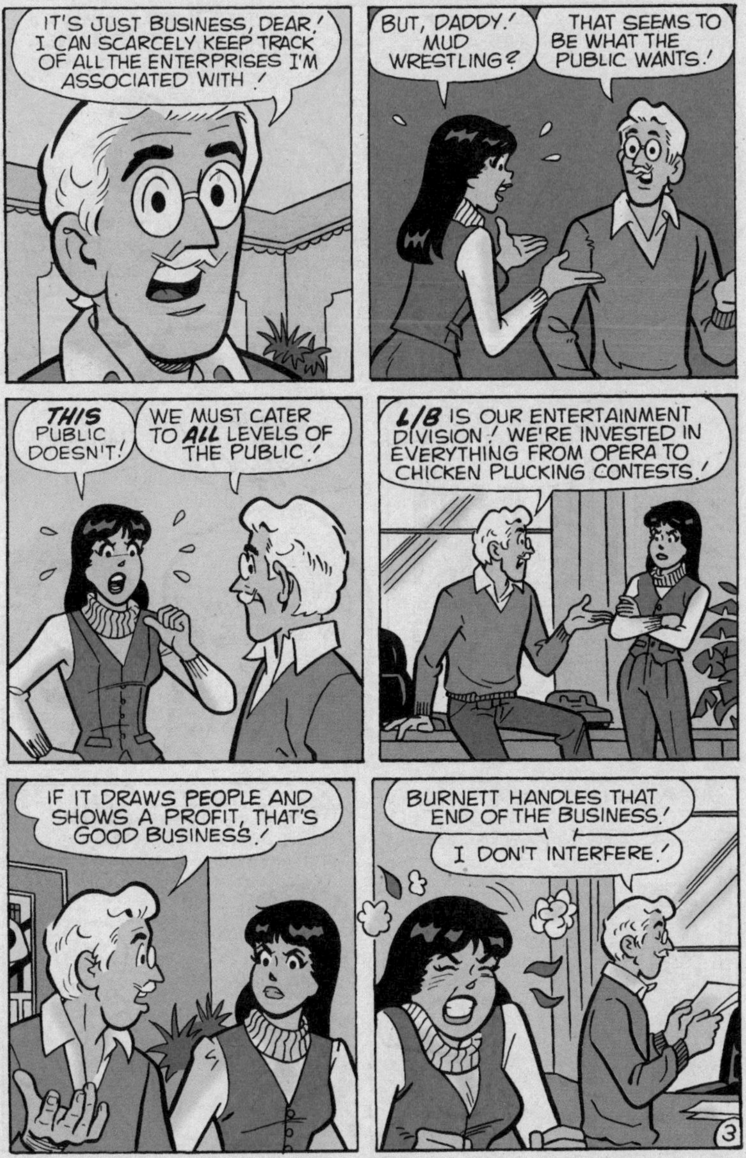

IT'S JUST BUSINESS, DEAR! I CAN SCARCELY KEEP TRACK OF ALL THE ENTERPRISES I'M ASSOCIATED WITH!
BUT, DADDY! MUD WRESTLING?
THAT SEEMS TO BE WHAT THE PUBLIC WANTS!
THIS PUBLIC DOESN'T!
WE MUST CATER TO ALL LEVELS OF THE PUBLIC!
L/B IS OUR ENTERTAINMENT DIVISION! WE'RE INVESTED IN EVERYTHING FROM OPERA TO CHICKEN PLUCKING CONTESTS!
IF IT DRAWS PEOPLE AND SHOWS A PROFIT, THAT'S GOOD BUSINESS!
BURNETT HANDLES THAT END OF THE BUSINESS!
I DON'T INTERFERE!
3

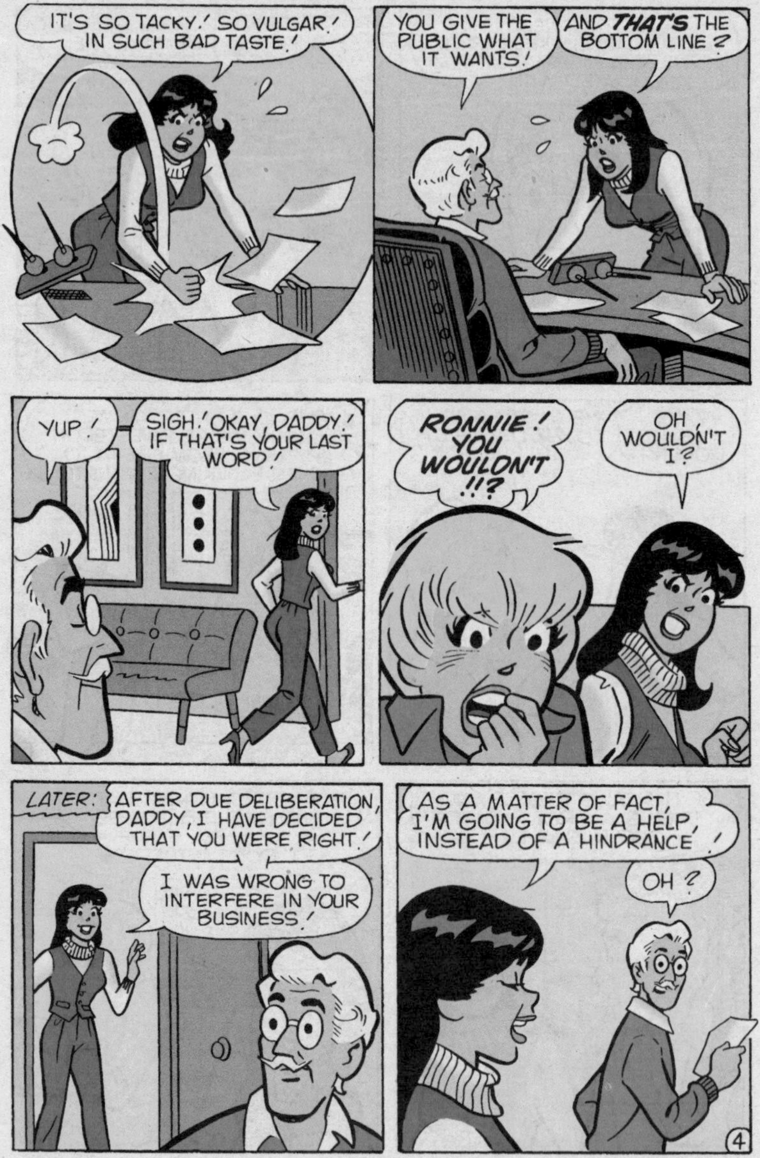
IT'S SO TACKY! SO VULGAR! IN SUCH BAD TASTE!
YOU GIVE THE PUBLIC WHAT IT WANTS!
AND THAT'S THE BOTTOM LINE?
YUP!
SIGH! OKAY, DADDY! IF THAT'S YOUR LAST WORD!
RONNIE! YOU WOULDN'T !!?
OH, WOULDN'T I?
LATER:
AFTER DUE DELIBERATION, DADDY, I HAVE DECIDED THAT YOU WERE RIGHT!
I WAS WRONG TO INTERFERE IN YOUR BUSINESS!
AS A MATTER OF FACT, I'M GOING TO BE A HELP, INSTEAD OF A HINDRANCE!
OH?
4

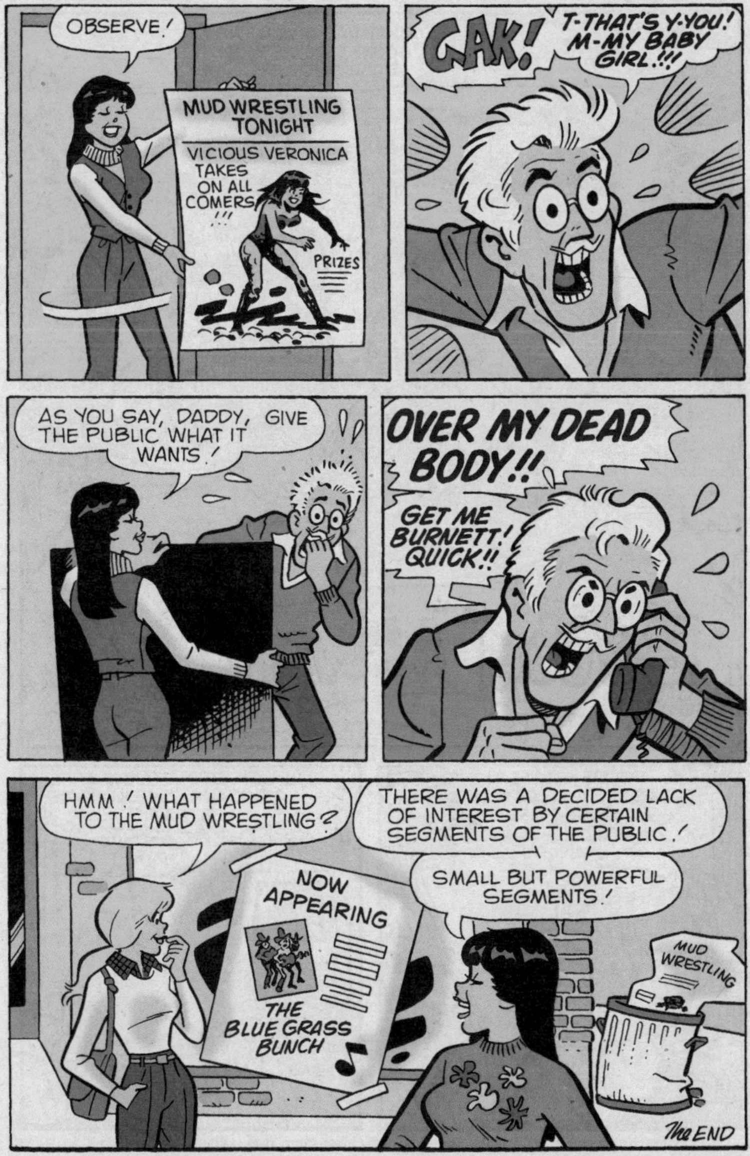
OBSERVE!
MUD WRESTLING TONIGHT
VICIOUS VERONICA TAKES ON ALL COMERS !!!
PRIZES
GAK!
T-THAT'S Y-YOU! M-MY BABY GIRL!!!
AS YOU SAY, DADDY, GIVE THE PUBLIC WHAT IT WANTS!
OVER MY DEAD BODY!!
GET ME BURNETT! QUICK!!
HMM! WHAT HAPPENED TO THE MUD WRESTLING?
THERE WAS A DECIDED LACK OF INTEREST BY CERTAIN SEGMENTS OF THE PUBLIC!
SMALL BUT POWERFUL SEGMENTS!
NOW APPEARING
THE BLUE GRASS BUNCH
MUD WRESTLING
The END

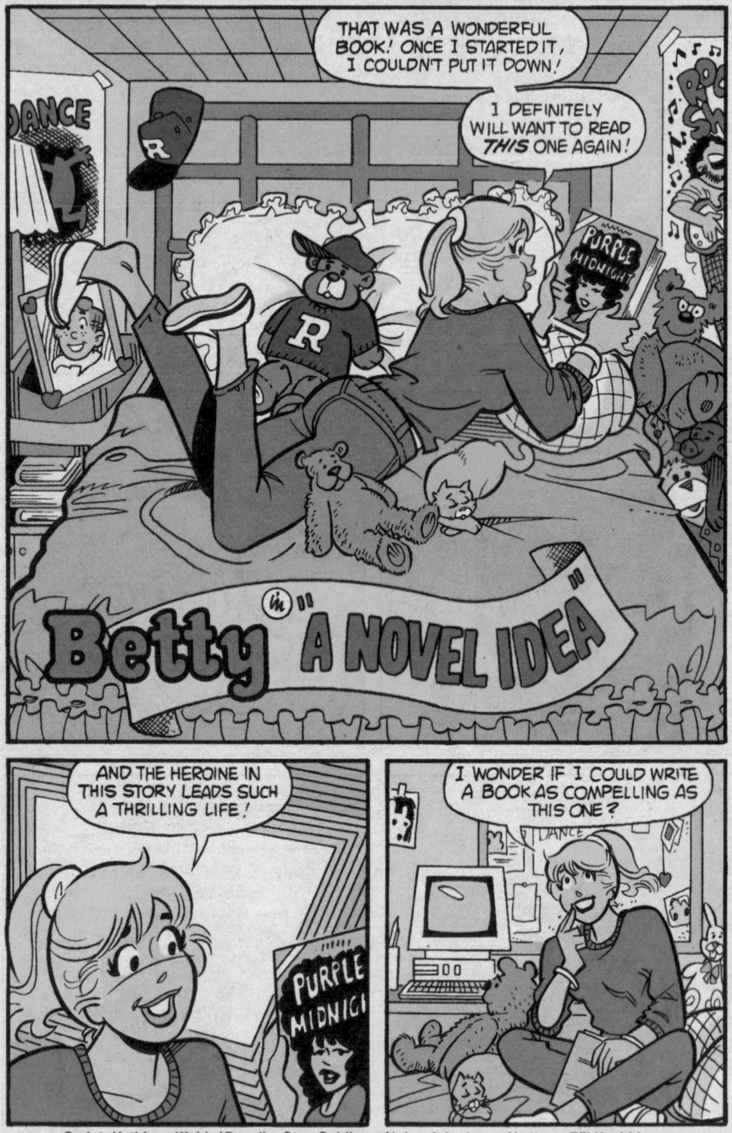
THAT WAS A WONDERFUL BOOK! ONCE I STARTED IT, I COULDN'T PUT IT DOWN!
I DEFINITELY WILL WANT TO READ *THIS* ONE AGAIN!
DANCE
PURPLE MIDNIGHT
Betty in "A NOVEL IDEA"
AND THE HEROINE IN THIS STORY LEADS SUCH A THRILLING LIFE!
I WONDER IF I COULD WRITE A BOOK AS COMPELLING AS THIS ONE?

Script: Kathleen Webb / Pencils: Stan Goldberg / Inks: John Lowe / Letters: Bill Yoshida

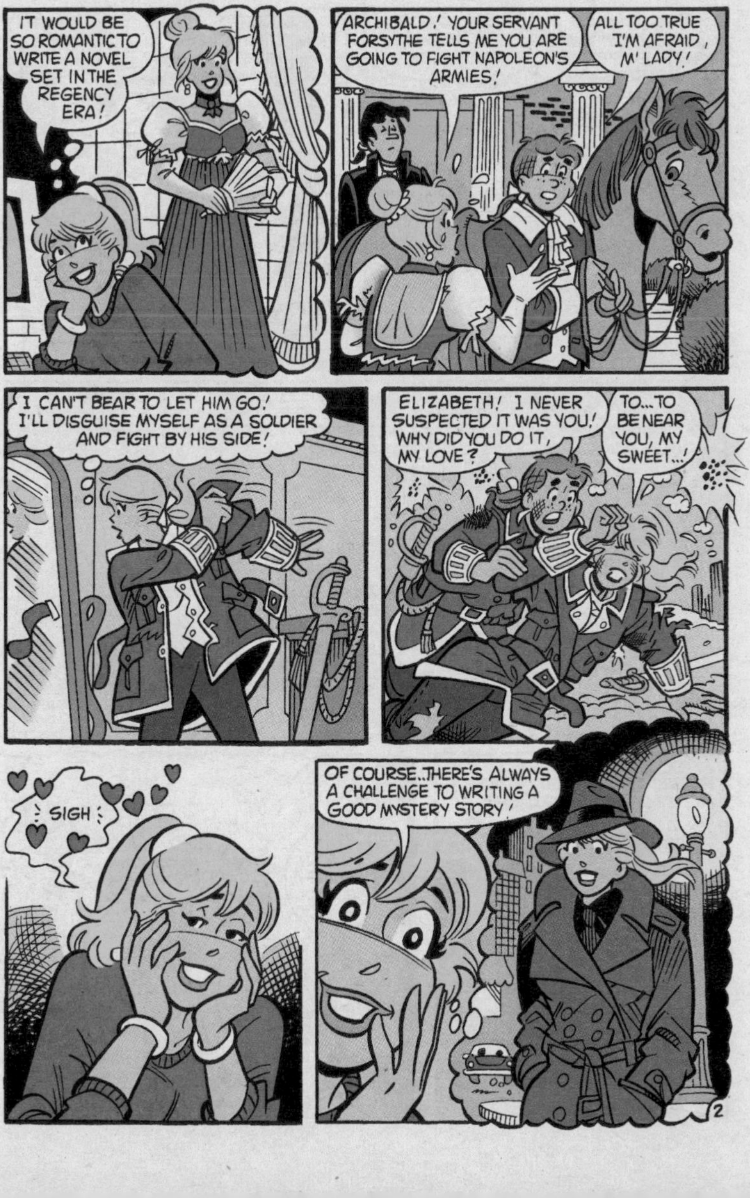

IT WOULD BE SO ROMANTIC TO WRITE A NOVEL SET IN THE REGENCY ERA!
ARCHIBALD! YOUR SERVANT FORSYTHE TELLS ME YOU ARE GOING TO FIGHT NAPOLEON'S ARMIES!
ALL TOO TRUE I'M AFRAID, M' LADY!
I CAN'T BEAR TO LET HIM GO! I'LL DISGUISE MYSELF AS A SOLDIER AND FIGHT BY HIS SIDE!
ELIZABETH! I NEVER SUSPECTED IT WAS YOU! WHY DID YOU DO IT, MY LOVE?
TO...TO BE NEAR YOU, MY SWEET...!
SIGH
OF COURSE..THERE'S ALWAYS A CHALLENGE TO WRITING A GOOD MYSTERY STORY!
2

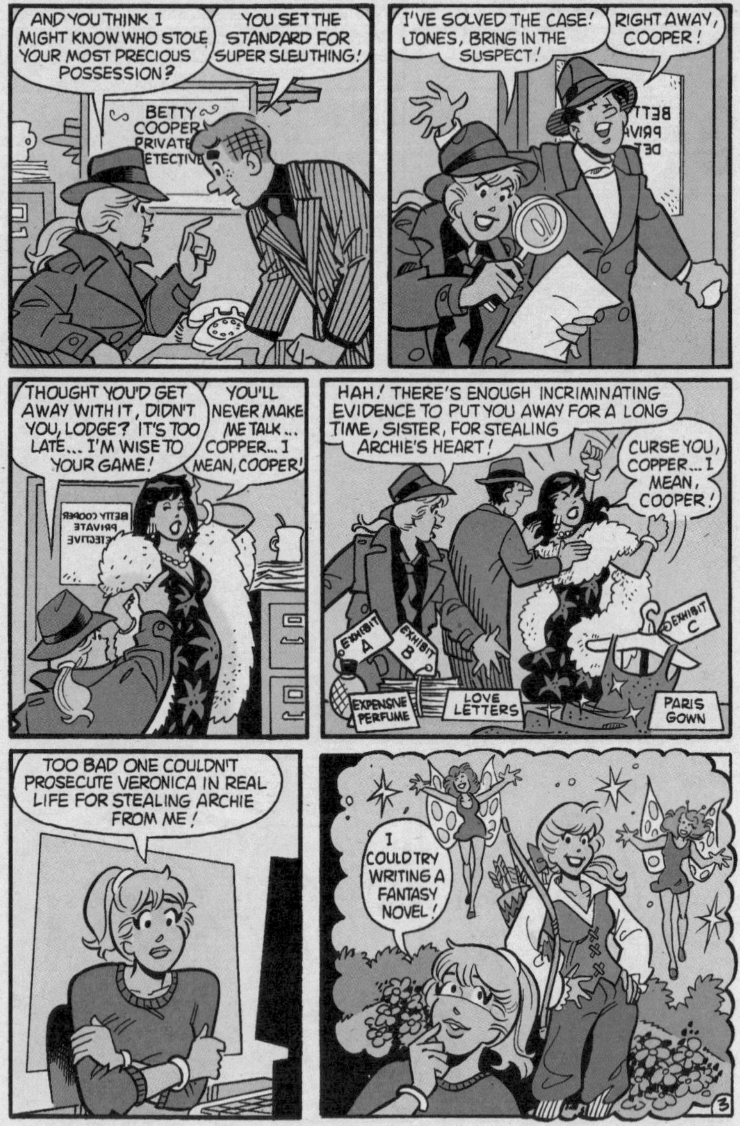
AND YOU THINK I MIGHT KNOW WHO STOLE YOUR MOST PRECIOUS POSSESSION?
YOU SET THE STANDARD FOR SUPER SLEUTHING!
BETTY COOPER PRIVATE DETECTIVE
I'VE SOLVED THE CASE! JONES, BRING IN THE SUSPECT!
RIGHT AWAY, COOPER!
THOUGHT YOU'D GET AWAY WITH IT, DIDN'T YOU, LODGE? IT'S TOO LATE... I'M WISE TO YOUR GAME!
YOU'LL NEVER MAKE ME TALK... COPPER... I MEAN, COOPER!
HAH! THERE'S ENOUGH INCRIMINATING EVIDENCE TO PUT YOU AWAY FOR A LONG TIME, SISTER, FOR STEALING ARCHIE'S HEART!
CURSE YOU, COPPER... I MEAN, COOPER!
EXHIBIT A
EXHIBIT B
EXHIBIT C
EXPENSIVE PERFUME
LOVE LETTERS
PARIS GOWN
TOO BAD ONE COULDN'T PROSECUTE VERONICA IN REAL LIFE FOR STEALING ARCHIE FROM ME!
I COULD TRY WRITING A FANTASY NOVEL!
3

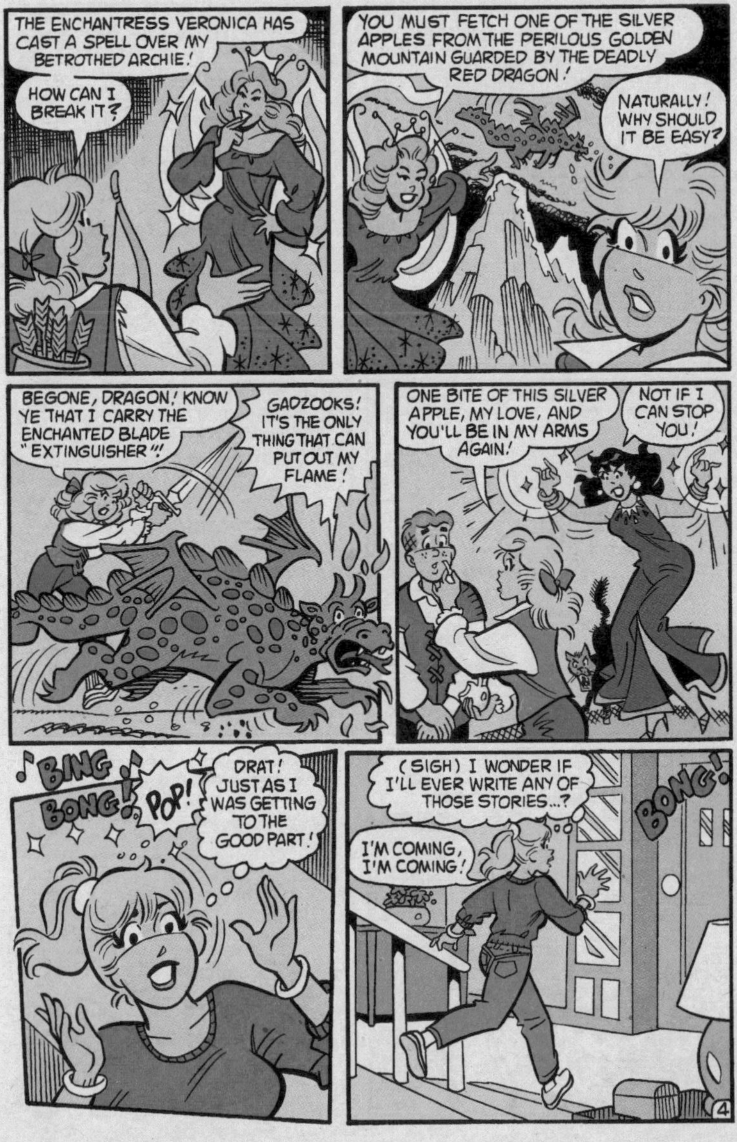
THE ENCHANTRESS VERONICA HAS CAST A SPELL OVER MY BETROTHED ARCHIE!
HOW CAN I BREAK IT?
YOU MUST FETCH ONE OF THE SILVER APPLES FROM THE PERILOUS GOLDEN MOUNTAIN GUARDED BY THE DEADLY RED DRAGON!
NATURALLY! WHY SHOULD IT BE EASY?
BEGONE, DRAGON! KNOW YE THAT I CARRY THE ENCHANTED BLADE "EXTINGUISHER"!
GADZOOKS! IT'S THE ONLY THING THAT CAN PUT OUT MY FLAME!
ONE BITE OF THIS SILVER APPLE, MY LOVE, AND YOU'LL BE IN MY ARMS AGAIN!
NOT IF I CAN STOP YOU!
BING BONG!
POP!
DRAT! JUST AS I WAS GETTING TO THE GOOD PART!
(SIGH) I WONDER IF I'LL EVER WRITE ANY OF THOSE STORIES...?
BONG!
I'M COMING, I'M COMING!
4

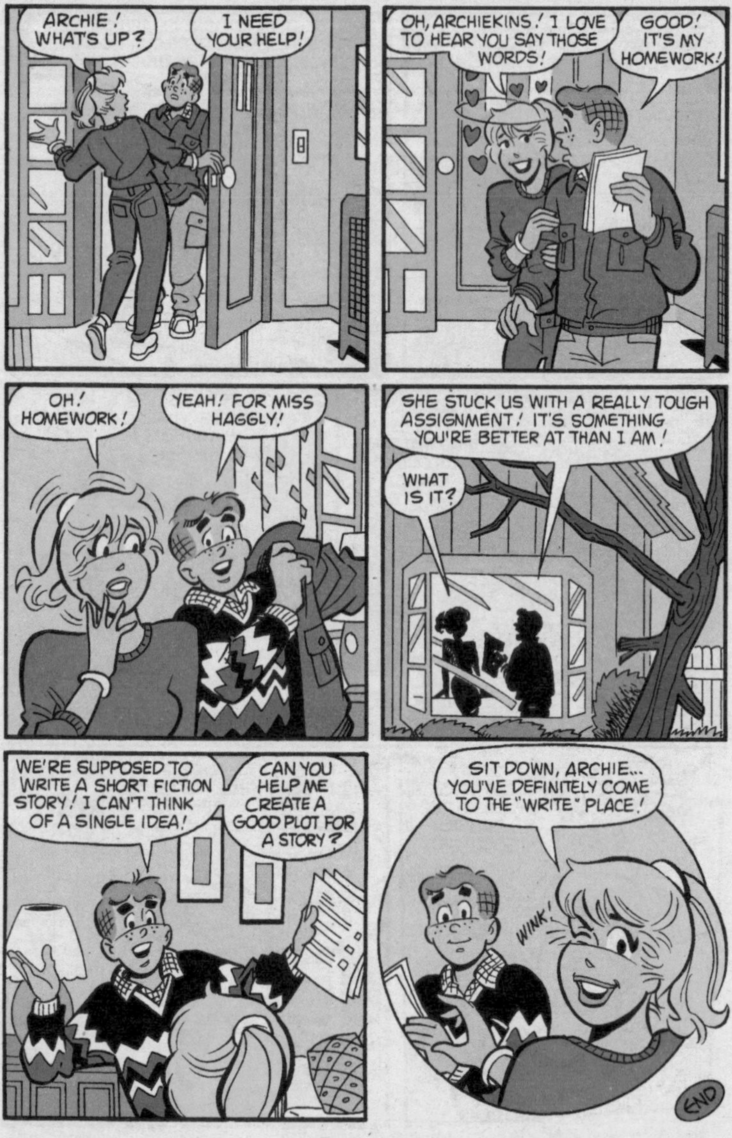
ARCHIE! WHAT'S UP?
I NEED YOUR HELP!
OH, ARCHIEKINS! I LOVE TO HEAR YOU SAY THOSE WORDS!
GOOD! IT'S MY HOMEWORK!
OH! HOMEWORK!
YEAH! FOR MISS HAGGLY!
SHE STUCK US WITH A REALLY TOUGH ASSIGNMENT! IT'S SOMETHING YOU'RE BETTER AT THAN I AM!
WHAT IS IT?
WE'RE SUPPOSED TO WRITE A SHORT FICTION STORY! I CAN'T THINK OF A SINGLE IDEA!
CAN YOU HELP ME CREATE A GOOD PLOT FOR A STORY?
SIT DOWN, ARCHIE... YOU'VE DEFINITELY COME TO THE "WRITE" PLACE!
WINK!
END

Veronica in "With Kid Gloves"

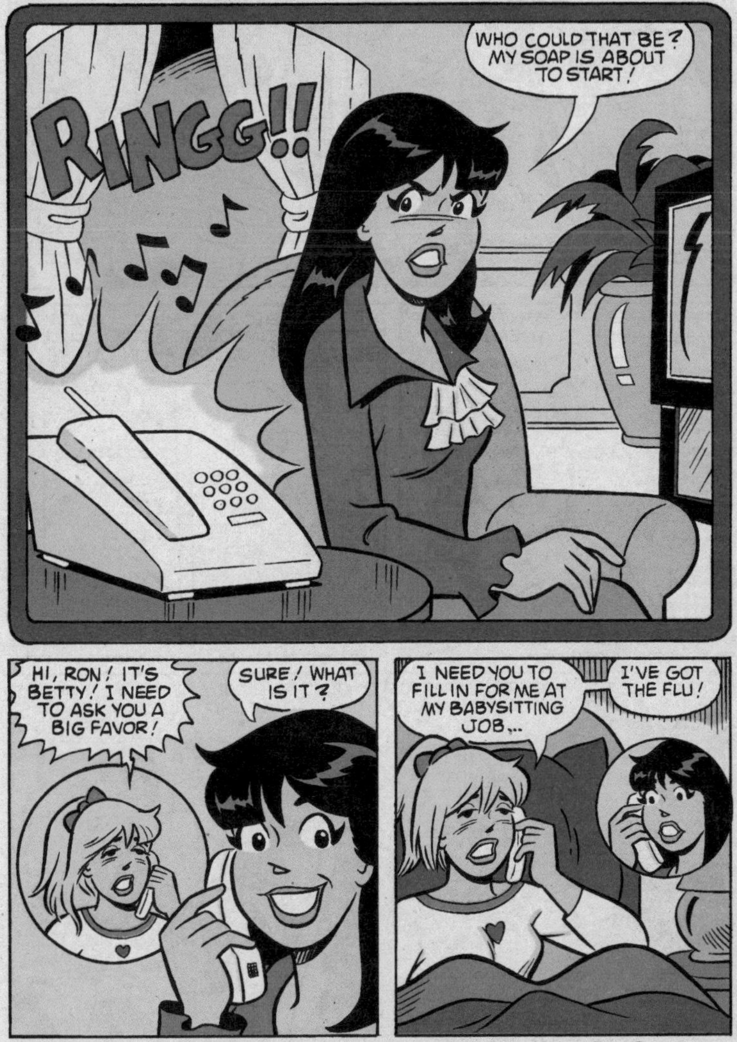
RINGG!!
WHO COULD THAT BE? MY SOAP IS ABOUT TO START!
HI, RON! IT'S BETTY! I NEED TO ASK YOU A BIG FAVOR!
SURE! WHAT IS IT?
I NEED YOU TO FILL IN FOR ME AT MY BABYSITTING JOB...
I'VE GOT THE FLU!

Script & Pencils: Dan Parent / Inks: Jon D'Agostino / Letters: Bill Yoshida / Colors: Barry Grossman

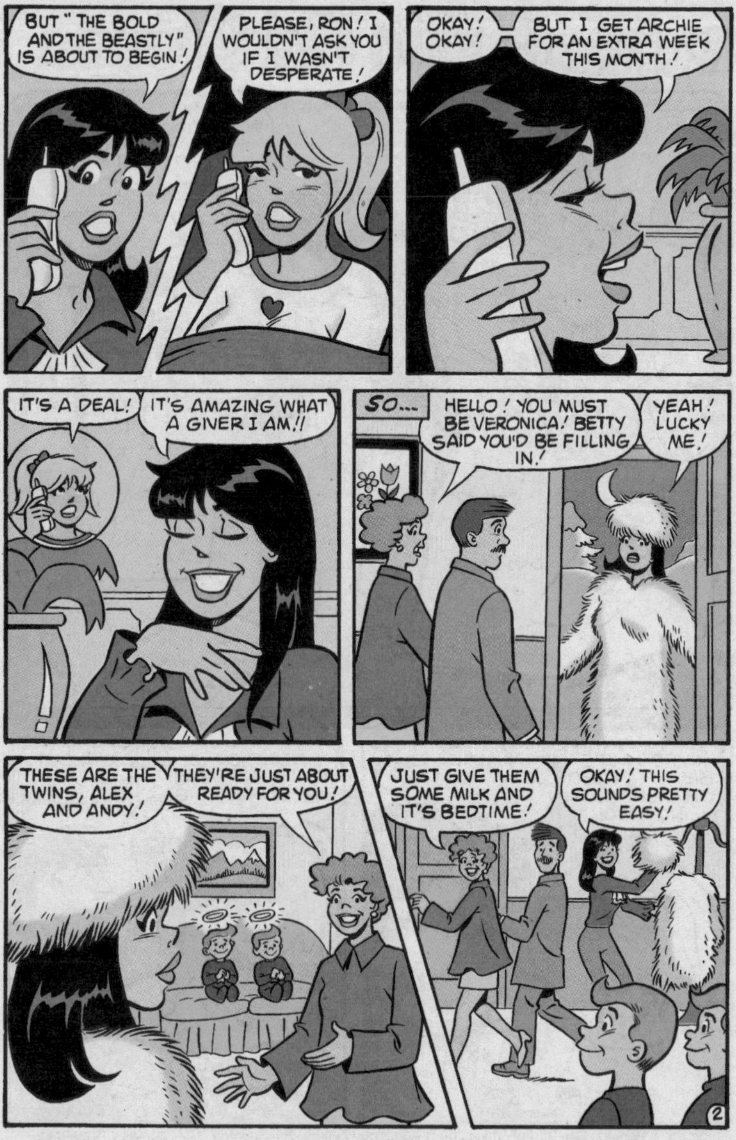
BUT "THE BOLD AND THE BEASTLY" IS ABOUT TO BEGIN!
PLEASE, RON! I WOULDN'T ASK YOU IF I WASN'T DESPERATE!
OKAY! OKAY!
BUT I GET ARCHIE FOR AN EXTRA WEEK THIS MONTH!
IT'S A DEAL!
IT'S AMAZING WHAT A GIVER I AM!!
SO...
HELLO! YOU MUST BE VERONICA! BETTY SAID YOU'D BE FILLING IN!
YEAH! LUCKY ME!
THESE ARE THE TWINS, ALEX AND ANDY!
THEY'RE JUST ABOUT READY FOR YOU!
JUST GIVE THEM SOME MILK AND IT'S BEDTIME!
OKAY! THIS SOUNDS PRETTY EASY!
2

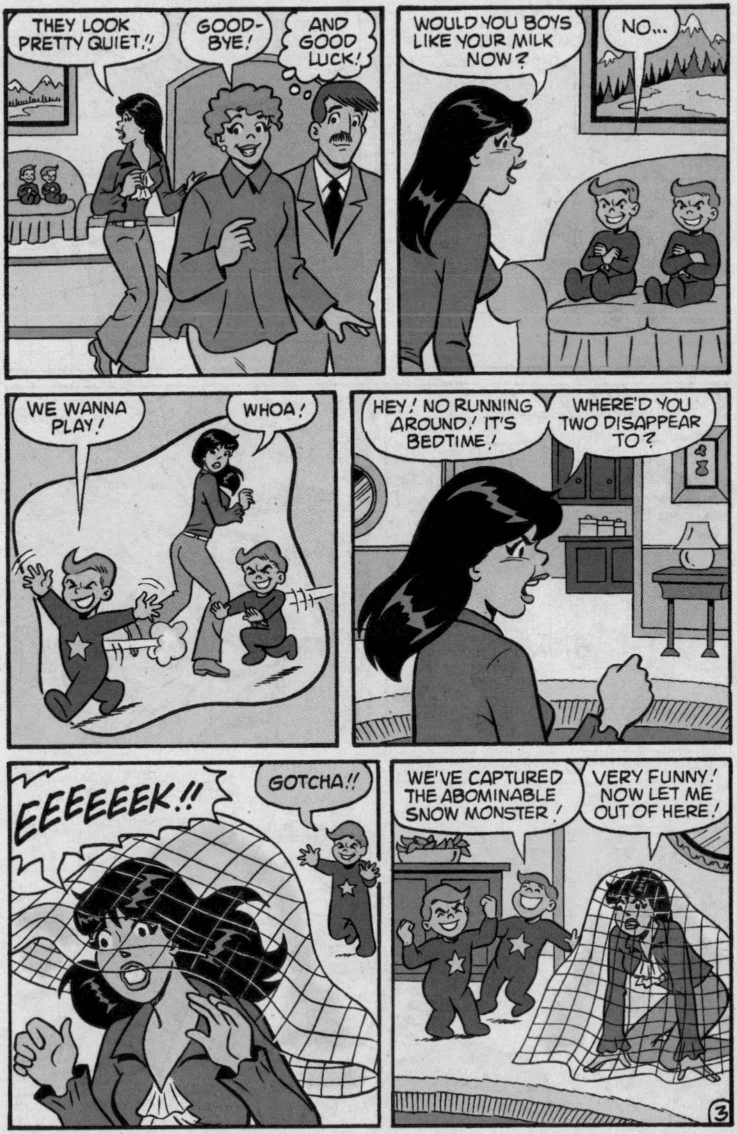
THEY LOOK PRETTY QUIET!!
GOOD-BYE!
AND GOOD LUCK!
WOULD YOU BOYS LIKE YOUR MILK NOW?
NO...
WE WANNA PLAY!
WHOA!
HEY! NO RUNNING AROUND! IT'S BEDTIME!
WHERE'D YOU TWO DISAPPEAR TO?
EEEEEEK!!
GOTCHA!!
WE'VE CAPTURED THE ABOMINABLE SNOW MONSTER!
VERY FUNNY! NOW LET ME OUT OF HERE!
3

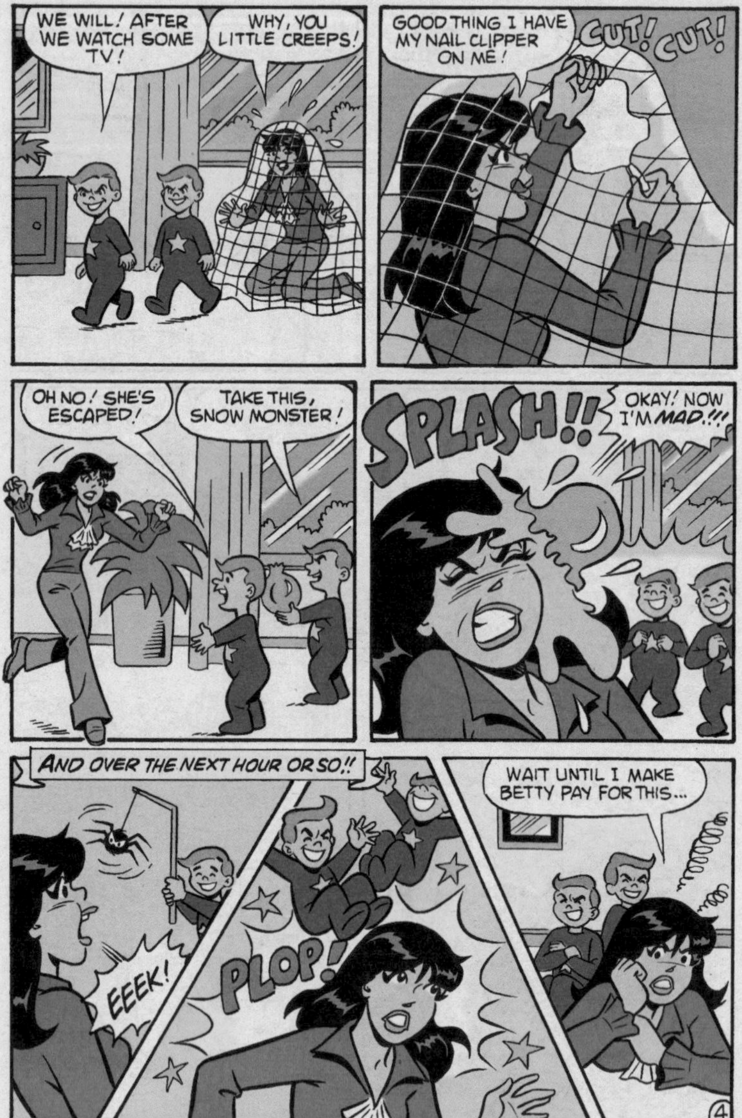
WE WILL! AFTER WE WATCH SOME TV!
WHY, YOU LITTLE CREEPS!
GOOD THING I HAVE MY NAIL CLIPPER ON ME!
CUT! CUT!
OH NO! SHE'S ESCAPED!
TAKE THIS, SNOW MONSTER!
SPLASH!!
OKAY! NOW I'M MAD!!!
AND OVER THE NEXT HOUR OR SO!!
EEEK!
PLOP!
WAIT UNTIL I MAKE BETTY PAY FOR THIS...
4

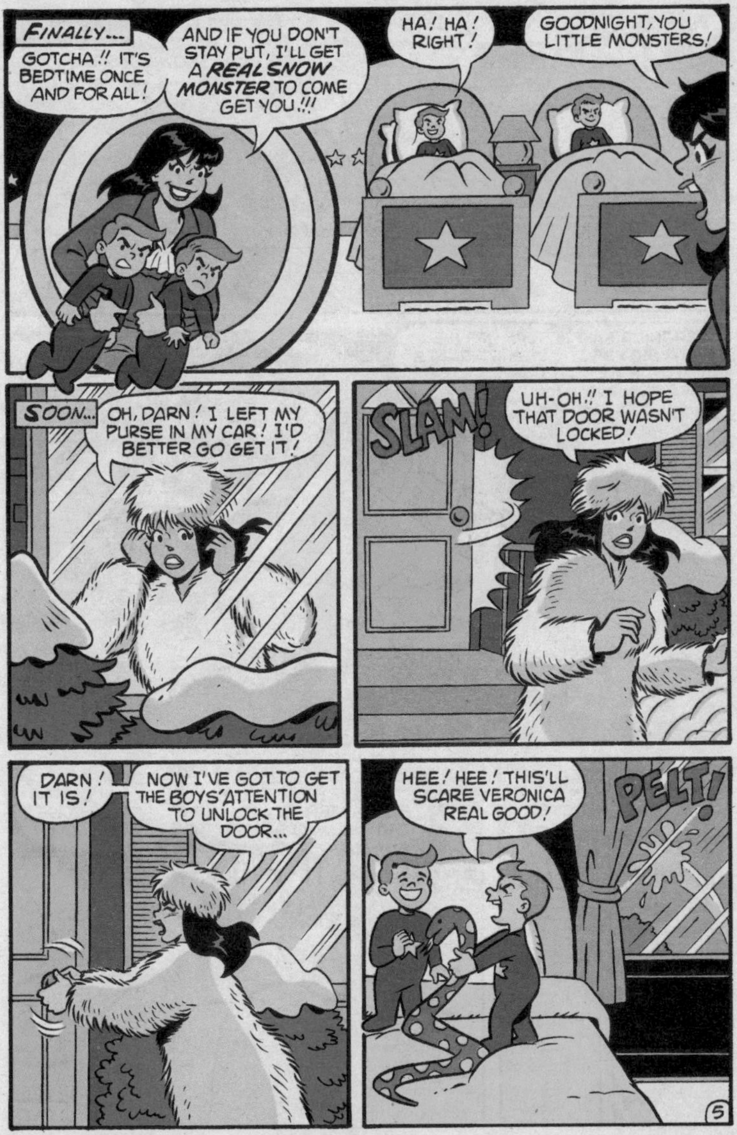
FINALLY...
GOTCHA!! IT'S BEDTIME ONCE AND FOR ALL!
AND IF YOU DON'T STAY PUT, I'LL GET A REAL SNOW MONSTER TO COME GET YOU!!!
HA! HA! RIGHT!
GOODNIGHT, YOU LITTLE MONSTERS!
SOON...
OH, DARN! I LEFT MY PURSE IN MY CAR! I'D BETTER GO GET IT!
SLAM!
UH-OH!! I HOPE THAT DOOR WASN'T LOCKED!
DARN! IT IS!
NOW I'VE GOT TO GET THE BOYS' ATTENTION TO UNLOCK THE DOOR...
HEE! HEE! THIS'LL SCARE VERONICA REAL GOOD!
PELT!
5

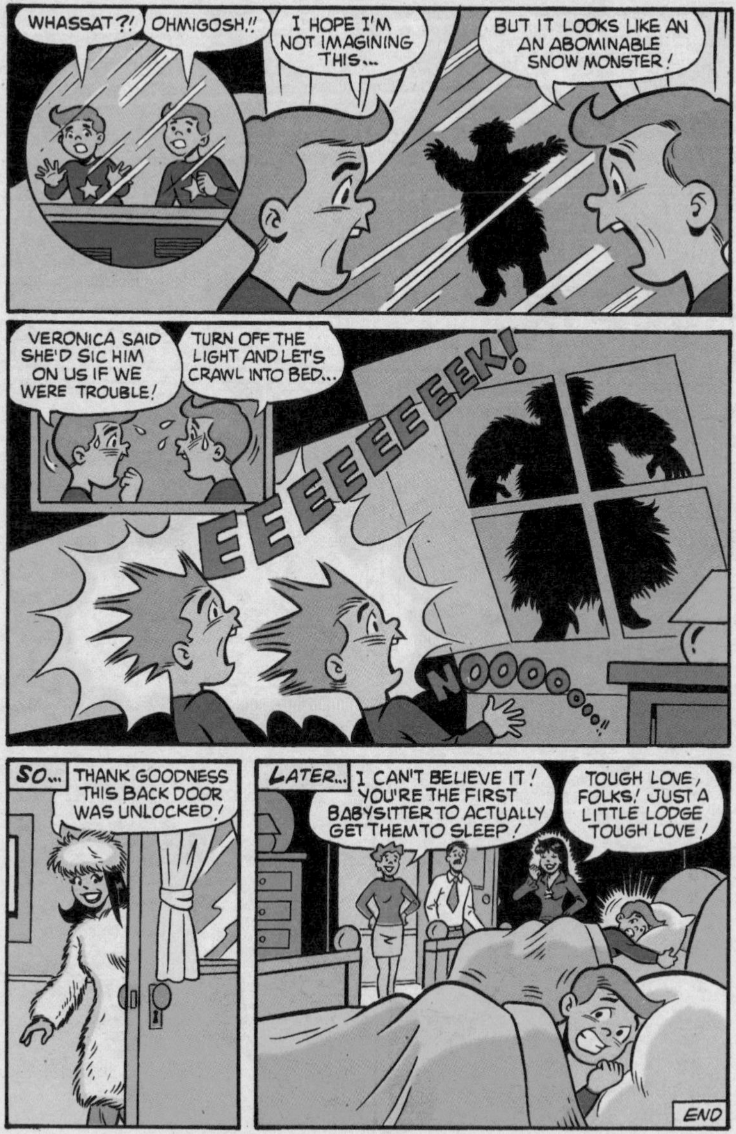
WHASSAT?!
OHMIGOSH!!
I HOPE I'M NOT IMAGINING THIS...
BUT IT LOOKS LIKE AN AN ABOMINABLE SNOW MONSTER!
VERONICA SAID SHE'D SIC HIM ON US IF WE WERE TROUBLE!
TURN OFF THE LIGHT AND LET'S CRAWL INTO BED...
EEEEEEEEEK!
NOOOOOOOO!!
SO...
THANK GOODNESS THIS BACK DOOR WAS UNLOCKED!
LATER...
I CAN'T BELIEVE IT! YOU'RE THE FIRST BABYSITTER TO ACTUALLY GET THEM TO SLEEP!
TOUGH LOVE, FOLKS! JUST A LITTLE LODGE TOUGH LOVE!
END

Archie in "BIG MOUTH"

Malmgren / D'Agostino / Yoshida

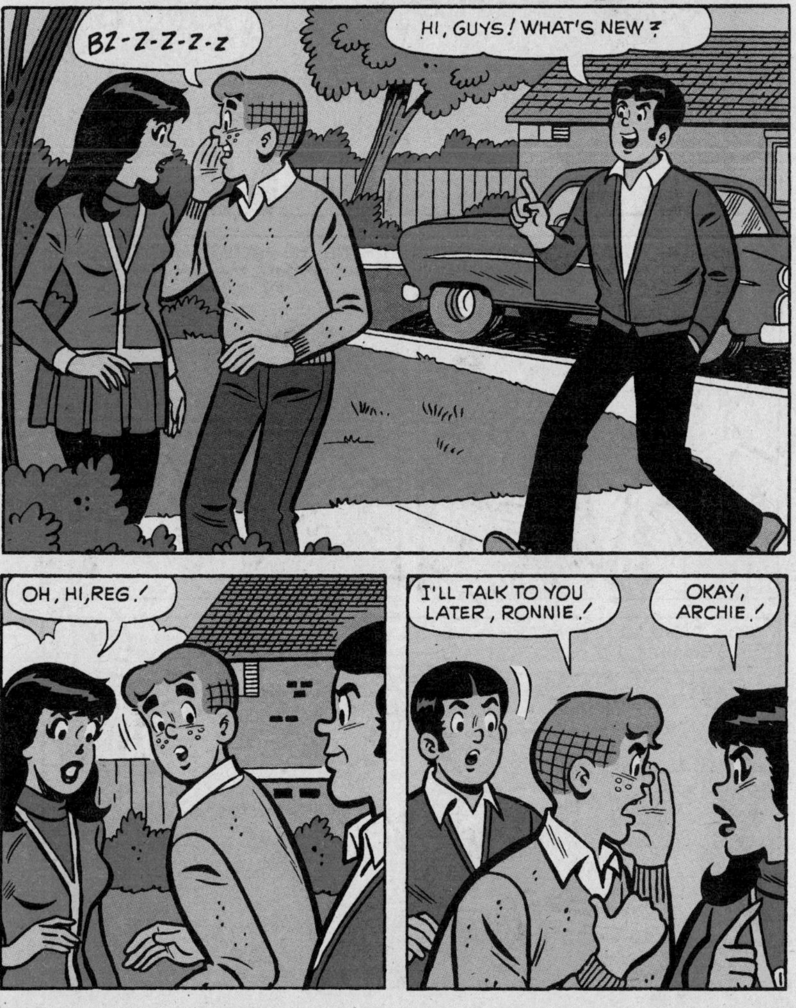
BZ-Z-Z-Z-z
HI, GUYS! WHAT'S NEW?
OH, HI, REG.!
I'LL TALK TO YOU LATER, RONNIE.!
OKAY, ARCHIE.!

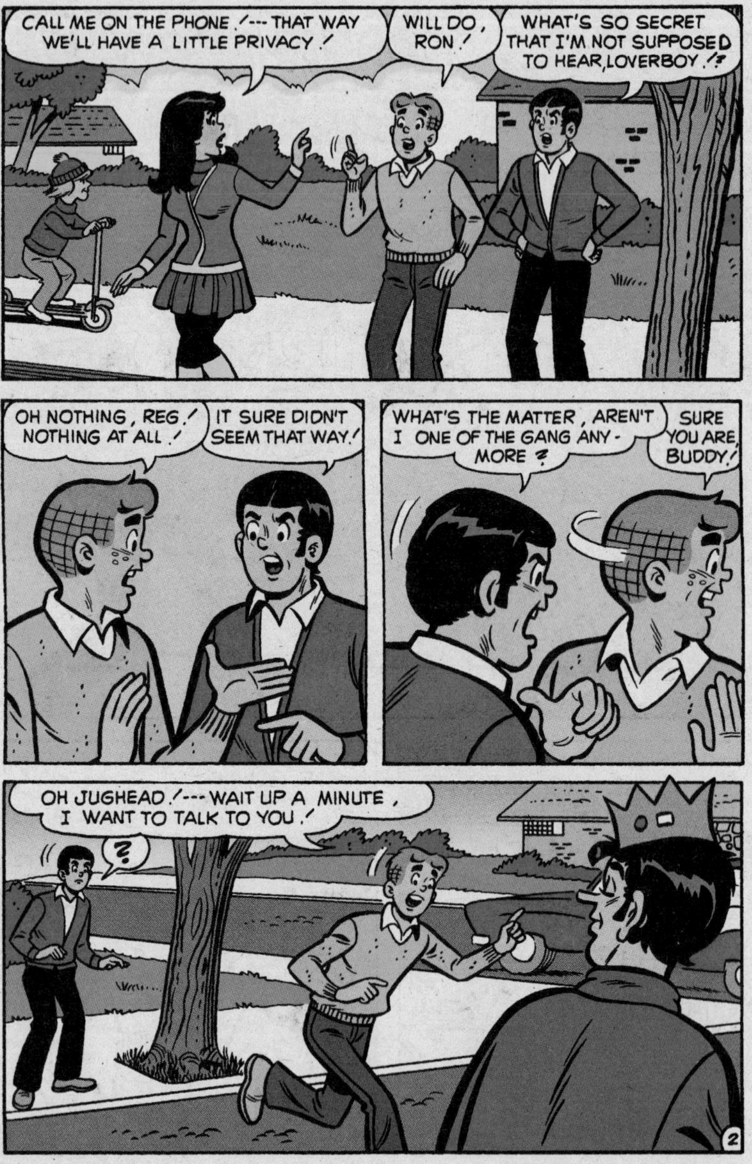
CALL ME ON THE PHONE !--- THAT WAY WE'LL HAVE A LITTLE PRIVACY !
WILL DO, RON !
WHAT'S SO SECRET THAT I'M NOT SUPPOSED TO HEAR, LOVERBOY !?
OH NOTHING, REG ! NOTHING AT ALL !
IT SURE DIDN'T SEEM THAT WAY !
WHAT'S THE MATTER, AREN'T I ONE OF THE GANG ANY-MORE ?
SURE YOU ARE, BUDDY !
OH JUGHEAD !--- WAIT UP A MINUTE, I WANT TO TALK TO YOU !
?
2

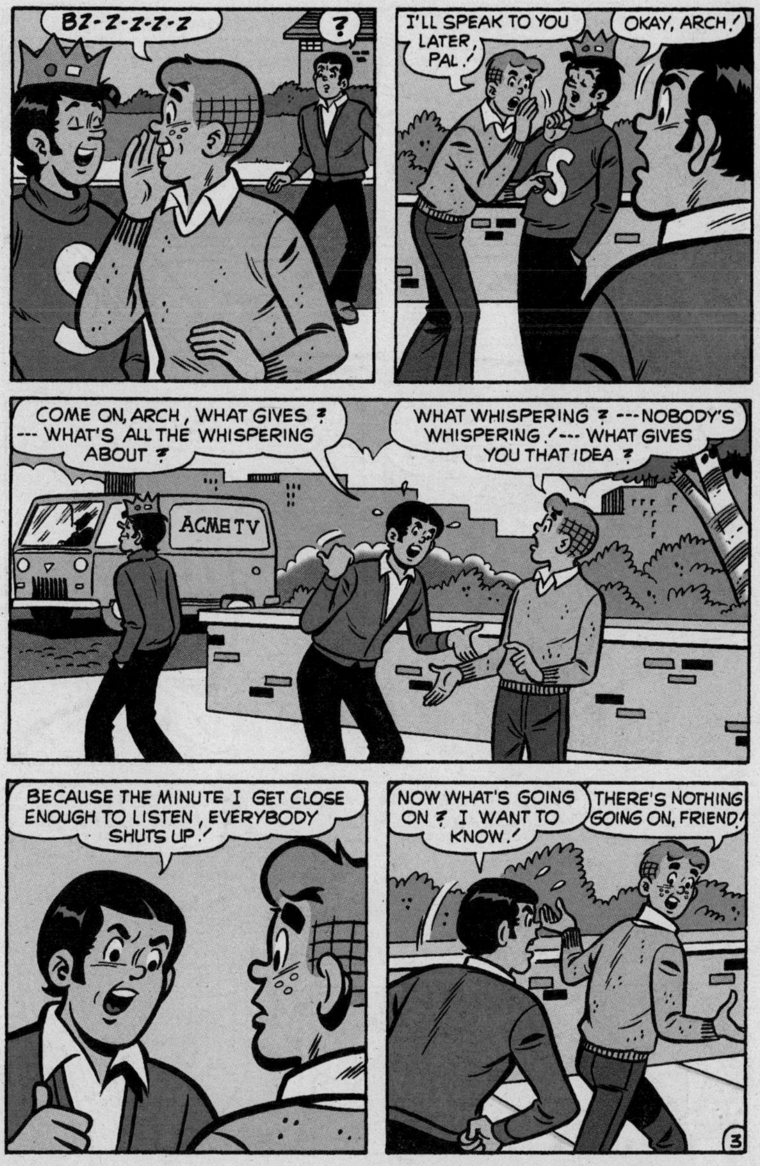
BZ-Z-Z-Z-Z
?
I'LL SPEAK TO YOU LATER, PAL!
OKAY, ARCH!
COME ON, ARCH, WHAT GIVES? --- WHAT'S ALL THE WHISPERING ABOUT?
WHAT WHISPERING? ---NOBODY'S WHISPERING! --- WHAT GIVES YOU THAT IDEA?
ACME TV
BECAUSE THE MINUTE I GET CLOSE ENOUGH TO LISTEN, EVERYBODY SHUTS UP!
NOW WHAT'S GOING ON? I WANT TO KNOW!
THERE'S NOTHING GOING ON, FRIEND!
3

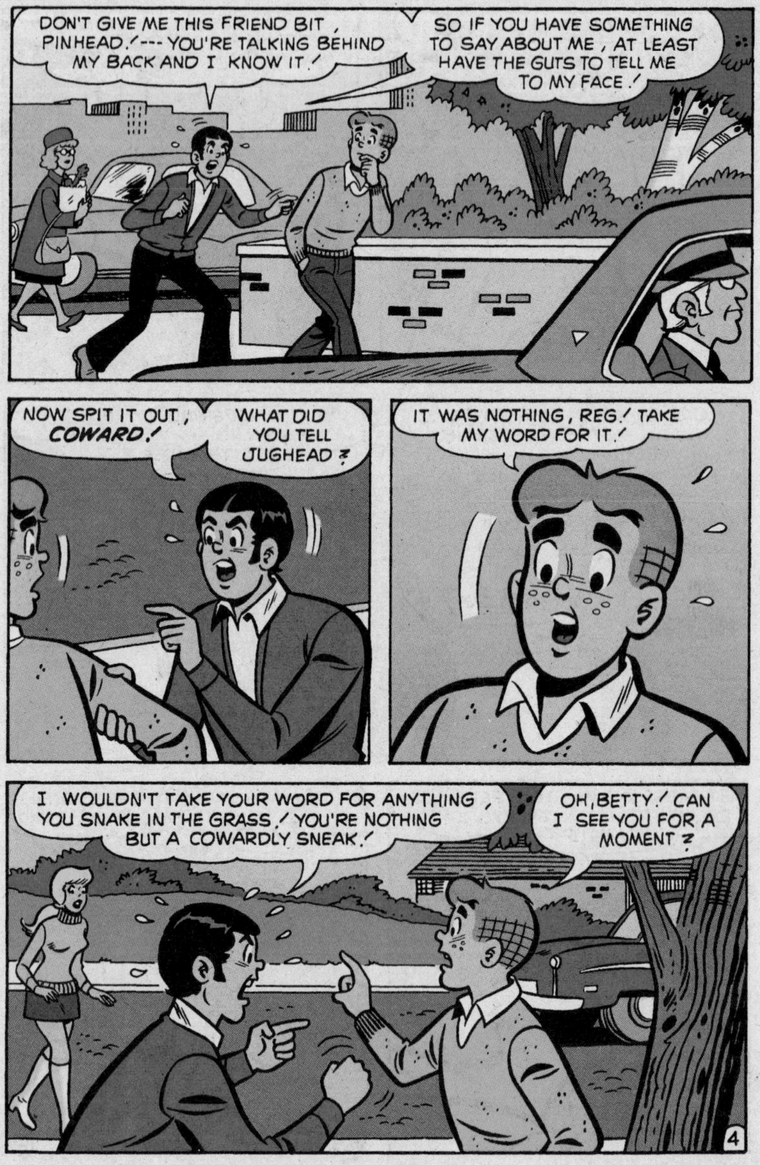
DON'T GIVE ME THIS FRIEND BIT, PINHEAD.! --- YOU'RE TALKING BEHIND MY BACK AND I KNOW IT!
SO IF YOU HAVE SOMETHING TO SAY ABOUT ME, AT LEAST HAVE THE GUTS TO TELL ME TO MY FACE!
NOW SPIT IT OUT, COWARD!
WHAT DID YOU TELL JUGHEAD?
IT WAS NOTHING, REG! TAKE MY WORD FOR IT!
I WOULDN'T TAKE YOUR WORD FOR ANYTHING, YOU SNAKE IN THE GRASS! YOU'RE NOTHING BUT A COWARDLY SNEAK!
OH, BETTY! CAN I SEE YOU FOR A MOMENT?
4

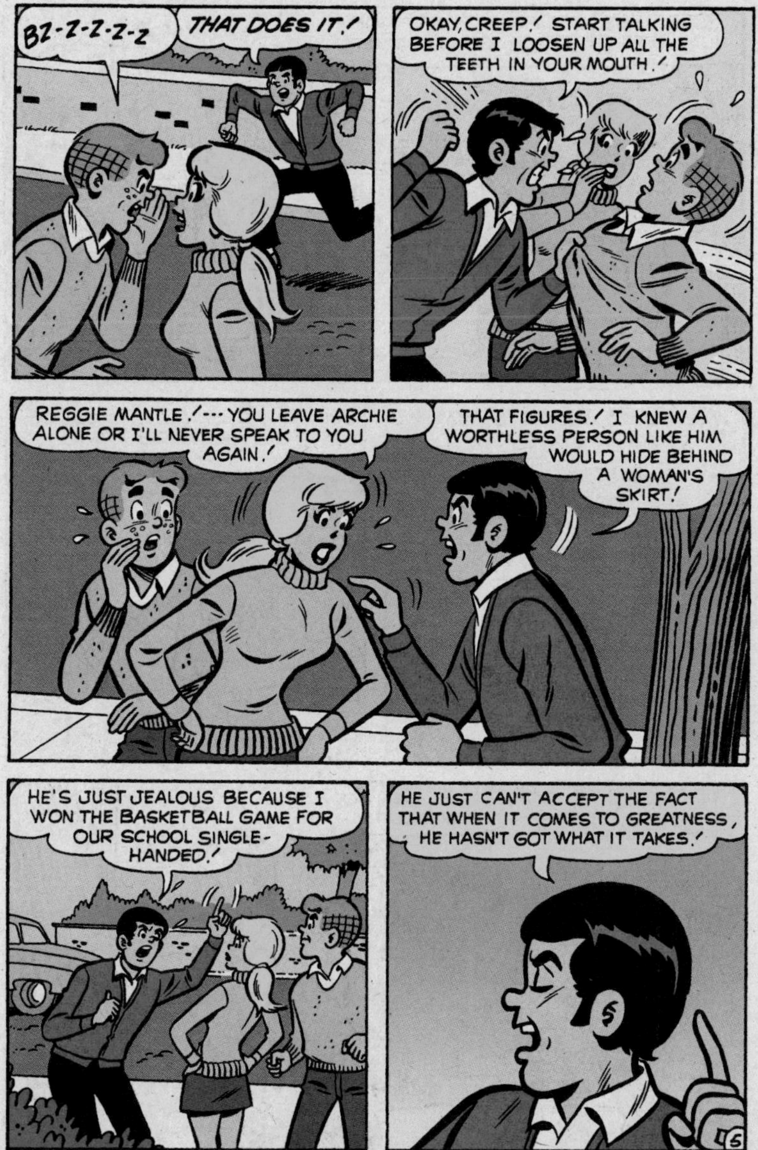
BZ-Z-Z-Z-Z
THAT DOES IT!
OKAY, CREEP! START TALKING BEFORE I LOOSEN UP ALL THE TEETH IN YOUR MOUTH!
REGGIE MANTLE!--- YOU LEAVE ARCHIE ALONE OR I'LL NEVER SPEAK TO YOU AGAIN!
THAT FIGURES! I KNEW A WORTHLESS PERSON LIKE HIM WOULD HIDE BEHIND A WOMAN'S SKIRT!
HE'S JUST JEALOUS BECAUSE I WON THE BASKETBALL GAME FOR OUR SCHOOL SINGLE-HANDED!
HE JUST CAN'T ACCEPT THE FACT THAT WHEN IT COMES TO GREATNESS, HE HASN'T GOT WHAT IT TAKES!
5

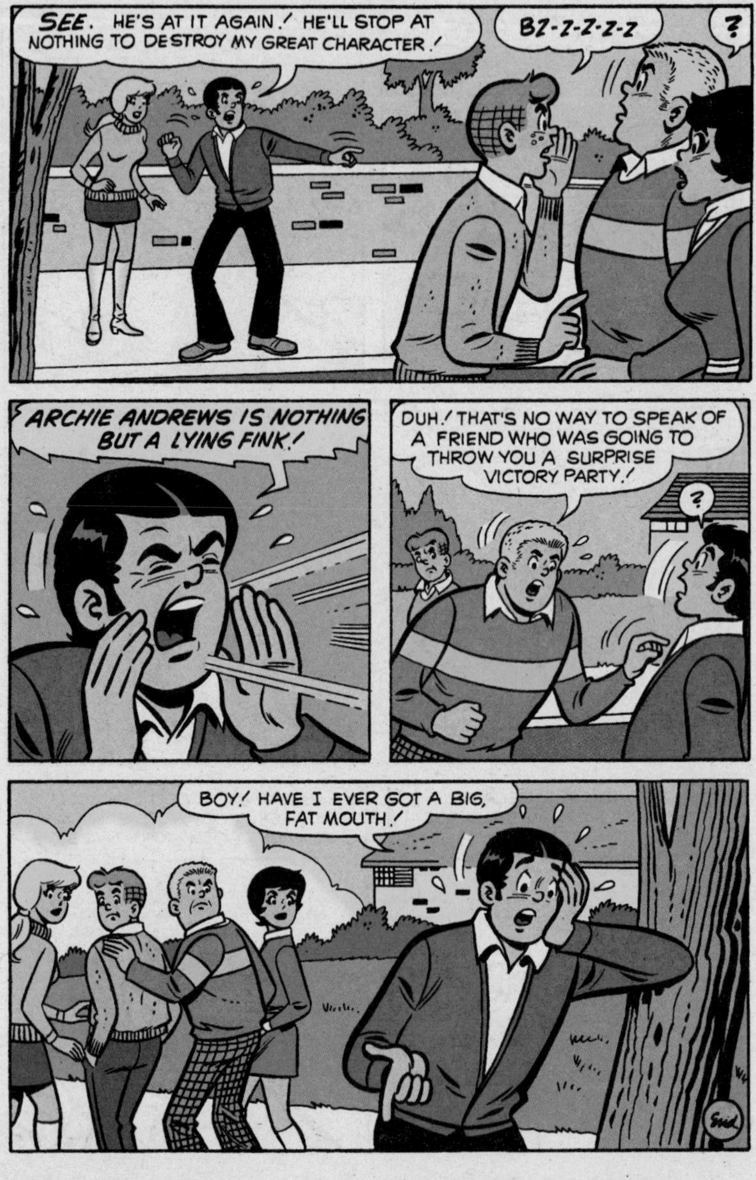

SEE. HE'S AT IT AGAIN! HE'LL STOP AT NOTHING TO DESTROY MY GREAT CHARACTER!
BZ-Z-Z-Z-Z
?
ARCHIE ANDREWS IS NOTHING BUT A LYING FINK!
DUH! THAT'S NO WAY TO SPEAK OF A FRIEND WHO WAS GOING TO THROW YOU A SURPRISE VICTORY PARTY!
?
BOY! HAVE I EVER GOT A BIG, FAT MOUTH!

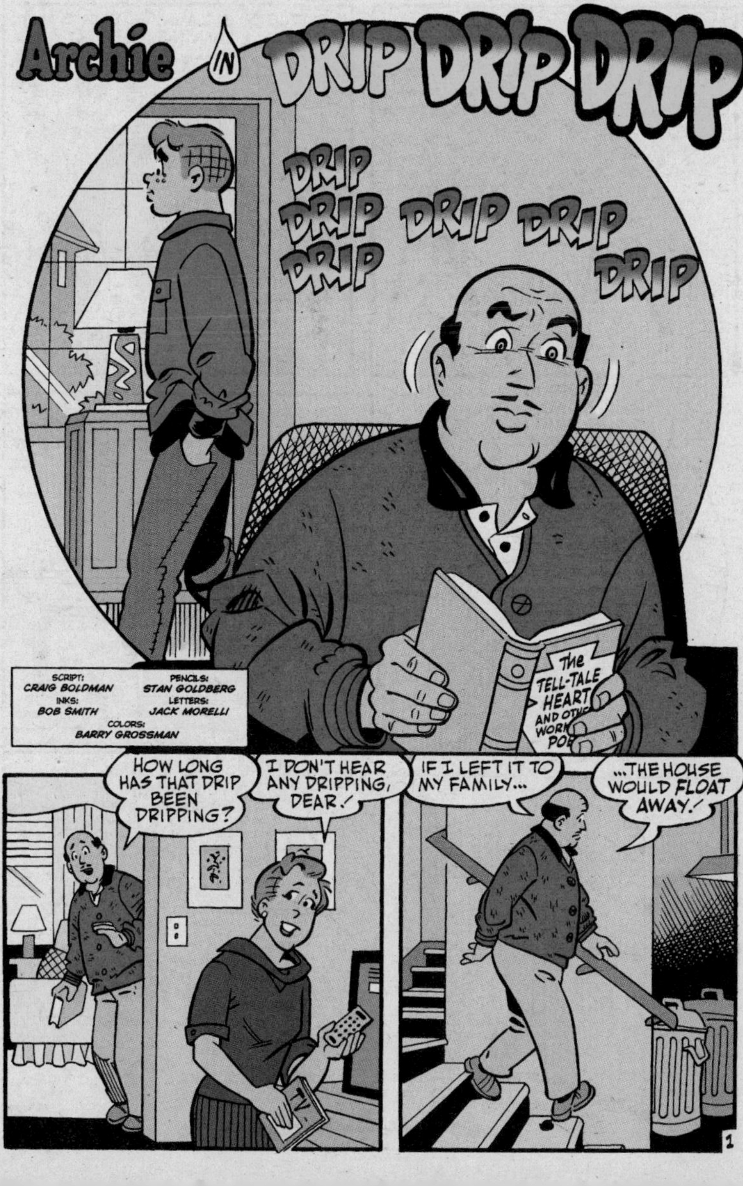
Archie in DRIP DRIP DRIP
DRIP DRIP DRIP DRIP DRIP DRIP
The TELL-TALE HEART AND OTHER WORK... PO...
SCRIPT: CRAIG BOLDMAN PENCILS: STAN GOLDBERG INKS: BOB SMITH LETTERS: JACK MORELLI COLORS: BARRY GROSSMAN
HOW LONG HAS THAT DRIP BEEN DRIPPING?
I DON'T HEAR ANY DRIPPING, DEAR!
TV
IF I LEFT IT TO MY FAMILY...
...THE HOUSE WOULD FLOAT AWAY!
1

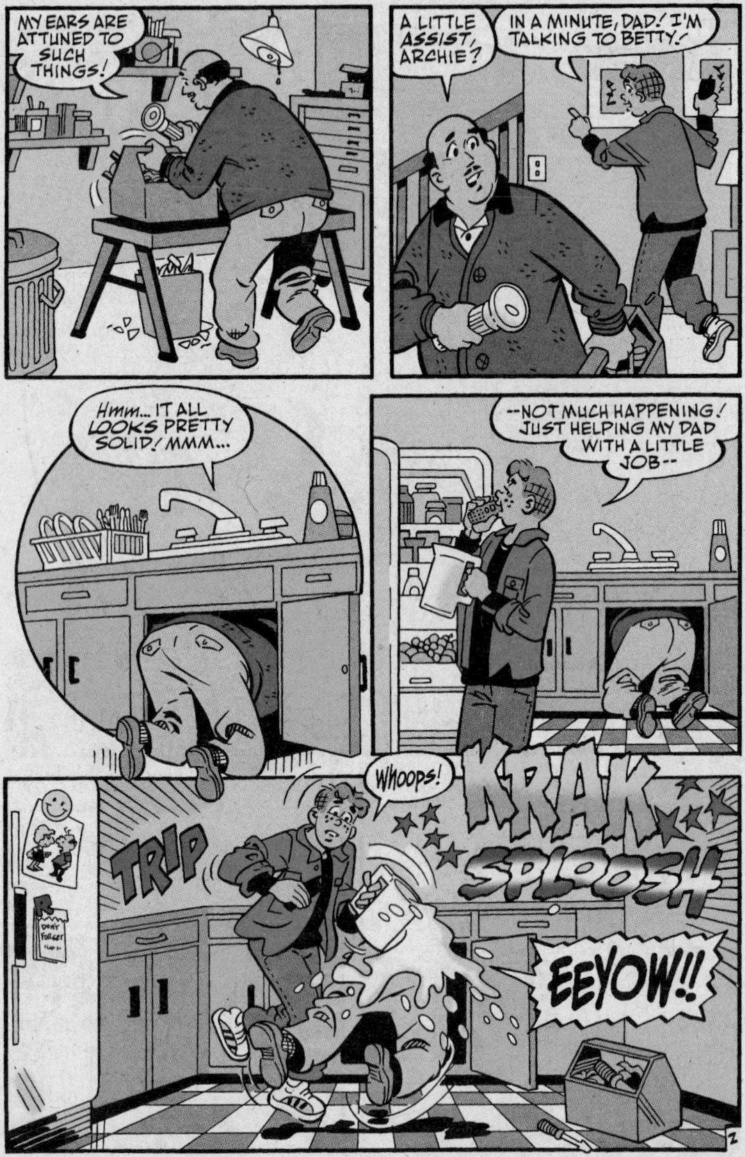
MY EARS ARE ATTUNED TO SUCH THINGS!
A LITTLE ASSIST, ARCHIE?
IN A MINUTE, DAD! I'M TALKING TO BETTY!
Hmm... IT ALL LOOKS PRETTY SOLID! MMM...
--NOT MUCH HAPPENING! JUST HELPING MY DAD WITH A LITTLE JOB--
Whoops!
KRAK
TRIP
SPLOOSH
EEYOW!!
2

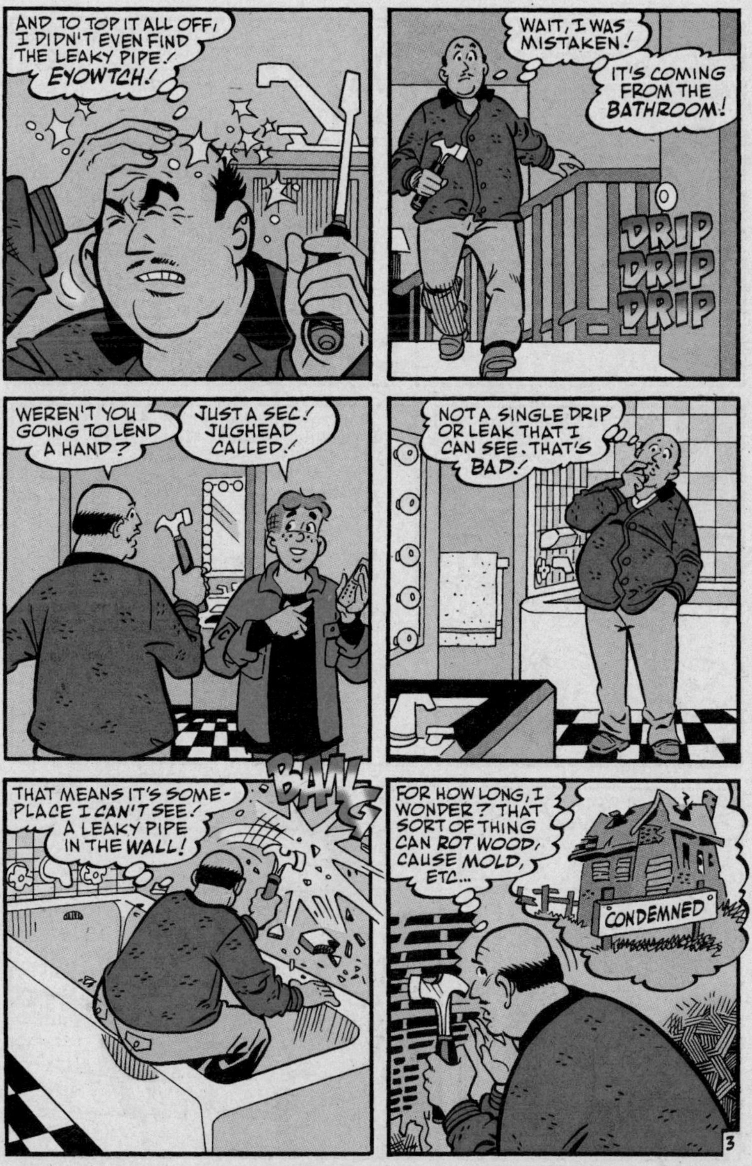
AND TO TOP IT ALL OFF, I DIDN'T EVEN FIND THE LEAKY PIPE! EYOWTCH!
WAIT, I WAS MISTAKEN!
IT'S COMING FROM THE BATHROOM!
DRIP DRIP DRIP
WEREN'T YOU GOING TO LEND A HAND?
JUST A SEC! JUGHEAD CALLED!
NOT A SINGLE DRIP OR LEAK THAT I CAN SEE. THAT'S BAD!
THAT MEANS IT'S SOME-PLACE I CAN'T SEE! A LEAKY PIPE IN THE WALL!
BANG
FOR HOW LONG, I WONDER? THAT SORT OF THING CAN ROT WOOD, CAUSE MOLD, ETC...
CONDEMNED
3

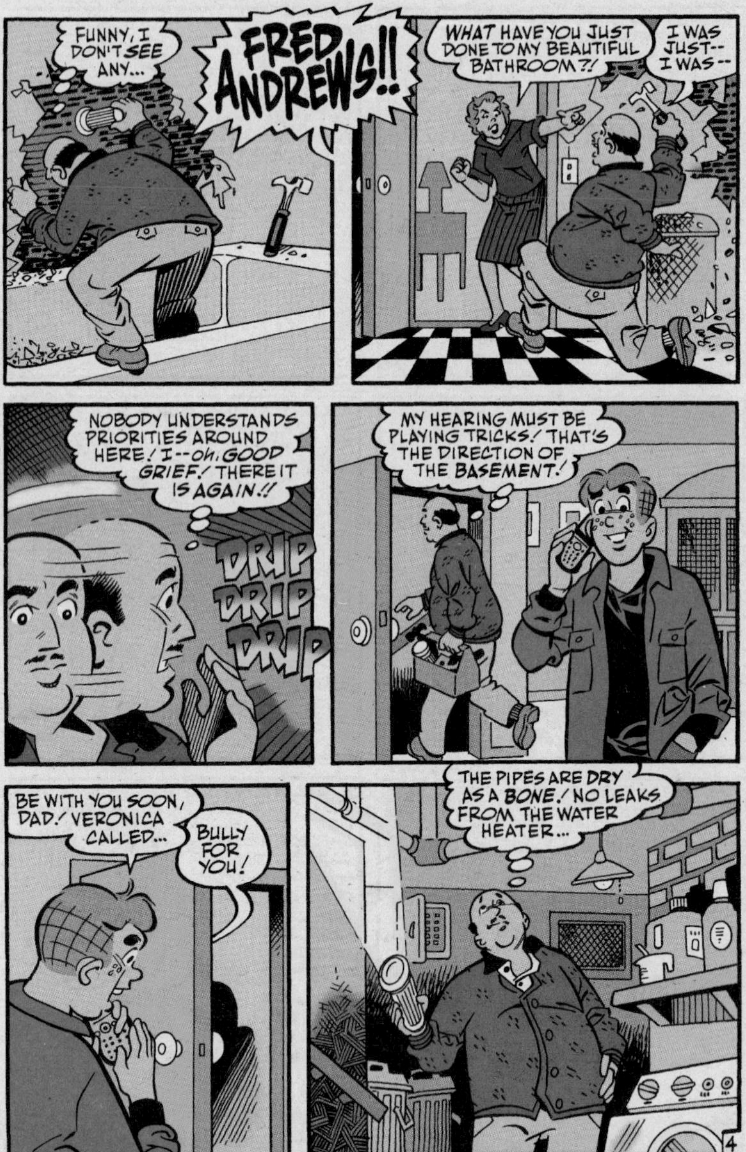
FUNNY, I DON'T SEE ANY...
FRED ANDREWS!!
WHAT HAVE YOU JUST DONE TO MY BEAUTIFUL BATHROOM?!
I WAS JUST-- I WAS--
NOBODY UNDERSTANDS PRIORITIES AROUND HERE! I--oh, GOOD GRIEF! THERE IT IS AGAIN!!
DRIP DRIP DRIP
MY HEARING MUST BE PLAYING TRICKS! THAT'S THE DIRECTION OF THE BASEMENT!
BE WITH YOU SOON, DAD! VERONICA CALLED...
BULLY FOR YOU!
THE PIPES ARE DRY AS A BONE! NO LEAKS FROM THE WATER HEATER...
4

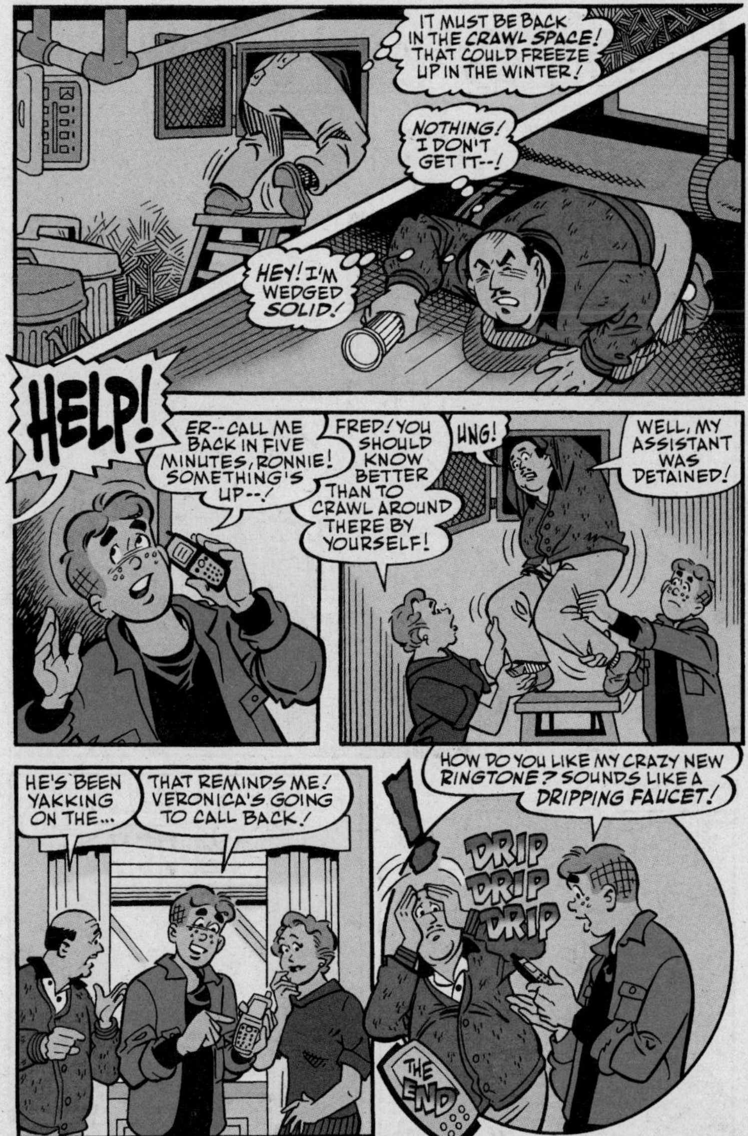
IT MUST BE BACK IN THE CRAWL SPACE! THAT COULD FREEZE UP IN THE WINTER!
NOTHING! I DON'T GET IT--!
HEY! I'M WEDGED SOLID!
HELP!
ER--CALL ME BACK IN FIVE MINUTES, RONNIE! SOMETHING'S UP--!
FRED! YOU SHOULD KNOW BETTER THAN TO CRAWL AROUND THERE BY YOURSELF!
UNG!
WELL, MY ASSISTANT WAS DETAINED!
HE'S BEEN YAKKING ON THE...
THAT REMINDS ME! VERONICA'S GOING TO CALL BACK!
HOW DO YOU LIKE MY CRAZY NEW RINGTONE? SOUNDS LIKE A DRIPPING FAUCET!
DRIP DRIP DRIP
THE END

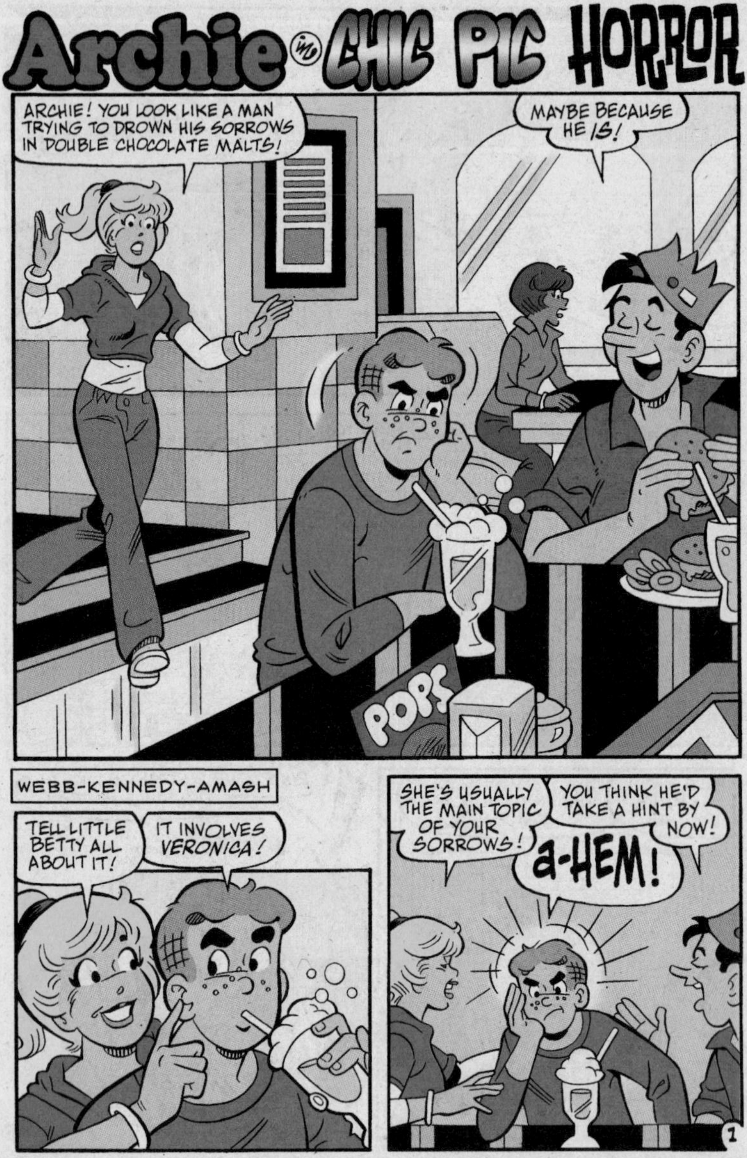

Archie in CHIC PIC HORROR
ARCHIE! YOU LOOK LIKE A MAN TRYING TO DROWN HIS SORROWS IN DOUBLE CHOCOLATE MALTS!
MAYBE BECAUSE HE IS!
POPS
WEBB-KENNEDY-AMASH
TELL LITTLE BETTY ALL ABOUT IT!
IT INVOLVES VERONICA!
SHE'S USUALLY THE MAIN TOPIC OF YOUR SORROWS!
YOU THINK HE'D TAKE A HINT BY NOW!
a-HEM!

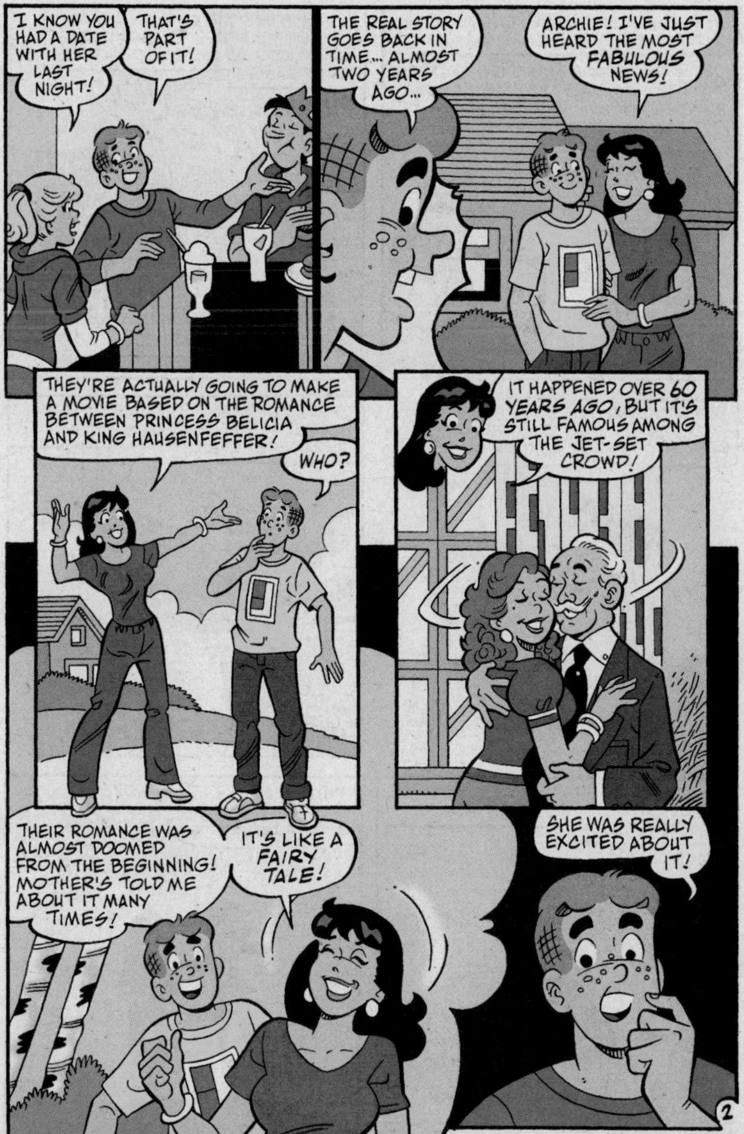
I KNOW YOU HAD A DATE WITH HER LAST NIGHT!
THAT'S PART OF IT!
THE REAL STORY GOES BACK IN TIME... ALMOST TWO YEARS AGO...
ARCHIE! I'VE JUST HEARD THE MOST FABULOUS NEWS!
THEY'RE ACTUALLY GOING TO MAKE A MOVIE BASED ON THE ROMANCE BETWEEN PRINCESS BELICIA AND KING HAUSENFEFFER!
WHO?
IT HAPPENED OVER 60 YEARS AGO, BUT IT'S STILL FAMOUS AMONG THE JET-SET CROWD!
THEIR ROMANCE WAS ALMOST DOOMED FROM THE BEGINNING! MOTHER'S TOLD ME ABOUT IT MANY TIMES!
IT'S LIKE A FAIRY TALE!
SHE WAS REALLY EXCITED ABOUT IT!
2

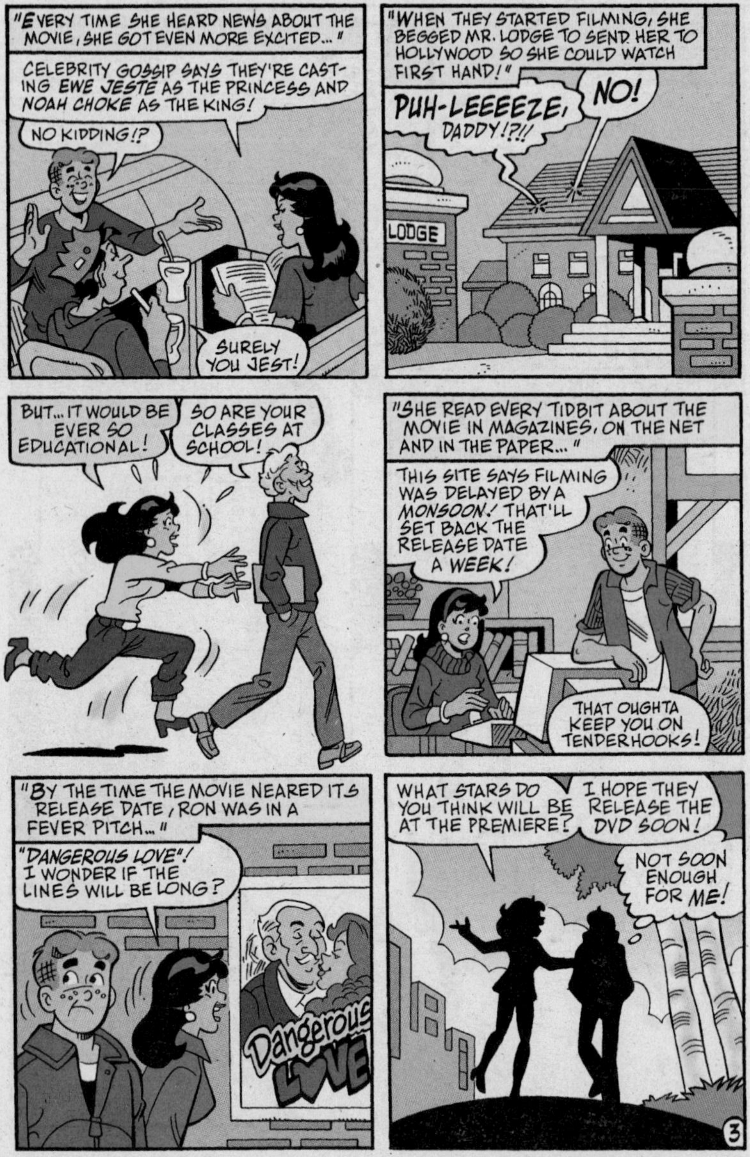

"EVERY TIME SHE HEARD NEWS ABOUT THE MOVIE, SHE GOT EVEN MORE EXCITED..."
CELEBRITY GOSSIP SAYS THEY'RE CASTING EWE JESTE AS THE PRINCESS AND NOAH CHOKE AS THE KING!
NO KIDDING!?
SURELY YOU JEST!
"WHEN THEY STARTED FILMING, SHE BEGGED MR. LODGE TO SEND HER TO HOLLYWOOD SO SHE COULD WATCH FIRST HAND!"
PUH-LEEEEZE, DADDY!?!!
NO!
LODGE
BUT... IT WOULD BE EVER SO EDUCATIONAL!
SO ARE YOUR CLASSES AT SCHOOL!
"SHE READ EVERY TIDBIT ABOUT THE MOVIE IN MAGAZINES, ON THE NET AND IN THE PAPER..."
THIS SITE SAYS FILMING WAS DELAYED BY A MONSOON! THAT'LL SET BACK THE RELEASE DATE A WEEK!
THAT OUGHTA KEEP YOU ON TENDERHOOKS!
"BY THE TIME THE MOVIE NEARED ITS RELEASE DATE, RON WAS IN A FEVER PITCH..."
"DANGEROUS LOVE"! I WONDER IF THE LINES WILL BE LONG?
Dangerous LOVE
WHAT STARS DO YOU THINK WILL BE AT THE PREMIERE?
I HOPE THEY RELEASE THE DVD SOON!
NOT SOON ENOUGH FOR ME!

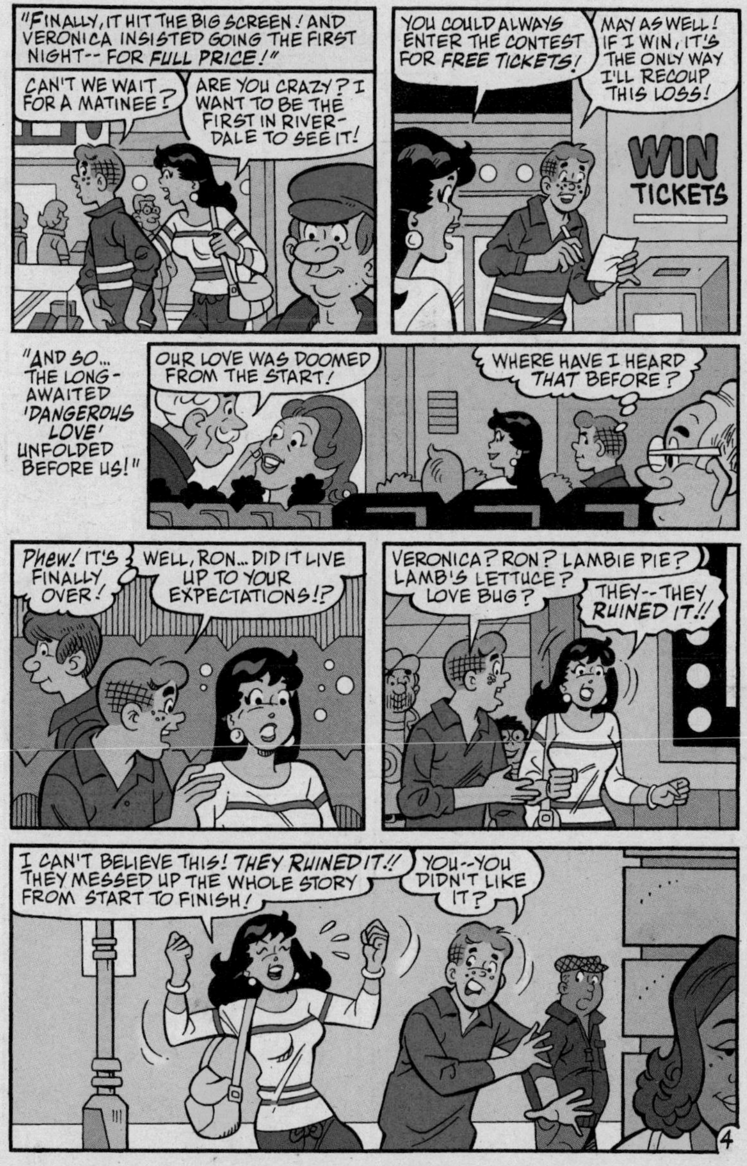
"FINALLY, IT HIT THE BIG SCREEN! AND VERONICA INSISTED GOING THE FIRST NIGHT-- FOR FULL PRICE!"
CAN'T WE WAIT FOR A MATINEE?
ARE YOU CRAZY? I WANT TO BE THE FIRST IN RIVER-DALE TO SEE IT!
YOU COULD ALWAYS ENTER THE CONTEST FOR FREE TICKETS!
MAY AS WELL! IF I WIN, IT'S THE ONLY WAY I'LL RECOUP THIS LOSS!
WIN TICKETS
"AND SO... THE LONG-AWAITED 'DANGEROUS LOVE' UNFOLDED BEFORE US!"
OUR LOVE WAS DOOMED FROM THE START!
WHERE HAVE I HEARD THAT BEFORE?
Phew! IT'S FINALLY OVER!
WELL, RON... DID IT LIVE UP TO YOUR EXPECTATIONS!?
VERONICA? RON? LAMBIE PIE? LAMB'S LETTUCE? LOVE BUG?
THEY--THEY RUINED IT!!
I CAN'T BELIEVE THIS! THEY RUINED IT!! THEY MESSED UP THE WHOLE STORY FROM START TO FINISH!
YOU--YOU DIDN'T LIKE IT?
4

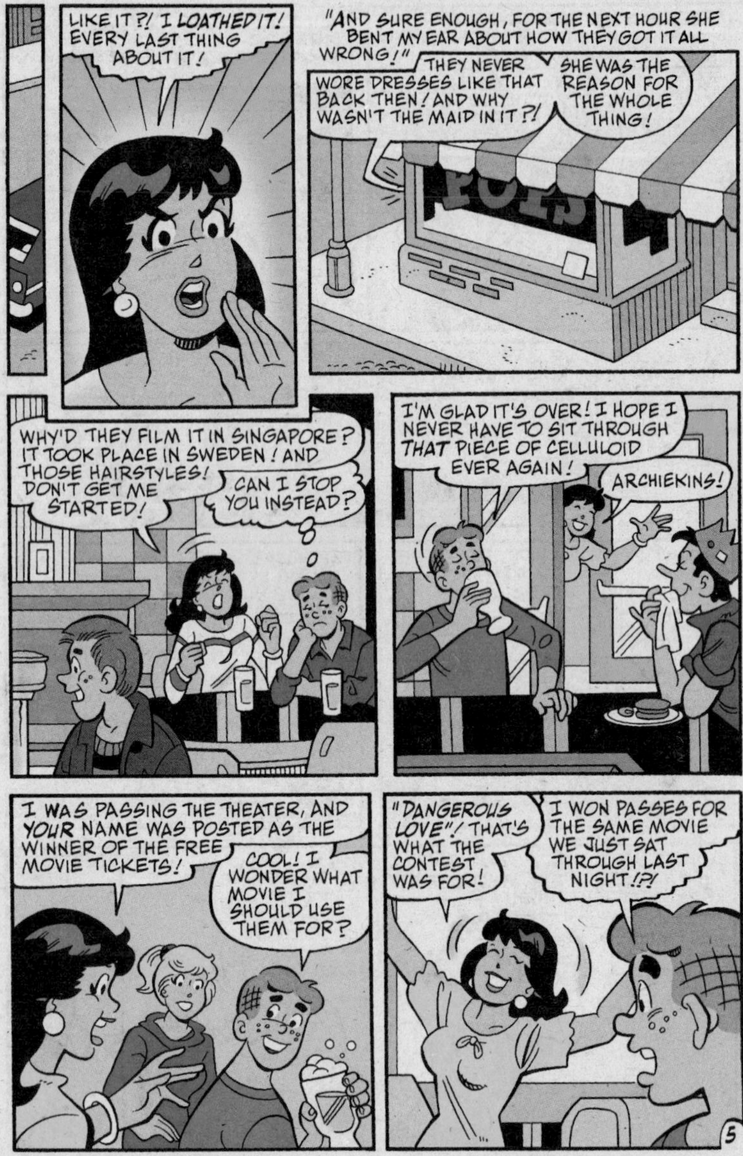

LIKE IT?! I LOATHED IT! EVERY LAST THING ABOUT IT!
"AND SURE ENOUGH, FOR THE NEXT HOUR SHE BENT MY EAR ABOUT HOW THEY GOT IT ALL WRONG!"
THEY NEVER WORE DRESSES LIKE THAT BACK THEN! AND WHY WASN'T THE MAID IN IT?!
SHE WAS THE REASON FOR THE WHOLE THING!
WHY'D THEY FILM IT IN SINGAPORE? IT TOOK PLACE IN SWEDEN! AND THOSE HAIRSTYLES! DON'T GET ME STARTED!
CAN I STOP YOU INSTEAD?
I'M GLAD IT'S OVER! I HOPE I NEVER HAVE TO SIT THROUGH THAT PIECE OF CELLULOID EVER AGAIN!
ARCHIEKINS!
I WAS PASSING THE THEATER, AND YOUR NAME WAS POSTED AS THE WINNER OF THE FREE MOVIE TICKETS!
COOL! I WONDER WHAT MOVIE I SHOULD USE THEM FOR?
"DANGEROUS LOVE"! THAT'S WHAT THE CONTEST WAS FOR!
I WON PASSES FOR THE SAME MOVIE WE JUST SAT THROUGH LAST NIGHT!?!

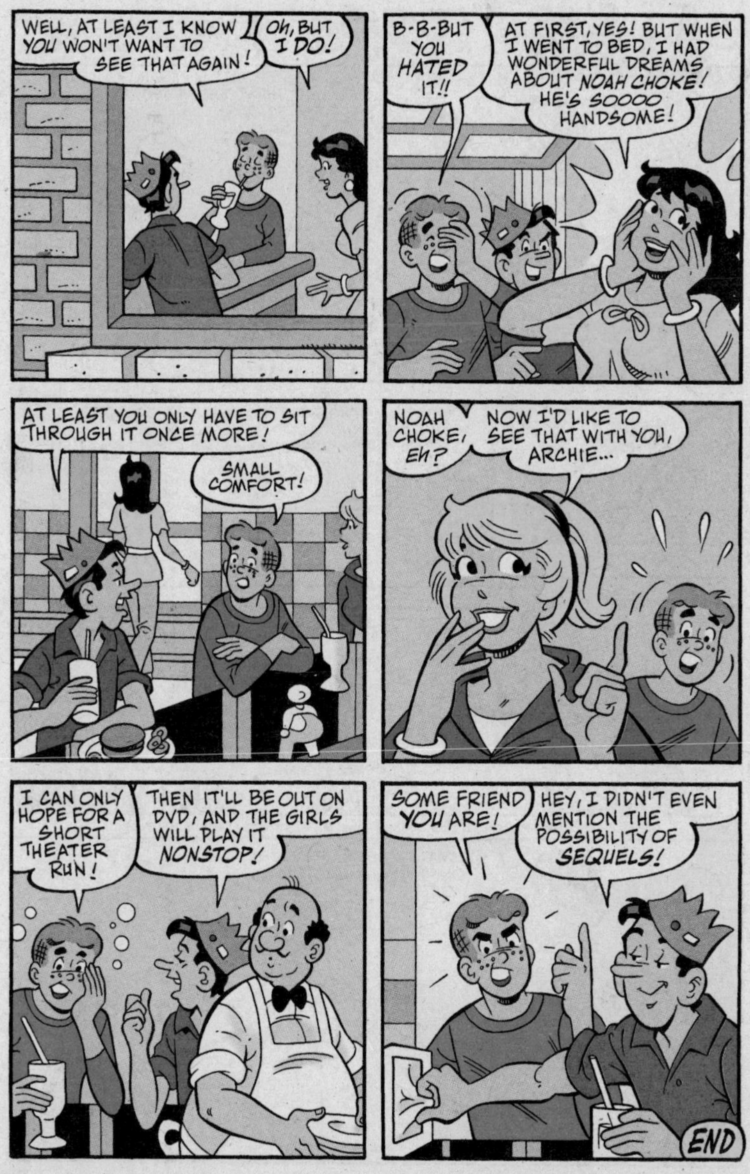

WELL, AT LEAST I KNOW YOU WON'T WANT TO SEE THAT AGAIN!
Oh, BUT I DO!
B-B-BUT YOU HATED IT!!
AT FIRST, YES! BUT WHEN I WENT TO BED, I HAD WONDERFUL DREAMS ABOUT NOAH CHOKE! HE'S SOOOO HANDSOME!
AT LEAST YOU ONLY HAVE TO SIT THROUGH IT ONCE MORE!
SMALL COMFORT!
NOAH CHOKE, Eh?
NOW I'D LIKE TO SEE THAT WITH YOU, ARCHIE...
I CAN ONLY HOPE FOR A SHORT THEATER RUN!
THEN IT'LL BE OUT ON DVD, AND THE GIRLS WILL PLAY IT NONSTOP!
SOME FRIEND YOU ARE!
HEY, I DIDN'T EVEN MENTION THE POSSIBILITY OF SEQUELS!
END

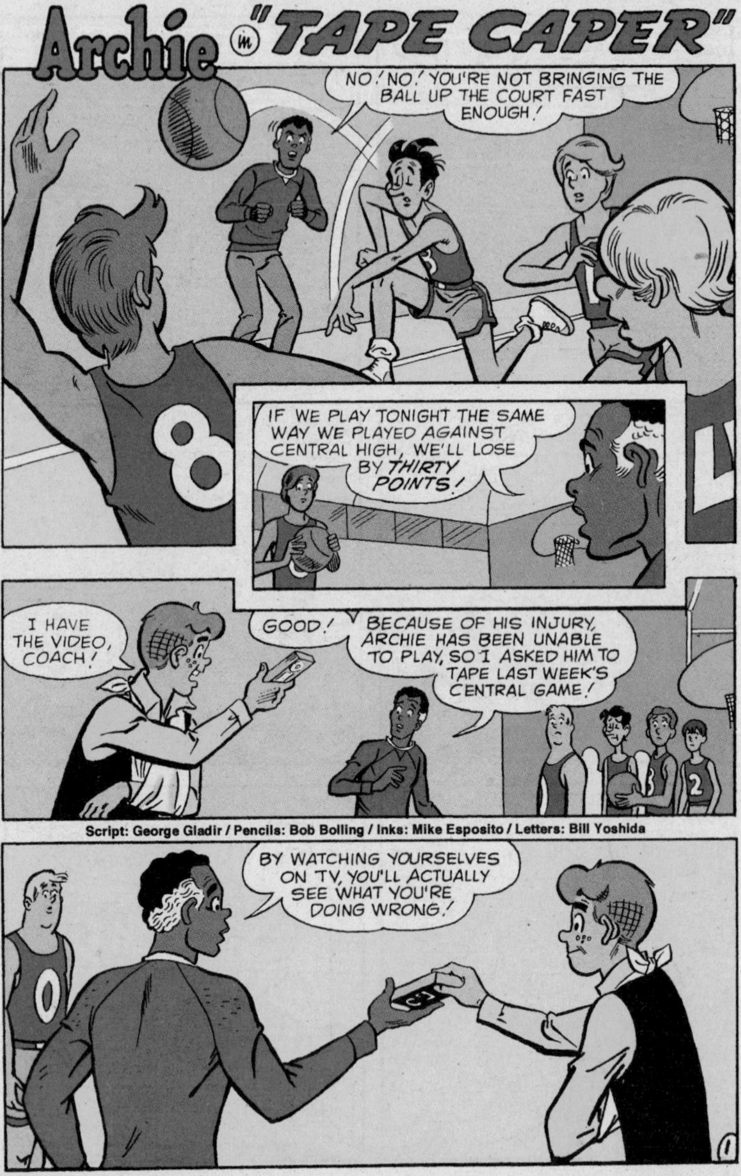
Archie in "TAPE CAPER"
NO! NO! YOU'RE NOT BRINGING THE BALL UP THE COURT FAST ENOUGH!
IF WE PLAY TONIGHT THE SAME WAY WE PLAYED AGAINST CENTRAL HIGH, WE'LL LOSE BY THIRTY POINTS!
I HAVE THE VIDEO, COACH!
GOOD!
BECAUSE OF HIS INJURY, ARCHIE HAS BEEN UNABLE TO PLAY, SO I ASKED HIM TO TAPE LAST WEEK'S CENTRAL GAME!
Script: George Gladir / Pencils: Bob Bolling / Inks: Mike Esposito / Letters: Bill Yoshida
BY WATCHING YOURSELVES ON TV, YOU'LL ACTUALLY SEE WHAT YOU'RE DOING WRONG!
1

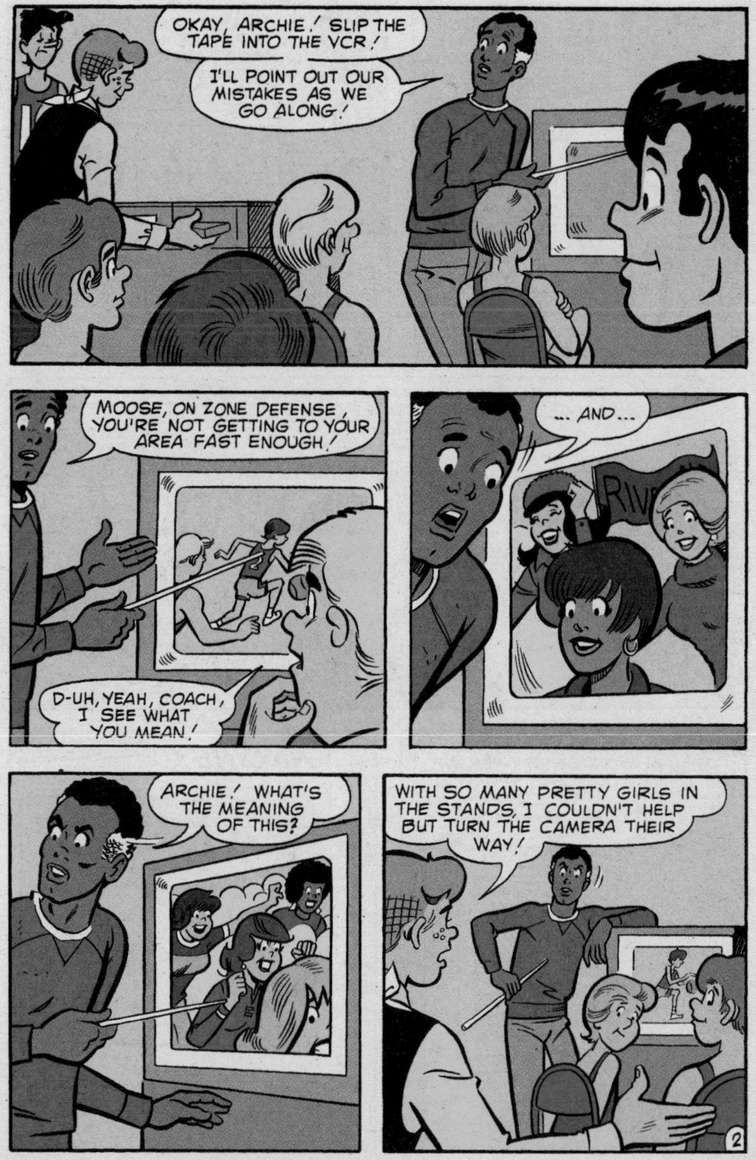
OKAY, ARCHIE! SLIP THE TAPE INTO THE VCR!
I'LL POINT OUT OUR MISTAKES AS WE GO ALONG!
MOOSE, ON ZONE DEFENSE, YOU'RE NOT GETTING TO YOUR AREA FAST ENOUGH!
D-UH, YEAH, COACH, I SEE WHAT YOU MEAN!
... AND ...
ARCHIE! WHAT'S THE MEANING OF THIS?
WITH SO MANY PRETTY GIRLS IN THE STANDS, I COULDN'T HELP BUT TURN THE CAMERA THEIR WAY!
2

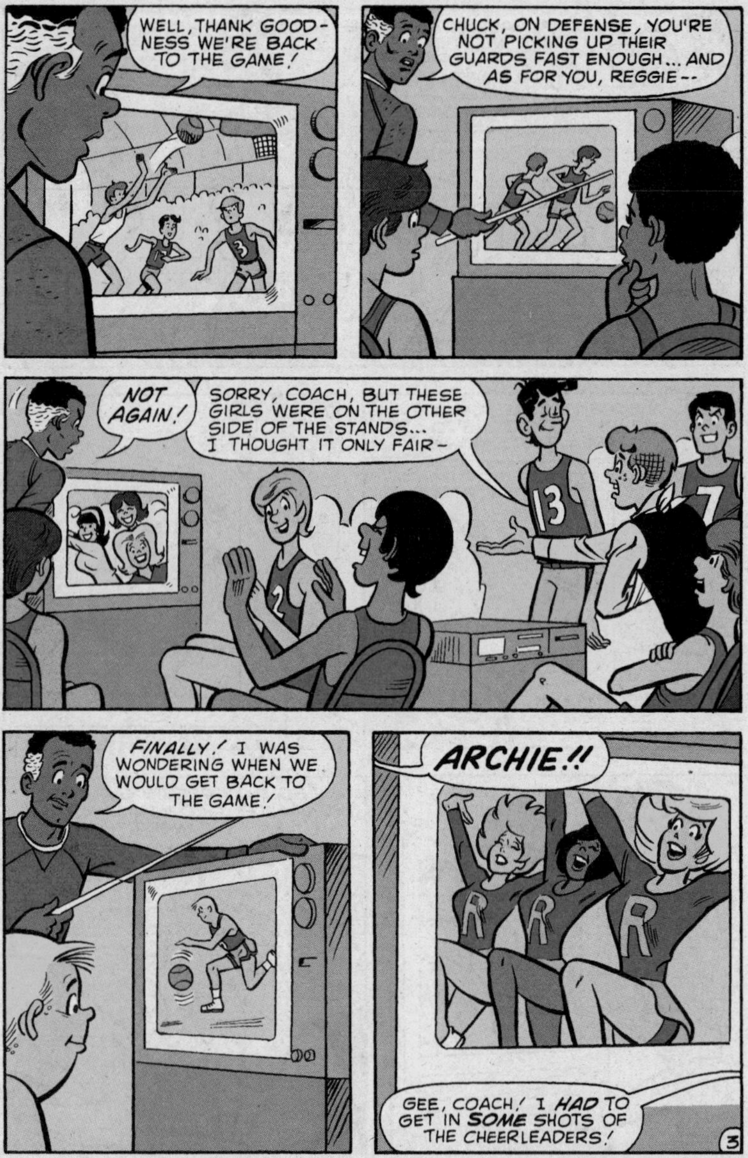
WELL, THANK GOOD-NESS WE'RE BACK TO THE GAME!
CHUCK, ON DEFENSE, YOU'RE NOT PICKING UP THEIR GUARDS FAST ENOUGH... AND AS FOR YOU, REGGIE--
NOT AGAIN!
SORRY, COACH, BUT THESE GIRLS WERE ON THE OTHER SIDE OF THE STANDS... I THOUGHT IT ONLY FAIR-
FINALLY! I WAS WONDERING WHEN WE WOULD GET BACK TO THE GAME!
ARCHIE!!
GEE, COACH! I *HAD* TO GET IN *SOME* SHOTS OF THE CHEERLEADERS!
3

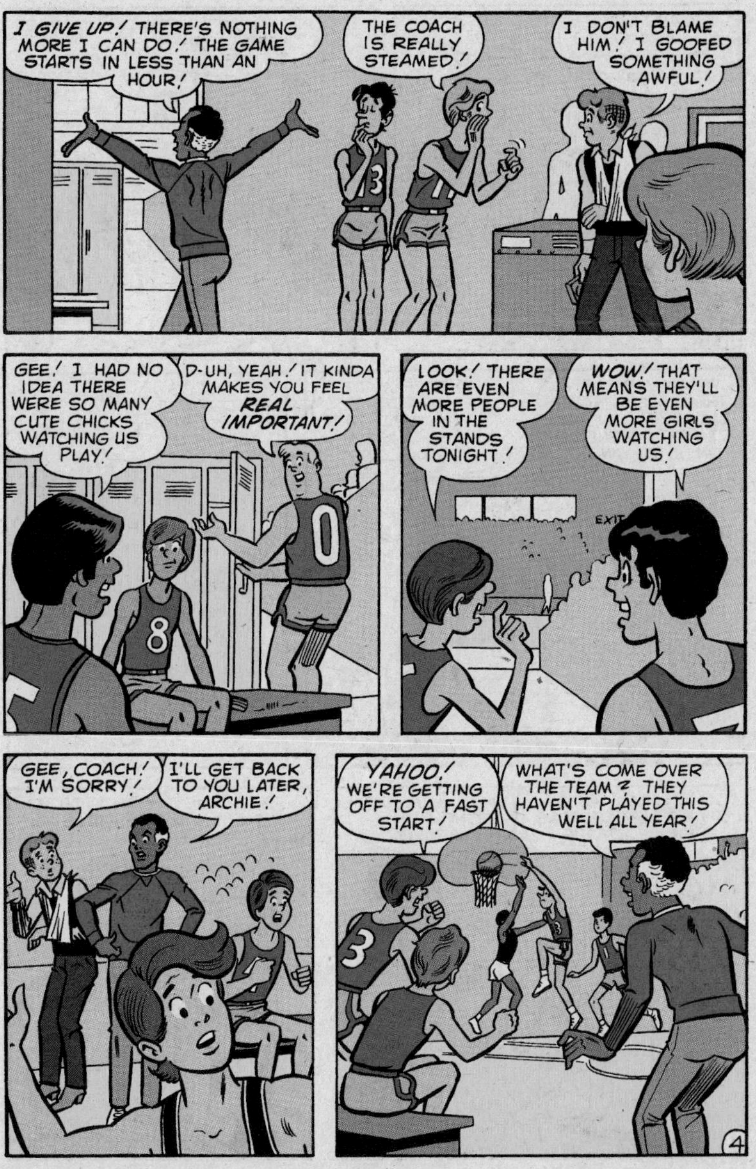
I GIVE UP! THERE'S NOTHING MORE I CAN DO! THE GAME STARTS IN LESS THAN AN HOUR!
THE COACH IS REALLY STEAMED!
I DON'T BLAME HIM! I GOOFED SOMETHING AWFUL!
GEE! I HAD NO IDEA THERE WERE SO MANY CUTE CHICKS WATCHING US PLAY!
D-UH, YEAH! IT KINDA MAKES YOU FEEL REAL IMPORTANT!
LOOK! THERE ARE EVEN MORE PEOPLE IN THE STANDS TONIGHT!
WOW! THAT MEANS THEY'LL BE EVEN MORE GIRLS WATCHING US!
EXIT
GEE, COACH! I'M SORRY!
I'LL GET BACK TO YOU LATER, ARCHIE!
YAHOO! WE'RE GETTING OFF TO A FAST START!
WHAT'S COME OVER THE TEAM? THEY HAVEN'T PLAYED THIS WELL ALL YEAR!
4

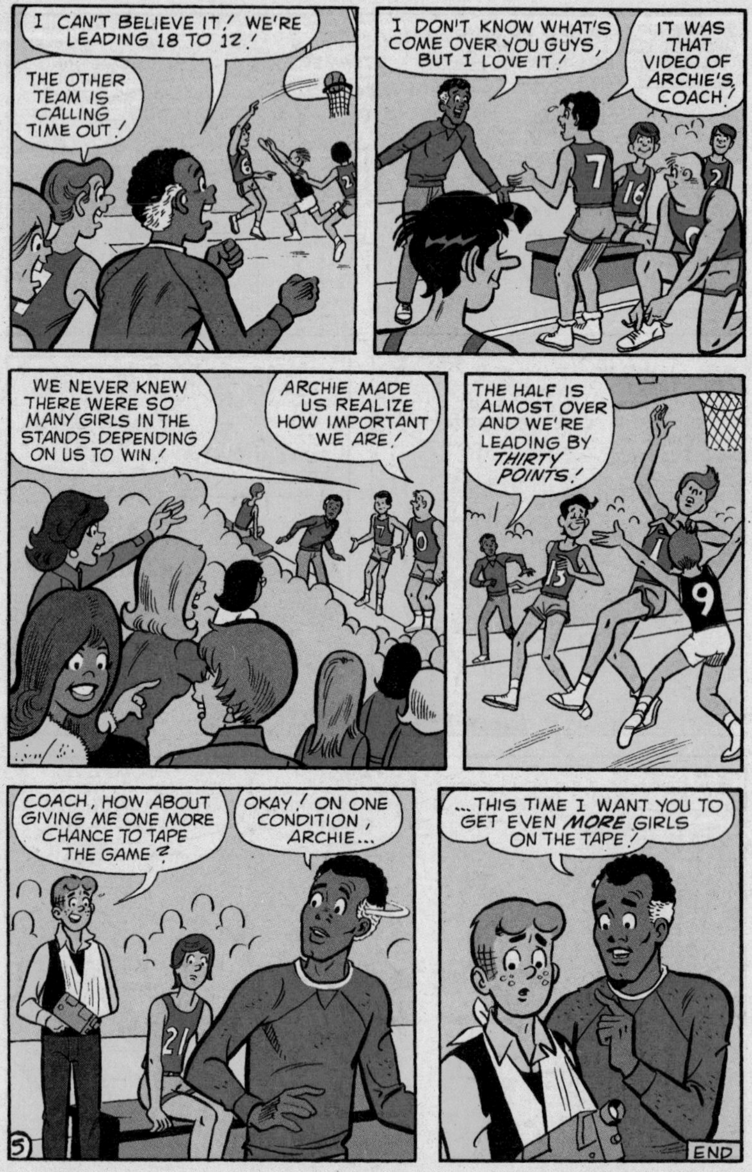
I CAN'T BELIEVE IT! WE'RE LEADING 18 TO 12!
THE OTHER TEAM IS CALLING TIME OUT!
I DON'T KNOW WHAT'S COME OVER YOU GUYS, BUT I LOVE IT!
IT WAS THAT VIDEO OF ARCHIE'S, COACH!
WE NEVER KNEW THERE WERE SO MANY GIRLS IN THE STANDS DEPENDING ON US TO WIN!
ARCHIE MADE US REALIZE HOW IMPORTANT WE ARE!
THE HALF IS ALMOST OVER AND WE'RE LEADING BY THIRTY POINTS!
COACH, HOW ABOUT GIVING ME ONE MORE CHANCE TO TAPE THE GAME?
OKAY! ON ONE CONDITION, ARCHIE...
...THIS TIME I WANT YOU TO GET EVEN MORE GIRLS ON THE TAPE!
5
END

Archie in "GYM DANDY"

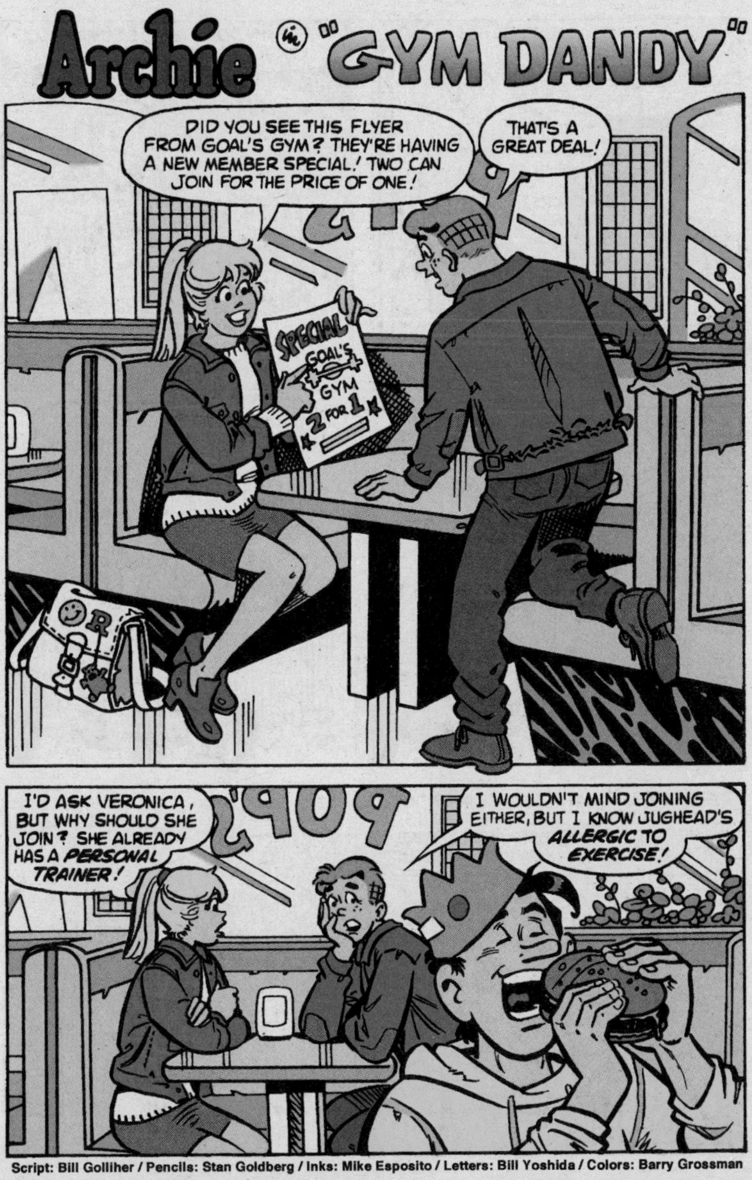
DID YOU SEE THIS FLYER FROM GOAL'S GYM? THEY'RE HAVING A NEW MEMBER SPECIAL! TWO CAN JOIN FOR THE PRICE OF ONE!
THAT'S A GREAT DEAL!
SPECIAL
GOAL'S GYM
2 FOR 1
I'D ASK VERONICA, BUT WHY SHOULD SHE JOIN? SHE ALREADY HAS A *PERSONAL TRAINER*!
I WOULDN'T MIND JOINING EITHER, BUT I KNOW JUGHEAD'S *ALLERGIC* TO *EXERCISE*!
POP'S

Script: Bill Golliher / Pencils: Stan Goldberg / Inks: Mike Esposito / Letters: Bill Yoshida / Colors: Barry Grossman

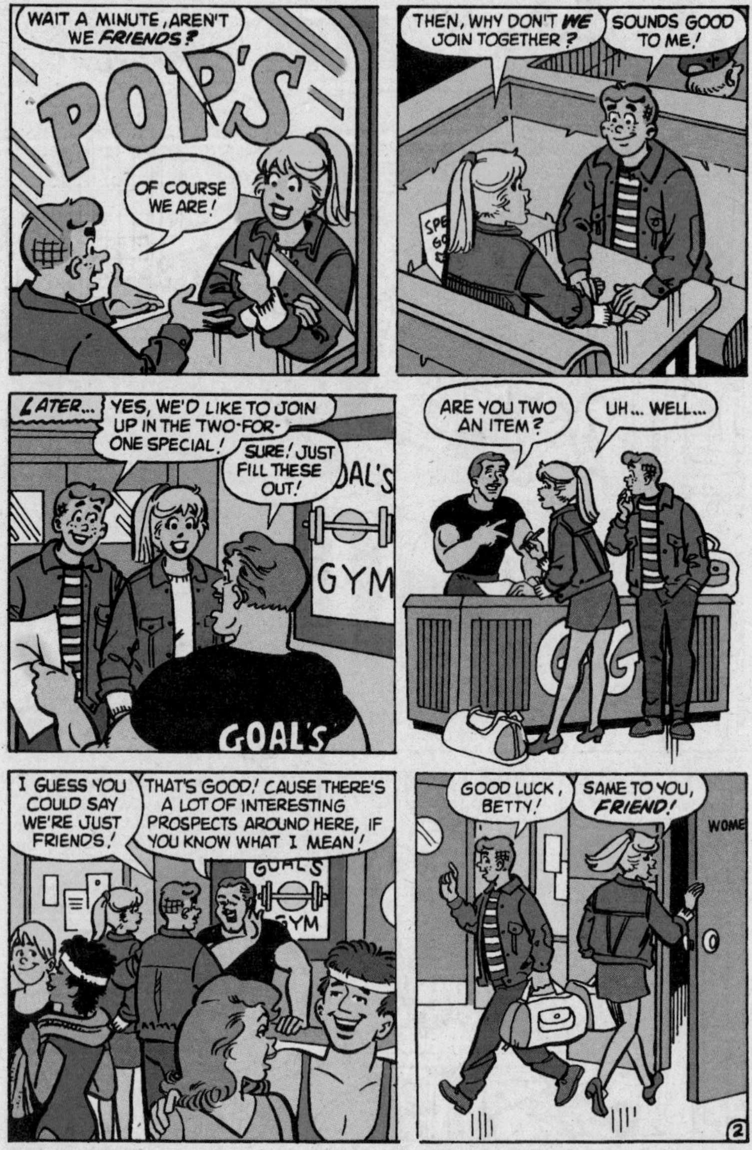
WAIT A MINUTE, AREN'T WE FRIENDS?
POP'S
OF COURSE WE ARE!
THEN, WHY DON'T WE JOIN TOGETHER?
SOUNDS GOOD TO ME!
LATER...
YES, WE'D LIKE TO JOIN UP IN THE TWO-FOR-ONE SPECIAL!
SURE! JUST FILL THESE OUT!
OAL'S
GYM
GOAL'S
ARE YOU TWO AN ITEM?
UH... WELL...
I GUESS YOU COULD SAY WE'RE JUST FRIENDS!
THAT'S GOOD! CAUSE THERE'S A LOT OF INTERESTING PROSPECTS AROUND HERE, IF YOU KNOW WHAT I MEAN!
GOAL'S
GYM
GOOD LUCK, BETTY!
SAME TO YOU, FRIEND!
WOME
2

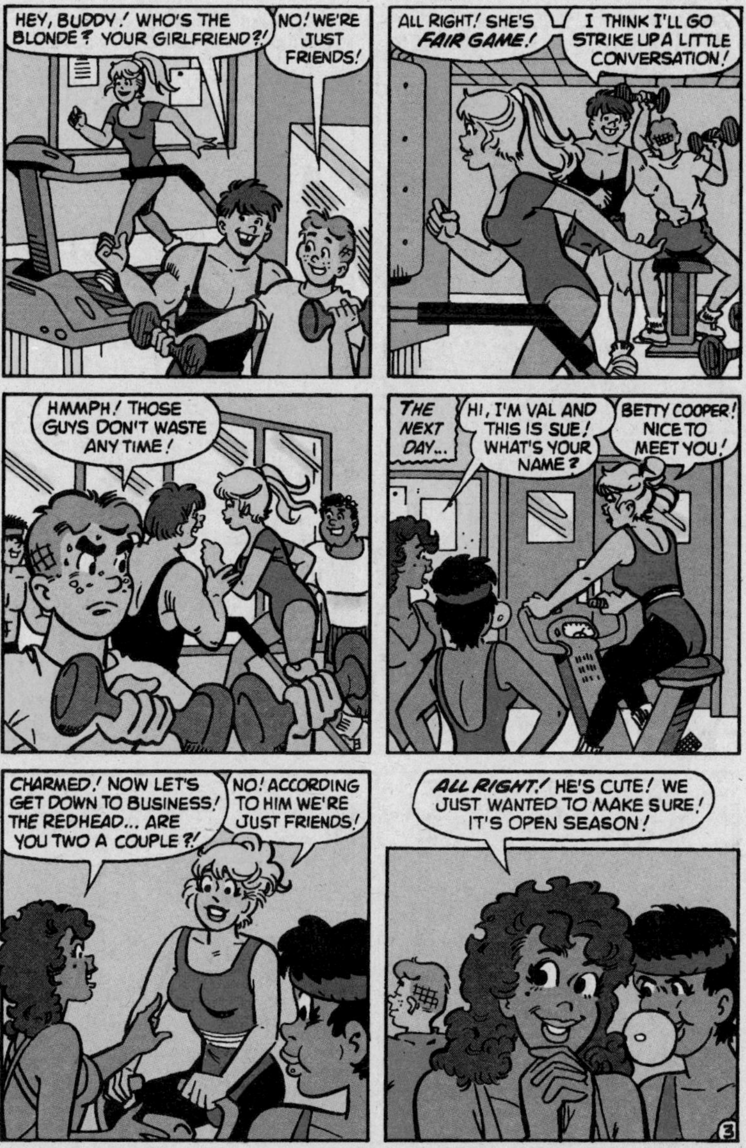
HEY, BUDDY! WHO'S THE BLONDE? YOUR GIRLFRIEND?!
NO! WE'RE JUST FRIENDS!
ALL RIGHT! SHE'S FAIR GAME!
I THINK I'LL GO STRIKE UP A LITTLE CONVERSATION!
HMMPH! THOSE GUYS DON'T WASTE ANY TIME!
THE NEXT DAY...
HI, I'M VAL AND THIS IS SUE! WHAT'S YOUR NAME?
BETTY COOPER! NICE TO MEET YOU!
CHARMED! NOW LET'S GET DOWN TO BUSINESS! THE REDHEAD... ARE YOU TWO A COUPLE?!
NO! ACCORDING TO HIM WE'RE JUST FRIENDS!
ALL RIGHT! HE'S CUTE! WE JUST WANTED TO MAKE SURE! IT'S OPEN SEASON!
3

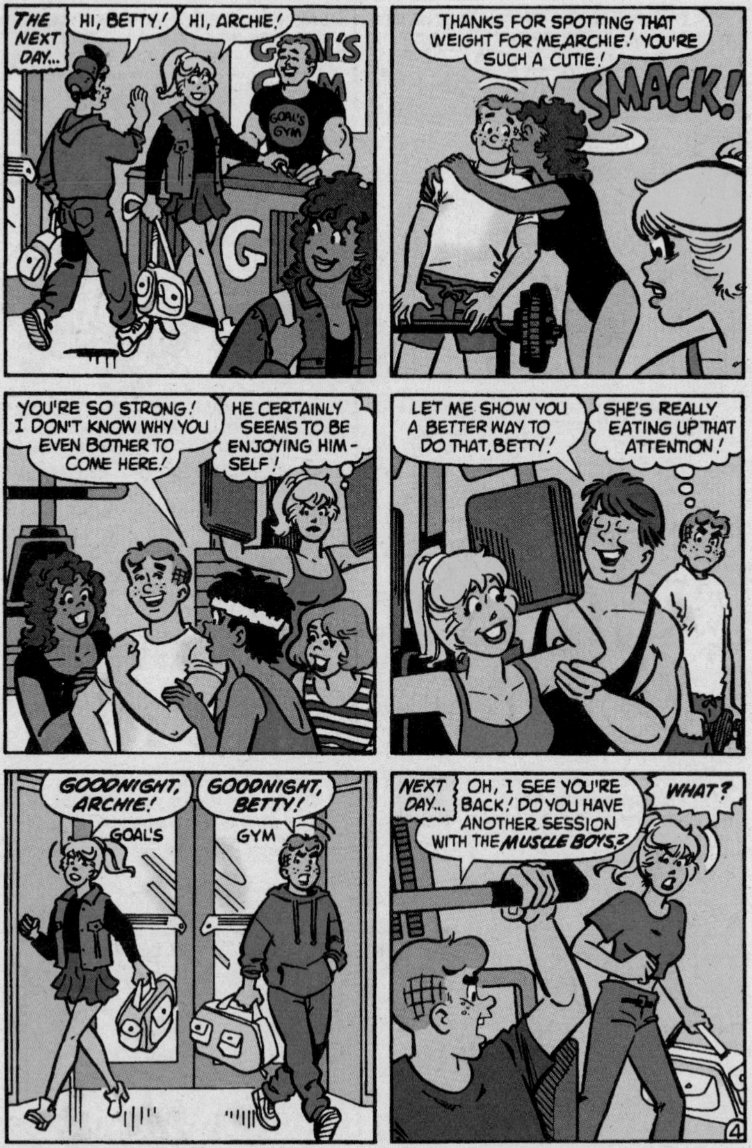
THE NEXT DAY...
HI, BETTY!
HI, ARCHIE!
GOAL'S GYM
GOAL'S GYM
THANKS FOR SPOTTING THAT WEIGHT FOR ME, ARCHIE! YOU'RE SUCH A CUTIE!
SMACK!
YOU'RE SO STRONG! I DON'T KNOW WHY YOU EVEN BOTHER TO COME HERE!
HE CERTAINLY SEEMS TO BE ENJOYING HIM-SELF!
LET ME SHOW YOU A BETTER WAY TO DO THAT, BETTY!
SHE'S REALLY EATING UP THAT ATTENTION!
GOODNIGHT, ARCHIE!
GOODNIGHT, BETTY!
GOAL'S
GYM
NEXT DAY...
OH, I SEE YOU'RE BACK! DO YOU HAVE ANOTHER SESSION WITH THE MUSCLE BOYS?
WHAT?
4

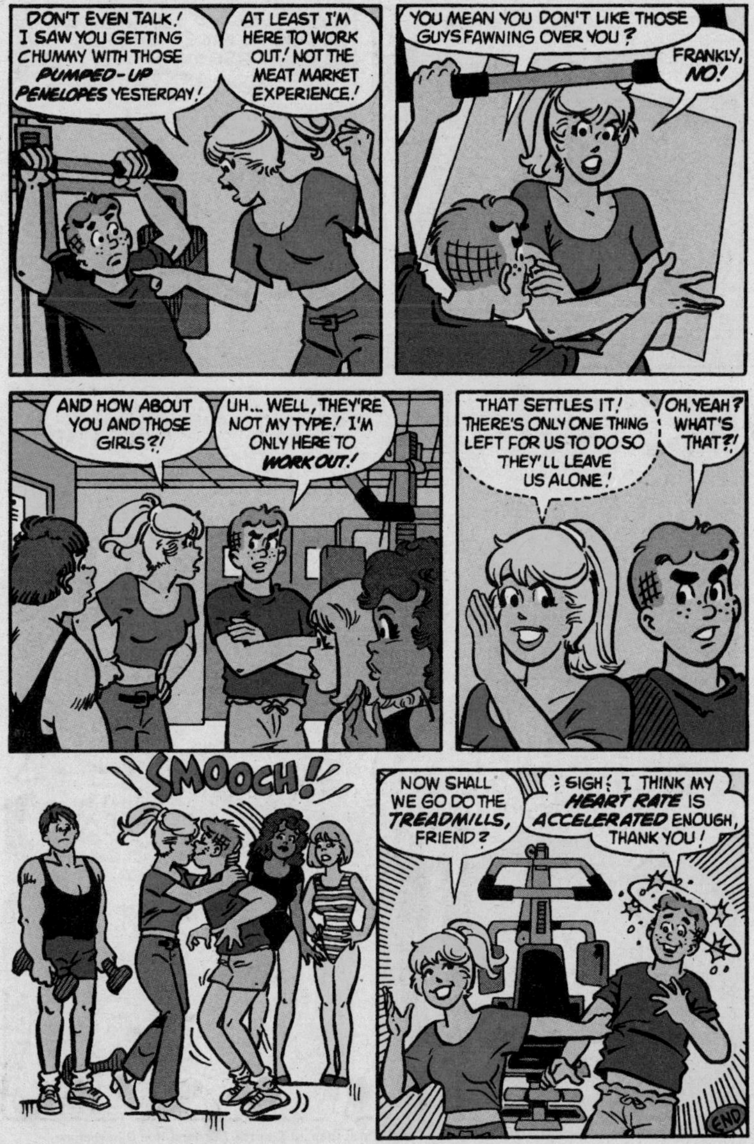

DON'T EVEN TALK! I SAW YOU GETTING CHUMMY WITH THOSE PUMPED-UP PENELOPES YESTERDAY!
AT LEAST I'M HERE TO WORK OUT! NOT THE MEAT MARKET EXPERIENCE!
YOU MEAN YOU DON'T LIKE THOSE GUYS FAWNING OVER YOU?
FRANKLY, NO!
AND HOW ABOUT YOU AND THOSE GIRLS?!
UH... WELL, THEY'RE NOT MY TYPE! I'M ONLY HERE TO WORK OUT!
THAT SETTLES IT! THERE'S ONLY ONE THING LEFT FOR US TO DO SO THEY'LL LEAVE US ALONE!
OH, YEAH? WHAT'S THAT?!
SMOOCH!
NOW SHALL WE GO DO THE TREADMILLS, FRIEND?
SIGH! I THINK MY HEART RATE IS ACCELERATED ENOUGH, THANK YOU!
END

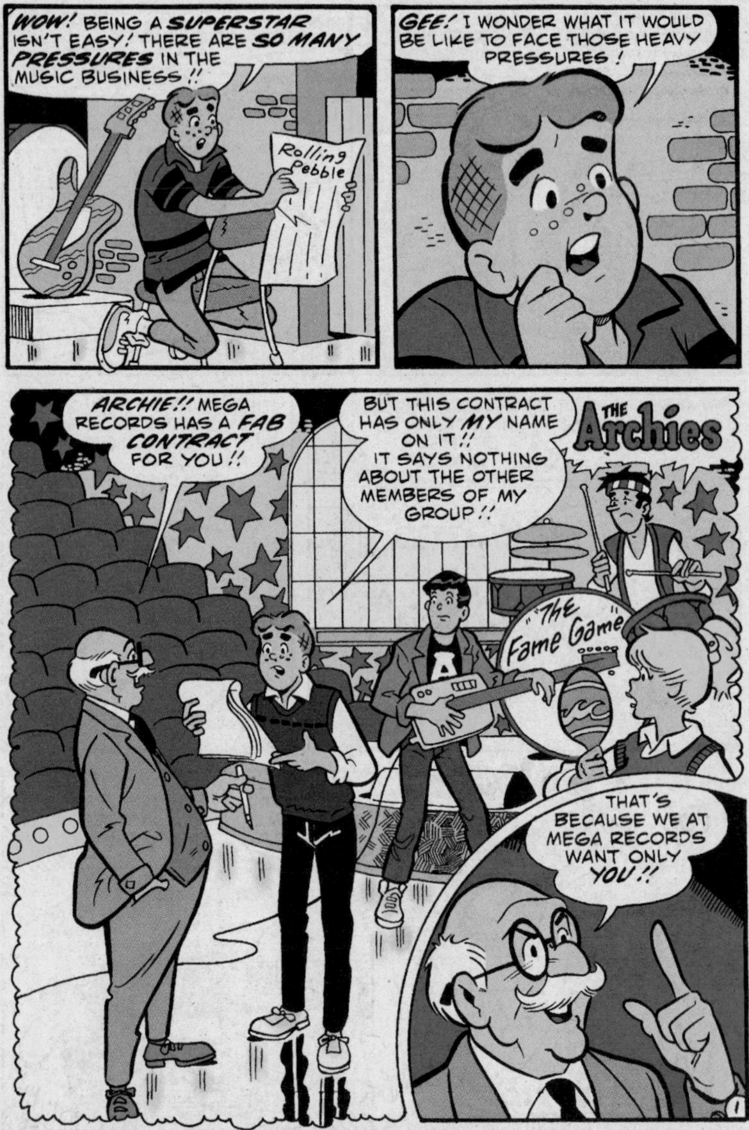

WOW! BEING A SUPERSTAR ISN'T EASY! THERE ARE SO MANY PRESSURES IN THE MUSIC BUSINESS!!
Rolling Pebble
GEE! I WONDER WHAT IT WOULD BE LIKE TO FACE THOSE HEAVY PRESSURES!
THE Archies
ARCHIE!! MEGA RECORDS HAS A FAB CONTRACT FOR YOU!!
BUT THIS CONTRACT HAS ONLY MY NAME ON IT!! IT SAYS NOTHING ABOUT THE OTHER MEMBERS OF MY GROUP!!
"The Fame Game"
THAT'S BECAUSE WE AT MEGA RECORDS WANT ONLY YOU!!
1

Script: George Gladir / Pencils: Doug Crane / Inks: Richard Maurizio / Letters: Rod Ollerenshaw

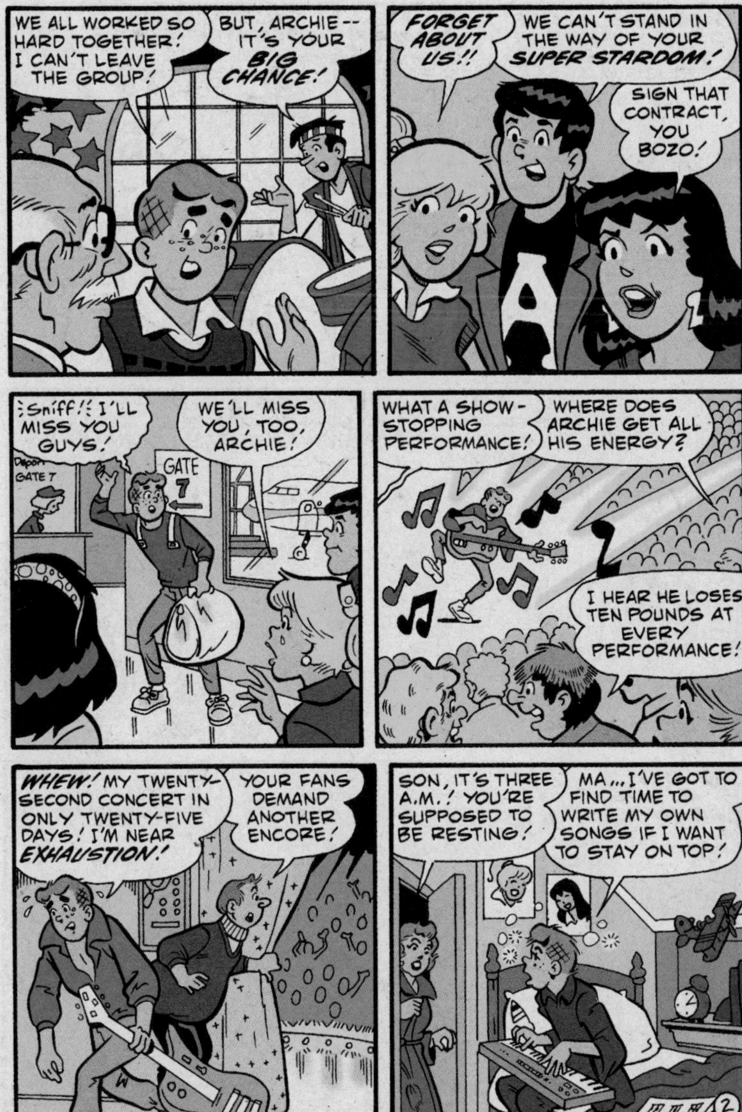
WE ALL WORKED SO HARD TOGETHER! I CAN'T LEAVE THE GROUP!
BUT, ARCHIE -- IT'S YOUR BIG CHANCE!
FORGET ABOUT US!!
WE CAN'T STAND IN THE WAY OF YOUR SUPER STARDOM!
SIGN THAT CONTRACT, YOU BOZO!
Sniff!! I'LL MISS YOU GUYS!
WE'LL MISS YOU, TOO, ARCHIE!
GATE 7
GATE 7
WHAT A SHOW-STOPPING PERFORMANCE!
WHERE DOES ARCHIE GET ALL HIS ENERGY?
I HEAR HE LOSES TEN POUNDS AT EVERY PERFORMANCE!
WHEW! MY TWENTY-SECOND CONCERT IN ONLY TWENTY-FIVE DAYS! I'M NEAR EXHAUSTION!
YOUR FANS DEMAND ANOTHER ENCORE!
SON, IT'S THREE A.M.! YOU'RE SUPPOSED TO BE RESTING!
MA... I'VE GOT TO FIND TIME TO WRITE MY OWN SONGS IF I WANT TO STAY ON TOP!
2

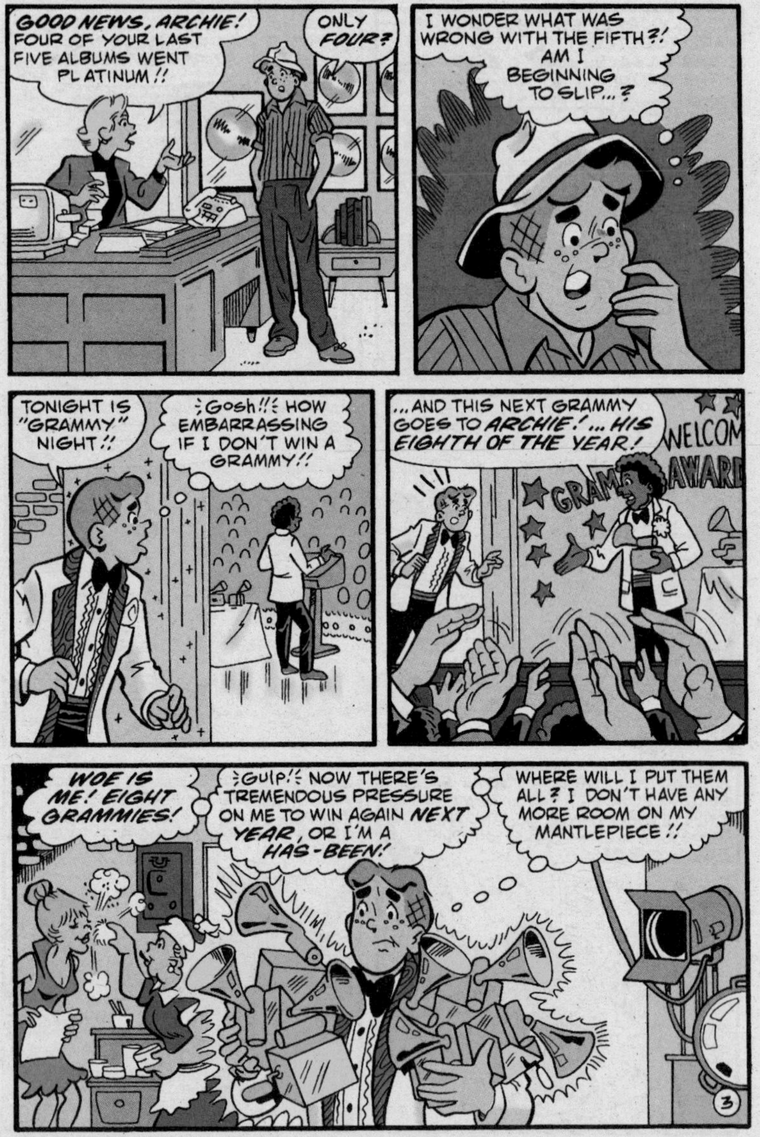
GOOD NEWS, ARCHIE! FOUR OF YOUR LAST FIVE ALBUMS WENT PLATINUM!!
ONLY FOUR?
I WONDER WHAT WAS WRONG WITH THE FIFTH?! AM I BEGINNING TO SLIP...?
TONIGHT IS "GRAMMY" NIGHT!!
Gosh!! HOW EMBARRASSING IF I DON'T WIN A GRAMMY!!
...AND THIS NEXT GRAMMY GOES TO ARCHIE! ...HIS EIGHTH OF THE YEAR!
WELCOM
AWARD
GRAM
WOE IS ME! EIGHT GRAMMIES!
Gulp! NOW THERE'S TREMENDOUS PRESSURE ON ME TO WIN AGAIN NEXT YEAR, OR I'M A HAS-BEEN!
WHERE WILL I PUT THEM ALL? I DON'T HAVE ANY MORE ROOM ON MY MANTLEPIECE!!
3

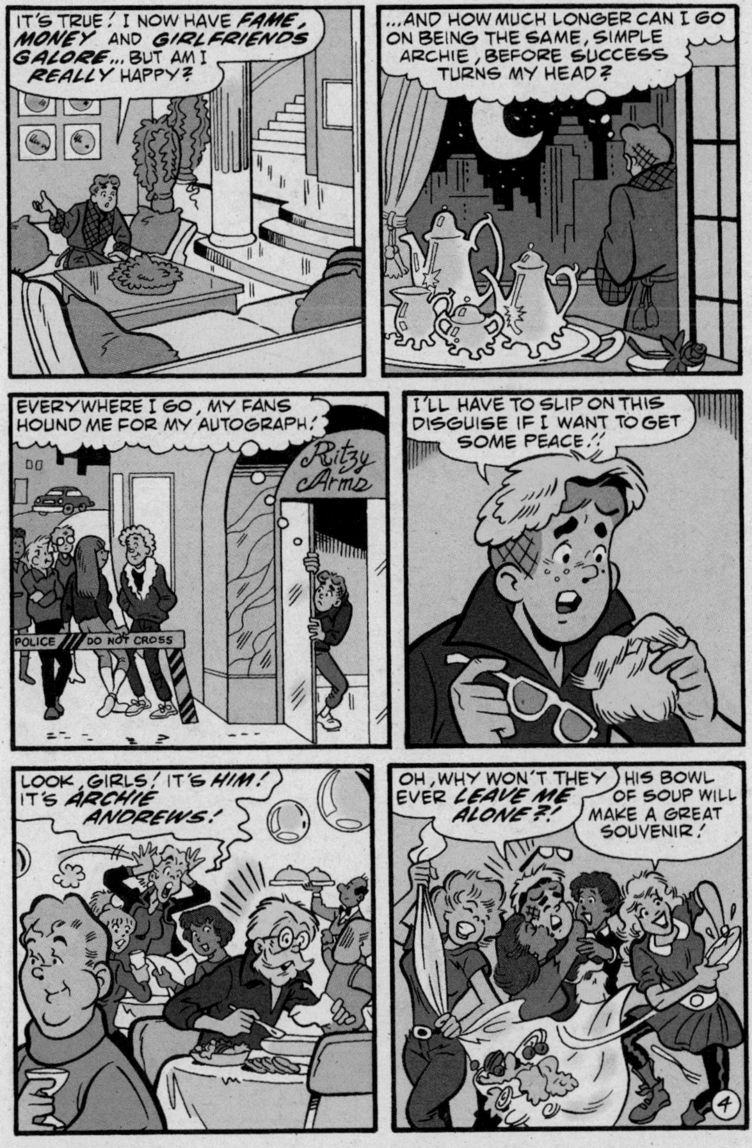
IT'S TRUE! I NOW HAVE FAME, MONEY AND GIRLFRIENDS GALORE... BUT AM I REALLY HAPPY?
...AND HOW MUCH LONGER CAN I GO ON BEING THE SAME, SIMPLE ARCHIE, BEFORE SUCCESS TURNS MY HEAD?
EVERYWHERE I GO, MY FANS HOUND ME FOR MY AUTOGRAPH!
Ritzy Arms
POLICE
DO NOT CROSS
I'LL HAVE TO SLIP ON THIS DISGUISE IF I WANT TO GET SOME PEACE!!
LOOK, GIRLS! IT'S HIM! IT'S ARCHIE ANDREWS!
OH, WHY WON'T THEY EVER LEAVE ME ALONE?!
HIS BOWL OF SOUP WILL MAKE A GREAT SOUVENIR!
4

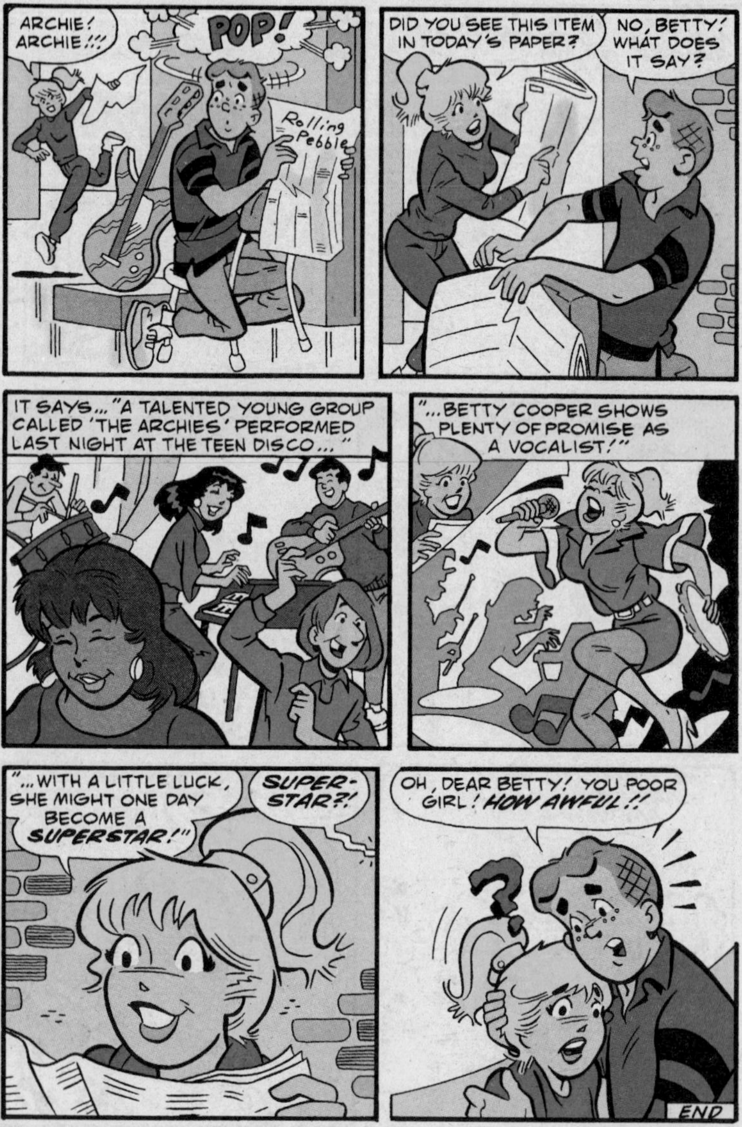
ARCHIE! ARCHIE!!!
POP!
Rolling Pebble
DID YOU SEE THIS ITEM IN TODAY'S PAPER?
NO, BETTY! WHAT DOES IT SAY?
IT SAYS... "A TALENTED YOUNG GROUP CALLED 'THE ARCHIES' PERFORMED LAST NIGHT AT THE TEEN DISCO..."
"...BETTY COOPER SHOWS PLENTY OF PROMISE AS A VOCALIST!"
"...WITH A LITTLE LUCK, SHE MIGHT ONE DAY BECOME A SUPERSTAR!"
SUPER-STAR?!
OH, DEAR BETTY! YOU POOR GIRL! HOW AWFUL!!
END

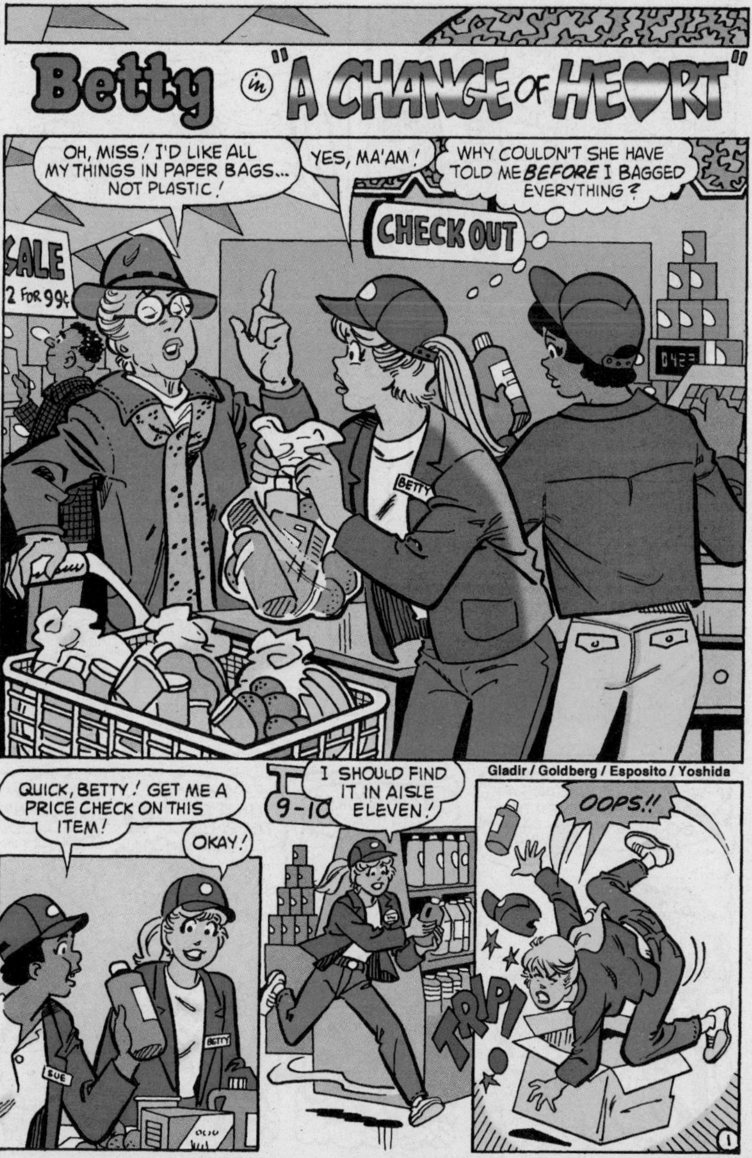

Betty in "A CHANGE OF HEART"
OH, MISS! I'D LIKE ALL MY THINGS IN PAPER BAGS... NOT PLASTIC!
YES, MA'AM!
WHY COULDN'T SHE HAVE TOLD ME BEFORE I BAGGED EVERYTHING?
CHECK OUT
SALE 2 FOR 99¢
BETTY
Gladir / Goldberg / Esposito / Yoshida
QUICK, BETTY! GET ME A PRICE CHECK ON THIS ITEM!
OKAY!
SUE
BETTY
I SHOULD FIND IT IN AISLE ELEVEN!
9-10
OOPS!!
TRIP!
1

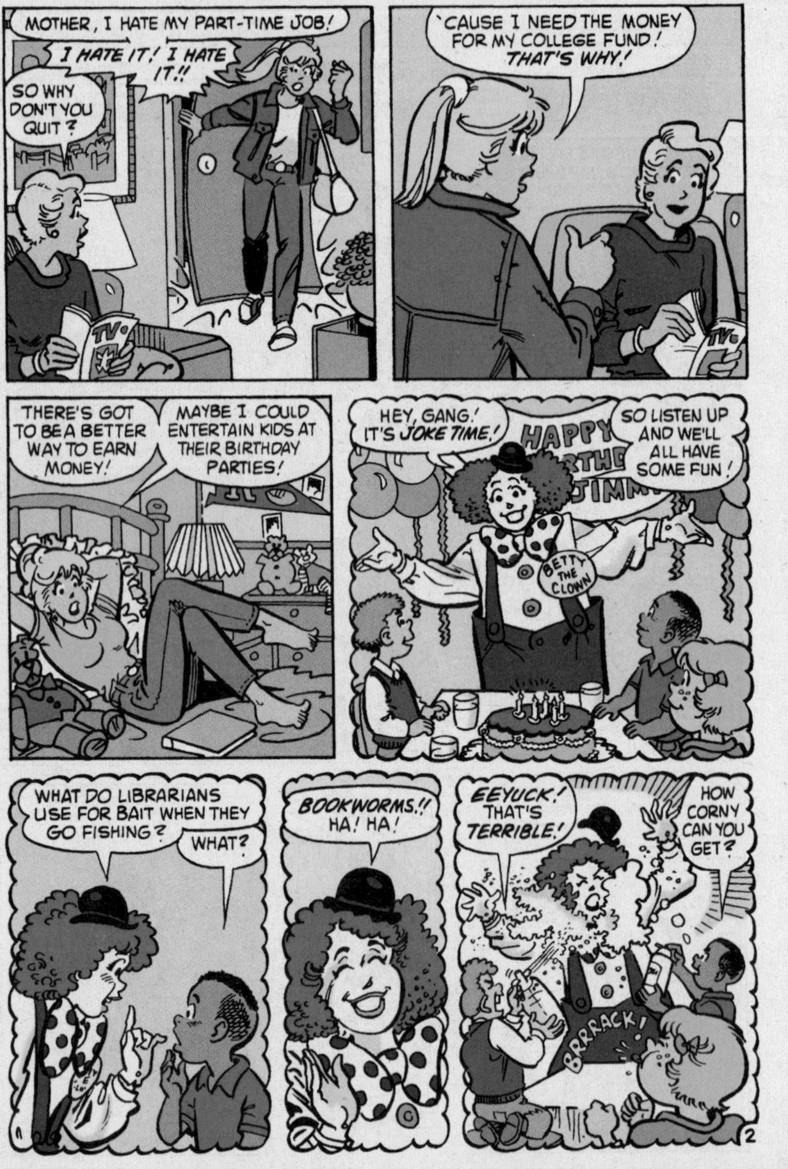
MOTHER, I HATE MY PART-TIME JOB!
I HATE IT! I HATE IT!!
SO WHY DON'T YOU QUIT?
'CAUSE I NEED THE MONEY FOR MY COLLEGE FUND! THAT'S WHY!
THERE'S GOT TO BE A BETTER WAY TO EARN MONEY!
MAYBE I COULD ENTERTAIN KIDS AT THEIR BIRTHDAY PARTIES!
HEY, GANG! IT'S JOKE TIME!
SO LISTEN UP AND WE'LL ALL HAVE SOME FUN!
BETTY THE CLOWN
WHAT DO LIBRARIANS USE FOR BAIT WHEN THEY GO FISHING?
WHAT?
BOOKWORMS!! HA! HA!
EEYUCK! THAT'S TERRIBLE!
HOW CORNY CAN YOU GET?
BRRRACK!

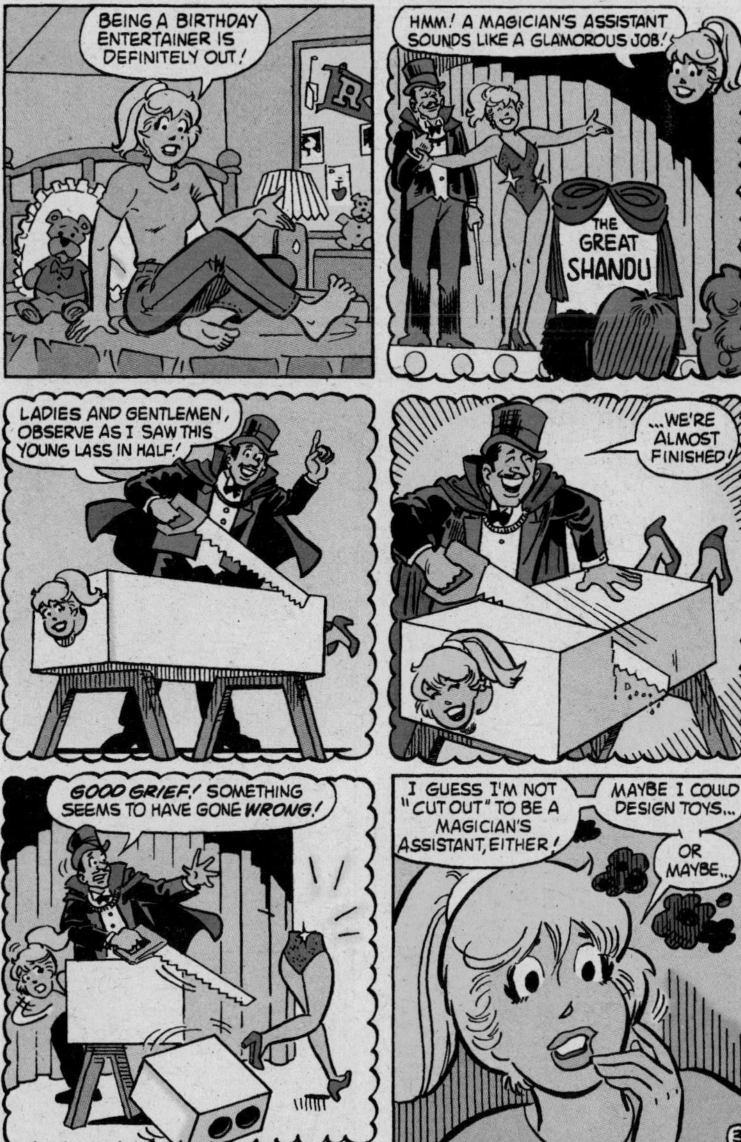

BEING A BIRTHDAY ENTERTAINER IS DEFINITELY OUT!
HMM! A MAGICIAN'S ASSISTANT SOUNDS LIKE A GLAMOROUS JOB!
THE GREAT SHANDU
LADIES AND GENTLEMEN, OBSERVE AS I SAW THIS YOUNG LASS IN HALF!
...WE'RE ALMOST FINISHED!
GOOD GRIEF! SOMETHING SEEMS TO HAVE GONE WRONG!
I GUESS I'M NOT "CUT OUT" TO BE A MAGICIAN'S ASSISTANT, EITHER!
MAYBE I COULD DESIGN TOYS...
OR MAYBE...
3

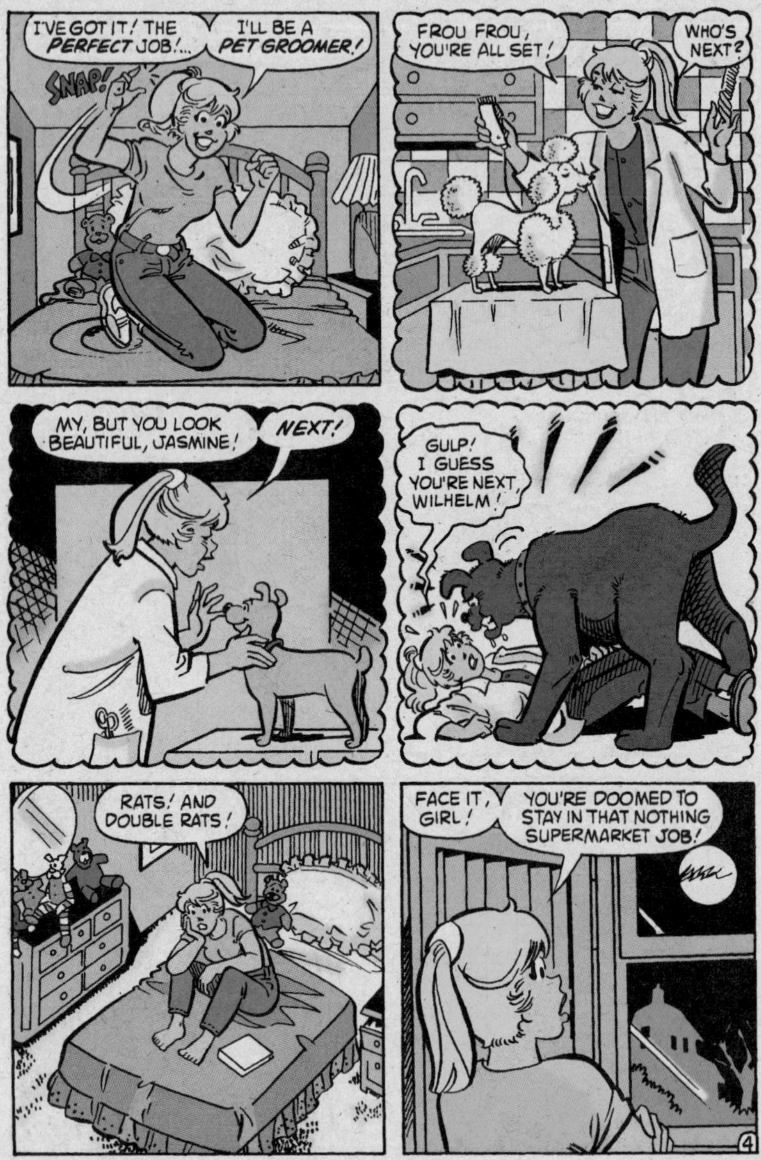

I'VE GOT IT! THE PERFECT JOB!...
I'LL BE A PET GROOMER!
SNAP!
FROU FROU, YOU'RE ALL SET!
WHO'S NEXT?
MY, BUT YOU LOOK BEAUTIFUL, JASMINE!
NEXT!
GULP! I GUESS YOU'RE NEXT, WILHELM!
RATS! AND DOUBLE RATS!
FACE IT, GIRL!
YOU'RE DOOMED TO STAY IN THAT NOTHING SUPERMARKET JOB!
4

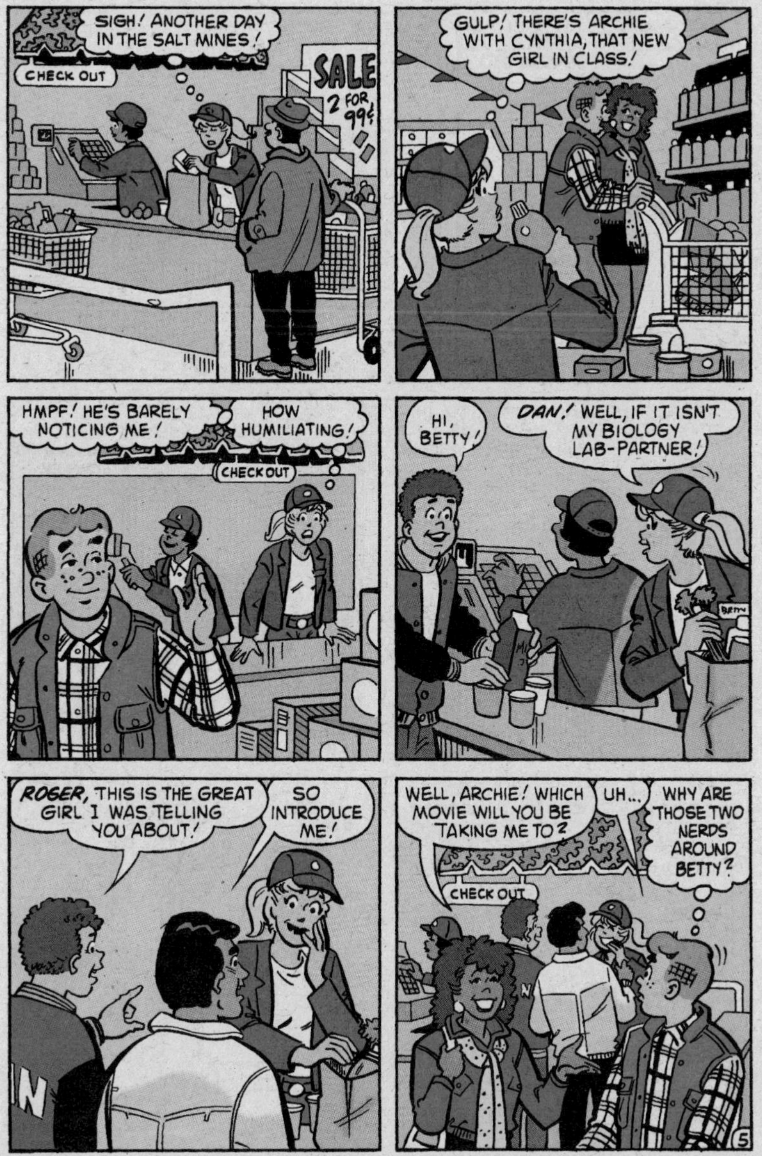
SIGH! ANOTHER DAY IN THE SALT MINES!
CHECK OUT
SALE 2 FOR 99¢
GULP! THERE'S ARCHIE WITH CYNTHIA, THAT NEW GIRL IN CLASS!
HMPF! HE'S BARELY NOTICING ME!
HOW HUMILIATING!
CHECK OUT
HI, BETTY!
DAN! WELL, IF IT ISN'T MY BIOLOGY LAB-PARTNER!
ROGER, THIS IS THE GREAT GIRL I WAS TELLING YOU ABOUT!
SO INTRODUCE ME!
WELL, ARCHIE! WHICH MOVIE WILL YOU BE TAKING ME TO?
UH...
WHY ARE THOSE TWO NERDS AROUND BETTY?
CHECK OUT
5

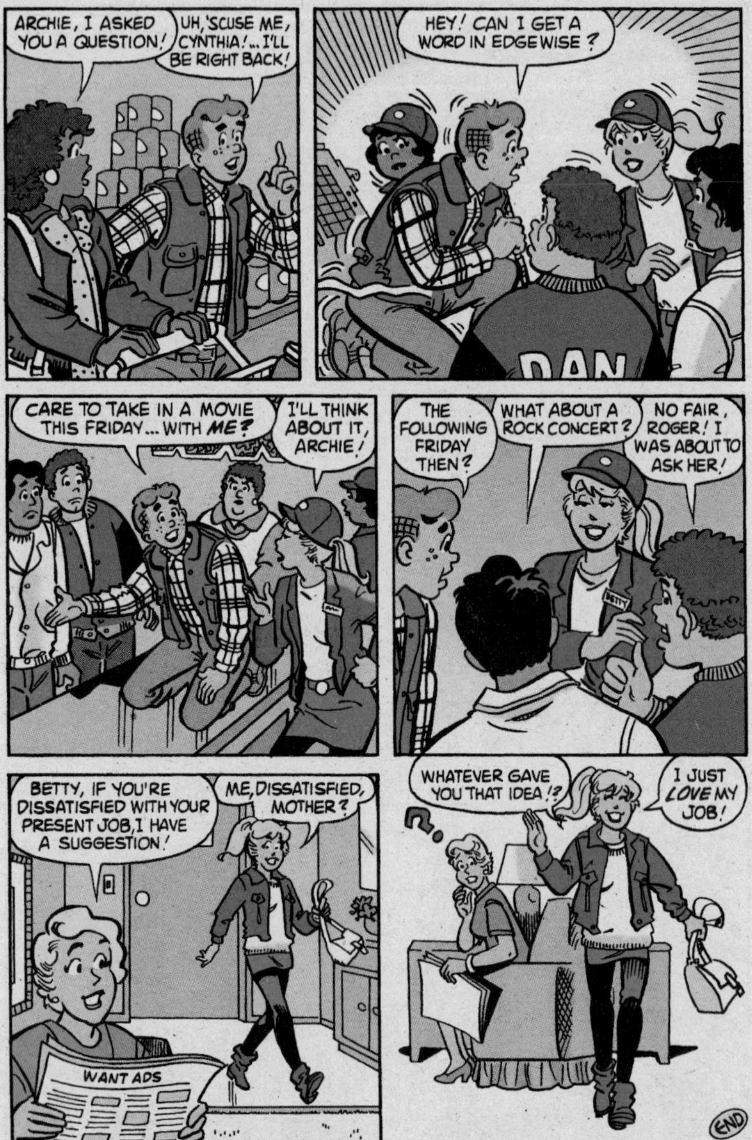

ARCHIE, I ASKED YOU A QUESTION!
UH, 'SCUSE ME, CYNTHIA!... I'LL BE RIGHT BACK!
HEY! CAN I GET A WORD IN EDGEWISE?
DAN
CARE TO TAKE IN A MOVIE THIS FRIDAY... WITH ME?
I'LL THINK ABOUT IT, ARCHIE!
THE FOLLOWING FRIDAY THEN?
WHAT ABOUT A ROCK CONCERT?
NO FAIR, ROGER! I WAS ABOUT TO ASK HER!
BETTY
BETTY, IF YOU'RE DISSATISFIED WITH YOUR PRESENT JOB, I HAVE A SUGGESTION!
ME, DISSATISFIED, MOTHER?
WANT ADS
WHATEVER GAVE YOU THAT IDEA!?
I JUST LOVE MY JOB!
END

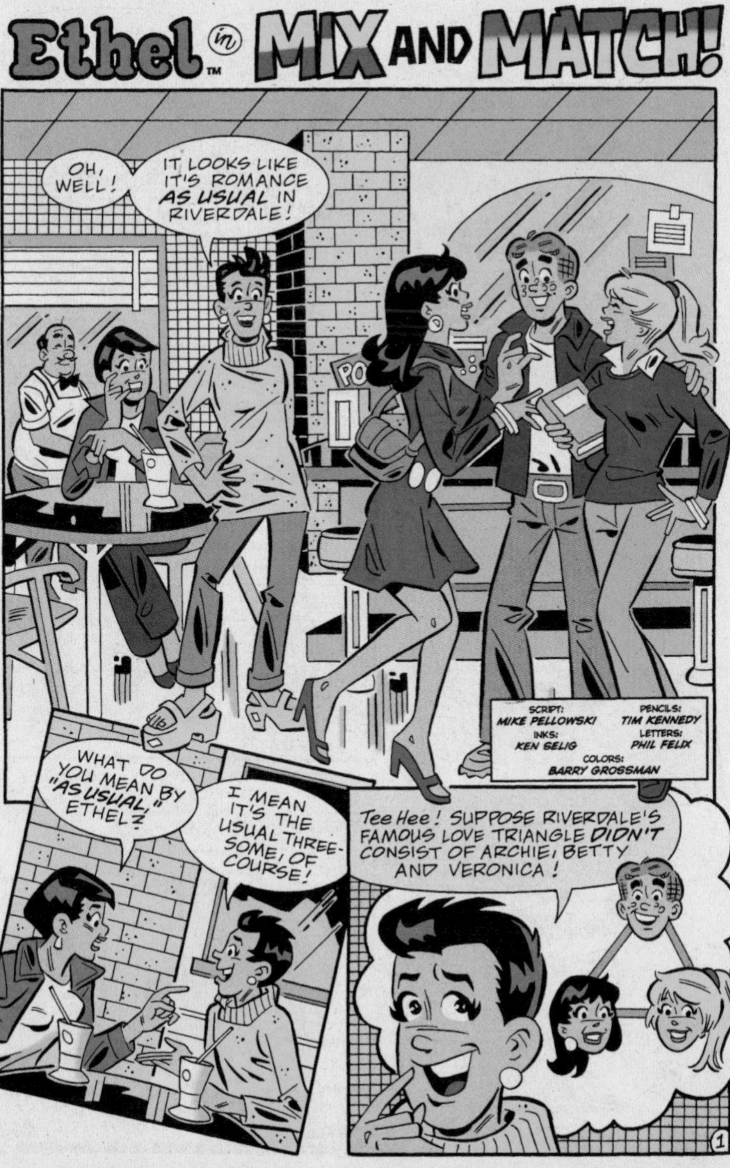
Ethel in MIX AND MATCH!
OH, WELL!
IT LOOKS LIKE IT'S ROMANCE AS USUAL IN RIVERDALE!
SCRIPT: MIKE PELLOWSKI PENCILS: TIM KENNEDY INKS: KEN SELIG LETTERS: PHIL FELIX COLORS: BARRY GROSSMAN
WHAT DO YOU MEAN BY "AS USUAL," ETHEL?
I MEAN IT'S THE USUAL THREESOME, OF COURSE!
Tee Hee! SUPPOSE RIVERDALE'S FAMOUS LOVE TRIANGLE DIDN'T CONSIST OF ARCHIE, BETTY AND VERONICA!
1

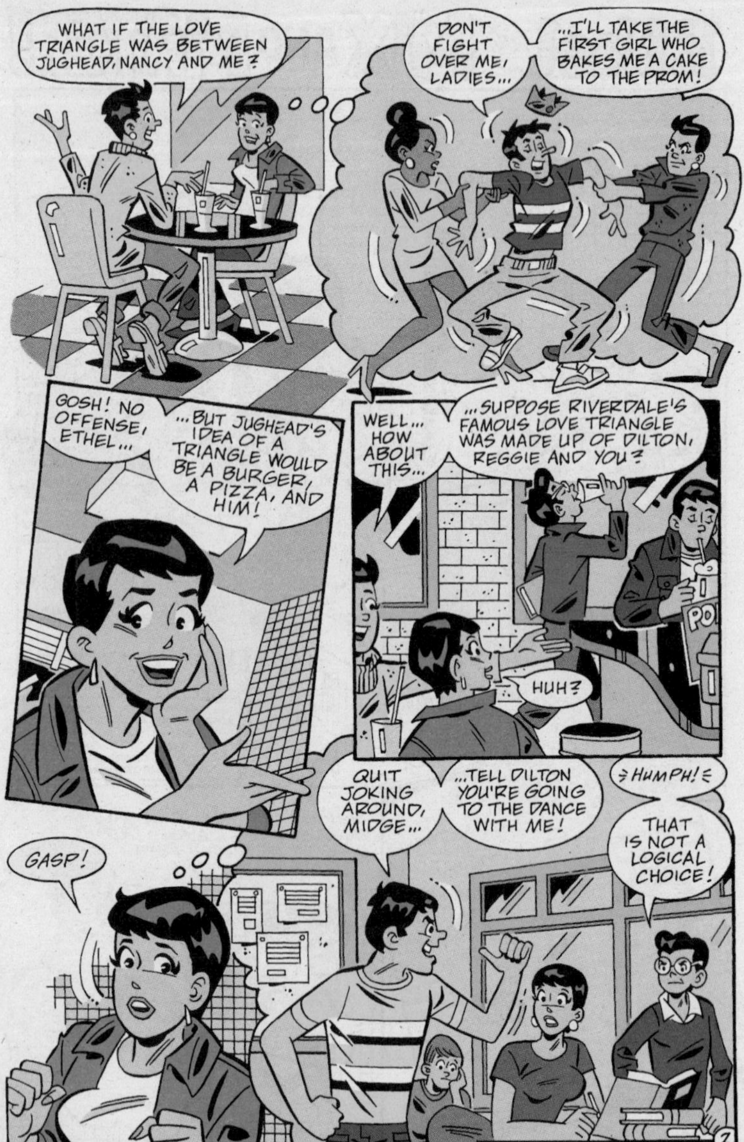

WHAT IF THE LOVE TRIANGLE WAS BETWEEN JUGHEAD, NANCY AND ME?
DON'T FIGHT OVER ME, LADIES...
...I'LL TAKE THE FIRST GIRL WHO BAKES ME A CAKE TO THE PROM!
GOSH! NO OFFENSE, ETHEL...
...BUT JUGHEAD'S IDEA OF A TRIANGLE WOULD BE A BURGER, A PIZZA, AND HIM!
WELL... HOW ABOUT THIS...
...SUPPOSE RIVERDALE'S FAMOUS LOVE TRIANGLE WAS MADE UP OF DILTON, REGGIE AND YOU?
HUH?
GASP!
QUIT JOKING AROUND, MIDGE...
...TELL DILTON YOU'RE GOING TO THE DANCE WITH ME!
HUMPH!
THAT IS NOT A LOGICAL CHOICE!
2

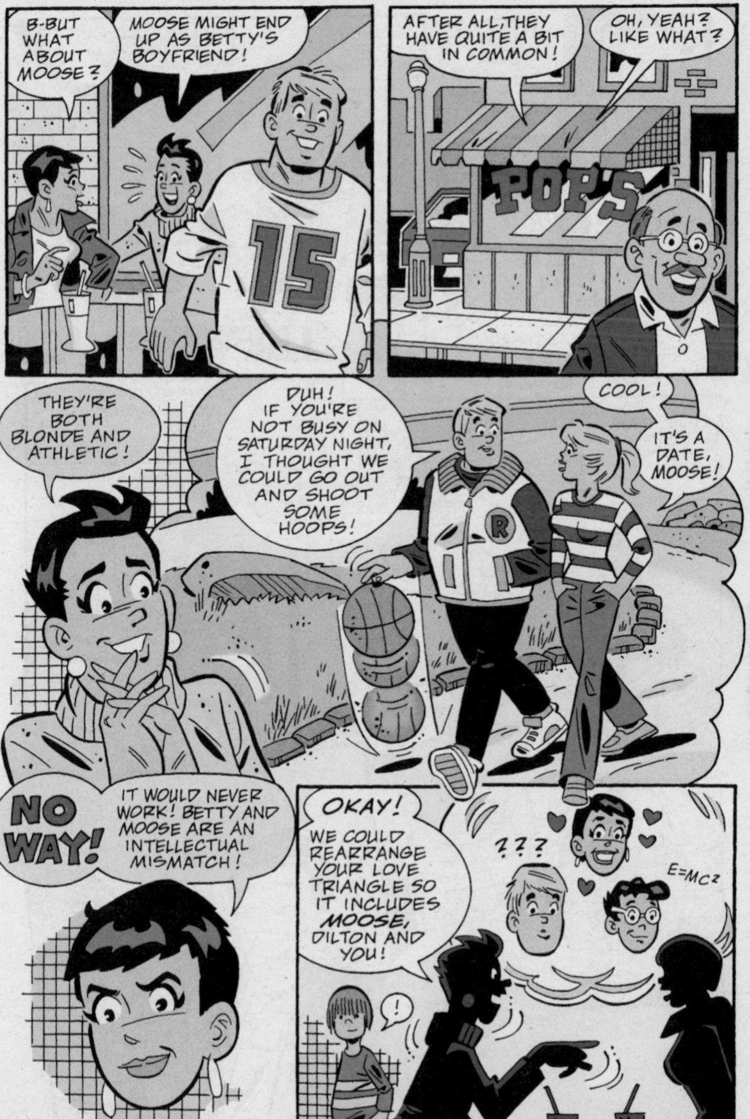
B-BUT WHAT ABOUT MOOSE?
MOOSE MIGHT END UP AS BETTY'S BOYFRIEND!
15
AFTER ALL, THEY HAVE QUITE A BIT IN COMMON!
OH, YEAH? LIKE WHAT?
POP'S
THEY'RE BOTH BLONDE AND ATHLETIC!
DUH! IF YOU'RE NOT BUSY ON SATURDAY NIGHT, I THOUGHT WE COULD GO OUT AND SHOOT SOME HOOPS!
COOL!
IT'S A DATE, MOOSE!
R
NO WAY!
IT WOULD NEVER WORK! BETTY AND MOOSE ARE AN INTELLECTUAL MISMATCH!
OKAY!
WE COULD REARRANGE YOUR LOVE TRIANGLE SO IT INCLUDES MOOSE, DILTON AND YOU!
???
E=MC²
!
3

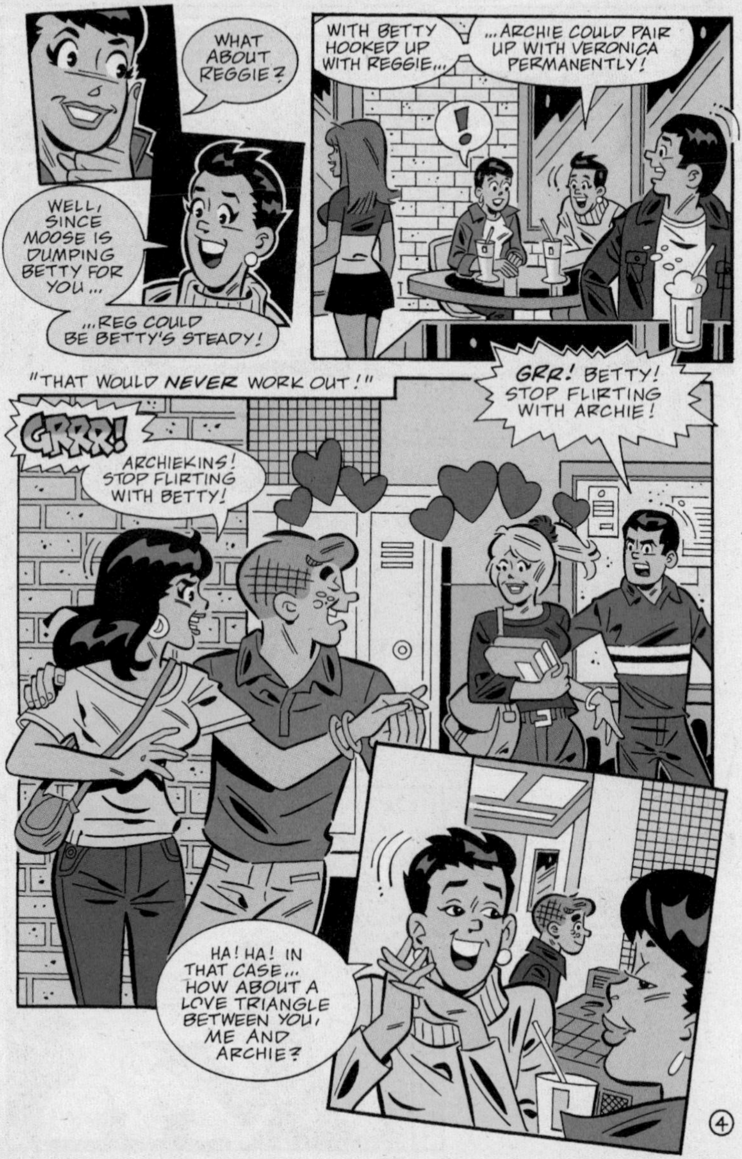

WHAT ABOUT REGGIE?
WELL, SINCE MOOSE IS DUMPING BETTY FOR YOU...
...REG COULD BE BETTY'S STEADY!
WITH BETTY HOOKED UP WITH REGGIE...
...ARCHIE COULD PAIR UP WITH VERONICA PERMANENTLY!
!
"THAT WOULD NEVER WORK OUT!"
GRRR!
ARCHIEKINS! STOP FLIRTING WITH BETTY!
GRR! BETTY! STOP FLIRTING WITH ARCHIE!
HA! HA! IN THAT CASE... HOW ABOUT A LOVE TRIANGLE BETWEEN YOU, ME AND ARCHIE?

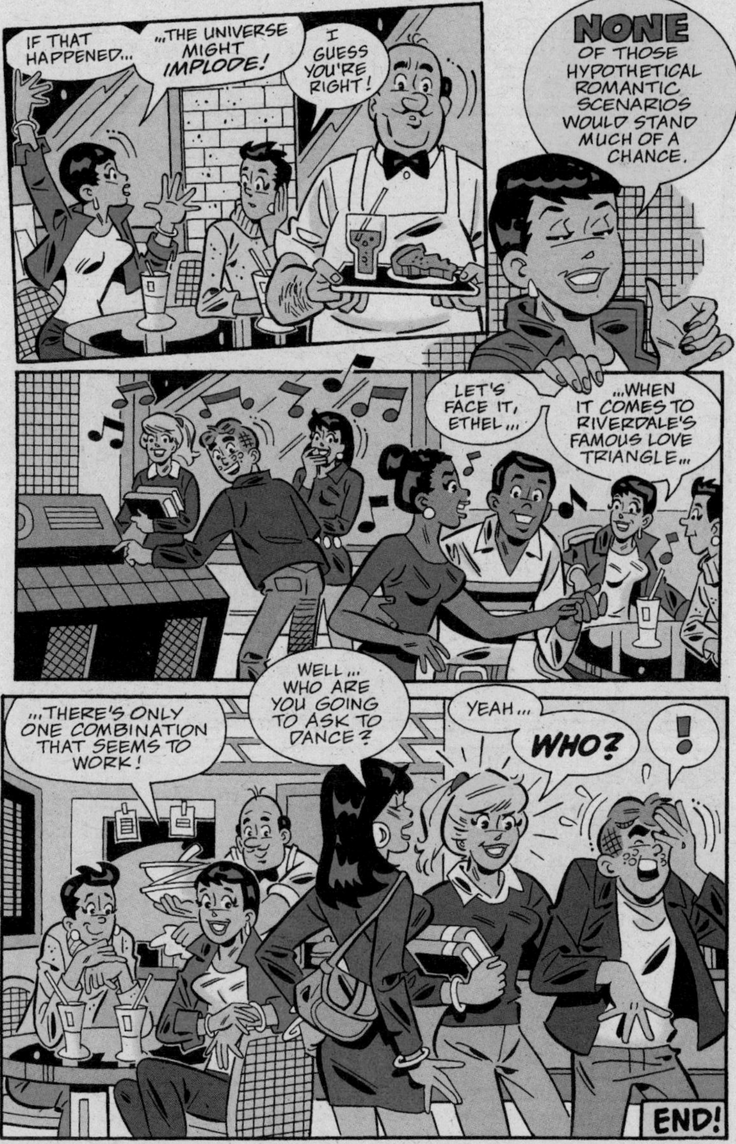
IF THAT HAPPENED...
...THE UNIVERSE MIGHT IMPLODE!
I GUESS YOU'RE RIGHT!
NONE OF THOSE HYPOTHETICAL ROMANTIC SCENARIOS WOULD STAND MUCH OF A CHANCE.
LET'S FACE IT, ETHEL...
...WHEN IT COMES TO RIVERDALE'S FAMOUS LOVE TRIANGLE...
...THERE'S ONLY ONE COMBINATION THAT SEEMS TO WORK!
WELL... WHO ARE YOU GOING TO ASK TO DANCE?
YEAH... WHO?
!
END!

Betty and Veronica in The Reading Lesson

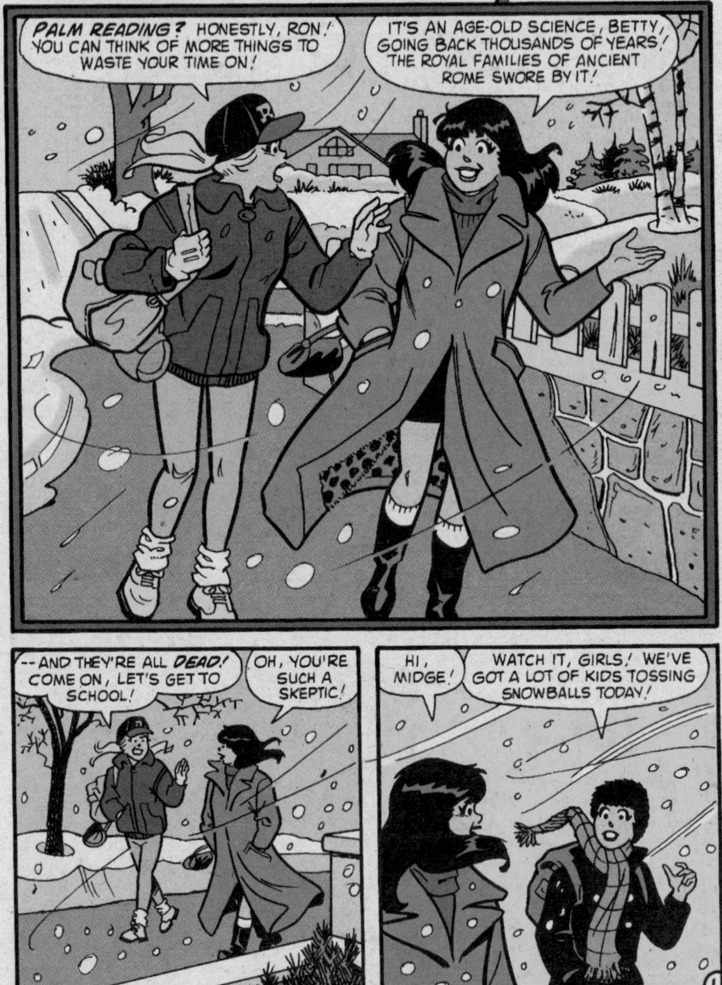
PALM READING? HONESTLY, RON! YOU CAN THINK OF MORE THINGS TO WASTE YOUR TIME ON!
IT'S AN AGE-OLD SCIENCE, BETTY, GOING BACK THOUSANDS OF YEARS! THE ROYAL FAMILIES OF ANCIENT ROME SWORE BY IT!
-- AND THEY'RE ALL DEAD! COME ON, LET'S GET TO SCHOOL!
OH, YOU'RE SUCH A SKEPTIC!
HI, MIDGE!
WATCH IT, GIRLS! WE'VE GOT A LOT OF KIDS TOSSING SNOWBALLS TODAY!
1

Script: Frank Doyle / Pencils: Dan DeCarlo / Inks: Alison Flood / Letters: Bill Yoshida / Colors: Barry Grossman

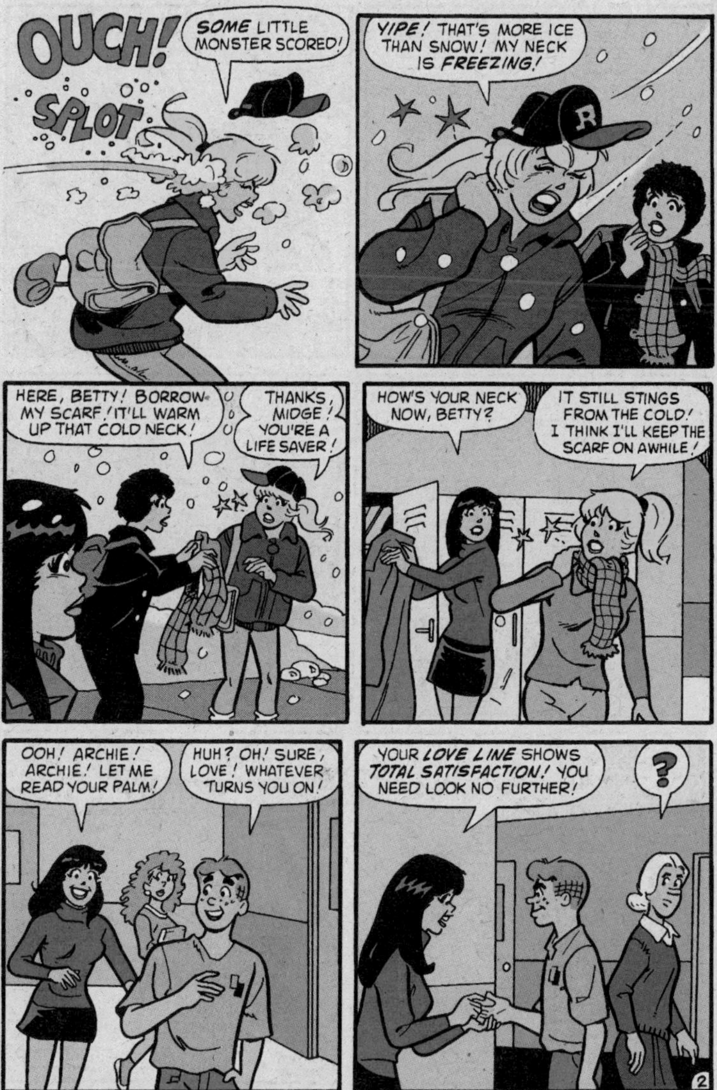
OUCH!
SOME LITTLE MONSTER SCORED!
SPLOT
YIPE! THAT'S MORE ICE THAN SNOW! MY NECK IS FREEZING!
R
HERE, BETTY! BORROW MY SCARF! IT'LL WARM UP THAT COLD NECK!
THANKS, MIDGE! YOU'RE A LIFE SAVER!
HOW'S YOUR NECK NOW, BETTY?
IT STILL STINGS FROM THE COLD! I THINK I'LL KEEP THE SCARF ON AWHILE!
OOH! ARCHIE! ARCHIE! LET ME READ YOUR PALM!
HUH? OH! SURE, LOVE! WHATEVER TURNS YOU ON!
YOUR LOVE LINE SHOWS TOTAL SATISFACTION! YOU NEED LOOK NO FURTHER!
?
2

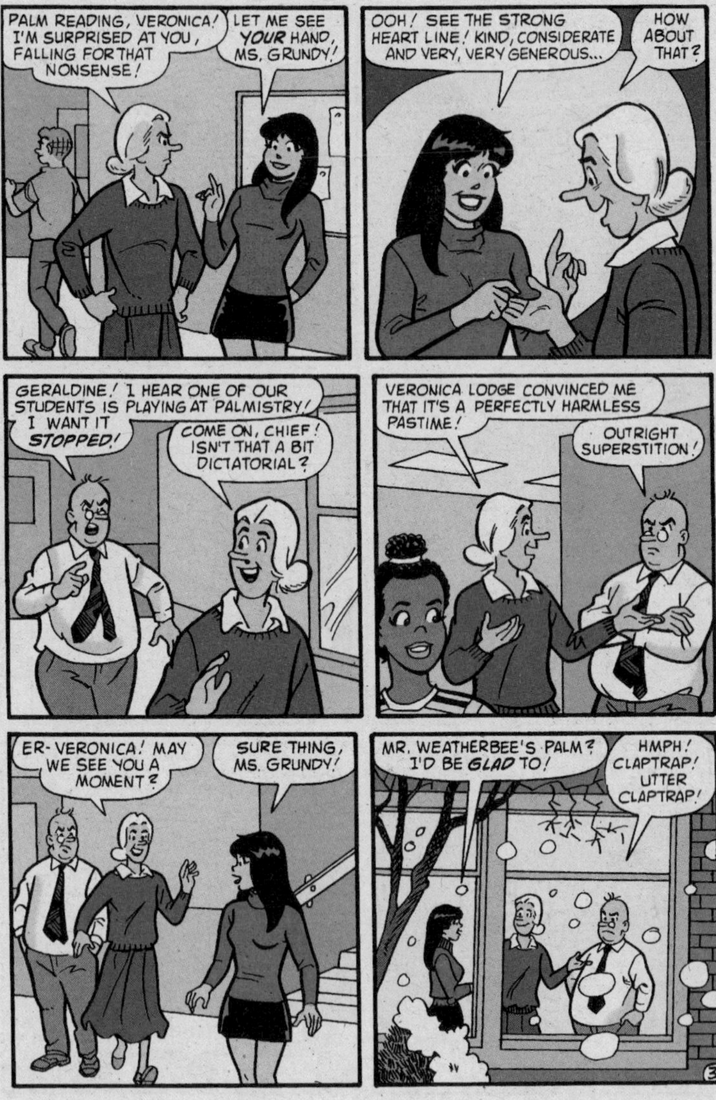
PALM READING, VERONICA! I'M SURPRISED AT YOU, FALLING FOR THAT NONSENSE!
LET ME SEE YOUR HAND, MS. GRUNDY!
OOH! SEE THE STRONG HEART LINE! KIND, CONSIDERATE AND VERY, VERY GENEROUS...
HOW ABOUT THAT?
GERALDINE! I HEAR ONE OF OUR STUDENTS IS PLAYING AT PALMISTRY! I WANT IT STOPPED!
COME ON, CHIEF! ISN'T THAT A BIT DICTATORIAL?
VERONICA LODGE CONVINCED ME THAT IT'S A PERFECTLY HARMLESS PASTIME!
OUTRIGHT SUPERSTITION!
ER- VERONICA! MAY WE SEE YOU A MOMENT?
SURE THING, MS. GRUNDY!
MR. WEATHERBEE'S PALM? I'D BE GLAD TO!
HMPH! CLAPTRAP! UTTER CLAPTRAP!
3

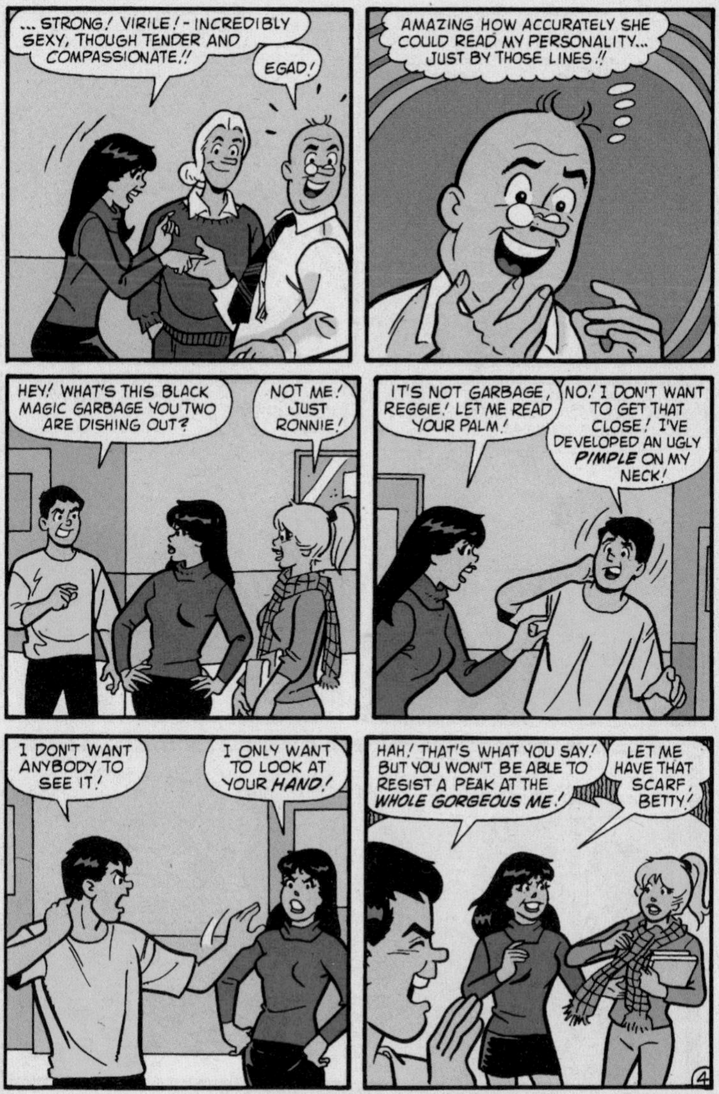
... STRONG! VIRILE! - INCREDIBLY SEXY, THOUGH TENDER AND COMPASSIONATE!!
EGAD!
AMAZING HOW ACCURATELY SHE COULD READ MY PERSONALITY... JUST BY THOSE LINES!!
HEY! WHAT'S THIS BLACK MAGIC GARBAGE YOU TWO ARE DISHING OUT?
NOT ME! JUST RONNIE!
IT'S NOT GARBAGE, REGGIE! LET ME READ YOUR PALM!
NO! I DON'T WANT TO GET THAT CLOSE! I'VE DEVELOPED AN UGLY PIMPLE ON MY NECK!
I DON'T WANT ANYBODY TO SEE IT!
I ONLY WANT TO LOOK AT YOUR HAND!
HAH! THAT'S WHAT YOU SAY! BUT YOU WON'T BE ABLE TO RESIST A PEAK AT THE WHOLE GORGEOUS ME!
LET ME HAVE THAT SCARF, BETTY!
4

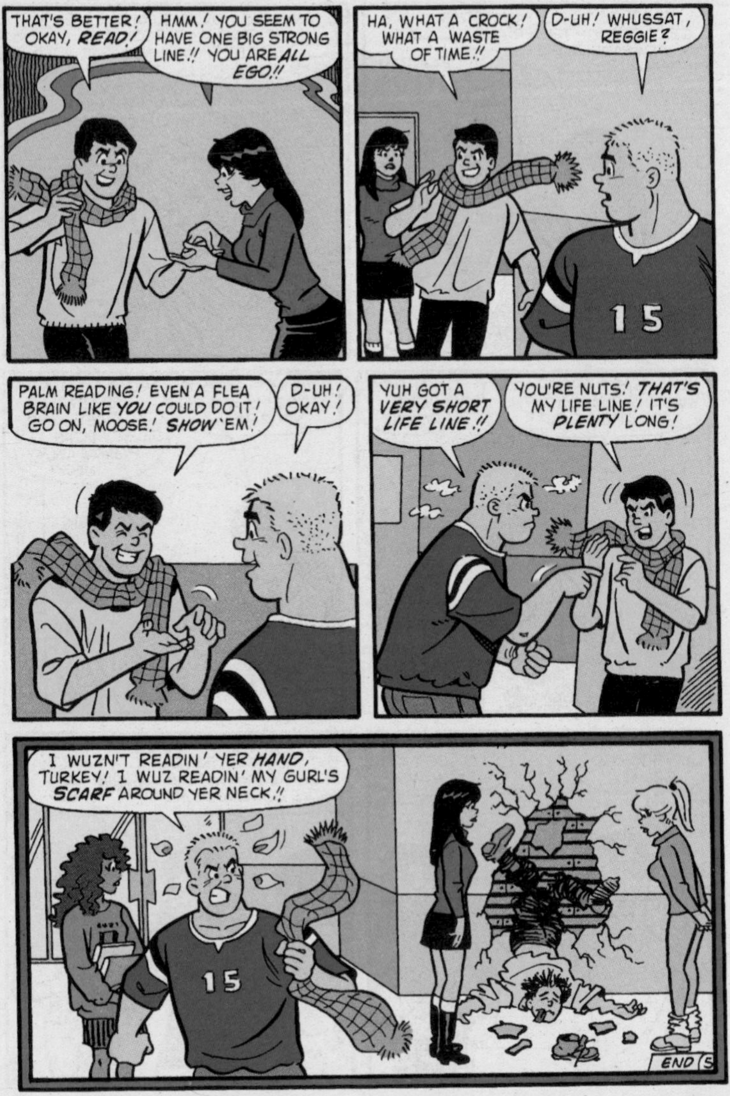
THAT'S BETTER! OKAY, READ!
HMM! YOU SEEM TO HAVE ONE BIG STRONG LINE!! YOU ARE ALL EGO!!
HA, WHAT A CROCK! WHAT A WASTE OF TIME!!
D-UH! WHUSSAT, REGGIE?
PALM READING! EVEN A FLEA BRAIN LIKE YOU COULD DO IT! GO ON, MOOSE! SHOW 'EM!
D-UH! OKAY!
YUH GOT A VERY SHORT LIFE LINE!!
YOU'RE NUTS! THAT'S MY LIFE LINE! IT'S PLENTY LONG!
I WUZN'T READIN' YER HAND, TURKEY! I WUZ READIN' MY GURL'S SCARF AROUND YER NECK!!
15
END 5

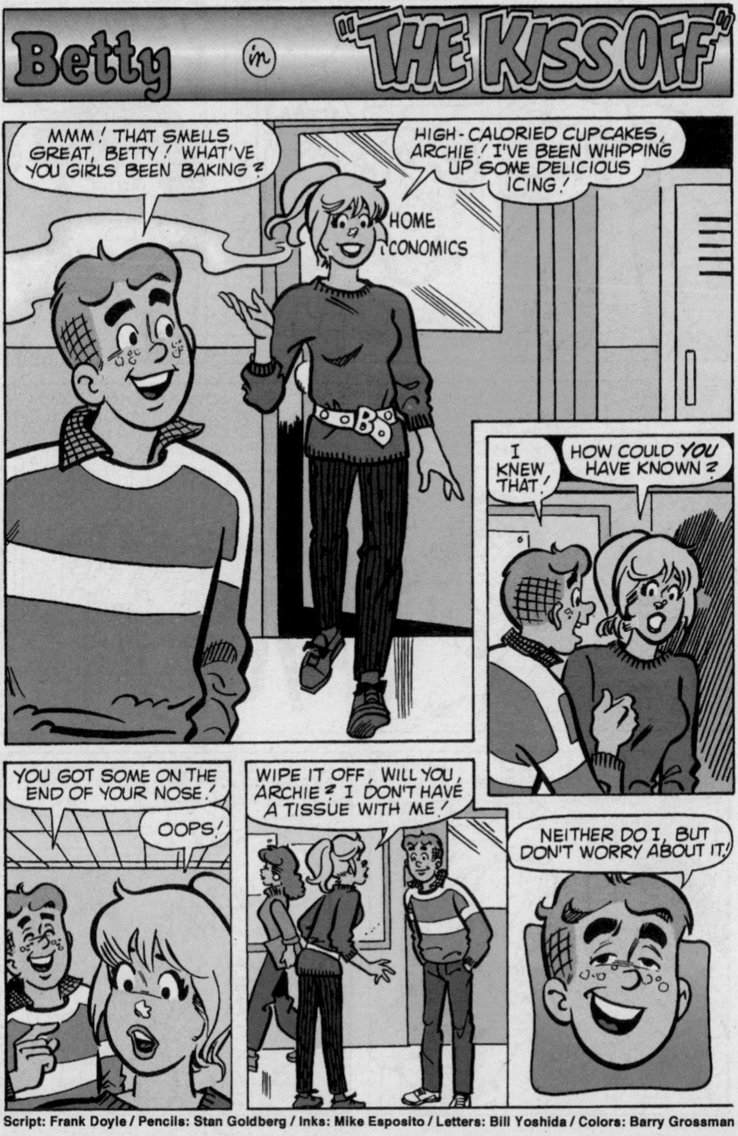
Betty in "THE KISS OFF"
MMM! THAT SMELLS GREAT, BETTY! WHAT'VE YOU GIRLS BEEN BAKING?
HIGH-CALORIED CUPCAKES, ARCHIE! I'VE BEEN WHIPPING UP SOME DELICIOUS ICING!
HOME ECONOMICS
I KNEW THAT!
HOW COULD YOU HAVE KNOWN?
YOU GOT SOME ON THE END OF YOUR NOSE!
OOPS!
WIPE IT OFF, WILL YOU, ARCHIE? I DON'T HAVE A TISSUE WITH ME!
NEITHER DO I, BUT DON'T WORRY ABOUT IT!

Script: Frank Doyle / Pencils: Stan Goldberg / Inks: Mike Esposito / Letters: Bill Yoshida / Colors: Barry Grossman

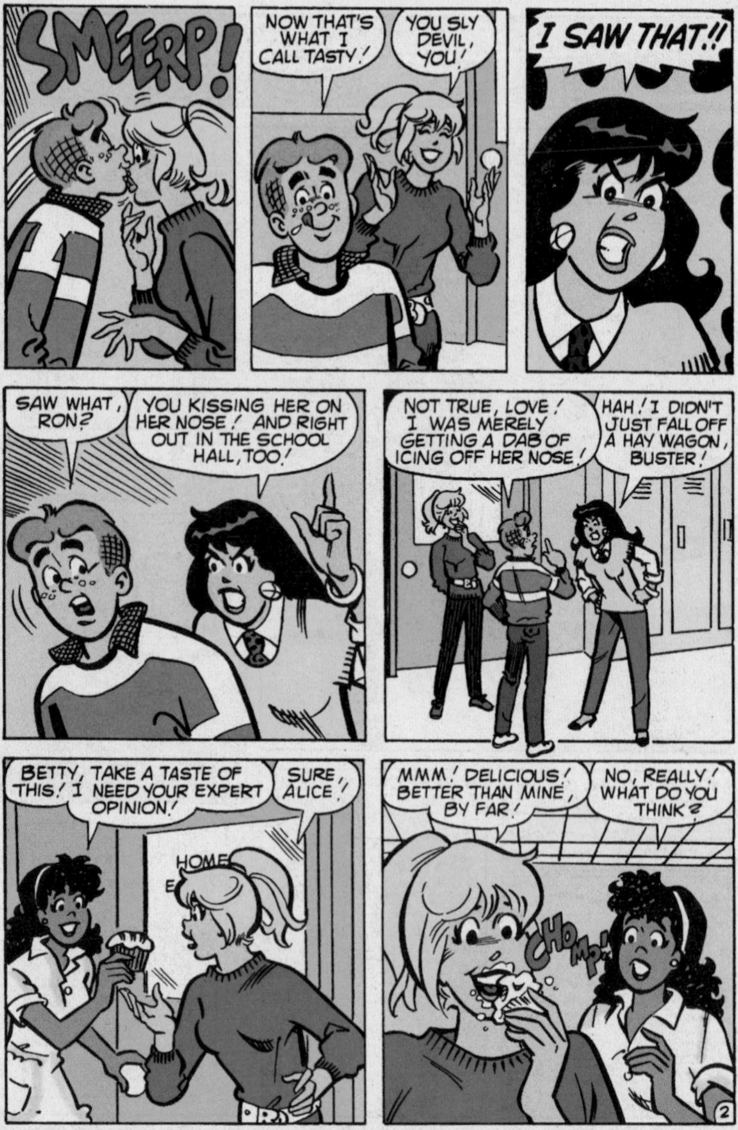
SMEERP!
NOW THAT'S WHAT I CALL TASTY!
YOU SLY DEVIL, YOU!
I SAW THAT!!
SAW WHAT, RON?
YOU KISSING HER ON HER NOSE! AND RIGHT OUT IN THE SCHOOL HALL, TOO!
NOT TRUE, LOVE! I WAS MERELY GETTING A DAB OF ICING OFF HER NOSE!
HAH! I DIDN'T JUST FALL OFF A HAY WAGON, BUSTER!
BETTY, TAKE A TASTE OF THIS! I NEED YOUR EXPERT OPINION!
SURE, ALICE!
HOME
MMM! DELICIOUS! BETTER THAN MINE, BY FAR!
NO, REALLY! WHAT DO YOU THINK?
CHOMP!
2

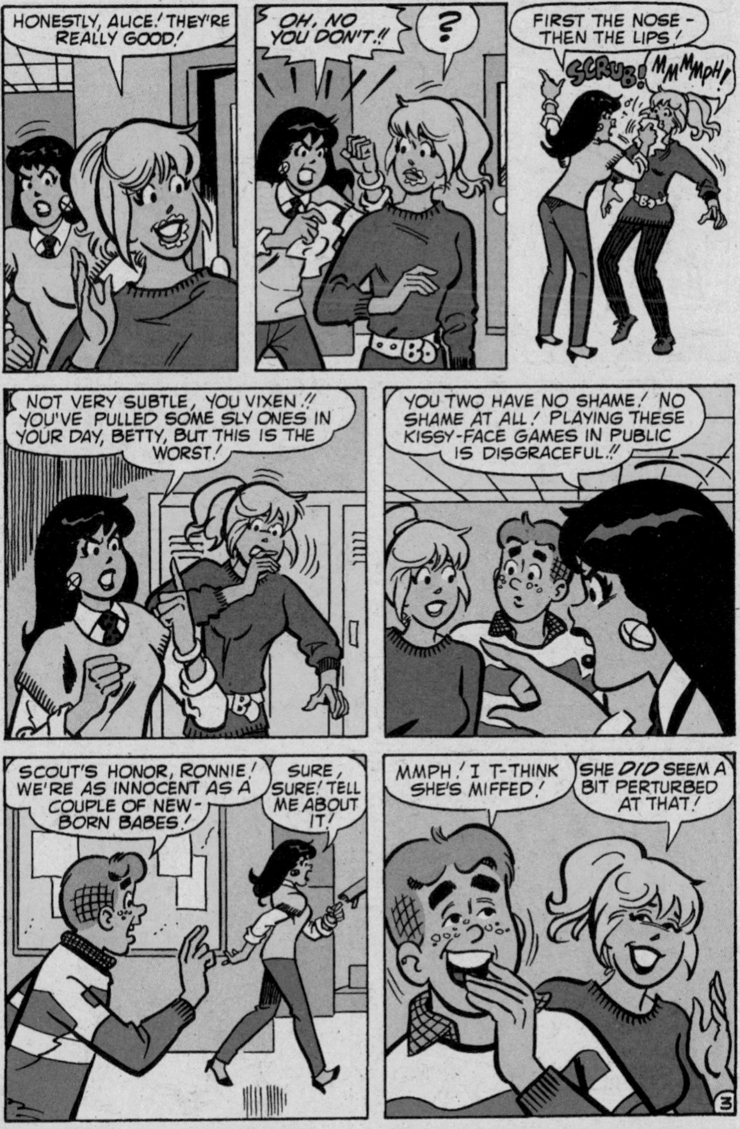
HONESTLY, ALICE! THEY'RE REALLY GOOD!
OH, NO YOU DON'T!!
?
FIRST THE NOSE - THEN THE LIPS!
SCRUB!
MMMMPH!
NOT VERY SUBTLE, YOU VIXEN!! YOU'VE PULLED SOME SLY ONES IN YOUR DAY, BETTY, BUT THIS IS THE WORST!
YOU TWO HAVE NO SHAME! NO SHAME AT ALL! PLAYING THESE KISSY-FACE GAMES IN PUBLIC IS DISGRACEFUL!!
SCOUT'S HONOR, RONNIE! WE'RE AS INNOCENT AS A COUPLE OF NEW-BORN BABES!
SURE, SURE! TELL ME ABOUT IT!
MMPH! I T-THINK SHE'S MIFFED!
SHE DID SEEM A BIT PERTURBED AT THAT!
3

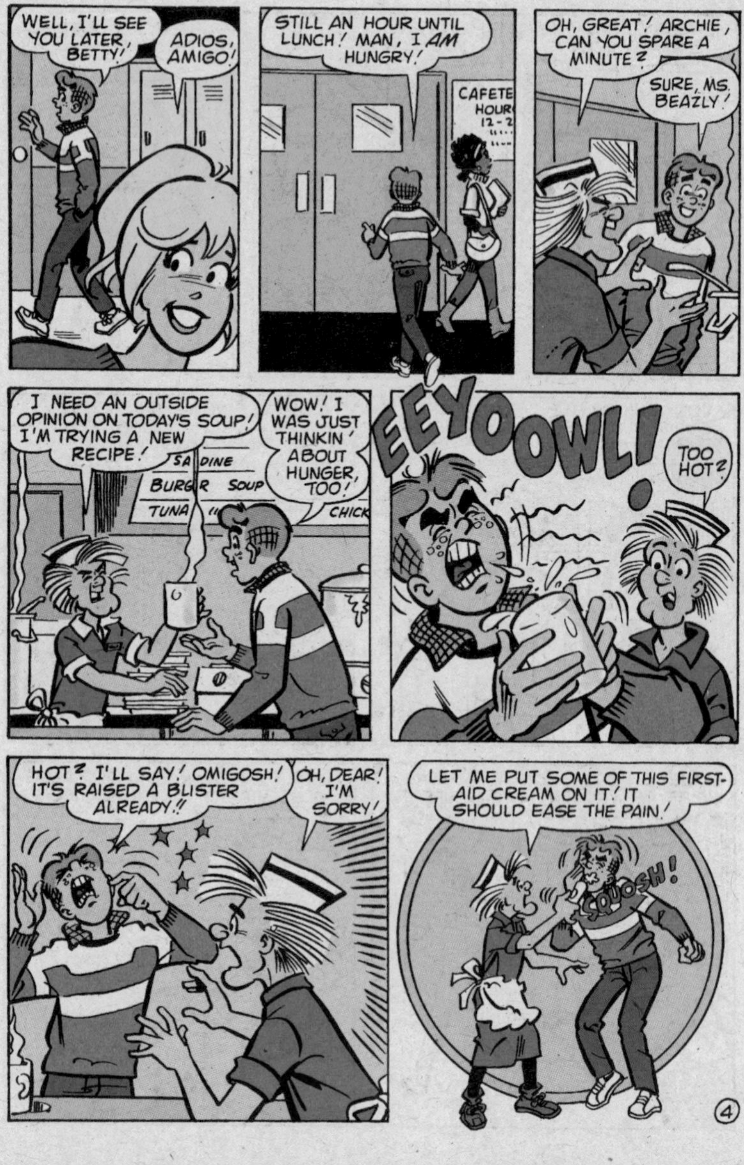
WELL, I'LL SEE YOU LATER, BETTY!
ADIOS, AMIGO!
STILL AN HOUR UNTIL LUNCH! MAN, I AM HUNGRY!
CAFETE HOUR 12-2
OH, GREAT! ARCHIE, CAN YOU SPARE A MINUTE?
SURE, MS. BEAZLY!
I NEED AN OUTSIDE OPINION ON TODAY'S SOUP! I'M TRYING A NEW RECIPE!
SA DINE
BURG R SOUP
TUNA
CHICK
WOW! I WAS JUST THINKIN' ABOUT HUNGER, TOO!
EEYOOOWL!
TOO HOT?
HOT? I'LL SAY! OMIGOSH! IT'S RAISED A BLISTER ALREADY!!
OH, DEAR! I'M SORRY!
LET ME PUT SOME OF THIS FIRST-AID CREAM ON IT! IT SHOULD EASE THE PAIN!
SQUOSH!

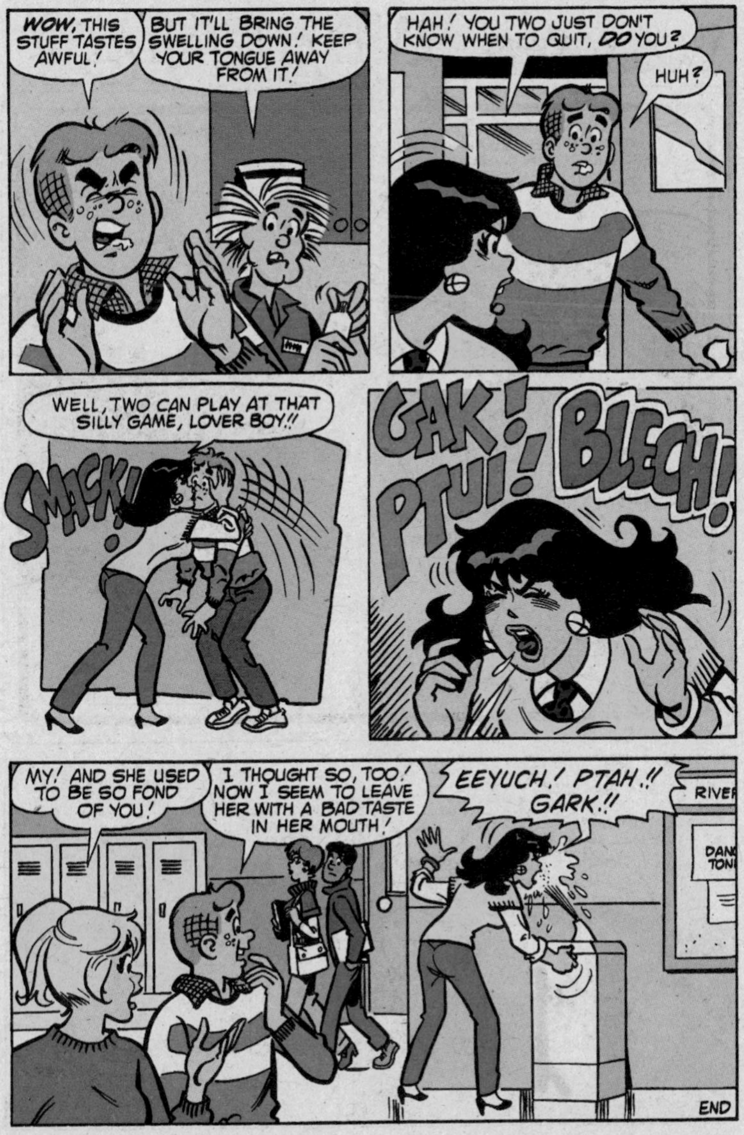
WOW, THIS STUFF TASTES AWFUL!
BUT IT'LL BRING THE SWELLING DOWN! KEEP YOUR TONGUE AWAY FROM IT!
HAH! YOU TWO JUST DON'T KNOW WHEN TO QUIT, DO YOU?
HUH?
WELL, TWO CAN PLAY AT THAT SILLY GAME, LOVER BOY!!
SMACK!
GAK! PTUI! BLECH!
MY! AND SHE USED TO BE SO FOND OF YOU!
I THOUGHT SO, TOO! NOW I SEEM TO LEAVE HER WITH A BAD TASTE IN HER MOUTH!
EEYUCH! PTAH!! GARK!!
END

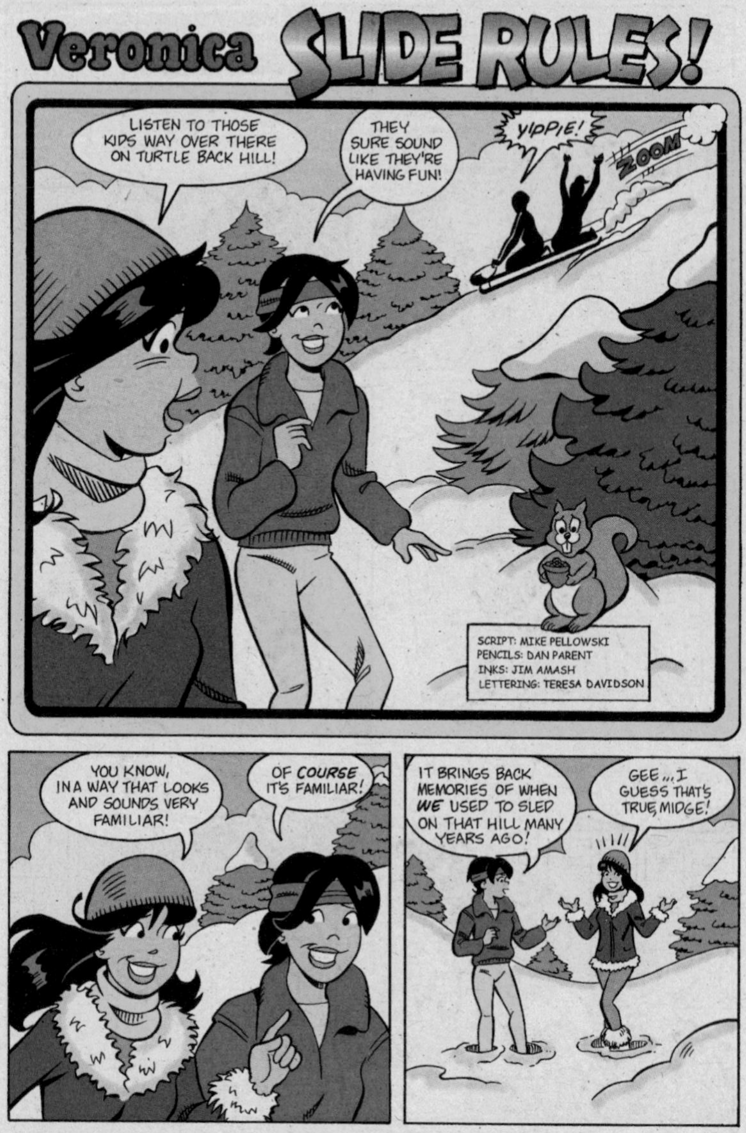
Veronica
SLIDE RULES!
LISTEN TO THOSE KIDS WAY OVER THERE ON TURTLE BACK HILL!
THEY SURE SOUND LIKE THEY'RE HAVING FUN!
YIPPIE!
ZOOM
SCRIPT: MIKE PELLOWSKI
PENCILS: DAN PARENT
INKS: JIM AMASH
LETTERING: TERESA DAVIDSON
YOU KNOW, IN A WAY THAT LOOKS AND SOUNDS VERY FAMILIAR!
OF COURSE IT'S FAMILIAR!
IT BRINGS BACK MEMORIES OF WHEN WE USED TO SLED ON THAT HILL MANY YEARS AGO!
GEE ... I GUESS THAT'S TRUE, MIDGE!

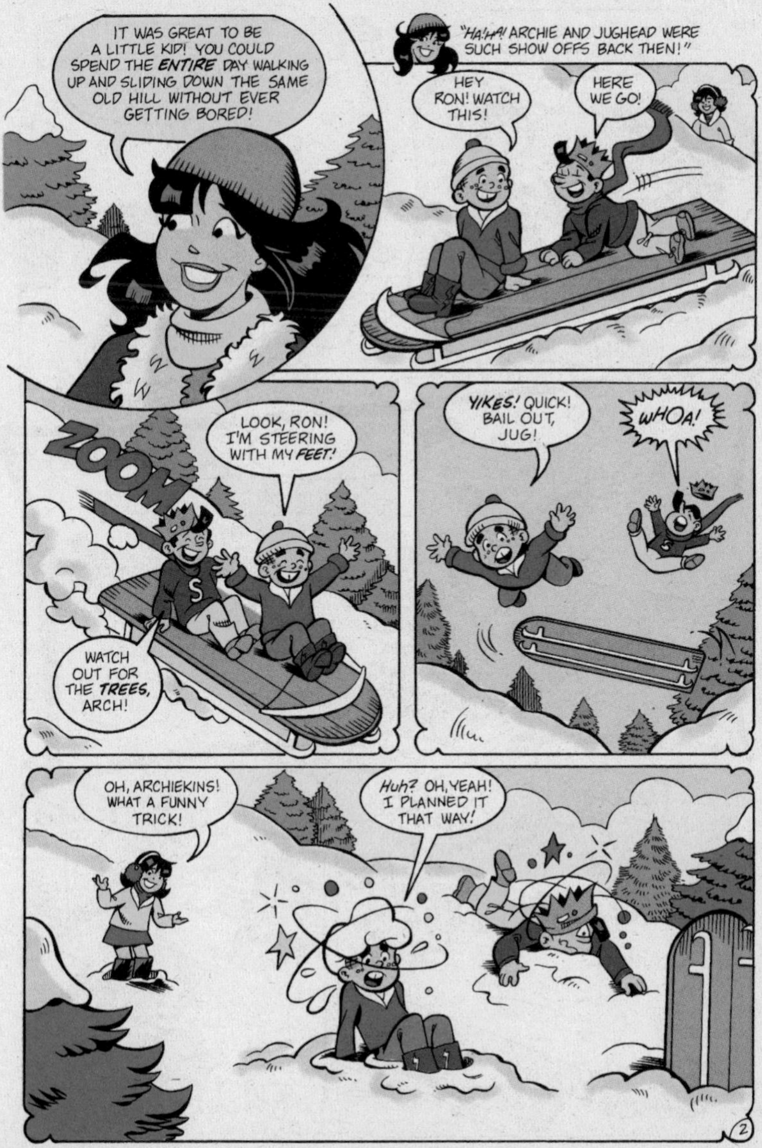

IT WAS GREAT TO BE A LITTLE KID! YOU COULD SPEND THE ENTIRE DAY WALKING UP AND SLIDING DOWN THE SAME OLD HILL WITHOUT EVER GETTING BORED!
"HA! HA! ARCHIE AND JUGHEAD WERE SUCH SHOW OFFS BACK THEN!"
HEY RON! WATCH THIS!
HERE WE GO!
ZOOM
LOOK, RON! I'M STEERING WITH MY FEET!
WATCH OUT FOR THE TREES, ARCH!
YIKES! QUICK! BAIL OUT, JUG!
WHOA!
OH, ARCHIEKINS! WHAT A FUNNY TRICK!
Huh? OH, YEAH! I PLANNED IT THAT WAY!

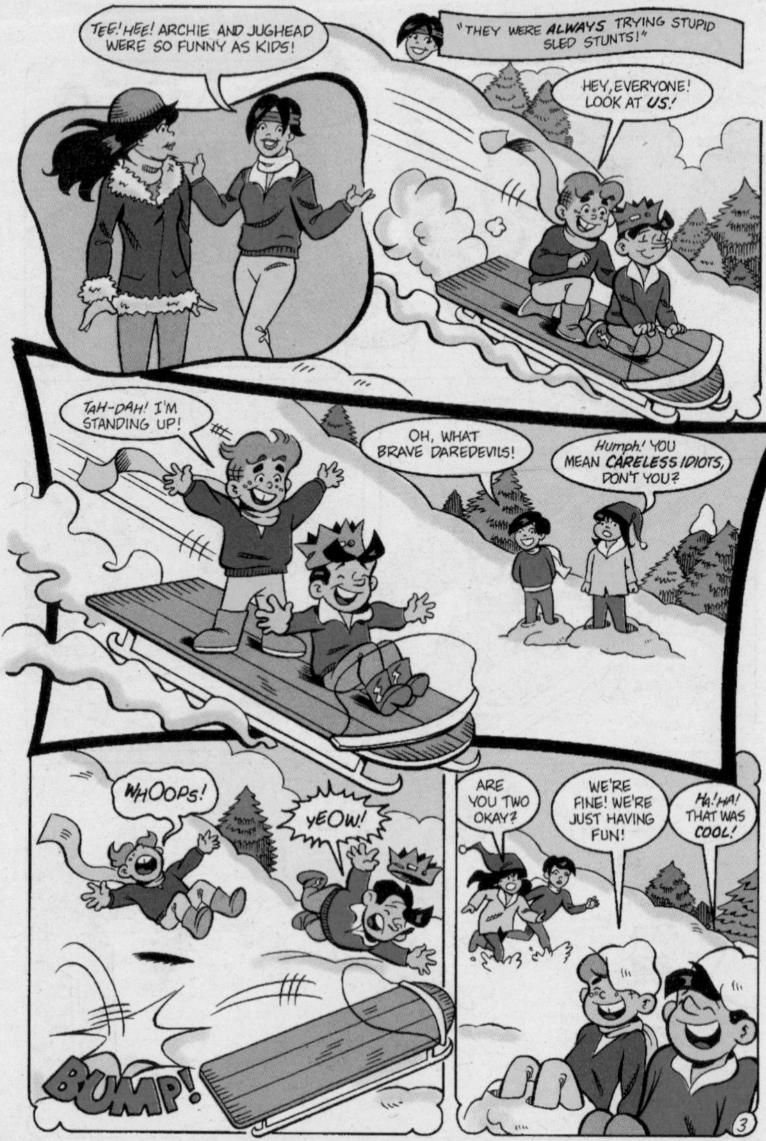
TEE! HEE! ARCHIE AND JUGHEAD WERE SO FUNNY AS KIDS!
"THEY WERE ALWAYS TRYING STUPID SLED STUNTS!"
HEY, EVERYONE! LOOK AT US!
TAH-DAH! I'M STANDING UP!
OH, WHAT BRAVE DAREDEVILS!
Humph! YOU MEAN CARELESS IDIOTS, DON'T YOU?
WHOOPS!
YEOW!
BUMP!
ARE YOU TWO OKAY?
WE'RE FINE! WE'RE JUST HAVING FUN!
HA! HA! THAT WAS COOL!
3

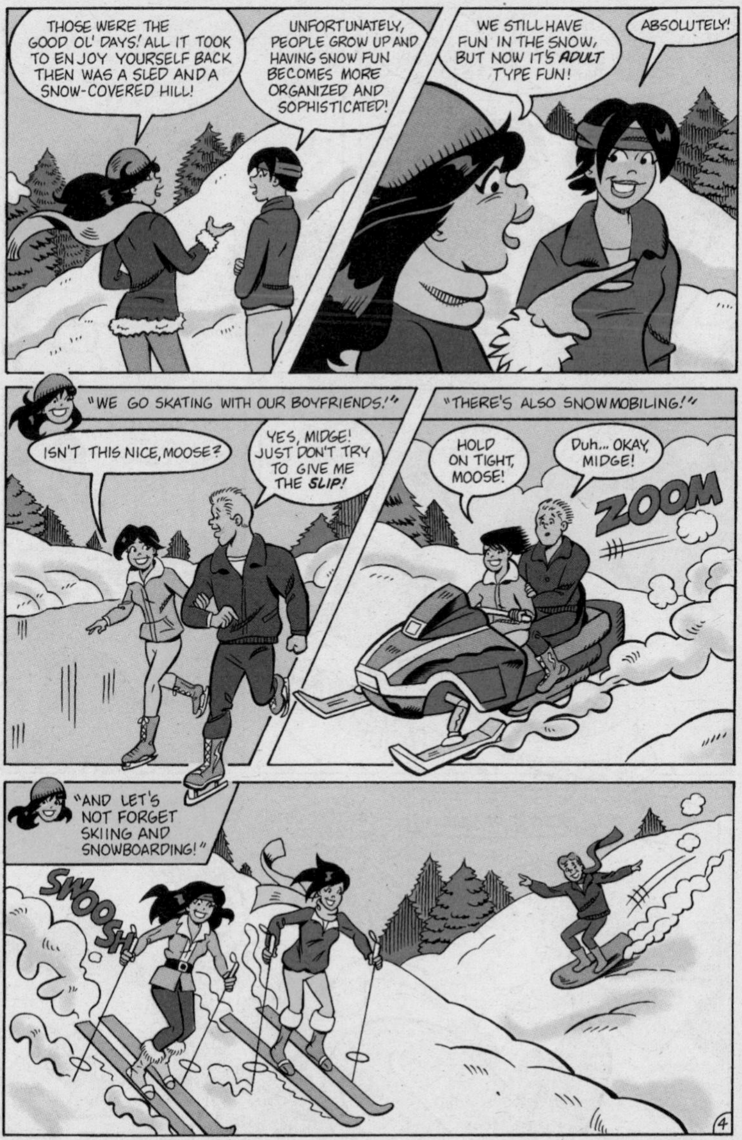
THOSE WERE THE GOOD OL' DAYS! ALL IT TOOK TO ENJOY YOURSELF BACK THEN WAS A SLED AND A SNOW-COVERED HILL!
UNFORTUNATELY, PEOPLE GROW UP AND HAVING SNOW FUN BECOMES MORE ORGANIZED AND SOPHISTICATED!
WE STILL HAVE FUN IN THE SNOW, BUT NOW IT'S ADULT TYPE FUN!
ABSOLUTELY!
"WE GO SKATING WITH OUR BOYFRIENDS!"
ISN'T THIS NICE, MOOSE?
YES, MIDGE! JUST DON'T TRY TO GIVE ME THE SLIP!
"THERE'S ALSO SNOWMOBILING!"
HOLD ON TIGHT, MOOSE!
Duh... OKAY, MIDGE!
ZOOM
"AND LET'S NOT FORGET SKIING AND SNOWBOARDING!"
SWOOSH
4

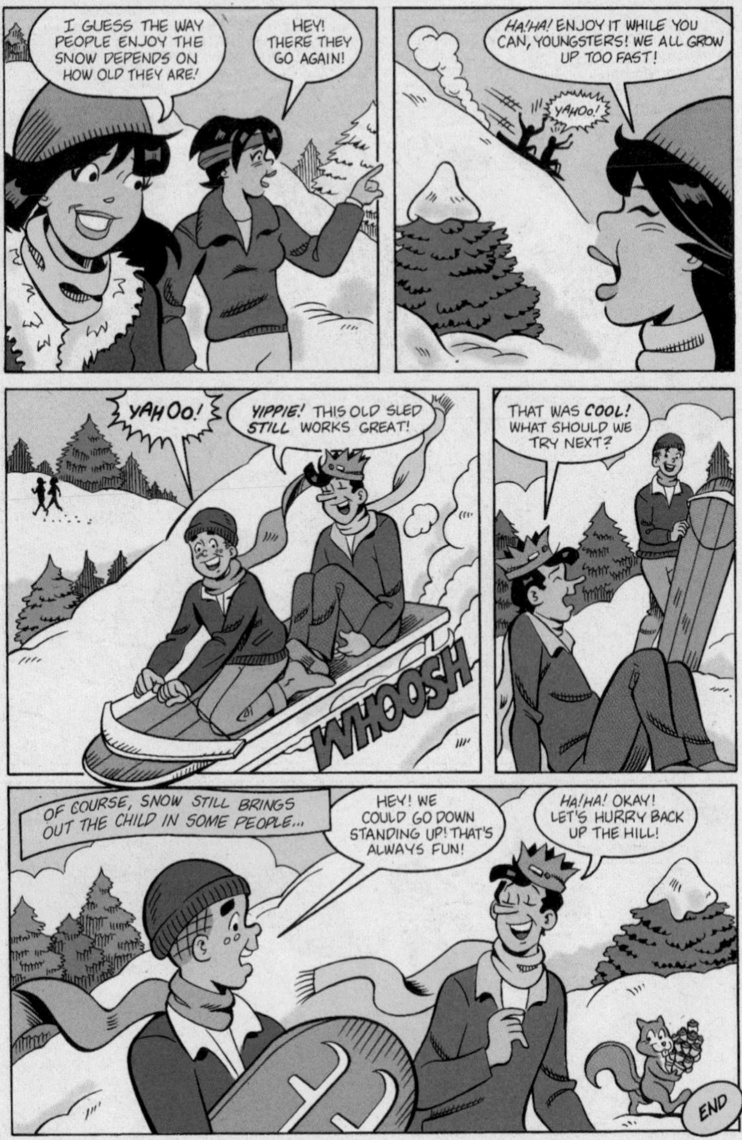

I GUESS THE WAY PEOPLE ENJOY THE SNOW DEPENDS ON HOW OLD THEY ARE!
HEY! THERE THEY GO AGAIN!
HA!HA! ENJOY IT WHILE YOU CAN, YOUNGSTERS! WE ALL GROW UP TOO FAST!
YAHOO!
YAHOO!
YIPPIE! THIS OLD SLED STILL WORKS GREAT!
WHOOSH
THAT WAS COOL! WHAT SHOULD WE TRY NEXT?
OF COURSE, SNOW STILL BRINGS OUT THE CHILD IN SOME PEOPLE...
HEY! WE COULD GO DOWN STANDING UP! THAT'S ALWAYS FUN!
HA!HA! OKAY! LET'S HURRY BACK UP THE HILL!
END

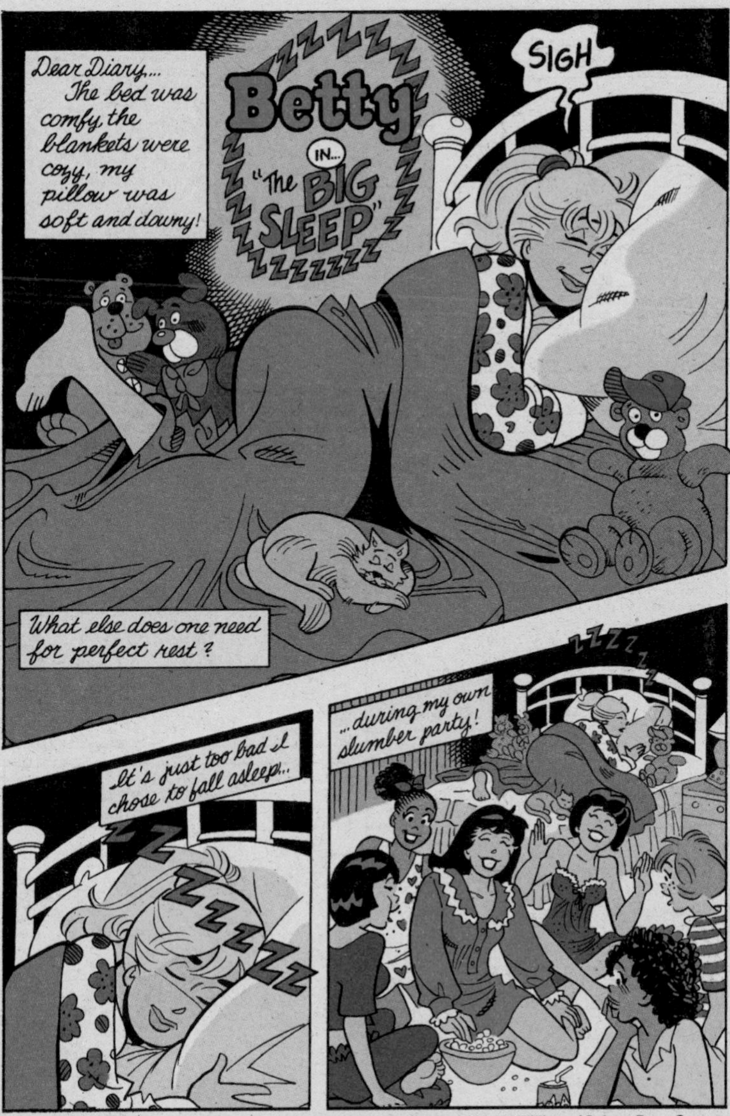
Dear Diary... The bed was comfy, the blankets were cozy, my pillow was soft and downy!
Betty
IN... "The BIG SLEEP"
ZZZZZZ
SIGH
What else does one need for perfect rest?
It's just too bad I chose to fall asleep...
ZZZZZ
...during my own slumber party!
ZZZZZ

Script: Kathleen Webb / Pencils: Stan Goldberg / Inks: John Lowe / Letters: Vickie Williams / Colors: Barry Grossman

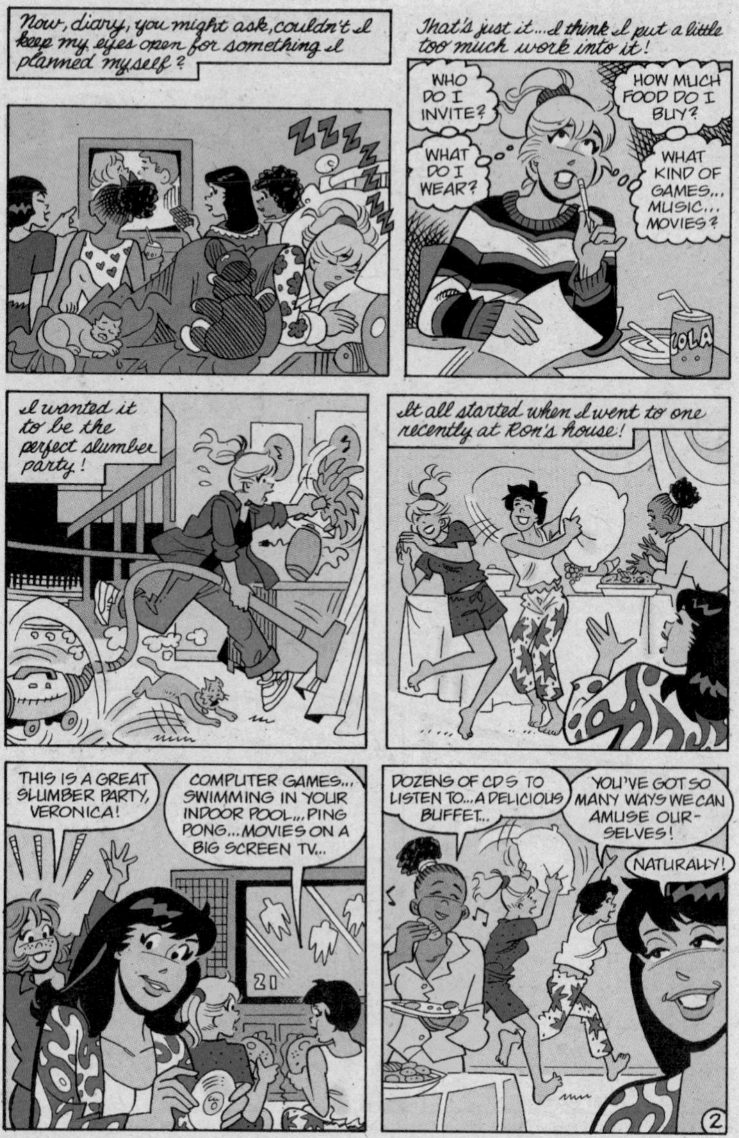
Now, diary, you might ask, couldn't I keep my eyes open for something I planned myself?
ZZZZZZ
That's just it... I think I put a little too much work into it!
WHO DO I INVITE?
HOW MUCH FOOD DO I BUY?
WHAT DO I WEAR?
WHAT KIND OF GAMES... MUSIC... MOVIES?
LOLA
I wanted it to be the perfect slumber party!
It all started when I went to one recently at Ron's house!
THIS IS A GREAT SLUMBER PARTY, VERONICA!
COMPUTER GAMES... SWIMMING IN YOUR INDOOR POOL... PING PONG... MOVIES ON A BIG SCREEN TV...
21
DOZENS OF CDS TO LISTEN TO... A DELICIOUS BUFFET...
YOU'VE GOT SO MANY WAYS WE CAN AMUSE OURSELVES!
NATURALLY!
2

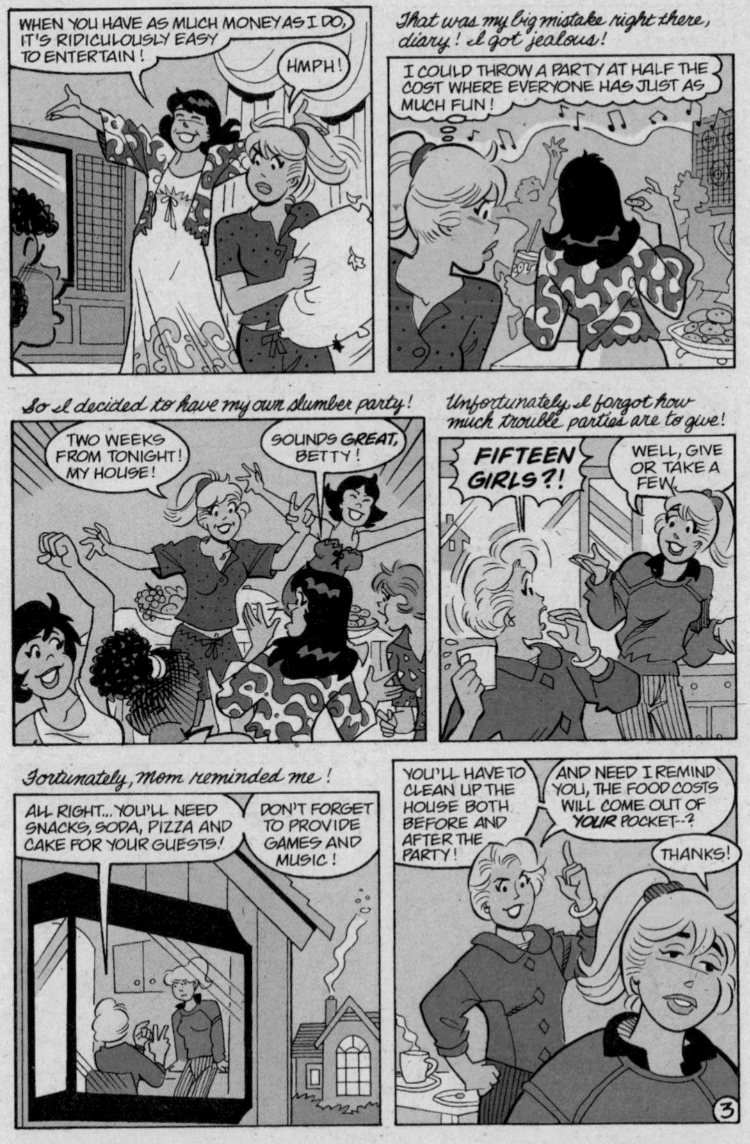

WHEN YOU HAVE AS MUCH MONEY AS I DO, IT'S RIDICULOUSLY EASY TO ENTERTAIN!
HMPH!
That was my big mistake right there, diary! I got jealous!
I COULD THROW A PARTY AT HALF THE COST WHERE EVERYONE HAS JUST AS MUCH FUN!
So I decided to have my own slumber party!
TWO WEEKS FROM TONIGHT! MY HOUSE!
SOUNDS GREAT, BETTY!
Unfortunately, I forgot how much trouble parties are to give!
FIFTEEN GIRLS?!
WELL, GIVE OR TAKE A FEW.
Fortunately, mom reminded me!
ALL RIGHT... YOU'LL NEED SNACKS, SODA, PIZZA AND CAKE FOR YOUR GUESTS!
DON'T FORGET TO PROVIDE GAMES AND MUSIC!
YOU'LL HAVE TO CLEAN UP THE HOUSE BOTH BEFORE AND AFTER THE PARTY!
AND NEED I REMIND YOU, THE FOOD COSTS WILL COME OUT OF YOUR POCKET--?
THANKS!
3

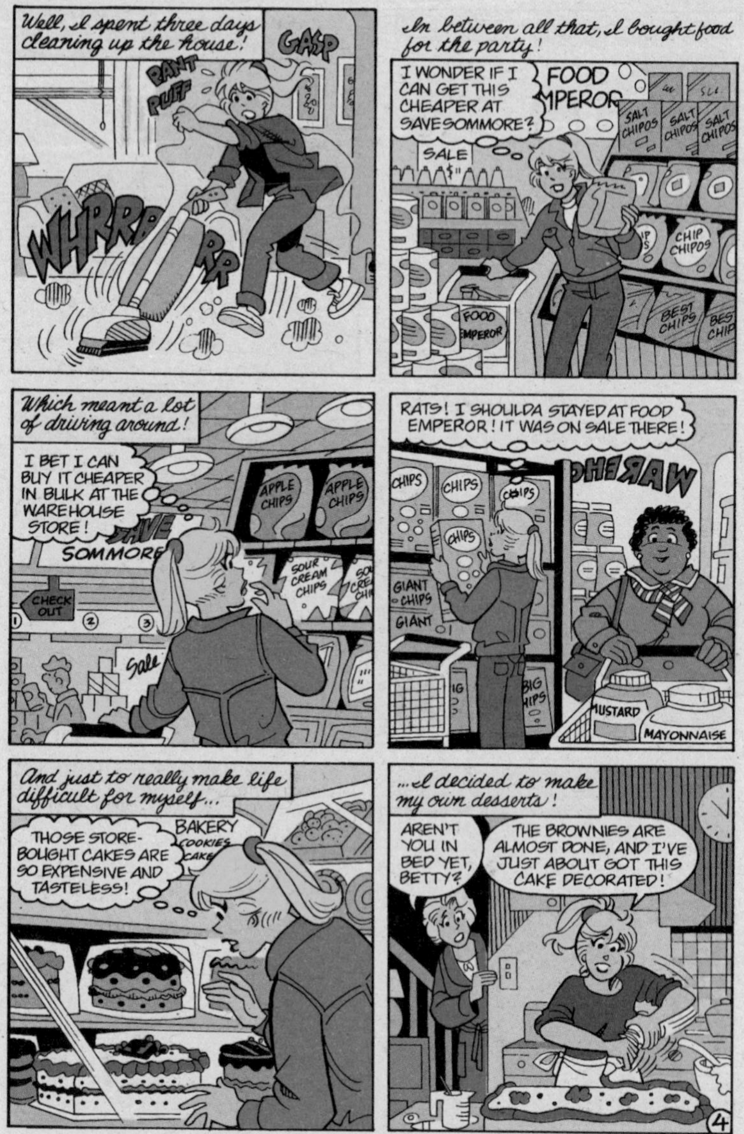

Well, I spent three days cleaning up the house!
GASP
PANT
PUFF
WHRRRRRRR
In between all that, I bought food for the party!
I WONDER IF I CAN GET THIS CHEAPER AT SAVESOMMORE?
FOOD EMPEROR
SALE
SALT CHIPOS
CHIP CHIPOS
BEST CHIPS
Which meant a lot of driving around!
I BET I CAN BUY IT CHEAPER IN BULK AT THE WAREHOUSE STORE!
SOMMORE
APPLE CHIPS
SOUR CREAM CHIPS
CHECK OUT
Sale
RATS! I SHOULDA STAYED AT FOOD EMPEROR! IT WAS ON SALE THERE!
CHIPS
GIANT CHIPS
MUSTARD
MAYONNAISE
And just to really make life difficult for myself...
THOSE STORE-BOUGHT CAKES ARE SO EXPENSIVE AND TASTELESS!
BAKERY
...I decided to make my own desserts!
AREN'T YOU IN BED YET, BETTY?
THE BROWNIES ARE ALMOST DONE, AND I'VE JUST ABOUT GOT THIS CAKE DECORATED!

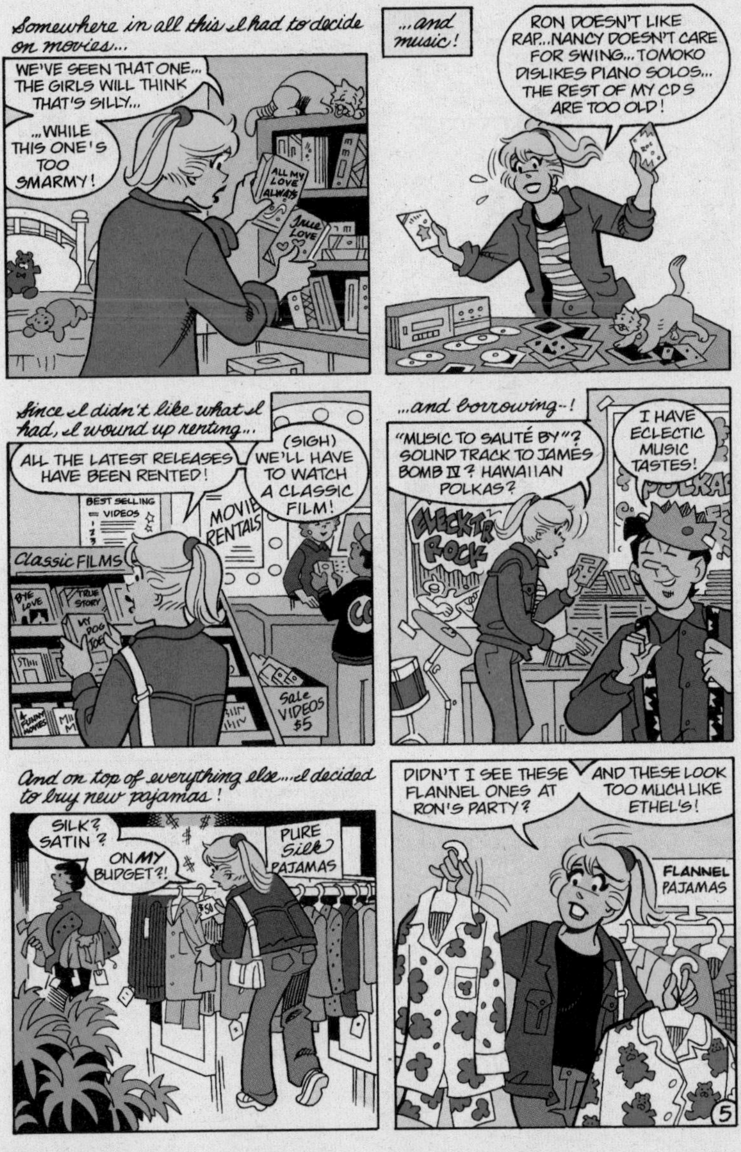
Somewhere in all this I had to decide on movies...
WE'VE SEEN THAT ONE... THE GIRLS WILL THINK THAT'S SILLY...
...WHILE THIS ONE'S TOO SMARMY!
ALL MY LOVE ALWAYS
TRUE LOVE
...and music!
RON DOESN'T LIKE RAP... NANCY DOESN'T CARE FOR SWING... TOMOKO DISLIKES PIANO SOLOS... THE REST OF MY CDS ARE TOO OLD!
Since I didn't like what I had, I wound up renting...
ALL THE LATEST RELEASES HAVE BEEN RENTED!
(SIGH) WE'LL HAVE TO WATCH A CLASSIC FILM!
BEST SELLING VIDEOS
MOVIE RENTALS
Classic FILMS
BYE LOVE
TRUE STORY
MY DOG JOE
FUNNY MOVIES
Sale VIDEOS $5
...and borrowing...!
"MUSIC TO SAUTÉ BY"? SOUND TRACK TO JAMES BOMB IV? HAWAIIAN POLKAS?
I HAVE ECLECTIC MUSIC TASTES!
ELECKTR ROCK
And on top of everything else... I decided to buy new pajamas!
SILK? SATIN?
ON MY BUDGET?!
PURE Silk PAJAMAS
$50
DIDN'T I SEE THESE FLANNEL ONES AT RON'S PARTY?
AND THESE LOOK TOO MUCH LIKE ETHEL'S!
FLANNEL PAJAMAS

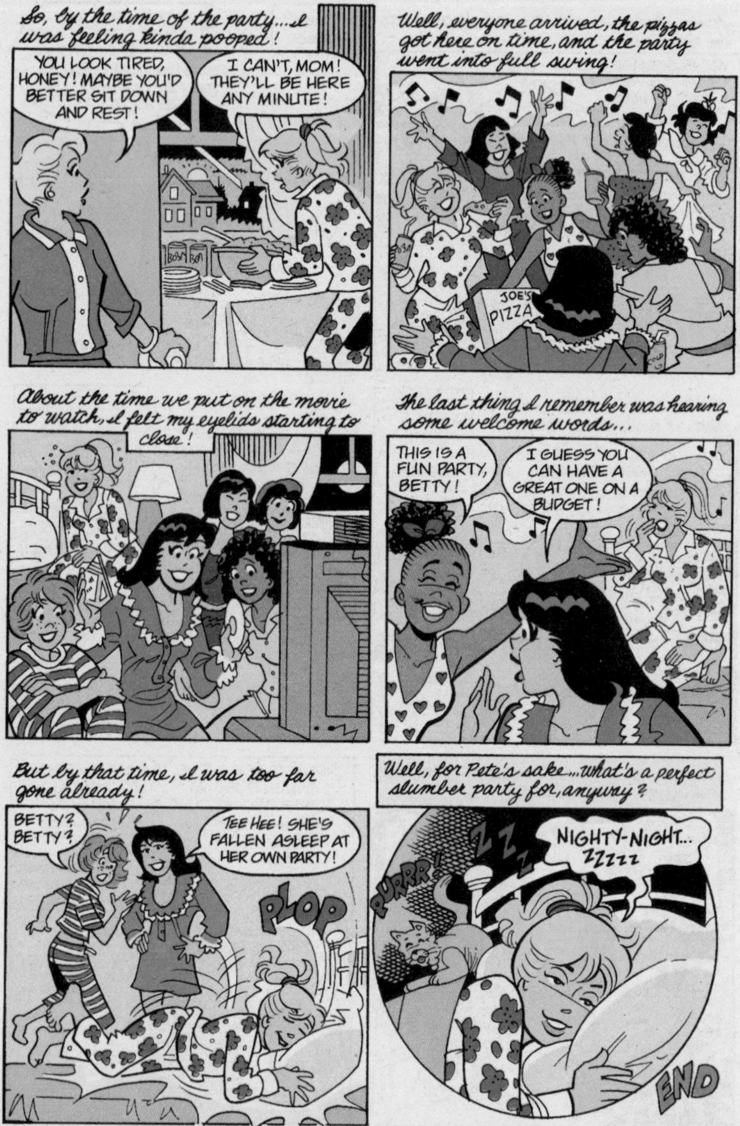
So, by the time of the party... I was feeling kinda pooped!
YOU LOOK TIRED, HONEY! MAYBE YOU'D BETTER SIT DOWN AND REST!
I CAN'T, MOM! THEY'LL BE HERE ANY MINUTE!
Well, everyone arrived, the pizzas got here on time, and the party went into full swing!
JOE'S PIZZA
About the time we put on the movie to watch, I felt my eyelids starting to close!
The last thing I remember was hearing some welcome words...
THIS IS A FUN PARTY, BETTY!
I GUESS YOU CAN HAVE A GREAT ONE ON A BUDGET!
But by that time, I was too far gone already!
BETTY? BETTY?
TEE HEE! SHE'S FALLEN ASLEEP AT HER OWN PARTY!
PLOP
Well, for Pete's sake... what's a perfect slumber party for, anyway?
ZZZ
NIGHTY-NIGHT... ZZzzz
PURRR!
END

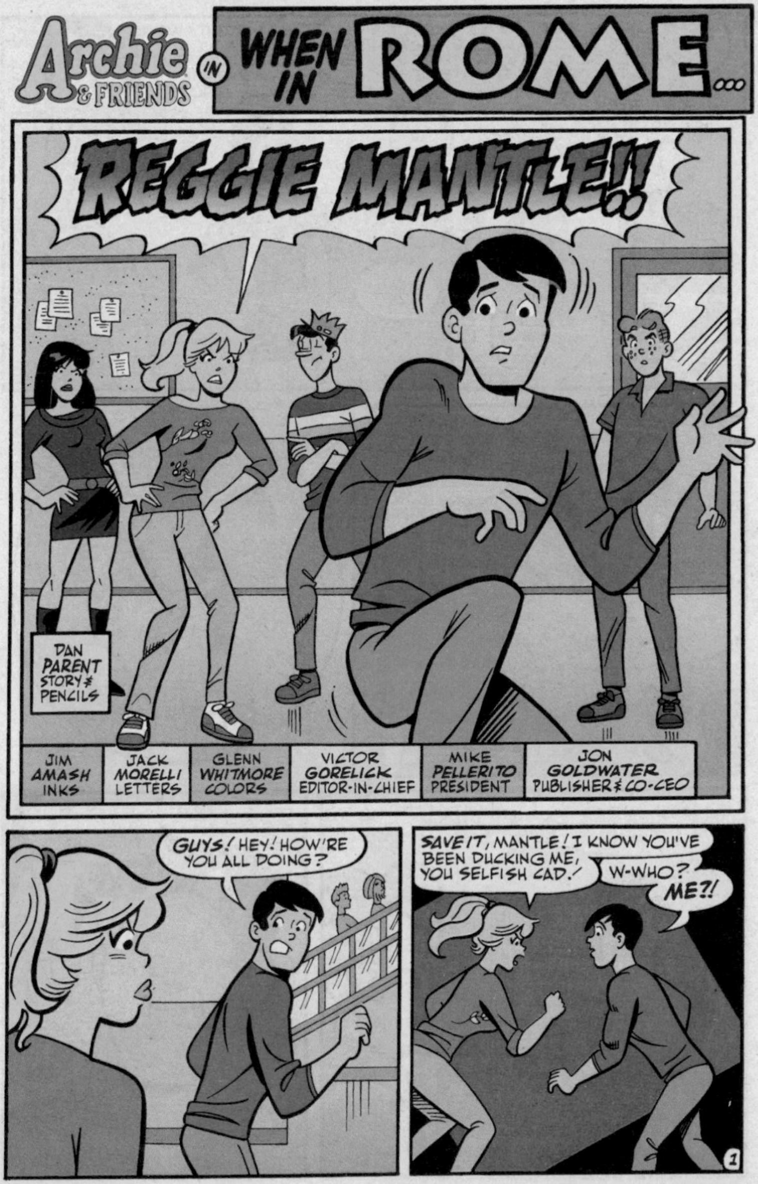

Archie & FRIENDS
IN
WHEN IN ROME...
REGGIE MANTLE!!
DAN PARENT STORY & PENCILS
JIM AMASH INKS
JACK MORELLI LETTERS
GLENN WHITMORE COLORS
VICTOR GORELICK EDITOR-IN-CHIEF
MIKE PELLERITO PRESIDENT
JON GOLDWATER PUBLISHER & CO-CEO
GUYS! HEY! HOW'RE YOU ALL DOING?
SAVE IT, MANTLE! I KNOW YOU'VE BEEN DUCKING ME, YOU SELFISH CAD!
W-WHO? ME?!
1

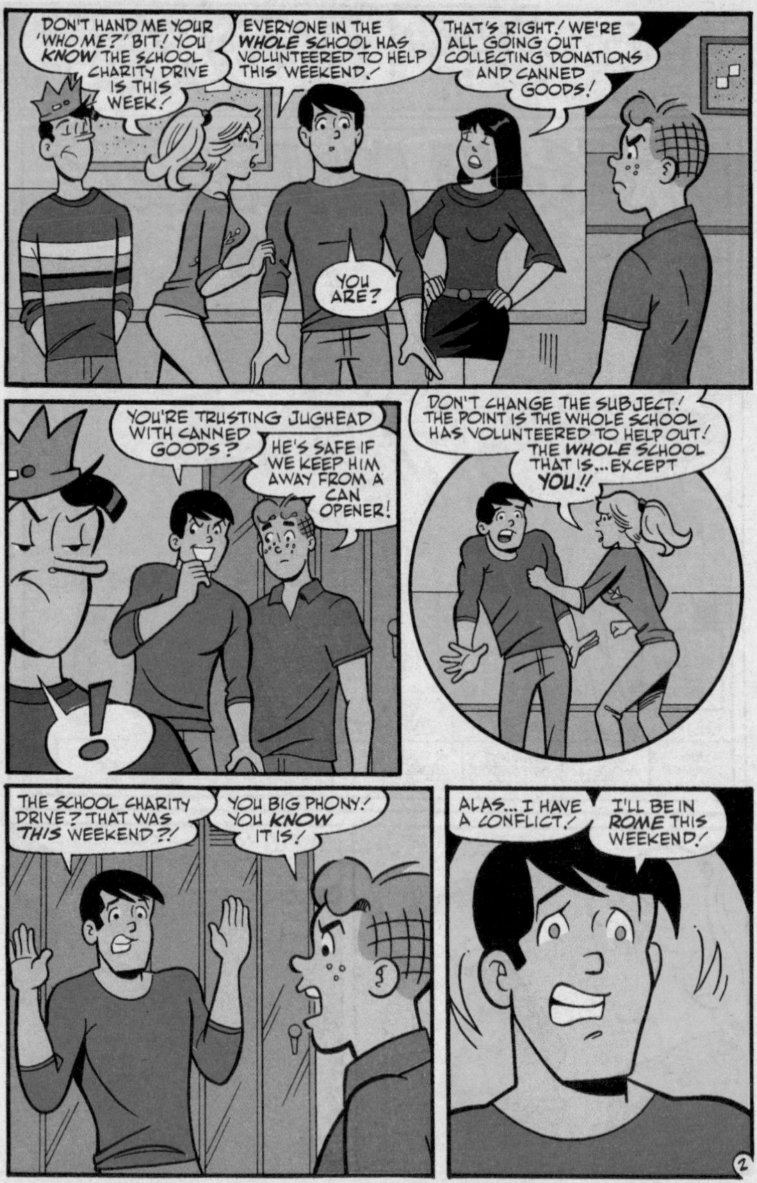
DON'T HAND ME YOUR 'WHO ME?' BIT! YOU KNOW THE SCHOOL CHARITY DRIVE IS THIS WEEK!
EVERYONE IN THE WHOLE SCHOOL HAS VOLUNTEERED TO HELP THIS WEEKEND!
THAT'S RIGHT! WE'RE ALL GOING OUT COLLECTING DONATIONS AND CANNED GOODS!
YOU ARE?
YOU'RE TRUSTING JUGHEAD WITH CANNED GOODS?
HE'S SAFE IF WE KEEP HIM AWAY FROM A CAN OPENER!
!
DON'T CHANGE THE SUBJECT! THE POINT IS THE WHOLE SCHOOL HAS VOLUNTEERED TO HELP OUT! THE WHOLE SCHOOL THAT IS... EXCEPT YOU!!
THE SCHOOL CHARITY DRIVE? THAT WAS THIS WEEKEND?!
YOU BIG PHONY! YOU KNOW IT IS!
ALAS... I HAVE A CONFLICT!
I'LL BE IN ROME THIS WEEKEND!
2

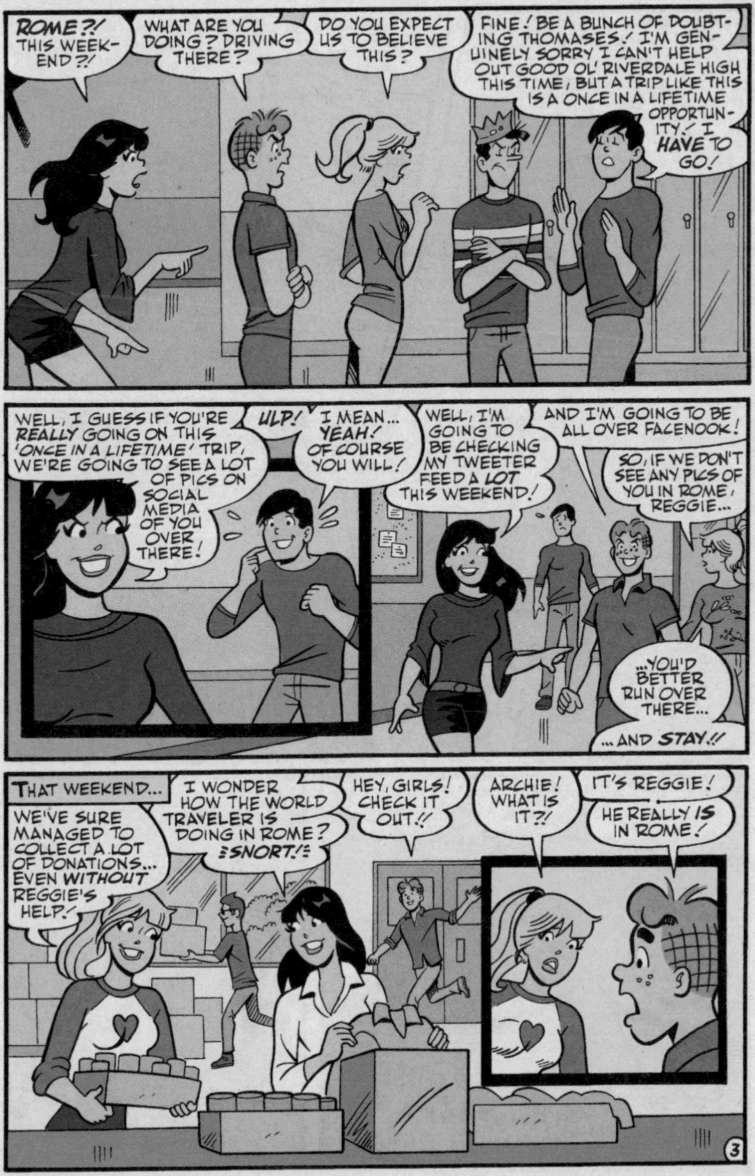
ROME?! THIS WEEKEND?!
WHAT ARE YOU DOING? DRIVING THERE?
DO YOU EXPECT US TO BELIEVE THIS?
FINE! BE A BUNCH OF DOUBTING THOMASES! I'M GENUINELY SORRY I CAN'T HELP OUT GOOD OL' RIVERDALE HIGH THIS TIME, BUT A TRIP LIKE THIS IS A ONCE IN A LIFETIME OPPORTUNITY! I HAVE TO GO!
WELL, I GUESS IF YOU'RE REALLY GOING ON THIS 'ONCE IN A LIFETIME' TRIP, WE'RE GOING TO SEE A LOT OF PICS ON SOCIAL MEDIA OF YOU OVER THERE!
ULP!
I MEAN... YEAH! OF COURSE YOU WILL!
WELL, I'M GOING TO BE CHECKING MY TWEETER FEED A LOT THIS WEEKEND!
AND I'M GOING TO BE ALL OVER FACENOOK!
SO, IF WE DON'T SEE ANY PICS OF YOU IN ROME, REGGIE...
...YOU'D BETTER RUN OVER THERE...
...AND STAY!!
THAT WEEKEND...
WE'VE SURE MANAGED TO COLLECT A LOT OF DONATIONS... EVEN WITHOUT REGGIE'S HELP!
I WONDER HOW THE WORLD TRAVELER IS DOING IN ROME? SNORT!
HEY, GIRLS! CHECK IT OUT!!
ARCHIE! WHAT IS IT?!
IT'S REGGIE!
HE REALLY IS IN ROME!
3

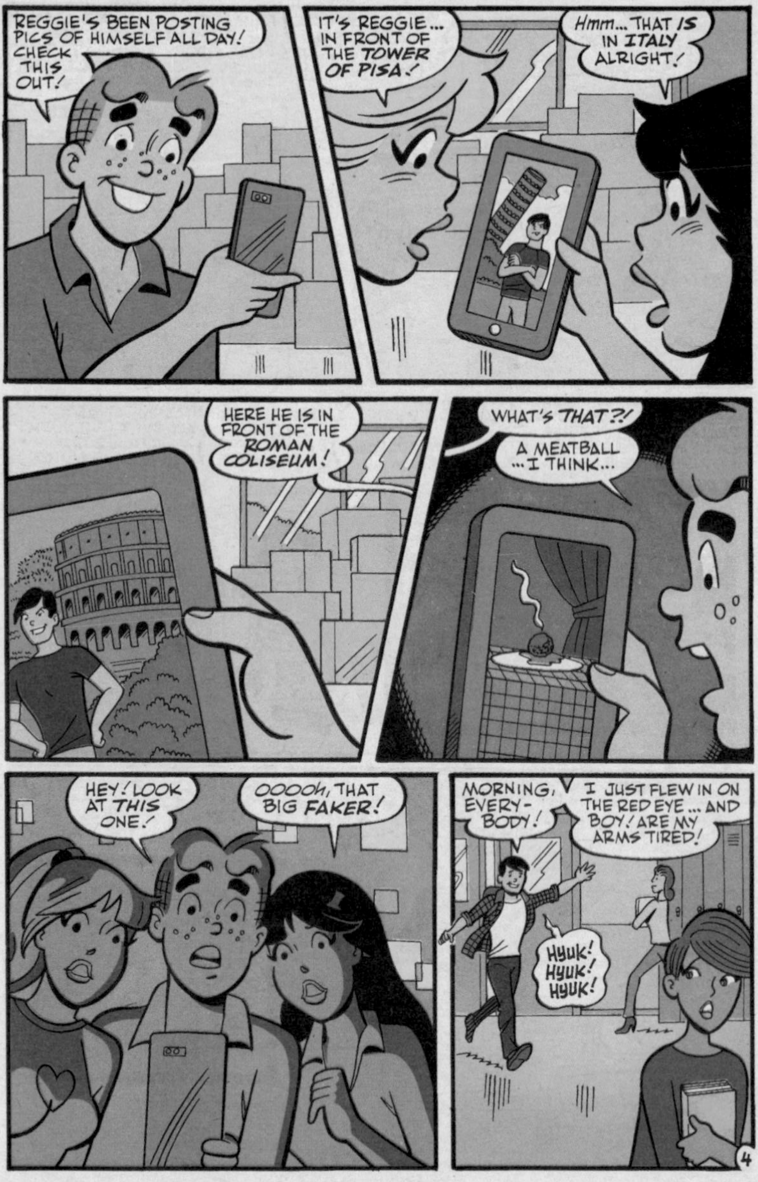
REGGIE'S BEEN POSTING PICS OF HIMSELF ALL DAY! CHECK THIS OUT!
IT'S REGGIE... IN FRONT OF THE TOWER OF PISA!
Hmm... THAT IS IN ITALY ALRIGHT!
HERE HE IS IN FRONT OF THE ROMAN COLISEUM!
WHAT'S THAT?!
A MEATBALL ...I THINK...
HEY! LOOK AT THIS ONE!
OOOOh, THAT BIG FAKER!
MORNING, EVERY-BODY!
I JUST FLEW IN ON THE RED EYE ... AND BOY! ARE MY ARMS TIRED!
HYUK! HYUK! HYUK!

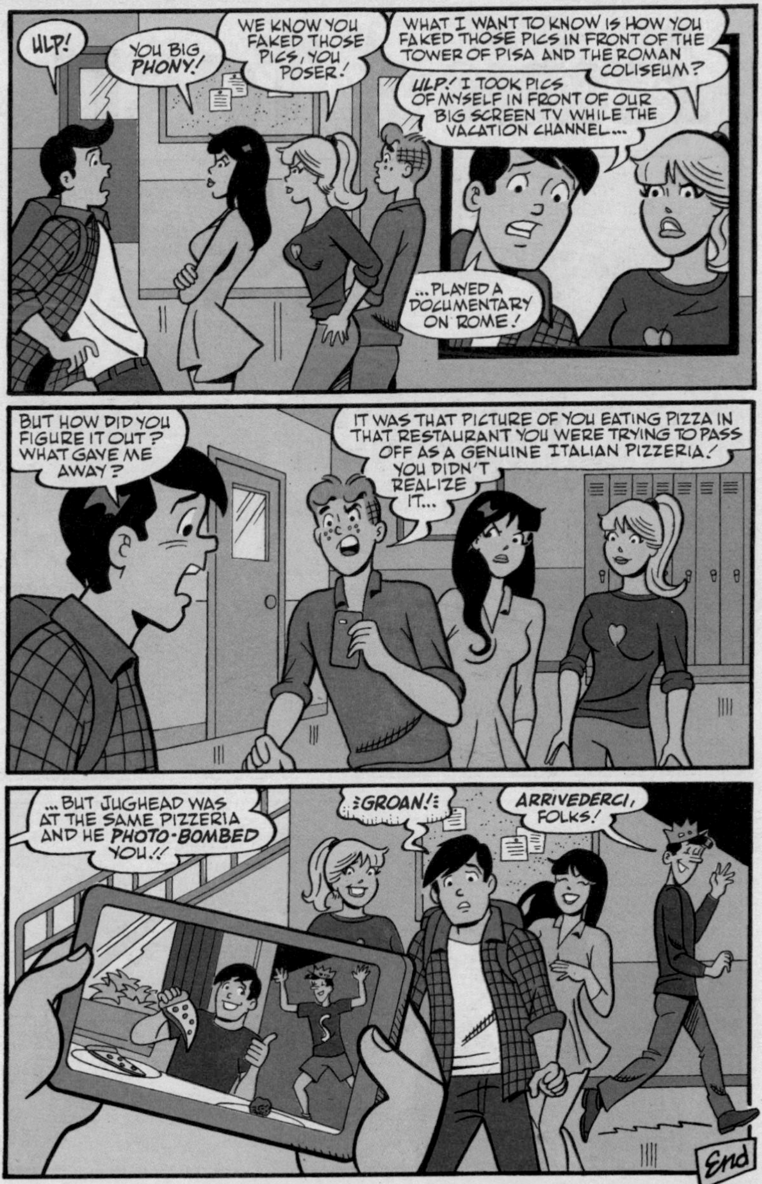
ULP!
YOU BIG PHONY!
WE KNOW YOU FAKED THOSE PICS, YOU POSER!
WHAT I WANT TO KNOW IS HOW YOU FAKED THOSE PICS IN FRONT OF THE TOWER OF PISA AND THE ROMAN COLISEUM?
ULP! I TOOK PICS OF MYSELF IN FRONT OF OUR BIG SCREEN TV WHILE THE VACATION CHANNEL...
...PLAYED A DOCUMENTARY ON ROME!
BUT HOW DID YOU FIGURE IT OUT? WHAT GAVE ME AWAY?
IT WAS THAT PICTURE OF YOU EATING PIZZA IN THAT RESTAURANT YOU WERE TRYING TO PASS OFF AS A GENUINE ITALIAN PIZZERIA!
YOU DIDN'T REALIZE IT...
...BUT JUGHEAD WAS AT THE SAME PIZZERIA AND HE PHOTO-BOMBED YOU!!
GROAN!
ARRIVEDERCI, FOLKS!
End

Archie in "The Test"

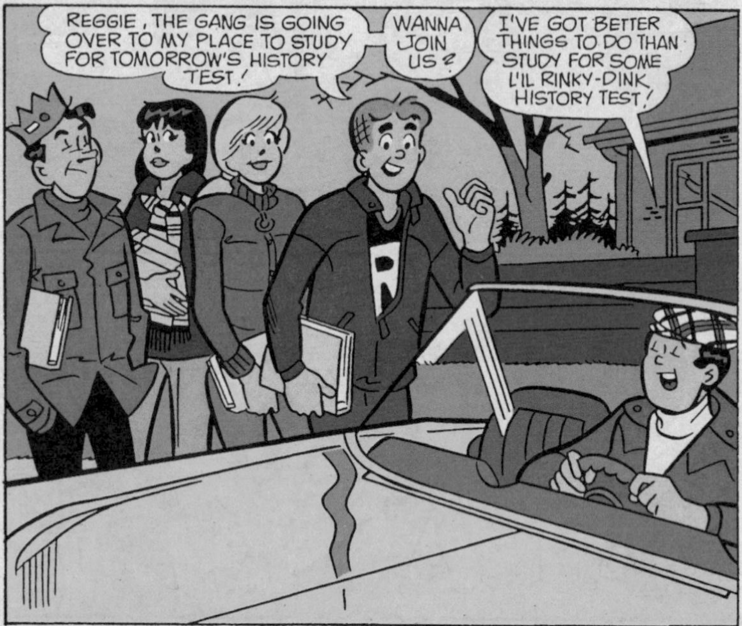
REGGIE, THE GANG IS GOING OVER TO MY PLACE TO STUDY FOR TOMORROW'S HISTORY TEST!
WANNA JOIN US?
I'VE GOT BETTER THINGS TO DO THAN STUDY FOR SOME L'IL RINKY-DINK HISTORY TEST!

Script: George Gladir / Pencils: Stan Goldberg / Inks: Henry Scarpelli / Letters: Bill Yoshida

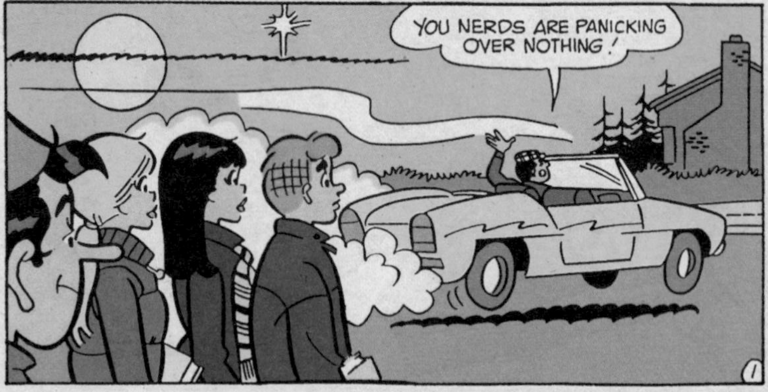
YOU NERDS ARE PANICKING OVER NOTHING!

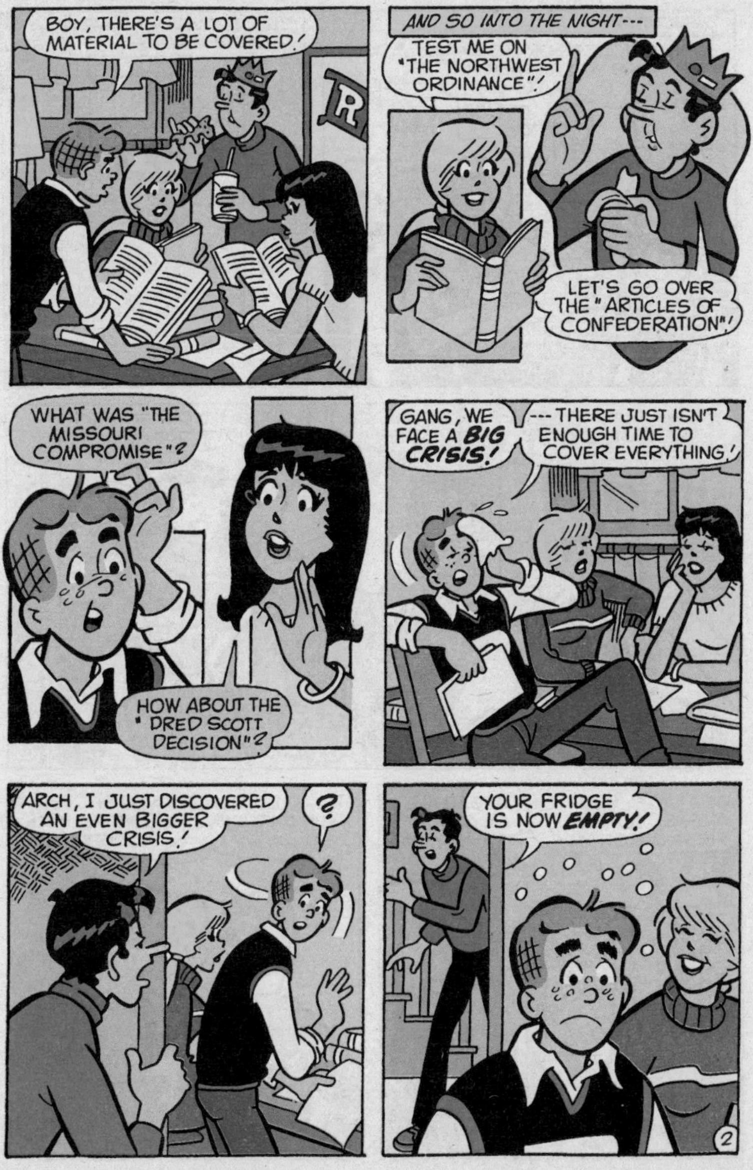
BOY, THERE'S A LOT OF MATERIAL TO BE COVERED!
AND SO INTO THE NIGHT---
TEST ME ON "THE NORTHWEST ORDINANCE"!
LET'S GO OVER THE "ARTICLES OF CONFEDERATION"!
WHAT WAS "THE MISSOURI COMPROMISE"?
HOW ABOUT THE "DRED SCOTT DECISION"?
GANG, WE FACE A BIG CRISIS!
---THERE JUST ISN'T ENOUGH TIME TO COVER EVERYTHING!
ARCH, I JUST DISCOVERED AN EVEN BIGGER CRISIS!
?
YOUR FRIDGE IS NOW EMPTY!
2

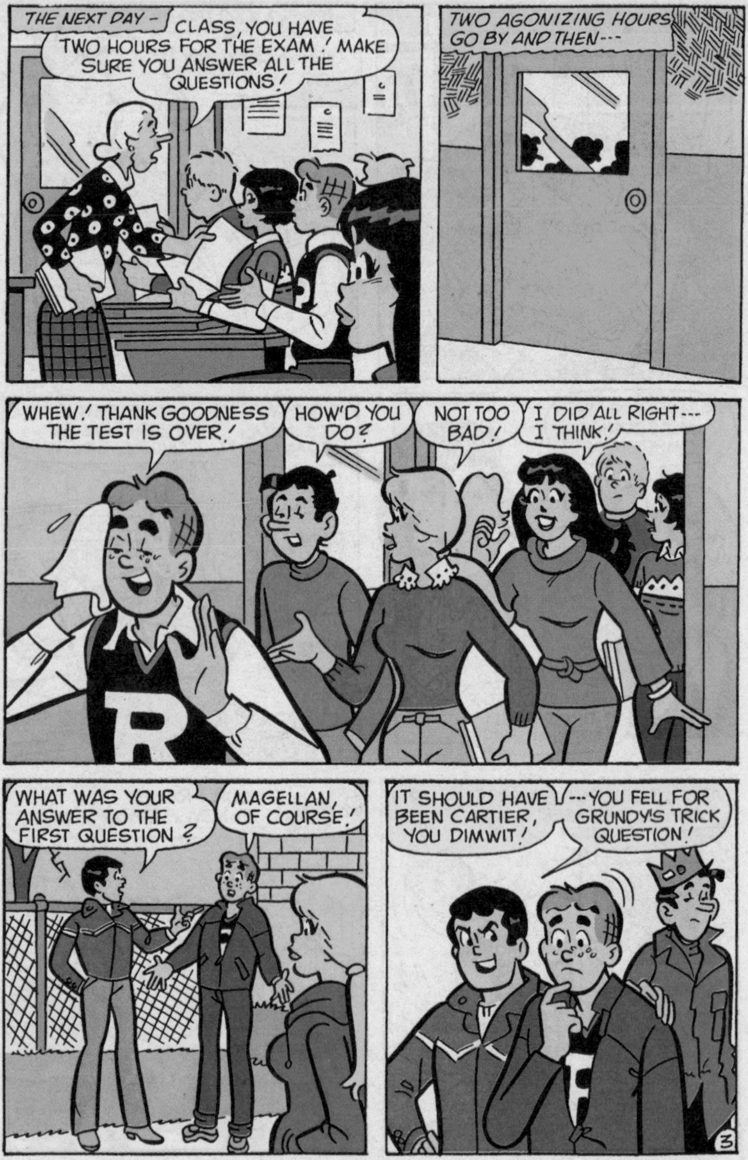
THE NEXT DAY -
CLASS, YOU HAVE TWO HOURS FOR THE EXAM! MAKE SURE YOU ANSWER ALL THE QUESTIONS!
TWO AGONIZING HOURS GO BY AND THEN---
WHEW! THANK GOODNESS THE TEST IS OVER!
HOW'D YOU DO?
NOT TOO BAD!
I DID ALL RIGHT--- I THINK!
WHAT WAS YOUR ANSWER TO THE FIRST QUESTION?
MAGELLAN, OF COURSE!
IT SHOULD HAVE BEEN CARTIER, YOU DIMWIT!
---YOU FELL FOR GRUNDY'S TRICK QUESTION!
3

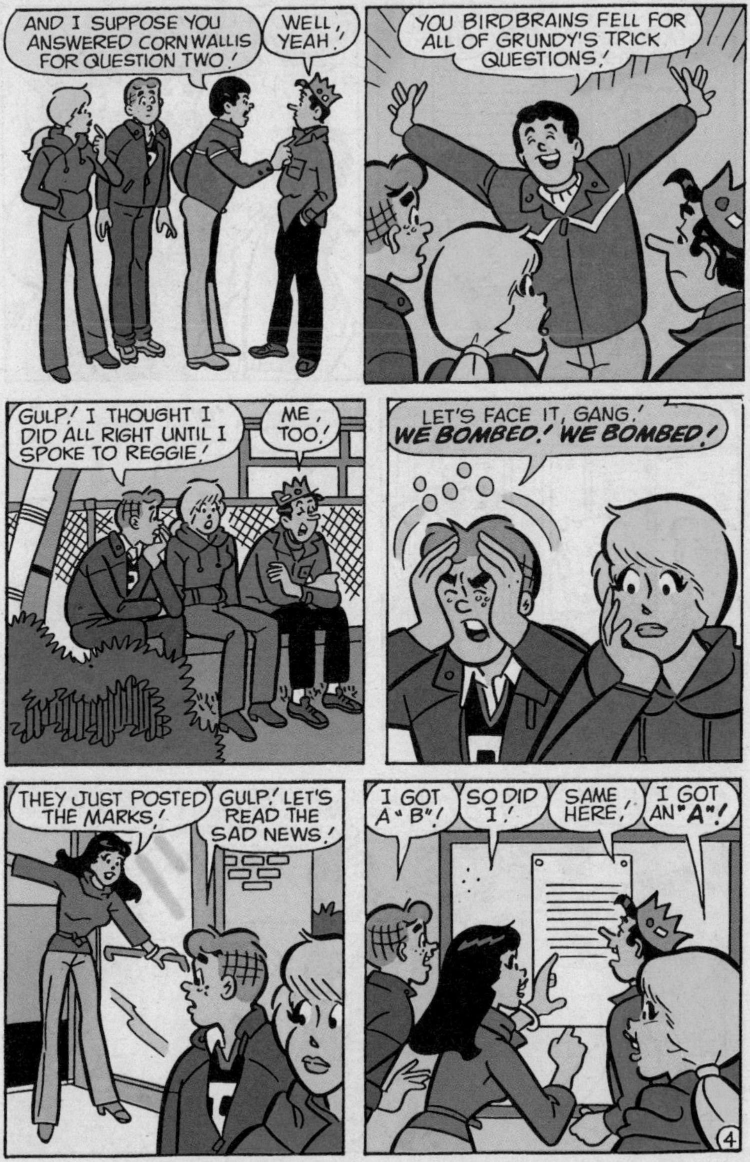
AND I SUPPOSE YOU ANSWERED CORNWALLIS FOR QUESTION TWO!
WELL, YEAH!
YOU BIRDBRAINS FELL FOR ALL OF GRUNDY'S TRICK QUESTIONS!
GULP! I THOUGHT I DID ALL RIGHT UNTIL I SPOKE TO REGGIE!
ME, TOO!
LET'S FACE IT, GANG! WE BOMBED! WE BOMBED!
THEY JUST POSTED THE MARKS!
GULP! LET'S READ THE SAD NEWS!
I GOT A "B"!
SO DID I!
SAME HERE!
I GOT AN "A"!
4

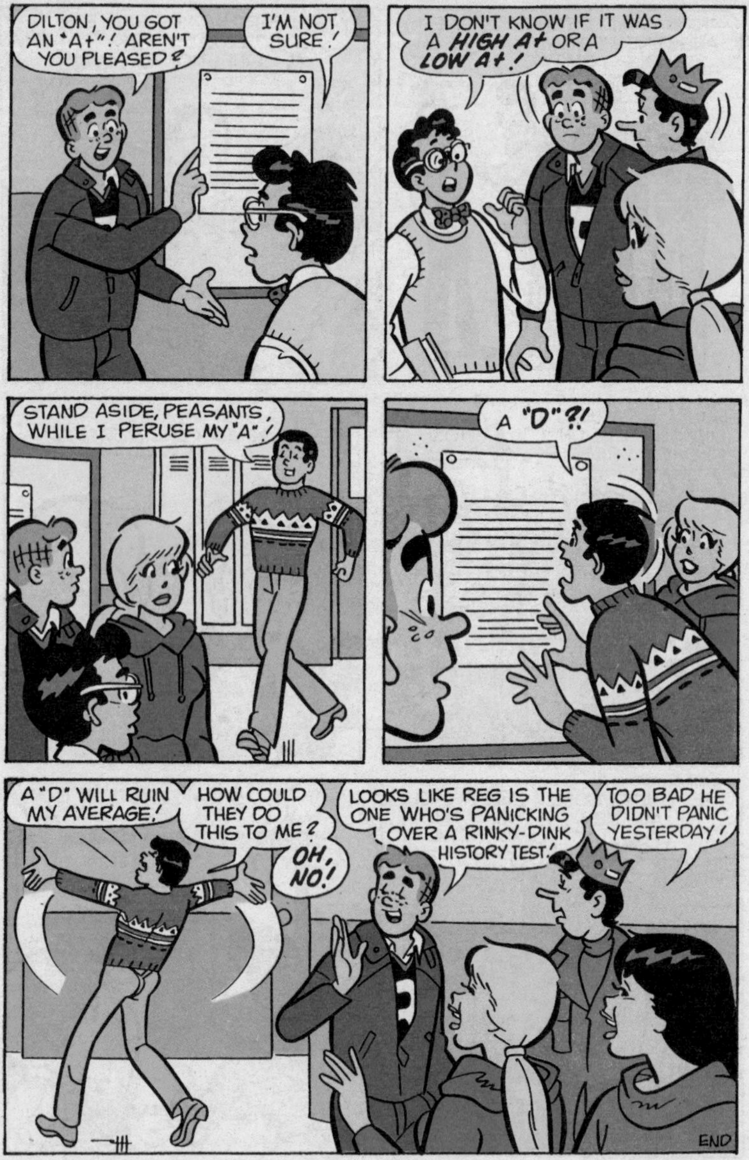
DILTON, YOU GOT AN "A+"! AREN'T YOU PLEASED?
I'M NOT SURE!
I DON'T KNOW IF IT WAS A HIGH A+ OR A LOW A+!
STAND ASIDE, PEASANTS, WHILE I PERUSE MY "A"!
A "D"?!
A "D" WILL RUIN MY AVERAGE!
HOW COULD THEY DO THIS TO ME?
OH, NO!
LOOKS LIKE REG IS THE ONE WHO'S PANICKING OVER A RINKY-DINK HISTORY TEST!
TOO BAD HE DIDN'T PANIC YESTERDAY!
END

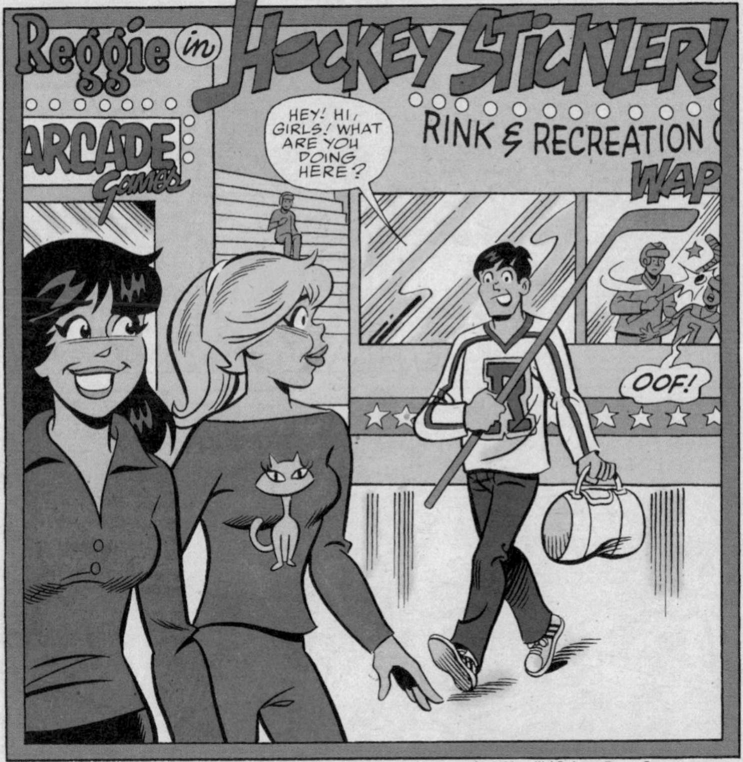
Reggie in Hockey Stickler!
ARCADE Games
RINK & RECREATION
WAP
HEY! HI, GIRLS! WHAT ARE YOU DOING HERE?
OOF!

Script: Mike Pellowski / Pencils: Dan Parent / Inks: Al Milgrom / Letters: Jack Morelli / Colors: Barry Grossman

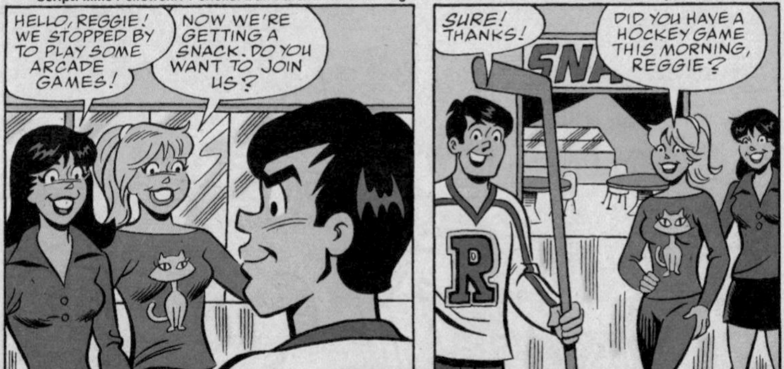
HELLO, REGGIE! WE STOPPED BY TO PLAY SOME ARCADE GAMES!
NOW WE'RE GETTING A SNACK. DO YOU WANT TO JOIN US?
SURE! THANKS!
SNA
DID YOU HAVE A HOCKEY GAME THIS MORNING, REGGIE?

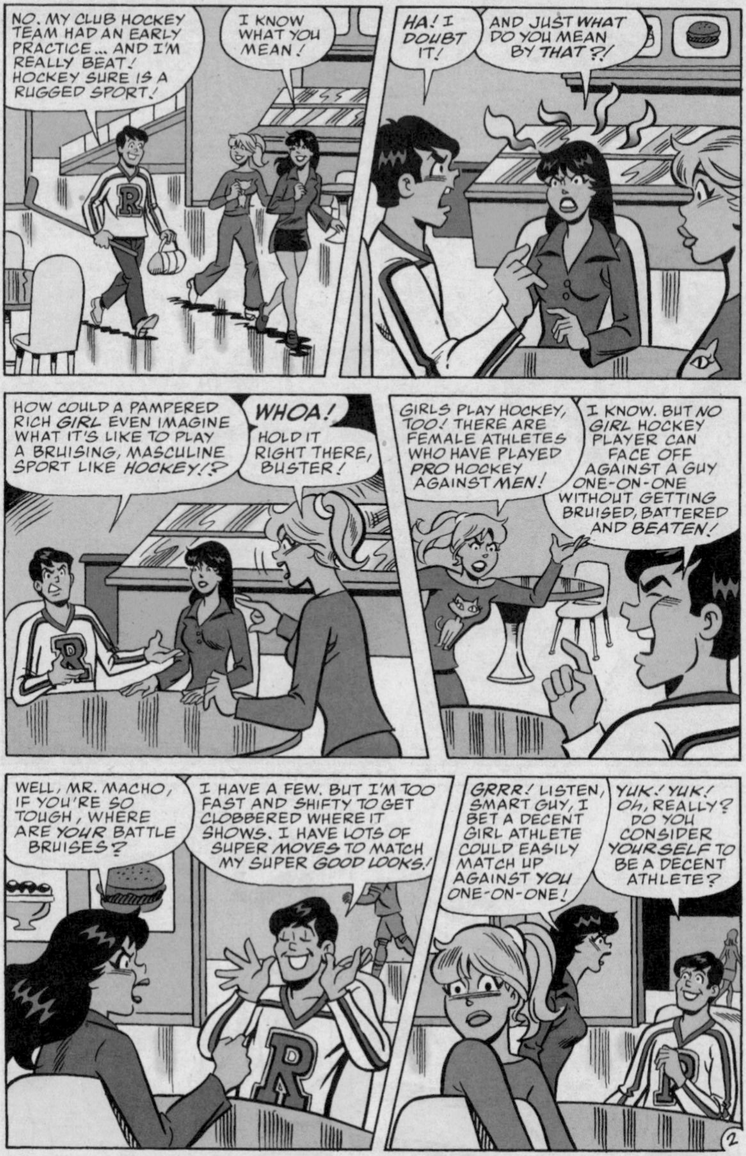
NO. MY CLUB HOCKEY TEAM HAD AN EARLY PRACTICE ... AND I'M REALLY BEAT! HOCKEY SURE IS A RUGGED SPORT!
I KNOW WHAT YOU MEAN!
HA! I DOUBT IT!
AND JUST WHAT DO YOU MEAN BY THAT ?!
HOW COULD A PAMPERED RICH GIRL EVEN IMAGINE WHAT IT'S LIKE TO PLAY A BRUISING, MASCULINE SPORT LIKE HOCKEY!?
WHOA! HOLD IT RIGHT THERE, BUSTER!
GIRLS PLAY HOCKEY, TOO! THERE ARE FEMALE ATHLETES WHO HAVE PLAYED PRO HOCKEY AGAINST MEN!
I KNOW. BUT NO GIRL HOCKEY PLAYER CAN FACE OFF AGAINST A GUY ONE-ON-ONE WITHOUT GETTING BRUISED, BATTERED AND BEATEN!
WELL, MR. MACHO, IF YOU'RE SO TOUGH, WHERE ARE YOUR BATTLE BRUISES?
I HAVE A FEW. BUT I'M TOO FAST AND SHIFTY TO GET CLOBBERED WHERE IT SHOWS. I HAVE LOTS OF SUPER MOVES TO MATCH MY SUPER GOOD LOOKS!
GRRR! LISTEN, SMART GUY, I BET A DECENT GIRL ATHLETE COULD EASILY MATCH UP AGAINST YOU ONE-ON-ONE!
YUK! YUK! OH, REALLY? DO YOU CONSIDER YOURSELF TO BE A DECENT ATHLETE?

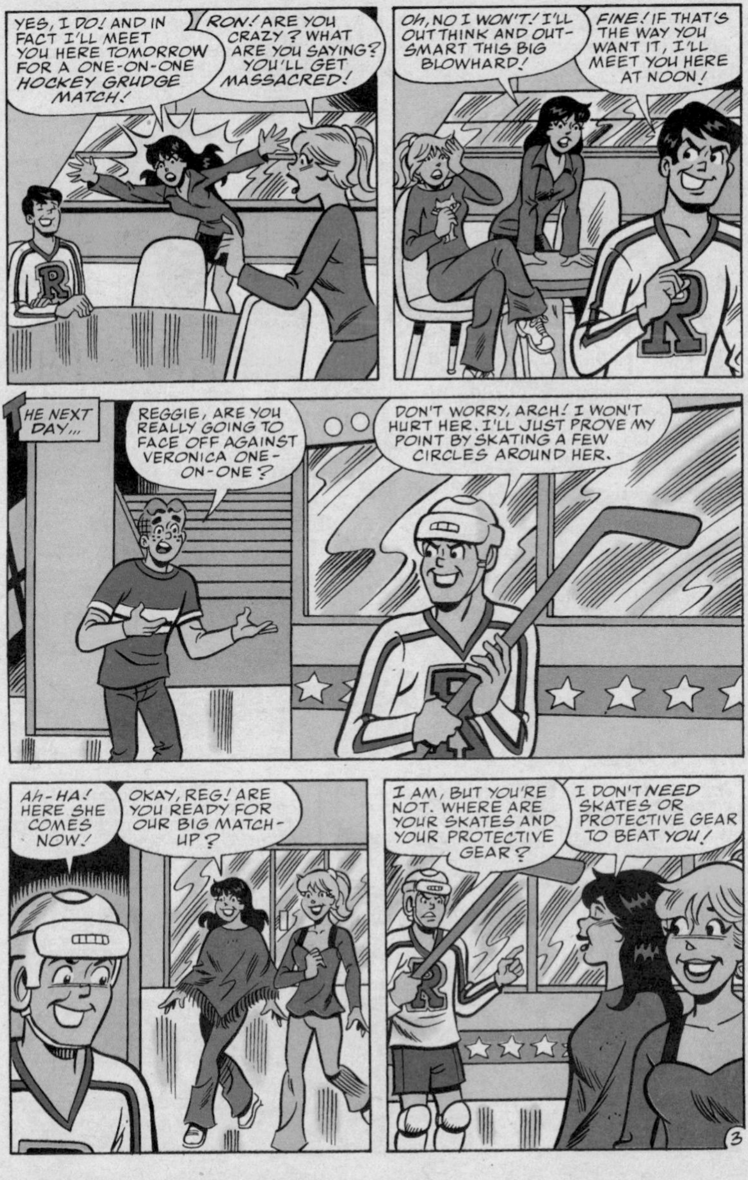
YES, I DO! AND IN FACT I'LL MEET YOU HERE TOMORROW FOR A ONE-ON-ONE HOCKEY GRUDGE MATCH!
RON! ARE YOU CRAZY? WHAT ARE YOU SAYING? YOU'LL GET MASSACRED!
OH, NO I WON'T! I'LL OUT THINK AND OUT-SMART THIS BIG BLOWHARD!
FINE! IF THAT'S THE WAY YOU WANT IT, I'LL MEET YOU HERE AT NOON!
THE NEXT DAY...
REGGIE, ARE YOU REALLY GOING TO FACE OFF AGAINST VERONICA ONE-ON-ONE?
DON'T WORRY, ARCH! I WON'T HURT HER. I'LL JUST PROVE MY POINT BY SKATING A FEW CIRCLES AROUND HER.
AH-HA! HERE SHE COMES NOW!
OKAY, REG! ARE YOU READY FOR OUR BIG MATCH-UP?
I AM, BUT YOU'RE NOT. WHERE ARE YOUR SKATES AND YOUR PROTECTIVE GEAR?
I DON'T NEED SKATES OR PROTECTIVE GEAR TO BEAT YOU!
3

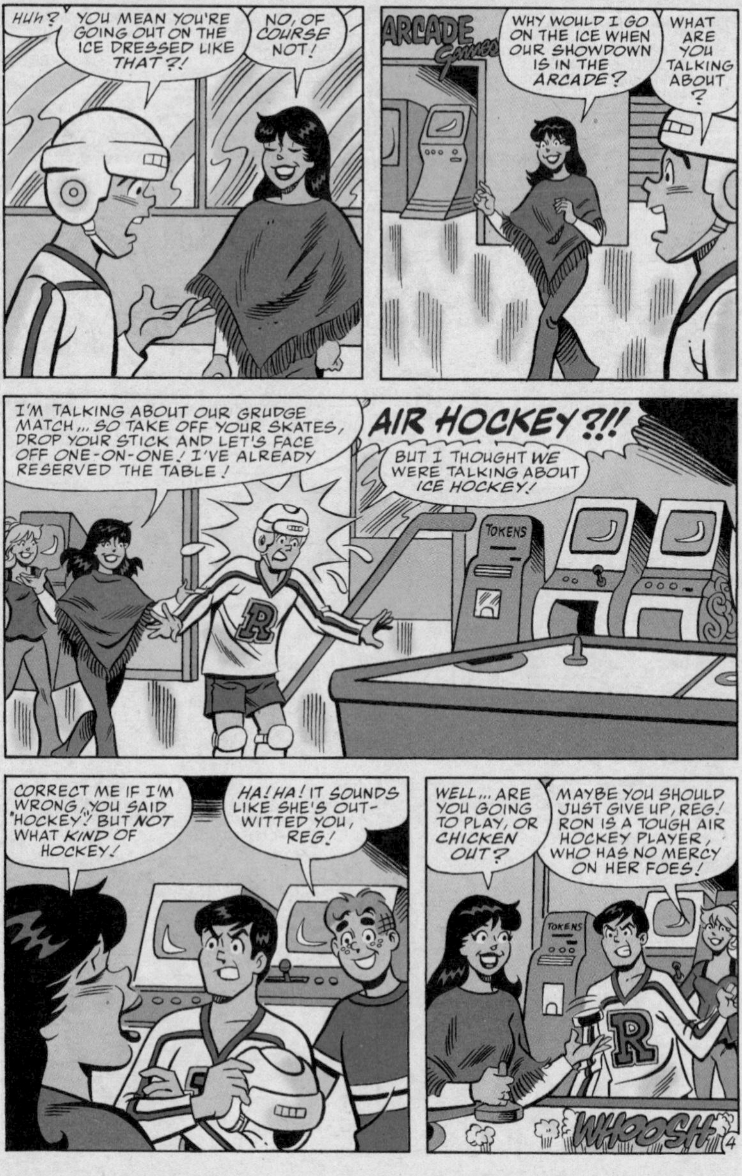
HUH?
YOU MEAN YOU'RE GOING OUT ON THE ICE DRESSED LIKE THAT?!
NO, OF COURSE NOT!
ARCADE Games
WHY WOULD I GO ON THE ICE WHEN OUR SHOWDOWN IS IN THE ARCADE?
WHAT ARE YOU TALKING ABOUT?
I'M TALKING ABOUT OUR GRUDGE MATCH... SO TAKE OFF YOUR SKATES, DROP YOUR STICK AND LET'S FACE OFF ONE-ON-ONE! I'VE ALREADY RESERVED THE TABLE!
AIR HOCKEY?!!
BUT I THOUGHT WE WERE TALKING ABOUT ICE HOCKEY!
TOKENS
R
CORRECT ME IF I'M WRONG... YOU SAID "HOCKEY"! BUT NOT WHAT KIND OF HOCKEY!
HA! HA! IT SOUNDS LIKE SHE'S OUT-WITTED YOU, REG!
WELL... ARE YOU GOING TO PLAY, OR CHICKEN OUT?
MAYBE YOU SHOULD JUST GIVE UP, REG! RON IS A TOUGH AIR HOCKEY PLAYER, WHO HAS NO MERCY ON HER FOES!
TOKENS
R
WHOOSH

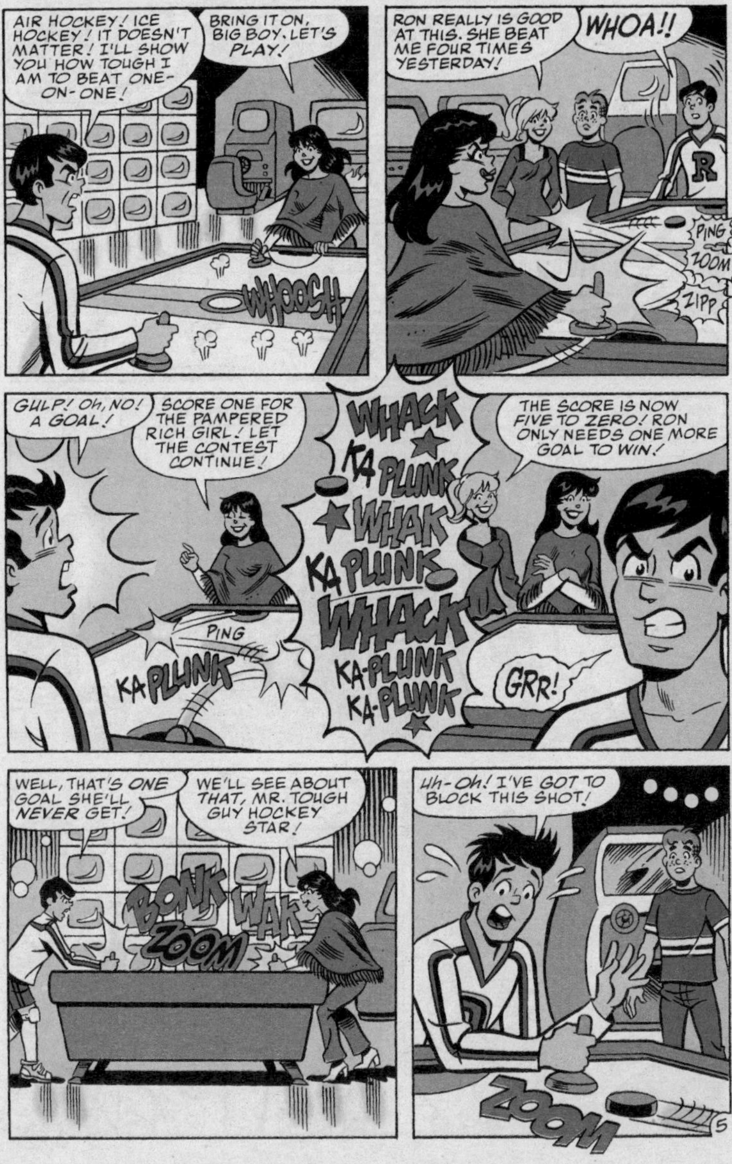
AIR HOCKEY! ICE HOCKEY! IT DOESN'T MATTER! I'LL SHOW YOU HOW TOUGH I AM TO BEAT ONE-ON-ONE!
BRING IT ON, BIG BOY. LET'S PLAY!
WHOOSH
RON REALLY IS GOOD AT THIS. SHE BEAT ME FOUR TIMES YESTERDAY!
WHOA!!
PING
ZOOM
ZIPP
GULP! Oh, NO! A GOAL!
SCORE ONE FOR THE PAMPERED RICH GIRL! LET THE CONTEST CONTINUE!
PING
KA PLUNK
WHACK
KA PLUNK
WHAK
KA PLUNK
WHACK
KA-PLUNK
KA-PLUNK
THE SCORE IS NOW FIVE TO ZERO! RON ONLY NEEDS ONE MORE GOAL TO WIN!
GRR!
WELL, THAT'S ONE GOAL SHE'LL NEVER GET!
WE'LL SEE ABOUT THAT, MR. TOUGH GUY HOCKEY STAR!
BONK
WAK
ZOOM
Uh-Oh! I'VE GOT TO BLOCK THIS SHOT!
ZOOM

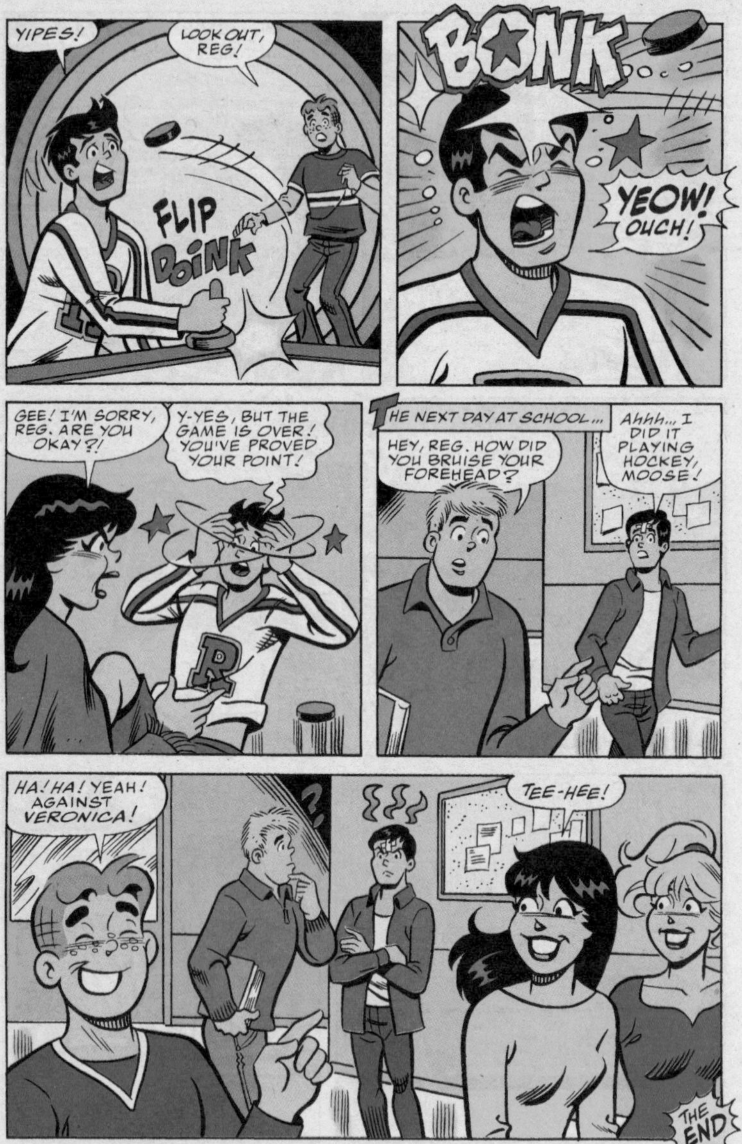
YIPES!
LOOK OUT, REG!
FLIP
DOINK
BONK
YEOW! OUCH!
GEE! I'M SORRY, REG. ARE YOU OKAY?!
Y-YES, BUT THE GAME IS OVER! YOU'VE PROVED YOUR POINT!
THE NEXT DAY AT SCHOOL...
HEY, REG. HOW DID YOU BRUISE YOUR FOREHEAD?
Ahhh... I DID IT PLAYING HOCKEY, MOOSE!
HA! HA! YEAH! AGAINST VERONICA!
TEE-HEE!
THE END

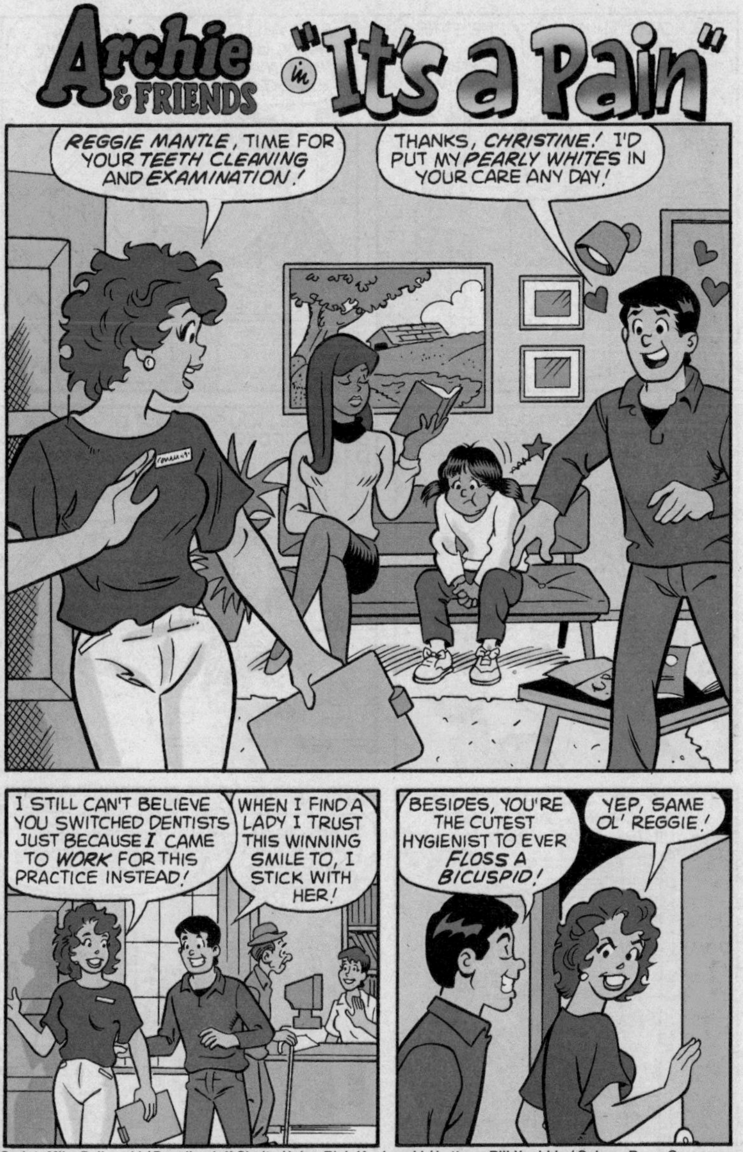
Archie & FRIENDS in "It's a Pain"
REGGIE MANTLE, TIME FOR YOUR TEETH CLEANING AND EXAMINATION!
THANKS, CHRISTINE! I'D PUT MY PEARLY WHITES IN YOUR CARE ANY DAY!
I STILL CAN'T BELIEVE YOU SWITCHED DENTISTS JUST BECAUSE I CAME TO WORK FOR THIS PRACTICE INSTEAD!
WHEN I FIND A LADY I TRUST THIS WINNING SMILE TO, I STICK WITH HER!
BESIDES, YOU'RE THE CUTEST HYGIENIST TO EVER FLOSS A BICUSPID!
YEP, SAME OL' REGGIE!

Script: Mike Pellowski / Pencils: Jeff Shultz / Inks: Rich Koslowski / Letters: Bill Yoshida / Colors: Barry Grossman

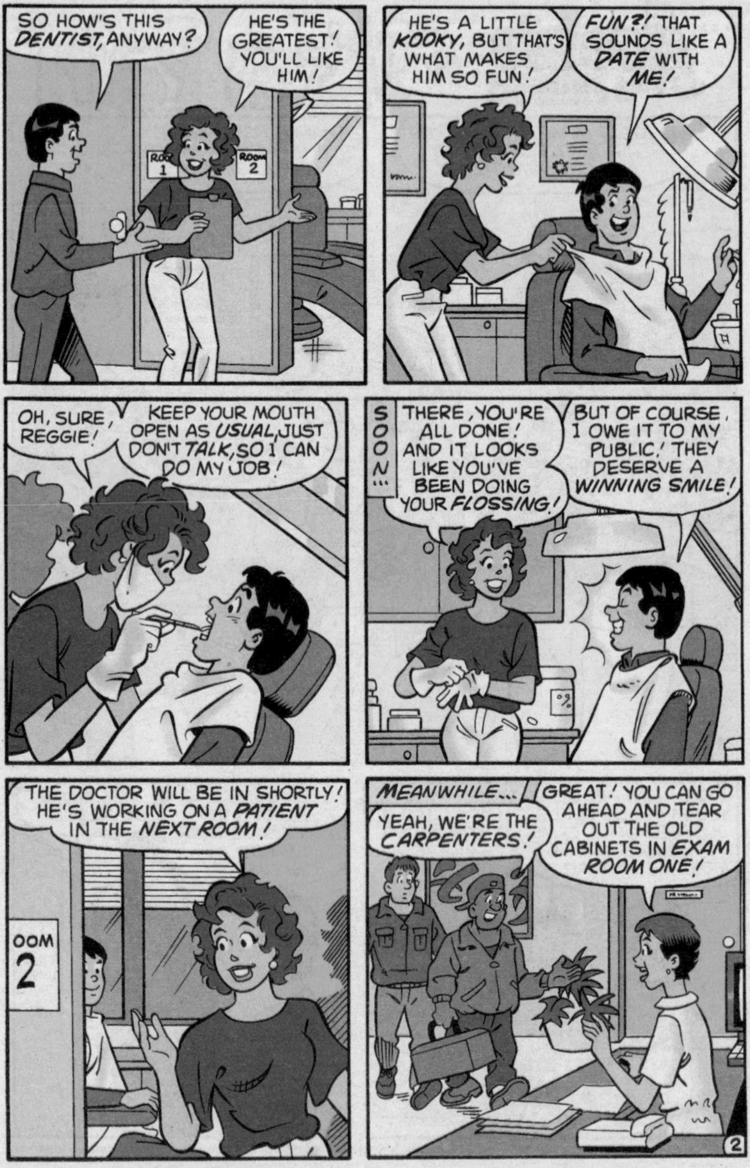
SO HOW'S THIS DENTIST, ANYWAY?
HE'S THE GREATEST! YOU'LL LIKE HIM!
ROOM 1
ROOM 2
HE'S A LITTLE KOOKY, BUT THAT'S WHAT MAKES HIM SO FUN!
FUN?! THAT SOUNDS LIKE A DATE WITH ME!
OH, SURE, REGGIE!
KEEP YOUR MOUTH OPEN AS USUAL, JUST DON'T TALK, SO I CAN DO MY JOB!
SOON...
THERE, YOU'RE ALL DONE! AND IT LOOKS LIKE YOU'VE BEEN DOING YOUR FLOSSING!
BUT OF COURSE, I OWE IT TO MY PUBLIC! THEY DESERVE A WINNING SMILE!
THE DOCTOR WILL BE IN SHORTLY! HE'S WORKING ON A PATIENT IN THE NEXT ROOM!
OOM 2
MEANWHILE...
YEAH, WE'RE THE CARPENTERS!
GREAT! YOU CAN GO AHEAD AND TEAR OUT THE OLD CABINETS IN EXAM ROOM ONE!
2

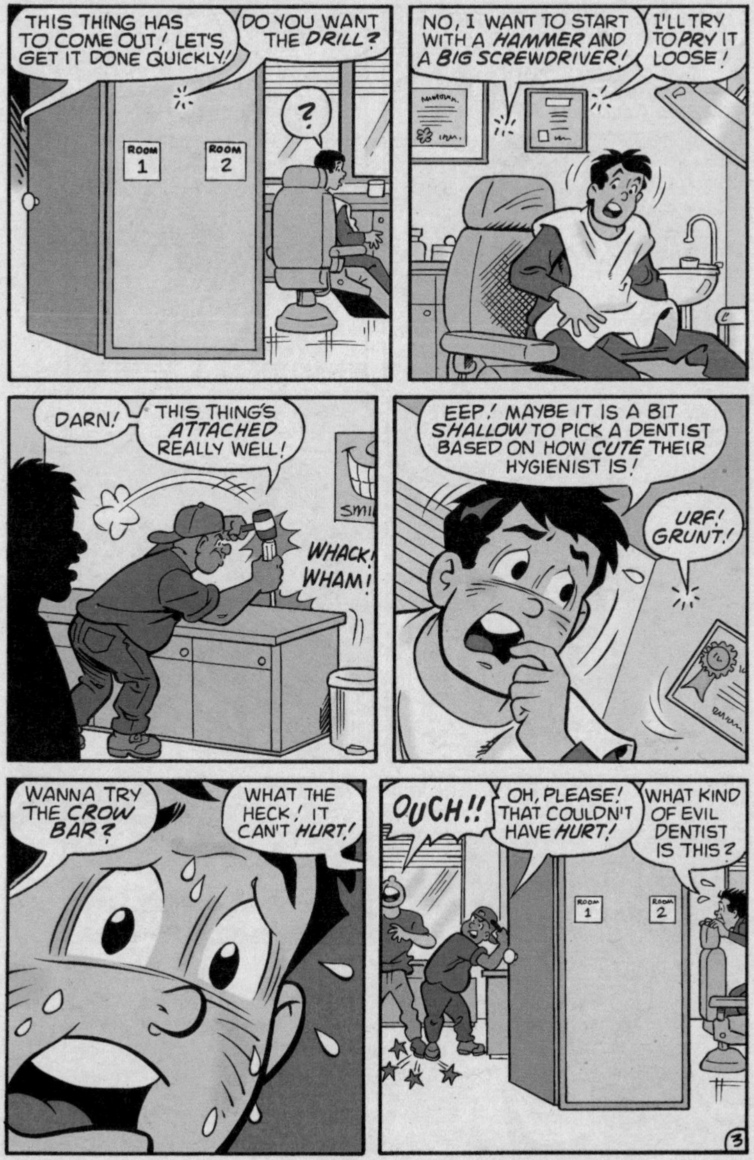
THIS THING HAS TO COME OUT! LET'S GET IT DONE QUICKLY!
DO YOU WANT THE DRILL?
?
NO, I WANT TO START WITH A HAMMER AND A BIG SCREWDRIVER!
I'LL TRY TO PRY IT LOOSE!
ROOM 1
ROOM 2
DARN!
THIS THING'S ATTACHED REALLY WELL!
WHACK! WHAM!
EEP! MAYBE IT IS A BIT SHALLOW TO PICK A DENTIST BASED ON HOW CUTE THEIR HYGIENIST IS!
URF! GRUNT!
WANNA TRY THE CROW BAR?
WHAT THE HECK! IT CAN'T HURT!
OUCH!!
OH, PLEASE! THAT COULDN'T HAVE HURT!
WHAT KIND OF EVIL DENTIST IS THIS?
3

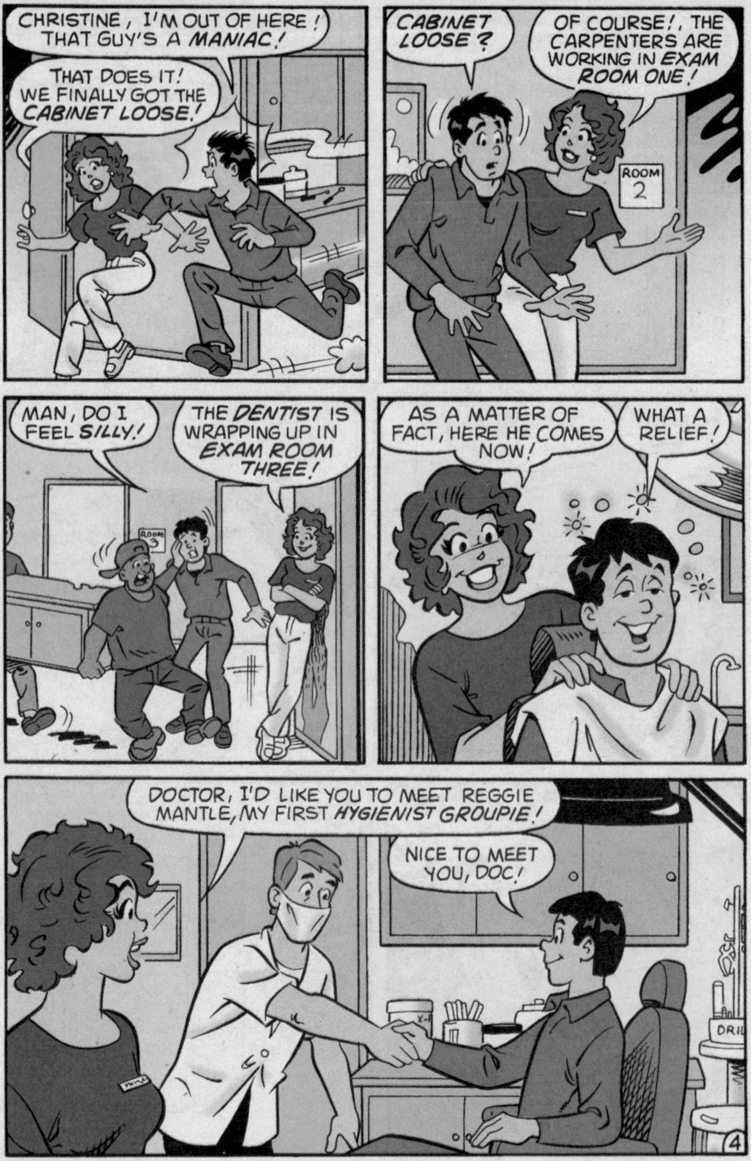

CHRISTINE, I'M OUT OF HERE! THAT GUY'S A MANIAC!
THAT DOES IT! WE FINALLY GOT THE CABINET LOOSE!
CABINET LOOSE?
OF COURSE!, THE CARPENTERS ARE WORKING IN EXAM ROOM ONE!
ROOM 2
MAN, DO I FEEL SILLY!
THE DENTIST IS WRAPPING UP IN EXAM ROOM THREE!
AS A MATTER OF FACT, HERE HE COMES NOW!
WHAT A RELIEF!
DOCTOR, I'D LIKE YOU TO MEET REGGIE MANTLE, MY FIRST HYGIENIST GROUPIE!
NICE TO MEET YOU, DOC!
4

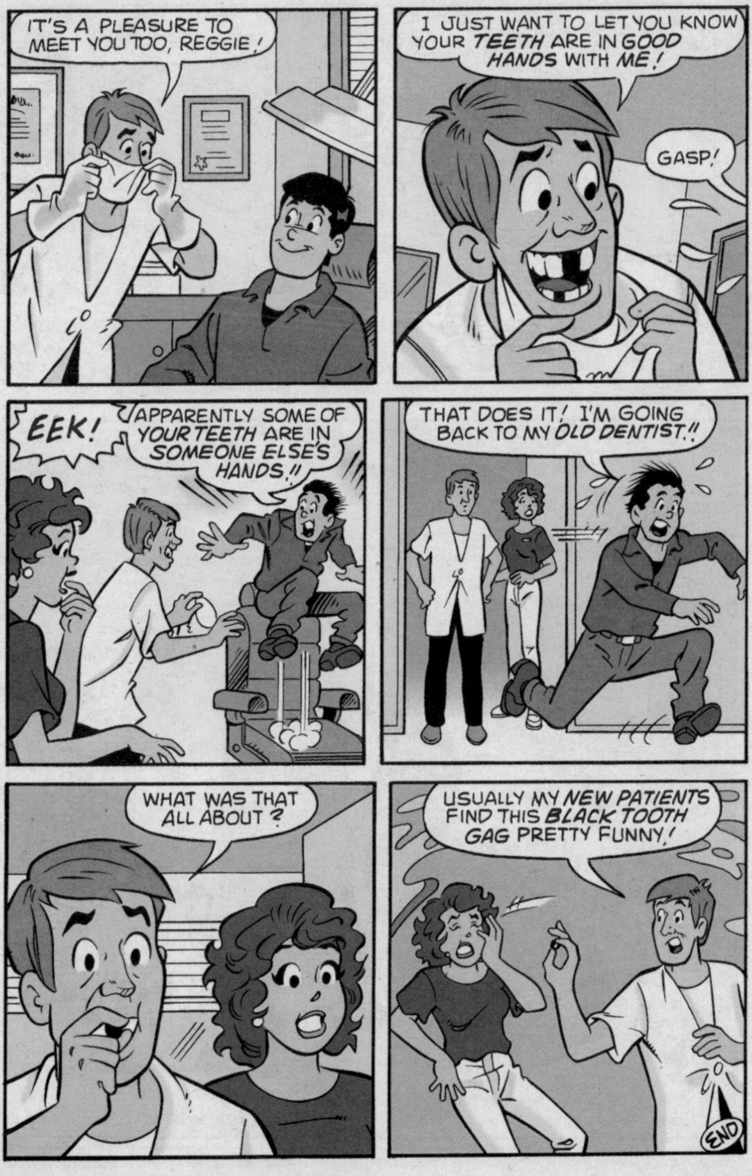
IT'S A PLEASURE TO MEET YOU TOO, REGGIE!
I JUST WANT TO LET YOU KNOW YOUR TEETH ARE IN GOOD HANDS WITH ME!
GASP!
EEK!
APPARENTLY SOME OF YOUR TEETH ARE IN SOMEONE ELSE'S HANDS!!
THAT DOES IT! I'M GOING BACK TO MY OLD DENTIST!!
WHAT WAS THAT ALL ABOUT?
USUALLY MY NEW PATIENTS FIND THIS BLACK TOOTH GAG PRETTY FUNNY!
END

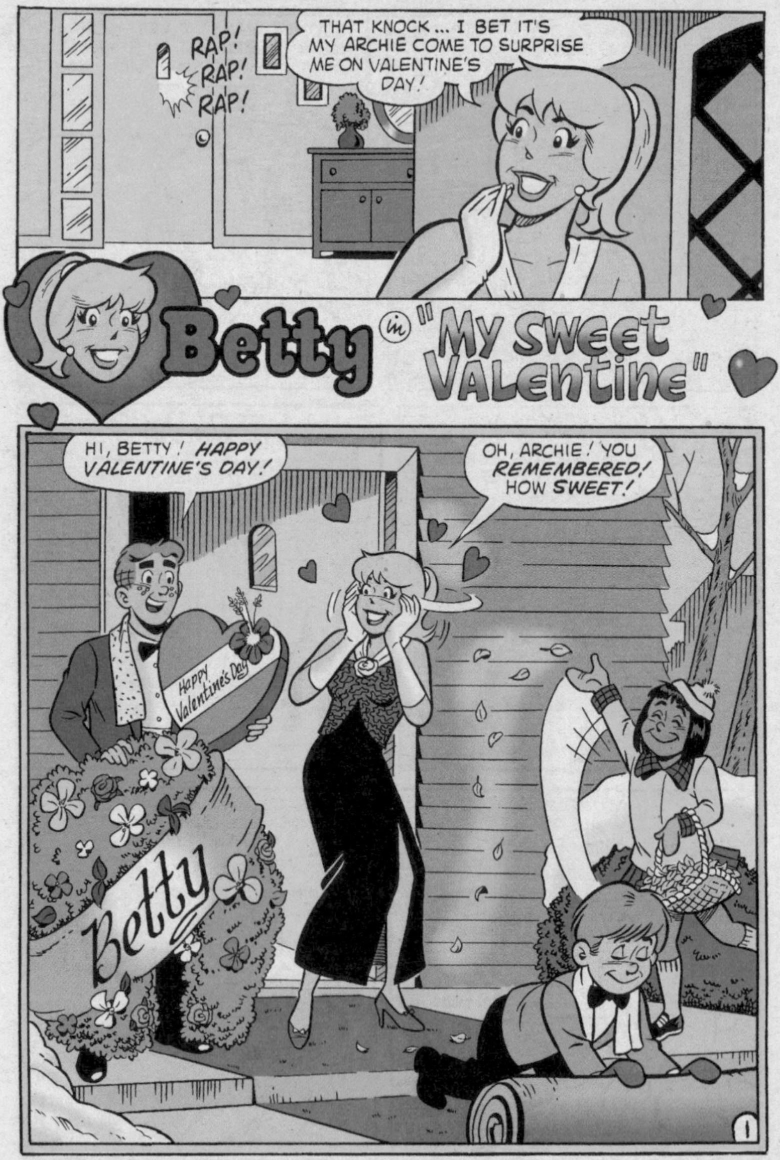
RAP! RAP! RAP!
THAT KNOCK ... I BET IT'S MY ARCHIE COME TO SURPRISE ME ON VALENTINE'S DAY!
Betty in "My Sweet Valentine"
HI, BETTY! HAPPY VALENTINE'S DAY!
OH, ARCHIE! YOU REMEMBERED! HOW SWEET!
Happy Valentine's Day
Betty
1

Script: George Gladir / Pencils: Fernando Ruiz / Inks: Jon D'Agostino / Letters: Bill Yoshida / Colors: Barrry Grossman

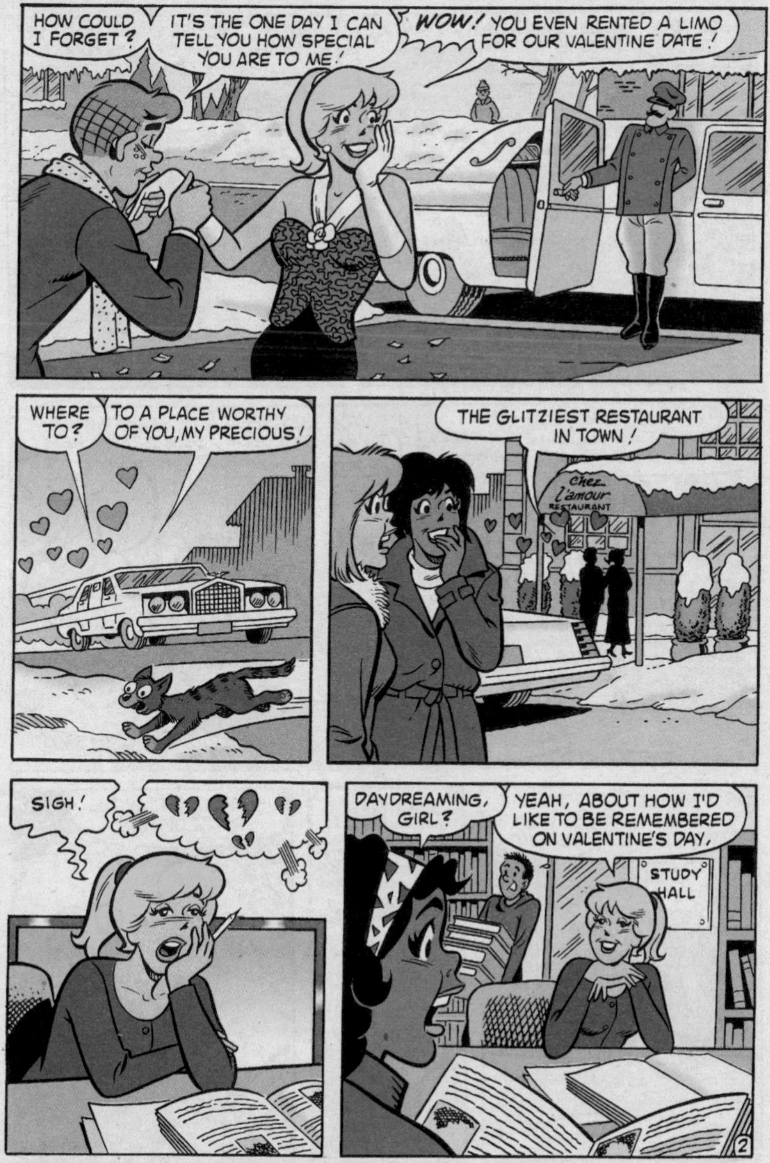
HOW COULD I FORGET?
IT'S THE ONE DAY I CAN TELL YOU HOW SPECIAL YOU ARE TO ME!
WOW! YOU EVEN RENTED A LIMO FOR OUR VALENTINE DATE!
WHERE TO?
TO A PLACE WORTHY OF YOU, MY PRECIOUS!
THE GLITZIEST RESTAURANT IN TOWN!
Chez l'amour RESTAURANT
SIGH!
DAYDREAMING, GIRL?
YEAH, ABOUT HOW I'D LIKE TO BE REMEMBERED ON VALENTINE'S DAY,
STUDY HALL
2

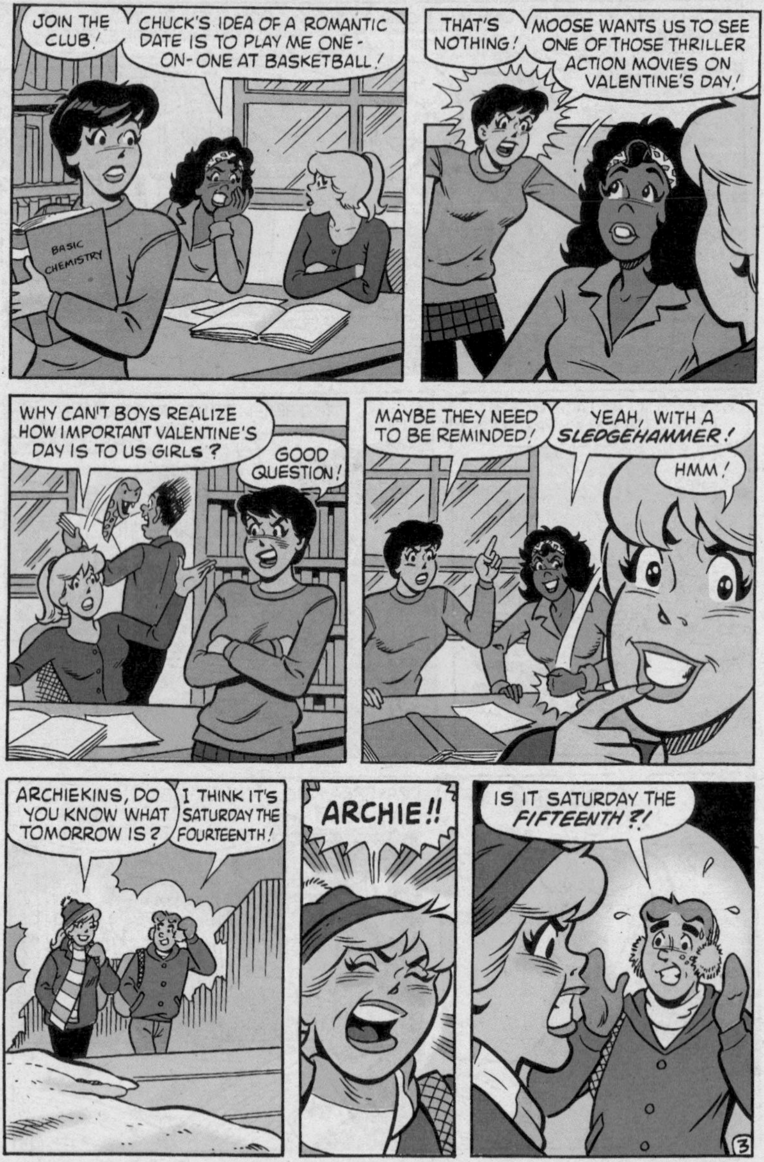
JOIN THE CLUB!
CHUCK'S IDEA OF A ROMANTIC DATE IS TO PLAY ME ONE-ON-ONE AT BASKETBALL!
BASIC CHEMISTRY
THAT'S NOTHING!
MOOSE WANTS US TO SEE ONE OF THOSE THRILLER ACTION MOVIES ON VALENTINE'S DAY!
WHY CAN'T BOYS REALIZE HOW IMPORTANT VALENTINE'S DAY IS TO US GIRLS?
GOOD QUESTION!
MAYBE THEY NEED TO BE REMINDED!
YEAH, WITH A SLEDGEHAMMER!
HMM!
ARCHIEKINS, DO YOU KNOW WHAT TOMORROW IS?
I THINK IT'S SATURDAY THE FOURTEENTH!
ARCHIE!!
IS IT SATURDAY THE FIFTEENTH?!
3

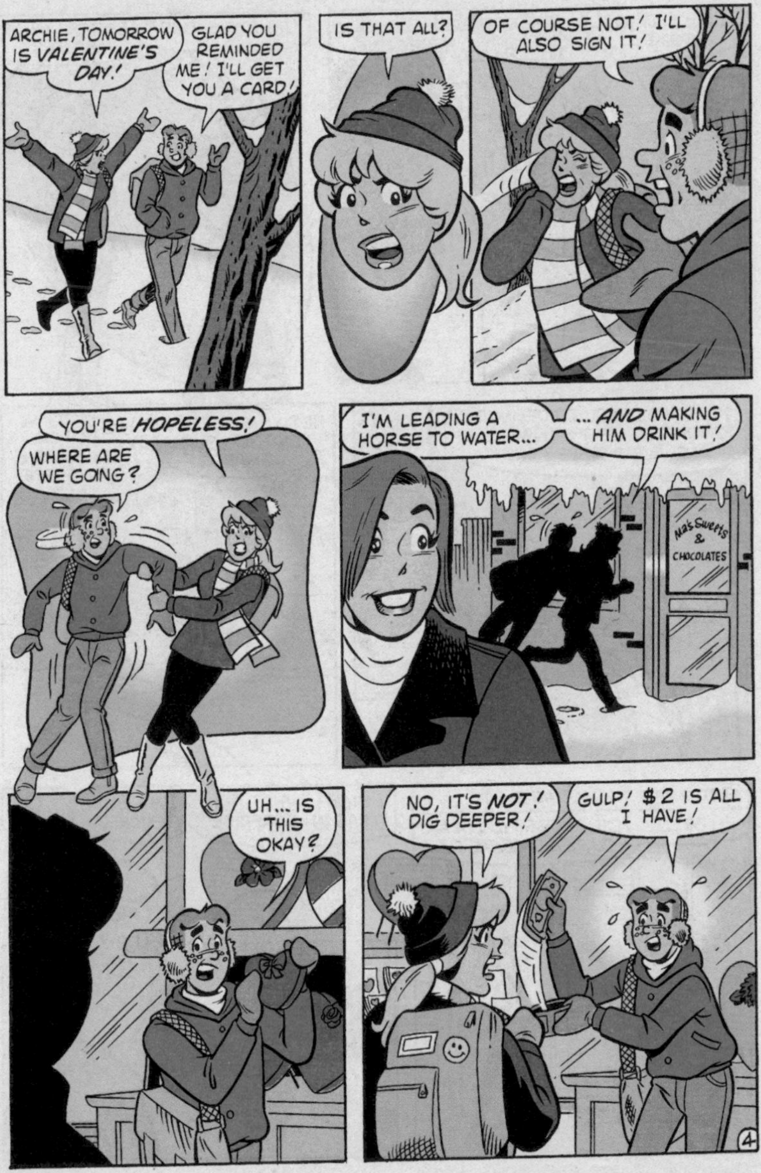
ARCHIE, TOMORROW IS VALENTINE'S DAY!
GLAD YOU REMINDED ME! I'LL GET YOU A CARD!
IS THAT ALL?
OF COURSE NOT! I'LL ALSO SIGN IT!
YOU'RE HOPELESS!
WHERE ARE WE GOING?
I'M LEADING A HORSE TO WATER...
... AND MAKING HIM DRINK IT!
Ma's Sweets & CHOCOLATES
UH... IS THIS OKAY?
NO, IT'S NOT! DIG DEEPER!
GULP! $2 IS ALL I HAVE!
4

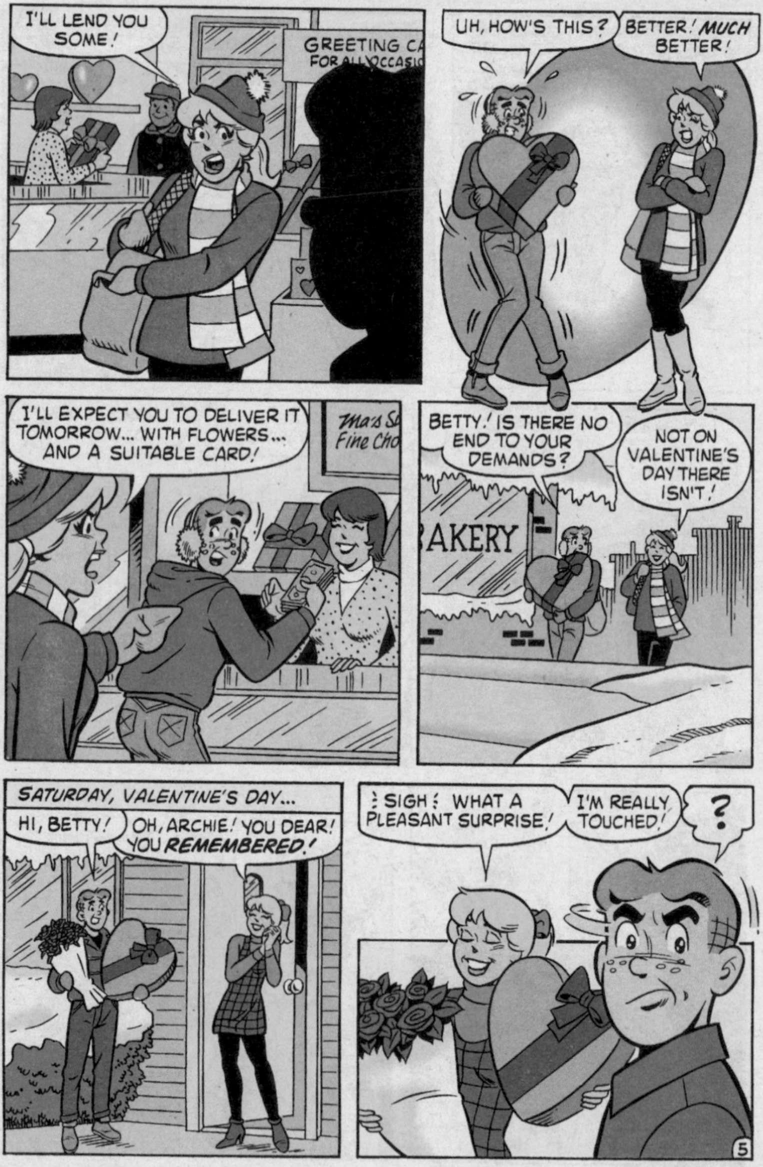
I'LL LEND YOU SOME!
GREETING CA
FOR ALL OCCASIO
UH, HOW'S THIS?
BETTER! MUCH BETTER!
I'LL EXPECT YOU TO DELIVER IT TOMORROW... WITH FLOWERS... AND A SUITABLE CARD!
BETTY! IS THERE NO END TO YOUR DEMANDS?
NOT ON VALENTINE'S DAY THERE ISN'T!
BAKERY
SATURDAY, VALENTINE'S DAY...
HI, BETTY!
OH, ARCHIE! YOU DEAR! YOU REMEMBERED!
SIGH WHAT A PLEASANT SURPRISE!
I'M REALLY TOUCHED!
?
5

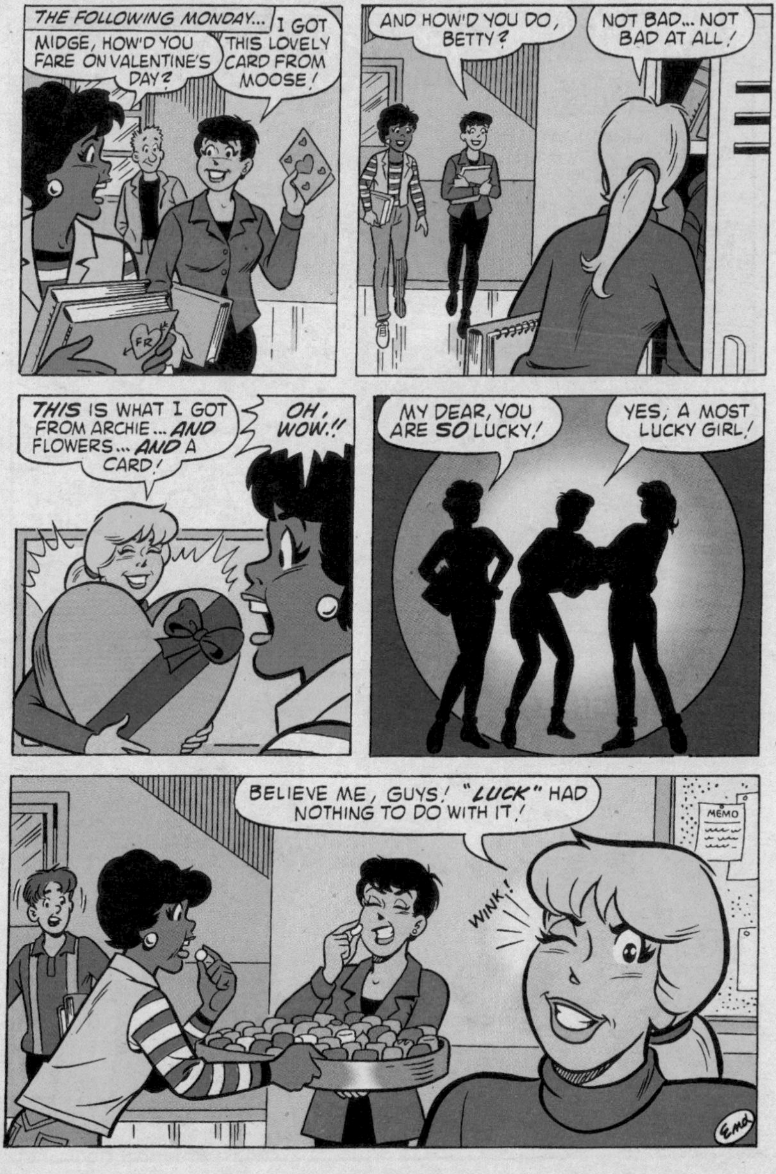
THE FOLLOWING MONDAY...
MIDGE, HOW'D YOU FARE ON VALENTINE'S DAY?
I GOT THIS LOVELY CARD FROM MOOSE!
AND HOW'D YOU DO, BETTY?
NOT BAD... NOT BAD AT ALL!
THIS IS WHAT I GOT FROM ARCHIE... AND FLOWERS... AND A CARD!
OH, WOW!!
MY DEAR, YOU ARE SO LUCKY!
YES, A MOST LUCKY GIRL!
BELIEVE ME, GUYS! "LUCK" HAD NOTHING TO DO WITH IT!
WINK!
MEMO
End

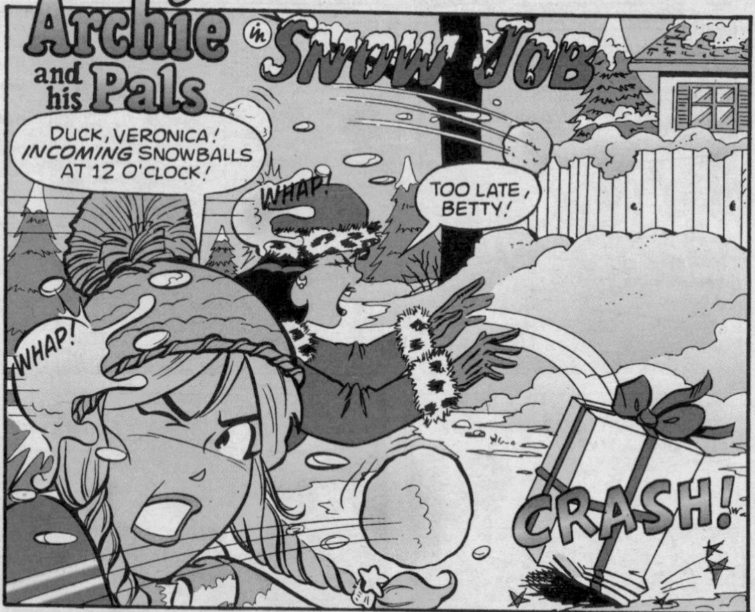
Archie and his Pals
in
SNOW JOB
DUCK, VERONICA! INCOMING SNOWBALLS AT 12 O'CLOCK!
WHAP!
TOO LATE, BETTY!
WHAP!
CRASH!

SCRIPT: JOE EDWARDS ARTWORK: HOLLY G!

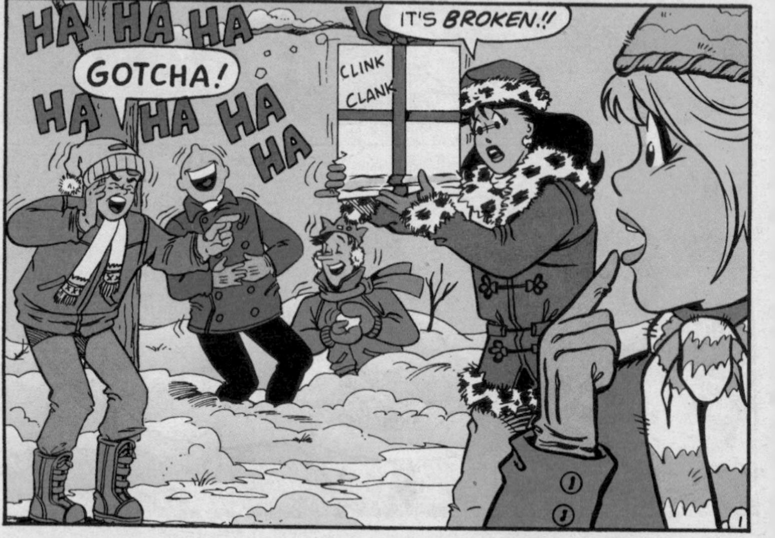
HA HA HA
IT'S BROKEN!!
GOTCHA!
CLINK
CLANK
HA HA HA HA HA
1

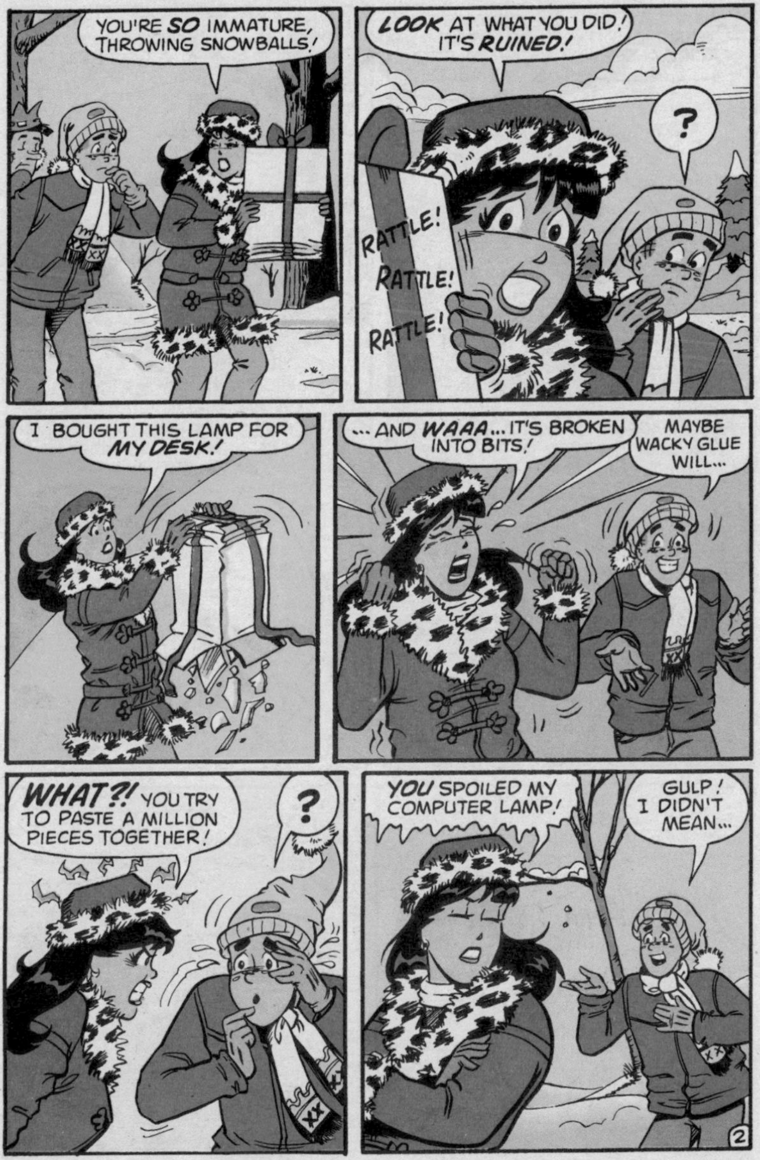

YOU'RE SO IMMATURE, THROWING SNOWBALLS!
LOOK AT WHAT YOU DID! IT'S RUINED!
?
RATTLE!
RATTLE!
RATTLE!
I BOUGHT THIS LAMP FOR MY DESK!
... AND WAAA... IT'S BROKEN INTO BITS!
MAYBE WACKY GLUE WILL...
WHAT?! YOU TRY TO PASTE A MILLION PIECES TOGETHER!
?
YOU SPOILED MY COMPUTER LAMP!
GULP! I DIDN'T MEAN...
2

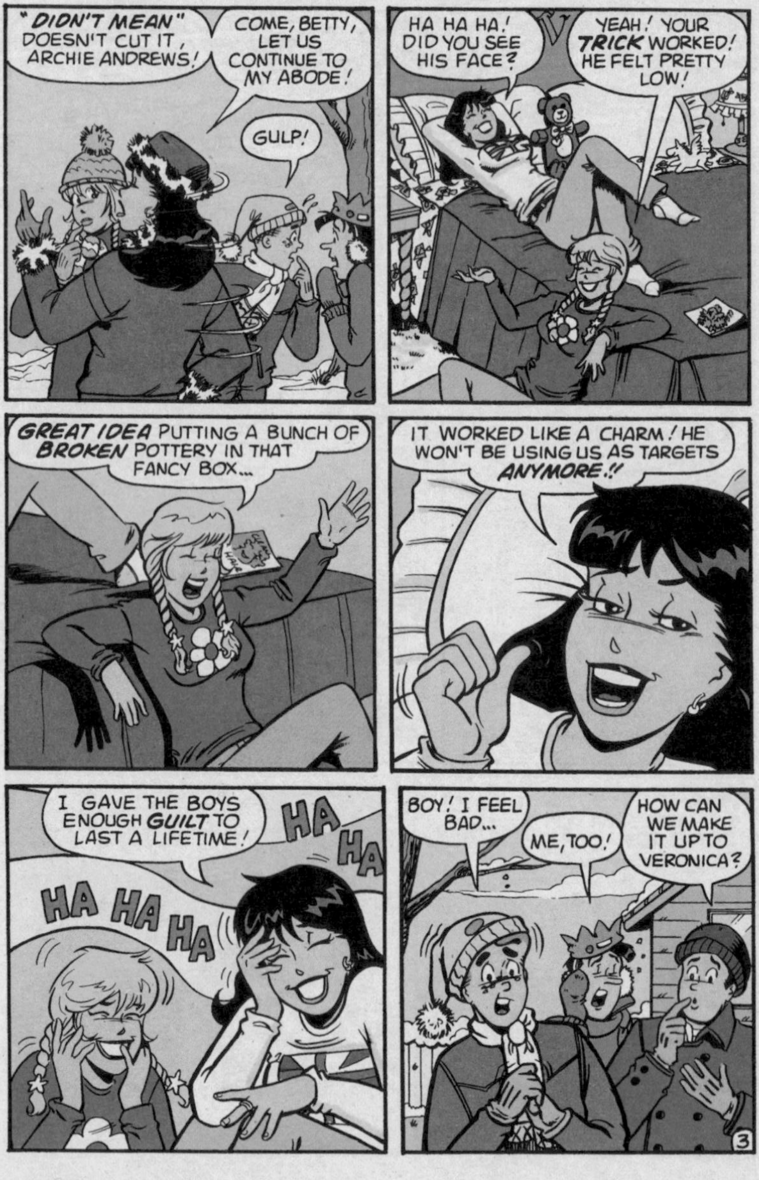

"DIDN'T MEAN" DOESN'T CUT IT, ARCHIE ANDREWS!
COME, BETTY, LET US CONTINUE TO MY ABODE!
GULP!
HA HA HA! DID YOU SEE HIS FACE?
YEAH! YOUR TRICK WORKED! HE FELT PRETTY LOW!
GREAT IDEA PUTTING A BUNCH OF BROKEN POTTERY IN THAT FANCY BOX...
IT WORKED LIKE A CHARM! HE WON'T BE USING US AS TARGETS ANYMORE!!
I GAVE THE BOYS ENOUGH GUILT TO LAST A LIFETIME!
HA HA
HA HA HA HA
BOY! I FEEL BAD...
ME, TOO!
HOW CAN WE MAKE IT UP TO VERONICA?
3

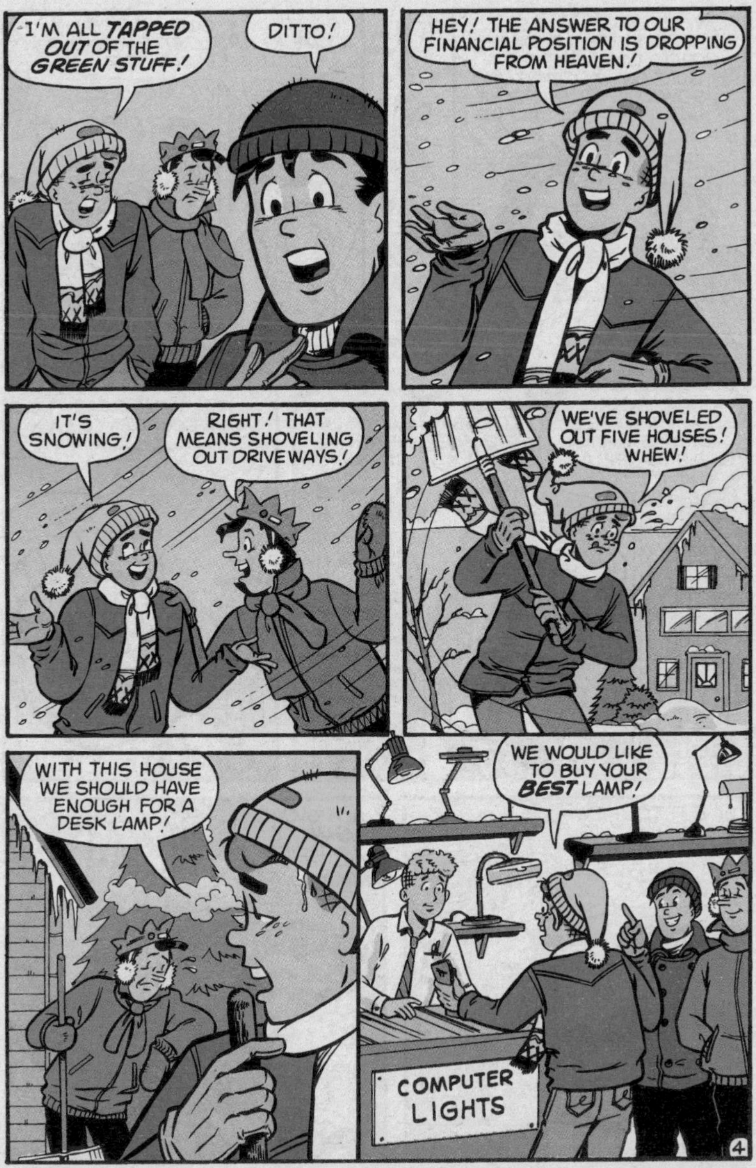
I'M ALL TAPPED OUT OF THE GREEN STUFF!
DITTO!
HEY! THE ANSWER TO OUR FINANCIAL POSITION IS DROPPING FROM HEAVEN!
IT'S SNOWING!
RIGHT! THAT MEANS SHOVELING OUT DRIVEWAYS!
WE'VE SHOVELED OUT FIVE HOUSES! WHEW!
WITH THIS HOUSE WE SHOULD HAVE ENOUGH FOR A DESK LAMP!
WE WOULD LIKE TO BUY YOUR BEST LAMP!
COMPUTER LIGHTS
4

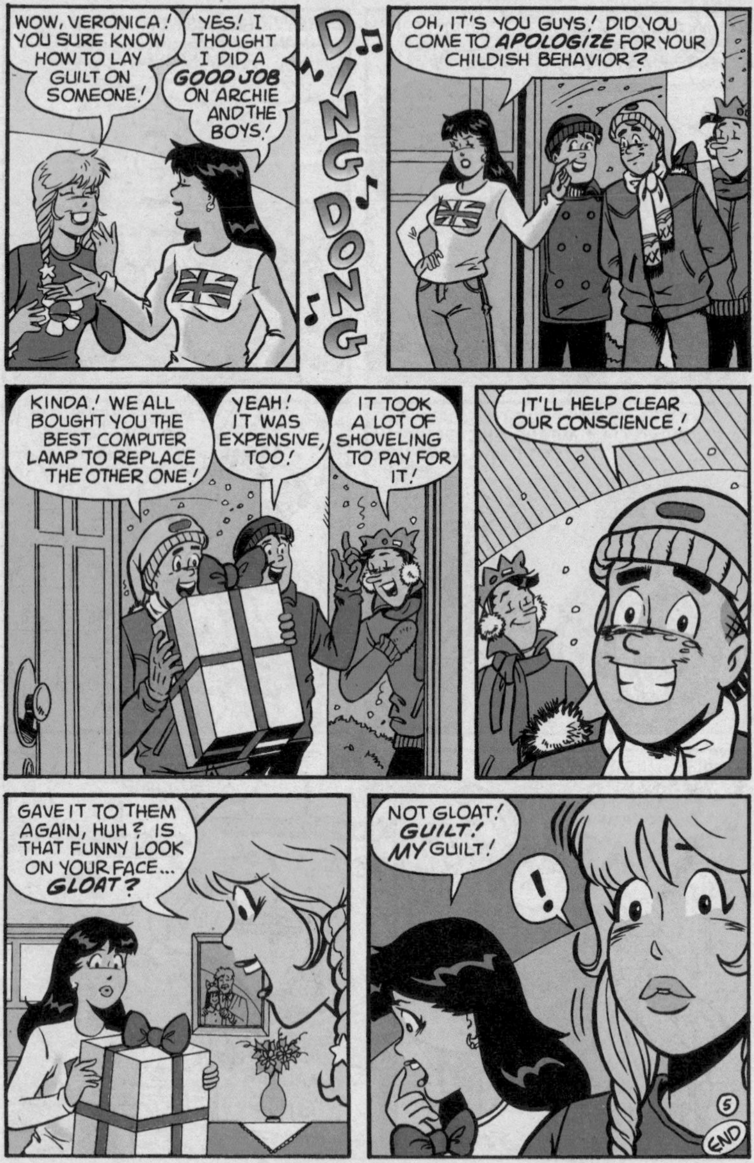
WOW, VERONICA! YOU SURE KNOW HOW TO LAY GUILT ON SOMEONE!
YES! I THOUGHT I DID A GOOD JOB ON ARCHIE AND THE BOYS!
DING DONG
OH, IT'S YOU GUYS! DID YOU COME TO APOLOGIZE FOR YOUR CHILDISH BEHAVIOR?
KINDA! WE ALL BOUGHT YOU THE BEST COMPUTER LAMP TO REPLACE THE OTHER ONE!
YEAH! IT WAS EXPENSIVE, TOO!
IT TOOK A LOT OF SHOVELING TO PAY FOR IT!
IT'LL HELP CLEAR OUR CONSCIENCE!
GAVE IT TO THEM AGAIN, HUH? IS THAT FUNNY LOOK ON YOUR FACE... GLOAT?
NOT GLOAT! GUILT! MY GUILT!
!
5
END

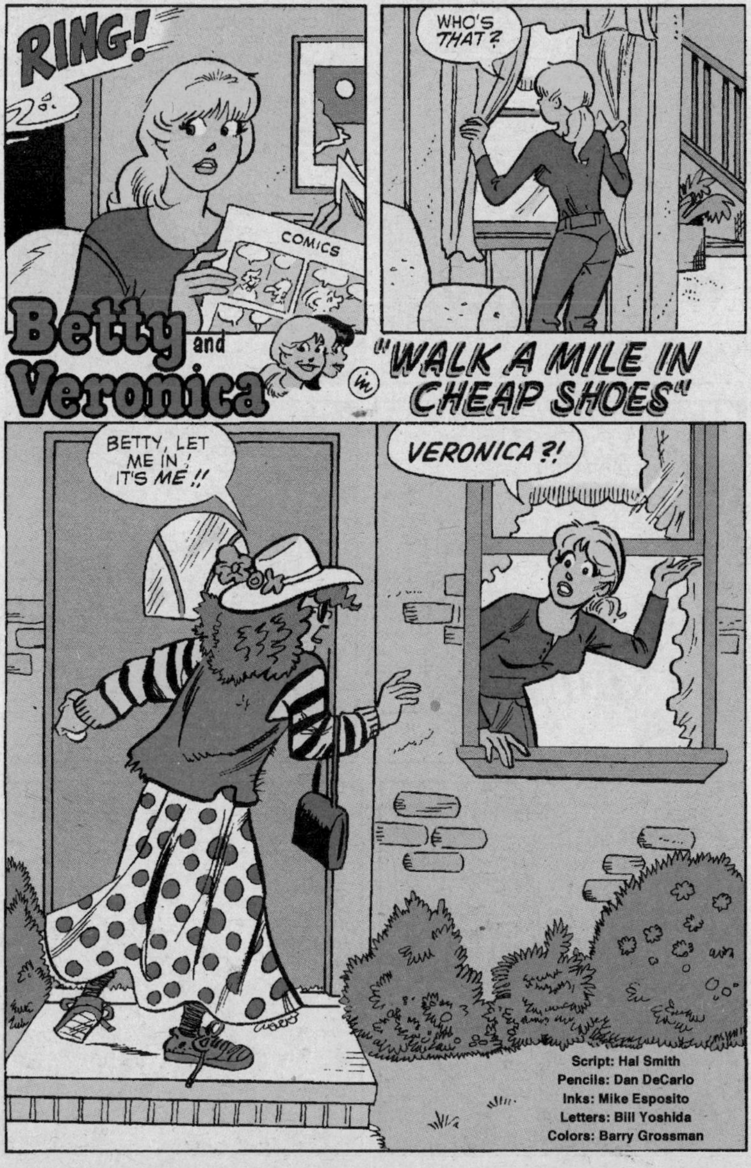
RING!
COMICS
WHO'S THAT?
Betty and Veronica in "WALK A MILE IN CHEAP SHOES"
BETTY, LET ME IN! IT'S ME!!
VERONICA?!
Script: Hal Smith
Pencils: Dan DeCarlo
Inks: Mike Esposito
Letters: Bill Yoshida
Colors: Barry Grossman

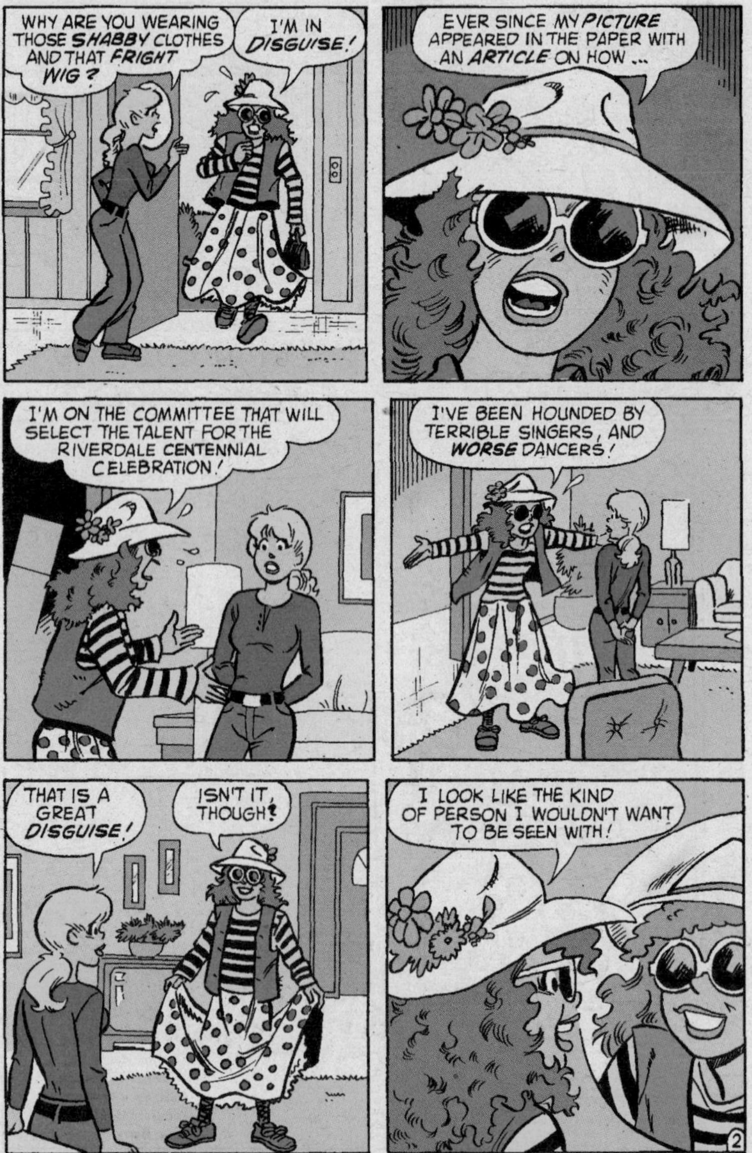
WHY ARE YOU WEARING THOSE SHABBY CLOTHES AND THAT FRIGHT WIG?
I'M IN DISGUISE!
EVER SINCE MY PICTURE APPEARED IN THE PAPER WITH AN ARTICLE ON HOW ...
I'M ON THE COMMITTEE THAT WILL SELECT THE TALENT FOR THE RIVERDALE CENTENNIAL CELEBRATION!
I'VE BEEN HOUNDED BY TERRIBLE SINGERS, AND WORSE DANCERS!
THAT IS A GREAT DISGUISE!
ISN'T IT, THOUGH?
I LOOK LIKE THE KIND OF PERSON I WOULDN'T WANT TO BE SEEN WITH!
2

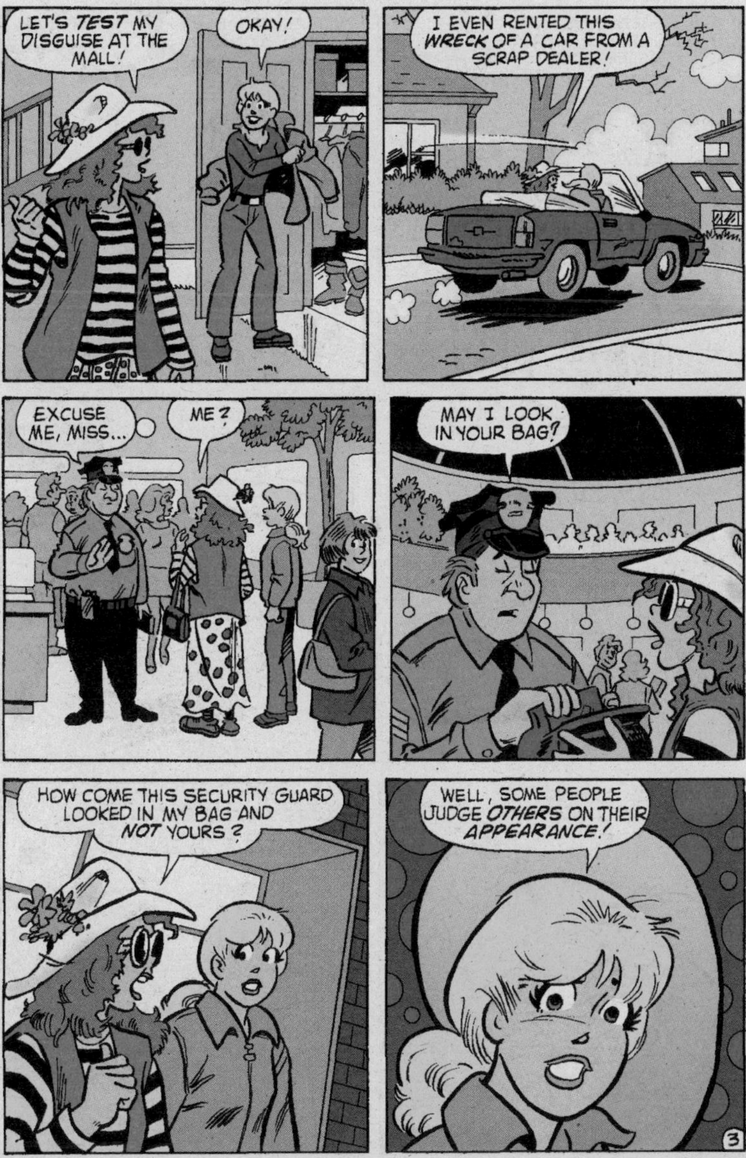
LET'S TEST MY DISGUISE AT THE MALL!
OKAY!
I EVEN RENTED THIS WRECK OF A CAR FROM A SCRAP DEALER!
EXCUSE ME, MISS...
ME?
MAY I LOOK IN YOUR BAG?
HOW COME THIS SECURITY GUARD LOOKED IN MY BAG AND NOT YOURS?
WELL, SOME PEOPLE JUDGE OTHERS ON THEIR APPEARANCE!
3

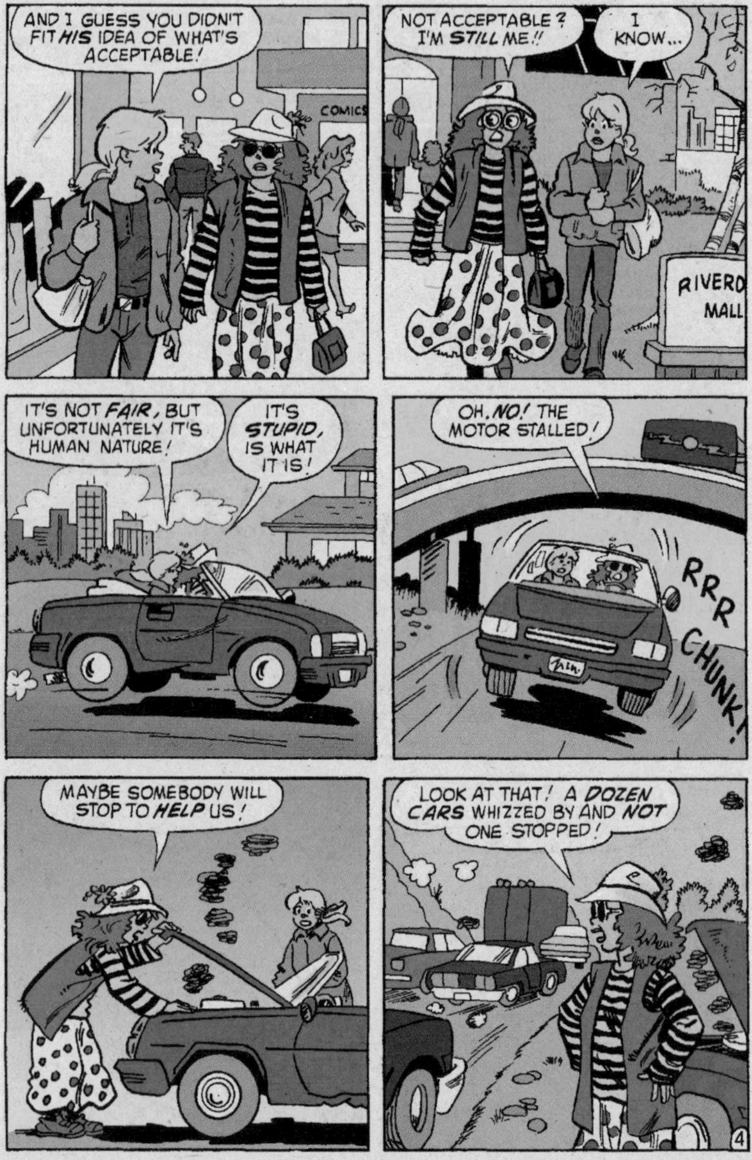
AND I GUESS YOU DIDN'T FIT HIS IDEA OF WHAT'S ACCEPTABLE!
COMICS
NOT ACCEPTABLE? I'M STILL ME!!
I KNOW...
RIVERD
MALL
IT'S NOT FAIR, BUT UNFORTUNATELY IT'S HUMAN NATURE!
IT'S STUPID, IS WHAT IT IS!
OH, NO! THE MOTOR STALLED!
RRR
CHUNK!
MAYBE SOMEBODY WILL STOP TO HELP US!
LOOK AT THAT! A DOZEN CARS WHIZZED BY AND NOT ONE STOPPED!
4

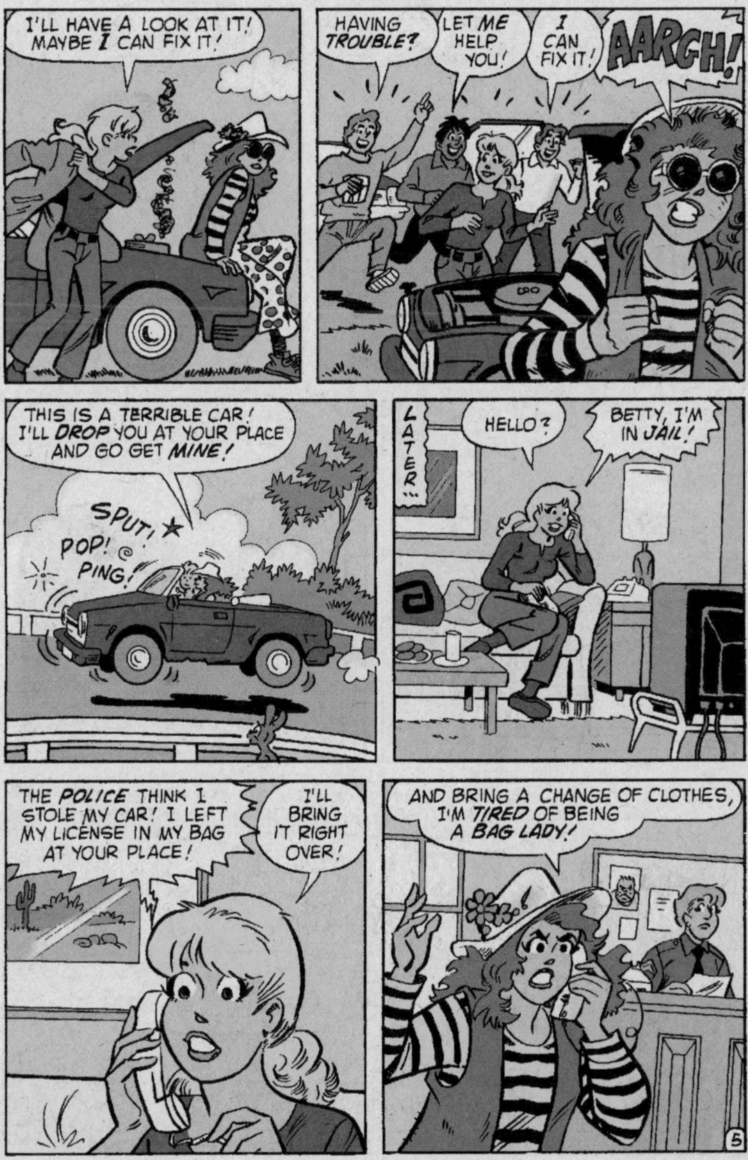
I'LL HAVE A LOOK AT IT! MAYBE I CAN FIX IT!
HAVING TROUBLE?
LET ME HELP YOU!
I CAN FIX IT!
AARGH!
THIS IS A TERRIBLE CAR! I'LL DROP YOU AT YOUR PLACE AND GO GET MINE!
SPUT!
POP!
PING!
LATER...
HELLO?
BETTY, I'M IN JAIL!
THE POLICE THINK I STOLE MY CAR! I LEFT MY LICENSE IN MY BAG AT YOUR PLACE!
I'LL BRING IT RIGHT OVER!
AND BRING A CHANGE OF CLOTHES, I'M TIRED OF BEING A BAG LADY!
5

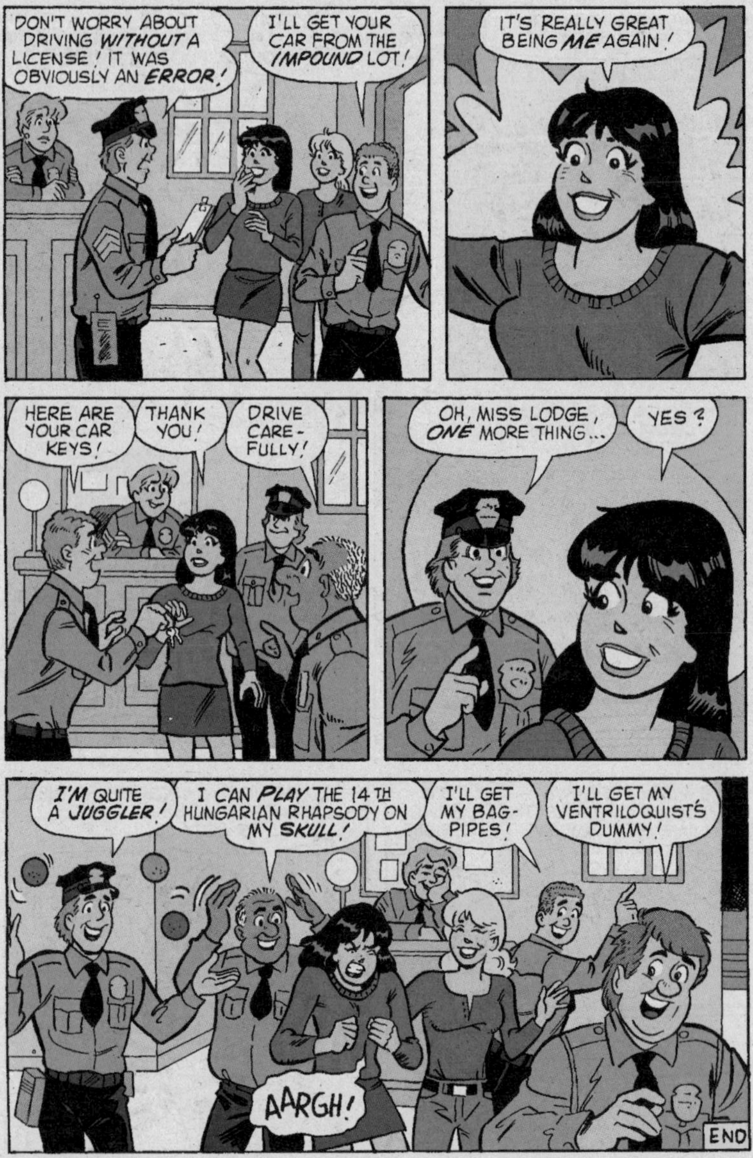
DON'T WORRY ABOUT DRIVING WITHOUT A LICENSE! IT WAS OBVIOUSLY AN ERROR!
I'LL GET YOUR CAR FROM THE IMPOUND LOT!
IT'S REALLY GREAT BEING ME AGAIN!
HERE ARE YOUR CAR KEYS!
THANK YOU!
DRIVE CARE-FULLY!
OH, MISS LODGE, ONE MORE THING...
YES?
I'M QUITE A JUGGLER!
I CAN PLAY THE 14TH HUNGARIAN RHAPSODY ON MY SKULL!
I'LL GET MY BAG-PIPES!
I'LL GET MY VENTRILOQUIST'S DUMMY!
AARGH!
END

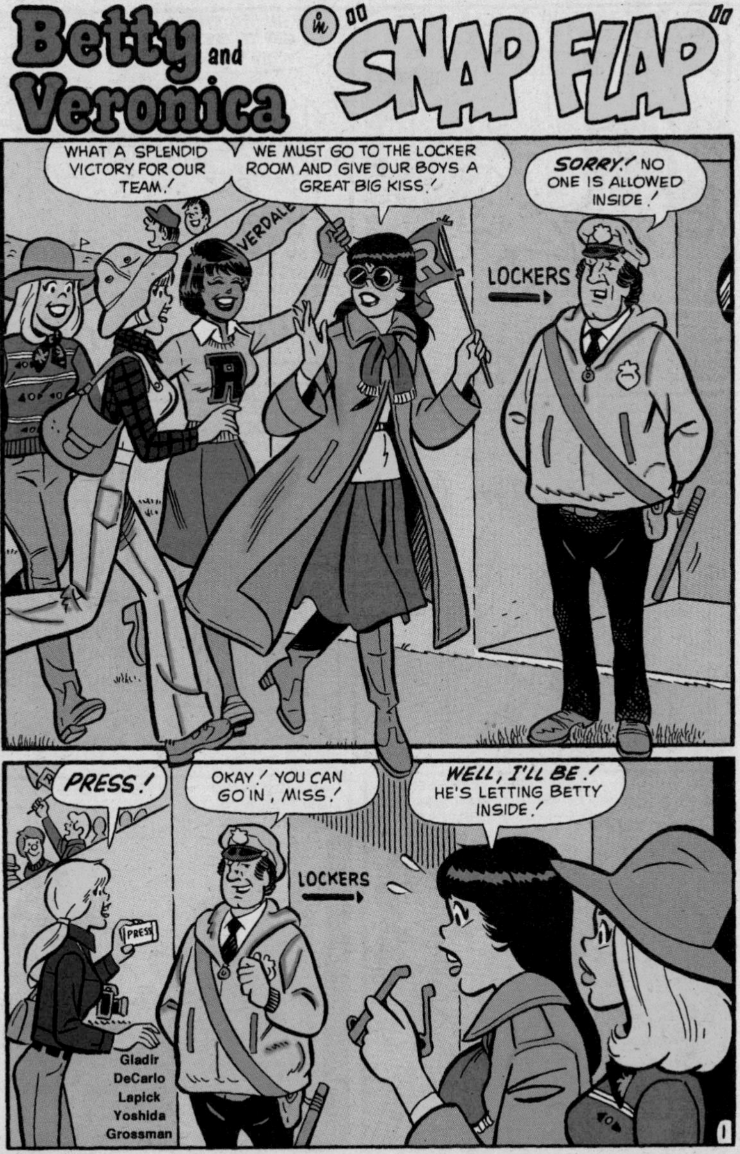
Betty and Veronica in "SNAP FLAP"
WHAT A SPLENDID VICTORY FOR OUR TEAM!
WE MUST GO TO THE LOCKER ROOM AND GIVE OUR BOYS A GREAT BIG KISS!
SORRY! NO ONE IS ALLOWED INSIDE!
RIVERDALE
LOCKERS
PRESS!
OKAY! YOU CAN GO IN, MISS!
WELL, I'LL BE! HE'S LETTING BETTY INSIDE!
PRESS
LOCKERS
Gladir
DeCarlo
Lapick
Yoshida
Grossman
1

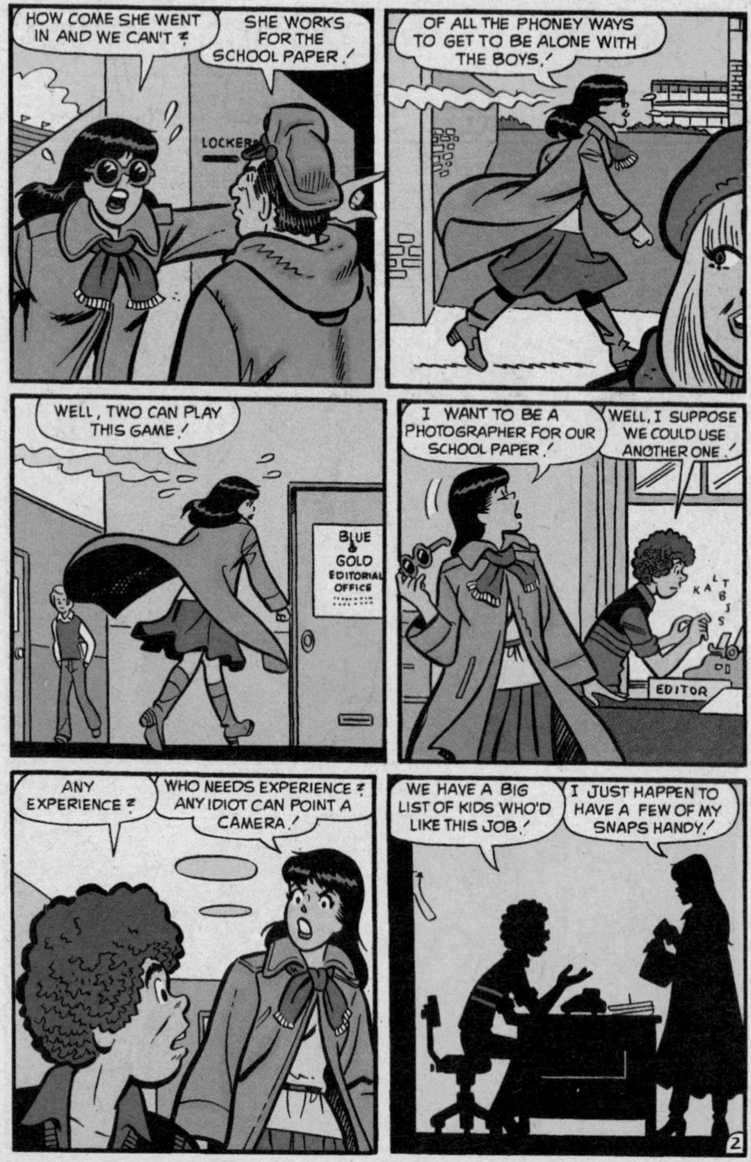
HOW COME SHE WENT IN AND WE CAN'T ?
SHE WORKS FOR THE SCHOOL PAPER !
LOCKER
OF ALL THE PHONEY WAYS TO GET TO BE ALONE WITH THE BOYS !
WELL, TWO CAN PLAY THIS GAME !
BLUE & GOLD EDITORIAL OFFICE
I WANT TO BE A PHOTOGRAPHER FOR OUR SCHOOL PAPER !
WELL, I SUPPOSE WE COULD USE ANOTHER ONE !
EDITOR
ANY EXPERIENCE ?
WHO NEEDS EXPERIENCE ? ANY IDIOT CAN POINT A CAMERA !
WE HAVE A BIG LIST OF KIDS WHO'D LIKE THIS JOB !
I JUST HAPPEN TO HAVE A FEW OF MY SNAPS HANDY !
2

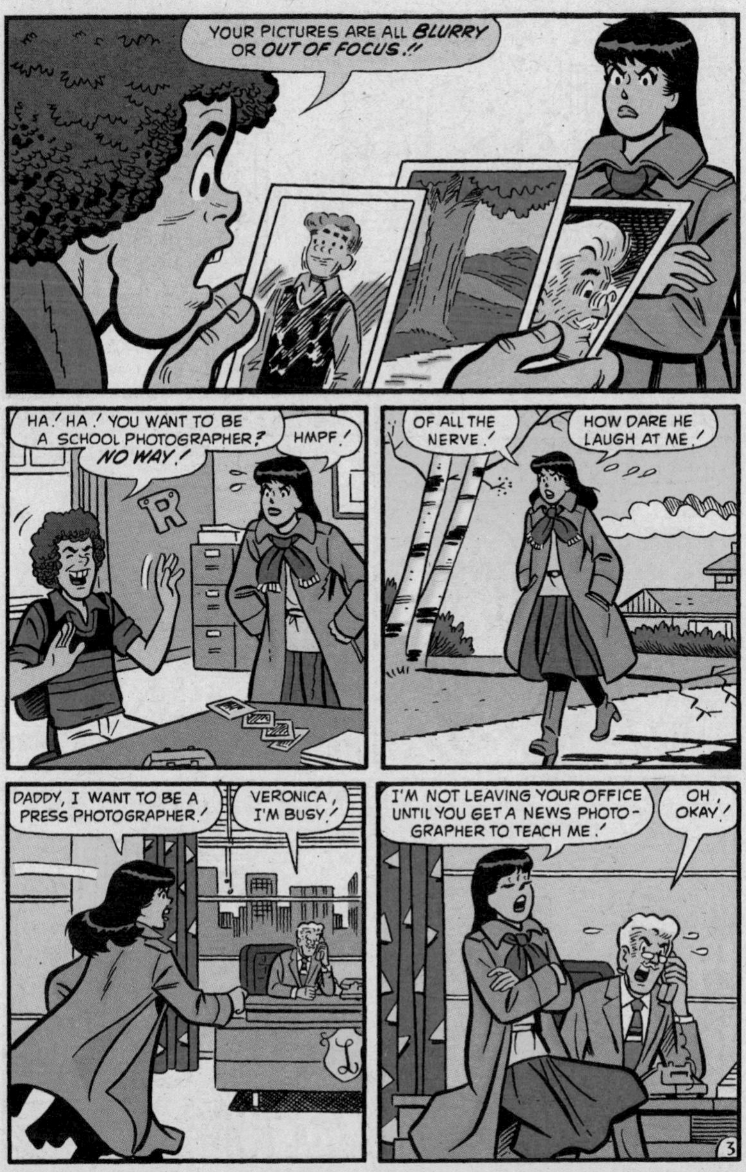

YOUR PICTURES ARE ALL BLURRY OR OUT OF FOCUS.!!
HA! HA! YOU WANT TO BE A SCHOOL PHOTOGRAPHER? NO WAY!
HMPF!
OF ALL THE NERVE!
HOW DARE HE LAUGH AT ME!
DADDY, I WANT TO BE A PRESS PHOTOGRAPHER!
VERONICA, I'M BUSY!
I'M NOT LEAVING YOUR OFFICE UNTIL YOU GET A NEWS PHOTOGRAPHER TO TEACH ME.
OH, OKAY!
3

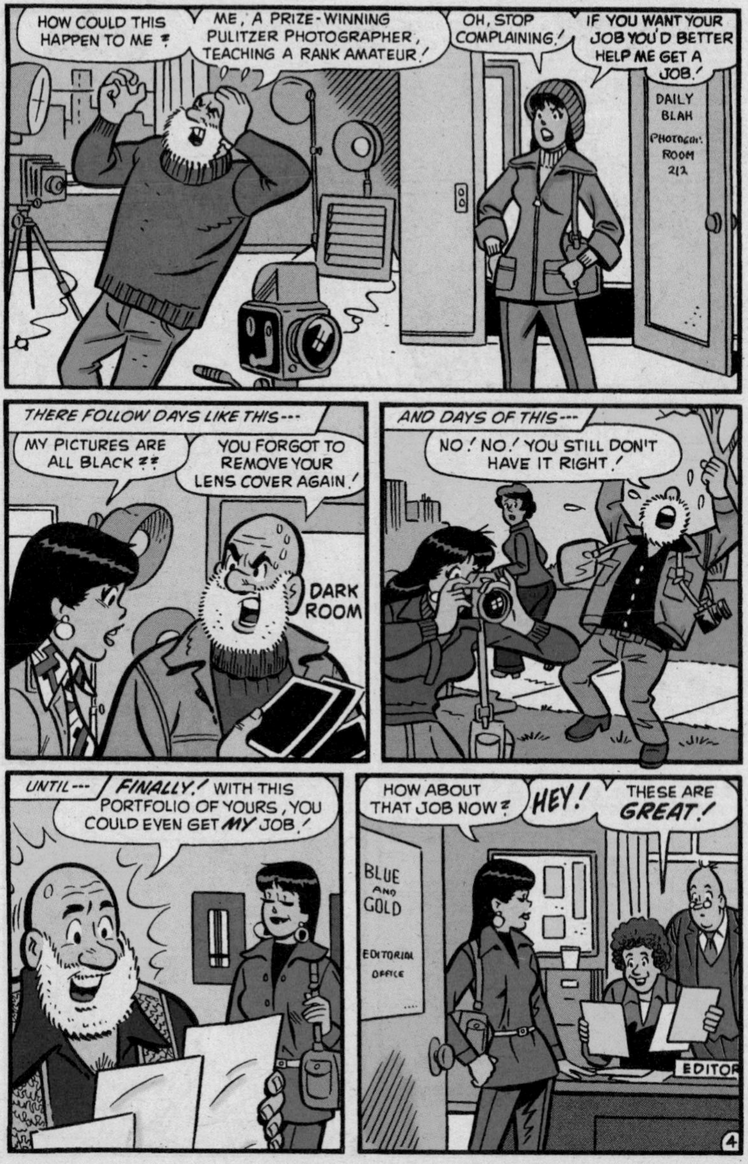
HOW COULD THIS HAPPEN TO ME ?
ME, A PRIZE-WINNING PULITZER PHOTOGRAPHER, TEACHING A RANK AMATEUR!
OH, STOP COMPLAINING!
IF YOU WANT YOUR JOB YOU'D BETTER HELP ME GET A JOB!
DAILY BLAH
ROOM 212
THERE FOLLOW DAYS LIKE THIS---
MY PICTURES ARE ALL BLACK ??
YOU FORGOT TO REMOVE YOUR LENS COVER AGAIN!
DARK ROOM
AND DAYS OF THIS---
NO! NO! YOU STILL DON'T HAVE IT RIGHT!
UNTIL---
FINALLY! WITH THIS PORTFOLIO OF YOURS, YOU COULD EVEN GET MY JOB!
HOW ABOUT THAT JOB NOW?
HEY!
THESE ARE GREAT!
BLUE AND GOLD
EDITORIAL OFFICE
EDITOR
4

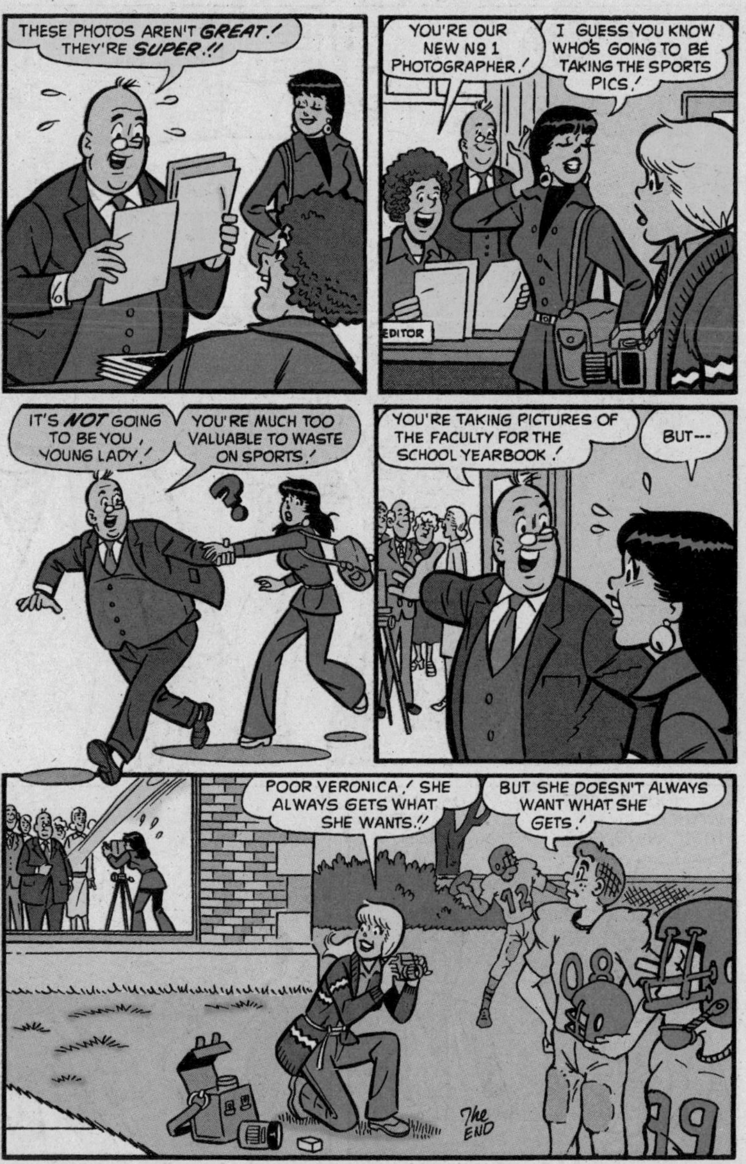
THESE PHOTOS AREN'T GREAT! THEY'RE SUPER!!
YOU'RE OUR NEW № 1 PHOTOGRAPHER!
I GUESS YOU KNOW WHO'S GOING TO BE TAKING THE SPORTS PICS!
EDITOR
IT'S NOT GOING TO BE YOU, YOUNG LADY!
YOU'RE MUCH TOO VALUABLE TO WASTE ON SPORTS!
YOU'RE TAKING PICTURES OF THE FACULTY FOR THE SCHOOL YEARBOOK!
BUT---
POOR VERONICA! SHE ALWAYS GETS WHAT SHE WANTS!!
BUT SHE DOESN'T ALWAYS WANT WHAT SHE GETS!
The END

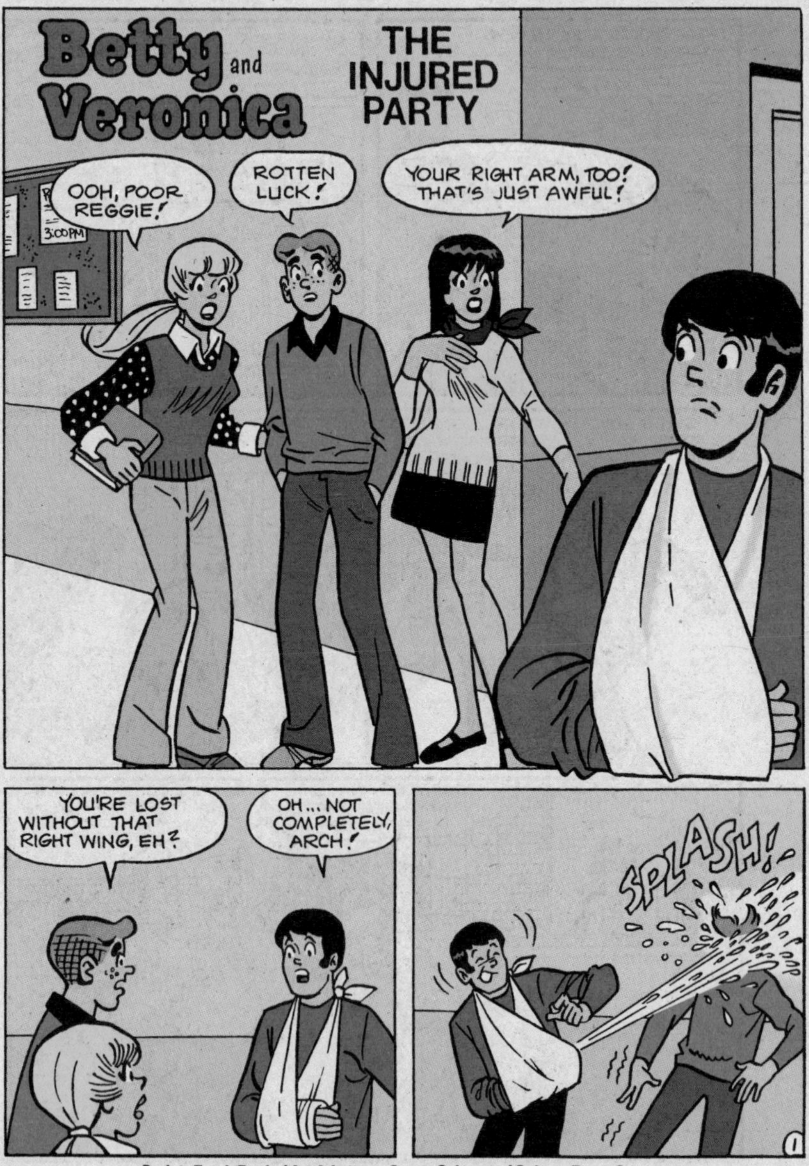
Betty and Veronica
THE INJURED PARTY
OOH, POOR REGGIE!
ROTTEN LUCK!
YOUR RIGHT ARM, TOO! THAT'S JUST AWFUL!
3:00PM
YOU'RE LOST WITHOUT THAT RIGHT WING, EH?
OH... NOT COMPLETELY, ARCH!
SPLASH!
1

Script: Frank Doyle / Art & Letters: Samm Schwartz / Colors: Barry Grossman

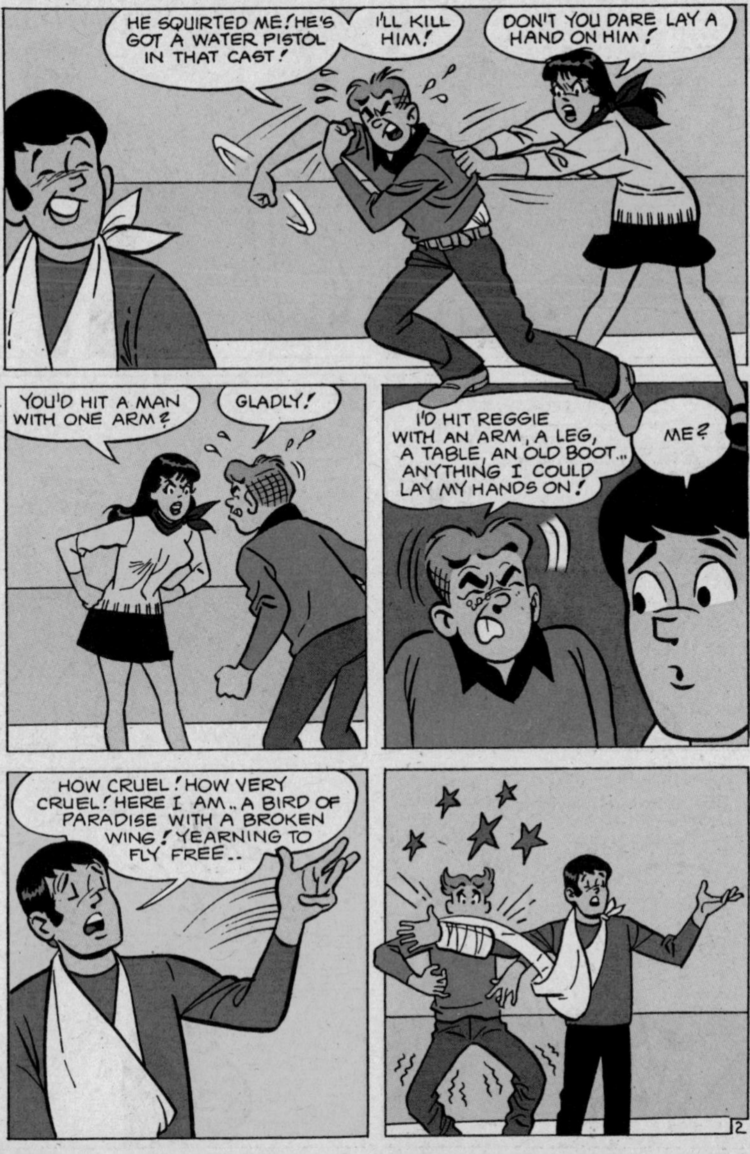
HE SQUIRTED ME! HE'S GOT A WATER PISTOL IN THAT CAST!
I'LL KILL HIM!
DON'T YOU DARE LAY A HAND ON HIM!
YOU'D HIT A MAN WITH ONE ARM?
GLADLY!
I'D HIT REGGIE WITH AN ARM, A LEG, A TABLE, AN OLD BOOT... ANYTHING I COULD LAY MY HANDS ON!
ME?
HOW CRUEL! HOW VERY CRUEL! HERE I AM.. A BIRD OF PARADISE WITH A BROKEN WING! YEARNING TO FLY FREE..

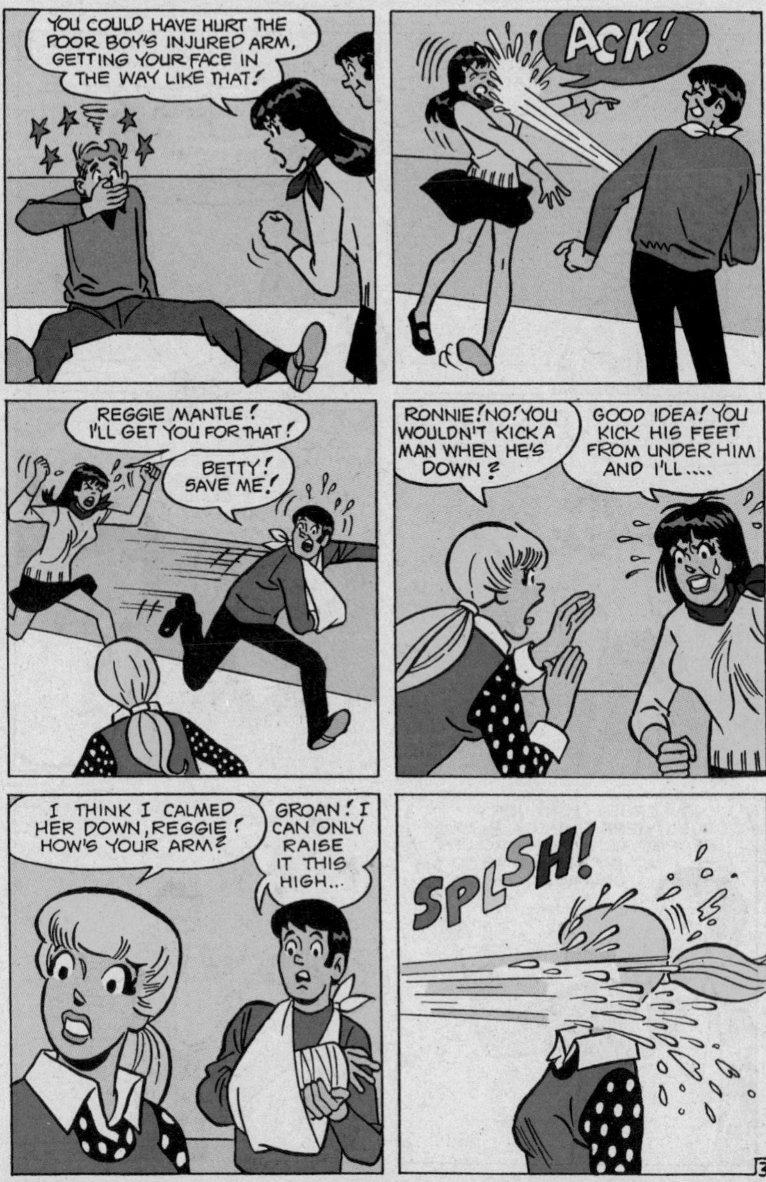
YOU COULD HAVE HURT THE POOR BOY'S INJURED ARM, GETTING YOUR FACE IN THE WAY LIKE THAT!
ACK!
REGGIE MANTLE! I'LL GET YOU FOR THAT!
BETTY! SAVE ME!
RONNIE! NO! YOU WOULDN'T KICK A MAN WHEN HE'S DOWN?
GOOD IDEA! YOU KICK HIS FEET FROM UNDER HIM AND I'LL....
I THINK I CALMED HER DOWN, REGGIE! HOW'S YOUR ARM?
GROAN! I CAN ONLY RAISE IT THIS HIGH...
SPLSH!
3

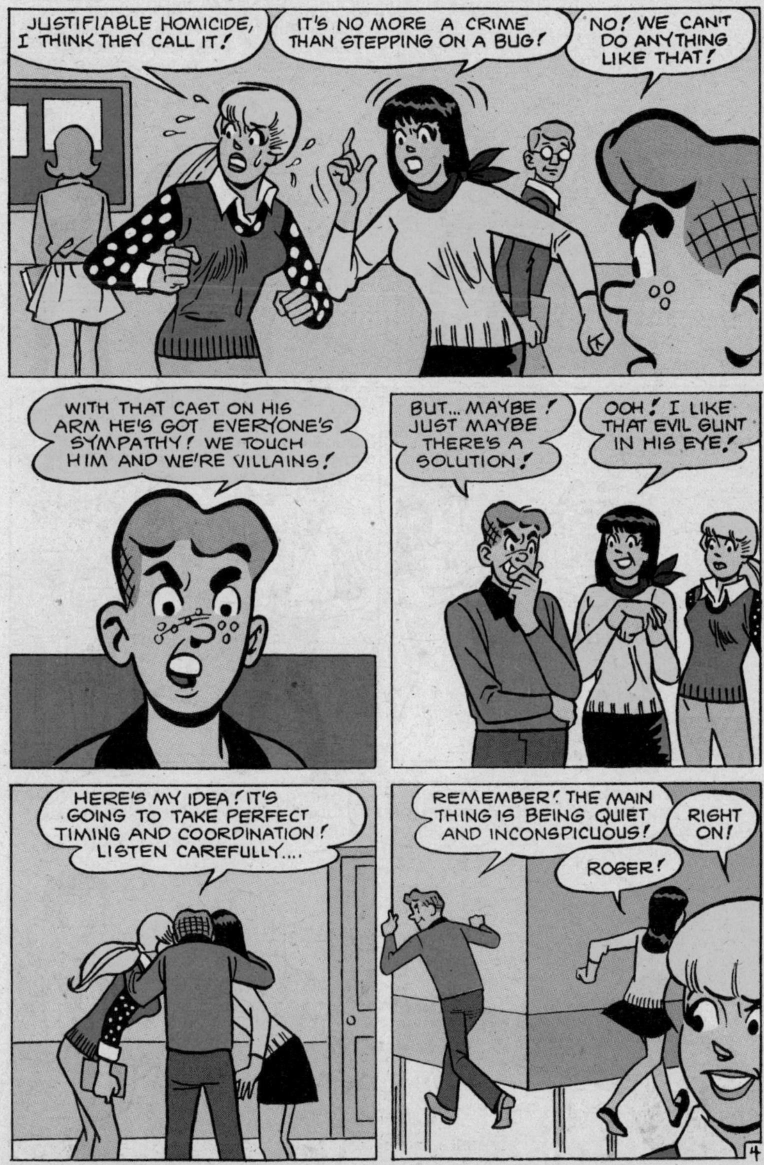
JUSTIFIABLE HOMICIDE, I THINK THEY CALL IT!
IT'S NO MORE A CRIME THAN STEPPING ON A BUG!
NO! WE CAN'T DO ANYTHING LIKE THAT!
WITH THAT CAST ON HIS ARM HE'S GOT EVERYONE'S SYMPATHY! WE TOUCH HIM AND WE'RE VILLAINS!
BUT... MAYBE! JUST MAYBE THERE'S A SOLUTION!
OOH! I LIKE THAT EVIL GLINT IN HIS EYE!
HERE'S MY IDEA! IT'S GOING TO TAKE PERFECT TIMING AND COORDINATION! LISTEN CAREFULLY....
REMEMBER! THE MAIN THING IS BEING QUIET AND INCONSPICUOUS!
RIGHT ON!
ROGER!
4

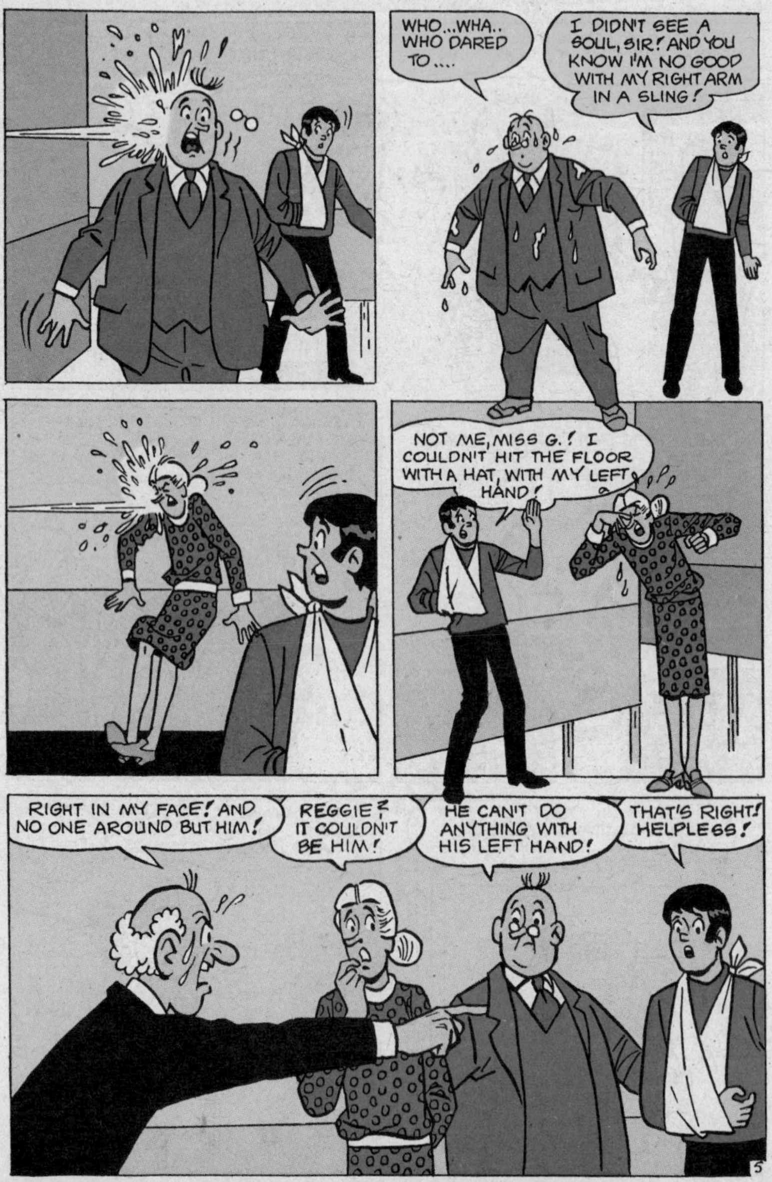
WHO...WHA.. WHO DARED TO....
I DIDN'T SEE A SOUL, SIR! AND YOU KNOW I'M NO GOOD WITH MY RIGHT ARM IN A SLING!
NOT ME, MISS G.! I COULDN'T HIT THE FLOOR WITH A HAT, WITH MY LEFT HAND!
RIGHT IN MY FACE! AND NO ONE AROUND BUT HIM!
REGGIE? IT COULDN'T BE HIM!
HE CAN'T DO ANYTHING WITH HIS LEFT HAND!
THAT'S RIGHT! HELPLESS!

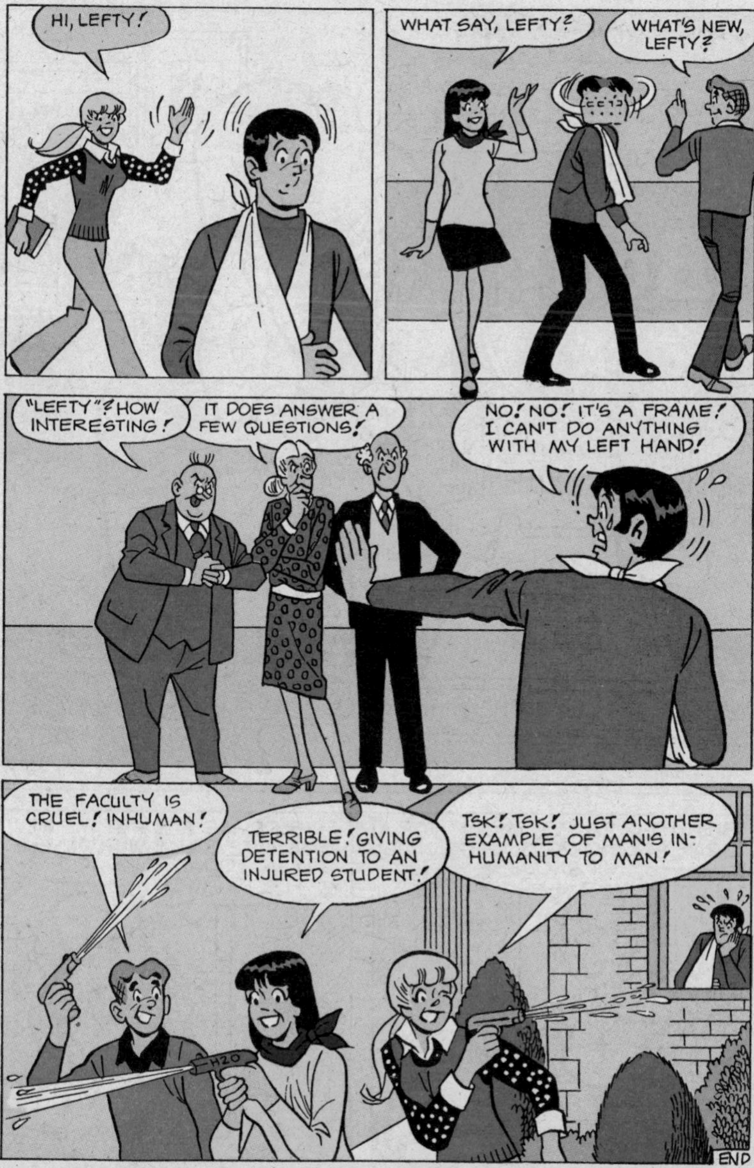
HI, LEFTY!
WHAT SAY, LEFTY?
WHAT'S NEW, LEFTY?
"LEFTY"? HOW INTERESTING!
IT DOES ANSWER A FEW QUESTIONS!
NO! NO! IT'S A FRAME! I CAN'T DO ANYTHING WITH MY LEFT HAND!
THE FACULTY IS CRUEL! INHUMAN!
TERRIBLE! GIVING DETENTION TO AN INJURED STUDENT!
TSK! TSK! JUST ANOTHER EXAMPLE OF MAN'S IN-HUMANITY TO MAN!
H2O
END

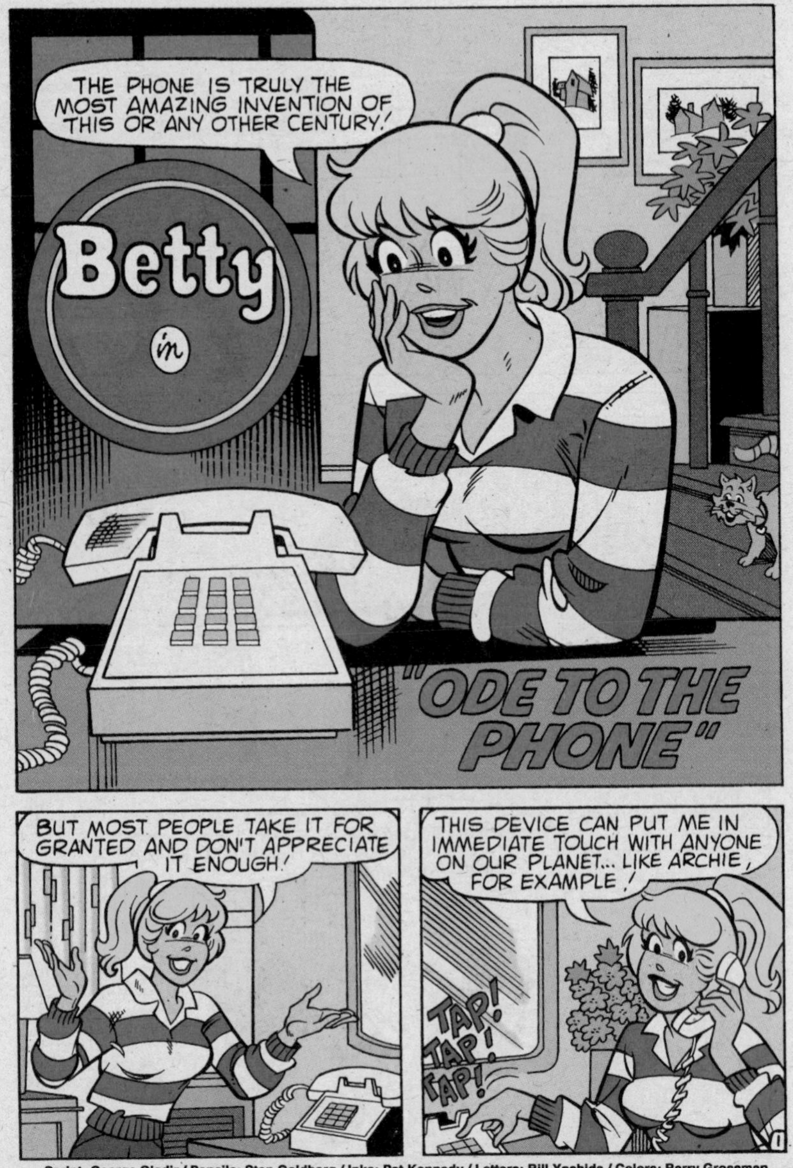
THE PHONE IS TRULY THE MOST AMAZING INVENTION OF THIS OR ANY OTHER CENTURY!
Betty
in
"ODE TO THE PHONE"
BUT MOST PEOPLE TAKE IT FOR GRANTED AND DON'T APPRECIATE IT ENOUGH!
THIS DEVICE CAN PUT ME IN IMMEDIATE TOUCH WITH ANYONE ON OUR PLANET... LIKE ARCHIE, FOR EXAMPLE!
TAP! TAP! TAP!
1

Script: George Gladir / Pencils: Stan Goldberg / Inks: Pat Kennedy / Letters: Bill Yoshida / Colors: Barry Grossman

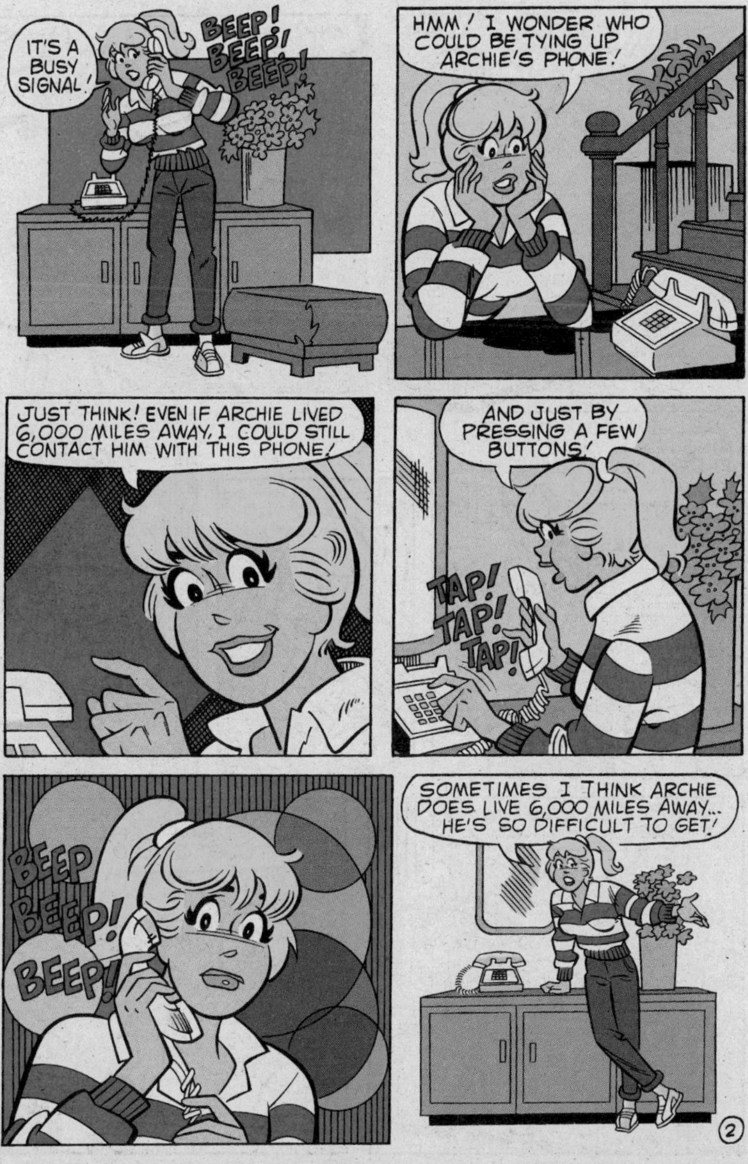

IT'S A BUSY SIGNAL!
BEEP! BEEP! BEEP!
HMM! I WONDER WHO COULD BE TYING UP ARCHIE'S PHONE!
JUST THINK! EVEN IF ARCHIE LIVED 6,000 MILES AWAY, I COULD STILL CONTACT HIM WITH THIS PHONE!
AND JUST BY PRESSING A FEW BUTTONS!
TAP! TAP! TAP!
BEEP BEEP! BEEP!
SOMETIMES I THINK ARCHIE DOES LIVE 6,000 MILES AWAY... HE'S SO DIFFICULT TO GET!
2

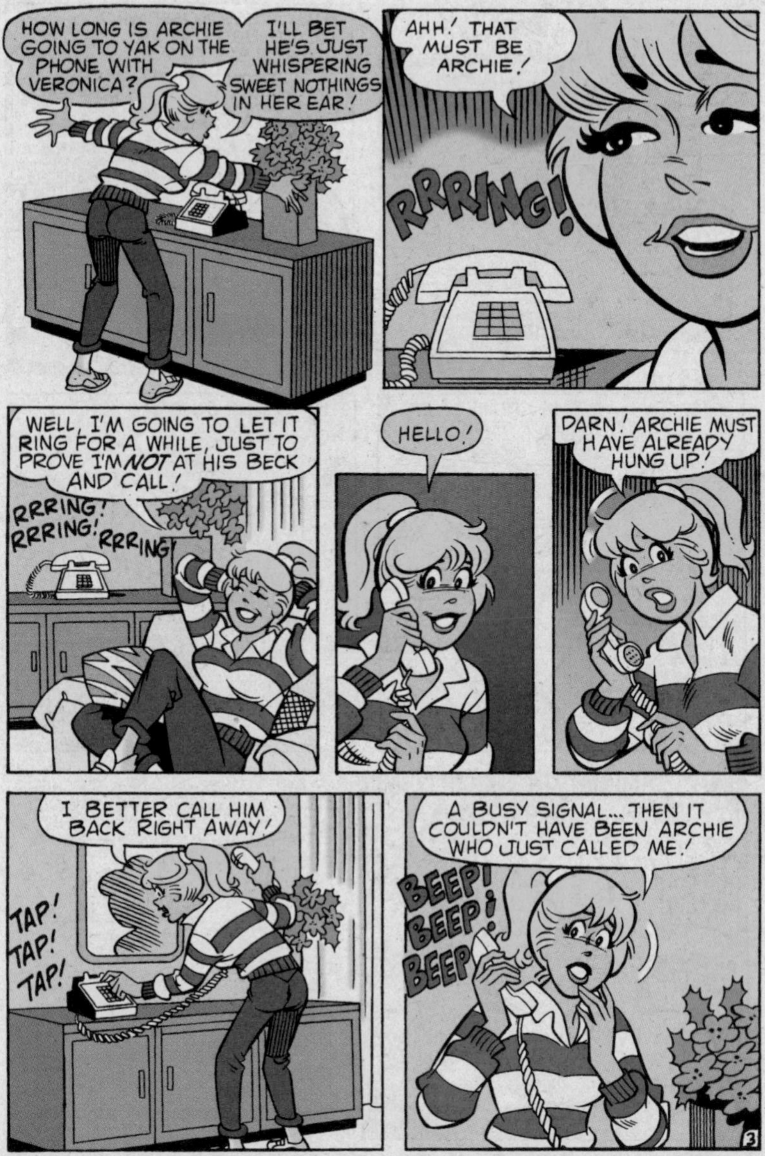
HOW LONG IS ARCHIE GOING TO YAK ON THE PHONE WITH VERONICA?
I'LL BET HE'S JUST WHISPERING SWEET NOTHINGS IN HER EAR!
AHH! THAT MUST BE ARCHIE!
RRRING!
WELL, I'M GOING TO LET IT RING FOR A WHILE, JUST TO PROVE I'M NOT AT HIS BECK AND CALL!
RRRING! RRRING! RRRING!
HELLO!
DARN! ARCHIE MUST HAVE ALREADY HUNG UP!
I BETTER CALL HIM BACK RIGHT AWAY!
TAP! TAP! TAP!
A BUSY SIGNAL... THEN IT COULDN'T HAVE BEEN ARCHIE WHO JUST CALLED ME!
BEEP! BEEP! BEEP
3

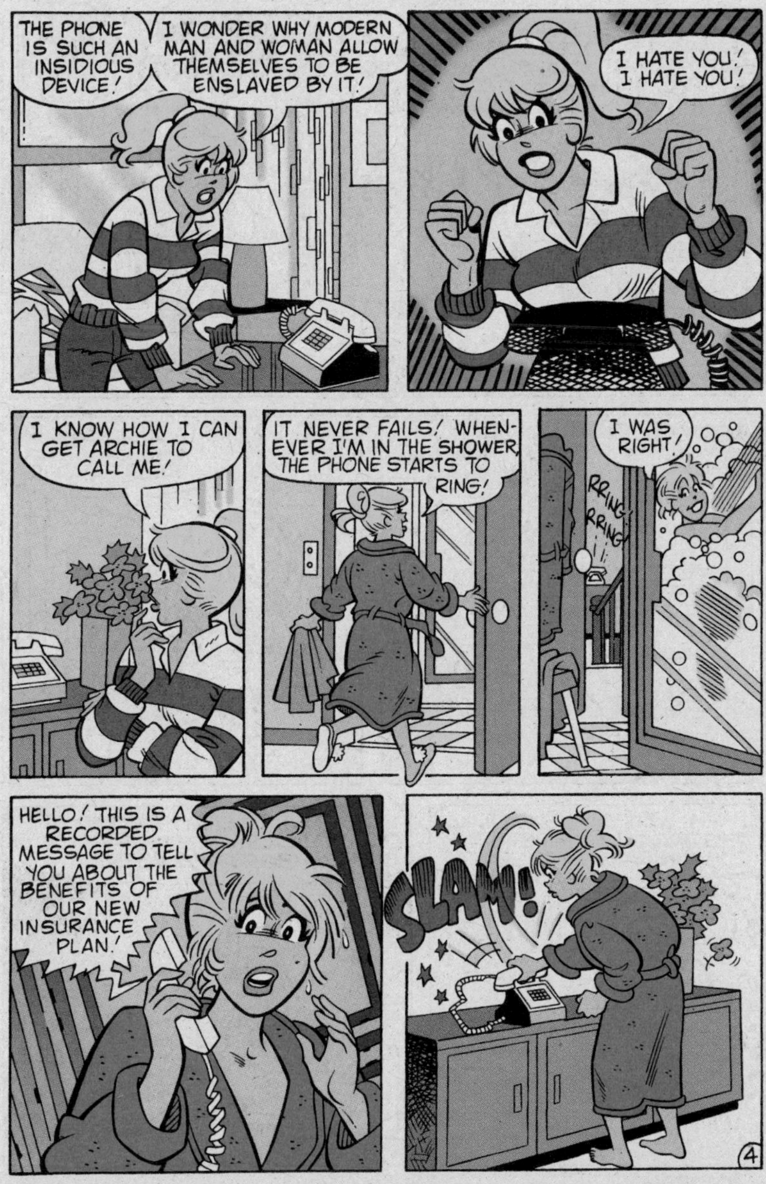
THE PHONE IS SUCH AN INSIDIOUS DEVICE!
I WONDER WHY MODERN MAN AND WOMAN ALLOW THEMSELVES TO BE ENSLAVED BY IT!
I HATE YOU! I HATE YOU!
I KNOW HOW I CAN GET ARCHIE TO CALL ME!
IT NEVER FAILS! WHENEVER I'M IN THE SHOWER, THE PHONE STARTS TO RING!
I WAS RIGHT!
RRING! RRING!
HELLO! THIS IS A RECORDED MESSAGE TO TELL YOU ABOUT THE BENEFITS OF OUR NEW INSURANCE PLAN!
SLAM!
4

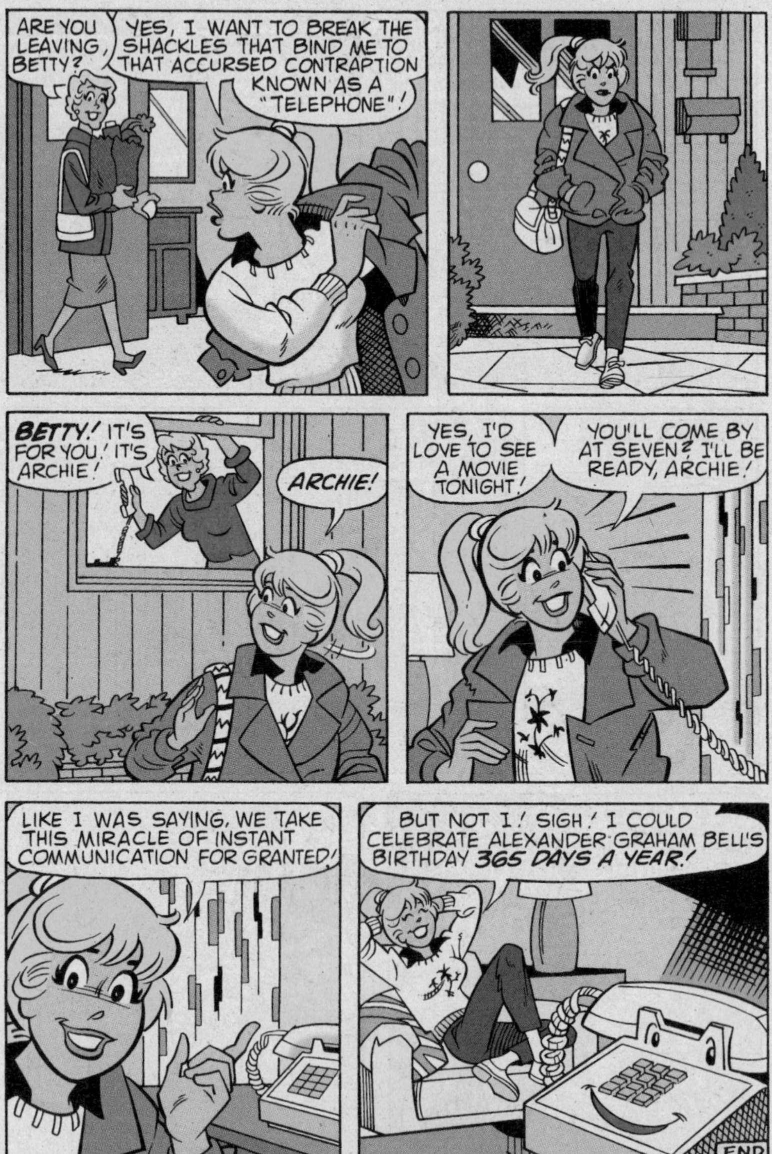
ARE YOU LEAVING, BETTY?
YES, I WANT TO BREAK THE SHACKLES THAT BIND ME TO THAT ACCURSED CONTRAPTION KNOWN AS A "TELEPHONE"!
BETTY! IT'S FOR YOU! IT'S ARCHIE!
ARCHIE!
YES, I'D LOVE TO SEE A MOVIE TONIGHT!
YOU'LL COME BY AT SEVEN? I'LL BE READY, ARCHIE!
LIKE I WAS SAYING, WE TAKE THIS MIRACLE OF INSTANT COMMUNICATION FOR GRANTED!
BUT NOT I! SIGH! I COULD CELEBRATE ALEXANDER GRAHAM BELL'S BIRTHDAY 365 DAYS A YEAR!
END

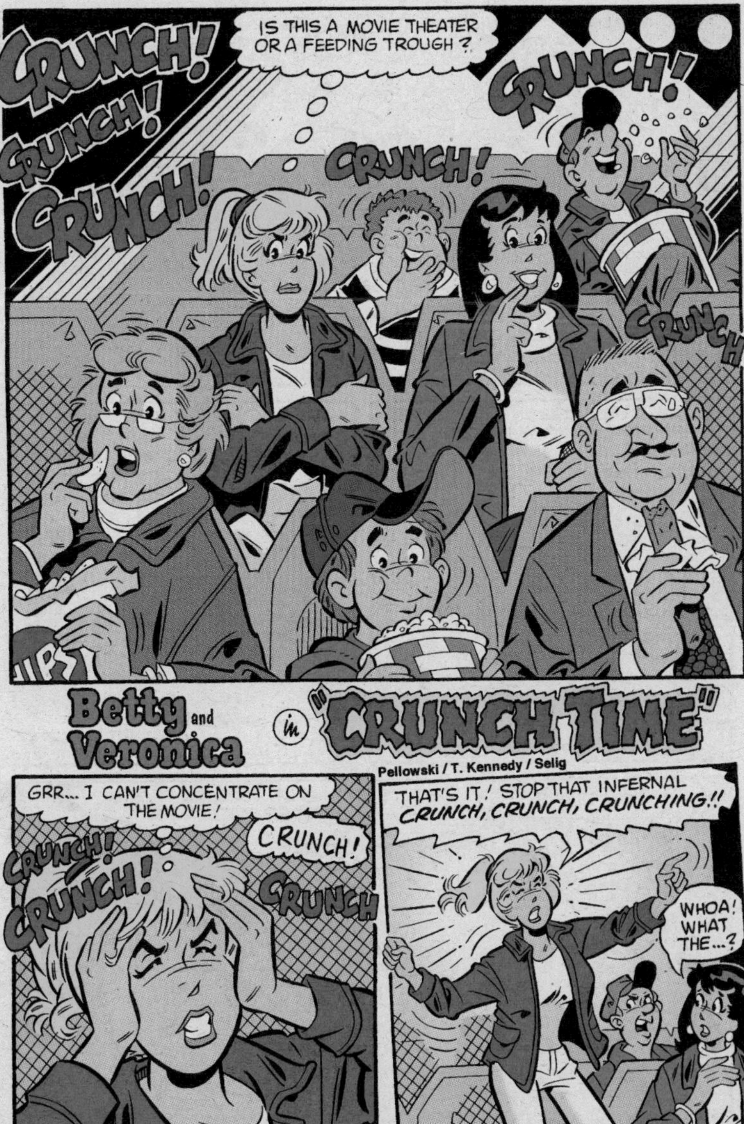
CRUNCH!
CRUNCH!
CRUNCH!
IS THIS A MOVIE THEATER OR A FEEDING TROUGH ?
CRUNCH!
CRUNCH!
CRUNCH
Betty and Veronica in "CRUNCH TIME"
Pellowski / T. Kennedy / Selig
GRR... I CAN'T CONCENTRATE ON THE MOVIE!
CRUNCH!
CRUNCH!
CRUNCH!
CRUNCH
THAT'S IT! STOP THAT INFERNAL CRUNCH, CRUNCH, CRUNCHING!!
WHOA! WHAT THE...?

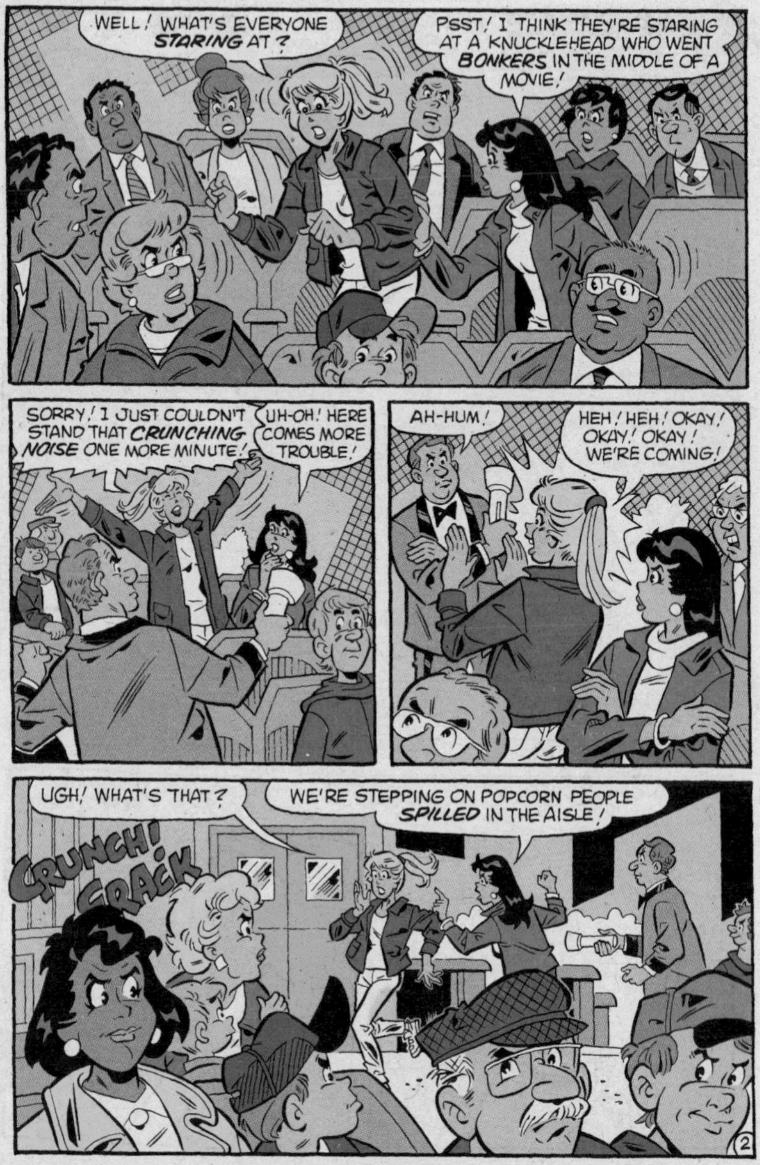
WELL! WHAT'S EVERYONE STARING AT?
PSST! I THINK THEY'RE STARING AT A KNUCKLEHEAD WHO WENT BONKERS IN THE MIDDLE OF A MOVIE!
SORRY! I JUST COULDN'T STAND THAT CRUNCHING NOISE ONE MORE MINUTE!
UH-OH! HERE COMES MORE TROUBLE!
AH-HUM!
HEH! HEH! OKAY! OKAY! OKAY! WE'RE COMING!
UGH! WHAT'S THAT?
WE'RE STEPPING ON POPCORN PEOPLE SPILLED IN THE AISLE!
CRUNCH! CRACK
2

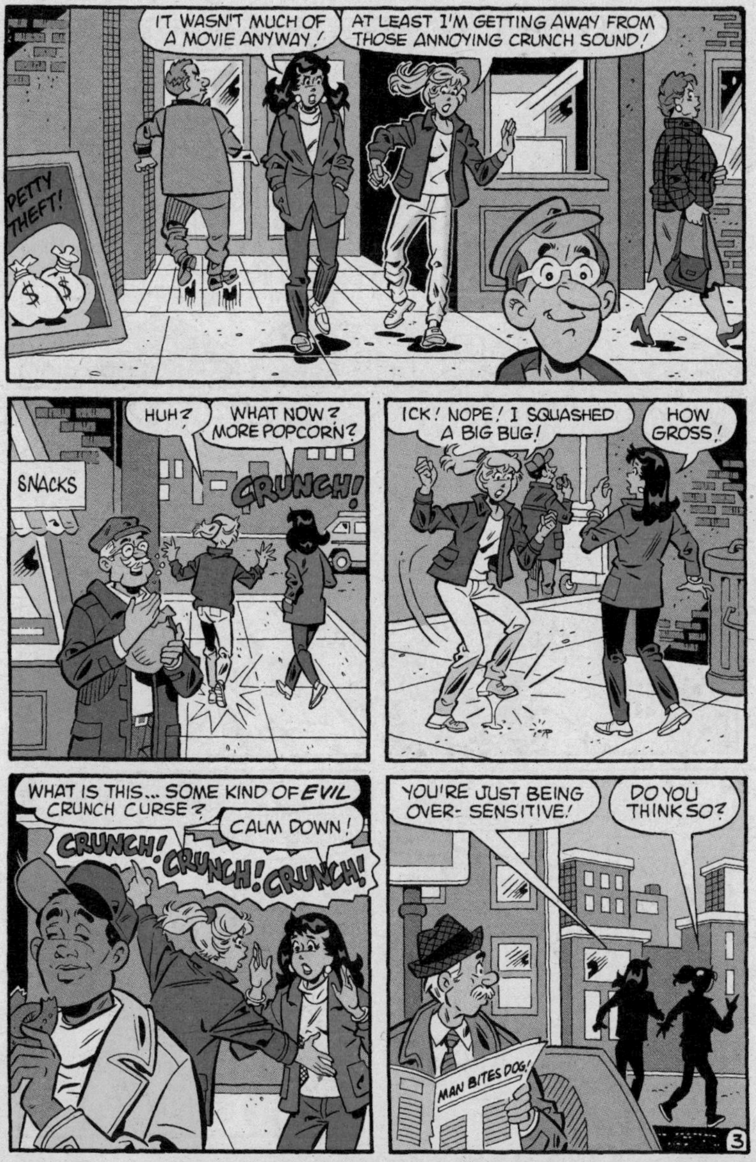
IT WASN'T MUCH OF A MOVIE ANYWAY!
AT LEAST I'M GETTING AWAY FROM THOSE ANNOYING CRUNCH SOUND!
PETTY THEFT!
HUH?
WHAT NOW? MORE POPCORN?
SNACKS
CRUNCH!
ICK! NOPE! I SQUASHED A BIG BUG!
HOW GROSS!
WHAT IS THIS... SOME KIND OF EVIL CRUNCH CURSE?
CALM DOWN!
CRUNCH! CRUNCH! CRUNCH!
YOU'RE JUST BEING OVER-SENSITIVE!
DO YOU THINK SO?
MAN BITES DOG!
3

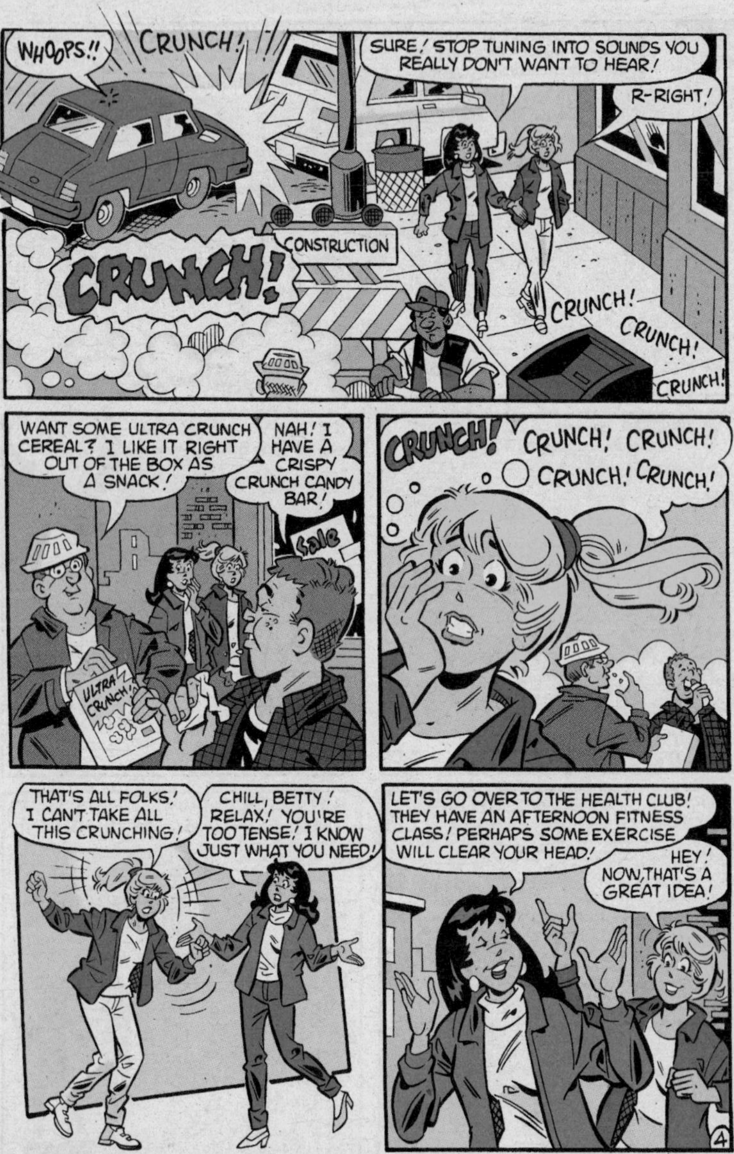
WHOOPS!!
CRUNCH!
SURE! STOP TUNING INTO SOUNDS YOU REALLY DON'T WANT TO HEAR!
R-RIGHT!
CONSTRUCTION
CRUNCH!
CRUNCH!
CRUNCH!
CRUNCH!
WANT SOME ULTRA CRUNCH CEREAL? I LIKE IT RIGHT OUT OF THE BOX AS A SNACK!
NAH! I HAVE A CRISPY CRUNCH CANDY BAR!
Sale
ULTRA CRUNCH!
CRUNCH!
CRUNCH! CRUNCH!
CRUNCH! CRUNCH!
THAT'S ALL FOLKS! I CAN'T TAKE ALL THIS CRUNCHING!
CHILL, BETTY! RELAX! YOU'RE TOO TENSE! I KNOW JUST WHAT YOU NEED!
LET'S GO OVER TO THE HEALTH CLUB! THEY HAVE AN AFTERNOON FITNESS CLASS! PERHAPS SOME EXERCISE WILL CLEAR YOUR HEAD!
HEY! NOW, THAT'S A GREAT IDEA!
4

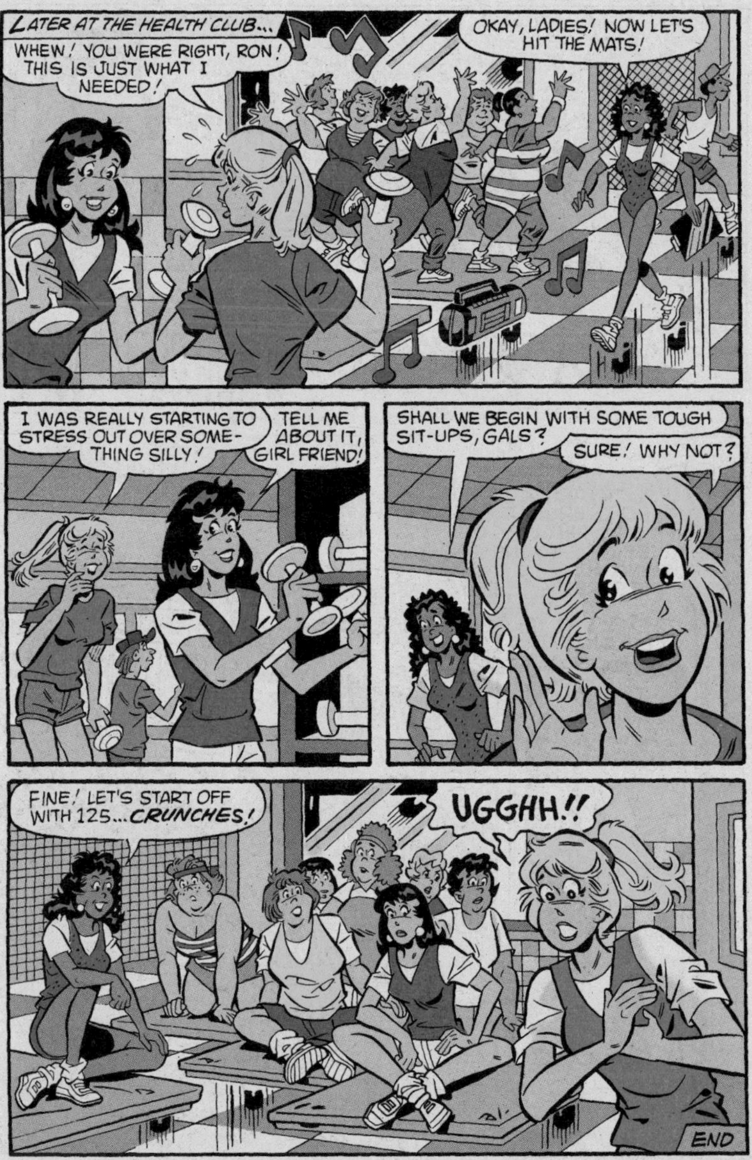
LATER AT THE HEALTH CLUB...
WHEW! YOU WERE RIGHT, RON! THIS IS JUST WHAT I NEEDED!
OKAY, LADIES! NOW LET'S HIT THE MATS!
I WAS REALLY STARTING TO STRESS OUT OVER SOME-THING SILLY!
TELL ME ABOUT IT, GIRL FRIEND!
SHALL WE BEGIN WITH SOME TOUGH SIT-UPS, GALS?
SURE! WHY NOT?
FINE! LET'S START OFF WITH 125... CRUNCHES!
UGGHH!!
END

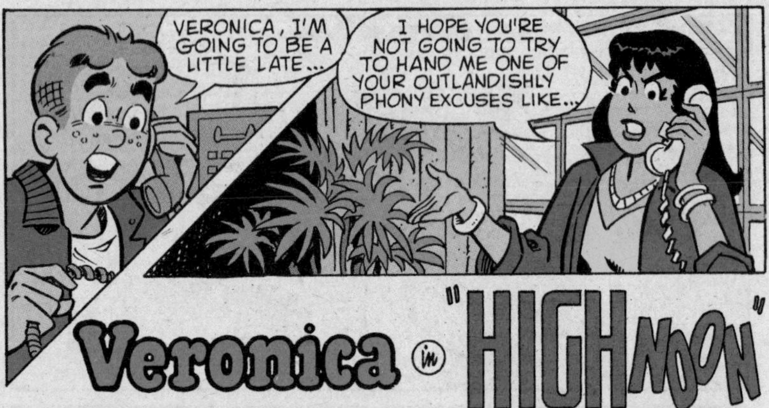
VERONICA, I'M GOING TO BE A LITTLE LATE...
I HOPE YOU'RE NOT GOING TO TRY TO HAND ME ONE OF YOUR OUTLANDISHLY PHONY EXCUSES LIKE...
Veronica in "HIGH NOON"

Script: George Gladir / Pencils: Stan Goldberg / Inks: Mike Esposito / Letters: Bill Yoshida

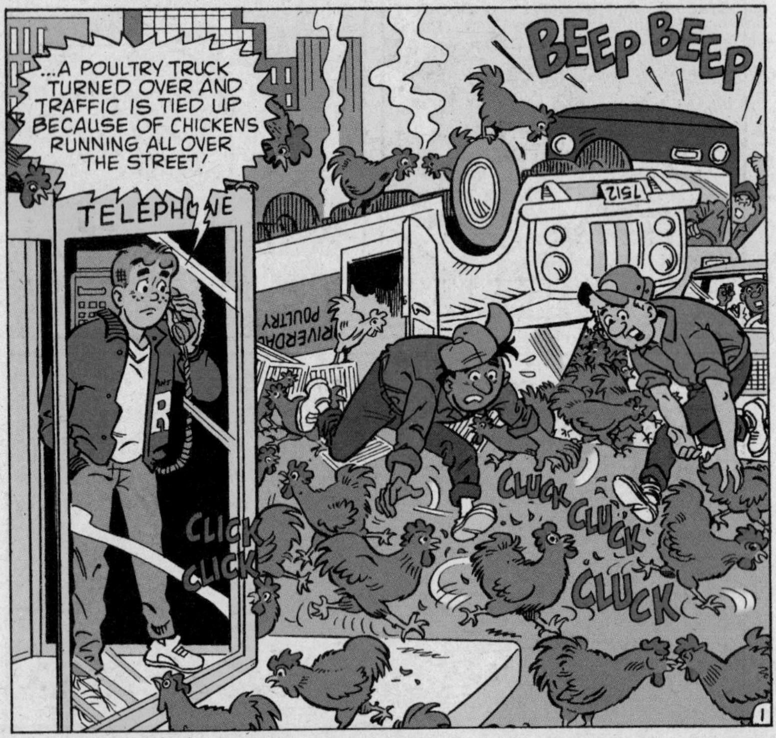
...A POULTRY TRUCK TURNED OVER AND TRAFFIC IS TIED UP BECAUSE OF CHICKENS RUNNING ALL OVER THE STREET!
BEEP BEEP
TELEPHONE
7512
CLICK CLICK
CLUCK CLUCK CLUCK
1

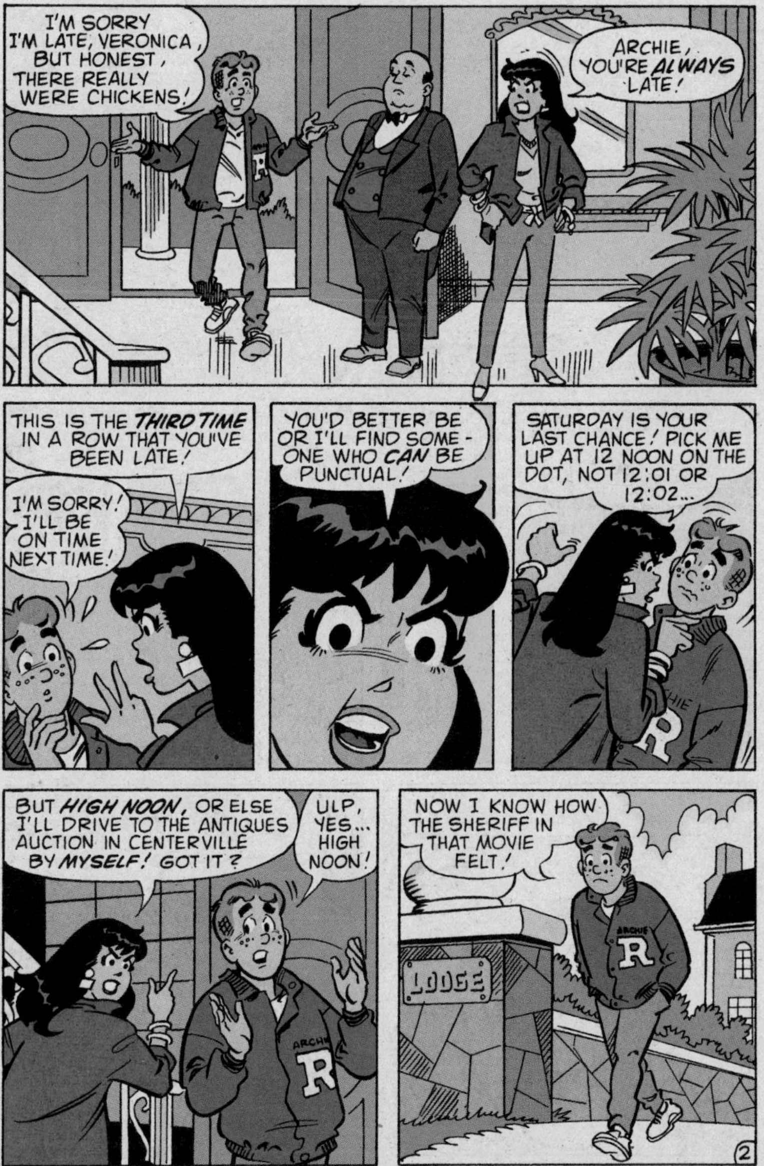
I'M SORRY I'M LATE, VERONICA, BUT HONEST, THERE REALLY WERE CHICKENS!
ARCHIE, YOU'RE ALWAYS LATE!
THIS IS THE THIRD TIME IN A ROW THAT YOU'VE BEEN LATE!
I'M SORRY! I'LL BE ON TIME NEXT TIME!
YOU'D BETTER BE OR I'LL FIND SOME-ONE WHO CAN BE PUNCTUAL!
SATURDAY IS YOUR LAST CHANCE! PICK ME UP AT 12 NOON ON THE DOT, NOT 12:01 OR 12:02...
BUT HIGH NOON, OR ELSE I'LL DRIVE TO THE ANTIQUES AUCTION IN CENTERVILLE BY MYSELF! GOT IT?
ULP, YES... HIGH NOON!
NOW I KNOW HOW THE SHERIFF IN THAT MOVIE FELT!
LODGE
2

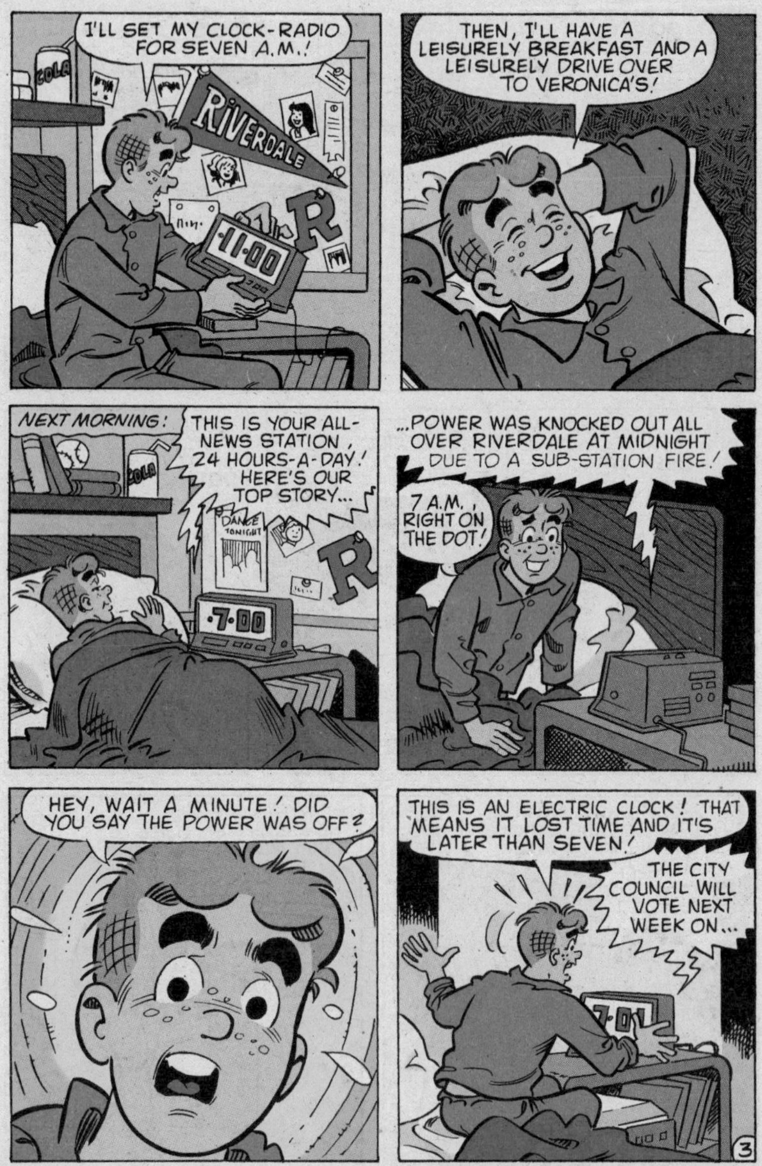
I'LL SET MY CLOCK-RADIO FOR SEVEN A.M.!
RIVERDALE
11:00
THEN, I'LL HAVE A LEISURELY BREAKFAST AND A LEISURELY DRIVE OVER TO VERONICA'S!
NEXT MORNING:
THIS IS YOUR ALL-NEWS STATION, 24 HOURS-A-DAY! HERE'S OUR TOP STORY...
DANCE TONIGHT
7:00
...POWER WAS KNOCKED OUT ALL OVER RIVERDALE AT MIDNIGHT DUE TO A SUB-STATION FIRE!
7 A.M., RIGHT ON THE DOT!
HEY, WAIT A MINUTE! DID YOU SAY THE POWER WAS OFF?
THIS IS AN ELECTRIC CLOCK! THAT MEANS IT LOST TIME AND IT'S LATER THAN SEVEN!
THE CITY COUNCIL WILL VOTE NEXT WEEK ON...
3

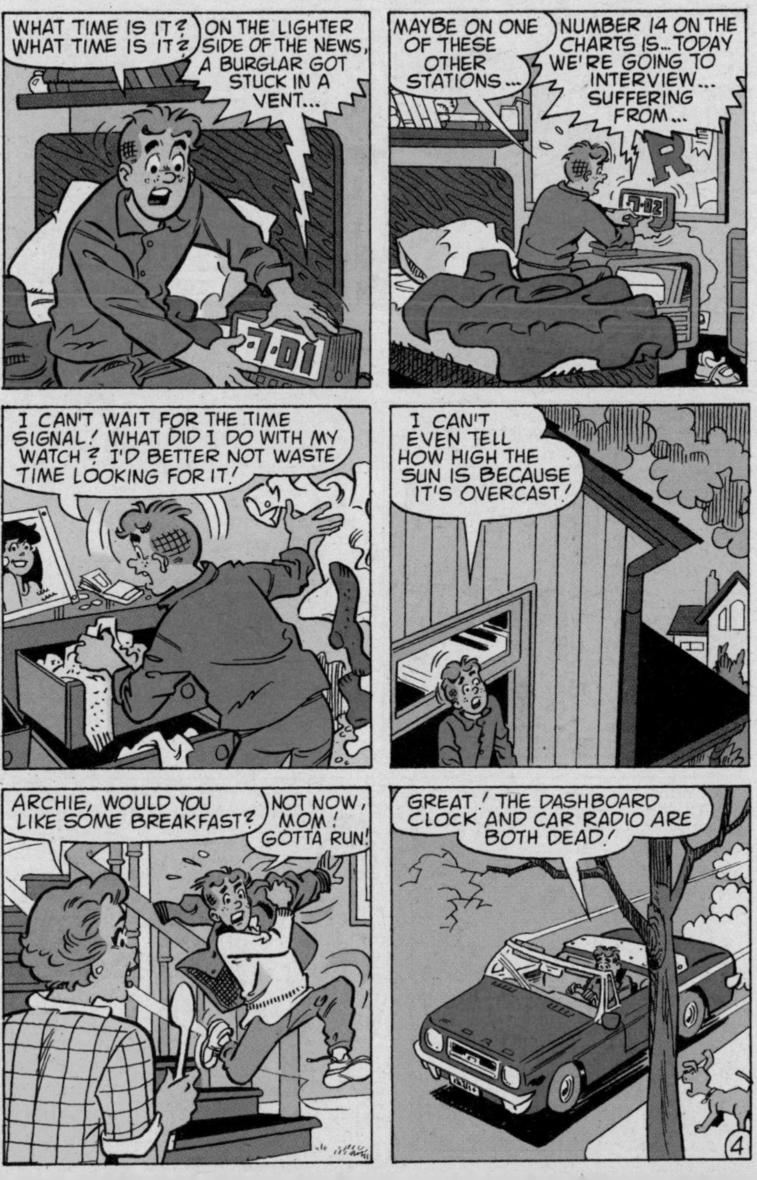
WHAT TIME IS IT? WHAT TIME IS IT?
ON THE LIGHTER SIDE OF THE NEWS, A BURGLAR GOT STUCK IN A VENT...
MAYBE ON ONE OF THESE OTHER STATIONS...
NUMBER 14 ON THE CHARTS IS... TODAY WE'RE GOING TO INTERVIEW... SUFFERING FROM...
7:01
7:02
I CAN'T WAIT FOR THE TIME SIGNAL! WHAT DID I DO WITH MY WATCH? I'D BETTER NOT WASTE TIME LOOKING FOR IT!
I CAN'T EVEN TELL HOW HIGH THE SUN IS BECAUSE IT'S OVERCAST!
ARCHIE, WOULD YOU LIKE SOME BREAKFAST?
NOT NOW, MOM! GOTTA RUN!
GREAT! THE DASHBOARD CLOCK AND CAR RADIO ARE BOTH DEAD!
4

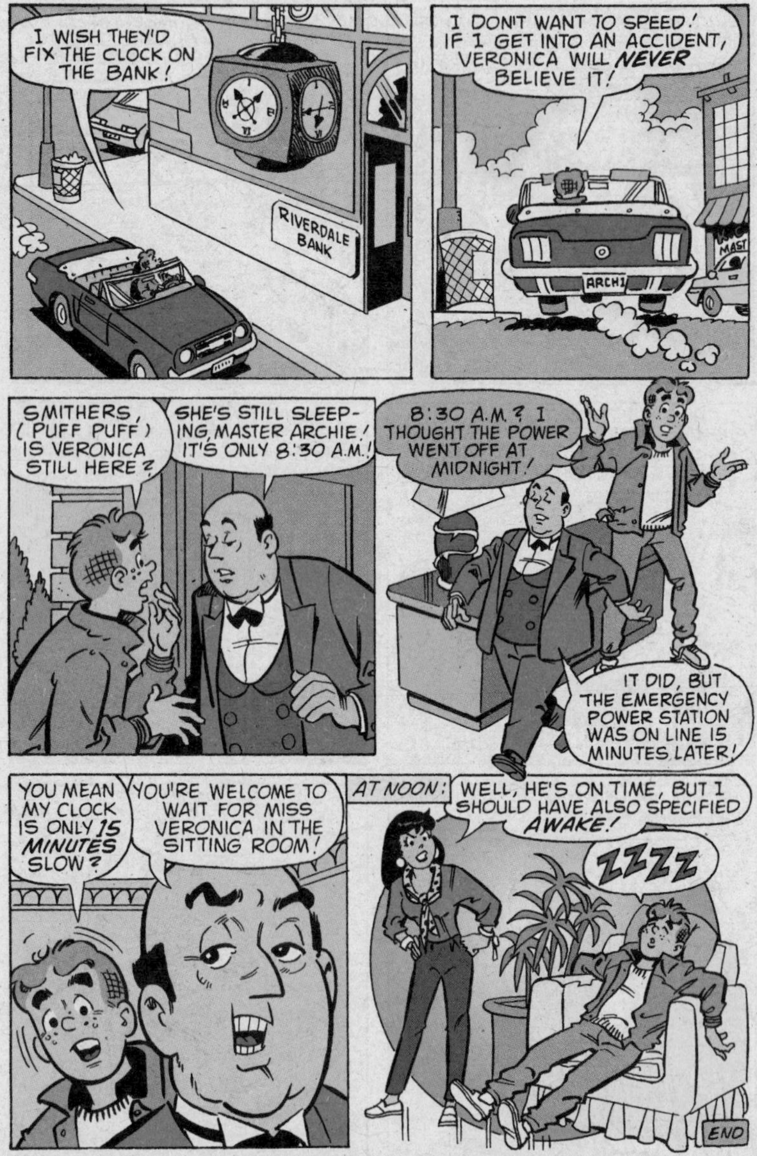

I WISH THEY'D FIX THE CLOCK ON THE BANK!
RIVERDALE BANK
I DON'T WANT TO SPEED! IF I GET INTO AN ACCIDENT, VERONICA WILL NEVER BELIEVE IT!
ARCH1
SMITHERS, (PUFF PUFF) IS VERONICA STILL HERE?
SHE'S STILL SLEEPING, MASTER ARCHIE! IT'S ONLY 8:30 A.M.!
8:30 A.M.? I THOUGHT THE POWER WENT OFF AT MIDNIGHT!
IT DID, BUT THE EMERGENCY POWER STATION WAS ON LINE 15 MINUTES LATER!
YOU MEAN MY CLOCK IS ONLY 15 MINUTES SLOW?
YOU'RE WELCOME TO WAIT FOR MISS VERONICA IN THE SITTING ROOM!
AT NOON:
WELL, HE'S ON TIME, BUT I SHOULD HAVE ALSO SPECIFIED AWAKE!
ZZZZ
END

Veronica in "Anniversary BLUES"

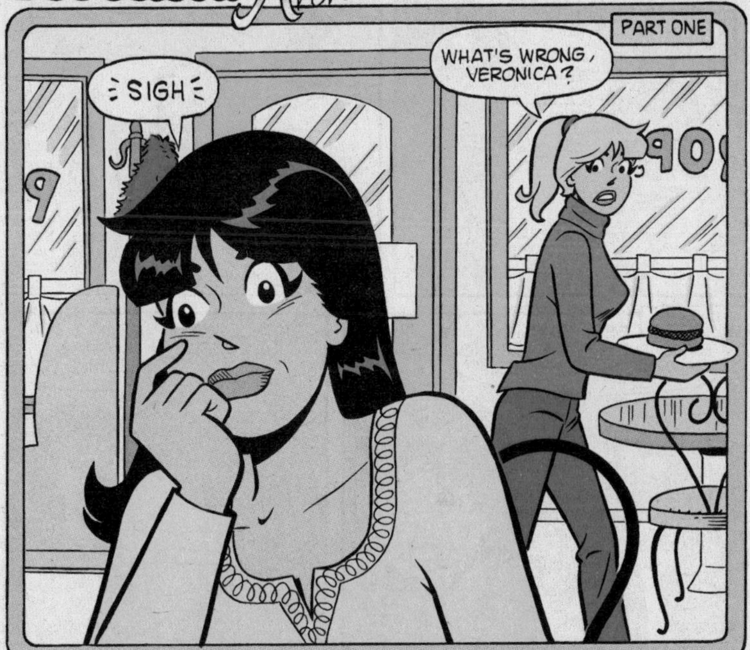
PART ONE
SIGH
WHAT'S WRONG, VERONICA?

Script & Pencils: Dan Parent / Inks: Jon D'Agostino / Letters: Bill Yoshida / Colors: Barry Grossman

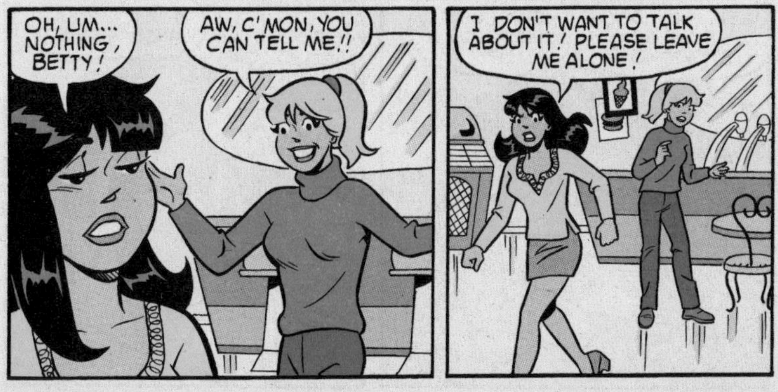
OH, UM... NOTHING, BETTY!
AW, C'MON, YOU CAN TELL ME!!
I DON'T WANT TO TALK ABOUT IT! PLEASE LEAVE ME ALONE!

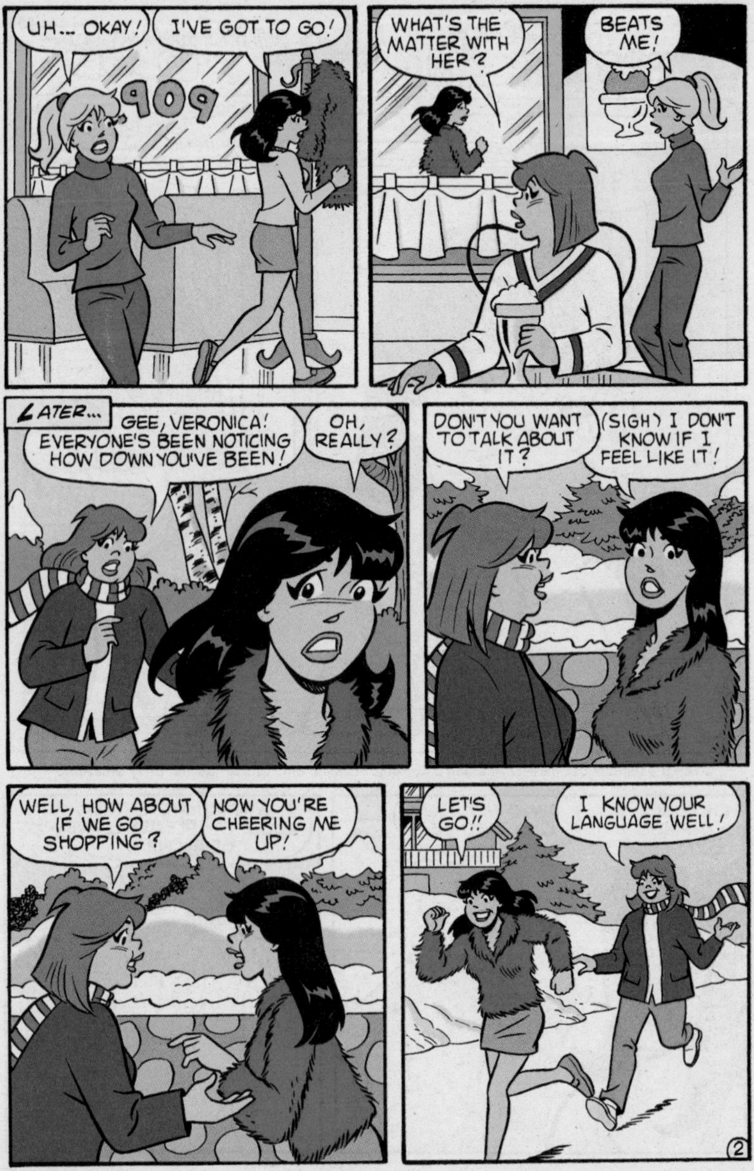
UH... OKAY!
I'VE GOT TO GO!
POP
WHAT'S THE MATTER WITH HER?
BEATS ME!
LATER...
GEE, VERONICA! EVERYONE'S BEEN NOTICING HOW DOWN YOU'VE BEEN!
OH, REALLY?
DON'T YOU WANT TO TALK ABOUT IT?
(SIGH) I DON'T KNOW IF I FEEL LIKE IT!
WELL, HOW ABOUT IF WE GO SHOPPING?
NOW YOU'RE CHEERING ME UP!
LET'S GO!!
I KNOW YOUR LANGUAGE WELL!

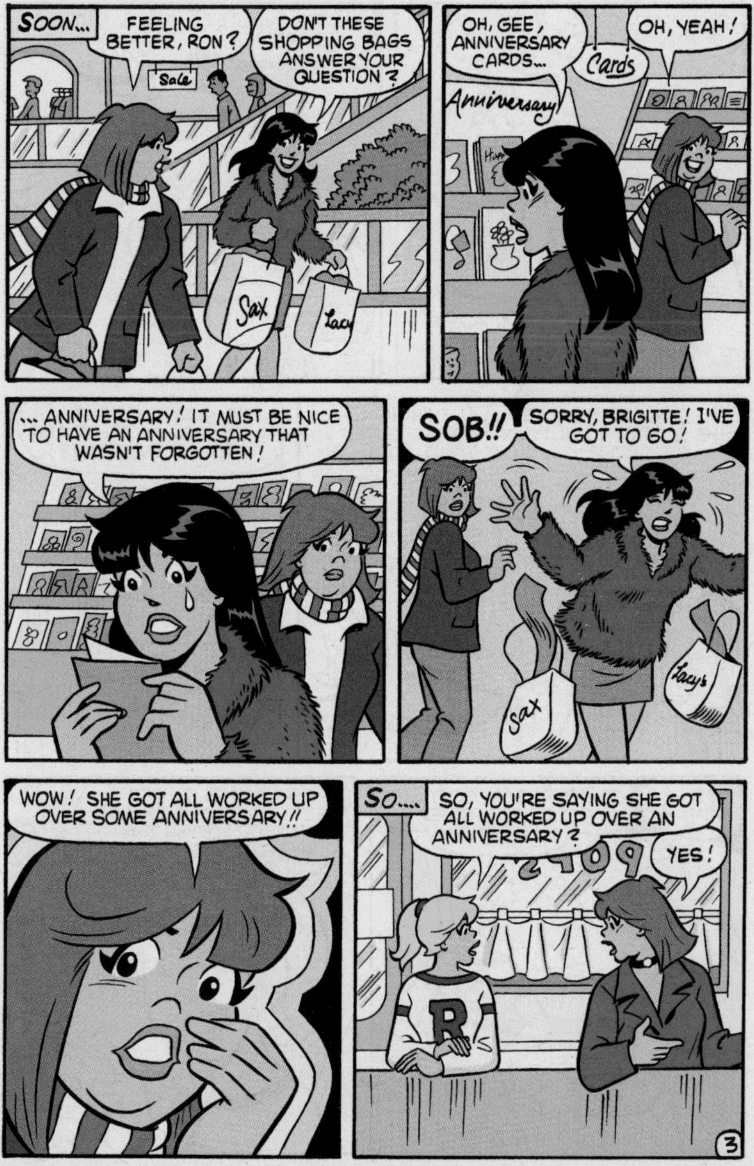
SOON...
FEELING BETTER, RON?
Sale
DON'T THESE SHOPPING BAGS ANSWER YOUR QUESTION?
Sax
Lacy
OH, GEE, ANNIVERSARY CARDS...
Cards
OH, YEAH!
Anniversary
... ANNIVERSARY! IT MUST BE NICE TO HAVE AN ANNIVERSARY THAT WASN'T FORGOTTEN!
SOB!!
SORRY, BRIGITTE! I'VE GOT TO GO!
Sax
Lacy's
WOW! SHE GOT ALL WORKED UP OVER SOME ANNIVERSARY!!
SO....
SO, YOU'RE SAYING SHE GOT ALL WORKED UP OVER AN ANNIVERSARY?
YES!
POP'S
R
3

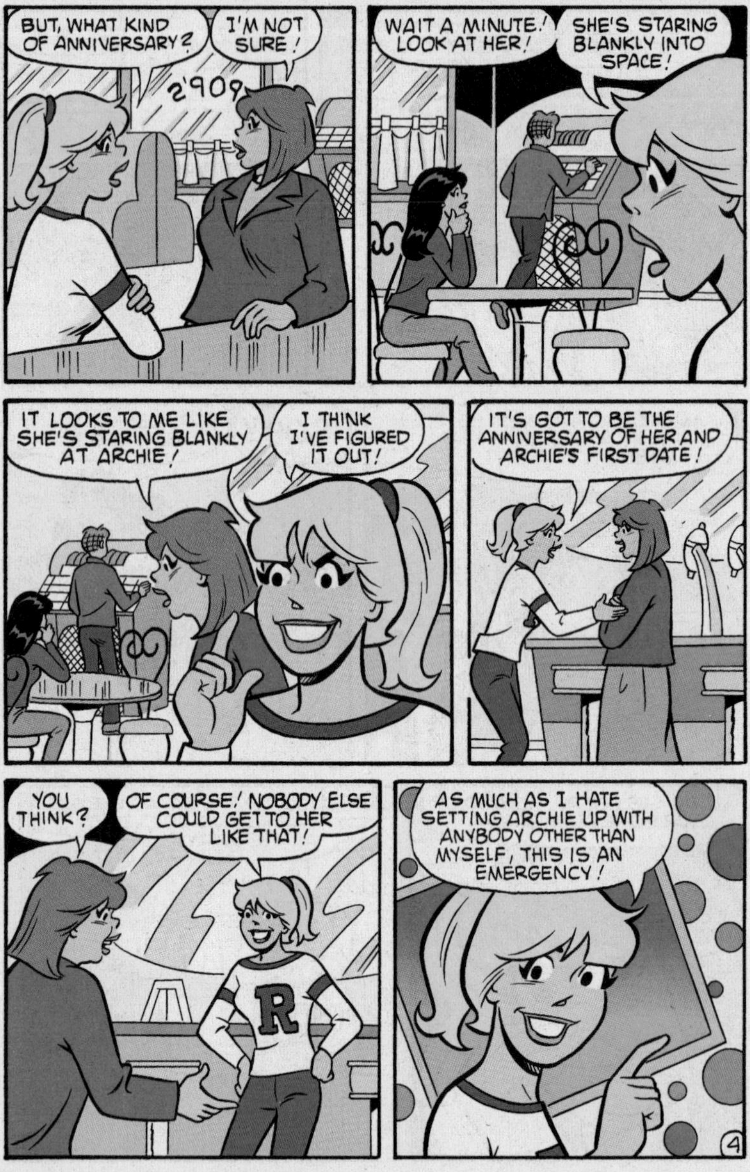
BUT, WHAT KIND OF ANNIVERSARY?
I'M NOT SURE!
WAIT A MINUTE! LOOK AT HER!
SHE'S STARING BLANKLY INTO SPACE!
IT LOOKS TO ME LIKE SHE'S STARING BLANKLY AT ARCHIE!
I THINK I'VE FIGURED IT OUT!
IT'S GOT TO BE THE ANNIVERSARY OF HER AND ARCHIE'S FIRST DATE!
YOU THINK?
OF COURSE! NOBODY ELSE COULD GET TO HER LIKE THAT!
AS MUCH AS I HATE SETTING ARCHIE UP WITH ANYBODY OTHER THAN MYSELF, THIS IS AN EMERGENCY!
R
4

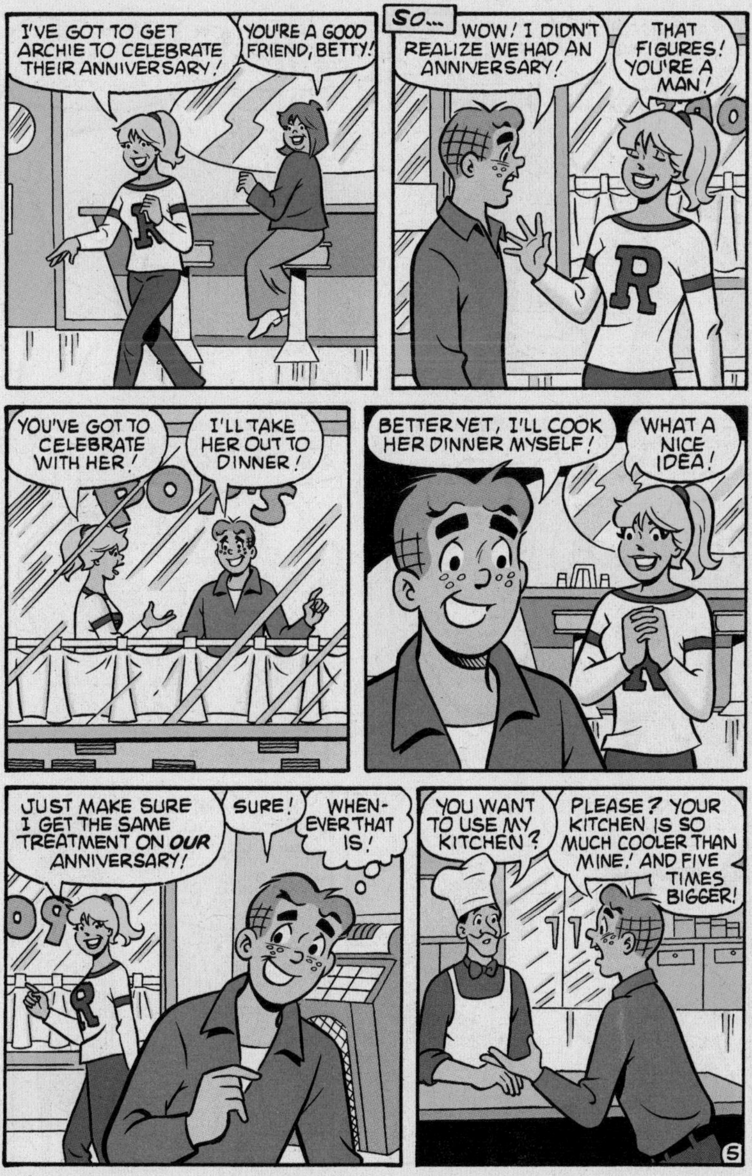

I'VE GOT TO GET ARCHIE TO CELEBRATE THEIR ANNIVERSARY!
YOU'RE A GOOD FRIEND, BETTY!
SO...
WOW! I DIDN'T REALIZE WE HAD AN ANNIVERSARY!
THAT FIGURES! YOU'RE A MAN!
YOU'VE GOT TO CELEBRATE WITH HER!
I'LL TAKE HER OUT TO DINNER!
BETTER YET, I'LL COOK HER DINNER MYSELF!
WHAT A NICE IDEA!
JUST MAKE SURE I GET THE SAME TREATMENT ON *OUR* ANNIVERSARY!
SURE!
WHEN-EVER THAT IS!
YOU WANT TO USE MY KITCHEN?
PLEASE? YOUR KITCHEN IS SO MUCH COOLER THAN MINE! AND FIVE TIMES BIGGER!
5

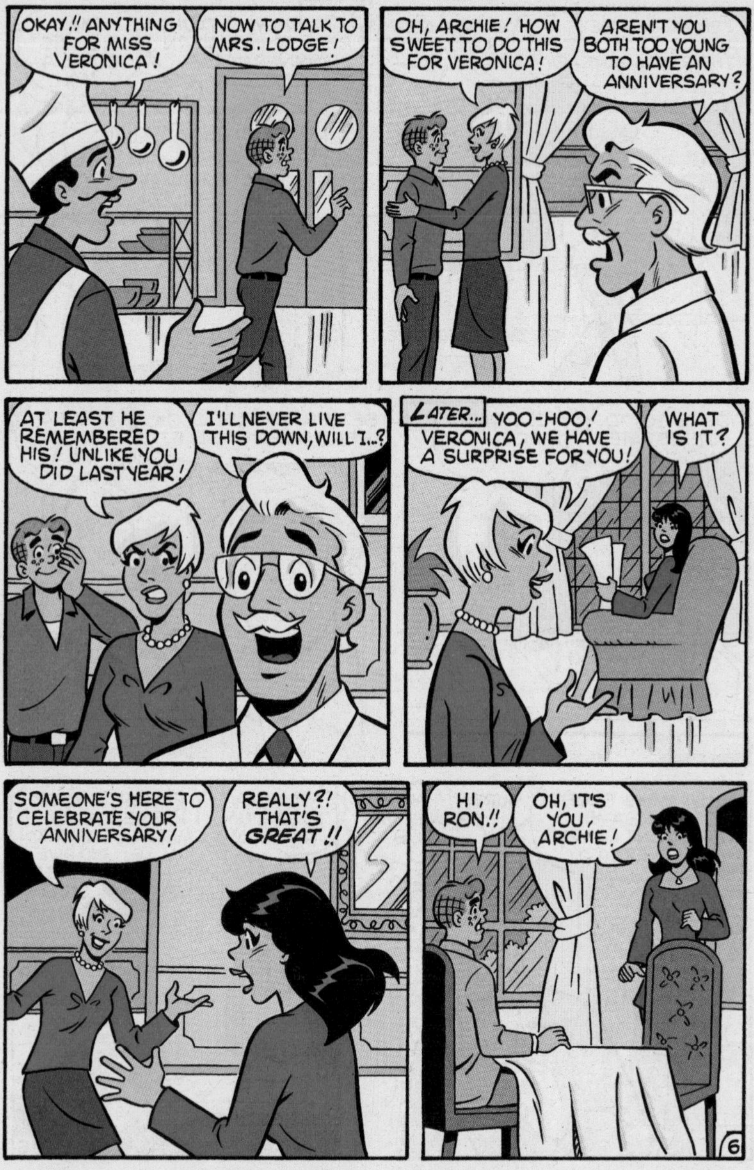
OKAY!! ANYTHING FOR MISS VERONICA!
NOW TO TALK TO MRS. LODGE!
OH, ARCHIE! HOW SWEET TO DO THIS FOR VERONICA!
AREN'T YOU BOTH TOO YOUNG TO HAVE AN ANNIVERSARY?
AT LEAST HE REMEMBERED HIS! UNLIKE YOU DID LAST YEAR!
I'LL NEVER LIVE THIS DOWN, WILL I...?
LATER...
YOO-HOO! VERONICA, WE HAVE A SURPRISE FOR YOU!
WHAT IS IT?
SOMEONE'S HERE TO CELEBRATE YOUR ANNIVERSARY!
REALLY?! THAT'S GREAT!!
HI, RON!!
OH, IT'S YOU, ARCHIE!
6

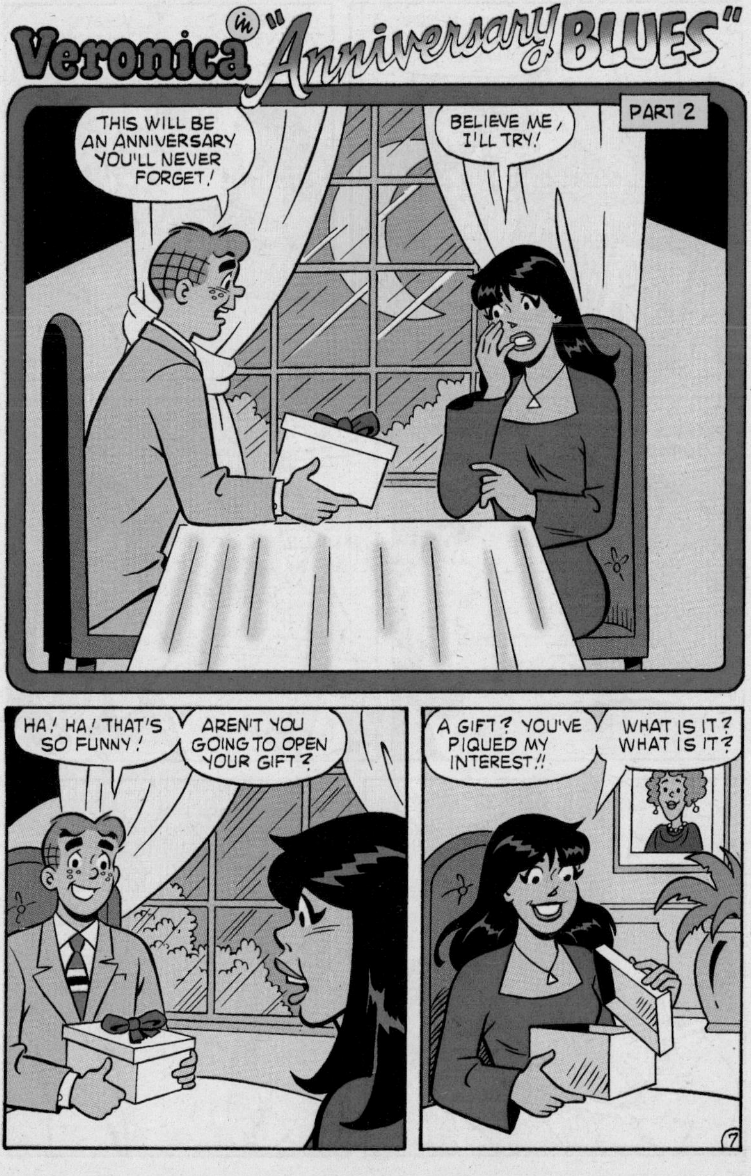

Veronica in "Anniversary BLUES"
PART 2
THIS WILL BE AN ANNIVERSARY YOU'LL NEVER FORGET!
BELIEVE ME, I'LL TRY!
HA! HA! THAT'S SO FUNNY!
AREN'T YOU GOING TO OPEN YOUR GIFT?
A GIFT? YOU'VE PIQUED MY INTEREST!!
WHAT IS IT? WHAT IS IT?

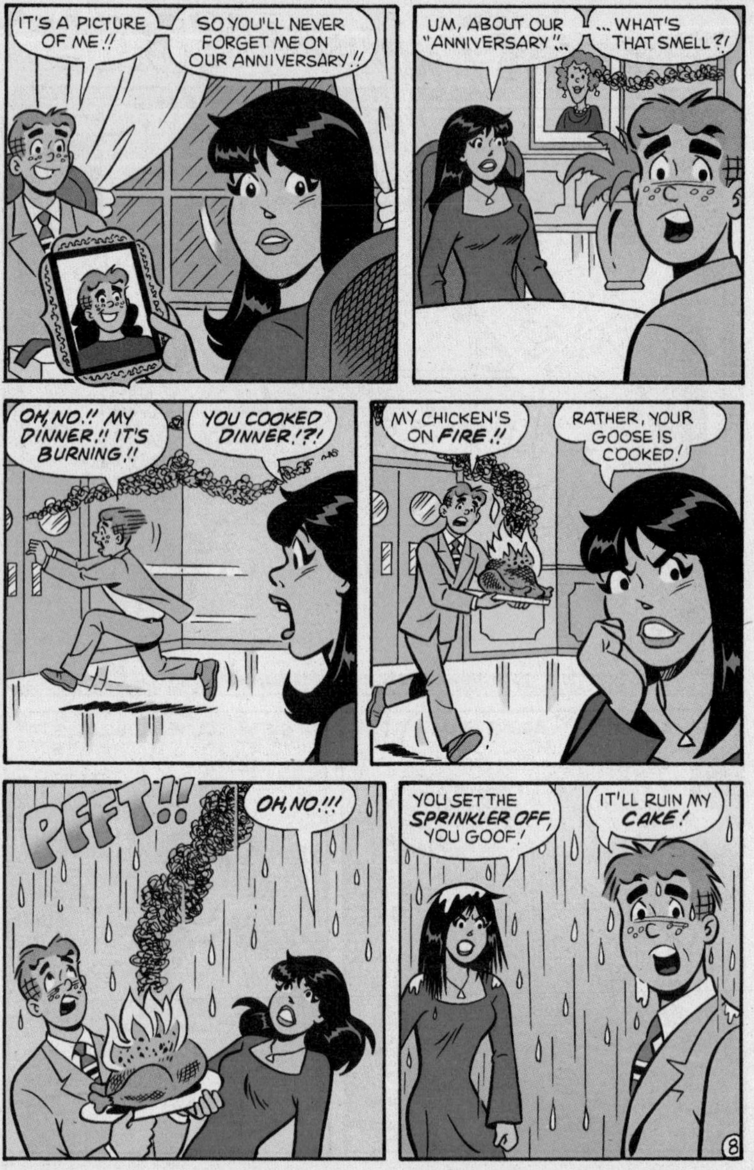
IT'S A PICTURE OF ME!!
SO YOU'LL NEVER FORGET ME ON OUR ANNIVERSARY!!
UM, ABOUT OUR "ANNIVERSARY"...
...WHAT'S THAT SMELL?!
OH, NO!! MY DINNER!! IT'S BURNING!!
YOU COOKED DINNER!?!
MY CHICKEN'S ON FIRE!!
RATHER, YOUR GOOSE IS COOKED!
PFFT!!
OH, NO!!!
YOU SET THE SPRINKLER OFF, YOU GOOF!
IT'LL RUIN MY CAKE!
8

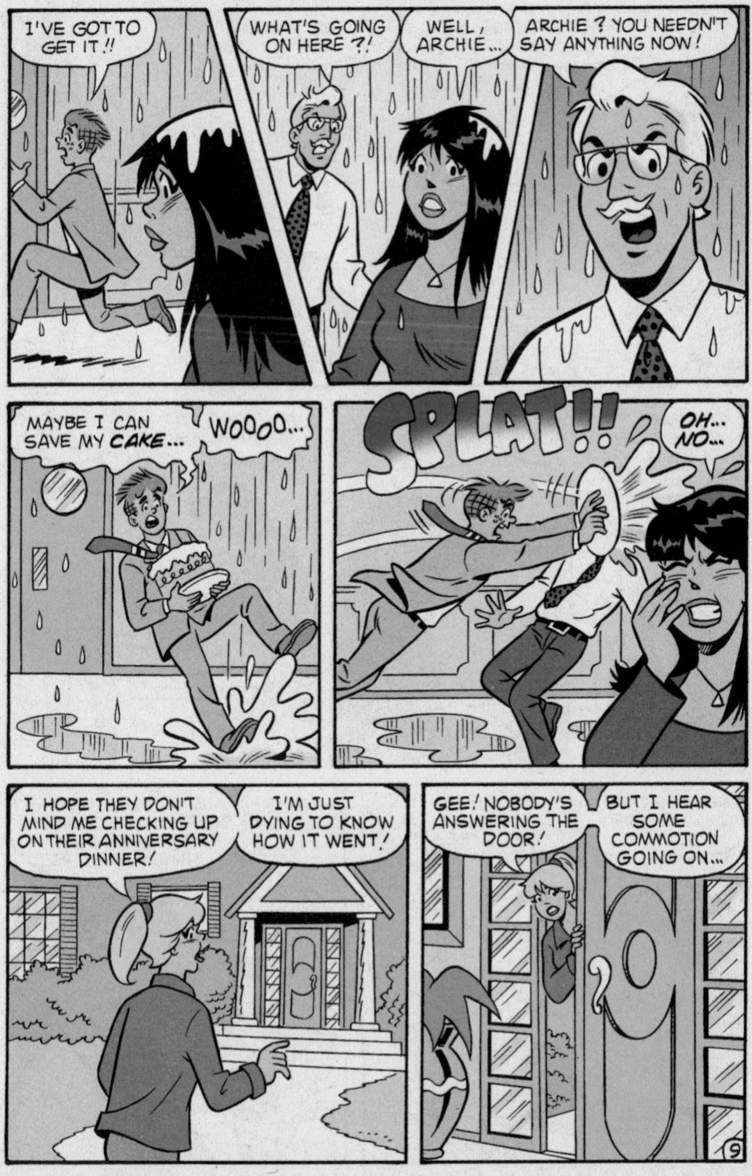
I'VE GOT TO GET IT!!
WHAT'S GOING ON HERE?!
WELL, ARCHIE...
ARCHIE? YOU NEEDN'T SAY ANYTHING NOW!
MAYBE I CAN SAVE MY CAKE...
WOOOO...
SPLAT!!
OH... NO...
I HOPE THEY DON'T MIND ME CHECKING UP ON THEIR ANNIVERSARY DINNER!
I'M JUST DYING TO KNOW HOW IT WENT!
GEE! NOBODY'S ANSWERING THE DOOR!
BUT I HEAR SOME COMMOTION GOING ON...
9

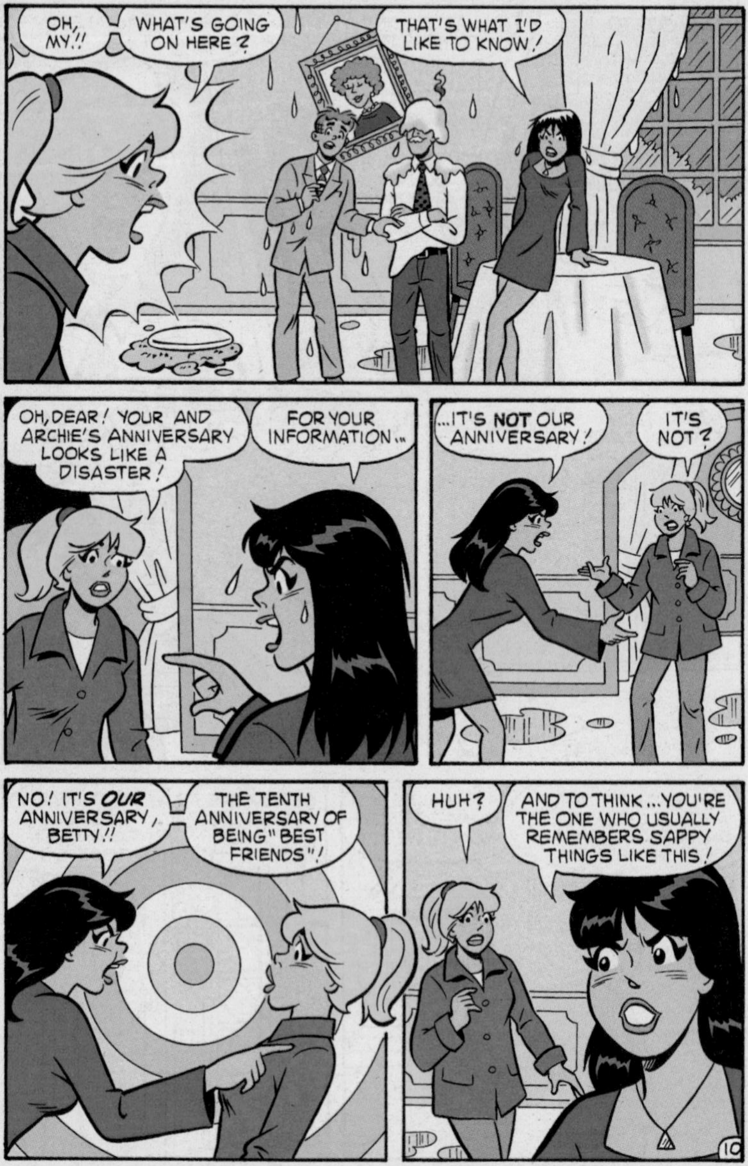
OH, MY!!
WHAT'S GOING ON HERE?
THAT'S WHAT I'D LIKE TO KNOW!
OH, DEAR! YOUR AND ARCHIE'S ANNIVERSARY LOOKS LIKE A DISASTER!
FOR YOUR INFORMATION...
...IT'S NOT OUR ANNIVERSARY!
IT'S NOT?
NO! IT'S OUR ANNIVERSARY, BETTY!!
THE TENTH ANNIVERSARY OF BEING "BEST FRIENDS"!
HUH?
AND TO THINK... YOU'RE THE ONE WHO USUALLY REMEMBERS SAPPY THINGS LIKE THIS!
10

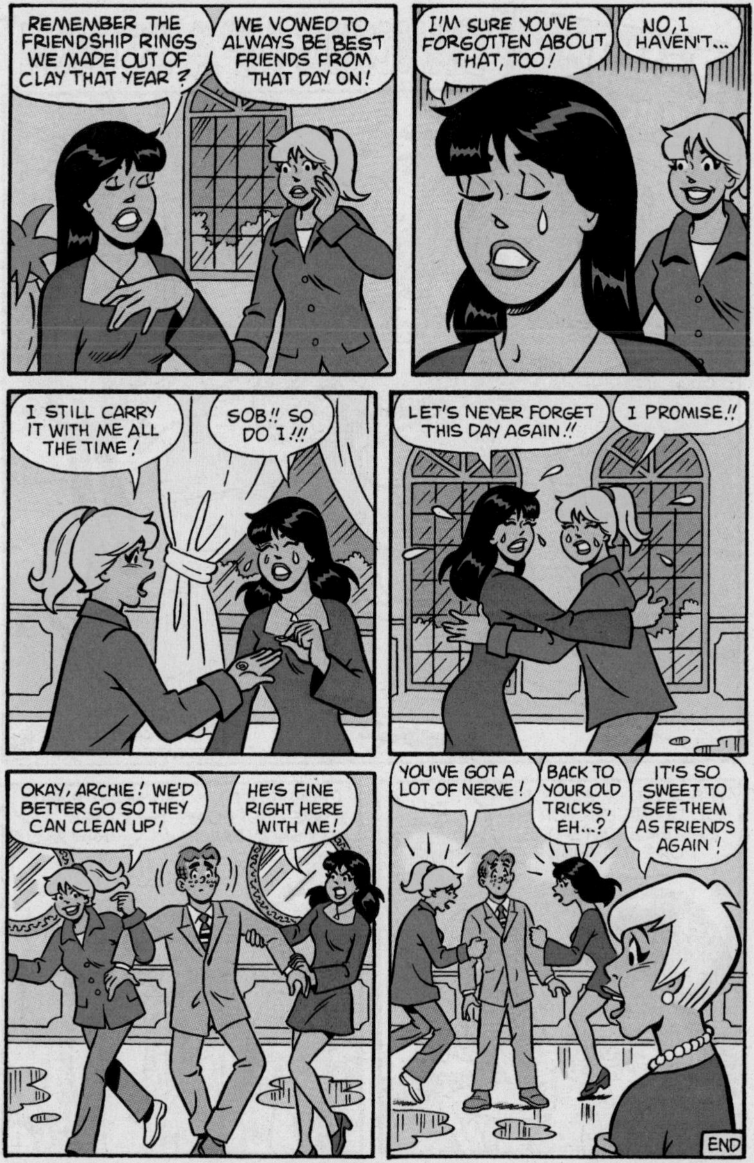
REMEMBER THE FRIENDSHIP RINGS WE MADE OUT OF CLAY THAT YEAR ?
WE VOWED TO ALWAYS BE BEST FRIENDS FROM THAT DAY ON!
I'M SURE YOU'VE FORGOTTEN ABOUT THAT, TOO!
NO, I HAVEN'T...
I STILL CARRY IT WITH ME ALL THE TIME!
SOB!! SO DO I!!!
LET'S NEVER FORGET THIS DAY AGAIN!!
I PROMISE!!
OKAY, ARCHIE! WE'D BETTER GO SO THEY CAN CLEAN UP!
HE'S FINE RIGHT HERE WITH ME!
YOU'VE GOT A LOT OF NERVE!
BACK TO YOUR OLD TRICKS, EH...?
IT'S SO SWEET TO SEE THEM AS FRIENDS AGAIN!
END

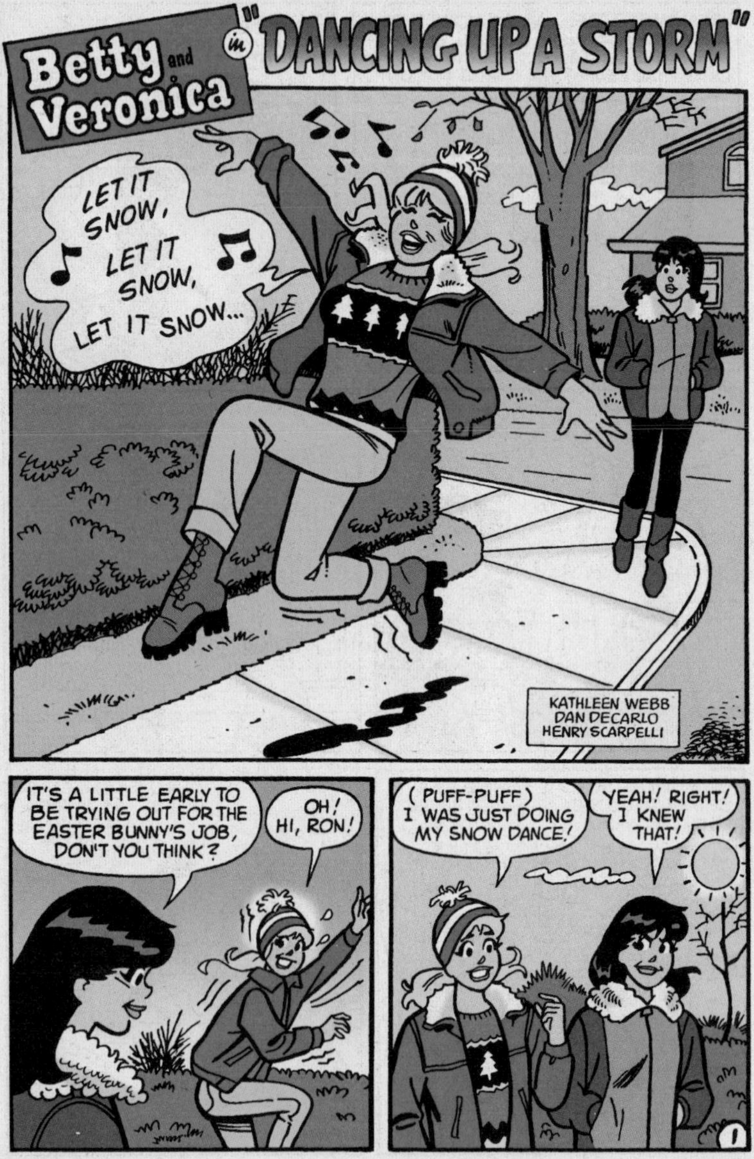
Betty and Veronica
in "DANCING UP A STORM"
LET IT SNOW, LET IT SNOW, LET IT SNOW...
KATHLEEN WEBB
DAN DECARLO
HENRY SCARPELLI
IT'S A LITTLE EARLY TO BE TRYING OUT FOR THE EASTER BUNNY'S JOB, DON'T YOU THINK?
OH! HI, RON!
(PUFF-PUFF) I WAS JUST DOING MY SNOW DANCE!
YEAH! RIGHT! I KNEW THAT!
1

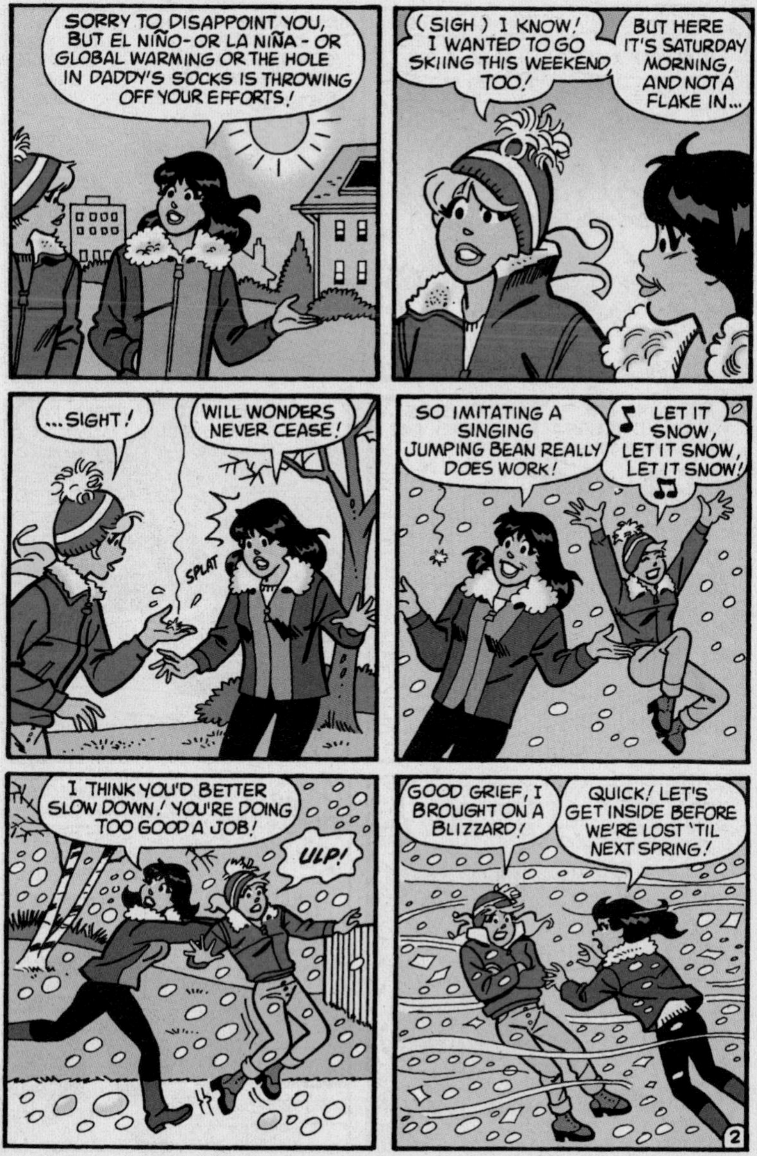
SORRY TO DISAPPOINT YOU, BUT EL NIÑO - OR LA NIÑA - OR GLOBAL WARMING OR THE HOLE IN DADDY'S SOCKS IS THROWING OFF YOUR EFFORTS!
(SIGH) I KNOW! I WANTED TO GO SKIING THIS WEEKEND, TOO!
BUT HERE IT'S SATURDAY MORNING, AND NOT A FLAKE IN...
...SIGHT!
WILL WONDERS NEVER CEASE!
SPLAT
SO IMITATING A SINGING JUMPING BEAN REALLY DOES WORK!
LET IT SNOW, LET IT SNOW, LET IT SNOW!
I THINK YOU'D BETTER SLOW DOWN! YOU'RE DOING TOO GOOD A JOB!
ULP!
GOOD GRIEF, I BROUGHT ON A BLIZZARD!
QUICK! LET'S GET INSIDE BEFORE WE'RE LOST 'TIL NEXT SPRING!
2

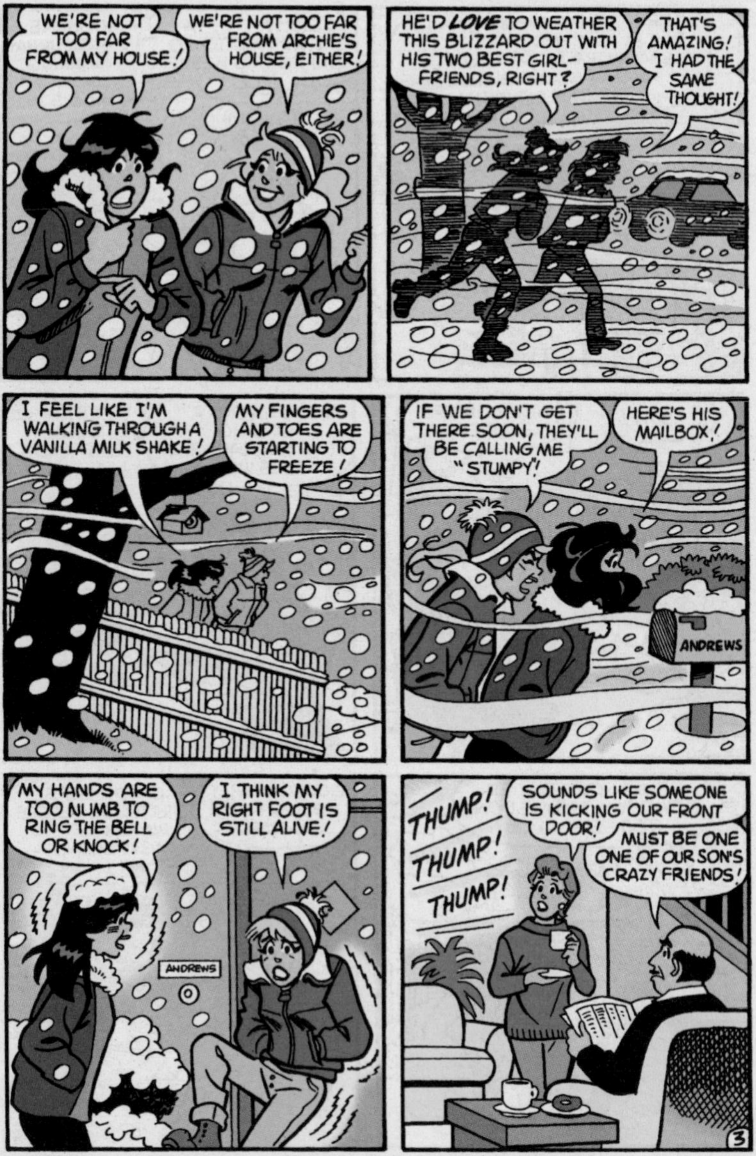
WE'RE NOT TOO FAR FROM MY HOUSE!
WE'RE NOT TOO FAR FROM ARCHIE'S HOUSE, EITHER!
HE'D LOVE TO WEATHER THIS BLIZZARD OUT WITH HIS TWO BEST GIRL-FRIENDS, RIGHT?
THAT'S AMAZING! I HAD THE SAME THOUGHT!
I FEEL LIKE I'M WALKING THROUGH A VANILLA MILK SHAKE!
MY FINGERS AND TOES ARE STARTING TO FREEZE!
IF WE DON'T GET THERE SOON, THEY'LL BE CALLING ME "STUMPY"!
HERE'S HIS MAILBOX!
ANDREWS
MY HANDS ARE TOO NUMB TO RING THE BELL OR KNOCK!
I THINK MY RIGHT FOOT IS STILL ALIVE!
ANDREWS
THUMP!
THUMP!
THUMP!
SOUNDS LIKE SOMEONE IS KICKING OUR FRONT DOOR!
MUST BE ONE ONE OF OUR SON'S CRAZY FRIENDS!

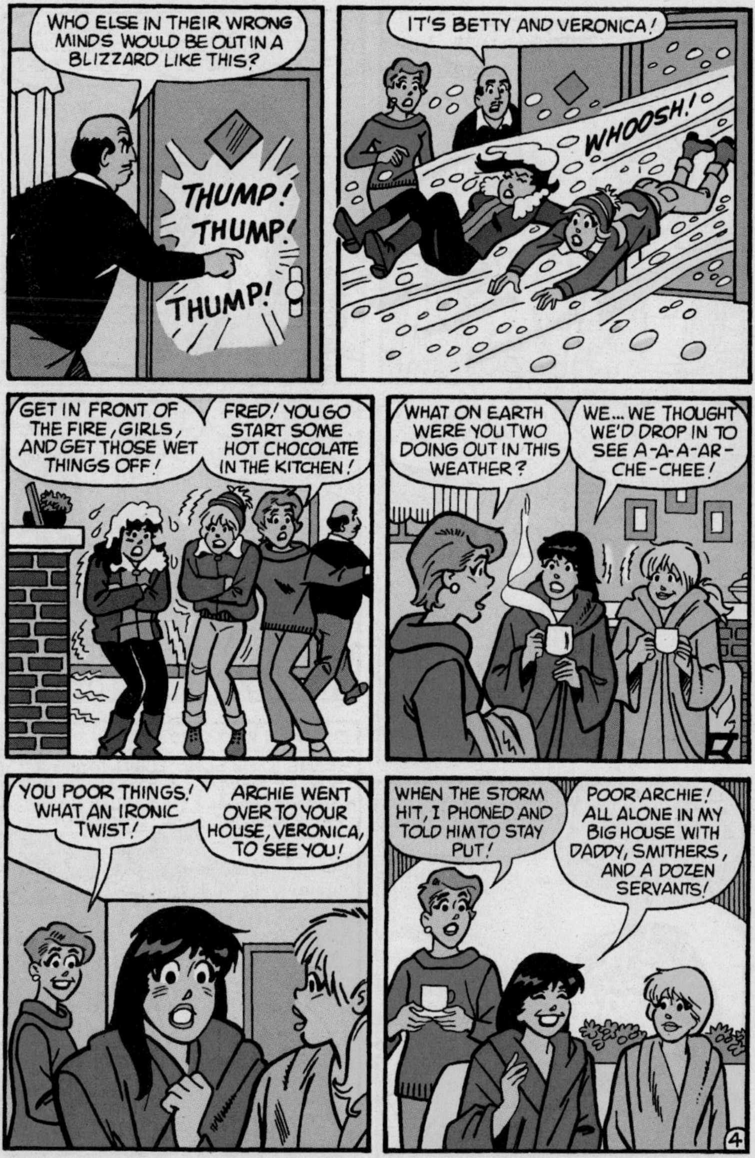
WHO ELSE IN THEIR WRONG MINDS WOULD BE OUT IN A BLIZZARD LIKE THIS?
THUMP! THUMP! THUMP!
IT'S BETTY AND VERONICA!
WHOOSH!
GET IN FRONT OF THE FIRE, GIRLS, AND GET THOSE WET THINGS OFF!
FRED! YOU GO START SOME HOT CHOCOLATE IN THE KITCHEN!
WHAT ON EARTH WERE YOU TWO DOING OUT IN THIS WEATHER?
WE... WE THOUGHT WE'D DROP IN TO SEE A-A-A-AR-CHE-CHEE!
YOU POOR THINGS! WHAT AN IRONIC TWIST!
ARCHIE WENT OVER TO YOUR HOUSE, VERONICA, TO SEE YOU!
WHEN THE STORM HIT, I PHONED AND TOLD HIM TO STAY PUT!
POOR ARCHIE! ALL ALONE IN MY BIG HOUSE WITH DADDY, SMITHERS, AND A DOZEN SERVANTS!
4

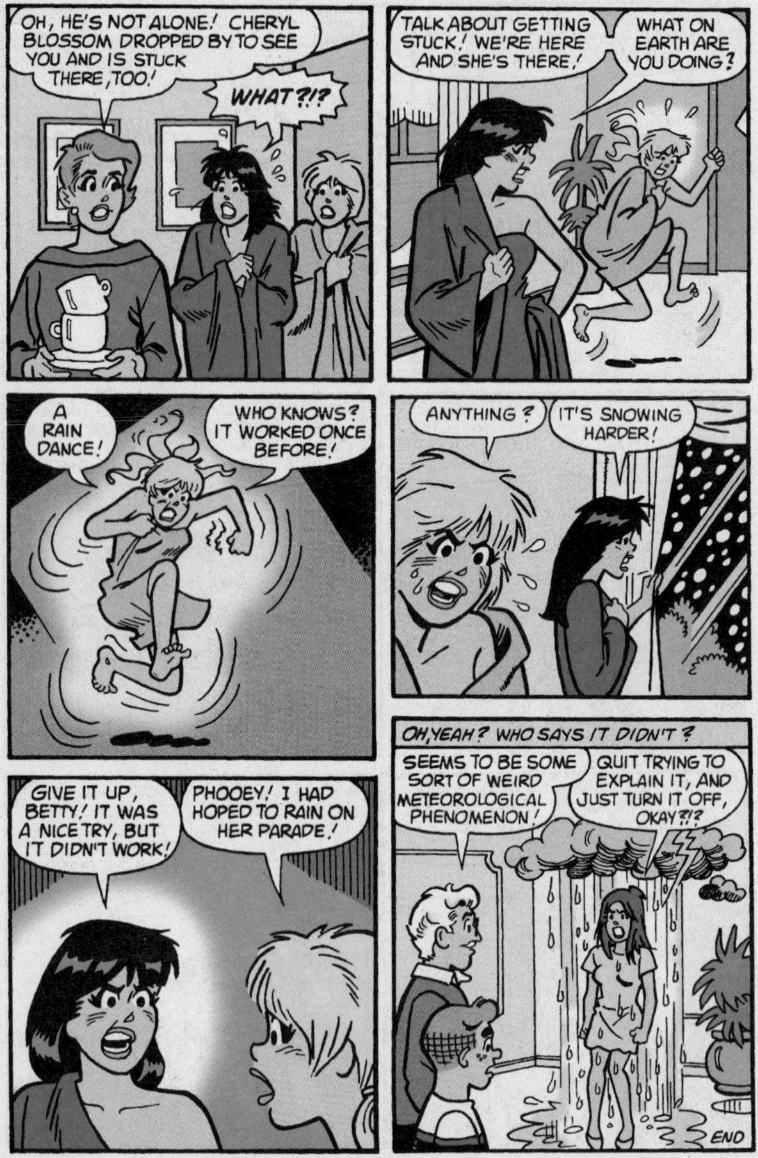
OH, HE'S NOT ALONE! CHERYL BLOSSOM DROPPED BY TO SEE YOU AND IS STUCK THERE, TOO!
WHAT?!?
TALK ABOUT GETTING STUCK! WE'RE HERE AND SHE'S THERE!
WHAT ON EARTH ARE YOU DOING?
A RAIN DANCE!
WHO KNOWS? IT WORKED ONCE BEFORE!
ANYTHING?
IT'S SNOWING HARDER!
GIVE IT UP, BETTY! IT WAS A NICE TRY, BUT IT DIDN'T WORK!
PHOOEY! I HAD HOPED TO RAIN ON HER PARADE!
OH, YEAH? WHO SAYS IT DIDN'T?
SEEMS TO BE SOME SORT OF WEIRD METEOROLOGICAL PHENOMENON!
QUIT TRYING TO EXPLAIN IT, AND JUST TURN IT OFF, OKAY?!?
END

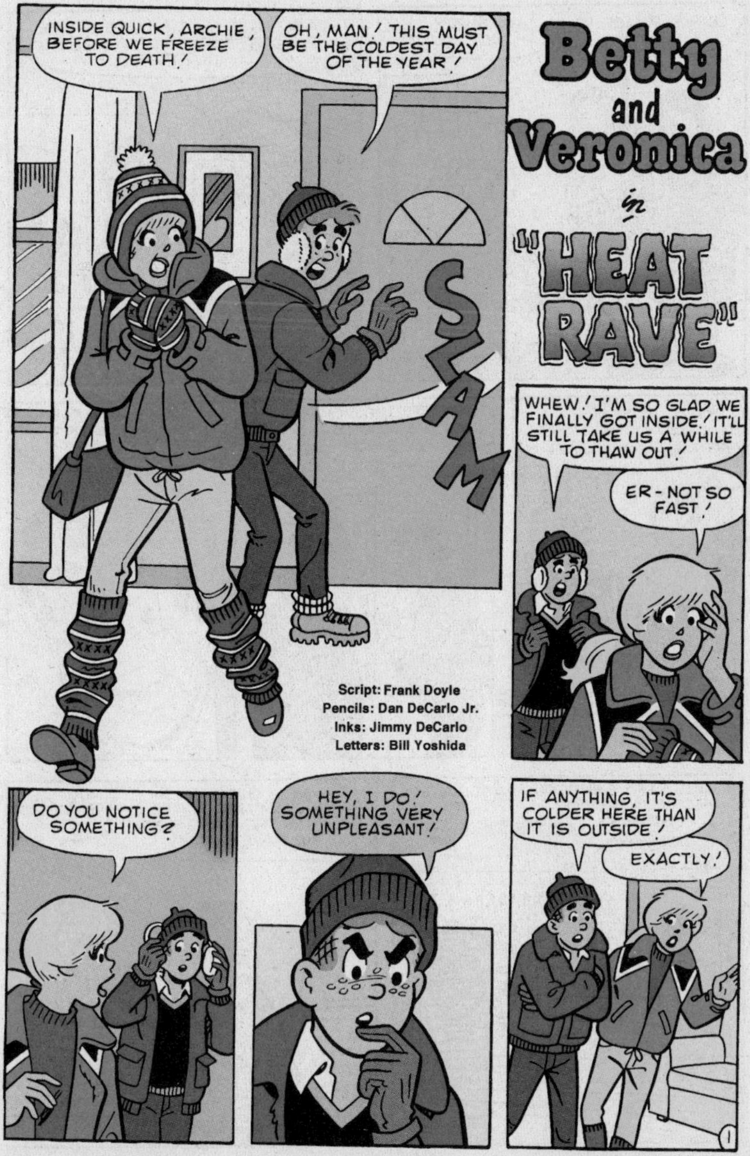
INSIDE QUICK, ARCHIE, BEFORE WE FREEZE TO DEATH!
OH, MAN! THIS MUST BE THE COLDEST DAY OF THE YEAR!
Betty and Veronica in "HEAT RAVE"
SLAM
Script: Frank Doyle
Pencils: Dan DeCarlo Jr.
Inks: Jimmy DeCarlo
Letters: Bill Yoshida
WHEW! I'M SO GLAD WE FINALLY GOT INSIDE! IT'LL STILL TAKE US A WHILE TO THAW OUT!
ER - NOT SO FAST!
DO YOU NOTICE SOMETHING?
HEY, I DO! SOMETHING VERY UNPLEASANT!
IF ANYTHING, IT'S COLDER HERE THAN IT IS OUTSIDE!
EXACTLY!
1

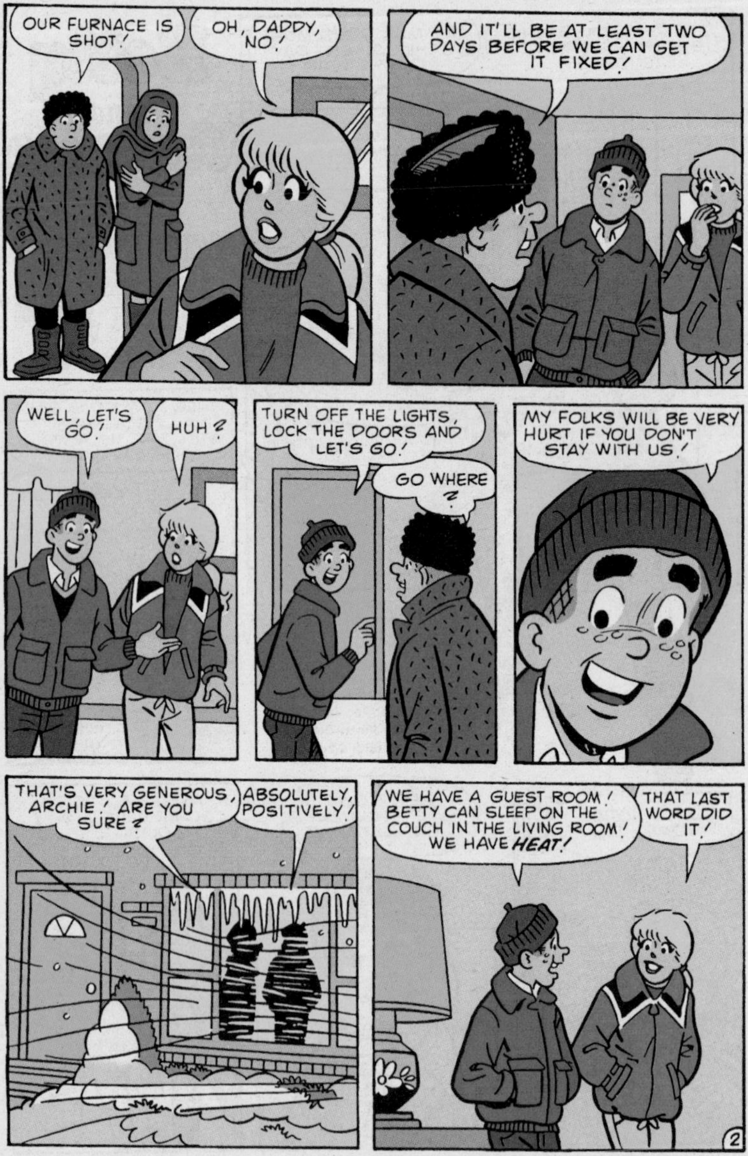
OUR FURNACE IS SHOT!
OH, DADDY, NO!
AND IT'LL BE AT LEAST TWO DAYS BEFORE WE CAN GET IT FIXED!
WELL, LET'S GO!
HUH?
TURN OFF THE LIGHTS, LOCK THE DOORS AND LET'S GO!
GO WHERE?
MY FOLKS WILL BE VERY HURT IF YOU DON'T STAY WITH US!
THAT'S VERY GENEROUS, ARCHIE! ARE YOU SURE?
ABSOLUTELY, POSITIVELY!
WE HAVE A GUEST ROOM! BETTY CAN SLEEP ON THE COUCH IN THE LIVING ROOM! WE HAVE HEAT!
THAT LAST WORD DID IT!
2

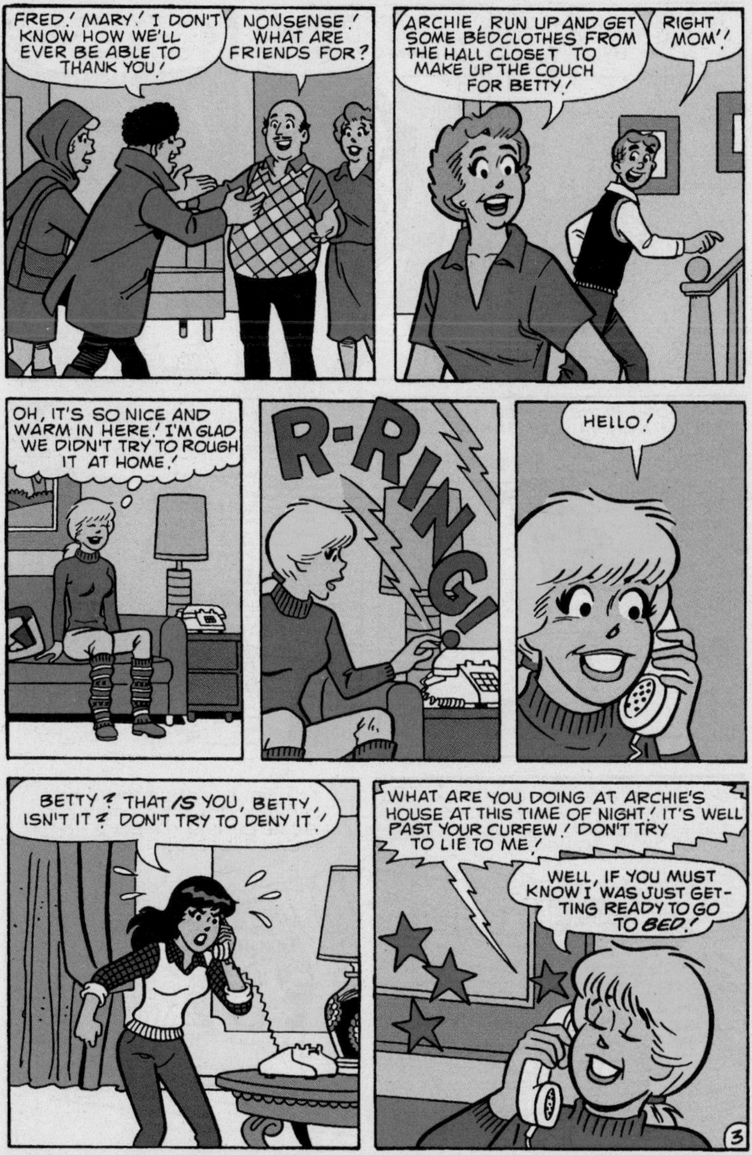
FRED! MARY! I DON'T KNOW HOW WE'LL EVER BE ABLE TO THANK YOU!
NONSENSE! WHAT ARE FRIENDS FOR?
ARCHIE, RUN UP AND GET SOME BEDCLOTHES FROM THE HALL CLOSET TO MAKE UP THE COUCH FOR BETTY!
RIGHT MOM'!
OH, IT'S SO NICE AND WARM IN HERE! I'M GLAD WE DIDN'T TRY TO ROUGH IT AT HOME!
R-RING!
HELLO!
BETTY? THAT IS YOU, BETTY, ISN'T IT? DON'T TRY TO DENY IT!
WHAT ARE YOU DOING AT ARCHIE'S HOUSE AT THIS TIME OF NIGHT! IT'S WELL PAST YOUR CURFEW! DON'T TRY TO LIE TO ME!
WELL, IF YOU MUST KNOW I WAS JUST GETTING READY TO GO TO BED!
3

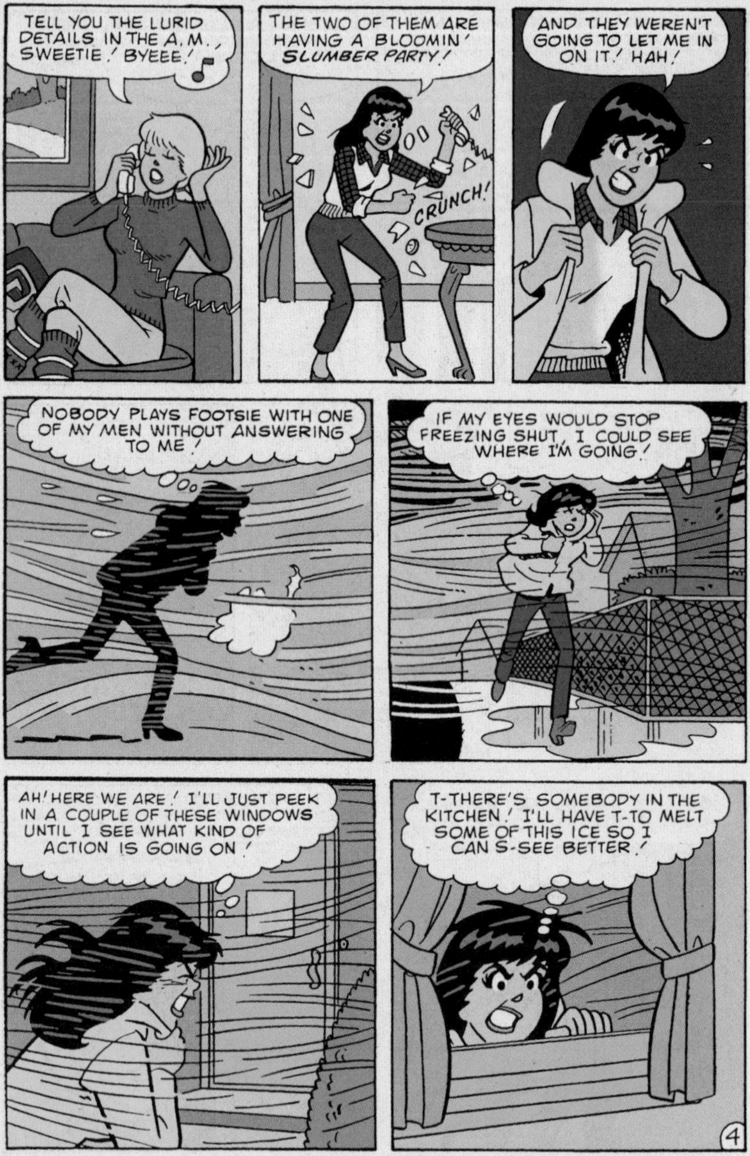

TELL YOU THE LURID DETAILS IN THE A.M., SWEETIE! BYEEE!
THE TWO OF THEM ARE HAVING A BLOOMIN' SLUMBER PARTY!
CRUNCH!
AND THEY WEREN'T GOING TO LET ME IN ON IT! HAH!
NOBODY PLAYS FOOTSIE WITH ONE OF MY MEN WITHOUT ANSWERING TO ME!
IF MY EYES WOULD STOP FREEZING SHUT, I COULD SEE WHERE I'M GOING!
AH! HERE WE ARE! I'LL JUST PEEK IN A COUPLE OF THESE WINDOWS UNTIL I SEE WHAT KIND OF ACTION IS GOING ON!
T-THERE'S SOMEBODY IN THE KITCHEN! I'LL HAVE T-TO MELT SOME OF THIS ICE SO I CAN S-SEE BETTER!
4

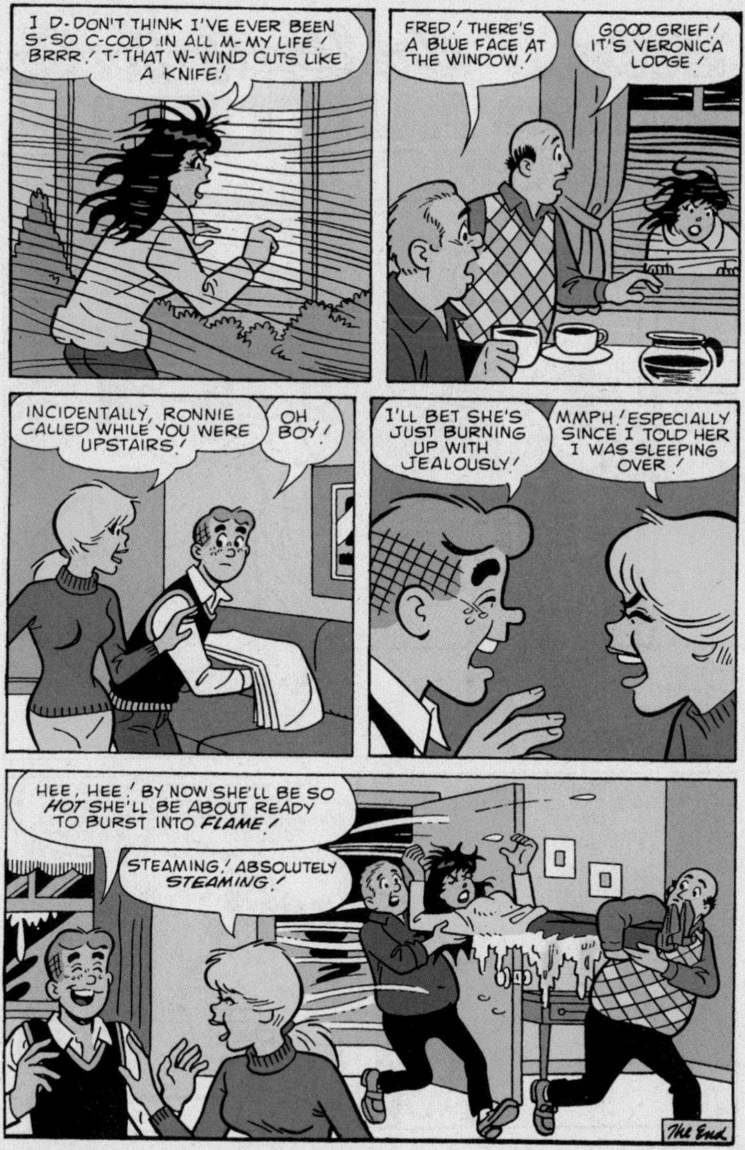
I D-DON'T THINK I'VE EVER BEEN S-SO C-COLD IN ALL M-MY LIFE! BRRR! T-THAT W-WIND CUTS LIKE A KNIFE!
FRED! THERE'S A BLUE FACE AT THE WINDOW!
GOOD GRIEF! IT'S VERONICA LODGE!
INCIDENTALLY, RONNIE CALLED WHILE YOU WERE UPSTAIRS!
OH BOY!
I'LL BET SHE'S JUST BURNING UP WITH JEALOUSLY!
MMPH! ESPECIALLY SINCE I TOLD HER I WAS SLEEPING OVER!
HEE, HEE! BY NOW SHE'LL BE SO *HOT* SHE'LL BE ABOUT READY TO BURST INTO *FLAME*!
STEAMING! ABSOLUTELY *STEAMING*!
The End

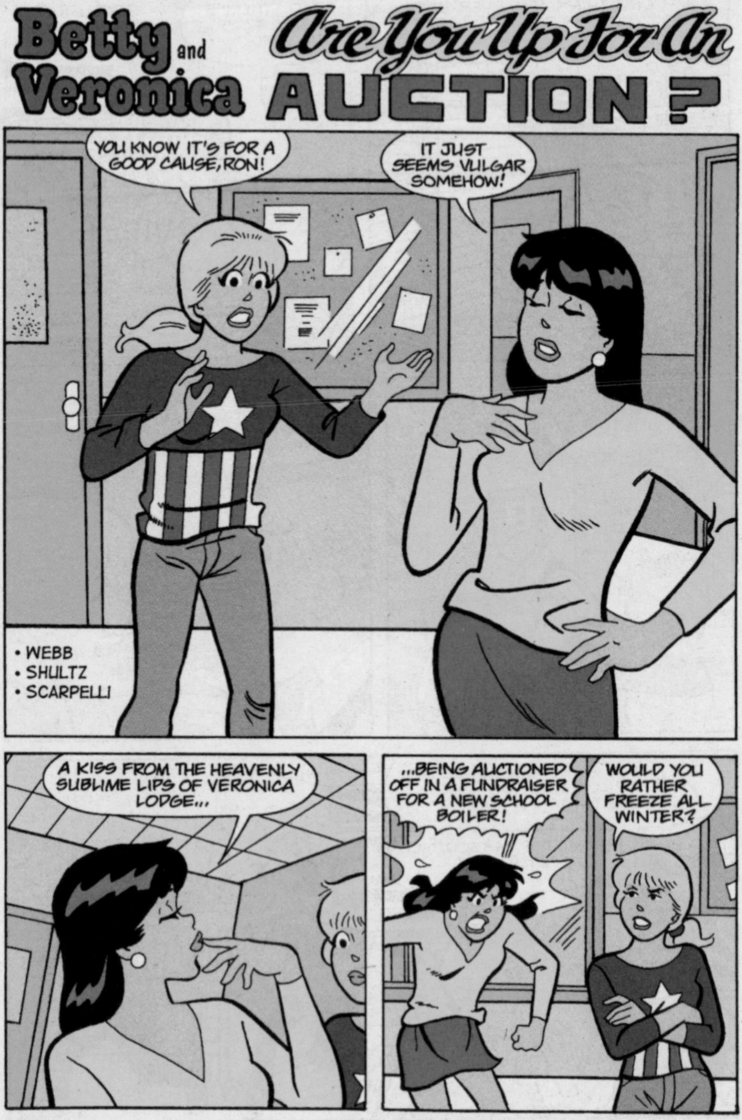
Betty and Veronica
Are You Up For An AUCTION?
YOU KNOW IT'S FOR A GOOD CAUSE, RON!
IT JUST SEEMS VULGAR SOMEHOW!
• WEBB
• SHULTZ
• SCARPELLI
A KISS FROM THE HEAVENLY SUBLIME LIPS OF VERONICA LODGE...
...BEING AUCTIONED OFF IN A FUNDRAISER FOR A NEW SCHOOL BOILER!
WOULD YOU RATHER FREEZE ALL WINTER?

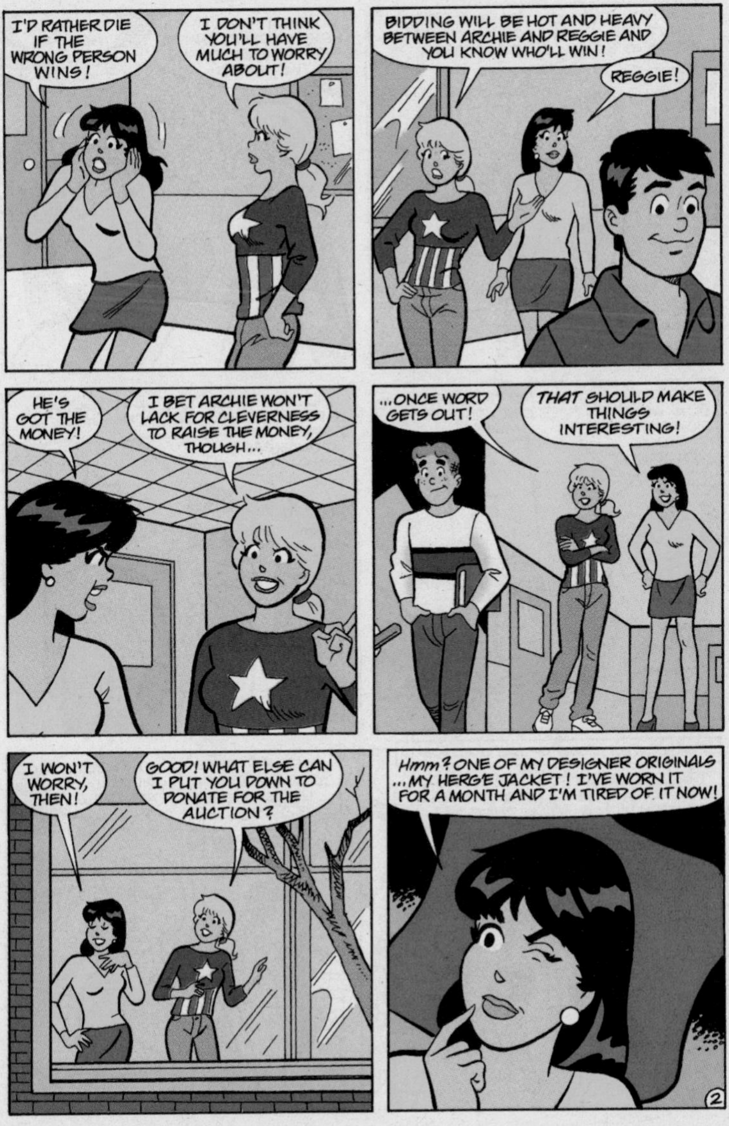
I'D RATHER DIE IF THE WRONG PERSON WINS!
I DON'T THINK YOU'LL HAVE MUCH TO WORRY ABOUT!
BIDDING WILL BE HOT AND HEAVY BETWEEN ARCHIE AND REGGIE AND YOU KNOW WHO'LL WIN!
REGGIE!
HE'S GOT THE MONEY!
I BET ARCHIE WON'T LACK FOR CLEVERNESS TO RAISE THE MONEY, THOUGH...
...ONCE WORD GETS OUT!
THAT SHOULD MAKE THINGS INTERESTING!
I WON'T WORRY, THEN!
GOOD! WHAT ELSE CAN I PUT YOU DOWN TO DONATE FOR THE AUCTION?
Hmm? ONE OF MY DESIGNER ORIGINALS ...MY HERG'E JACKET! I'VE WORN IT FOR A MONTH AND I'M TIRED OF IT NOW!
2

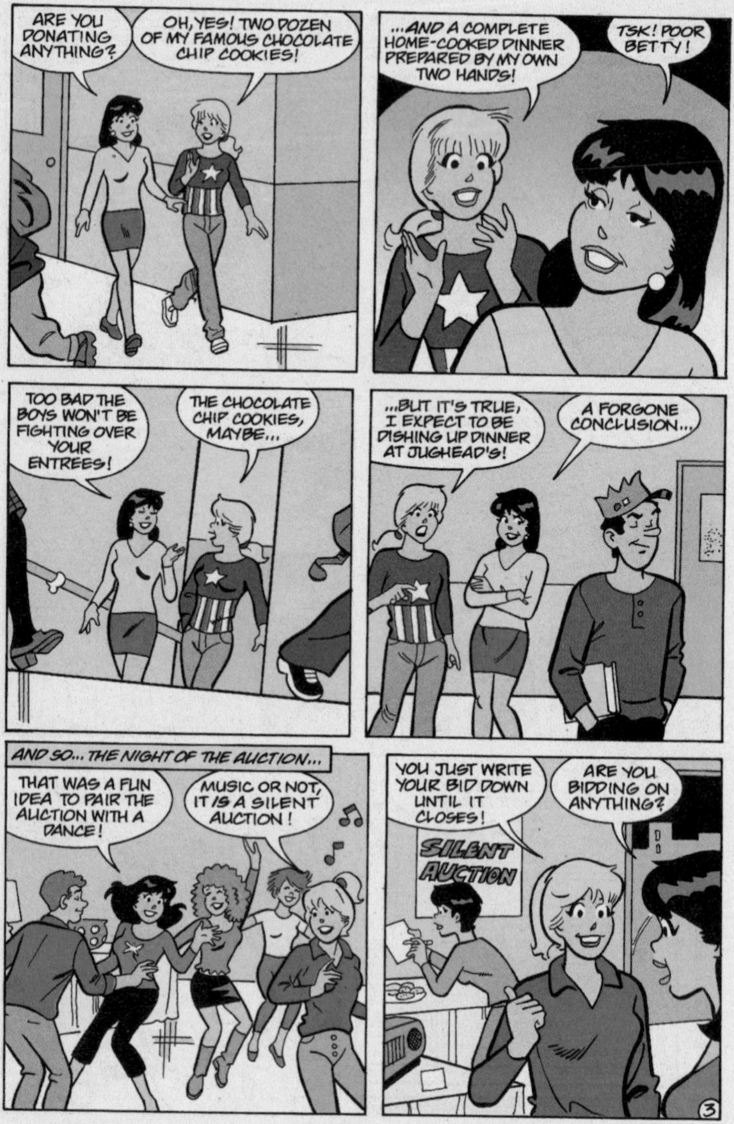
ARE YOU DONATING ANYTHING?
OH, YES! TWO DOZEN OF MY FAMOUS CHOCOLATE CHIP COOKIES!
...AND A COMPLETE HOME-COOKED DINNER PREPARED BY MY OWN TWO HANDS!
TSK! POOR BETTY!
TOO BAD THE BOYS WON'T BE FIGHTING OVER YOUR ENTREES!
THE CHOCOLATE CHIP COOKIES, MAYBE...
...BUT IT'S TRUE, I EXPECT TO BE DISHING UP DINNER AT JUGHEAD'S!
A FORGONE CONCLUSION...
AND SO... THE NIGHT OF THE AUCTION...
THAT WAS A FUN IDEA TO PAIR THE AUCTION WITH A DANCE!
MUSIC OR NOT, IT IS A SILENT AUCTION!
YOU JUST WRITE YOUR BID DOWN UNTIL IT CLOSES!
SILENT AUCTION
ARE YOU BIDDING ON ANYTHING?
3

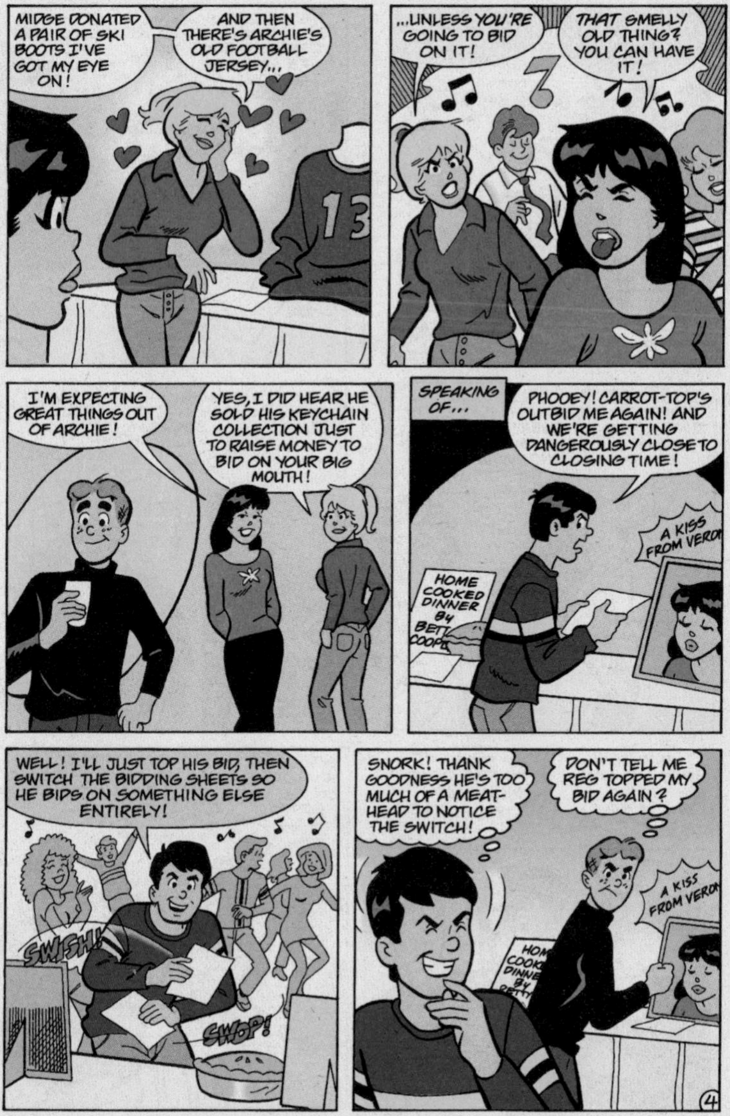
MIDGE DONATED A PAIR OF SKI BOOTS I'VE GOT MY EYE ON!
AND THEN THERE'S ARCHIE'S OLD FOOTBALL JERSEY...
...UNLESS YOU'RE GOING TO BID ON IT!
THAT SMELLY OLD THING? YOU CAN HAVE IT!
I'M EXPECTING GREAT THINGS OUT OF ARCHIE!
YES, I DID HEAR HE SOLD HIS KEYCHAIN COLLECTION JUST TO RAISE MONEY TO BID ON YOUR BIG MOUTH!
SPEAKING OF...
PHOOEY! CARROT-TOP'S OUTBID ME AGAIN! AND WE'RE GETTING DANGEROUSLY CLOSE TO CLOSING TIME!
HOME COOKED DINNER BY
WELL! I'LL JUST TOP HIS BID, THEN SWITCH THE BIDDING SHEETS SO HE BIDS ON SOMETHING ELSE ENTIRELY!
SWISH!
SWOOP!
SNORK! THANK GOODNESS HE'S TOO MUCH OF A MEAT-HEAD TO NOTICE THE SWITCH!
DON'T TELL ME REG TOPPED MY BID AGAIN?
4

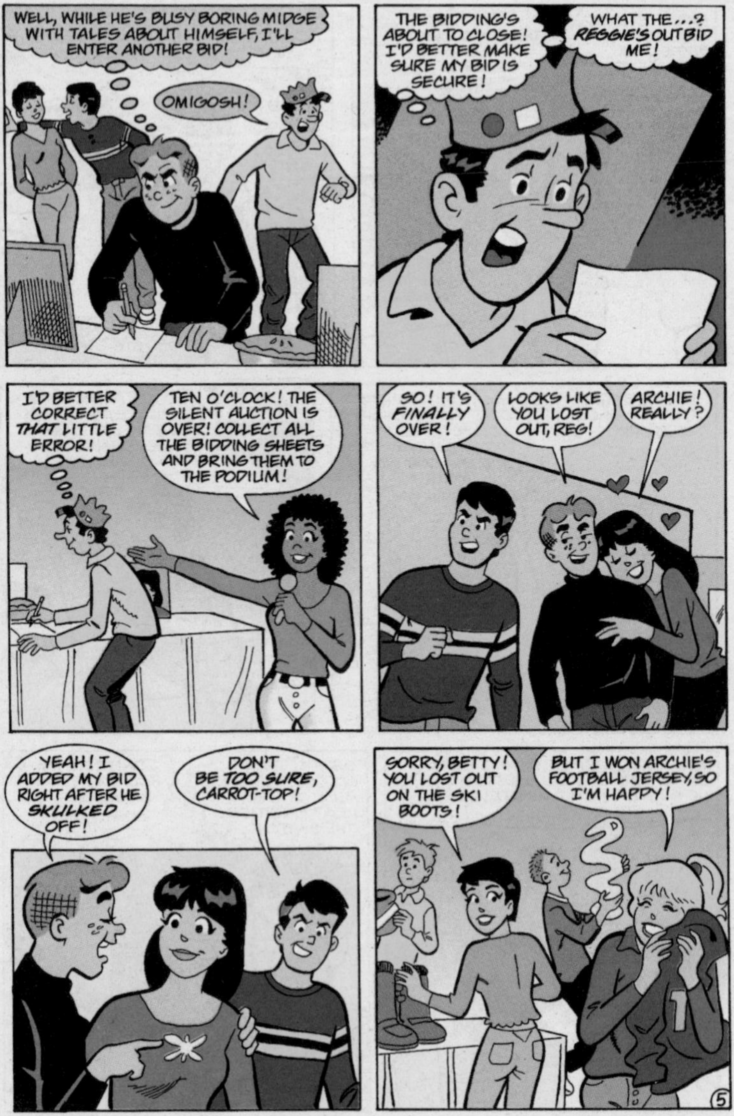
WELL, WHILE HE'S BUSY BORING MIDGE WITH TALES ABOUT HIMSELF, I'LL ENTER ANOTHER BID!
OMIGOSH!
THE BIDDING'S ABOUT TO CLOSE! I'D BETTER MAKE SURE MY BID IS SECURE!
WHAT THE...? REGGIE'S OUTBID ME!
I'D BETTER CORRECT THAT LITTLE ERROR!
TEN O'CLOCK! THE SILENT AUCTION IS OVER! COLLECT ALL THE BIDDING SHEETS AND BRING THEM TO THE PODIUM!
SO! IT'S FINALLY OVER!
LOOKS LIKE YOU LOST OUT, REG!
ARCHIE! REALLY?
YEAH! I ADDED MY BID RIGHT AFTER HE SKULKED OFF!
DON'T BE TOO SURE, CARROT-TOP!
SORRY, BETTY! YOU LOST OUT ON THE SKI BOOTS!
BUT I WON ARCHIE'S FOOTBALL JERSEY, SO I'M HAPPY!
5

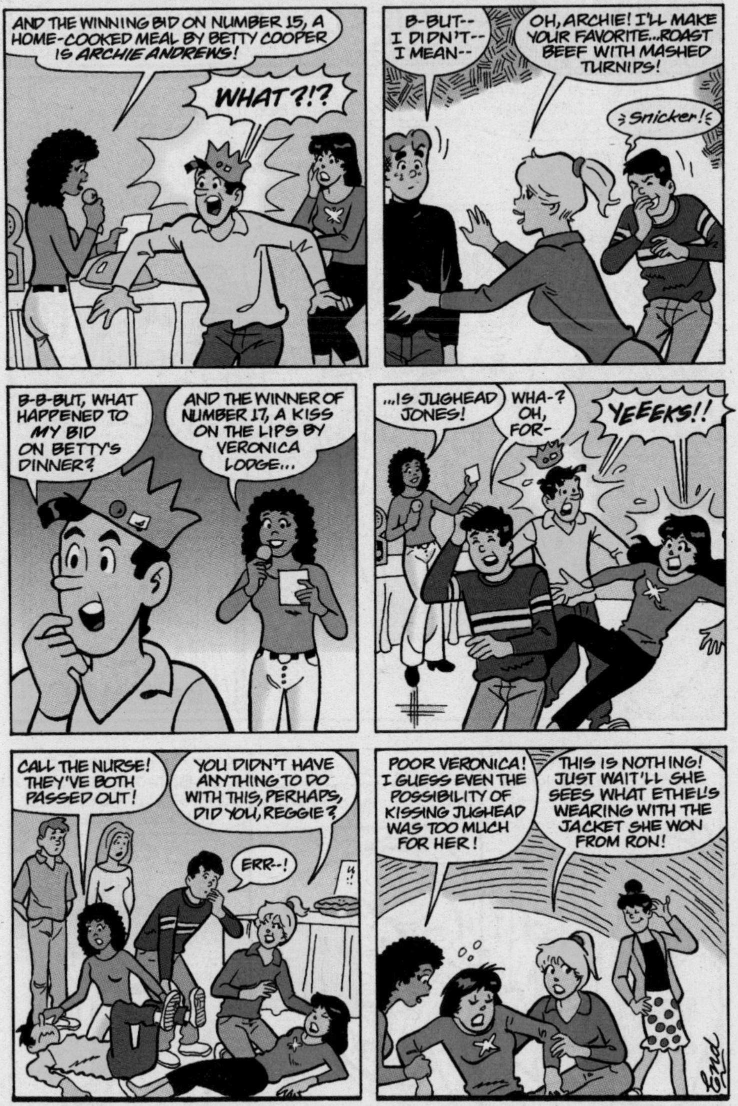
AND THE WINNING BID ON NUMBER 15, A HOME-COOKED MEAL BY BETTY COOPER IS ARCHIE ANDREWS!
WHAT?!?
B-BUT-- I DIDN'T-- I MEAN--
OH, ARCHIE! I'LL MAKE YOUR FAVORITE...ROAST BEEF WITH MASHED TURNIPS!
Snicker!
B-B-BUT, WHAT HAPPENED TO MY BID ON BETTY'S DINNER?
AND THE WINNER OF NUMBER 17, A KISS ON THE LIPS BY VERONICA LODGE...
...IS JUGHEAD JONES!
WHA-? OH, FOR-
YEEEKS!!
CALL THE NURSE! THEY'VE BOTH PASSED OUT!
YOU DIDN'T HAVE ANYTHING TO DO WITH THIS, PERHAPS, DID YOU, REGGIE?
ERR--!
POOR VERONICA! I GUESS EVEN THE POSSIBILITY OF KISSING JUGHEAD WAS TOO MUCH FOR HER!
THIS IS NOTHING! JUST WAIT'LL SHE SEES WHAT ETHEL'S WEARING WITH THE JACKET SHE WON FROM RON!
End

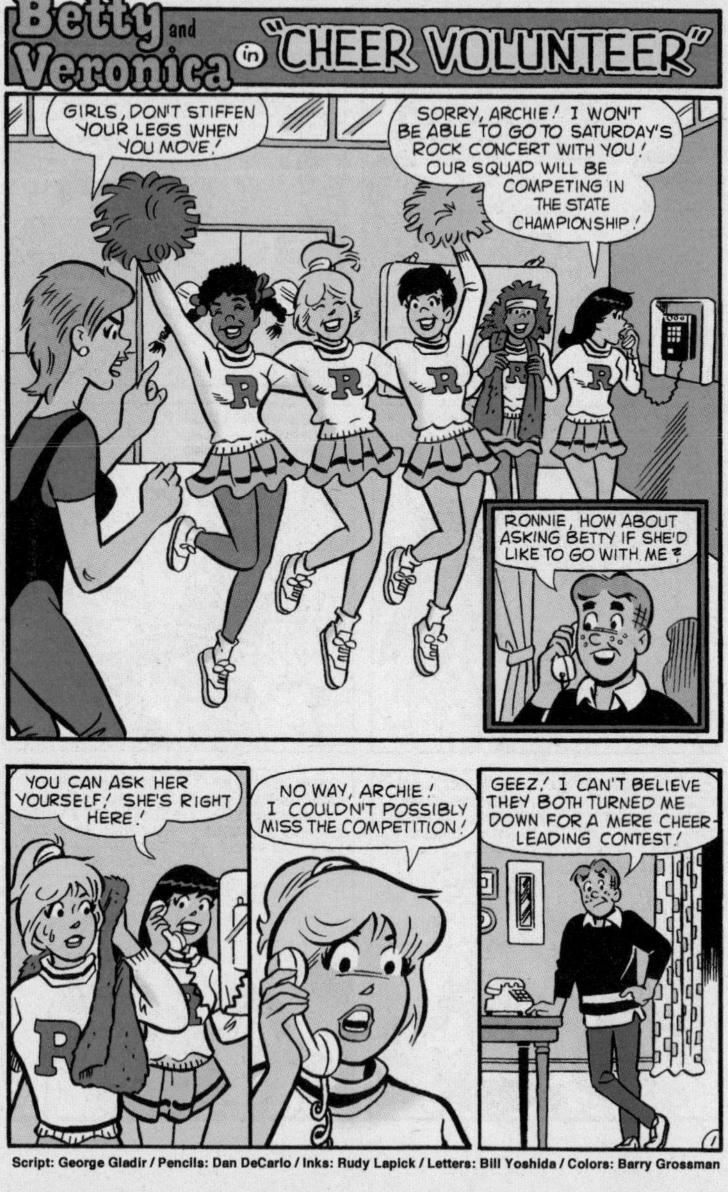
Betty and Veronica in "CHEER VOLUNTEER"
GIRLS, DON'T STIFFEN YOUR LEGS WHEN YOU MOVE!
SORRY, ARCHIE! I WON'T BE ABLE TO GO TO SATURDAY'S ROCK CONCERT WITH YOU! OUR SQUAD WILL BE COMPETING IN THE STATE CHAMPIONSHIP!
RONNIE, HOW ABOUT ASKING BETTY IF SHE'D LIKE TO GO WITH ME?
YOU CAN ASK HER YOURSELF! SHE'S RIGHT HERE!
NO WAY, ARCHIE! I COULDN'T POSSIBLY MISS THE COMPETITION!
GEEZ! I CAN'T BELIEVE THEY BOTH TURNED ME DOWN FOR A MERE CHEER-LEADING CONTEST!
1

Script: George Gladir / Pencils: Dan DeCarlo / Inks: Rudy Lapick / Letters: Bill Yoshida / Colors: Barry Grossman

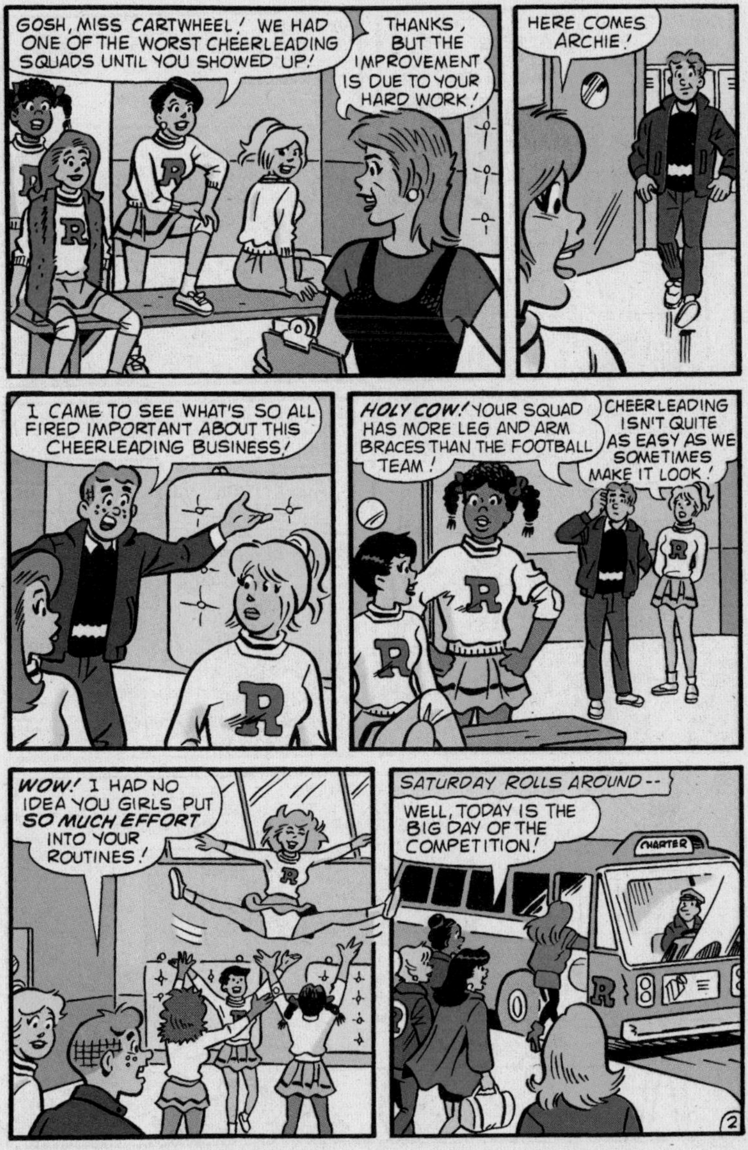
GOSH, MISS CARTWHEEL! WE HAD ONE OF THE WORST CHEERLEADING SQUADS UNTIL YOU SHOWED UP!
THANKS, BUT THE IMPROVEMENT IS DUE TO YOUR HARD WORK!
HERE COMES ARCHIE!
I CAME TO SEE WHAT'S SO ALL FIRED IMPORTANT ABOUT THIS CHEERLEADING BUSINESS!
HOLY COW! YOUR SQUAD HAS MORE LEG AND ARM BRACES THAN THE FOOTBALL TEAM!
CHEERLEADING ISN'T QUITE AS EASY AS WE SOMETIMES MAKE IT LOOK!
WOW! I HAD NO IDEA YOU GIRLS PUT SO MUCH EFFORT INTO YOUR ROUTINES!
SATURDAY ROLLS AROUND--
WELL, TODAY IS THE BIG DAY OF THE COMPETITION!
CHARTER
2

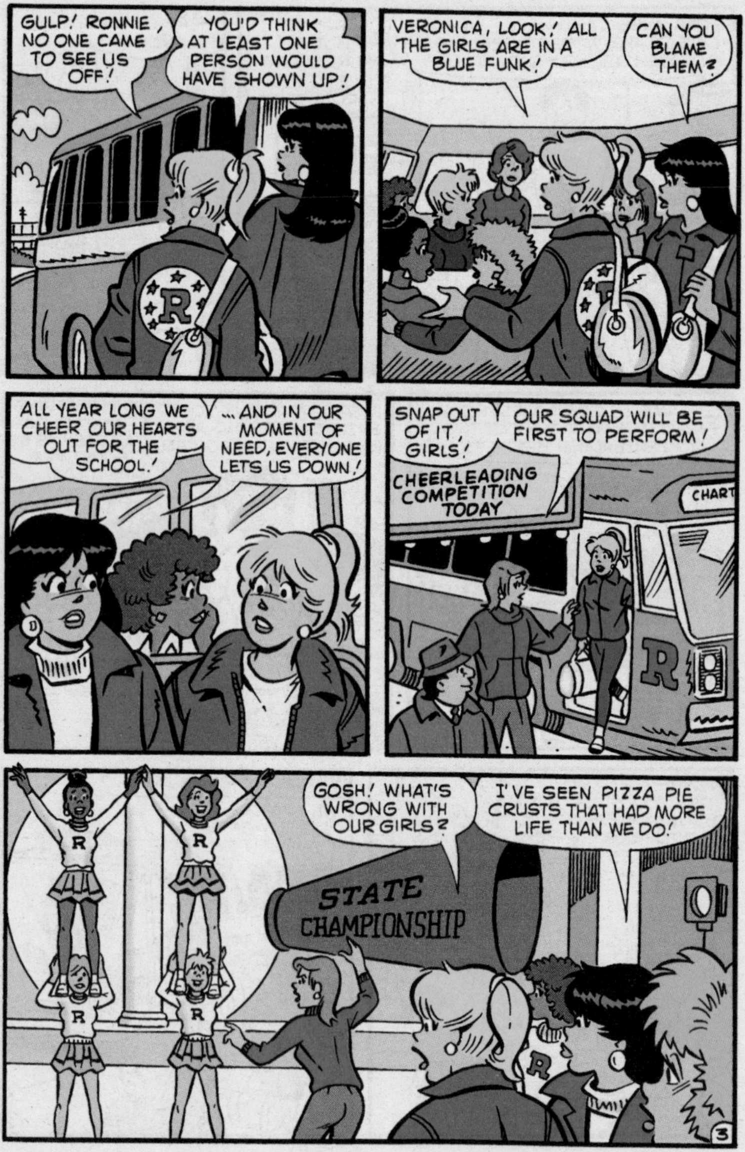
GULP! RONNIE, NO ONE CAME TO SEE US OFF!
YOU'D THINK AT LEAST ONE PERSON WOULD HAVE SHOWN UP!
VERONICA, LOOK! ALL THE GIRLS ARE IN A BLUE FUNK!
CAN YOU BLAME THEM?
ALL YEAR LONG WE CHEER OUR HEARTS OUT FOR THE SCHOOL!
...AND IN OUR MOMENT OF NEED, EVERYONE LETS US DOWN!
SNAP OUT OF IT, GIRLS!
OUR SQUAD WILL BE FIRST TO PERFORM!
CHEERLEADING COMPETITION TODAY
CHART
GOSH! WHAT'S WRONG WITH OUR GIRLS?
I'VE SEEN PIZZA PIE CRUSTS THAT HAD MORE LIFE THAN WE DO!
STATE CHAMPIONSHIP
3

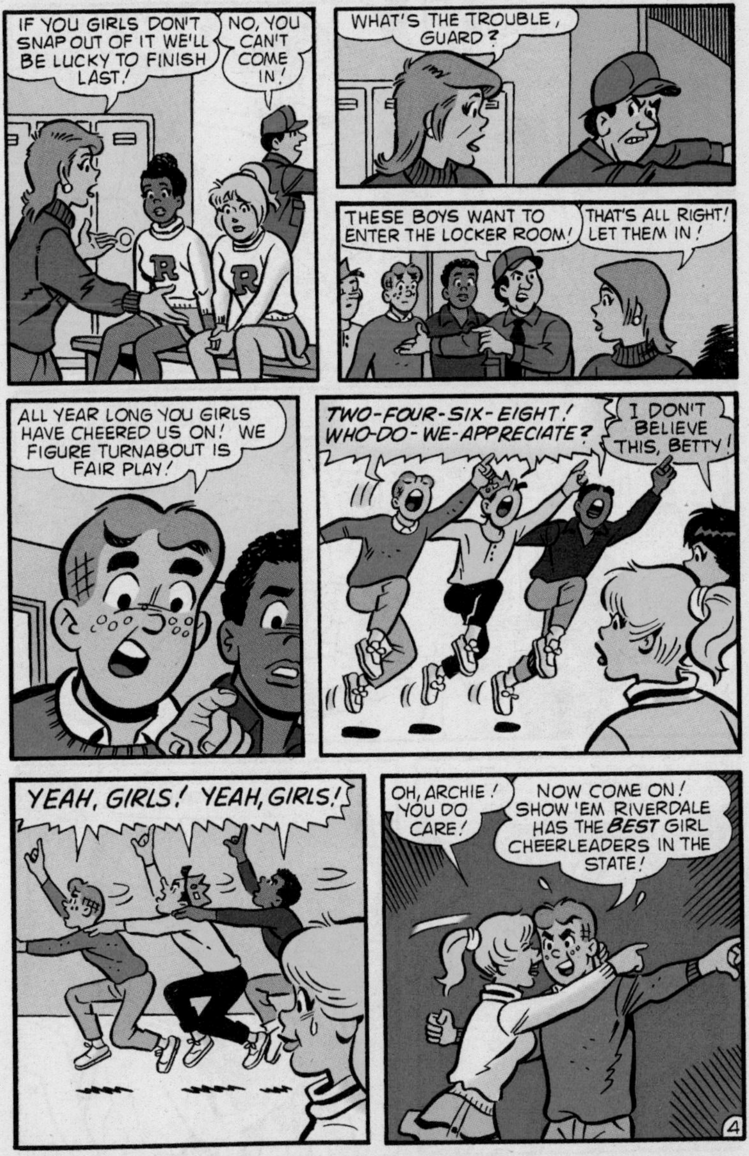

IF YOU GIRLS DON'T SNAP OUT OF IT WE'LL BE LUCKY TO FINISH LAST!
NO, YOU CAN'T COME IN!
WHAT'S THE TROUBLE, GUARD?
THESE BOYS WANT TO ENTER THE LOCKER ROOM!
THAT'S ALL RIGHT! LET THEM IN!
ALL YEAR LONG YOU GIRLS HAVE CHEERED US ON! WE FIGURE TURNABOUT IS FAIR PLAY!
TWO-FOUR-SIX-EIGHT! WHO-DO-WE-APPRECIATE?
I DON'T BELIEVE THIS, BETTY!
YEAH, GIRLS! YEAH, GIRLS!
OH, ARCHIE! YOU DO CARE!
NOW COME ON! SHOW 'EM RIVERDALE HAS THE BEST GIRL CHEERLEADERS IN THE STATE!
4

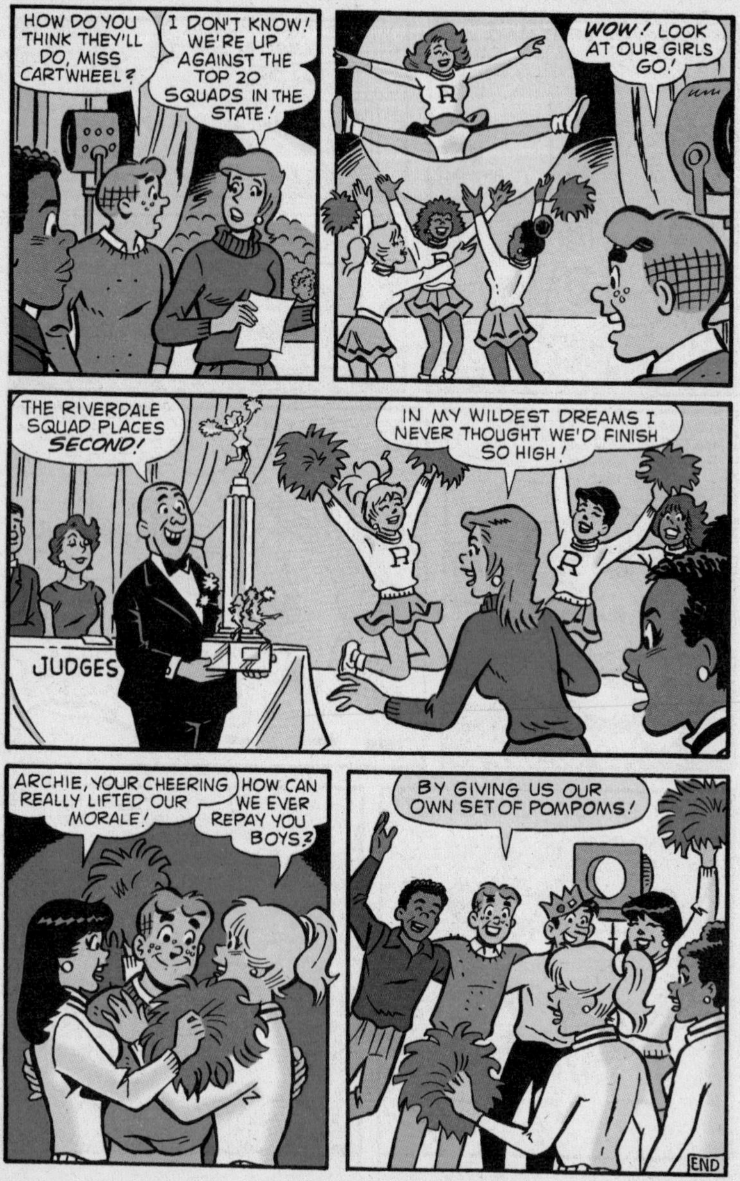
HOW DO YOU THINK THEY'LL DO, MISS CARTWHEEL?
I DON'T KNOW! WE'RE UP AGAINST THE TOP 20 SQUADS IN THE STATE!
WOW! LOOK AT OUR GIRLS GO!
THE RIVERDALE SQUAD PLACES SECOND!
JUDGES
IN MY WILDEST DREAMS I NEVER THOUGHT WE'D FINISH SO HIGH!
ARCHIE, YOUR CHEERING REALLY LIFTED OUR MORALE!
HOW CAN WE EVER REPAY YOU BOYS?
BY GIVING US OUR OWN SET OF POMPOMS!
END

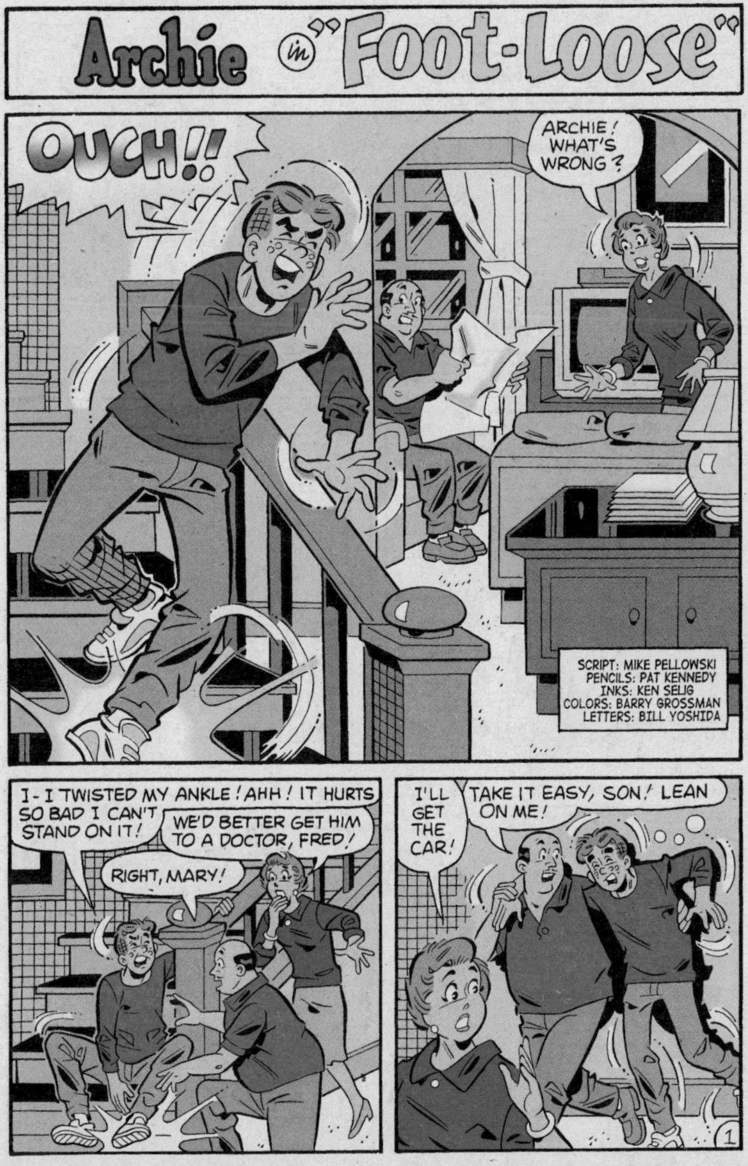
Archie in "Foot-Loose"
OUCH!!
ARCHIE! WHAT'S WRONG?
SCRIPT: MIKE PELLOWSKI
PENCILS: PAT KENNEDY
INKS: KEN SELIG
COLORS: BARRY GROSSMAN
LETTERS: BILL YOSHIDA
I-I TWISTED MY ANKLE! AHH! IT HURTS SO BAD I CAN'T STAND ON IT!
WE'D BETTER GET HIM TO A DOCTOR, FRED!
RIGHT, MARY!
TAKE IT EASY, SON! LEAN ON ME!
I'LL GET THE CAR!
1

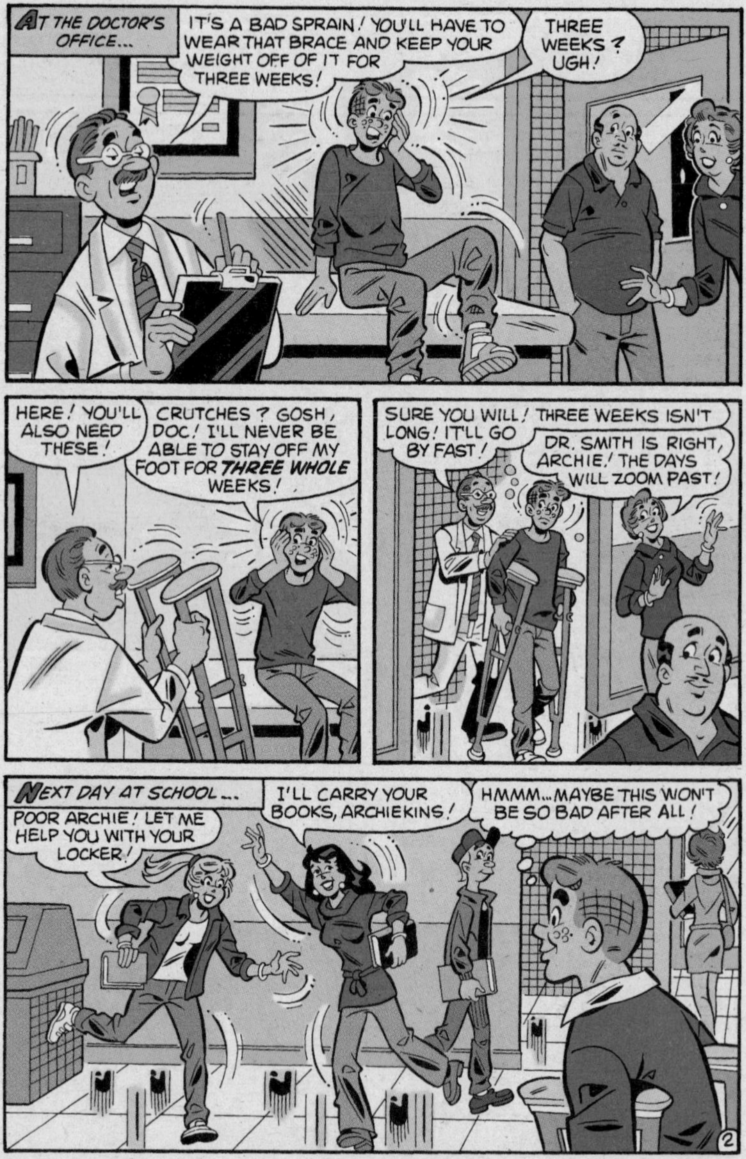
AT THE DOCTOR'S OFFICE...
IT'S A BAD SPRAIN! YOU'LL HAVE TO WEAR THAT BRACE AND KEEP YOUR WEIGHT OFF OF IT FOR THREE WEEKS!
THREE WEEKS? UGH!
HERE! YOU'LL ALSO NEED THESE!
CRUTCHES? GOSH, DOC! I'LL NEVER BE ABLE TO STAY OFF MY FOOT FOR THREE WHOLE WEEKS!
SURE YOU WILL! THREE WEEKS ISN'T LONG! IT'LL GO BY FAST!
DR. SMITH IS RIGHT, ARCHIE! THE DAYS WILL ZOOM PAST!
NEXT DAY AT SCHOOL...
POOR ARCHIE! LET ME HELP YOU WITH YOUR LOCKER!
I'LL CARRY YOUR BOOKS, ARCHIEKINS!
HMMM...MAYBE THIS WON'T BE SO BAD AFTER ALL!
2

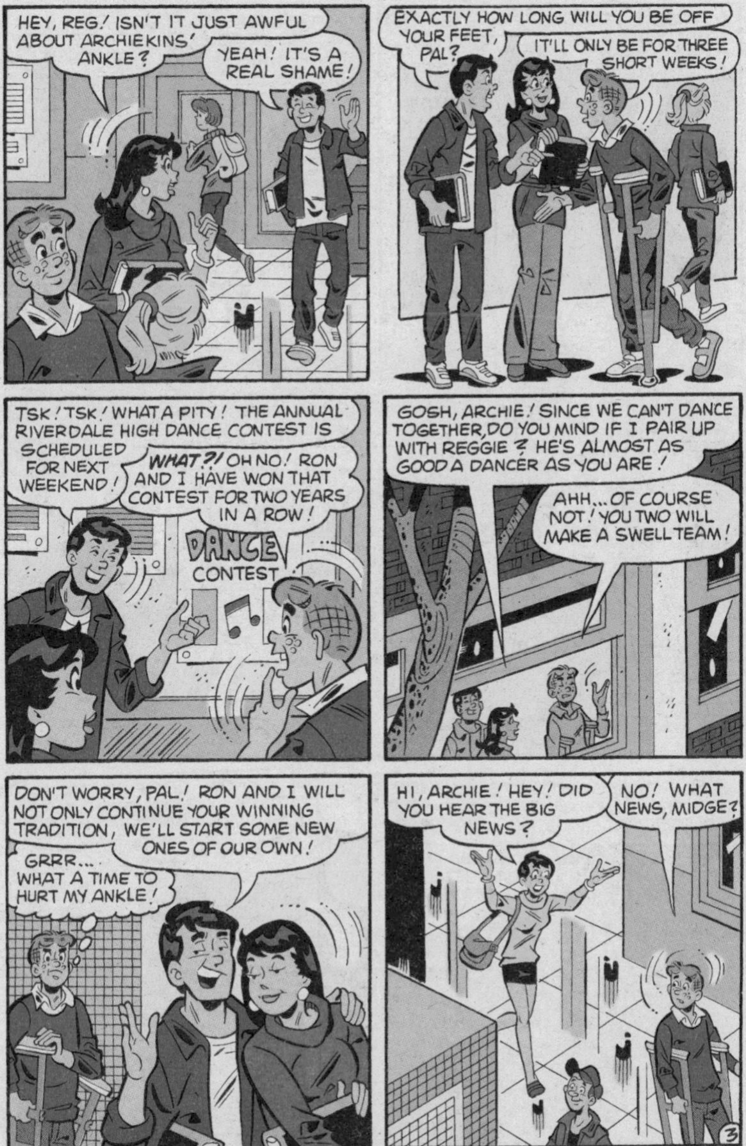
HEY, REG! ISN'T IT JUST AWFUL ABOUT ARCHIEKINS' ANKLE?
YEAH! IT'S A REAL SHAME!
EXACTLY HOW LONG WILL YOU BE OFF YOUR FEET, PAL?
IT'LL ONLY BE FOR THREE SHORT WEEKS!
TSK! TSK! WHAT A PITY! THE ANNUAL RIVERDALE HIGH DANCE CONTEST IS SCHEDULED FOR NEXT WEEKEND!
WHAT?! OH NO! RON AND I HAVE WON THAT CONTEST FOR TWO YEARS IN A ROW!
DANCE CONTEST
GOSH, ARCHIE! SINCE WE CAN'T DANCE TOGETHER, DO YOU MIND IF I PAIR UP WITH REGGIE? HE'S ALMOST AS GOOD A DANCER AS YOU ARE!
AHH... OF COURSE NOT! YOU TWO WILL MAKE A SWELL TEAM!
DON'T WORRY, PAL! RON AND I WILL NOT ONLY CONTINUE YOUR WINNING TRADITION, WE'LL START SOME NEW ONES OF OUR OWN!
GRRR... WHAT A TIME TO HURT MY ANKLE!
HI, ARCHIE! HEY! DID YOU HEAR THE BIG NEWS?
NO! WHAT NEWS, MIDGE?
3

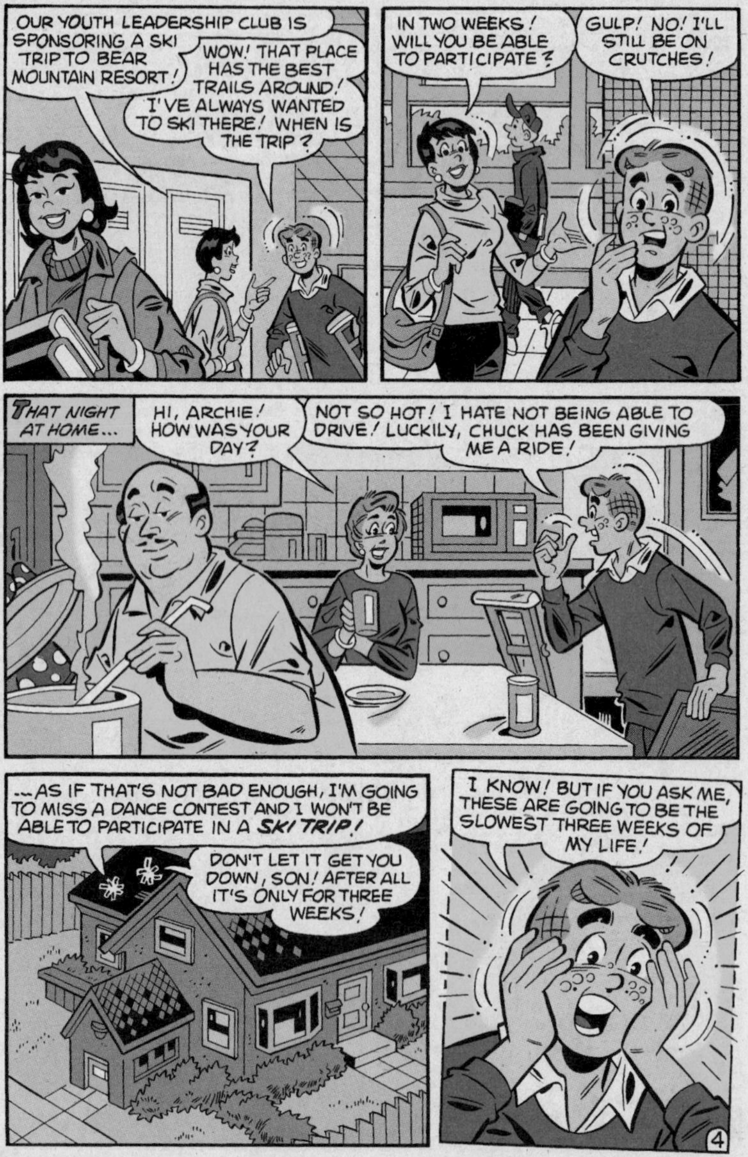
OUR YOUTH LEADERSHIP CLUB IS SPONSORING A SKI TRIP TO BEAR MOUNTAIN RESORT!
WOW! THAT PLACE HAS THE BEST TRAILS AROUND! I'VE ALWAYS WANTED TO SKI THERE! WHEN IS THE TRIP?
IN TWO WEEKS! WILL YOU BE ABLE TO PARTICIPATE?
GULP! NO! I'LL STILL BE ON CRUTCHES!
THAT NIGHT AT HOME...
HI, ARCHIE! HOW WAS YOUR DAY?
NOT SO HOT! I HATE NOT BEING ABLE TO DRIVE! LUCKILY, CHUCK HAS BEEN GIVING ME A RIDE!
...AS IF THAT'S NOT BAD ENOUGH, I'M GOING TO MISS A DANCE CONTEST AND I WON'T BE ABLE TO PARTICIPATE IN A SKI TRIP!
DON'T LET IT GET YOU DOWN, SON! AFTER ALL IT'S ONLY FOR THREE WEEKS!
I KNOW! BUT IF YOU ASK ME, THESE ARE GOING TO BE THE SLOWEST THREE WEEKS OF MY LIFE!
4

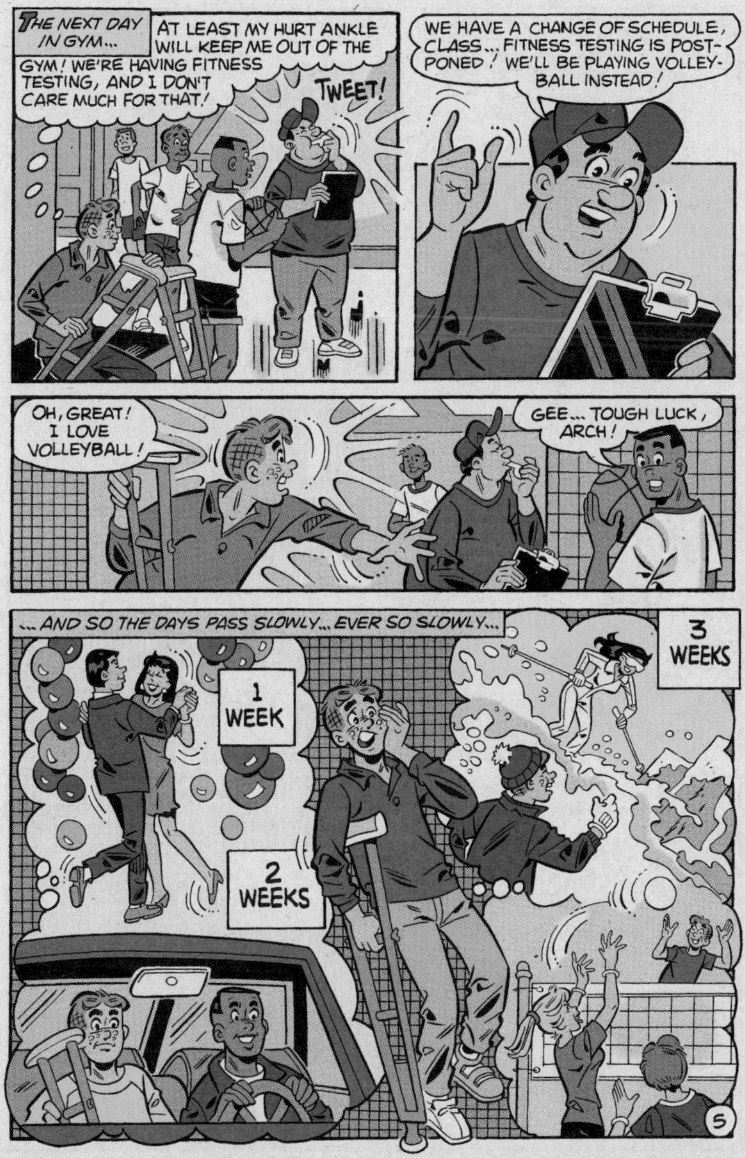
THE NEXT DAY IN GYM...
AT LEAST MY HURT ANKLE WILL KEEP ME OUT OF THE GYM! WE'RE HAVING FITNESS TESTING, AND I DON'T CARE MUCH FOR THAT!
TWEET!
WE HAVE A CHANGE OF SCHEDULE, CLASS... FITNESS TESTING IS POSTPONED! WE'LL BE PLAYING VOLLEYBALL INSTEAD!
OH, GREAT! I LOVE VOLLEYBALL!
GEE... TOUGH LUCK, ARCH!
...AND SO THE DAYS PASS SLOWLY... EVER SO SLOWLY...
1 WEEK
2 WEEKS
3 WEEKS
5

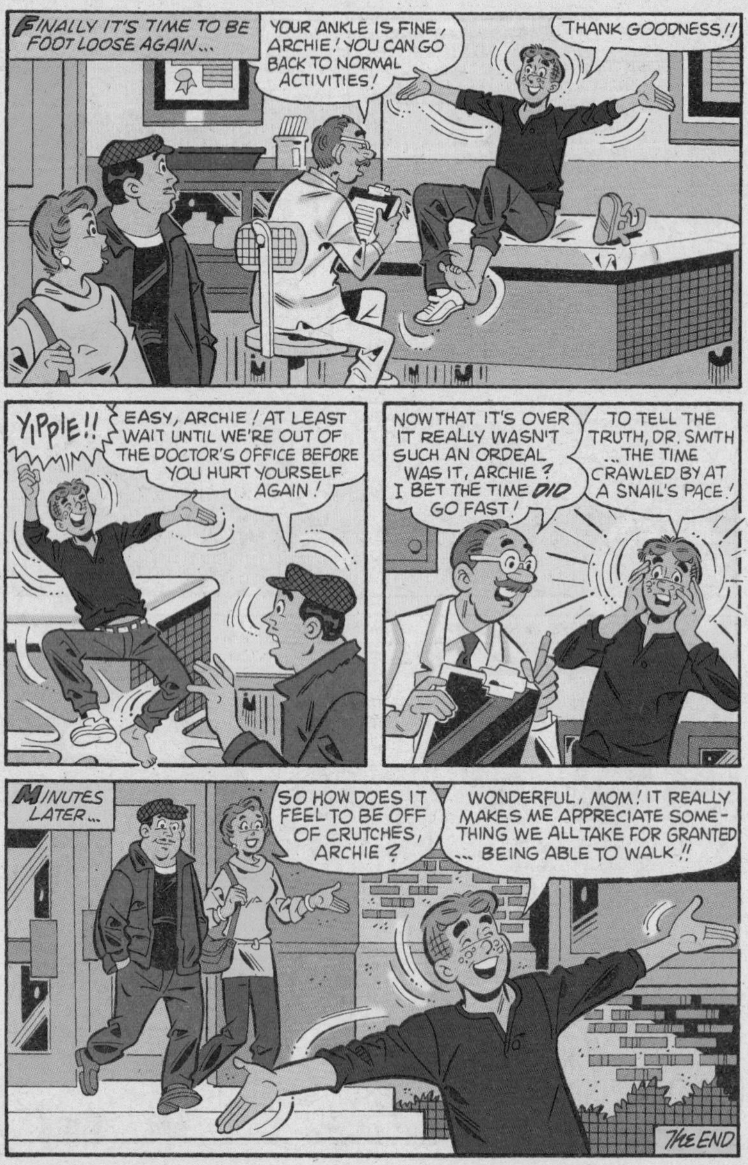
FINALLY IT'S TIME TO BE FOOT LOOSE AGAIN...
YOUR ANKLE IS FINE, ARCHIE! YOU CAN GO BACK TO NORMAL ACTIVITIES!
THANK GOODNESS!!
YIPPIE!!
EASY, ARCHIE! AT LEAST WAIT UNTIL WE'RE OUT OF THE DOCTOR'S OFFICE BEFORE YOU HURT YOURSELF AGAIN!
NOW THAT IT'S OVER IT REALLY WASN'T SUCH AN ORDEAL WAS IT, ARCHIE? I BET THE TIME DID GO FAST!
TO TELL THE TRUTH, DR. SMITH ...THE TIME CRAWLED BY AT A SNAIL'S PACE!
MINUTES LATER...
SO HOW DOES IT FEEL TO BE OFF OF CRUTCHES, ARCHIE?
WONDERFUL, MOM! IT REALLY MAKES ME APPRECIATE SOME-THING WE ALL TAKE FOR GRANTED ... BEING ABLE TO WALK!!
THE END

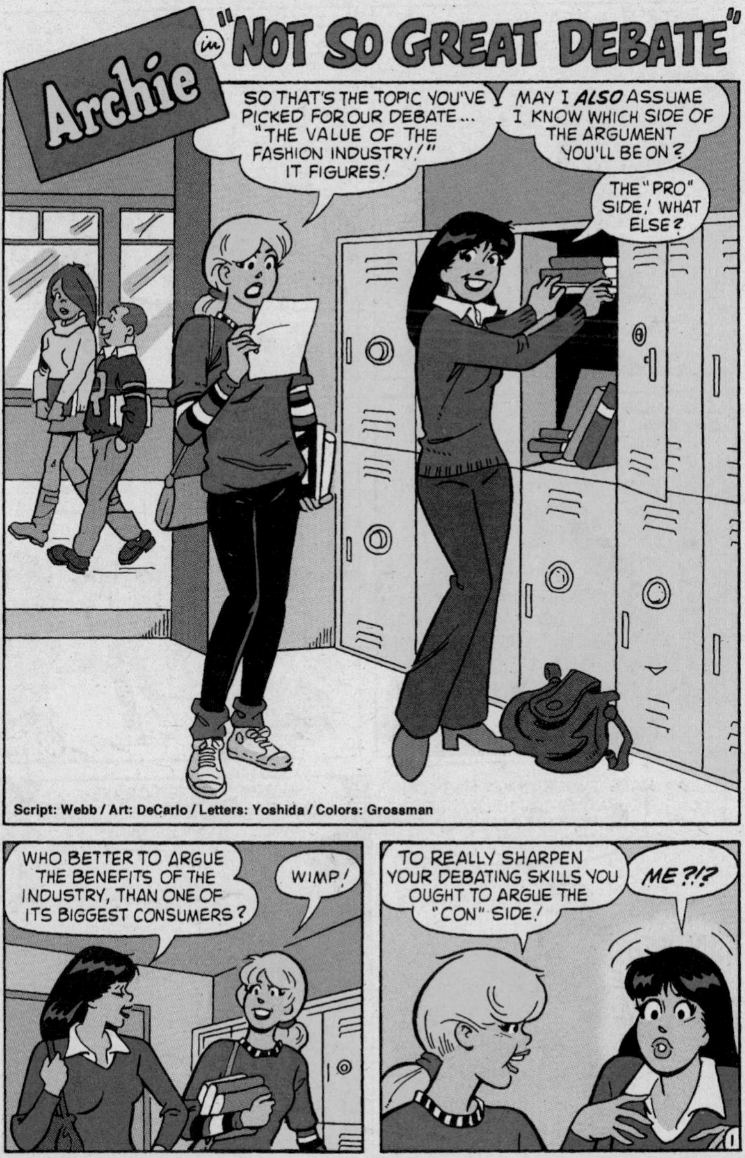
Archie in "NOT SO GREAT DEBATE"
SO THAT'S THE TOPIC YOU'VE PICKED FOR OUR DEBATE... "THE VALUE OF THE FASHION INDUSTRY!" IT FIGURES!
MAY I ALSO ASSUME I KNOW WHICH SIDE OF THE ARGUMENT YOU'LL BE ON?
THE "PRO" SIDE! WHAT ELSE?
Script: Webb / Art: DeCarlo / Letters: Yoshida / Colors: Grossman
WHO BETTER TO ARGUE THE BENEFITS OF THE INDUSTRY, THAN ONE OF ITS BIGGEST CONSUMERS?
WIMP!
TO REALLY SHARPEN YOUR DEBATING SKILLS YOU OUGHT TO ARGUE THE "CON" SIDE!
ME?!?
1

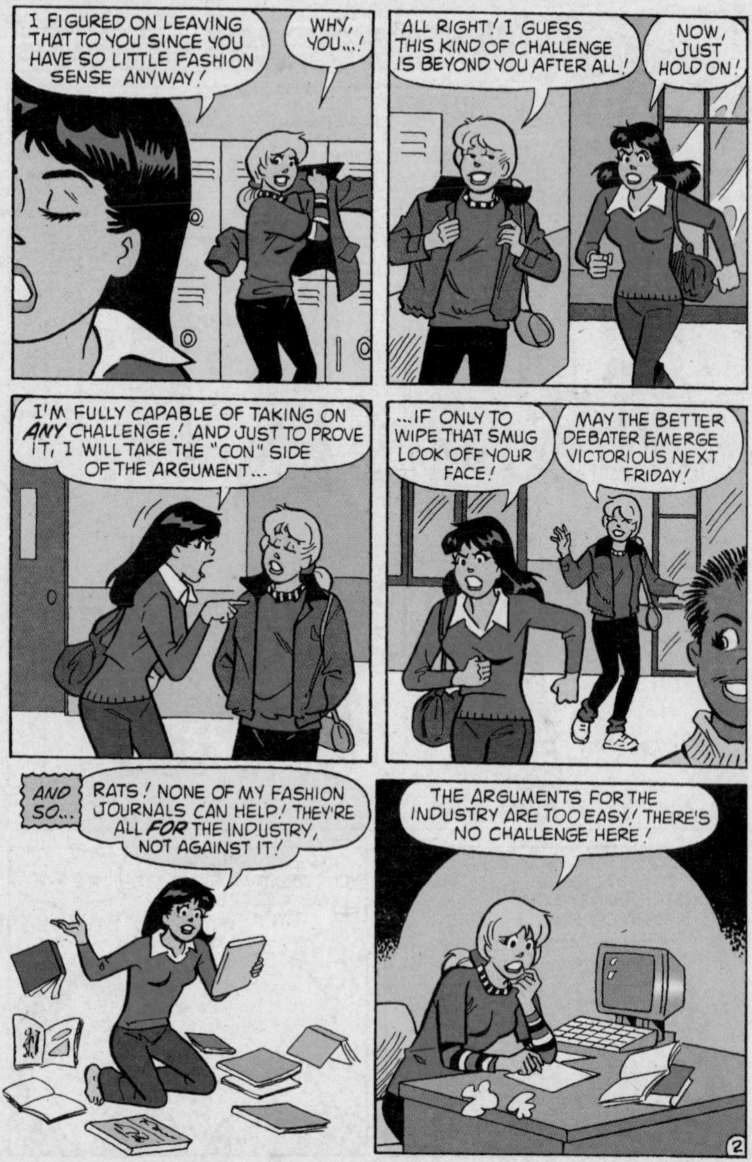
I FIGURED ON LEAVING THAT TO YOU SINCE YOU HAVE SO LITTLE FASHION SENSE ANYWAY!
WHY, YOU...!
ALL RIGHT! I GUESS THIS KIND OF CHALLENGE IS BEYOND YOU AFTER ALL!
NOW, JUST HOLD ON!
I'M FULLY CAPABLE OF TAKING ON ANY CHALLENGE! AND JUST TO PROVE IT, I WILL TAKE THE "CON" SIDE OF THE ARGUMENT...
...IF ONLY TO WIPE THAT SMUG LOOK OFF YOUR FACE!
MAY THE BETTER DEBATER EMERGE VICTORIOUS NEXT FRIDAY!
AND SO...
RATS! NONE OF MY FASHION JOURNALS CAN HELP! THEY'RE ALL FOR THE INDUSTRY, NOT AGAINST IT!
THE ARGUMENTS FOR THE INDUSTRY ARE TOO EASY! THERE'S NO CHALLENGE HERE!
2

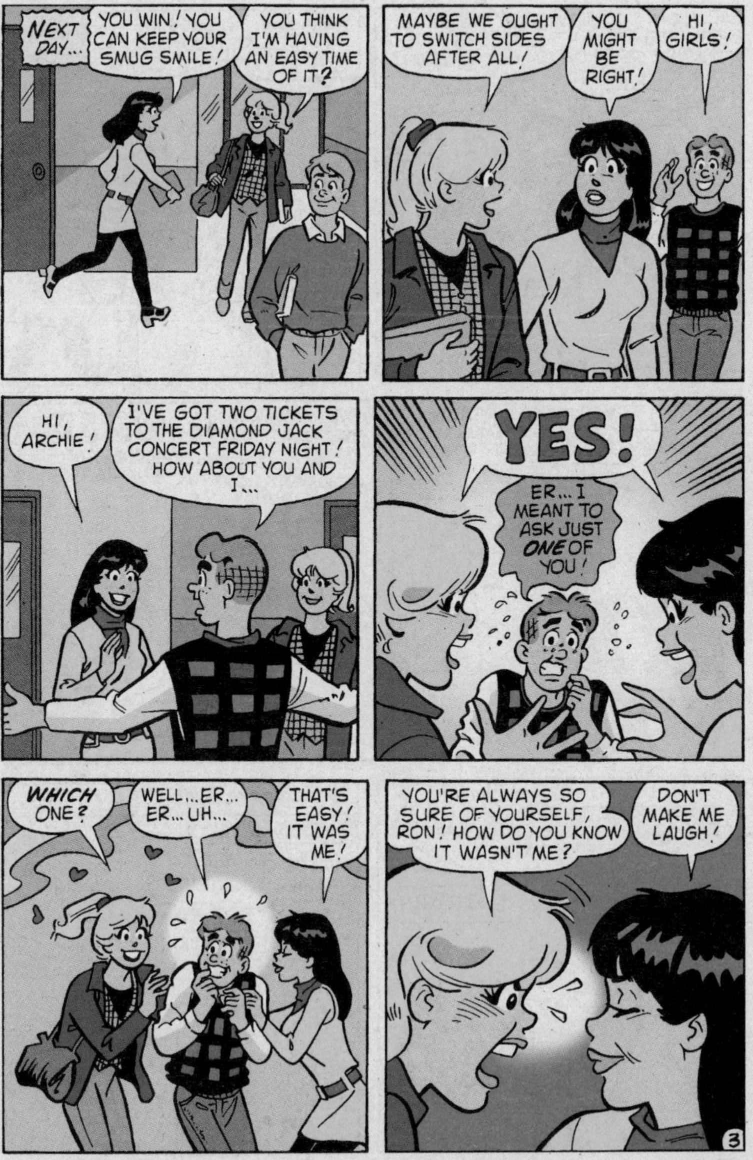
NEXT DAY...
YOU WIN! YOU CAN KEEP YOUR SMUG SMILE!
YOU THINK I'M HAVING AN EASY TIME OF IT?
MAYBE WE OUGHT TO SWITCH SIDES AFTER ALL!
YOU MIGHT BE RIGHT!
HI, GIRLS!
HI, ARCHIE!
I'VE GOT TWO TICKETS TO THE DIAMOND JACK CONCERT FRIDAY NIGHT! HOW ABOUT YOU AND I...
YES!
ER... I MEANT TO ASK JUST ONE OF YOU!
WHICH ONE?
WELL...ER... ER...UH...
THAT'S EASY! IT WAS ME!
YOU'RE ALWAYS SO SURE OF YOURSELF, RON! HOW DO YOU KNOW IT WASN'T ME?
DON'T MAKE ME LAUGH!
3

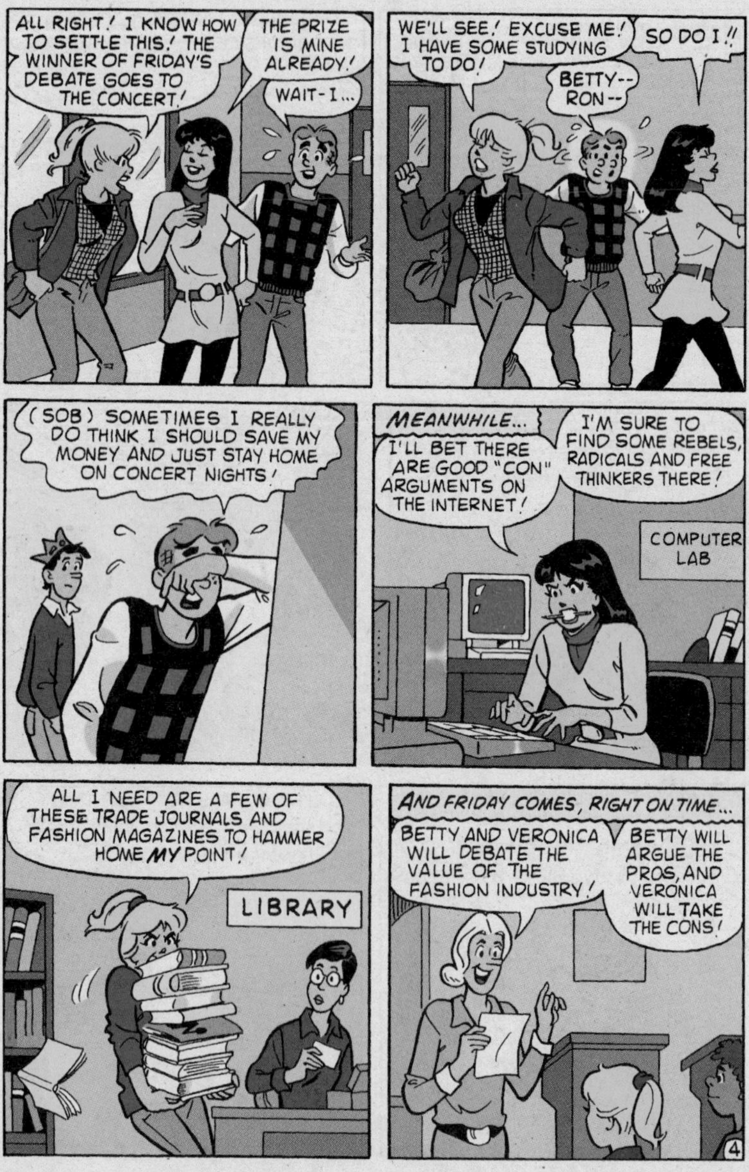
ALL RIGHT! I KNOW HOW TO SETTLE THIS! THE WINNER OF FRIDAY'S DEBATE GOES TO THE CONCERT!
THE PRIZE IS MINE ALREADY!
WAIT-I...
WE'LL SEE! EXCUSE ME! I HAVE SOME STUDYING TO DO!
BETTY-- RON--
SO DO I!!
(SOB) SOMETIMES I REALLY DO THINK I SHOULD SAVE MY MONEY AND JUST STAY HOME ON CONCERT NIGHTS!
MEANWHILE...
I'LL BET THERE ARE GOOD "CON" ARGUMENTS ON THE INTERNET!
I'M SURE TO FIND SOME REBELS, RADICALS AND FREE THINKERS THERE!
COMPUTER LAB
ALL I NEED ARE A FEW OF THESE TRADE JOURNALS AND FASHION MAGAZINES TO HAMMER HOME MY POINT!
LIBRARY
AND FRIDAY COMES, RIGHT ON TIME...
BETTY AND VERONICA WILL DEBATE THE VALUE OF THE FASHION INDUSTRY!
BETTY WILL ARGUE THE PROS, AND VERONICA WILL TAKE THE CONS!
4

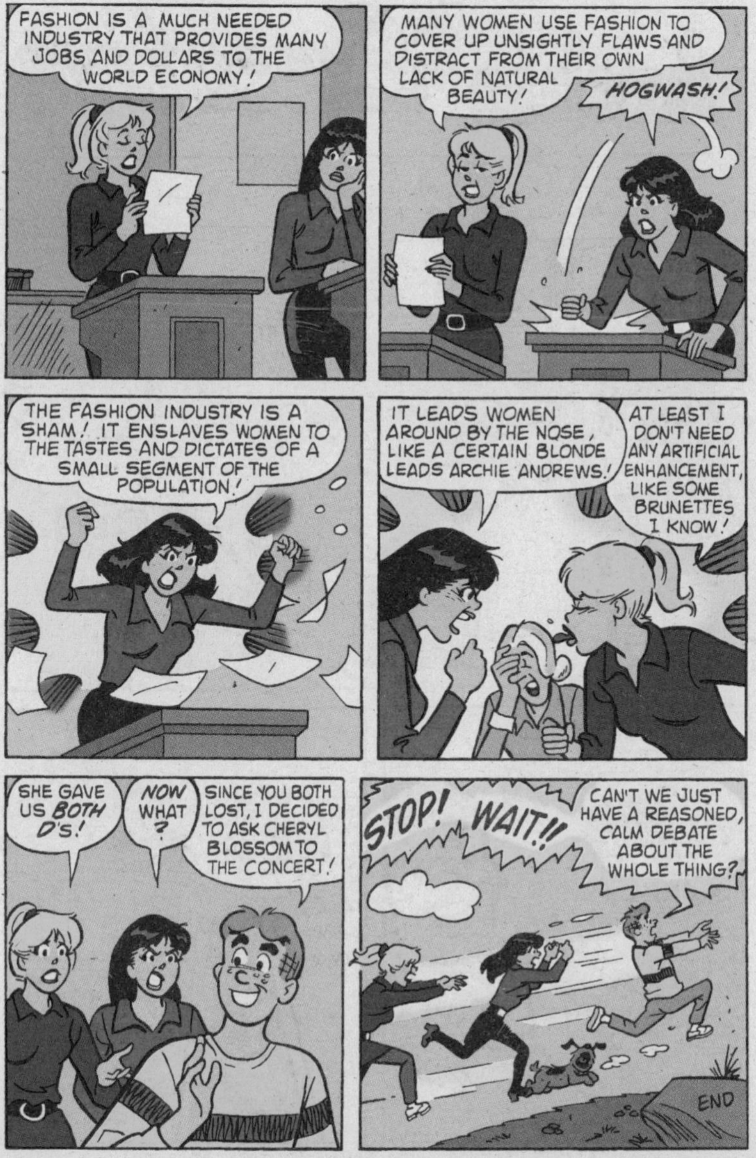
FASHION IS A MUCH NEEDED INDUSTRY THAT PROVIDES MANY JOBS AND DOLLARS TO THE WORLD ECONOMY!
MANY WOMEN USE FASHION TO COVER UP UNSIGHTLY FLAWS AND DISTRACT FROM THEIR OWN LACK OF NATURAL BEAUTY!
HOGWASH!
THE FASHION INDUSTRY IS A SHAM! IT ENSLAVES WOMEN TO THE TASTES AND DICTATES OF A SMALL SEGMENT OF THE POPULATION!
IT LEADS WOMEN AROUND BY THE NOSE, LIKE A CERTAIN BLONDE LEADS ARCHIE ANDREWS!
AT LEAST I DON'T NEED ANY ARTIFICIAL ENHANCEMENT, LIKE SOME BRUNETTES I KNOW!
SHE GAVE US BOTH D's!
NOW WHAT?
SINCE YOU BOTH LOST, I DECIDED TO ASK CHERYL BLOSSOM TO THE CONCERT!
STOP!
WAIT!!
CAN'T WE JUST HAVE A REASONED, CALM DEBATE ABOUT THE WHOLE THING?
END

Archie *The* Executive

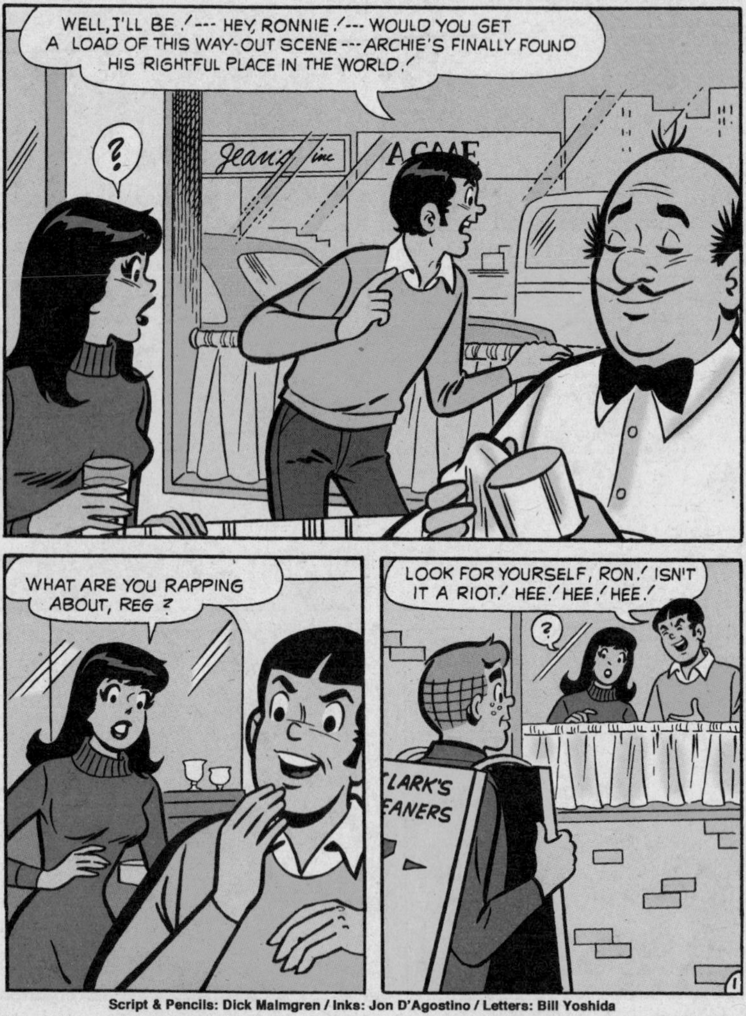

WELL, I'LL BE!--- HEY, RONNIE!--- WOULD YOU GET A LOAD OF THIS WAY-OUT SCENE --- ARCHIE'S FINALLY FOUND HIS RIGHTFUL PLACE IN THE WORLD!
?
Jean's Inc
ACME
WHAT ARE YOU RAPPING ABOUT, REG?
LOOK FOR YOURSELF, RON! ISN'T IT A RIOT! HEE! HEE! HEE!
?
LARK'S
EANERS
1

Script & Pencils: Dick Malmgren / Inks: Jon D'Agostino / Letters: Bill Yoshida

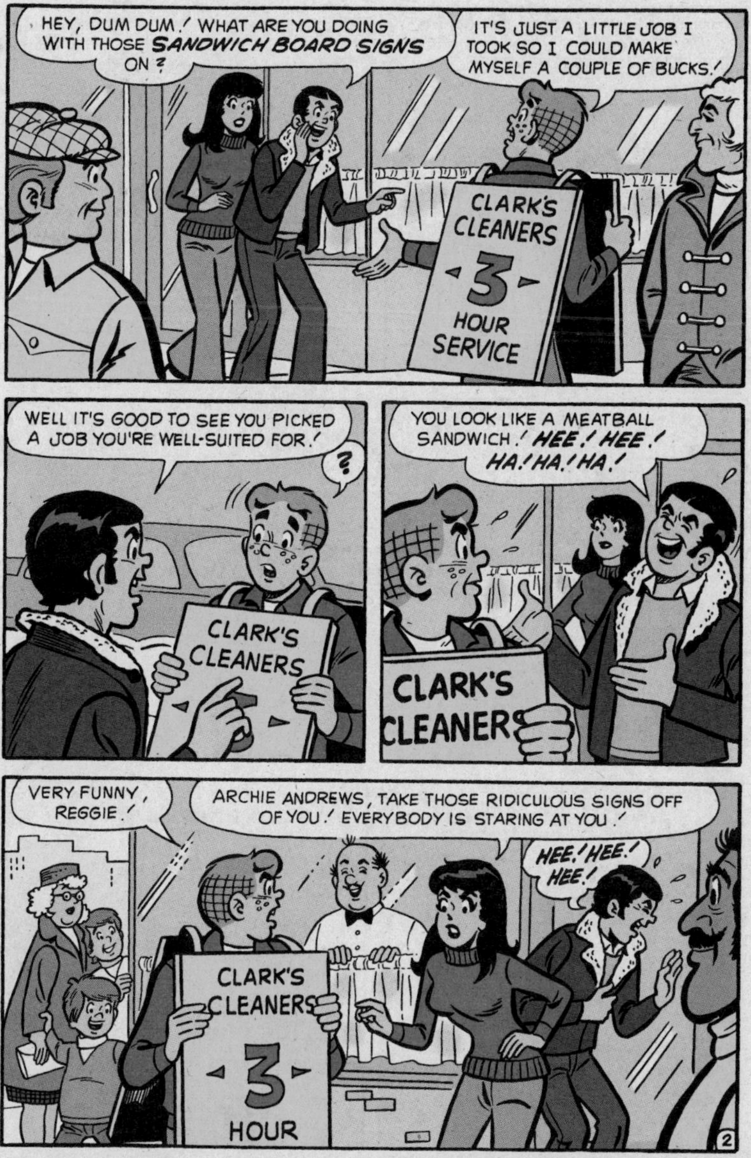
HEY, DUM DUM.! WHAT ARE YOU DOING WITH THOSE SANDWICH BOARD SIGNS ON ?
IT'S JUST A LITTLE JOB I TOOK SO I COULD MAKE MYSELF A COUPLE OF BUCKS.!
CLARK'S CLEANERS 3 HOUR SERVICE
WELL IT'S GOOD TO SEE YOU PICKED A JOB YOU'RE WELL-SUITED FOR.!
?
CLARK'S CLEANERS
YOU LOOK LIKE A MEATBALL SANDWICH.! HEE.! HEE.! HA.! HA.! HA.!
CLARK'S CLEANERS
VERY FUNNY, REGGIE.!
ARCHIE ANDREWS, TAKE THOSE RIDICULOUS SIGNS OFF OF YOU.! EVERYBODY IS STARING AT YOU.!
HEE.! HEE.! HEE.!
CLARK'S CLEANERS 3 HOUR
2

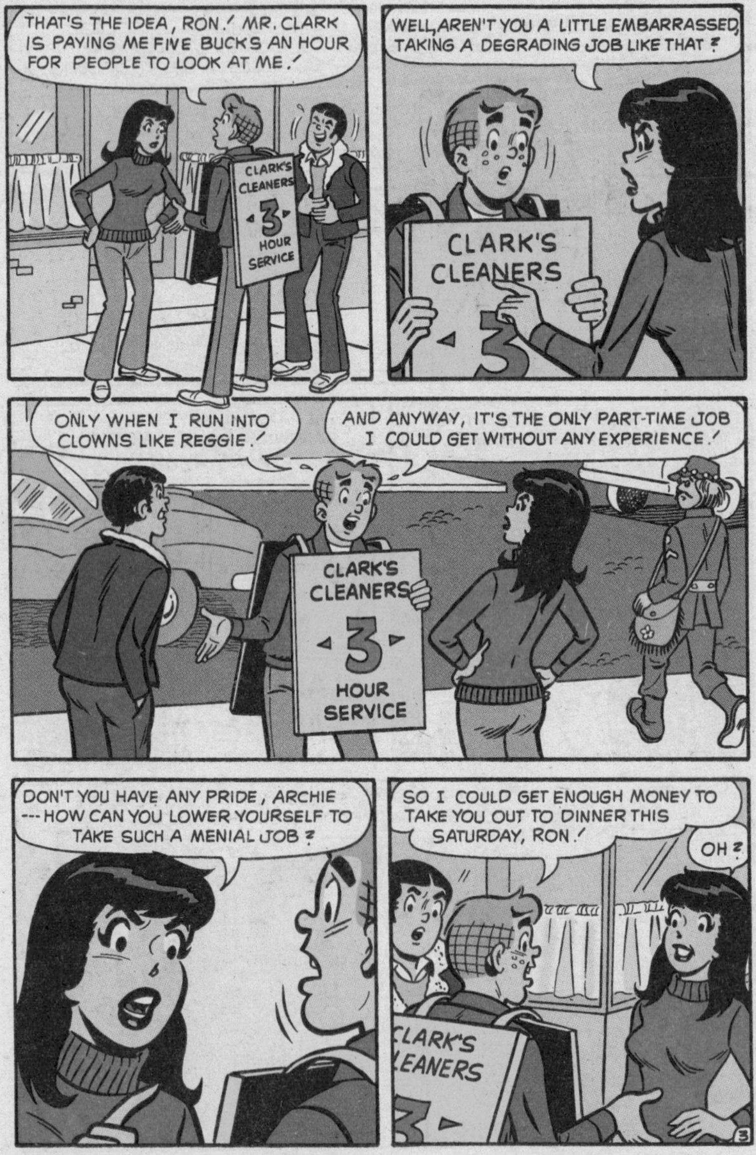
THAT'S THE IDEA, RON.! MR. CLARK IS PAYING ME FIVE BUCKS AN HOUR FOR PEOPLE TO LOOK AT ME.!
CLARK'S CLEANERS 3 HOUR SERVICE
WELL, AREN'T YOU A LITTLE EMBARRASSED, TAKING A DEGRADING JOB LIKE THAT?
CLARK'S CLEANERS 3
ONLY WHEN I RUN INTO CLOWNS LIKE REGGIE.!
AND ANYWAY, IT'S THE ONLY PART-TIME JOB I COULD GET WITHOUT ANY EXPERIENCE.!
CLARK'S CLEANERS 3 HOUR SERVICE
DON'T YOU HAVE ANY PRIDE, ARCHIE --- HOW CAN YOU LOWER YOURSELF TO TAKE SUCH A MENIAL JOB?
SO I COULD GET ENOUGH MONEY TO TAKE YOU OUT TO DINNER THIS SATURDAY, RON.!
OH?
LARK'S LEANERS 3
3

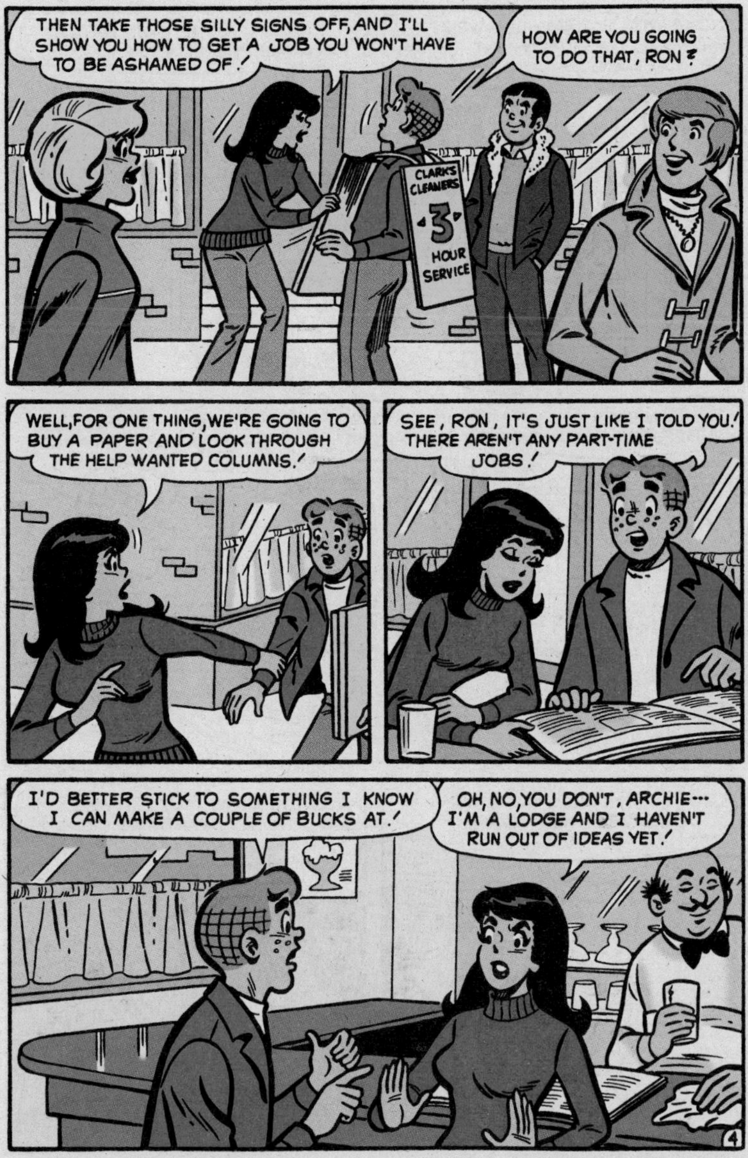
THEN TAKE THOSE SILLY SIGNS OFF, AND I'LL SHOW YOU HOW TO GET A JOB YOU WON'T HAVE TO BE ASHAMED OF!
HOW ARE YOU GOING TO DO THAT, RON?
CLARK'S CLEANERS 3 HOUR SERVICE
WELL, FOR ONE THING, WE'RE GOING TO BUY A PAPER AND LOOK THROUGH THE HELP WANTED COLUMNS!
SEE, RON, IT'S JUST LIKE I TOLD YOU! THERE AREN'T ANY PART-TIME JOBS!
I'D BETTER STICK TO SOMETHING I KNOW I CAN MAKE A COUPLE OF BUCKS AT!
OH, NO, YOU DON'T, ARCHIE--- I'M A LODGE AND I HAVEN'T RUN OUT OF IDEAS YET!
4

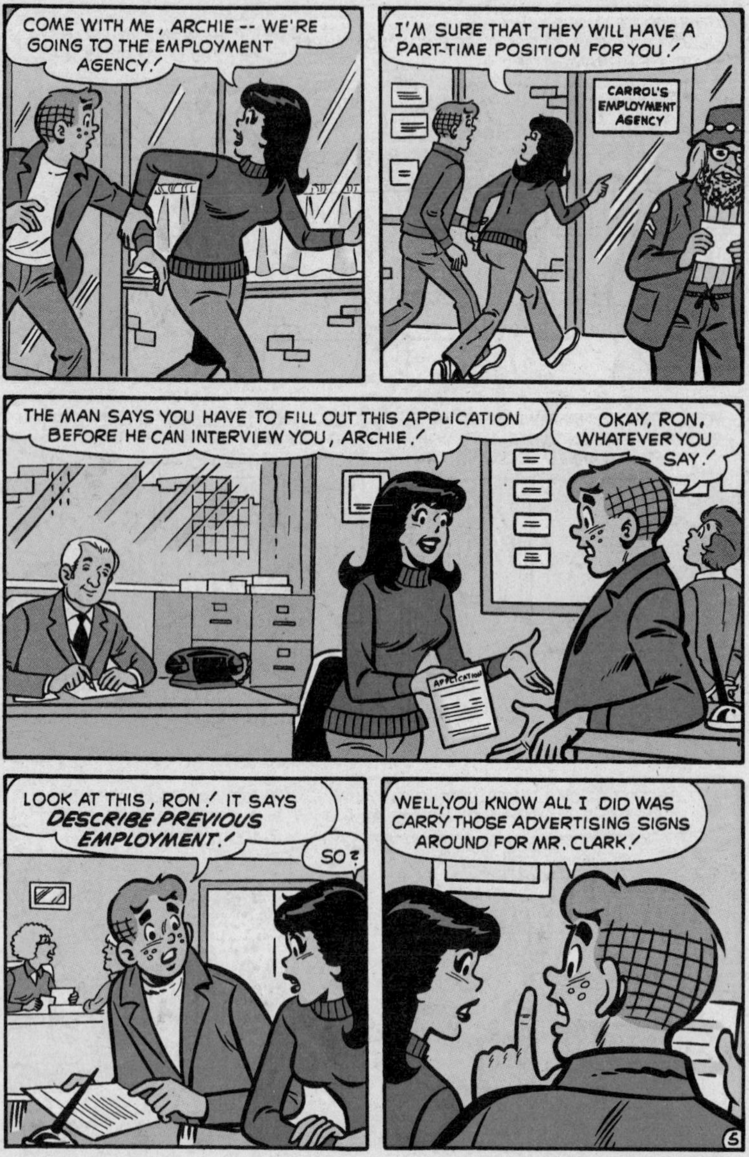
COME WITH ME, ARCHIE -- WE'RE GOING TO THE EMPLOYMENT AGENCY.!
I'M SURE THAT THEY WILL HAVE A PART-TIME POSITION FOR YOU.!
CARROL'S EMPLOYMENT AGENCY
THE MAN SAYS YOU HAVE TO FILL OUT THIS APPLICATION BEFORE HE CAN INTERVIEW YOU, ARCHIE.!
OKAY, RON, WHATEVER YOU SAY.!
APPLICATION
LOOK AT THIS, RON.! IT SAYS *DESCRIBE PREVIOUS EMPLOYMENT*.!
SO?
WELL, YOU KNOW ALL I DID WAS CARRY THOSE ADVERTISING SIGNS AROUND FOR MR. CLARK.!
5

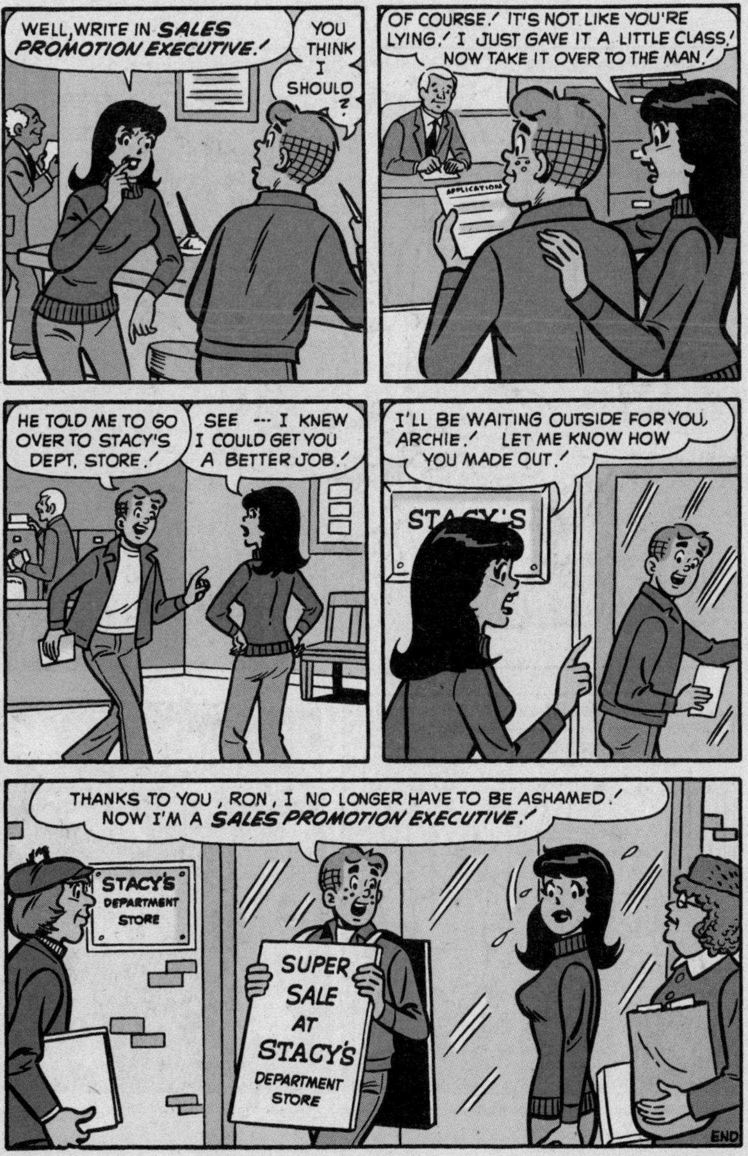
WELL, WRITE IN SALES PROMOTION EXECUTIVE!
YOU THINK I SHOULD?
OF COURSE! IT'S NOT LIKE YOU'RE LYING! I JUST GAVE IT A LITTLE CLASS! NOW TAKE IT OVER TO THE MAN!
APPLICATION
HE TOLD ME TO GO OVER TO STACY'S DEPT. STORE!
SEE --- I KNEW I COULD GET YOU A BETTER JOB!
I'LL BE WAITING OUTSIDE FOR YOU, ARCHIE! LET ME KNOW HOW YOU MADE OUT!
THANKS TO YOU, RON, I NO LONGER HAVE TO BE ASHAMED! NOW I'M A SALES PROMOTION EXECUTIVE!
STACY'S DEPARTMENT STORE
SUPER SALE AT STACY'S DEPARTMENT STORE
END

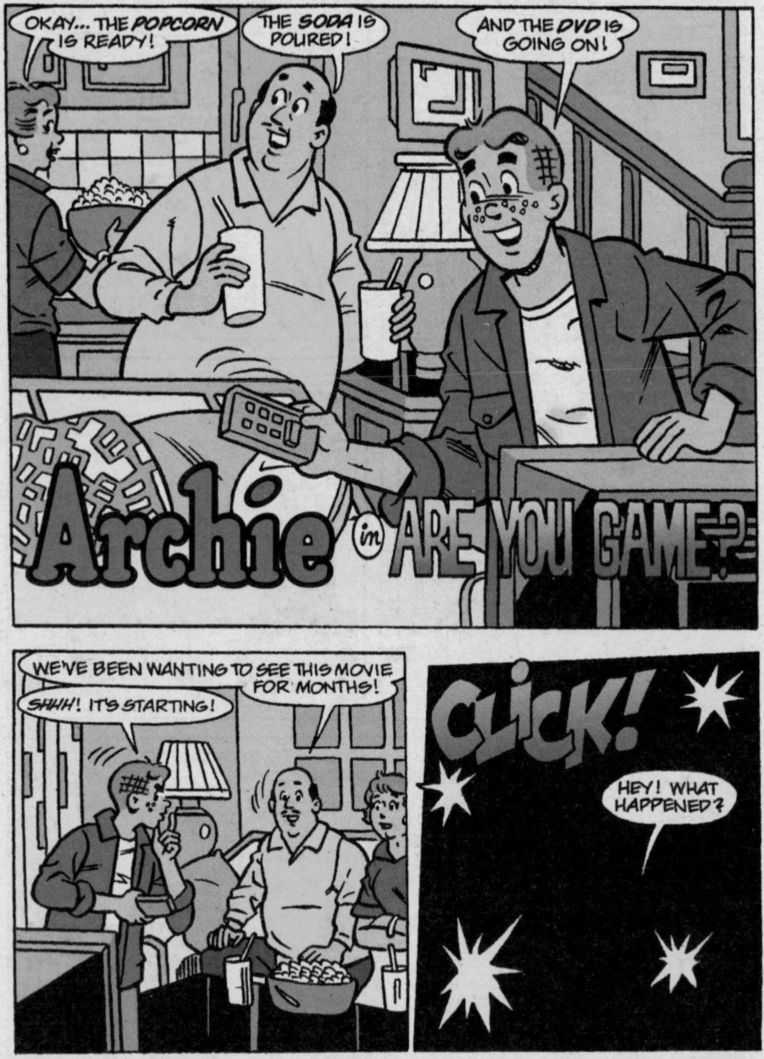
OKAY... THE POPCORN IS READY!
THE SODA IS POURED!
AND THE DVD IS GOING ON!
Archie in ARE YOU GAME?
WE'VE BEEN WANTING TO SEE THIS MOVIE FOR MONTHS!
SHHH! IT'S STARTING!
CLICK!
HEY! WHAT HAPPENED?

Script: Bill Golliher / Pencils: Tim Kennedy / Inks: Rudy Lapick / Letters: Vickie Williams / Colors: Barry Grossman

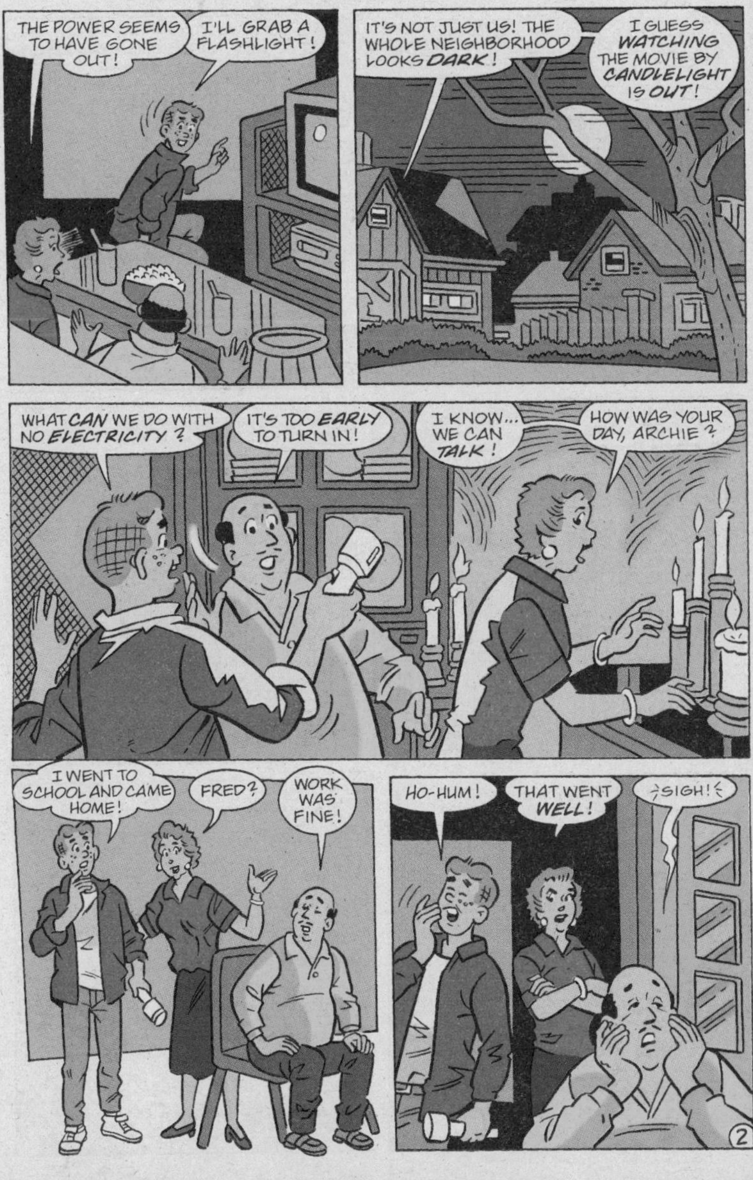
THE POWER SEEMS TO HAVE GONE OUT!
I'LL GRAB A FLASHLIGHT!
IT'S NOT JUST US! THE WHOLE NEIGHBORHOOD LOOKS DARK!
I GUESS WATCHING THE MOVIE BY CANDLELIGHT IS OUT!
WHAT CAN WE DO WITH NO ELECTRICITY?
IT'S TOO EARLY TO TURN IN!
I KNOW... WE CAN TALK!
HOW WAS YOUR DAY, ARCHIE?
I WENT TO SCHOOL AND CAME HOME!
FRED?
WORK WAS FINE!
HO-HUM!
THAT WENT WELL!
SIGH!

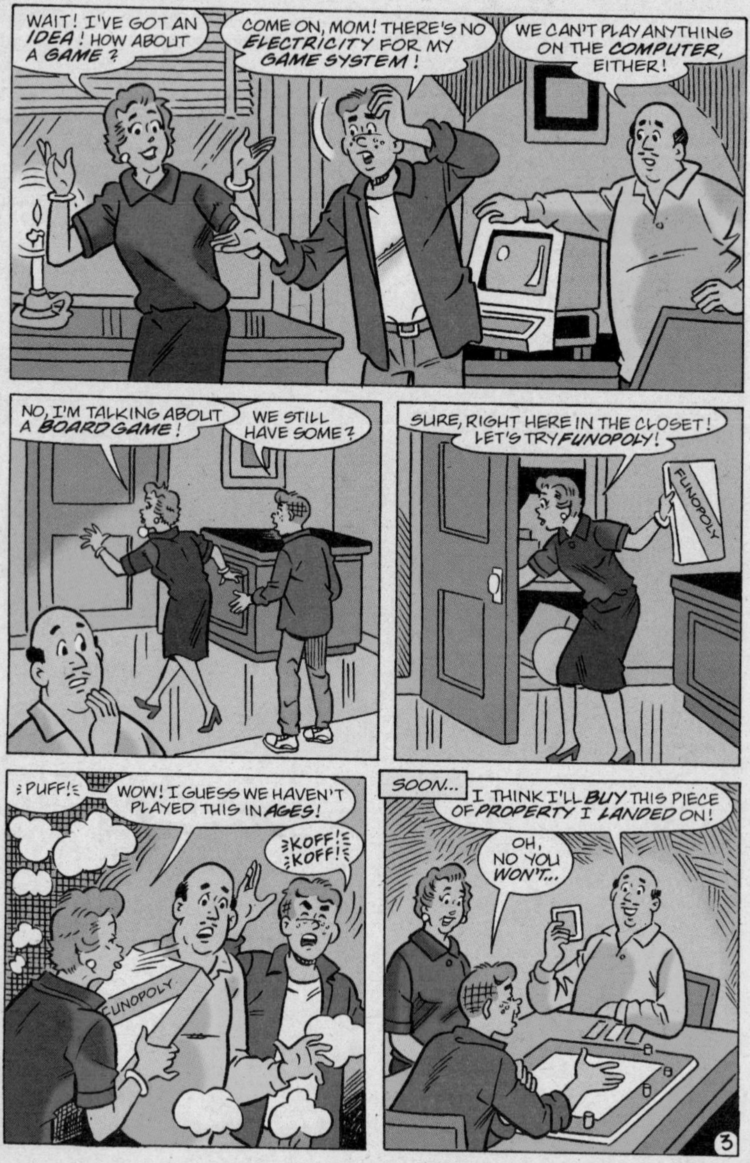
WAIT! I'VE GOT AN IDEA! HOW ABOUT A GAME?
COME ON, MOM! THERE'S NO ELECTRICITY FOR MY GAME SYSTEM!
WE CAN'T PLAY ANYTHING ON THE COMPUTER, EITHER!
NO, I'M TALKING ABOUT A BOARD GAME!
WE STILL HAVE SOME?
SURE, RIGHT HERE IN THE CLOSET! LET'S TRY FUNOPOLY!
FUNOPOLY
PUFF!
WOW! I GUESS WE HAVEN'T PLAYED THIS IN AGES!
KOFF! KOFF!
FUNOPOLY
SOON...
I THINK I'LL BUY THIS PIECE OF PROPERTY I LANDED ON!
OH, NO YOU WON'T...
3

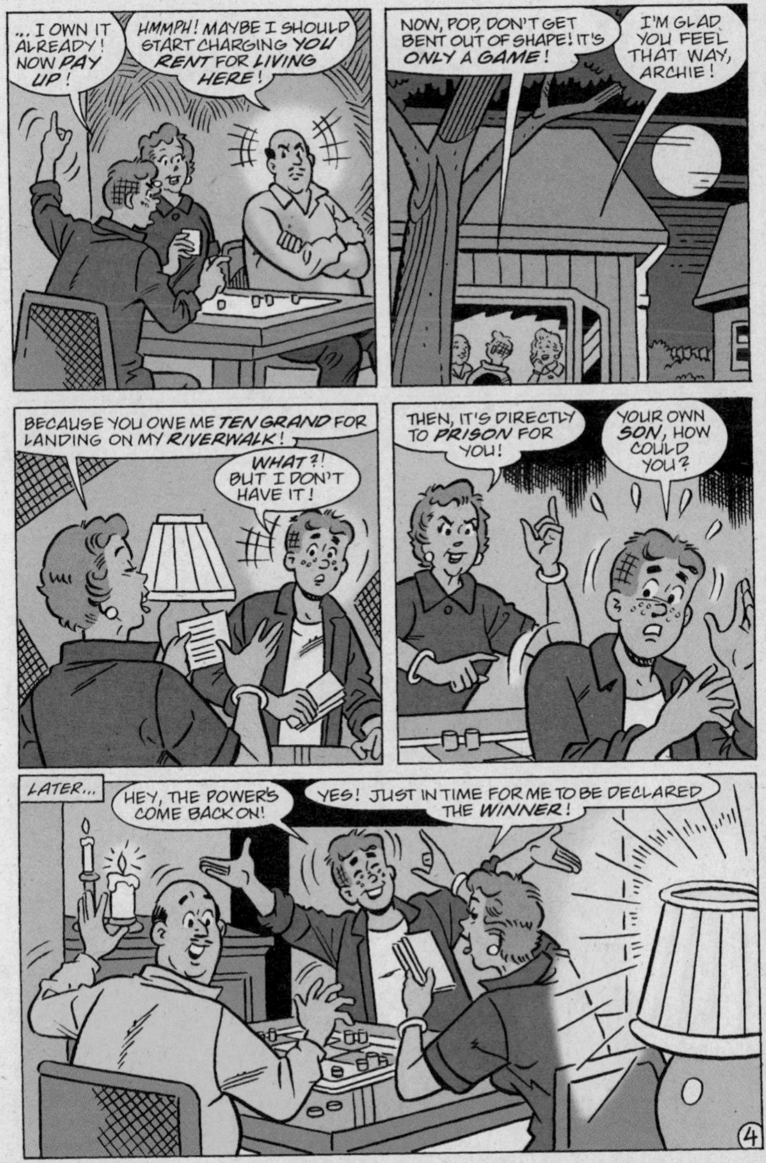

... I OWN IT ALREADY! NOW PAY UP!
HMMPH! MAYBE I SHOULD START CHARGING YOU RENT FOR LIVING HERE!
NOW, POP, DON'T GET BENT OUT OF SHAPE! IT'S ONLY A GAME!
I'M GLAD YOU FEEL THAT WAY, ARCHIE!
BECAUSE YOU OWE ME TEN GRAND FOR LANDING ON MY RIVERWALK!
WHAT?! BUT I DON'T HAVE IT!
THEN, IT'S DIRECTLY TO PRISON FOR YOU!
YOUR OWN SON, HOW COULD YOU?
LATER...
HEY, THE POWER'S COME BACK ON!
YES! JUST IN TIME FOR ME TO BE DECLARED THE WINNER!
4

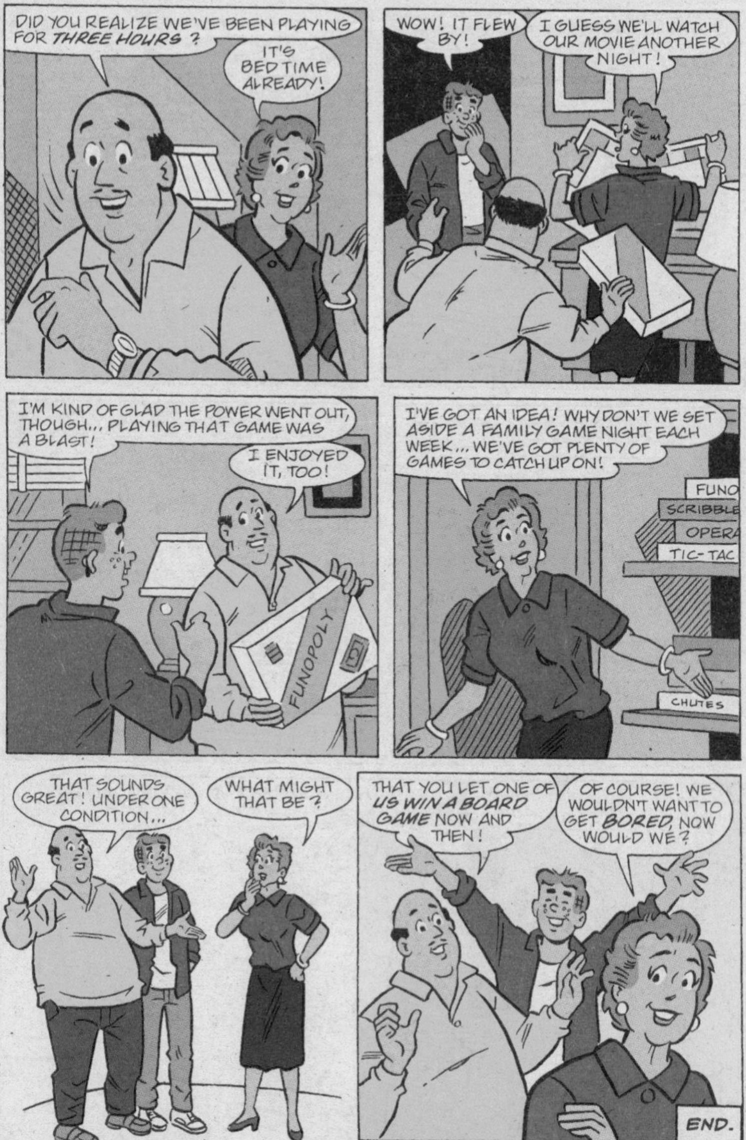

DID YOU REALIZE WE'VE BEEN PLAYING FOR THREE HOURS ?
IT'S BED TIME ALREADY!
WOW! IT FLEW BY!
I GUESS WE'LL WATCH OUR MOVIE ANOTHER NIGHT!
I'M KIND OF GLAD THE POWER WENT OUT, THOUGH... PLAYING THAT GAME WAS A BLAST!
I ENJOYED IT, TOO!
FUNOPOLY
I'VE GOT AN IDEA! WHY DON'T WE SET ASIDE A FAMILY GAME NIGHT EACH WEEK... WE'VE GOT PLENTY OF GAMES TO CATCH UP ON!
FUNO
SCRIBBLE
OPERA
TIC-TAC
CHUTES
THAT SOUNDS GREAT! UNDER ONE CONDITION...
WHAT MIGHT THAT BE ?
THAT YOU LET ONE OF US WIN A BOARD GAME NOW AND THEN!
OF COURSE! WE WOULDN'T WANT TO GET BORED, NOW WOULD WE ?
END.

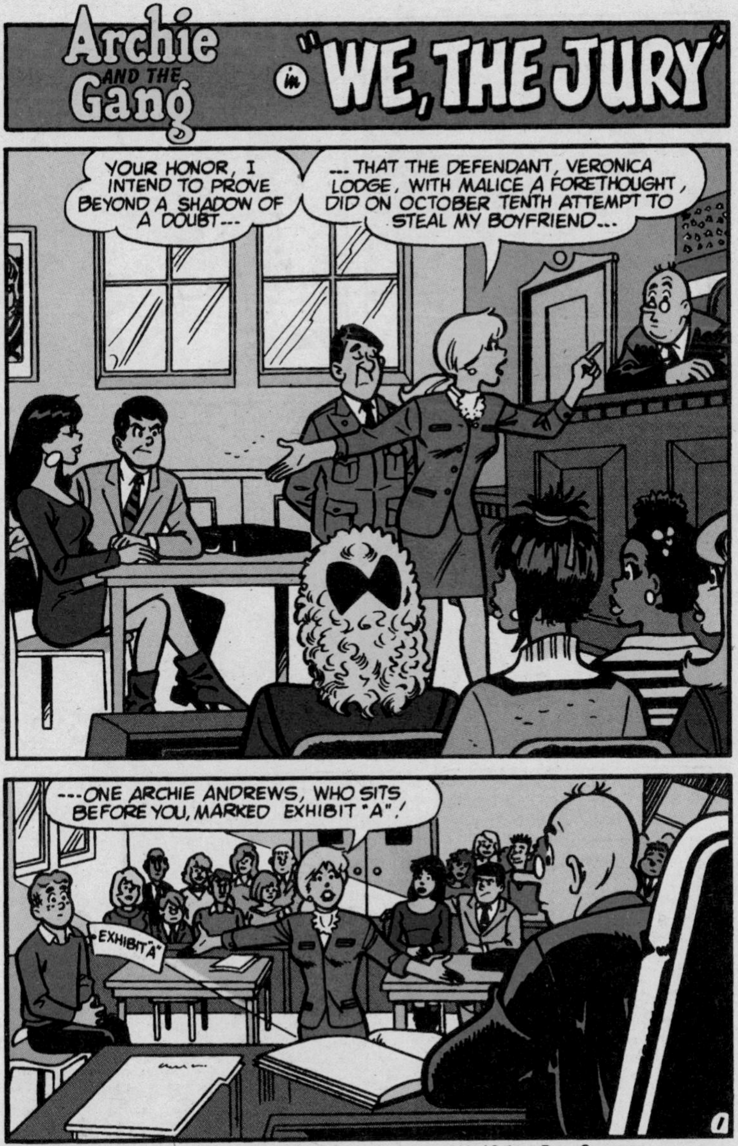
Archie AND THE Gang
in "WE, THE JURY"
YOUR HONOR, I INTEND TO PROVE BEYOND A SHADOW OF A DOUBT---
--- THAT THE DEFENDANT, VERONICA LODGE, WITH MALICE A FORETHOUGHT, DID ON OCTOBER TENTH ATTEMPT TO STEAL MY BOYFRIEND...
---ONE ARCHIE ANDREWS, WHO SITS BEFORE YOU, MARKED EXHIBIT "A"!
EXHIBIT "A"
0

Script: George Gladir / Art: Dan DeCarlo / Letters: Bill Yoshida / Colors: Barry Grossman

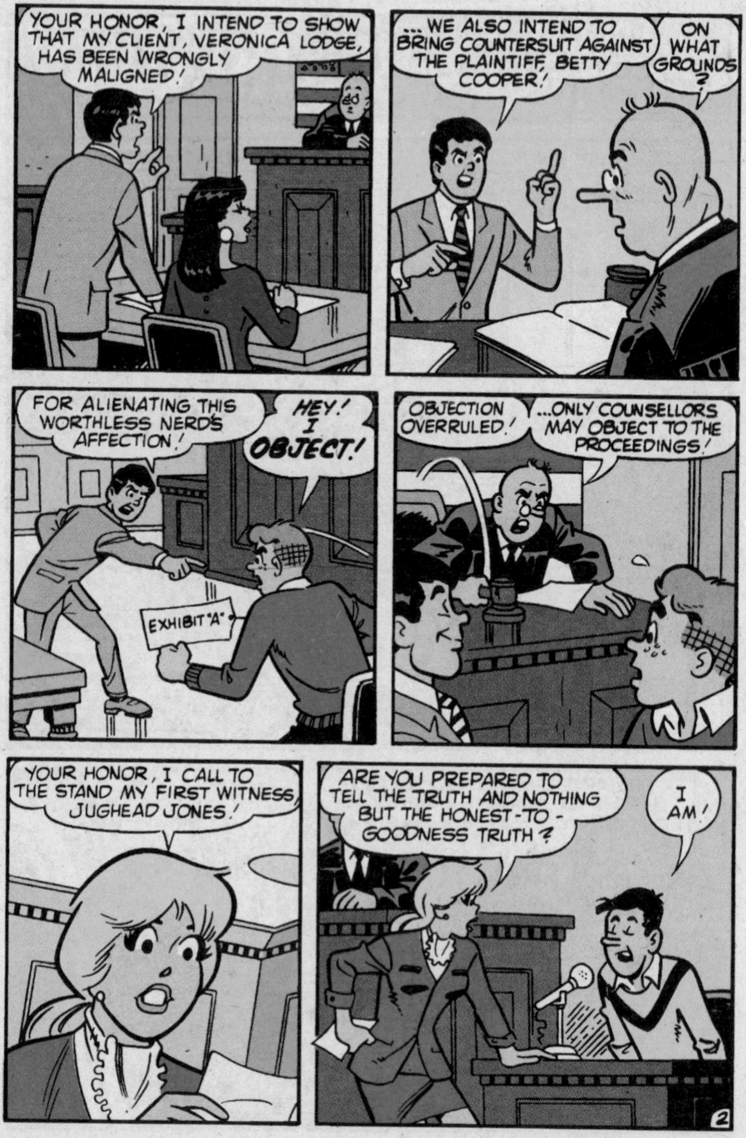
YOUR HONOR, I INTEND TO SHOW THAT MY CLIENT, VERONICA LODGE, HAS BEEN WRONGLY MALIGNED!
...WE ALSO INTEND TO BRING COUNTERSUIT AGAINST THE PLAINTIFF, BETTY COOPER!
ON WHAT GROUNDS?
FOR ALIENATING THIS WORTHLESS NERD'S AFFECTION!
HEY! I OBJECT!
EXHIBIT "A"
OBJECTION OVERRULED!
...ONLY COUNSELLORS MAY OBJECT TO THE PROCEEDINGS!
YOUR HONOR, I CALL TO THE STAND MY FIRST WITNESS, JUGHEAD JONES!
ARE YOU PREPARED TO TELL THE TRUTH AND NOTHING BUT THE HONEST-TO-GOODNESS TRUTH?
I AM!
2

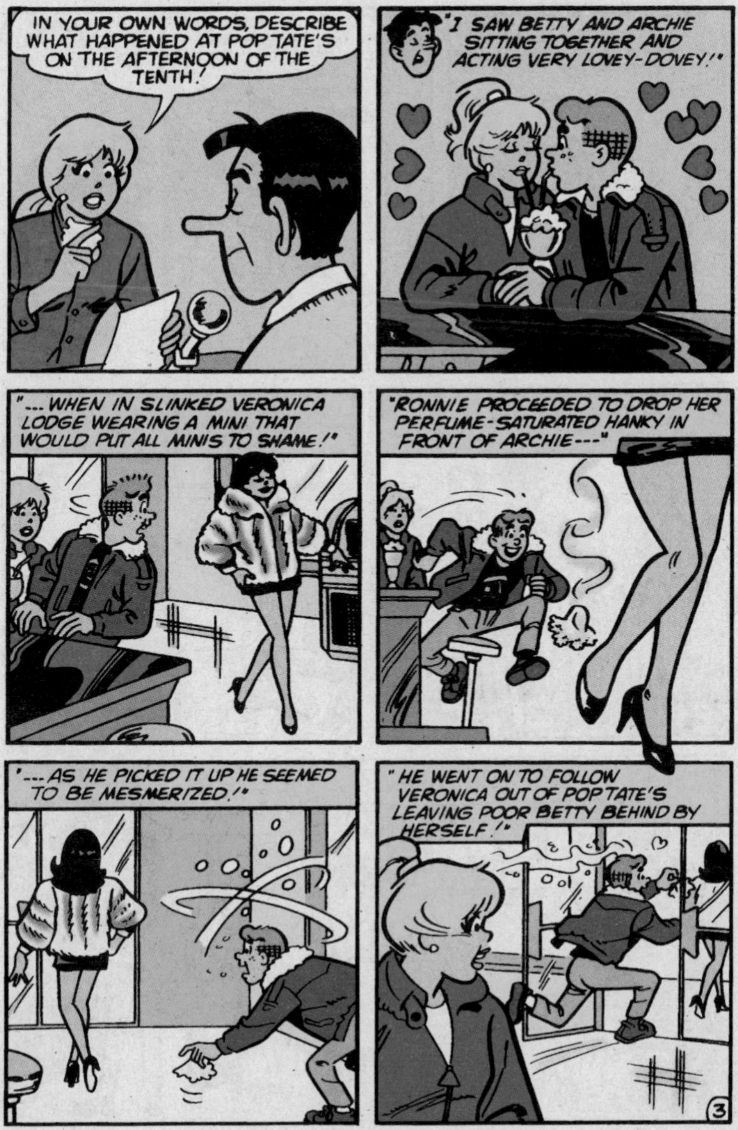
IN YOUR OWN WORDS, DESCRIBE WHAT HAPPENED AT POP TATE'S ON THE AFTERNOON OF THE TENTH!
"I SAW BETTY AND ARCHIE SITTING TOGETHER AND ACTING VERY LOVEY-DOVEY!"
"...WHEN IN SLINKED VERONICA LODGE WEARING A MINI THAT WOULD PUT ALL MINIS TO SHAME!"
"RONNIE PROCEEDED TO DROP HER PERFUME-SATURATED HANKY IN FRONT OF ARCHIE---"
"...AS HE PICKED IT UP HE SEEMED TO BE MESMERIZED!"
"HE WENT ON TO FOLLOW VERONICA OUT OF POP TATE'S LEAVING POOR BETTY BEHIND BY HERSELF!"
3

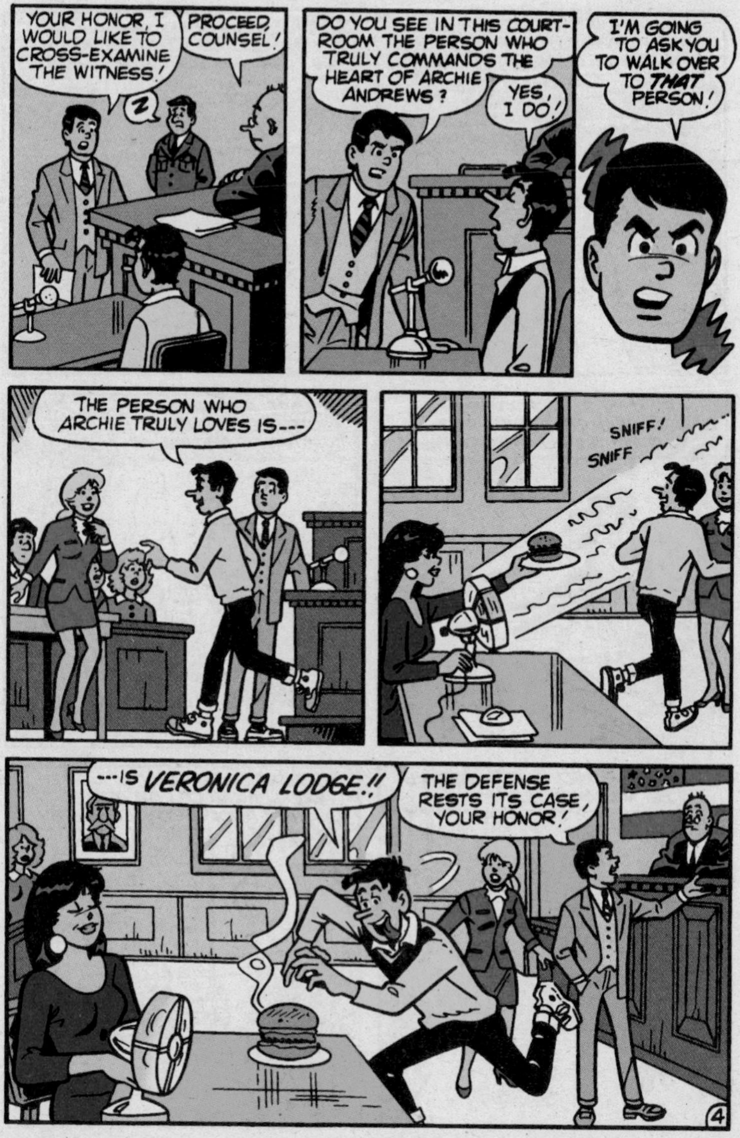
YOUR HONOR, I WOULD LIKE TO CROSS-EXAMINE THE WITNESS!
PROCEED, COUNSEL!
Z
DO YOU SEE IN THIS COURTROOM THE PERSON WHO TRULY COMMANDS THE HEART OF ARCHIE ANDREWS?
YES, I DO!
I'M GOING TO ASK YOU TO WALK OVER TO *THAT* PERSON!
THE PERSON WHO ARCHIE TRULY LOVES IS---
SNIFF!
SNIFF
---IS *VERONICA LODGE!!*
THE DEFENSE RESTS ITS CASE, YOUR HONOR!
4

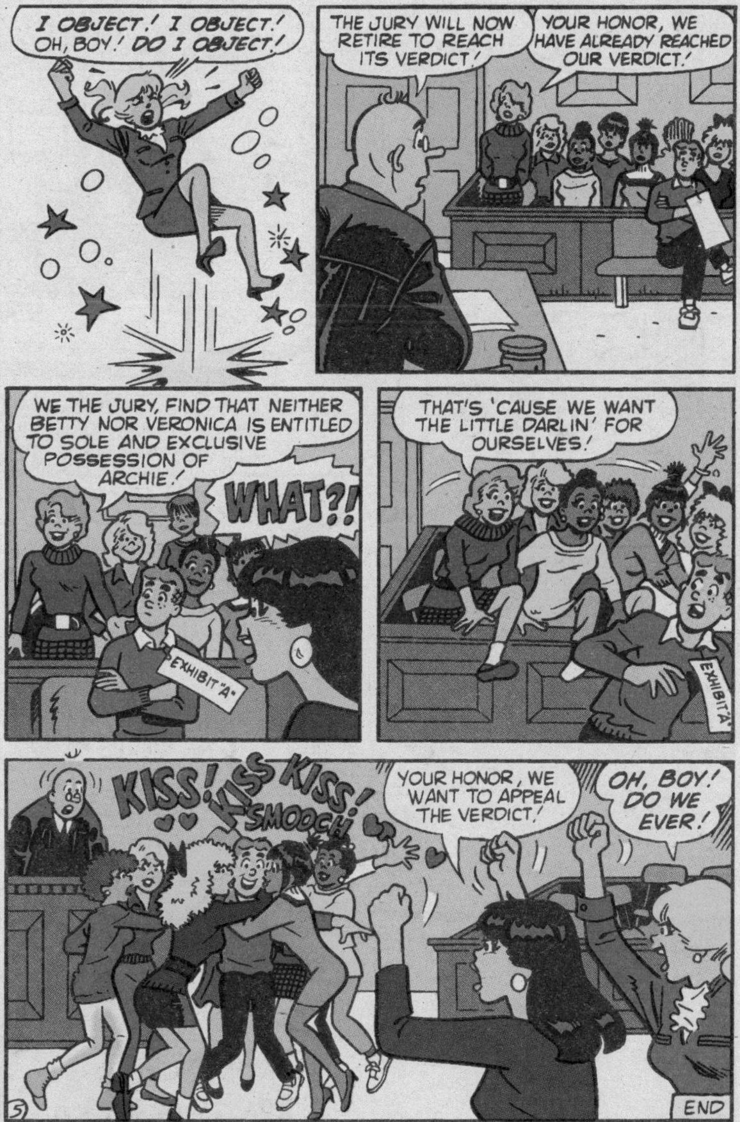
I OBJECT! I OBJECT! OH, BOY! DO I OBJECT!
THE JURY WILL NOW RETIRE TO REACH ITS VERDICT!
YOUR HONOR, WE HAVE ALREADY REACHED OUR VERDICT!
WE THE JURY, FIND THAT NEITHER BETTY NOR VERONICA IS ENTITLED TO SOLE AND EXCLUSIVE POSSESSION OF ARCHIE!
WHAT?!
EXHIBIT "A"
THAT'S 'CAUSE WE WANT THE LITTLE DARLIN' FOR OURSELVES!
EXHIBIT "A"
KISS! KISS KISS! SMOOCH
YOUR HONOR, WE WANT TO APPEAL THE VERDICT!
OH, BOY! DO WE EVER!
5
END

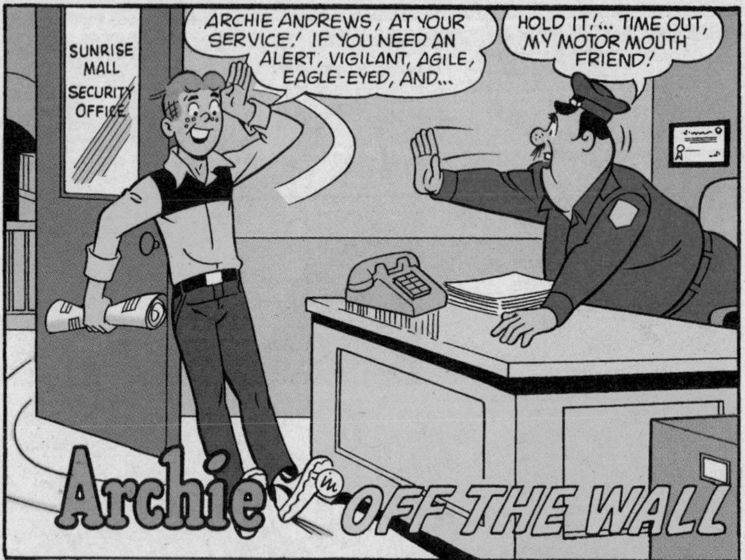
SUNRISE MALL SECURITY OFFICE
ARCHIE ANDREWS, AT YOUR SERVICE! IF YOU NEED AN ALERT, VIGILANT, AGILE, EAGLE-EYED, AND...
HOLD IT!... TIME OUT, MY MOTOR MOUTH FRIEND!
Archie in OFF THE WALL

Script & Pencils: Bob Bolling / Inks: Jim Amash / Letters: Bill Yoshida

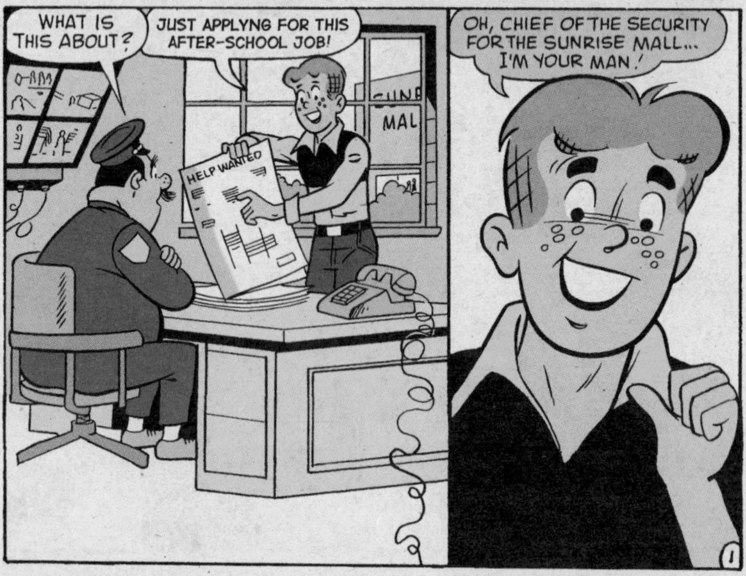
WHAT IS THIS ABOUT?
JUST APPLYNG FOR THIS AFTER-SCHOOL JOB!
HELP WANTED
OH, CHIEF OF THE SECURITY FOR THE SUNRISE MALL... I'M YOUR MAN!
1

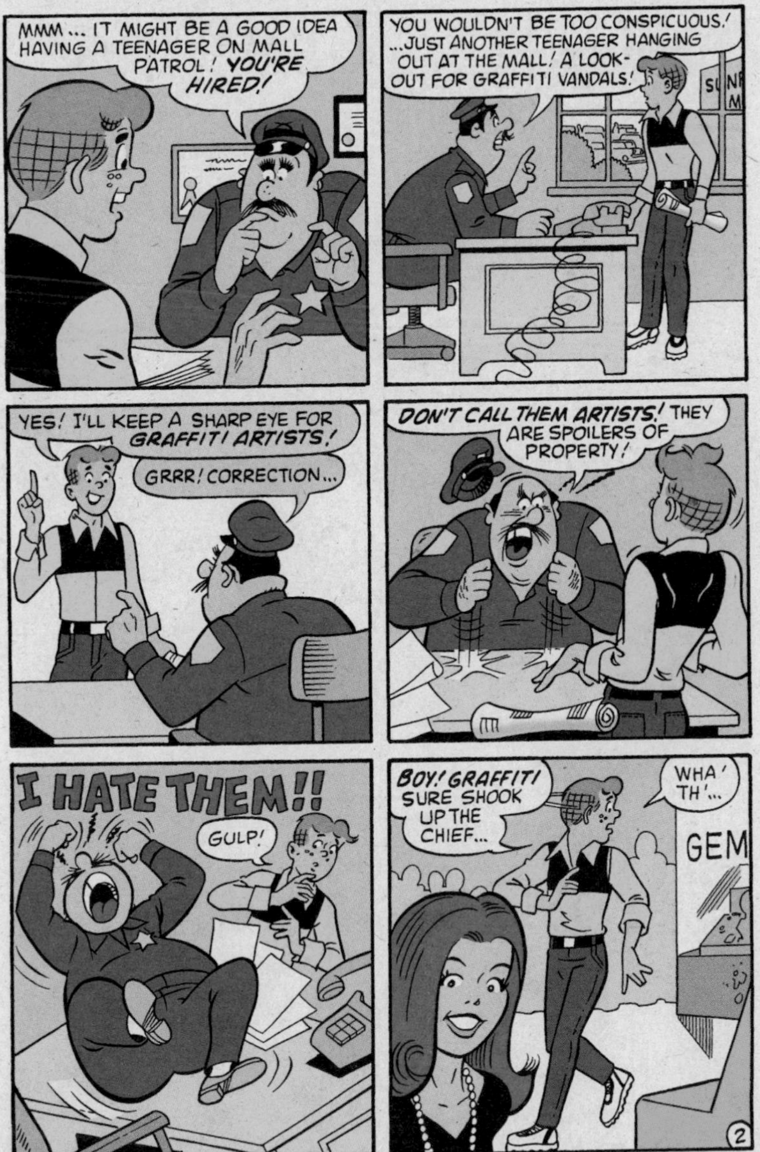
MMM... IT MIGHT BE A GOOD IDEA HAVING A TEENAGER ON MALL PATROL! YOU'RE HIRED!
YOU WOULDN'T BE TOO CONSPICUOUS! ...JUST ANOTHER TEENAGER HANGING OUT AT THE MALL! A LOOK-OUT FOR GRAFFITI VANDALS!
YES! I'LL KEEP A SHARP EYE FOR GRAFFITI ARTISTS!
GRRR! CORRECTION...
DON'T CALL THEM ARTISTS! THEY ARE SPOILERS OF PROPERTY!
I HATE THEM!!
GULP!
BOY! GRAFFITI SURE SHOOK UP THE CHIEF...
WHA' TH'...
GEM
2

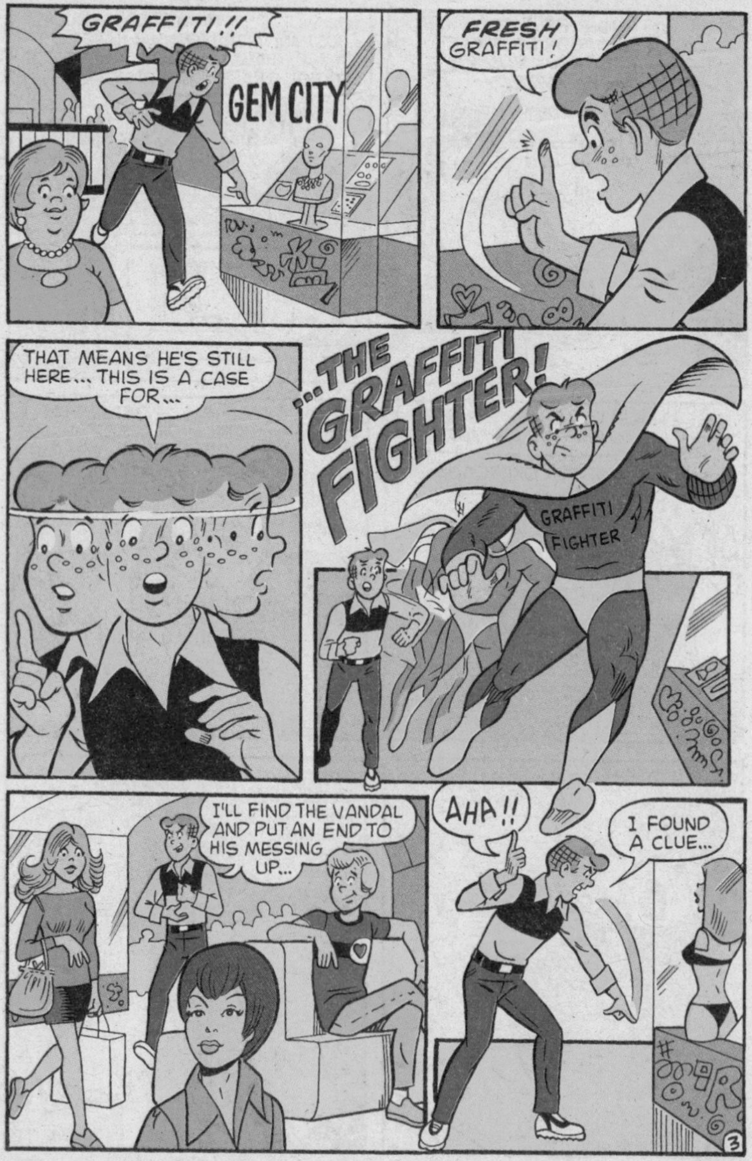

GRAFFITI!!
GEM CITY
FRESH GRAFFITI!
THAT MEANS HE'S STILL HERE... THIS IS A CASE FOR...
...THE GRAFFITI FIGHTER!
GRAFFITI FIGHTER
I'LL FIND THE VANDAL AND PUT AN END TO HIS MESSING UP...
AHA!!
I FOUND A CLUE...
3

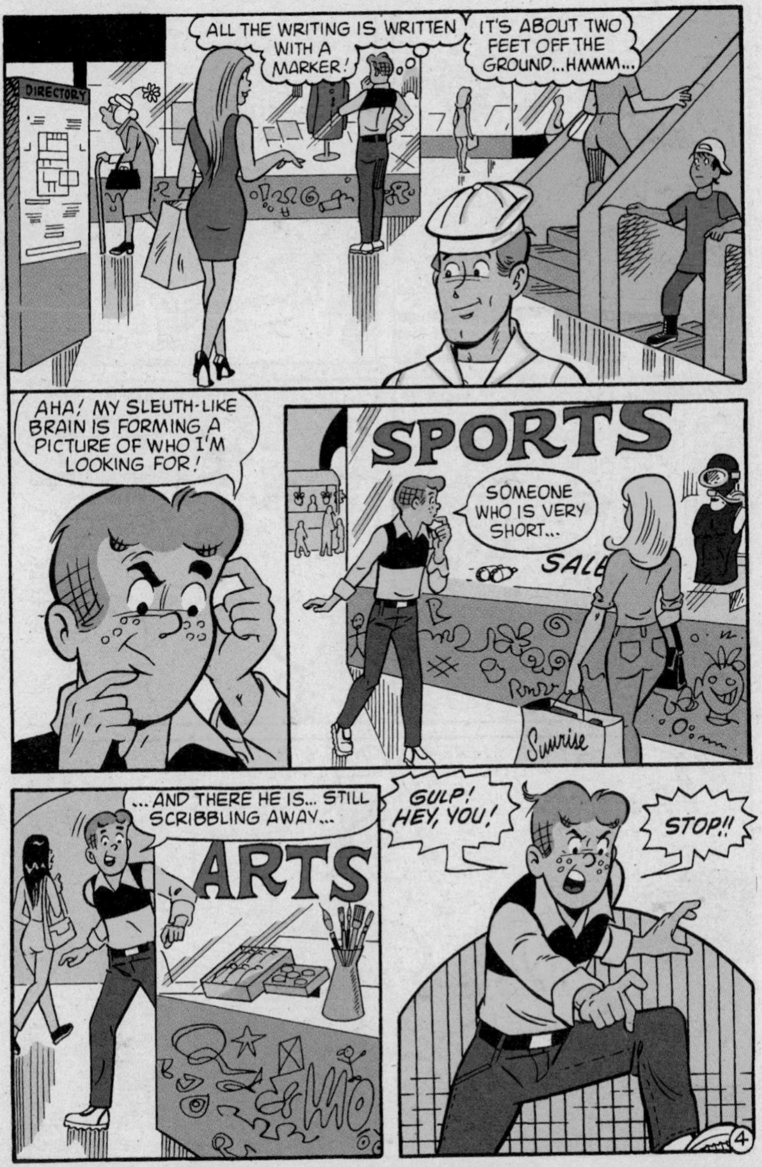
ALL THE WRITING IS WRITTEN WITH A MARKER!
IT'S ABOUT TWO FEET OFF THE GROUND...HMMM...
DIRECTORY
AHA! MY SLEUTH-LIKE BRAIN IS FORMING A PICTURE OF WHO I'M LOOKING FOR!
SPORTS
SOMEONE WHO IS VERY SHORT...
SALE
Sunrise
...AND THERE HE IS... STILL SCRIBBLING AWAY...
ARTS
GULP! HEY, YOU!
STOP!!
4

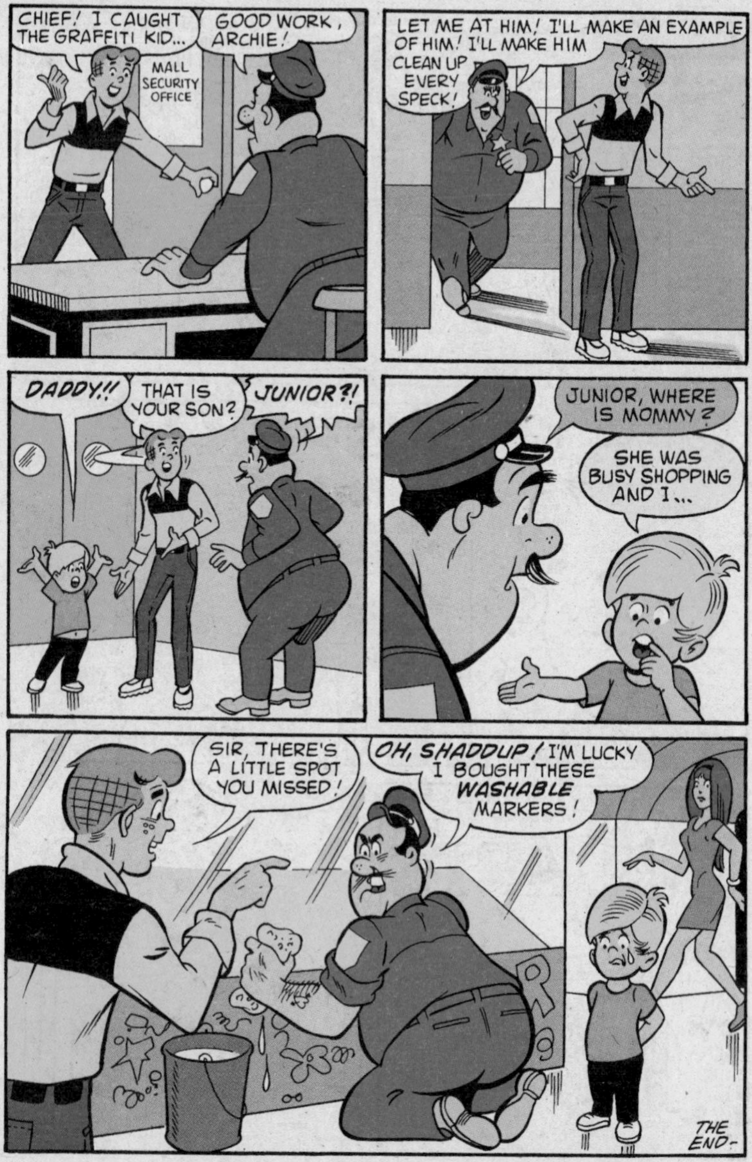
CHIEF! I CAUGHT THE GRAFFITI KID...
GOOD WORK, ARCHIE!
MALL SECURITY OFFICE
LET ME AT HIM! I'LL MAKE AN EXAMPLE OF HIM! I'LL MAKE HIM CLEAN UP EVERY SPECK!
DADDY!!
THAT IS YOUR SON?
JUNIOR?!
JUNIOR, WHERE IS MOMMY?
SHE WAS BUSY SHOPPING AND I...
SIR, THERE'S A LITTLE SPOT YOU MISSED!
OH, SHADDUP! I'M LUCKY I BOUGHT THESE WASHABLE MARKERS!
THE END-

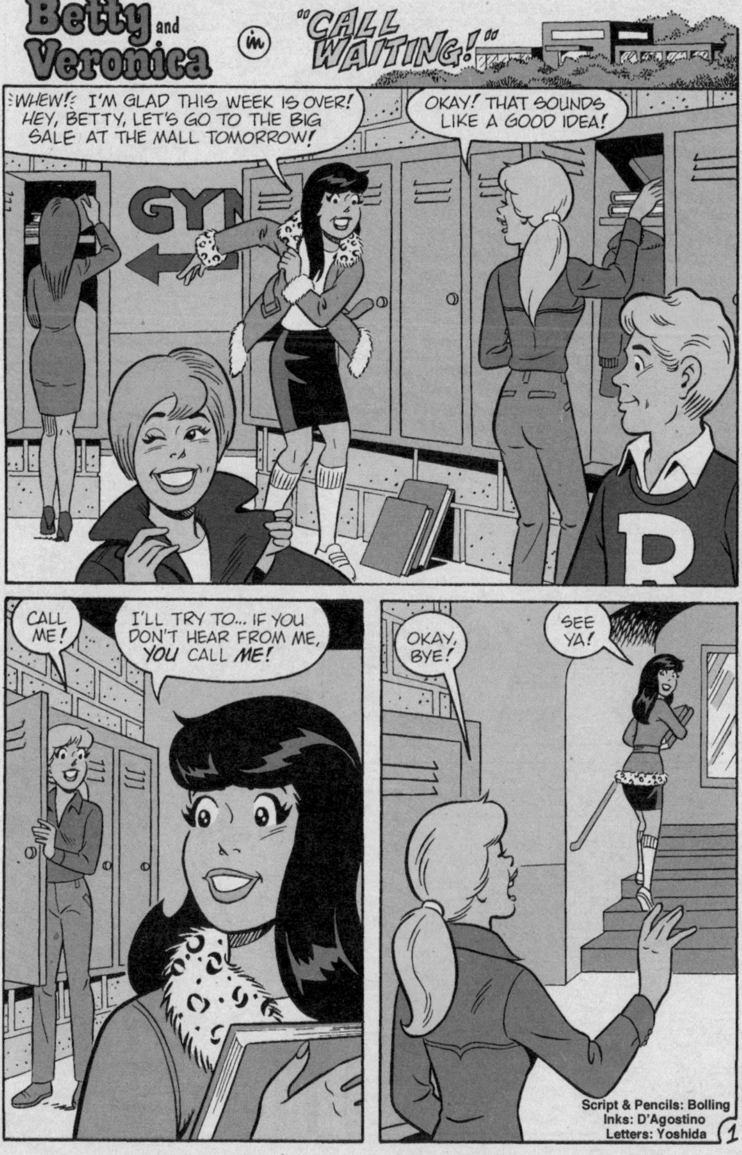
Betty and Veronica in "CALL WAITING!"
WHEW! I'M GLAD THIS WEEK IS OVER! HEY, BETTY, LET'S GO TO THE BIG SALE AT THE MALL TOMORROW!
OKAY! THAT SOUNDS LIKE A GOOD IDEA!
GYM
R
CALL ME!
I'LL TRY TO... IF YOU DON'T HEAR FROM ME, YOU CALL ME!
OKAY, BYE!
SEE YA!
Script & Pencils: Bolling
Inks: D'Agostino
Letters: Yoshida
1

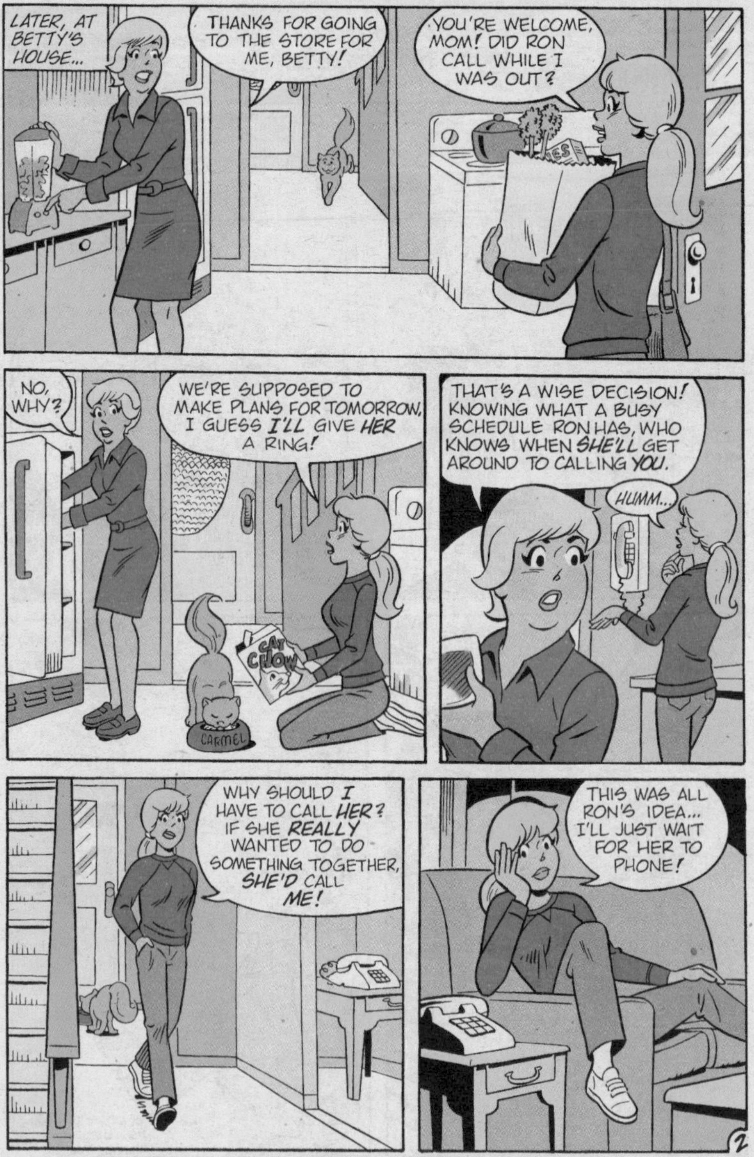

LATER, AT BETTY'S HOUSE...
THANKS FOR GOING TO THE STORE FOR ME, BETTY!
YOU'RE WELCOME, MOM! DID RON CALL WHILE I WAS OUT?
NO, WHY?
WE'RE SUPPOSED TO MAKE PLANS FOR TOMORROW. I GUESS I'LL GIVE HER A RING!
CAT CHOW
CARMEL
THAT'S A WISE DECISION! KNOWING WHAT A BUSY SCHEDULE RON HAS, WHO KNOWS WHEN SHE'LL GET AROUND TO CALLING YOU.
HUMM...
WHY SHOULD I HAVE TO CALL HER? IF SHE REALLY WANTED TO DO SOMETHING TOGETHER, SHE'D CALL ME!
THIS WAS ALL RON'S IDEA... I'LL JUST WAIT FOR HER TO PHONE!
2

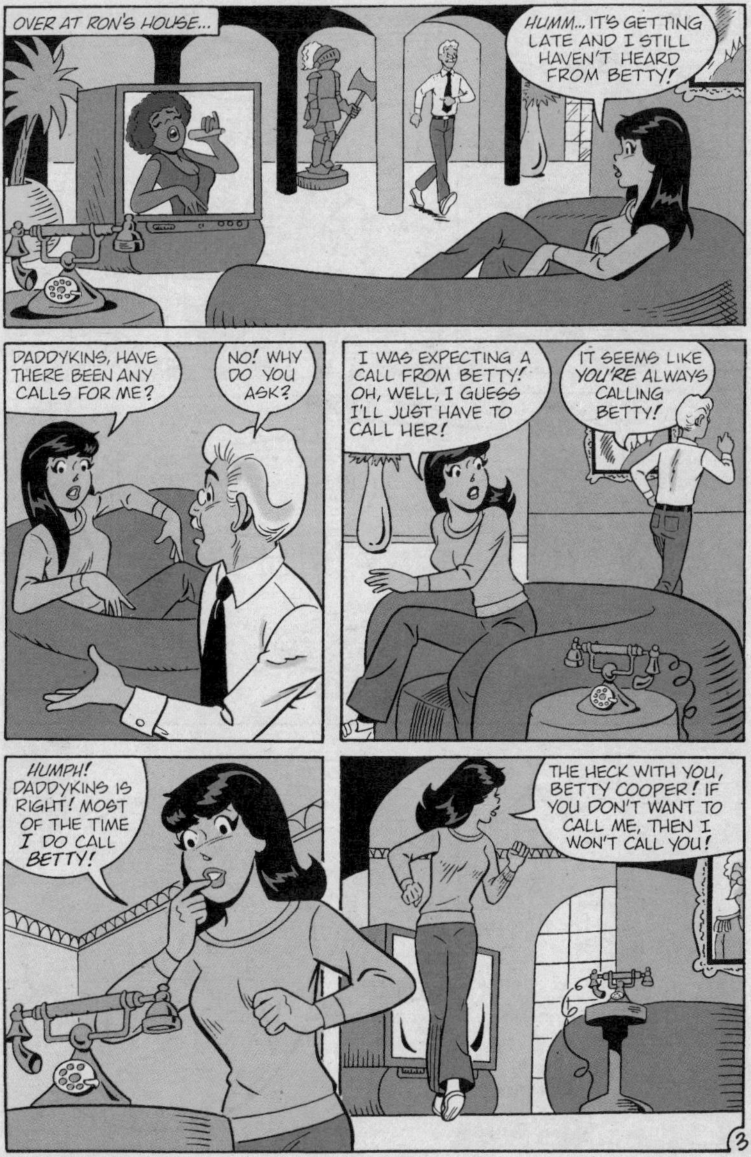
OVER AT RON'S HOUSE...
HUMM... IT'S GETTING LATE AND I STILL HAVEN'T HEARD FROM BETTY!
DADDYKINS, HAVE THERE BEEN ANY CALLS FOR ME?
NO! WHY DO YOU ASK?
I WAS EXPECTING A CALL FROM BETTY! OH, WELL, I GUESS I'LL JUST HAVE TO CALL HER!
IT SEEMS LIKE YOU'RE ALWAYS CALLING BETTY!
HUMPH! DADDYKINS IS RIGHT! MOST OF THE TIME I DO CALL BETTY!
THE HECK WITH YOU, BETTY COOPER! IF YOU DON'T WANT TO CALL ME, THEN I WON'T CALL YOU!
3

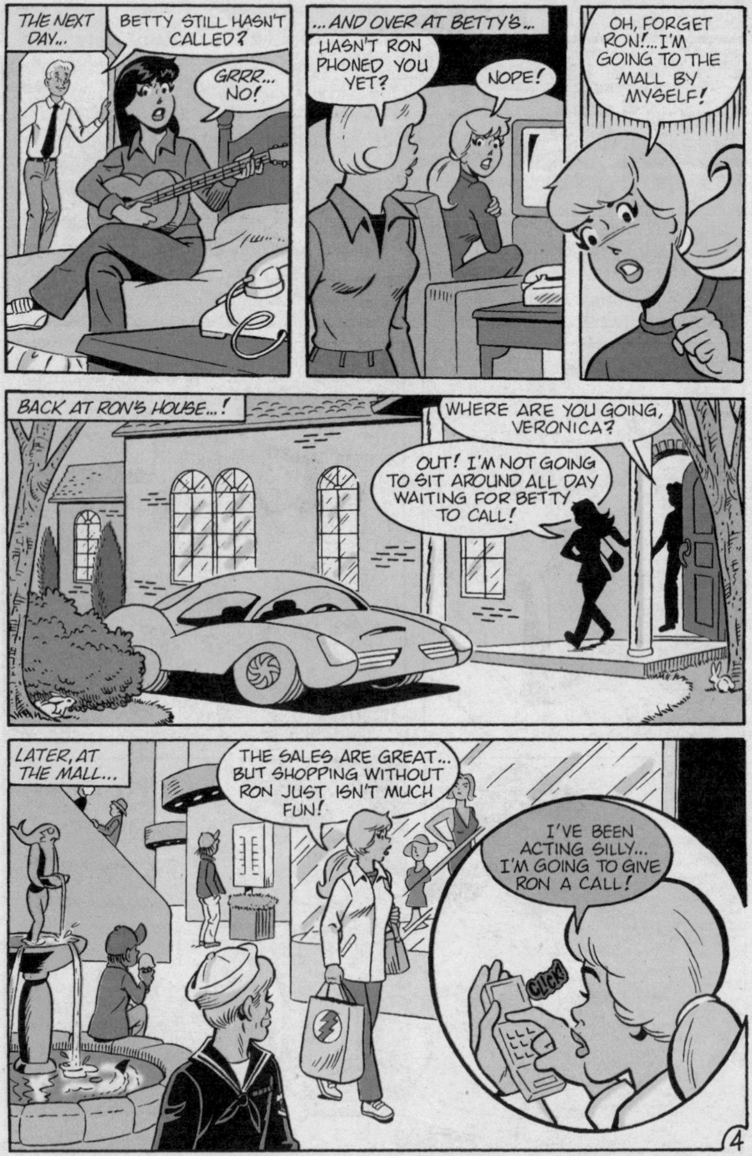
THE NEXT DAY...
BETTY STILL HASN'T CALLED?
GRRR... NO!
...AND OVER AT BETTY'S...
HASN'T RON PHONED YOU YET?
NOPE!
OH, FORGET RON!...I'M GOING TO THE MALL BY MYSELF!
BACK AT RON'S HOUSE...!
WHERE ARE YOU GOING, VERONICA?
OUT! I'M NOT GOING TO SIT AROUND ALL DAY WAITING FOR BETTY TO CALL!
LATER, AT THE MALL...
THE SALES ARE GREAT... BUT SHOPPING WITHOUT RON JUST ISN'T MUCH FUN!
I'VE BEEN ACTING SILLY... I'M GOING TO GIVE RON A CALL!
CLICK!
4

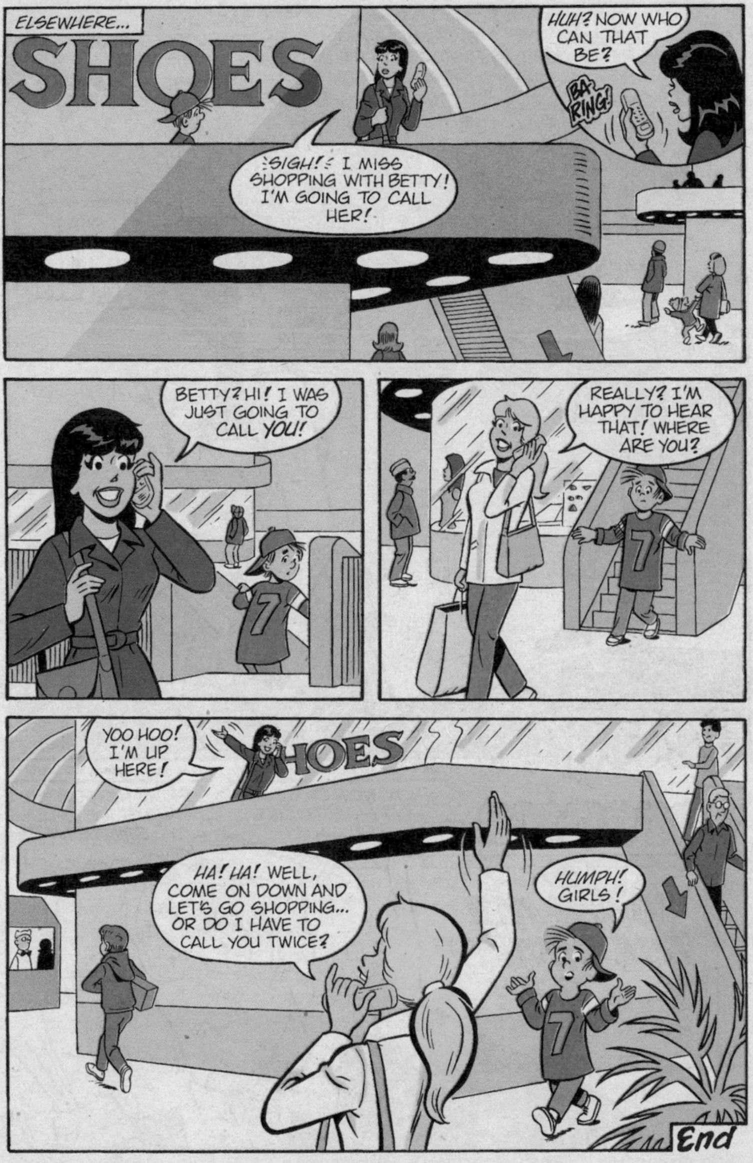
ELSEWHERE...
SHOES
HUH? NOW WHO CAN THAT BE?
BA RING!
SIGH! I MISS SHOPPING WITH BETTY! I'M GOING TO CALL HER!
BETTY? HI! I WAS JUST GOING TO CALL YOU!
REALLY? I'M HAPPY TO HEAR THAT! WHERE ARE YOU?
YOO HOO! I'M UP HERE!
HOES
HA! HA! WELL, COME ON DOWN AND LET'S GO SHOPPING... OR DO I HAVE TO CALL YOU TWICE?
HUMPH! GIRLS!
End

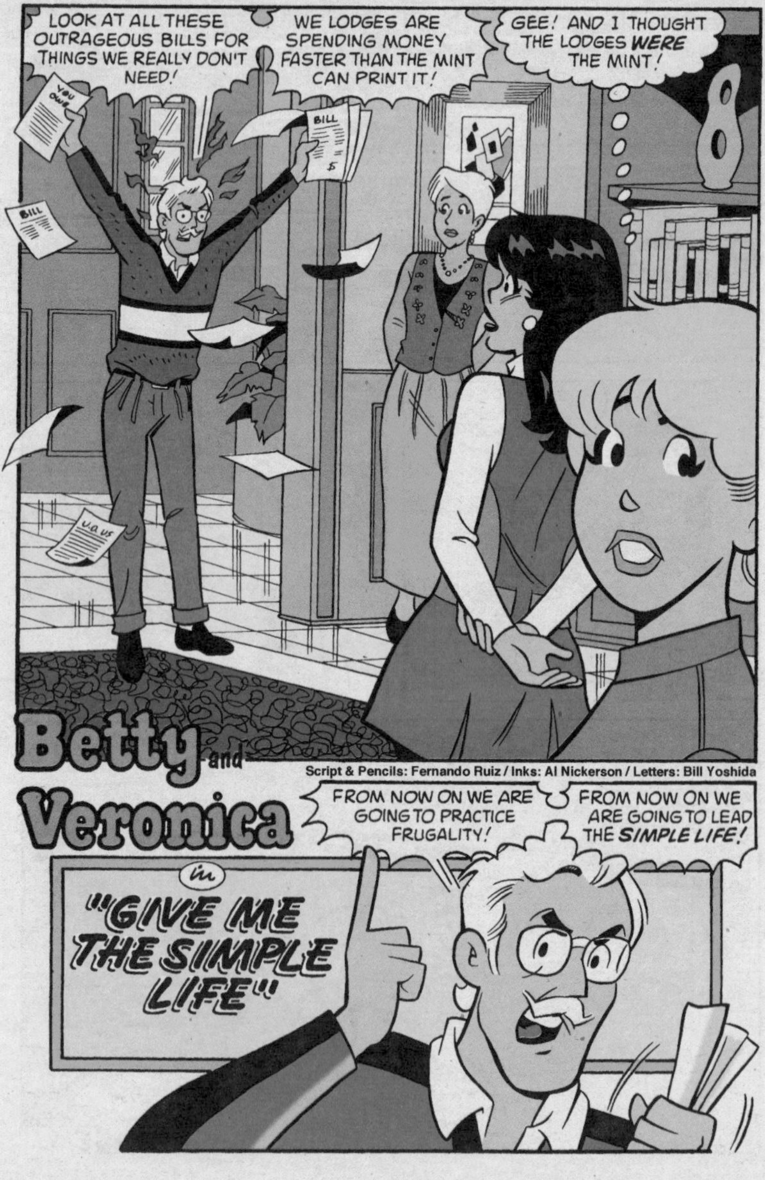
LOOK AT ALL THESE OUTRAGEOUS BILLS FOR THINGS WE REALLY DON'T NEED!
WE LODGES ARE SPENDING MONEY FASTER THAN THE MINT CAN PRINT IT!
GEE! AND I THOUGHT THE LODGES WERE THE MINT!
BILL
BILL
Betty and Veronica
Script & Pencils: Fernando Ruiz / Inks: Al Nickerson / Letters: Bill Yoshida
FROM NOW ON WE ARE GOING TO PRACTICE FRUGALITY!
FROM NOW ON WE ARE GOING TO LEAD THE SIMPLE LIFE!
in
"GIVE ME THE SIMPLE LIFE"

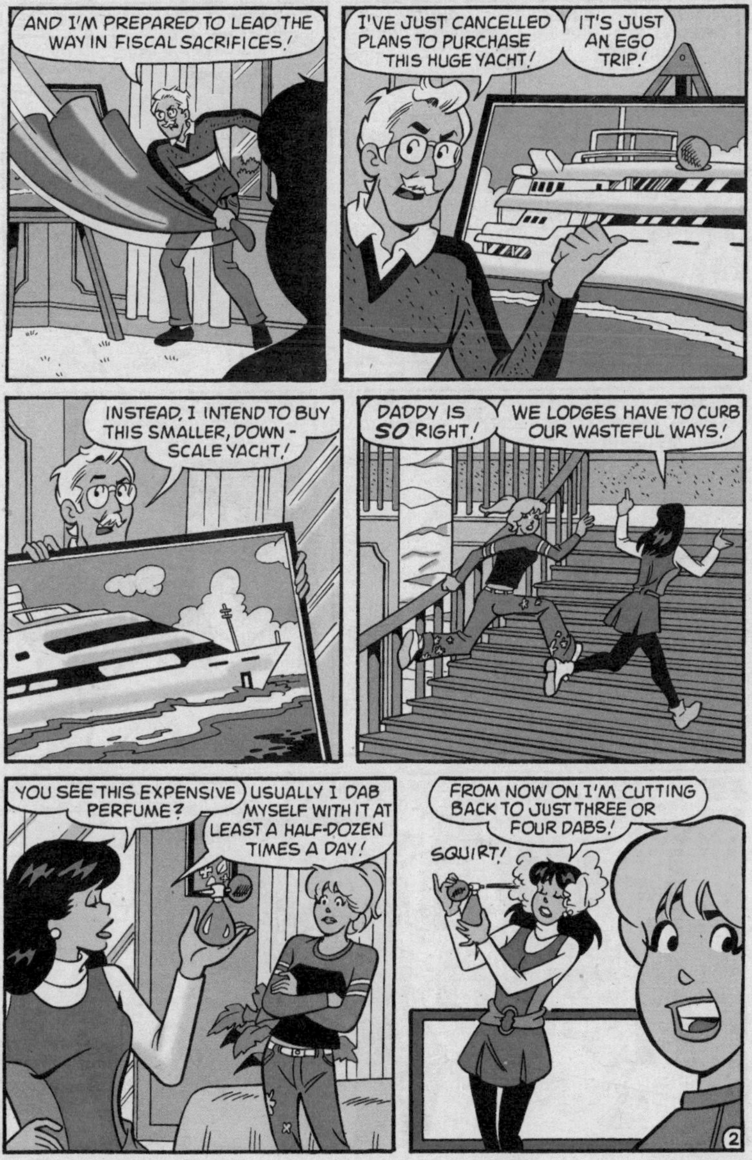
AND I'M PREPARED TO LEAD THE WAY IN FISCAL SACRIFICES!
I'VE JUST CANCELLED PLANS TO PURCHASE THIS HUGE YACHT!
IT'S JUST AN EGO TRIP!
INSTEAD, I INTEND TO BUY THIS SMALLER, DOWN-SCALE YACHT!
DADDY IS SO RIGHT!
WE LODGES HAVE TO CURB OUR WASTEFUL WAYS!
YOU SEE THIS EXPENSIVE PERFUME?
USUALLY I DAB MYSELF WITH IT AT LEAST A HALF-DOZEN TIMES A DAY!
FROM NOW ON I'M CUTTING BACK TO JUST THREE OR FOUR DABS!
SQUIRT!
2

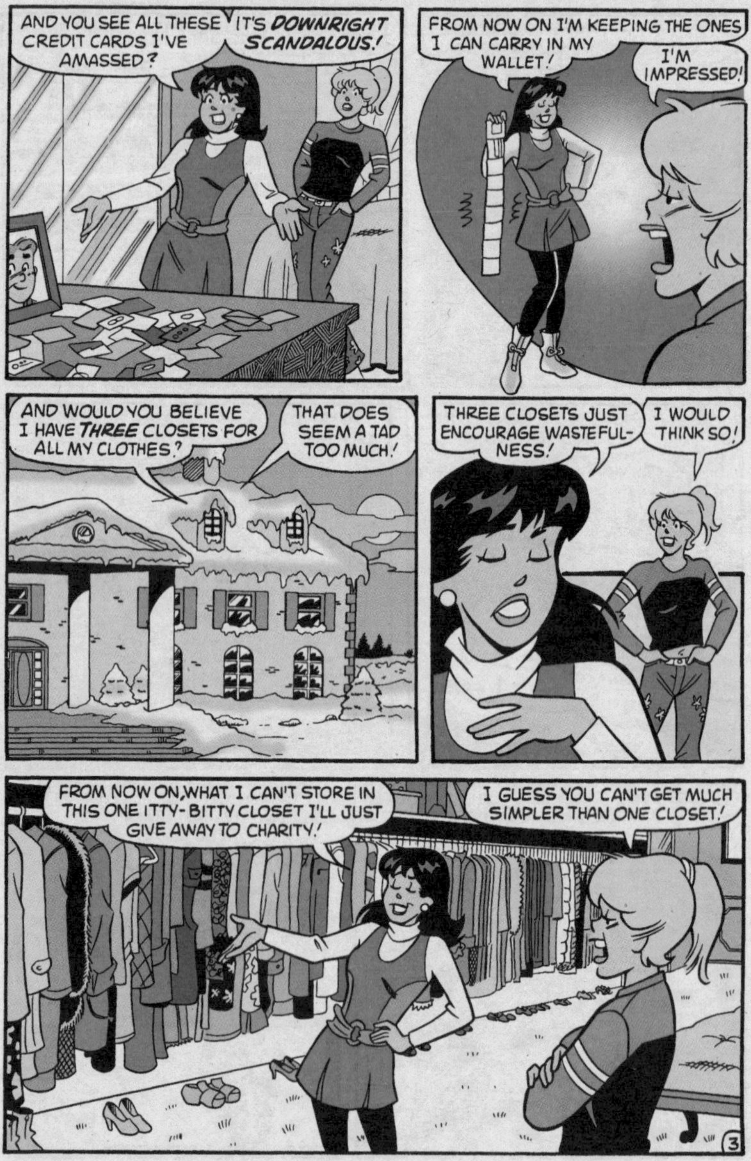

AND YOU SEE ALL THESE CREDIT CARDS I'VE AMASSED?
IT'S DOWNRIGHT SCANDALOUS!
FROM NOW ON I'M KEEPING THE ONES I CAN CARRY IN MY WALLET!
I'M IMPRESSED!
AND WOULD YOU BELIEVE I HAVE THREE CLOSETS FOR ALL MY CLOTHES?
THAT DOES SEEM A TAD TOO MUCH!
THREE CLOSETS JUST ENCOURAGE WASTEFUL-NESS!
I WOULD THINK SO!
FROM NOW ON, WHAT I CAN'T STORE IN THIS ONE ITTY-BITTY CLOSET I'LL JUST GIVE AWAY TO CHARITY!
I GUESS YOU CAN'T GET MUCH SIMPLER THAN ONE CLOSET!
3

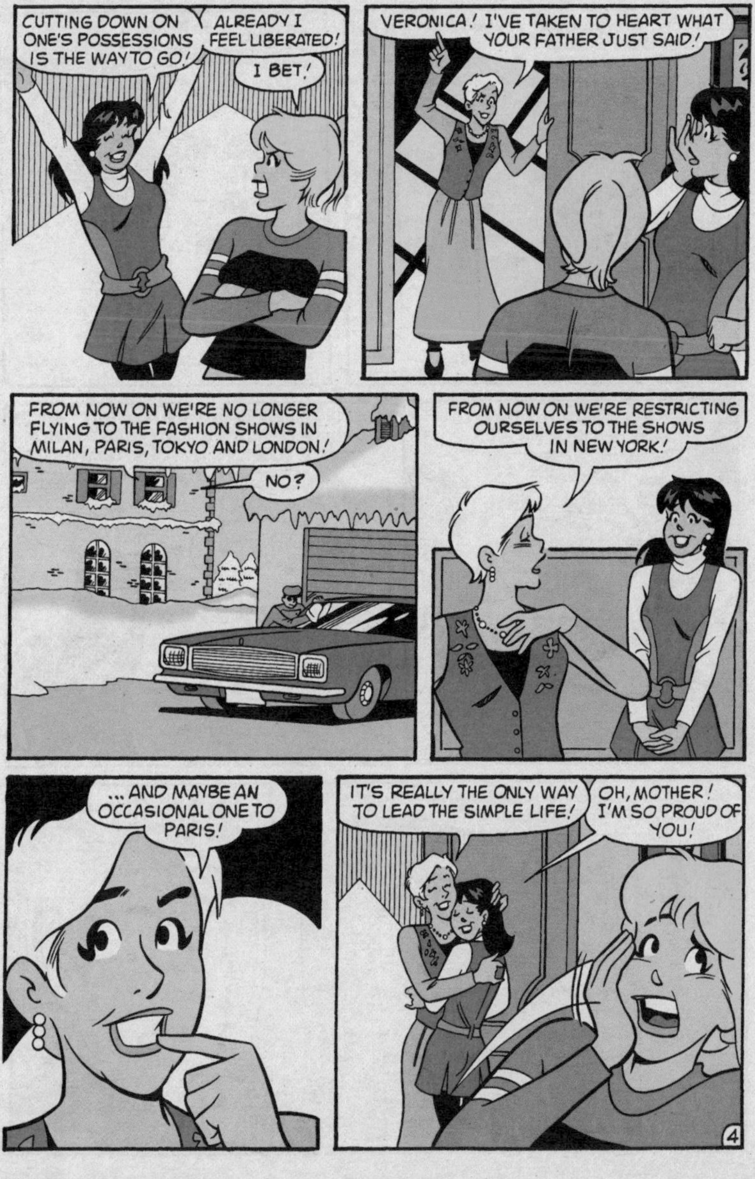
CUTTING DOWN ON ONE'S POSSESSIONS IS THE WAY TO GO!
ALREADY I FEEL LIBERATED!
I BET!
VERONICA! I'VE TAKEN TO HEART WHAT YOUR FATHER JUST SAID!
FROM NOW ON WE'RE NO LONGER FLYING TO THE FASHION SHOWS IN MILAN, PARIS, TOKYO AND LONDON!
NO?
FROM NOW ON WE'RE RESTRICTING OURSELVES TO THE SHOWS IN NEW YORK!
... AND MAYBE AN OCCASIONAL ONE TO PARIS!
IT'S REALLY THE ONLY WAY TO LEAD THE SIMPLE LIFE!
OH, MOTHER! I'M SO PROUD OF YOU!
4

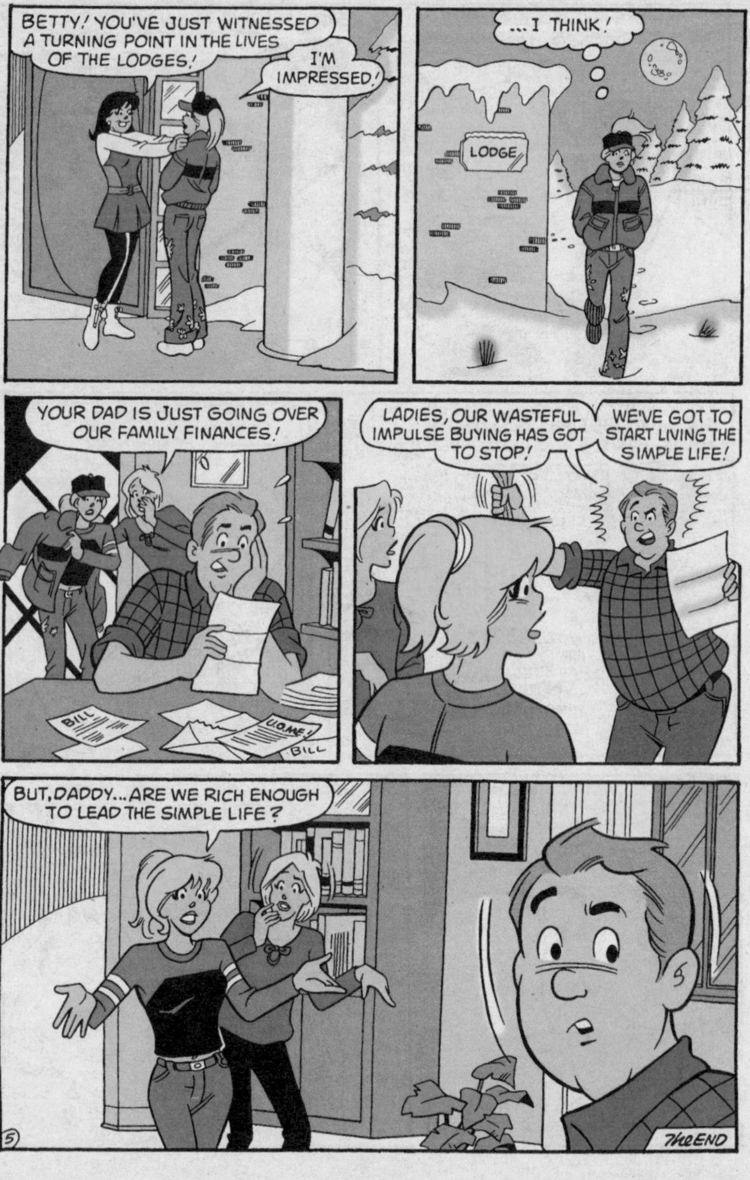
BETTY! YOU'VE JUST WITNESSED A TURNING POINT IN THE LIVES OF THE LODGES!
I'M IMPRESSED!
...I THINK!
LODGE
YOUR DAD IS JUST GOING OVER OUR FAMILY FINANCES!
BILL
U.O.ME!
BILL
LADIES, OUR WASTEFUL IMPULSE BUYING HAS GOT TO STOP!
WE'VE GOT TO START LIVING THE SIMPLE LIFE!
BUT, DADDY... ARE WE RICH ENOUGH TO LEAD THE SIMPLE LIFE?
5
The END

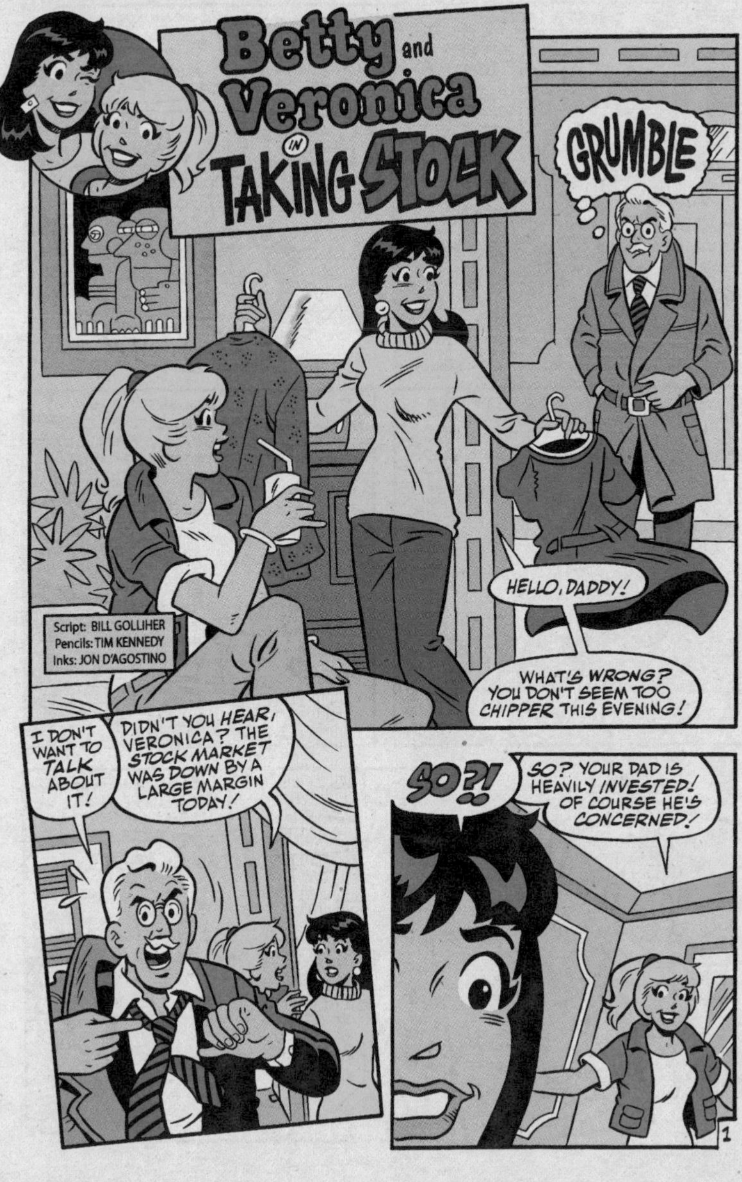
Betty and Veronica in TAKING STOCK
GRUMBLE
Script: BILL GOLLIHER
Pencils: TIM KENNEDY
Inks: JON D'AGOSTINO
HELLO, DADDY!
WHAT'S WRONG? YOU DON'T SEEM TOO CHIPPER THIS EVENING!
DIDN'T YOU HEAR, VERONICA? THE STOCK MARKET WAS DOWN BY A LARGE MARGIN TODAY!
I DON'T WANT TO TALK ABOUT IT!
SO?!
SO? YOUR DAD IS HEAVILY INVESTED! OF COURSE HE'S CONCERNED!
1

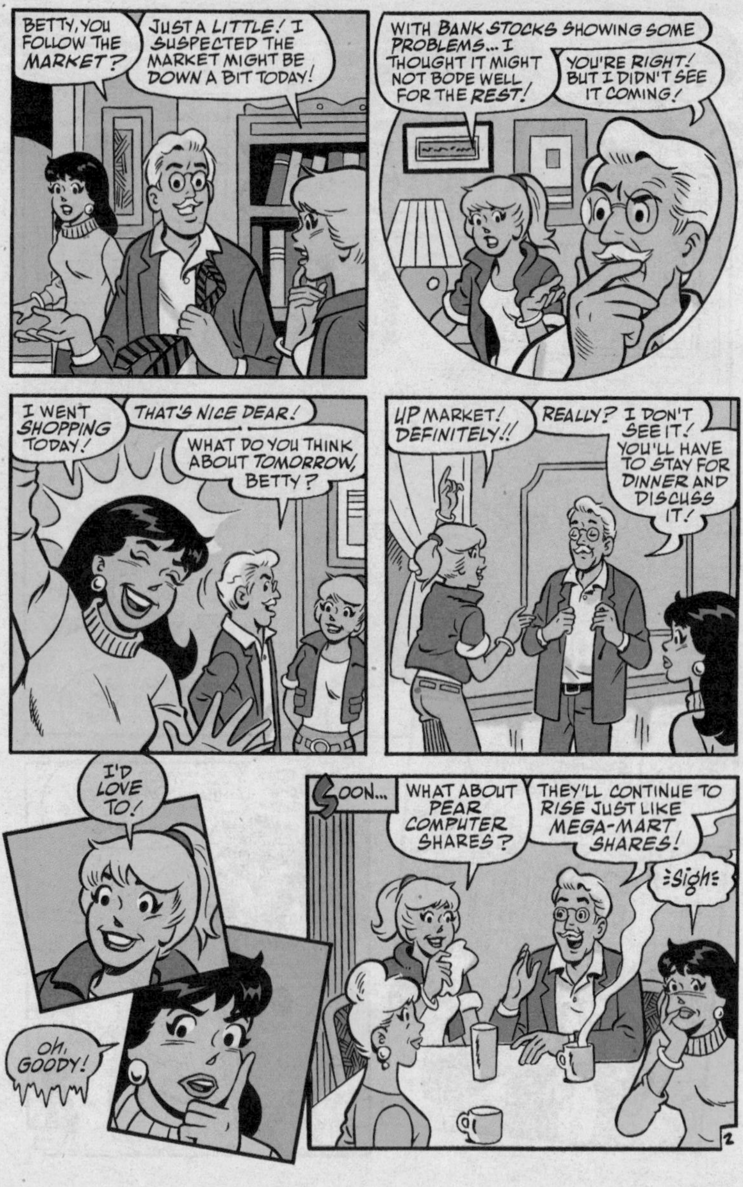

BETTY, YOU FOLLOW THE MARKET?
JUST A LITTLE! I SUSPECTED THE MARKET MIGHT BE DOWN A BIT TODAY!
WITH BANK STOCKS SHOWING SOME PROBLEMS... I THOUGHT IT MIGHT NOT BODE WELL FOR THE REST!
YOU'RE RIGHT! BUT I DIDN'T SEE IT COMING!
I WENT SHOPPING TODAY!
THAT'S NICE DEAR!
WHAT DO YOU THINK ABOUT TOMORROW, BETTY?
UP MARKET! DEFINITELY!!
REALLY? I DON'T SEE IT! YOU'LL HAVE TO STAY FOR DINNER AND DISCUSS IT!
I'D LOVE TO!
OH, GOODY!
SOON...
WHAT ABOUT PEAR COMPUTER SHARES?
THEY'LL CONTINUE TO RISE JUST LIKE MEGA-MART SHARES!
SIGH

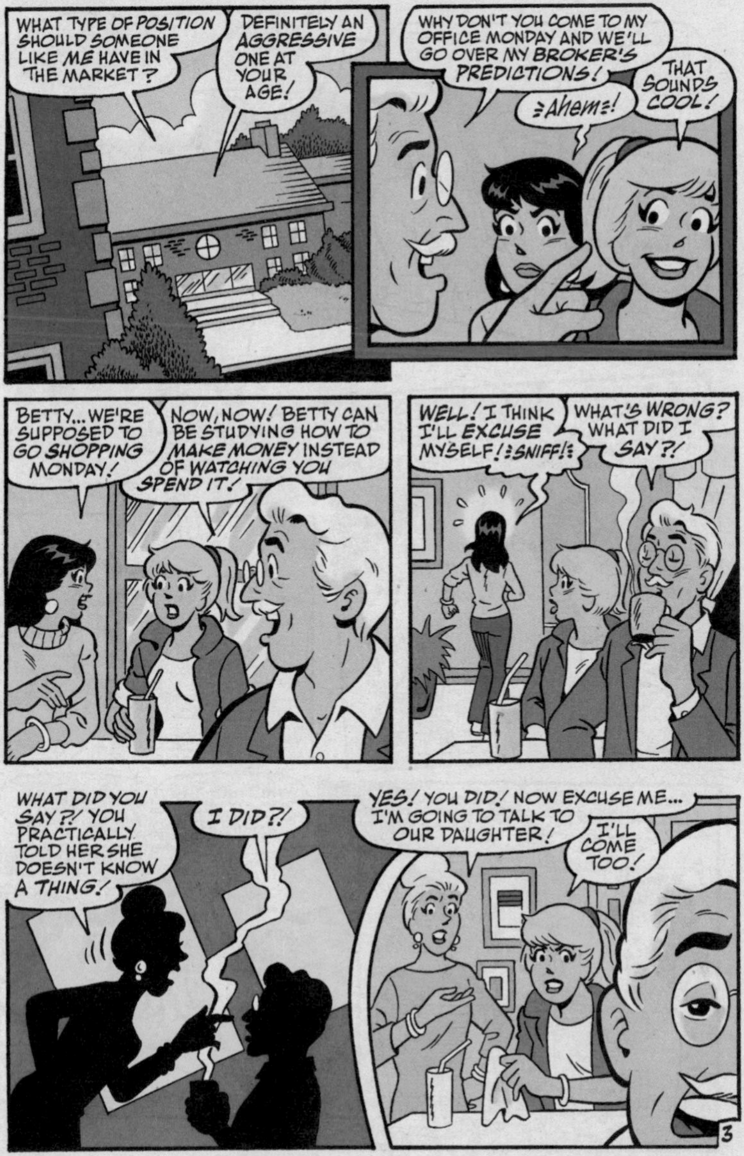
WHAT TYPE OF POSITION SHOULD SOMEONE LIKE ME HAVE IN THE MARKET?
DEFINITELY AN AGGRESSIVE ONE AT YOUR AGE!
WHY DON'T YOU COME TO MY OFFICE MONDAY AND WE'LL GO OVER MY BROKER'S PREDICTIONS!
AHEM!
THAT SOUNDS COOL!
BETTY... WE'RE SUPPOSED TO GO SHOPPING MONDAY!
NOW, NOW! BETTY CAN BE STUDYING HOW TO MAKE MONEY INSTEAD OF WATCHING YOU SPEND IT!
WELL! I THINK I'LL EXCUSE MYSELF! SNIFF!
WHAT'S WRONG? WHAT DID I SAY?!
WHAT DID YOU SAY?! YOU PRACTICALLY TOLD HER SHE DOESN'T KNOW A THING!
I DID?!
YES! YOU DID! NOW EXCUSE ME... I'M GOING TO TALK TO OUR DAUGHTER!
I'LL COME TOO!

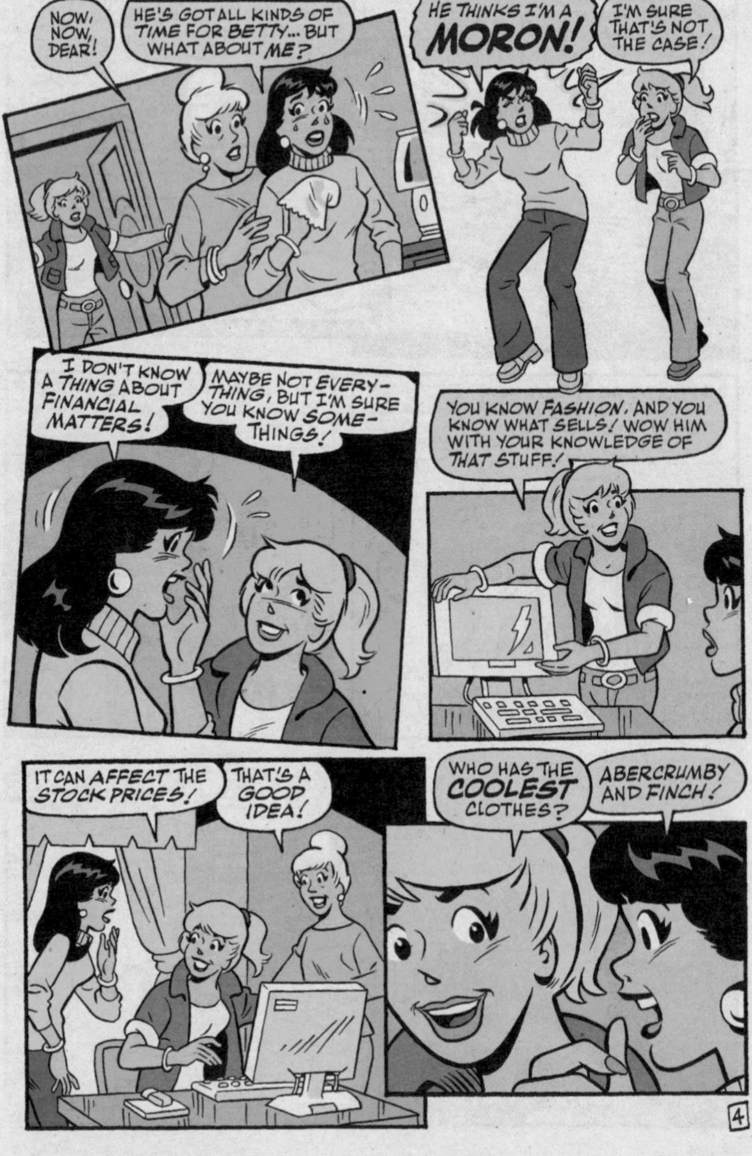
NOW, NOW, DEAR!
HE'S GOT ALL KINDS OF TIME FOR BETTY... BUT WHAT ABOUT ME?
HE THINKS I'M A MORON!
I'M SURE THAT'S NOT THE CASE!
I DON'T KNOW A THING ABOUT FINANCIAL MATTERS!
MAYBE NOT EVERY-THING, BUT I'M SURE YOU KNOW SOME-THINGS!
YOU KNOW FASHION, AND YOU KNOW WHAT SELLS! WOW HIM WITH YOUR KNOWLEDGE OF THAT STUFF!
IT CAN AFFECT THE STOCK PRICES!
THAT'S A GOOD IDEA!
WHO HAS THE COOLEST CLOTHES?
ABERCRUMBY AND FINCH!

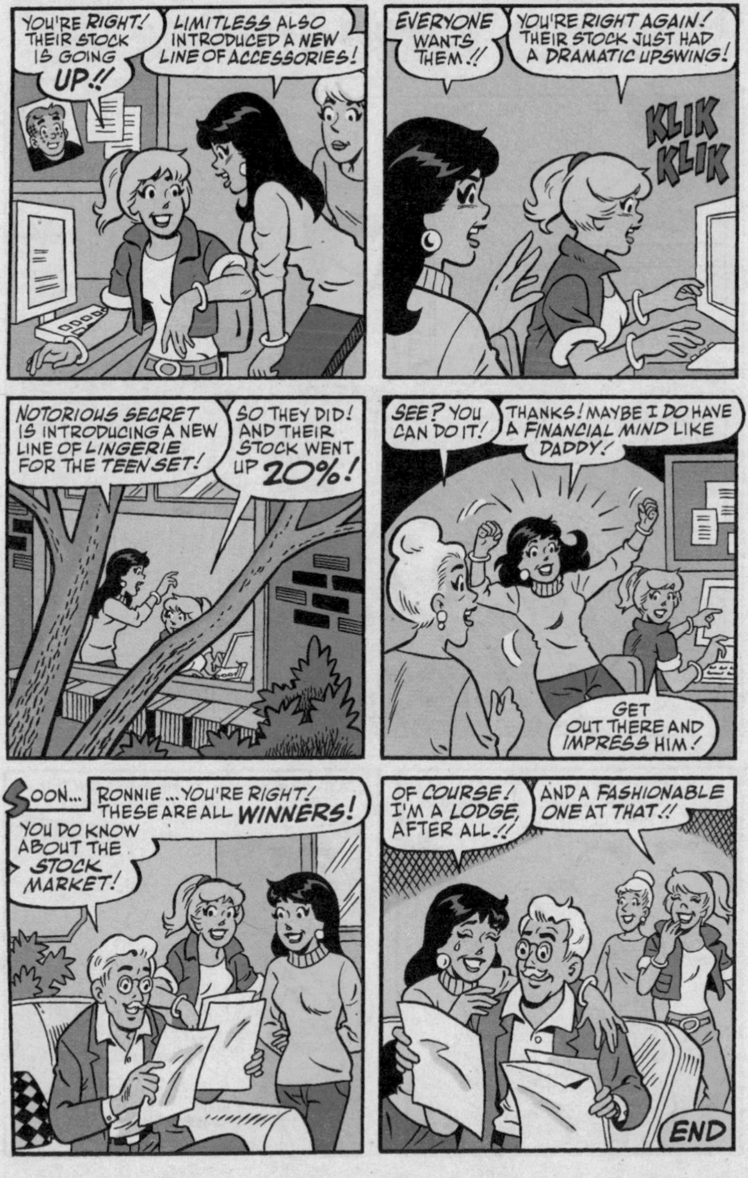
YOU'RE RIGHT! THEIR STOCK IS GOING UP!!
LIMITLESS ALSO INTRODUCED A NEW LINE OF ACCESSORIES!
EVERYONE WANTS THEM!!
YOU'RE RIGHT AGAIN! THEIR STOCK JUST HAD A DRAMATIC UPSWING!
KLIK KLIK
NOTORIOUS SECRET IS INTRODUCING A NEW LINE OF LINGERIE FOR THE TEEN SET!
SO THEY DID! AND THEIR STOCK WENT UP 20%!
SEE? YOU CAN DO IT!
THANKS! MAYBE I DO HAVE A FINANCIAL MIND LIKE DADDY!
GET OUT THERE AND IMPRESS HIM!
SOON...
RONNIE ...YOU'RE RIGHT! THESE ARE ALL WINNERS!
YOU DO KNOW ABOUT THE STOCK MARKET!
OF COURSE! I'M A LODGE, AFTER ALL!!
AND A FASHIONABLE ONE AT THAT!!
END

Veronica "LURE of the ARCADE"

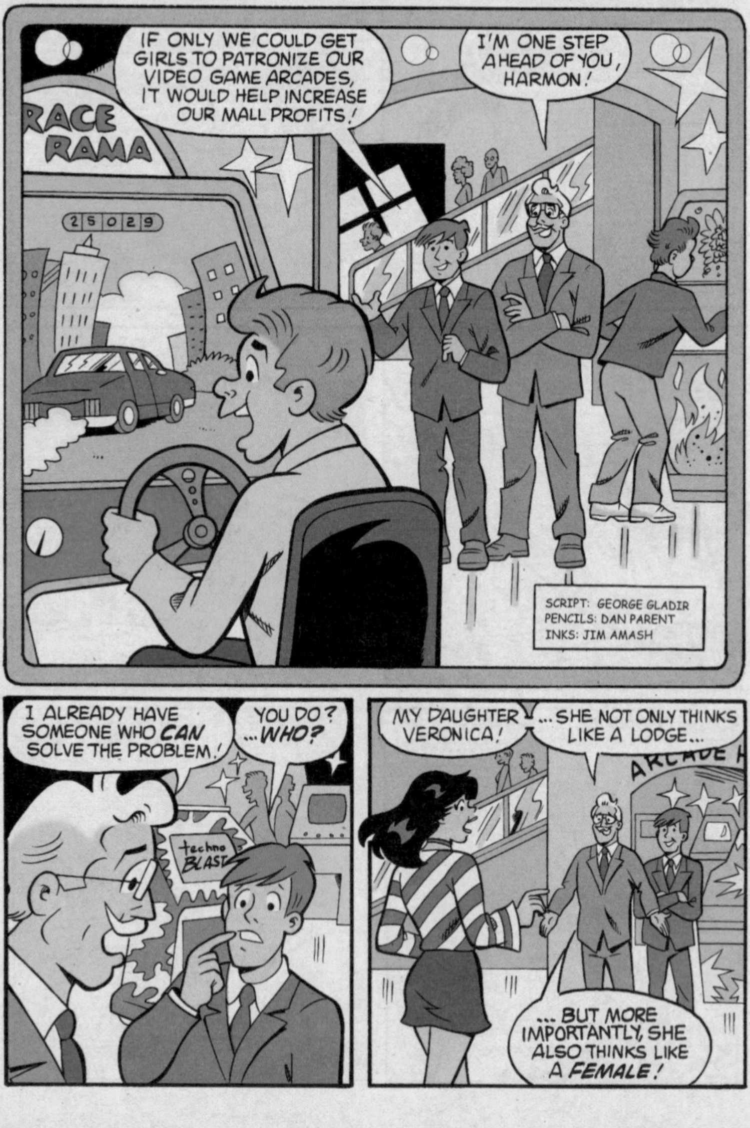
RACE RAMA
25029
IF ONLY WE COULD GET GIRLS TO PATRONIZE OUR VIDEO GAME ARCADES, IT WOULD HELP INCREASE OUR MALL PROFITS!
I'M ONE STEP AHEAD OF YOU, HARMON!
SCRIPT: GEORGE GLADIR
PENCILS: DAN PARENT
INKS: JIM AMASH
I ALREADY HAVE SOMEONE WHO CAN SOLVE THE PROBLEM!
YOU DO? ...WHO?
techno BLAST
MY DAUGHTER VERONICA!
...SHE NOT ONLY THINKS LIKE A LODGE...
...BUT MORE IMPORTANTLY, SHE ALSO THINKS LIKE A FEMALE!

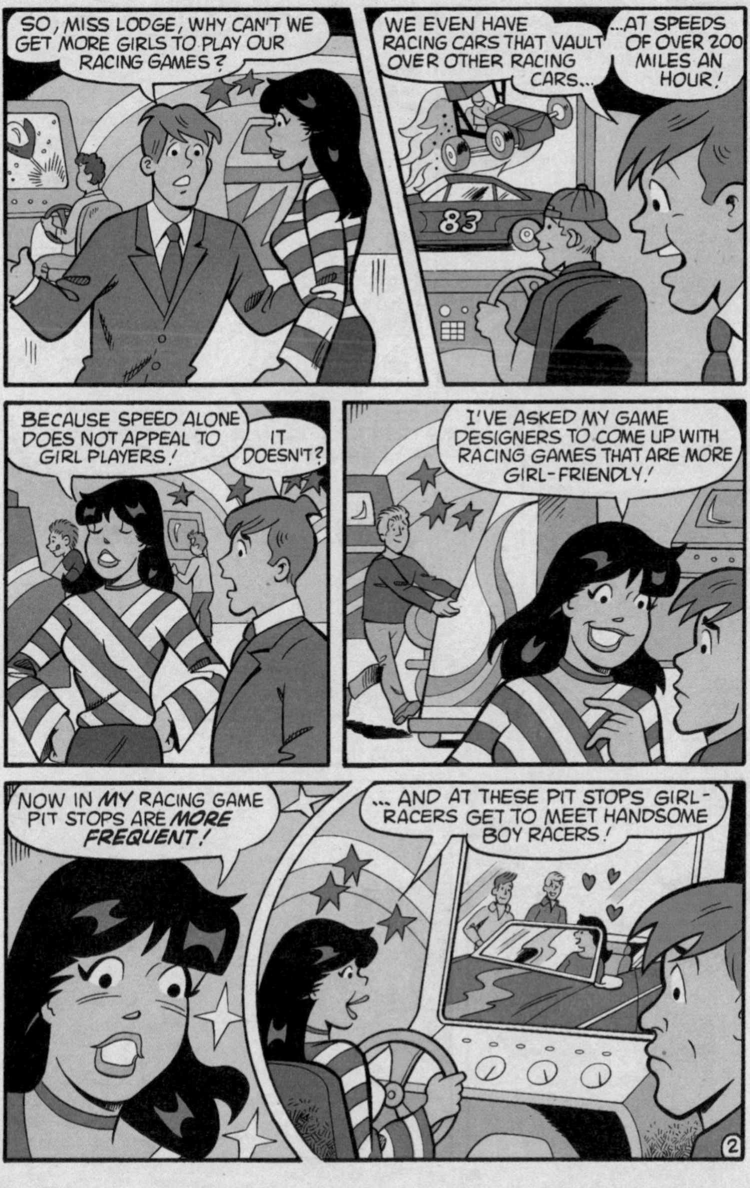
SO, MISS LODGE, WHY CAN'T WE GET MORE GIRLS TO PLAY OUR RACING GAMES?
WE EVEN HAVE RACING CARS THAT VAULT OVER OTHER RACING CARS...
...AT SPEEDS OF OVER 200 MILES AN HOUR!
83
BECAUSE SPEED ALONE DOES NOT APPEAL TO GIRL PLAYERS!
IT DOESN'T?
I'VE ASKED MY GAME DESIGNERS TO COME UP WITH RACING GAMES THAT ARE MORE GIRL-FRIENDLY!
NOW IN MY RACING GAME PIT STOPS ARE MORE FREQUENT!
... AND AT THESE PIT STOPS GIRL-RACERS GET TO MEET HANDSOME BOY RACERS!
2

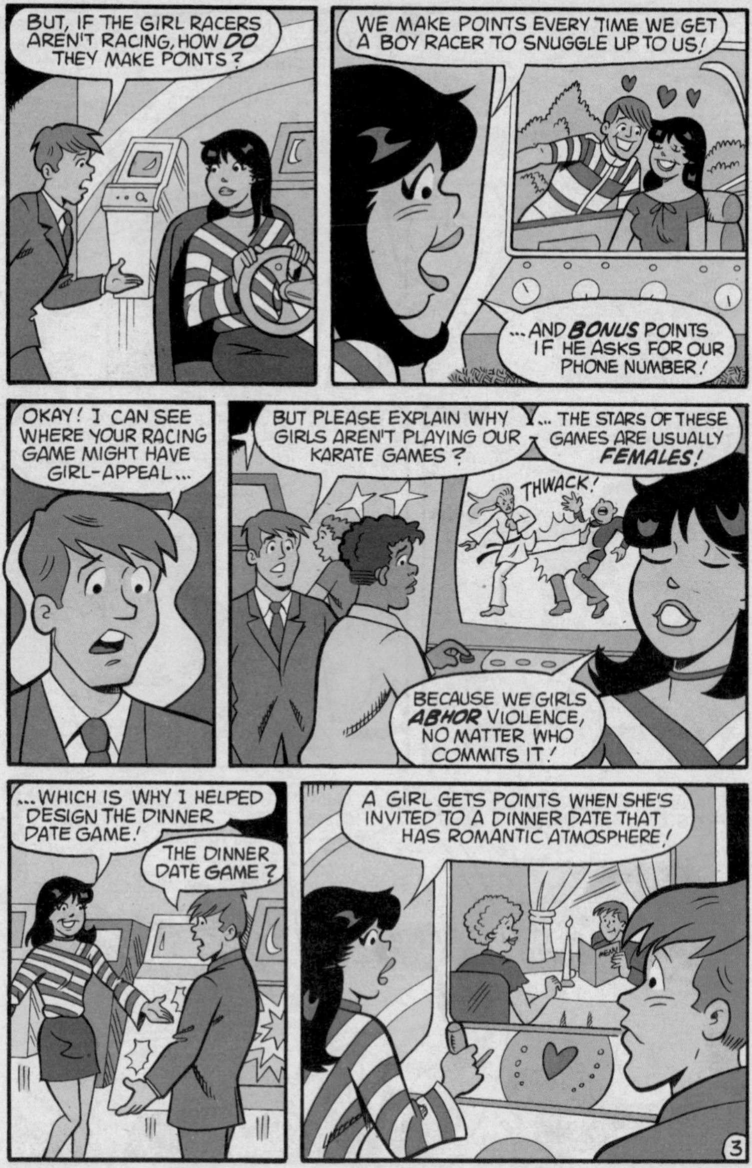

BUT, IF THE GIRL RACERS AREN'T RACING, HOW *DO* THEY MAKE POINTS?
WE MAKE POINTS EVERY TIME WE GET A BOY RACER TO SNUGGLE UP TO US!
...AND *BONUS* POINTS IF HE ASKS FOR OUR PHONE NUMBER!
OKAY! I CAN SEE WHERE YOUR RACING GAME MIGHT HAVE GIRL-APPEAL...
BUT PLEASE EXPLAIN WHY GIRLS AREN'T PLAYING OUR KARATE GAMES?
... THE STARS OF THESE GAMES ARE USUALLY *FEMALES!*
THWACK!
BECAUSE WE GIRLS *ABHOR* VIOLENCE, NO MATTER WHO COMMITS IT!
...WHICH IS WHY I HELPED DESIGN THE DINNER DATE GAME!
THE DINNER DATE GAME?
A GIRL GETS POINTS WHEN SHE'S INVITED TO A DINNER DATE THAT HAS ROMANTIC ATMOSPHERE!
3

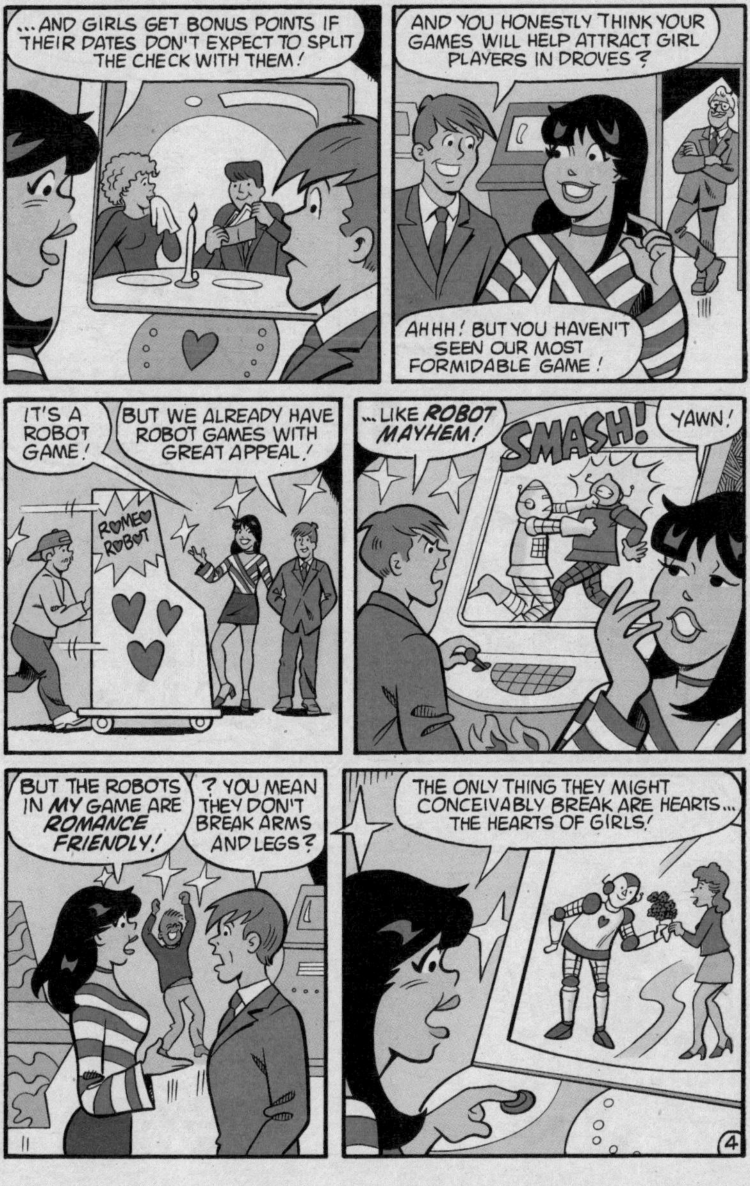
...AND GIRLS GET BONUS POINTS IF THEIR DATES DON'T EXPECT TO SPLIT THE CHECK WITH THEM!
AND YOU HONESTLY THINK YOUR GAMES WILL HELP ATTRACT GIRL PLAYERS IN DROVES?
AHHH! BUT YOU HAVEN'T SEEN OUR MOST FORMIDABLE GAME!
IT'S A ROBOT GAME!
BUT WE ALREADY HAVE ROBOT GAMES WITH GREAT APPEAL!
ROMEO ROBOT
...LIKE ROBOT MAYHEM!
SMASH!
YAWN!
BUT THE ROBOTS IN MY GAME ARE ROMANCE FRIENDLY!
? YOU MEAN THEY DON'T BREAK ARMS AND LEGS?
THE ONLY THING THEY MIGHT CONCEIVABLY BREAK ARE HEARTS... THE HEARTS OF GIRLS!
4

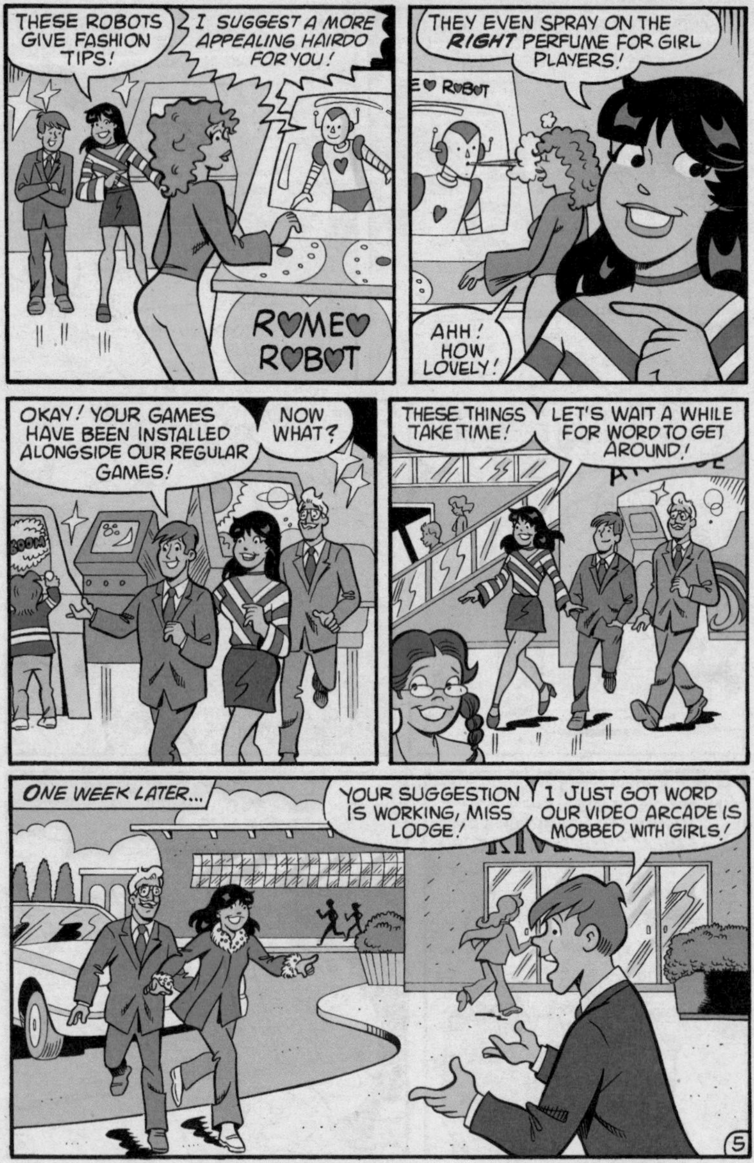

THESE ROBOTS GIVE FASHION TIPS!
I SUGGEST A MORE APPEALING HAIRDO FOR YOU!
ROMEO ROBOT
THEY EVEN SPRAY ON THE RIGHT PERFUME FOR GIRL PLAYERS!
AHH! HOW LOVELY!
OKAY! YOUR GAMES HAVE BEEN INSTALLED ALONGSIDE OUR REGULAR GAMES!
NOW WHAT?
THESE THINGS TAKE TIME!
LET'S WAIT A WHILE FOR WORD TO GET AROUND!
ONE WEEK LATER...
YOUR SUGGESTION IS WORKING, MISS LODGE!
I JUST GOT WORD OUR VIDEO ARCADE IS MOBBED WITH GIRLS!
5

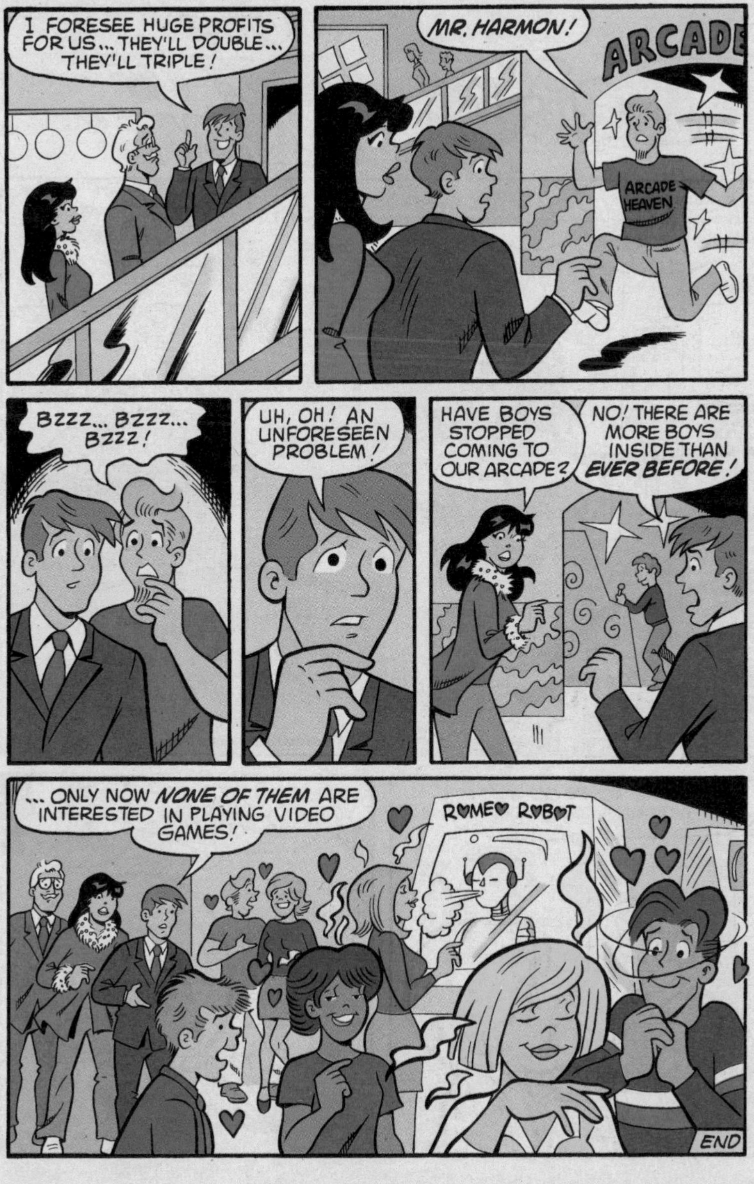
I FORESEE HUGE PROFITS FOR US... THEY'LL DOUBLE... THEY'LL TRIPLE!
MR. HARMON!
ARCADE
ARCADE HEAVEN
BZZZ... BZZZ... BZZZ!
UH, OH! AN UNFORESEEN PROBLEM!
HAVE BOYS STOPPED COMING TO OUR ARCADE?
NO! THERE ARE MORE BOYS INSIDE THAN EVER BEFORE!
... ONLY NOW NONE OF THEM ARE INTERESTED IN PLAYING VIDEO GAMES!
ROMEO ROBOT
END

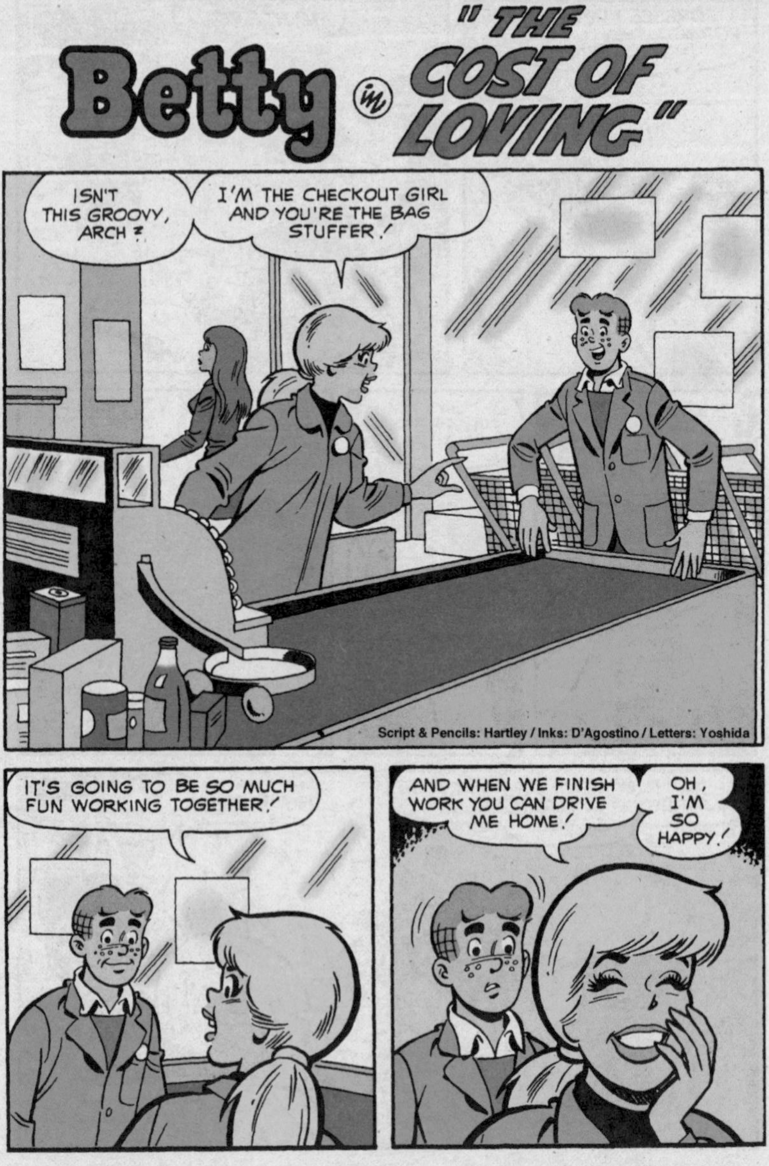
Betty in "THE COST OF LOVING"
ISN'T THIS GROOVY, ARCH?
I'M THE CHECKOUT GIRL AND YOU'RE THE BAG STUFFER!
Script & Pencils: Hartley / Inks: D'Agostino / Letters: Yoshida
IT'S GOING TO BE SO MUCH FUN WORKING TOGETHER!
AND WHEN WE FINISH WORK YOU CAN DRIVE ME HOME!
OH, I'M SO HAPPY!

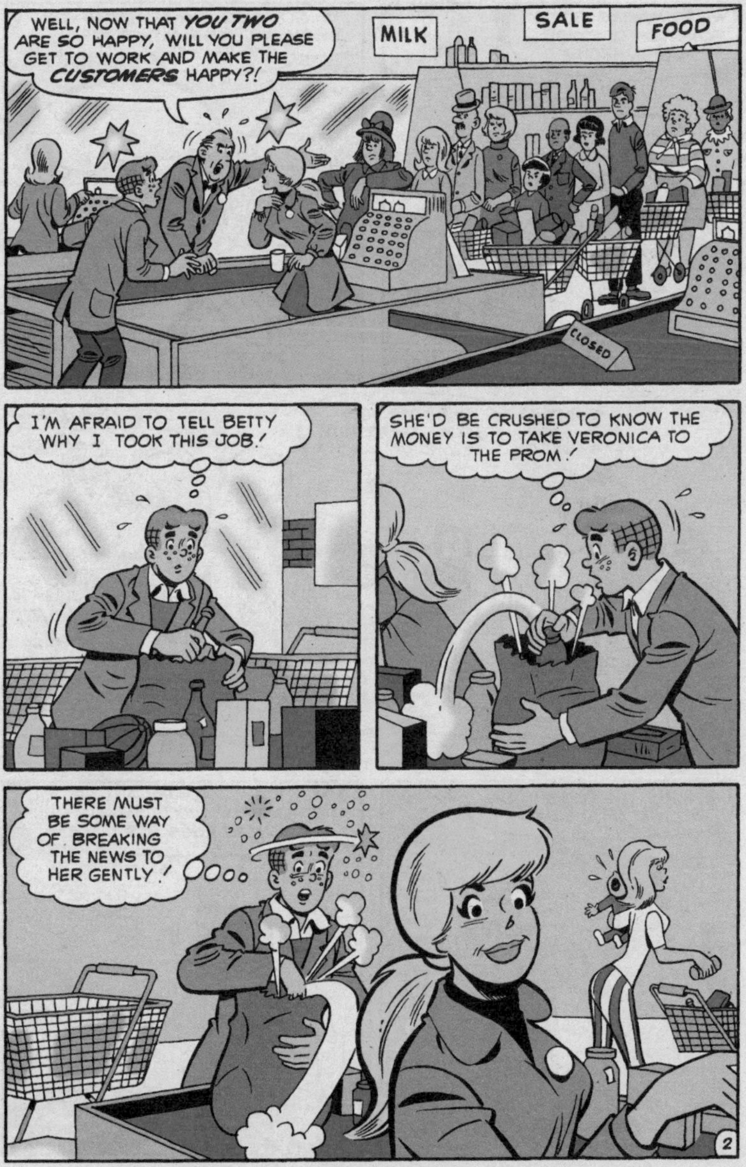

MILK
SALE
FOOD
WELL, NOW THAT YOU TWO ARE SO HAPPY, WILL YOU PLEASE GET TO WORK AND MAKE THE CUSTOMERS HAPPY?!
CLOSED
I'M AFRAID TO TELL BETTY WHY I TOOK THIS JOB!
SHE'D BE CRUSHED TO KNOW THE MONEY IS TO TAKE VERONICA TO THE PROM!
THERE MUST BE SOME WAY OF BREAKING THE NEWS TO HER GENTLY!
2

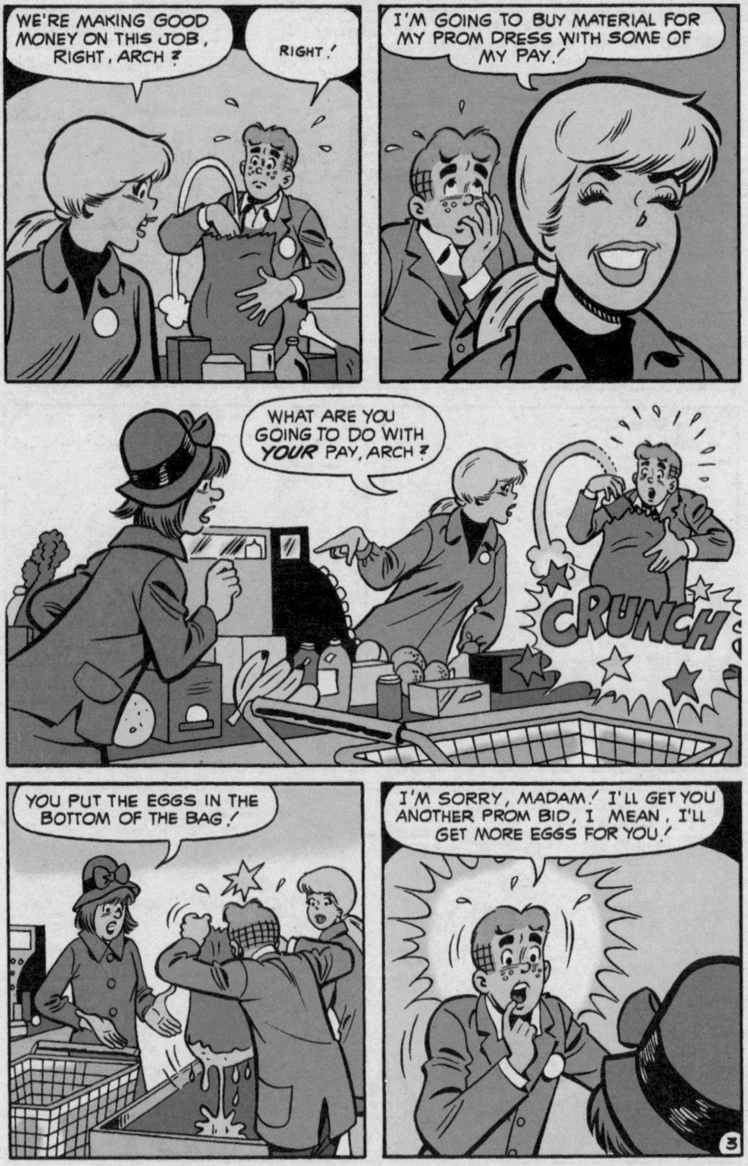
WE'RE MAKING GOOD MONEY ON THIS JOB, RIGHT, ARCH ?
RIGHT!
I'M GOING TO BUY MATERIAL FOR MY PROM DRESS WITH SOME OF MY PAY!
WHAT ARE YOU GOING TO DO WITH YOUR PAY, ARCH ?
CRUNCH
YOU PUT THE EGGS IN THE BOTTOM OF THE BAG!
I'M SORRY, MADAM! I'LL GET YOU ANOTHER PROM BID, I MEAN, I'LL GET MORE EGGS FOR YOU!
3

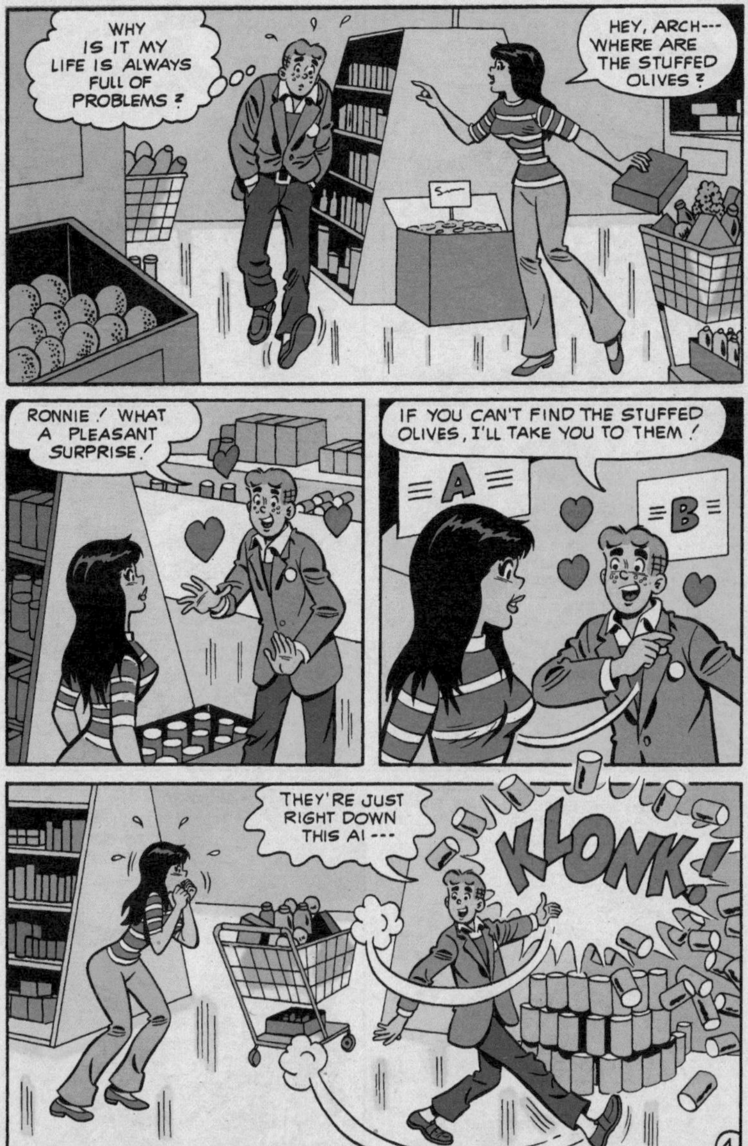
WHY IS IT MY LIFE IS ALWAYS FULL OF PROBLEMS?
HEY, ARCH--- WHERE ARE THE STUFFED OLIVES?
RONNIE! WHAT A PLEASANT SURPRISE!
IF YOU CAN'T FIND THE STUFFED OLIVES, I'LL TAKE YOU TO THEM!
A
B
THEY'RE JUST RIGHT DOWN THIS AI ---
KLONK!
4

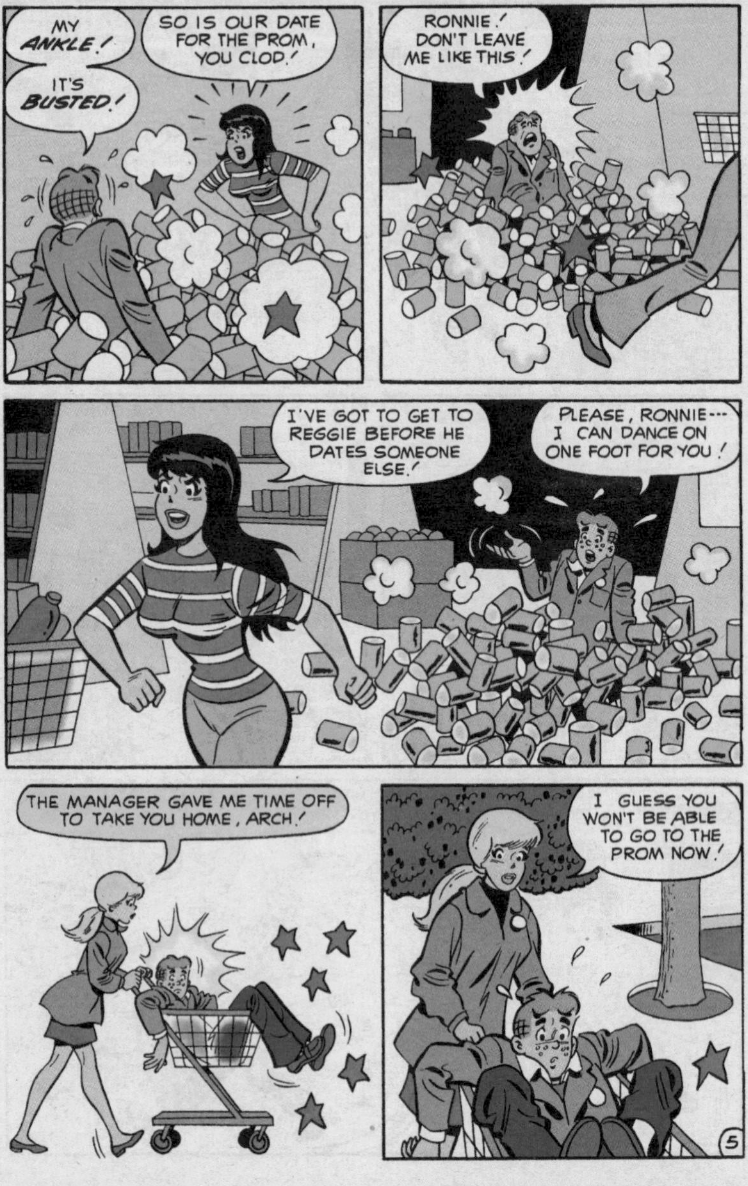

MY ANKLE!
IT'S BUSTED!
SO IS OUR DATE FOR THE PROM, YOU CLOD!
RONNIE! DON'T LEAVE ME LIKE THIS!
I'VE GOT TO GET TO REGGIE BEFORE HE DATES SOMEONE ELSE!
PLEASE, RONNIE--- I CAN DANCE ON ONE FOOT FOR YOU!
THE MANAGER GAVE ME TIME OFF TO TAKE YOU HOME, ARCH!
I GUESS YOU WON'T BE ABLE TO GO TO THE PROM NOW!

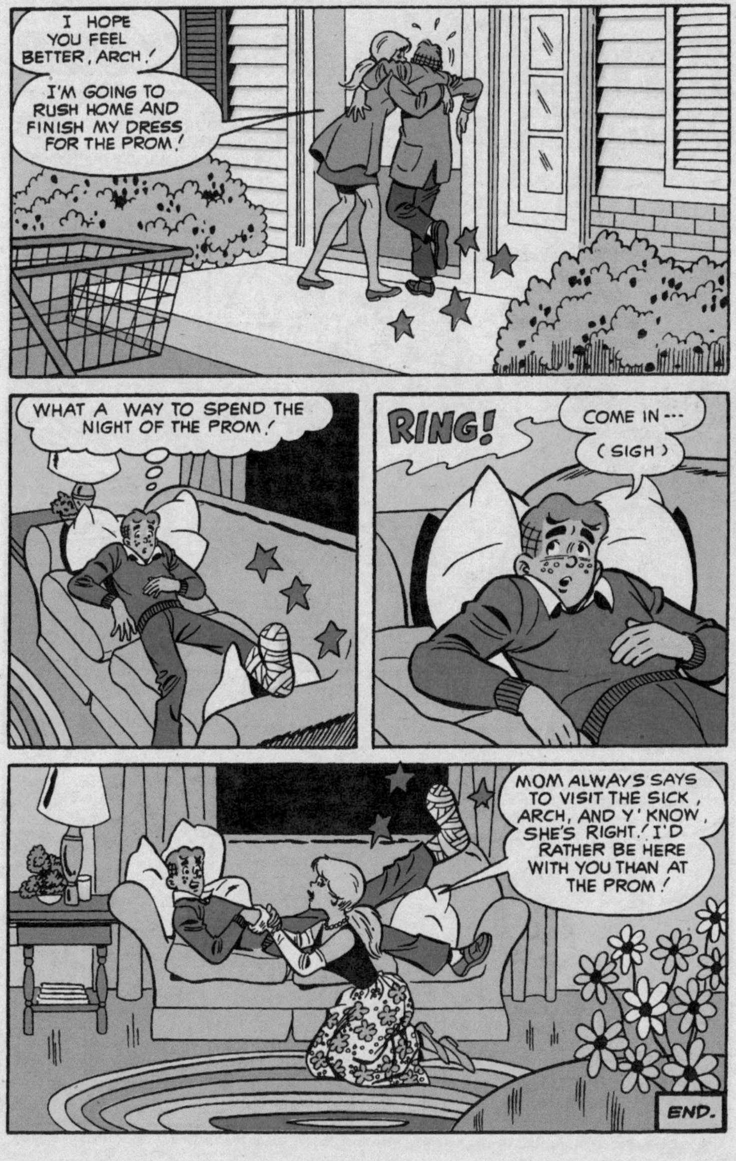
I HOPE YOU FEEL BETTER, ARCH!
I'M GOING TO RUSH HOME AND FINISH MY DRESS FOR THE PROM!
WHAT A WAY TO SPEND THE NIGHT OF THE PROM!
RING!
COME IN --- (SIGH)
MOM ALWAYS SAYS TO VISIT THE SICK, ARCH, AND Y'KNOW, SHE'S RIGHT! I'D RATHER BE HERE WITH YOU THAN AT THE PROM!
END.

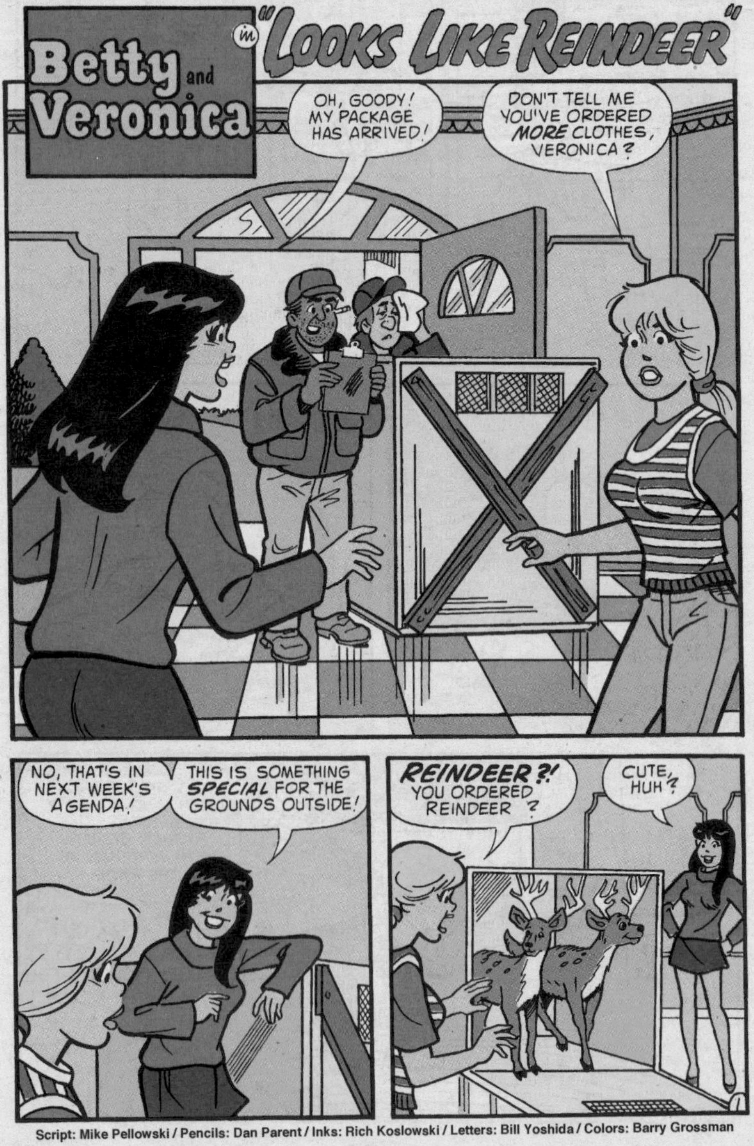
Betty and Veronica
in "LOOKS LIKE REINDEER"
OH, GOODY! MY PACKAGE HAS ARRIVED!
DON'T TELL ME YOU'VE ORDERED MORE CLOTHES, VERONICA?
NO, THAT'S IN NEXT WEEK'S AGENDA!
THIS IS SOMETHING SPECIAL FOR THE GROUNDS OUTSIDE!
REINDEER?! YOU ORDERED REINDEER?
CUTE, HUH?

Script: Mike Pellowski / Pencils: Dan Parent / Inks: Rich Koslowski / Letters: Bill Yoshida / Colors: Barry Grossman

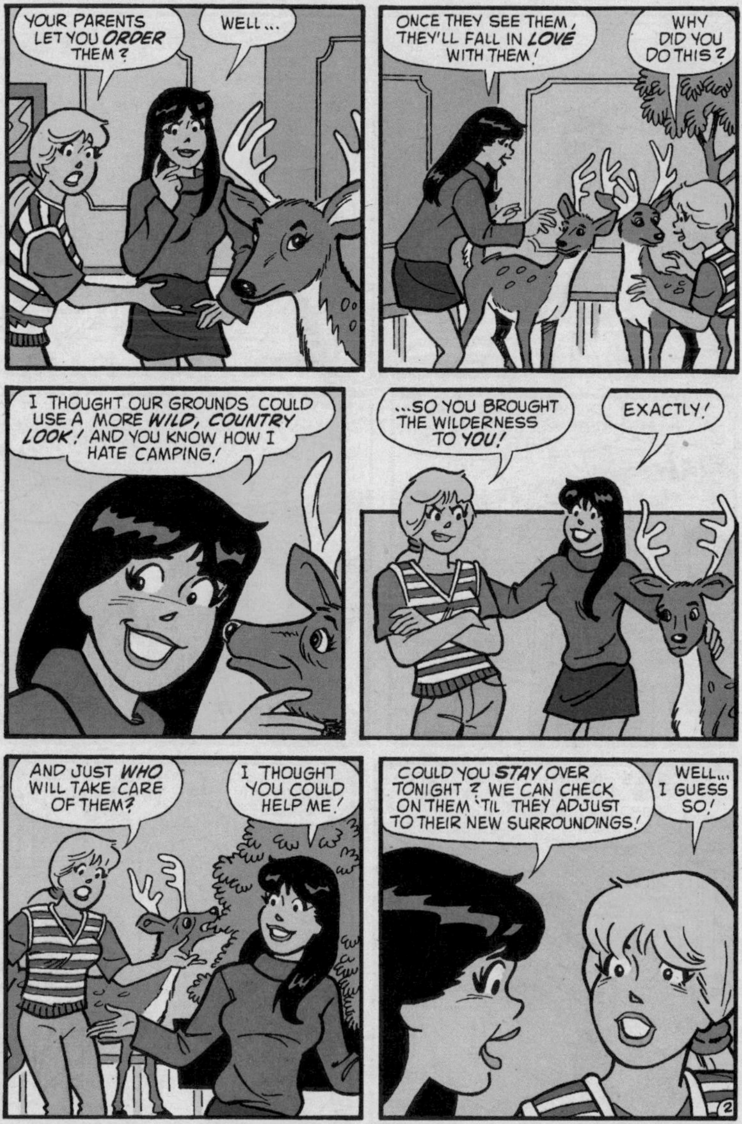
YOUR PARENTS LET YOU ORDER THEM?
WELL...
ONCE THEY SEE THEM, THEY'LL FALL IN LOVE WITH THEM!
WHY DID YOU DO THIS?
I THOUGHT OUR GROUNDS COULD USE A MORE WILD, COUNTRY LOOK! AND YOU KNOW HOW I HATE CAMPING!
...SO YOU BROUGHT THE WILDERNESS TO YOU!
EXACTLY!
AND JUST WHO WILL TAKE CARE OF THEM?
I THOUGHT YOU COULD HELP ME!
COULD YOU STAY OVER TONIGHT? WE CAN CHECK ON THEM 'TIL THEY ADJUST TO THEIR NEW SURROUNDINGS!
WELL... I GUESS SO!
2

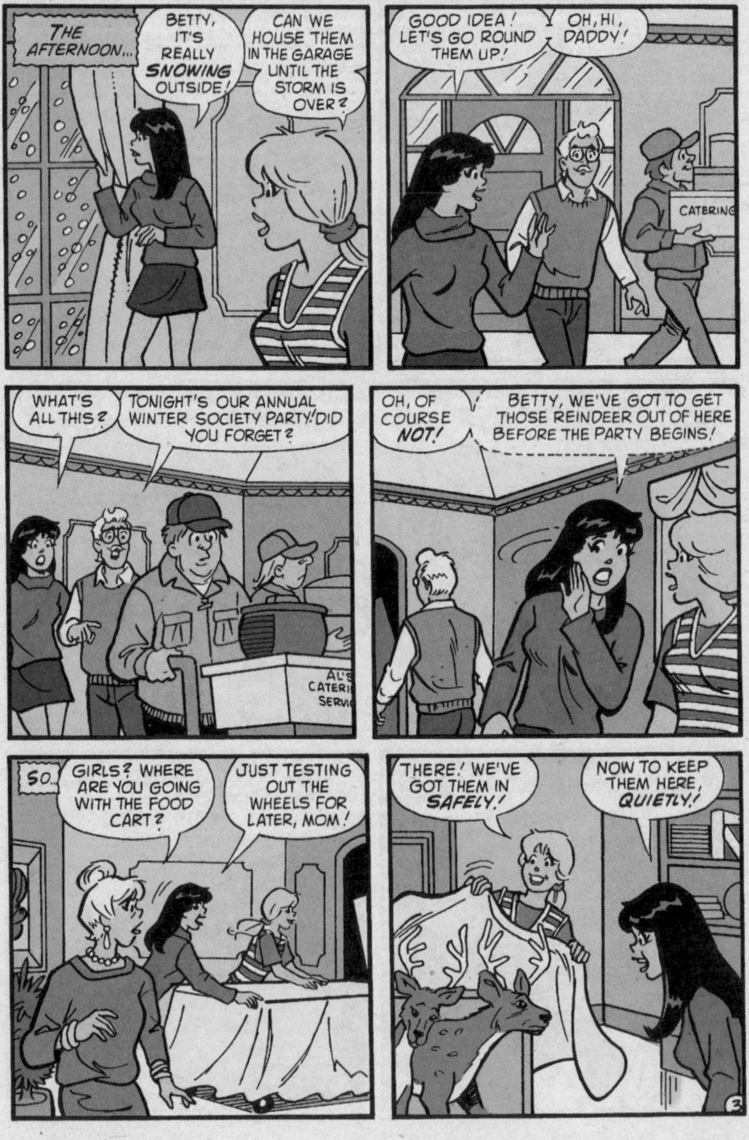

THE AFTERNOON...
BETTY, IT'S REALLY SNOWING OUTSIDE!
CAN WE HOUSE THEM IN THE GARAGE UNTIL THE STORM IS OVER?
GOOD IDEA! LET'S GO ROUND THEM UP!
OH, HI, DADDY!
CATERING
WHAT'S ALL THIS?
TONIGHT'S OUR ANNUAL WINTER SOCIETY PARTY! DID YOU FORGET?
AL'S CATERI SERVI
OH, OF COURSE NOT!
BETTY, WE'VE GOT TO GET THOSE REINDEER OUT OF HERE BEFORE THE PARTY BEGINS!
SO...
GIRLS? WHERE ARE YOU GOING WITH THE FOOD CART?
JUST TESTING OUT THE WHEELS FOR LATER, MOM!
THERE! WE'VE GOT THEM IN SAFELY!
NOW TO KEEP THEM HERE, QUIETLY!
3

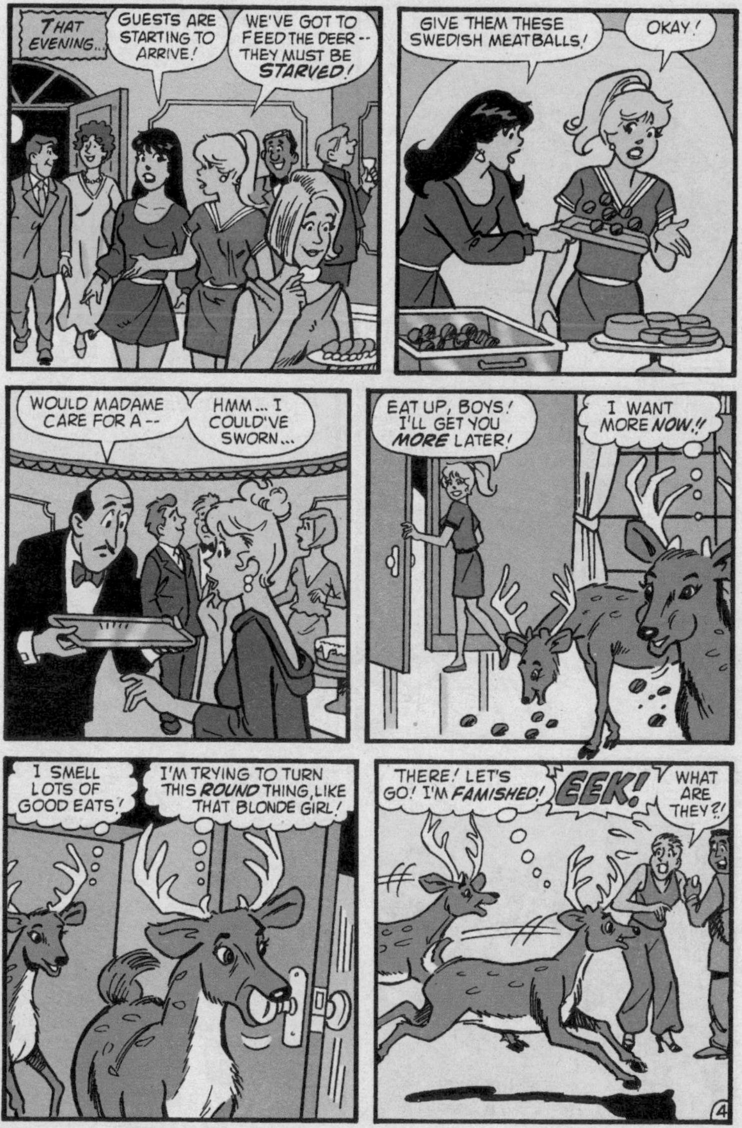
THAT EVENING...
GUESTS ARE STARTING TO ARRIVE!
WE'VE GOT TO FEED THE DEER -- THEY MUST BE STARVED!
GIVE THEM THESE SWEDISH MEATBALLS!
OKAY!
WOULD MADAME CARE FOR A --
HMM ... I COULD'VE SWORN ...
EAT UP, BOYS! I'LL GET YOU MORE LATER!
I WANT MORE NOW!!
I SMELL LOTS OF GOOD EATS!
I'M TRYING TO TURN THIS ROUND THING, LIKE THAT BLONDE GIRL!
THERE! LET'S GO! I'M FAMISHED!
EEK!
WHAT ARE THEY?!
4

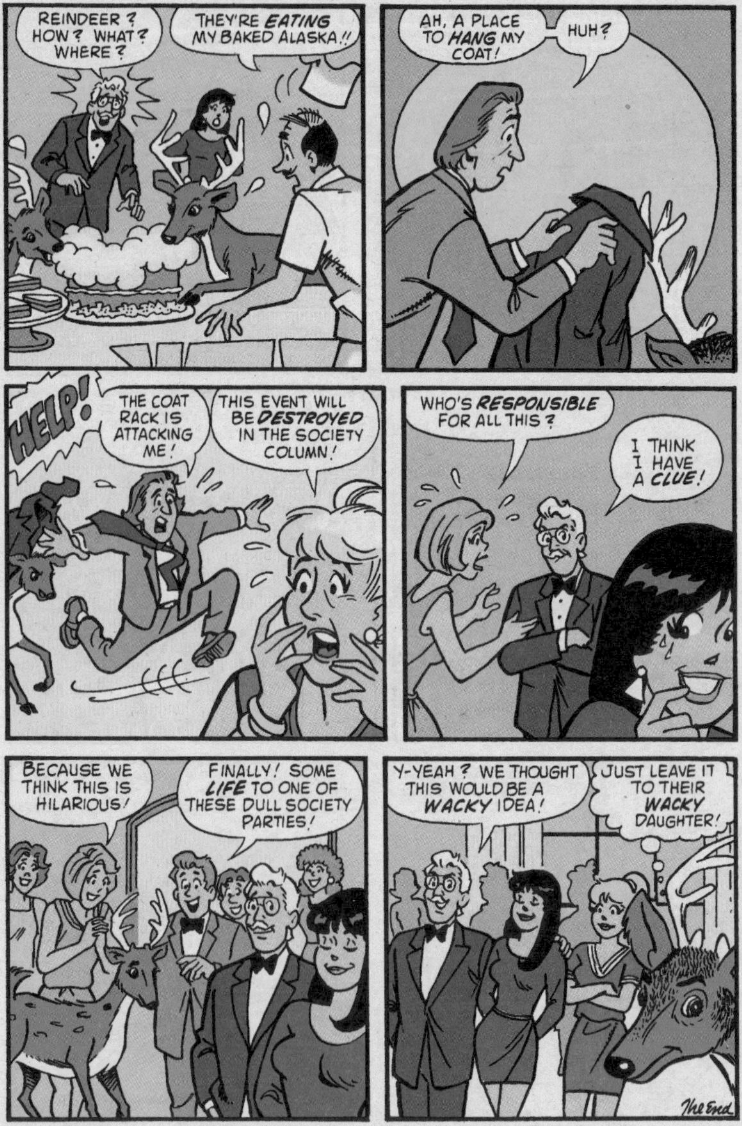
REINDEER? HOW? WHAT? WHERE?
THEY'RE EATING MY BAKED ALASKA!!
AH, A PLACE TO HANG MY COAT!
HUH?
HELP!
THE COAT RACK IS ATTACKING ME!
THIS EVENT WILL BE DESTROYED IN THE SOCIETY COLUMN!
WHO'S RESPONSIBLE FOR ALL THIS?
I THINK I HAVE A CLUE!
BECAUSE WE THINK THIS IS HILARIOUS!
FINALLY! SOME LIFE TO ONE OF THESE DULL SOCIETY PARTIES!
Y-YEAH? WE THOUGHT THIS WOULD BE A WACKY IDEA!
JUST LEAVE IT TO THEIR WACKY DAUGHTER!
The End

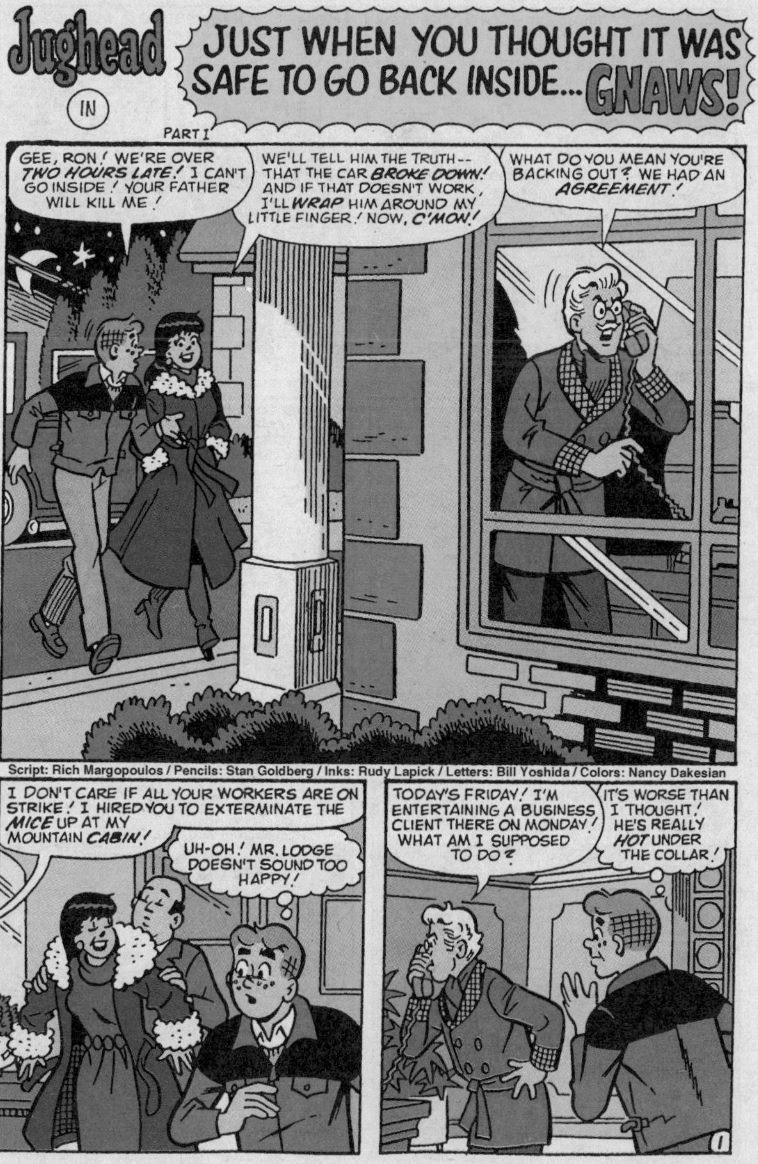
Jughead
IN
JUST WHEN YOU THOUGHT IT WAS SAFE TO GO BACK INSIDE... GNAWS!
PART I
GEE, RON! WE'RE OVER TWO HOURS LATE! I CAN'T GO INSIDE! YOUR FATHER WILL KILL ME!
WE'LL TELL HIM THE TRUTH -- THAT THE CAR BROKE DOWN! AND IF THAT DOESN'T WORK, I'LL WRAP HIM AROUND MY LITTLE FINGER! NOW, C'MON!
WHAT DO YOU MEAN YOU'RE BACKING OUT? WE HAD AN AGREEMENT!
Script: Rich Margopoulos / Pencils: Stan Goldberg / Inks: Rudy Lapick / Letters: Bill Yoshida / Colors: Nancy Dakesian
I DON'T CARE IF ALL YOUR WORKERS ARE ON STRIKE! I HIRED YOU TO EXTERMINATE THE MICE UP AT MY MOUNTAIN CABIN!
UH-OH! MR. LODGE DOESN'T SOUND TOO HAPPY!
TODAY'S FRIDAY! I'M ENTERTAINING A BUSINESS CLIENT THERE ON MONDAY! WHAT AM I SUPPOSED TO DO?
IT'S WORSE THAN I THOUGHT! HE'S REALLY HOT UNDER THE COLLAR!
1

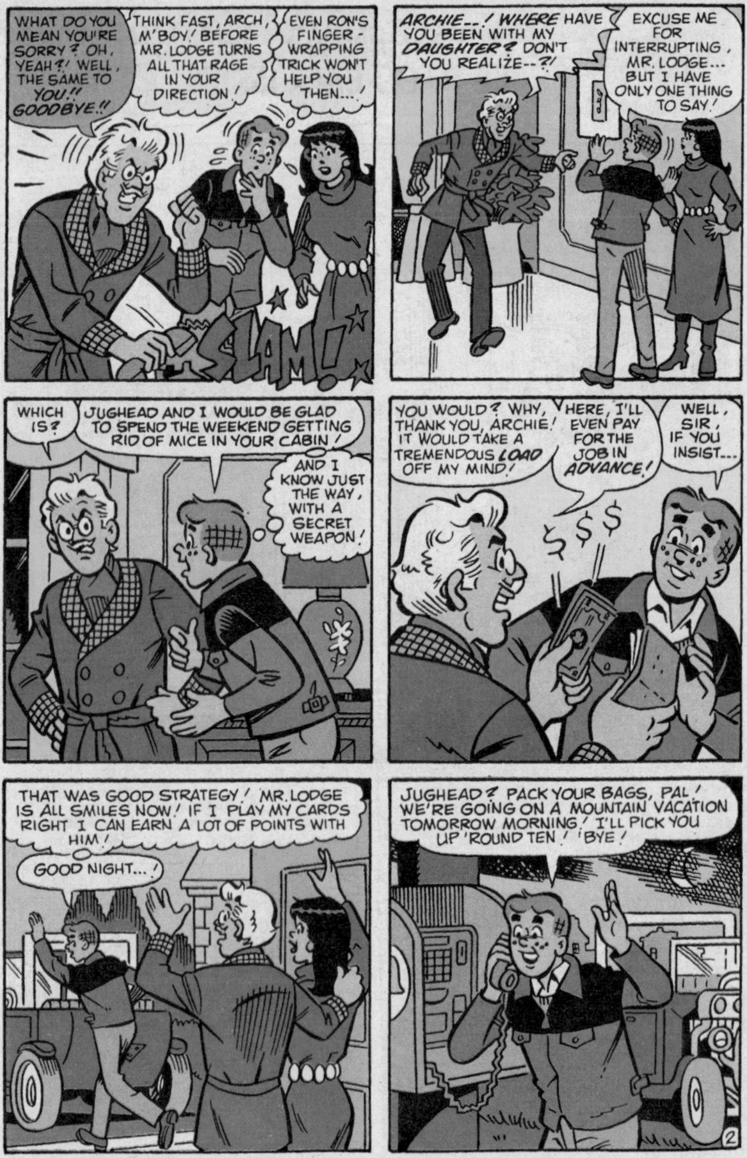
WHAT DO YOU MEAN YOU'RE SORRY? OH, YEAH?! WELL, THE SAME TO YOU!! GOODBYE!!
THINK FAST, ARCH, M'BOY! BEFORE MR. LODGE TURNS ALL THAT RAGE IN YOUR DIRECTION!
EVEN RON'S FINGER-WRAPPING TRICK WON'T HELP YOU THEN...!
SLAM!
ARCHIE--! WHERE HAVE YOU BEEN WITH MY DAUGHTER? DON'T YOU REALIZE--?!
EXCUSE ME FOR INTERRUPTING, MR. LODGE... BUT I HAVE ONLY ONE THING TO SAY!
WHICH IS?
JUGHEAD AND I WOULD BE GLAD TO SPEND THE WEEKEND GETTING RID OF MICE IN YOUR CABIN!
AND I KNOW JUST THE WAY, WITH A SECRET WEAPON!
YOU WOULD? WHY, THANK YOU, ARCHIE! IT WOULD TAKE A TREMENDOUS LOAD OFF MY MIND!
HERE, I'LL EVEN PAY FOR THE JOB IN ADVANCE!
WELL, SIR, IF YOU INSIST...
THAT WAS GOOD STRATEGY! MR. LODGE IS ALL SMILES NOW! IF I PLAY MY CARDS RIGHT I CAN EARN A LOT OF POINTS WITH HIM!
GOOD NIGHT...!
JUGHEAD? PACK YOUR BAGS, PAL! WE'RE GOING ON A MOUNTAIN VACATION TOMORROW MORNING! I'LL PICK YOU UP 'ROUND TEN! 'BYE!
2

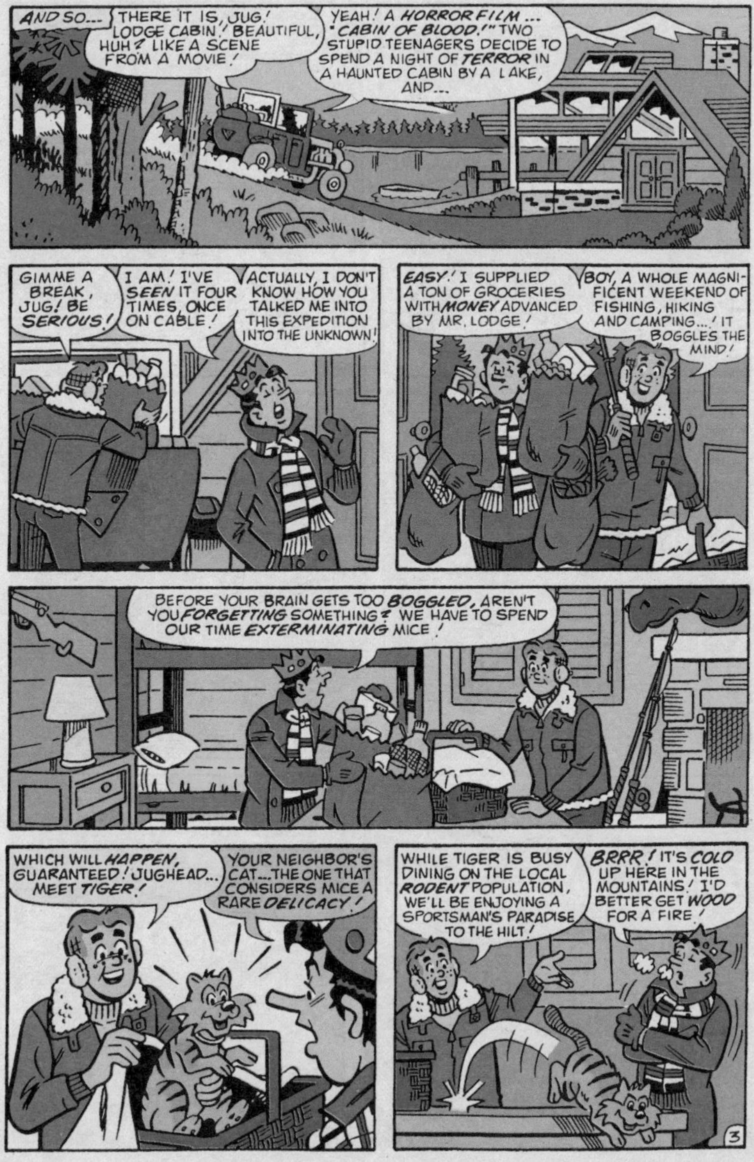
AND SO...
THERE IT IS, JUG! LODGE CABIN! BEAUTIFUL, HUH? LIKE A SCENE FROM A MOVIE!
YEAH! A HORROR FILM ... "CABIN OF BLOOD!" TWO STUPID TEENAGERS DECIDE TO SPEND A NIGHT OF TERROR IN A HAUNTED CABIN BY A LAKE, AND...
GIMME A BREAK, JUG! BE SERIOUS!
I AM! I'VE SEEN IT FOUR TIMES, ONCE ON CABLE!
ACTUALLY, I DON'T KNOW HOW YOU TALKED ME INTO THIS EXPEDITION INTO THE UNKNOWN!
EASY! I SUPPLIED A TON OF GROCERIES WITH MONEY ADVANCED BY MR. LODGE!
BOY, A WHOLE MAGNIFICENT WEEKEND OF FISHING, HIKING AND CAMPING...! IT BOGGLES THE MIND!
BEFORE YOUR BRAIN GETS TOO BOGGLED, AREN'T YOU FORGETTING SOMETHING? WE HAVE TO SPEND OUR TIME EXTERMINATING MICE!
WHICH WILL HAPPEN, GUARANTEED! JUGHEAD... MEET TIGER!
YOUR NEIGHBOR'S CAT...THE ONE THAT CONSIDERS MICE A RARE DELICACY!
WHILE TIGER IS BUSY DINING ON THE LOCAL RODENT POPULATION, WE'LL BE ENJOYING A SPORTSMAN'S PARADISE TO THE HILT!
BRRR! IT'S COLD UP HERE IN THE MOUNTAINS! I'D BETTER GET WOOD FOR A FIRE!
3

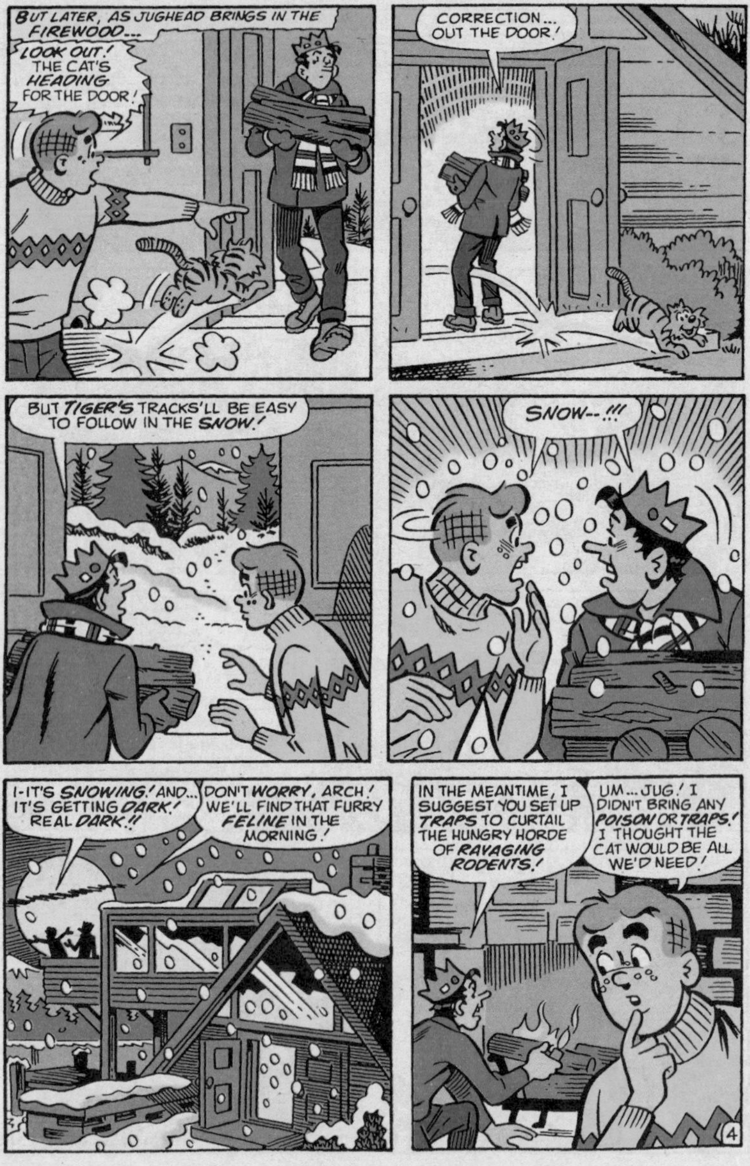
BUT LATER, AS JUGHEAD BRINGS IN THE FIREWOOD...
LOOK OUT! THE CAT'S HEADING FOR THE DOOR!
CORRECTION... OUT THE DOOR!
BUT TIGER'S TRACKS'LL BE EASY TO FOLLOW IN THE SNOW!
SNOW--!!!
I-IT'S SNOWING! AND... IT'S GETTING DARK! REAL DARK!!
DON'T WORRY, ARCH! WE'LL FIND THAT FURRY FELINE IN THE MORNING!
IN THE MEANTIME, I SUGGEST YOU SET UP TRAPS TO CURTAIL THE HUNGRY HORDE OF RAVAGING RODENTS!
UM... JUG! I DIDN'T BRING ANY POISON OR TRAPS! I THOUGHT THE CAT WOULD BE ALL WE'D NEED!
4

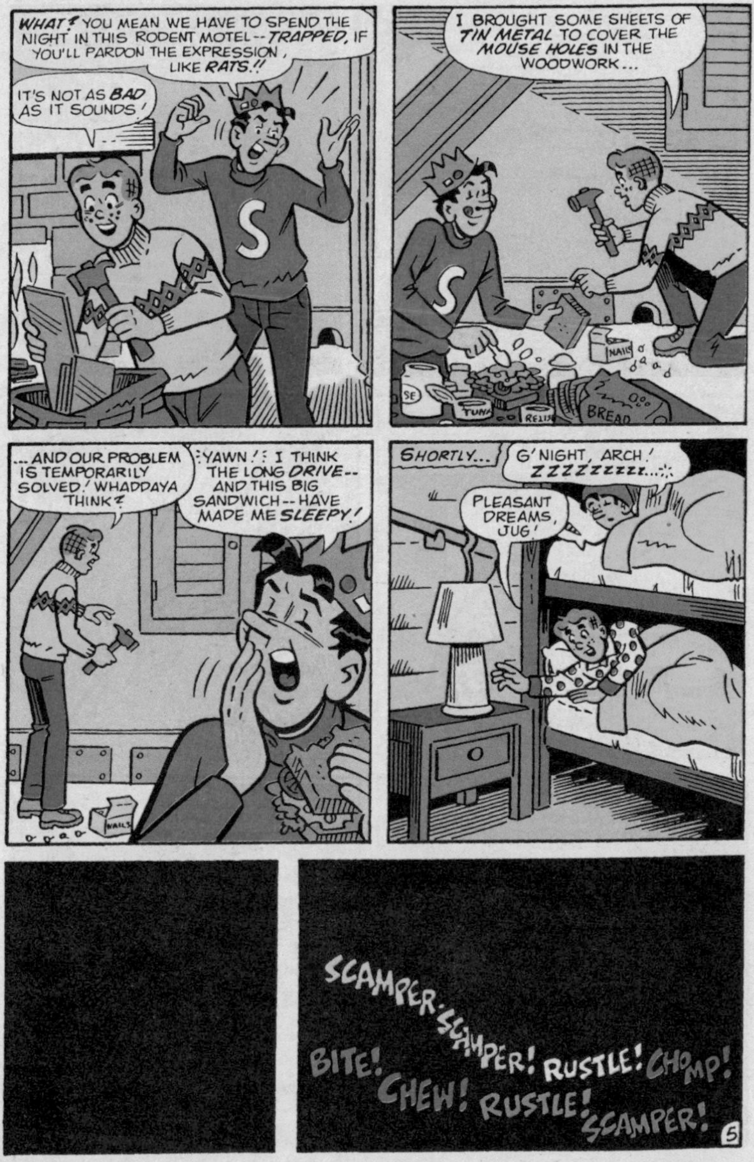
WHAT? YOU MEAN WE HAVE TO SPEND THE NIGHT IN THIS RODENT MOTEL -- TRAPPED, IF YOU'LL PARDON THE EXPRESSION, LIKE RATS.!!
IT'S NOT AS BAD AS IT SOUNDS!
I BROUGHT SOME SHEETS OF TIN METAL TO COVER THE MOUSE HOLES IN THE WOODWORK...
NAILS
BREAD
TUNA
RELISH
... AND OUR PROBLEM IS TEMPORARILY SOLVED! WHADDAYA THINK?
YAWN! I THINK THE LONG DRIVE -- AND THIS BIG SANDWICH -- HAVE MADE ME SLEEPY!
NAILS
SHORTLY...
G' NIGHT, ARCH! ZZZZZZZZZ...
PLEASANT DREAMS, JUG!
SCAMPER-SCAMPER! RUSTLE! CHOMP!
BITE! CHEW! RUSTLE! SCAMPER!
5

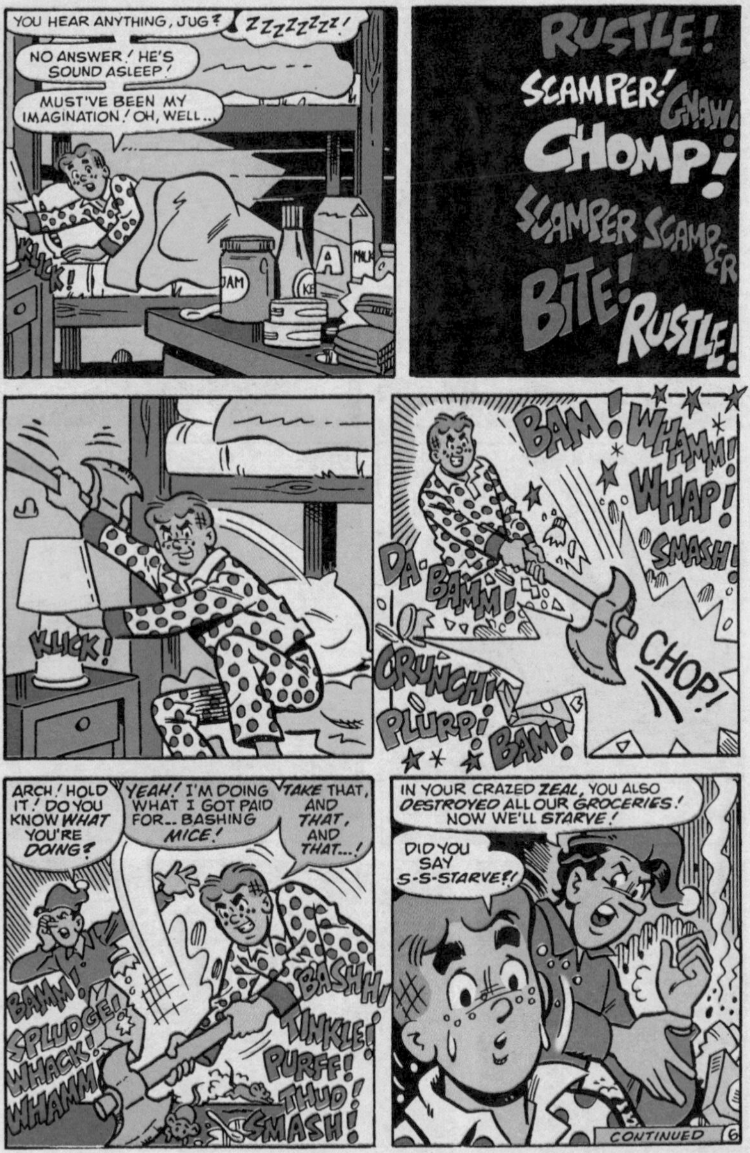

YOU HEAR ANYTHING, JUG?
ZZZZZZZZ!
NO ANSWER! HE'S SOUND ASLEEP!
MUST'VE BEEN MY IMAGINATION! OH, WELL...
KLICK!
JAM
A
MILK
RUSTLE!
SCAMPER!
GNAW!
CHOMP!
SCAMPER SCAMPER SCAMPER
BITE!
RUSTLE!
KLICK!
BAM! WHAMM! WHAP! SMASH!
DA-BAMM!
CRUNCH! PLURP! BAM!
CHOP!
ARCH! HOLD IT! DO YOU KNOW WHAT YOU'RE DOING?
YEAH! I'M DOING WHAT I GOT PAID FOR.. BASHING MICE!
TAKE THAT, AND THAT, AND THAT...!
BAMM! SPLUDGE! WHACK! WHAMM!
BASHH! TINKLE! PURFF! THUD! SMASH!
IN YOUR CRAZED ZEAL, YOU ALSO DESTROYED ALL OUR GROCERIES! NOW WE'LL STARVE!
DID YOU SAY S-S-STARVE?!
CONTINUED

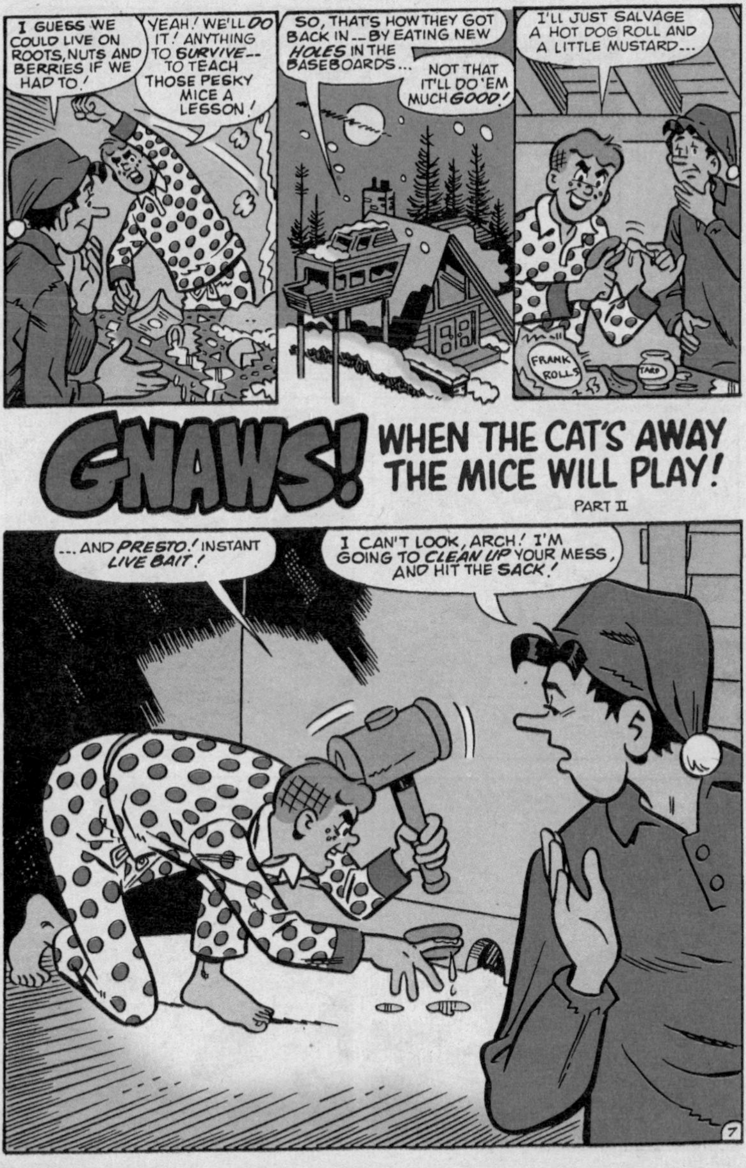
I GUESS WE COULD LIVE ON ROOTS, NUTS AND BERRIES IF WE HAD TO!
YEAH! WE'LL DO IT! ANYTHING TO SURVIVE-- TO TEACH THOSE PESKY MICE A LESSON!
SO, THAT'S HOW THEY GOT BACK IN -- BY EATING NEW HOLES IN THE BASEBOARDS...
NOT THAT IT'LL DO 'EM MUCH GOOD!
I'LL JUST SALVAGE A HOT DOG ROLL AND A LITTLE MUSTARD...
FRANK ROLLS
GNAWS!
WHEN THE CAT'S AWAY THE MICE WILL PLAY!
PART II
...AND PRESTO! INSTANT LIVE BAIT!
I CAN'T LOOK, ARCH! I'M GOING TO CLEAN UP YOUR MESS, AND HIT THE SACK!
7

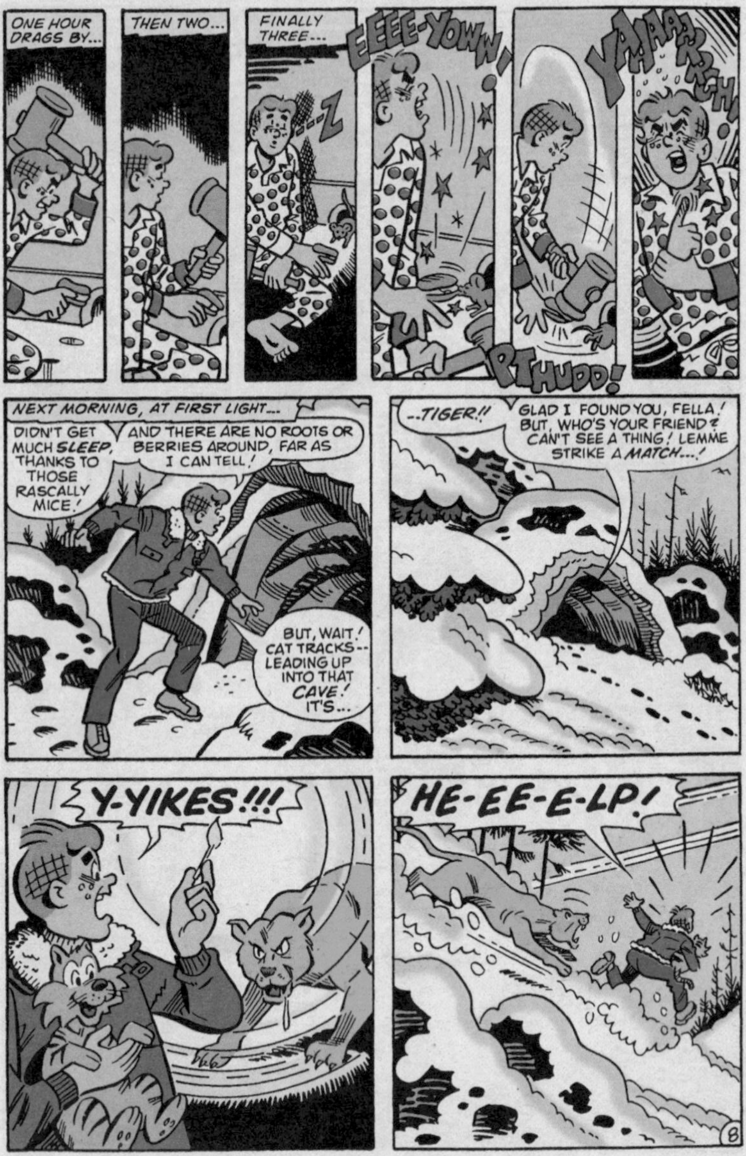
ONE HOUR DRAGS BY...
THEN TWO...
FINALLY THREE...
Z-Z-Z
EEEE-YOWW!
YAAARRGH!
PTHUDD!
NEXT MORNING, AT FIRST LIGHT...
DIDN'T GET MUCH SLEEP, THANKS TO THOSE RASCALLY MICE!
AND THERE ARE NO ROOTS OR BERRIES AROUND, FAR AS I CAN TELL!
BUT, WAIT! CAT TRACKS-- LEADING UP INTO THAT CAVE! IT'S...
--TIGER!!
GLAD I FOUND YOU, FELLA! BUT, WHO'S YOUR FRIEND? CAN'T SEE A THING! LEMME STRIKE A MATCH...!
Y-YIKES!!!
HE-EE-E-LP!
8

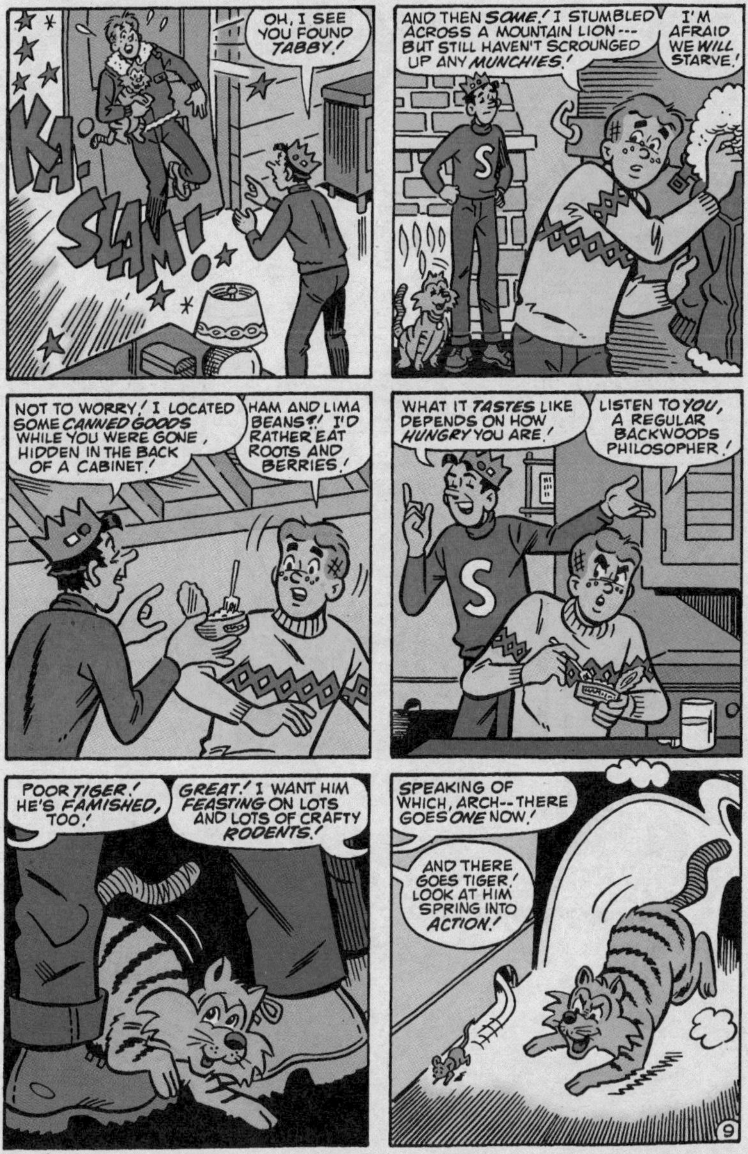
KA-SLAM!
OH, I SEE YOU FOUND TABBY!
AND THEN SOME! I STUMBLED ACROSS A MOUNTAIN LION--- BUT STILL HAVEN'T SCROUNGED UP ANY MUNCHIES!
I'M AFRAID WE WILL STARVE!
NOT TO WORRY! I LOCATED SOME CANNED GOODS WHILE YOU WERE GONE, HIDDEN IN THE BACK OF A CABINET!
HAM AND LIMA BEANS?! I'D RATHER EAT ROOTS AND BERRIES!
WHAT IT TASTES LIKE DEPENDS ON HOW HUNGRY YOU ARE!
LISTEN TO YOU, A REGULAR BACKWOODS PHILOSOPHER!
POOR TIGER! HE'S FAMISHED, TOO!
GREAT! I WANT HIM FEASTING ON LOTS AND LOTS OF CRAFTY RODENTS!
SPEAKING OF WHICH, ARCH-- THERE GOES ONE NOW!
AND THERE GOES TIGER! LOOK AT HIM SPRING INTO ACTION!
9

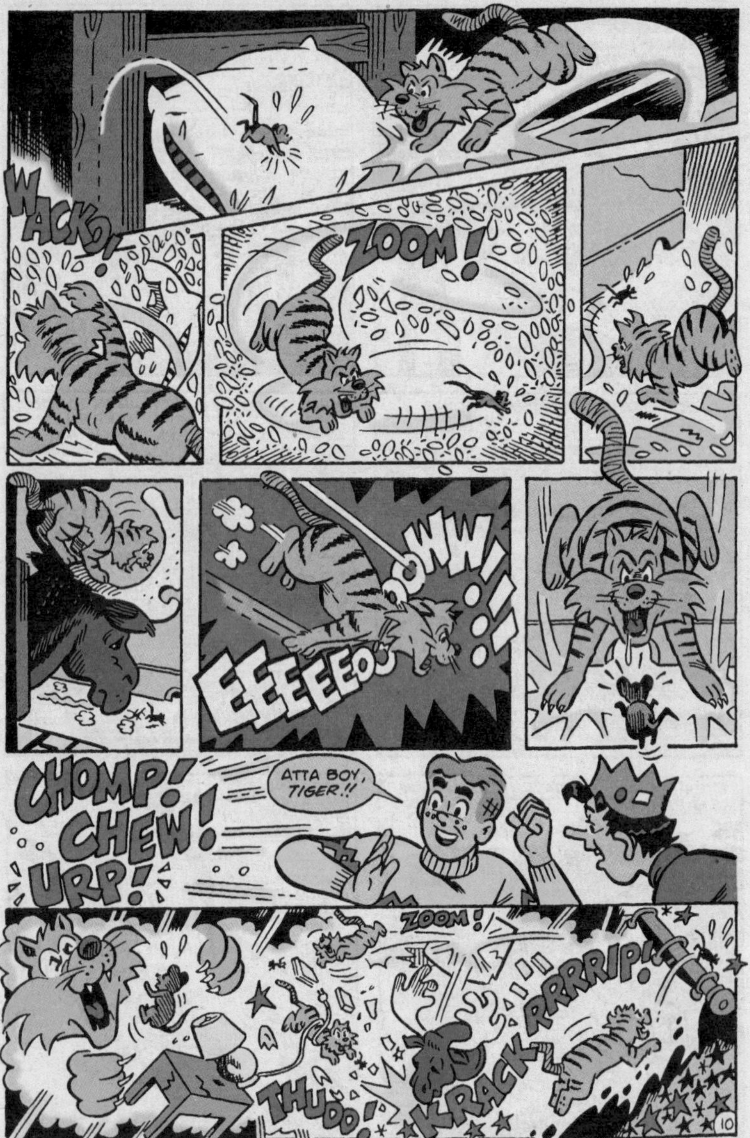
WACK!
ZOOM!
OWW!!
EEEEEOOO!!
CHOMP! CHEW! URP!
ATTA BOY, TIGER!!
ZOOM!
RRRRIP!
THUDD!
KRACK
10

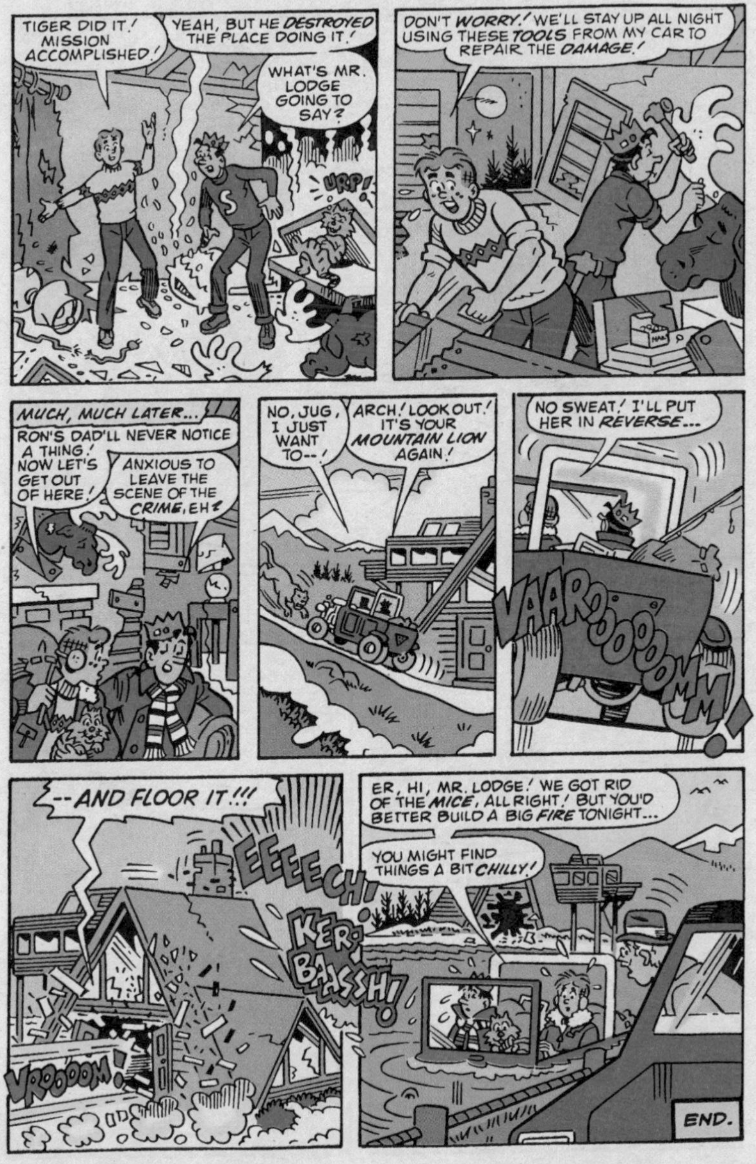

TIGER DID IT! MISSION ACCOMPLISHED!
YEAH, BUT HE DESTROYED THE PLACE DOING IT!
WHAT'S MR. LODGE GOING TO SAY?
URP!
DON'T WORRY! WE'LL STAY UP ALL NIGHT USING THESE TOOLS FROM MY CAR TO REPAIR THE DAMAGE!
MUCH, MUCH LATER...
RON'S DAD'LL NEVER NOTICE A THING! NOW LET'S GET OUT OF HERE!
ANXIOUS TO LEAVE THE SCENE OF THE CRIME, EH?
NO, JUG, I JUST WANT TO--!
ARCH! LOOK OUT! IT'S YOUR MOUNTAIN LION AGAIN!
NO SWEAT! I'LL PUT HER IN REVERSE...
VAAROOOOOOOMM!
--AND FLOOR IT!!!
EEEEECH!
KER-BAASSH!
VROOOOM!
ER, HI, MR. LODGE! WE GOT RID OF THE MICE, ALL RIGHT! BUT YOU'D BETTER BUILD A BIG FIRE TONIGHT...
YOU MIGHT FIND THINGS A BIT CHILLY!
END.

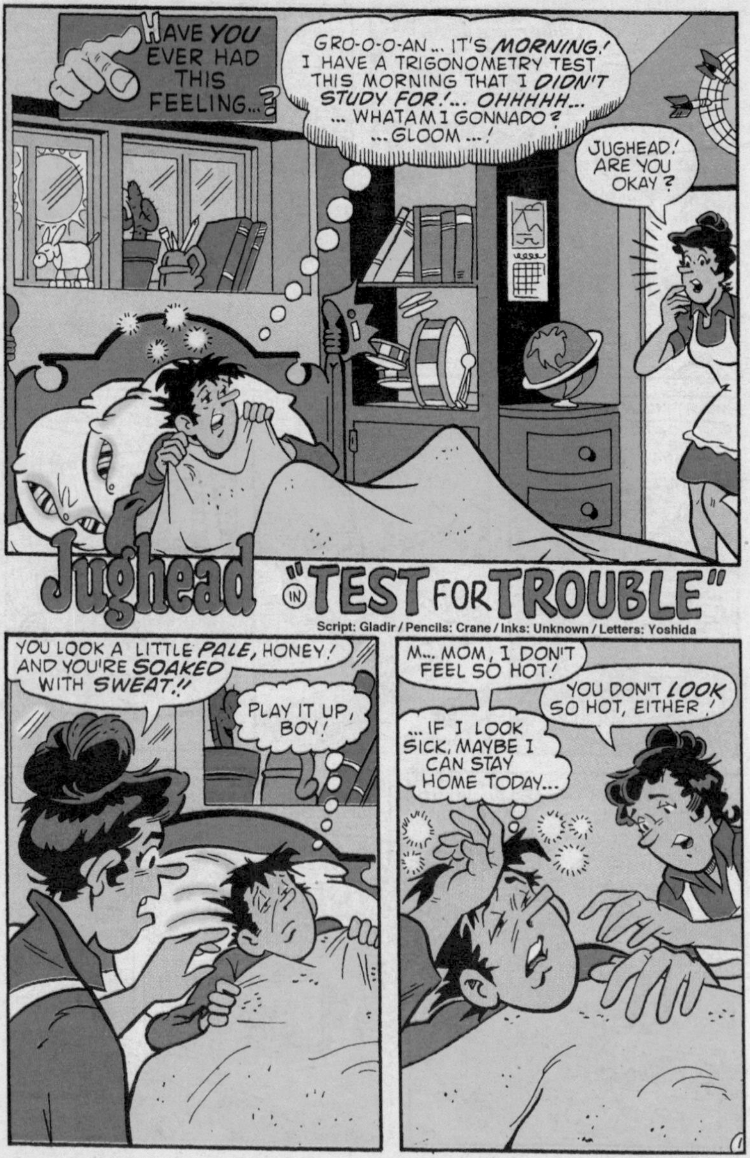
HAVE YOU EVER HAD THIS FEELING...?
GRO-O-O-AN... IT'S MORNING! I HAVE A TRIGONOMETRY TEST THIS MORNING THAT I DIDN'T STUDY FOR!... OHHHHH... ... WHATAM I GONNADO? ...GLOOM...!
JUGHEAD! ARE YOU OKAY?
Jughead IN "TEST FOR TROUBLE"
Script: Gladir / Pencils: Crane / Inks: Unknown / Letters: Yoshida
YOU LOOK A LITTLE PALE, HONEY! AND YOU'RE SOAKED WITH SWEAT!!
PLAY IT UP, BOY!
M... MOM, I DON'T FEEL SO HOT!
YOU DON'T LOOK SO HOT, EITHER!
...IF I LOOK SICK, MAYBE I CAN STAY HOME TODAY...
1

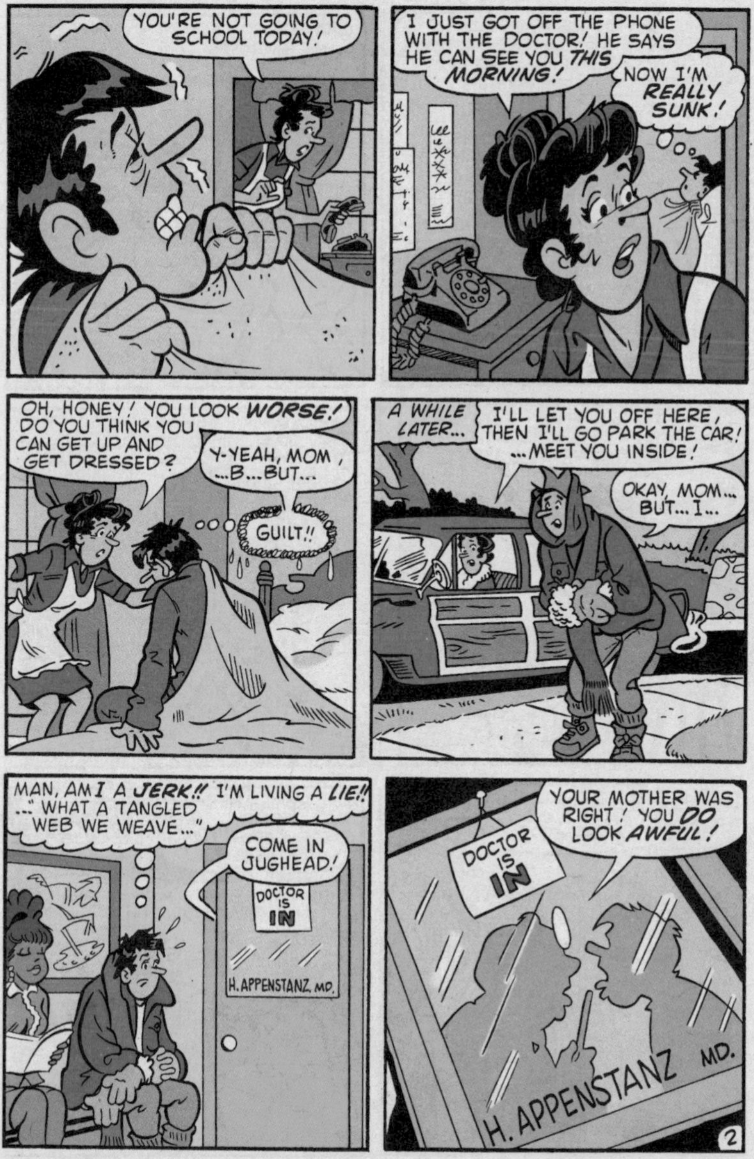
YOU'RE NOT GOING TO SCHOOL TODAY!
I JUST GOT OFF THE PHONE WITH THE DOCTOR! HE SAYS HE CAN SEE YOU THIS MORNING!
NOW I'M REALLY SUNK!
OH, HONEY! YOU LOOK WORSE! DO YOU THINK YOU CAN GET UP AND GET DRESSED?
Y-YEAH, MOM, ...B...BUT...
GUILT!!
A WHILE LATER...
I'LL LET YOU OFF HERE, THEN I'LL GO PARK THE CAR! ...MEET YOU INSIDE!
OKAY, MOM... BUT... I...
MAN, AM I A JERK!! I'M LIVING A LIE!! ..."WHAT A TANGLED WEB WE WEAVE..."
COME IN JUGHEAD!
DOCTOR IS IN
H. APPENSTANZ, MD.
YOUR MOTHER WAS RIGHT! YOU DO LOOK AWFUL!
DOCTOR IS IN
H. APPENSTANZ MD.
2

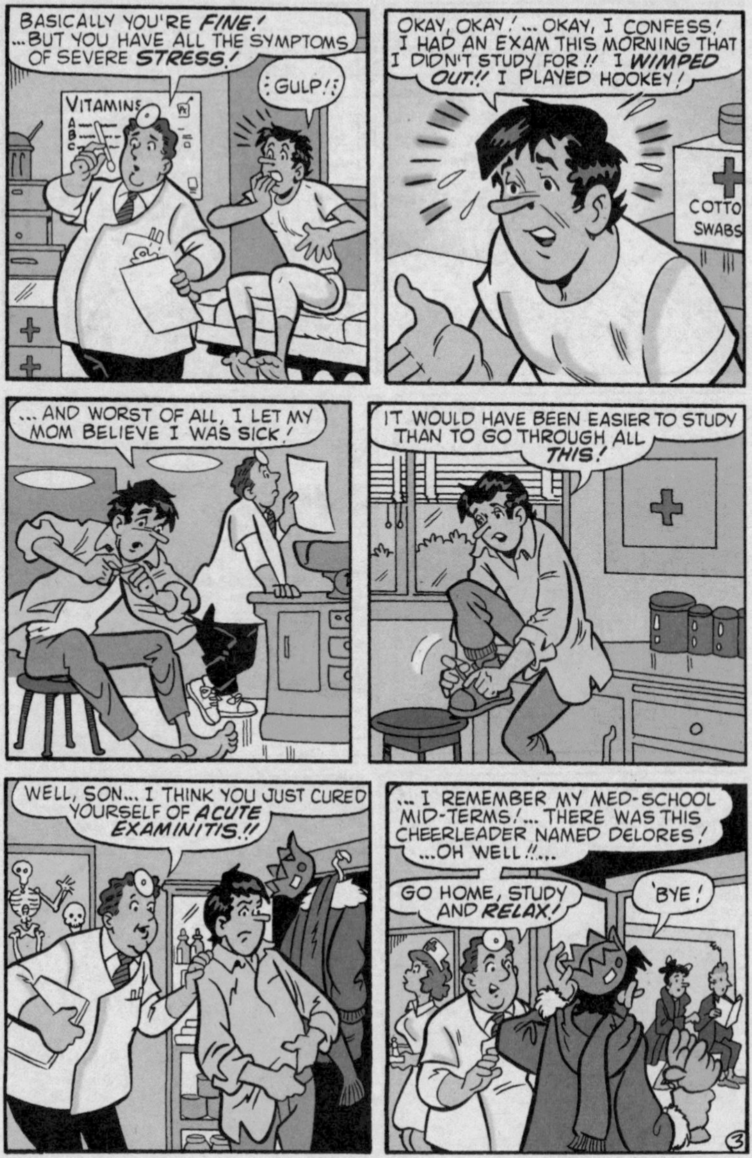
BASICALLY YOU'RE FINE! ...BUT YOU HAVE ALL THE SYMPTOMS OF SEVERE STRESS!
VITAMINS
A
B
C
GULP!
OKAY, OKAY! ... OKAY, I CONFESS! I HAD AN EXAM THIS MORNING THAT I DIDN'T STUDY FOR!! I WIMPED OUT!! I PLAYED HOOKEY!
COTTO SWABS
... AND WORST OF ALL, I LET MY MOM BELIEVE I WAS SICK!
IT WOULD HAVE BEEN EASIER TO STUDY THAN TO GO THROUGH ALL THIS!
WELL, SON... I THINK YOU JUST CURED YOURSELF OF ACUTE EXAMINITIS!!
... I REMEMBER MY MED-SCHOOL MID-TERMS! ... THERE WAS THIS CHEERLEADER NAMED DELORES! ...OH WELL!!...
GO HOME, STUDY AND RELAX!
'BYE!
3

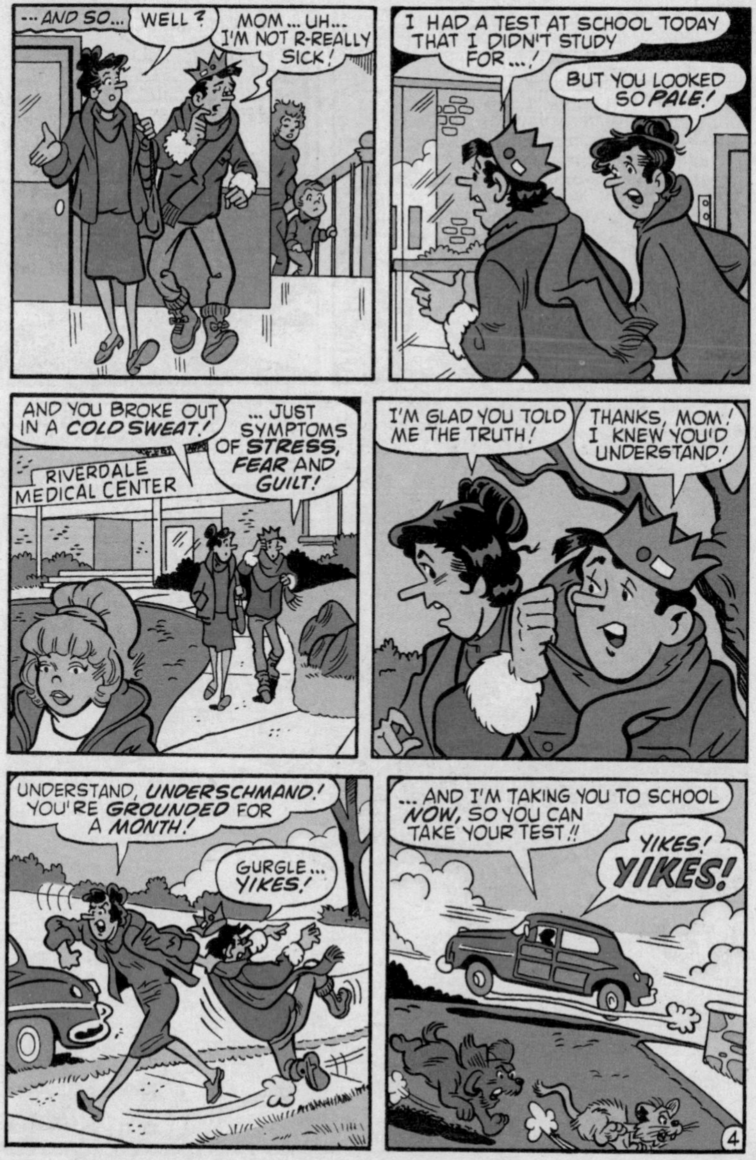
...AND SO...
WELL?
MOM... UH... I'M NOT R-REALLY SICK!
I HAD A TEST AT SCHOOL TODAY THAT I DIDN'T STUDY FOR...!
BUT YOU LOOKED SO PALE!
AND YOU BROKE OUT IN A COLD SWEAT!
... JUST SYMPTOMS OF STRESS, FEAR AND GUILT!
RIVERDALE MEDICAL CENTER
I'M GLAD YOU TOLD ME THE TRUTH!
THANKS, MOM! I KNEW YOU'D UNDERSTAND!
UNDERSTAND, UNDERSCHMAND! YOU'RE GROUNDED FOR A MONTH!
GURGLE... YIKES!
... AND I'M TAKING YOU TO SCHOOL NOW, SO YOU CAN TAKE YOUR TEST!!
YIKES! YIKES!
4

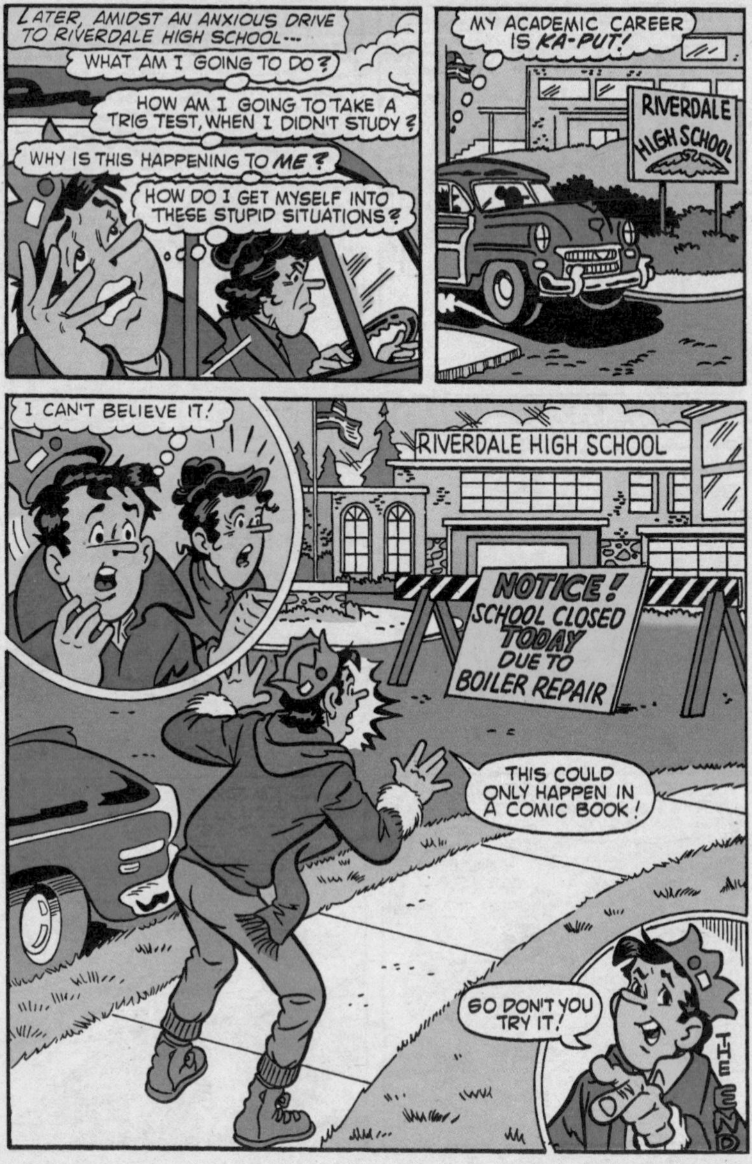
LATER, AMIDST AN ANXIOUS DRIVE TO RIVERDALE HIGH SCHOOL---
WHAT AM I GOING TO DO?
HOW AM I GOING TO TAKE A TRIG TEST, WHEN I DIDN'T STUDY?
WHY IS THIS HAPPENING TO ME?
HOW DO I GET MYSELF INTO THESE STUPID SITUATIONS?
MY ACADEMIC CAREER IS KA-PUT!
RIVERDALE HIGH SCHOOL
I CAN'T BELIEVE IT!
RIVERDALE HIGH SCHOOL
NOTICE! SCHOOL CLOSED TODAY DUE TO BOILER REPAIR
THIS COULD ONLY HAPPEN IN A COMIC BOOK!
SO DON'T YOU TRY IT!
THE END

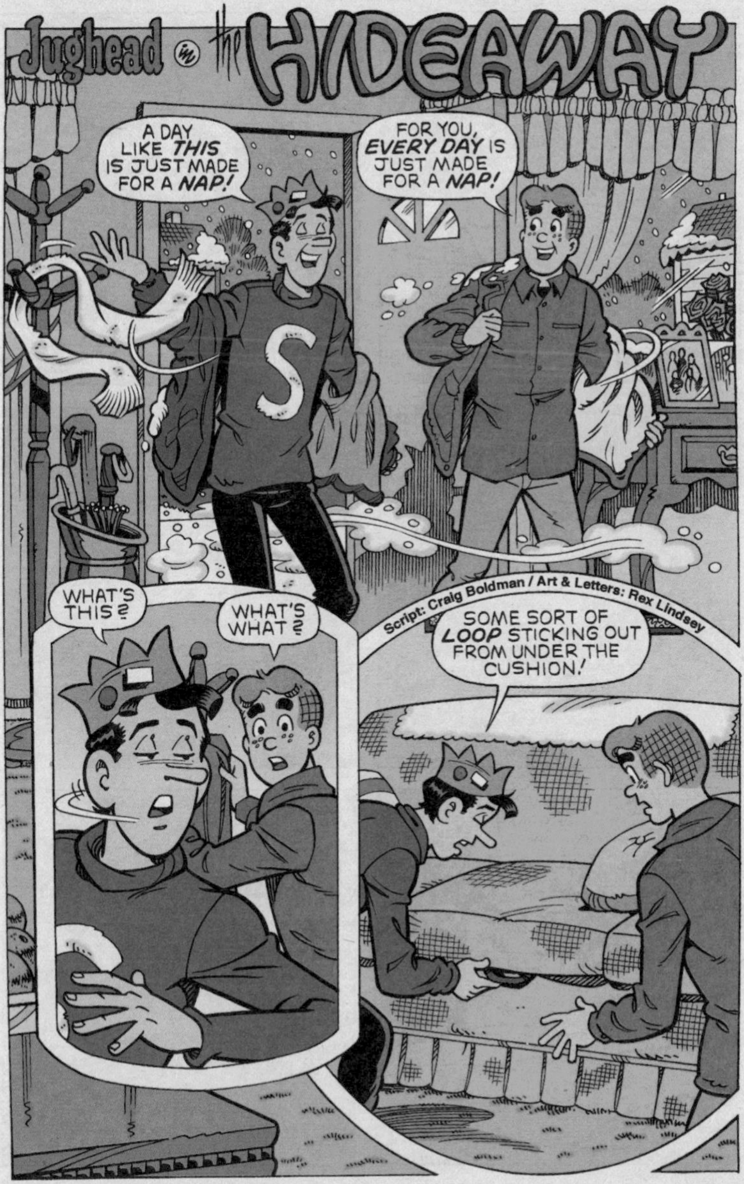
Jughead in the HIDEAWAY
A DAY LIKE THIS IS JUST MADE FOR A NAP!
FOR YOU, EVERY DAY IS JUST MADE FOR A NAP!
Script: Craig Boldman / Art & Letters: Rex Lindsey
WHAT'S THIS?
WHAT'S WHAT?
SOME SORT OF LOOP STICKING OUT FROM UNDER THE CUSHION!

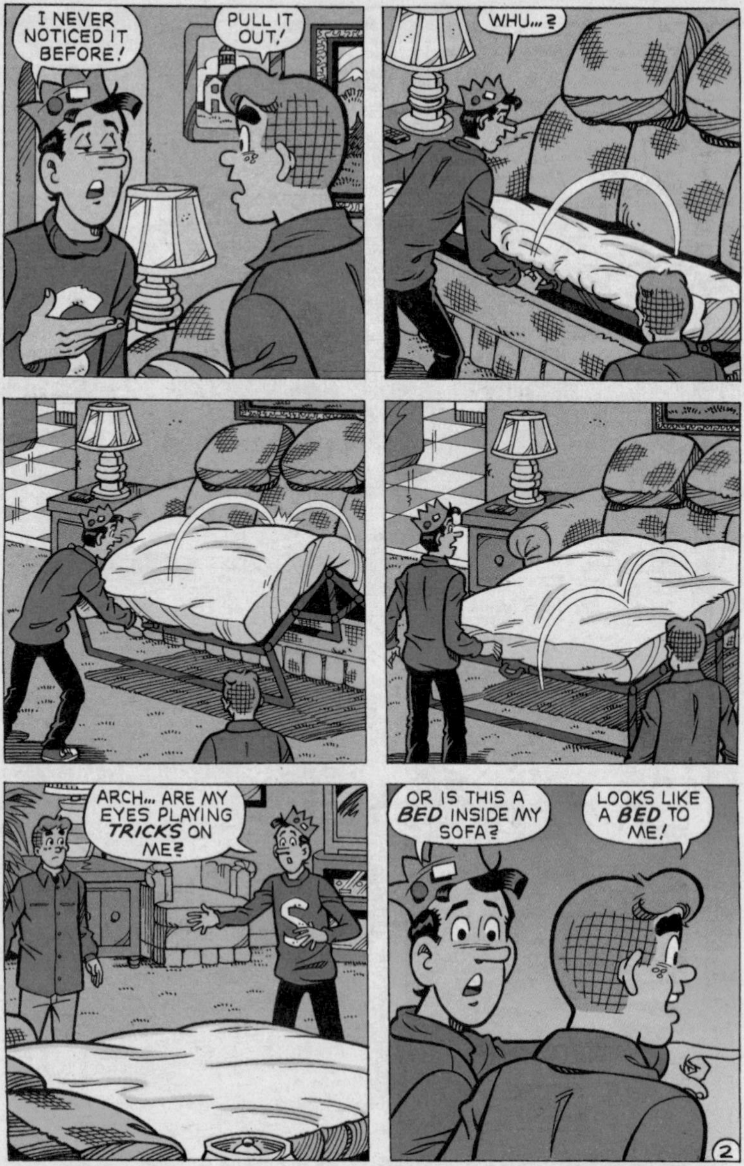
I NEVER NOTICED IT BEFORE!
PULL IT OUT!
WHU...?
ARCH... ARE MY EYES PLAYING *TRICKS* ON ME?
OR IS THIS A *BED* INSIDE MY SOFA?
LOOKS LIKE A *BED* TO ME!
2

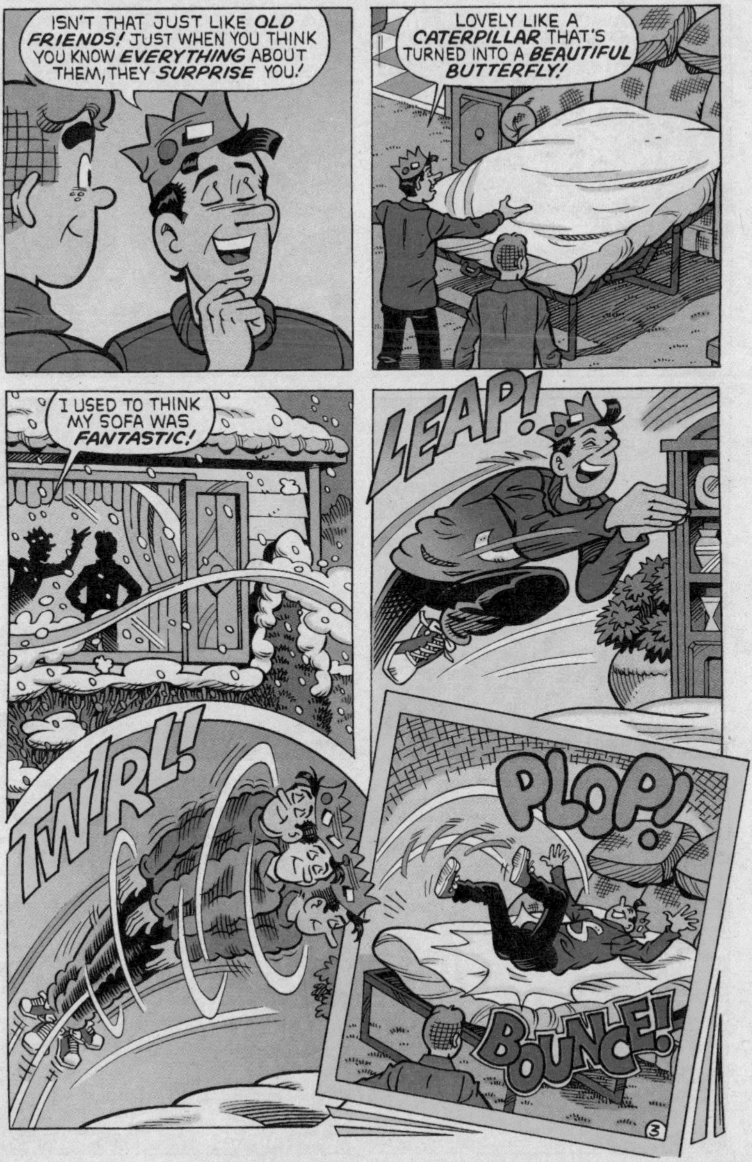

ISN'T THAT JUST LIKE OLD FRIENDS! JUST WHEN YOU THINK YOU KNOW EVERYTHING ABOUT THEM, THEY SURPRISE YOU!
LOVELY LIKE A CATERPILLAR THAT'S TURNED INTO A BEAUTIFUL BUTTERFLY!
I USED TO THINK MY SOFA WAS FANTASTIC!
LEAP!
TWIRL!
PLOP!
BOUNCE!
3

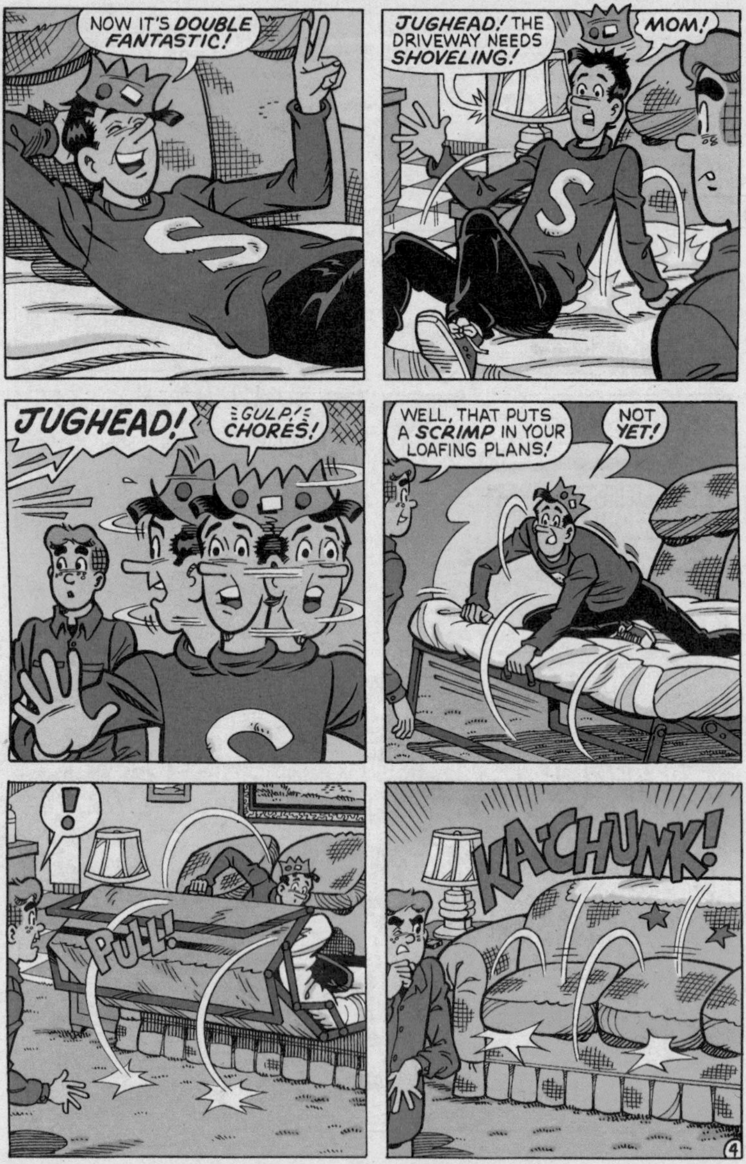
NOW IT'S DOUBLE FANTASTIC!
JUGHEAD! THE DRIVEWAY NEEDS SHOVELING!
MOM!
JUGHEAD!
GULP! CHORES!
WELL, THAT PUTS A SCRIMP IN YOUR LOAFING PLANS!
NOT YET!
!
PULL!
KA-CHUNK!
4

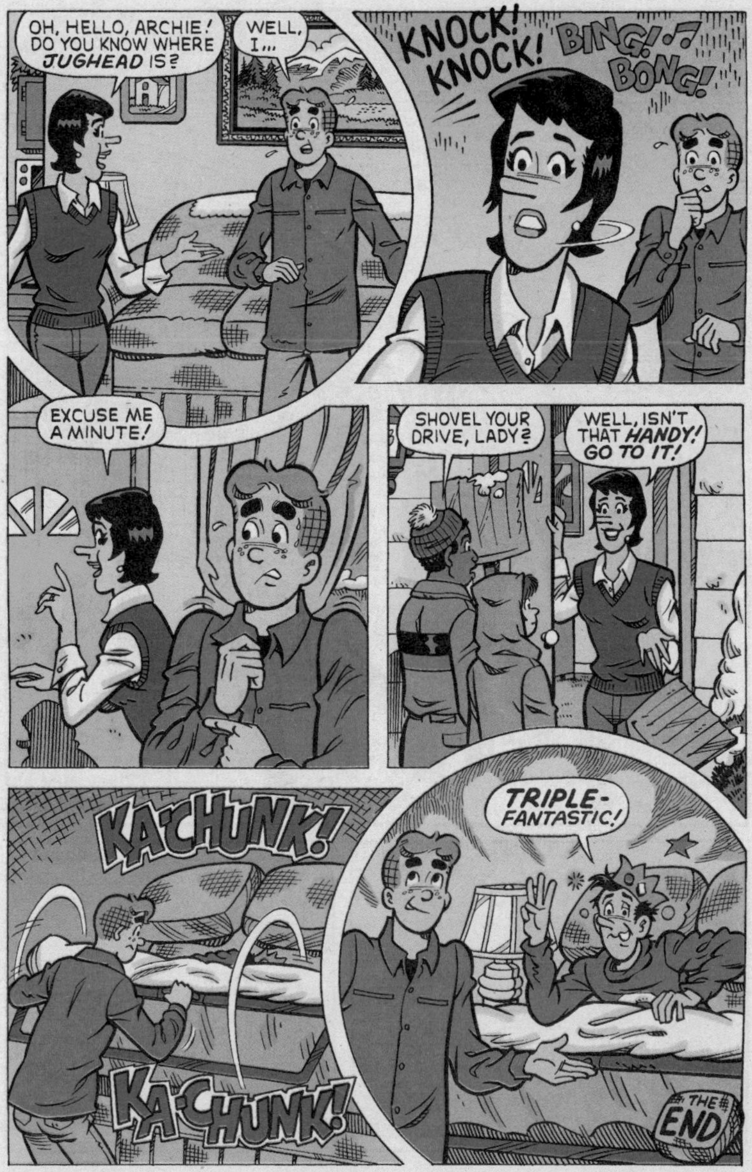
OH, HELLO, ARCHIE! DO YOU KNOW WHERE JUGHEAD IS?
WELL, I...
KNOCK! KNOCK!
BING! BONG!
EXCUSE ME A MINUTE!
SHOVEL YOUR DRIVE, LADY?
WELL, ISN'T THAT HANDY! GO TO IT!
KA-CHUNK!
KA-CHUNK!
TRIPLE-FANTASTIC!
THE END

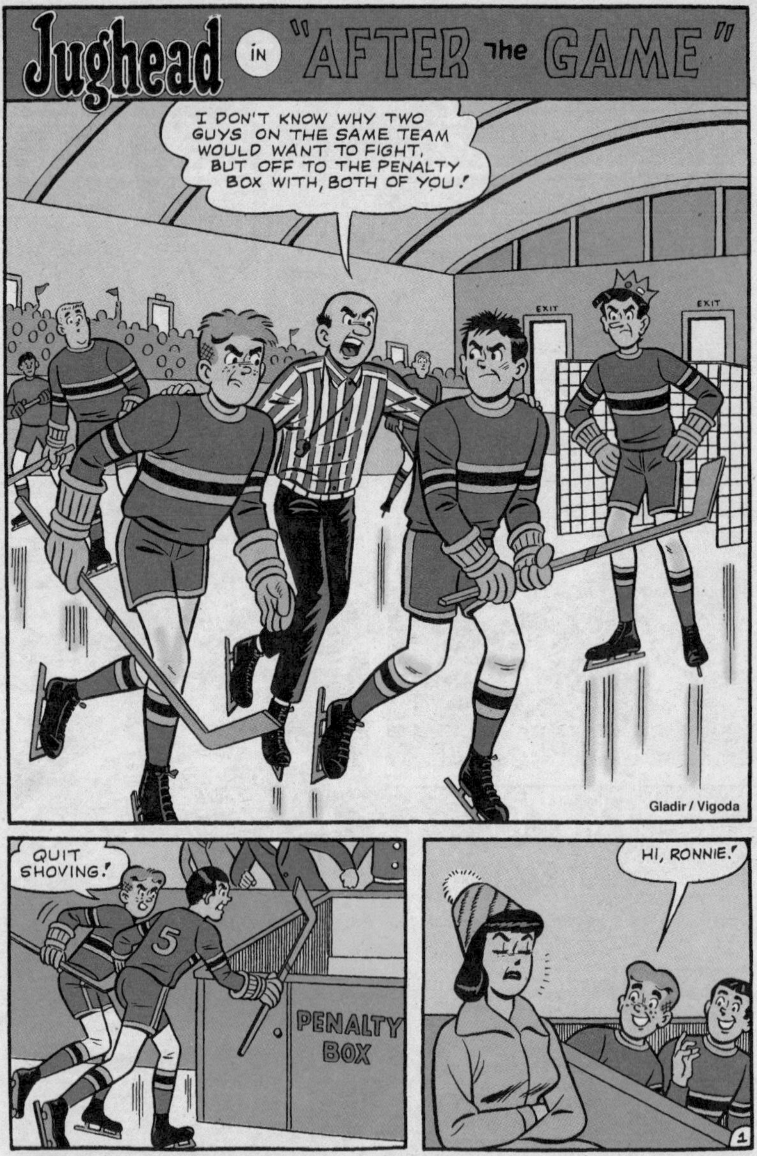
Jughead in "AFTER the GAME"
I DON'T KNOW WHY TWO GUYS ON THE SAME TEAM WOULD WANT TO FIGHT, BUT OFF TO THE PENALTY BOX WITH, BOTH OF YOU!
EXIT
EXIT
Gladir / Vigoda
QUIT SHOVING!
5
PENALTY BOX
HI, RONNIE!
1

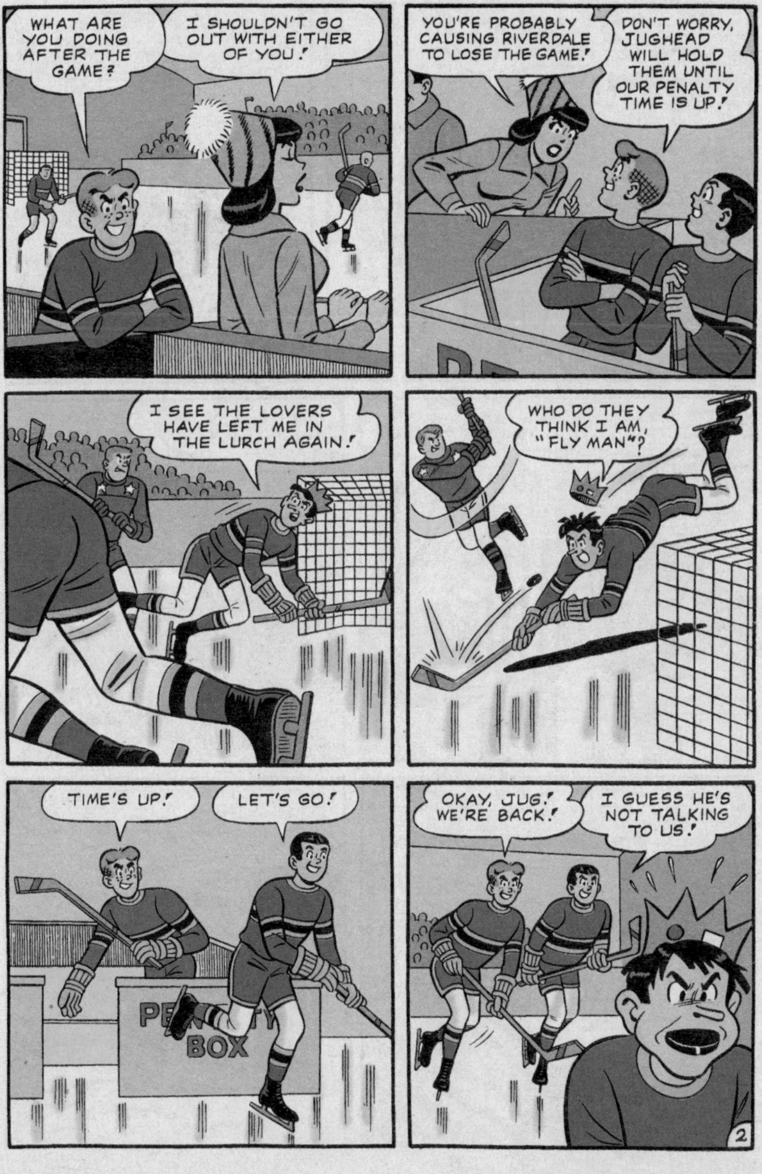
WHAT ARE YOU DOING AFTER THE GAME?
I SHOULDN'T GO OUT WITH EITHER OF YOU!
YOU'RE PROBABLY CAUSING RIVERDALE TO LOSE THE GAME!
DON'T WORRY, JUGHEAD WILL HOLD THEM UNTIL OUR PENALTY TIME IS UP!
I SEE THE LOVERS HAVE LEFT ME IN THE LURCH AGAIN!
WHO DO THEY THINK I AM, "FLY MAN"?
TIME'S UP!
LET'S GO!
BOX
OKAY, JUG! WE'RE BACK!
I GUESS HE'S NOT TALKING TO US!
2

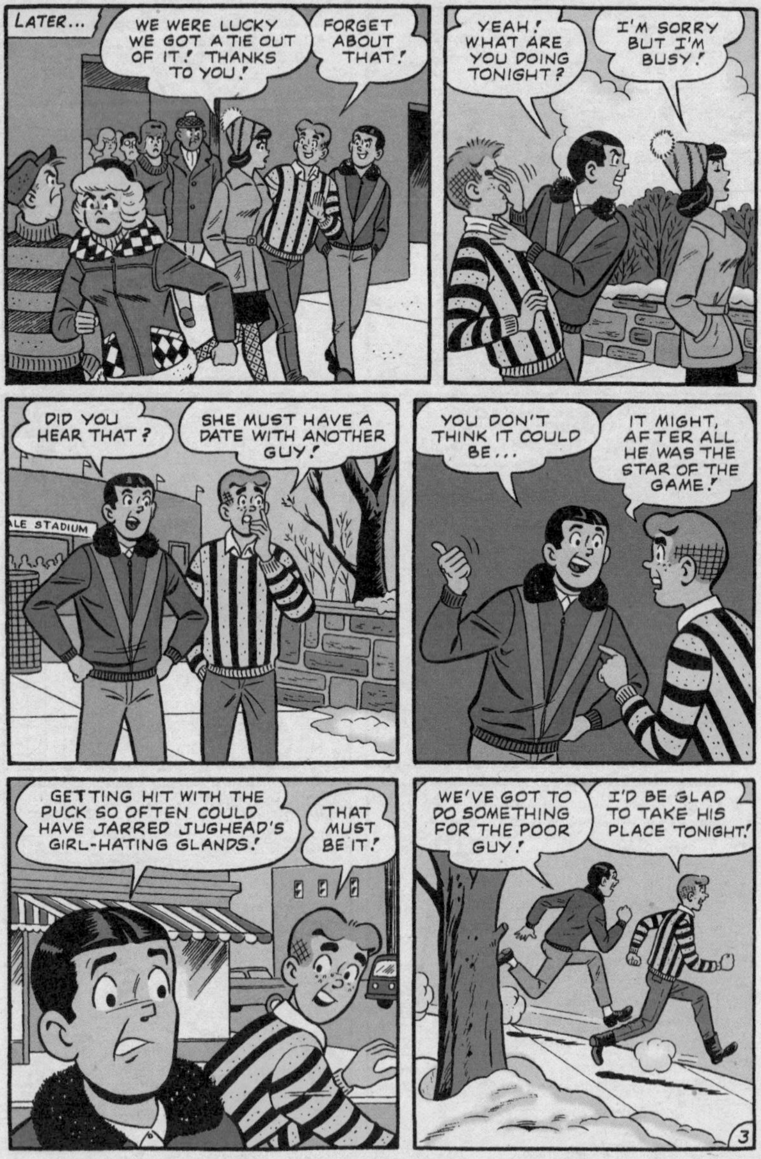
LATER...
WE WERE LUCKY WE GOT A TIE OUT OF IT! THANKS TO YOU!
FORGET ABOUT THAT!
YEAH! WHAT ARE YOU DOING TONIGHT?
I'M SORRY BUT I'M BUSY!
DID YOU HEAR THAT?
SHE MUST HAVE A DATE WITH ANOTHER GUY!
ALE STADIUM
YOU DON'T THINK IT COULD BE...
IT MIGHT, AFTER ALL HE WAS THE STAR OF THE GAME!
GETTING HIT WITH THE PUCK SO OFTEN COULD HAVE JARRED JUGHEAD'S GIRL-HATING GLANDS!
THAT MUST BE IT!
WE'VE GOT TO DO SOMETHING FOR THE POOR GUY!
I'D BE GLAD TO TAKE HIS PLACE TONIGHT!
3

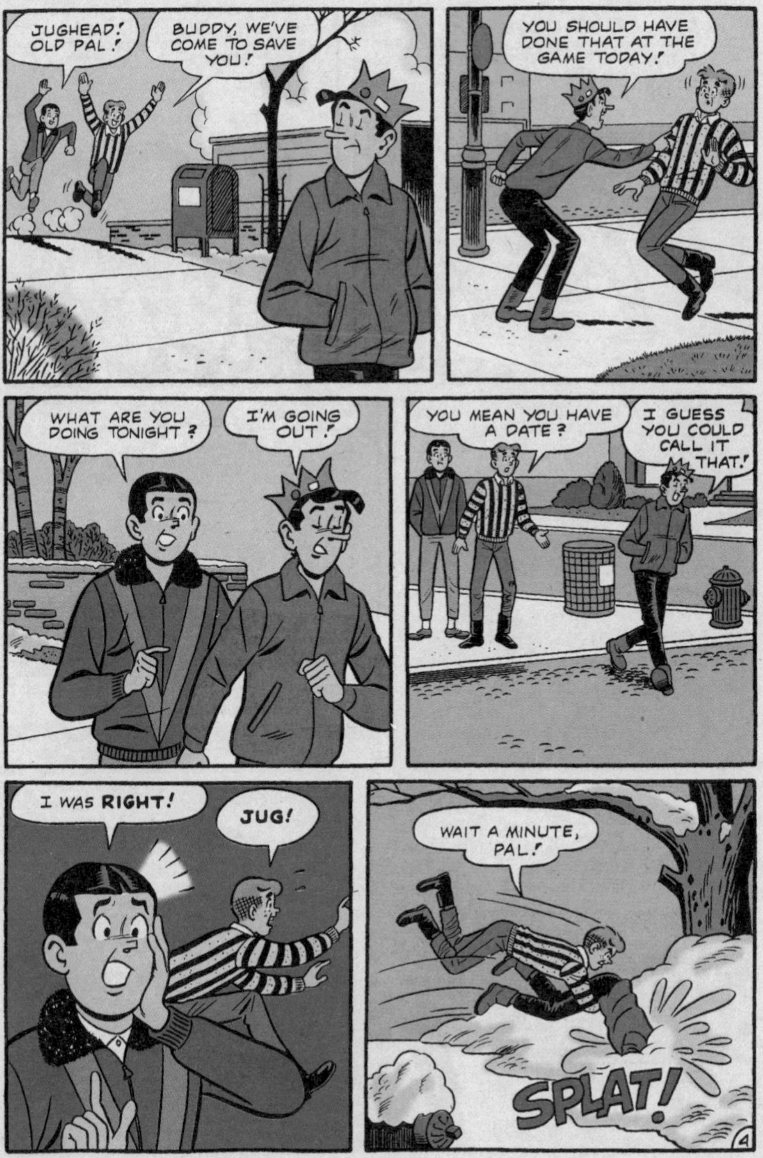
JUGHEAD! OLD PAL!
BUDDY, WE'VE COME TO SAVE YOU!
YOU SHOULD HAVE DONE THAT AT THE GAME TODAY!
WHAT ARE YOU DOING TONIGHT?
I'M GOING OUT!
YOU MEAN YOU HAVE A DATE?
I GUESS YOU COULD CALL IT THAT!
I WAS RIGHT!
JUG!
WAIT A MINUTE, PAL!
SPLAT!
4

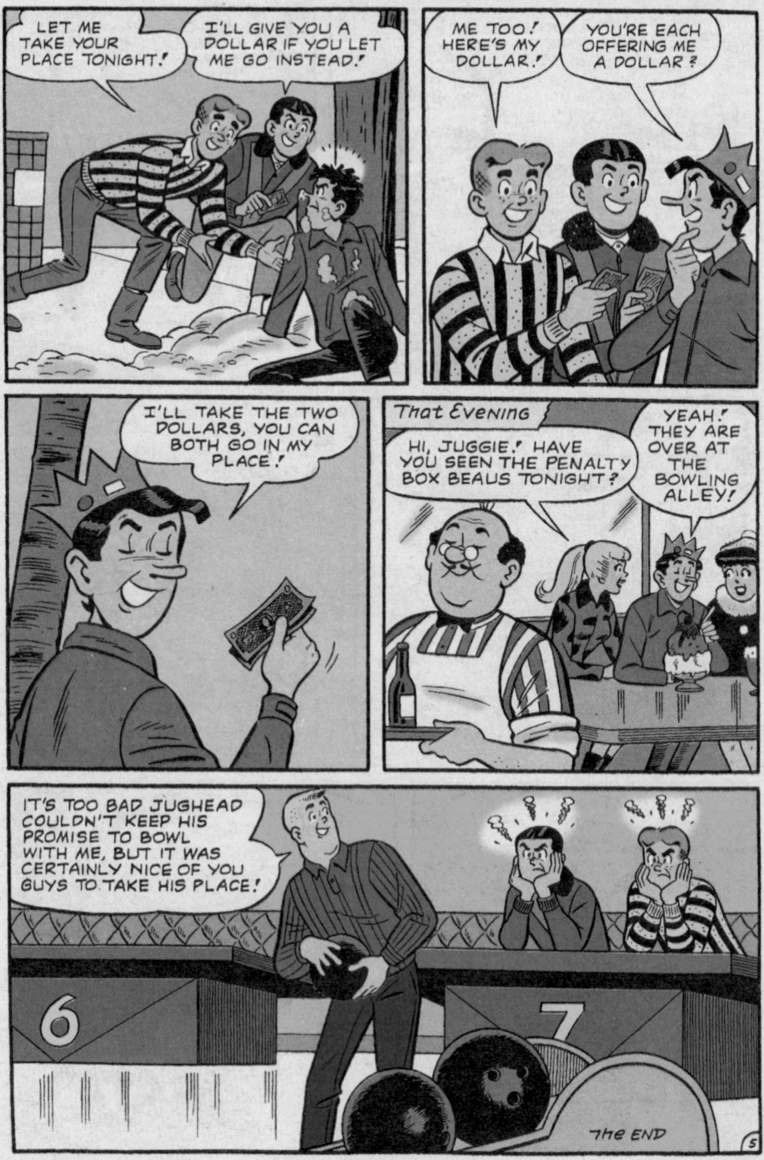
LET ME TAKE YOUR PLACE TONIGHT!
I'LL GIVE YOU A DOLLAR IF YOU LET ME GO INSTEAD!
ME TOO! HERE'S MY DOLLAR!
YOU'RE EACH OFFERING ME A DOLLAR?
I'LL TAKE THE TWO DOLLARS, YOU CAN BOTH GO IN MY PLACE!
That Evening
HI, JUGGIE! HAVE YOU SEEN THE PENALTY BOX BEAUS TONIGHT?
YEAH! THEY ARE OVER AT THE BOWLING ALLEY!
IT'S TOO BAD JUGHEAD COULDN'T KEEP HIS PROMISE TO BOWL WITH ME, BUT IT WAS CERTAINLY NICE OF YOU GUYS TO TAKE HIS PLACE!
6
7
THE END
5

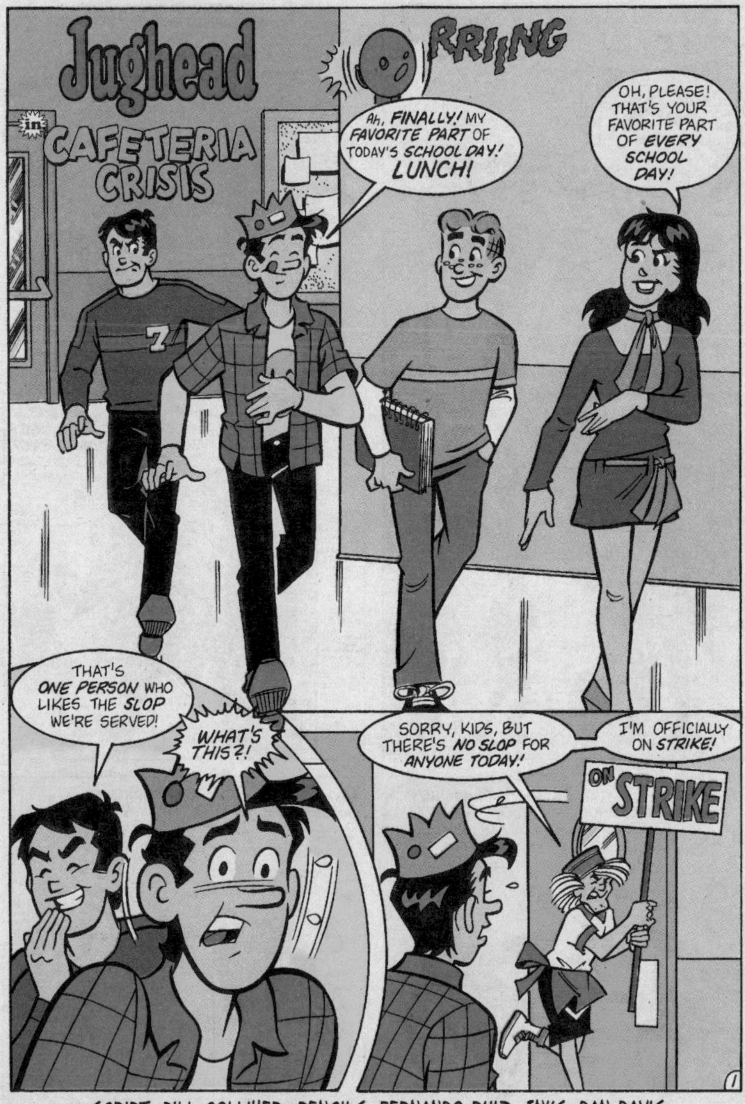
Jughead
in
CAFETERIA CRISIS
RRIING
Ah, FINALLY! MY FAVORITE PART OF TODAY'S SCHOOL DAY! LUNCH!
OH, PLEASE! THAT'S YOUR FAVORITE PART OF EVERY SCHOOL DAY!
THAT'S ONE PERSON WHO LIKES THE SLOP WE'RE SERVED!
WHAT'S THIS?!
SORRY, KIDS, BUT THERE'S NO SLOP FOR ANYONE TODAY!
I'M OFFICIALLY ON STRIKE!
ON STRIKE
1

SCRIPT: BILL GOLLIHER PENCILS: FERNANDO RUIZ INKS: DAN DAVIS
COLORS: CARLOS ANTUNES LETTERS: TERESA DAVIDSON

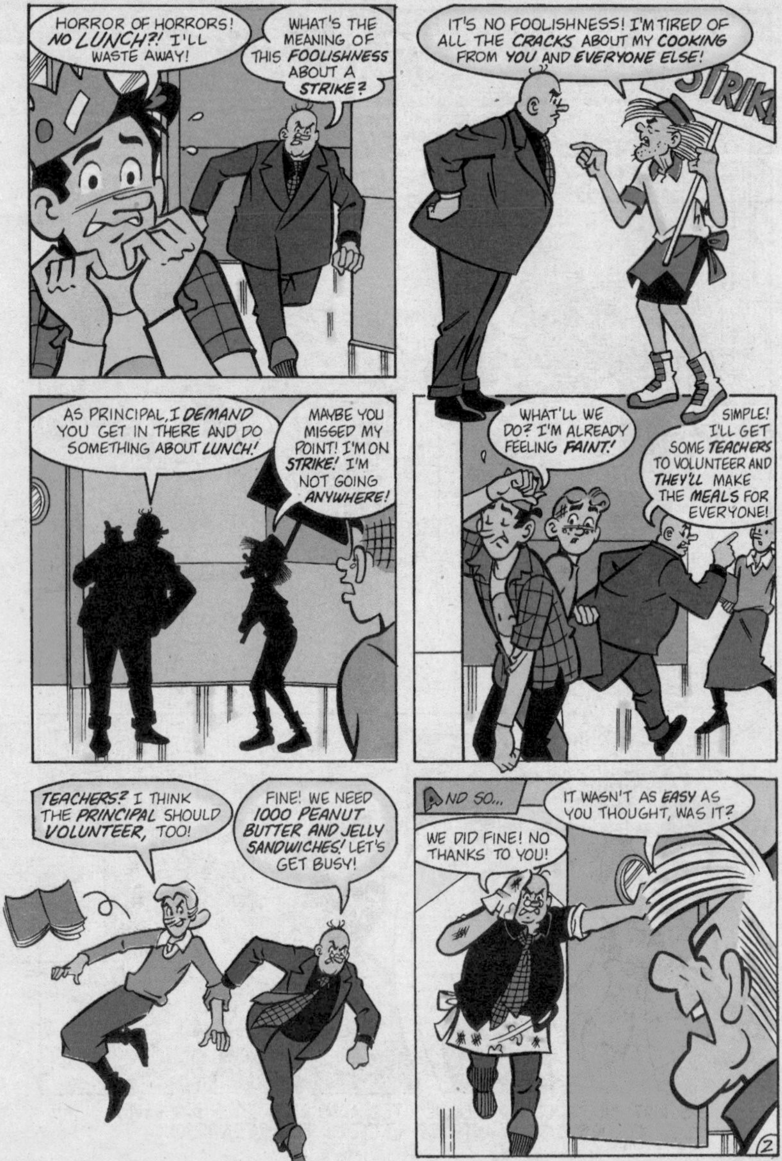
HORROR OF HORRORS! NO LUNCH?! I'LL WASTE AWAY!
WHAT'S THE MEANING OF THIS FOOLISHNESS ABOUT A STRIKE?
IT'S NO FOOLISHNESS! I'M TIRED OF ALL THE CRACKS ABOUT MY COOKING FROM YOU AND EVERYONE ELSE!
STRIKE
AS PRINCIPAL, I DEMAND YOU GET IN THERE AND DO SOMETHING ABOUT LUNCH!
MAYBE YOU MISSED MY POINT! I'M ON STRIKE! I'M NOT GOING ANYWHERE!
WHAT'LL WE DO? I'M ALREADY FEELING FAINT!
SIMPLE! I'LL GET SOME TEACHERS TO VOLUNTEER AND THEY'LL MAKE THE MEALS FOR EVERYONE!
TEACHERS? I THINK THE PRINCIPAL SHOULD VOLUNTEER, TOO!
FINE! WE NEED 1000 PEANUT BUTTER AND JELLY SANDWICHES! LET'S GET BUSY!
AND SO...
IT WASN'T AS EASY AS YOU THOUGHT, WAS IT?
WE DID FINE! NO THANKS TO YOU!
2

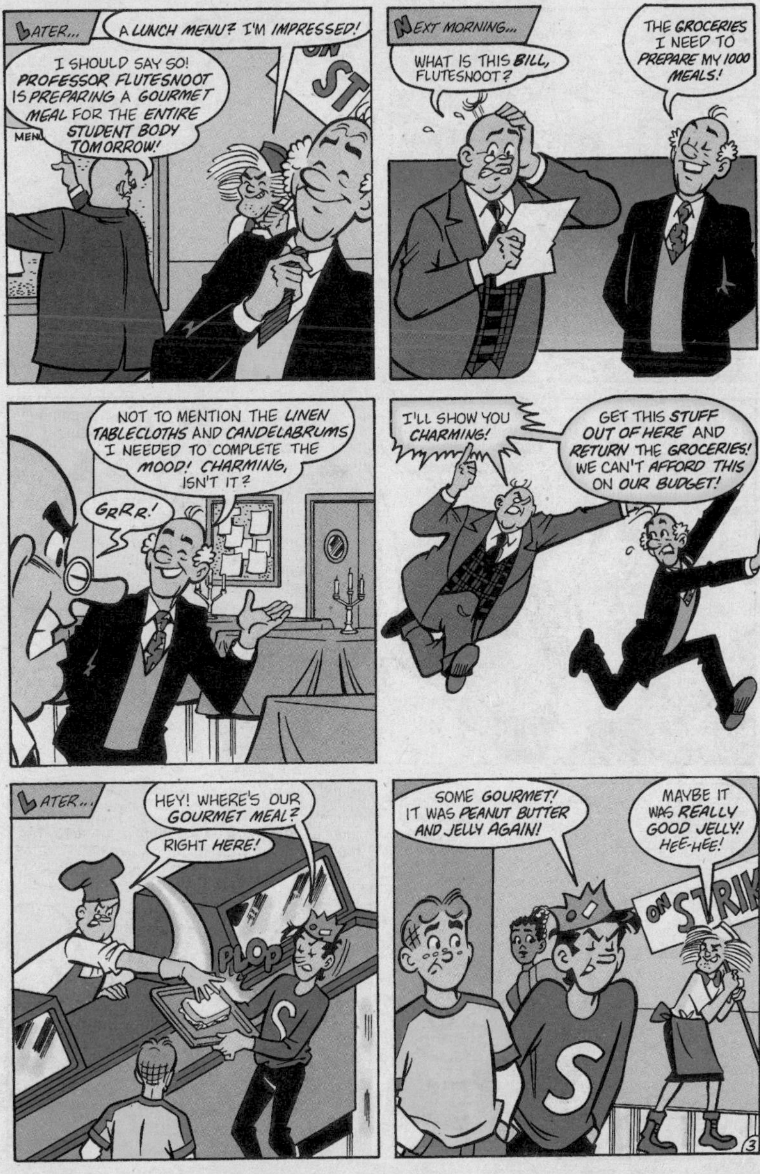
LATER...
A LUNCH MENU? I'M IMPRESSED!
I SHOULD SAY SO! PROFESSOR FLUTESNOOT IS PREPARING A GOURMET MEAL FOR THE ENTIRE STUDENT BODY TOMORROW!
MENU
ON ST
NEXT MORNING...
WHAT IS THIS BILL, FLUTESNOOT?
THE GROCERIES I NEED TO PREPARE MY 1000 MEALS!
NOT TO MENTION THE LINEN TABLECLOTHS AND CANDELABRUMS I NEEDED TO COMPLETE THE MOOD! CHARMING, ISN'T IT?
GRRR!
I'LL SHOW YOU CHARMING!
GET THIS STUFF OUT OF HERE AND RETURN THE GROCERIES! WE CAN'T AFFORD THIS ON OUR BUDGET!
LATER...
HEY! WHERE'S OUR GOURMET MEAL?
RIGHT HERE!
PLOP
SOME GOURMET! IT WAS PEANUT BUTTER AND JELLY AGAIN!
MAYBE IT WAS REALLY GOOD JELLY! HEE-HEE!
ON STRIK
3

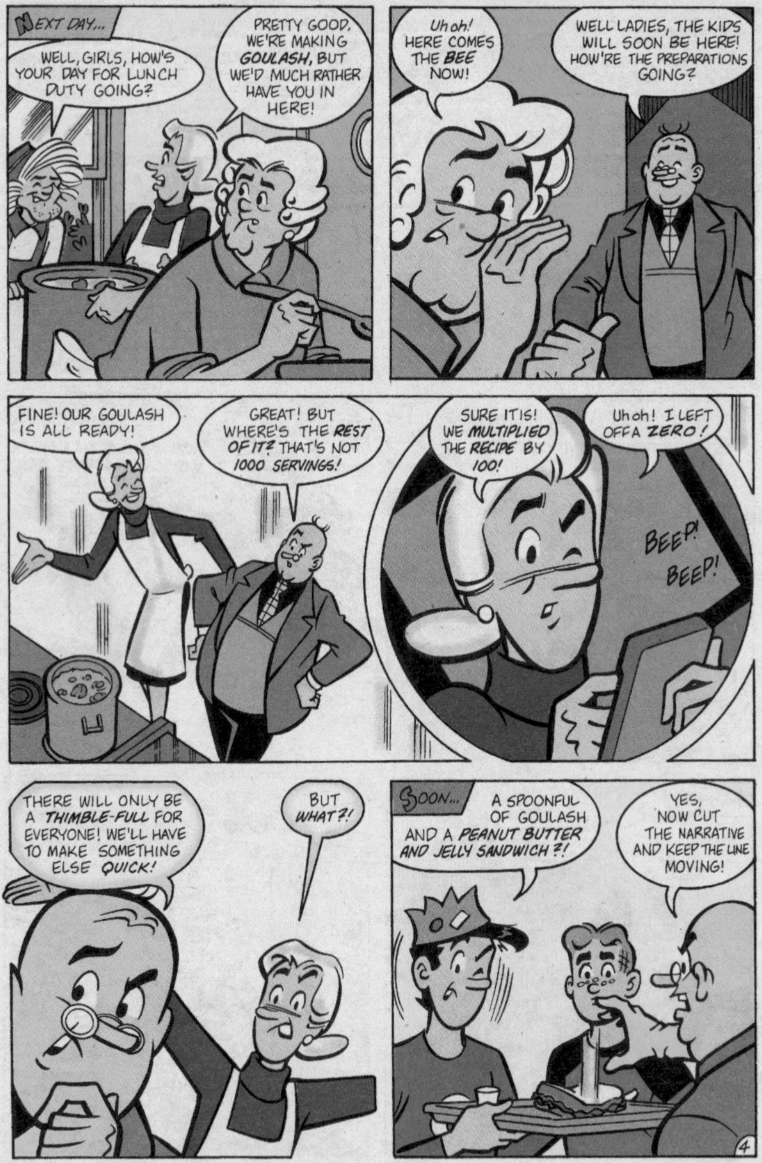
NEXT DAY...
WELL, GIRLS, HOW'S YOUR DAY FOR LUNCH DUTY GOING?
PRETTY GOOD. WE'RE MAKING GOULASH, BUT WE'D MUCH RATHER HAVE YOU IN HERE!
Uh oh! HERE COMES THE BEE NOW!
WELL LADIES, THE KIDS WILL SOON BE HERE! HOW'RE THE PREPARATIONS GOING?
FINE! OUR GOULASH IS ALL READY!
GREAT! BUT WHERE'S THE REST OF IT? THAT'S NOT 1000 SERVINGS!
SURE IT IS! WE MULTIPLIED THE RECIPE BY 100!
Uh oh! I LEFT OFFA ZERO!
BEEP! BEEP!
THERE WILL ONLY BE A THIMBLE-FULL FOR EVERYONE! WE'LL HAVE TO MAKE SOMETHING ELSE QUICK!
BUT WHAT?!
SOON...
A SPOONFUL OF GOULASH AND A PEANUT BUTTER AND JELLY SANDWICH?!
YES, NOW CUT THE NARRATIVE AND KEEP THE LINE MOVING!

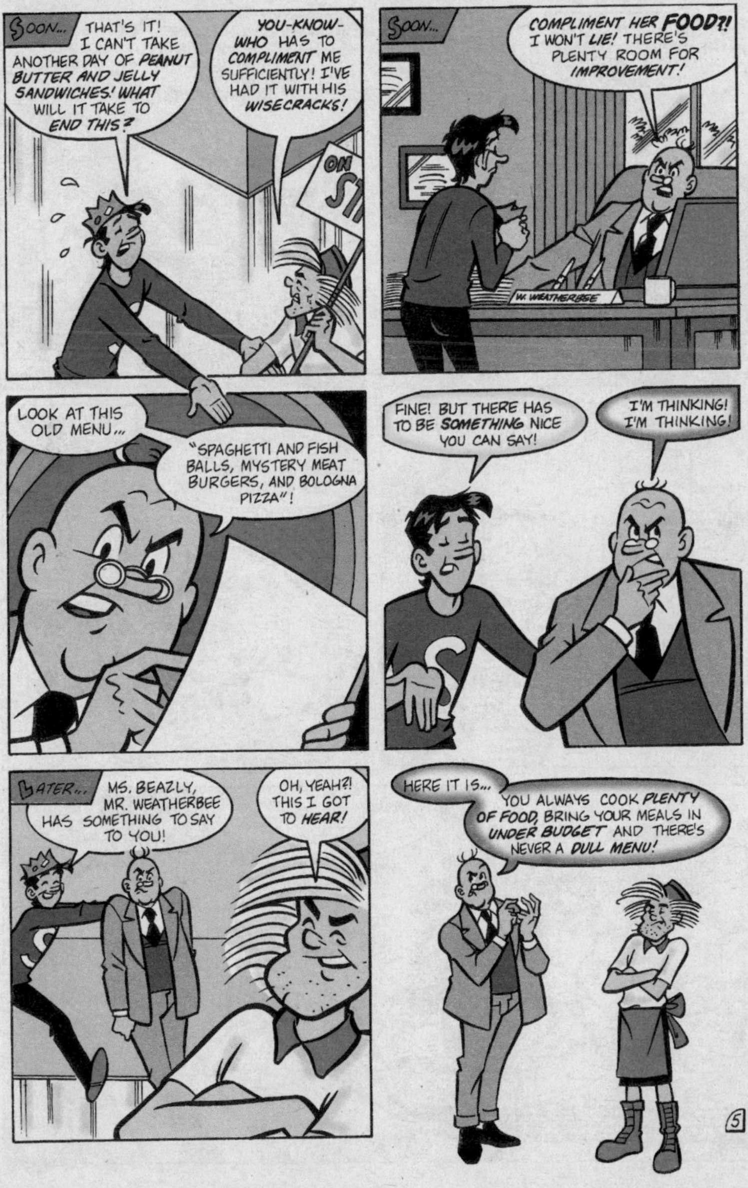
SOON...
THAT'S IT! I CAN'T TAKE ANOTHER DAY OF PEANUT BUTTER AND JELLY SANDWICHES! WHAT WILL IT TAKE TO END THIS?
YOU-KNOW-WHO HAS TO COMPLIMENT ME SUFFICIENTLY! I'VE HAD IT WITH HIS WISECRACKS!
ON ST
SOON...
COMPLIMENT HER FOOD?! I WON'T LIE! THERE'S PLENTY ROOM FOR IMPROVEMENT!
W. WEATHERBEE
LOOK AT THIS OLD MENU...
"SPAGHETTI AND FISH BALLS, MYSTERY MEAT BURGERS, AND BOLOGNA PIZZA"!
FINE! BUT THERE HAS TO BE SOMETHING NICE YOU CAN SAY!
I'M THINKING! I'M THINKING!
LATER...
MS. BEAZLY, MR. WEATHERBEE HAS SOMETHING TO SAY TO YOU!
OH, YEAH?! THIS I GOT TO HEAR!
HERE IT IS...
YOU ALWAYS COOK PLENTY OF FOOD, BRING YOUR MEALS IN UNDER BUDGET AND THERE'S NEVER A DULL MENU!
5

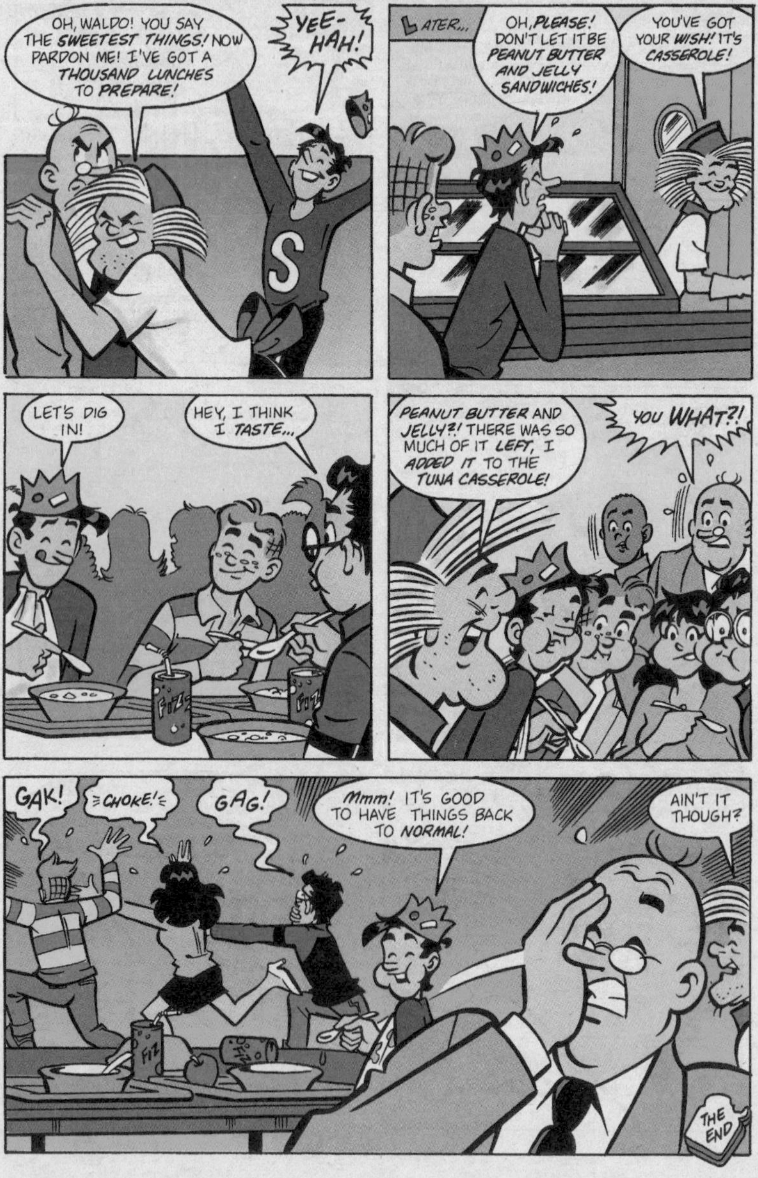
OH, WALDO! YOU SAY THE SWEETEST THINGS! NOW PARDON ME! I'VE GOT A THOUSAND LUNCHES TO PREPARE!
YEE-HAH!
LATER...
OH, PLEASE! DON'T LET IT BE PEANUT BUTTER AND JELLY SANDWICHES!
YOU'VE GOT YOUR WISH! IT'S CASSEROLE!
LET'S DIG IN!
HEY, I THINK I TASTE...
FIZZ
FIZZ
PEANUT BUTTER AND JELLY?! THERE WAS SO MUCH OF IT LEFT, I ADDED IT TO THE TUNA CASSEROLE!
YOU WHAT?!
GAK!
CHOKE!
GAG!
Mmm! IT'S GOOD TO HAVE THINGS BACK TO NORMAL!
AIN'T IT THOUGH?
FIZ
FIZ
THE END

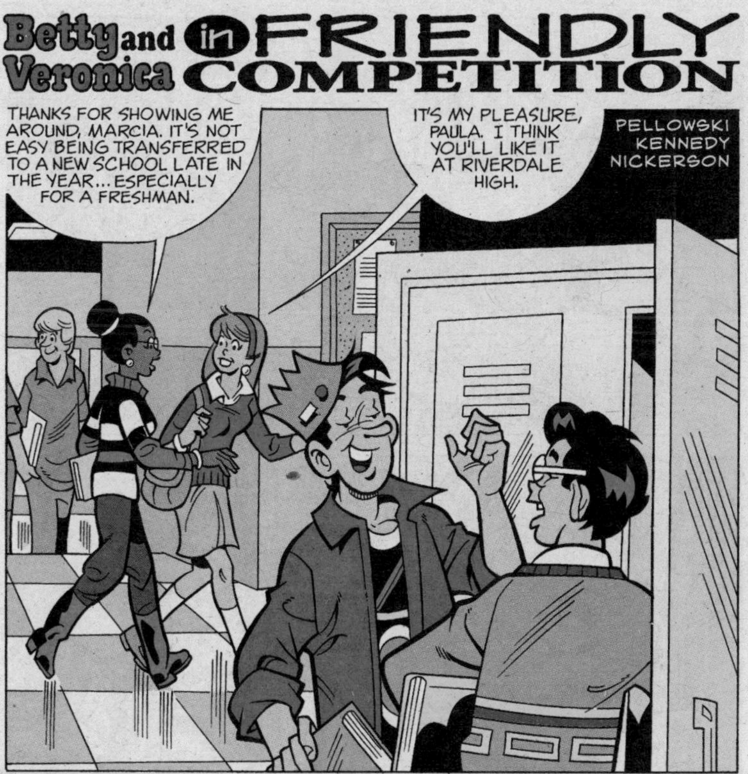
Betty and Veronica in FRIENDLY COMPETITION
THANKS FOR SHOWING ME AROUND, MARCIA. IT'S NOT EASY BEING TRANSFERRED TO A NEW SCHOOL LATE IN THE YEAR... ESPECIALLY FOR A FRESHMAN.
IT'S MY PLEASURE, PAULA. I THINK YOU'LL LIKE IT AT RIVERDALE HIGH.
PELLOWSKI KENNEDY NICKERSON

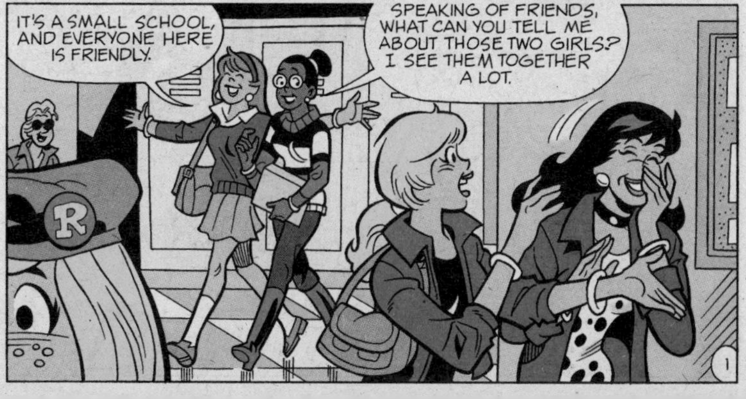
IT'S A SMALL SCHOOL, AND EVERYONE HERE IS FRIENDLY.
SPEAKING OF FRIENDS, WHAT CAN YOU TELL ME ABOUT THOSE TWO GIRLS? I SEE THEM TOGETHER A LOT.
R

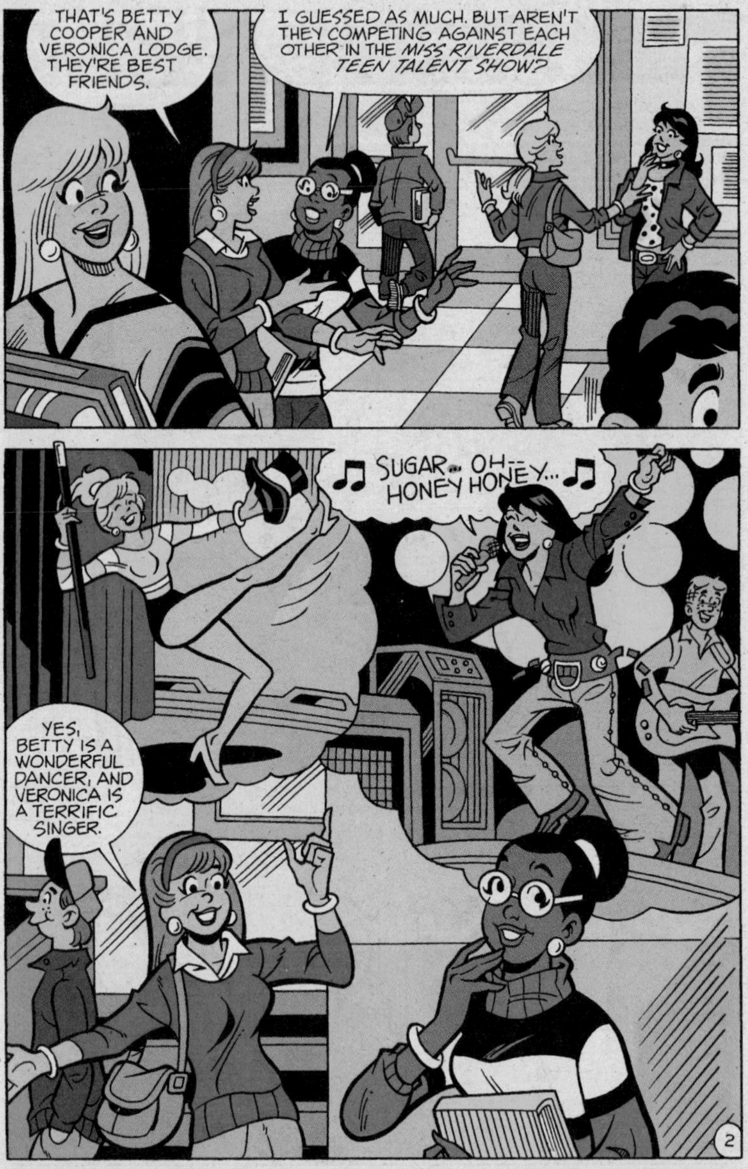
THAT'S BETTY COOPER AND VERONICA LODGE. THEY'RE BEST FRIENDS.
I GUESSED AS MUCH. BUT AREN'T THEY COMPETING AGAINST EACH OTHER IN THE *MISS RIVERDALE TEEN TALENT SHOW?*
♫ SUGAR... OH-- HONEY HONEY... ♫
YES, BETTY IS A WONDERFUL DANCER, AND VERONICA IS A TERRIFIC SINGER.

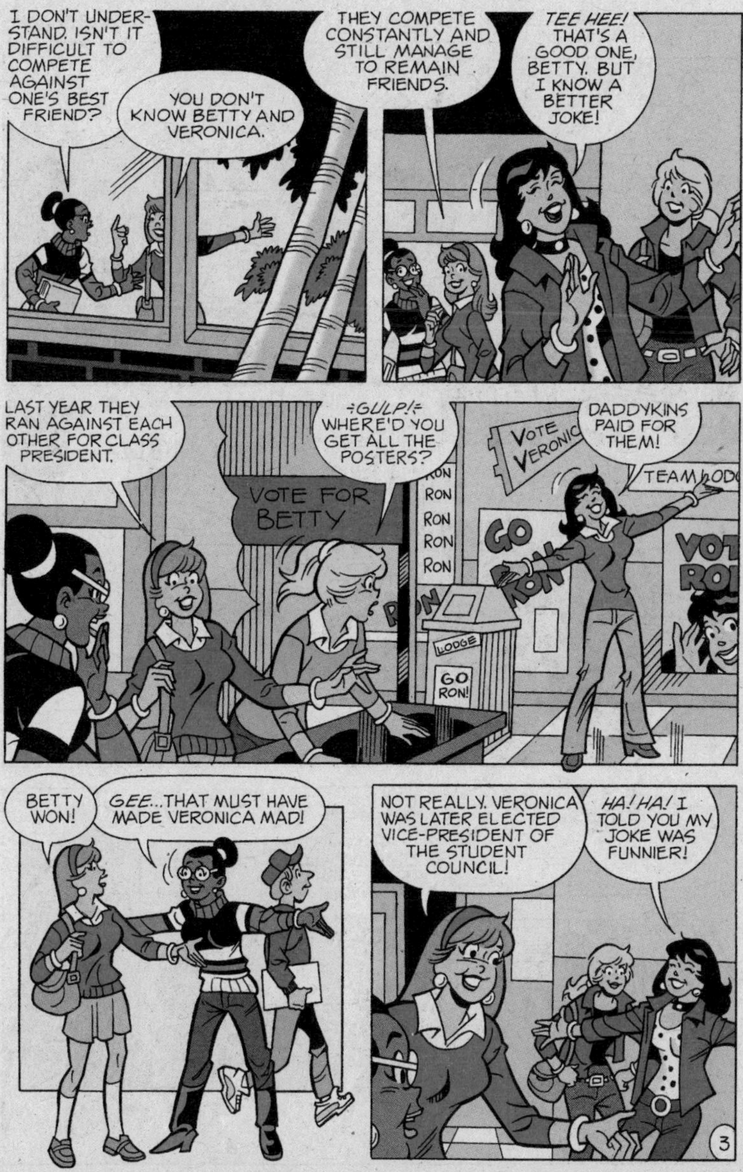
I DON'T UNDERSTAND. ISN'T IT DIFFICULT TO COMPETE AGAINST ONE'S BEST FRIEND?
YOU DON'T KNOW BETTY AND VERONICA.
THEY COMPETE CONSTANTLY AND STILL MANAGE TO REMAIN FRIENDS.
TEE HEE! THAT'S A GOOD ONE, BETTY. BUT I KNOW A BETTER JOKE!
LAST YEAR THEY RAN AGAINST EACH OTHER FOR CLASS PRESIDENT.
GULP! WHERE'D YOU GET ALL THE POSTERS?
VOTE FOR BETTY
RON RON RON RON RON
VOTE VERONIC
DADDYKINS PAID FOR THEM!
TEAM LODG
GO RON
LODGE
GO RON!
BETTY WON!
GEE...THAT MUST HAVE MADE VERONICA MAD!
NOT REALLY. VERONICA WAS LATER ELECTED VICE-PRESIDENT OF THE STUDENT COUNCIL!
HA! HA! I TOLD YOU MY JOKE WAS FUNNIER!

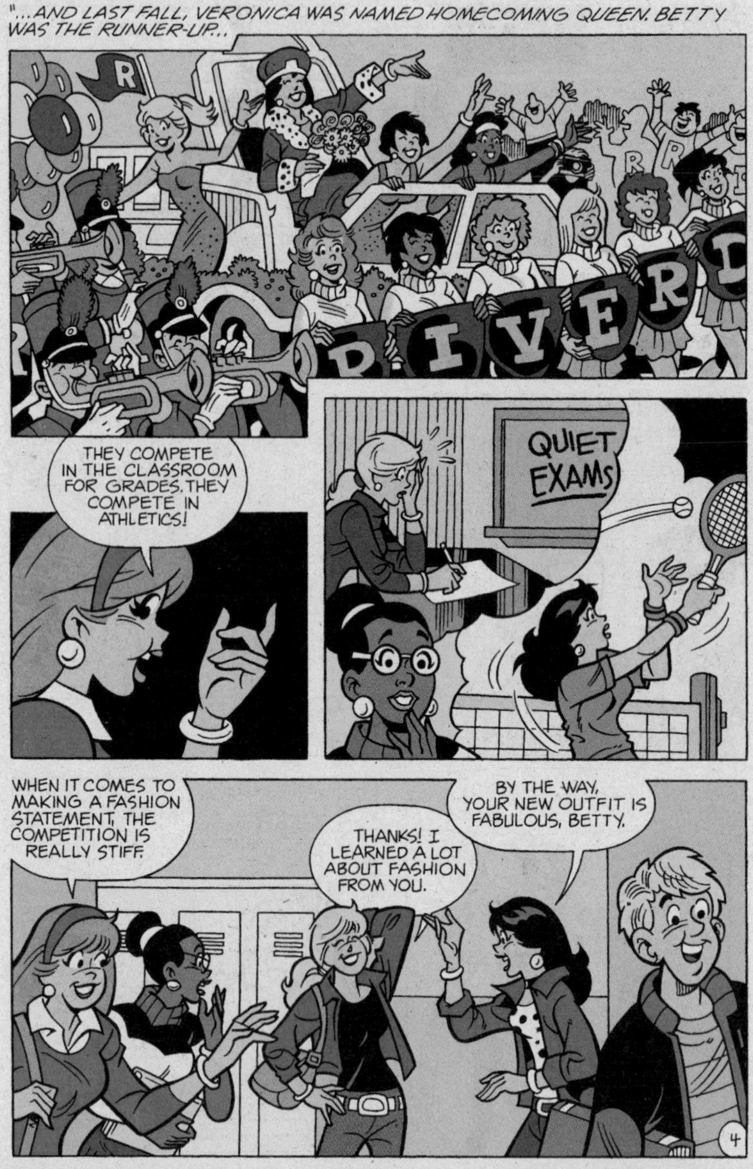
"...AND LAST FALL, VERONICA WAS NAMED HOMECOMING QUEEN. BETTY WAS THE RUNNER-UP...
THEY COMPETE IN THE CLASSROOM FOR GRADES. THEY COMPETE IN ATHLETICS!
QUIET EXAMS
WHEN IT COMES TO MAKING A FASHION STATEMENT, THE COMPETITION IS REALLY STIFF.
BY THE WAY, YOUR NEW OUTFIT IS FABULOUS, BETTY.
THANKS! I LEARNED A LOT ABOUT FASHION FROM YOU.

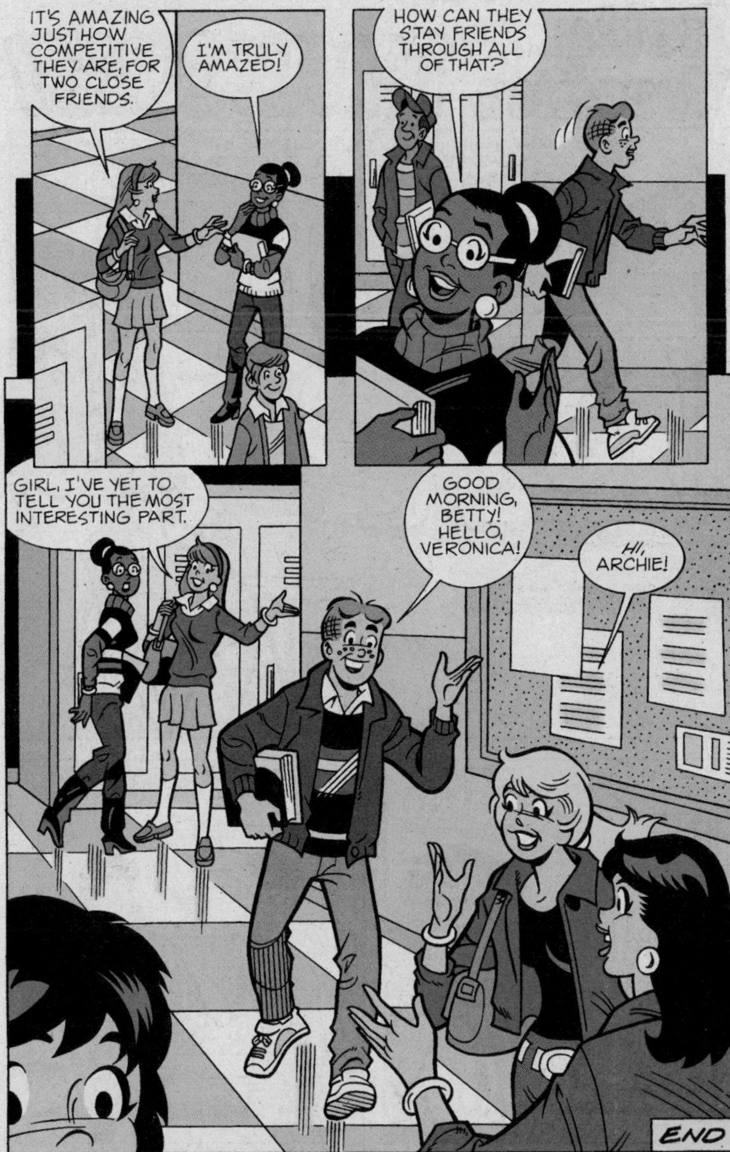
IT'S AMAZING JUST HOW COMPETITIVE THEY ARE, FOR TWO CLOSE FRIENDS.
I'M TRULY AMAZED!
HOW CAN THEY STAY FRIENDS THROUGH ALL OF THAT?
GIRL, I'VE YET TO TELL YOU THE MOST INTERESTING PART.
GOOD MORNING, BETTY! HELLO, VERONICA!
HI, ARCHIE!
END

Betty and Veronica in DRASTIC SURGERY

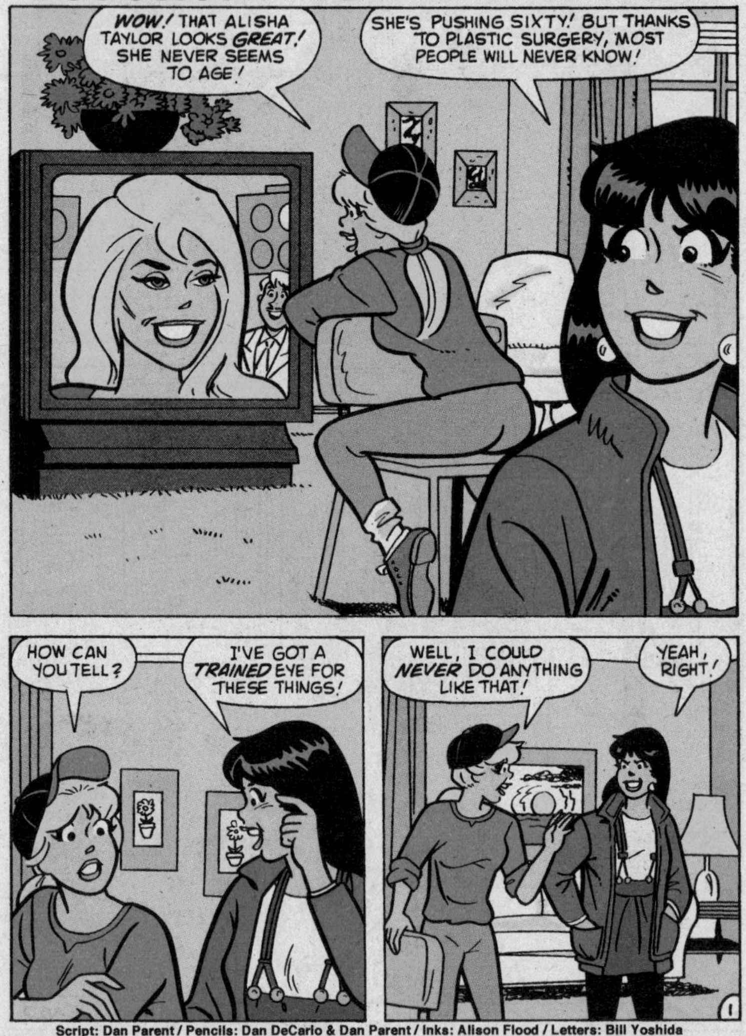
WOW! THAT ALISHA TAYLOR LOOKS GREAT! SHE NEVER SEEMS TO AGE!
SHE'S PUSHING SIXTY! BUT THANKS TO PLASTIC SURGERY, MOST PEOPLE WILL NEVER KNOW!
HOW CAN YOU TELL?
I'VE GOT A TRAINED EYE FOR THESE THINGS!
WELL, I COULD NEVER DO ANYTHING LIKE THAT!
YEAH, RIGHT!
1

Script: Dan Parent / Pencils: Dan DeCarlo & Dan Parent / Inks: Alison Flood / Letters: Bill Yoshida

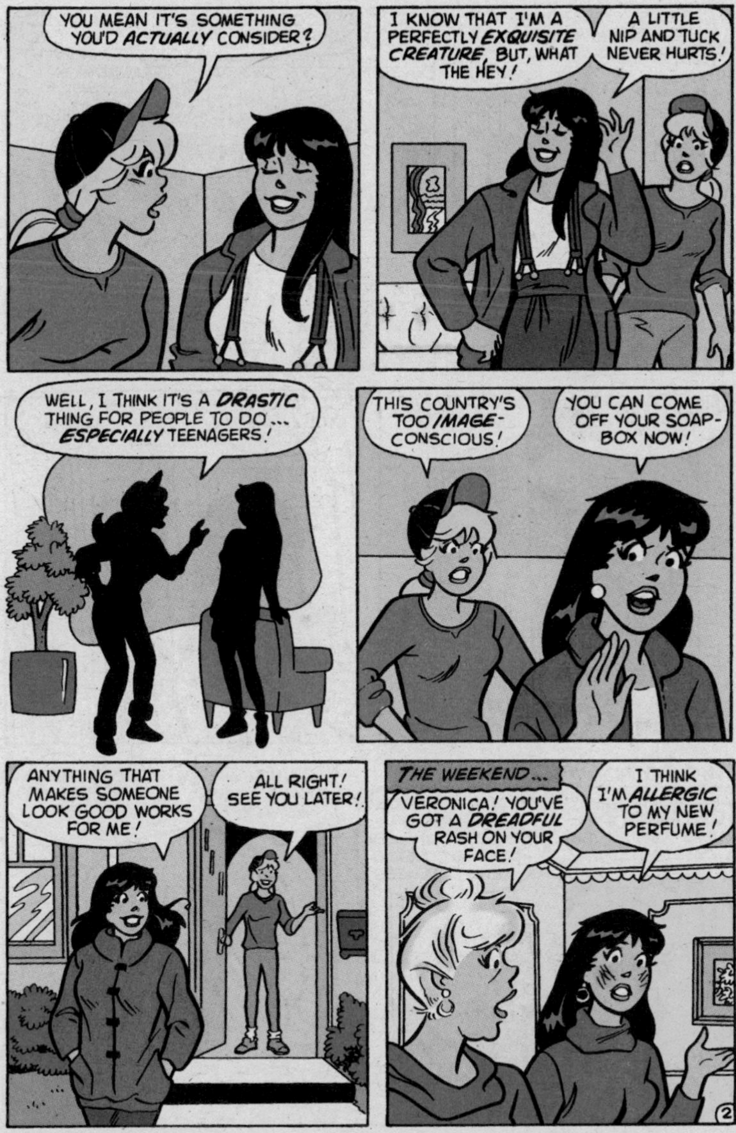
YOU MEAN IT'S SOMETHING YOU'D ACTUALLY CONSIDER?
I KNOW THAT I'M A PERFECTLY EXQUISITE CREATURE, BUT, WHAT THE HEY!
A LITTLE NIP AND TUCK NEVER HURTS!
WELL, I THINK IT'S A DRASTIC THING FOR PEOPLE TO DO... ESPECIALLY TEENAGERS!
THIS COUNTRY'S TOO IMAGE-CONSCIOUS!
YOU CAN COME OFF YOUR SOAP-BOX NOW!
ANYTHING THAT MAKES SOMEONE LOOK GOOD WORKS FOR ME!
ALL RIGHT! SEE YOU LATER!
THE WEEKEND...
VERONICA! YOU'VE GOT A DREADFUL RASH ON YOUR FACE!
I THINK I'M ALLERGIC TO MY NEW PERFUME!
2

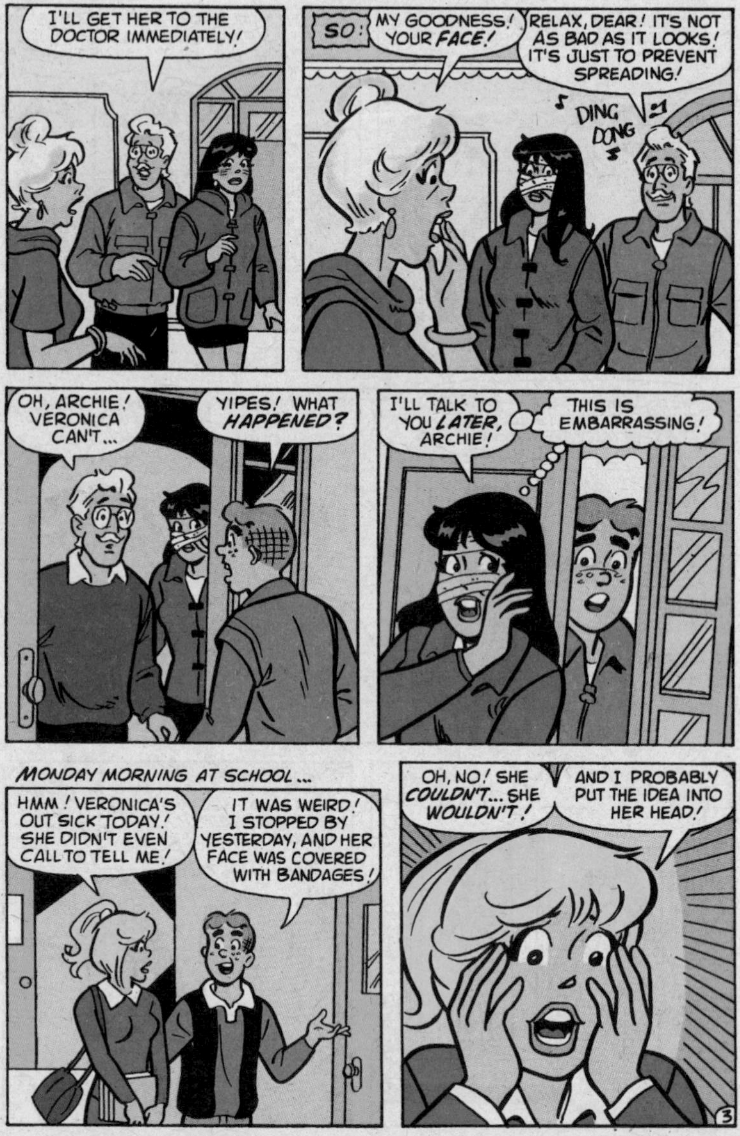

I'LL GET HER TO THE DOCTOR IMMEDIATELY!
SO:
MY GOODNESS! YOUR FACE!
RELAX, DEAR! IT'S NOT AS BAD AS IT LOOKS! IT'S JUST TO PREVENT SPREADING!
DING DONG
OH, ARCHIE! VERONICA CAN'T...
YIPES! WHAT HAPPENED?
I'LL TALK TO YOU LATER, ARCHIE!
THIS IS EMBARRASSING!
MONDAY MORNING AT SCHOOL...
HMM! VERONICA'S OUT SICK TODAY! SHE DIDN'T EVEN CALL TO TELL ME!
IT WAS WEIRD! I STOPPED BY YESTERDAY, AND HER FACE WAS COVERED WITH BANDAGES!
OH, NO! SHE COULDN'T... SHE WOULDN'T!
AND I PROBABLY PUT THE IDEA INTO HER HEAD!
3

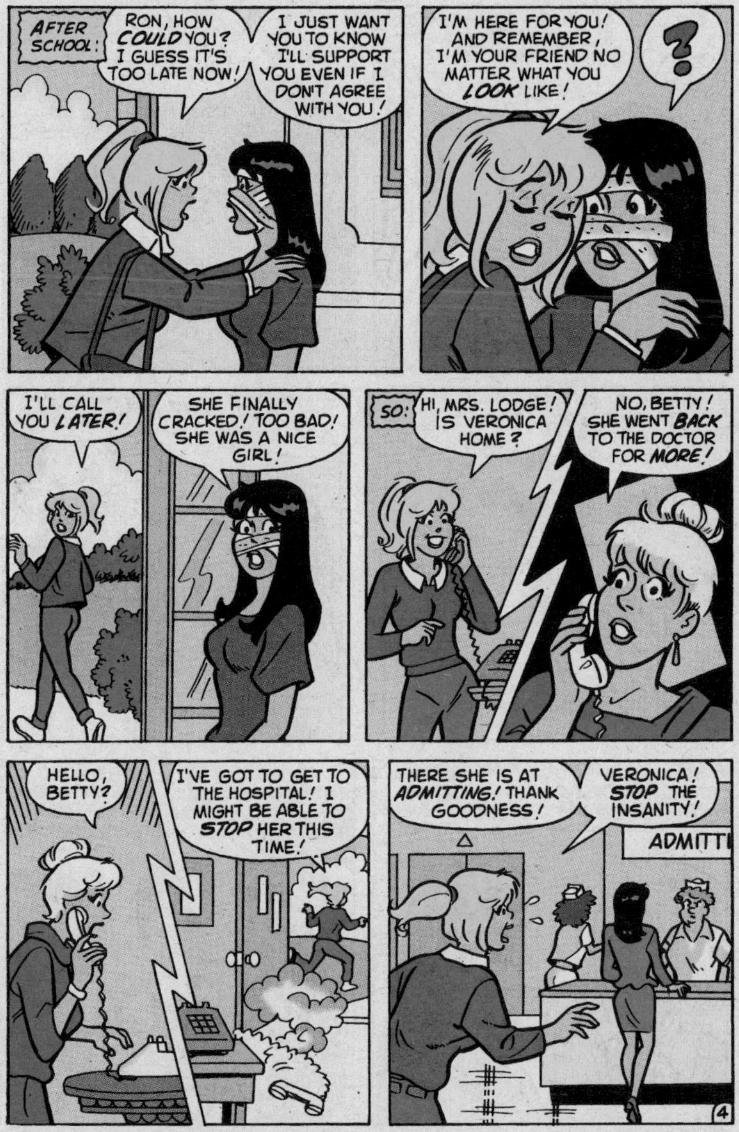

AFTER SCHOOL:
RON, HOW COULD YOU? I GUESS IT'S TOO LATE NOW!
I JUST WANT YOU TO KNOW I'LL SUPPORT YOU EVEN IF I DON'T AGREE WITH YOU!
I'M HERE FOR YOU! AND REMEMBER, I'M YOUR FRIEND NO MATTER WHAT YOU LOOK LIKE!
?
I'LL CALL YOU LATER!
SHE FINALLY CRACKED! TOO BAD! SHE WAS A NICE GIRL!
SO:
HI, MRS. LODGE! IS VERONICA HOME?
NO, BETTY! SHE WENT BACK TO THE DOCTOR FOR MORE!
HELLO, BETTY?
I'VE GOT TO GET TO THE HOSPITAL! I MIGHT BE ABLE TO STOP HER THIS TIME!
THERE SHE IS AT ADMITTING! THANK GOODNESS!
VERONICA! STOP THE INSANITY!
ADMITTI
4

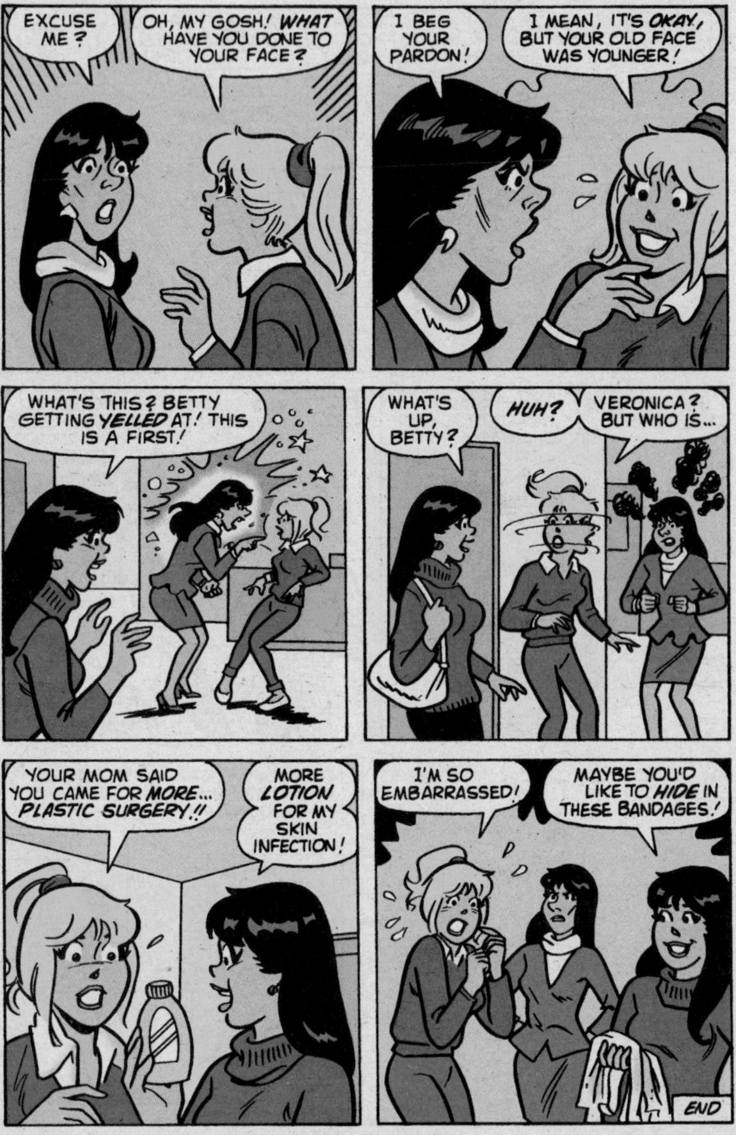
EXCUSE ME?
OH, MY GOSH! WHAT HAVE YOU DONE TO YOUR FACE?
I BEG YOUR PARDON!
I MEAN, IT'S OKAY, BUT YOUR OLD FACE WAS YOUNGER!
WHAT'S THIS? BETTY GETTING YELLED AT! THIS IS A FIRST!
WHAT'S UP, BETTY?
HUH?
VERONICA? BUT WHO IS...
YOUR MOM SAID YOU CAME FOR MORE... PLASTIC SURGERY!!
MORE LOTION FOR MY SKIN INFECTION!
I'M SO EMBARRASSED!
MAYBE YOU'D LIKE TO HIDE IN THESE BANDAGES!
END

Betty and Veronica in "THE SNOOP"

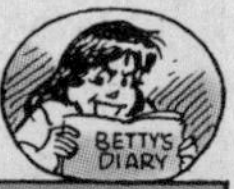
BETTY'S DIARY

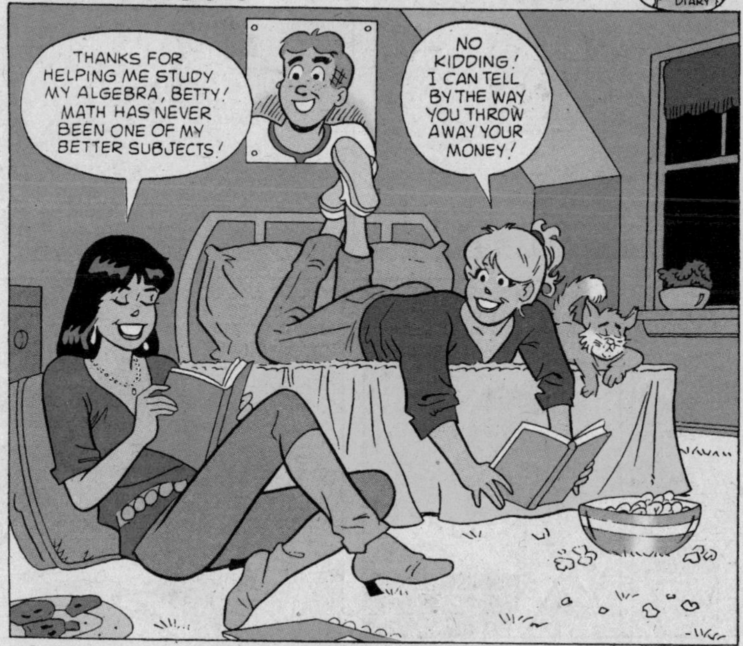
THANKS FOR HELPING ME STUDY MY ALGEBRA, BETTY! MATH HAS NEVER BEEN ONE OF MY BETTER SUBJECTS!
NO KIDDING! I CAN TELL BY THE WAY YOU THROW AWAY YOUR MONEY!

Script: Kathleen Webb / Art: Dan DeCarlo / Letters: Bill Yoshida / Colors: Barry Grossman

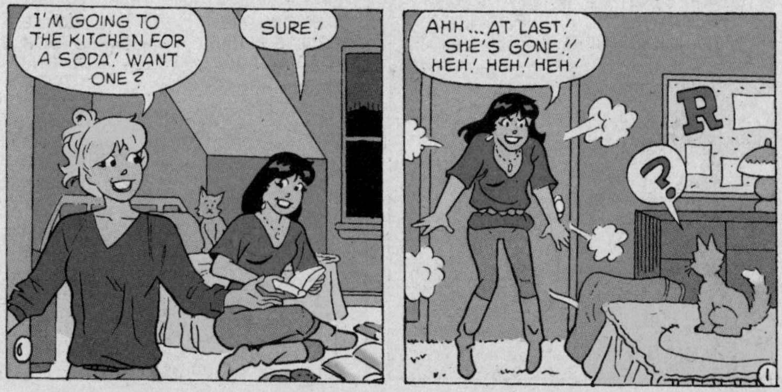
I'M GOING TO THE KITCHEN FOR A SODA! WANT ONE?
SURE!
AHH... AT LAST! SHE'S GONE!! HEH! HEH! HEH!
R
?

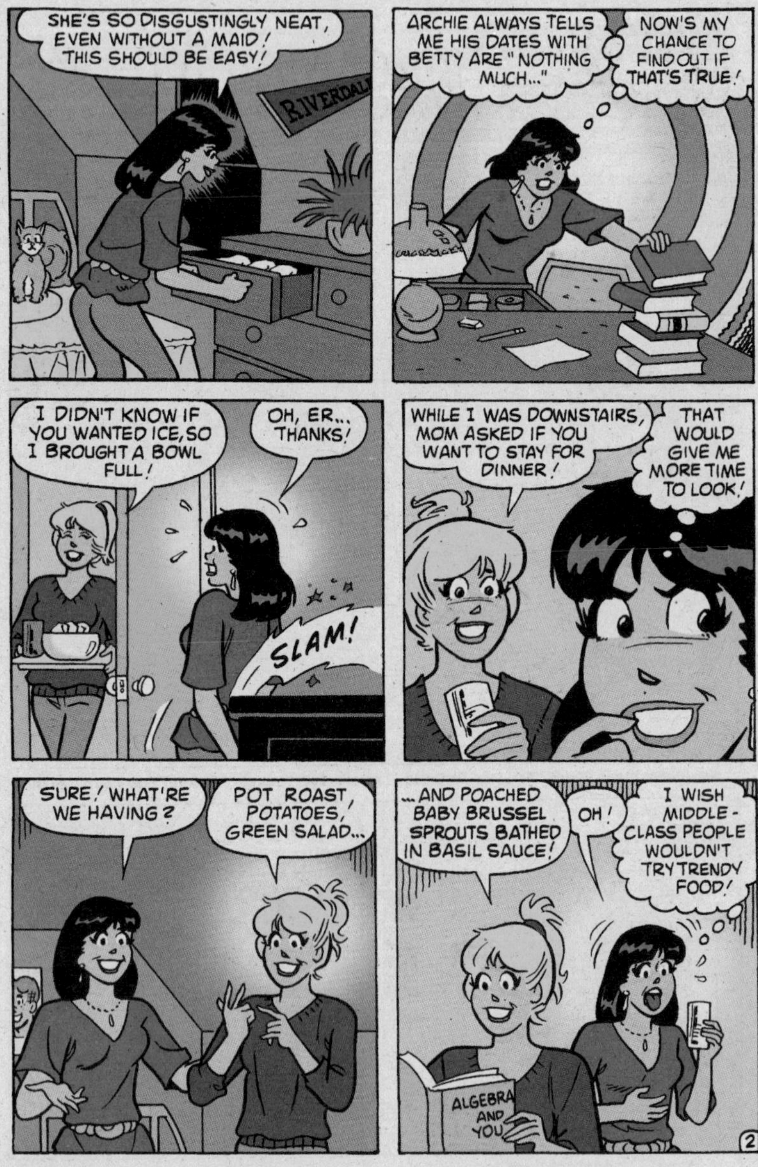
SHE'S SO DISGUSTINGLY NEAT, EVEN WITHOUT A MAID! THIS SHOULD BE EASY!
RIVERDALE
ARCHIE ALWAYS TELLS ME HIS DATES WITH BETTY ARE "NOTHING MUCH..."
NOW'S MY CHANCE TO FIND OUT IF THAT'S TRUE!
I DIDN'T KNOW IF YOU WANTED ICE, SO I BROUGHT A BOWL FULL!
OH, ER... THANKS!
SLAM!
WHILE I WAS DOWNSTAIRS, MOM ASKED IF YOU WANT TO STAY FOR DINNER!
THAT WOULD GIVE ME MORE TIME TO LOOK!
SURE! WHAT'RE WE HAVING?
POT ROAST, POTATOES, GREEN SALAD...
...AND POACHED BABY BRUSSEL SPROUTS BATHED IN BASIL SAUCE!
OH!
I WISH MIDDLE-CLASS PEOPLE WOULDN'T TRY TRENDY FOOD!
ALGEBRA AND YOU
2

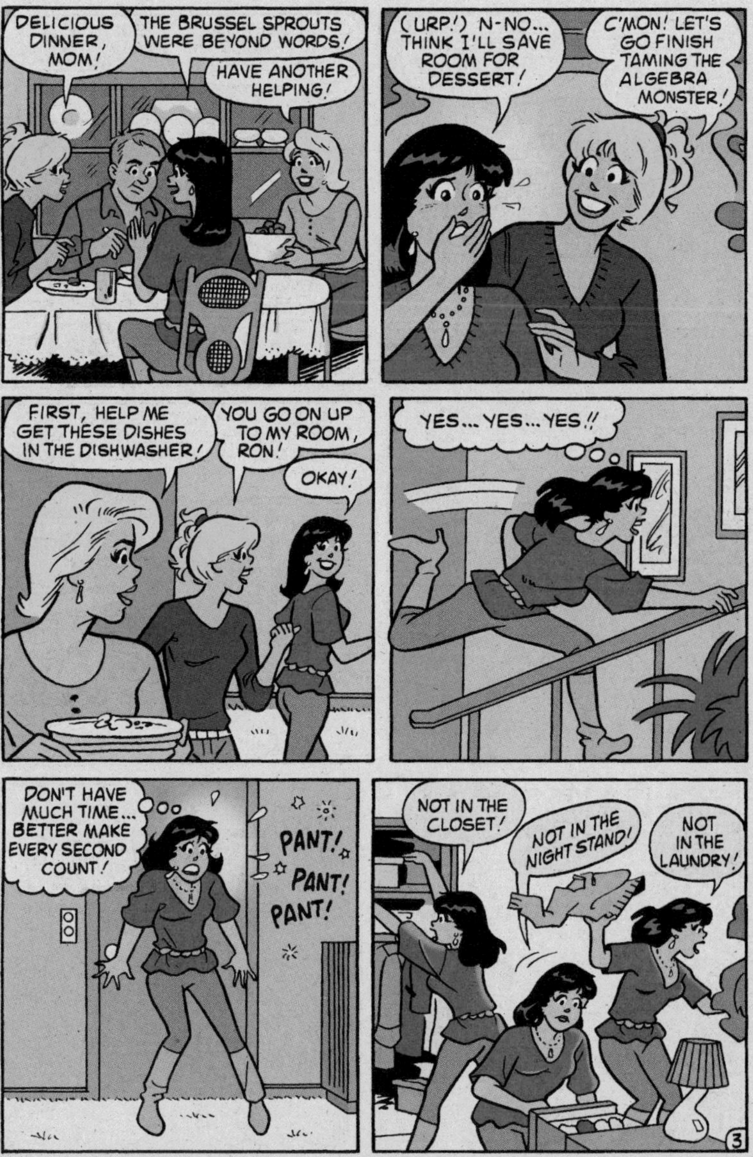
DELICIOUS DINNER, MOM!
THE BRUSSEL SPROUTS WERE BEYOND WORDS!
HAVE ANOTHER HELPING!
(URP!) N-NO... THINK I'LL SAVE ROOM FOR DESSERT!
C'MON! LET'S GO FINISH TAMING THE ALGEBRA MONSTER!
FIRST, HELP ME GET THESE DISHES IN THE DISHWASHER!
YOU GO ON UP TO MY ROOM, RON!
OKAY!
YES... YES... YES!!
DON'T HAVE MUCH TIME... BETTER MAKE EVERY SECOND COUNT!
PANT! PANT! PANT!
NOT IN THE CLOSET!
NOT IN THE NIGHT STAND!
NOT IN THE LAUNDRY!
3

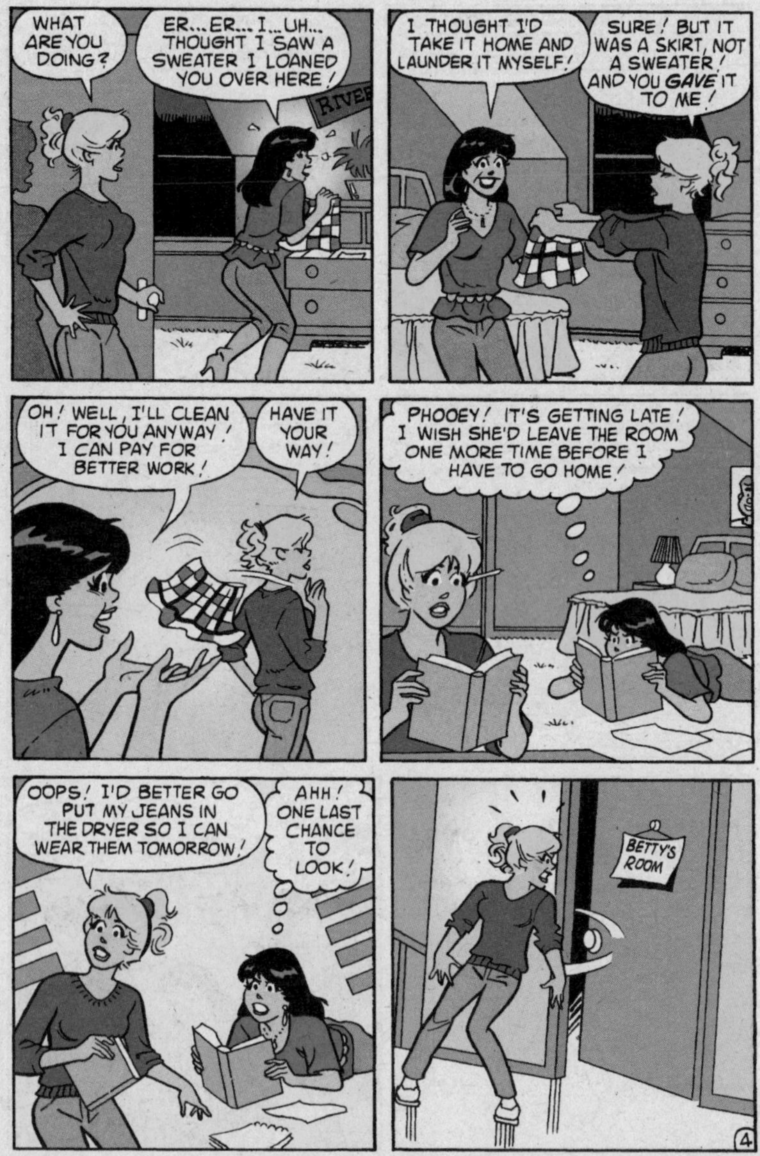

WHAT ARE YOU DOING?
ER...ER... I...UH... THOUGHT I SAW A SWEATER I LOANED YOU OVER HERE!
RIVER
I THOUGHT I'D TAKE IT HOME AND LAUNDER IT MYSELF!
SURE! BUT IT WAS A SKIRT, NOT A SWEATER! AND YOU GAVE IT TO ME!
OH! WELL, I'LL CLEAN IT FOR YOU ANYWAY! I CAN PAY FOR BETTER WORK!
HAVE IT YOUR WAY!
PHOOEY! IT'S GETTING LATE! I WISH SHE'D LEAVE THE ROOM ONE MORE TIME BEFORE I HAVE TO GO HOME!
OOPS! I'D BETTER GO PUT MY JEANS IN THE DRYER SO I CAN WEAR THEM TOMORROW!
AHH! ONE LAST CHANCE TO LOOK!
BETTY'S ROOM
4

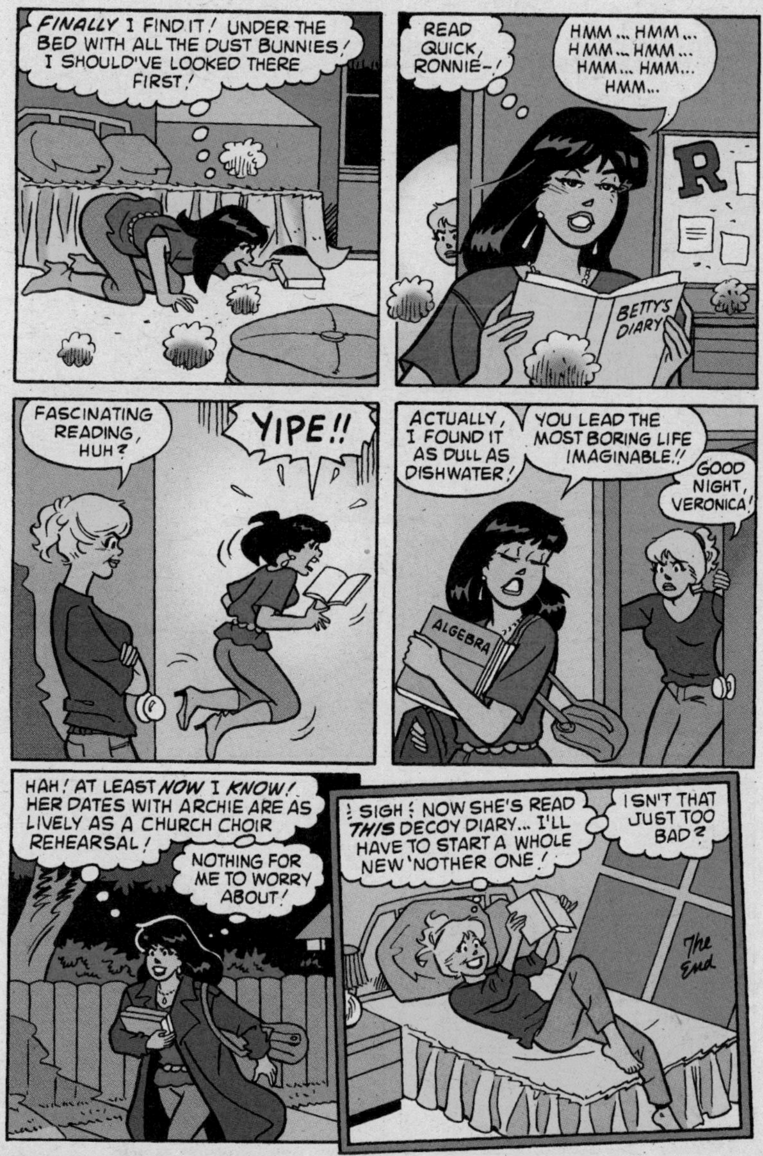
FINALLY I FIND IT! UNDER THE BED WITH ALL THE DUST BUNNIES! I SHOULD'VE LOOKED THERE FIRST!
READ QUICK, RONNIE-!
HMM... HMM... HMM... HMM... HMM... HMM... HMM...
BETTY'S DIARY
FASCINATING READING, HUH?
YIPE!!
ACTUALLY, I FOUND IT AS DULL AS DISHWATER!
YOU LEAD THE MOST BORING LIFE IMAGINABLE!!
ALGEBRA
GOOD NIGHT, VERONICA!
HAH! AT LEAST NOW I KNOW! HER DATES WITH ARCHIE ARE AS LIVELY AS A CHURCH CHOIR REHEARSAL!
NOTHING FOR ME TO WORRY ABOUT!
! SIGH ! NOW SHE'S READ THIS DECOY DIARY... I'LL HAVE TO START A WHOLE NEW 'NOTHER ONE!
ISN'T THAT JUST TOO BAD?
The End

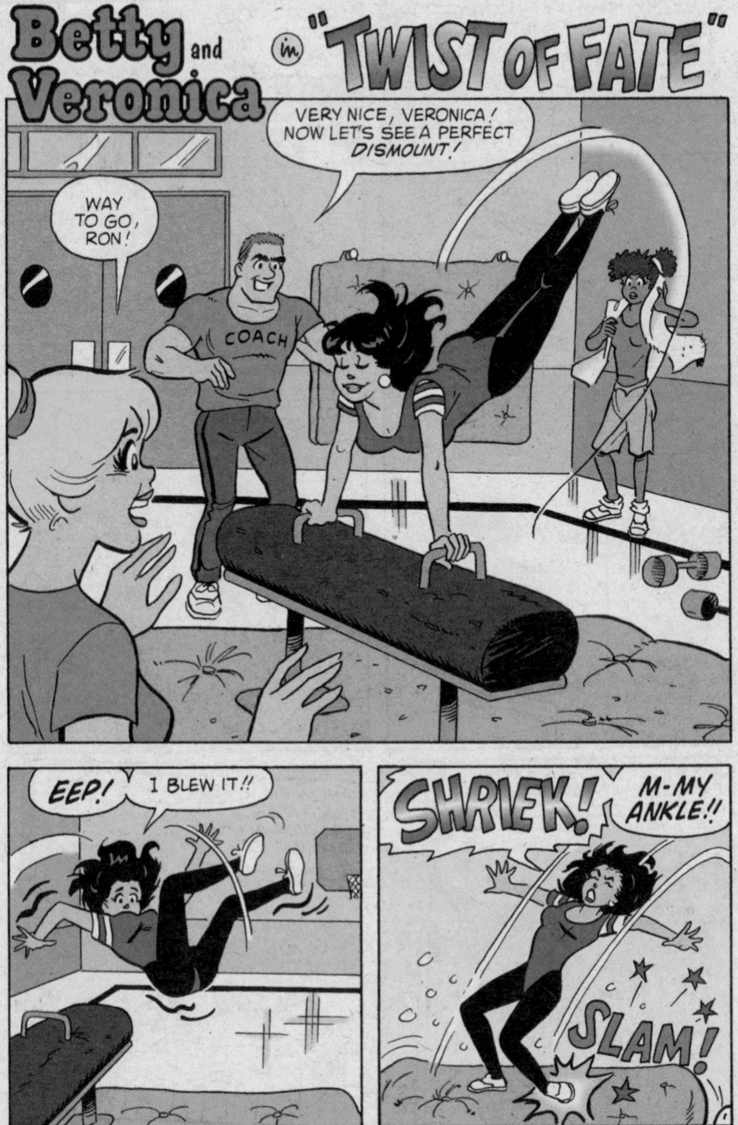
Betty and Veronica
in
"TWIST OF FATE"
VERY NICE, VERONICA! NOW LET'S SEE A PERFECT DISMOUNT!
WAY TO GO, RON!
COACH
EEP!
I BLEW IT!!
SHRIEK!
M-MY ANKLE!!
SLAM!
1

Script: Frank Doyle / Art: Dan DeCarlo / Letters: Bill Yoshida / Colors: Barry Grossman

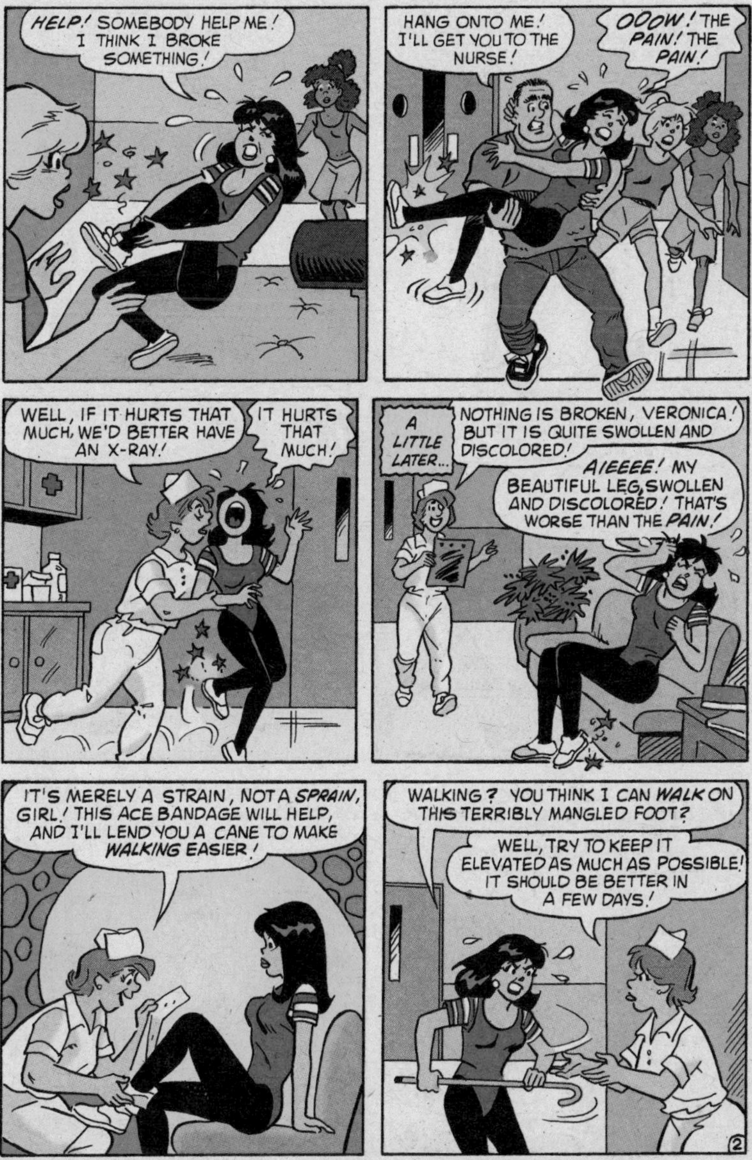
HELP! SOMEBODY HELP ME! I THINK I BROKE SOMETHING!
HANG ONTO ME! I'LL GET YOU TO THE NURSE!
OOOW! THE PAIN! THE PAIN!
WELL, IF IT HURTS THAT MUCH, WE'D BETTER HAVE AN X-RAY!
IT HURTS THAT MUCH!
A LITTLE LATER...
NOTHING IS BROKEN, VERONICA! BUT IT IS QUITE SWOLLEN AND DISCOLORED!
AIEEEE! MY BEAUTIFUL LEG, SWOLLEN AND DISCOLORED! THAT'S WORSE THAN THE PAIN!
IT'S MERELY A STRAIN, NOT A SPRAIN, GIRL! THIS ACE BANDAGE WILL HELP, AND I'LL LEND YOU A CANE TO MAKE WALKING EASIER!
WALKING? YOU THINK I CAN WALK ON THIS TERRIBLY MANGLED FOOT?
WELL, TRY TO KEEP IT ELEVATED AS MUCH AS POSSIBLE! IT SHOULD BE BETTER IN A FEW DAYS!
2

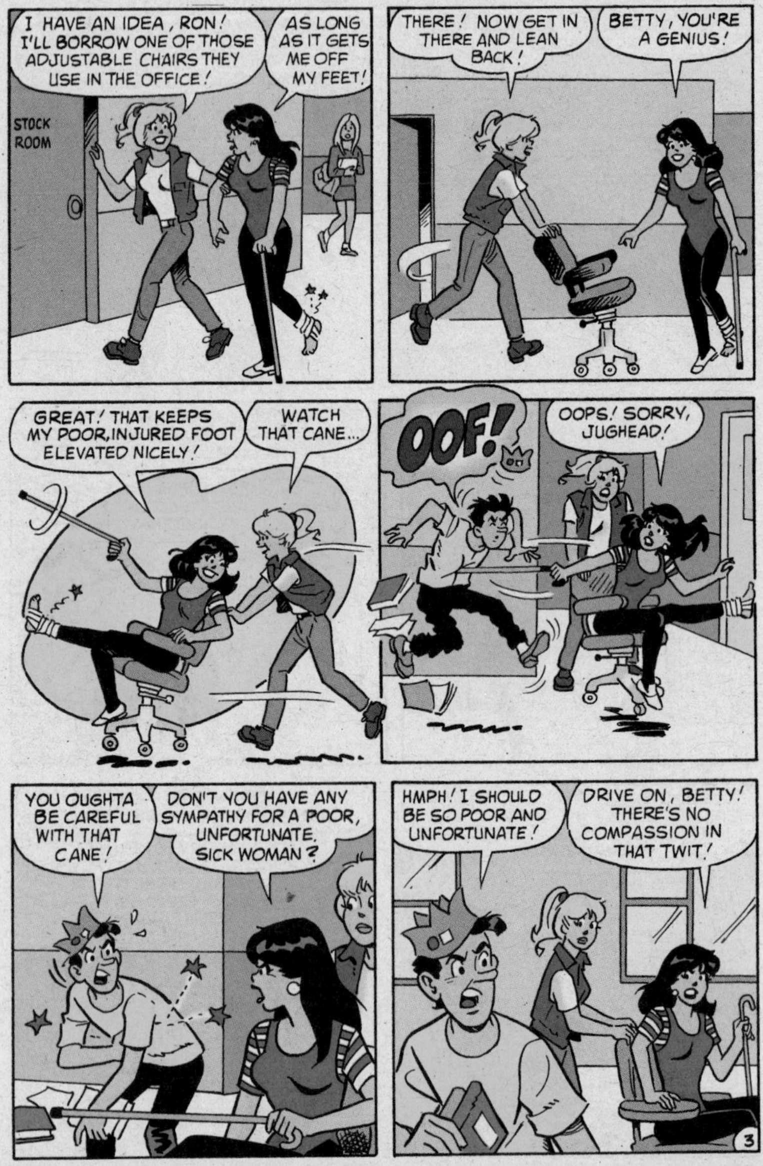
I HAVE AN IDEA, RON! I'LL BORROW ONE OF THOSE ADJUSTABLE CHAIRS THEY USE IN THE OFFICE!
AS LONG AS IT GETS ME OFF MY FEET!
STOCK ROOM
THERE! NOW GET IN THERE AND LEAN BACK!
BETTY, YOU'RE A GENIUS!
GREAT! THAT KEEPS MY POOR, INJURED FOOT ELEVATED NICELY!
WATCH THAT CANE...
OOF!
OOPS! SORRY, JUGHEAD!
YOU OUGHTA BE CAREFUL WITH THAT CANE!
DON'T YOU HAVE ANY SYMPATHY FOR A POOR, UNFORTUNATE, SICK WOMAN?
HMPH! I SHOULD BE SO POOR AND UNFORTUNATE!
DRIVE ON, BETTY! THERE'S NO COMPASSION IN THAT TWIT!
3

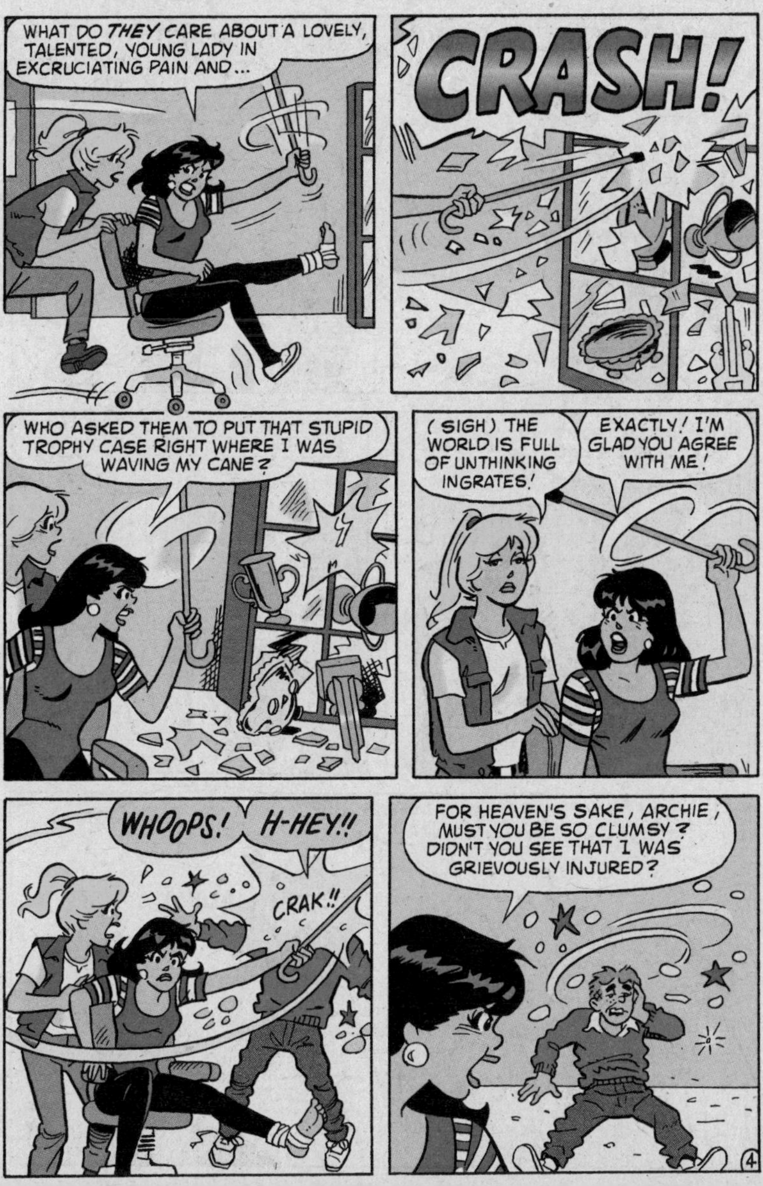
WHAT DO THEY CARE ABOUT A LOVELY, TALENTED, YOUNG LADY IN EXCRUCIATING PAIN AND...
CRASH!
WHO ASKED THEM TO PUT THAT STUPID TROPHY CASE RIGHT WHERE I WAS WAVING MY CANE?
(SIGH) THE WORLD IS FULL OF UNTHINKING INGRATES!
EXACTLY! I'M GLAD YOU AGREE WITH ME!
WHOOPS!
H-HEY!!
CRAK!!
FOR HEAVEN'S SAKE, ARCHIE, MUST YOU BE SO CLUMSY? DIDN'T YOU SEE THAT I WAS GRIEVOUSLY INJURED?
4

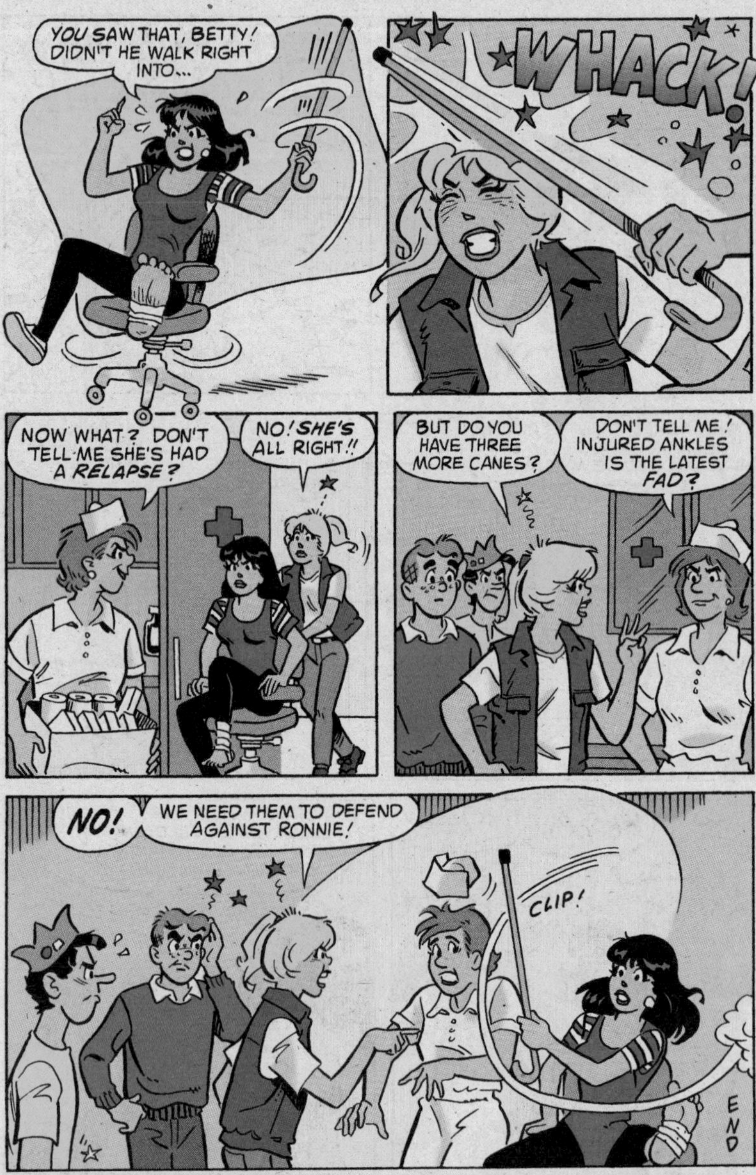
YOU SAW THAT, BETTY! DIDN'T HE WALK RIGHT INTO...
WHACK!
NOW WHAT? DON'T TELL ME SHE'S HAD A RELAPSE?
NO! SHE'S ALL RIGHT!!
BUT DO YOU HAVE THREE MORE CANES?
DON'T TELL ME! INJURED ANKLES IS THE LATEST FAD?
NO!
WE NEED THEM TO DEFEND AGAINST RONNIE!
CLIP!
END

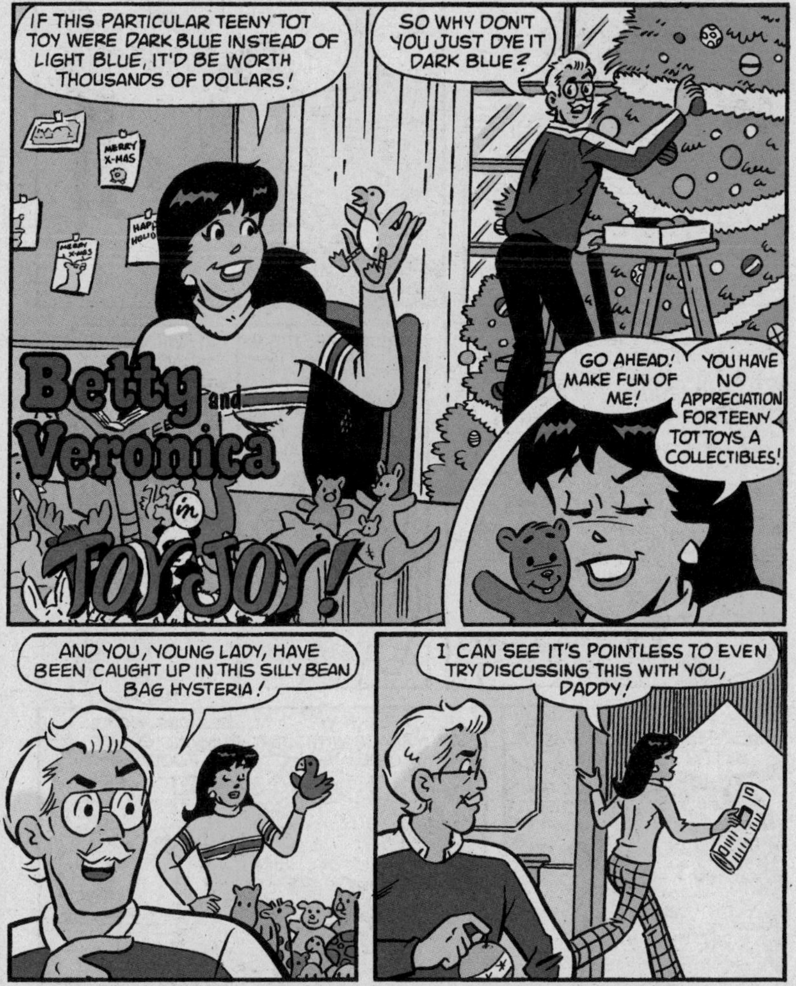
IF THIS PARTICULAR TEENY TOT TOY WERE DARK BLUE INSTEAD OF LIGHT BLUE, IT'D BE WORTH THOUSANDS OF DOLLARS!
SO WHY DON'T YOU JUST DYE IT DARK BLUE?
MERRY X-MAS
Betty and Veronica in TOY JOY!
GO AHEAD! MAKE FUN OF ME!
YOU HAVE NO APPRECIATION FOR TEENY TOT TOYS A COLLECTIBLES!
AND YOU, YOUNG LADY, HAVE BEEN CAUGHT UP IN THIS SILLY BEAN BAG HYSTERIA!
I CAN SEE IT'S POINTLESS TO EVEN TRY DISCUSSING THIS WITH YOU, DADDY!

SCRIPT: GEORGE GLADIR PENCILS: FERNANDO RUIZ INKS: RUDY LAPICK
COLORS: BARRY GROSSMAN LETTERS: BILL YOSHIDA

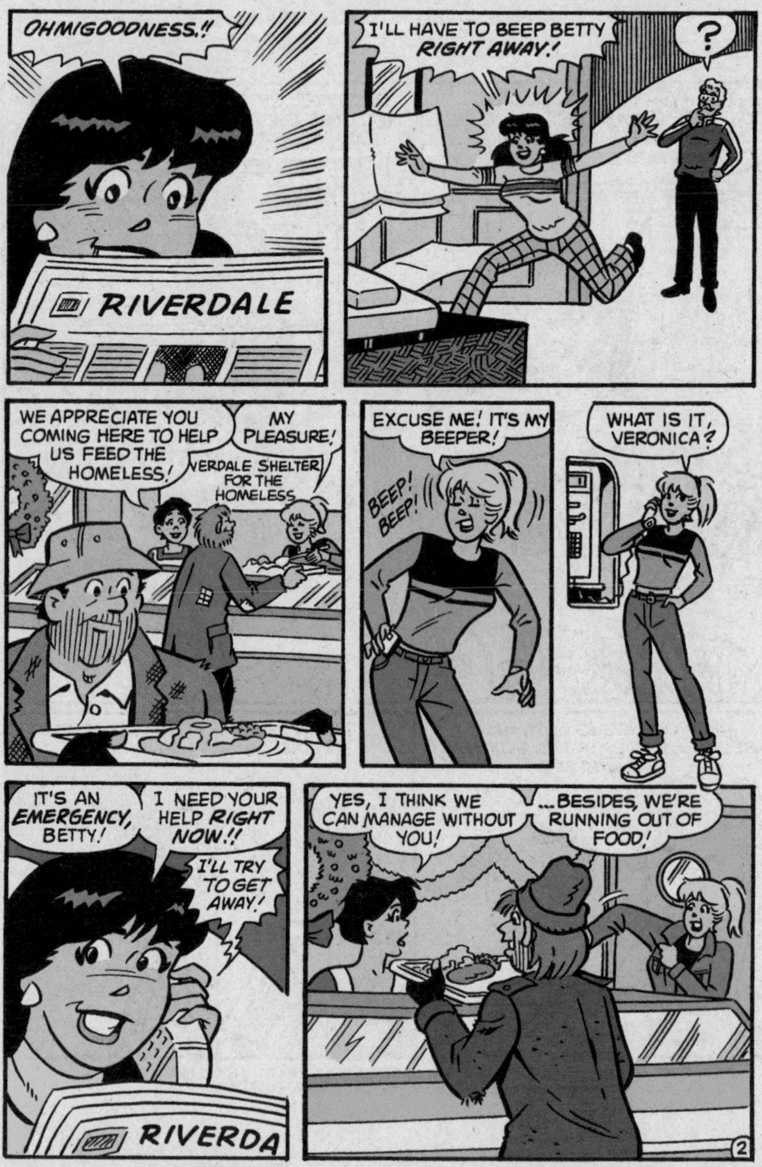
OHMIGOODNESS.!!
RIVERDALE
I'LL HAVE TO BEEP BETTY RIGHT AWAY.!
?
WE APPRECIATE YOU COMING HERE TO HELP US FEED THE HOMELESS!
MY PLEASURE!
VERDALE SHELTER FOR THE HOMELESS
EXCUSE ME! IT'S MY BEEPER!
BEEP! BEEP!
WHAT IS IT, VERONICA?
IT'S AN EMERGENCY, BETTY!
I NEED YOUR HELP RIGHT NOW.!!
I'LL TRY TO GET AWAY!
RIVERDA
YES, I THINK WE CAN MANAGE WITHOUT YOU!
...BESIDES, WE'RE RUNNING OUT OF FOOD!
2

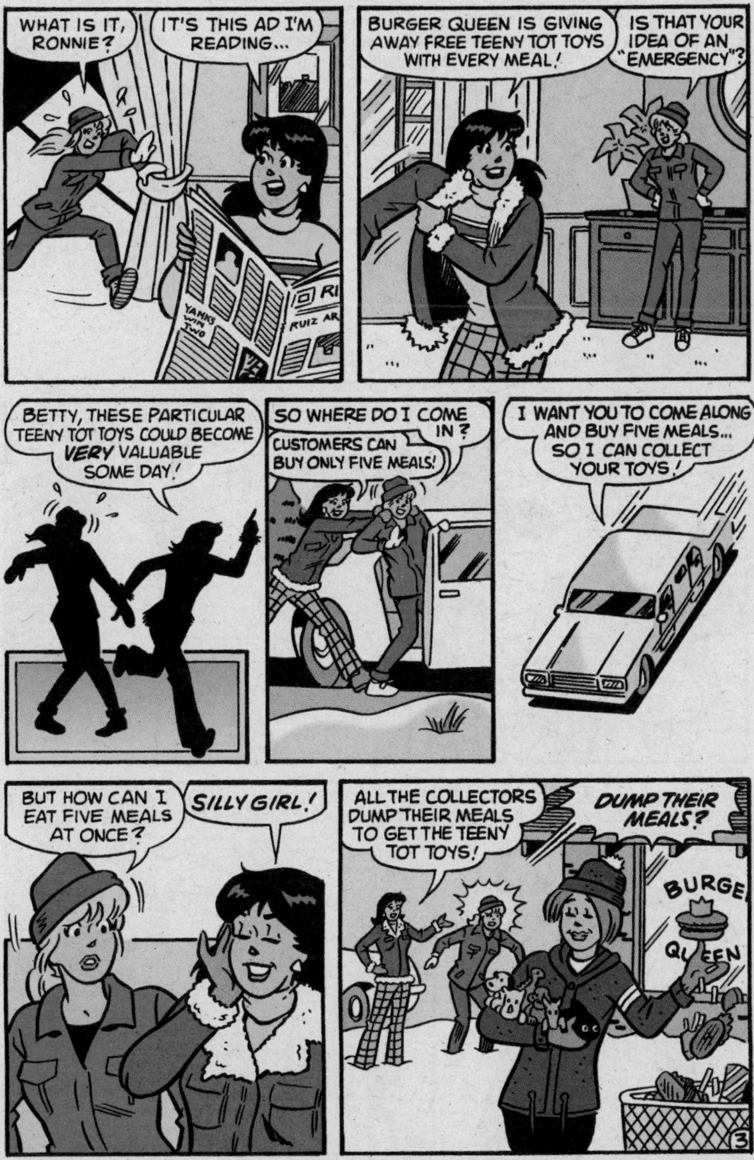
WHAT IS IT, RONNIE?
IT'S THIS AD I'M READING...
YANKS WIN TWO
RUIZ AR
BURGER QUEEN IS GIVING AWAY FREE TEENY TOT TOYS WITH EVERY MEAL!
IS THAT YOUR IDEA OF AN "EMERGENCY"?
BETTY, THESE PARTICULAR TEENY TOT TOYS COULD BECOME VERY VALUABLE SOME DAY!
SO WHERE DO I COME IN?
CUSTOMERS CAN BUY ONLY FIVE MEALS!
I WANT YOU TO COME ALONG AND BUY FIVE MEALS... SO I CAN COLLECT YOUR TOYS!
BUT HOW CAN I EAT FIVE MEALS AT ONCE?
SILLY GIRL!
ALL THE COLLECTORS DUMP THEIR MEALS TO GET THE TEENY TOT TOYS!
DUMP THEIR MEALS?
BURGE
QUEEN
3

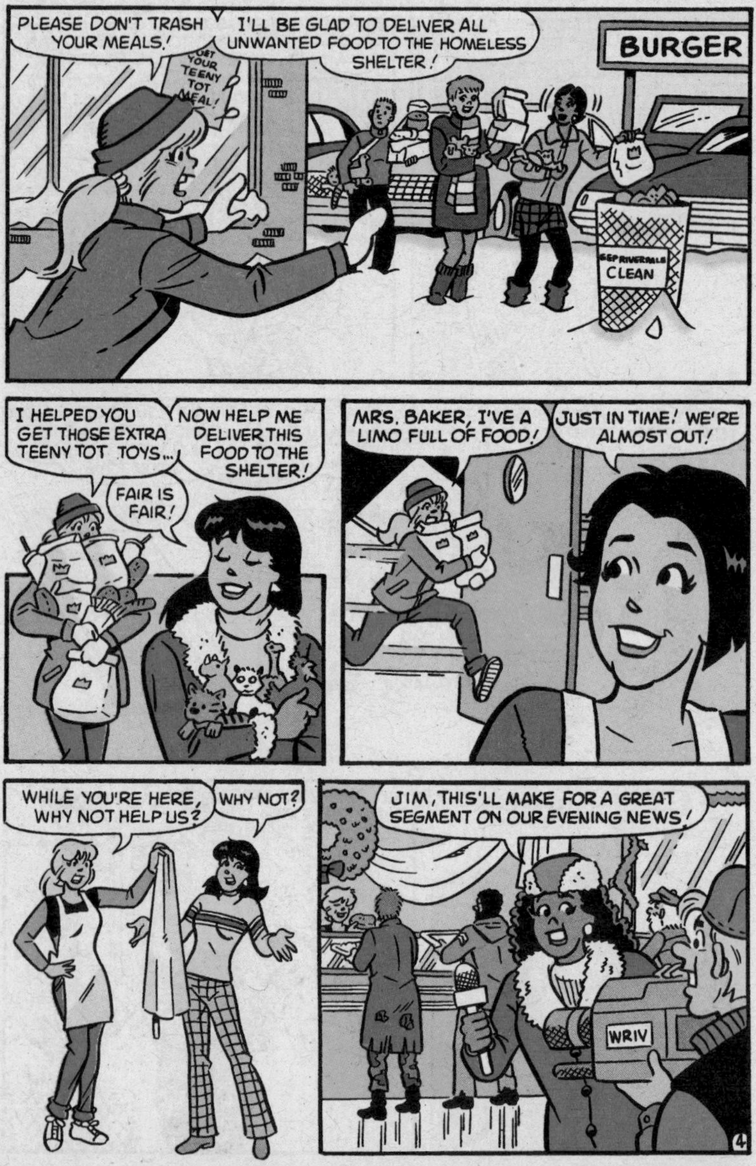
PLEASE DON'T TRASH YOUR MEALS!
I'LL BE GLAD TO DELIVER ALL UNWANTED FOOD TO THE HOMELESS SHELTER!
BURGER
GET YOUR TEENY TOT MEAL!
CLEAN
I HELPED YOU GET THOSE EXTRA TEENY TOT TOYS...
NOW HELP ME DELIVER THIS FOOD TO THE SHELTER!
FAIR IS FAIR!
MRS. BAKER, I'VE A LIMO FULL OF FOOD!
JUST IN TIME! WE'RE ALMOST OUT!
WHILE YOU'RE HERE, WHY NOT HELP US?
WHY NOT?
JIM, THIS'LL MAKE FOR A GREAT SEGMENT ON OUR EVENING NEWS!
WRIV
4

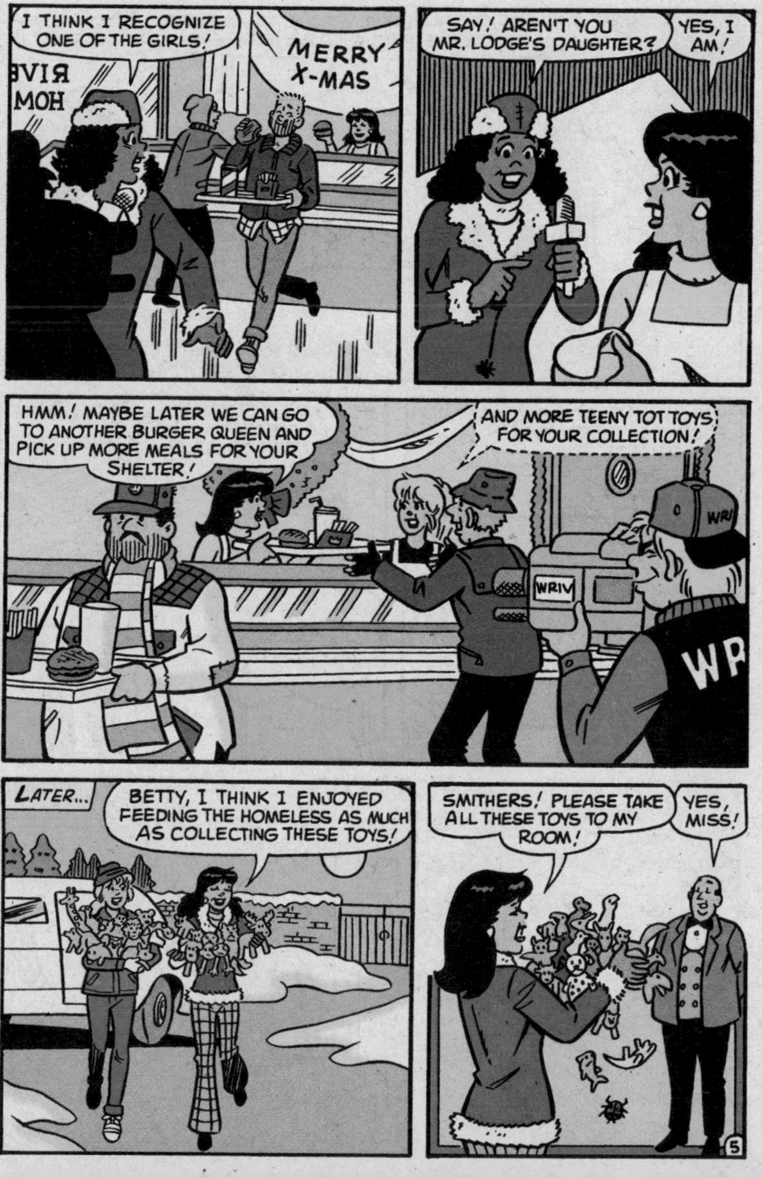
I THINK I RECOGNIZE ONE OF THE GIRLS!
MERRY X-MAS
SAY! AREN'T YOU MR. LODGE'S DAUGHTER?
YES, I AM!
HMM! MAYBE LATER WE CAN GO TO ANOTHER BURGER QUEEN AND PICK UP MORE MEALS FOR YOUR SHELTER!
AND MORE TEENY TOT TOYS FOR YOUR COLLECTION!
WRIV
LATER...
BETTY, I THINK I ENJOYED FEEDING THE HOMELESS AS MUCH AS COLLECTING THESE TOYS!
SMITHERS! PLEASE TAKE ALL THESE TOYS TO MY ROOM!
YES, MISS!
5

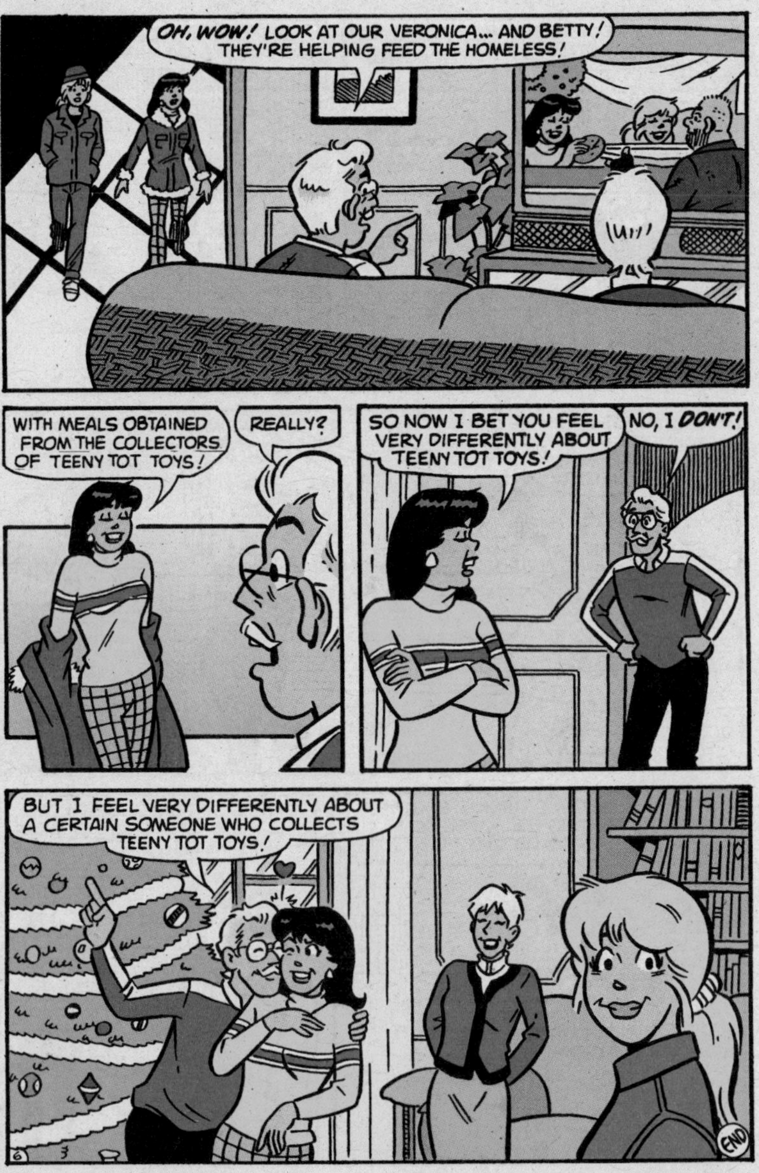

OH, WOW! LOOK AT OUR VERONICA... AND BETTY! THEY'RE HELPING FEED THE HOMELESS!
WITH MEALS OBTAINED FROM THE COLLECTORS OF TEENY TOT TOYS!
REALLY?
SO NOW I BET YOU FEEL VERY DIFFERENTLY ABOUT TEENY TOT TOYS!
NO, I DON'T!
BUT I FEEL VERY DIFFERENTLY ABOUT A CERTAIN SOMEONE WHO COLLECTS TEENY TOT TOYS!
END

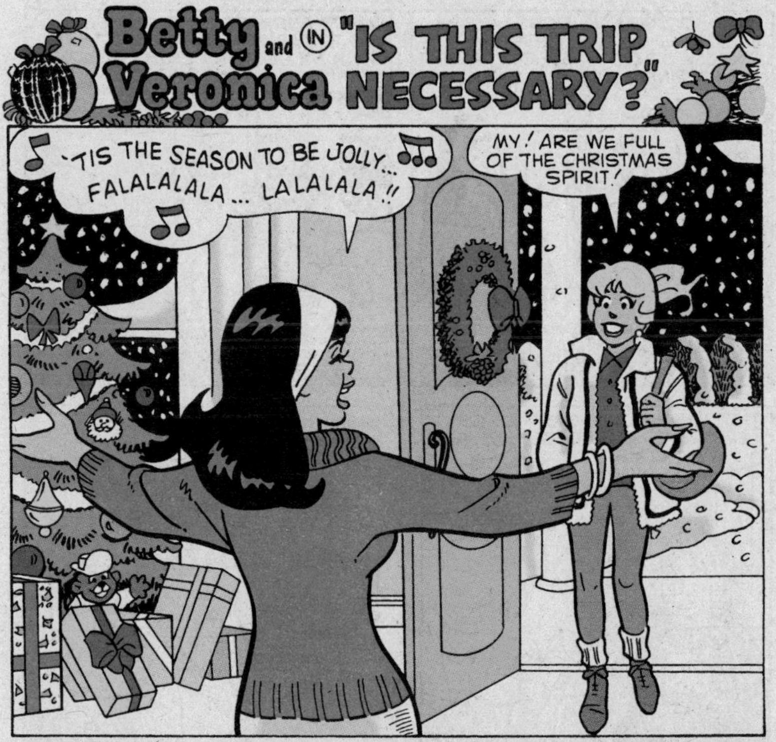
Betty and Veronica IN "IS THIS TRIP NECESSARY?"
'TIS THE SEASON TO BE JOLLY... FALALALALA... LALALALA!!
MY! ARE WE FULL OF THE CHRISTMAS SPIRIT!

Script: Kathleen Webb / Pencils: Dan DeCarlo / Inks: Alison Flood / Letters: Bill Yoshida / Colors: Barry Grossman

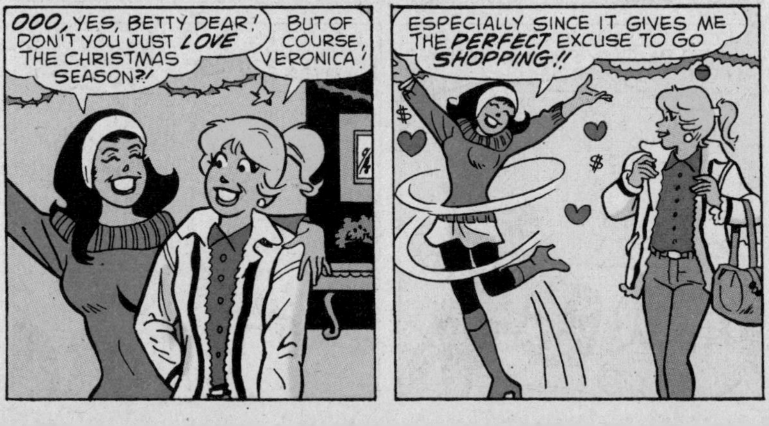
OOO, YES, BETTY DEAR! DON'T YOU JUST *LOVE* THE CHRISTMAS SEASON?!
BUT OF COURSE, VERONICA!
ESPECIALLY SINCE IT GIVES ME THE *PERFECT* EXCUSE TO GO *SHOPPING*!!

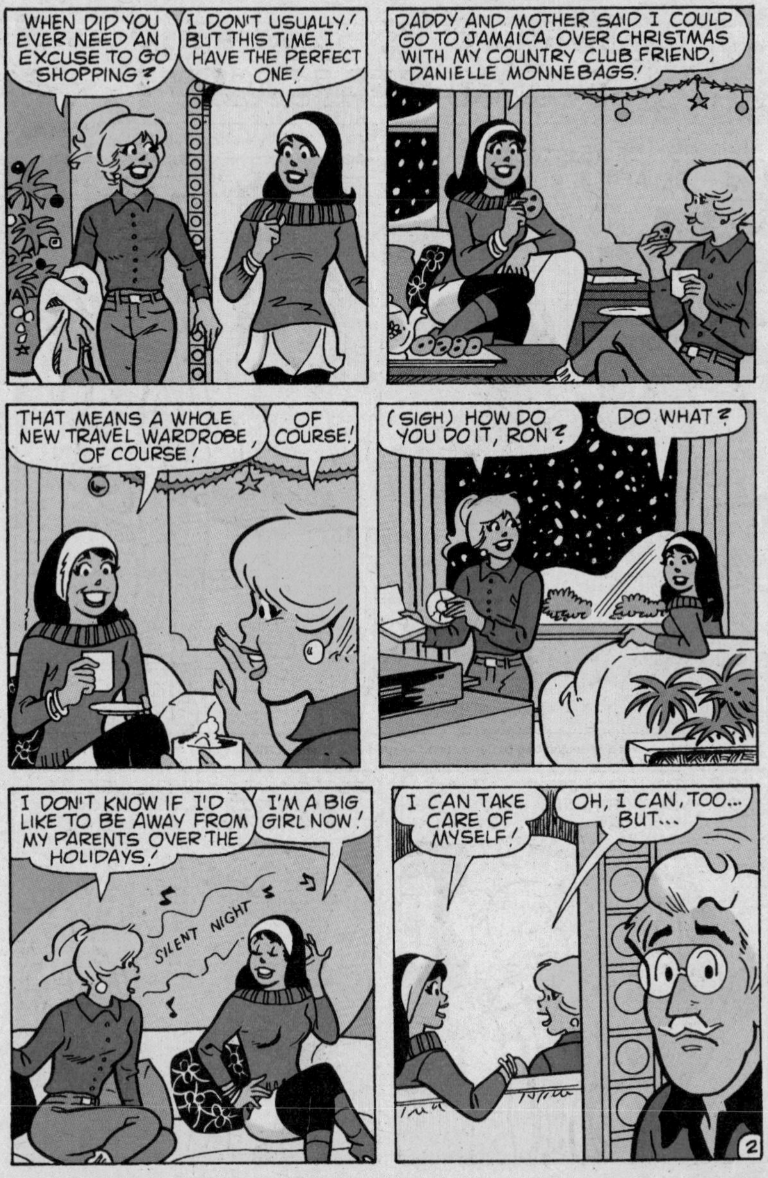
WHEN DID YOU EVER NEED AN EXCUSE TO GO SHOPPING?
I DON'T USUALLY! BUT THIS TIME I HAVE THE PERFECT ONE!
DADDY AND MOTHER SAID I COULD GO TO JAMAICA OVER CHRISTMAS WITH MY COUNTRY CLUB FRIEND, DANIELLE MONNEBAGS!
THAT MEANS A WHOLE NEW TRAVEL WARDROBE, OF COURSE!
OF COURSE!
(SIGH) HOW DO YOU DO IT, RON?
DO WHAT?
I DON'T KNOW IF I'D LIKE TO BE AWAY FROM MY PARENTS OVER THE HOLIDAYS!
I'M A BIG GIRL NOW!
SILENT NIGHT
I CAN TAKE CARE OF MYSELF!
OH, I CAN, TOO... BUT...
2

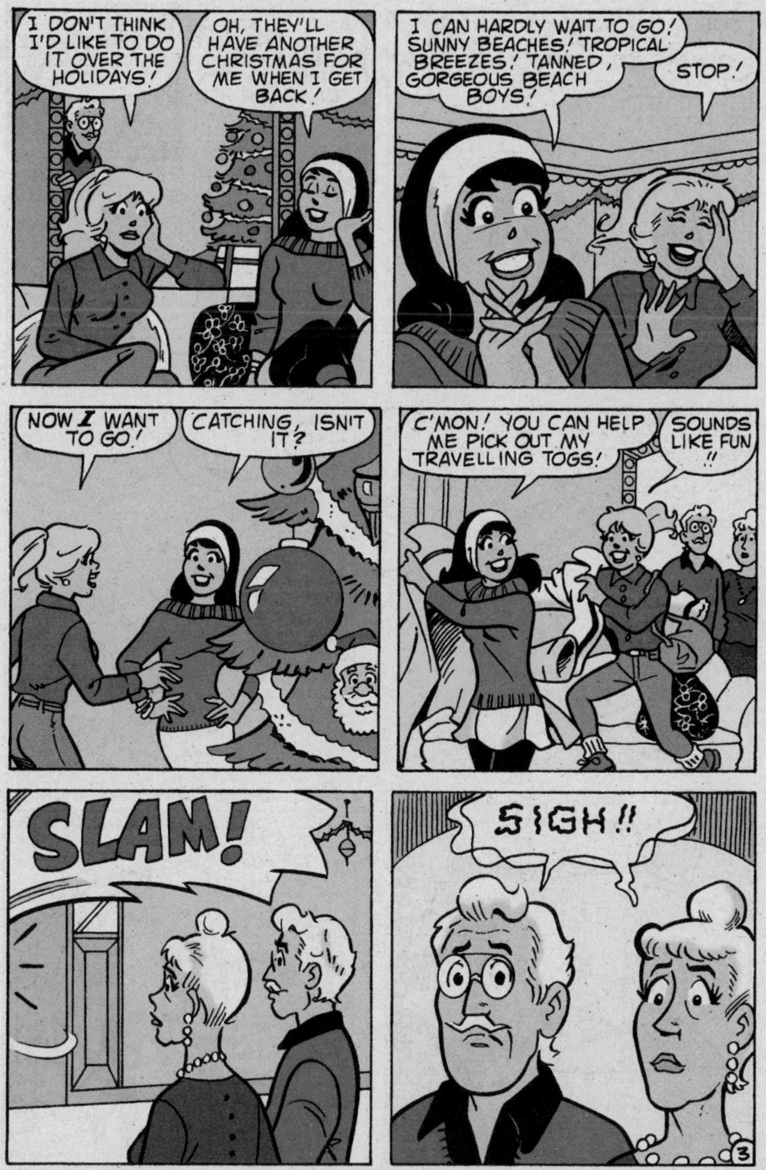
I DON'T THINK I'D LIKE TO DO IT OVER THE HOLIDAYS!
OH, THEY'LL HAVE ANOTHER CHRISTMAS FOR ME WHEN I GET BACK!
I CAN HARDLY WAIT TO GO! SUNNY BEACHES! TROPICAL BREEZES! TANNED, GORGEOUS BEACH BOYS!
STOP!
NOW I WANT TO GO!
CATCHING, ISN'T IT?
C'MON! YOU CAN HELP ME PICK OUT MY TRAVELLING TOGS!
SOUNDS LIKE FUN!!
SLAM!
SIGH!!
3

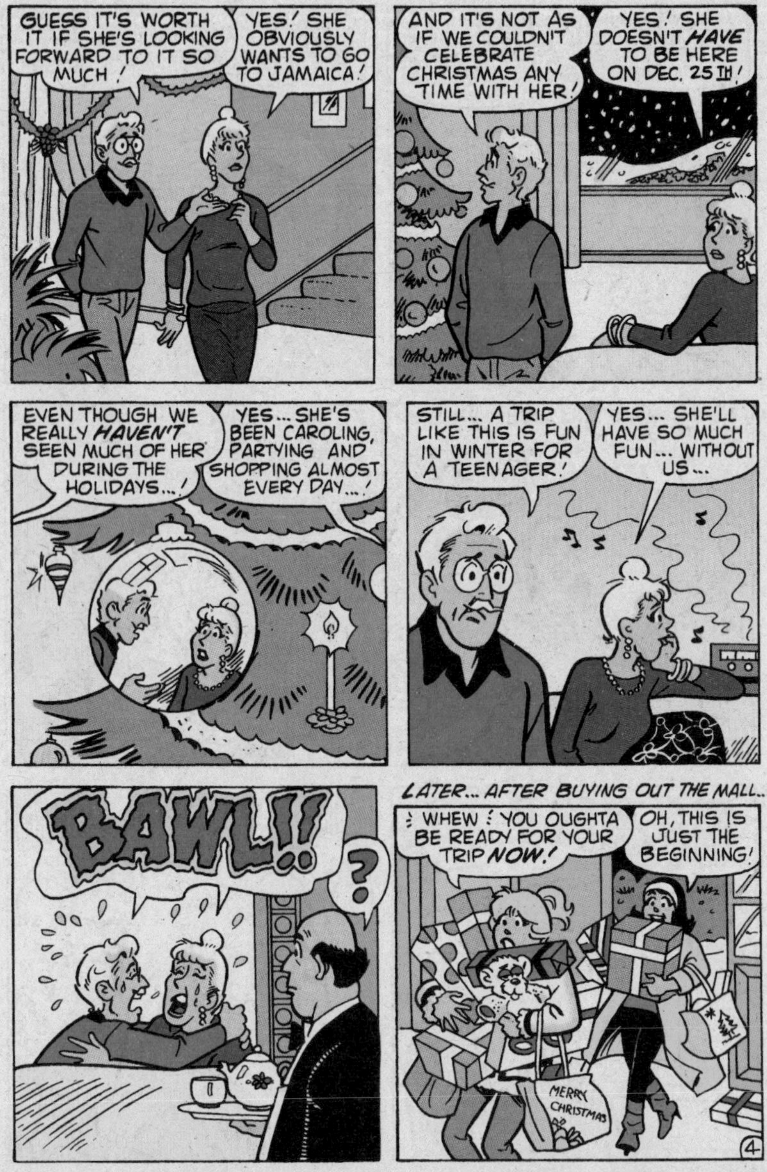
GUESS IT'S WORTH IT IF SHE'S LOOKING FORWARD TO IT SO MUCH!
YES! SHE OBVIOUSLY WANTS TO GO TO JAMAICA!
AND IT'S NOT AS IF WE COULDN'T CELEBRATE CHRISTMAS ANY TIME WITH HER!
YES! SHE DOESN'T *HAVE* TO BE HERE ON DEC. 25TH!
EVEN THOUGH WE REALLY *HAVEN'T* SEEN MUCH OF HER DURING THE HOLIDAYS...!
YES... SHE'S BEEN CAROLING, PARTYING AND SHOPPING ALMOST EVERY DAY...!
STILL... A TRIP LIKE THIS IS FUN IN WINTER FOR A TEENAGER!
YES... SHE'LL HAVE SO MUCH FUN... WITHOUT US...
BAWL!!
?
LATER... AFTER BUYING OUT THE MALL...
WHEW! YOU OUGHTA BE READY FOR YOUR TRIP *NOW*!
OH, THIS IS JUST THE BEGINNING!
MERRY CHRISTMAS
4

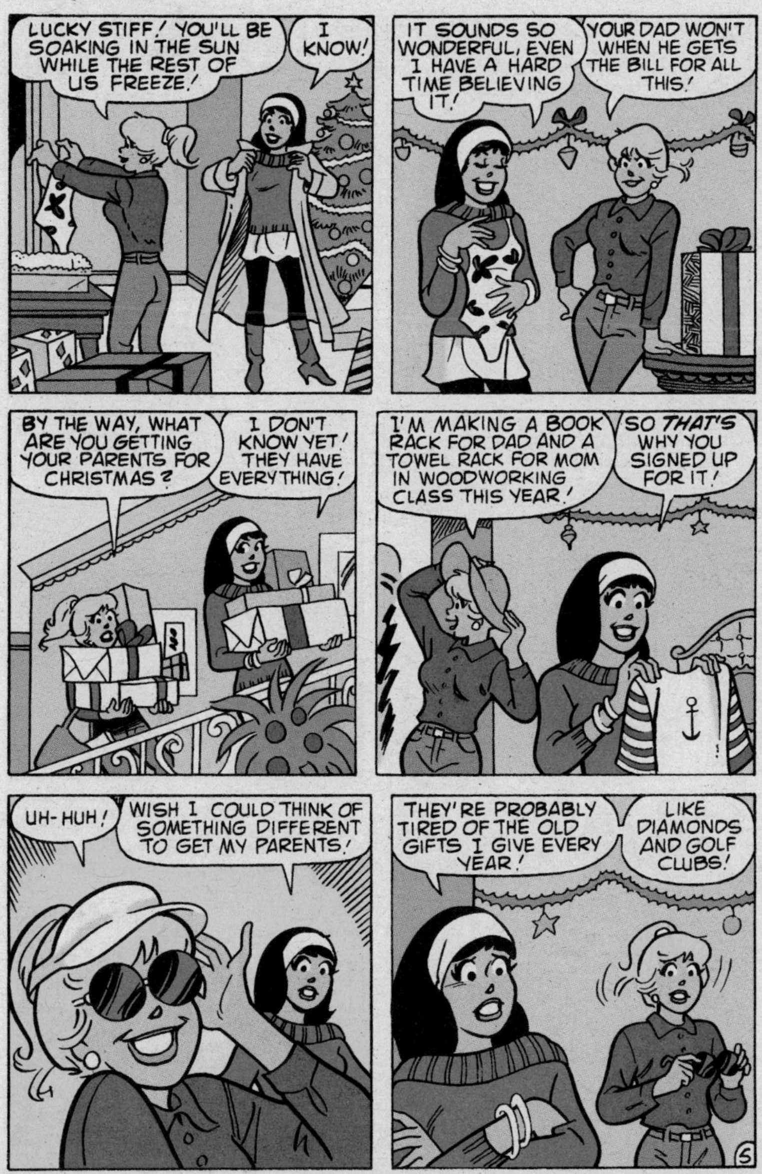
LUCKY STIFF! YOU'LL BE SOAKING IN THE SUN WHILE THE REST OF US FREEZE!
I KNOW!
IT SOUNDS SO WONDERFUL, EVEN I HAVE A HARD TIME BELIEVING IT!
YOUR DAD WON'T WHEN HE GETS THE BILL FOR ALL THIS!
BY THE WAY, WHAT ARE YOU GETTING YOUR PARENTS FOR CHRISTMAS?
I DON'T KNOW YET! THEY HAVE EVERYTHING!
I'M MAKING A BOOK RACK FOR DAD AND A TOWEL RACK FOR MOM IN WOODWORKING CLASS THIS YEAR!
SO *THAT'S* WHY YOU SIGNED UP FOR IT!
UH-HUH!
WISH I COULD THINK OF SOMETHING DIFFERENT TO GET MY PARENTS!
THEY'RE PROBABLY TIRED OF THE OLD GIFTS I GIVE EVERY YEAR!
LIKE DIAMONDS AND GOLF CLUBS!
5

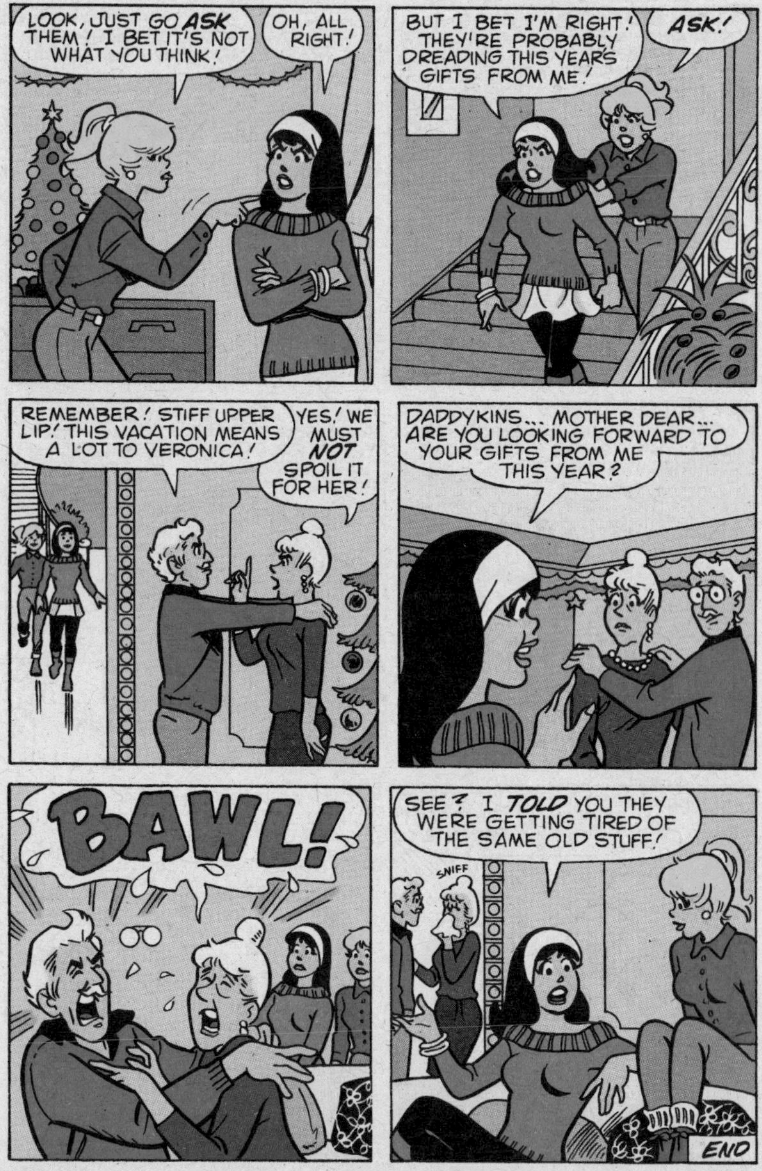

LOOK, JUST GO ASK THEM! I BET IT'S NOT WHAT YOU THINK!
OH, ALL RIGHT!
BUT I BET I'M RIGHT! THEY'RE PROBABLY DREADING THIS YEAR'S GIFTS FROM ME!
ASK!
REMEMBER! STIFF UPPER LIP! THIS VACATION MEANS A LOT TO VERONICA!
YES! WE MUST NOT SPOIL IT FOR HER!
DADDYKINS... MOTHER DEAR... ARE YOU LOOKING FORWARD TO YOUR GIFTS FROM ME THIS YEAR?
BAWL!
SEE? I TOLD YOU THEY WERE GETTING TIRED OF THE SAME OLD STUFF!
SNIFF
END

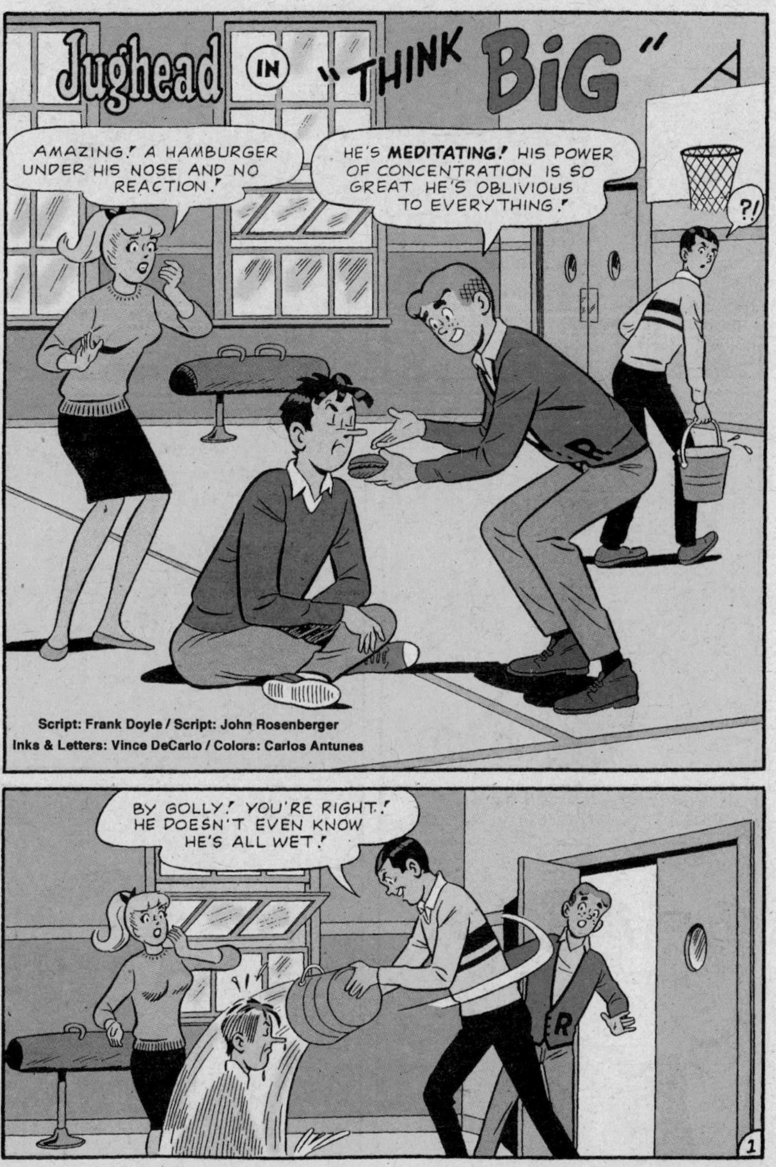
Jughead IN "THINK BiG"
AMAZING! A HAMBURGER UNDER HIS NOSE AND NO REACTION!
HE'S MEDITATING! HIS POWER OF CONCENTRATION IS SO GREAT HE'S OBLIVIOUS TO EVERYTHING!
?!
Script: Frank Doyle / Script: John Rosenberger
Inks & Letters: Vince DeCarlo / Colors: Carlos Antunes
BY GOLLY! YOU'RE RIGHT! HE DOESN'T EVEN KNOW HE'S ALL WET!

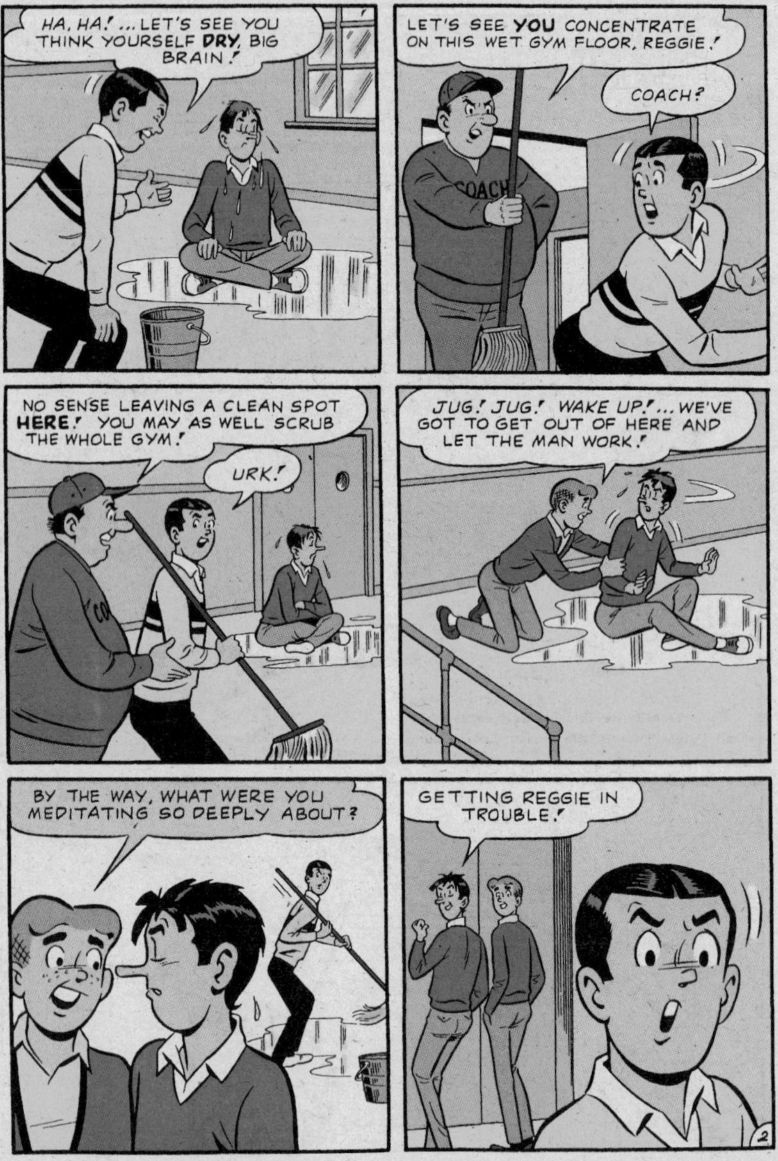
HA, HA! ... LET'S SEE YOU THINK YOURSELF DRY, BIG BRAIN!
LET'S SEE YOU CONCENTRATE ON THIS WET GYM FLOOR, REGGIE!
COACH?
COACH
NO SENSE LEAVING A CLEAN SPOT HERE! YOU MAY AS WELL SCRUB THE WHOLE GYM!
URK!
JUG! JUG! WAKE UP! ... WE'VE GOT TO GET OUT OF HERE AND LET THE MAN WORK!
BY THE WAY, WHAT WERE YOU MEDITATING SO DEEPLY ABOUT?
GETTING REGGIE IN TROUBLE!
2

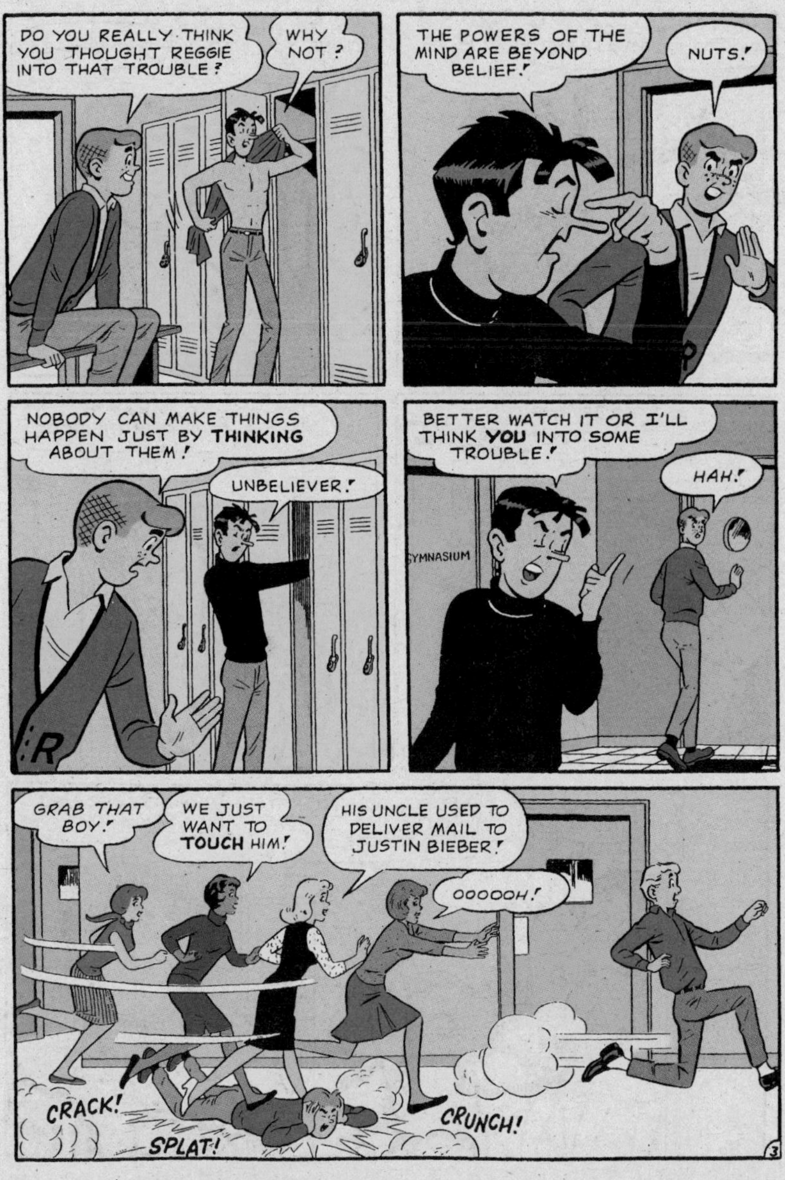
DO YOU REALLY THINK YOU THOUGHT REGGIE INTO THAT TROUBLE?
WHY NOT?
THE POWERS OF THE MIND ARE BEYOND BELIEF!
NUTS!
NOBODY CAN MAKE THINGS HAPPEN JUST BY THINKING ABOUT THEM!
UNBELIEVER!
BETTER WATCH IT OR I'LL THINK YOU INTO SOME TROUBLE!
HAH!
GYMNASIUM
GRAB THAT BOY!
WE JUST WANT TO TOUCH HIM!
HIS UNCLE USED TO DELIVER MAIL TO JUSTIN BIEBER!
OOOOOH!
CRACK!
SPLAT!
CRUNCH!

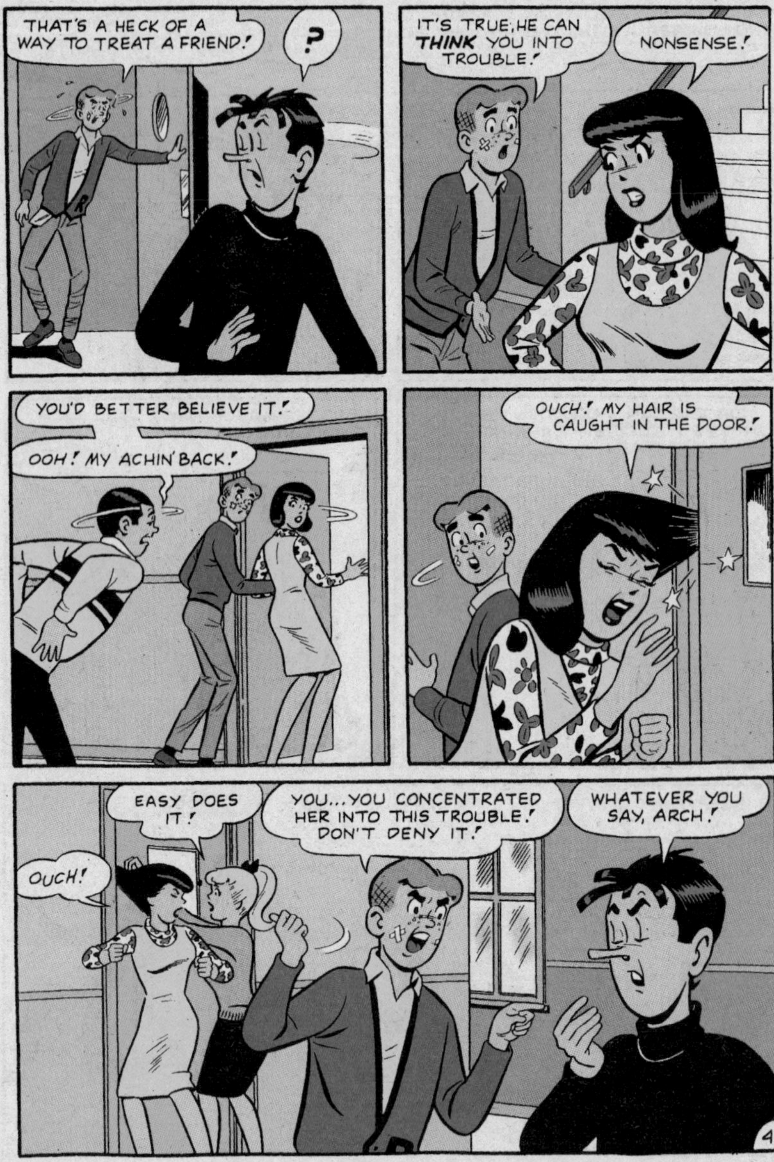

THAT'S A HECK OF A WAY TO TREAT A FRIEND!
?
IT'S TRUE; HE CAN THINK YOU INTO TROUBLE!
NONSENSE!
YOU'D BETTER BELIEVE IT!
OOH! MY ACHIN' BACK!
OUCH! MY HAIR IS CAUGHT IN THE DOOR!
EASY DOES IT!
OUCH!
YOU...YOU CONCENTRATED HER INTO THIS TROUBLE! DON'T DENY IT!
WHATEVER YOU SAY, ARCH!
4

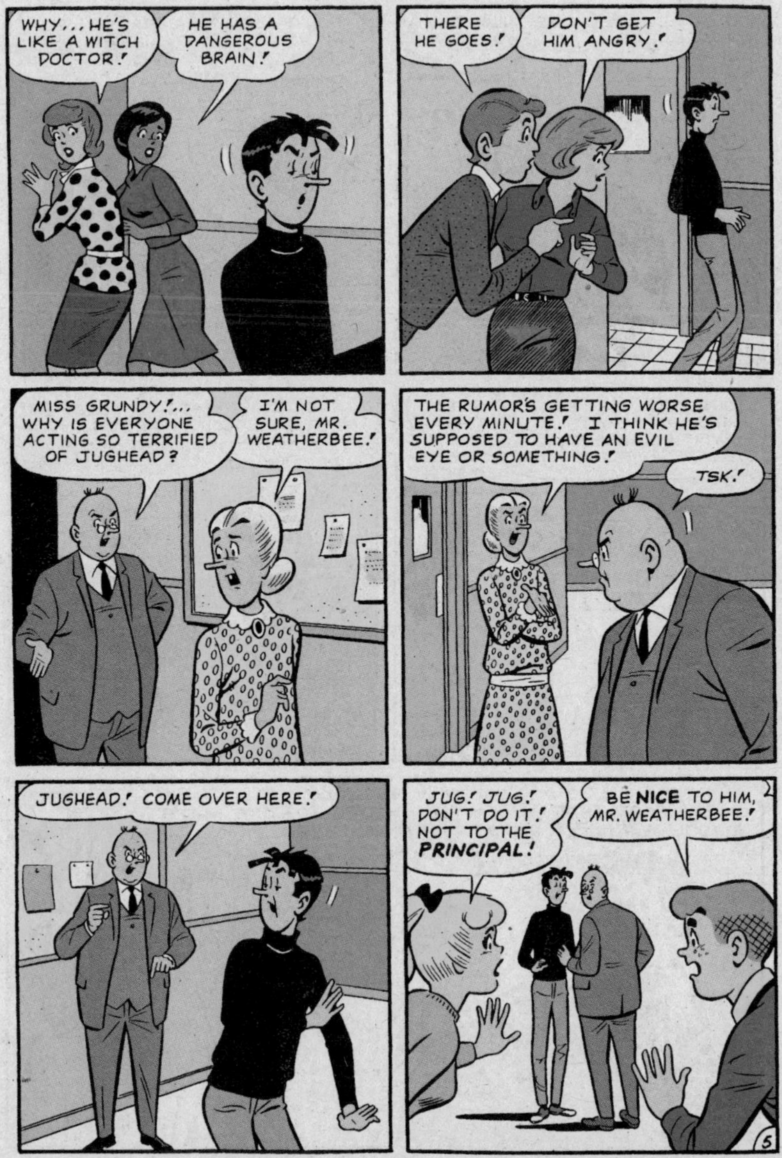
WHY... HE'S LIKE A WITCH DOCTOR!
HE HAS A DANGEROUS BRAIN!
THERE HE GOES!
DON'T GET HIM ANGRY!
MISS GRUNDY!... WHY IS EVERYONE ACTING SO TERRIFIED OF JUGHEAD?
I'M NOT SURE, MR. WEATHERBEE!
THE RUMOR'S GETTING WORSE EVERY MINUTE! I THINK HE'S SUPPOSED TO HAVE AN EVIL EYE OR SOMETHING!
TSK!
JUGHEAD! COME OVER HERE!
JUG! JUG! DON'T DO IT! NOT TO THE **PRINCIPAL**!
BE **NICE** TO HIM, MR. WEATHERBEE!
5

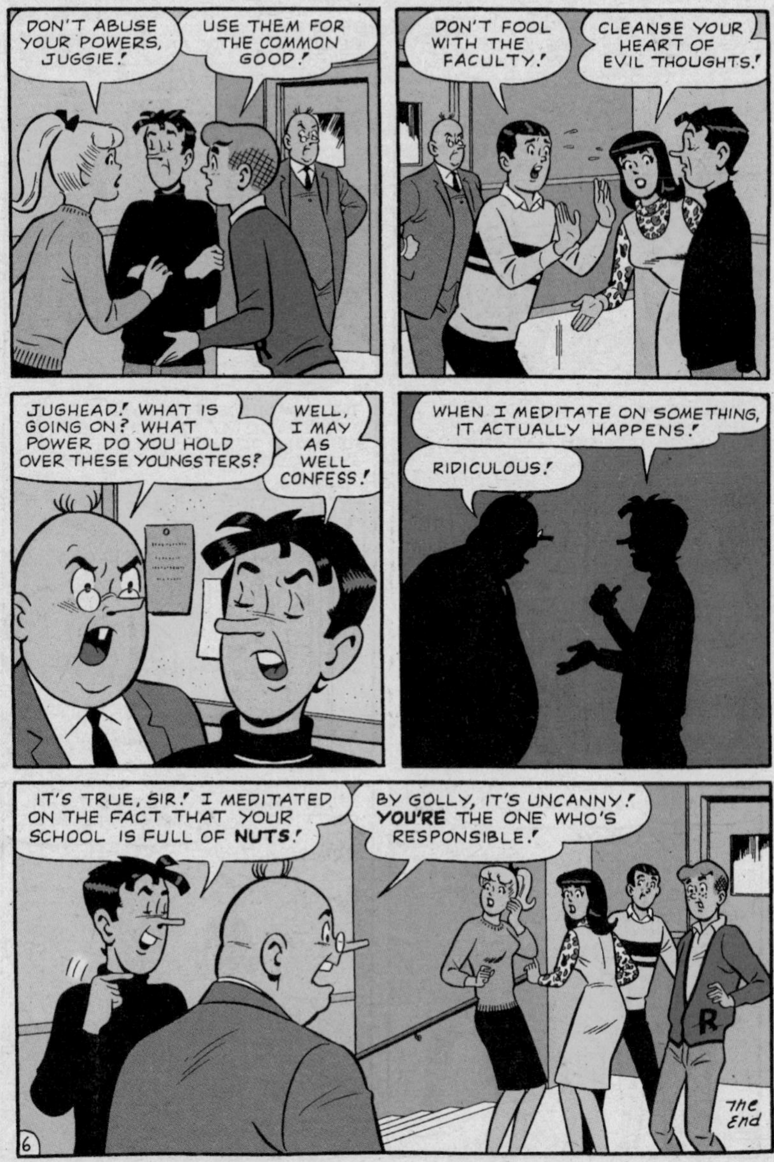
DON'T ABUSE YOUR POWERS, JUGGIE!
USE THEM FOR THE COMMON GOOD!
DON'T FOOL WITH THE FACULTY!
CLEANSE YOUR HEART OF EVIL THOUGHTS!
JUGHEAD! WHAT IS GOING ON? WHAT POWER DO YOU HOLD OVER THESE YOUNGSTERS?
WELL, I MAY AS WELL CONFESS!
WHEN I MEDITATE ON SOMETHING, IT ACTUALLY HAPPENS!
RIDICULOUS!
IT'S TRUE, SIR! I MEDITATED ON THE FACT THAT YOUR SCHOOL IS FULL OF NUTS!
BY GOLLY, IT'S UNCANNY! YOU'RE THE ONE WHO'S RESPONSIBLE!
R
The End
6

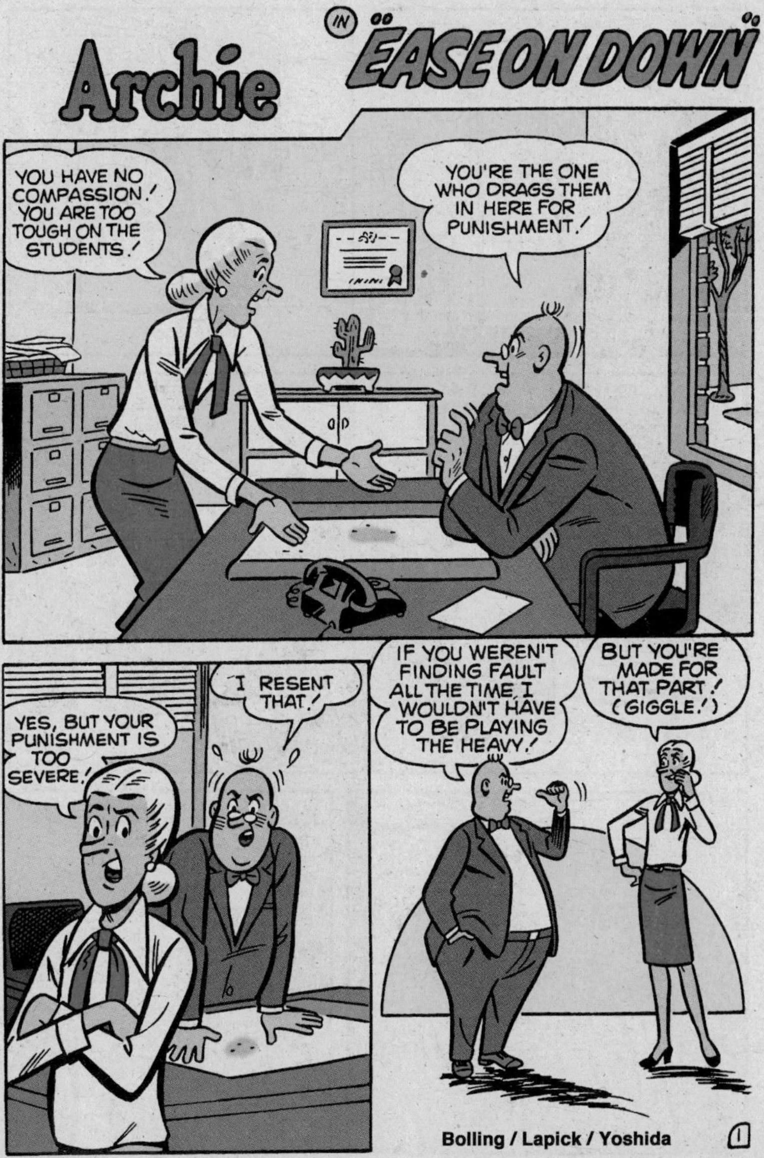
Archie
IN
EASE ON DOWN
YOU HAVE NO COMPASSION! YOU ARE TOO TOUGH ON THE STUDENTS!
YOU'RE THE ONE WHO DRAGS THEM IN HERE FOR PUNISHMENT!
YES, BUT YOUR PUNISHMENT IS TOO SEVERE!
I RESENT THAT!
IF YOU WEREN'T FINDING FAULT ALL THE TIME, I WOULDN'T HAVE TO BE PLAYING THE HEAVY!
BUT YOU'RE MADE FOR THAT PART! (GIGGLE!)
Bolling / Lapick / Yoshida
1

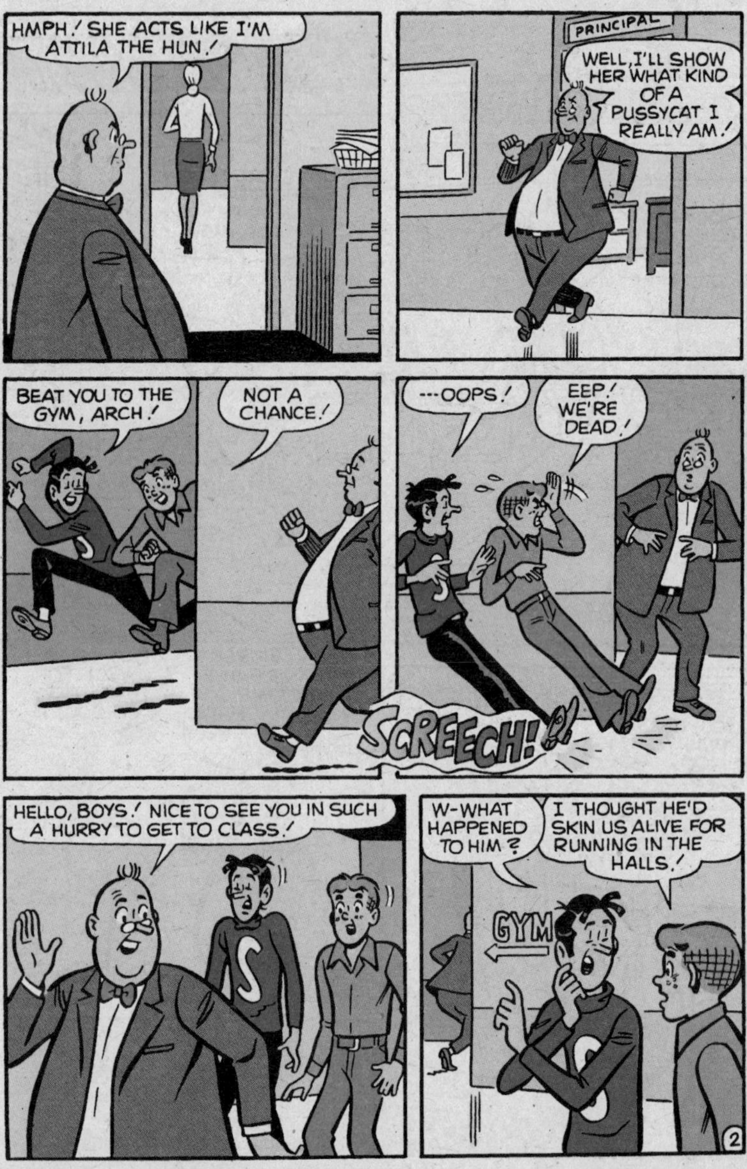
HMPH! SHE ACTS LIKE I'M ATTILA THE HUN!
PRINCIPAL
WELL, I'LL SHOW HER WHAT KIND OF A PUSSYCAT I REALLY AM!
BEAT YOU TO THE GYM, ARCH!
NOT A CHANCE!
---OOPS!
EEP! WE'RE DEAD!
SCREECH!
HELLO, BOYS! NICE TO SEE YOU IN SUCH A HURRY TO GET TO CLASS!
W-WHAT HAPPENED TO HIM?
I THOUGHT HE'D SKIN US ALIVE FOR RUNNING IN THE HALLS!
GYM
2

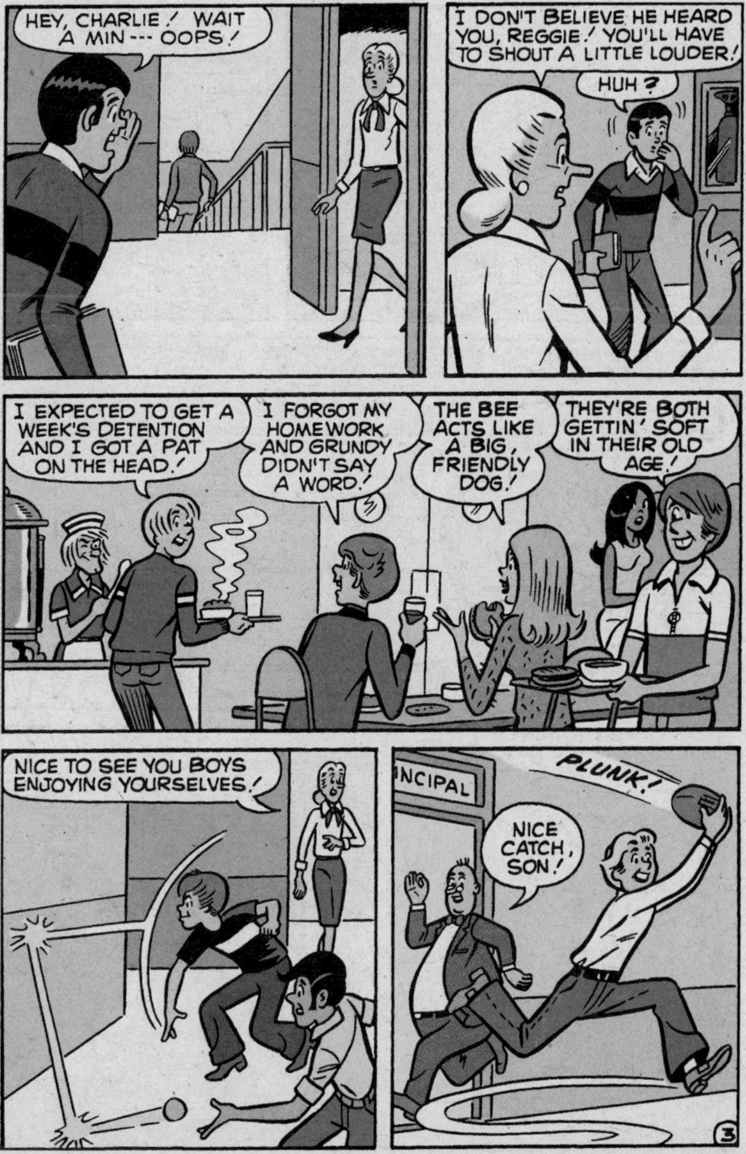
HEY, CHARLIE! WAIT A MIN--- OOPS!
I DON'T BELIEVE HE HEARD YOU, REGGIE! YOU'LL HAVE TO SHOUT A LITTLE LOUDER!
HUH?
I EXPECTED TO GET A WEEK'S DETENTION AND I GOT A PAT ON THE HEAD!
I FORGOT MY HOMEWORK AND GRUNDY DIDN'T SAY A WORD!
THE BEE ACTS LIKE A BIG, FRIENDLY DOG!
THEY'RE BOTH GETTIN' SOFT IN THEIR OLD AGE!
NICE TO SEE YOU BOYS ENJOYING YOURSELVES!
INCIPAL
PLUNK!
NICE CATCH, SON!
3

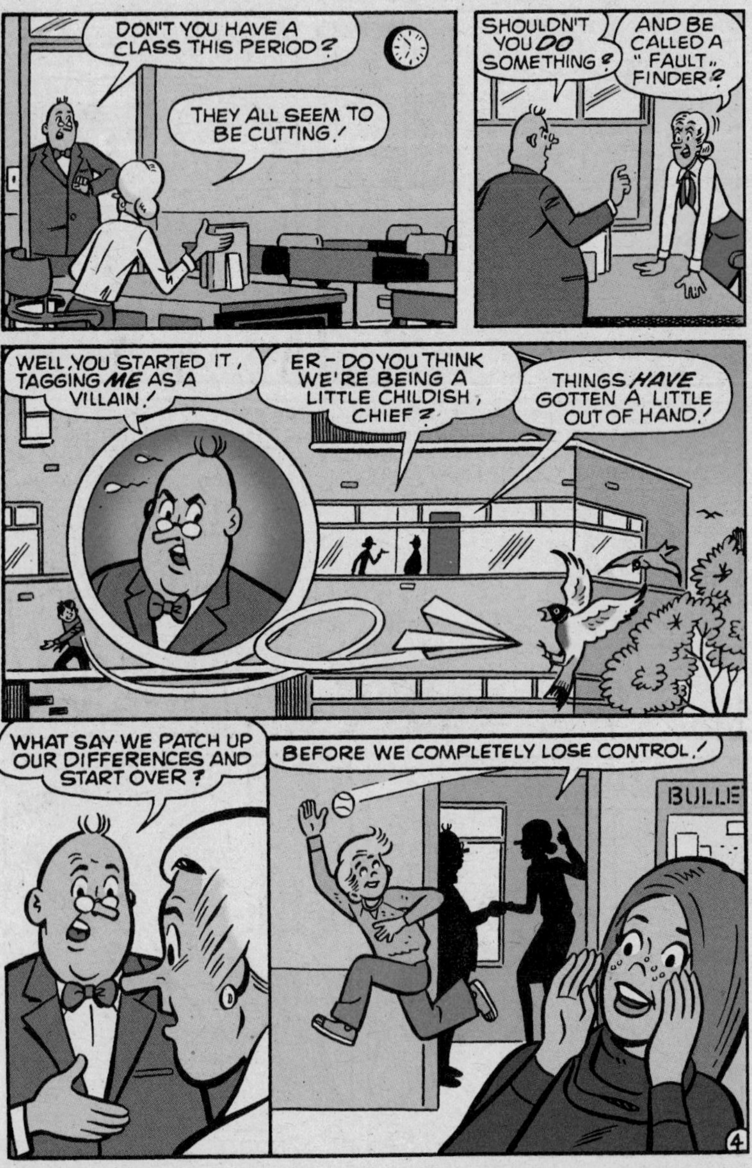
DON'T YOU HAVE A CLASS THIS PERIOD?
THEY ALL SEEM TO BE CUTTING!
SHOULDN'T YOU DO SOMETHING?
AND BE CALLED A "FAULT" FINDER?
WELL, YOU STARTED IT, TAGGING ME AS A VILLAIN!
ER - DO YOU THINK WE'RE BEING A LITTLE CHILDISH, CHIEF?
THINGS HAVE GOTTEN A LITTLE OUT OF HAND!
WHAT SAY WE PATCH UP OUR DIFFERENCES AND START OVER?
BEFORE WE COMPLETELY LOSE CONTROL!
BULLE
4

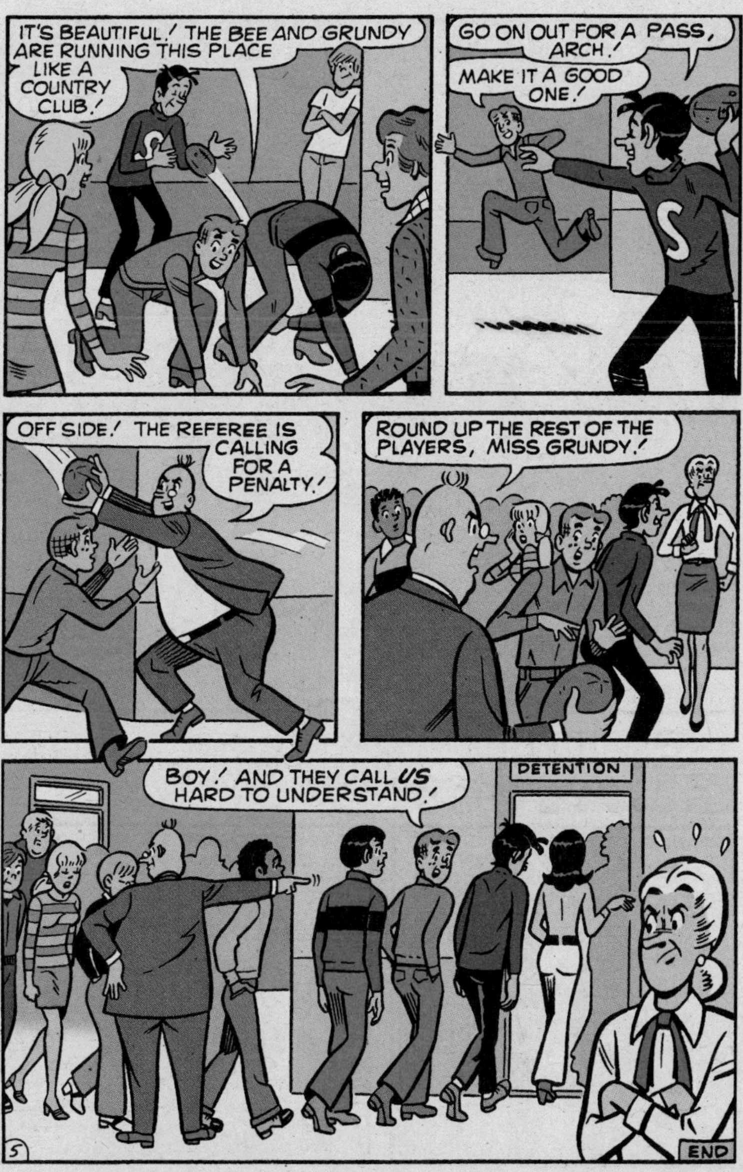
IT'S BEAUTIFUL! THE BEE AND GRUNDY ARE RUNNING THIS PLACE
LIKE A COUNTRY CLUB!
GO ON OUT FOR A PASS, ARCH!
MAKE IT A GOOD ONE!
OFF SIDE! THE REFEREE IS CALLING FOR A PENALTY!
ROUND UP THE REST OF THE PLAYERS, MISS GRUNDY!
BOY! AND THEY CALL US HARD TO UNDERSTAND!
DETENTION
5
END

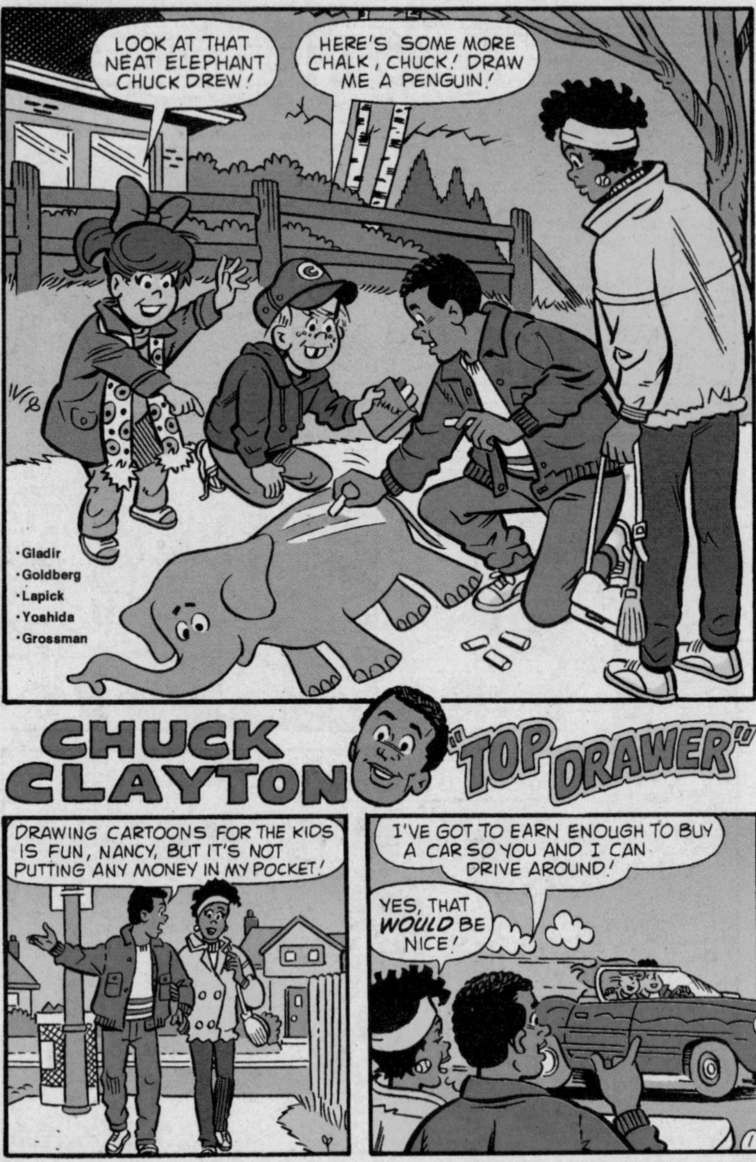
LOOK AT THAT NEAT ELEPHANT CHUCK DREW!
HERE'S SOME MORE CHALK, CHUCK! DRAW ME A PENGUIN!
CHALK
•Gladir
•Goldberg
•Lapick
•Yoshida
•Grossman
CHUCK CLAYTON
"TOP DRAWER"
DRAWING CARTOONS FOR THE KIDS IS FUN, NANCY, BUT IT'S NOT PUTTING ANY MONEY IN MY POCKET!
I'VE GOT TO EARN ENOUGH TO BUY A CAR SO YOU AND I CAN DRIVE AROUND!
YES, THAT WOULD BE NICE!
1

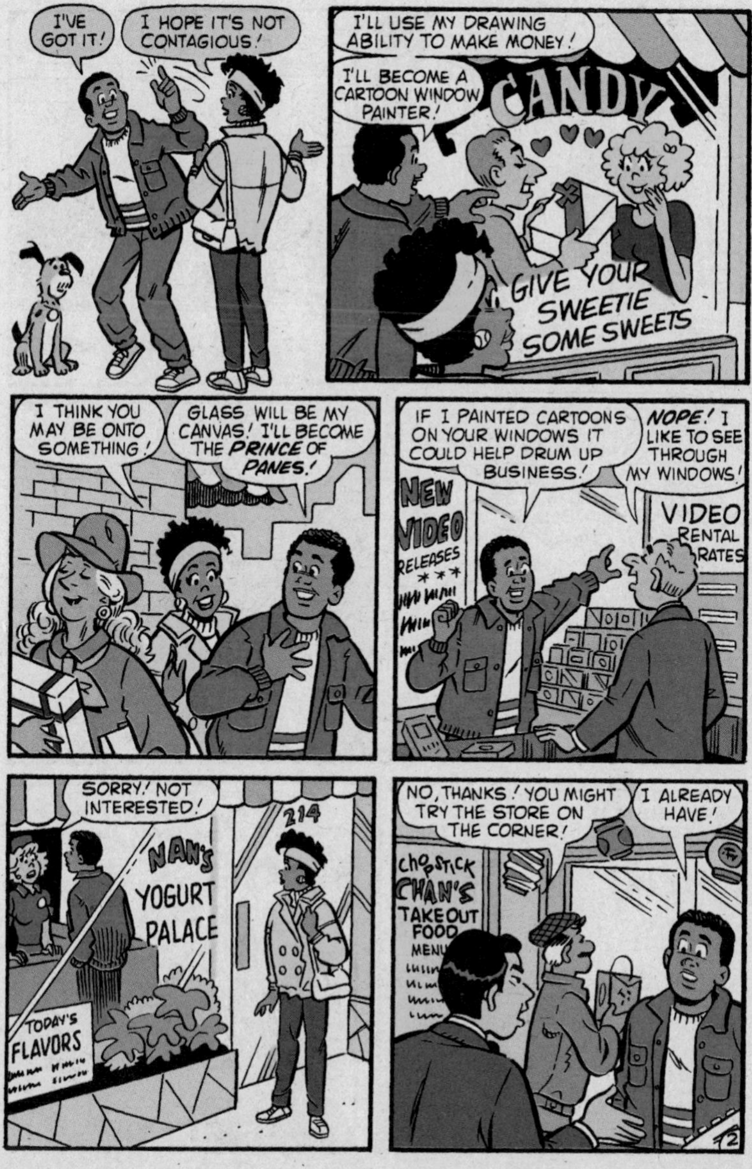
I'VE GOT IT!
I HOPE IT'S NOT CONTAGIOUS!
I'LL USE MY DRAWING ABILITY TO MAKE MONEY!
I'LL BECOME A CARTOON WINDOW PAINTER!
CANDY
GIVE YOUR SWEETIE SOME SWEETS
I THINK YOU MAY BE ONTO SOMETHING!
GLASS WILL BE MY CANVAS! I'LL BECOME THE *PRINCE* OF *PANES*!
IF I PAINTED CARTOONS ON YOUR WINDOWS IT COULD HELP DRUM UP BUSINESS!
NOPE! I LIKE TO SEE THROUGH MY WINDOWS!
NEW VIDEO RELEASES
VIDEO RENTAL RATES
SORRY! NOT INTERESTED!
214
NAN'S YOGURT PALACE
TODAY'S FLAVORS
NO, THANKS! YOU MIGHT TRY THE STORE ON THE CORNER!
I ALREADY HAVE!
CHOPSTICK CHAN'S TAKEOUT FOOD MENU
2

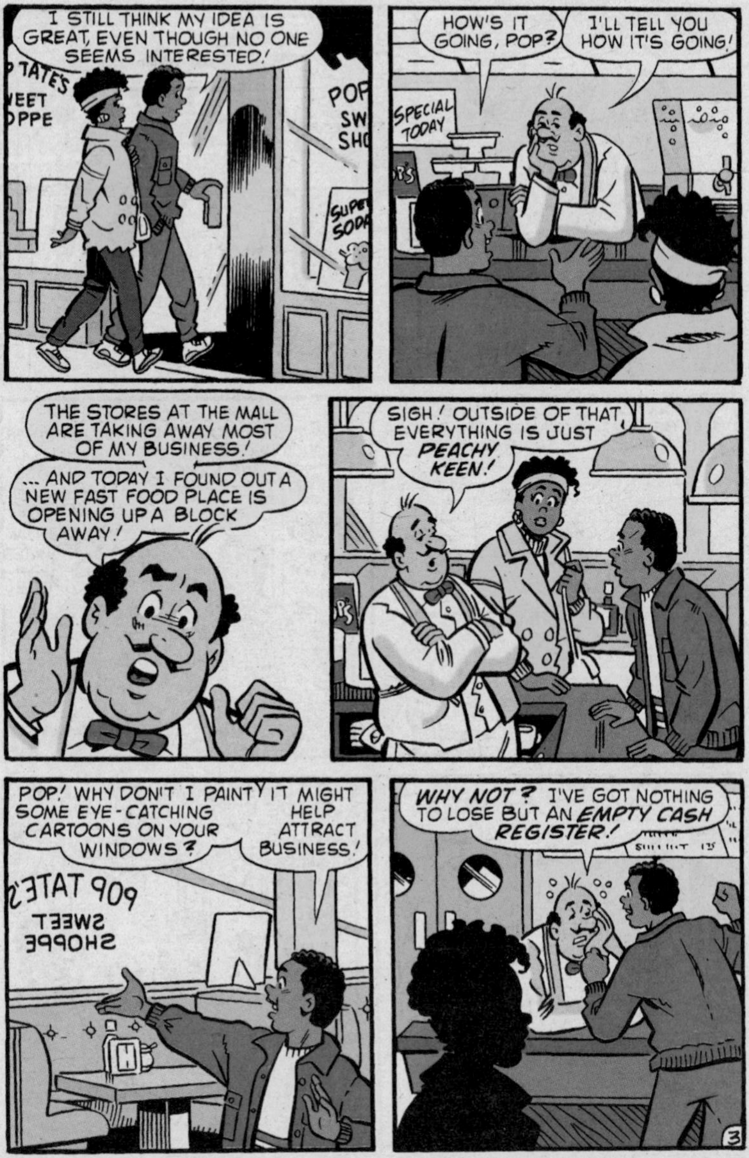

I STILL THINK MY IDEA IS GREAT, EVEN THOUGH NO ONE SEEMS INTERESTED!
HOW'S IT GOING, POP?
I'LL TELL YOU HOW IT'S GOING!
SPECIAL TODAY
THE STORES AT THE MALL ARE TAKING AWAY MOST OF MY BUSINESS!
... AND TODAY I FOUND OUT A NEW FAST FOOD PLACE IS OPENING UP A BLOCK AWAY!
SIGH! OUTSIDE OF THAT, EVERYTHING IS JUST *PEACHY KEEN!*
POP! WHY DON'T I PAINT SOME EYE-CATCHING CARTOONS ON YOUR WINDOWS?
IT MIGHT HELP ATTRACT BUSINESS!
POP TATE'S SWEET SHOPPE
WHY NOT? I'VE GOT NOTHING TO LOSE BUT AN *EMPTY CASH REGISTER!*
3

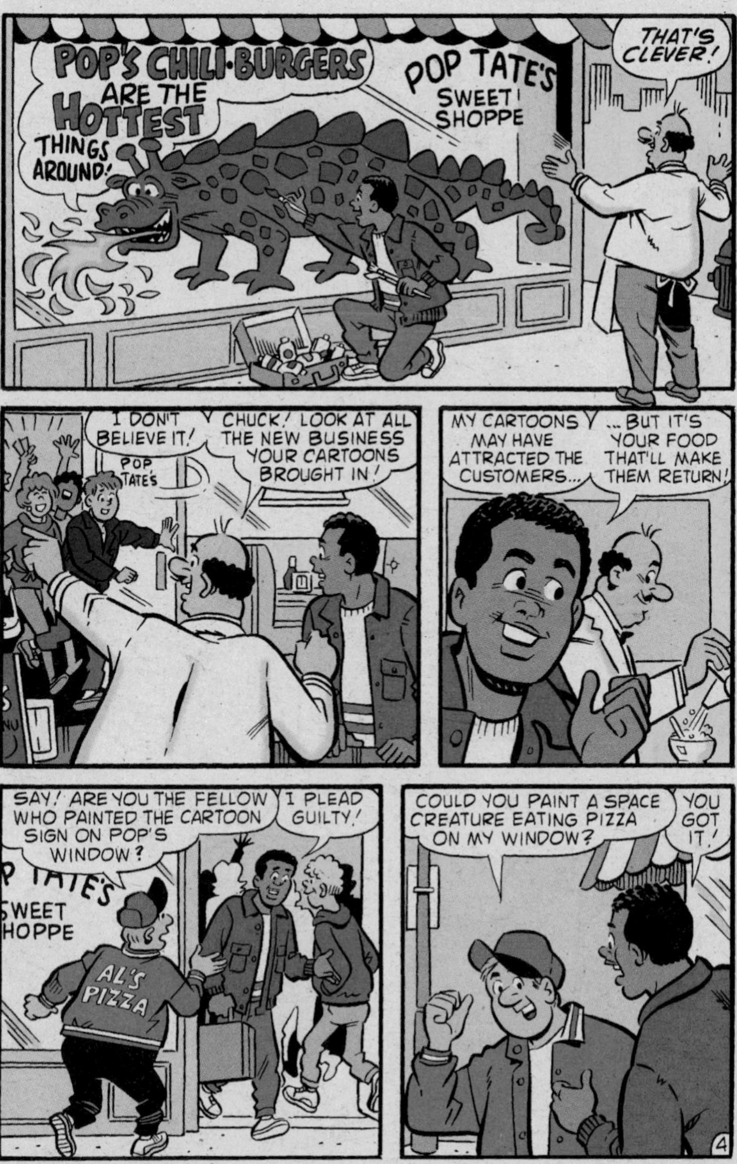
POP'S CHILI·BURGERS ARE THE HOTTEST THINGS AROUND!
POP TATE'S
SWEET SHOPPE
THAT'S CLEVER!
I DON'T BELIEVE IT!
CHUCK! LOOK AT ALL THE NEW BUSINESS YOUR CARTOONS BROUGHT IN!
POP TATE'S
MY CARTOONS MAY HAVE ATTRACTED THE CUSTOMERS...
... BUT IT'S YOUR FOOD THAT'LL MAKE THEM RETURN!
SAY! ARE YOU THE FELLOW WHO PAINTED THE CARTOON SIGN ON POP'S WINDOW?
I PLEAD GUILTY!
AL'S PIZZA
COULD YOU PAINT A SPACE CREATURE EATING PIZZA ON MY WINDOW?
YOU GOT IT!
4

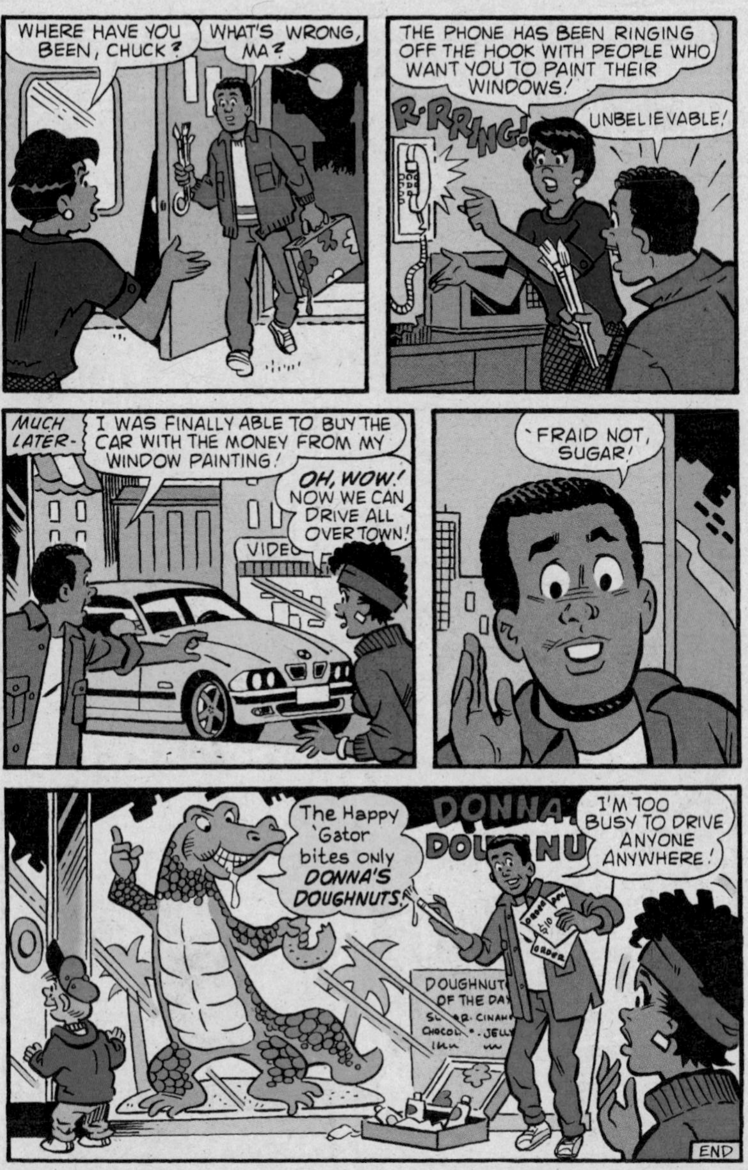
WHERE HAVE YOU BEEN, CHUCK?
WHAT'S WRONG, MA?
THE PHONE HAS BEEN RINGING OFF THE HOOK WITH PEOPLE WHO WANT YOU TO PAINT THEIR WINDOWS!
R-RRING!
UNBELIEVABLE!
MUCH LATER-
I WAS FINALLY ABLE TO BUY THE CAR WITH THE MONEY FROM MY WINDOW PAINTING!
OH, WOW! NOW WE CAN DRIVE ALL OVER TOWN!
'FRAID NOT, SUGAR!
The Happy 'Gator bites only DONNA'S DOUGHNUTS.
I'M TOO BUSY TO DRIVE ANYONE ANYWHERE!
END

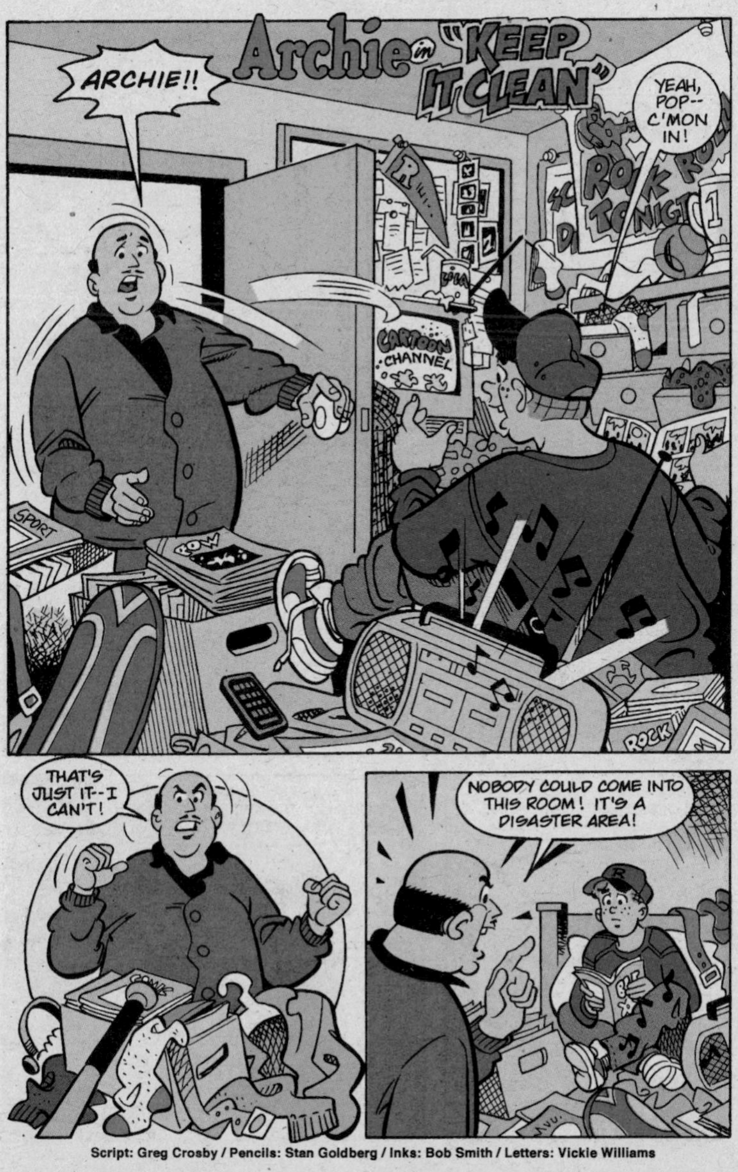
Archie in "KEEP IT CLEAN"
ARCHIE!!
YEAH, POP-- C'MON IN!
CARTOON CHANNEL
SPORT
ROCK
THAT'S JUST IT--I CAN'T!
NOBODY COULD COME INTO THIS ROOM! IT'S A DISASTER AREA!

Script: Greg Crosby / Pencils: Stan Goldberg / Inks: Bob Smith / Letters: Vickie Williams

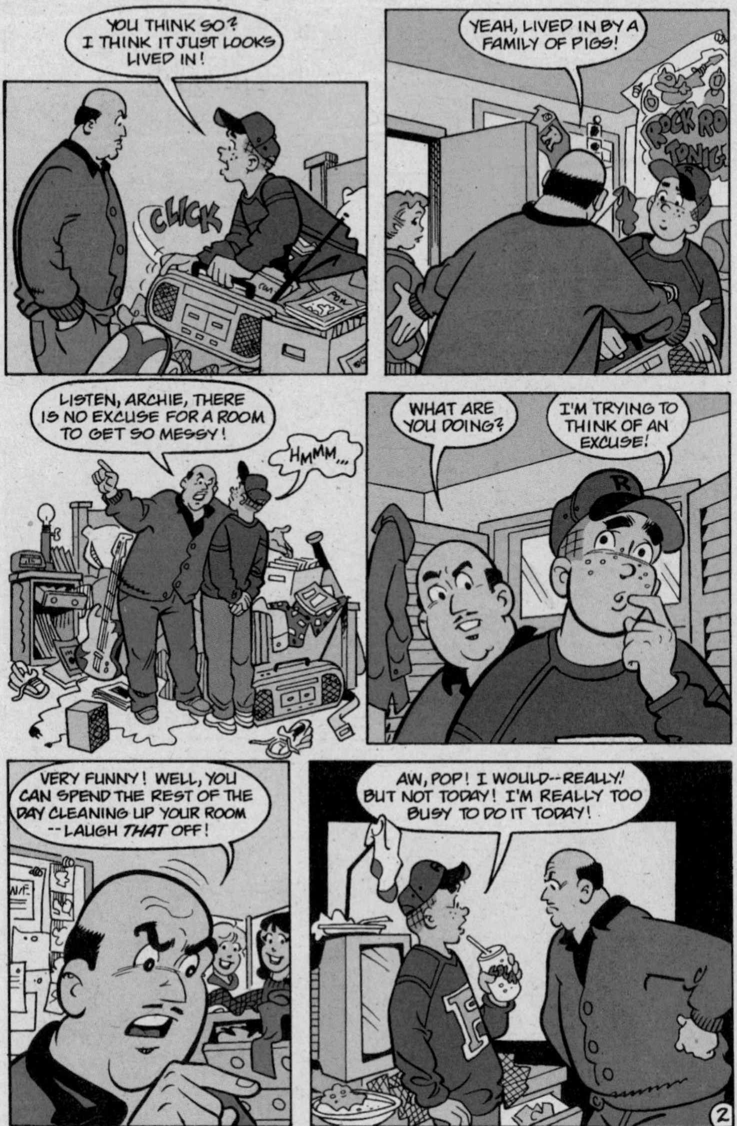

YOU THINK SO? I THINK IT JUST LOOKS LIVED IN!
CLICK
YEAH, LIVED IN BY A FAMILY OF PIGS!
LISTEN, ARCHIE, THERE IS NO EXCUSE FOR A ROOM TO GET SO MESSY!
HMMM...
WHAT ARE YOU DOING?
I'M TRYING TO THINK OF AN EXCUSE!
VERY FUNNY! WELL, YOU CAN SPEND THE REST OF THE DAY CLEANING UP YOUR ROOM --LAUGH THAT OFF!
AW, POP! I WOULD--REALLY! BUT NOT TODAY! I'M REALLY TOO BUSY TO DO IT TODAY!
2

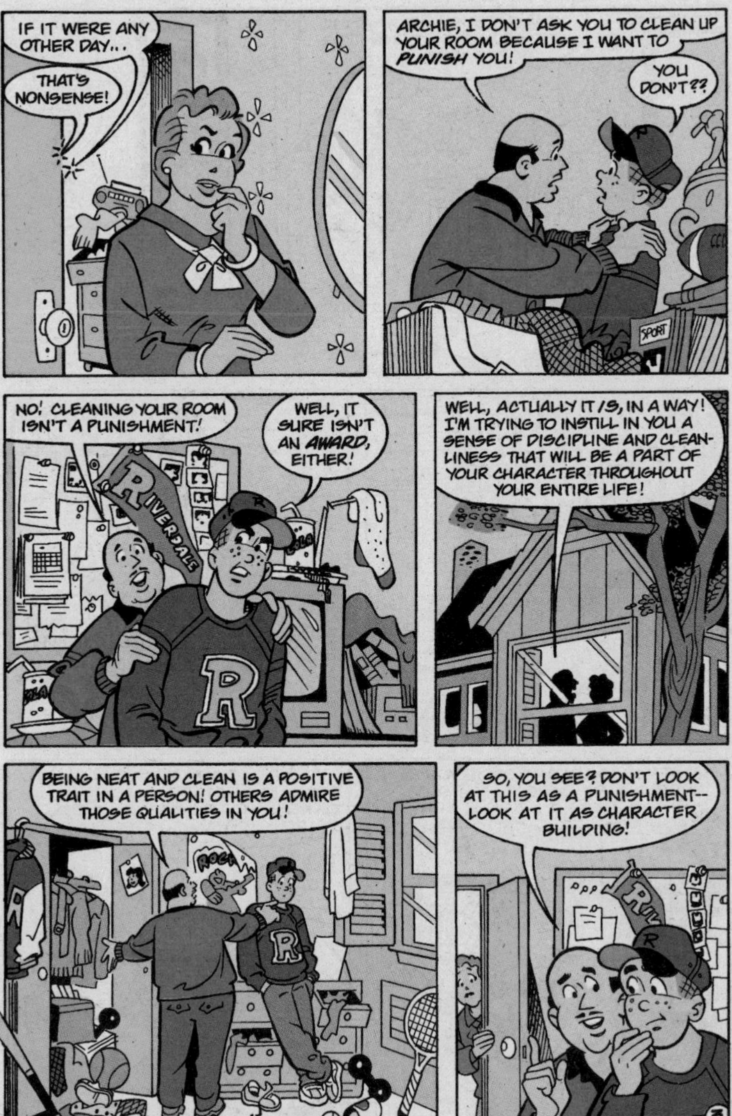
IF IT WERE ANY OTHER DAY...
THAT'S NONSENSE!
ARCHIE, I DON'T ASK YOU TO CLEAN UP YOUR ROOM BECAUSE I WANT TO *PUNISH* YOU!
YOU DON'T??
SPORT
NO! CLEANING YOUR ROOM ISN'T A PUNISHMENT!
WELL, IT SURE ISN'T AN *AWARD*, EITHER!
RIVERDALE
WELL, ACTUALLY IT *IS*, IN A WAY! I'M TRYING TO INSTILL IN YOU A SENSE OF DISCIPLINE AND CLEANLINESS THAT WILL BE A PART OF YOUR CHARACTER THROUGHOUT YOUR ENTIRE LIFE!
BEING NEAT AND CLEAN IS A POSITIVE TRAIT IN A PERSON! OTHERS ADMIRE THOSE QUALITIES IN YOU!
SO, YOU SEE? DON'T LOOK AT THIS AS A PUNISHMENT-- LOOK AT IT AS CHARACTER BUILDING!
3

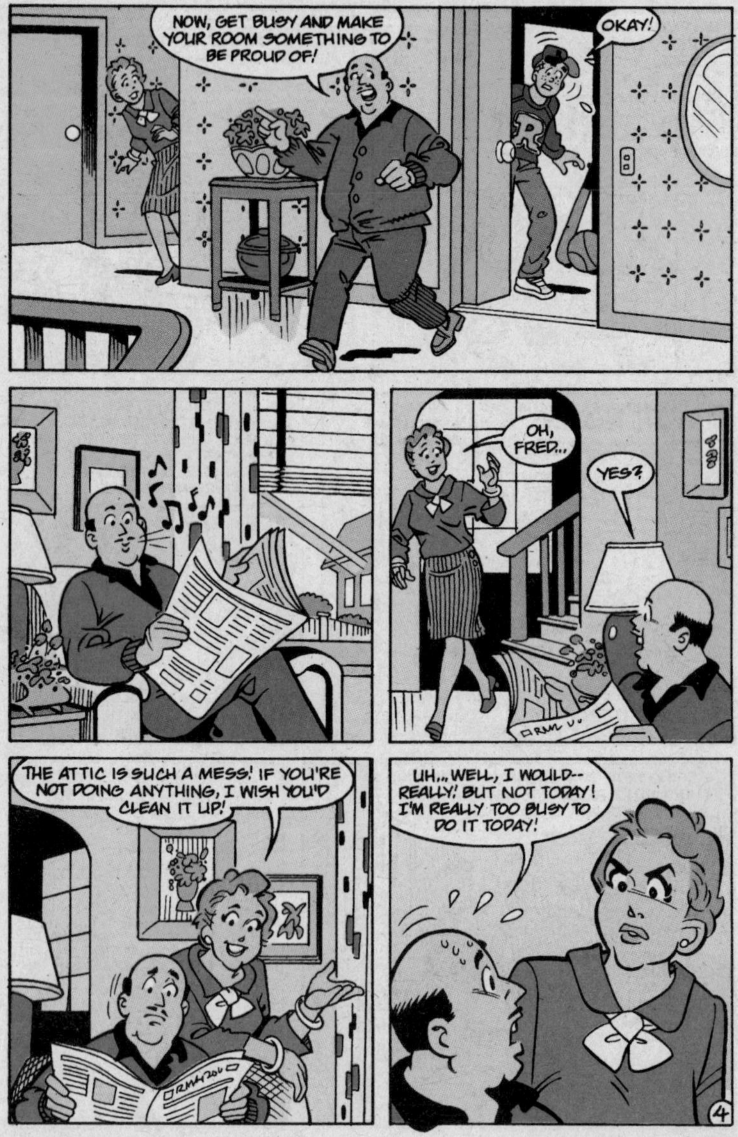
NOW, GET BUSY AND MAKE YOUR ROOM SOMETHING TO BE PROUD OF!
OKAY!
OH, FRED...
YES?
THE ATTIC IS SUCH A MESS! IF YOU'RE NOT DOING ANYTHING, I WISH YOU'D CLEAN IT UP!
UH... WELL, I WOULD-- REALLY! BUT NOT TODAY! I'M REALLY TOO BUSY TO DO IT TODAY!
4

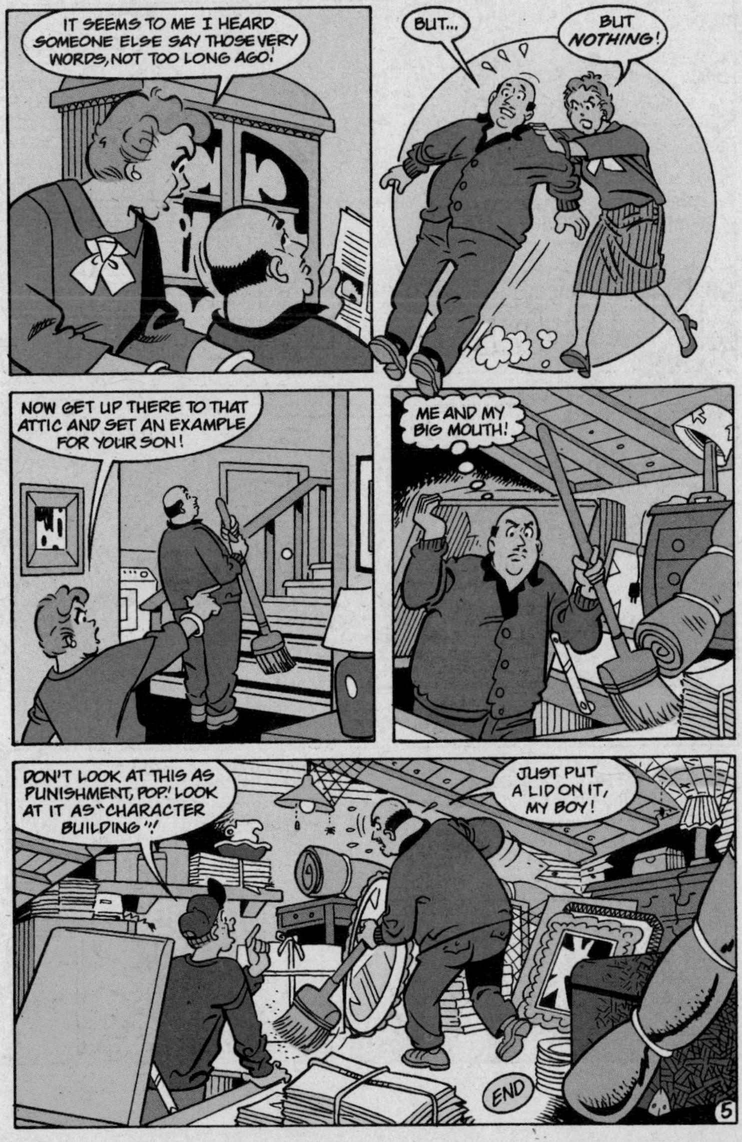

IT SEEMS TO ME I HEARD SOMEONE ELSE SAY THOSE VERY WORDS, NOT TOO LONG AGO!
BUT...
BUT NOTHING!
NOW GET UP THERE TO THAT ATTIC AND SET AN EXAMPLE FOR YOUR SON!
ME AND MY BIG MOUTH!
DON'T LOOK AT THIS AS PUNISHMENT, POP! LOOK AT IT AS "CHARACTER BUILDING"!
JUST PUT A LID ON IT, MY BOY!
END

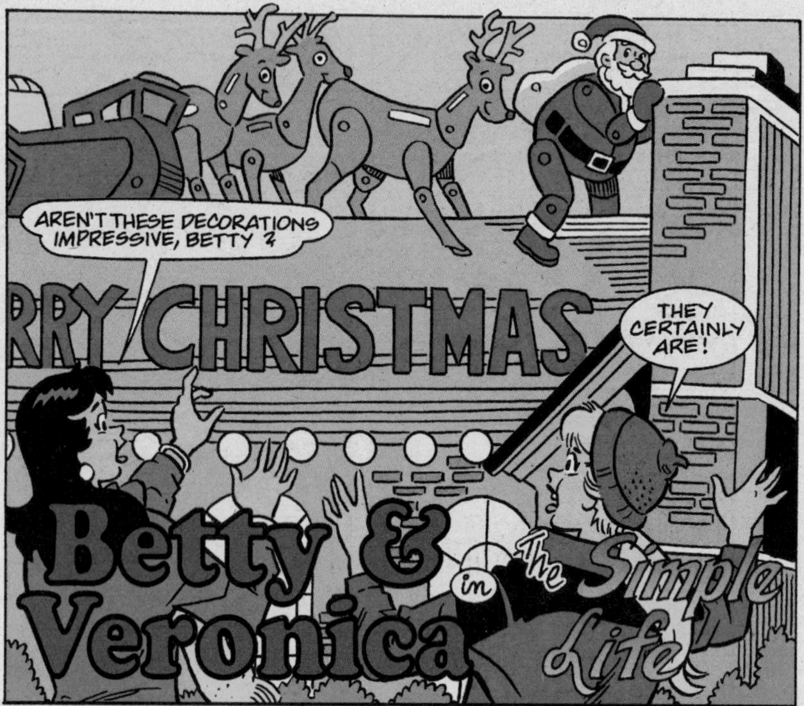

RRY CHRISTMAS
AREN'T THESE DECORATIONS IMPRESSIVE, BETTY ?
THEY CERTAINLY ARE!
Betty & Veronica in The Simple Life

SCRIPT: GEORGE GLADIR PENCILS: TIM KENNEDY INKS: RUDY LAPICK
COLORS: BARRY GROSSMAN LETTERS: VICKIE WILLIAMS

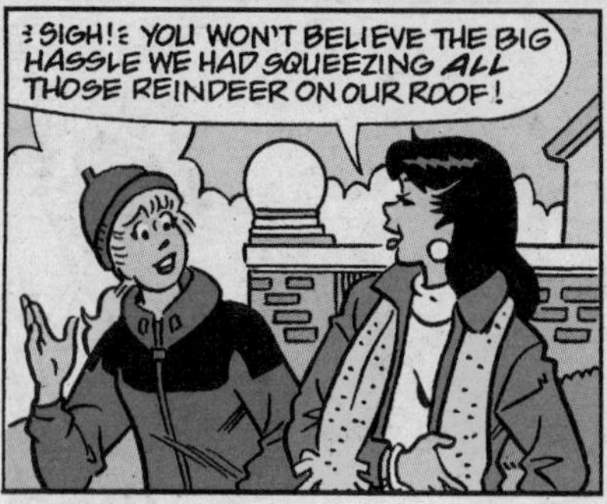

: SIGH! : YOU WON'T BELIEVE THE BIG HASSLE WE HAD SQUEEZING *ALL* THOSE REINDEER ON OUR ROOF!

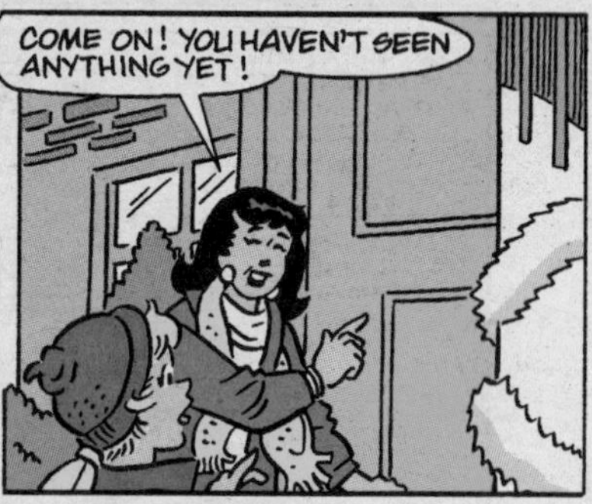

COME ON! YOU HAVEN'T SEEN ANYTHING YET!

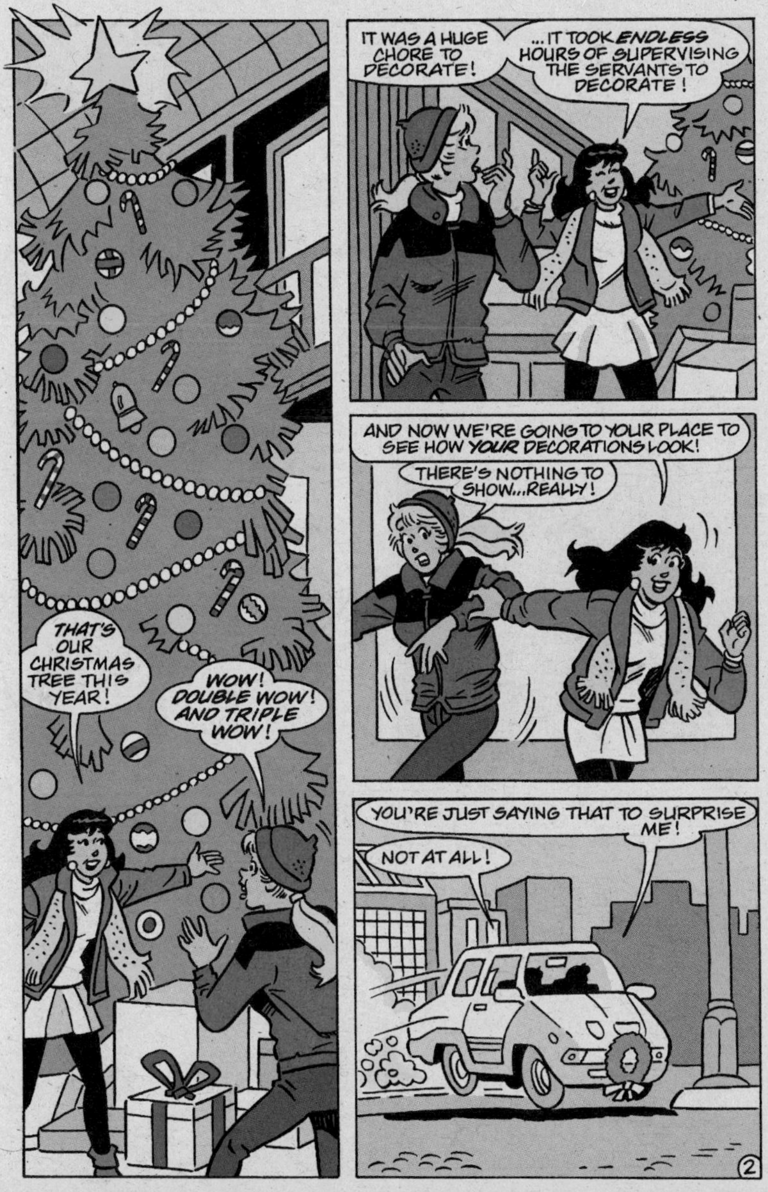
THAT'S OUR CHRISTMAS TREE THIS YEAR!
WOW! DOUBLE WOW! AND TRIPLE WOW!
IT WAS A HUGE CHORE TO DECORATE!
...IT TOOK ENDLESS HOURS OF SUPERVISING THE SERVANTS TO DECORATE!
AND NOW WE'RE GOING TO YOUR PLACE TO SEE HOW YOUR DECORATIONS LOOK!
THERE'S NOTHING TO SHOW...REALLY!
YOU'RE JUST SAYING THAT TO SURPRISE ME!
NOT AT ALL!
2

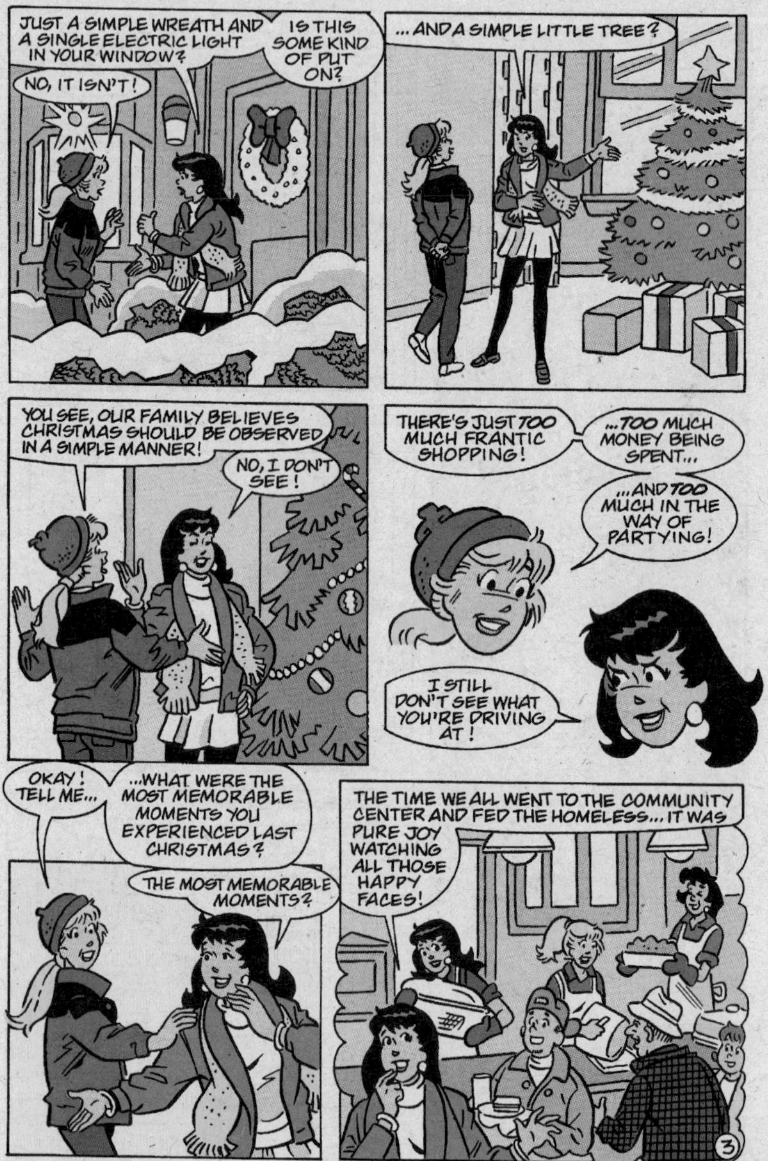

JUST A SIMPLE WREATH AND A SINGLE ELECTRIC LIGHT IN YOUR WINDOW?
IS THIS SOME KIND OF PUT ON?
NO, IT ISN'T!
... AND A SIMPLE LITTLE TREE?
YOU SEE, OUR FAMILY BELIEVES CHRISTMAS SHOULD BE OBSERVED IN A SIMPLE MANNER!
NO, I DON'T SEE!
THERE'S JUST TOO MUCH FRANTIC SHOPPING!
...TOO MUCH MONEY BEING SPENT...
...AND TOO MUCH IN THE WAY OF PARTYING!
I STILL DON'T SEE WHAT YOU'RE DRIVING AT!
OKAY! TELL ME...
...WHAT WERE THE MOST MEMORABLE MOMENTS YOU EXPERIENCED LAST CHRISTMAS?
THE MOST MEMORABLE MOMENTS?
THE TIME WE ALL WENT TO THE COMMUNITY CENTER AND FED THE HOMELESS... IT WAS PURE JOY WATCHING ALL THOSE HAPPY FACES!

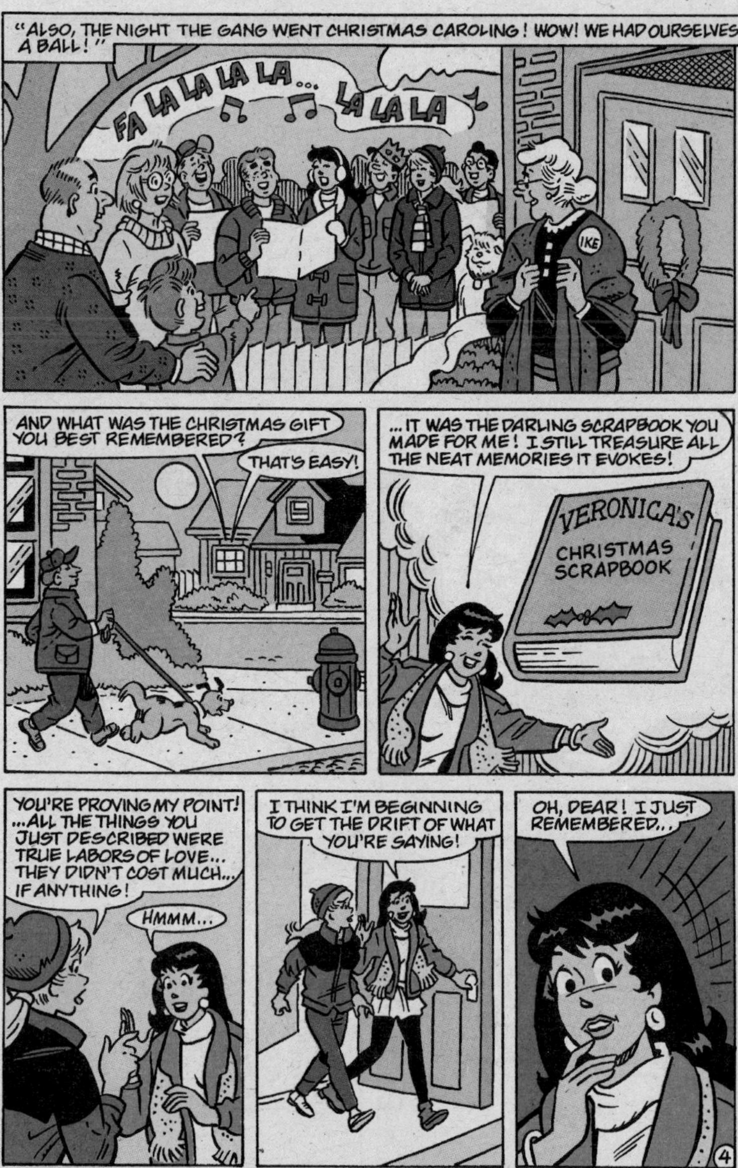
"ALSO, THE NIGHT THE GANG WENT CHRISTMAS CAROLING! WOW! WE HAD OURSELVES A BALL!"
FA LA LA LA LA... LA LA LA
IKE
AND WHAT WAS THE CHRISTMAS GIFT YOU BEST REMEMBERED?
THAT'S EASY!
...IT WAS THE DARLING SCRAPBOOK YOU MADE FOR ME! I STILL TREASURE ALL THE NEAT MEMORIES IT EVOKES!
VERONICA'S CHRISTMAS SCRAPBOOK
YOU'RE PROVING MY POINT! ...ALL THE THINGS YOU JUST DESCRIBED WERE TRUE LABORS OF LOVE... THEY DIDN'T COST MUCH... IF ANYTHING!
HMMM...
I THINK I'M BEGINNING TO GET THE DRIFT OF WHAT YOU'RE SAYING!
OH, DEAR! I JUST REMEMBERED...
4

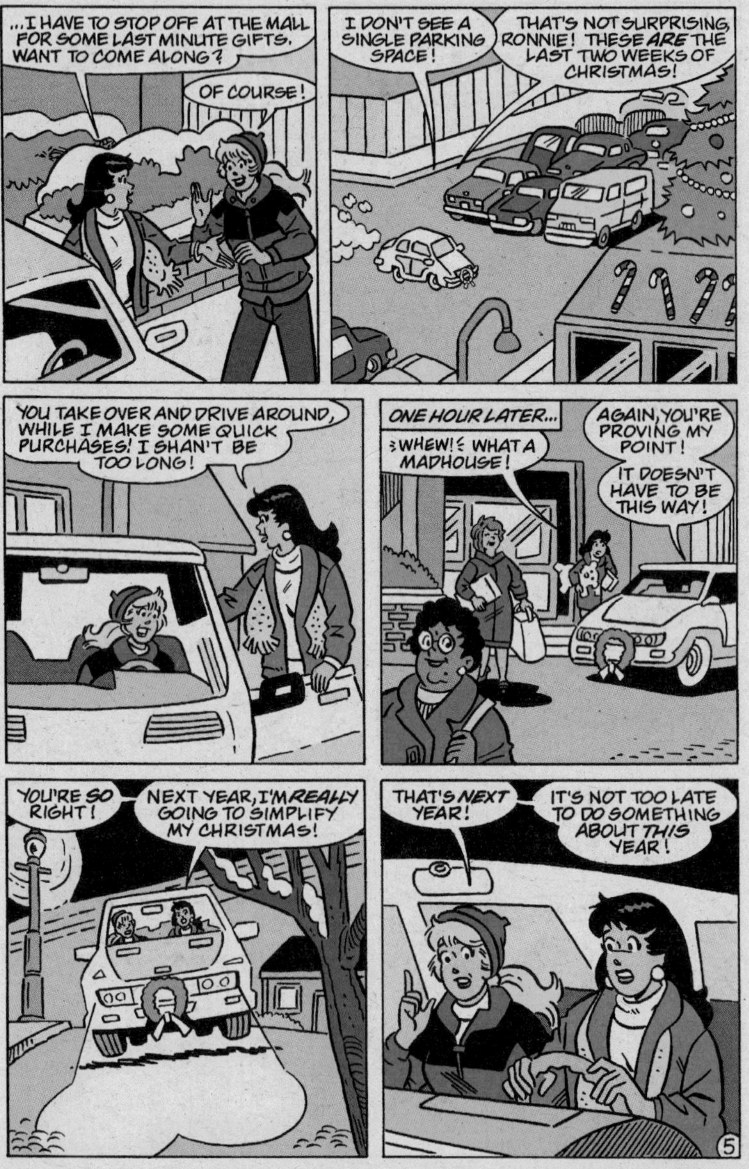
...I HAVE TO STOP OFF AT THE MALL FOR SOME LAST MINUTE GIFTS. WANT TO COME ALONG?
OF COURSE!
I DON'T SEE A SINGLE PARKING SPACE!
THAT'S NOT SURPRISING, RONNIE! THESE ARE THE LAST TWO WEEKS OF CHRISTMAS!
YOU TAKE OVER AND DRIVE AROUND, WHILE I MAKE SOME QUICK PURCHASES! I SHAN'T BE TOO LONG!
ONE HOUR LATER...
WHEW! WHAT A MADHOUSE!
AGAIN, YOU'RE PROVING MY POINT!
IT DOESN'T HAVE TO BE THIS WAY!
YOU'RE SO RIGHT!
NEXT YEAR, I'M REALLY GOING TO SIMPLIFY MY CHRISTMAS!
THAT'S NEXT YEAR!
IT'S NOT TOO LATE TO DO SOMETHING ABOUT THIS YEAR!
5

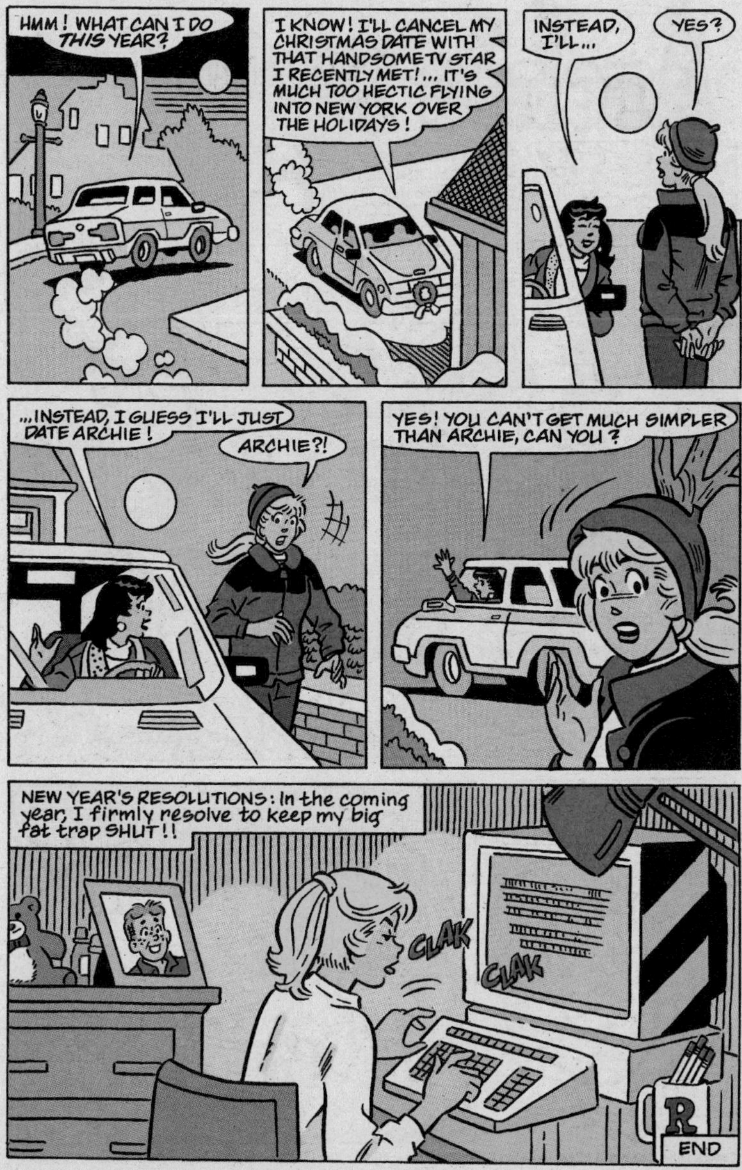

HMM! WHAT CAN I DO THIS YEAR?
I KNOW! I'LL CANCEL MY CHRISTMAS DATE WITH THAT HANDSOME TV STAR I RECENTLY MET! ... IT'S MUCH TOO HECTIC FLYING INTO NEW YORK OVER THE HOLIDAYS!
INSTEAD, I'LL...
YES?
...INSTEAD, I GUESS I'LL JUST DATE ARCHIE!
ARCHIE?!
YES! YOU CAN'T GET MUCH SIMPLER THAN ARCHIE, CAN YOU?
NEW YEAR'S RESOLUTIONS: In the coming year, I firmly resolve to keep my big fat trap SHUT!!
CLAK
CLAK
R
END

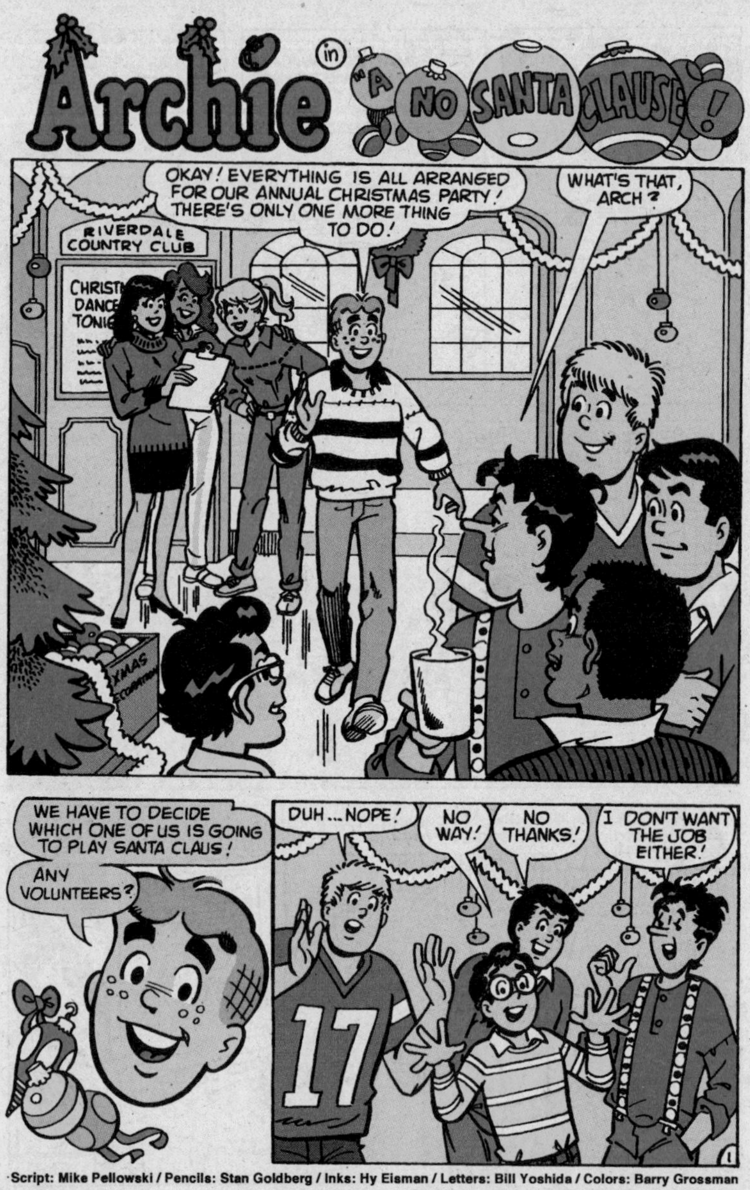
Archie in "A NO SANTA CLAUSE!"
OKAY! EVERYTHING IS ALL ARRANGED FOR OUR ANNUAL CHRISTMAS PARTY! THERE'S ONLY ONE MORE THING TO DO!
WHAT'S THAT, ARCH?
RIVERDALE COUNTRY CLUB
XMAS
WE HAVE TO DECIDE WHICH ONE OF US IS GOING TO PLAY SANTA CLAUS!
ANY VOLUNTEERS?
DUH... NOPE!
NO WAY!
NO THANKS!
I DON'T WANT THE JOB EITHER!
17

Script: Mike Pellowski / Pencils: Stan Goldberg / Inks: Hy Eisman / Letters: Bill Yoshida / Colors: Barry Grossman

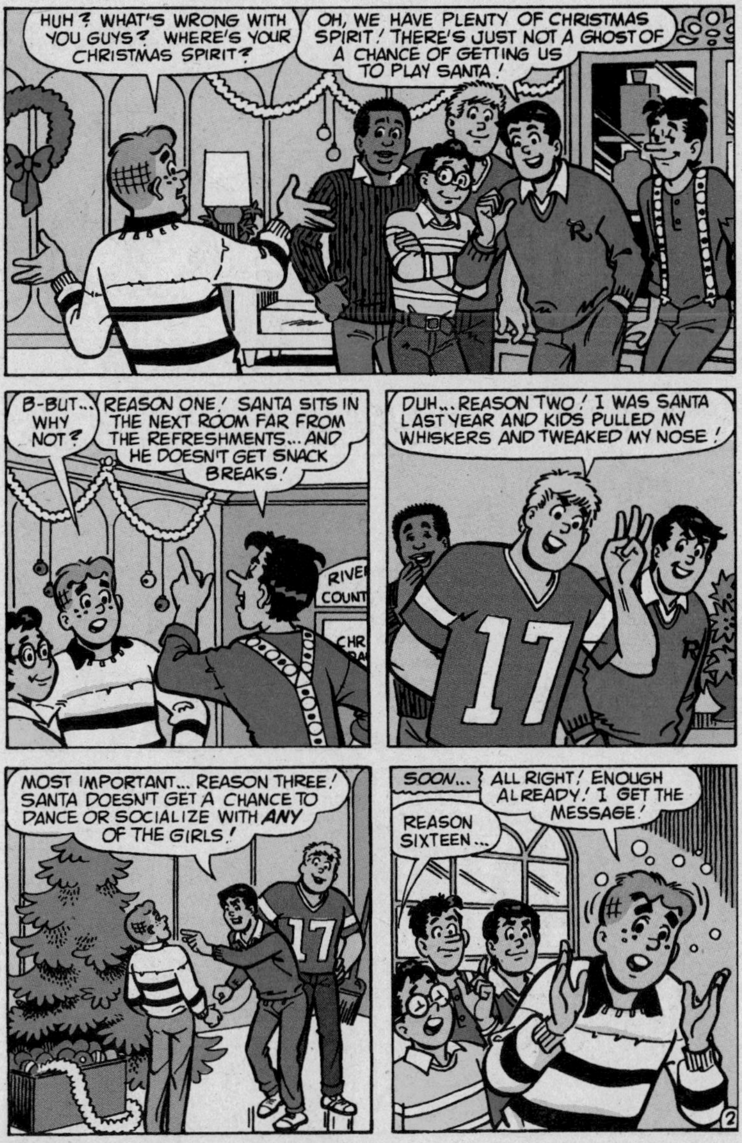
HUH? WHAT'S WRONG WITH YOU GUYS? WHERE'S YOUR CHRISTMAS SPIRIT?
OH, WE HAVE PLENTY OF CHRISTMAS SPIRIT! THERE'S JUST NOT A GHOST OF A CHANCE OF GETTING US TO PLAY SANTA!
B-BUT... WHY NOT?
REASON ONE! SANTA SITS IN THE NEXT ROOM FAR FROM THE REFRESHMENTS... AND HE DOESN'T GET SNACK BREAKS!
DUH... REASON TWO! I WAS SANTA LAST YEAR AND KIDS PULLED MY WHISKERS AND TWEAKED MY NOSE!
17
MOST IMPORTANT... REASON THREE! SANTA DOESN'T GET A CHANCE TO DANCE OR SOCIALIZE WITH ANY OF THE GIRLS!
17
SOON...
REASON SIXTEEN...
ALL RIGHT! ENOUGH ALREADY! I GET THE MESSAGE!
2

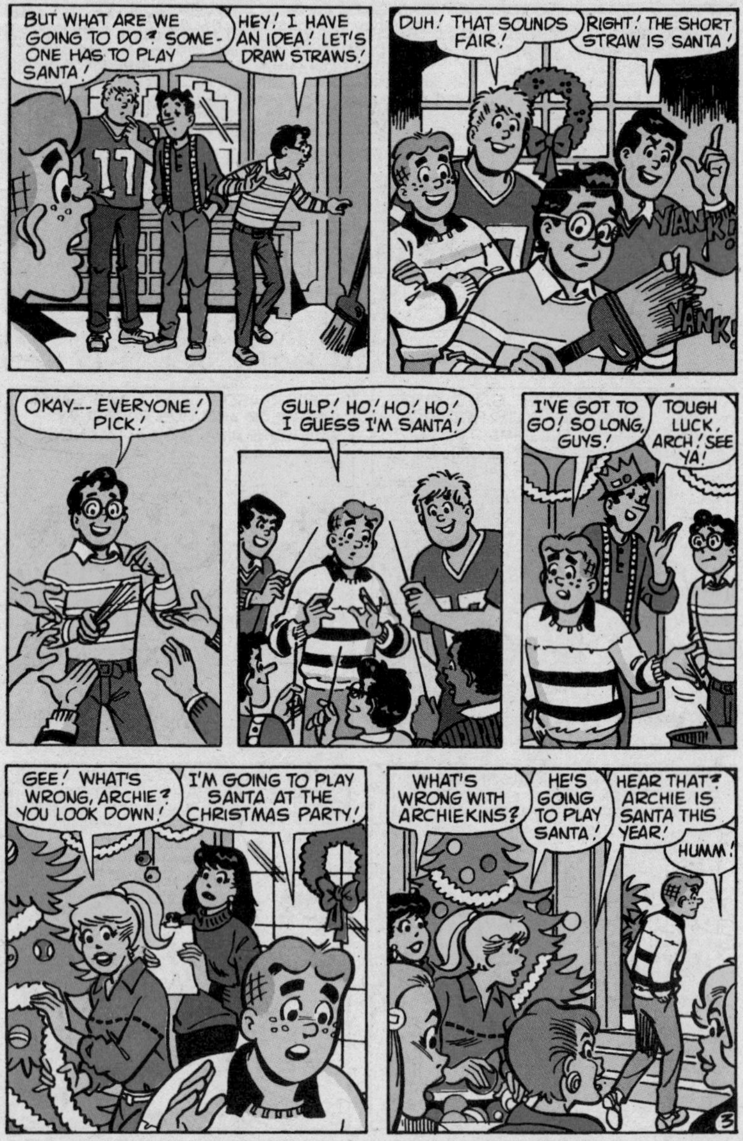
BUT WHAT ARE WE GOING TO DO? SOME-ONE HAS TO PLAY SANTA!
HEY! I HAVE AN IDEA! LET'S DRAW STRAWS!
DUH! THAT SOUNDS FAIR!
RIGHT! THE SHORT STRAW IS SANTA!
YANK!
YANK!
OKAY--- EVERYONE! PICK!
GULP! HO! HO! HO! I GUESS I'M SANTA!
I'VE GOT TO GO! SO LONG, GUYS!
TOUGH LUCK, ARCH! SEE YA!
GEE! WHAT'S WRONG, ARCHIE? YOU LOOK DOWN!
I'M GOING TO PLAY SANTA AT THE CHRISTMAS PARTY!
WHAT'S WRONG WITH ARCHIEKINS?
HE'S GOING TO PLAY SANTA!
HEAR THAT? ARCHIE IS SANTA THIS YEAR!
HUMM!
3

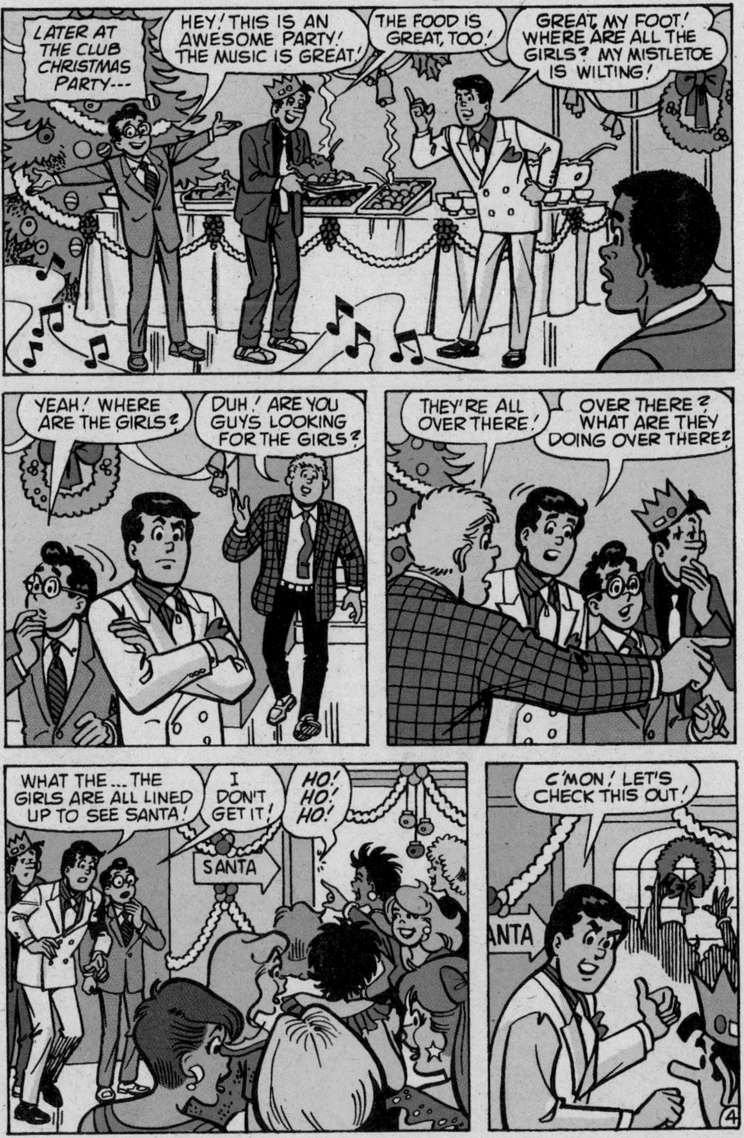
LATER AT THE CLUB CHRISTMAS PARTY---
HEY! THIS IS AN AWESOME PARTY! THE MUSIC IS GREAT!
THE FOOD IS GREAT, TOO!
GREAT, MY FOOT! WHERE ARE ALL THE GIRLS? MY MISTLETOE IS WILTING!
YEAH! WHERE ARE THE GIRLS?
DUH! ARE YOU GUYS LOOKING FOR THE GIRLS?
THEY'RE ALL OVER THERE!
OVER THERE? WHAT ARE THEY DOING OVER THERE?
WHAT THE ... THE GIRLS ARE ALL LINED UP TO SEE SANTA!
I DON'T GET IT!
HO! HO! HO!
SANTA
C'MON! LET'S CHECK THIS OUT!
4

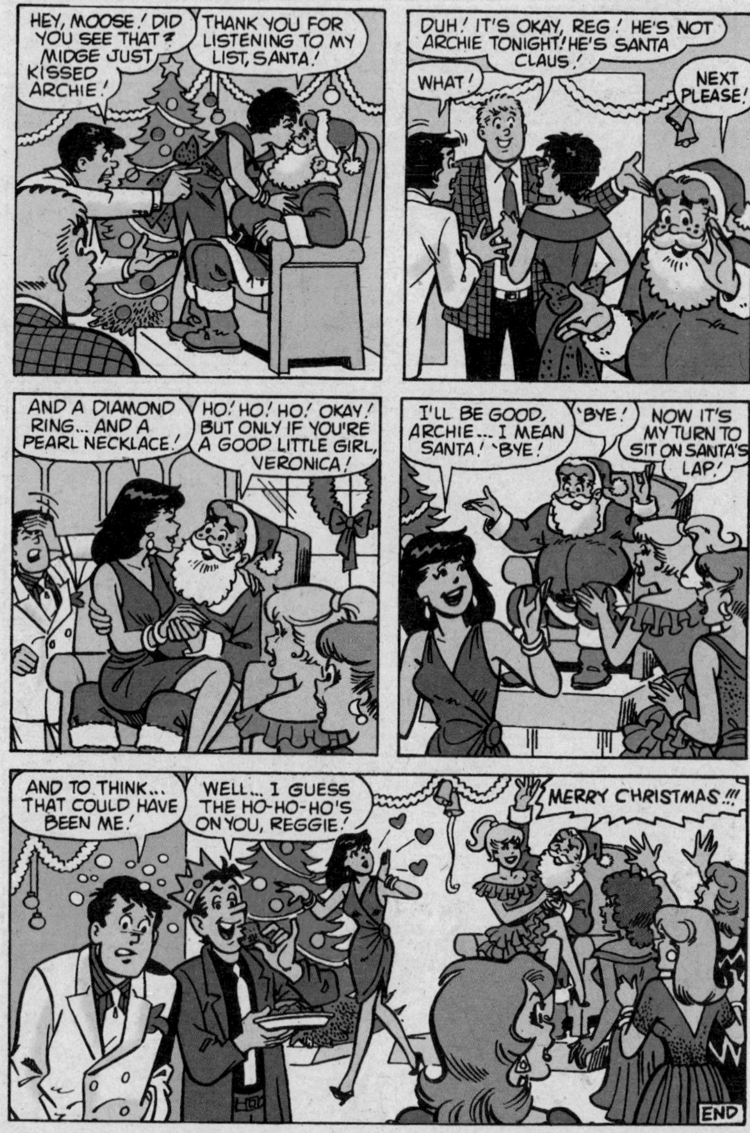
HEY, MOOSE! DID YOU SEE THAT? MIDGE JUST KISSED ARCHIE!
THANK YOU FOR LISTENING TO MY LIST, SANTA!
DUH! IT'S OKAY, REG! HE'S NOT ARCHIE TONIGHT! HE'S SANTA CLAUS!
WHAT!
NEXT PLEASE!
AND A DIAMOND RING... AND A PEARL NECKLACE!
HO! HO! HO! OKAY! BUT ONLY IF YOU'RE A GOOD LITTLE GIRL, VERONICA!
I'LL BE GOOD, ARCHIE... I MEAN SANTA! 'BYE!
'BYE!
NOW IT'S MY TURN TO SIT ON SANTA'S LAP!
AND TO THINK... THAT COULD HAVE BEEN ME!
WELL... I GUESS THE HO-HO-HO'S ON YOU, REGGIE!
MERRY CHRISTMAS!!!
END

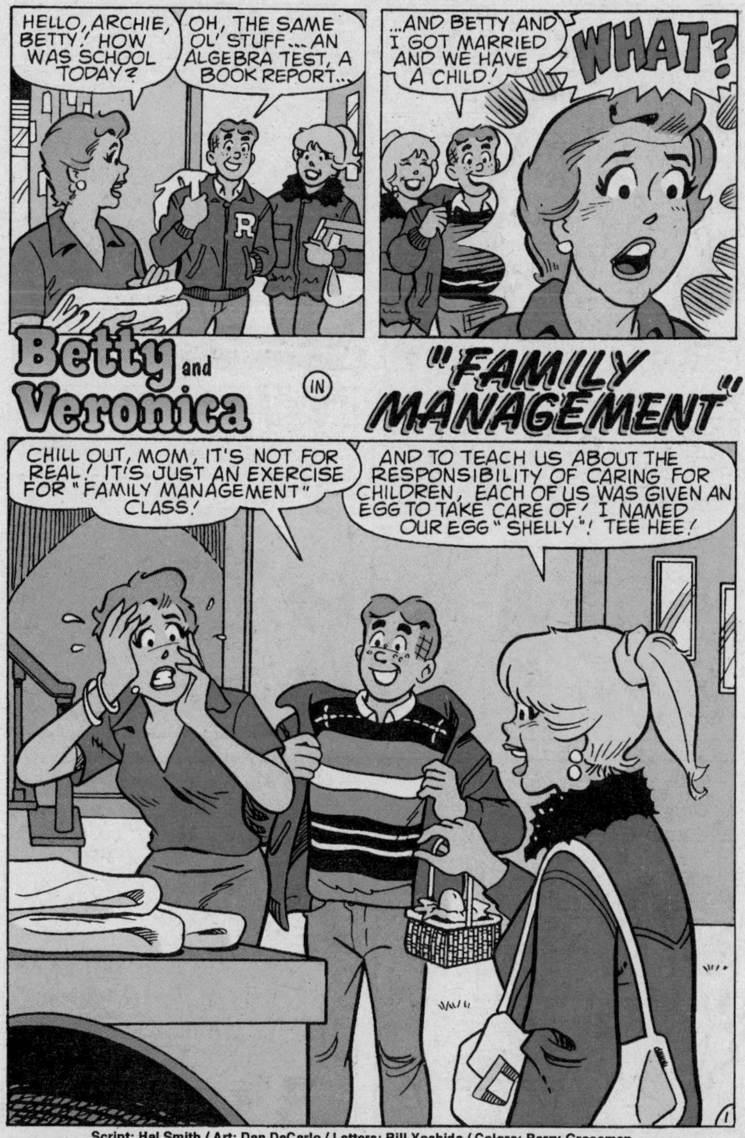
HELLO, ARCHIE, BETTY! HOW WAS SCHOOL TODAY?
OH, THE SAME OL' STUFF... AN ALGEBRA TEST, A BOOK REPORT...
...AND BETTY AND I GOT MARRIED AND WE HAVE A CHILD!
WHAT?
Betty and Veronica IN "FAMILY MANAGEMENT"
CHILL OUT, MOM, IT'S NOT FOR REAL! IT'S JUST AN EXERCISE FOR "FAMILY MANAGEMENT" CLASS!
AND TO TEACH US ABOUT THE RESPONSIBILITY OF CARING FOR CHILDREN, EACH OF US WAS GIVEN AN EGG TO TAKE CARE OF! I NAMED OUR EGG "SHELLY"! TEE HEE!
1

Script: Hal Smith / Art: Dan DeCarlo / Letters: Bill Yoshida / Colors: Barry Grossman

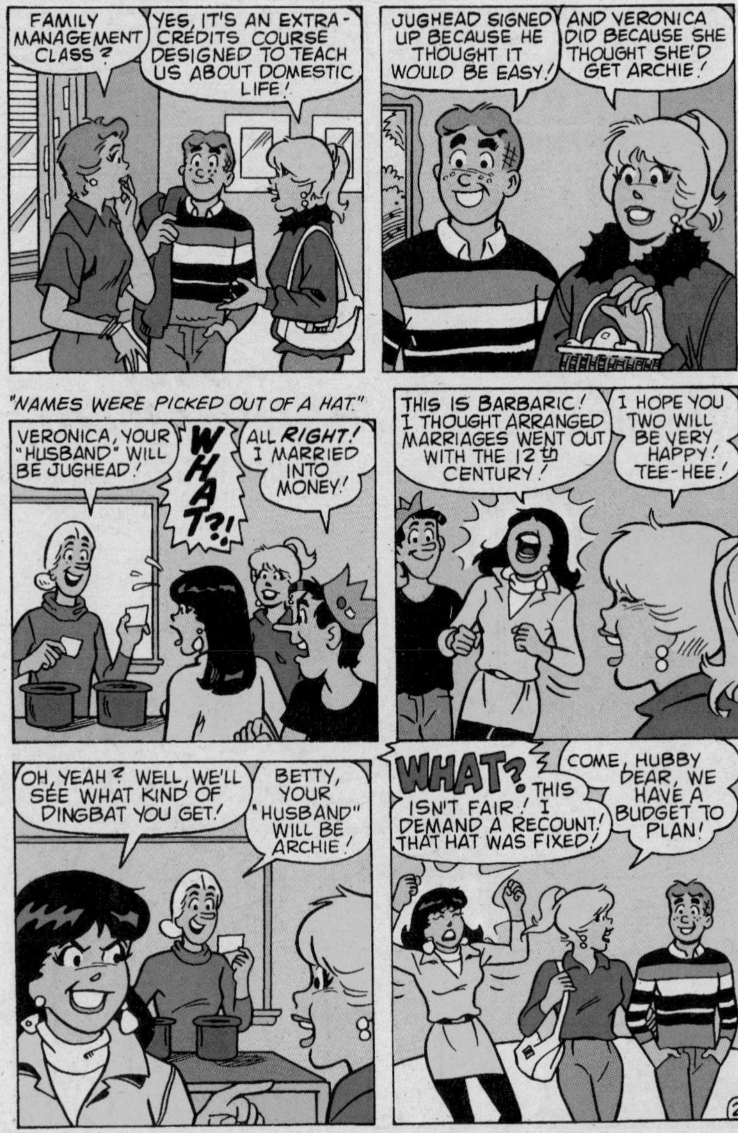
FAMILY MANAGEMENT CLASS?
YES, IT'S AN EXTRA-CREDITS COURSE DESIGNED TO TEACH US ABOUT DOMESTIC LIFE!
JUGHEAD SIGNED UP BECAUSE HE THOUGHT IT WOULD BE EASY!
AND VERONICA DID BECAUSE SHE THOUGHT SHE'D GET ARCHIE!
"NAMES WERE PICKED OUT OF A HAT."
VERONICA, YOUR "HUSBAND" WILL BE JUGHEAD!
WHAT?!
ALL RIGHT! I MARRIED INTO MONEY!
THIS IS BARBARIC! I THOUGHT ARRANGED MARRIAGES WENT OUT WITH THE 12th CENTURY!
I HOPE YOU TWO WILL BE VERY HAPPY! TEE-HEE!
OH, YEAH? WELL, WE'LL SEE WHAT KIND OF DINGBAT YOU GET!
BETTY, YOUR "HUSBAND" WILL BE ARCHIE!
WHAT? THIS ISN'T FAIR! I DEMAND A RECOUNT! THAT HAT WAS FIXED!
COME, HUBBY DEAR, WE HAVE A BUDGET TO PLAN!
2

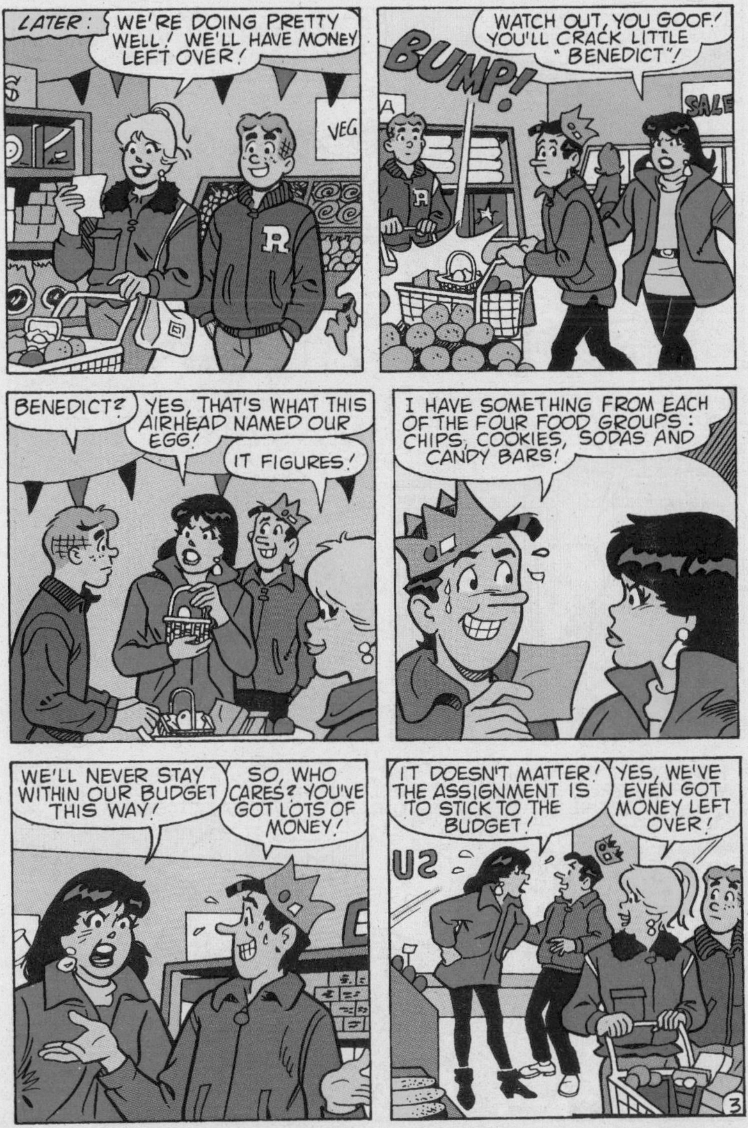
LATER:
WE'RE DOING PRETTY WELL! WE'LL HAVE MONEY LEFT OVER!
VEG
BUMP!
WATCH OUT, YOU GOOF! YOU'LL CRACK LITTLE "BENEDICT"!
SALE
BENEDICT?
YES, THAT'S WHAT THIS AIRHEAD NAMED OUR EGG!
IT FIGURES!
I HAVE SOMETHING FROM EACH OF THE FOUR FOOD GROUPS: CHIPS, COOKIES, SODAS AND CANDY BARS!
WE'LL NEVER STAY WITHIN OUR BUDGET THIS WAY!
SO, WHO CARES? YOU'VE GOT LOTS OF MONEY!
IT DOESN'T MATTER! THE ASSIGNMENT IS TO STICK TO THE BUDGET!
YES, WE'VE EVEN GOT MONEY LEFT OVER!
3

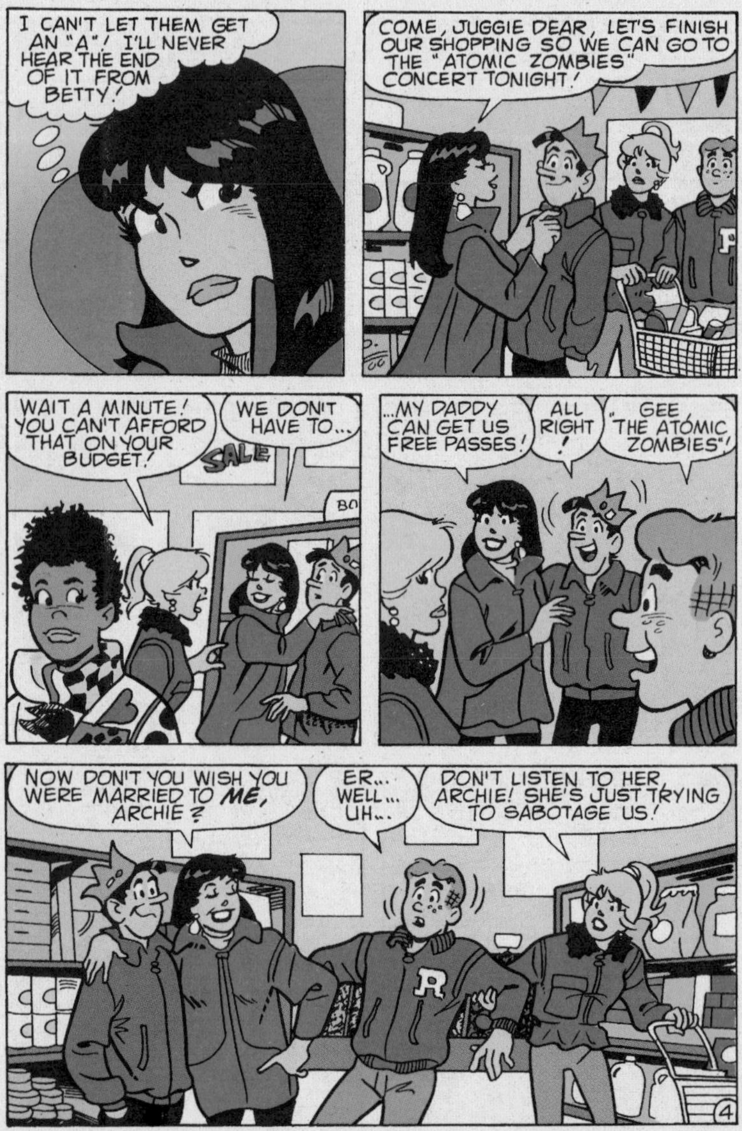
I CAN'T LET THEM GET AN "A"! I'LL NEVER HEAR THE END OF IT FROM BETTY!
COME, JUGGIE DEAR, LET'S FINISH OUR SHOPPING SO WE CAN GO TO THE "ATOMIC ZOMBIES" CONCERT TONIGHT!
WAIT A MINUTE! YOU CAN'T AFFORD THAT ON YOUR BUDGET!
WE DON'T HAVE TO...
SALE
...MY DADDY CAN GET US FREE PASSES!
ALL RIGHT!
GEE, "THE ATOMIC ZOMBIES"!
NOW DON'T YOU WISH YOU WERE MARRIED TO *ME*, ARCHIE?
ER... WELL... UH...
DON'T LISTEN TO HER, ARCHIE! SHE'S JUST TRYING TO SABOTAGE US!
4

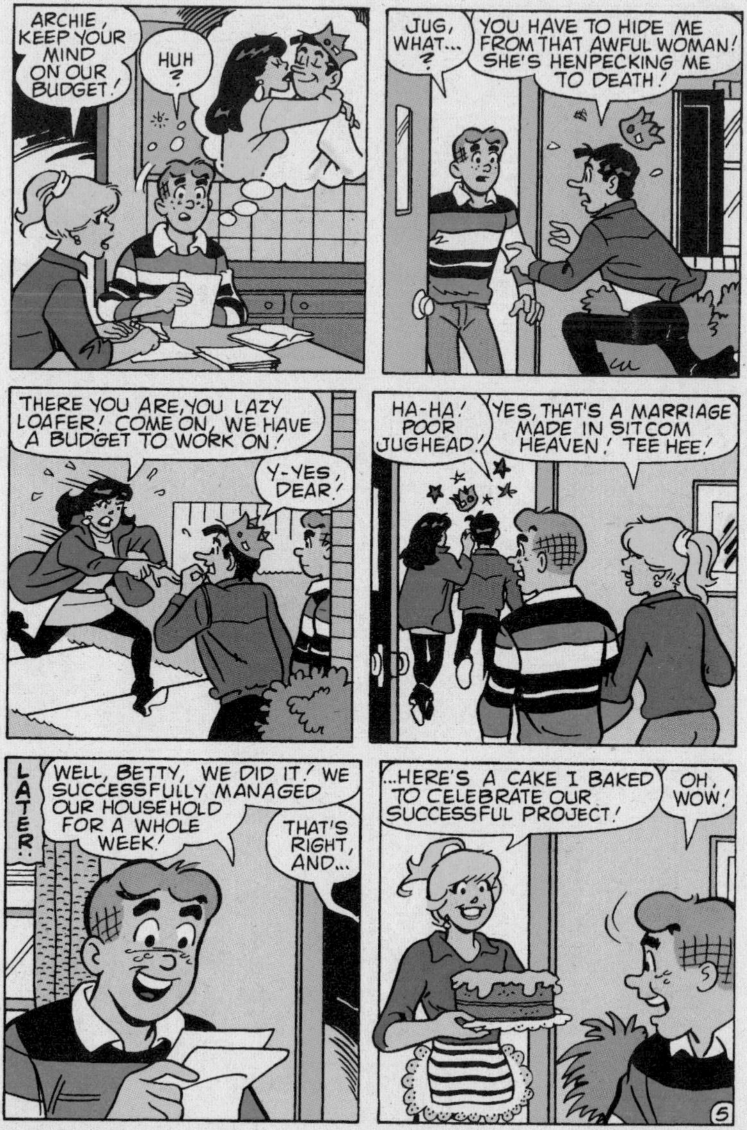
ARCHIE, KEEP YOUR MIND ON OUR BUDGET!
HUH?
JUG, WHAT...?
YOU HAVE TO HIDE ME FROM THAT AWFUL WOMAN! SHE'S HENPECKING ME TO DEATH!
THERE YOU ARE, YOU LAZY LOAFER! COME ON, WE HAVE A BUDGET TO WORK ON!
Y-YES, DEAR!
HA-HA! POOR JUGHEAD!
YES, THAT'S A MARRIAGE MADE IN SITCOM HEAVEN! TEE HEE!
LATER:
WELL, BETTY, WE DID IT! WE SUCCESSFULLY MANAGED OUR HOUSEHOLD FOR A WHOLE WEEK!
THAT'S RIGHT, AND...
...HERE'S A CAKE I BAKED TO CELEBRATE OUR SUCCESSFUL PROJECT!
OH, WOW!
5

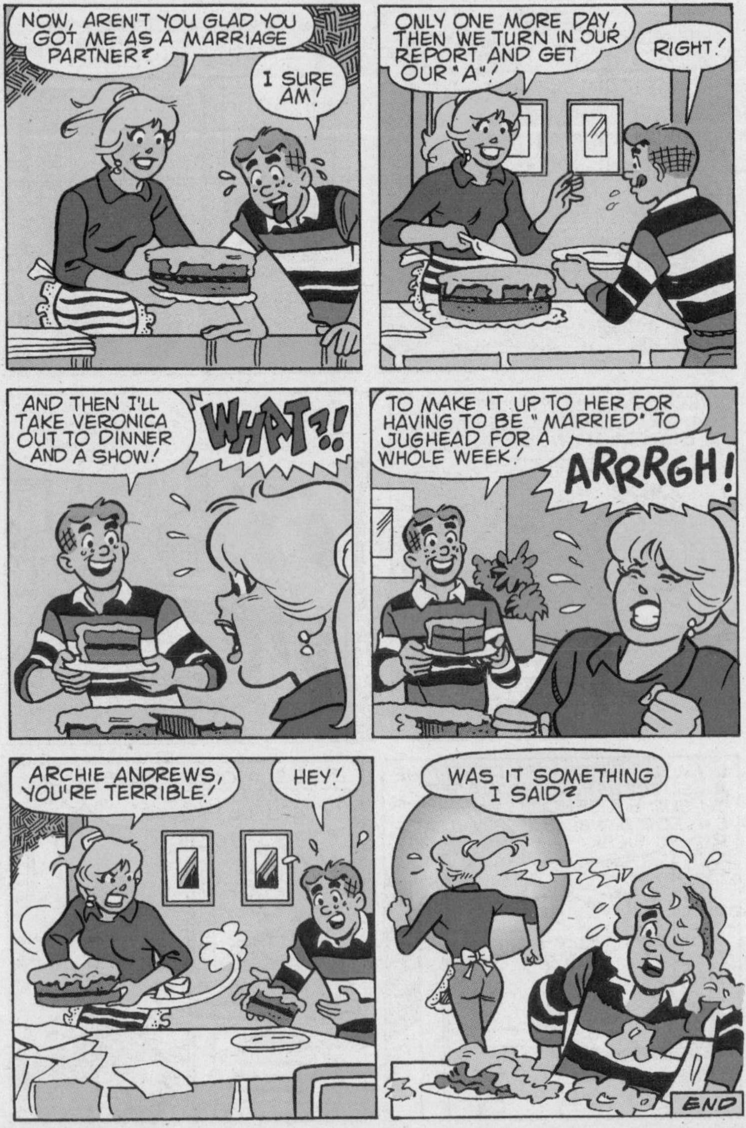
NOW, AREN'T YOU GLAD YOU GOT ME AS A MARRIAGE PARTNER?
I SURE AM!
ONLY ONE MORE DAY, THEN WE TURN IN OUR REPORT AND GET OUR "A"!
RIGHT!
AND THEN I'LL TAKE VERONICA OUT TO DINNER AND A SHOW!
WHAT?!
TO MAKE IT UP TO HER FOR HAVING TO BE "MARRIED" TO JUGHEAD FOR A WHOLE WEEK!
ARRRGH!
ARCHIE ANDREWS, YOU'RE TERRIBLE!
HEY!
WAS IT SOMETHING I SAID?
END

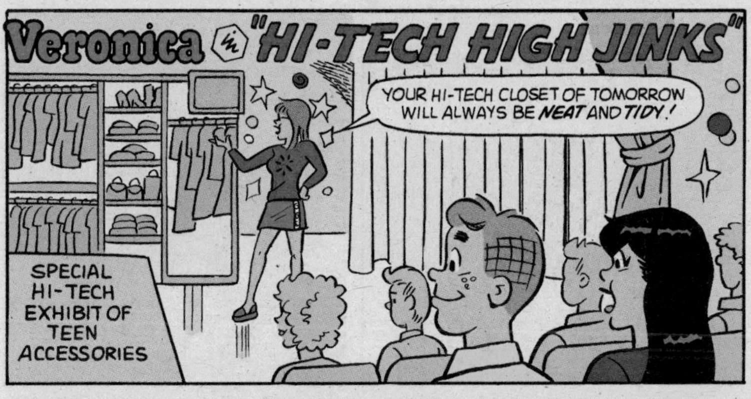
Veronica in "HI-TECH HIGH JINKS"
YOUR HI-TECH CLOSET OF TOMORROW WILL ALWAYS BE NEAT AND TIDY!
SPECIAL HI-TECH EXHIBIT OF TEEN ACCESSORIES

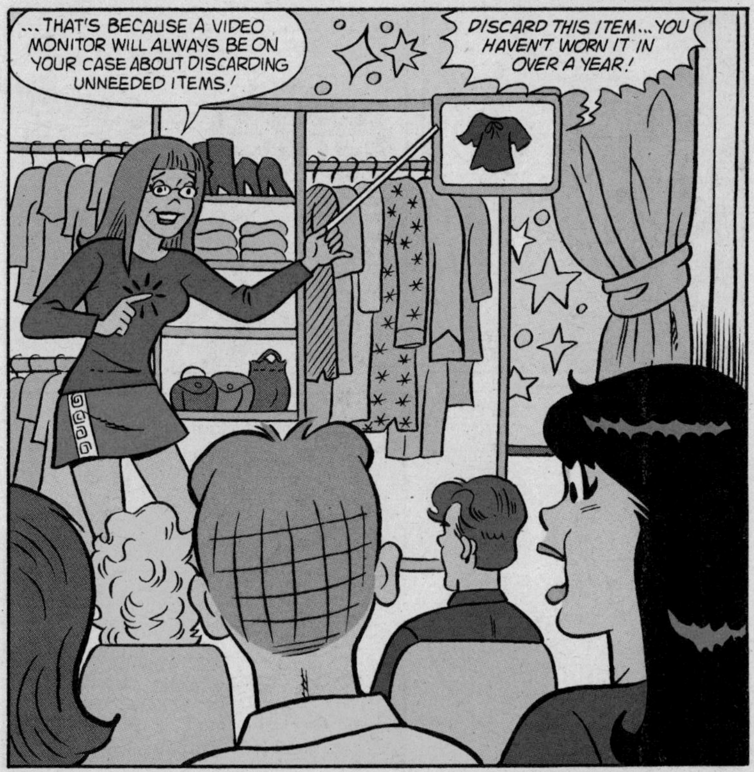
...THAT'S BECAUSE A VIDEO MONITOR WILL ALWAYS BE ON YOUR CASE ABOUT DISCARDING UNNEEDED ITEMS!
DISCARD THIS ITEM... YOU HAVEN'T WORN IT IN OVER A YEAR!

Script: George Gladir / Pencils: Dan Parent / Inks: Rudy Lapick / Letters: Bill Yoshida

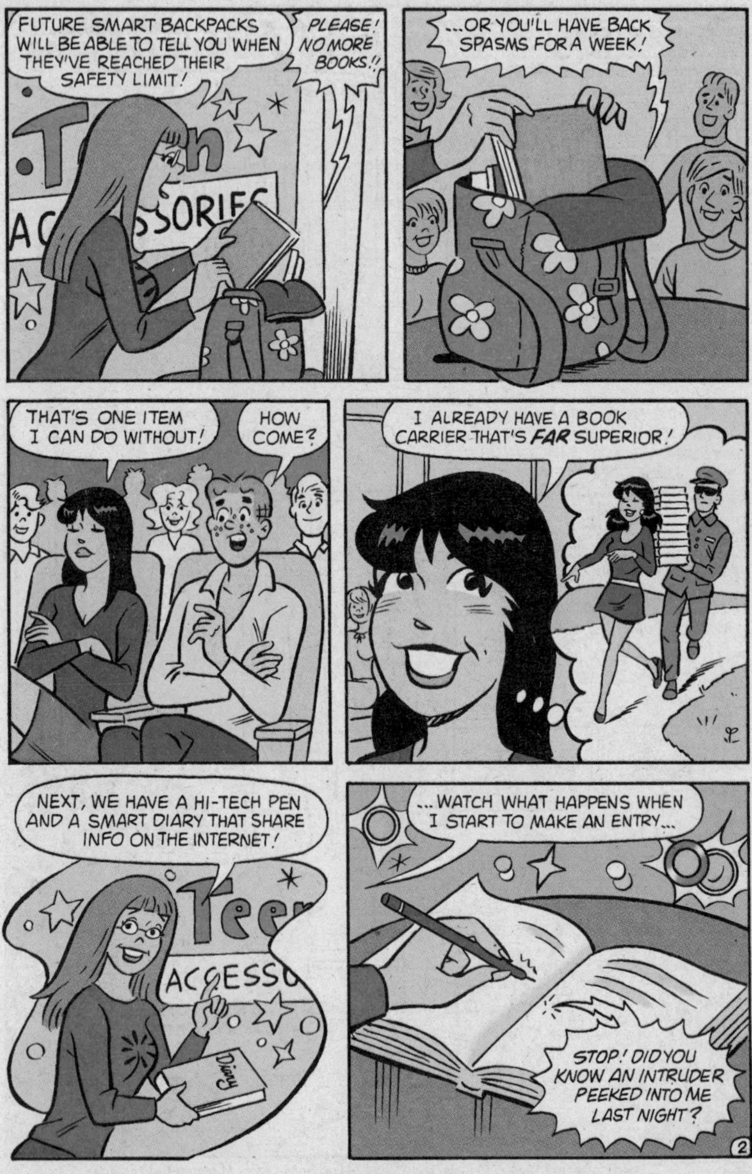

FUTURE SMART BACKPACKS WILL BE ABLE TO TELL YOU WHEN THEY'VE REACHED THEIR SAFETY LIMIT!
PLEASE! NO MORE BOOKS!!
...OR YOU'LL HAVE BACK SPASMS FOR A WEEK!
THAT'S ONE ITEM I CAN DO WITHOUT!
HOW COME?
I ALREADY HAVE A BOOK CARRIER THAT'S **FAR** SUPERIOR!
NEXT, WE HAVE A HI-TECH PEN AND A SMART DIARY THAT SHARE INFO ON THE INTERNET!
ACCESSO
Diary
...WATCH WHAT HAPPENS WHEN I START TO MAKE AN ENTRY...
STOP! DID YOU KNOW AN INTRUDER PEEKED INTO ME LAST NIGHT?
2

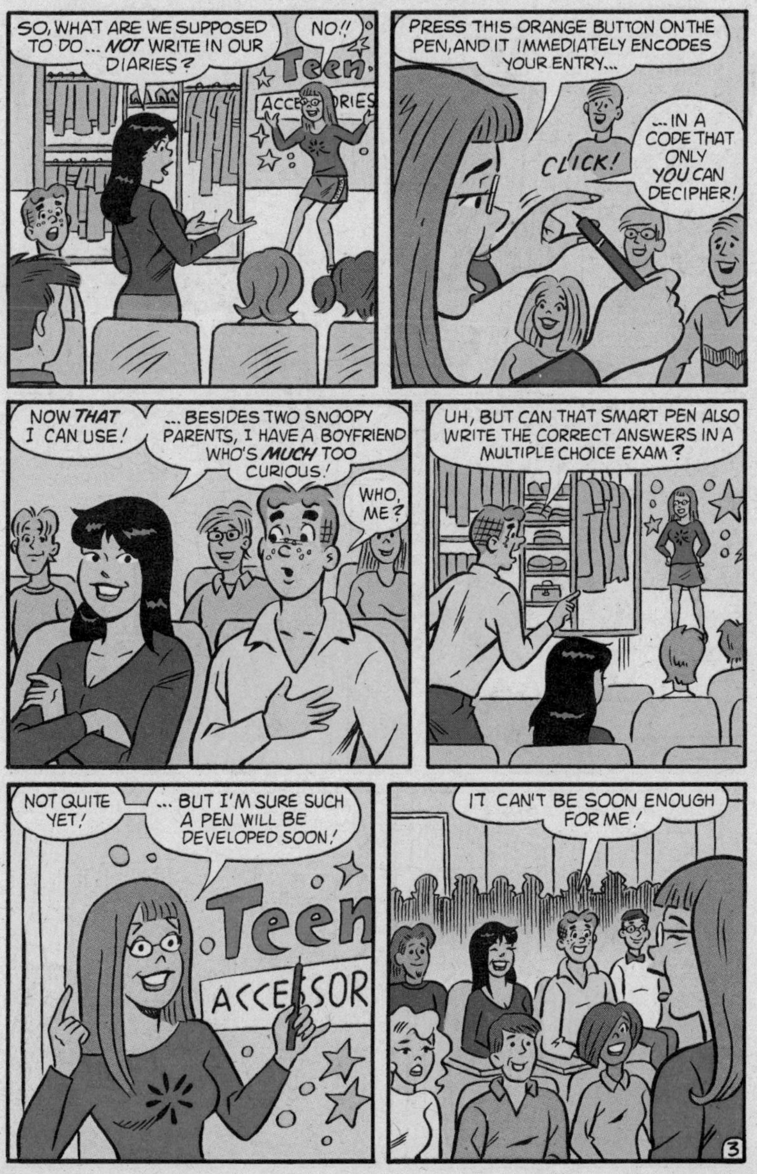

SO, WHAT ARE WE SUPPOSED TO DO... NOT WRITE IN OUR DIARIES?
NO!!
Teen
ACCESSORIES
PRESS THIS ORANGE BUTTON ON THE PEN, AND IT IMMEDIATELY ENCODES YOUR ENTRY...
CLICK!
...IN A CODE THAT ONLY YOU CAN DECIPHER!
NOW THAT I CAN USE!
...BESIDES TWO SNOOPY PARENTS, I HAVE A BOYFRIEND WHO'S MUCH TOO CURIOUS!
WHO, ME?
UH, BUT CAN THAT SMART PEN ALSO WRITE THE CORRECT ANSWERS IN A MULTIPLE CHOICE EXAM?
NOT QUITE YET!
...BUT I'M SURE SUCH A PEN WILL BE DEVELOPED SOON!
Teen
ACCESSOR
IT CAN'T BE SOON ENOUGH FOR ME!
3

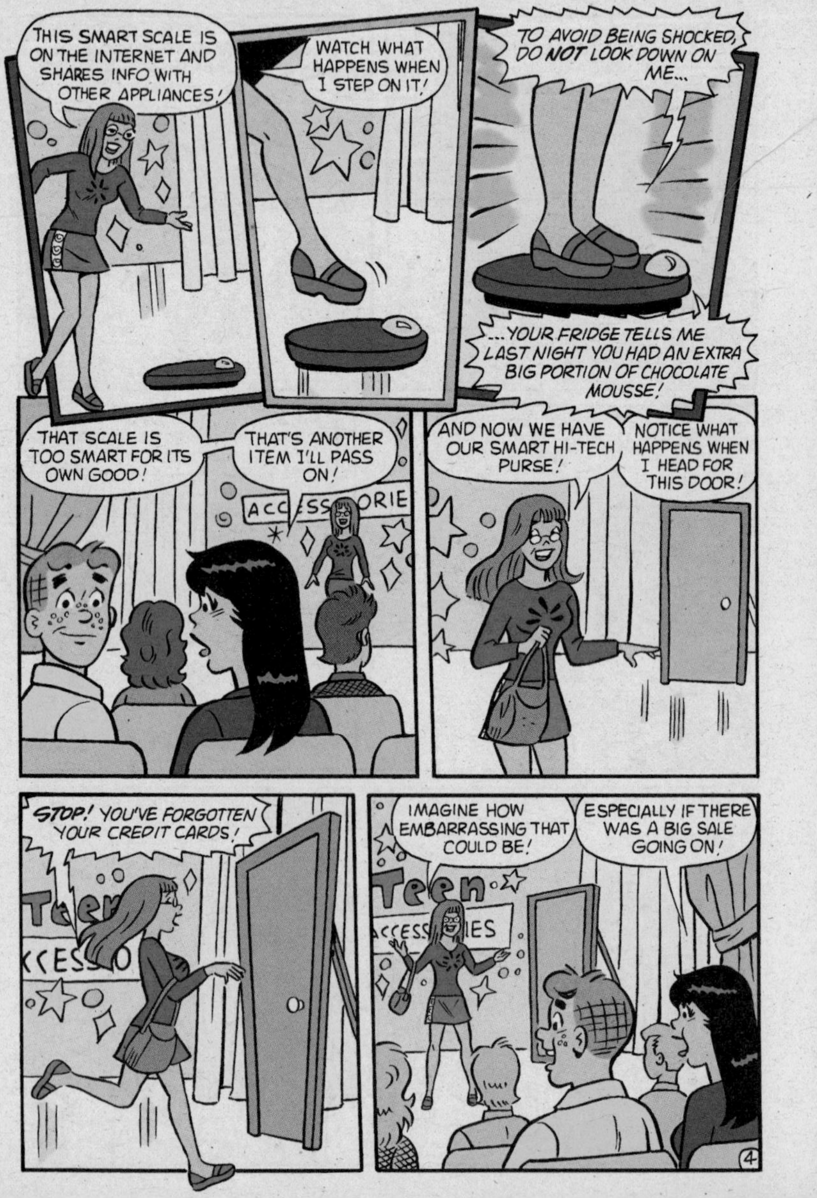
THIS SMART SCALE IS ON THE INTERNET AND SHARES INFO WITH OTHER APPLIANCES!
WATCH WHAT HAPPENS WHEN I STEP ON IT!
TO AVOID BEING SHOCKED, DO **NOT** LOOK DOWN ON ME...
...YOUR FRIDGE TELLS ME LAST NIGHT YOU HAD AN EXTRA BIG PORTION OF CHOCOLATE MOUSSE!
THAT SCALE IS TOO SMART FOR ITS OWN GOOD!
THAT'S ANOTHER ITEM I'LL PASS ON!
AND NOW WE HAVE OUR SMART HI-TECH PURSE!
NOTICE WHAT HAPPENS WHEN I HEAD FOR THIS DOOR!
STOP! YOU'VE FORGOTTEN YOUR CREDIT CARDS!
IMAGINE HOW EMBARRASSING THAT COULD BE!
ESPECIALLY IF THERE WAS A BIG SALE GOING ON!
4

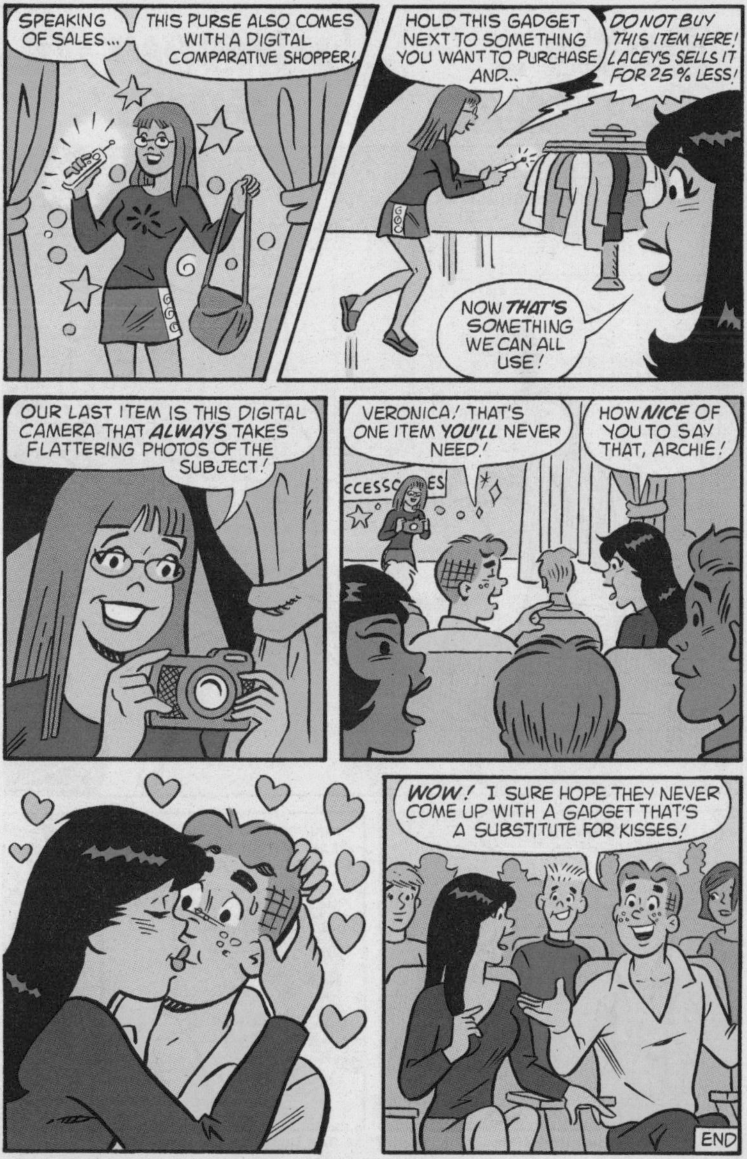
SPEAKING OF SALES...
THIS PURSE ALSO COMES WITH A DIGITAL COMPARATIVE SHOPPER!
HOLD THIS GADGET NEXT TO SOMETHING YOU WANT TO PURCHASE AND...
DO NOT BUY THIS ITEM HERE! LACEY'S SELLS IT FOR 25% LESS!
NOW THAT'S SOMETHING WE CAN ALL USE!
OUR LAST ITEM IS THIS DIGITAL CAMERA THAT ALWAYS TAKES FLATTERING PHOTOS OF THE SUBJECT!
VERONICA! THAT'S ONE ITEM YOU'LL NEVER NEED!
HOW NICE OF YOU TO SAY THAT, ARCHIE!
WOW! I SURE HOPE THEY NEVER COME UP WITH A GADGET THAT'S A SUBSTITUTE FOR KISSES!
END

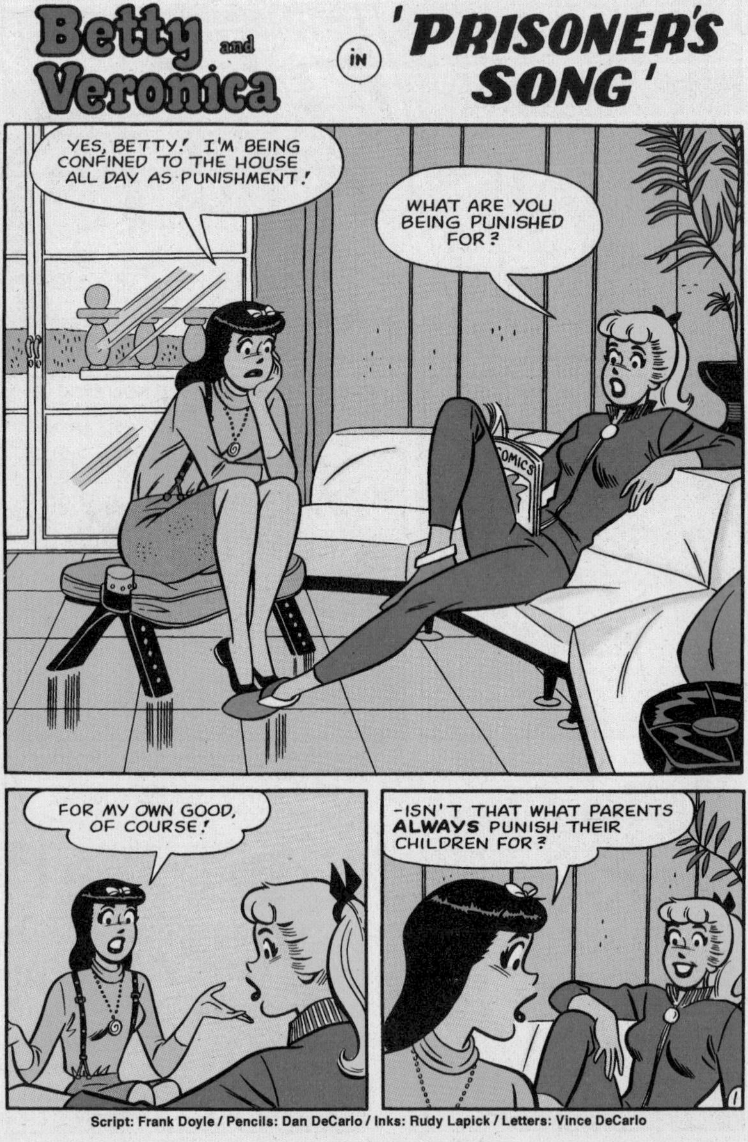
Betty and Veronica in 'PRISONER'S SONG'
YES, BETTY! I'M BEING CONFINED TO THE HOUSE ALL DAY AS PUNISHMENT!
WHAT ARE YOU BEING PUNISHED FOR?
COMICS
FOR MY OWN GOOD, OF COURSE!
-ISN'T THAT WHAT PARENTS **ALWAYS** PUNISH THEIR CHILDREN FOR?
1

Script: Frank Doyle / Pencils: Dan DeCarlo / Inks: Rudy Lapick / Letters: Vince DeCarlo

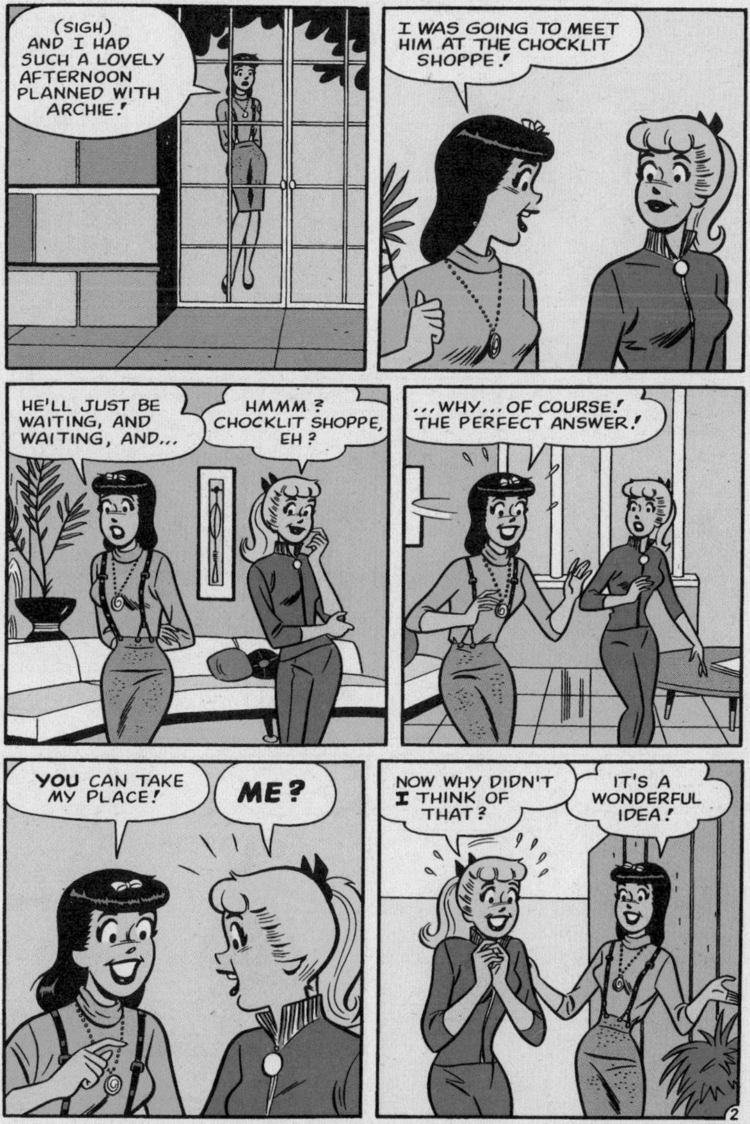

(SIGH) AND I HAD SUCH A LOVELY AFTERNOON PLANNED WITH ARCHIE!
I WAS GOING TO MEET HIM AT THE CHOCKLIT SHOPPE!
HE'LL JUST BE WAITING, AND WAITING, AND...
HMMM? CHOCKLIT SHOPPE, EH?
...WHY...OF COURSE! THE PERFECT ANSWER!
YOU CAN TAKE MY PLACE!
ME?
NOW WHY DIDN'T I THINK OF THAT?
IT'S A WONDERFUL IDEA!

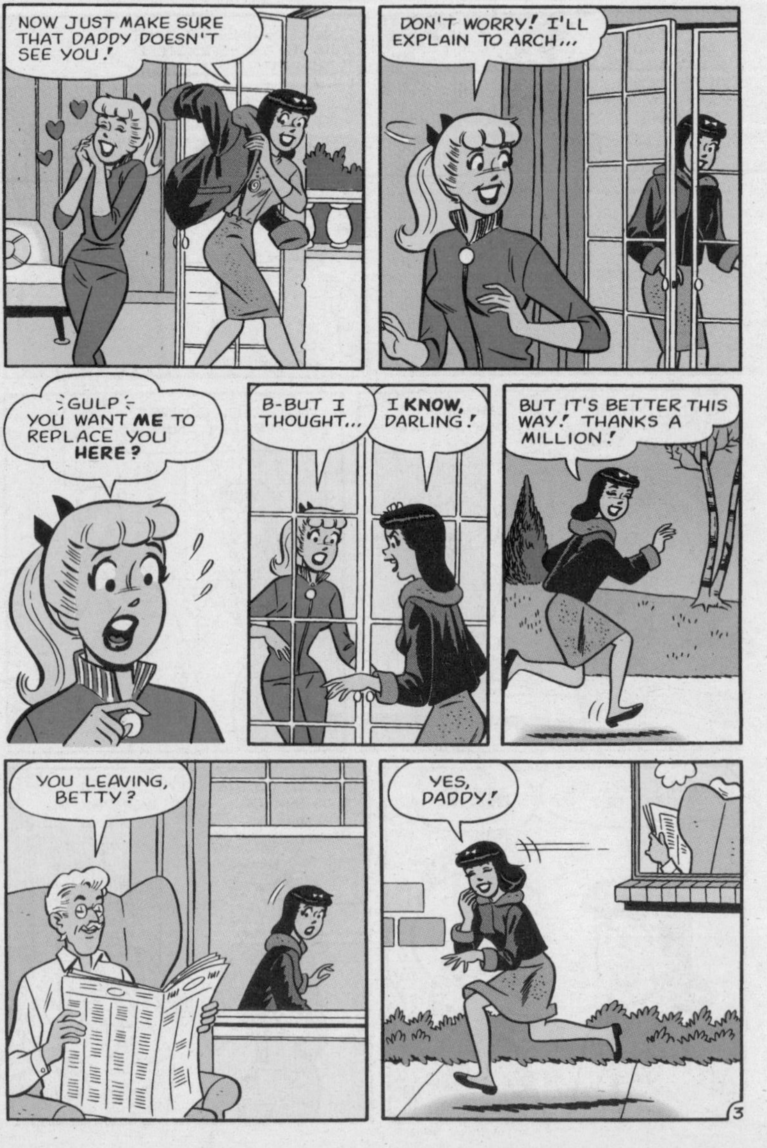

NOW JUST MAKE SURE THAT DADDY DOESN'T SEE YOU!
DON'T WORRY! I'LL EXPLAIN TO ARCH...
GULP YOU WANT ME TO REPLACE YOU HERE?
B-BUT I THOUGHT...
I KNOW, DARLING!
BUT IT'S BETTER THIS WAY! THANKS A MILLION!
YOU LEAVING, BETTY?
YES, DADDY!
3

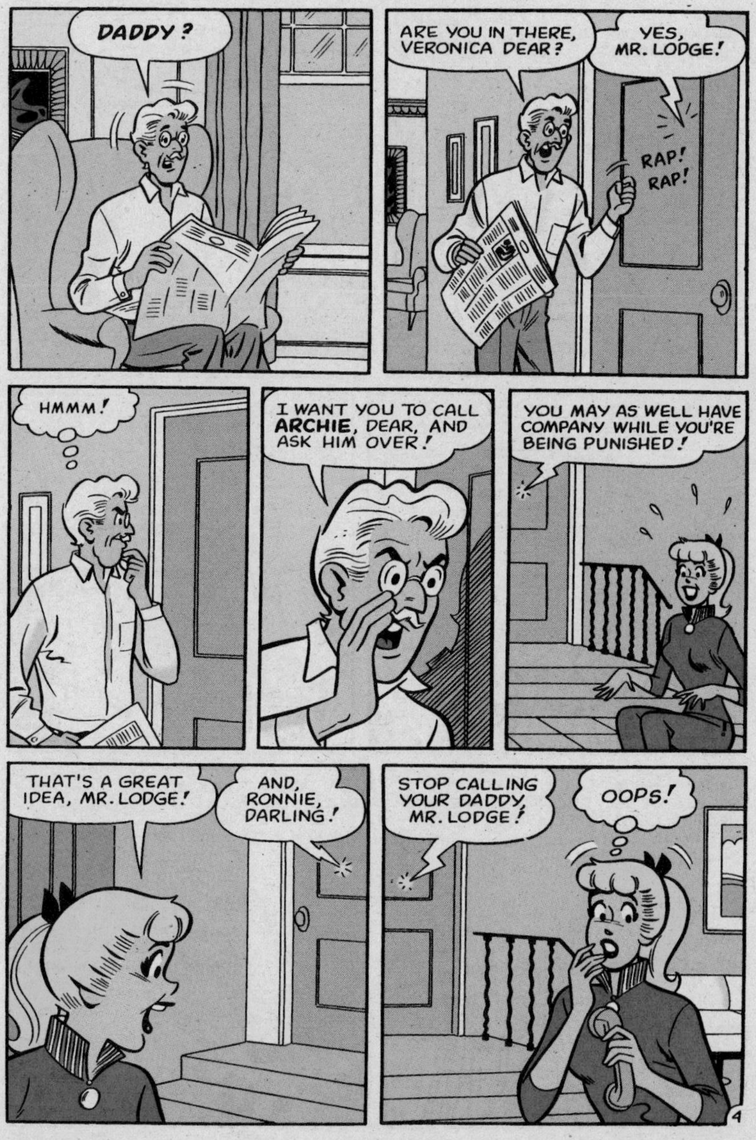
DADDY?
ARE YOU IN THERE, VERONICA DEAR?
YES, MR. LODGE!
RAP! RAP!
HMMM!
I WANT YOU TO CALL ARCHIE, DEAR, AND ASK HIM OVER!
YOU MAY AS WELL HAVE COMPANY WHILE YOU'RE BEING PUNISHED!
THAT'S A GREAT IDEA, MR. LODGE!
AND, RONNIE, DARLING!
STOP CALLING YOUR DADDY, MR. LODGE!
OOPS!
4

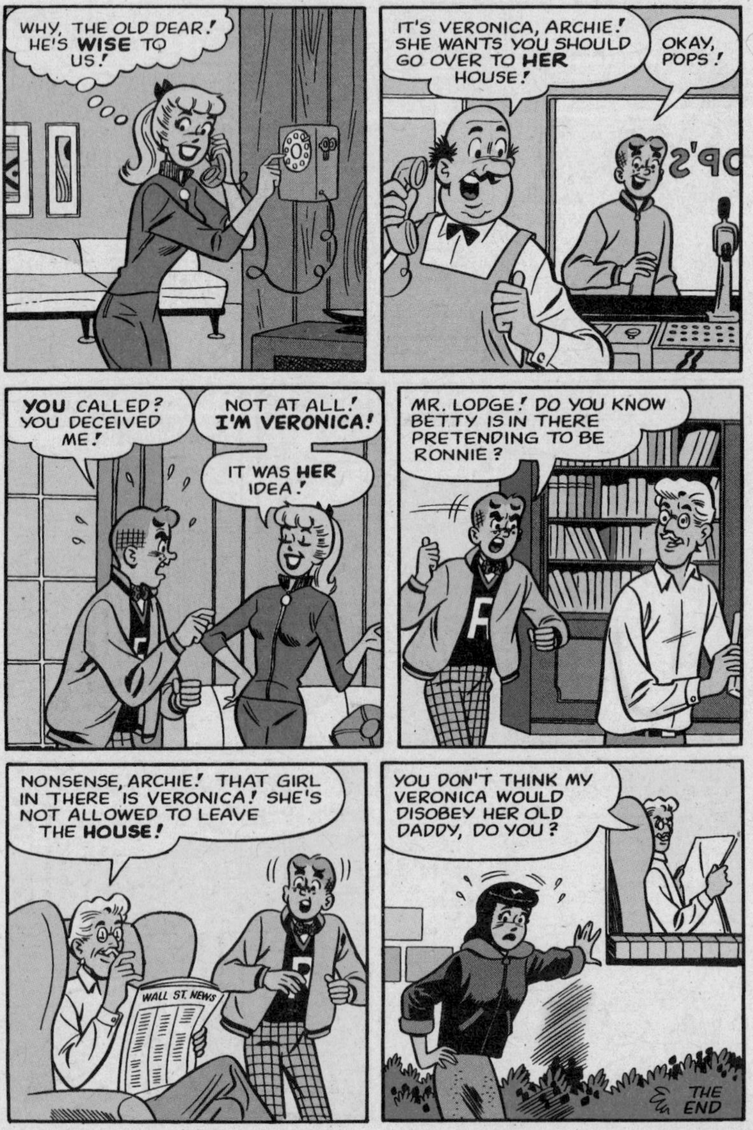
WHY, THE OLD DEAR! HE'S WISE TO US!
IT'S VERONICA, ARCHIE! SHE WANTS YOU SHOULD GO OVER TO HER HOUSE!
OKAY, POPS!
POP'S
YOU CALLED? YOU DECEIVED ME!
NOT AT ALL! I'M VERONICA!
IT WAS HER IDEA!
MR. LODGE! DO YOU KNOW BETTY IS IN THERE PRETENDING TO BE RONNIE?
NONSENSE, ARCHIE! THAT GIRL IN THERE IS VERONICA! SHE'S NOT ALLOWED TO LEAVE THE HOUSE!
WALL ST. NEWS
YOU DON'T THINK MY VERONICA WOULD DISOBEY HER OLD DADDY, DO YOU?
THE END

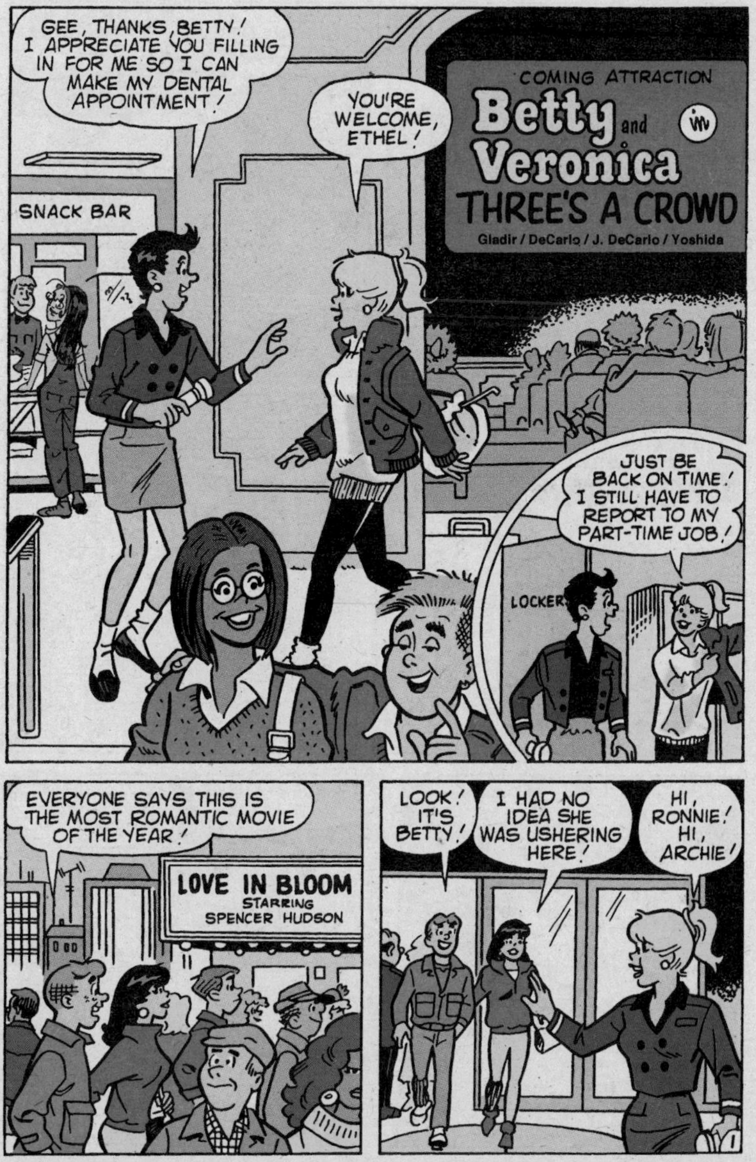
GEE, THANKS, BETTY! I APPRECIATE YOU FILLING IN FOR ME SO I CAN MAKE MY DENTAL APPOINTMENT!
YOU'RE WELCOME, ETHEL!
COMING ATTRACTION
Betty and Veronica
THREE'S A CROWD
Gladir / DeCarlo / J. DeCarlo / Yoshida
SNACK BAR
JUST BE BACK ON TIME! I STILL HAVE TO REPORT TO MY PART-TIME JOB!
LOCKER
EVERYONE SAYS THIS IS THE MOST ROMANTIC MOVIE OF THE YEAR!
LOVE IN BLOOM
STARRING
SPENCER HUDSON
LOOK! IT'S BETTY!
I HAD NO IDEA SHE WAS USHERING HERE!
HI, RONNIE! HI, ARCHIE!

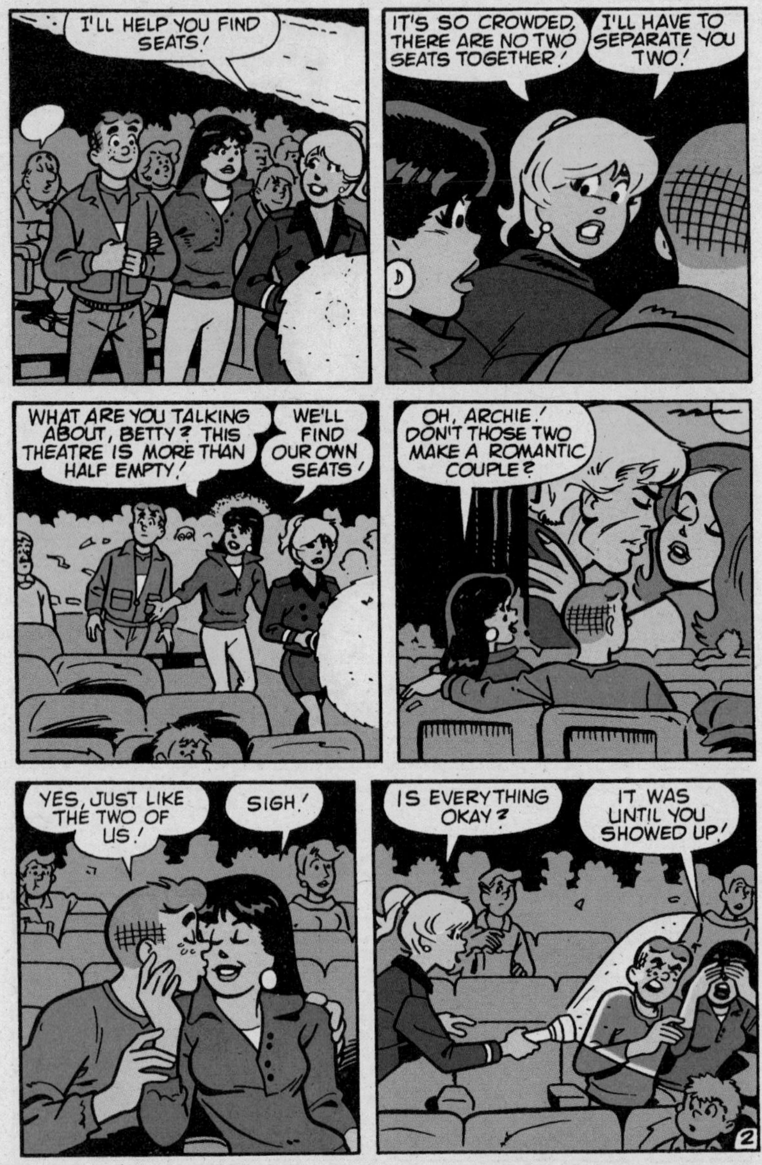
I'LL HELP YOU FIND SEATS!
IT'S SO CROWDED, THERE ARE NO TWO SEATS TOGETHER!
I'LL HAVE TO SEPARATE YOU TWO!
WHAT ARE YOU TALKING ABOUT, BETTY? THIS THEATRE IS MORE THAN HALF EMPTY!
WE'LL FIND OUR OWN SEATS!
OH, ARCHIE! DON'T THOSE TWO MAKE A ROMANTIC COUPLE?
YES, JUST LIKE THE TWO OF US!
SIGH!
IS EVERYTHING OKAY?
IT WAS UNTIL YOU SHOWED UP!
2

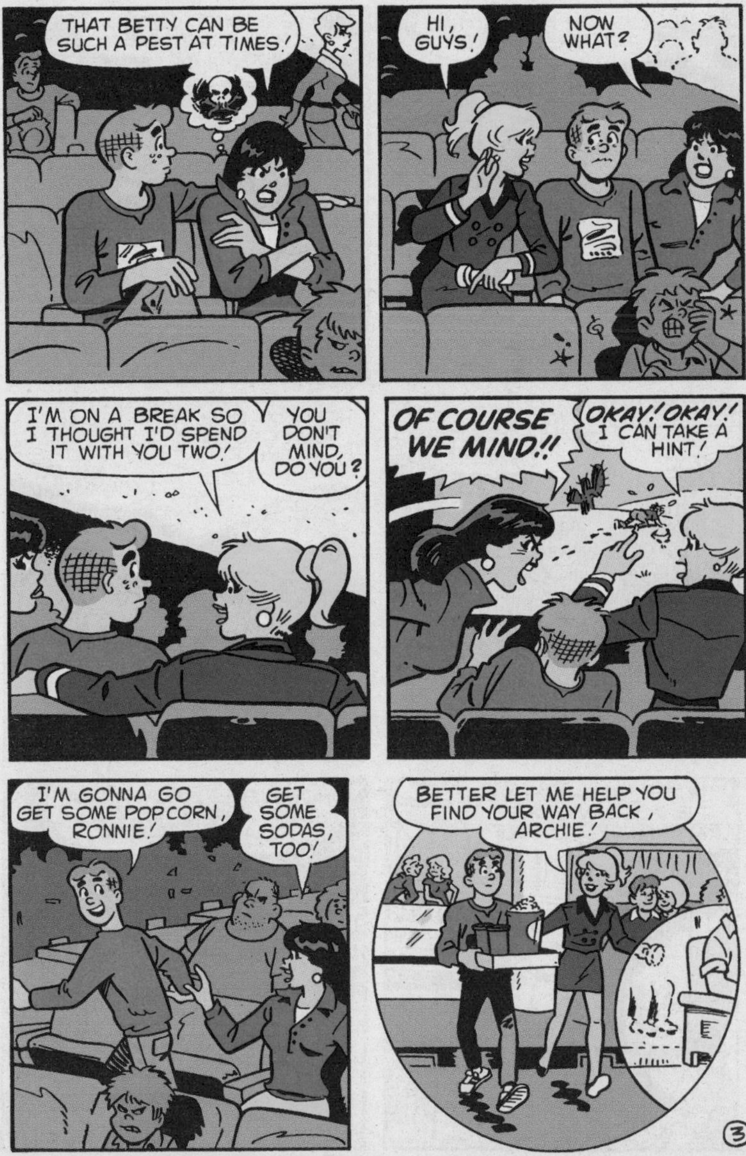
THAT BETTY CAN BE SUCH A PEST AT TIMES!
HI, GUYS!
NOW WHAT?
I'M ON A BREAK SO I THOUGHT I'D SPEND IT WITH YOU TWO!
YOU DON'T MIND, DO YOU?
OF COURSE WE MIND!!
OKAY! OKAY! I CAN TAKE A HINT!
I'M GONNA GO GET SOME POPCORN, RONNIE!
GET SOME SODAS, TOO!
BETTER LET ME HELP YOU FIND YOUR WAY BACK, ARCHIE!

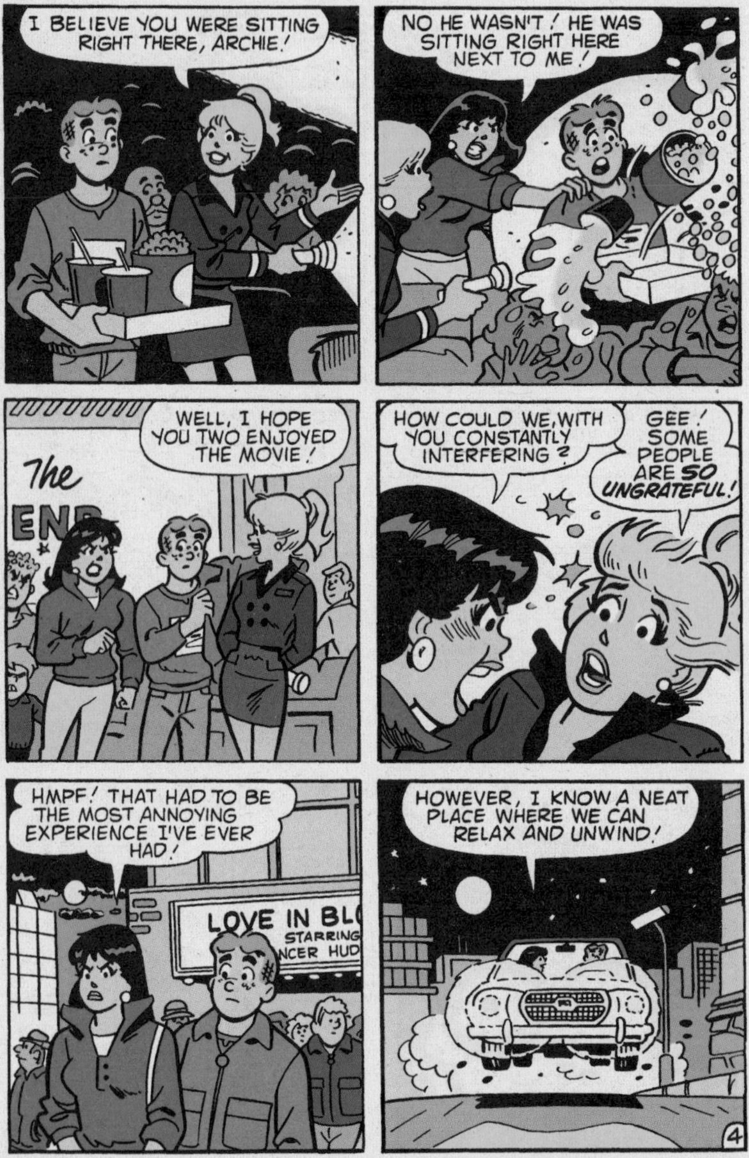
I BELIEVE YOU WERE SITTING RIGHT THERE, ARCHIE!
NO HE WASN'T! HE WAS SITTING RIGHT HERE NEXT TO ME!
WELL, I HOPE YOU TWO ENJOYED THE MOVIE!
The END
HOW COULD WE, WITH YOU CONSTANTLY INTERFERING?
GEE! SOME PEOPLE ARE SO UNGRATEFUL!
HMPF! THAT HAD TO BE THE MOST ANNOYING EXPERIENCE I'VE EVER HAD!
LOVE IN BL
STARRING
NCER HUD
HOWEVER, I KNOW A NEAT PLACE WHERE WE CAN RELAX AND UNWIND!
4

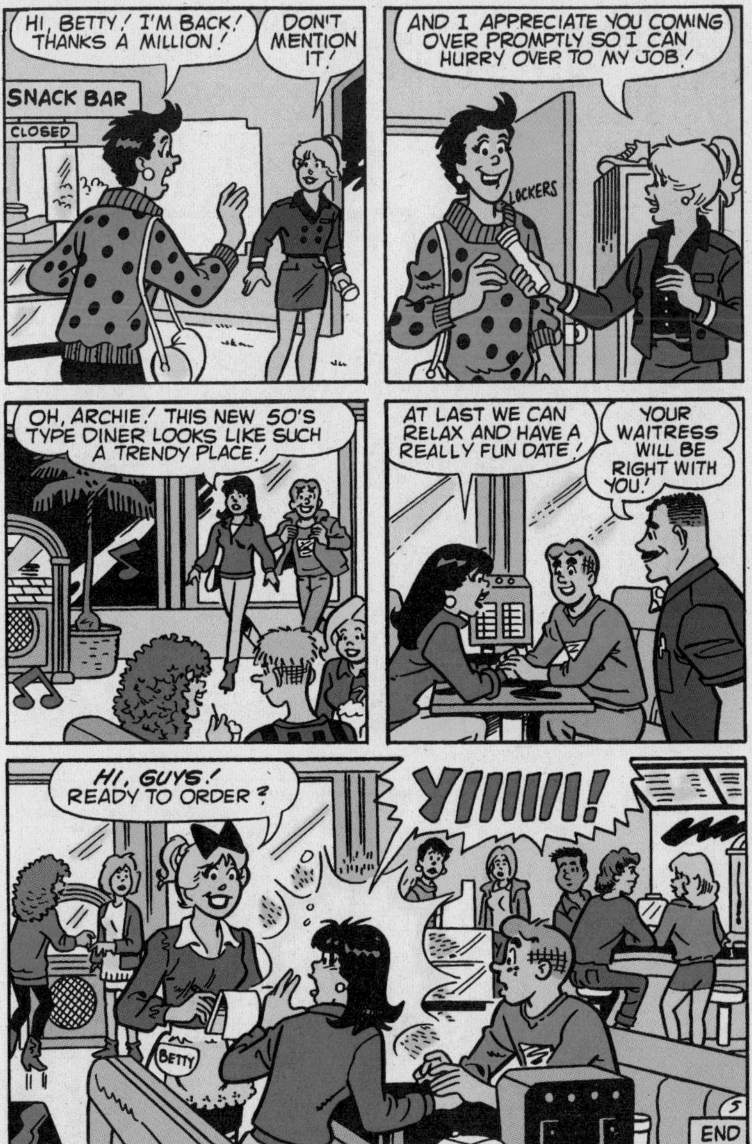

SNACK BAR
CLOSED
HI, BETTY! I'M BACK! THANKS A MILLION!
DON'T MENTION IT!
AND I APPRECIATE YOU COMING OVER PROMPTLY SO I CAN HURRY OVER TO MY JOB!
LOCKERS
OH, ARCHIE! THIS NEW 50'S TYPE DINER LOOKS LIKE SUCH A TRENDY PLACE!
AT LAST WE CAN RELAX AND HAVE A REALLY FUN DATE!
YOUR WAITRESS WILL BE RIGHT WITH YOU!
HI, GUYS! READY TO ORDER?
YIIIII!
BETTY
5
END

Betty and Veronica in Famous Name Game

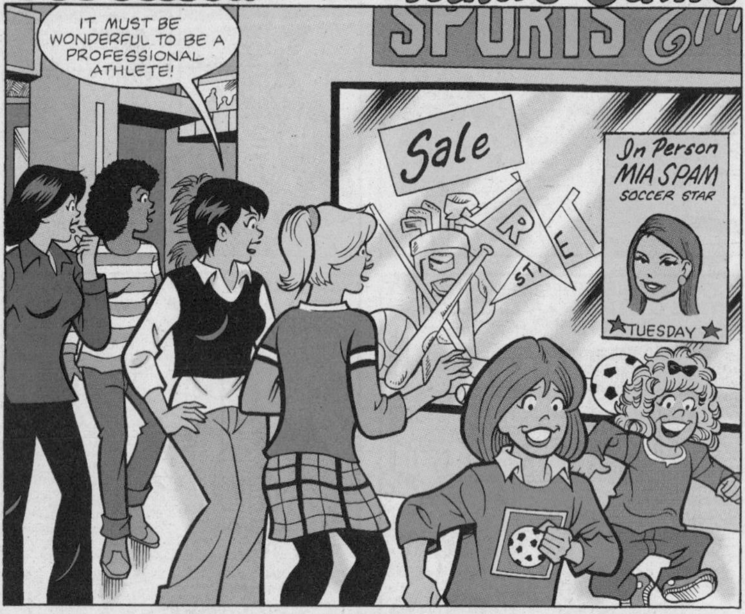
IT MUST BE WONDERFUL TO BE A PROFESSIONAL ATHLETE!
SPORTS
Sale
In Person
MIA SPAM
SOCCER STAR
TUESDAY

Script: MIKE PELLOWSKI   Pencils: JEFF SHULTZ   Inks: AL NICKERSON

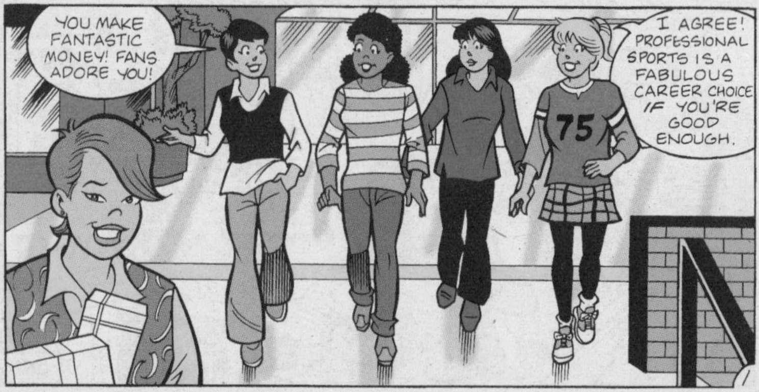
YOU MAKE FANTASTIC MONEY! FANS ADORE YOU!
I AGREE! PROFESSIONAL SPORTS IS A FABULOUS CAREER CHOICE IF YOU'RE GOOD ENOUGH.
75
1

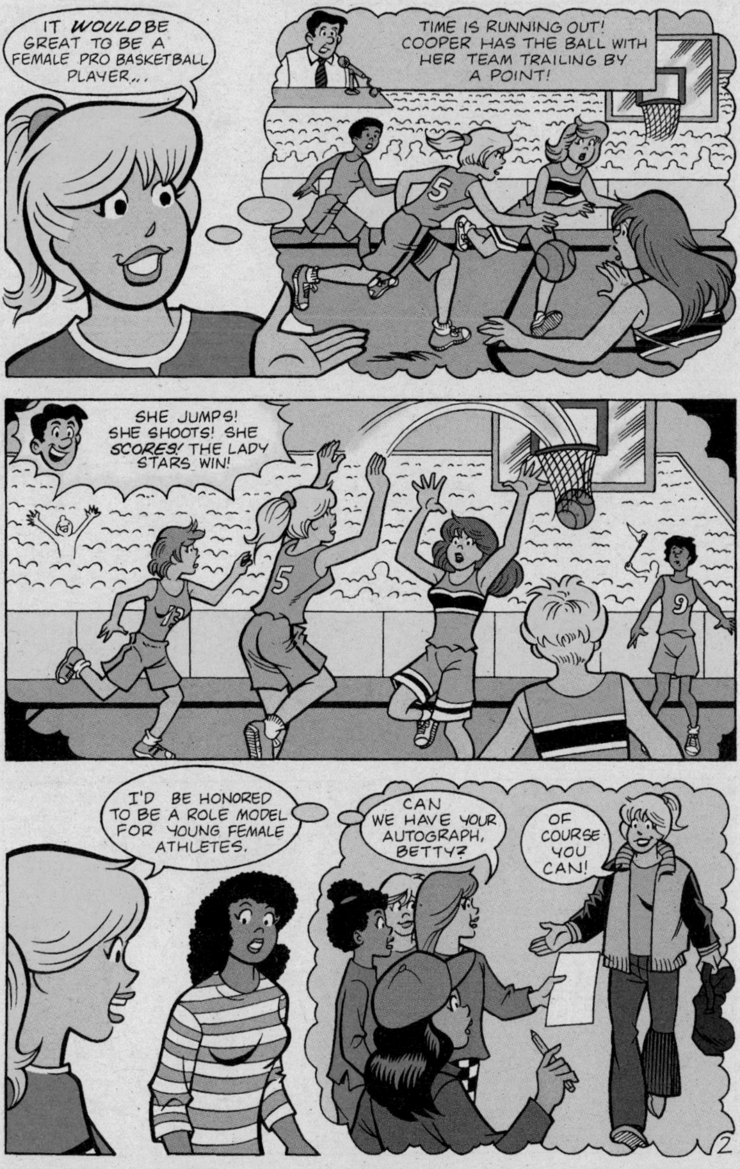
IT WOULD BE GREAT TO BE A FEMALE PRO BASKETBALL PLAYER...
TIME IS RUNNING OUT! COOPER HAS THE BALL WITH HER TEAM TRAILING BY A POINT!
SHE JUMPS! SHE SHOOTS! SHE SCORES! THE LADY STARS WIN!
I'D BE HONORED TO BE A ROLE MODEL FOR YOUNG FEMALE ATHLETES.
CAN WE HAVE YOUR AUTOGRAPH, BETTY?
OF COURSE YOU CAN!
2

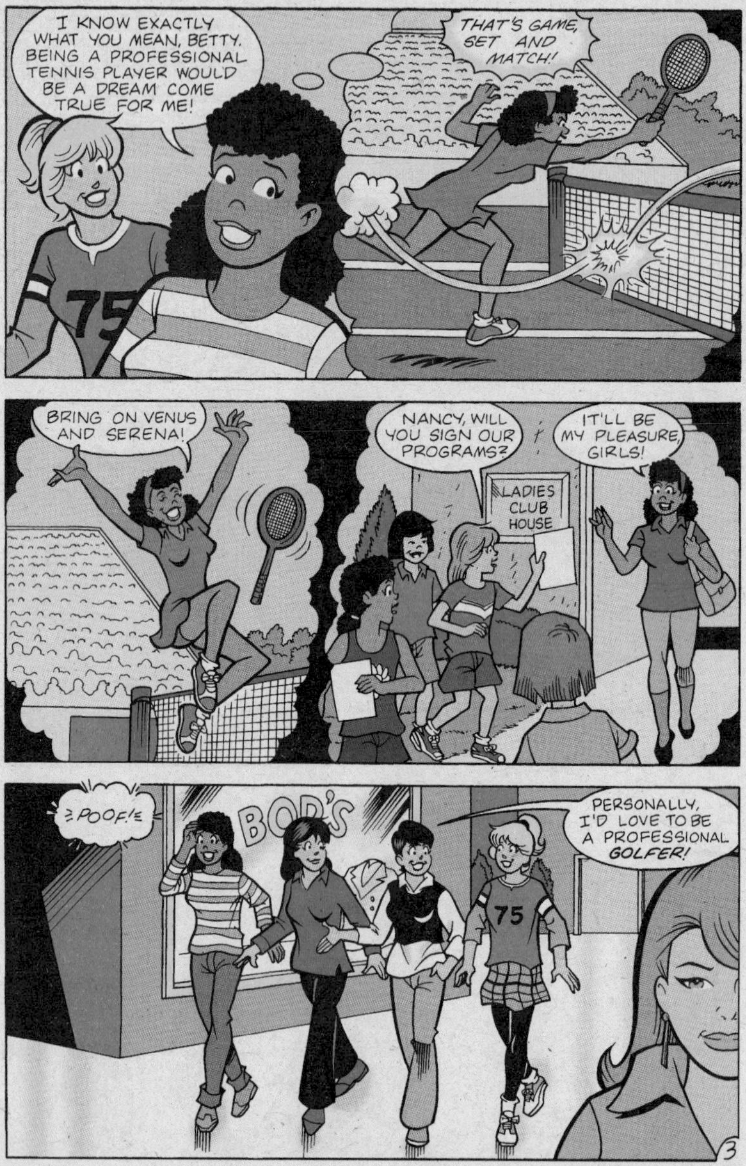

I KNOW EXACTLY WHAT YOU MEAN, BETTY. BEING A PROFESSIONAL TENNIS PLAYER WOULD BE A DREAM COME TRUE FOR ME!
THAT'S GAME, SET AND MATCH!
75
BRING ON VENUS AND SERENA!
NANCY, WILL YOU SIGN OUR PROGRAMS?
IT'LL BE MY PLEASURE, GIRLS!
LADIES CLUB HOUSE
POOF!
BOB'S
PERSONALLY, I'D LOVE TO BE A PROFESSIONAL *GOLFER!*
75

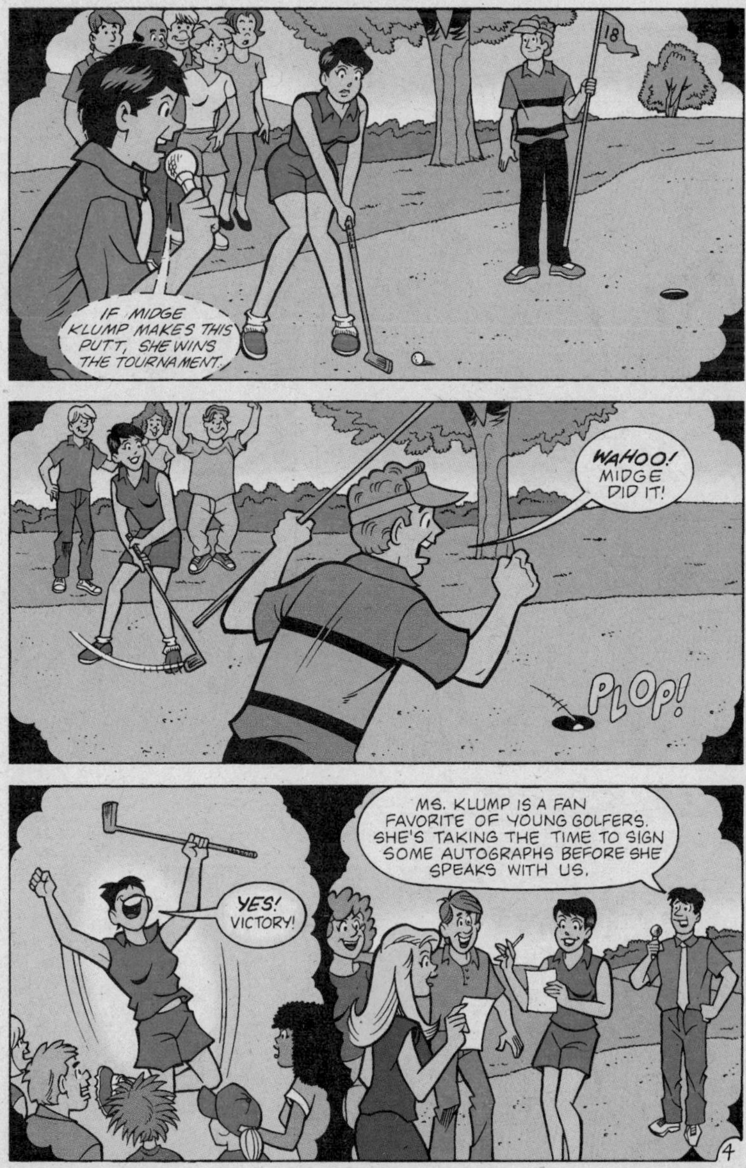

IF MIDGE KLUMP MAKES THIS PUTT, SHE WINS THE TOURNAMENT.
WAHOO! MIDGE DID IT!
PLOP!
YES! VICTORY!
MS. KLUMP IS A FAN FAVORITE OF YOUNG GOLFERS. SHE'S TAKING THE TIME TO SIGN SOME AUTOGRAPHS BEFORE SHE SPEAKS WITH US.
4

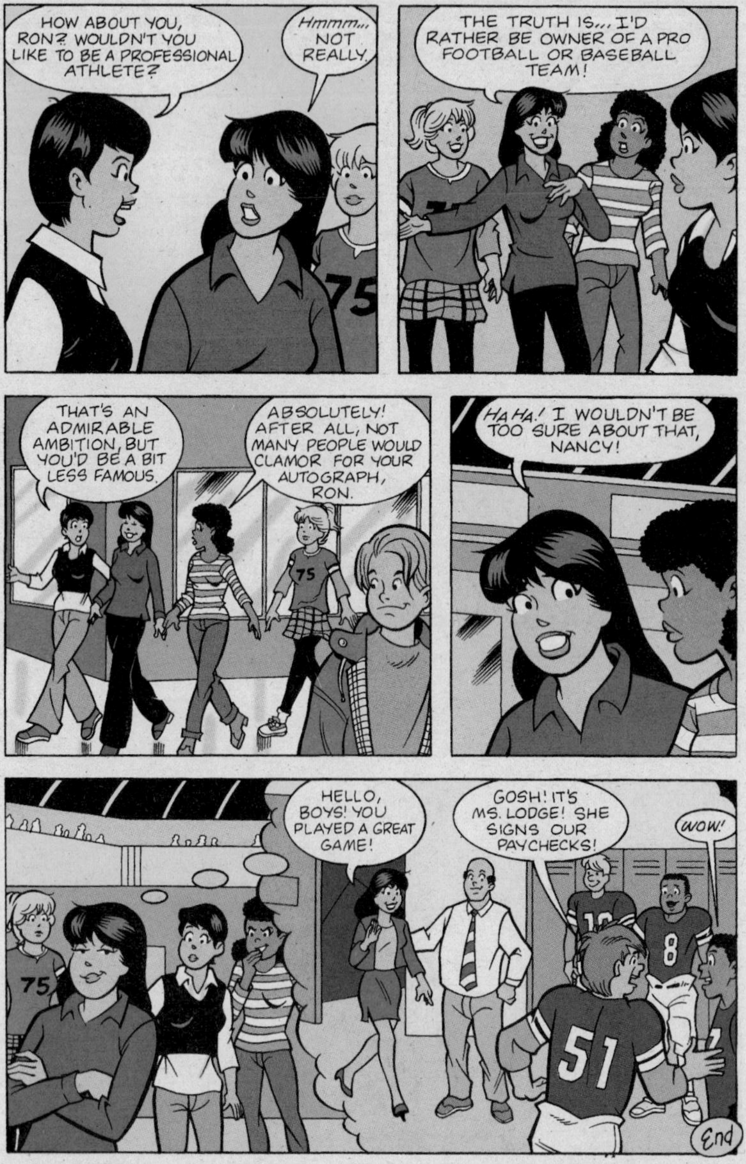

HOW ABOUT YOU, RON? WOULDN'T YOU LIKE TO BE A PROFESSIONAL ATHLETE?
Hmmm... NOT REALLY.
THE TRUTH IS... I'D RATHER BE OWNER OF A PRO FOOTBALL OR BASEBALL TEAM!
THAT'S AN ADMIRABLE AMBITION, BUT YOU'D BE A BIT LESS FAMOUS.
ABSOLUTELY! AFTER ALL, NOT MANY PEOPLE WOULD CLAMOR FOR YOUR AUTOGRAPH, RON.
HA HA! I WOULDN'T BE TOO SURE ABOUT THAT, NANCY!
HELLO, BOYS! YOU PLAYED A GREAT GAME!
GOSH! IT'S MS. LODGE! SHE SIGNS OUR PAYCHECKS!
WOW!
End

Veronica in "The Sound of Music?"

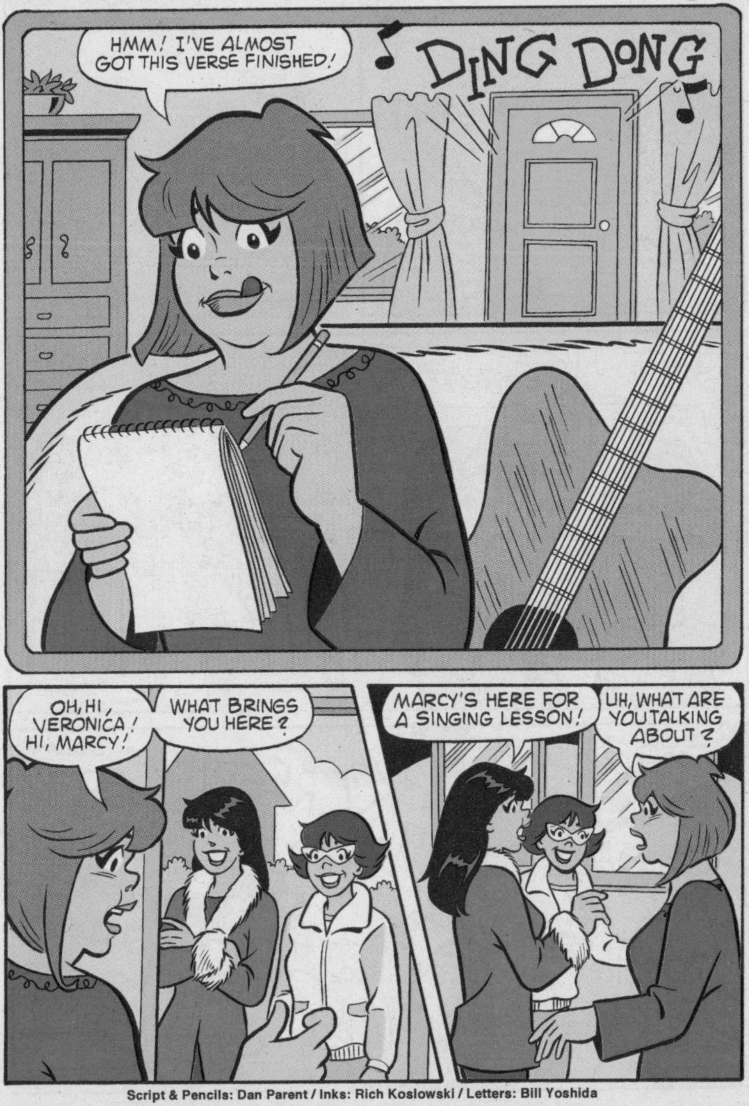
HMM! I'VE ALMOST GOT THIS VERSE FINISHED!
DING DONG
OH, HI, VERONICA! HI, MARCY!
WHAT BRINGS YOU HERE?
MARCY'S HERE FOR A SINGING LESSON!
UH, WHAT ARE YOU TALKING ABOUT?

Script & Pencils: Dan Parent / Inks: Rich Koslowski / Letters: Bill Yoshida

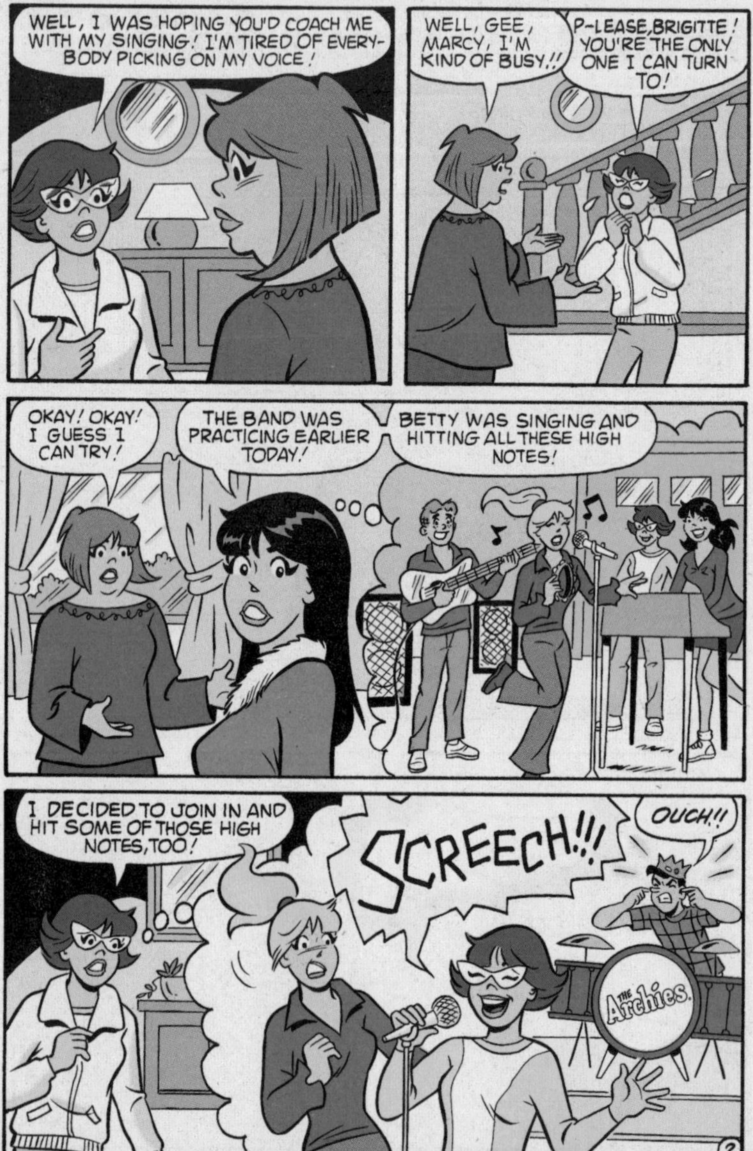
WELL, I WAS HOPING YOU'D COACH ME WITH MY SINGING! I'M TIRED OF EVERY-BODY PICKING ON MY VOICE!
WELL, GEE, MARCY, I'M KIND OF BUSY!!
P-LEASE, BRIGITTE! YOU'RE THE ONLY ONE I CAN TURN TO!
OKAY! OKAY! I GUESS I CAN TRY!
THE BAND WAS PRACTICING EARLIER TODAY!
BETTY WAS SINGING AND HITTING ALL THESE HIGH NOTES!
I DECIDED TO JOIN IN AND HIT SOME OF THOSE HIGH NOTES, TOO!
SCREECH!!!
OUCH!!
THE Archies
2

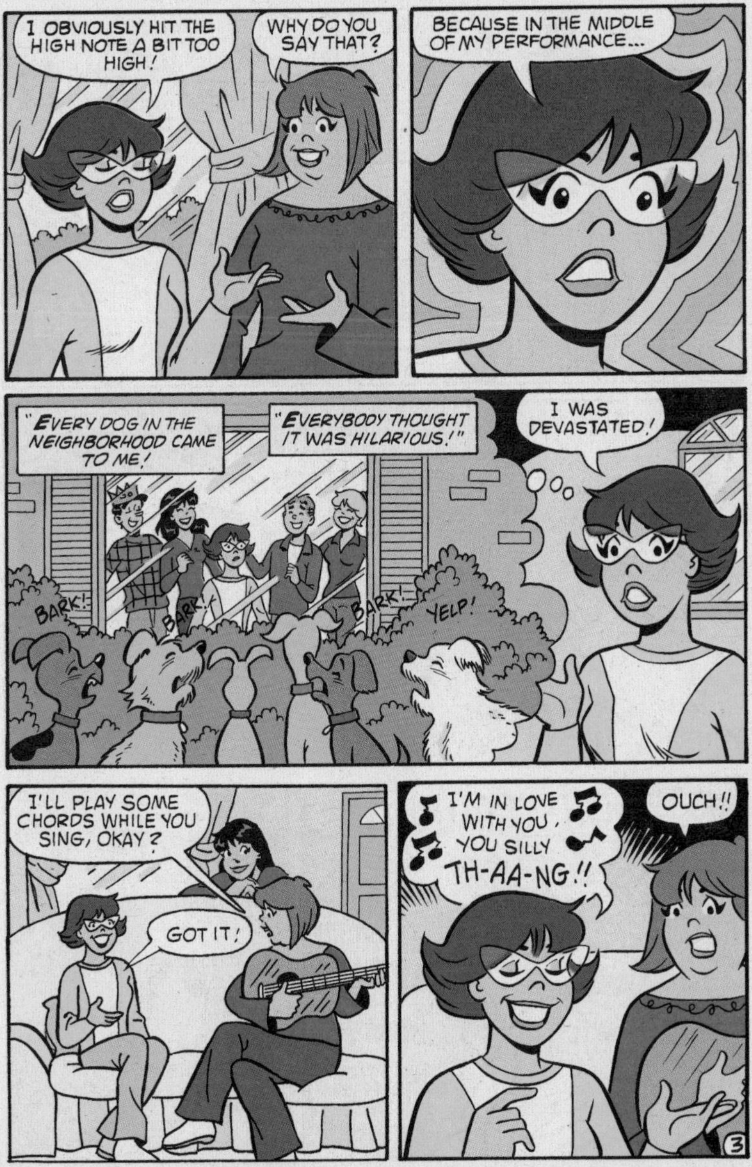

I OBVIOUSLY HIT THE HIGH NOTE A BIT TOO HIGH!
WHY DO YOU SAY THAT?
BECAUSE IN THE MIDDLE OF MY PERFORMANCE...
"EVERY DOG IN THE NEIGHBORHOOD CAME TO ME!
"EVERYBODY THOUGHT IT WAS HILARIOUS!"
I WAS DEVASTATED!
BARK!
BARK!
BARK!
YELP!
I'LL PLAY SOME CHORDS WHILE YOU SING, OKAY?
GOT IT!
I'M IN LOVE WITH YOU, YOU SILLY TH-AA-NG!!
OUCH!!
3

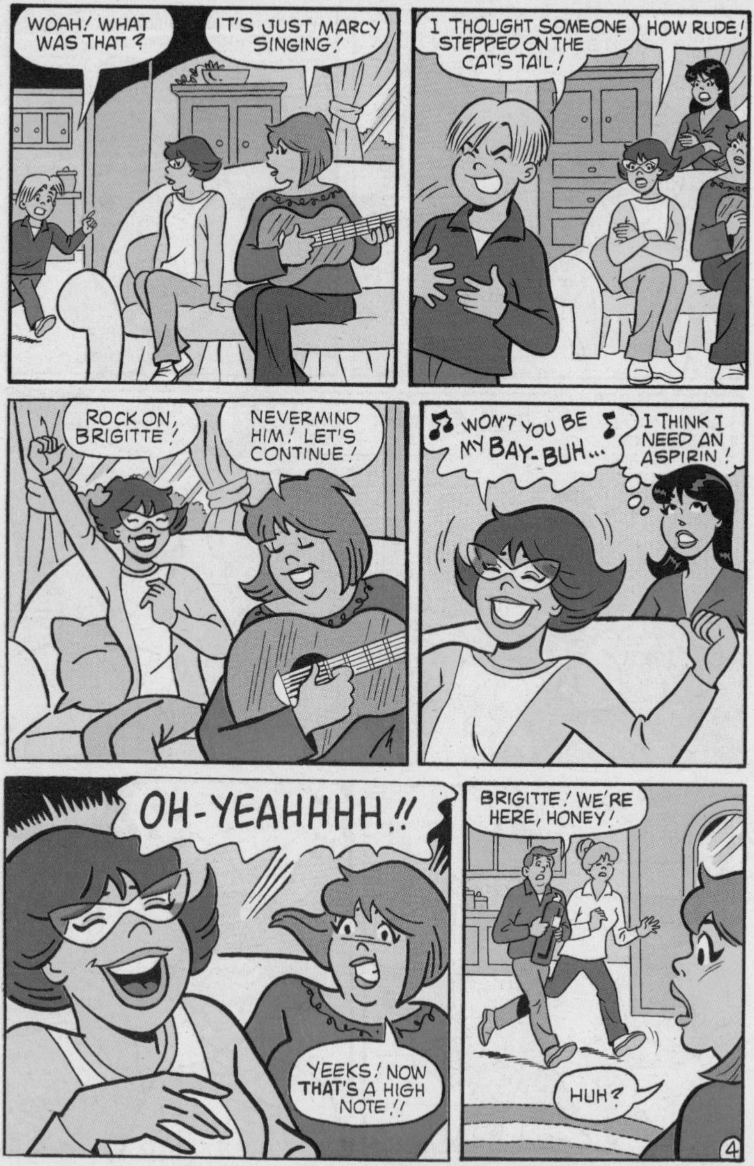
WOAH! WHAT WAS THAT?
IT'S JUST MARCY SINGING!
I THOUGHT SOMEONE STEPPED ON THE CAT'S TAIL!
HOW RUDE!
ROCK ON, BRIGITTE!
NEVERMIND HIM! LET'S CONTINUE!
WON'T YOU BE MY BAY-BUH...
I THINK I NEED AN ASPIRIN!
OH-YEAHHHH!!
YEEKS! NOW THAT'S A HIGH NOTE!!
BRIGITTE! WE'RE HERE, HONEY!
HUH?
4

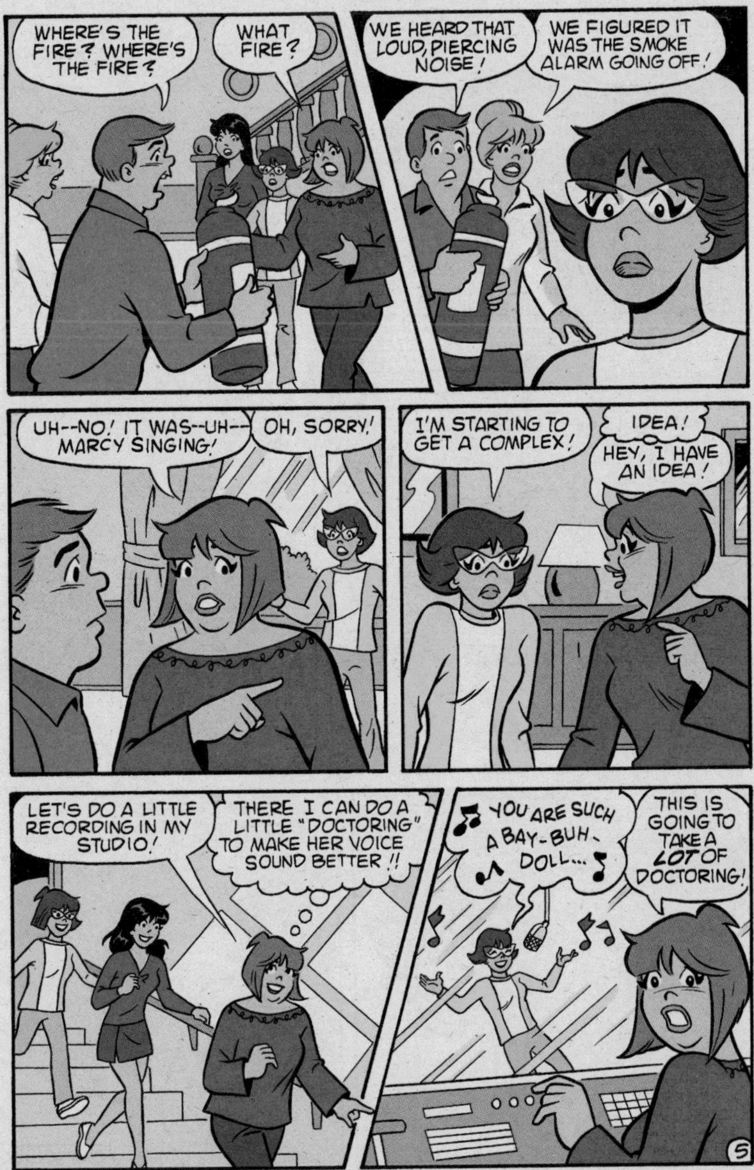
WHERE'S THE FIRE? WHERE'S THE FIRE?
WHAT FIRE?
WE HEARD THAT LOUD, PIERCING NOISE!
WE FIGURED IT WAS THE SMOKE ALARM GOING OFF!
UH--NO! IT WAS--UH-- MARCY SINGING!
OH, SORRY!
I'M STARTING TO GET A COMPLEX!
IDEA!
HEY, I HAVE AN IDEA!
LET'S DO A LITTLE RECORDING IN MY STUDIO!
THERE I CAN DO A LITTLE "DOCTORING" TO MAKE HER VOICE SOUND BETTER!!
YOU ARE SUCH A BAY-BUH-DOLL...
THIS IS GOING TO TAKE A LOT OF DOCTORING!
5

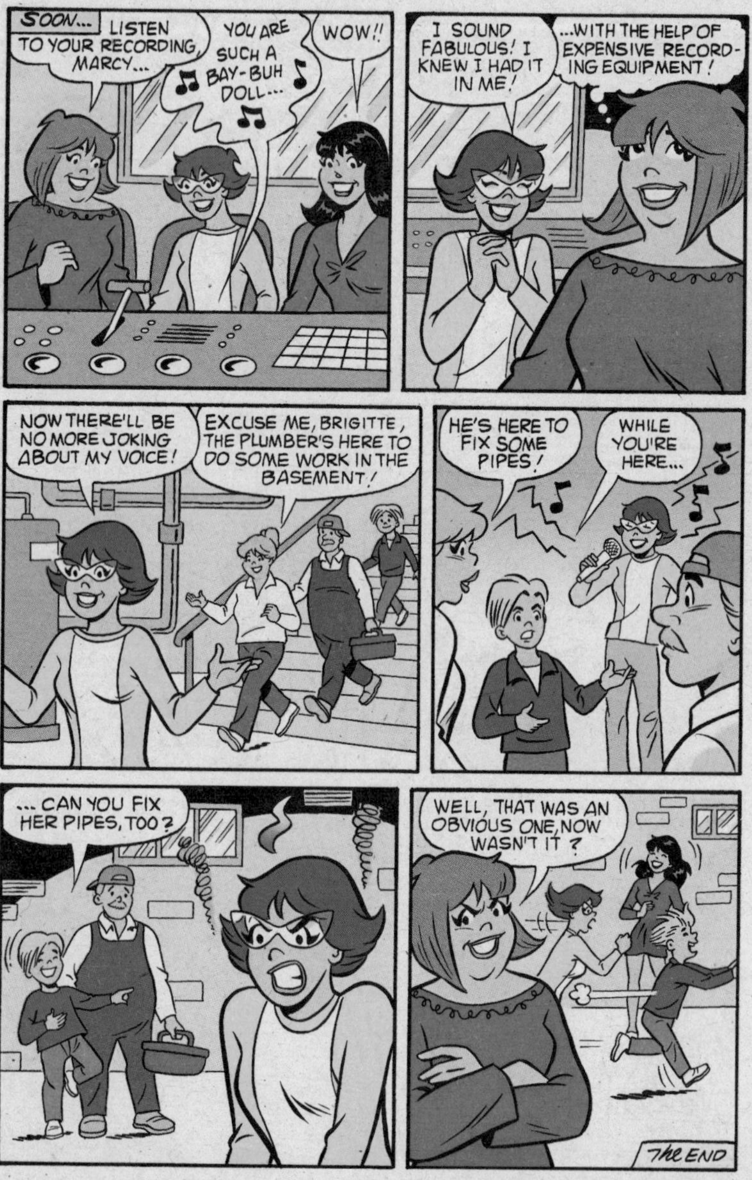
SOON...
LISTEN TO YOUR RECORDING, MARCY...
YOU ARE SUCH A BAY-BUH DOLL...
WOW!!
I SOUND FABULOUS! I KNEW I HAD IT IN ME!
...WITH THE HELP OF EXPENSIVE RECORDING EQUIPMENT!
NOW THERE'LL BE NO MORE JOKING ABOUT MY VOICE!
EXCUSE ME, BRIGITTE, THE PLUMBER'S HERE TO DO SOME WORK IN THE BASEMENT!
HE'S HERE TO FIX SOME PIPES!
WHILE YOU'RE HERE...
... CAN YOU FIX HER PIPES, TOO?
WELL, THAT WAS AN OBVIOUS ONE, NOW WASN'T IT?
THE END

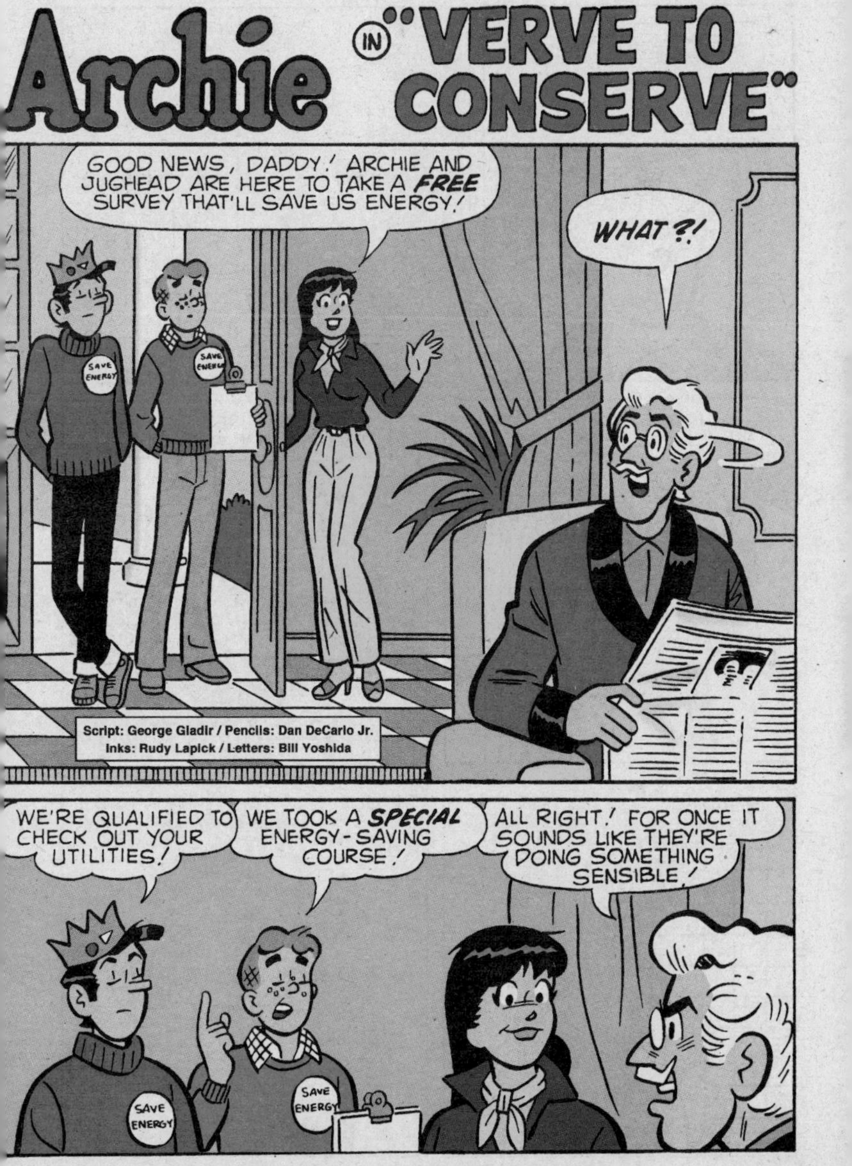
Archie
IN "VERVE TO CONSERVE"
GOOD NEWS, DADDY! ARCHIE AND JUGHEAD ARE HERE TO TAKE A FREE SURVEY THAT'LL SAVE US ENERGY!
WHAT?!
SAVE ENERGY
SAVE ENERGY
Script: George Gladir / Pencils: Dan DeCarlo Jr.
Inks: Rudy Lapick / Letters: Bill Yoshida
WE'RE QUALIFIED TO CHECK OUT YOUR UTILITIES!
WE TOOK A SPECIAL ENERGY-SAVING COURSE!
ALL RIGHT! FOR ONCE IT SOUNDS LIKE THEY'RE DOING SOMETHING SENSIBLE!
SAVE ENERGY
SAVE ENERGY

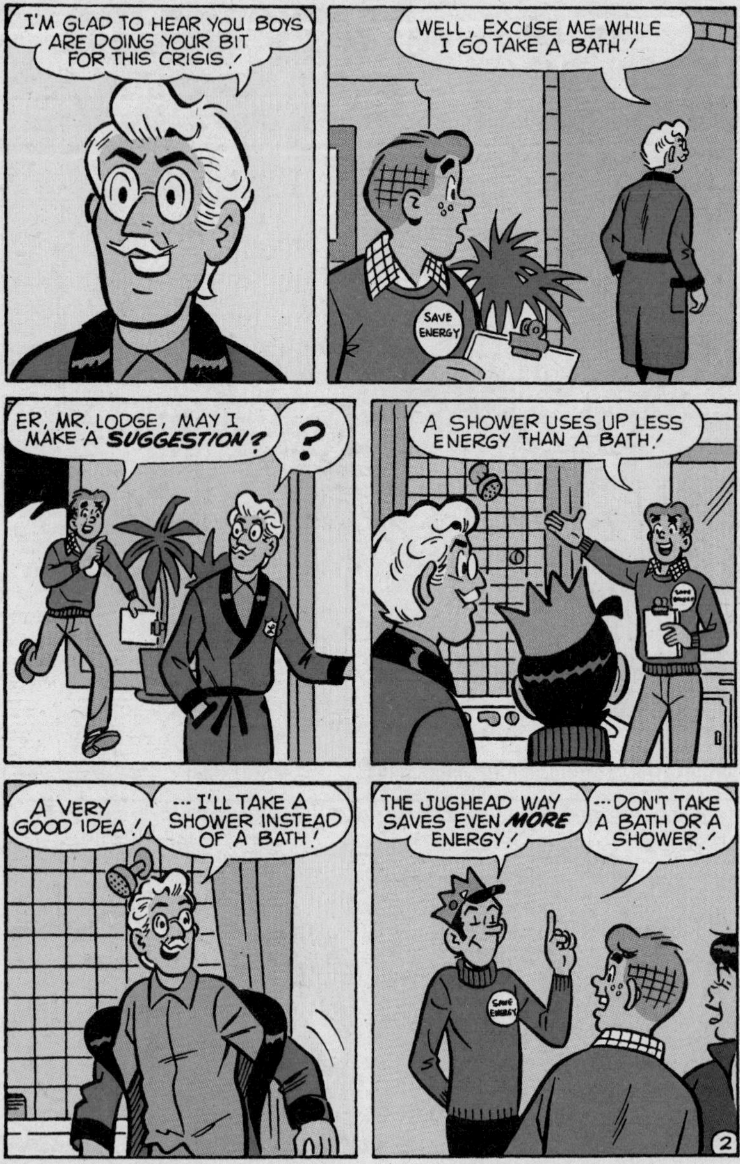

I'M GLAD TO HEAR YOU BOYS ARE DOING YOUR BIT FOR THIS CRISIS!
WELL, EXCUSE ME WHILE I GO TAKE A BATH!
SAVE ENERGY
ER, MR. LODGE, MAY I MAKE A SUGGESTION?
?
A SHOWER USES UP LESS ENERGY THAN A BATH!
A VERY GOOD IDEA!
--- I'LL TAKE A SHOWER INSTEAD OF A BATH!
THE JUGHEAD WAY SAVES EVEN MORE ENERGY!
--- DON'T TAKE A BATH OR A SHOWER!
2

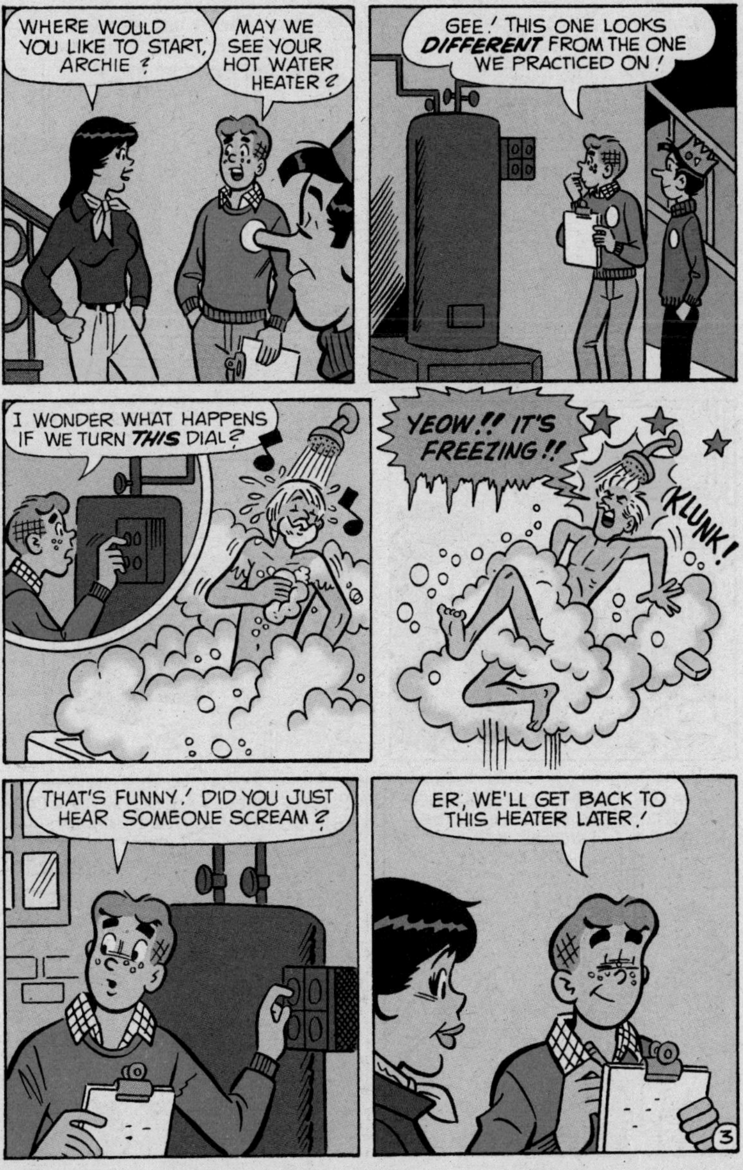

WHERE WOULD YOU LIKE TO START, ARCHIE ?
MAY WE SEE YOUR HOT WATER HEATER ?
GEE! THIS ONE LOOKS DIFFERENT FROM THE ONE WE PRACTICED ON!
I WONDER WHAT HAPPENS IF WE TURN THIS DIAL?
YEOW!! IT'S FREEZING!!
KLUNK!
THAT'S FUNNY! DID YOU JUST HEAR SOMEONE SCREAM ?
ER, WE'LL GET BACK TO THIS HEATER LATER!
3

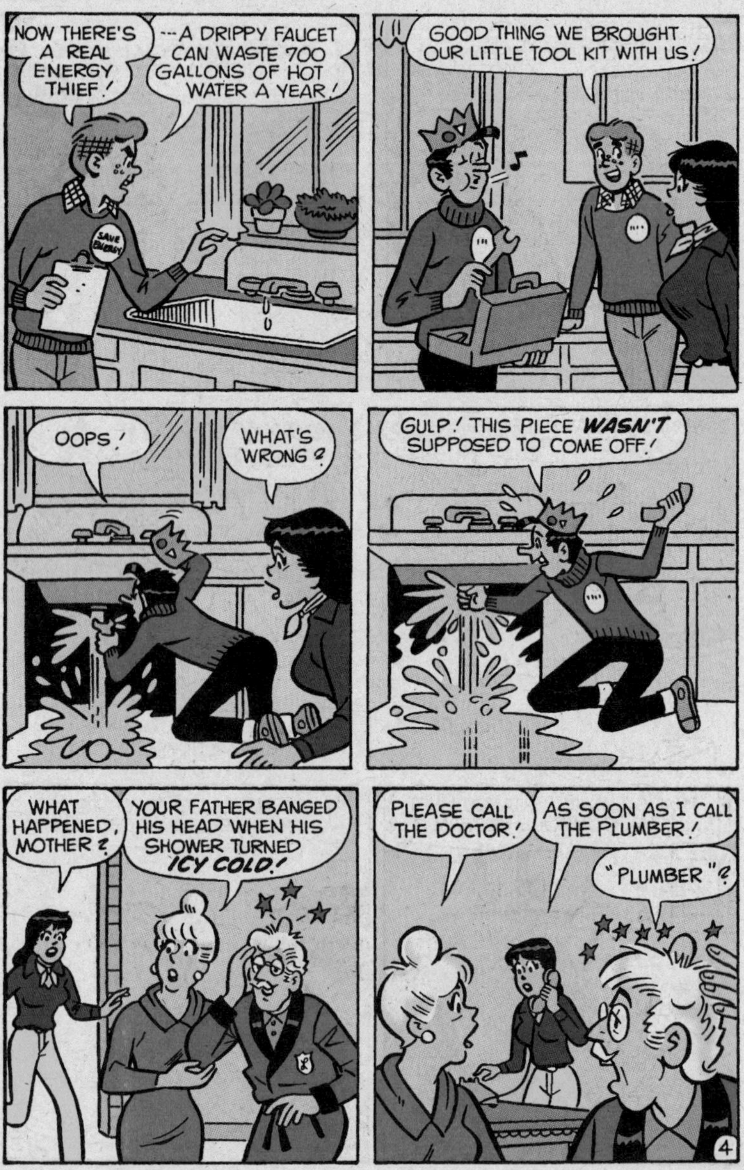
NOW THERE'S A REAL ENERGY THIEF!
---A DRIPPY FAUCET CAN WASTE 700 GALLONS OF HOT WATER A YEAR!
SAVE ENERGY
GOOD THING WE BROUGHT OUR LITTLE TOOL KIT WITH US!
OOPS!
WHAT'S WRONG?
GULP! THIS PIECE WASN'T SUPPOSED TO COME OFF!
WHAT HAPPENED, MOTHER?
YOUR FATHER BANGED HIS HEAD WHEN HIS SHOWER TURNED ICY COLD!
PLEASE CALL THE DOCTOR!
AS SOON AS I CALL THE PLUMBER!
"PLUMBER"?
4

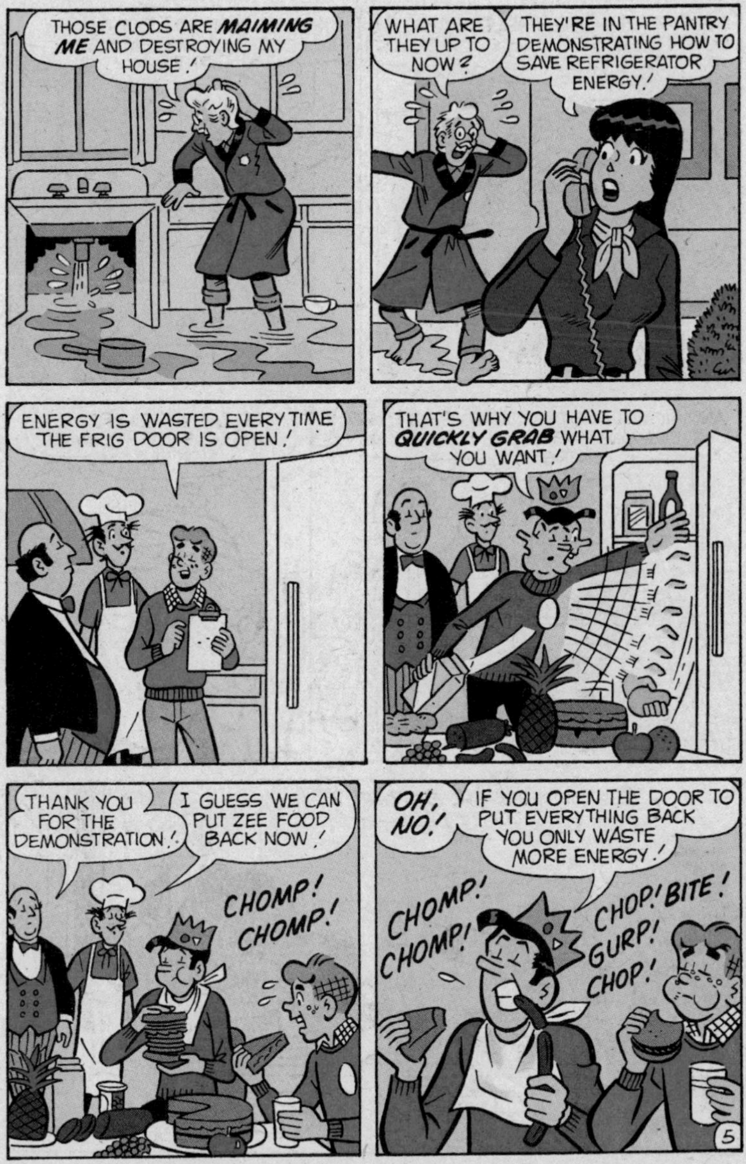
THOSE CLODS ARE MAIMING ME AND DESTROYING MY HOUSE!
WHAT ARE THEY UP TO NOW?
THEY'RE IN THE PANTRY DEMONSTRATING HOW TO SAVE REFRIGERATOR ENERGY!
ENERGY IS WASTED EVERY TIME THE FRIG DOOR IS OPEN!
THAT'S WHY YOU HAVE TO QUICKLY GRAB WHAT YOU WANT!
THANK YOU FOR THE DEMONSTRATION!
I GUESS WE CAN PUT ZEE FOOD BACK NOW!
CHOMP! CHOMP!
OH, NO!
IF YOU OPEN THE DOOR TO PUT EVERYTHING BACK YOU ONLY WASTE MORE ENERGY!
CHOMP! CHOMP!
CHOP! BITE! GURP! CHOP!

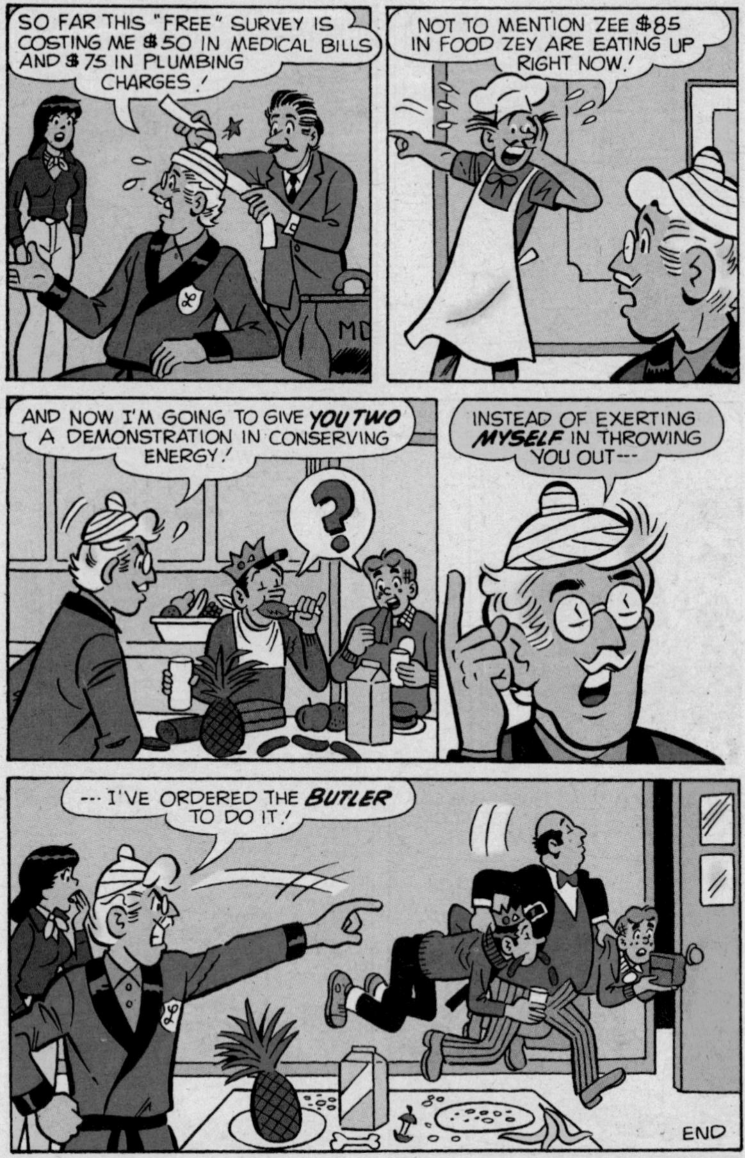
SO FAR THIS "FREE" SURVEY IS COSTING ME $50 IN MEDICAL BILLS AND $75 IN PLUMBING CHARGES!
MD
NOT TO MENTION ZEE $85 IN FOOD ZEY ARE EATING UP RIGHT NOW!
AND NOW I'M GOING TO GIVE YOU TWO A DEMONSTRATION IN CONSERVING ENERGY!
?
INSTEAD OF EXERTING MYSELF IN THROWING YOU OUT---
--- I'VE ORDERED THE BUTLER TO DO IT!
END

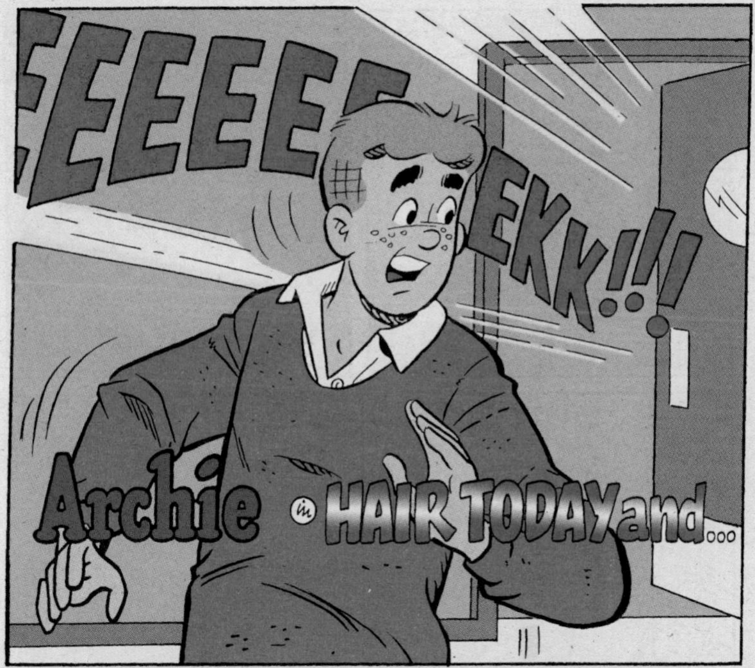
EEEEEEEEKK!!!
Archie in HAIR TODAY and...

Script: Mike Pellowski / Pencils: Tim Kennedy / Inks: Rudy Lapick / Letters: Bill Yoshida

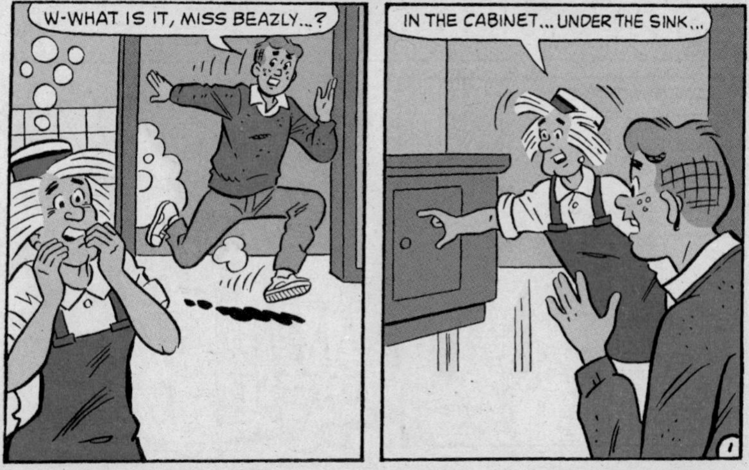
W-WHAT IS IT, MISS BEAZLY...?
IN THE CABINET... UNDER THE SINK...
1

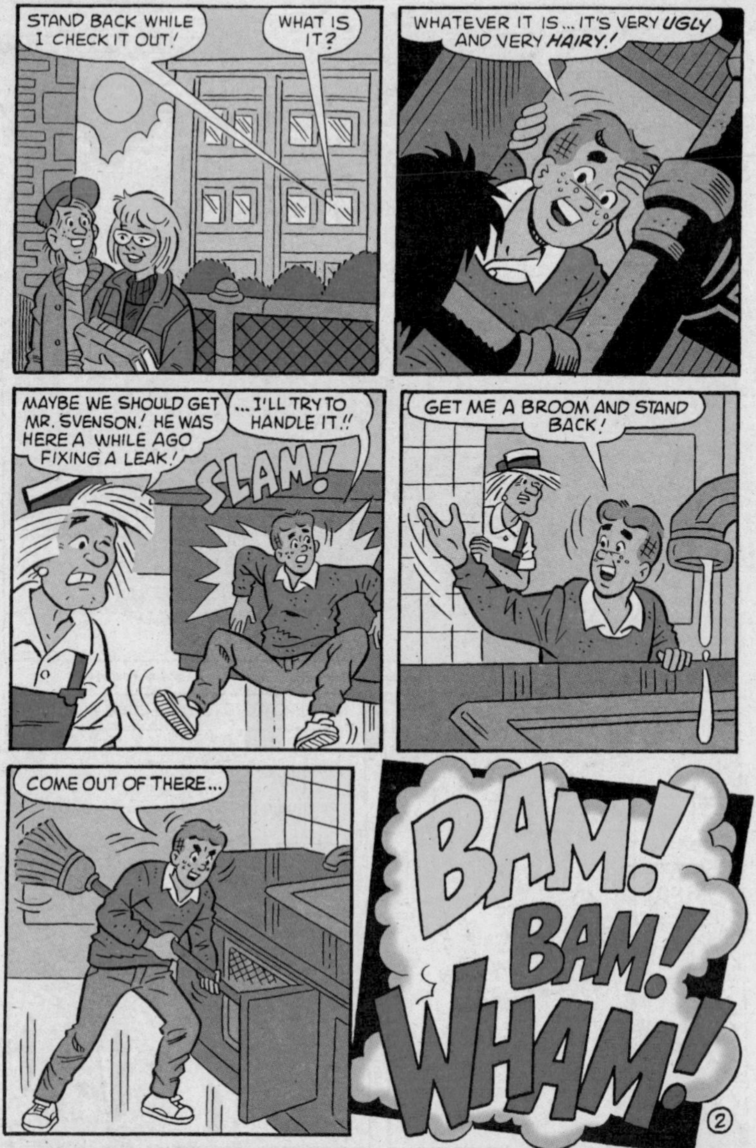
STAND BACK WHILE I CHECK IT OUT!
WHAT IS IT?
WHATEVER IT IS... IT'S VERY UGLY AND VERY HAIRY!
MAYBE WE SHOULD GET MR. SVENSON! HE WAS HERE A WHILE AGO FIXING A LEAK!
...I'LL TRY TO HANDLE IT.!!
SLAM!
GET ME A BROOM AND STAND BACK!
COME OUT OF THERE...
BAM! BAM! WHAM!
2

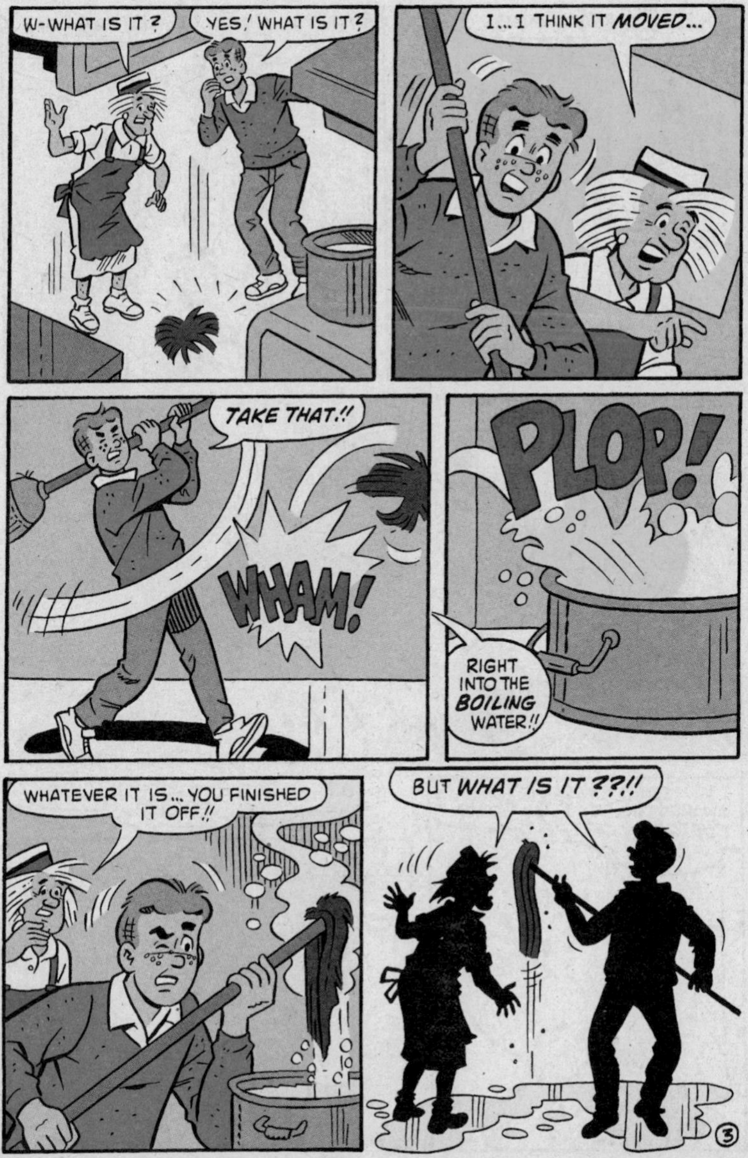
W-WHAT IS IT ?
YES! WHAT IS IT ?
I... I THINK IT MOVED...
TAKE THAT.!!
WHAM!
PLOP!
RIGHT INTO THE BOILING WATER!!
WHATEVER IT IS... YOU FINISHED IT OFF!!
BUT WHAT IS IT ??!!
3

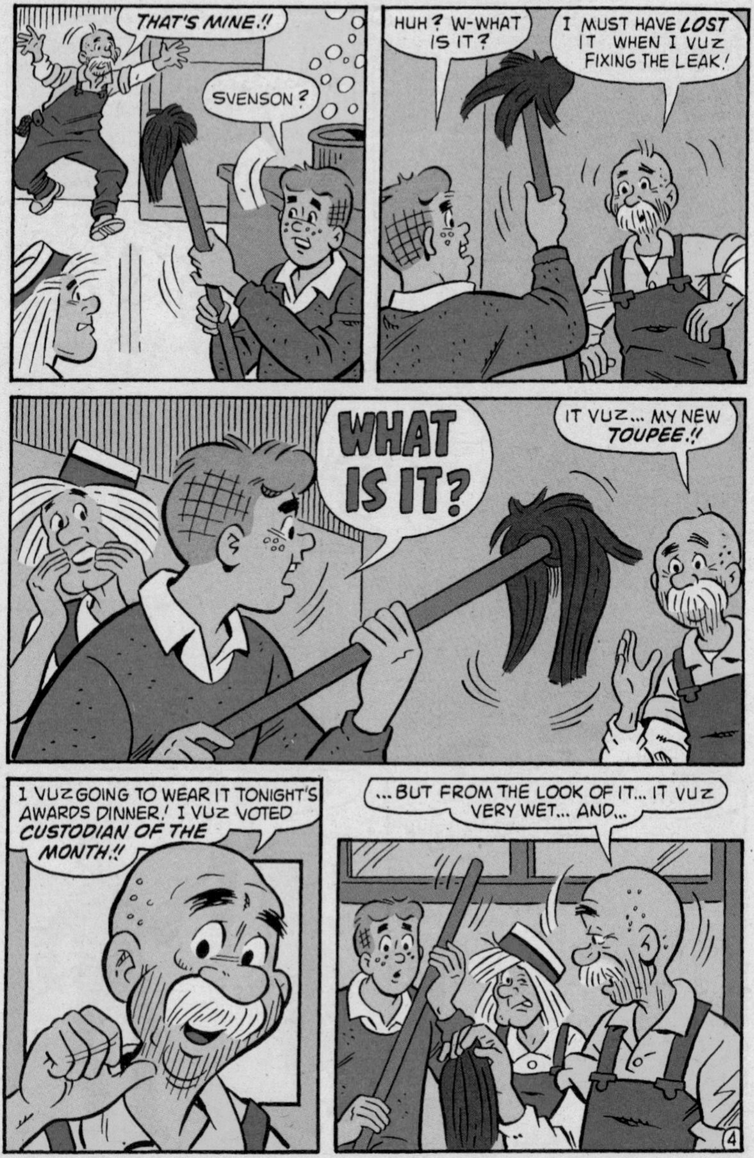
THAT'S MINE.!!
SVENSON?
HUH? W-WHAT IS IT?
I MUST HAVE LOST IT WHEN I VUZ FIXING THE LEAK!
WHAT IS IT?
IT VUZ... MY NEW TOUPEE.!!
I VUZ GOING TO WEAR IT TONIGHT'S AWARDS DINNER! I VUZ VOTED CUSTODIAN OF THE MONTH.!!
...BUT FROM THE LOOK OF IT... IT VUZ VERY WET... AND...
4

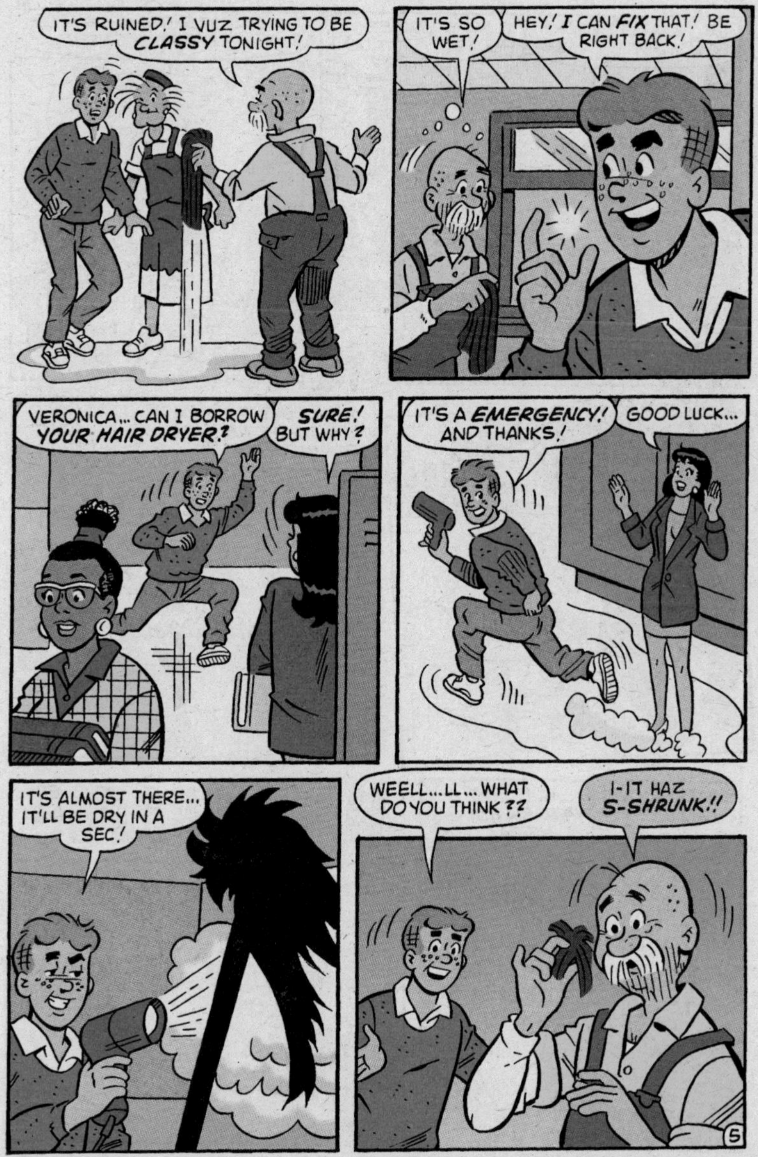
IT'S RUINED! I VUZ TRYING TO BE CLASSY TONIGHT!
IT'S SO WET!
HEY! I CAN FIX THAT! BE RIGHT BACK!
VERONICA... CAN I BORROW YOUR HAIR DRYER?
SURE! BUT WHY?
IT'S A EMERGENCY! AND THANKS!
GOOD LUCK...
IT'S ALMOST THERE... IT'LL BE DRY IN A SEC!
WEELL...LL... WHAT DO YOU THINK??
I-IT HAZ S-SHRUNK!!
5

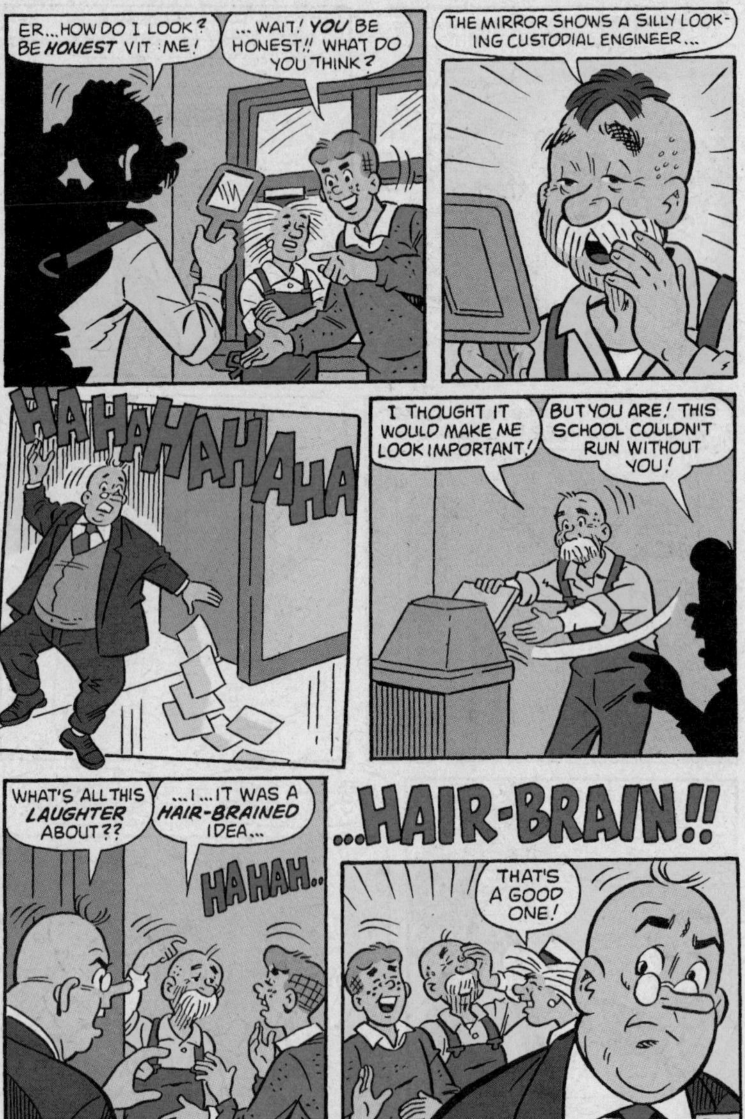
ER...HOW DO I LOOK? BE HONEST VIT ME!
...WAIT! YOU BE HONEST!! WHAT DO YOU THINK?
THE MIRROR SHOWS A SILLY LOOKING CUSTODIAL ENGINEER...
HAHAHAHAHAHAHA
I THOUGHT IT WOULD MAKE ME LOOK IMPORTANT!
BUT YOU ARE! THIS SCHOOL COULDN'T RUN WITHOUT YOU!
WHAT'S ALL THIS LAUGHTER ABOUT??
...I...IT WAS A HAIR-BRAINED IDEA...
HAHAH..
...HAIR-BRAIN!!
THAT'S A GOOD ONE!
END

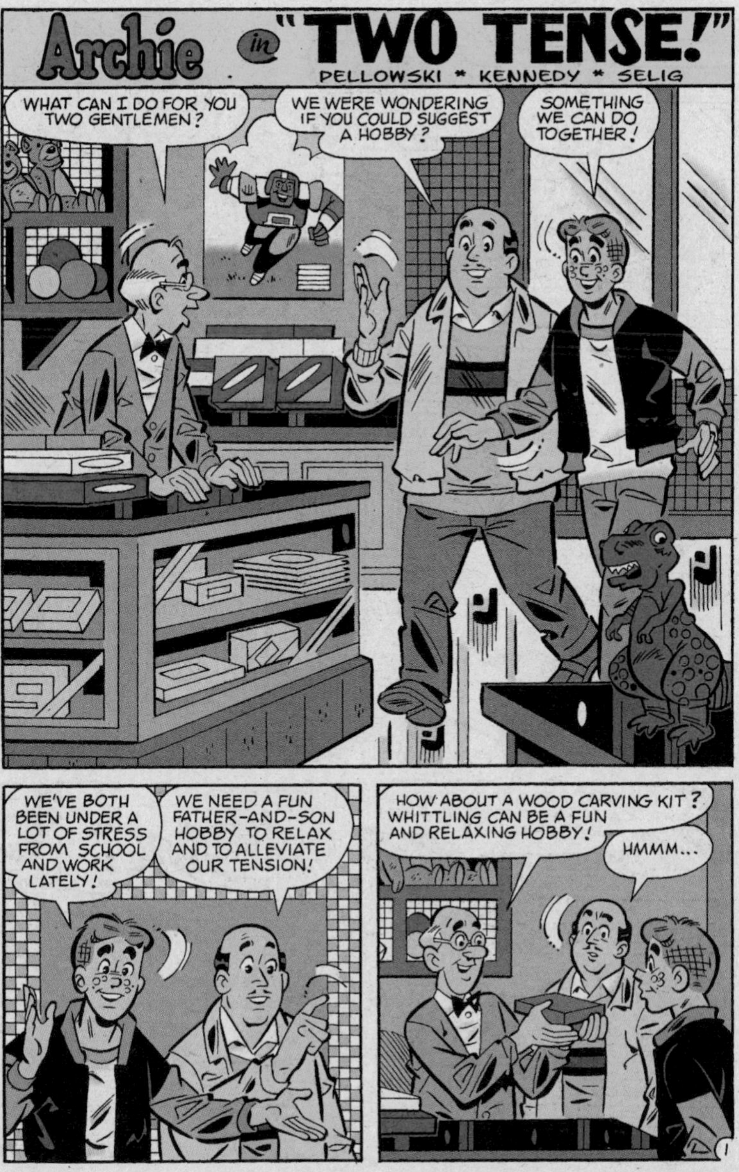
Archie in "TWO TENSE!"
PELLOWSKI * KENNEDY * SELIG
WHAT CAN I DO FOR YOU TWO GENTLEMEN?
WE WERE WONDERING IF YOU COULD SUGGEST A HOBBY?
SOMETHING WE CAN DO TOGETHER!
WE'VE BOTH BEEN UNDER A LOT OF STRESS FROM SCHOOL AND WORK LATELY!
WE NEED A FUN FATHER-AND-SON HOBBY TO RELAX AND TO ALLEVIATE OUR TENSION!
HOW ABOUT A WOOD CARVING KIT? WHITTLING CAN BE A FUN AND RELAXING HOBBY!
HMMM...
1

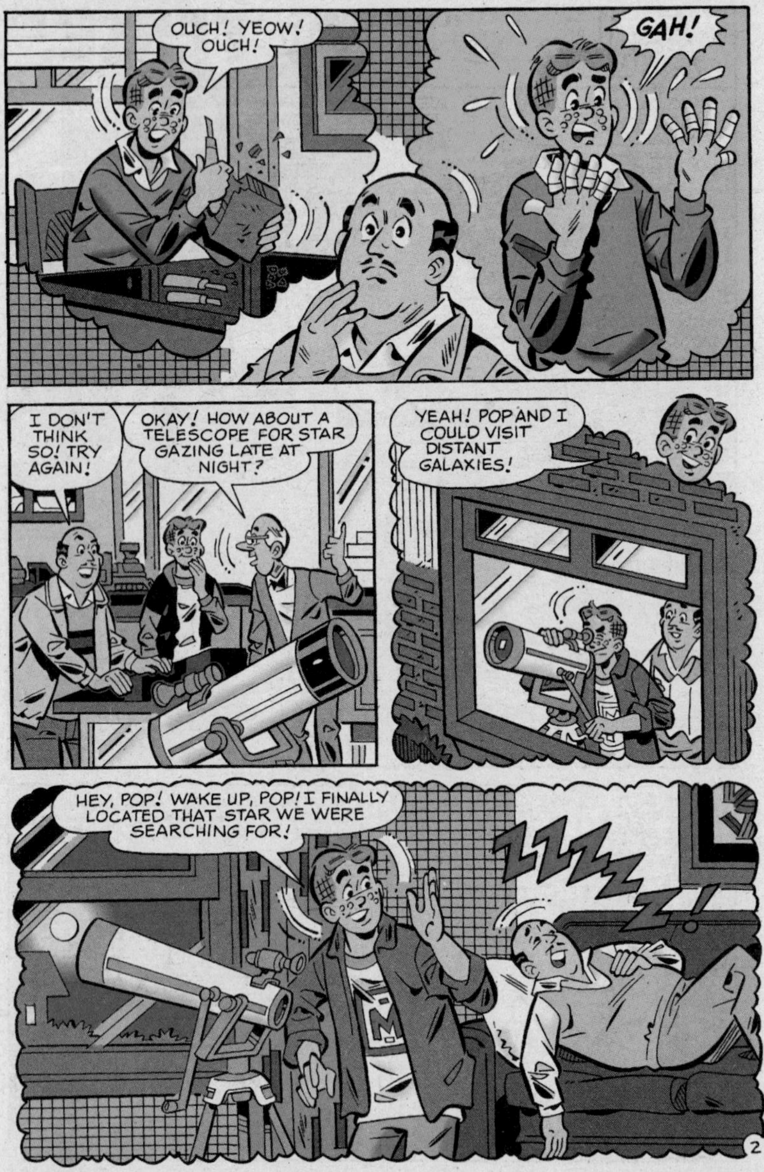
OUCH! YEOW! OUCH!
GAH!
I DON'T THINK SO! TRY AGAIN!
OKAY! HOW ABOUT A TELESCOPE FOR STAR GAZING LATE AT NIGHT?
YEAH! POP AND I COULD VISIT DISTANT GALAXIES!
HEY, POP! WAKE UP, POP! I FINALLY LOCATED THAT STAR WE WERE SEARCHING FOR!
ZZZZZ!

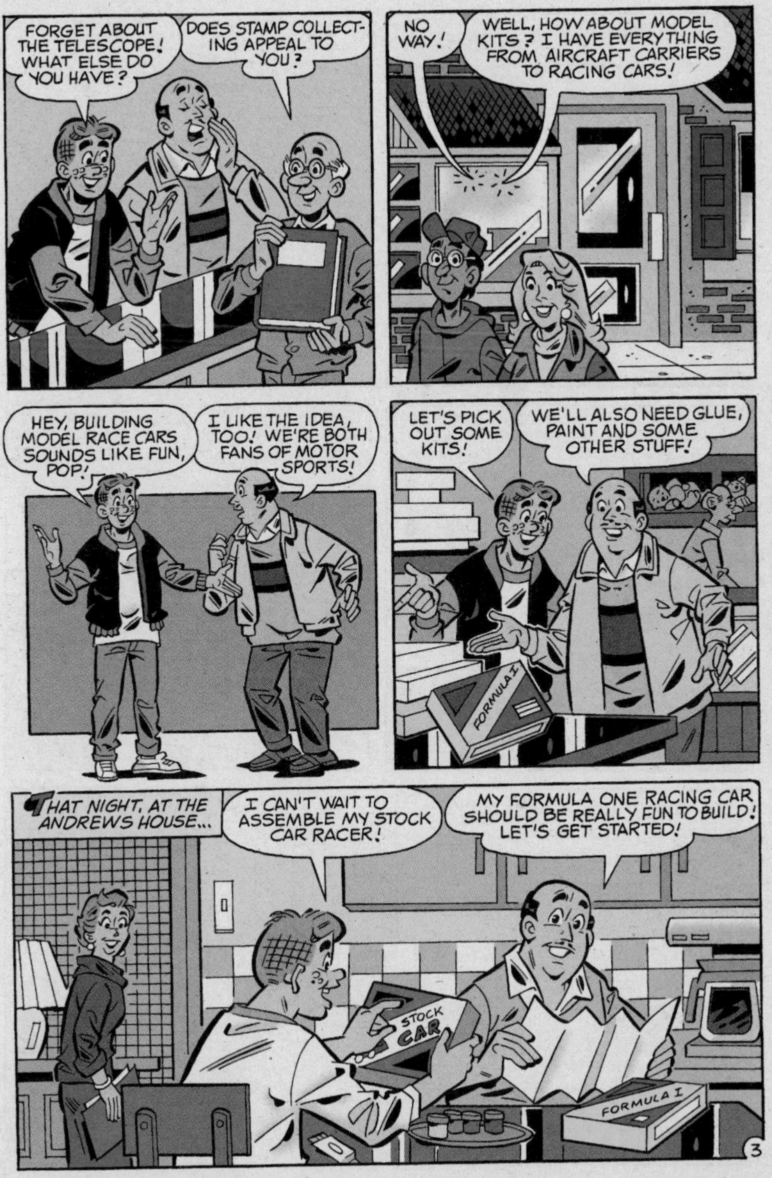

FORGET ABOUT THE TELESCOPE! WHAT ELSE DO YOU HAVE?
DOES STAMP COLLECTING APPEAL TO YOU?
NO WAY!
WELL, HOW ABOUT MODEL KITS? I HAVE EVERYTHING FROM AIRCRAFT CARRIERS TO RACING CARS!
HEY, BUILDING MODEL RACE CARS SOUNDS LIKE FUN, POP!
I LIKE THE IDEA, TOO! WE'RE BOTH FANS OF MOTOR SPORTS!
LET'S PICK OUT SOME KITS!
WE'LL ALSO NEED GLUE, PAINT AND SOME OTHER STUFF!
FORMULA I
THAT NIGHT, AT THE ANDREWS HOUSE...
I CAN'T WAIT TO ASSEMBLE MY STOCK CAR RACER!
MY FORMULA ONE RACING CAR SHOULD BE REALLY FUN TO BUILD! LET'S GET STARTED!
STOCK CAR
FORMULA I

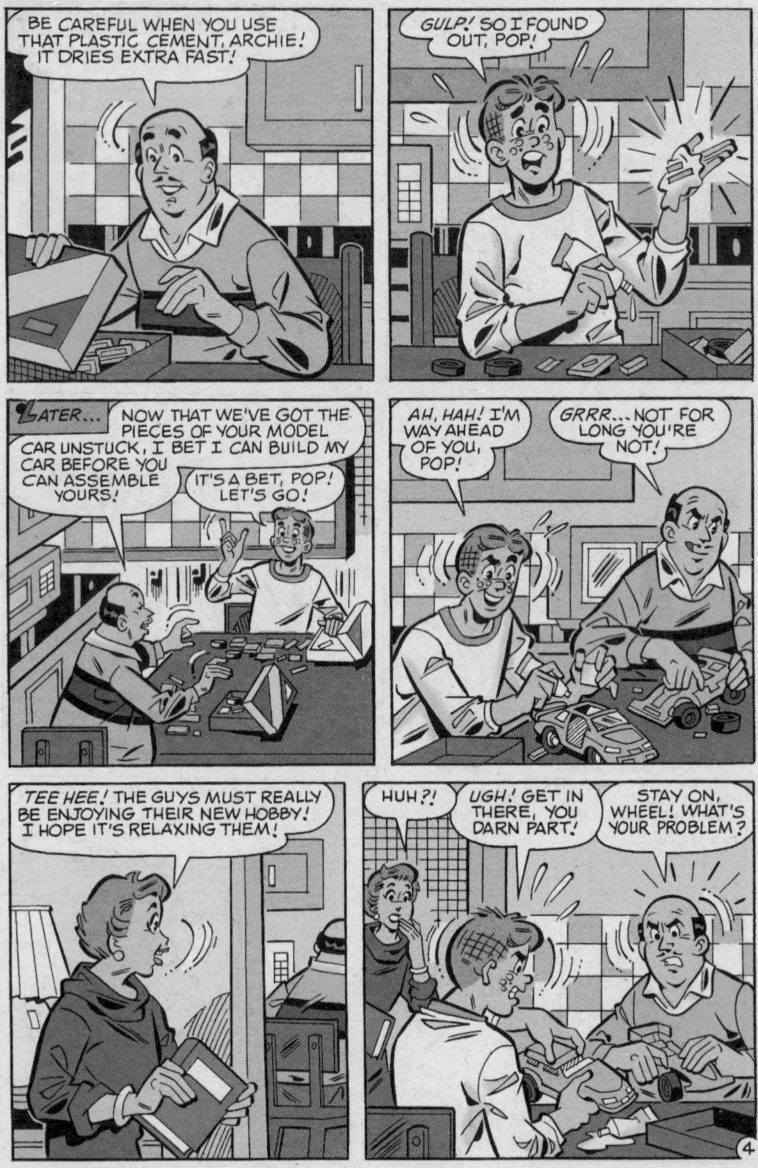
BE CAREFUL WHEN YOU USE THAT PLASTIC CEMENT, ARCHIE! IT DRIES EXTRA FAST!
GULP! SO I FOUND OUT, POP!
LATER...
NOW THAT WE'VE GOT THE PIECES OF YOUR MODEL CAR UNSTUCK, I BET I CAN BUILD MY CAR BEFORE YOU CAN ASSEMBLE YOURS!
IT'S A BET, POP! LET'S GO!
AH, HAH! I'M WAY AHEAD OF YOU, POP!
GRRR... NOT FOR LONG YOU'RE NOT!
TEE HEE! THE GUYS MUST REALLY BE ENJOYING THEIR NEW HOBBY! I HOPE IT'S RELAXING THEM!
HUH?!
UGH! GET IN THERE, YOU DARN PART!
STAY ON, WHEEL! WHAT'S YOUR PROBLEM?
4

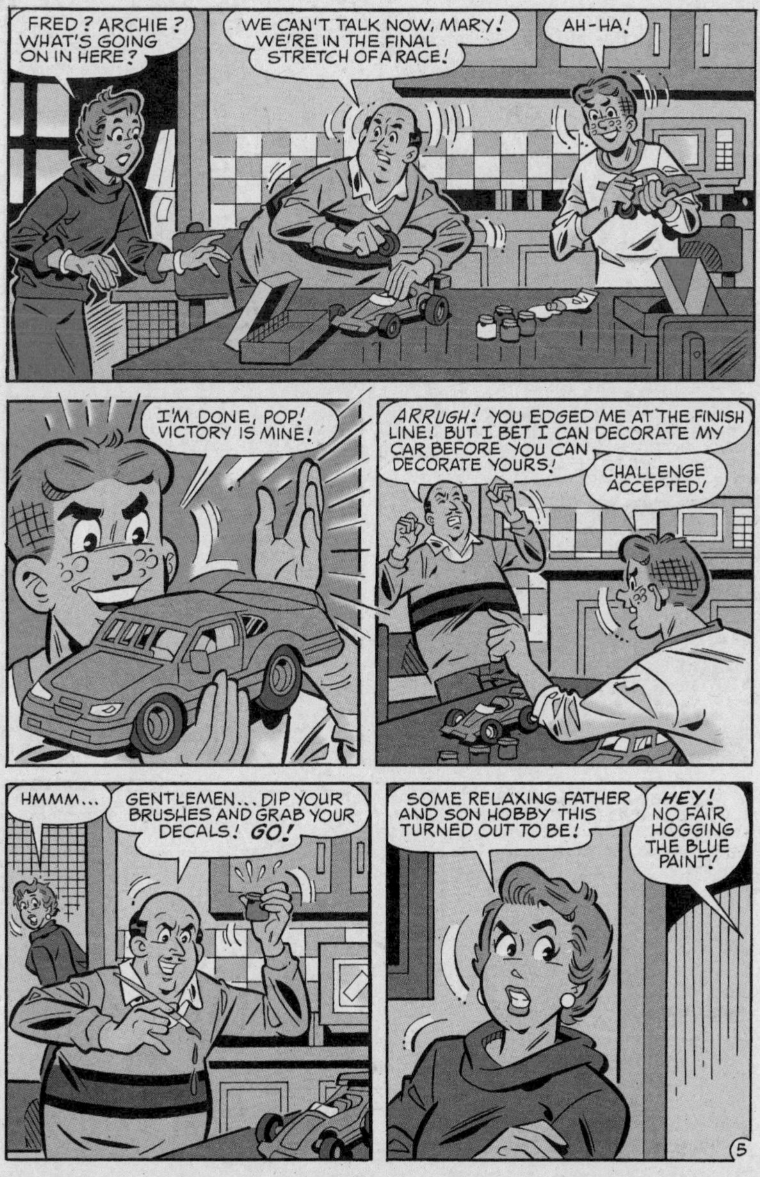
FRED? ARCHIE? WHAT'S GOING ON IN HERE?
WE CAN'T TALK NOW, MARY! WE'RE IN THE FINAL STRETCH OF A RACE!
AH-HA!
I'M DONE, POP! VICTORY IS MINE!
ARRUGH! YOU EDGED ME AT THE FINISH LINE! BUT I BET I CAN DECORATE MY CAR BEFORE YOU CAN DECORATE YOURS!
CHALLENGE ACCEPTED!
HMMM...
GENTLEMEN... DIP YOUR BRUSHES AND GRAB YOUR DECALS! GO!
SOME RELAXING FATHER AND SON HOBBY THIS TURNED OUT TO BE!
HEY! NO FAIR HOGGING THE BLUE PAINT!
5

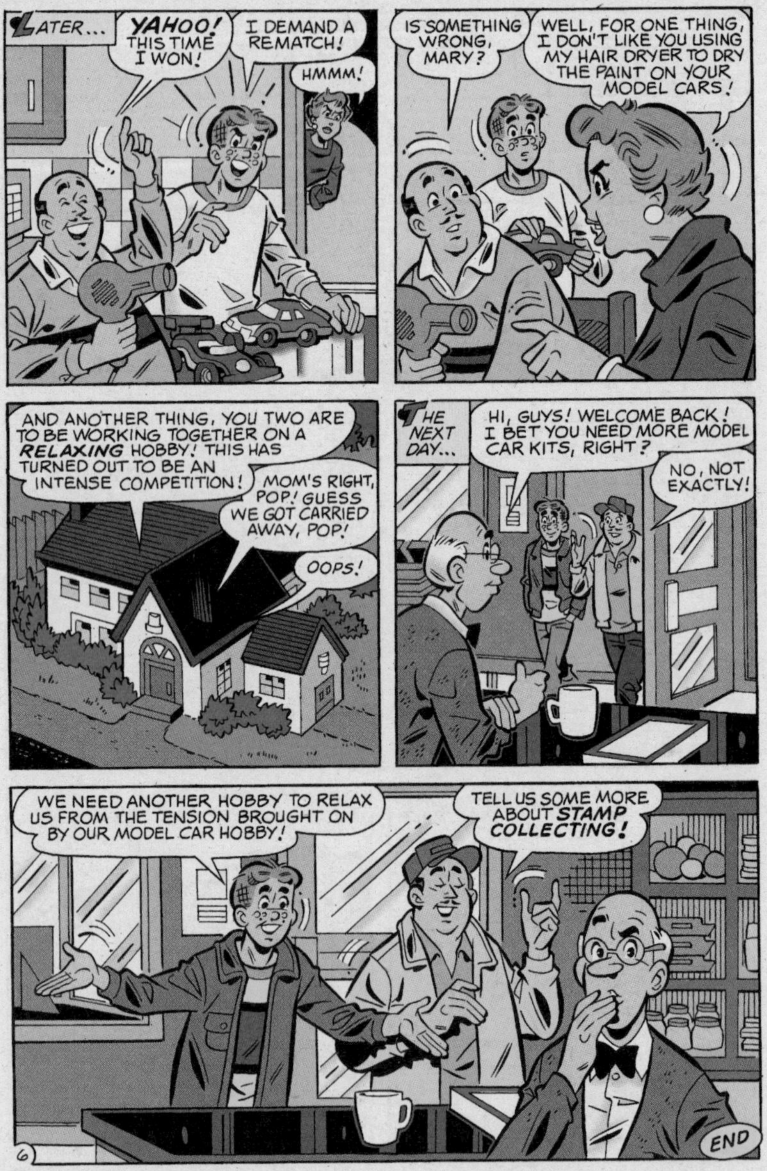
LATER...
YAHOO! THIS TIME I WON!
I DEMAND A REMATCH!
HMMM!
IS SOMETHING WRONG, MARY?
WELL, FOR ONE THING, I DON'T LIKE YOU USING MY HAIR DRYER TO DRY THE PAINT ON YOUR MODEL CARS!
AND ANOTHER THING, YOU TWO ARE TO BE WORKING TOGETHER ON A RELAXING HOBBY! THIS HAS TURNED OUT TO BE AN INTENSE COMPETITION!
MOM'S RIGHT, POP! GUESS WE GOT CARRIED AWAY, POP!
OOPS!
THE NEXT DAY...
HI, GUYS! WELCOME BACK! I BET YOU NEED MORE MODEL CAR KITS, RIGHT?
NO, NOT EXACTLY!
WE NEED ANOTHER HOBBY TO RELAX US FROM THE TENSION BROUGHT ON BY OUR MODEL CAR HOBBY!
TELL US SOME MORE ABOUT STAMP COLLECTING!
END
6

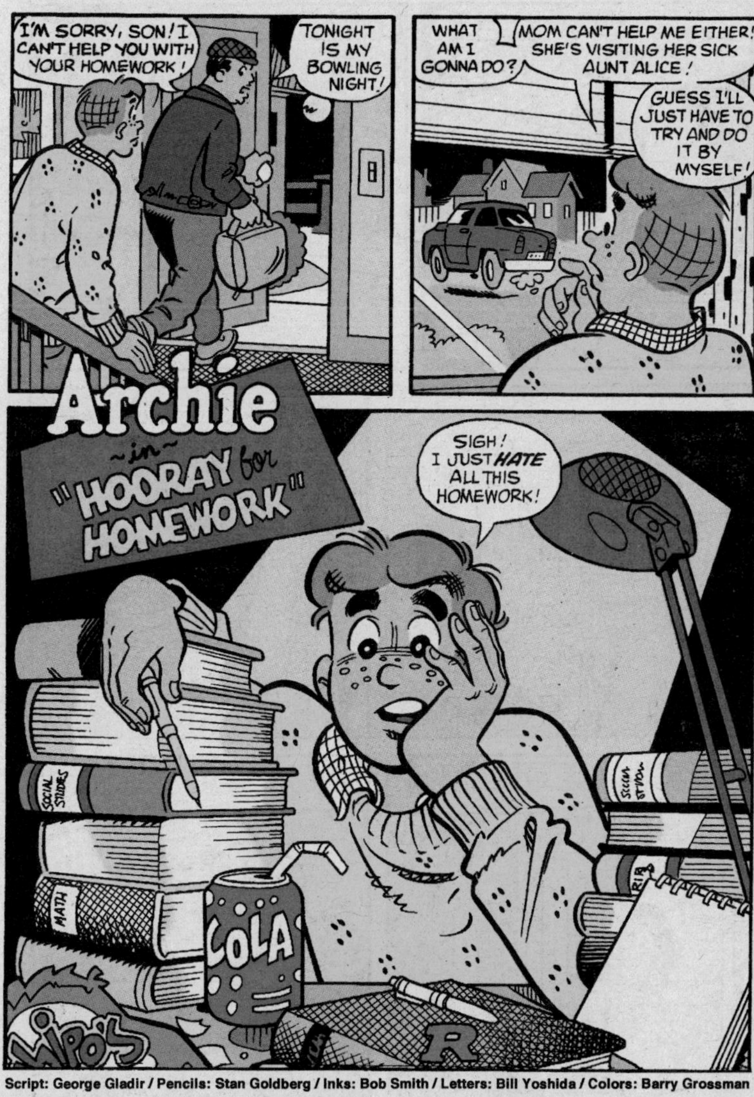
I'M SORRY, SON! I CAN'T HELP YOU WITH YOUR HOMEWORK!
TONIGHT IS MY BOWLING NIGHT!
WHAT AM I GONNA DO?
MOM CAN'T HELP ME EITHER! SHE'S VISITING HER SICK AUNT ALICE!
GUESS I'LL JUST HAVE TO TRY AND DO IT BY MYSELF!
Archie
~in~
"HOORAY for HOMEWORK"
SIGH! I JUST HATE ALL THIS HOMEWORK!
SOCIAL STUDIES
MATH
COLA
R

Script: George Gladir / Pencils: Stan Goldberg / Inks: Bob Smith / Letters: Bill Yoshida / Colors: Barry Grossman

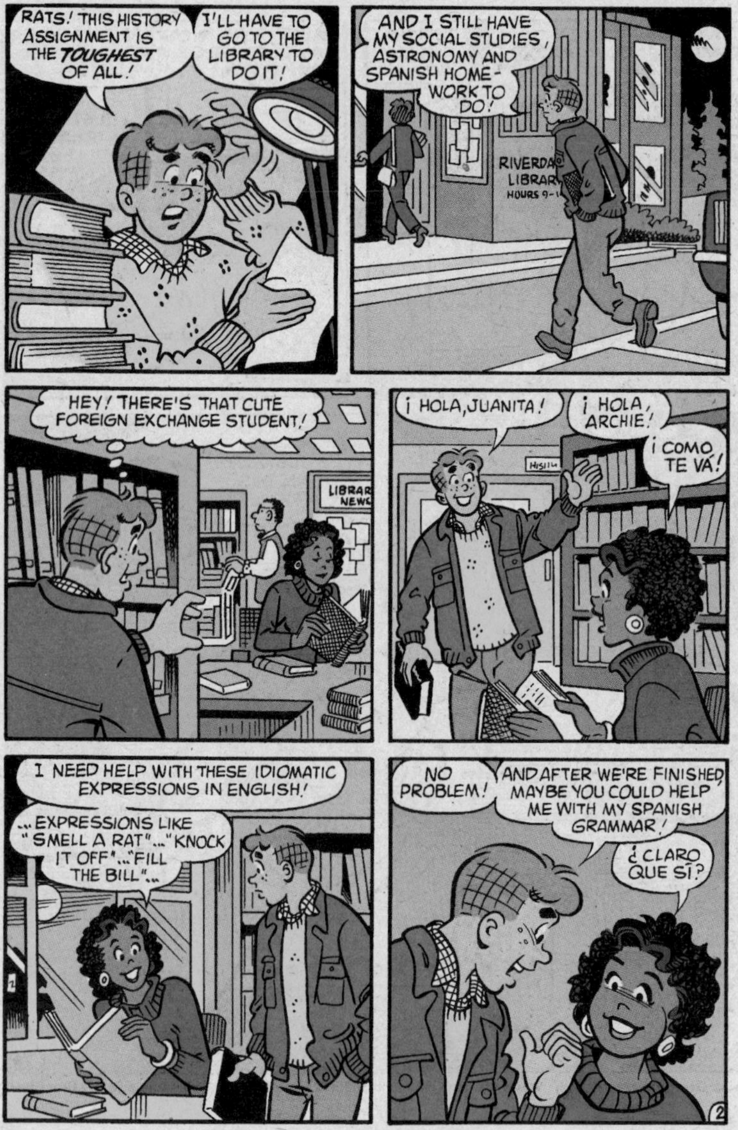
RATS! THIS HISTORY ASSIGNMENT IS THE *TOUGHEST* OF ALL!
I'LL HAVE TO GO TO THE LIBRARY TO DO IT!
AND I STILL HAVE MY SOCIAL STUDIES, ASTRONOMY AND SPANISH HOME-WORK TO DO!
RIVERDA LIBRAR HOURS 9-1
HEY! THERE'S THAT CUTE FOREIGN EXCHANGE STUDENT!
LIBRAR NEWS
¡ HOLA, JUANITA!
¡ HOLA, ARCHIE!
¡ COMO TE VÁ!
I NEED HELP WITH THESE IDIOMATIC EXPRESSIONS IN ENGLISH!
... EXPRESSIONS LIKE "SMELL A RAT"..."KNOCK IT OFF"..."FILL THE BILL"...
NO PROBLEM!
AND AFTER WE'RE FINISHED, MAYBE YOU COULD HELP ME WITH MY SPANISH GRAMMAR!
¿ CLARO QUE SÍ?
2

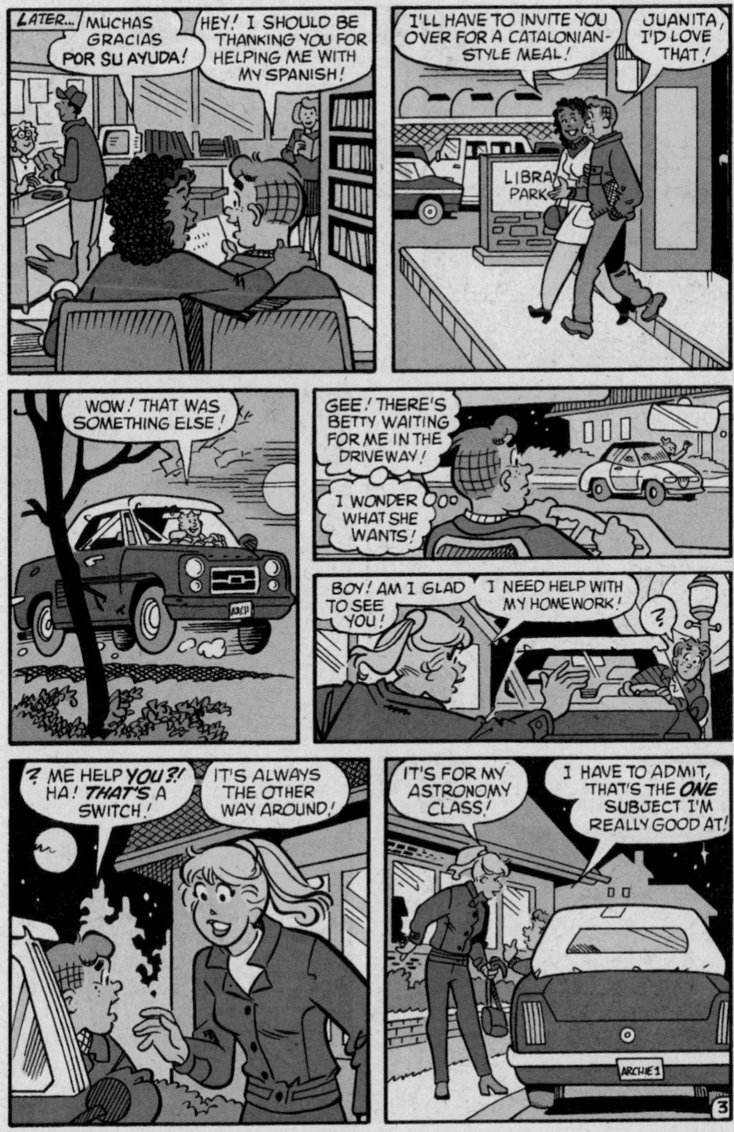
LATER...
MUCHAS GRACIAS POR SU AYUDA!
HEY! I SHOULD BE THANKING YOU FOR HELPING ME WITH MY SPANISH!
I'LL HAVE TO INVITE YOU OVER FOR A CATALONIAN-STYLE MEAL!
JUANITA, I'D LOVE THAT!
WOW! THAT WAS SOMETHING ELSE!
GEE! THERE'S BETTY WAITING FOR ME IN THE DRIVEWAY!
I WONDER WHAT SHE WANTS!
BOY! AM I GLAD TO SEE YOU!
I NEED HELP WITH MY HOMEWORK!
?
? ME HELP YOU?! HA! THAT'S A SWITCH!
IT'S ALWAYS THE OTHER WAY AROUND!
IT'S FOR MY ASTRONOMY CLASS!
I HAVE TO ADMIT, THAT'S THE ONE SUBJECT I'M REALLY GOOD AT!
ARCHIE 1

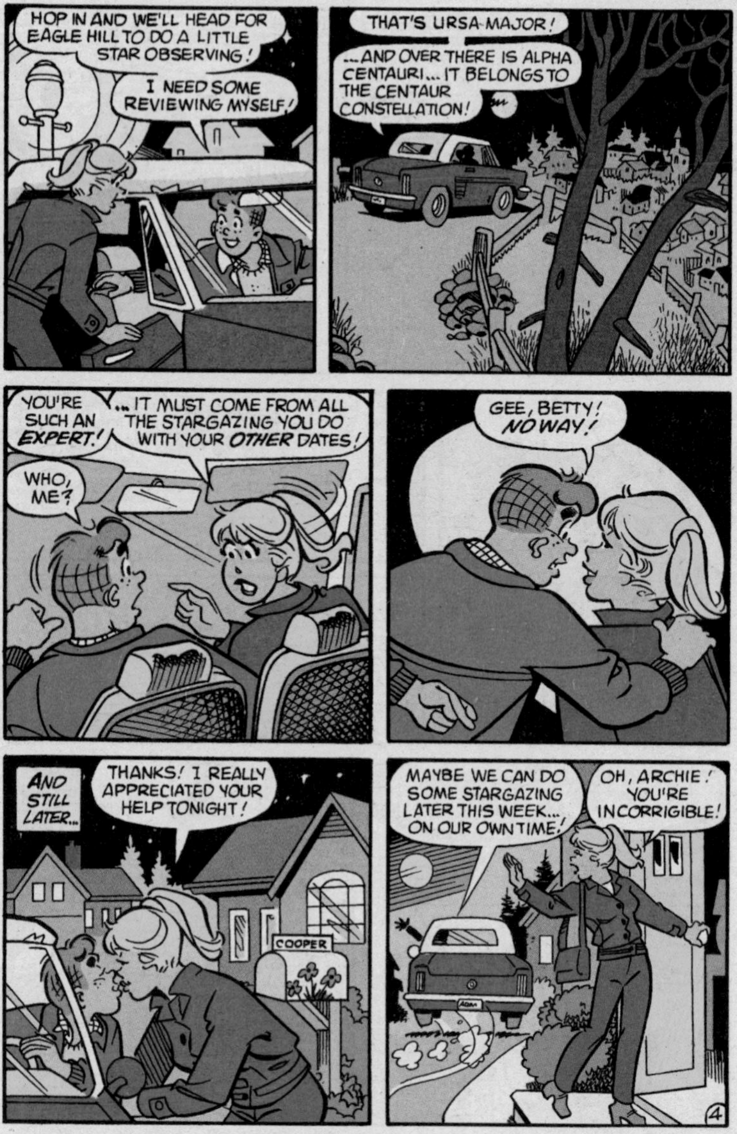

HOP IN AND WE'LL HEAD FOR EAGLE HILL TO DO A LITTLE STAR OBSERVING!
I NEED SOME REVIEWING MYSELF!
THAT'S URSA-MAJOR!
...AND OVER THERE IS ALPHA CENTAURI... IT BELONGS TO THE CENTAUR CONSTELLATION!
YOU'RE SUCH AN EXPERT!
...IT MUST COME FROM ALL THE STARGAZING YOU DO WITH YOUR OTHER DATES!
WHO, ME?
GEE, BETTY! NO WAY!
AND STILL LATER...
THANKS! I REALLY APPRECIATED YOUR HELP TONIGHT!
COOPER
MAYBE WE CAN DO SOME STARGAZING LATER THIS WEEK... ON OUR OWN TIME!
OH, ARCHIE! YOU'RE INCORRIGIBLE!
4

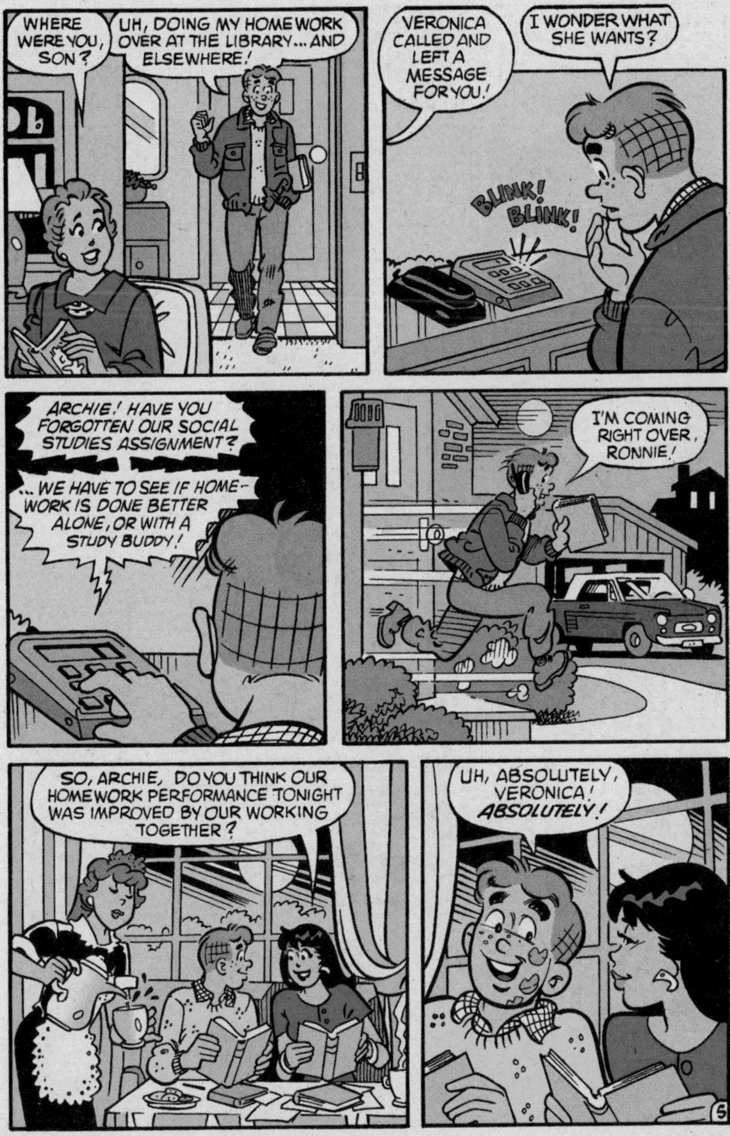
WHERE WERE YOU, SON?
UH, DOING MY HOMEWORK OVER AT THE LIBRARY... AND ELSEWHERE!
VERONICA CALLED AND LEFT A MESSAGE FOR YOU!
I WONDER WHAT SHE WANTS?
BLINK! BLINK!
ARCHIE! HAVE YOU FORGOTTEN OUR SOCIAL STUDIES ASSIGNMENT?
...WE HAVE TO SEE IF HOME-WORK IS DONE BETTER ALONE, OR WITH A STUDY BUDDY!
I'M COMING RIGHT OVER, RONNIE!
SO, ARCHIE, DO YOU THINK OUR HOMEWORK PERFORMANCE TONIGHT WAS IMPROVED BY OUR WORKING TOGETHER?
UH, ABSOLUTELY, VERONICA! ABSOLUTELY!
5

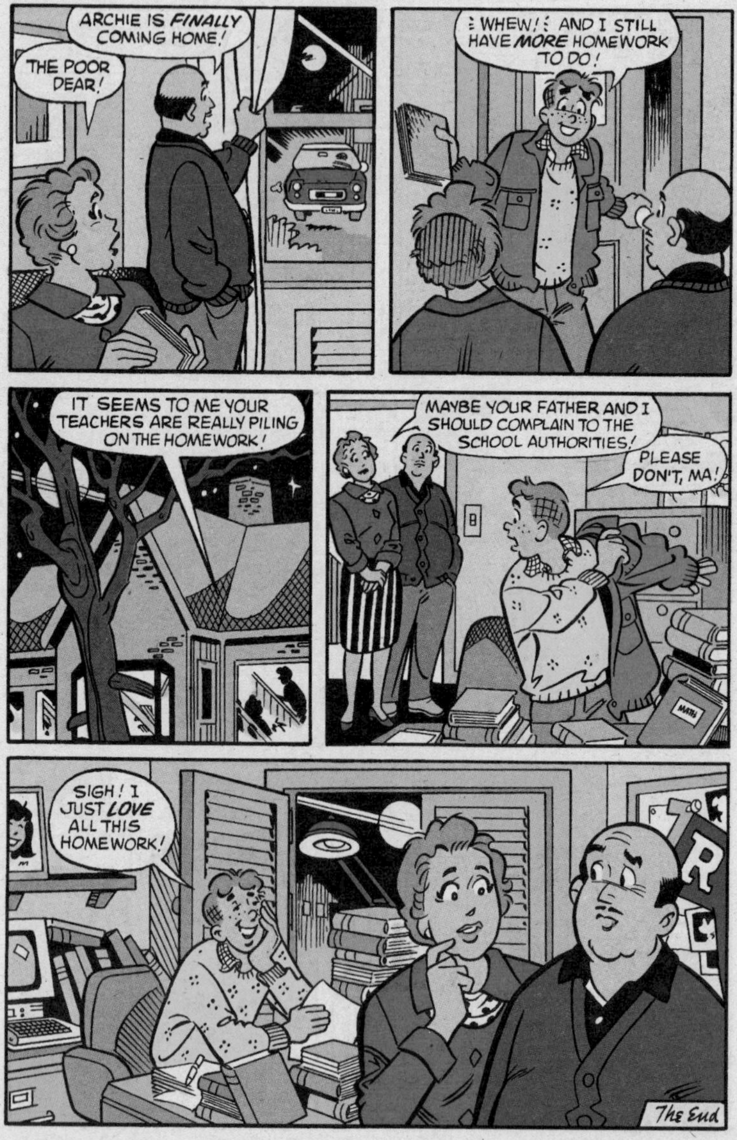
ARCHIE IS *FINALLY* COMING HOME!
THE POOR DEAR!
WHEW! AND I STILL HAVE *MORE* HOMEWORK TO DO!
IT SEEMS TO ME YOUR TEACHERS ARE REALLY PILING ON THE HOMEWORK!
MAYBE YOUR FATHER AND I SHOULD COMPLAIN TO THE SCHOOL AUTHORITIES!
PLEASE DON'T, MA!
MATHS
SIGH! I JUST *LOVE* ALL THIS HOMEWORK!
The End

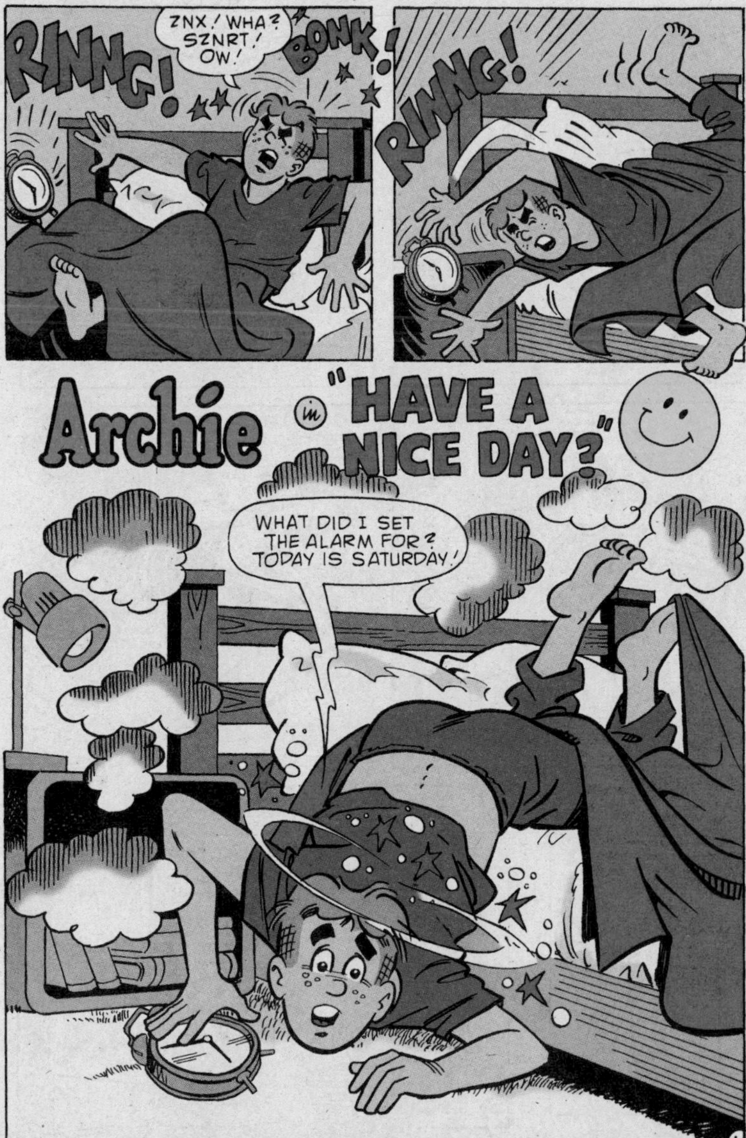
RINNG!
ZNX! WHA? SZNRT! OW!
BONK!
RINNG!
Archie in "HAVE A NICE DAY?"
WHAT DID I SET THE ALARM FOR? TODAY IS SATURDAY!
1

Script: Hal Smith / Pencils: Stan Goldberg / Inks: Mike Esposito / Letters: Bill Yoshida / Colors: Barry Grossman

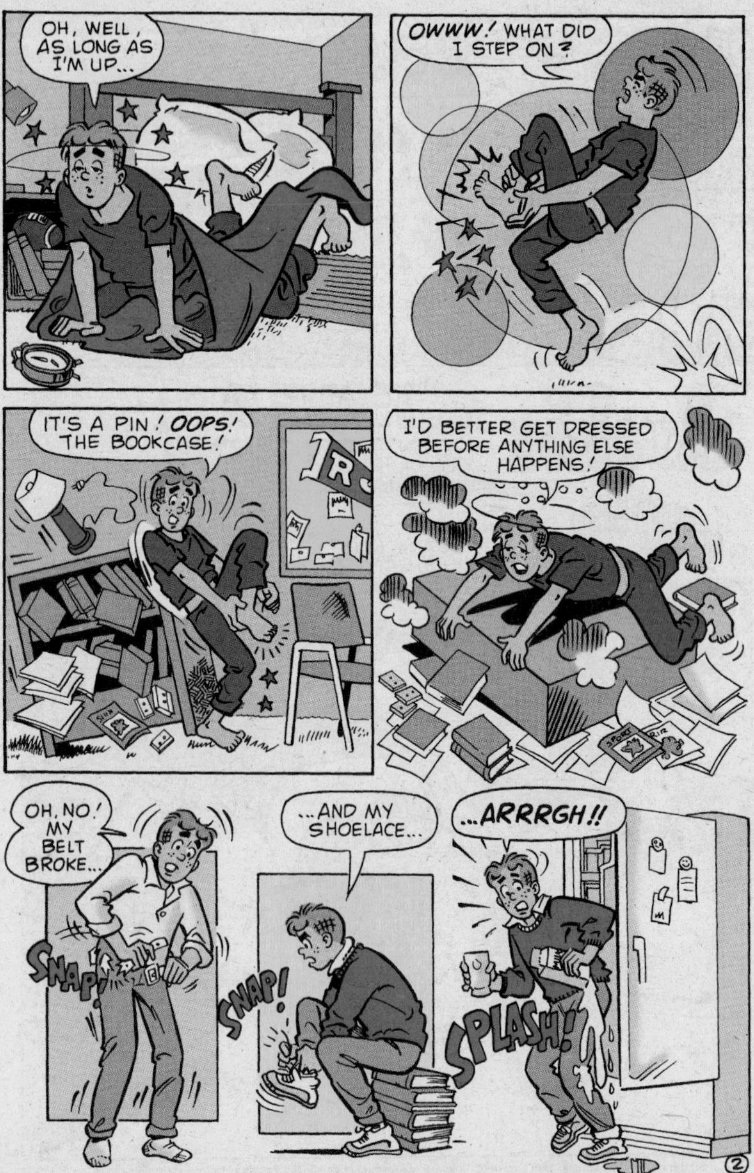
OH, WELL, AS LONG AS I'M UP...
OWWW! WHAT DID I STEP ON?
IT'S A PIN! OOPS! THE BOOKCASE!
I'D BETTER GET DRESSED BEFORE ANYTHING ELSE HAPPENS!
OH, NO! MY BELT BROKE...
SNAP!
...AND MY SHOELACE...
SNAP!
...ARRRGH!!
SPLASH!

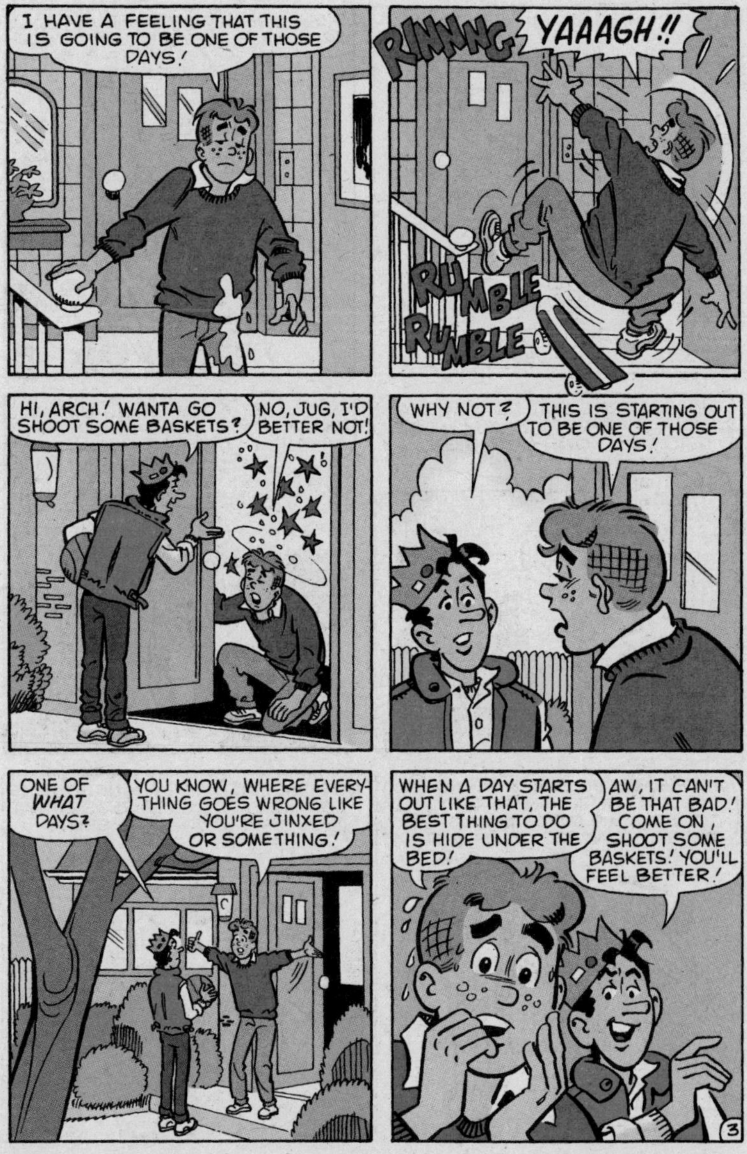

I HAVE A FEELING THAT THIS IS GOING TO BE ONE OF THOSE DAYS!
RINNNG
YAAAGH!!
RUMBLE RUMBLE
HI, ARCH! WANTA GO SHOOT SOME BASKETS?
NO, JUG, I'D BETTER NOT!
WHY NOT?
THIS IS STARTING OUT TO BE ONE OF THOSE DAYS!
ONE OF *WHAT* DAYS?
YOU KNOW, WHERE EVERYTHING GOES WRONG LIKE YOU'RE JINXED OR SOMETHING!
WHEN A DAY STARTS OUT LIKE THAT, THE BEST THING TO DO IS HIDE UNDER THE BED!
AW, IT CAN'T BE THAT BAD! COME ON, SHOOT SOME BASKETS! YOU'LL FEEL BETTER!
3

I REALLY SHOULDN'T! I'M COURTING DISASTER! I JUST KNOW IT!

IT'S BEEN TWO MINUTES AND NOTHING'S HAPPENED YET!

DUH-H...HEY, ARCH, WAIT UP!

UH-OH! DID YOU INCUR MOOSE'S WRATH?

I DON'T THINK SO!

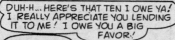

DUH-H...HERE'S THAT TEN I OWE YA! I REALLY APPRECIATE YOU LENDING IT TO ME! I OWE YOU A BIG FAVOR!

ER...THANKS, MOOSE!

WELL, THAT WASN'T SO TERRIBLE!

SOMETHING BAD WILL HAPPEN! YOU'LL SEE!

RIVERDALE

ARCHIE, I'M SO GLAD I FOUND YOU! I'VE GOT TWO TICKETS TO THE COUNTRY CLUB DANCE TONIGHT! WANT TO TAKE ME?

OH, *WOW!* SURE!

NOTHING TOO HORRIBLE ABOUT THAT!

WAIT A MINUTE! HERE COMES REGGIE! THAT ALWAYS SPELLS TROUBLE!

4

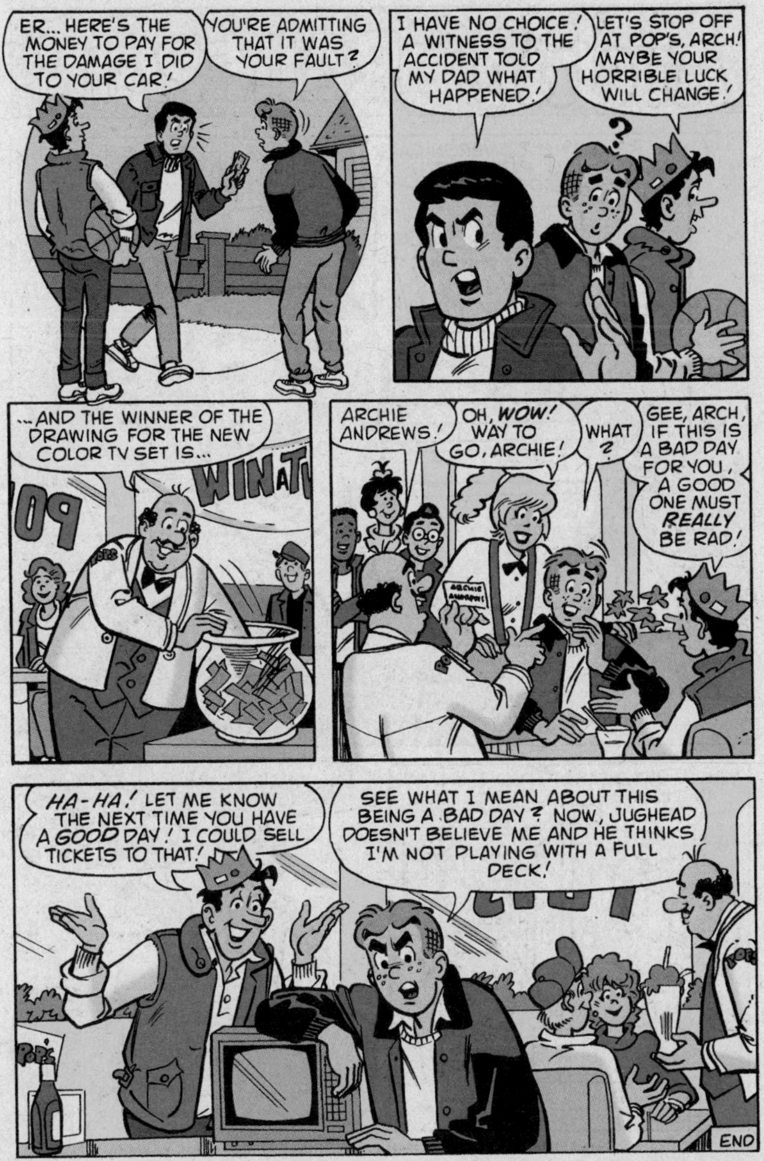

ER... HERE'S THE MONEY TO PAY FOR THE DAMAGE I DID TO YOUR CAR!
YOU'RE ADMITTING THAT IT WAS YOUR FAULT?
I HAVE NO CHOICE! A WITNESS TO THE ACCIDENT TOLD MY DAD WHAT HAPPENED!
LET'S STOP OFF AT POP'S, ARCH! MAYBE YOUR HORRIBLE LUCK WILL CHANGE!
?
...AND THE WINNER OF THE DRAWING FOR THE NEW COLOR TV SET IS...
WIN A T
POP
ARCHIE ANDREWS!
OH, WOW! WAY TO GO, ARCHIE!
WHAT?
GEE, ARCH, IF THIS IS A BAD DAY FOR YOU, A GOOD ONE MUST REALLY BE RAD!
HA-HA! LET ME KNOW THE NEXT TIME YOU HAVE A GOOD DAY! I COULD SELL TICKETS TO THAT!
SEE WHAT I MEAN ABOUT THIS BEING A BAD DAY? NOW, JUGHEAD DOESN'T BELIEVE ME AND HE THINKS I'M NOT PLAYING WITH A FULL DECK!
POP'S
END

Archie in "RAIN PAIN"

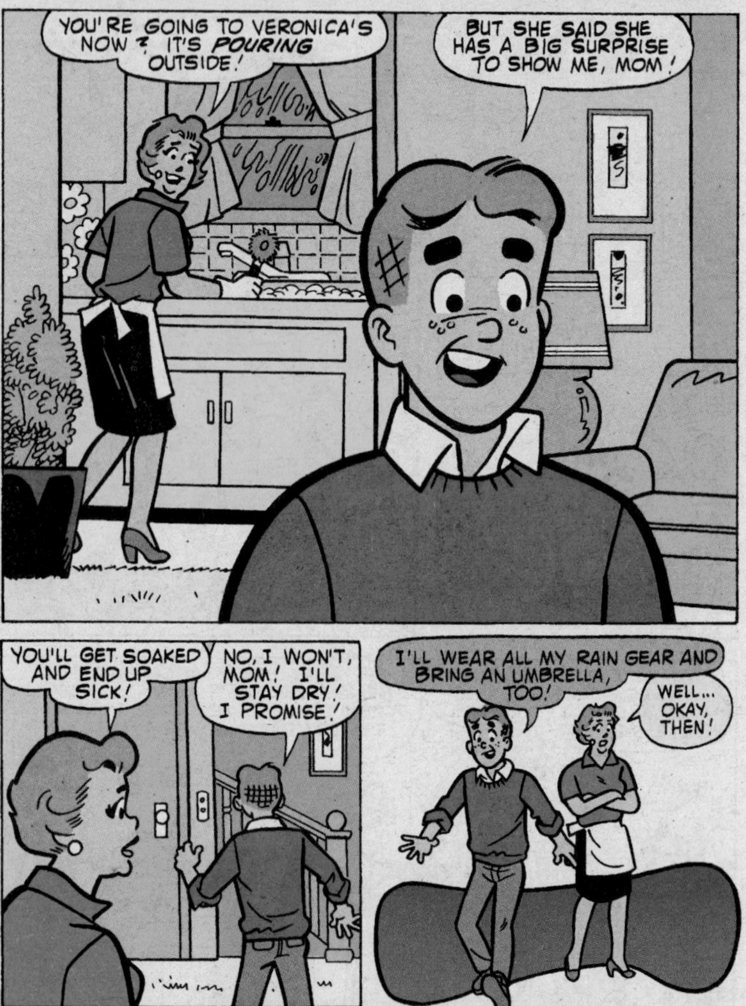
YOU'RE GOING TO VERONICA'S NOW? IT'S POURING OUTSIDE!
BUT SHE SAID SHE HAS A BIG SURPRISE TO SHOW ME, MOM!
YOU'LL GET SOAKED AND END UP SICK!
NO, I WON'T, MOM! I'LL STAY DRY! I PROMISE!
I'LL WEAR ALL MY RAIN GEAR AND BRING AN UMBRELLA, TOO!
WELL... OKAY, THEN!

Script: Mike Pellowski / Art: Henry Scarpelli / Letters: Bill Yoshida

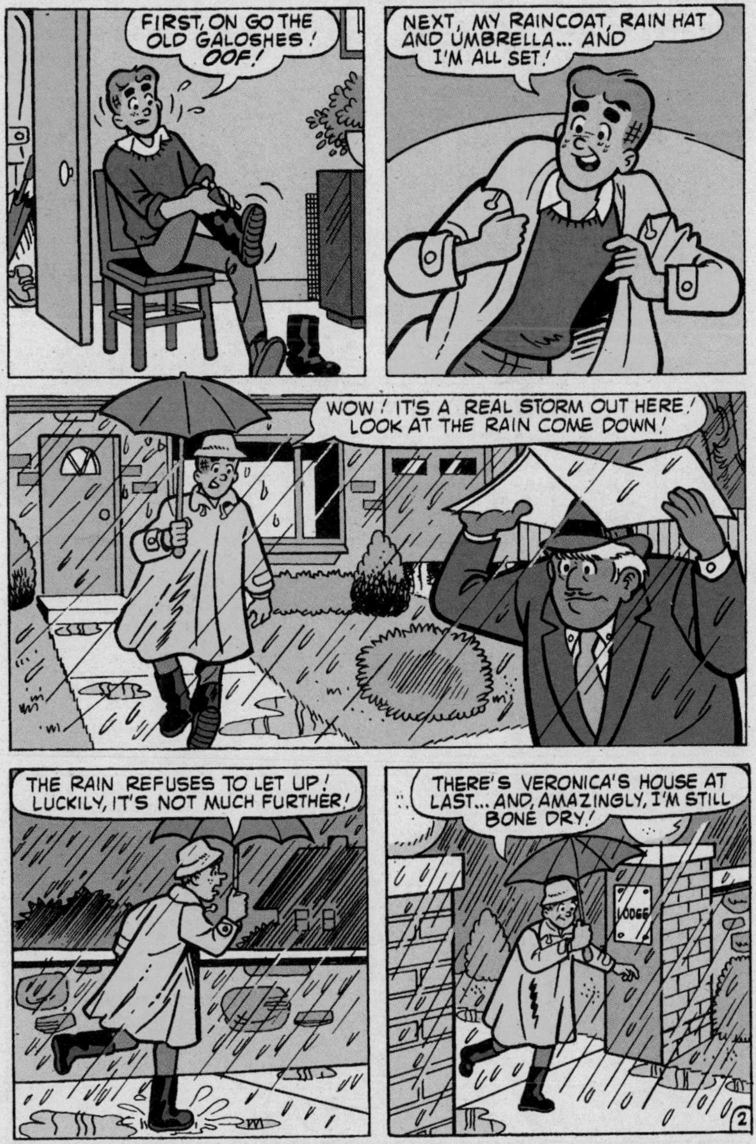
FIRST, ON GO THE OLD GALOSHES! OOF!
NEXT, MY RAINCOAT, RAIN HAT AND UMBRELLA... AND I'M ALL SET!
WOW! IT'S A REAL STORM OUT HERE! LOOK AT THE RAIN COME DOWN!
THE RAIN REFUSES TO LET UP! LUCKILY, IT'S NOT MUCH FURTHER!
THERE'S VERONICA'S HOUSE AT LAST... AND, AMAZINGLY, I'M STILL BONE DRY!
LODGE
2

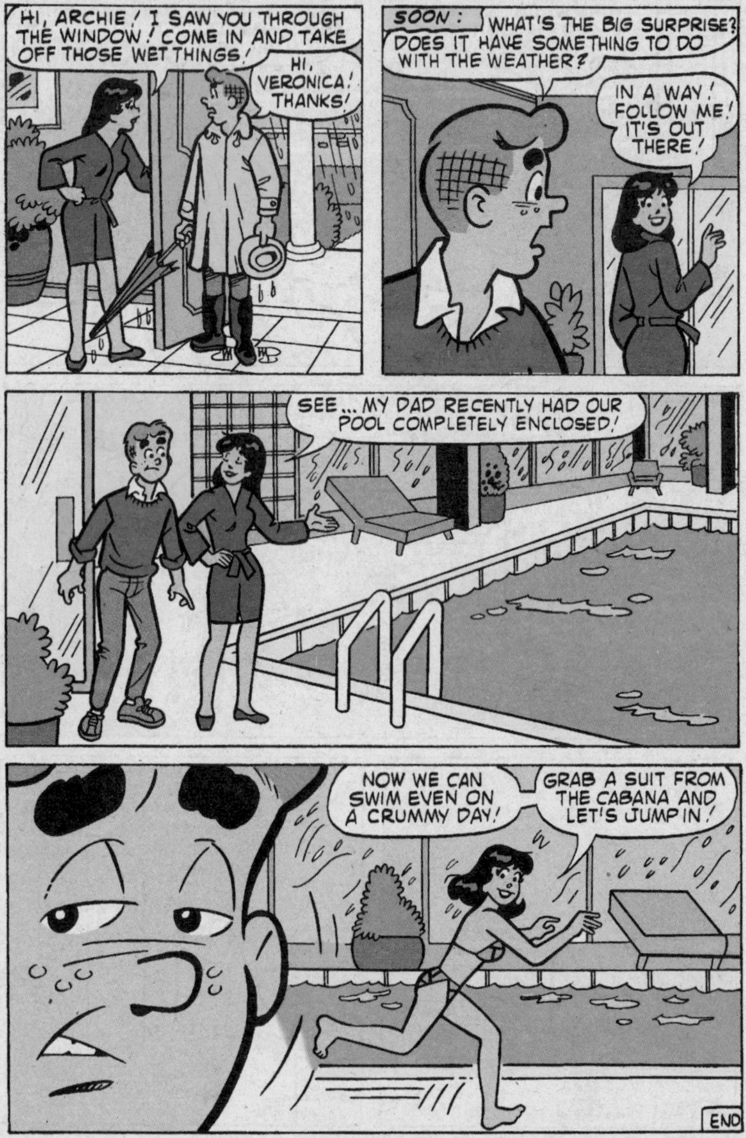
HI, ARCHIE! I SAW YOU THROUGH THE WINDOW! COME IN AND TAKE OFF THOSE WET THINGS!
HI, VERONICA! THANKS!
SOON:
WHAT'S THE BIG SURPRISE? DOES IT HAVE SOMETHING TO DO WITH THE WEATHER?
IN A WAY! FOLLOW ME! IT'S OUT THERE!
SEE... MY DAD RECENTLY HAD OUR POOL COMPLETELY ENCLOSED!
NOW WE CAN SWIM EVEN ON A CRUMMY DAY!
GRAB A SUIT FROM THE CABANA AND LET'S JUMP IN!
END

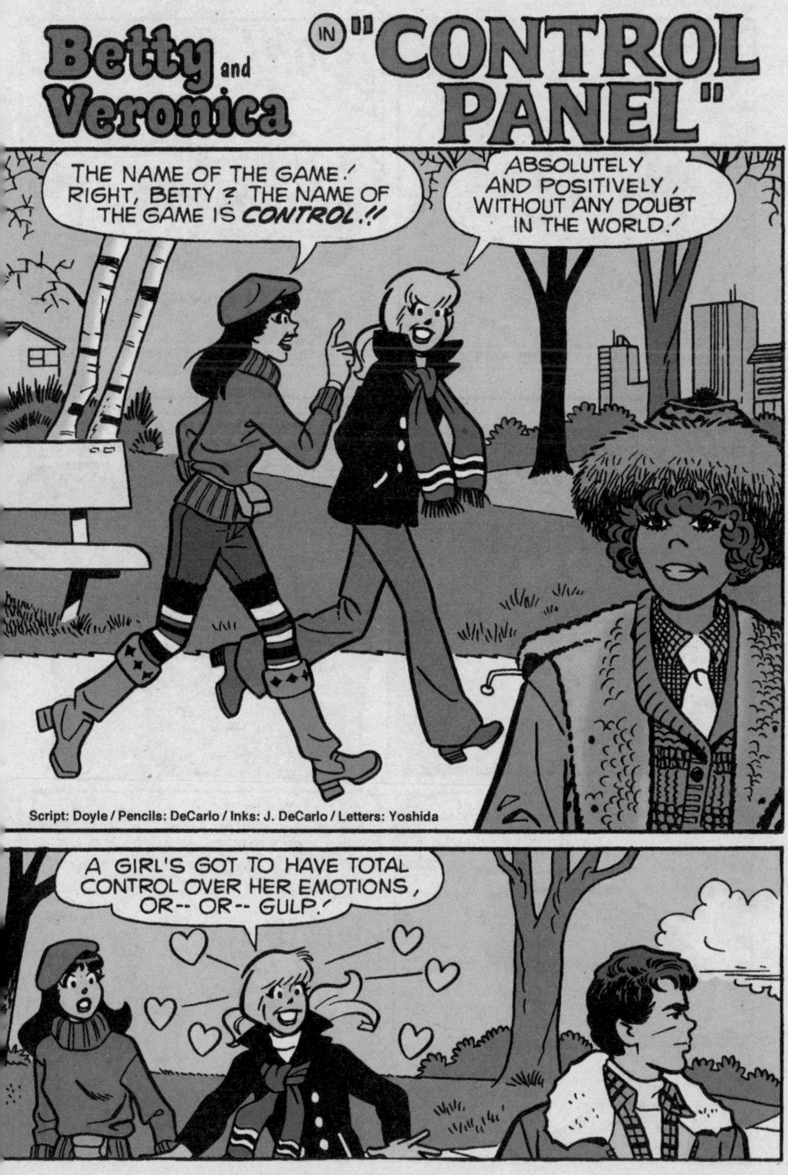
Betty and Veronica
IN "CONTROL PANEL"
THE NAME OF THE GAME! RIGHT, BETTY? THE NAME OF THE GAME IS CONTROL!!
ABSOLUTELY AND POSITIVELY, WITHOUT ANY DOUBT IN THE WORLD!
Script: Doyle / Pencils: DeCarlo / Inks: J. DeCarlo / Letters: Yoshida
A GIRL'S GOT TO HAVE TOTAL CONTROL OVER HER EMOTIONS, OR-- OR-- GULP!

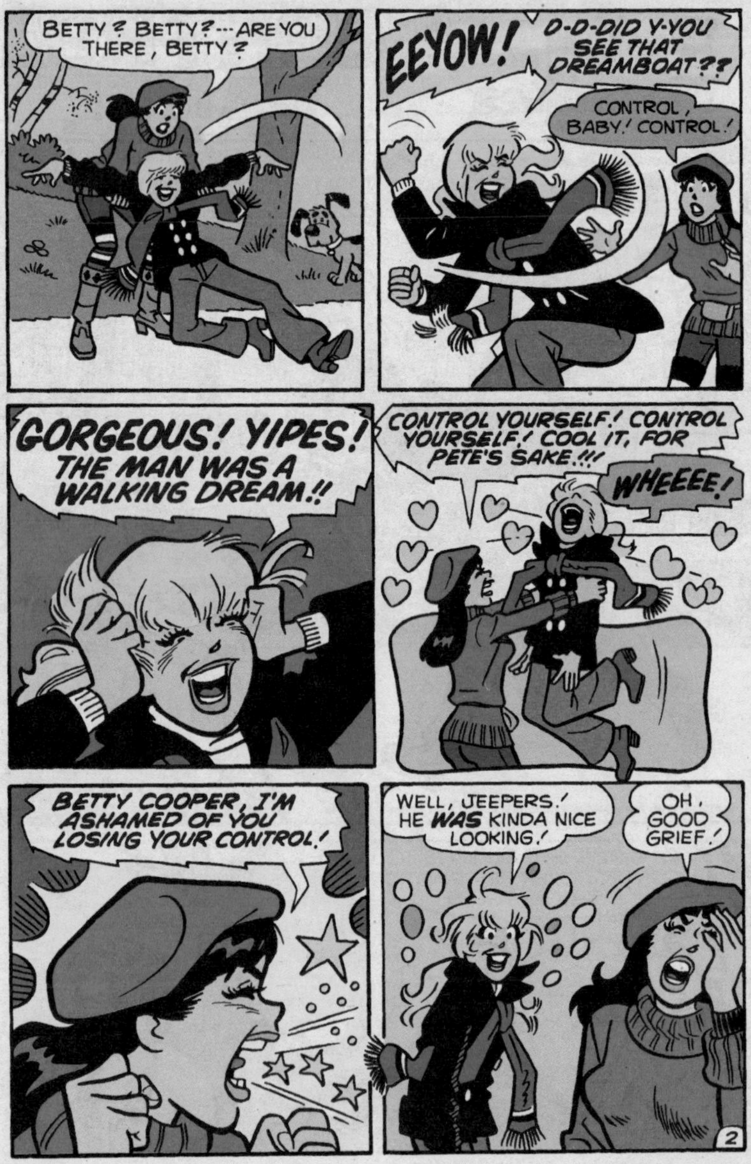
BETTY ? BETTY ? --- ARE YOU THERE, BETTY ?
EEYOW!
D-D-DID Y-YOU SEE THAT DREAMBOAT ??
CONTROL, BABY! CONTROL!
GORGEOUS! YIPES! THE MAN WAS A WALKING DREAM!!
CONTROL YOURSELF! CONTROL YOURSELF! COOL IT, FOR PETE'S SAKE!!!
WHEEEEE!
BETTY COOPER, I'M ASHAMED OF YOU LOSING YOUR CONTROL!
WELL, JEEPERS! HE WAS KINDA NICE LOOKING!
OH, GOOD GRIEF!
2

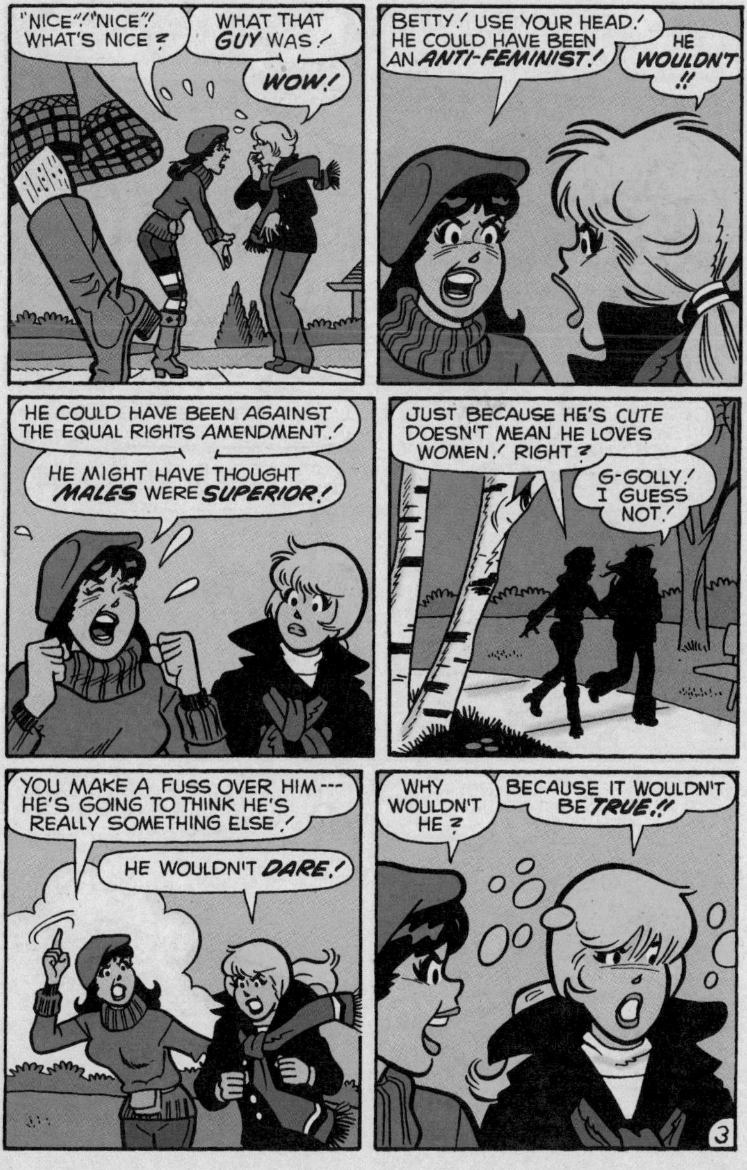
"NICE"! "NICE"! WHAT'S NICE ?
WHAT THAT GUY WAS!
WOW!
BETTY! USE YOUR HEAD! HE COULD HAVE BEEN AN ANTI-FEMINIST!
HE WOULDN'T !!
HE COULD HAVE BEEN AGAINST THE EQUAL RIGHTS AMENDMENT!
HE MIGHT HAVE THOUGHT MALES WERE SUPERIOR!
JUST BECAUSE HE'S CUTE DOESN'T MEAN HE LOVES WOMEN! RIGHT ?
G-GOLLY! I GUESS NOT!
YOU MAKE A FUSS OVER HIM--- HE'S GOING TO THINK HE'S REALLY SOMETHING ELSE!
HE WOULDN'T DARE!
WHY WOULDN'T HE ?
BECAUSE IT WOULDN'T BE TRUE!!
3

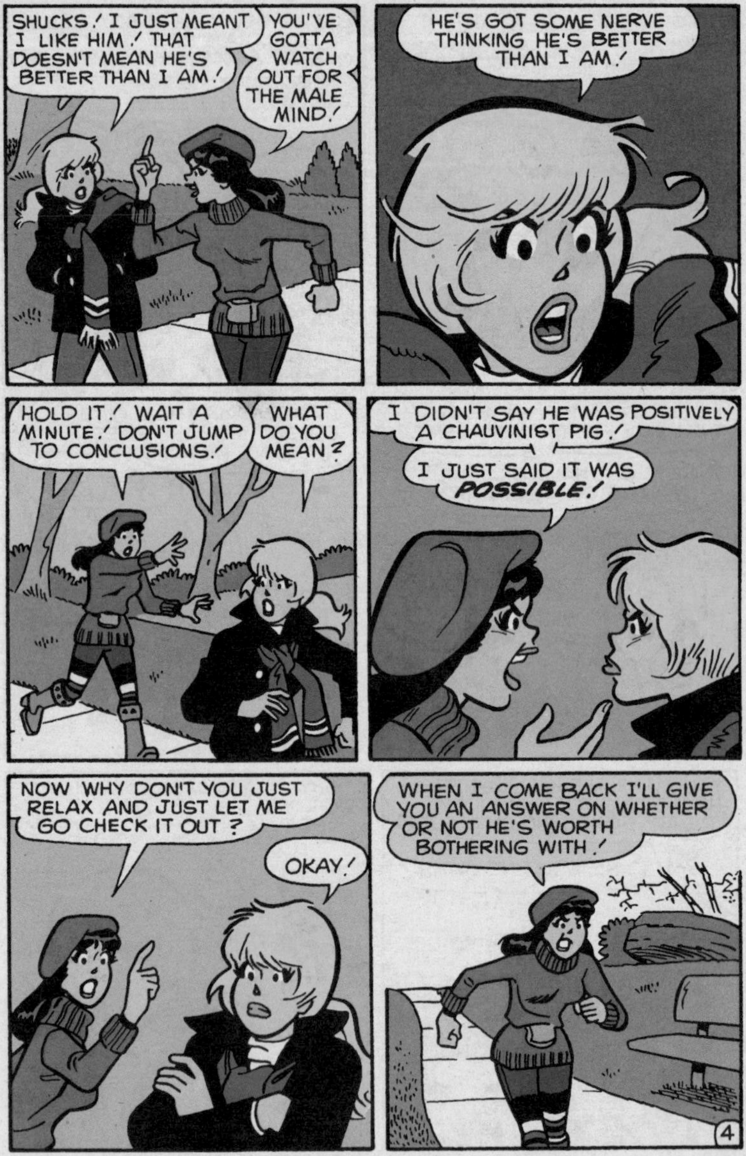

SHUCKS! I JUST MEANT I LIKE HIM! THAT DOESN'T MEAN HE'S BETTER THAN I AM!
YOU'VE GOTTA WATCH OUT FOR THE MALE MIND!
HE'S GOT SOME NERVE THINKING HE'S BETTER THAN I AM!
HOLD IT! WAIT A MINUTE! DON'T JUMP TO CONCLUSIONS!
WHAT DO YOU MEAN?
I DIDN'T SAY HE WAS POSITIVELY A CHAUVINIST PIG!
I JUST SAID IT WAS *POSSIBLE!*
NOW WHY DON'T YOU JUST RELAX AND JUST LET ME GO CHECK IT OUT?
OKAY!
WHEN I COME BACK I'LL GIVE YOU AN ANSWER ON WHETHER OR NOT HE'S WORTH BOTHERING WITH!
4

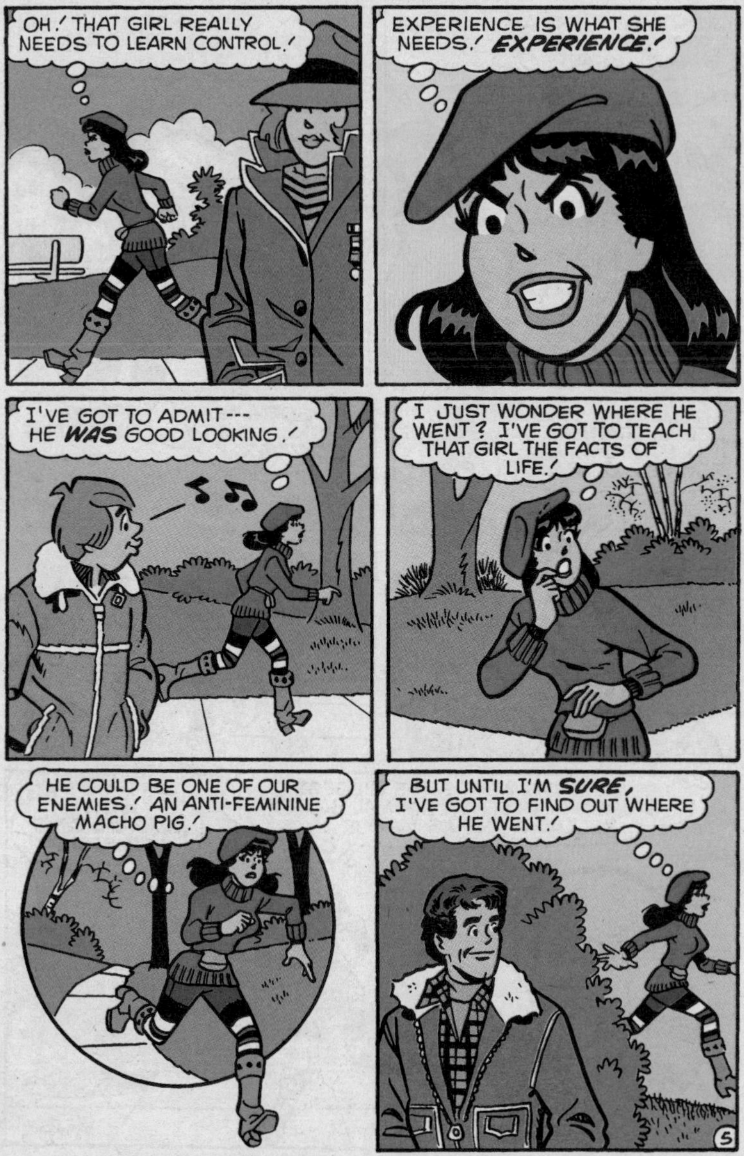
OH.! THAT GIRL REALLY NEEDS TO LEARN CONTROL.!
EXPERIENCE IS WHAT SHE NEEDS.! EXPERIENCE.!
I'VE GOT TO ADMIT--- HE WAS GOOD LOOKING.!
I JUST WONDER WHERE HE WENT? I'VE GOT TO TEACH THAT GIRL THE FACTS OF LIFE.!
HE COULD BE ONE OF OUR ENEMIES.! AN ANTI-FEMININE MACHO PIG.!
BUT UNTIL I'M SURE, I'VE GOT TO FIND OUT WHERE HE WENT.!
5

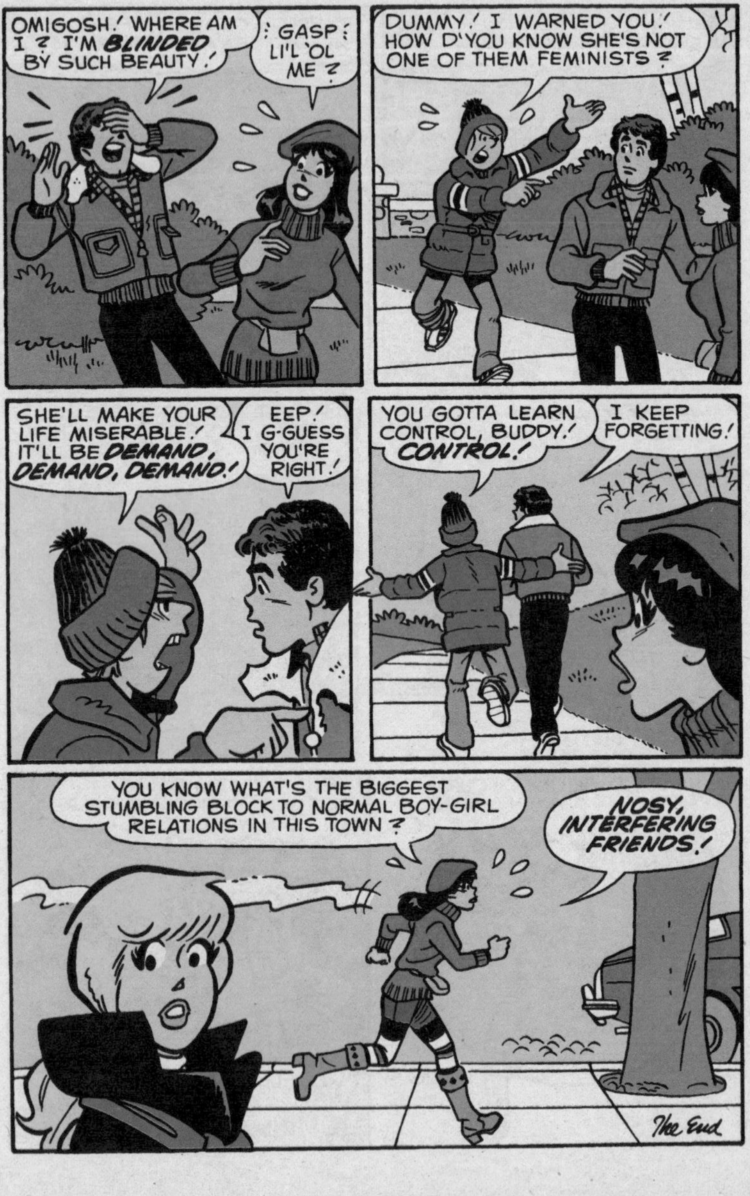

OMIGOSH! WHERE AM I? I'M BLINDED BY SUCH BEAUTY!
GASP! LI'L 'OL ME?
DUMMY! I WARNED YOU! HOW D'YOU KNOW SHE'S NOT ONE OF THEM FEMINISTS?
SHE'LL MAKE YOUR LIFE MISERABLE! IT'LL BE DEMAND, DEMAND, DEMAND!
EEP! I G-GUESS YOU'RE RIGHT!
YOU GOTTA LEARN CONTROL, BUDDY! CONTROL!
I KEEP FORGETTING!
YOU KNOW WHAT'S THE BIGGEST STUMBLING BLOCK TO NORMAL BOY-GIRL RELATIONS IN THIS TOWN?
NOSY, INTERFERING FRIENDS!
The End

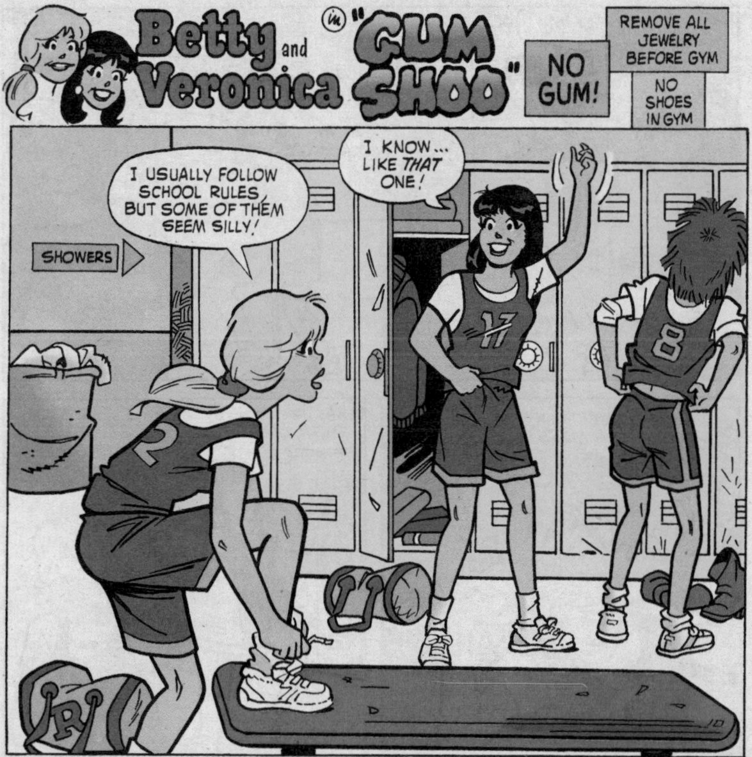
Betty and Veronica in "GUM SHOO"
NO GUM!
REMOVE ALL JEWELRY BEFORE GYM
NO SHOES IN GYM
SHOWERS
I USUALLY FOLLOW SCHOOL RULES, BUT SOME OF THEM SEEM SILLY!
I KNOW... LIKE *THAT* ONE!

Script: Mike Pellowski / Pencils: Dan DeCarlo / Inks: Henry Scarpelli / Letters: Bill Yoshida / Colors: Barry Grossman

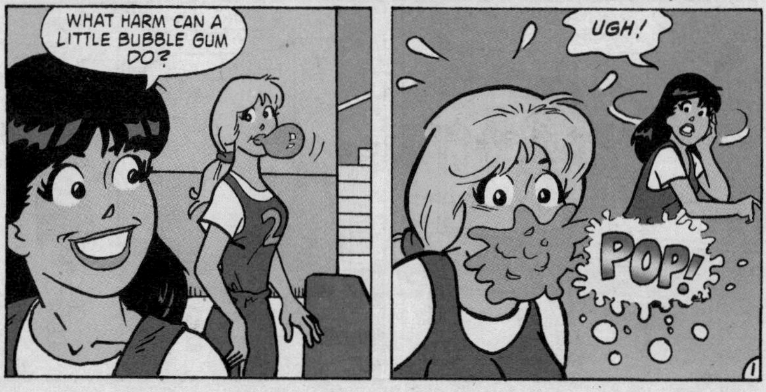
WHAT HARM CAN A LITTLE BUBBLE GUM DO?
UGH!
POP!
1

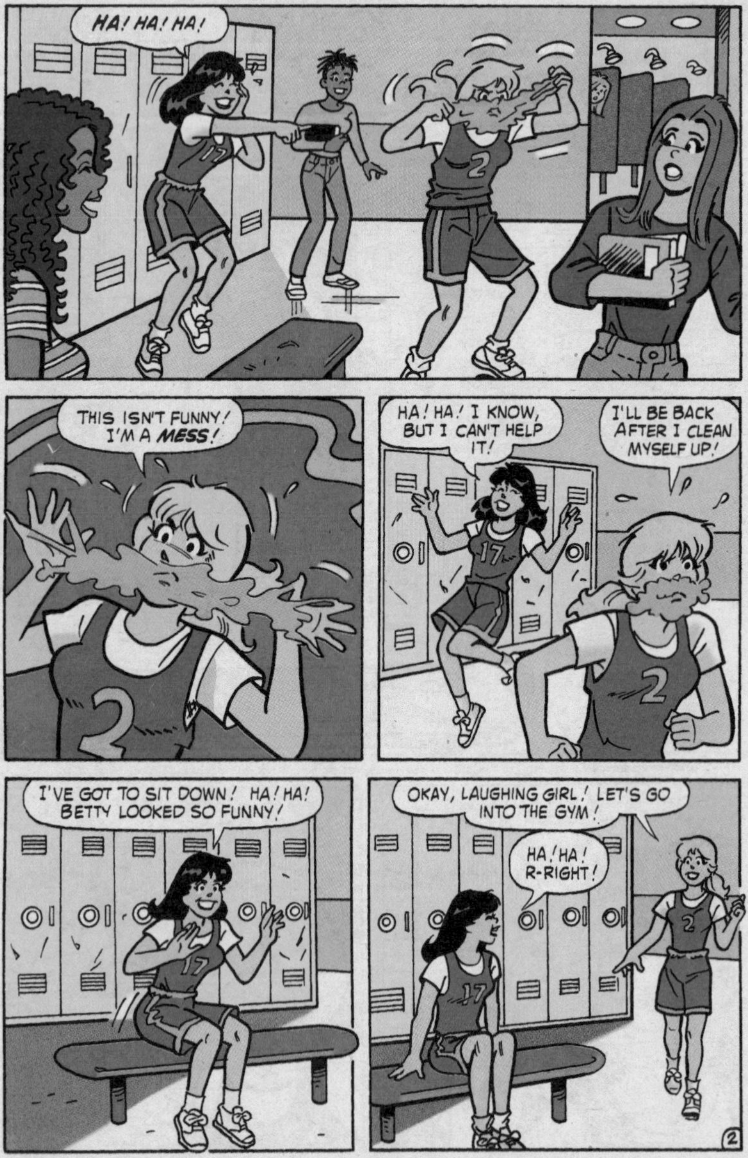

HA! HA! HA!
THIS ISN'T FUNNY! I'M A MESS!
HA! HA! I KNOW, BUT I CAN'T HELP IT!
I'LL BE BACK AFTER I CLEAN MYSELF UP!
I'VE GOT TO SIT DOWN! HA! HA! BETTY LOOKED SO FUNNY!
OKAY, LAUGHING GIRL! LET'S GO INTO THE GYM!
HA! HA! R-RIGHT!
2

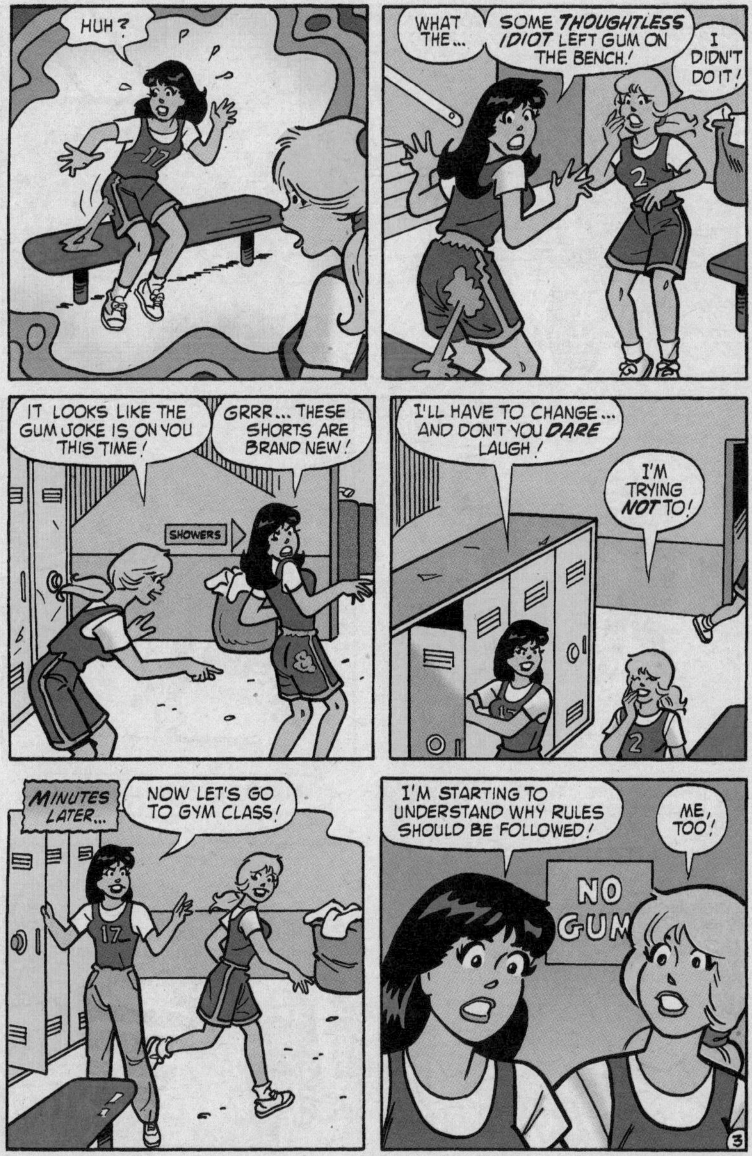
HUH?
WHAT THE...
SOME THOUGHTLESS IDIOT LEFT GUM ON THE BENCH!
I DIDN'T DO IT!
IT LOOKS LIKE THE GUM JOKE IS ON YOU THIS TIME!
GRRR... THESE SHORTS ARE BRAND NEW!
SHOWERS
I'LL HAVE TO CHANGE... AND DON'T YOU DARE LAUGH!
I'M TRYING NOT TO!
MINUTES LATER...
NOW LET'S GO TO GYM CLASS!
I'M STARTING TO UNDERSTAND WHY RULES SHOULD BE FOLLOWED!
ME, TOO!
NO GUM
3

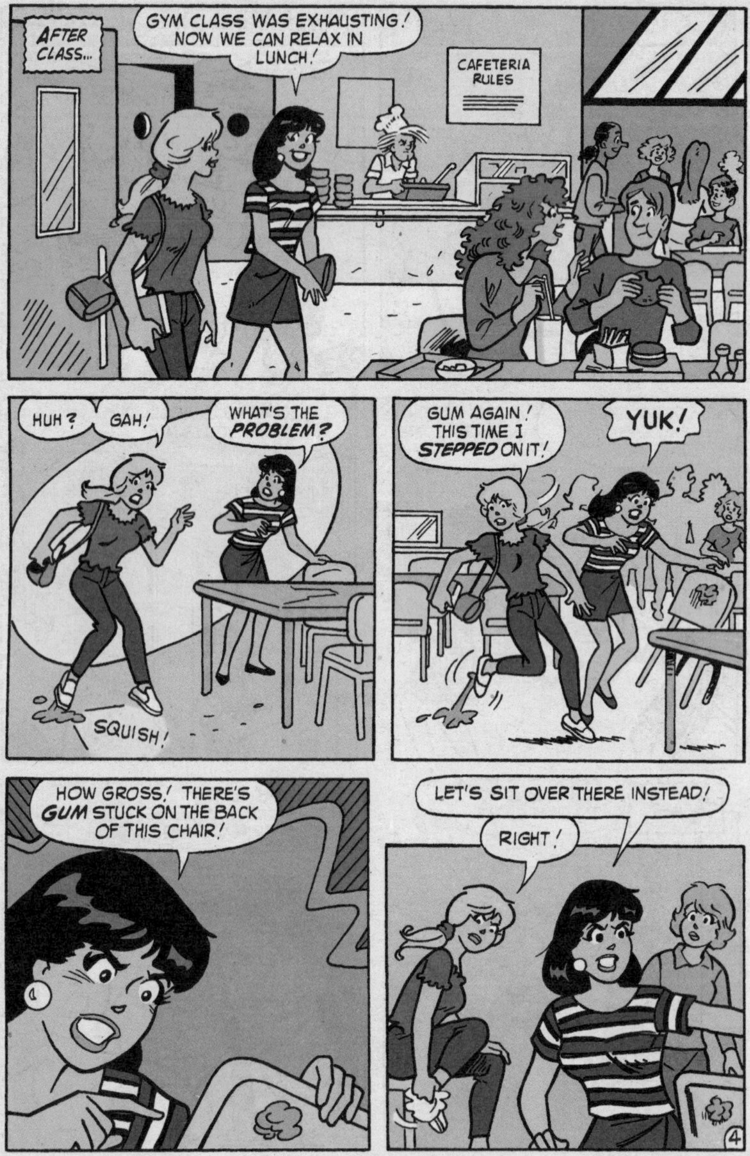
AFTER CLASS...
GYM CLASS WAS EXHAUSTING! NOW WE CAN RELAX IN LUNCH!
CAFETERIA RULES
HUH?
GAH!
WHAT'S THE PROBLEM?
SQUISH!
GUM AGAIN! THIS TIME I STEPPED ON IT!
YUK!
HOW GROSS! THERE'S GUM STUCK ON THE BACK OF THIS CHAIR!
LET'S SIT OVER THERE INSTEAD!
RIGHT!
4

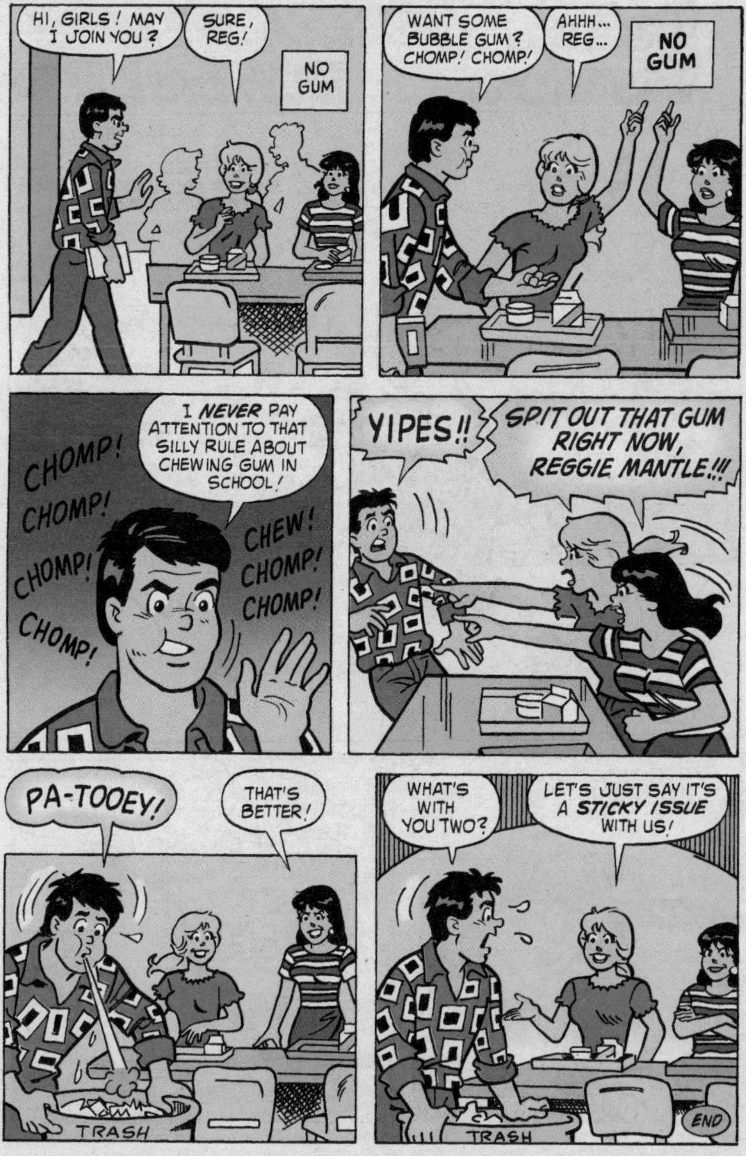
HI, GIRLS! MAY I JOIN YOU?
SURE, REG!
NO GUM
WANT SOME BUBBLE GUM? CHOMP! CHOMP!
AHHH... REG...
NO GUM
I NEVER PAY ATTENTION TO THAT SILLY RULE ABOUT CHEWING GUM IN SCHOOL!
CHOMP! CHOMP! CHOMP! CHOMP!
CHEW! CHOMP! CHOMP!
YIPES!!
SPIT OUT THAT GUM RIGHT NOW, REGGIE MANTLE!!!
PA-TOOEY!
THAT'S BETTER!
TRASH
WHAT'S WITH YOU TWO?
LET'S JUST SAY IT'S A STICKY ISSUE WITH US!
TRASH
END

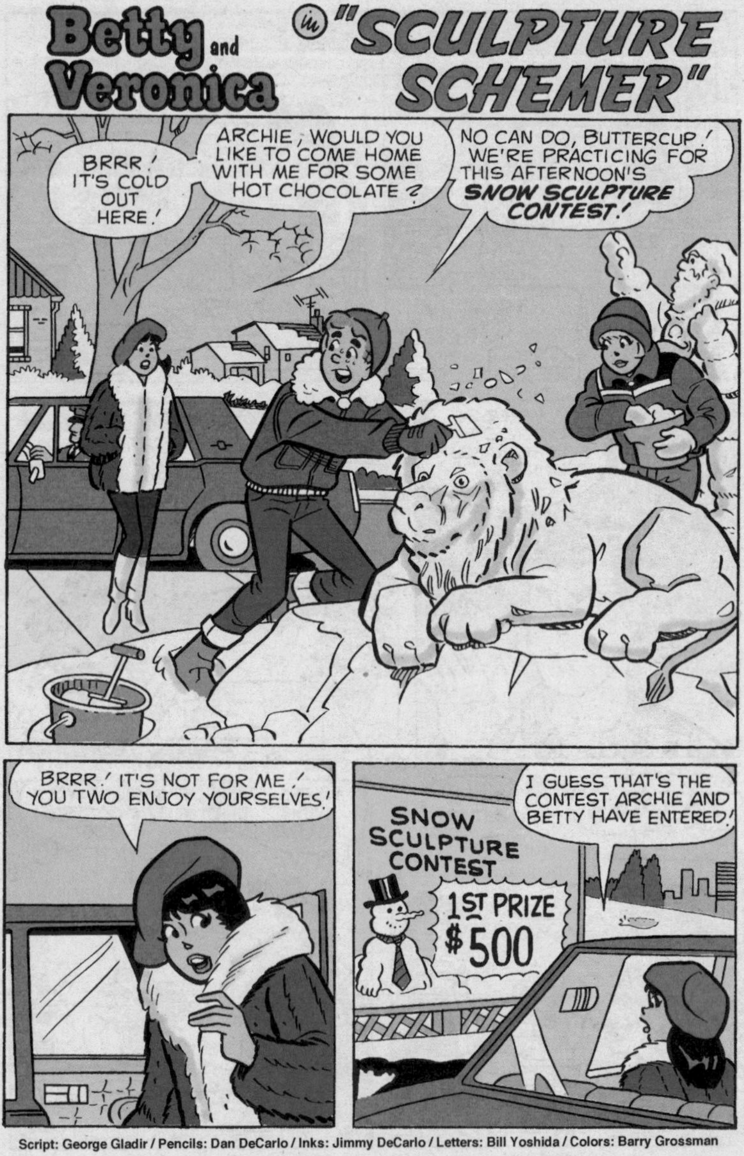
Betty and Veronica
in "SCULPTURE SCHEMER"
BRRR! IT'S COLD OUT HERE!
ARCHIE, WOULD YOU LIKE TO COME HOME WITH ME FOR SOME HOT CHOCOLATE?
NO CAN DO, BUTTERCUP! WE'RE PRACTICING FOR THIS AFTERNOON'S SNOW SCULPTURE CONTEST!
BRRR! IT'S NOT FOR ME! YOU TWO ENJOY YOURSELVES!
I GUESS THAT'S THE CONTEST ARCHIE AND BETTY HAVE ENTERED!
SNOW SCULPTURE CONTEST
1ST PRIZE $500

Script: George Gladir / Pencils: Dan DeCarlo / Inks: Jimmy DeCarlo / Letters: Bill Yoshida / Colors: Barry Grossman

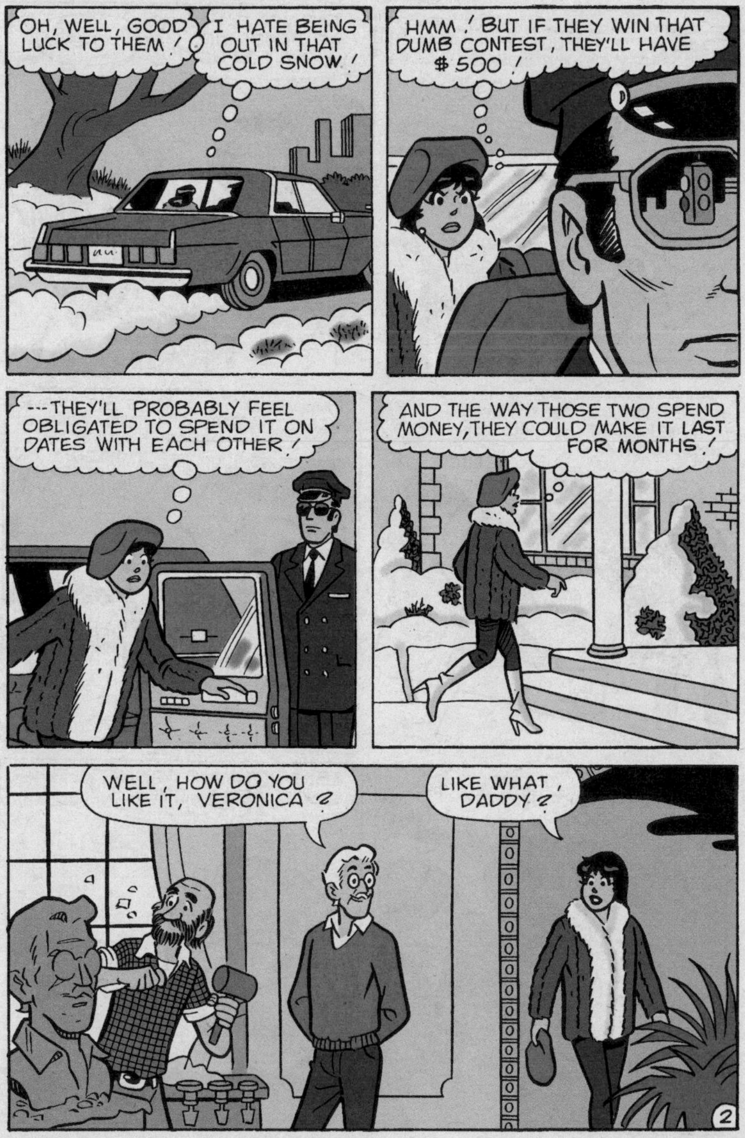

OH, WELL, GOOD LUCK TO THEM !
I HATE BEING OUT IN THAT COLD SNOW !
HMM ! BUT IF THEY WIN THAT DUMB CONTEST, THEY'LL HAVE $ 500 !
---THEY'LL PROBABLY FEEL OBLIGATED TO SPEND IT ON DATES WITH EACH OTHER !
AND THE WAY THOSE TWO SPEND MONEY, THEY COULD MAKE IT LAST FOR MONTHS !
WELL, HOW DO YOU LIKE IT, VERONICA ?
LIKE WHAT, DADDY ?
2

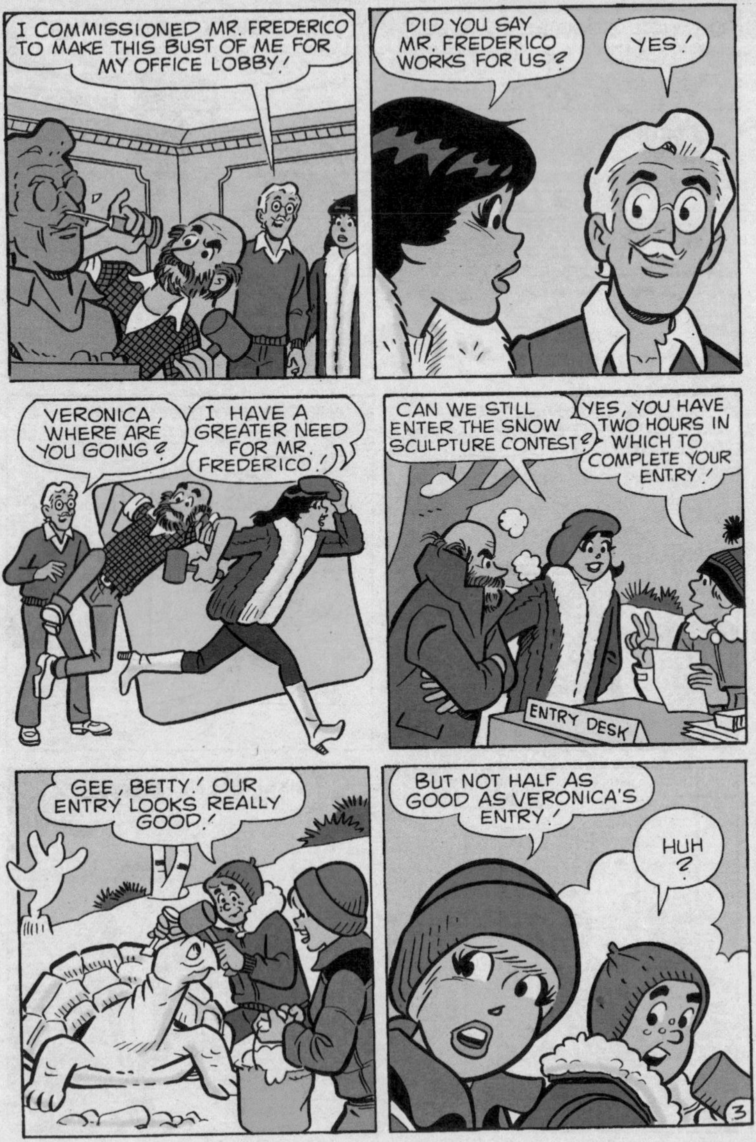

I COMMISSIONED MR. FREDERICO TO MAKE THIS BUST OF ME FOR MY OFFICE LOBBY!
DID YOU SAY MR. FREDERICO WORKS FOR US?
YES!
VERONICA, WHERE ARE YOU GOING?
I HAVE A GREATER NEED FOR MR. FREDERICO!
CAN WE STILL ENTER THE SNOW SCULPTURE CONTEST?
YES, YOU HAVE TWO HOURS IN WHICH TO COMPLETE YOUR ENTRY!
ENTRY DESK
GEE, BETTY! OUR ENTRY LOOKS REALLY GOOD!
BUT NOT HALF AS GOOD AS VERONICA'S ENTRY!
HUH?
3

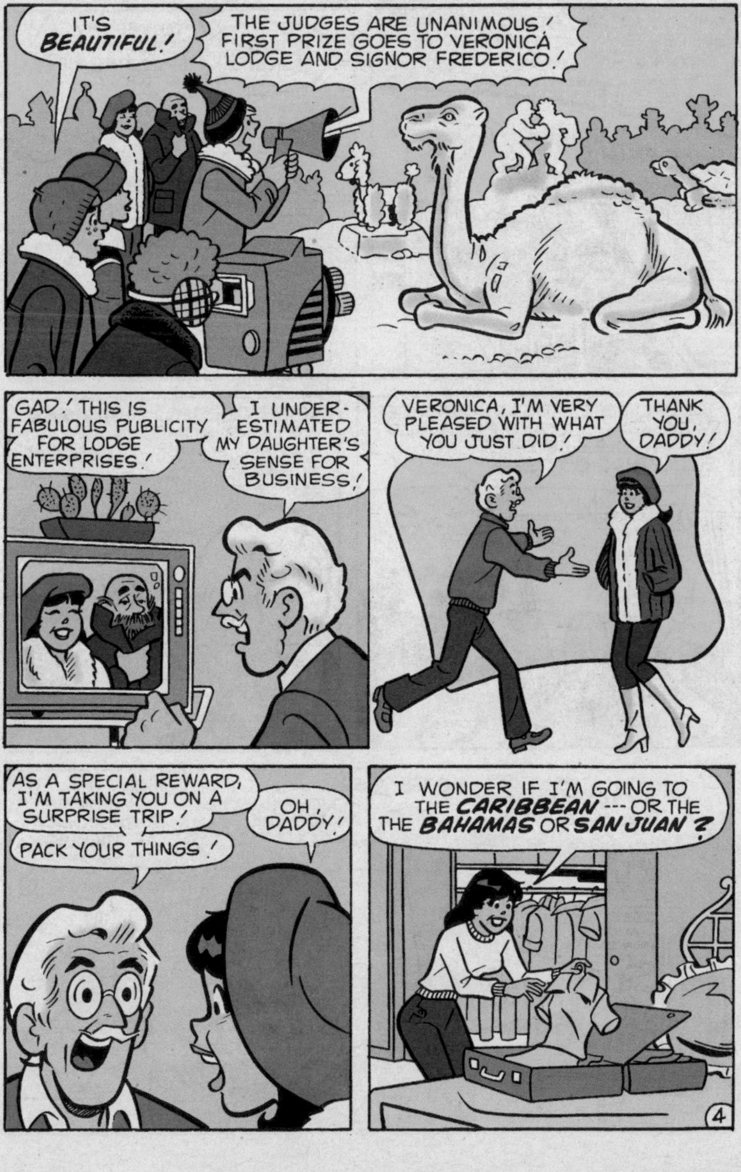

IT'S BEAUTIFUL!
THE JUDGES ARE UNANIMOUS! FIRST PRIZE GOES TO VERONICA LODGE AND SIGNOR FREDERICO!
GAD! THIS IS FABULOUS PUBLICITY FOR LODGE ENTERPRISES!
I UNDER-ESTIMATED MY DAUGHTER'S SENSE FOR BUSINESS!
VERONICA, I'M VERY PLEASED WITH WHAT YOU JUST DID!
THANK YOU, DADDY!
AS A SPECIAL REWARD, I'M TAKING YOU ON A SURPRISE TRIP!
PACK YOUR THINGS!
OH, DADDY!
I WONDER IF I'M GOING TO THE CARIBBEAN --- OR THE THE BAHAMAS OR SAN JUAN?
4

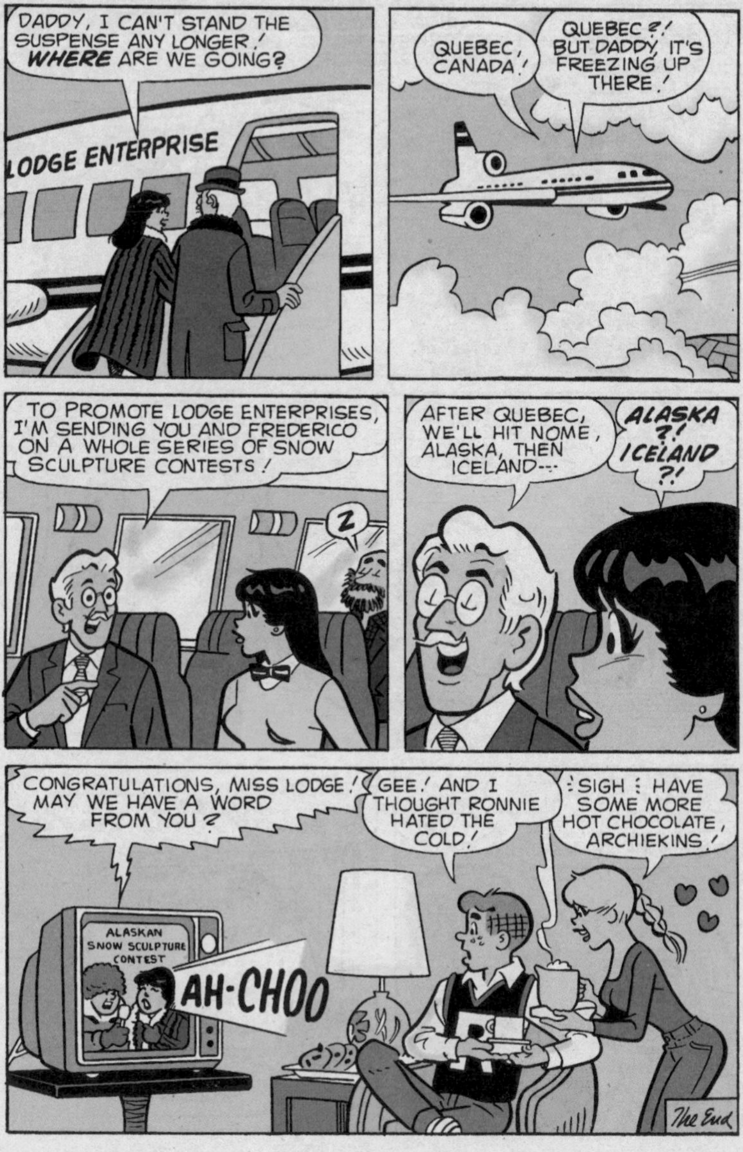

DADDY, I CAN'T STAND THE SUSPENSE ANY LONGER! WHERE ARE WE GOING?
LODGE ENTERPRISE
QUEBEC, CANADA!
QUEBEC?! BUT DADDY, IT'S FREEZING UP THERE!
TO PROMOTE LODGE ENTERPRISES, I'M SENDING YOU AND FREDERICO ON A WHOLE SERIES OF SNOW SCULPTURE CONTESTS!
Z
AFTER QUEBEC, WE'LL HIT NOME, ALASKA, THEN ICELAND---
ALASKA?! ICELAND?!
CONGRATULATIONS, MISS LODGE! MAY WE HAVE A WORD FROM YOU?
GEE! AND I THOUGHT RONNIE HATED THE COLD!
:SIGH: HAVE SOME MORE HOT CHOCOLATE, ARCHIEKINS!
ALASKAN SNOW SCULPTURE CONTEST
AH-CHOO
The End

Betty and Veronica in "A GUEST IN THE HOUSE"

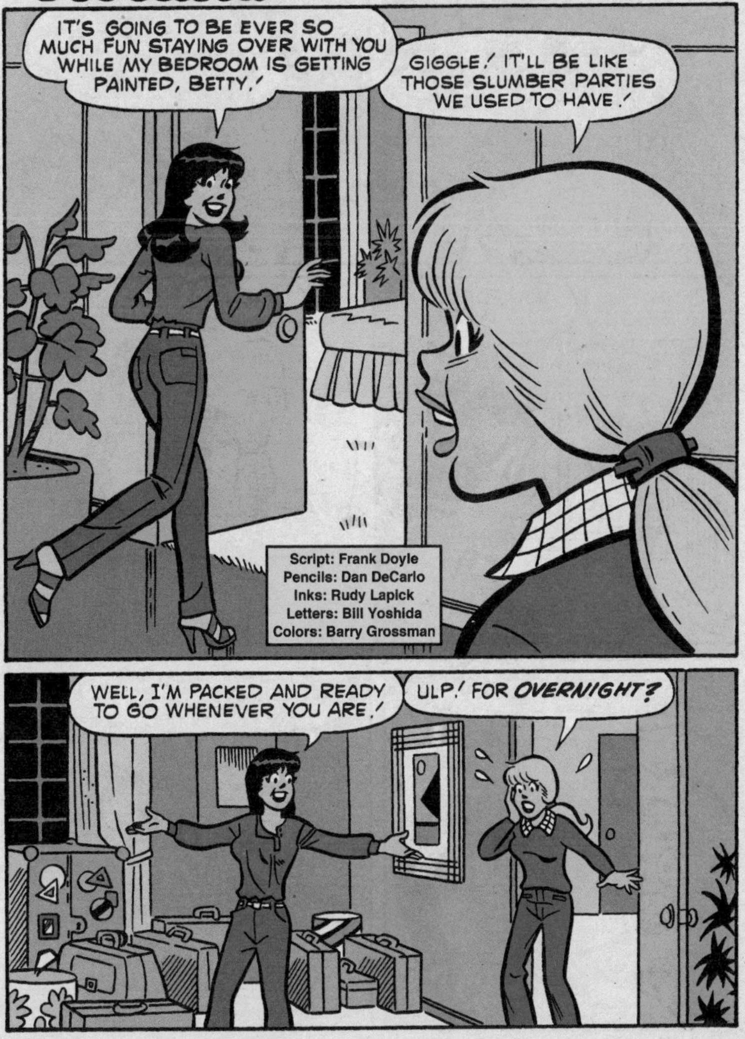
IT'S GOING TO BE EVER SO MUCH FUN STAYING OVER WITH YOU WHILE MY BEDROOM IS GETTING PAINTED, BETTY.!
GIGGLE! IT'LL BE LIKE THOSE SLUMBER PARTIES WE USED TO HAVE.!
Script: Frank Doyle
Pencils: Dan DeCarlo
Inks: Rudy Lapick
Letters: Bill Yoshida
Colors: Barry Grossman
WELL, I'M PACKED AND READY TO GO WHENEVER YOU ARE.!
ULP! FOR *OVERNIGHT?*

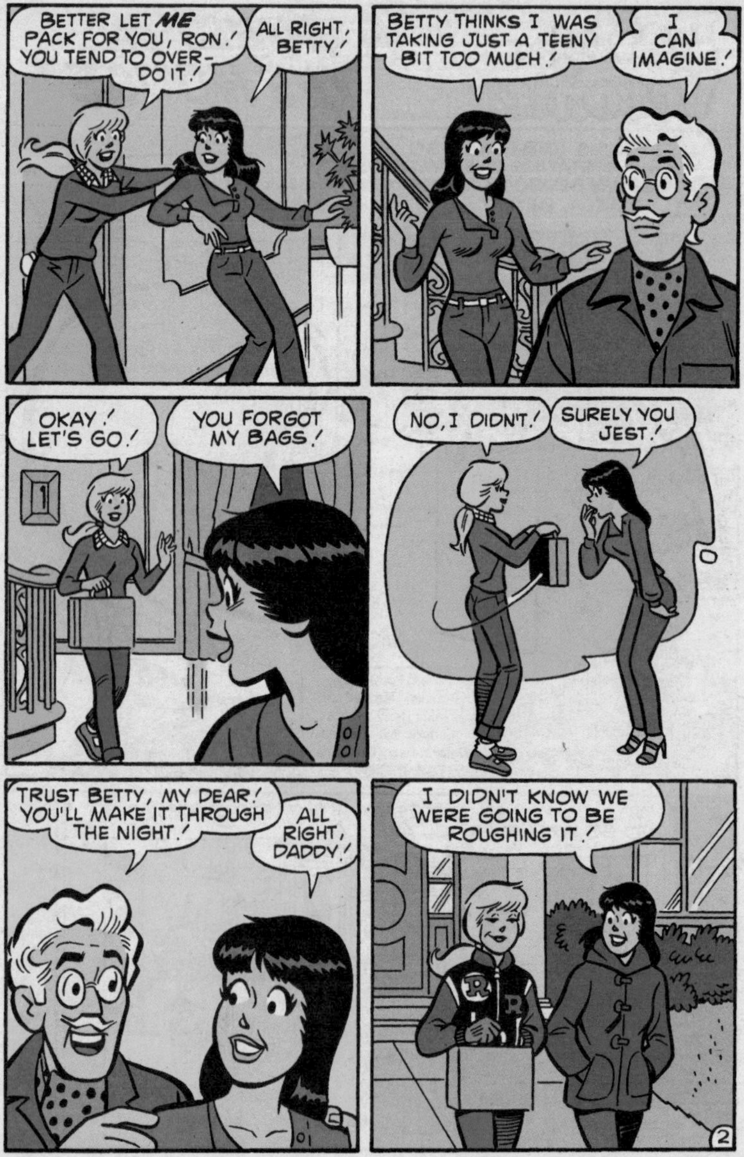

BETTER LET ME PACK FOR YOU, RON.! YOU TEND TO OVER-DO IT.!
ALL RIGHT, BETTY.!
BETTY THINKS I WAS TAKING JUST A TEENY BIT TOO MUCH.!
I CAN IMAGINE.!
OKAY.! LET'S GO.!
YOU FORGOT MY BAGS.!
NO, I DIDN'T.!
SURELY YOU JEST.!
TRUST BETTY, MY DEAR.! YOU'LL MAKE IT THROUGH THE NIGHT.!
ALL RIGHT, DADDY.!
I DIDN'T KNOW WE WERE GOING TO BE ROUGHING IT.!
2

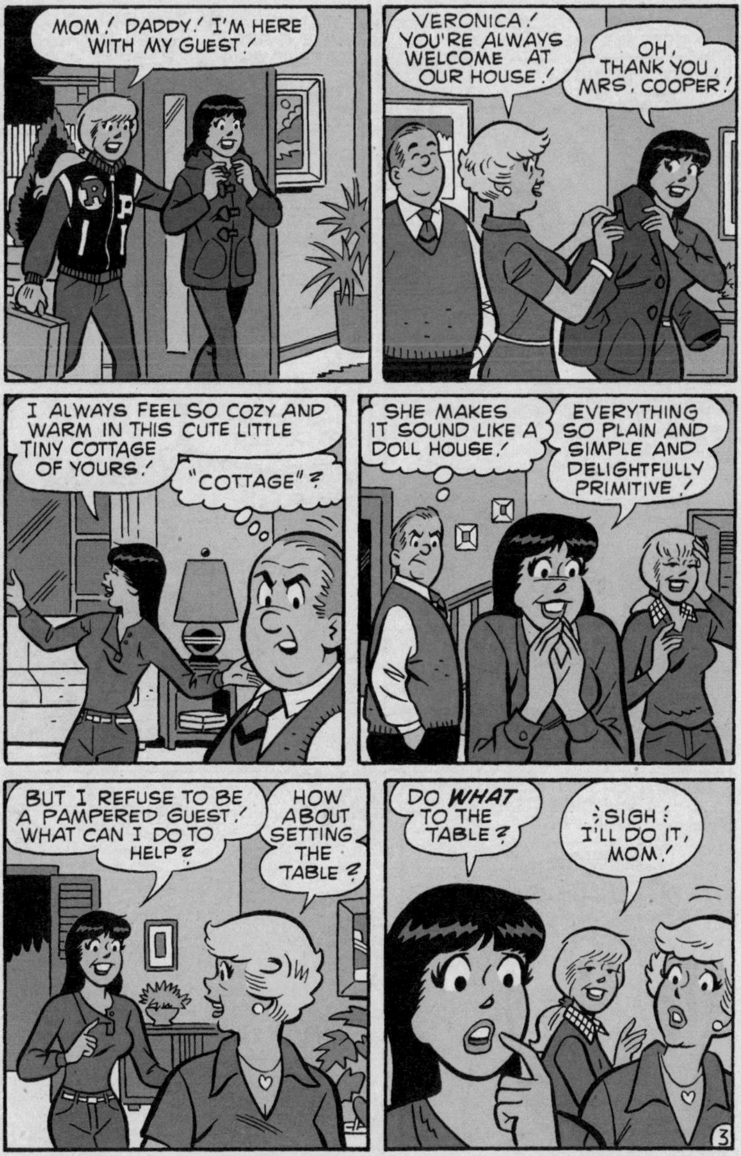
MOM! DADDY! I'M HERE WITH MY GUEST!
VERONICA! YOU'RE ALWAYS WELCOME AT OUR HOUSE!
OH, THANK YOU, MRS. COOPER!
I ALWAYS FEEL SO COZY AND WARM IN THIS CUTE LITTLE TINY COTTAGE OF YOURS!
"COTTAGE"?
SHE MAKES IT SOUND LIKE A DOLL HOUSE!
EVERYTHING SO PLAIN AND SIMPLE AND DELIGHTFULLY PRIMITIVE!
BUT I REFUSE TO BE A PAMPERED GUEST! WHAT CAN I DO TO HELP?
HOW ABOUT SETTING THE TABLE?
DO *WHAT* TO THE TABLE?
:SIGH: I'LL DO IT, MOM!
3

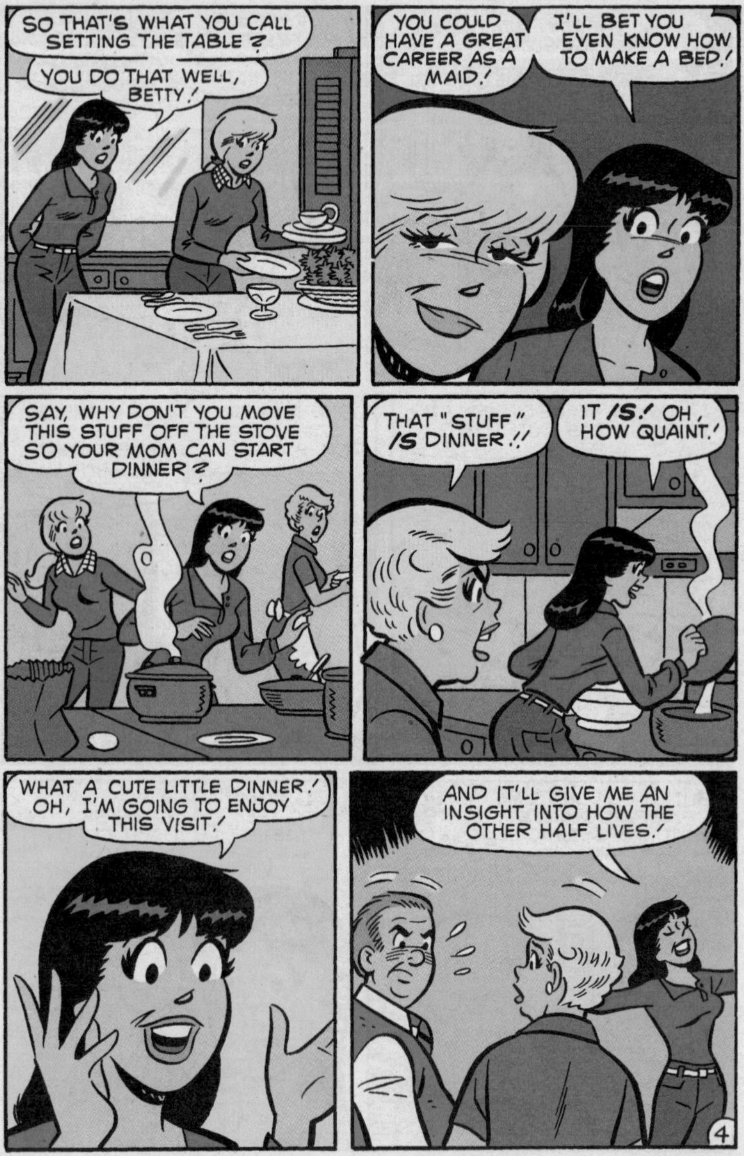
SO THAT'S WHAT YOU CALL SETTING THE TABLE ?
YOU DO THAT WELL, BETTY!
YOU COULD HAVE A GREAT CAREER AS A MAID!
I'LL BET YOU EVEN KNOW HOW TO MAKE A BED!
SAY, WHY DON'T YOU MOVE THIS STUFF OFF THE STOVE SO YOUR MOM CAN START DINNER ?
THAT "STUFF" IS DINNER!!
IT IS! OH, HOW QUAINT!
WHAT A CUTE LITTLE DINNER! OH, I'M GOING TO ENJOY THIS VISIT!
AND IT'LL GIVE ME AN INSIGHT INTO HOW THE OTHER HALF LIVES!
4

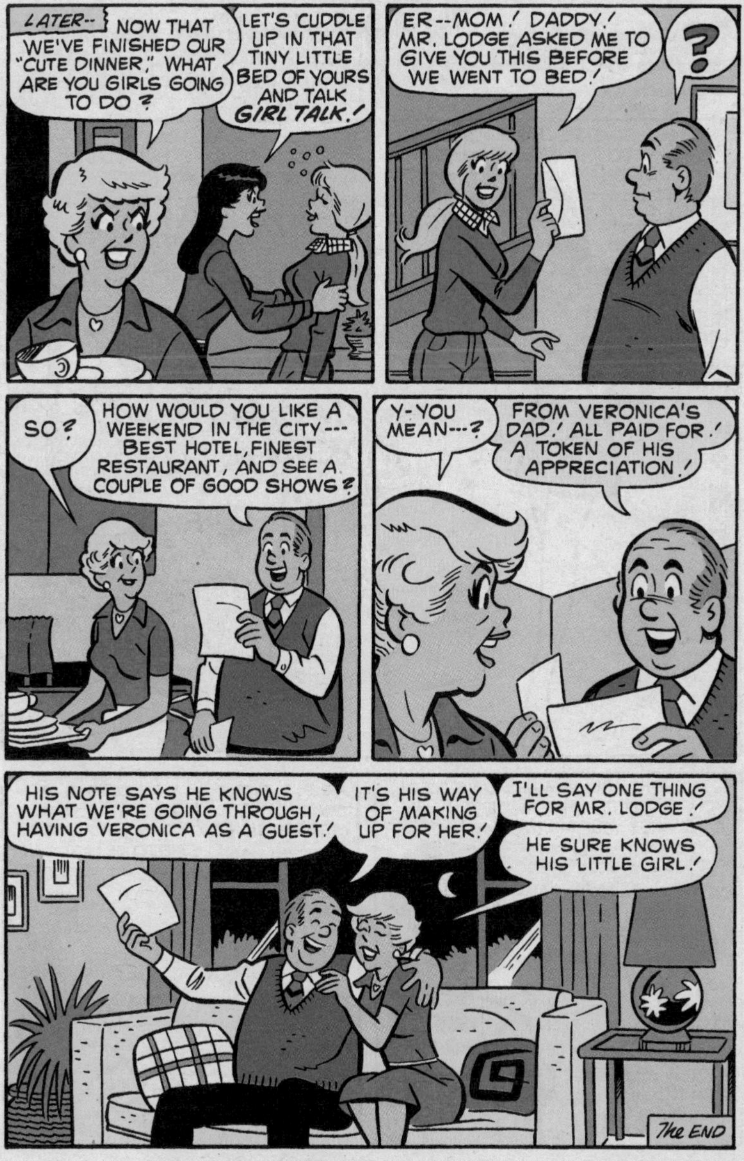
LATER--
NOW THAT WE'VE FINISHED OUR "CUTE DINNER," WHAT ARE YOU GIRLS GOING TO DO?
LET'S CUDDLE UP IN THAT TINY LITTLE BED OF YOURS AND TALK GIRL TALK!
ER--MOM! DADDY! MR. LODGE ASKED ME TO GIVE YOU THIS BEFORE WE WENT TO BED!
?
SO?
HOW WOULD YOU LIKE A WEEKEND IN THE CITY--- BEST HOTEL, FINEST RESTAURANT, AND SEE A COUPLE OF GOOD SHOWS?
Y-YOU MEAN---?
FROM VERONICA'S DAD! ALL PAID FOR! A TOKEN OF HIS APPRECIATION!
HIS NOTE SAYS HE KNOWS WHAT WE'RE GOING THROUGH, HAVING VERONICA AS A GUEST!
IT'S HIS WAY OF MAKING UP FOR HER!
I'LL SAY ONE THING FOR MR. LODGE!
HE SURE KNOWS HIS LITTLE GIRL!
The END

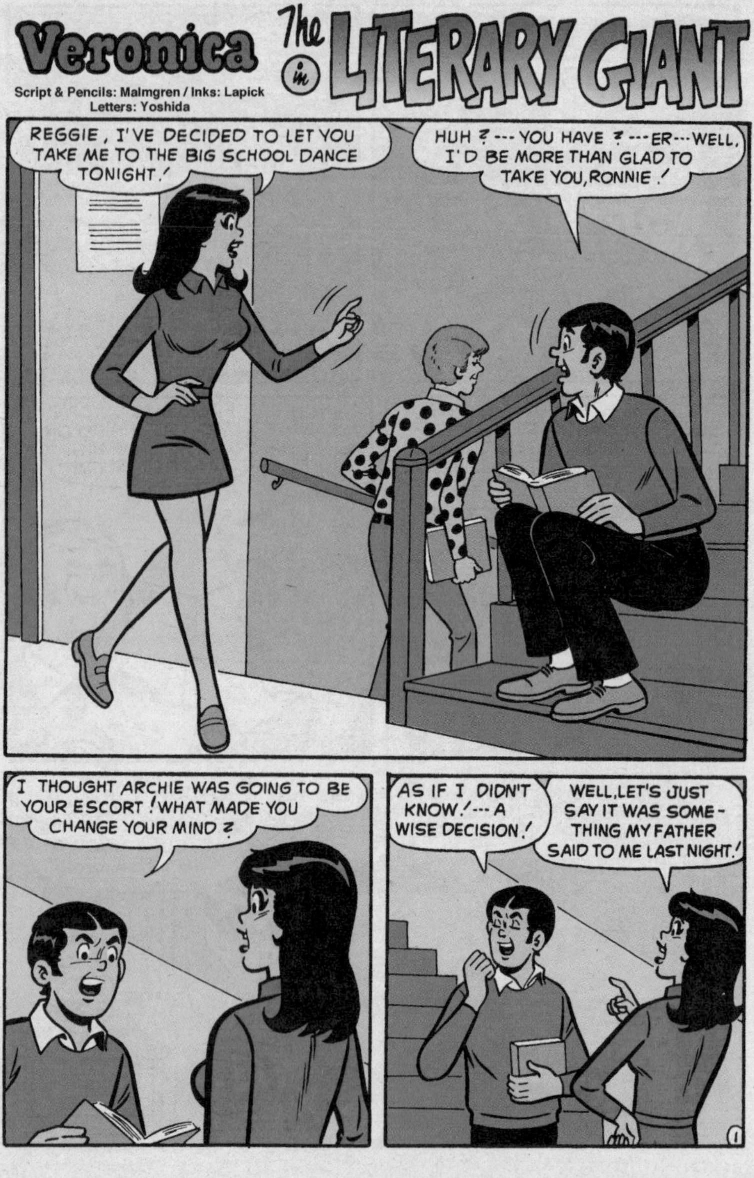

Veronica in The LITERARY GIANT
Script & Pencils: Malmgren / Inks: Lapick
Letters: Yoshida
REGGIE, I'VE DECIDED TO LET YOU TAKE ME TO THE BIG SCHOOL DANCE TONIGHT!
HUH ? --- YOU HAVE ? --- ER --- WELL, I'D BE MORE THAN GLAD TO TAKE YOU, RONNIE!
I THOUGHT ARCHIE WAS GOING TO BE YOUR ESCORT! WHAT MADE YOU CHANGE YOUR MIND ?
AS IF I DIDN'T KNOW! --- A WISE DECISION!
WELL, LET'S JUST SAY IT WAS SOMETHING MY FATHER SAID TO ME LAST NIGHT!
1

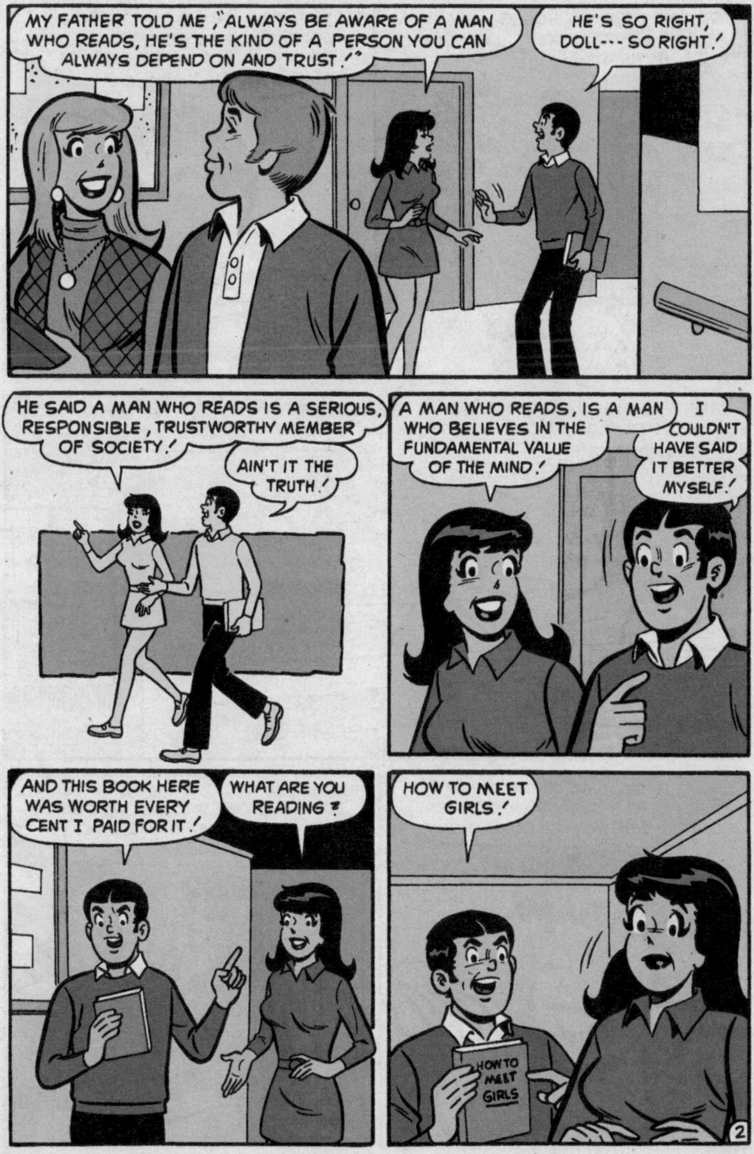
MY FATHER TOLD ME, "ALWAYS BE AWARE OF A MAN WHO READS, HE'S THE KIND OF A PERSON YOU CAN ALWAYS DEPEND ON AND TRUST!"
HE'S SO RIGHT, DOLL--- SO RIGHT!
HE SAID A MAN WHO READS IS A SERIOUS, RESPONSIBLE, TRUSTWORTHY MEMBER OF SOCIETY!
AIN'T IT THE TRUTH!
A MAN WHO READS, IS A MAN WHO BELIEVES IN THE FUNDAMENTAL VALUE OF THE MIND!
I COULDN'T HAVE SAID IT BETTER MYSELF!
AND THIS BOOK HERE WAS WORTH EVERY CENT I PAID FOR IT!
WHAT ARE YOU READING?
HOW TO MEET GIRLS!
HOW TO MEET GIRLS
2

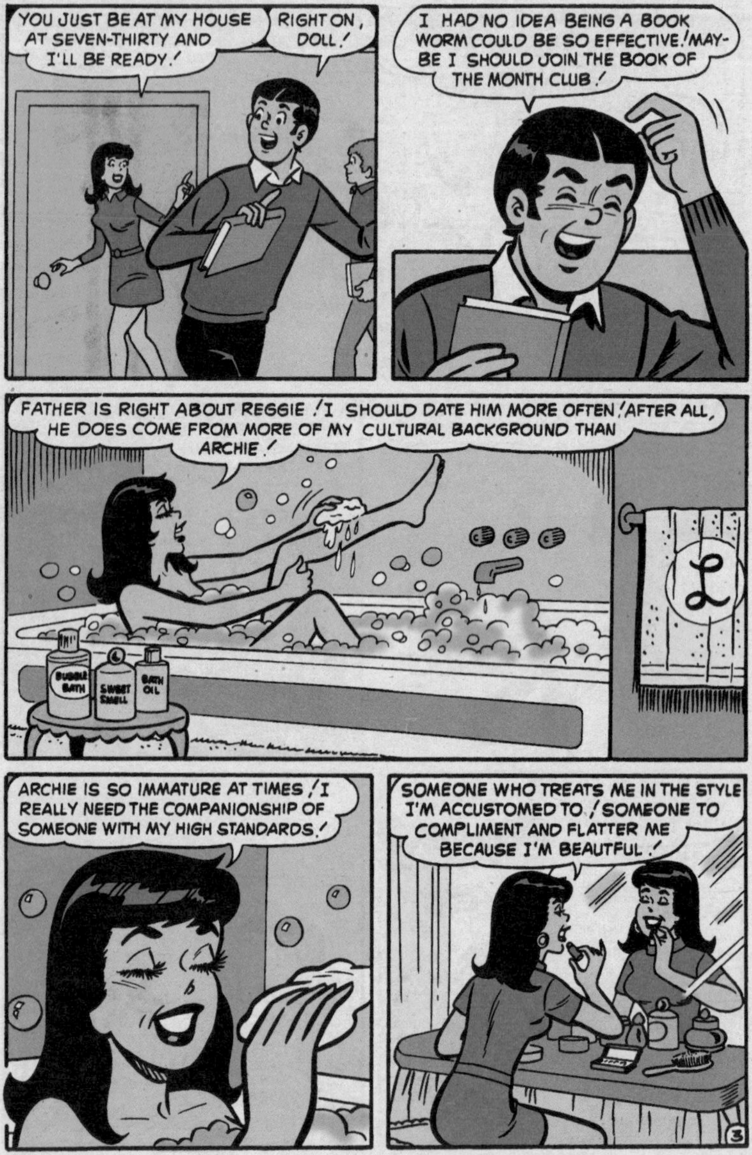
YOU JUST BE AT MY HOUSE AT SEVEN-THIRTY AND I'LL BE READY!
RIGHT ON, DOLL!
I HAD NO IDEA BEING A BOOK WORM COULD BE SO EFFECTIVE! MAY-BE I SHOULD JOIN THE BOOK OF THE MONTH CLUB!
FATHER IS RIGHT ABOUT REGGIE! I SHOULD DATE HIM MORE OFTEN! AFTER ALL, HE DOES COME FROM MORE OF MY CULTURAL BACKGROUND THAN ARCHIE!
BUBBLE BATH
SWEET SMELL
BATH OIL
ARCHIE IS SO IMMATURE AT TIMES! I REALLY NEED THE COMPANIONSHIP OF SOMEONE WITH MY HIGH STANDARDS!
SOMEONE WHO TREATS ME IN THE STYLE I'M ACCUSTOMED TO! SOMEONE TO COMPLIMENT AND FLATTER ME BECAUSE I'M BEAUTFUL!
3

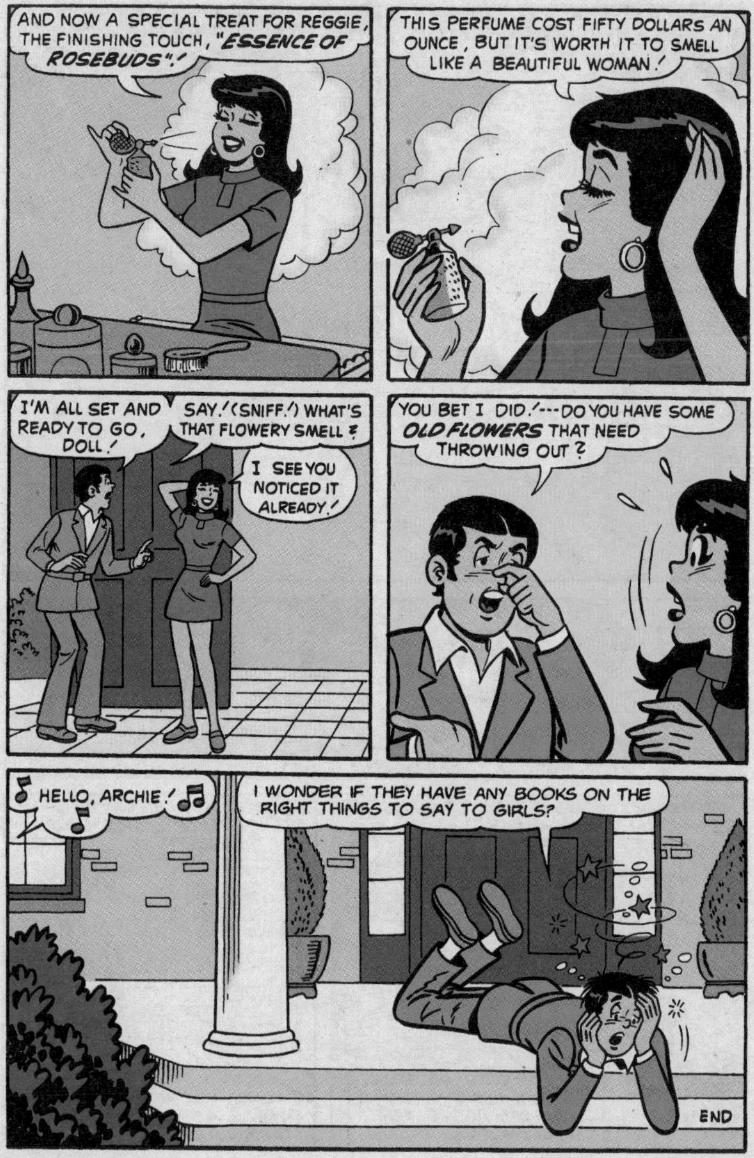
AND NOW A SPECIAL TREAT FOR REGGIE, THE FINISHING TOUCH, "ESSENCE OF ROSEBUDS"!
THIS PERFUME COST FIFTY DOLLARS AN OUNCE, BUT IT'S WORTH IT TO SMELL LIKE A BEAUTIFUL WOMAN!
I'M ALL SET AND READY TO GO, DOLL!
SAY! (SNIFF!) WHAT'S THAT FLOWERY SMELL?
I SEE YOU NOTICED IT ALREADY!
YOU BET I DID!---DO YOU HAVE SOME OLD FLOWERS THAT NEED THROWING OUT?
HELLO, ARCHIE!
I WONDER IF THEY HAVE ANY BOOKS ON THE RIGHT THINGS TO SAY TO GIRLS?
END

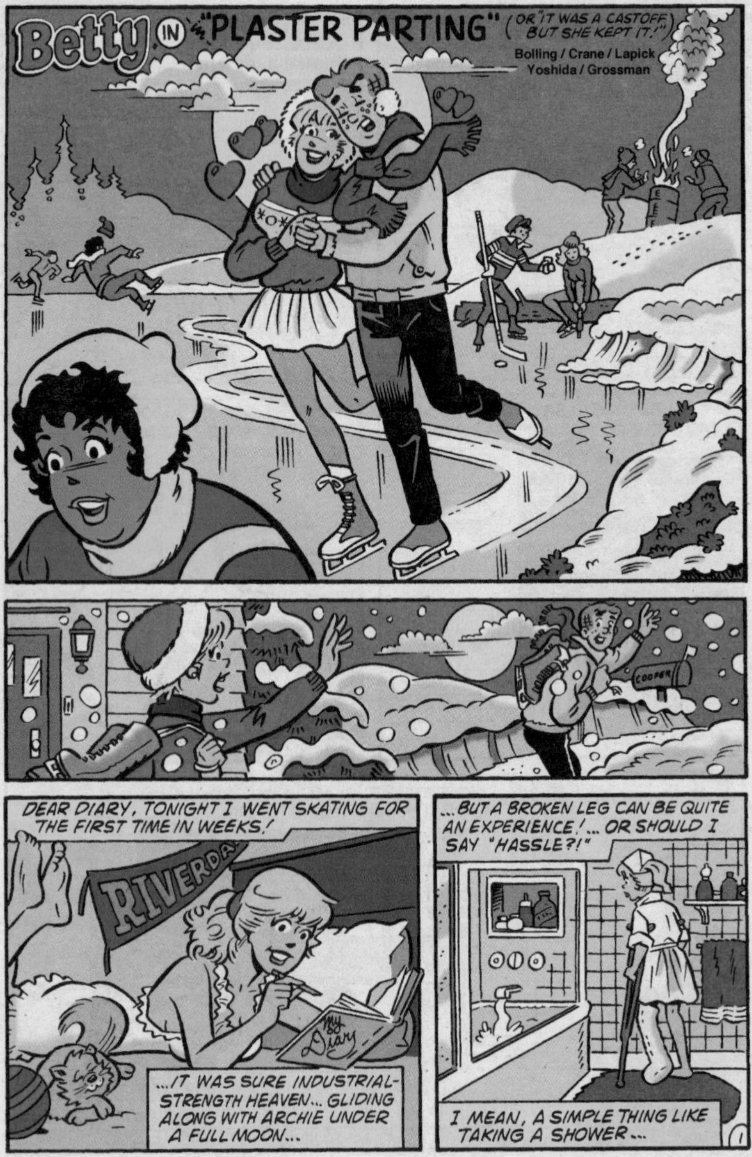
Betty IN "PLASTER PARTING" (OR "IT WAS A CASTOFF BUT SHE KEPT IT!")
Bolling / Crane / Lapick
Yoshida / Grossman
COOPER
RIVERDA
DEAR DIARY, TONIGHT I WENT SKATING FOR THE FIRST TIME IN WEEKS!
...IT WAS SURE INDUSTRIAL-STRENGTH HEAVEN... GLIDING ALONG WITH ARCHIE UNDER A FULL MOON...
...BUT A BROKEN LEG CAN BE QUITE AN EXPERIENCE!... OR SHOULD I SAY "HASSLE?!"
I MEAN, A SIMPLE THING LIKE TAKING A SHOWER...
1

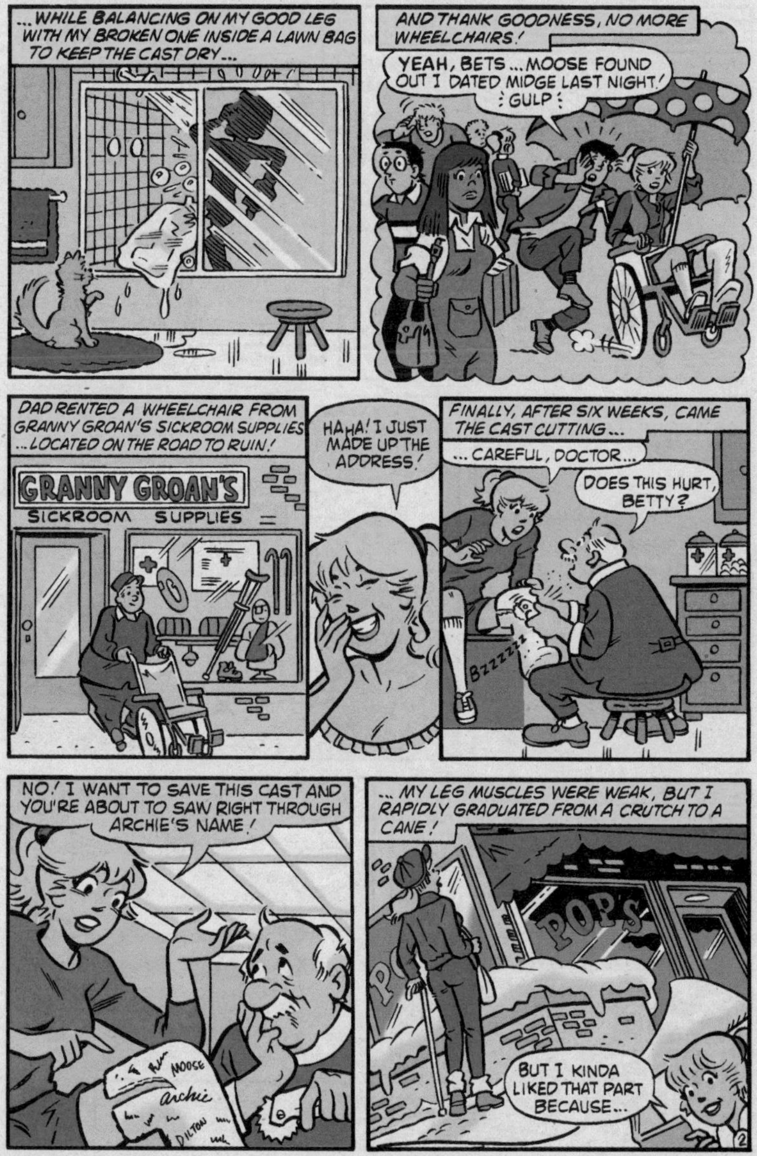
...WHILE BALANCING ON MY GOOD LEG WITH MY BROKEN ONE INSIDE A LAWN BAG TO KEEP THE CAST DRY...
AND THANK GOODNESS, NO MORE WHEELCHAIRS!
YEAH, BETS ...MOOSE FOUND OUT I DATED MIDGE LAST NIGHT! GULP
DAD RENTED A WHEELCHAIR FROM GRANNY GROAN'S SICKROOM SUPPLIES ...LOCATED ON THE ROAD TO RUIN!
GRANNY GROAN'S
SICKROOM SUPPLIES
HA HA! I JUST MADE UP THE ADDRESS!
FINALLY, AFTER SIX WEEKS, CAME THE CAST CUTTING...
...CAREFUL, DOCTOR...
DOES THIS HURT, BETTY?
Bzzzzzz
NO! I WANT TO SAVE THIS CAST AND YOU'RE ABOUT TO SAW RIGHT THROUGH ARCHIE'S NAME!
MOOSE
Archie
DILTON
...MY LEG MUSCLES WERE WEAK, BUT I RAPIDLY GRADUATED FROM A CRUTCH TO A CANE!
POP'S
BUT I KINDA LIKED THAT PART BECAUSE...
2

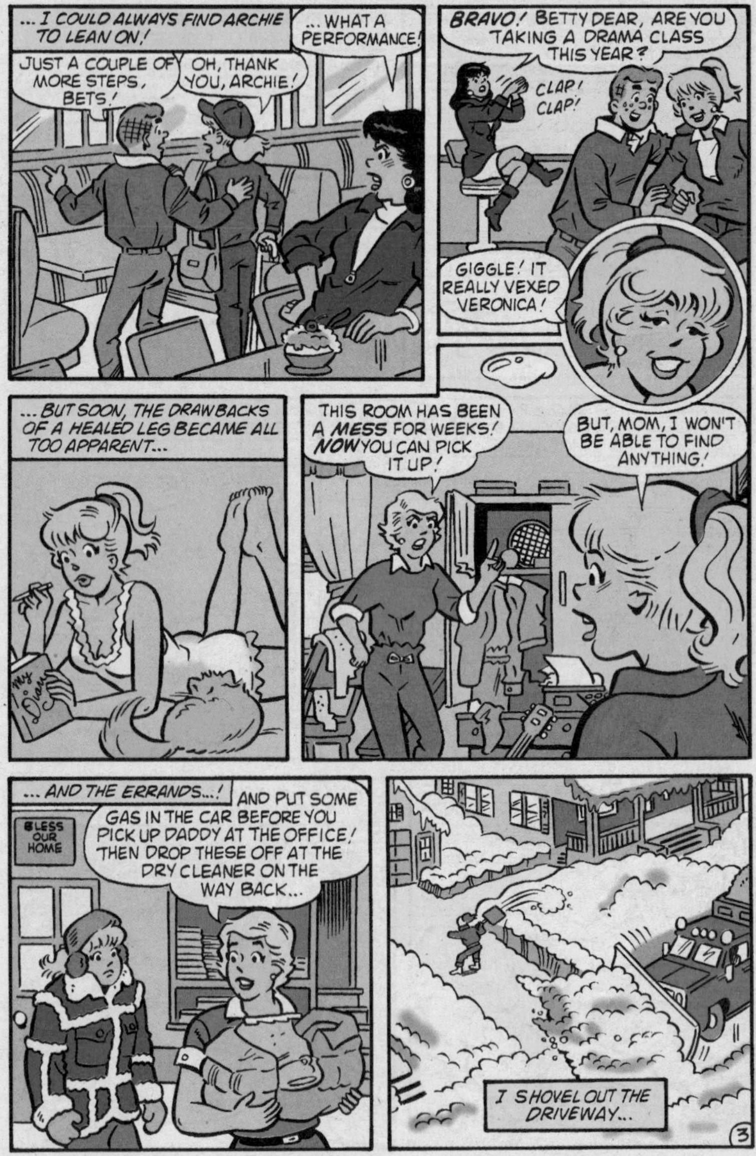

...I COULD ALWAYS FIND ARCHIE TO LEAN ON!
JUST A COUPLE OF MORE STEPS, BETS!
OH, THANK YOU, ARCHIE!
...WHAT A PERFORMANCE!
BRAVO! BETTY DEAR, ARE YOU TAKING A DRAMA CLASS THIS YEAR?
CLAP! CLAP!
GIGGLE! IT REALLY VEXED VERONICA!
...BUT SOON, THE DRAWBACKS OF A HEALED LEG BECAME ALL TOO APPARENT...
My Diary
THIS ROOM HAS BEEN A MESS FOR WEEKS! NOW YOU CAN PICK IT UP!
BUT, MOM, I WON'T BE ABLE TO FIND ANYTHING!
...AND THE ERRANDS...!
BLESS OUR HOME
AND PUT SOME GAS IN THE CAR BEFORE YOU PICK UP DADDY AT THE OFFICE! THEN DROP THESE OFF AT THE DRY CLEANER ON THE WAY BACK...
I SHOVEL OUT THE DRIVEWAY...

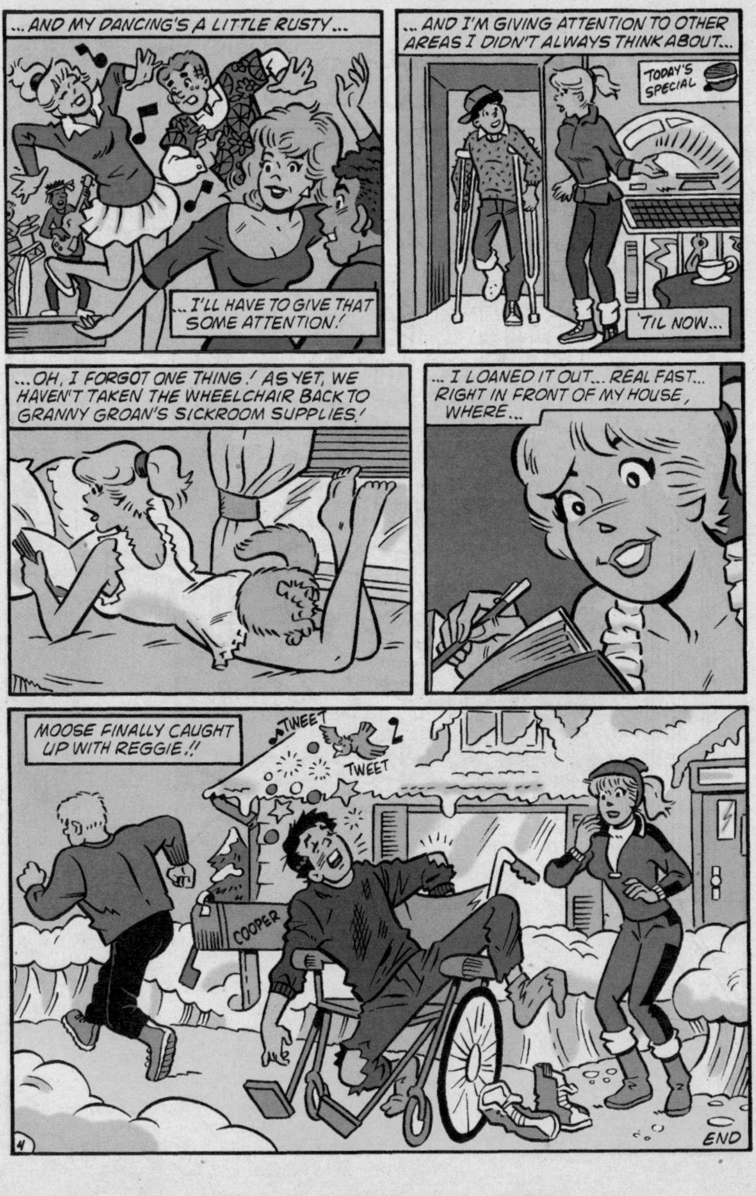

...AND MY DANCING'S A LITTLE RUSTY...
...I'LL HAVE TO GIVE THAT SOME ATTENTION!
...AND I'M GIVING ATTENTION TO OTHER AREAS I DIDN'T ALWAYS THINK ABOUT...
TODAY'S SPECIAL
'TIL NOW...
...OH, I FORGOT ONE THING! AS YET, WE HAVEN'T TAKEN THE WHEELCHAIR BACK TO GRANNY GROAN'S SICKROOM SUPPLIES!
...I LOANED IT OUT... REAL FAST... RIGHT IN FRONT OF MY HOUSE, WHERE...
MOOSE FINALLY CAUGHT UP WITH REGGIE!!
TWEET
TWEET
COOPER
4
END

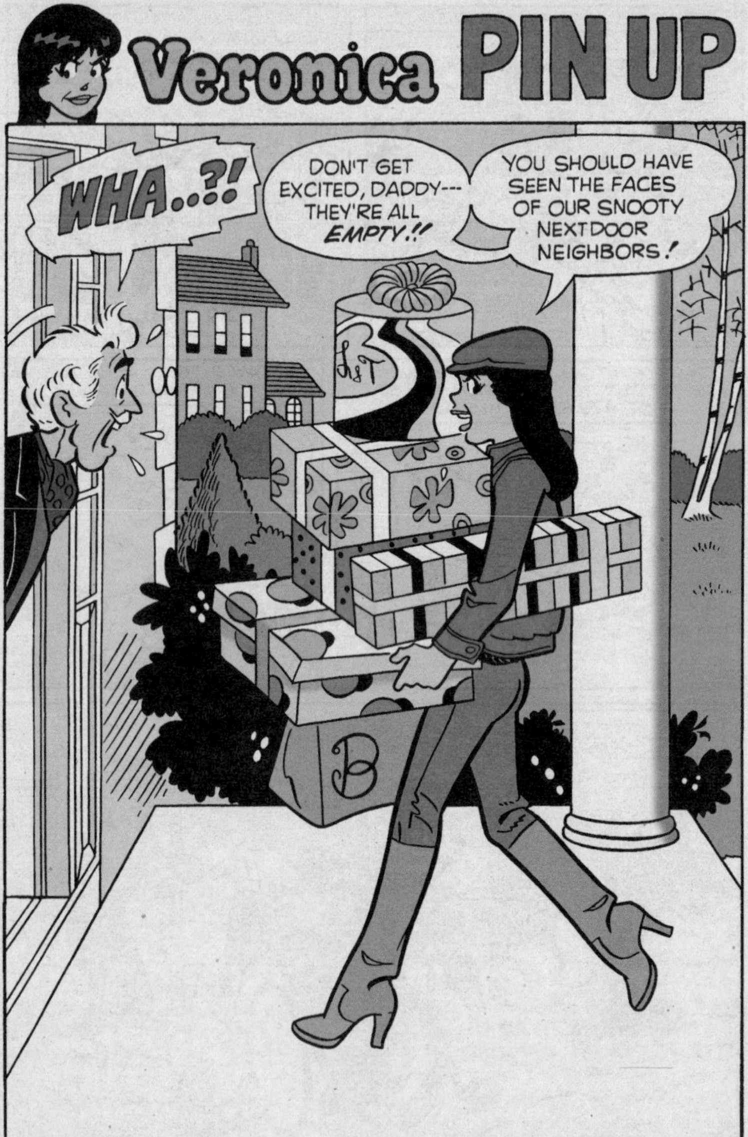
Veronica PIN UP
WHA..?!
DON'T GET EXCITED, DADDY--- THEY'RE ALL EMPTY.!!
YOU SHOULD HAVE SEEN THE FACES OF OUR SNOOTY NEXTDOOR NEIGHBORS!

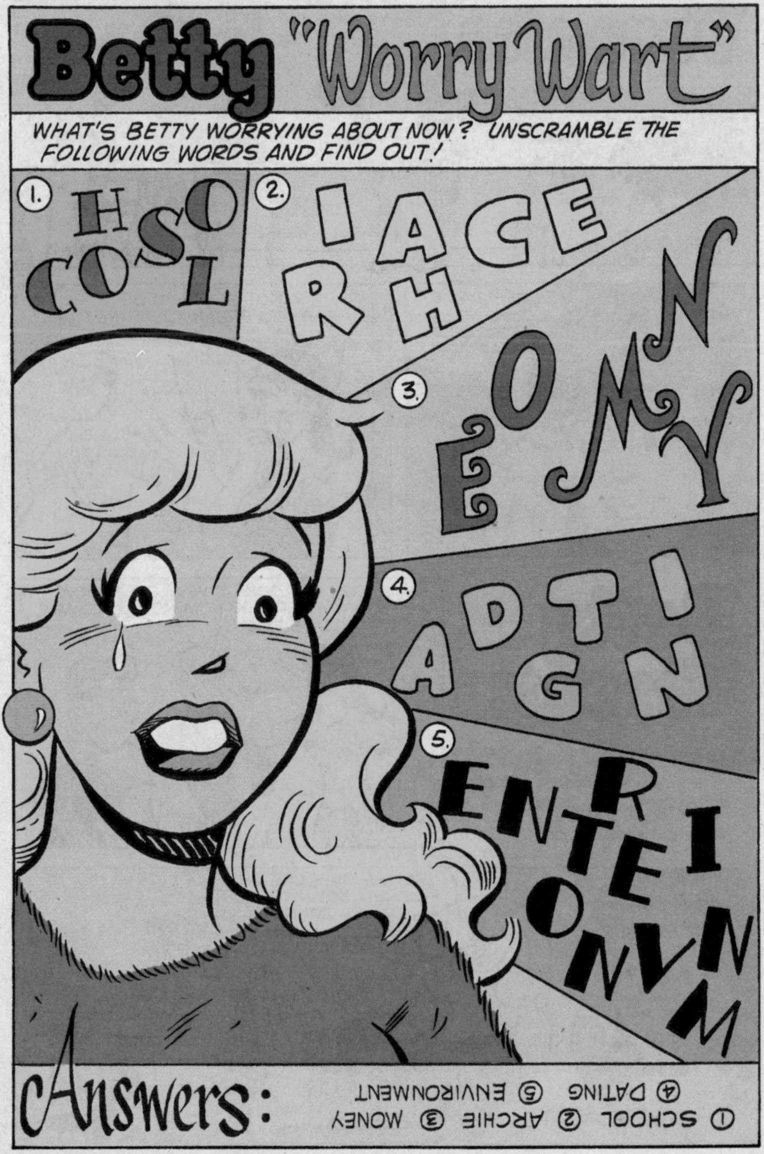
Betty "Worry Wart"
WHAT'S BETTY WORRYING ABOUT NOW? UNSCRAMBLE THE FOLLOWING WORDS AND FIND OUT!
1. H S O O C L
2. I A C E R H
3. E O M N M Y
4. A D T I A G N
5. E N T R N T E I O N V M N
Answers:
1 SCHOOL 2 ARCHIE 3 MONEY
4 DATING 5 ENVIRONMENT

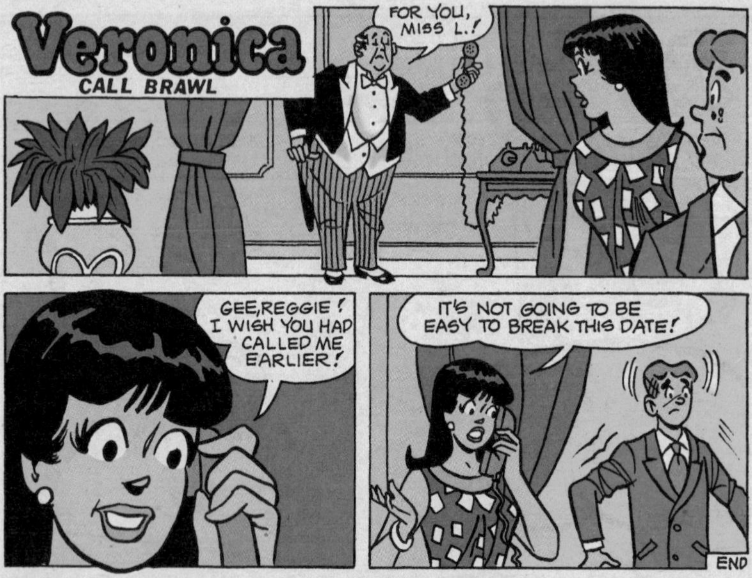
Veronica
CALL BRAWL
FOR YOU, MISS L.!
GEE, REGGIE! I WISH YOU HAD CALLED ME EARLIER!
IT'S NOT GOING TO BE EASY TO BREAK THIS DATE!
END

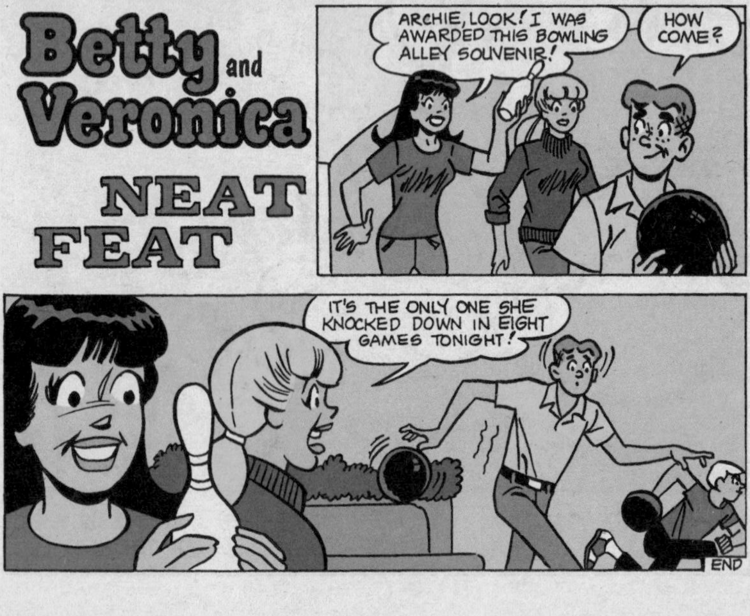
Betty and Veronica
NEAT FEAT
ARCHIE, LOOK! I WAS AWARDED THIS BOWLING ALLEY SOUVENIR!
HOW COME?
IT'S THE ONLY ONE SHE KNOCKED DOWN IN EIGHT GAMES TONIGHT!
END

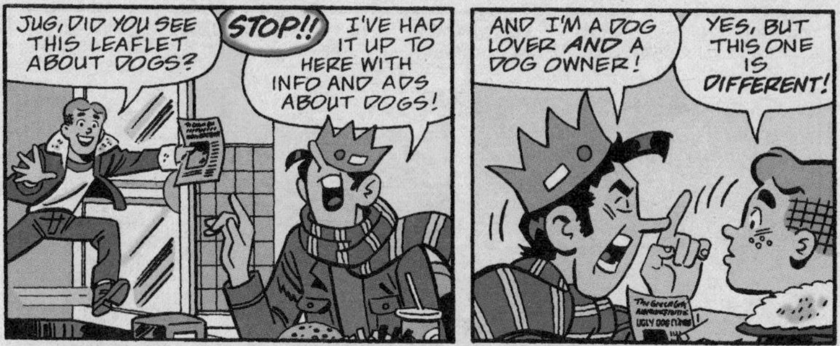
JUG, DID YOU SEE THIS LEAFLET ABOUT DOGS?
STOP!!
I'VE HAD IT UP TO HERE WITH INFO AND ADS ABOUT DOGS!
AND I'M A DOG LOVER AND A DOG OWNER!
YES, BUT THIS ONE IS DIFFERENT!

Jughead IN GOING to the DOGS

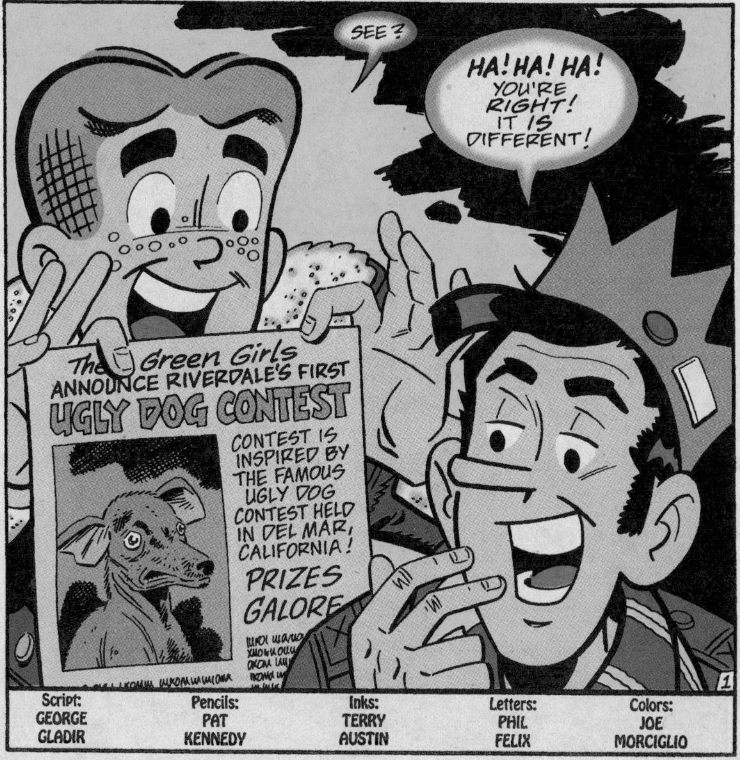
SEE?
HA! HA! HA! YOU'RE RIGHT! IT IS DIFFERENT!
The Green Girls ANNOUNCE RIVERDALE'S FIRST
UGLY DOG CONTEST
CONTEST IS INSPIRED BY THE FAMOUS UGLY DOG CONTEST HELD IN DEL MAR, CALIFORNIA!
PRIZES GALORE
1

Script: GEORGE GLADIR | Pencils: PAT KENNEDY | Inks: TERRY AUSTIN | Letters: PHIL FELIX | Colors: JOE MORCIGLIO

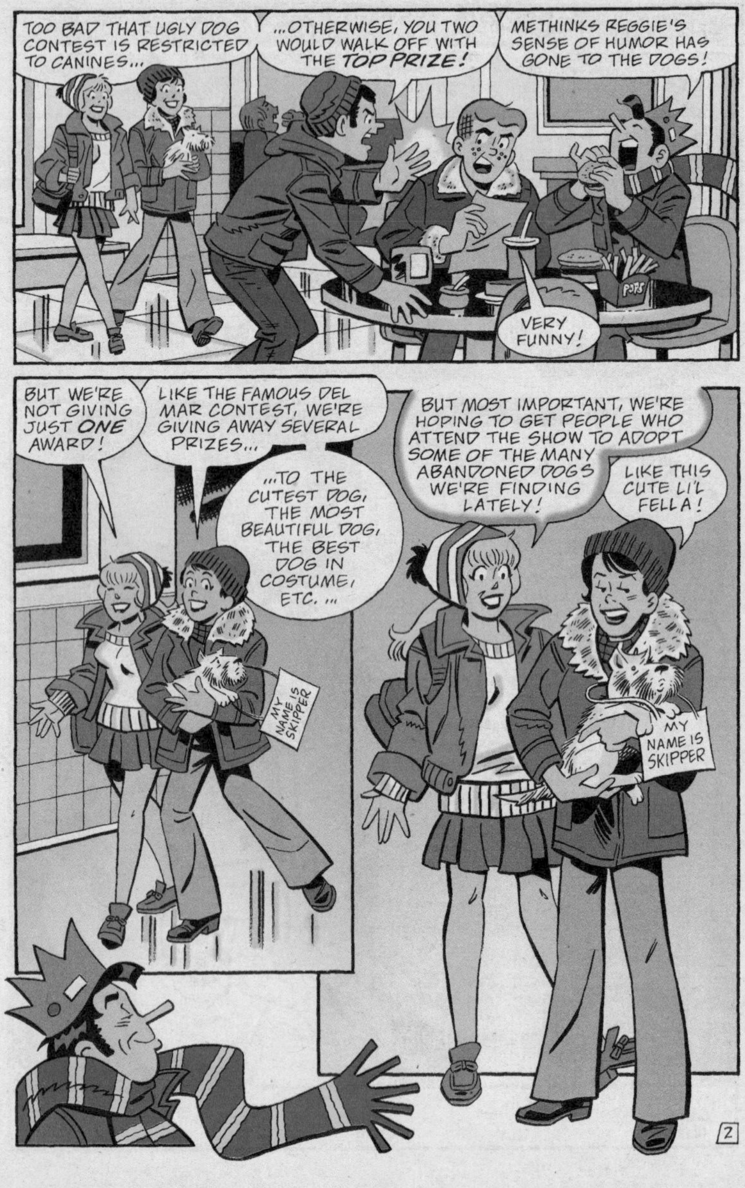
TOO BAD THAT UGLY DOG CONTEST IS RESTRICTED TO CANINES...
...OTHERWISE, YOU TWO WOULD WALK OFF WITH THE TOP PRIZE!
METHINKS REGGIE'S SENSE OF HUMOR HAS GONE TO THE DOGS!
VERY FUNNY!
POPS
BUT WE'RE NOT GIVING JUST ONE AWARD!
LIKE THE FAMOUS DEL MAR CONTEST, WE'RE GIVING AWAY SEVERAL PRIZES...
...TO THE CUTEST DOG, THE MOST BEAUTIFUL DOG, THE BEST DOG IN COSTUME, ETC. ...
MY NAME IS SKIPPER
BUT MOST IMPORTANT, WE'RE HOPING TO GET PEOPLE WHO ATTEND THE SHOW TO ADOPT SOME OF THE MANY ABANDONED DOGS WE'RE FINDING LATELY!
LIKE THIS CUTE LI'L FELLA!
MY NAME IS SKIPPER

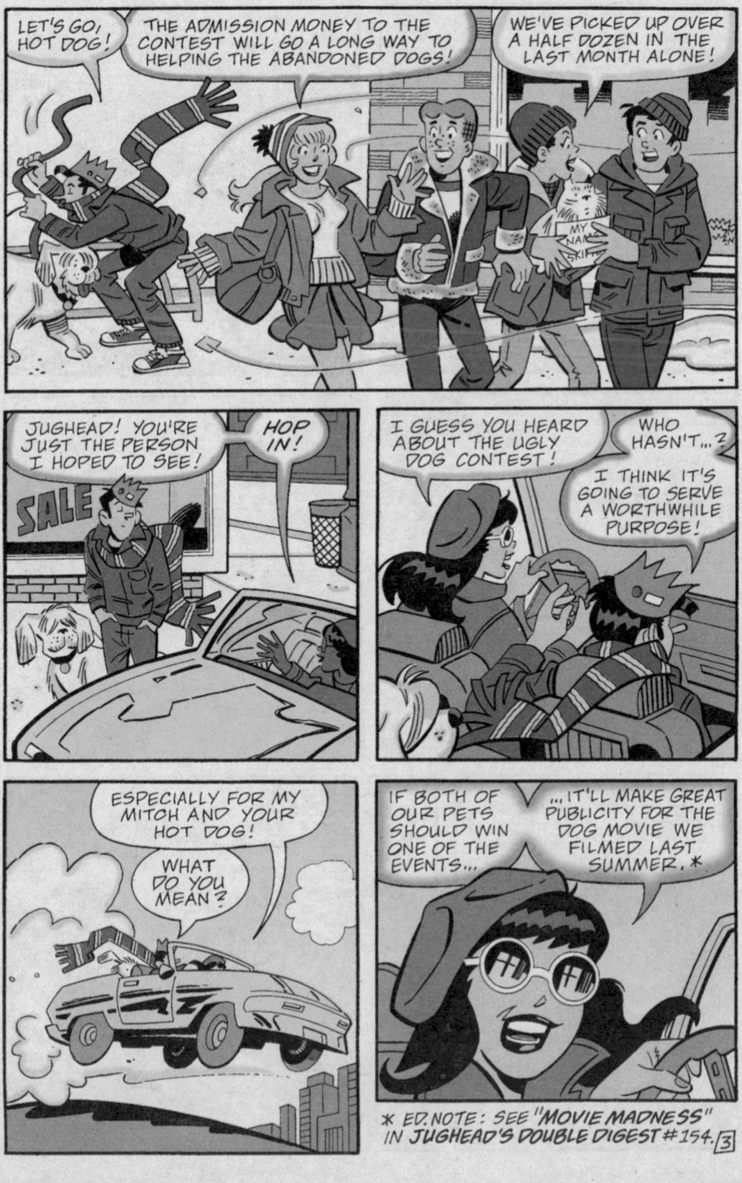
LET'S GO, HOT DOG!
THE ADMISSION MONEY TO THE CONTEST WILL GO A LONG WAY TO HELPING THE ABANDONED DOGS!
WE'VE PICKED UP OVER A HALF DOZEN IN THE LAST MONTH ALONE!
JUGHEAD! YOU'RE JUST THE PERSON I HOPED TO SEE!
HOP IN!
SALE
I GUESS YOU HEARD ABOUT THE UGLY DOG CONTEST!
WHO HASN'T...?
I THINK IT'S GOING TO SERVE A WORTHWHILE PURPOSE!
ESPECIALLY FOR MY MITCH AND YOUR HOT DOG!
WHAT DO YOU MEAN?
IF BOTH OF OUR PETS SHOULD WIN ONE OF THE EVENTS...
...IT'LL MAKE GREAT PUBLICITY FOR THE DOG MOVIE WE FILMED LAST SUMMER.*
* ED. NOTE: SEE "MOVIE MADNESS" IN JUGHEAD'S DOUBLE DIGEST #154.
3

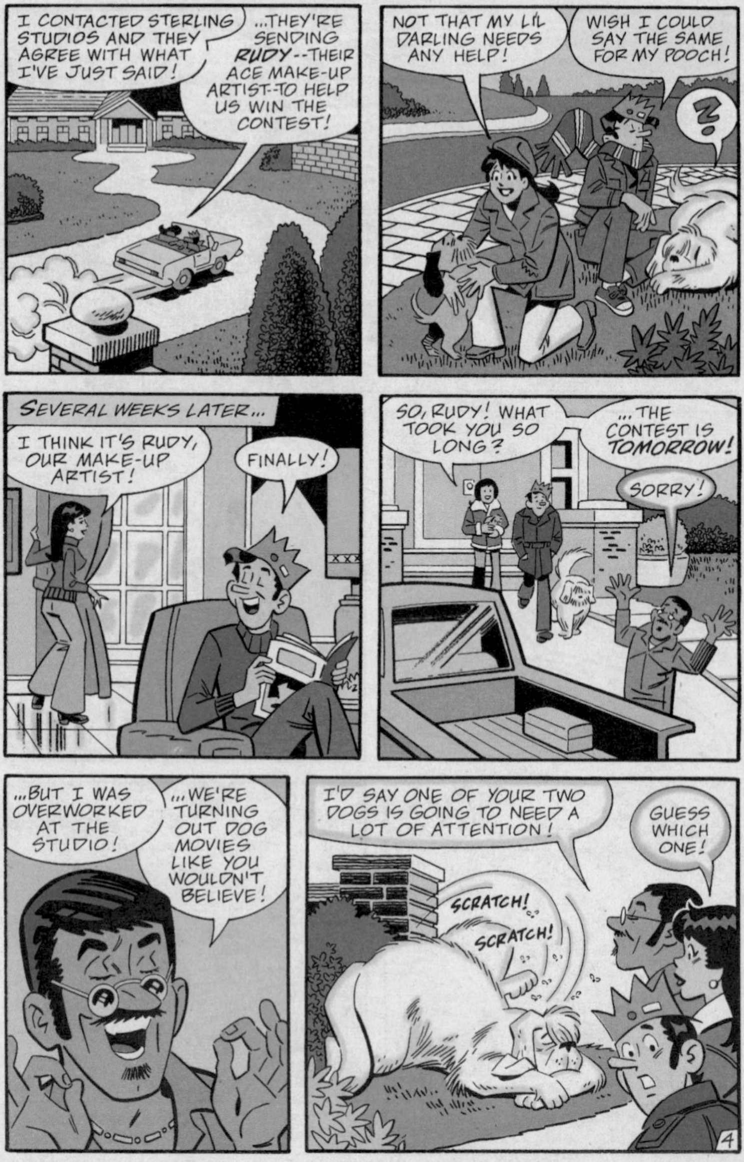
I CONTACTED STERLING STUDIOS AND THEY AGREE WITH WHAT I'VE JUST SAID!
...THEY'RE SENDING RUDY--THEIR ACE MAKE-UP ARTIST--TO HELP US WIN THE CONTEST!
NOT THAT MY LI'L DARLING NEEDS ANY HELP!
WISH I COULD SAY THE SAME FOR MY POOCH!
?
SEVERAL WEEKS LATER...
I THINK IT'S RUDY, OUR MAKE-UP ARTIST!
FINALLY!
SO, RUDY! WHAT TOOK YOU SO LONG?
...THE CONTEST IS TOMORROW!
SORRY!
...BUT I WAS OVERWORKED AT THE STUDIO!
...WE'RE TURNING OUT DOG MOVIES LIKE YOU WOULDN'T BELIEVE!
I'D SAY ONE OF YOUR TWO DOGS IS GOING TO NEED A LOT OF ATTENTION!
GUESS WHICH ONE!
SCRATCH!
SCRATCH!
4

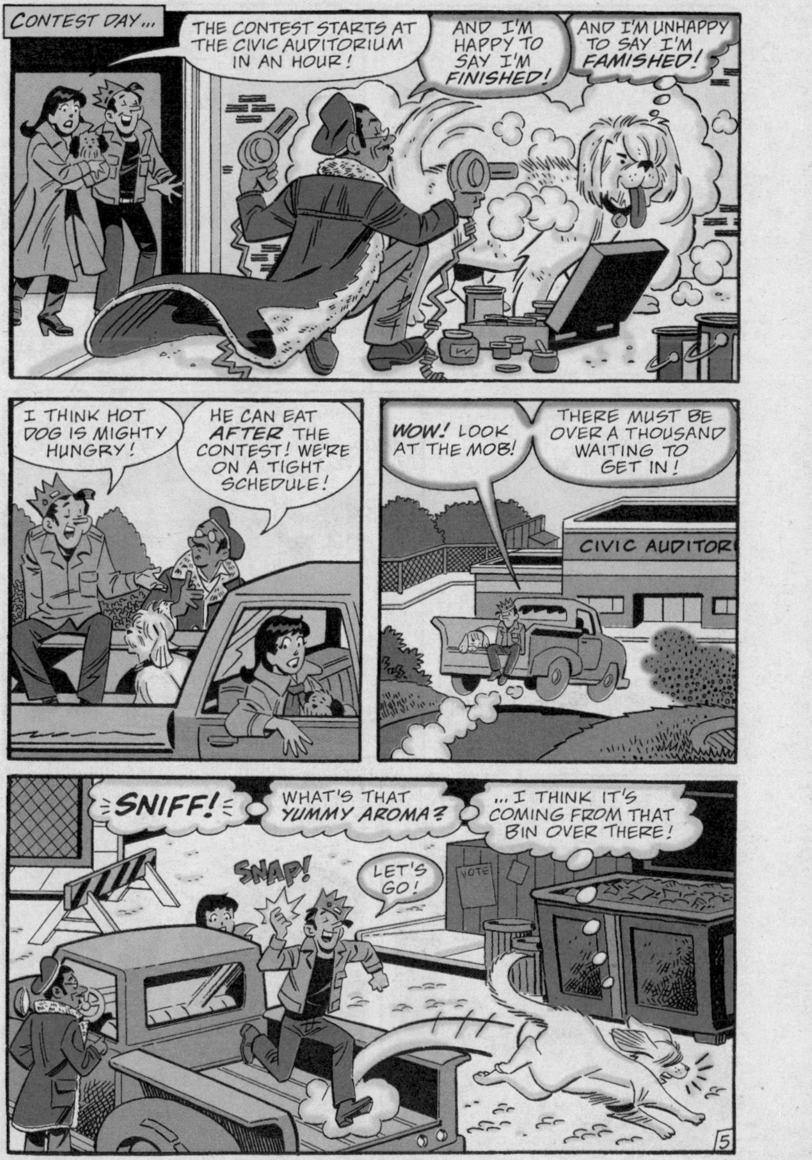
CONTEST DAY...
THE CONTEST STARTS AT THE CIVIC AUDITORIUM IN AN HOUR!
AND I'M HAPPY TO SAY I'M FINISHED!
AND I'M UNHAPPY TO SAY I'M FAMISHED!
I THINK HOT DOG IS MIGHTY HUNGRY!
HE CAN EAT AFTER THE CONTEST! WE'RE ON A TIGHT SCHEDULE!
WOW! LOOK AT THE MOB!
THERE MUST BE OVER A THOUSAND WAITING TO GET IN!
CIVIC AUDITOR
SNIFF!
WHAT'S THAT YUMMY AROMA?
...I THINK IT'S COMING FROM THAT BIN OVER THERE!
SNAP!
LET'S GO!
VOTE
5

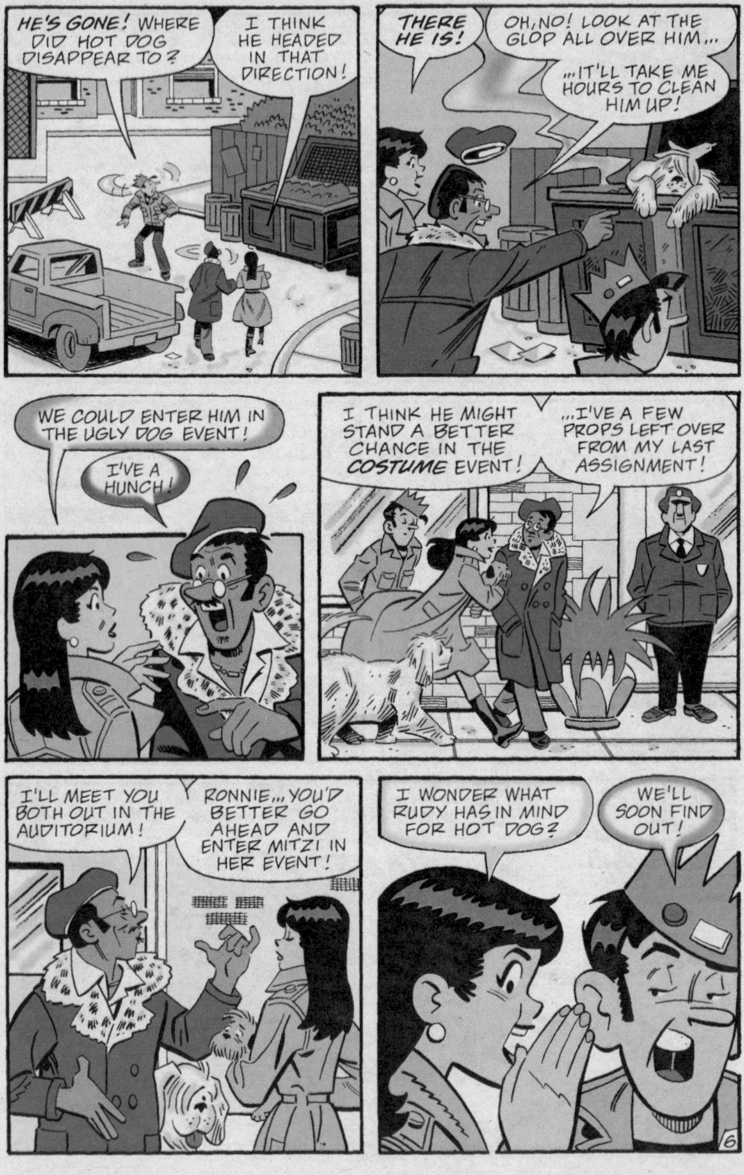
HE'S GONE! WHERE DID HOT DOG DISAPPEAR TO?
I THINK HE HEADED IN THAT DIRECTION!
THERE HE IS!
OH, NO! LOOK AT THE GLOP ALL OVER HIM...
...IT'LL TAKE ME HOURS TO CLEAN HIM UP!
WE COULD ENTER HIM IN THE UGLY DOG EVENT!
I'VE A HUNCH!
I THINK HE MIGHT STAND A BETTER CHANCE IN THE COSTUME EVENT!
...I'VE A FEW PROPS LEFT OVER FROM MY LAST ASSIGNMENT!
I'LL MEET YOU BOTH OUT IN THE AUDITORIUM!
RONNIE... YOU'D BETTER GO AHEAD AND ENTER MITZI IN HER EVENT!
I WONDER WHAT RUDY HAS IN MIND FOR HOT DOG?
WE'LL SOON FIND OUT!
6

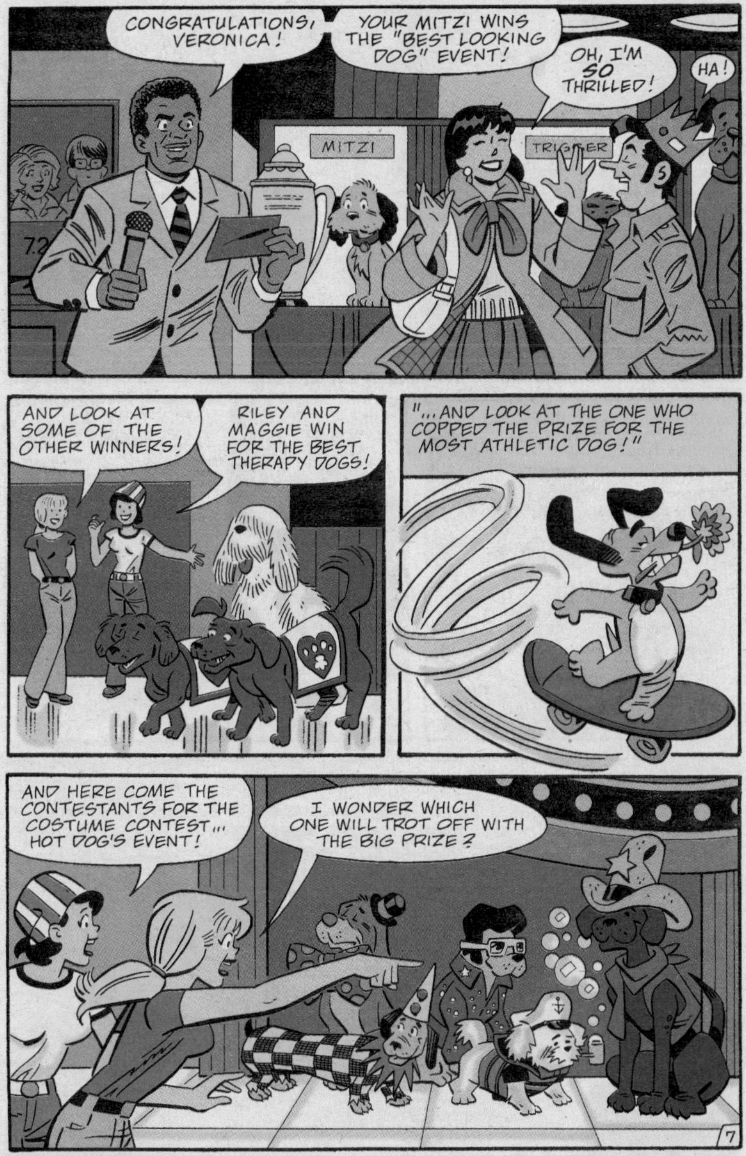
CONGRATULATIONS, VERONICA!
YOUR MITZI WINS THE "BEST LOOKING DOG" EVENT!
OH, I'M SO THRILLED!
HA!
MITZI
AND LOOK AT SOME OF THE OTHER WINNERS!
RILEY AND MAGGIE WIN FOR THE BEST THERAPY DOGS!
"...AND LOOK AT THE ONE WHO COPPED THE PRIZE FOR THE MOST ATHLETIC DOG!"
AND HERE COME THE CONTESTANTS FOR THE COSTUME CONTEST... HOT DOG'S EVENT!
I WONDER WHICH ONE WILL TROT OFF WITH THE BIG PRIZE?
7

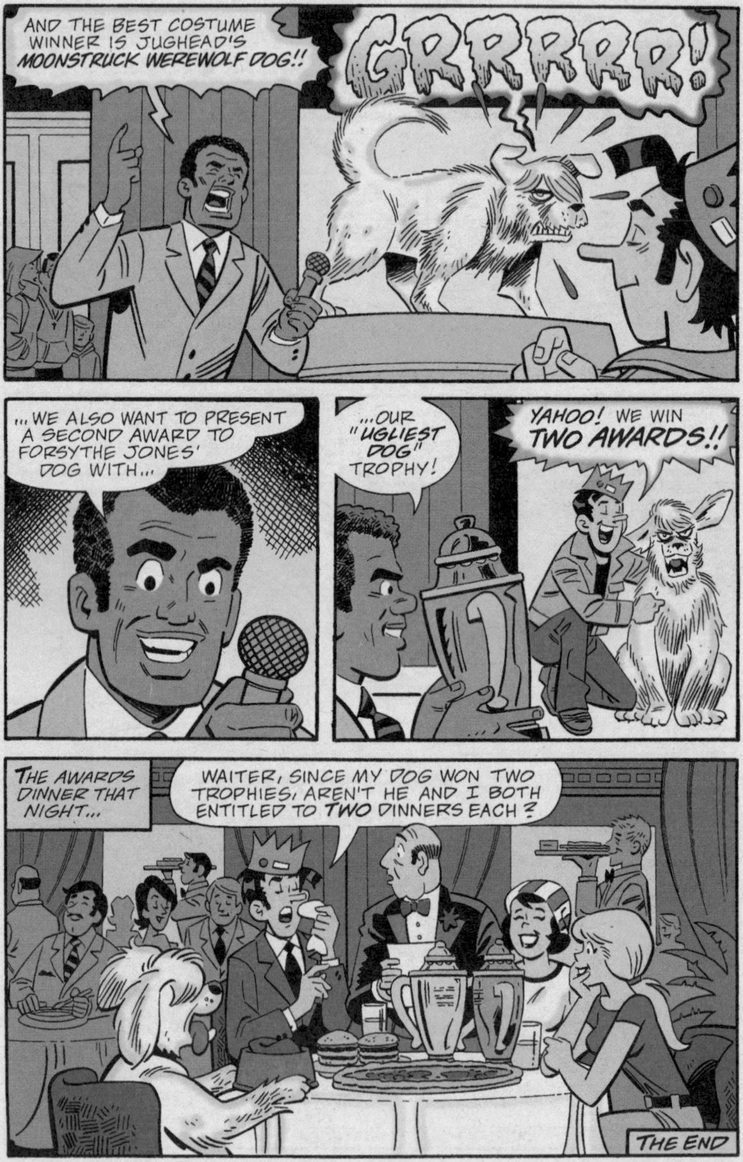
AND THE BEST COSTUME WINNER IS JUGHEAD'S MOONSTRUCK WEREWOLF DOG!!
GRRRRR!
...WE ALSO WANT TO PRESENT A SECOND AWARD TO FORSYTHE JONES' DOG WITH...
...OUR "UGLIEST DOG" TROPHY!
YAHOO! WE WIN TWO AWARDS!!
THE AWARDS DINNER THAT NIGHT...
WAITER, SINCE MY DOG WON TWO TROPHIES, AREN'T HE AND I BOTH ENTITLED TO TWO DINNERS EACH?
THE END

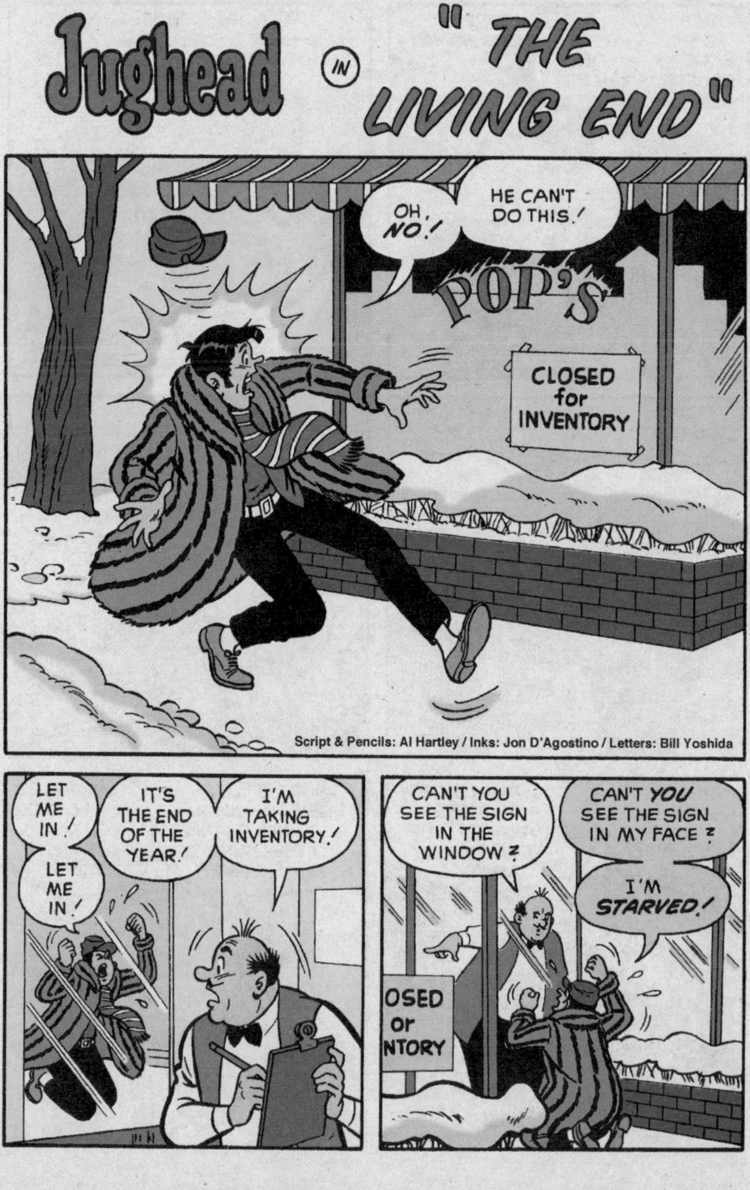
Jughead IN "THE LIVING END"
OH, NO!
HE CAN'T DO THIS!
POP'S
CLOSED for INVENTORY
Script & Pencils: Al Hartley / Inks: Jon D'Agostino / Letters: Bill Yoshida
LET ME IN!
LET ME IN!
IT'S THE END OF THE YEAR!
I'M TAKING INVENTORY!
CAN'T YOU SEE THE SIGN IN THE WINDOW?
CAN'T YOU SEE THE SIGN IN MY FACE?
I'M STARVED!
OSED or NTORY

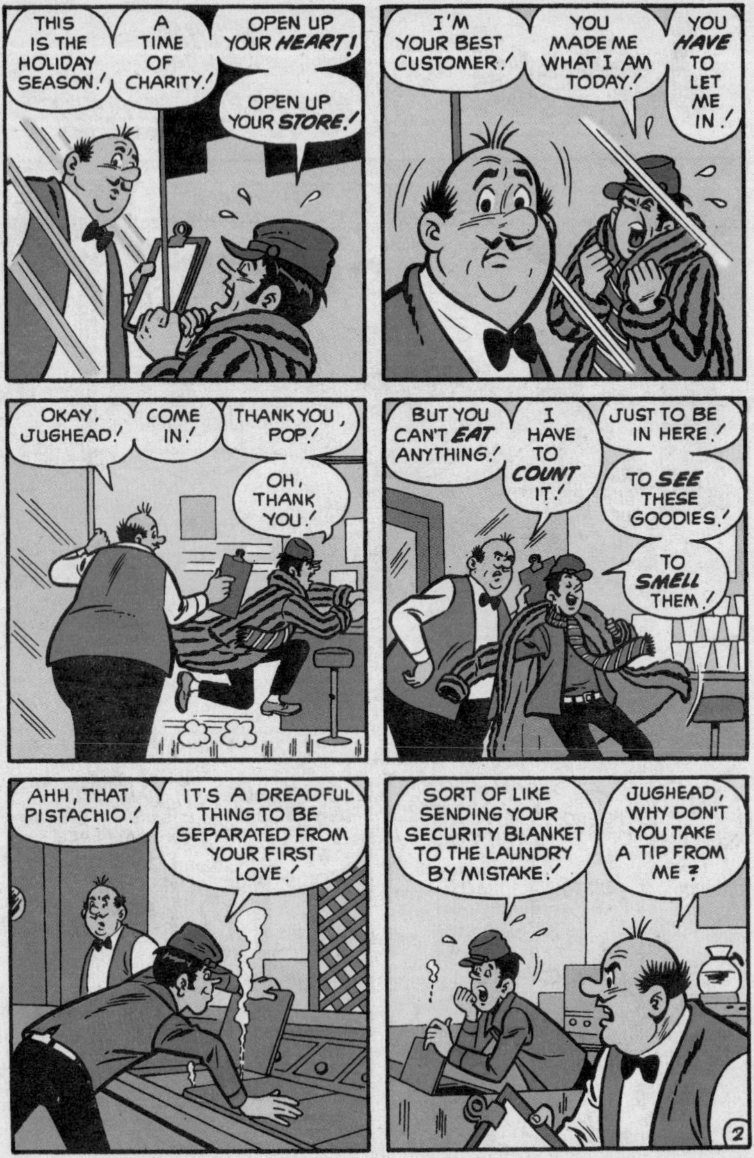
THIS IS THE HOLIDAY SEASON!
A TIME OF CHARITY!
OPEN UP YOUR HEART!
OPEN UP YOUR STORE!
I'M YOUR BEST CUSTOMER!
YOU MADE ME WHAT I AM TODAY!
YOU HAVE TO LET ME IN!
OKAY, JUGHEAD!
COME IN!
THANK YOU, POP!
OH, THANK YOU!
BUT YOU CAN'T EAT ANYTHING!
I HAVE TO COUNT IT!
JUST TO BE IN HERE!
TO SEE THESE GOODIES!
TO SMELL THEM!
AHH, THAT PISTACHIO!
IT'S A DREADFUL THING TO BE SEPARATED FROM YOUR FIRST LOVE!
SORT OF LIKE SENDING YOUR SECURITY BLANKET TO THE LAUNDRY BY MISTAKE!
JUGHEAD, WHY DON'T YOU TAKE A TIP FROM ME?
2

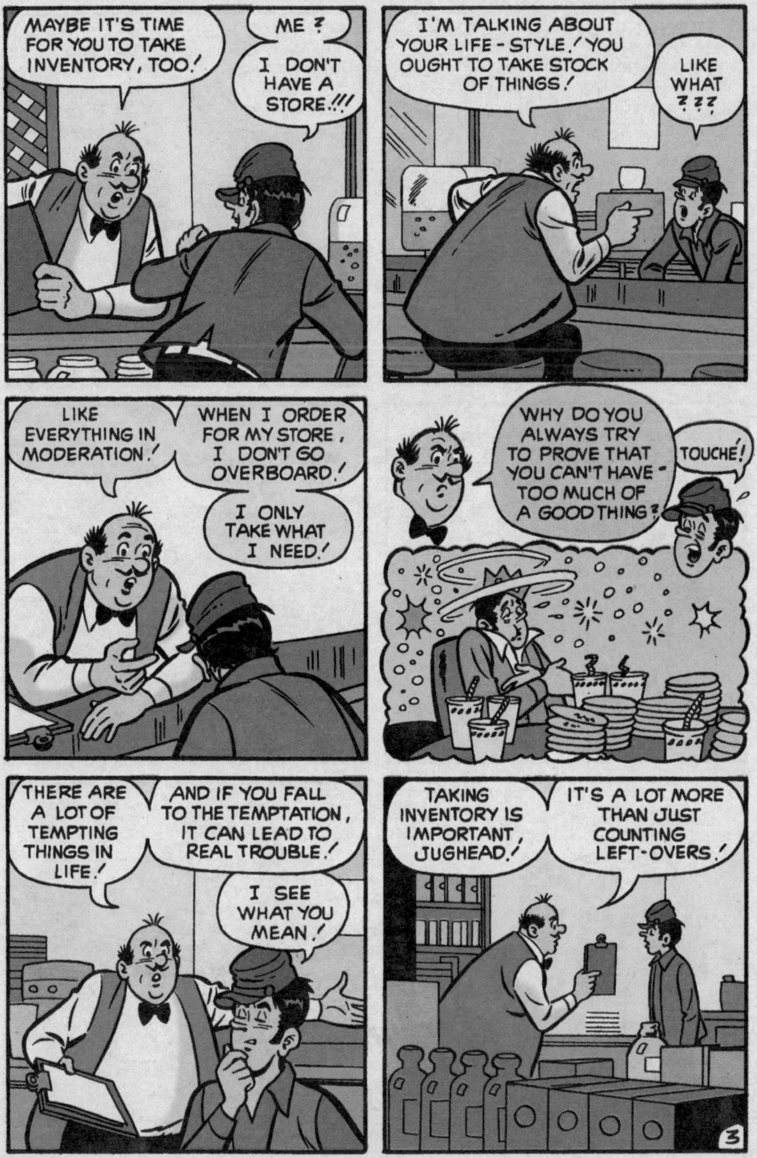
MAYBE IT'S TIME FOR YOU TO TAKE INVENTORY, TOO!
ME ?
I DON'T HAVE A STORE!!!
I'M TALKING ABOUT YOUR LIFE-STYLE! YOU OUGHT TO TAKE STOCK OF THINGS!
LIKE WHAT ???
LIKE EVERYTHING IN MODERATION!
WHEN I ORDER FOR MY STORE, I DON'T GO OVERBOARD!
I ONLY TAKE WHAT I NEED!
WHY DO YOU ALWAYS TRY TO PROVE THAT YOU CAN'T HAVE TOO MUCH OF A GOOD THING?
TOUCHÉ!
THERE ARE A LOT OF TEMPTING THINGS IN LIFE!
AND IF YOU FALL TO THE TEMPTATION, IT CAN LEAD TO REAL TROUBLE!
I SEE WHAT YOU MEAN!
TAKING INVENTORY IS IMPORTANT, JUGHEAD!
IT'S A LOT MORE THAN JUST COUNTING LEFT-OVERS!
3

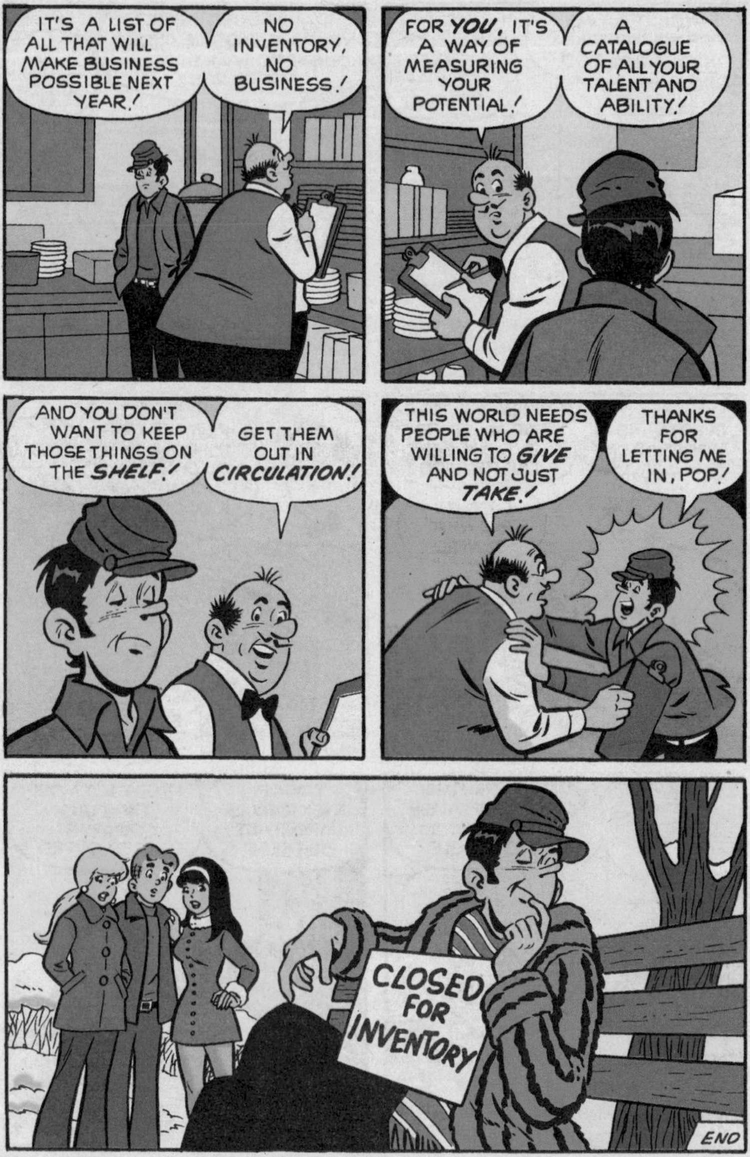
IT'S A LIST OF ALL THAT WILL MAKE BUSINESS POSSIBLE NEXT YEAR!
NO INVENTORY, NO BUSINESS!
FOR YOU, IT'S A WAY OF MEASURING YOUR POTENTIAL!
A CATALOGUE OF ALL YOUR TALENT AND ABILITY!
AND YOU DON'T WANT TO KEEP THOSE THINGS ON THE SHELF!
GET THEM OUT IN CIRCULATION!
THIS WORLD NEEDS PEOPLE WHO ARE WILLING TO GIVE AND NOT JUST TAKE!
THANKS FOR LETTING ME IN, POP!
CLOSED FOR INVENTORY
END

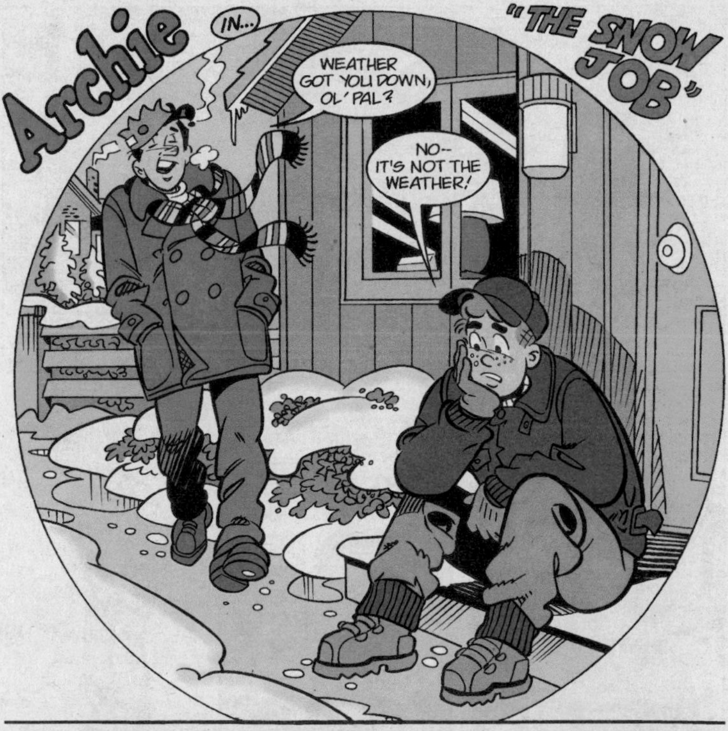
Archie
IN...
"THE SNOW JOB"
WEATHER GOT YOU DOWN, OL' PAL?
NO-- IT'S NOT THE WEATHER!

Script: Greg Crosby / Pencils: Stan Goldberg / Inks: Bob Smith / Letters: Vickie Williams / Colors: Barry Grossman

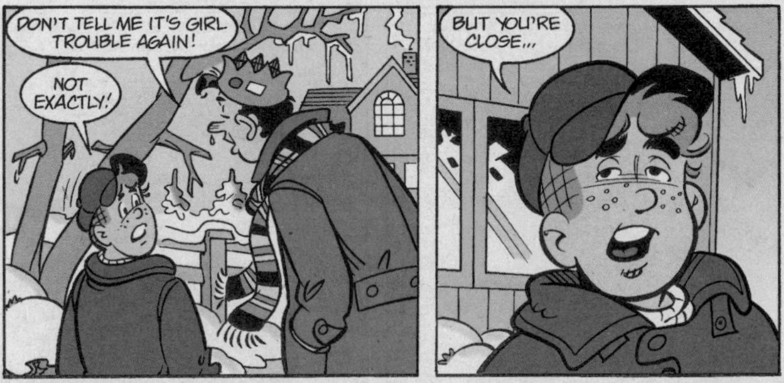
DON'T TELL ME IT'S GIRL TROUBLE AGAIN!
NOT EXACTLY!
BUT YOU'RE CLOSE...

WELL, THEN IT MUST BE MONEY PROBLEMS!

THAT'S RIGHT! HOW'D YOU KNOW?

WITH YOU, ARCHIE, MY BOY, GIRL TROUBLES AND MONEY PROBLEMS GO HAND IN HAND!

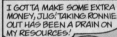

I GOTTA MAKE SOME EXTRA MONEY, JUG! TAKING RONNIE OUT HAS BEEN A DRAIN ON MY RESOURCES!

THAT GIRL CAN BE EXPENSIVE, ALL RIGHT!

YEAH... BUT SHE'S WORTH IT!

IF YOU NEED SOME FAST CASH, WHY DON'T YOU GO INTO SNOW BUSINESS?

SHOW BUSINESS?

NO-- *SNOW* BUSINESS! SHOVELING PEOPLE'S WALKS AND DRIVE-WAYS AND STUFF!

2

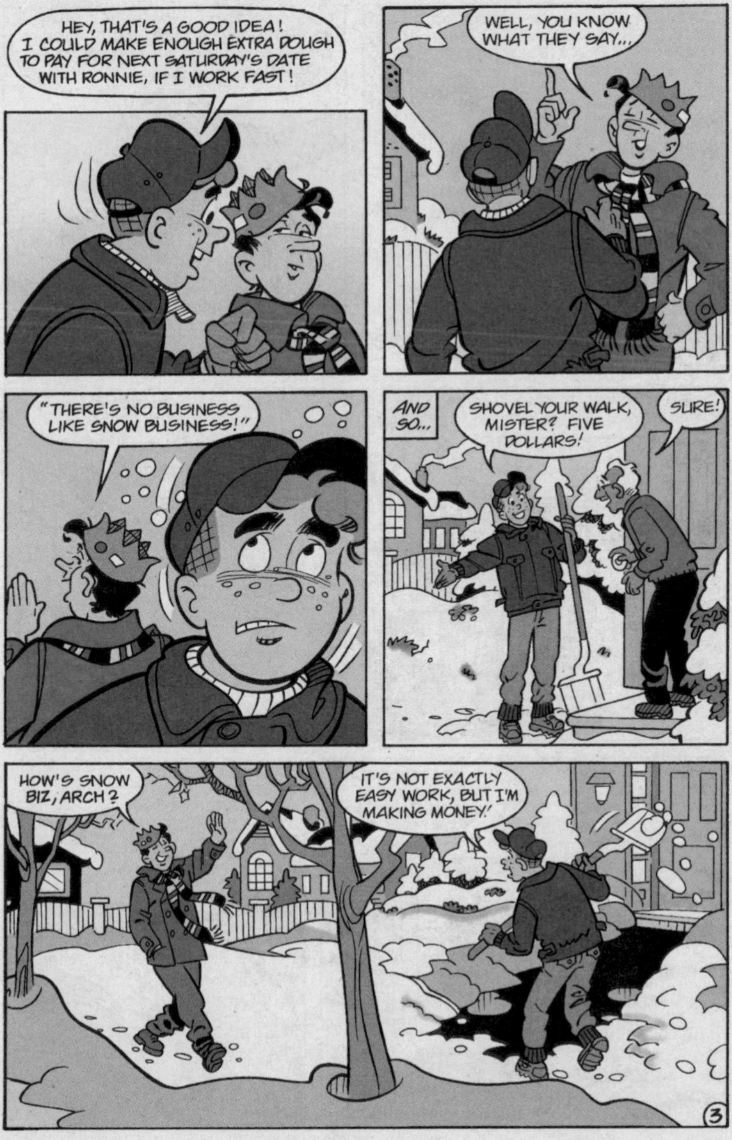
HEY, THAT'S A GOOD IDEA! I COULD MAKE ENOUGH EXTRA DOUGH TO PAY FOR NEXT SATURDAY'S DATE WITH RONNIE, IF I WORK FAST!
WELL, YOU KNOW WHAT THEY SAY...
"THERE'S NO BUSINESS LIKE SNOW BUSINESS!"
AND SO...
SHOVEL YOUR WALK, MISTER? FIVE DOLLARS!
SURE!
HOW'S SNOW BIZ, ARCH?
IT'S NOT EXACTLY EASY WORK, BUT I'M MAKING MONEY!

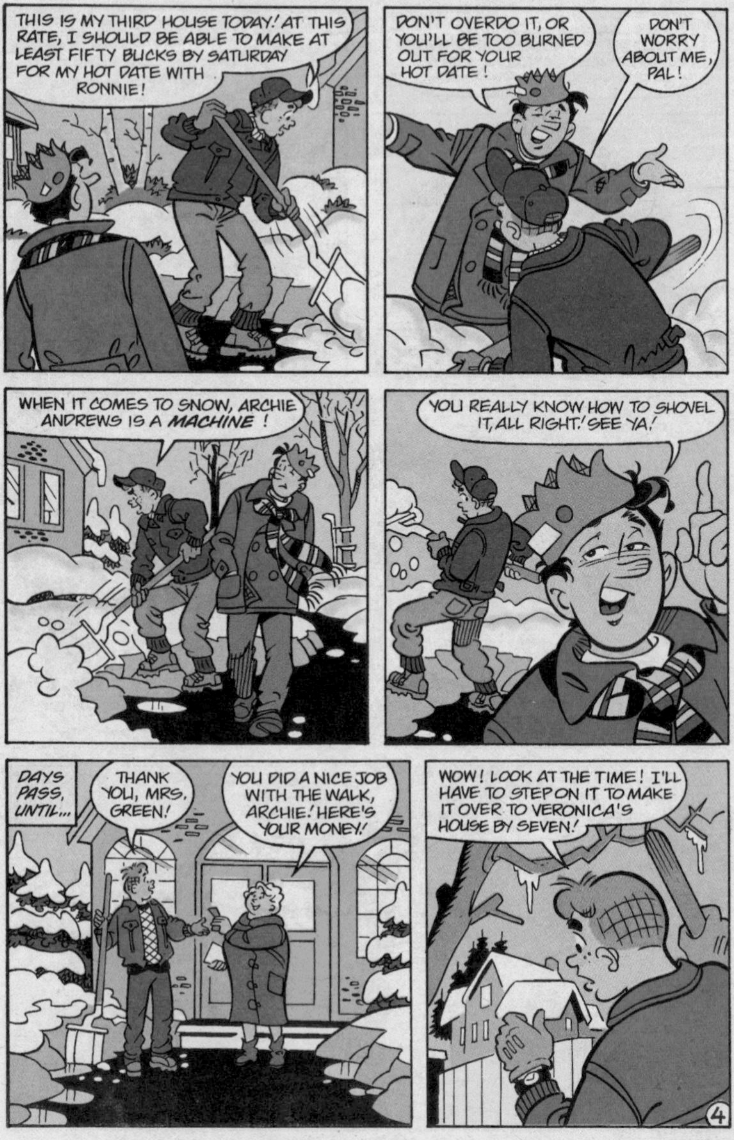
THIS IS MY THIRD HOUSE TODAY! AT THIS RATE, I SHOULD BE ABLE TO MAKE AT LEAST FIFTY BUCKS BY SATURDAY FOR MY HOT DATE WITH RONNIE!
DON'T OVERDO IT, OR YOU'LL BE TOO BURNED OUT FOR YOUR HOT DATE!
DON'T WORRY ABOUT ME, PAL!
WHEN IT COMES TO SNOW, ARCHIE ANDREWS IS A MACHINE!
YOU REALLY KNOW HOW TO SHOVEL IT, ALL RIGHT! SEE YA!
DAYS PASS, UNTIL...
THANK YOU, MRS. GREEN!
YOU DID A NICE JOB WITH THE WALK, ARCHIE! HERE'S YOUR MONEY!
WOW! LOOK AT THE TIME! I'LL HAVE TO STEP ON IT TO MAKE IT OVER TO VERONICA'S HOUSE BY SEVEN!
4

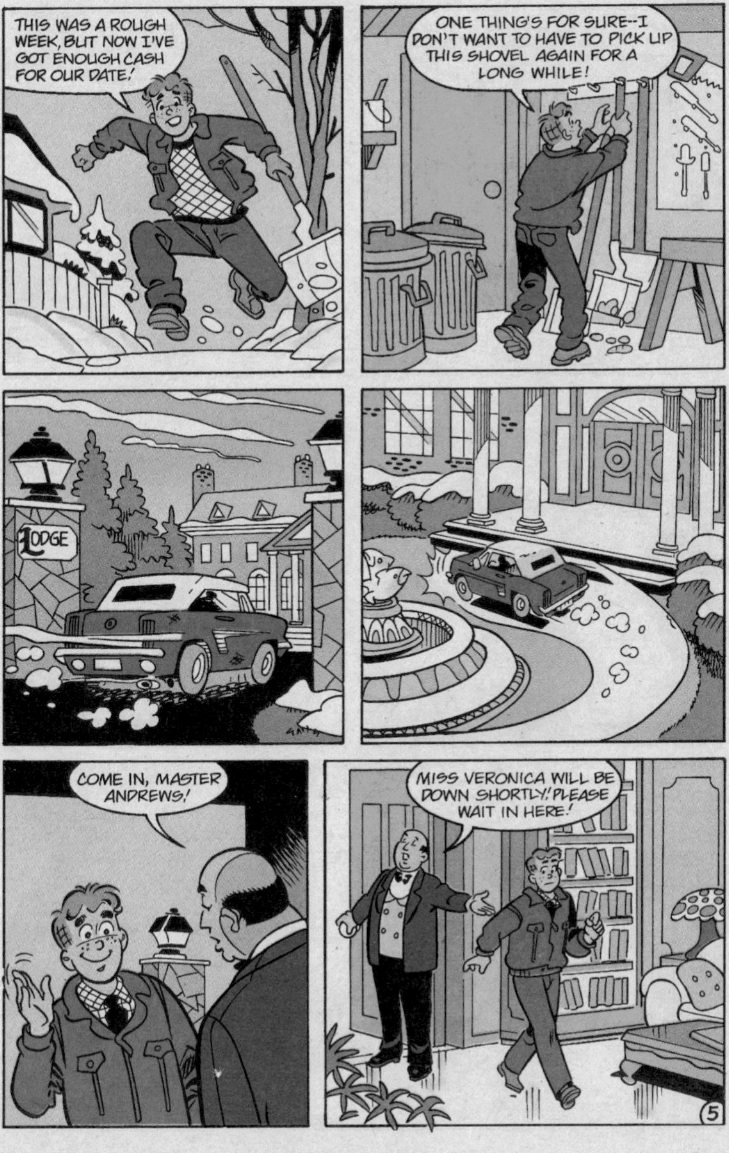
THIS WAS A ROUGH WEEK, BUT NOW I'VE GOT ENOUGH CASH FOR OUR DATE!
ONE THING'S FOR SURE--I DON'T WANT TO HAVE TO PICK UP THIS SHOVEL AGAIN FOR A LONG WHILE!
LODGE
COME IN, MASTER ANDREWS!
MISS VERONICA WILL BE DOWN SHORTLY! PLEASE WAIT IN HERE!
5

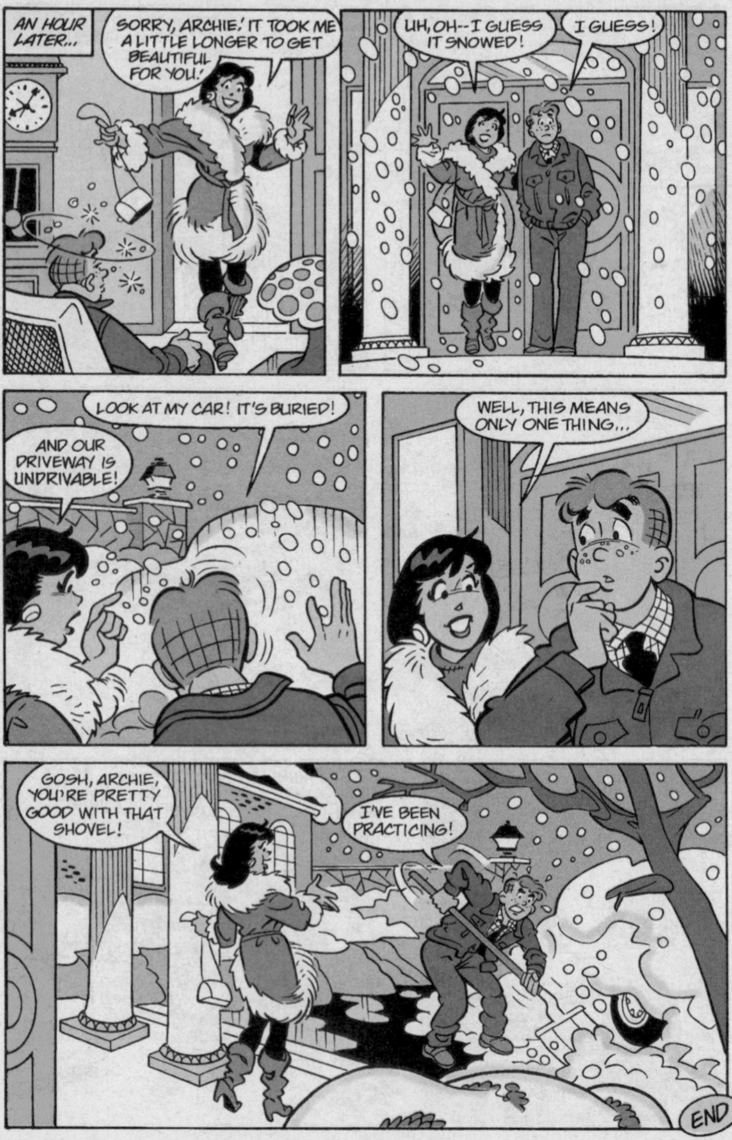
AN HOUR LATER...
SORRY, ARCHIE! IT TOOK ME A LITTLE LONGER TO GET BEAUTIFUL FOR YOU!
UH, OH--I GUESS IT SNOWED!
I GUESS!
LOOK AT MY CAR! IT'S BURIED!
AND OUR DRIVEWAY IS UNDRIVABLE!
WELL, THIS MEANS ONLY ONE THING...
GOSH, ARCHIE, YOU'RE PRETTY GOOD WITH THAT SHOVEL!
I'VE BEEN PRACTICING!
END

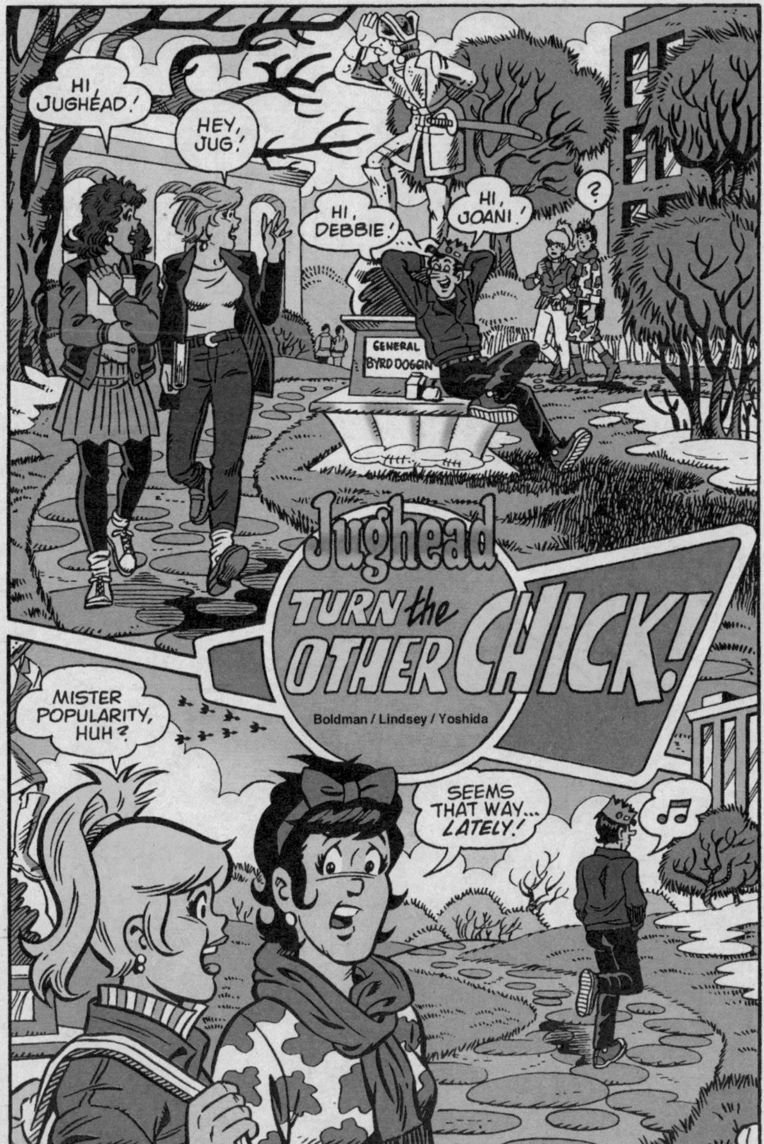

HI, JUGHEAD!
HEY, JUG!
HI, DEBBIE!
HI, JOANI!
?
GENERAL BYRD DOGGIN
Jughead
TURN the OTHER CHICK!
Boldman / Lindsey / Yoshida
MISTER POPULARITY, HUH?
SEEMS THAT WAY... LATELY!
1

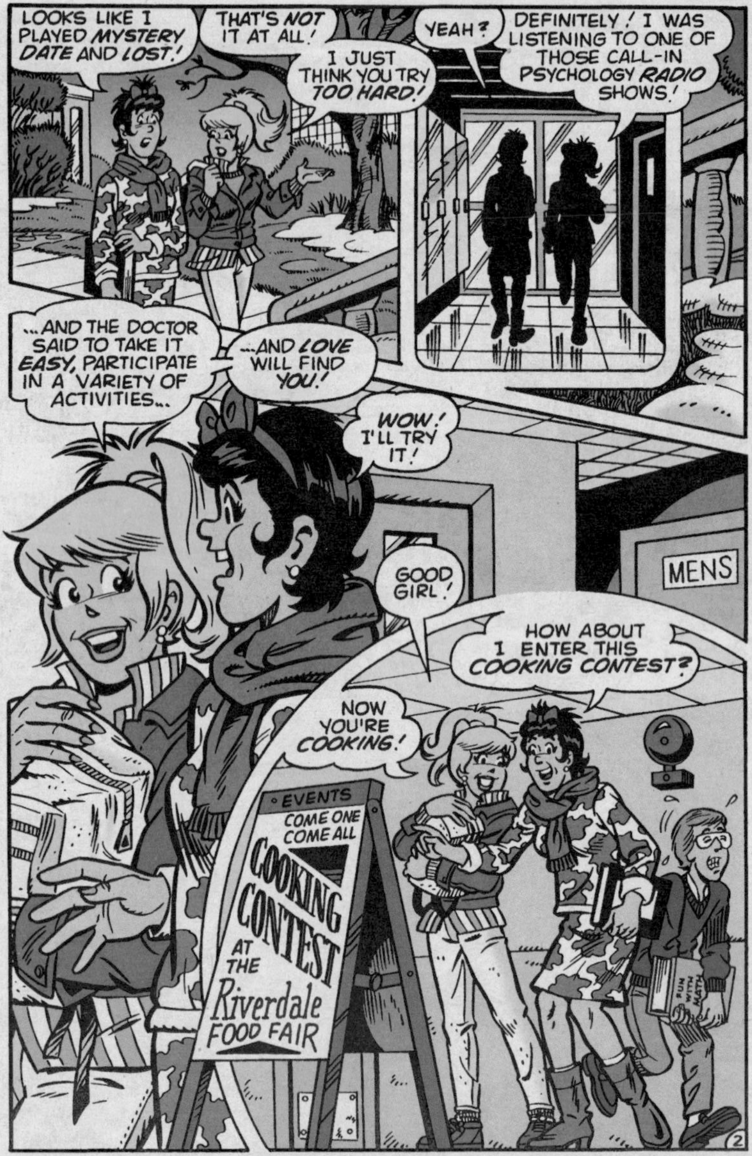
LOOKS LIKE I PLAYED MYSTERY DATE AND LOST!
THAT'S NOT IT AT ALL!
I JUST THINK YOU TRY TOO HARD!
YEAH?
DEFINITELY! I WAS LISTENING TO ONE OF THOSE CALL-IN PSYCHOLOGY RADIO SHOWS!
...AND THE DOCTOR SAID TO TAKE IT EASY, PARTICIPATE IN A VARIETY OF ACTIVITIES...
...AND LOVE WILL FIND YOU!
WOW! I'LL TRY IT!
MENS
GOOD GIRL!
HOW ABOUT I ENTER THIS COOKING CONTEST?
NOW YOU'RE COOKING!
EVENTS
COME ONE COME ALL
COOKING CONTEST AT THE Riverdale FOOD FAIR
FUN WITH MATH
2

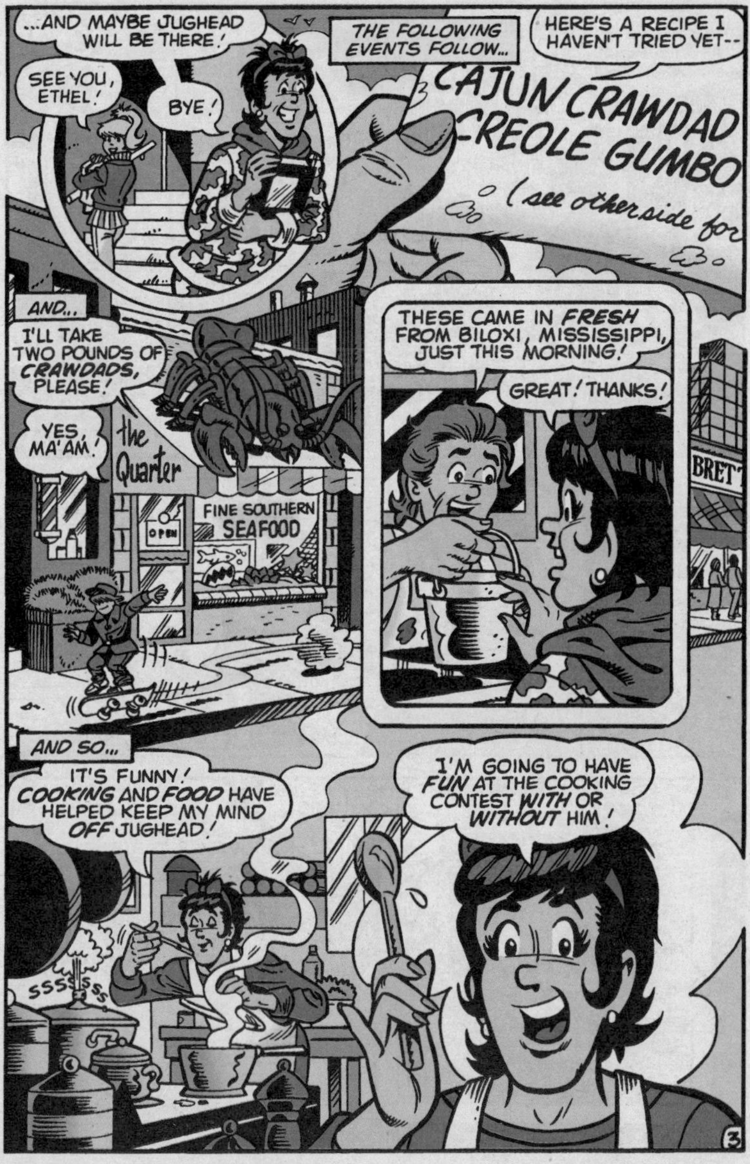
...AND MAYBE JUGHEAD WILL BE THERE!
SEE YOU, ETHEL!
BYE!
THE FOLLOWING EVENTS FOLLOW...
HERE'S A RECIPE I HAVEN'T TRIED YET--
CAJUN CRAWDAD CREOLE GUMBO
(see other side for
AND...
I'LL TAKE TWO POUNDS OF CRAWDADS, PLEASE!
YES, MA'AM!
the Quarter
FINE SOUTHERN SEAFOOD
OPEN
THESE CAME IN FRESH FROM BILOXI, MISSISSIPPI, JUST THIS MORNING!
GREAT! THANKS!
BRETT
AND SO...
IT'S FUNNY! COOKING AND FOOD HAVE HELPED KEEP MY MIND OFF JUGHEAD!
I'M GOING TO HAVE FUN AT THE COOKING CONTEST WITH OR WITHOUT HIM!
SSSSSSS
3

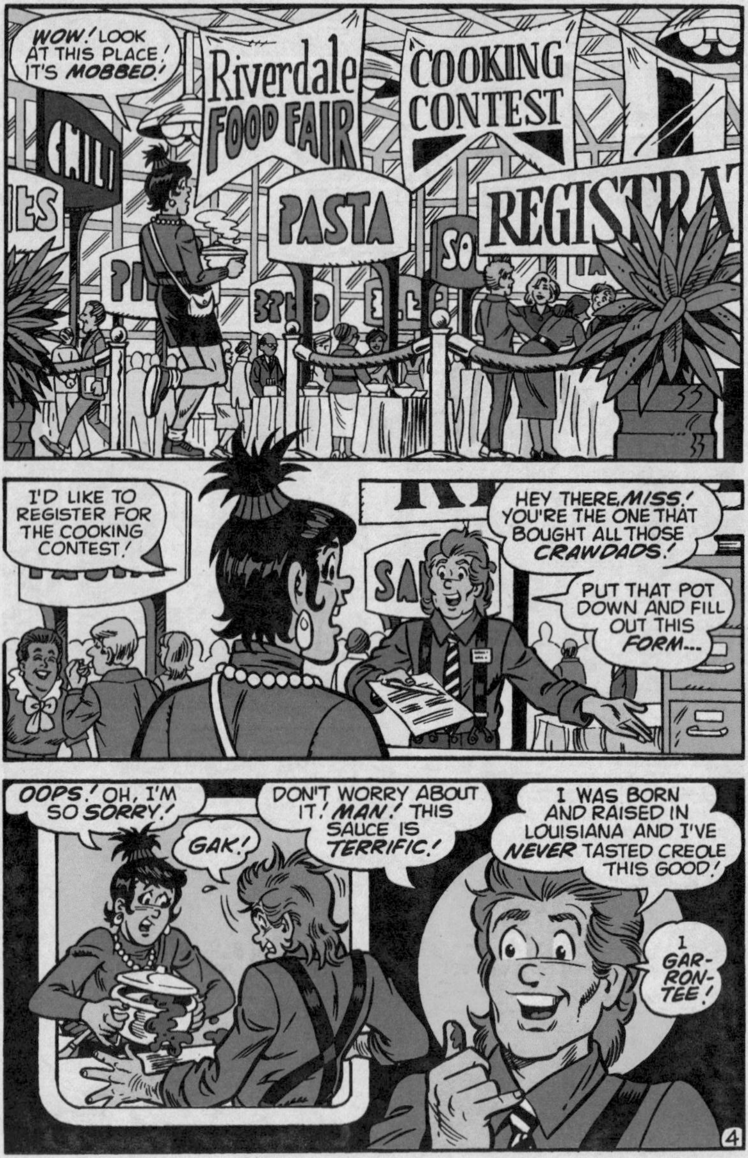
WOW! LOOK AT THIS PLACE! IT'S MOBBED!
Riverdale FOOD FAIR
COOKING CONTEST
CHILI
PASTA
REGISTRAT
I'D LIKE TO REGISTER FOR THE COOKING CONTEST!
HEY THERE, MISS! YOU'RE THE ONE THAT BOUGHT ALL THOSE CRAWDADS!
PUT THAT POT DOWN AND FILL OUT THIS FORM...
OOPS! OH, I'M SO SORRY!
GAK!
DON'T WORRY ABOUT IT! MAN! THIS SAUCE IS TERRIFIC!
I WAS BORN AND RAISED IN LOUISIANA AND I'VE NEVER TASTED CREOLE THIS GOOD!
I GAR-RON-TEE!
4

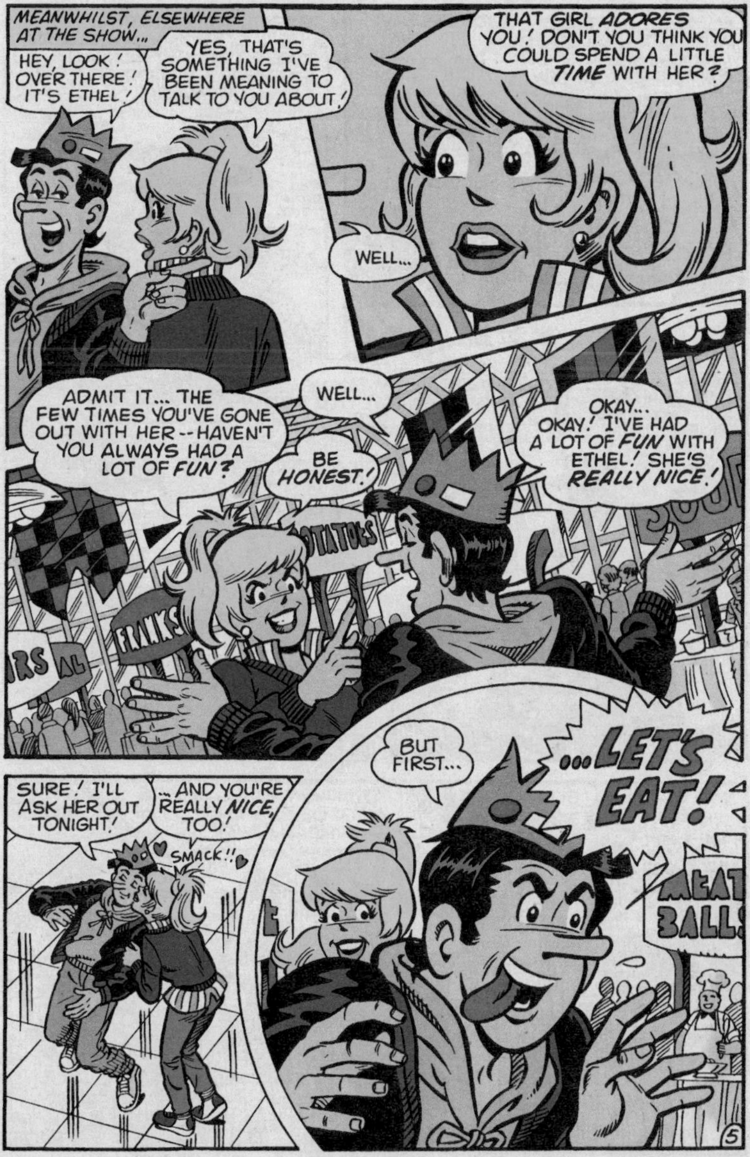
MEANWHILST, ELSEWHERE AT THE SHOW...
HEY, LOOK! OVER THERE! IT'S ETHEL!
YES, THAT'S SOMETHING I'VE BEEN MEANING TO TALK TO YOU ABOUT!
THAT GIRL ADORES YOU! DON'T YOU THINK YOU COULD SPEND A LITTLE TIME WITH HER?
WELL...
ADMIT IT... THE FEW TIMES YOU'VE GONE OUT WITH HER--HAVEN'T YOU ALWAYS HAD A LOT OF FUN?
WELL...
BE HONEST!
OKAY... OKAY! I'VE HAD A LOT OF FUN WITH ETHEL! SHE'S REALLY NICE!
POTATOES
FRANKS
SURE! I'LL ASK HER OUT TONIGHT!
...AND YOU'RE REALLY NICE, TOO!
SMACK!!
BUT FIRST...
...LET'S EAT!
MEAT BALLS

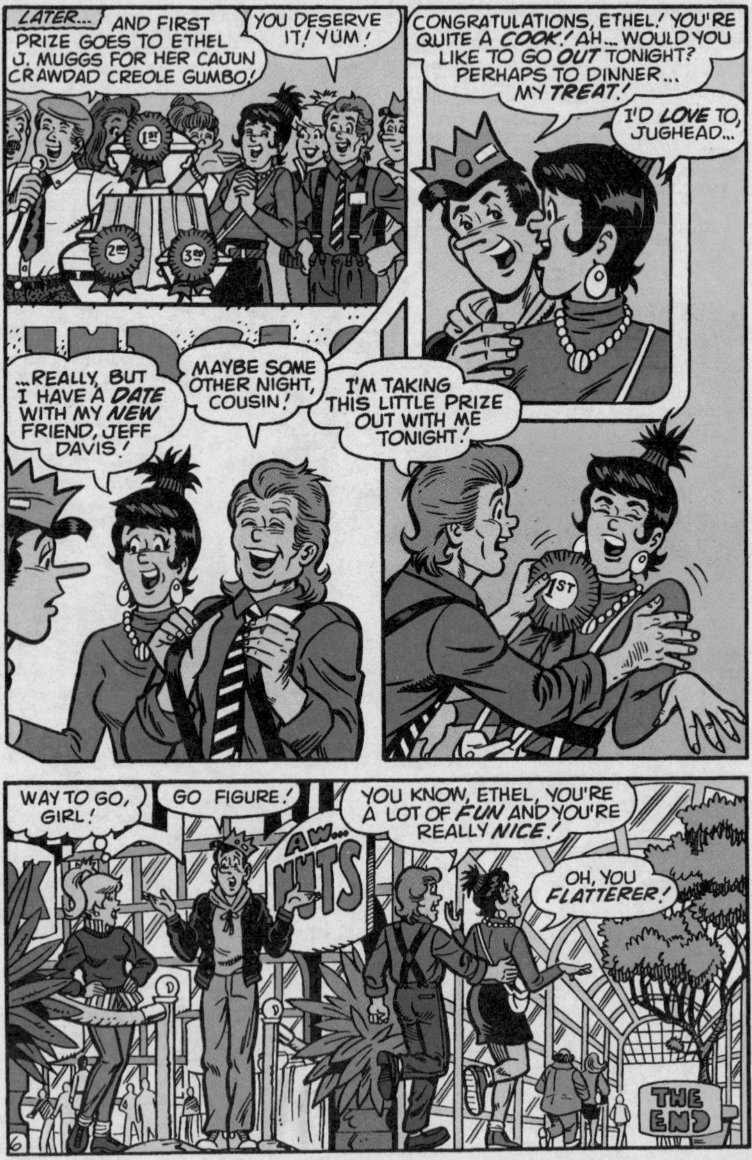
LATER...
AND FIRST PRIZE GOES TO ETHEL J. MUGGS FOR HER CAJUN CRAWDAD CREOLE GUMBO!
YOU DESERVE IT! YUM!
1ST
2ND
3RD
CONGRATULATIONS, ETHEL! YOU'RE QUITE A COOK! AH... WOULD YOU LIKE TO GO OUT TONIGHT? PERHAPS TO DINNER... MY TREAT!
I'D LOVE TO, JUGHEAD...
...REALLY, BUT I HAVE A DATE WITH MY NEW FRIEND, JEFF DAVIS!
MAYBE SOME OTHER NIGHT, COUSIN!
I'M TAKING THIS LITTLE PRIZE OUT WITH ME TONIGHT!
1ST
WAY TO GO, GIRL!
GO FIGURE!
AW... NUTS
YOU KNOW, ETHEL, YOU'RE A LOT OF FUN AND YOU'RE REALLY NICE!
OH, YOU FLATTERER!
THE END

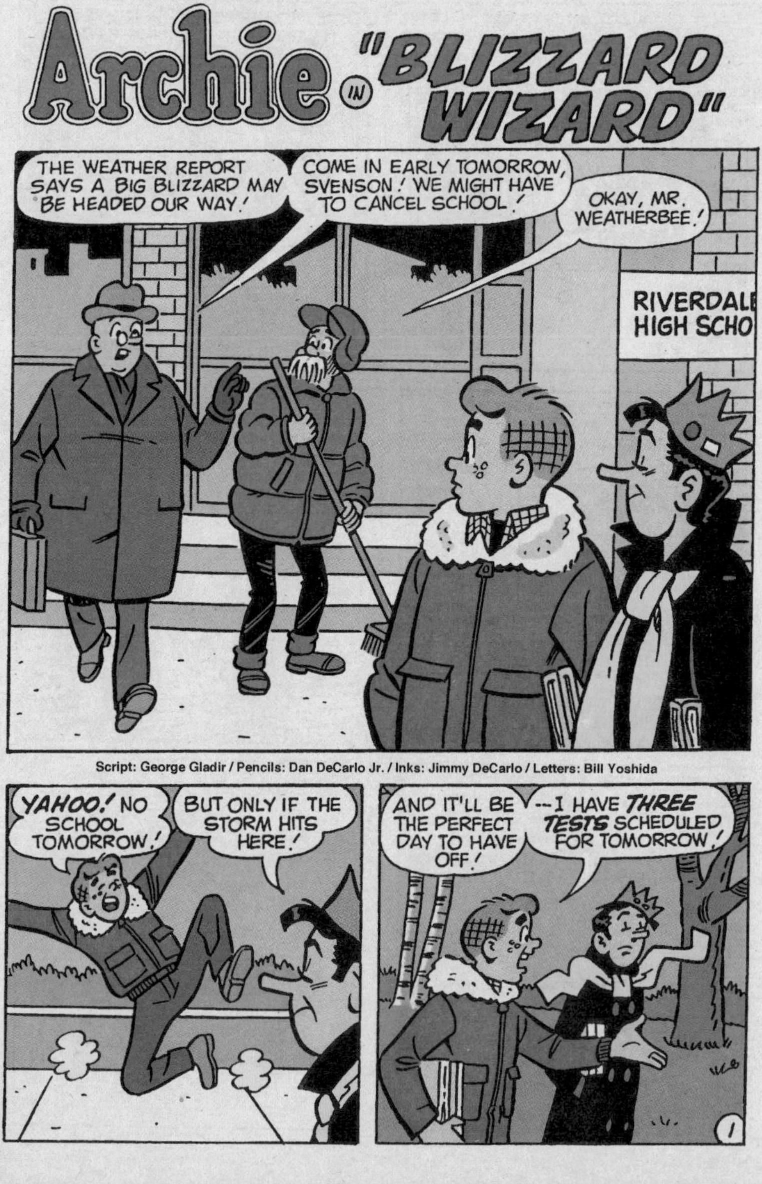

Archie IN "BLIZZARD WIZARD"
THE WEATHER REPORT SAYS A BIG BLIZZARD MAY BE HEADED OUR WAY!
COME IN EARLY TOMORROW, SVENSON! WE MIGHT HAVE TO CANCEL SCHOOL!
OKAY, MR. WEATHERBEE!
RIVERDALE HIGH SCHO
Script: George Gladir / Pencils: Dan DeCarlo Jr. / Inks: Jimmy DeCarlo / Letters: Bill Yoshida
YAHOO! NO SCHOOL TOMORROW!
BUT ONLY IF THE STORM HITS HERE!
AND IT'LL BE THE PERFECT DAY TO HAVE OFF!
--I HAVE THREE TESTS SCHEDULED FOR TOMORROW!
1

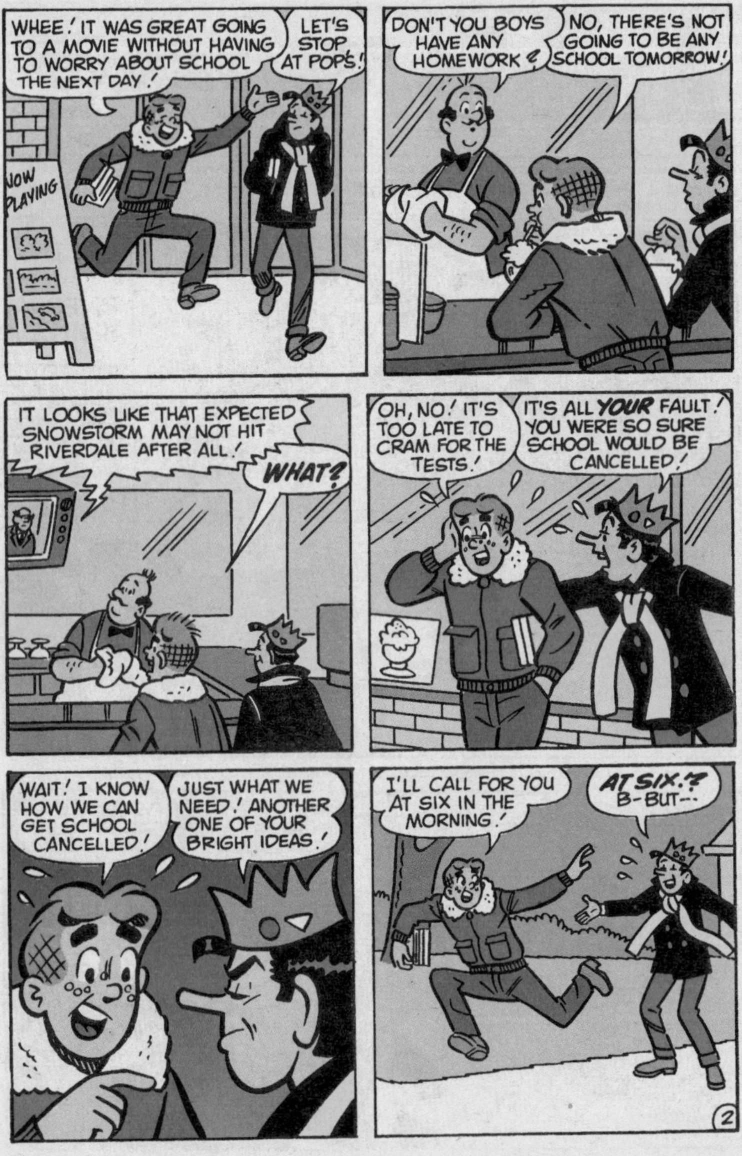

WHEE! IT WAS GREAT GOING TO A MOVIE WITHOUT HAVING TO WORRY ABOUT SCHOOL THE NEXT DAY!
LET'S STOP AT POP'S!
NOW PLAYING
DON'T YOU BOYS HAVE ANY HOMEWORK?
NO, THERE'S NOT GOING TO BE ANY SCHOOL TOMORROW!
IT LOOKS LIKE THAT EXPECTED SNOWSTORM MAY NOT HIT RIVERDALE AFTER ALL!
WHAT?
OH, NO! IT'S TOO LATE TO CRAM FOR THE TESTS!
IT'S ALL **YOUR** FAULT! YOU WERE SO SURE SCHOOL WOULD BE CANCELLED!
WAIT! I KNOW HOW WE CAN GET SCHOOL CANCELLED!
JUST WHAT WE NEED! ANOTHER ONE OF YOUR BRIGHT IDEAS!
I'LL CALL FOR YOU AT SIX IN THE MORNING!
AT SIX!? B-BUT--
2

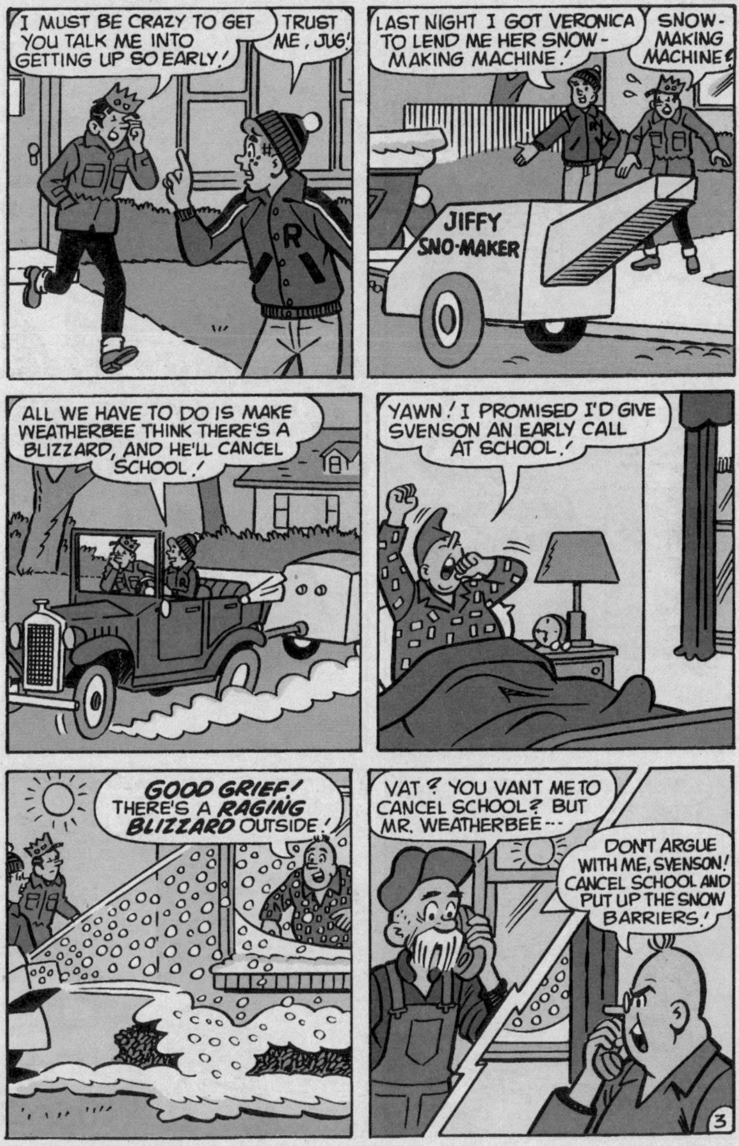
I MUST BE CRAZY TO GET YOU TALK ME INTO GETTING UP SO EARLY!
TRUST ME, JUG!
LAST NIGHT I GOT VERONICA TO LEND ME HER SNOW-MAKING MACHINE!
SNOW-MAKING MACHINE?
JIFFY SNO-MAKER
ALL WE HAVE TO DO IS MAKE WEATHERBEE THINK THERE'S A BLIZZARD, AND HE'LL CANCEL SCHOOL!
YAWN! I PROMISED I'D GIVE SVENSON AN EARLY CALL AT SCHOOL!
GOOD GRIEF! THERE'S A RAGING BLIZZARD OUTSIDE!
VAT? YOU VANT ME TO CANCEL SCHOOL? BUT MR. WEATHERBEE---
DON'T ARGUE WITH ME, SVENSON! CANCEL SCHOOL AND PUT UP THE SNOW BARRIERS!
3

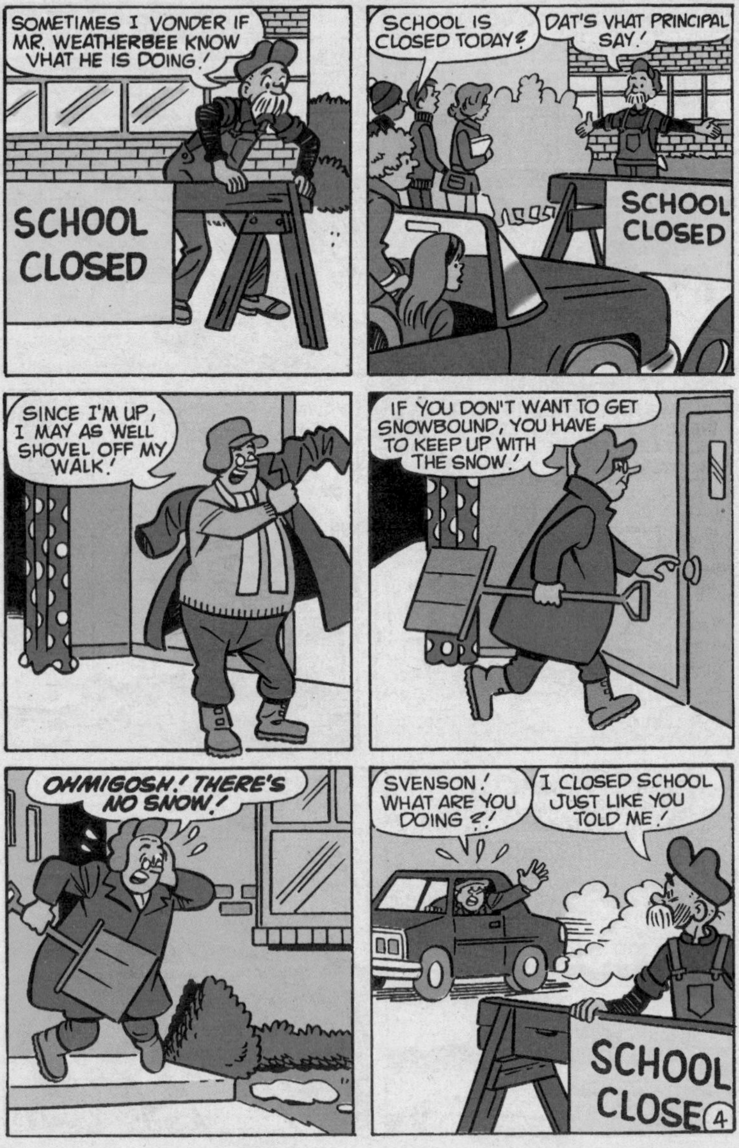
SOMETIMES I VONDER IF MR. WEATHERBEE KNOW VHAT HE IS DOING!
SCHOOL CLOSED
SCHOOL IS CLOSED TODAY?
DAT'S VHAT PRINCIPAL SAY!
SCHOOL CLOSED
SINCE I'M UP, I MAY AS WELL SHOVEL OFF MY WALK!
IF YOU DON'T WANT TO GET SNOWBOUND, YOU HAVE TO KEEP UP WITH THE SNOW!
OHMIGOSH! THERE'S NO SNOW!
SVENSON! WHAT ARE YOU DOING?!
I CLOSED SCHOOL JUST LIKE YOU TOLD ME!
SCHOOL CLOSE
4

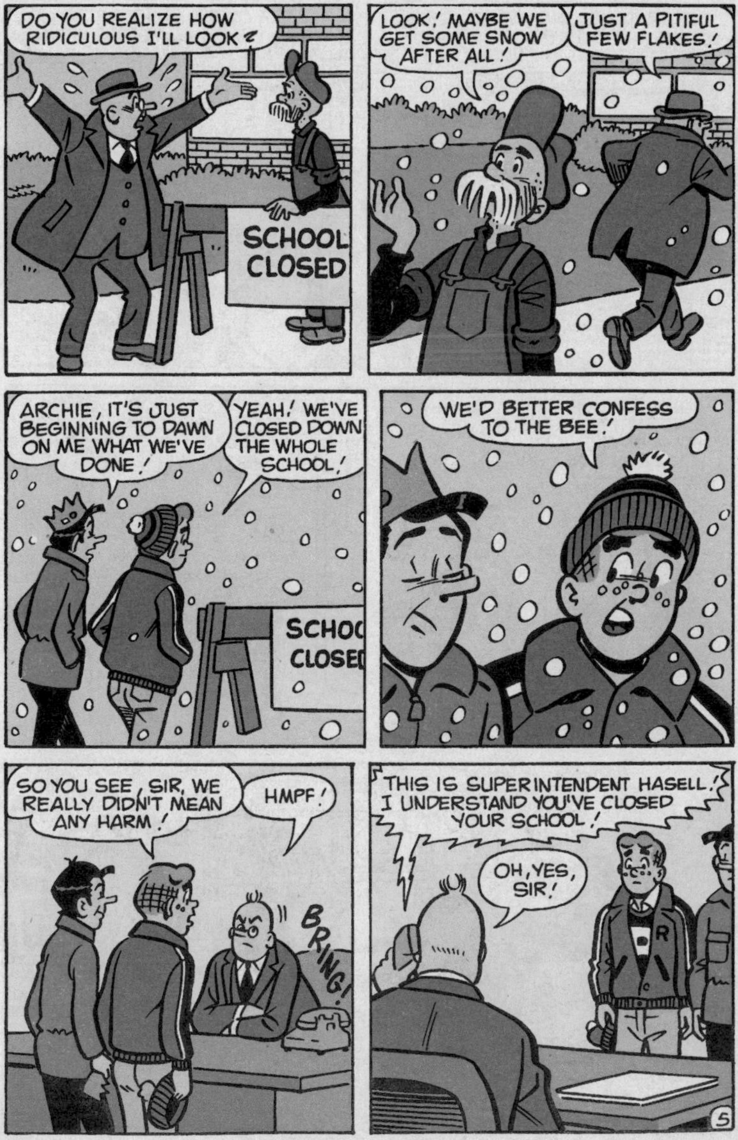
DO YOU REALIZE HOW RIDICULOUS I'LL LOOK?
SCHOOL CLOSED
LOOK! MAYBE WE GET SOME SNOW AFTER ALL!
JUST A PITIFUL FEW FLAKES!
ARCHIE, IT'S JUST BEGINNING TO DAWN ON ME WHAT WE'VE DONE!
YEAH! WE'VE CLOSED DOWN THE WHOLE SCHOOL!
WE'D BETTER CONFESS TO THE BEE!
SO YOU SEE, SIR, WE REALLY DIDN'T MEAN ANY HARM!
HMPF!
BRING!
THIS IS SUPERINTENDENT HASELL! I UNDERSTAND YOU'VE CLOSED YOUR SCHOOL!
OH, YES, SIR!
5

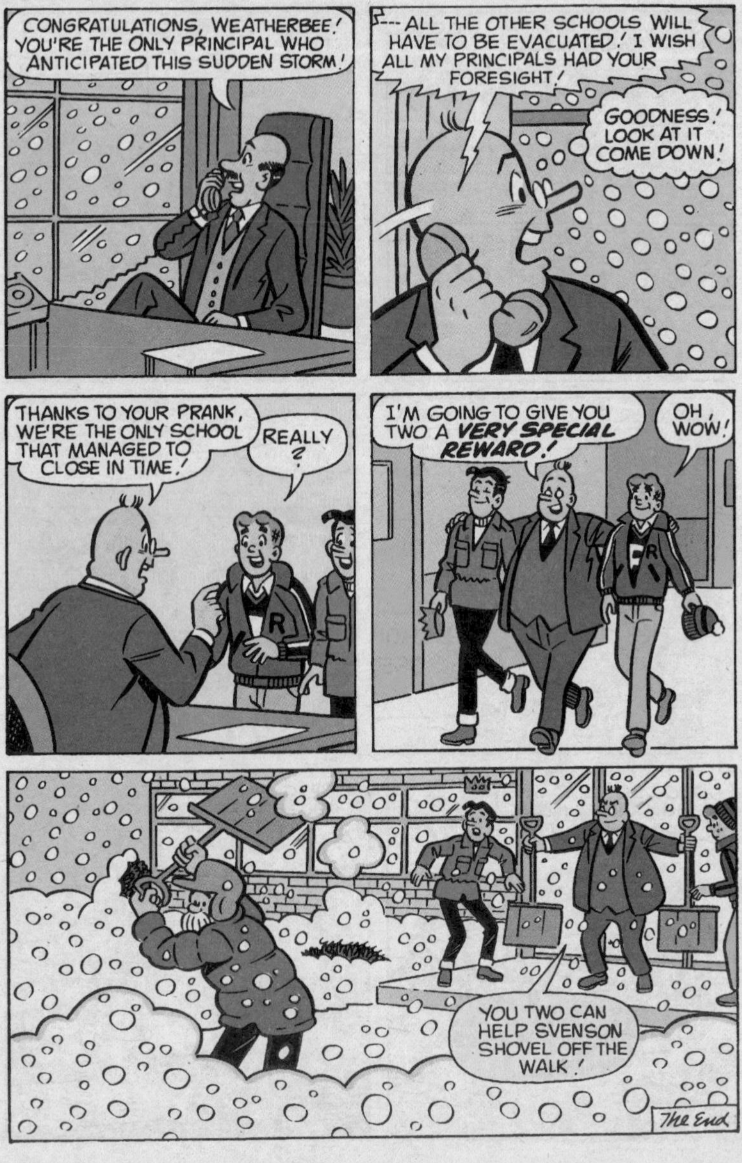

CONGRATULATIONS, WEATHERBEE! YOU'RE THE ONLY PRINCIPAL WHO ANTICIPATED THIS SUDDEN STORM!
--- ALL THE OTHER SCHOOLS WILL HAVE TO BE EVACUATED! I WISH ALL MY PRINCIPALS HAD YOUR FORESIGHT!
GOODNESS! LOOK AT IT COME DOWN!
THANKS TO YOUR PRANK, WE'RE THE ONLY SCHOOL THAT MANAGED TO CLOSE IN TIME!
REALLY ?
I'M GOING TO GIVE YOU TWO A VERY SPECIAL REWARD!
OH, WOW!
YOU TWO CAN HELP SVENSON SHOVEL OFF THE WALK!
The End

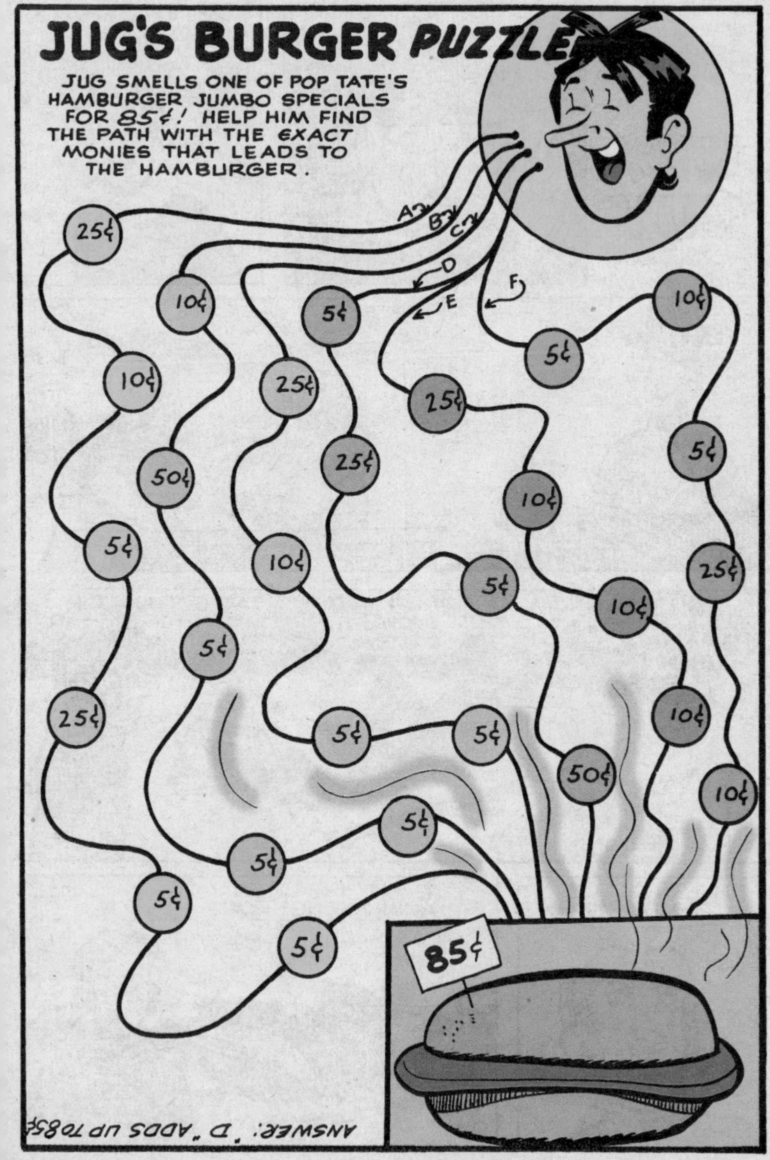
JUG'S BURGER PUZZLE
JUG SMELLS ONE OF POP TATE'S HAMBURGER JUMBO SPECIALS FOR 85¢! HELP HIM FIND THE PATH WITH THE EXACT MONIES THAT LEADS TO THE HAMBURGER.
A
B
C
D
E
F
85¢
ANSWER: "D" ADDS UP TO 85¢

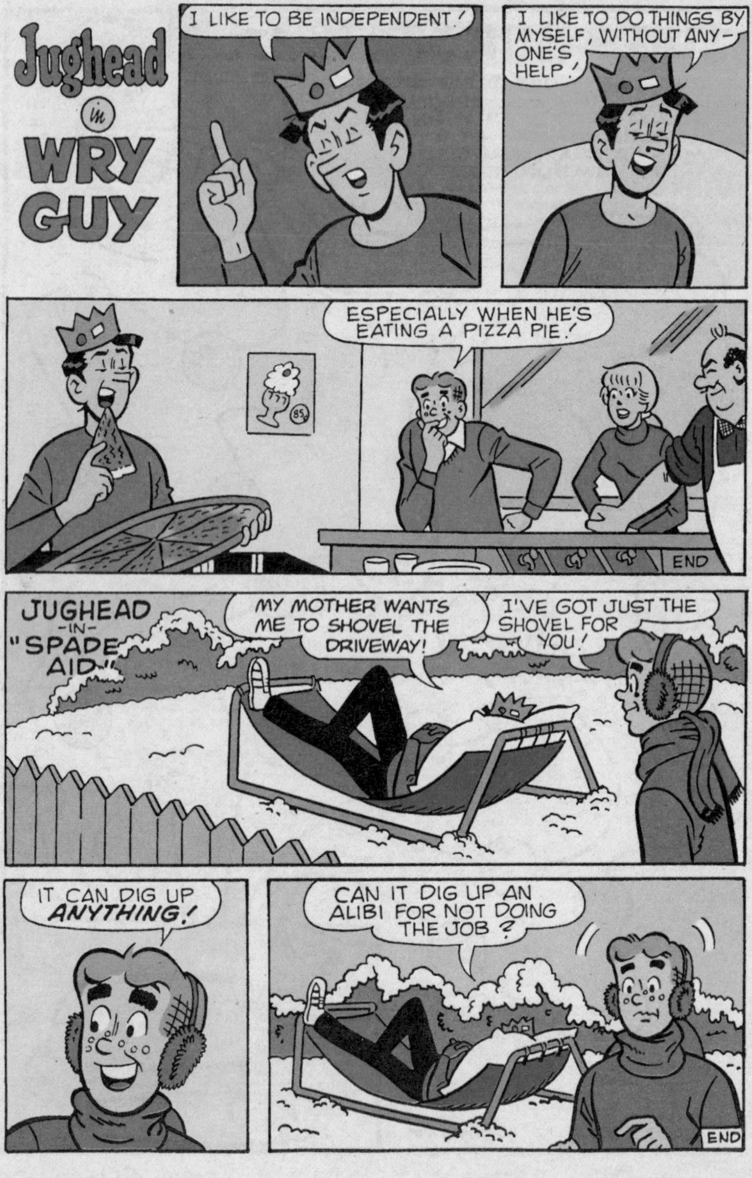
Jughead
in
WRY GUY
I LIKE TO BE INDEPENDENT!
I LIKE TO DO THINGS BY MYSELF, WITHOUT ANY-ONE'S HELP!
ESPECIALLY WHEN HE'S EATING A PIZZA PIE!
85¢
END
JUGHEAD -IN- "SPADE AID"
MY MOTHER WANTS ME TO SHOVEL THE DRIVEWAY!
I'VE GOT JUST THE SHOVEL FOR YOU!
IT CAN DIG UP ANYTHING!
CAN IT DIG UP AN ALIBI FOR NOT DOING THE JOB?
END

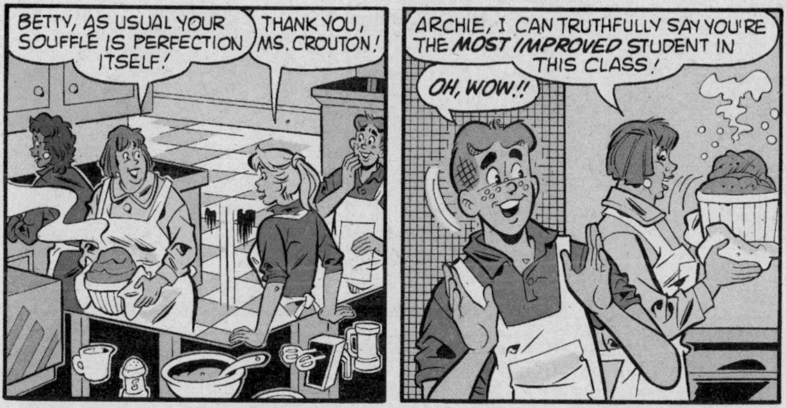
BETTY, AS USUAL YOUR SOUFFLÉ IS PERFECTION ITSELF!
THANK YOU, MS. CROUTON!
ARCHIE, I CAN TRUTHFULLY SAY YOU'RE THE *MOST IMPROVED* STUDENT IN THIS CLASS!
OH, WOW!!

SCRIPT: GEORGE GLADIR PENCILS: TIM KENNEDY INKS: KEN SELIG
COLORS: BARRY GROSSMAN LETTERS: BILL YOSHIDA

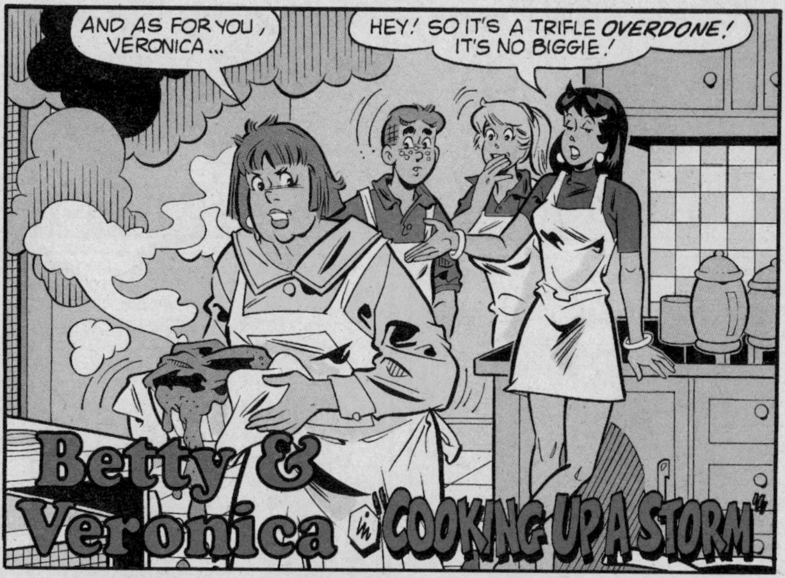
AND AS FOR YOU, VERONICA...
HEY! SO IT'S A TRIFLE *OVERDONE*! IT'S NO BIGGIE!
Betty & Veronica in "COOKING UP A STORM"

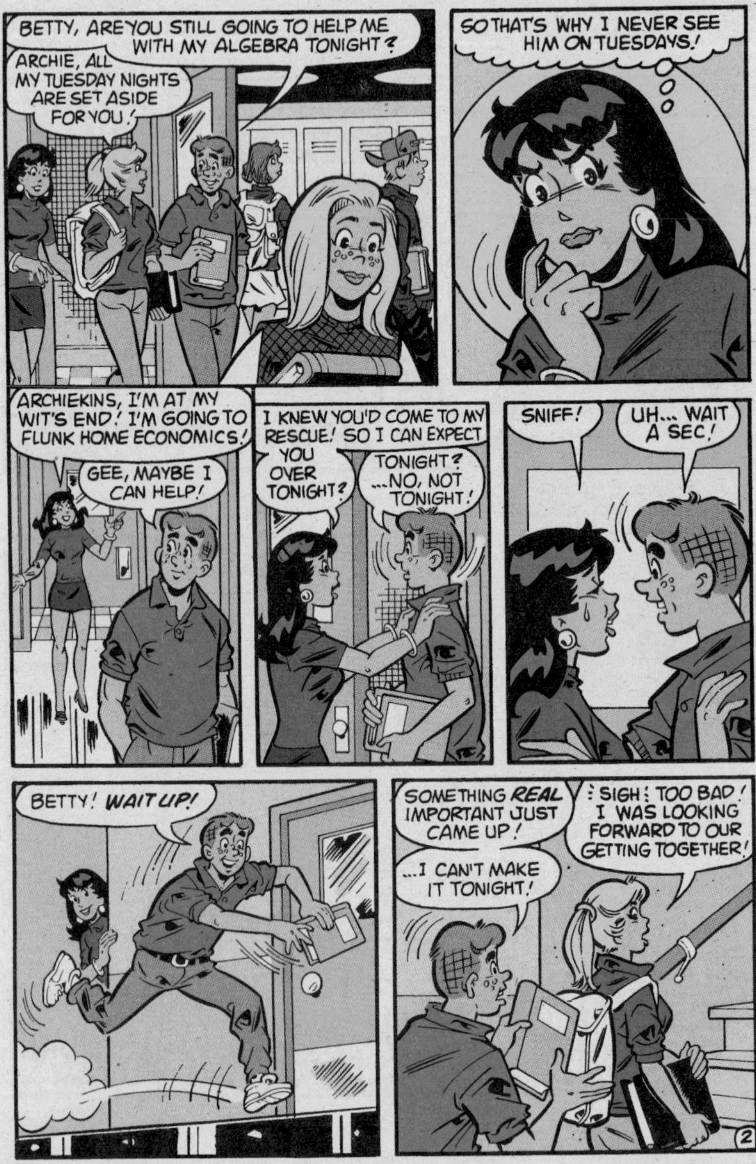
BETTY, ARE YOU STILL GOING TO HELP ME WITH MY ALGEBRA TONIGHT?
ARCHIE, ALL MY TUESDAY NIGHTS ARE SET ASIDE FOR YOU!
SO THAT'S WHY I NEVER SEE HIM ON TUESDAYS!
ARCHIEKINS, I'M AT MY WIT'S END! I'M GOING TO FLUNK HOME ECONOMICS!
GEE, MAYBE I CAN HELP!
I KNEW YOU'D COME TO MY RESCUE! SO I CAN EXPECT YOU OVER TONIGHT?
TONIGHT? ...NO, NOT TONIGHT!
SNIFF!
UH... WAIT A SEC!
BETTY! WAIT UP!
SOMETHING REAL IMPORTANT JUST CAME UP!
...I CAN'T MAKE IT TONIGHT!
: SIGH : TOO BAD! I WAS LOOKING FORWARD TO OUR GETTING TOGETHER!
2

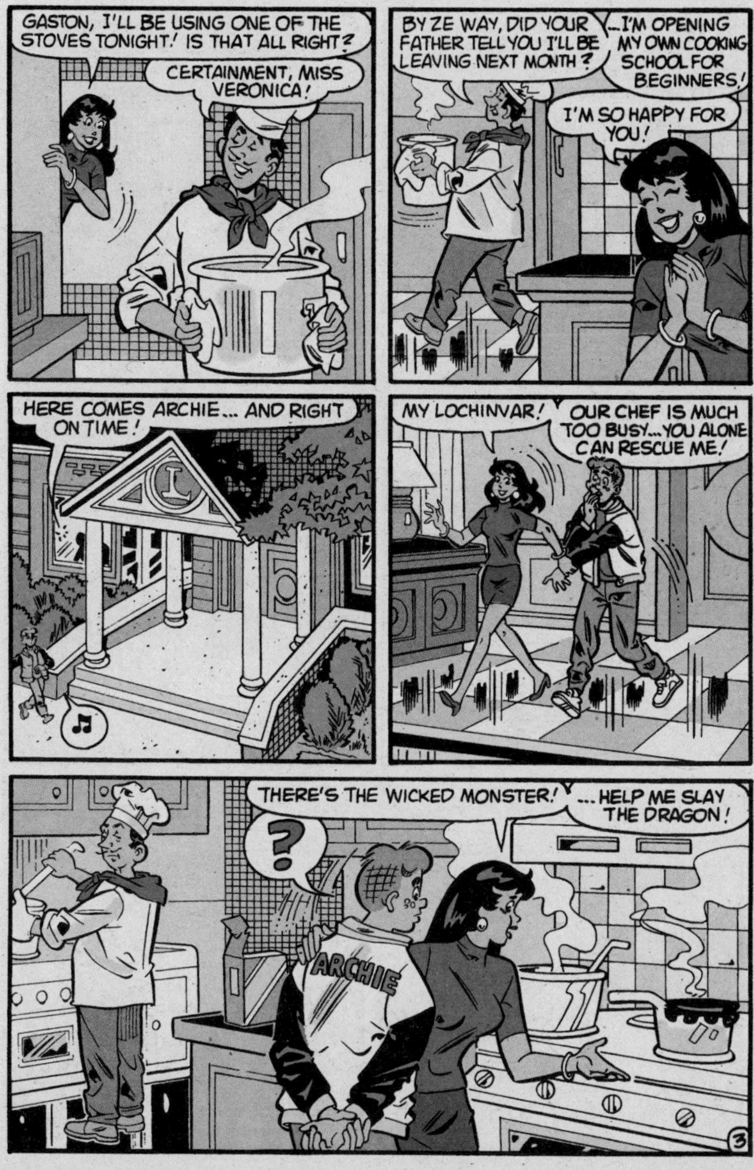
GASTON, I'LL BE USING ONE OF THE STOVES TONIGHT! IS THAT ALL RIGHT?
CERTAINMENT, MISS VERONICA!
BY ZE WAY, DID YOUR FATHER TELL YOU I'LL BE LEAVING NEXT MONTH?
...I'M OPENING MY OWN COOKING SCHOOL FOR BEGINNERS!
I'M SO HAPPY FOR YOU!
HERE COMES ARCHIE... AND RIGHT ON TIME!
MY LOCHINVAR!
OUR CHEF IS MUCH TOO BUSY... YOU ALONE CAN RESCUE ME!
?
THERE'S THE WICKED MONSTER!
... HELP ME SLAY THE DRAGON!
ARCHIE
3

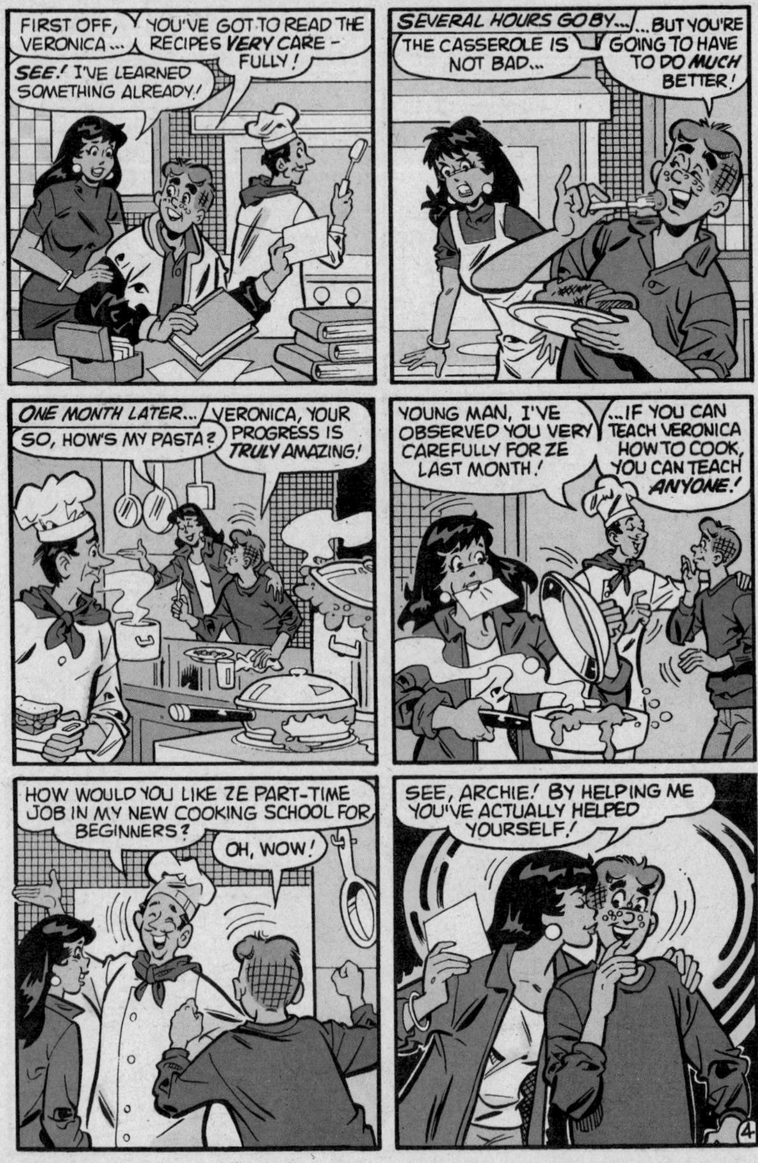
FIRST OFF, VERONICA...
YOU'VE GOT TO READ THE RECIPES VERY CARE - FULLY!
SEE! I'VE LEARNED SOMETHING ALREADY!
SEVERAL HOURS GO BY...
THE CASSEROLE IS NOT BAD...
...BUT YOU'RE GOING TO HAVE TO DO MUCH BETTER!
ONE MONTH LATER...
SO, HOW'S MY PASTA?
VERONICA, YOUR PROGRESS IS TRULY AMAZING!
YOUNG MAN, I'VE OBSERVED YOU VERY CAREFULLY FOR ZE LAST MONTH!
...IF YOU CAN TEACH VERONICA HOW TO COOK, YOU CAN TEACH ANYONE!
HOW WOULD YOU LIKE ZE PART-TIME JOB IN MY NEW COOKING SCHOOL FOR BEGINNERS?
OH, WOW!
SEE, ARCHIE! BY HELPING ME YOU'VE ACTUALLY HELPED YOURSELF!
4

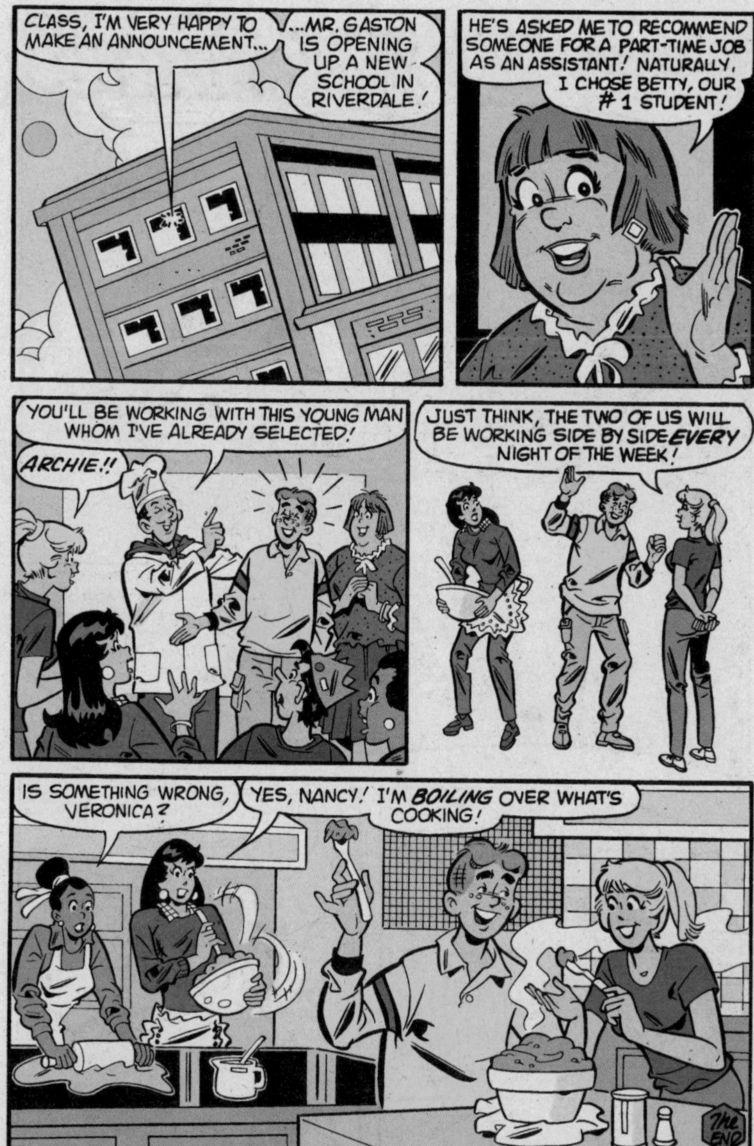
CLASS, I'M VERY HAPPY TO MAKE AN ANNOUNCEMENT...
...MR. GASTON IS OPENING UP A NEW SCHOOL IN RIVERDALE!
HE'S ASKED ME TO RECOMMEND SOMEONE FOR A PART-TIME JOB AS AN ASSISTANT! NATURALLY, I CHOSE BETTY, OUR #1 STUDENT!
YOU'LL BE WORKING WITH THIS YOUNG MAN WHOM I'VE ALREADY SELECTED!
ARCHIE!!
JUST THINK, THE TWO OF US WILL BE WORKING SIDE BY SIDE EVERY NIGHT OF THE WEEK!
IS SOMETHING WRONG, VERONICA?
YES, NANCY! I'M BOILING OVER WHAT'S COOKING!
THE END

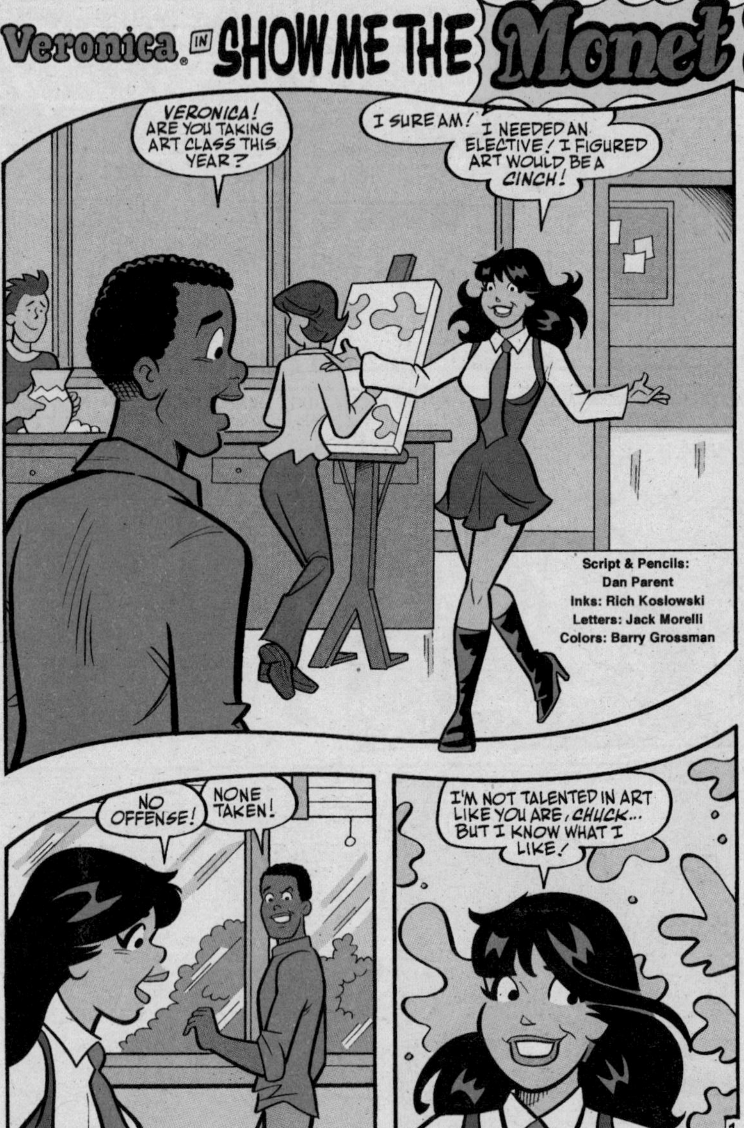

Veronica IN SHOW ME THE Monet
VERONICA! ARE YOU TAKING ART CLASS THIS YEAR?
I SURE AM!
I NEEDED AN ELECTIVE! I FIGURED ART WOULD BE A CINCH!
Script & Pencils: Dan Parent
Inks: Rich Koslowski
Letters: Jack Morelli
Colors: Barry Grossman
NO OFFENSE!
NONE TAKEN!
I'M NOT TALENTED IN ART LIKE YOU ARE, CHUCK... BUT I KNOW WHAT I LIKE!

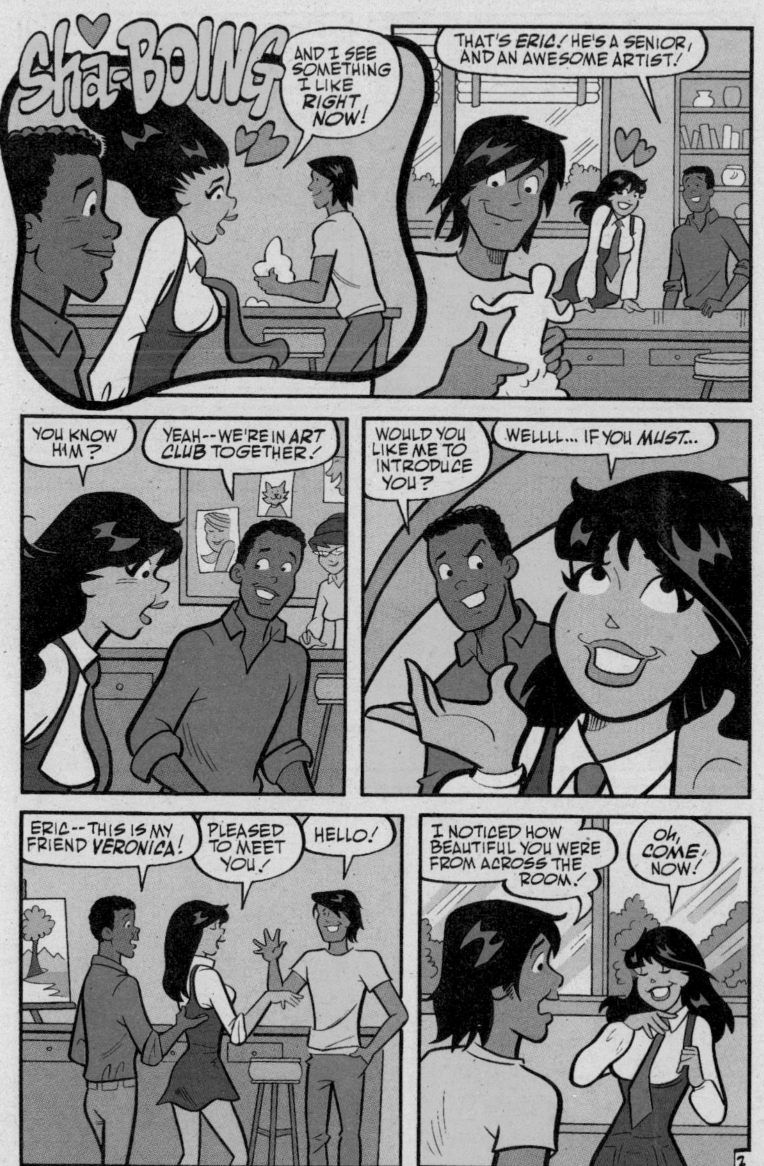
Sha-BOING
AND I SEE SOMETHING I LIKE RIGHT NOW!
THAT'S ERIC! HE'S A SENIOR, AND AN AWESOME ARTIST!
YOU KNOW HIM?
YEAH--WE'RE IN ART CLUB TOGETHER!
WOULD YOU LIKE ME TO INTRODUCE YOU?
WELLLL... IF YOU MUST...
ERIC--THIS IS MY FRIEND VERONICA!
PLEASED TO MEET YOU!
HELLO!
I NOTICED HOW BEAUTIFUL YOU WERE FROM ACROSS THE ROOM!
Oh, COME NOW!
2

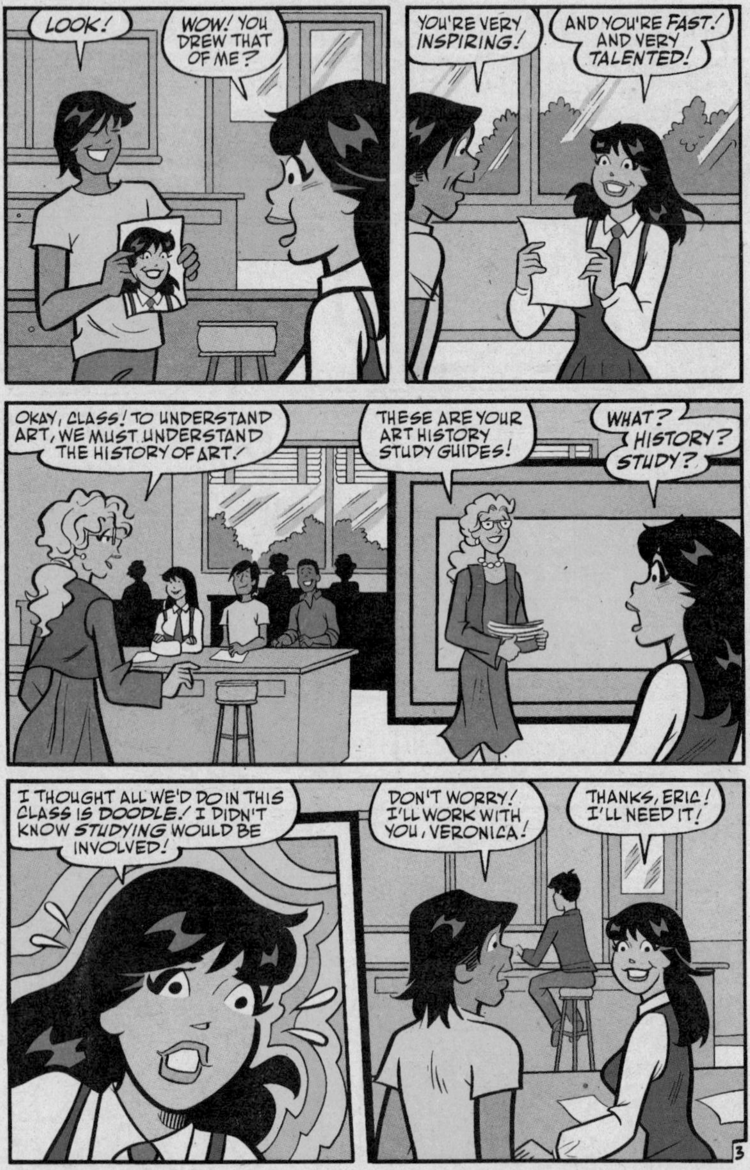

LOOK!
WOW! YOU DREW THAT OF ME?
YOU'RE VERY INSPIRING!
AND YOU'RE FAST! AND VERY TALENTED!
OKAY, CLASS! TO UNDERSTAND ART, WE MUST UNDERSTAND THE HISTORY OF ART!
THESE ARE YOUR ART HISTORY STUDY GUIDES!
WHAT? HISTORY? STUDY?
I THOUGHT ALL WE'D DO IN THIS CLASS IS DOODLE! I DIDN'T KNOW STUDYING WOULD BE INVOLVED!
DON'T WORRY! I'LL WORK WITH YOU, VERONICA!
THANKS, ERIC! I'LL NEED IT!

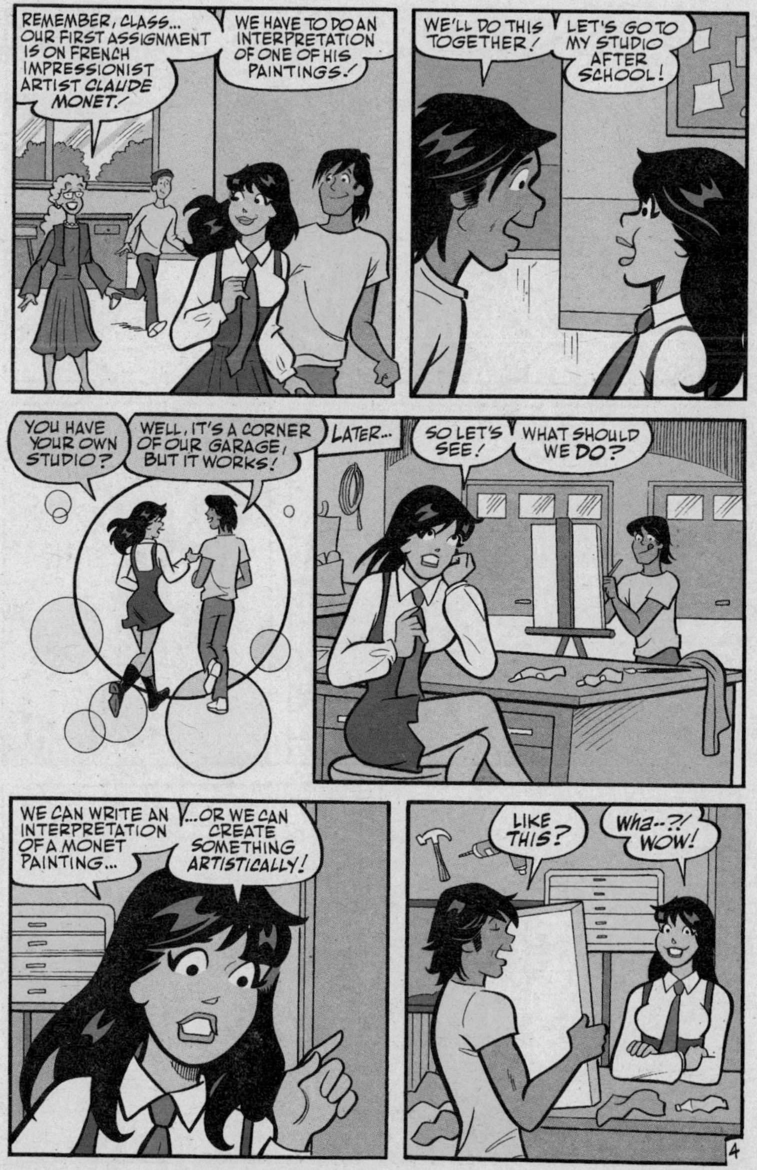
REMEMBER, CLASS... OUR FIRST ASSIGNMENT IS ON FRENCH IMPRESSIONIST ARTIST CLAUDE MONET!
WE HAVE TO DO AN INTERPRETATION OF ONE OF HIS PAINTINGS!
WE'LL DO THIS TOGETHER!
LET'S GO TO MY STUDIO AFTER SCHOOL!
YOU HAVE YOUR OWN STUDIO?
WELL, IT'S A CORNER OF OUR GARAGE, BUT IT WORKS!
LATER...
SO LET'S SEE!
WHAT SHOULD WE DO?
WE CAN WRITE AN INTERPRETATION OF A MONET PAINTING...
...OR WE CAN CREATE SOMETHING ARTISTICALLY!
LIKE THIS?
Wha--?! WOW!

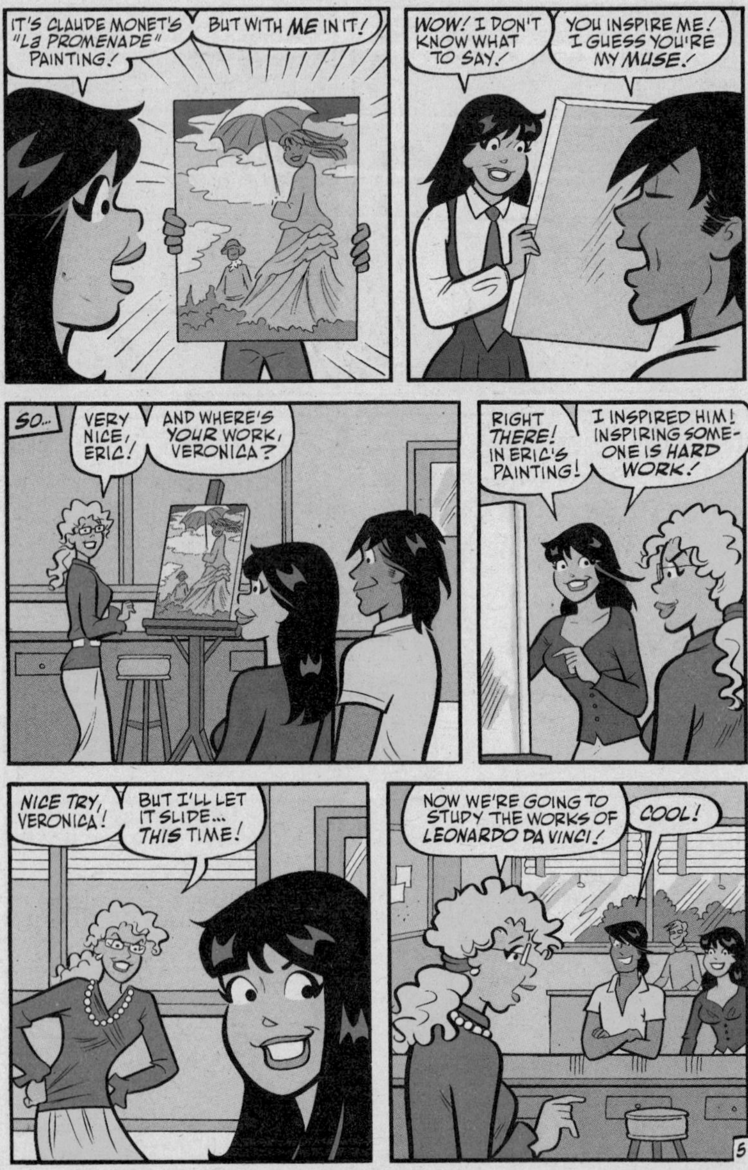
IT'S CLAUDE MONET'S "La PROMENADE" PAINTING!
BUT WITH ME IN IT!
WOW! I DON'T KNOW WHAT TO SAY!
YOU INSPIRE ME! I GUESS YOU'RE MY MUSE!
SO...
VERY NICE, ERIC!
AND WHERE'S YOUR WORK, VERONICA?
RIGHT THERE! IN ERIC'S PAINTING!
I INSPIRED HIM! INSPIRING SOME-ONE IS HARD WORK!
NICE TRY, VERONICA!
BUT I'LL LET IT SLIDE... THIS TIME!
NOW WE'RE GOING TO STUDY THE WORKS OF LEONARDO DA VINCI!
COOL!
5

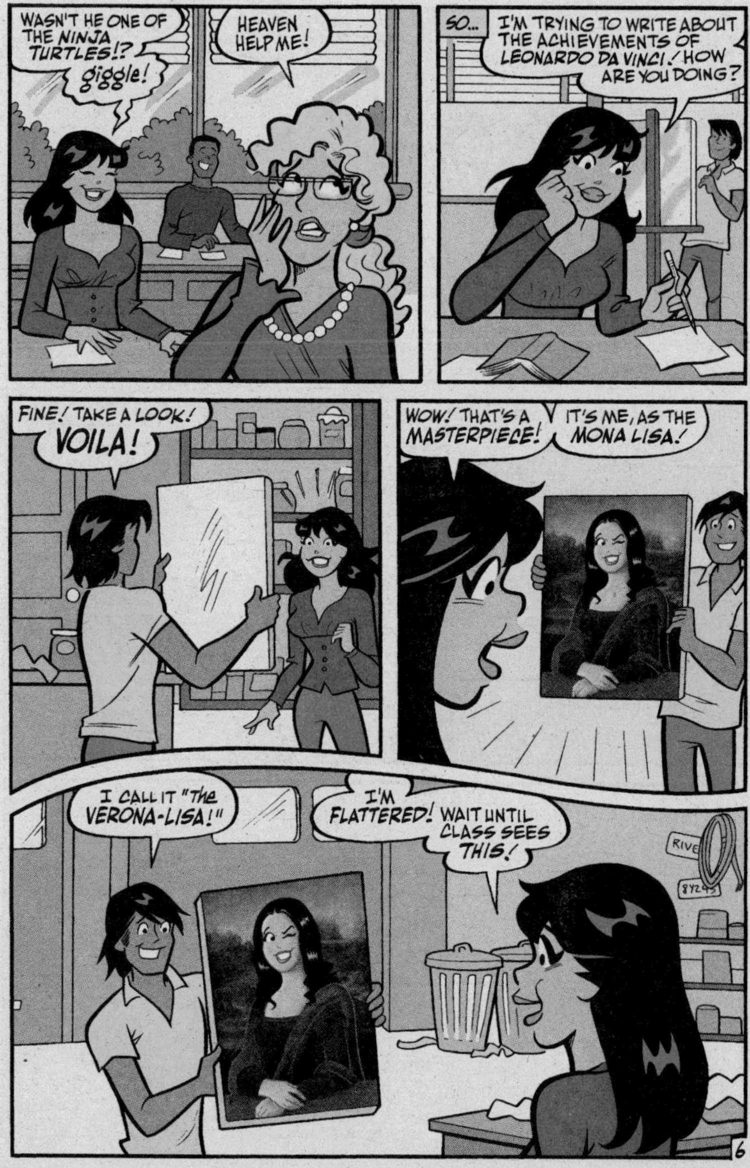
WASN'T HE ONE OF THE NINJA TURTLES!?
giggle!
HEAVEN HELP ME!
SO...
I'M TRYING TO WRITE ABOUT THE ACHIEVEMENTS OF LEONARDO DA VINCI! HOW ARE YOU DOING?
FINE! TAKE A LOOK! VOILA!
WOW! THAT'S A MASTERPIECE!
IT'S ME, AS THE MONA LISA!
I CALL IT "The VERONA-LISA!"
I'M FLATTERED! WAIT UNTIL CLASS SEES THIS!
RIVE
8YZ45

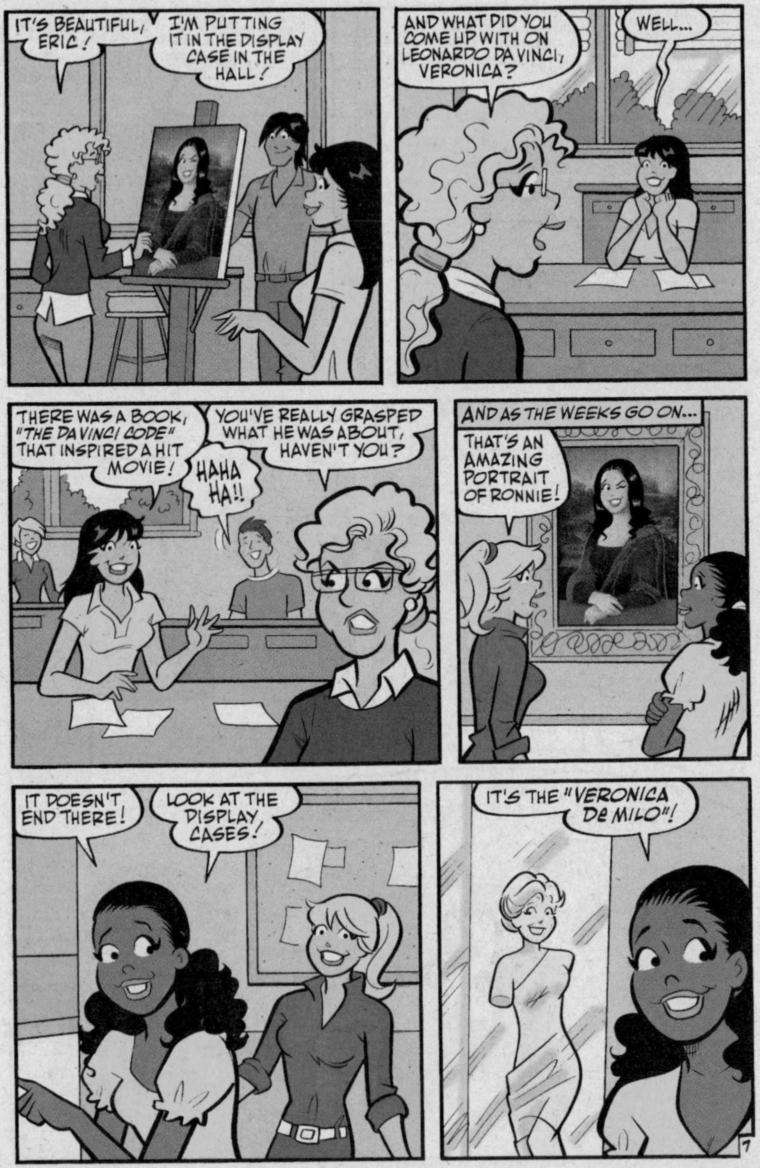
IT'S BEAUTIFUL, ERIC!
I'M PUTTING IT IN THE DISPLAY CASE IN THE HALL!
AND WHAT DID YOU COME UP WITH ON LEONARDO DA VINCI, VERONICA?
WELL...
THERE WAS A BOOK, "THE DA VINCI CODE" THAT INSPIRED A HIT MOVIE!
HAHA HA!!
YOU'VE REALLY GRASPED WHAT HE WAS ABOUT, HAVEN'T YOU?
AND AS THE WEEKS GO ON...
THAT'S AN AMAZING PORTRAIT OF RONNIE!
IT DOESN'T END THERE!
LOOK AT THE DISPLAY CASES!
IT'S THE "VERONICA DE MILO"!
7

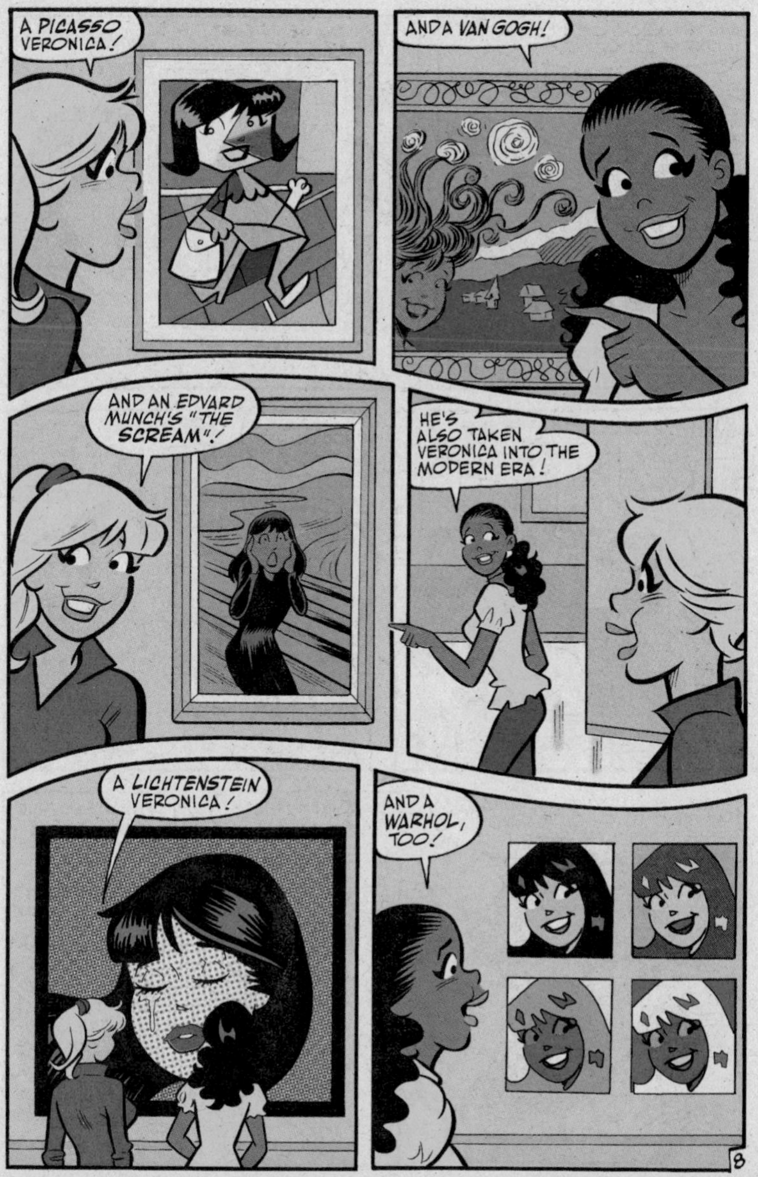
A PICASSO VERONICA!
AND A VAN GOGH!
AND AN EDVARD MUNCH'S "THE SCREAM"!
HE'S ALSO TAKEN VERONICA INTO THE MODERN ERA!
A LICHTENSTEIN VERONICA!
AND A WARHOL, TOO!

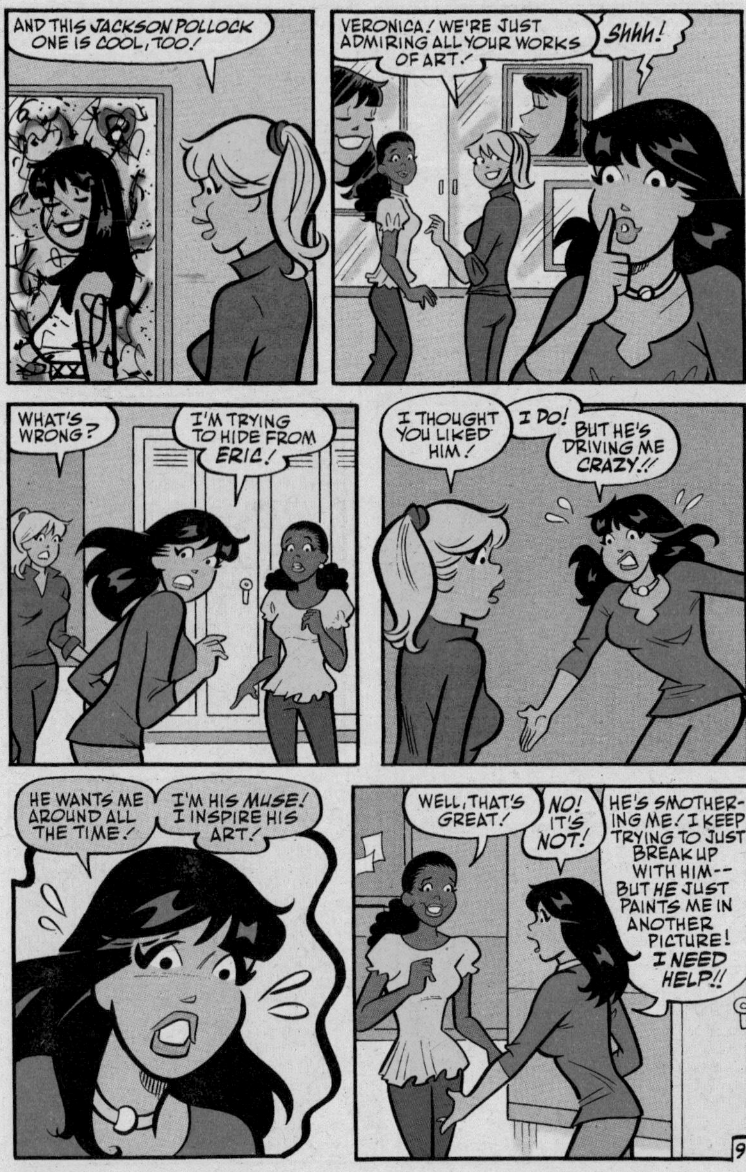
AND THIS JACKSON POLLOCK ONE IS COOL, TOO!
VERONICA! WE'RE JUST ADMIRING ALL YOUR WORKS OF ART!
Shhh!
WHAT'S WRONG?
I'M TRYING TO HIDE FROM ERIC!
I THOUGHT YOU LIKED HIM!
I DO!
BUT HE'S DRIVING ME CRAZY!!
HE WANTS ME AROUND ALL THE TIME!
I'M HIS MUSE! I INSPIRE HIS ART!
WELL, THAT'S GREAT!
NO! IT'S NOT!
HE'S SMOTHERING ME! I KEEP TRYING TO JUST BREAK UP WITH HIM-- BUT HE JUST PAINTS ME IN ANOTHER PICTURE! I NEED HELP!!

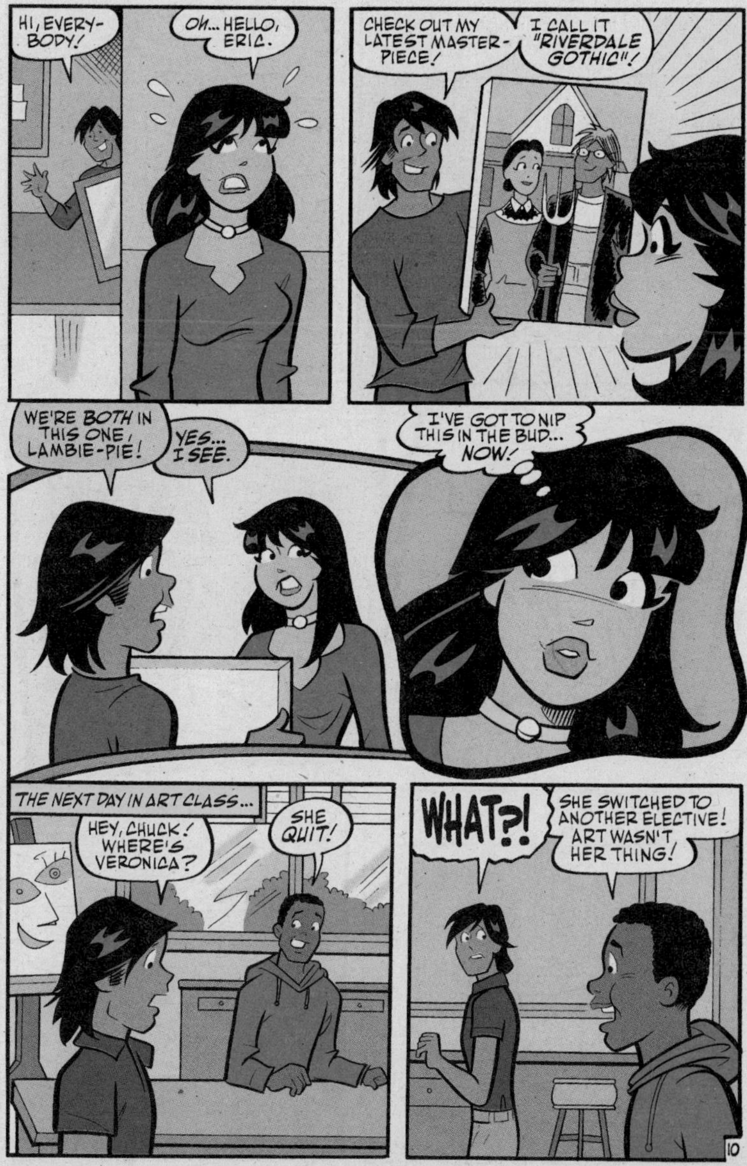
HI, EVERY-BODY!
OH... HELLO, ERIC.
CHECK OUT MY LATEST MASTER-PIECE!
I CALL IT "RIVERDALE GOTHIC"!
WE'RE BOTH IN THIS ONE, LAMBIE-PIE!
YES... I SEE.
I'VE GOT TO NIP THIS IN THE BUD... NOW!
THE NEXT DAY IN ART CLASS...
HEY, CHUCK! WHERE'S VERONICA?
SHE QUIT!
WHAT?!
SHE SWITCHED TO ANOTHER ELECTIVE! ART WASN'T HER THING!

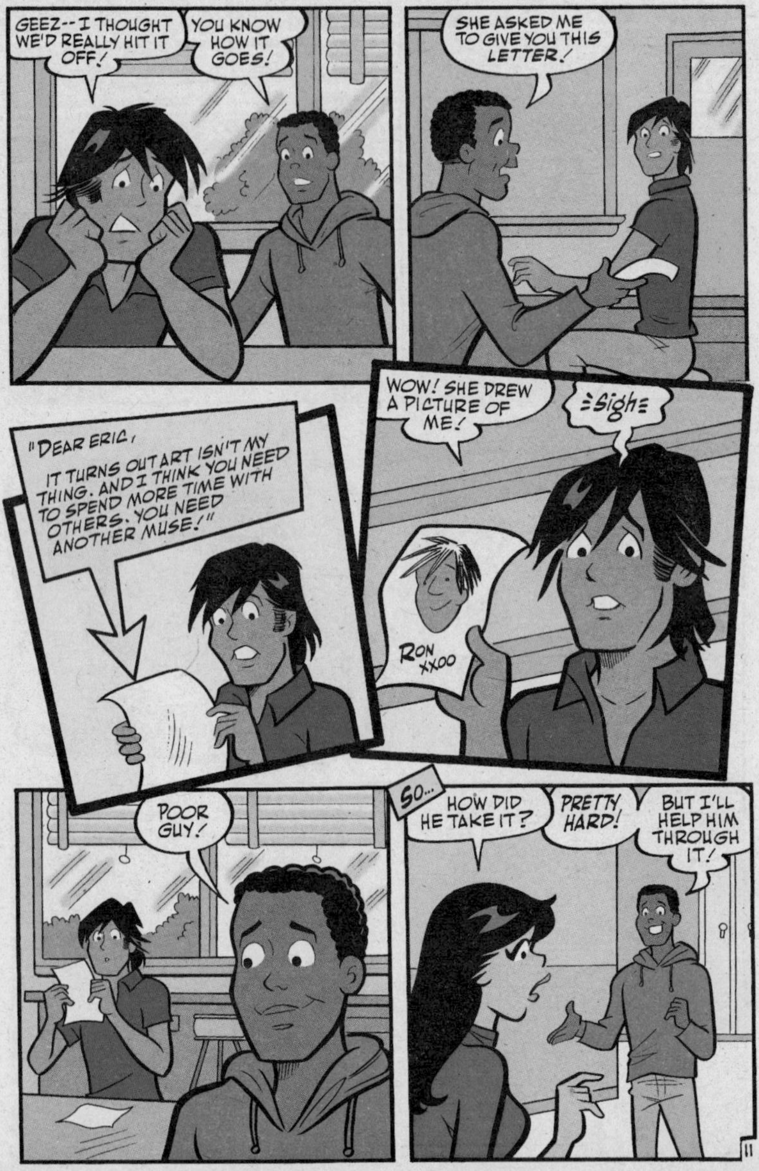

GEEZ--I THOUGHT WE'D REALLY HIT IT OFF!
YOU KNOW HOW IT GOES!
SHE ASKED ME TO GIVE YOU THIS LETTER!
"DEAR ERIC, IT TURNS OUT ART ISN'T MY THING. AND I THINK YOU NEED TO SPEND MORE TIME WITH OTHERS. YOU NEED ANOTHER MUSE!"
WOW! SHE DREW A PICTURE OF ME!
Sigh
RON XXOO
POOR GUY!
SO...
HOW DID HE TAKE IT?
PRETTY HARD!
BUT I'LL HELP HIM THROUGH IT!

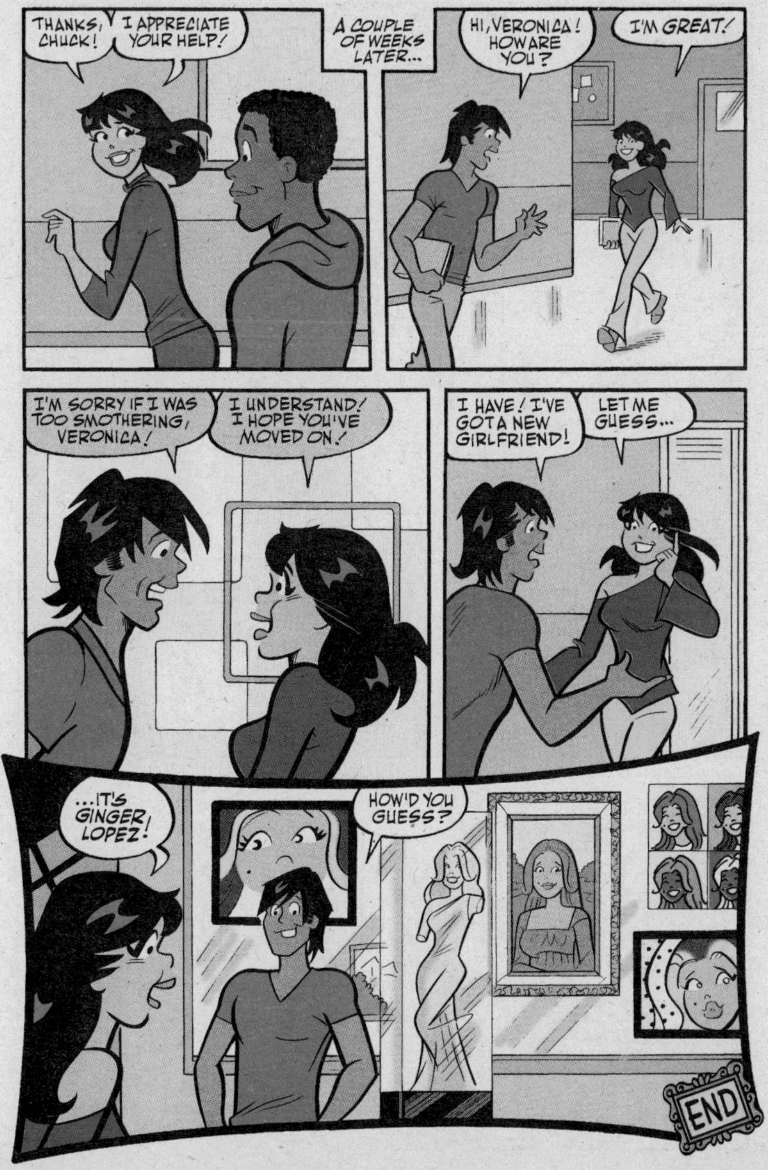
THANKS, CHUCK!
I APPRECIATE YOUR HELP!
A COUPLE OF WEEKS LATER...
HI, VERONICA! HOW ARE YOU?
I'M GREAT!
I'M SORRY IF I WAS TOO SMOTHERING, VERONICA!
I UNDERSTAND! I HOPE YOU'VE MOVED ON!
I HAVE! I'VE GOT A NEW GIRLFRIEND!
LET ME GUESS...
...IT'S GINGER LOPEZ!
HOW'D YOU GUESS?
END

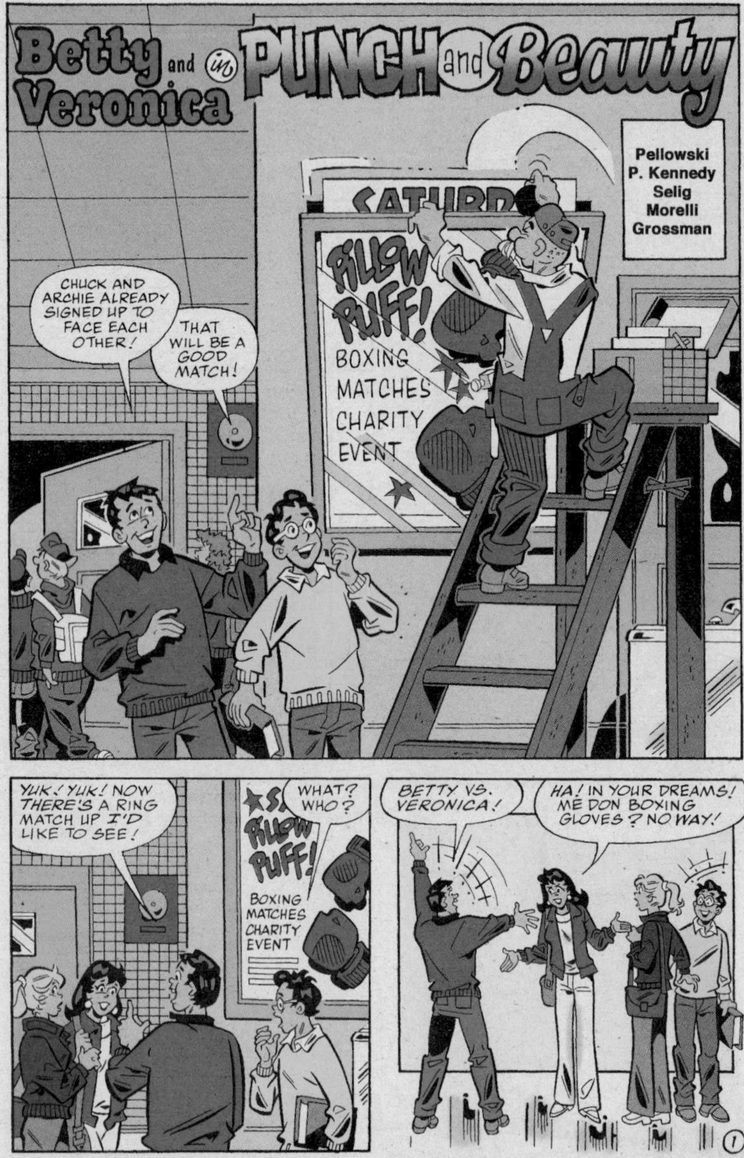
Betty and Veronica in PUNCH and Beauty
Pellowski
P. Kennedy
Selig
Morelli
Grossman
SATURD
PILLOW PUFF!
BOXING
MATCHES
CHARITY
EVENT
CHUCK AND ARCHIE ALREADY SIGNED UP TO FACE EACH OTHER!
THAT WILL BE A GOOD MATCH!
YUK! YUK! NOW THERE'S A RING MATCH UP I'D LIKE TO SEE!
WHAT? WHO?
PILLOW PUFF!
BOXING
MATCHES
CHARITY
EVENT
BETTY VS. VERONICA!
HA! IN YOUR DREAMS! ME DON BOXING GLOVES? NO WAY!
1

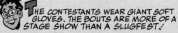

I'D NEVER RISK MARRING *THIS* PERFECT PROFILE IN A BOXING RING!

PILLOW PUFF BOXING IS TOTALLY SAFE, RON!

XING CHES RITY EVENT

THE CONTESTANTS WEAR GIANT SOFT GLOVES. THE BOUTS ARE MORE OF A STAGE SHOW THAN A SLUGFEST!

SWIPE!

THAT'S RIGHT, RON. THERE'S NOTHING TO BE AFRAID OF. MIDGE AND NANCY HAVE SIGNED UP!

IT'S FOR CHARITY, RON!

BO MATCH CHARITY EVENT

Hmmm... I GUESS WE COULD TASTEFULLY FAKE A GOOD FIGHT!

ABSOLUTELY!

NOW THAT'S A BOUT I'LL GLADLY PAY TO SEE!

OKAY, BETTY, SIGN US UP!

BO MATCH CHARITY EVENT

LET'S MEET AT MY HOUSE TONIGHT TO START REHEARSING OUR SO-CALLED "FIGHT"!

HEE HEE! RIGHT!

2

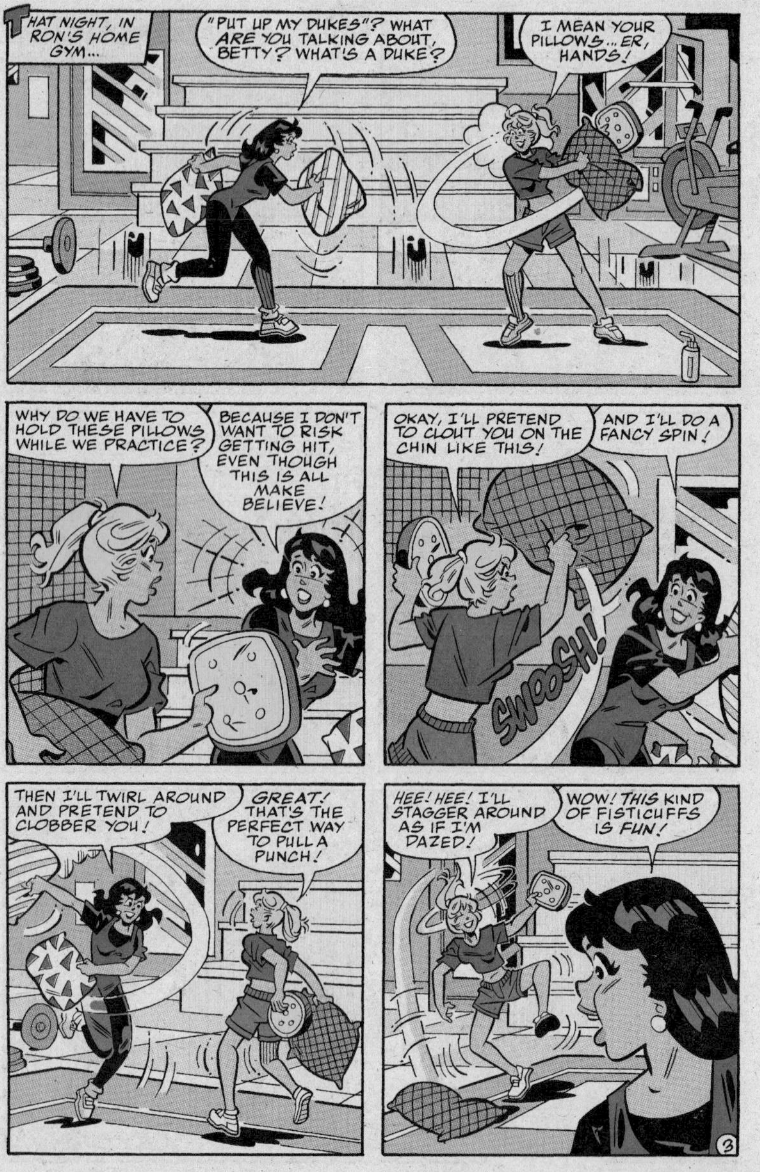
THAT NIGHT, IN RON'S HOME GYM...
"PUT UP MY DUKES"? WHAT ARE YOU TALKING ABOUT, BETTY? WHAT'S A DUKE?
I MEAN YOUR PILLOWS... ER, HANDS!
WHY DO WE HAVE TO HOLD THESE PILLOWS WHILE WE PRACTICE?
BECAUSE I DON'T WANT TO RISK GETTING HIT, EVEN THOUGH THIS IS ALL MAKE BELIEVE!
OKAY, I'LL PRETEND TO CLOUT YOU ON THE CHIN LIKE THIS!
AND I'LL DO A FANCY SPIN!
SWOOSH!
THEN I'LL TWIRL AROUND AND PRETEND TO CLOBBER YOU!
GREAT! THAT'S THE PERFECT WAY TO PULL A PUNCH!
HEE! HEE! I'LL STAGGER AROUND AS IF I'M DAZED!
WOW! THIS KIND OF FISTICUFFS IS FUN!
3

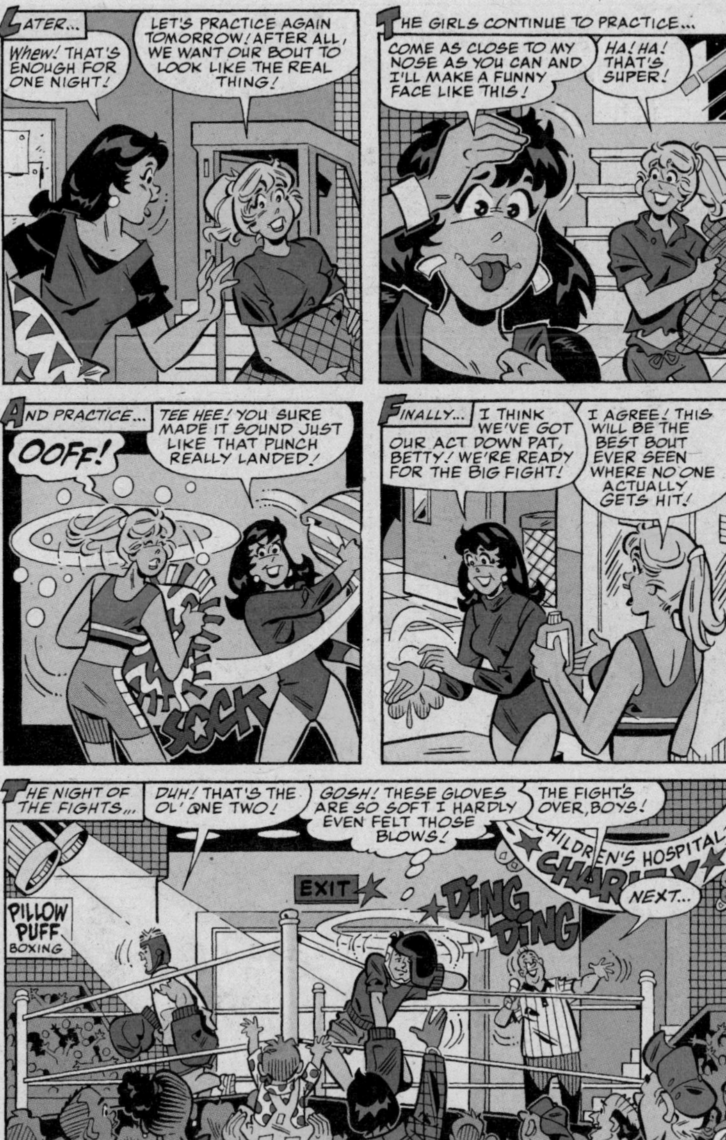
LATER...
Whew! THAT'S ENOUGH FOR ONE NIGHT!
LET'S PRACTICE AGAIN TOMORROW! AFTER ALL, WE WANT OUR BOUT TO LOOK LIKE THE REAL THING!
THE GIRLS CONTINUE TO PRACTICE...
COME AS CLOSE TO MY NOSE AS YOU CAN AND I'LL MAKE A FUNNY FACE LIKE THIS!
HA! HA! THAT'S SUPER!
AND PRACTICE...
OOFF!
TEE HEE! YOU SURE MADE IT SOUND JUST LIKE THAT PUNCH REALLY LANDED!
SOCK
FINALLY...
I THINK WE'VE GOT OUR ACT DOWN PAT, BETTY! WE'RE READY FOR THE BIG FIGHT!
I AGREE! THIS WILL BE THE BEST BOUT EVER SEEN WHERE NO ONE ACTUALLY GETS HIT!
THE NIGHT OF THE FIGHTS...
DUH! THAT'S THE OL' ONE TWO!
GOSH! THESE GLOVES ARE SO SOFT I HARDLY EVEN FELT THOSE BLOWS!
THE FIGHT'S OVER, BOYS!
NEXT...
CHILDREN'S HOSPITAL CHARITY
EXIT
DING DING
PILLOW PUFF BOXING
4

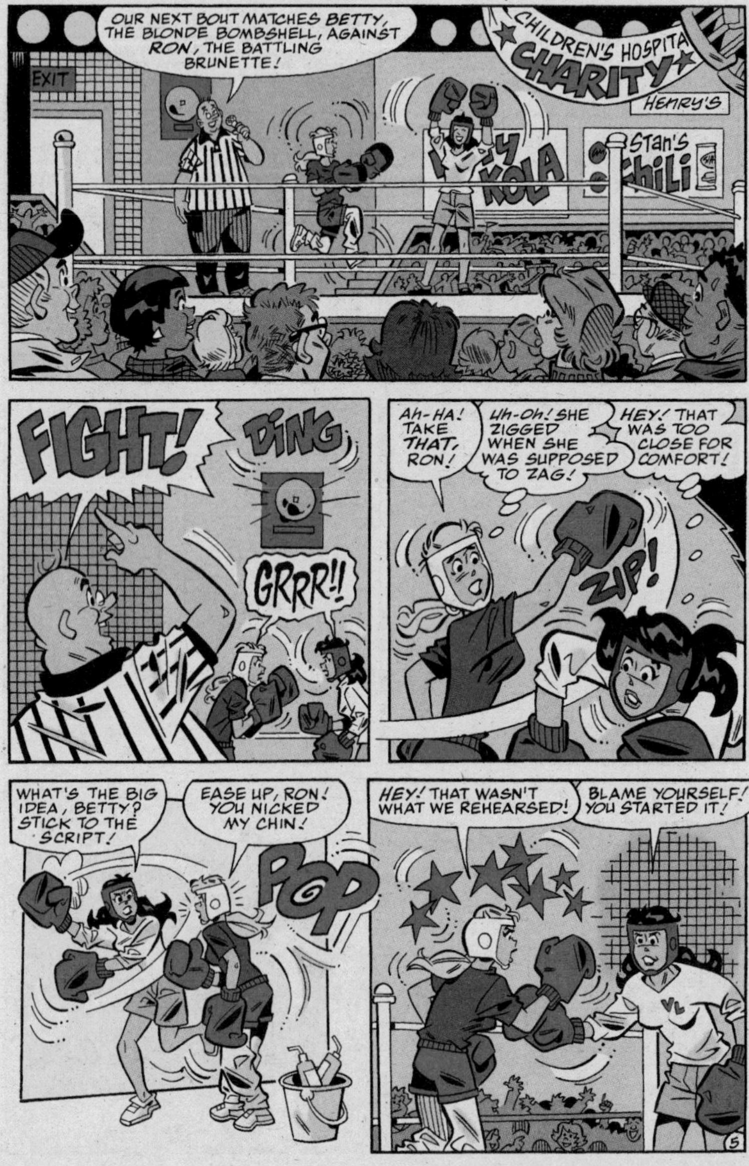
OUR NEXT BOUT MATCHES BETTY, THE BLONDE BOMBSHELL, AGAINST RON, THE BATTLING BRUNETTE!
CHILDREN'S HOSPITA
CHARITY
HENRY'S
EXIT
KOLA
Stan's
CHILI
FIGHT!
DING
GRRR!!
Ah-HA! TAKE THAT, RON!
Uh-Oh! SHE ZIGGED WHEN SHE WAS SUPPOSED TO ZAG!
HEY! THAT WAS TOO CLOSE FOR COMFORT!
ZIP!
WHAT'S THE BIG IDEA, BETTY? STICK TO THE SCRIPT!
EASE UP, RON! YOU NICKED MY CHIN!
POP
HEY! THAT WASN'T WHAT WE REHEARSED!
BLAME YOURSELF! YOU STARTED IT!
5

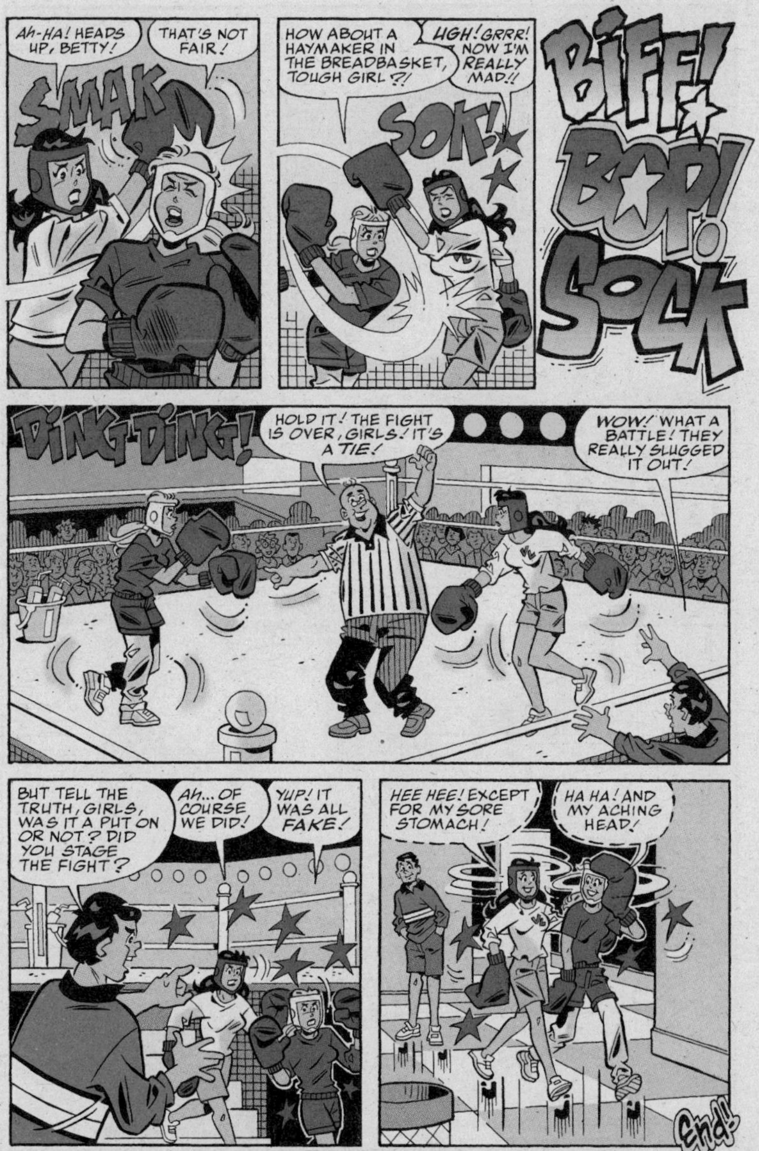
AH-HA! HEADS UP, BETTY!
THAT'S NOT FAIR!
SMAK
HOW ABOUT A HAYMAKER IN THE BREADBASKET, TOUGH GIRL?!
UGH! GRRR! NOW I'M REALLY MAD!!
SOK!
BIFF! BOP! SOCK
DING DING!
HOLD IT! THE FIGHT IS OVER, GIRLS! IT'S A TIE!
WOW! WHAT A BATTLE! THEY REALLY SLUGGED IT OUT!
BUT TELL THE TRUTH, GIRLS, WAS IT A PUT ON OR NOT? DID YOU STAGE THE FIGHT?
AH... OF COURSE WE DID!
YUP! IT WAS ALL FAKE!
HEE HEE! EXCEPT FOR MY SORE STOMACH!
HA HA! AND MY ACHING HEAD!
End!

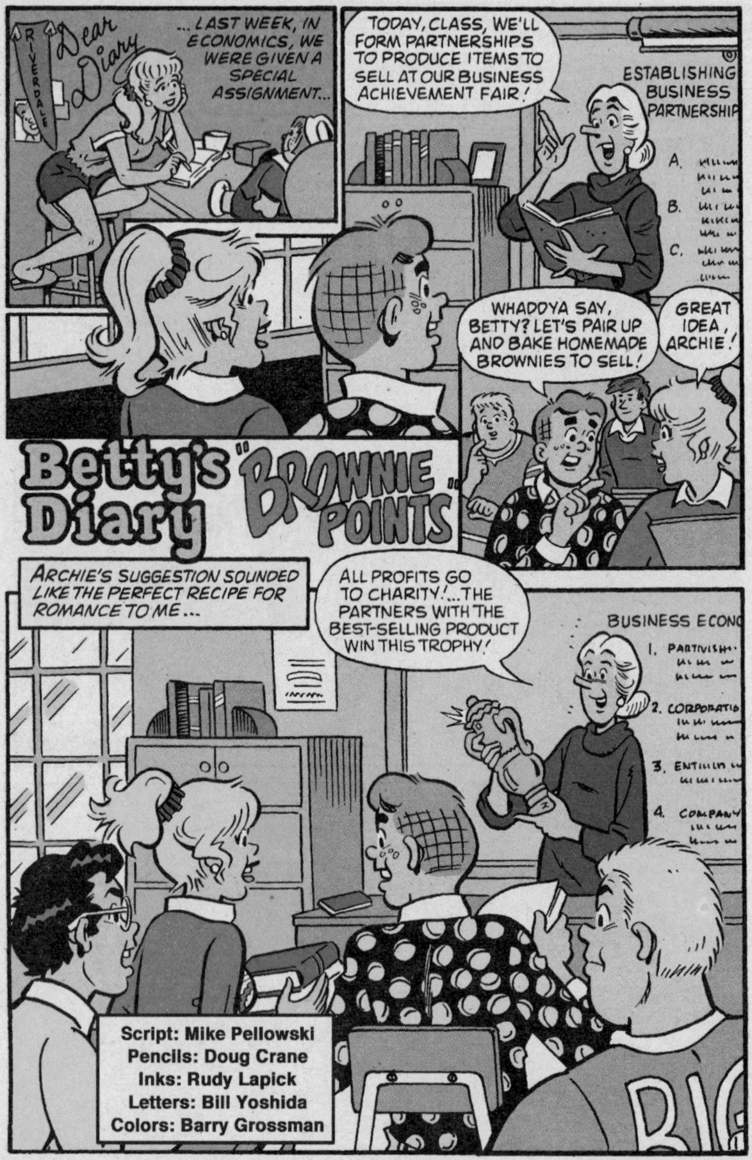
Dear Diary
RIVERDALE
... LAST WEEK, IN ECONOMICS, WE WERE GIVEN A SPECIAL ASSIGNMENT...
TODAY, CLASS, WE'LL FORM PARTNERSHIPS TO PRODUCE ITEMS TO SELL AT OUR BUSINESS ACHIEVEMENT FAIR!
ESTABLISHING BUSINESS PARTNERSHIP
A.
B.
C.
WHADDYA SAY, BETTY? LET'S PAIR UP AND BAKE HOMEMADE BROWNIES TO SELL!
GREAT IDEA, ARCHIE!
Betty's Diary
"BROWNIE POINTS"
ARCHIE'S SUGGESTION SOUNDED LIKE THE PERFECT RECIPE FOR ROMANCE TO ME...
ALL PROFITS GO TO CHARITY!...THE PARTNERS WITH THE BEST-SELLING PRODUCT WIN THIS TROPHY!
BUSINESS ECONO
1. PARTNERSH
2. CORPORATIO
3. ENTI
4. COMPANY
Script: Mike Pellowski
Pencils: Doug Crane
Inks: Rudy Lapick
Letters: Bill Yoshida
Colors: Barry Grossman
BIG

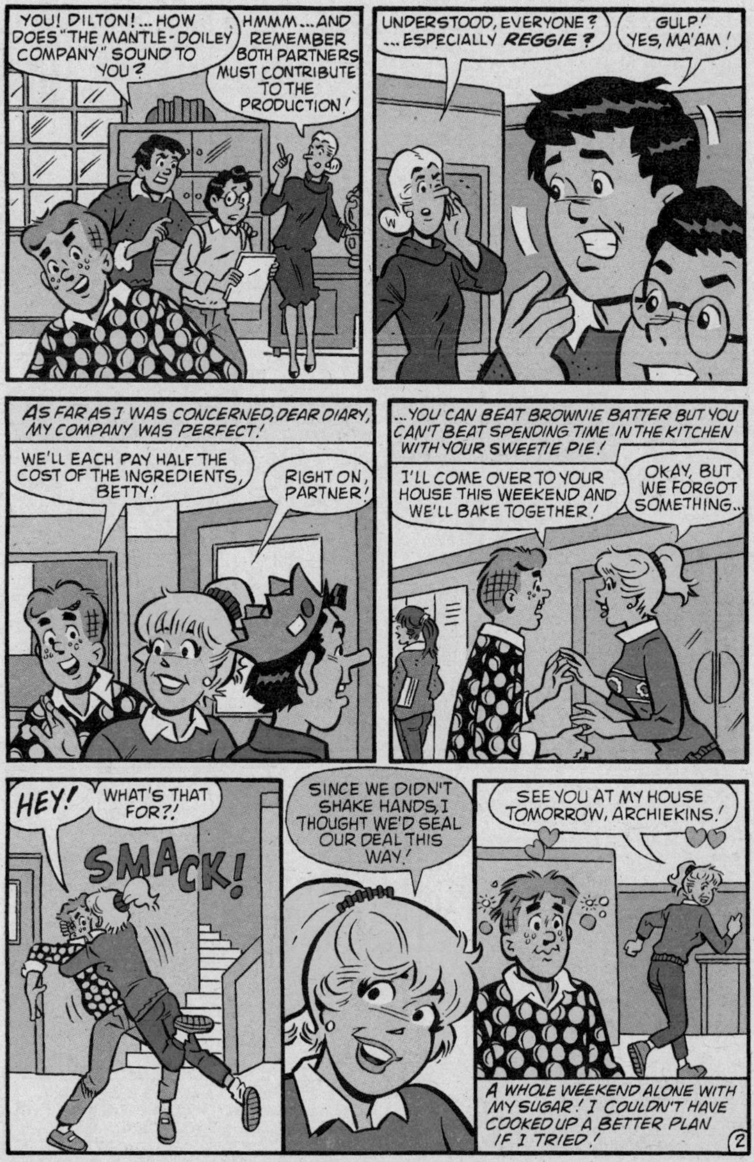
YOU! DILTON!... HOW DOES "THE MANTLE-DOILEY COMPANY" SOUND TO YOU?
HMMM... AND REMEMBER BOTH PARTNERS MUST CONTRIBUTE TO THE PRODUCTION!
UNDERSTOOD, EVERYONE? ...ESPECIALLY REGGIE?
GULP! YES, MA'AM!
AS FAR AS I WAS CONCERNED, DEAR DIARY, MY COMPANY WAS PERFECT!
WE'LL EACH PAY HALF THE COST OF THE INGREDIENTS, BETTY!
RIGHT ON, PARTNER!
...YOU CAN BEAT BROWNIE BATTER BUT YOU CAN'T BEAT SPENDING TIME IN THE KITCHEN WITH YOUR SWEETIE PIE!
I'LL COME OVER TO YOUR HOUSE THIS WEEKEND AND WE'LL BAKE TOGETHER!
OKAY, BUT WE FORGOT SOMETHING...
HEY!
WHAT'S THAT FOR?!
SMACK!
SINCE WE DIDN'T SHAKE HANDS, I THOUGHT WE'D SEAL OUR DEAL THIS WAY!
SEE YOU AT MY HOUSE TOMORROW, ARCHIEKINS!
A WHOLE WEEKEND ALONE WITH MY SUGAR! I COULDN'T HAVE COOKED UP A BETTER PLAN IF I TRIED!
2

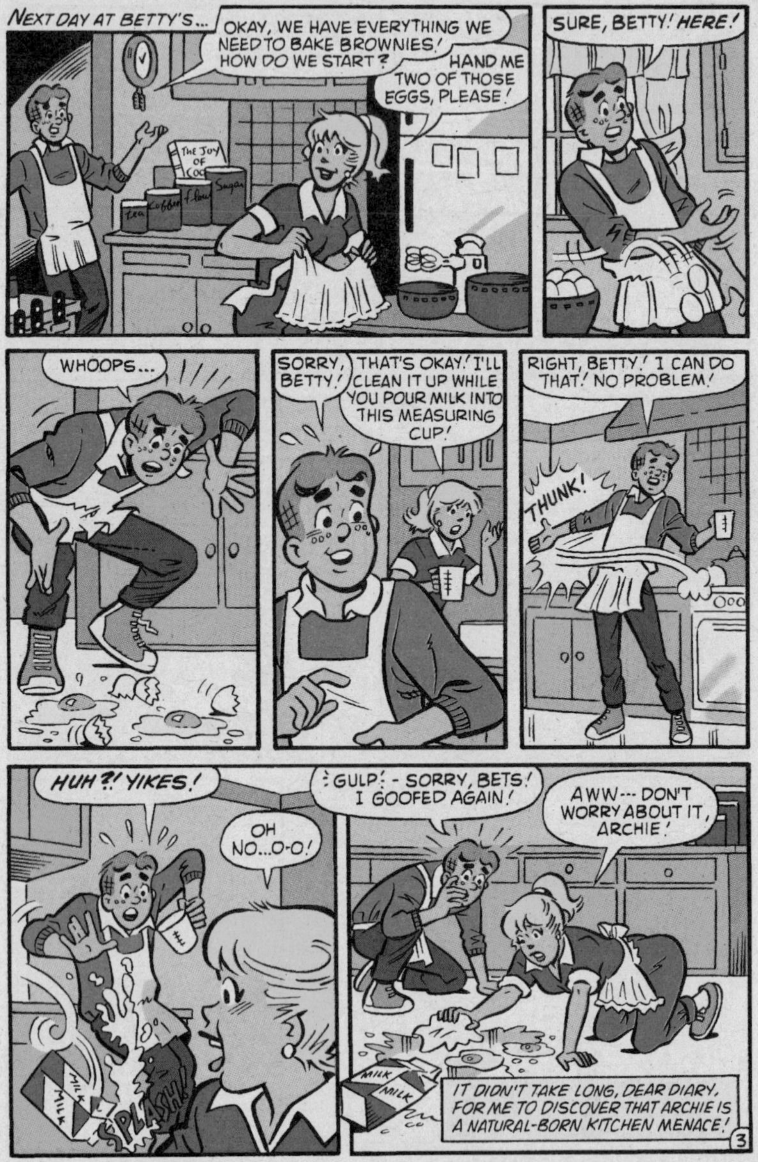
NEXT DAY AT BETTY'S...
OKAY, WE HAVE EVERYTHING WE NEED TO BAKE BROWNIES! HOW DO WE START?
HAND ME TWO OF THOSE EGGS, PLEASE!
THE JOY OF COO
TEA
COFFEE
FLOUR
SUGAR
SURE, BETTY! HERE!
WHOOPS...
SORRY, BETTY!
THAT'S OKAY! I'LL CLEAN IT UP WHILE YOU POUR MILK INTO THIS MEASURING CUP!
RIGHT, BETTY! I CAN DO THAT! NO PROBLEM!
THUNK!
HUH?! YIKES!
OH NO...O-O!
MILK
SPLASH!
:GULP: - SORRY, BETS! I GOOFED AGAIN!
AWW--- DON'T WORRY ABOUT IT, ARCHIE!
MILK
IT DIDN'T TAKE LONG, DEAR DIARY, FOR ME TO DISCOVER THAT ARCHIE IS A NATURAL-BORN KITCHEN MENACE!
3

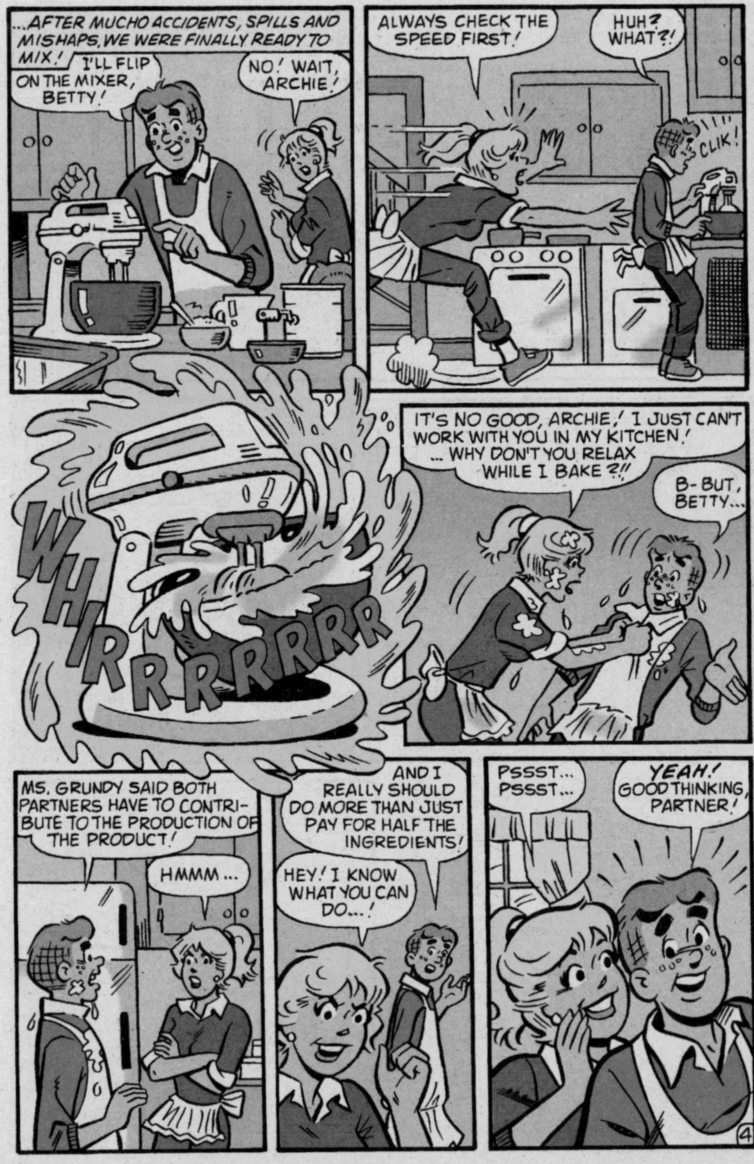
...AFTER MUCHO ACCIDENTS, SPILLS AND MISHAPS, WE WERE FINALLY READY TO MIX!
I'LL FLIP ON THE MIXER, BETTY!
NO! WAIT, ARCHIE!
ALWAYS CHECK THE SPEED FIRST!
HUH? WHAT?!
CLIK!
WHIRRRRRRR
IT'S NO GOOD, ARCHIE! I JUST CAN'T WORK WITH YOU IN MY KITCHEN! ... WHY DON'T YOU RELAX WHILE I BAKE?!!
B-BUT, BETTY...
MS. GRUNDY SAID BOTH PARTNERS HAVE TO CONTRIBUTE TO THE PRODUCTION OF THE PRODUCT!
HMMM...
AND I REALLY SHOULD DO MORE THAN JUST PAY FOR HALF THE INGREDIENTS!
HEY! I KNOW WHAT YOU CAN DO...!
PSSST... PSSST...
YEAH! GOOD THINKING, PARTNER!
4

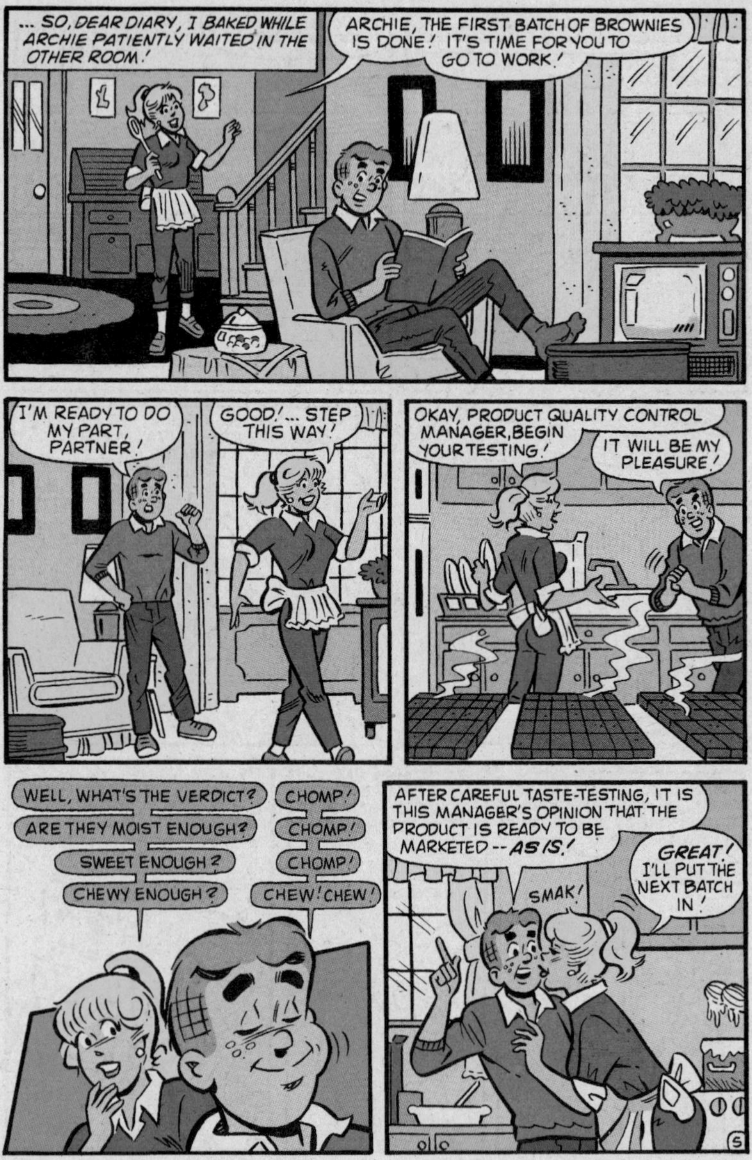

... SO, DEAR DIARY, I BAKED WHILE ARCHIE PATIENTLY WAITED IN THE OTHER ROOM!
ARCHIE, THE FIRST BATCH OF BROWNIES IS DONE! IT'S TIME FOR YOU TO GO TO WORK!
I'M READY TO DO MY PART, PARTNER!
GOOD! ... STEP THIS WAY!
OKAY, PRODUCT QUALITY CONTROL MANAGER, BEGIN YOUR TESTING!
IT WILL BE MY PLEASURE!
WELL, WHAT'S THE VERDICT?
ARE THEY MOIST ENOUGH?
SWEET ENOUGH?
CHEWY ENOUGH?
CHOMP!
CHOMP!
CHOMP!
CHEW! CHEW!
AFTER CAREFUL TASTE-TESTING, IT IS THIS MANAGER'S OPINION THAT THE PRODUCT IS READY TO BE MARKETED -- AS IS!
SMAK!
GREAT! I'LL PUT THE NEXT BATCH IN!
5

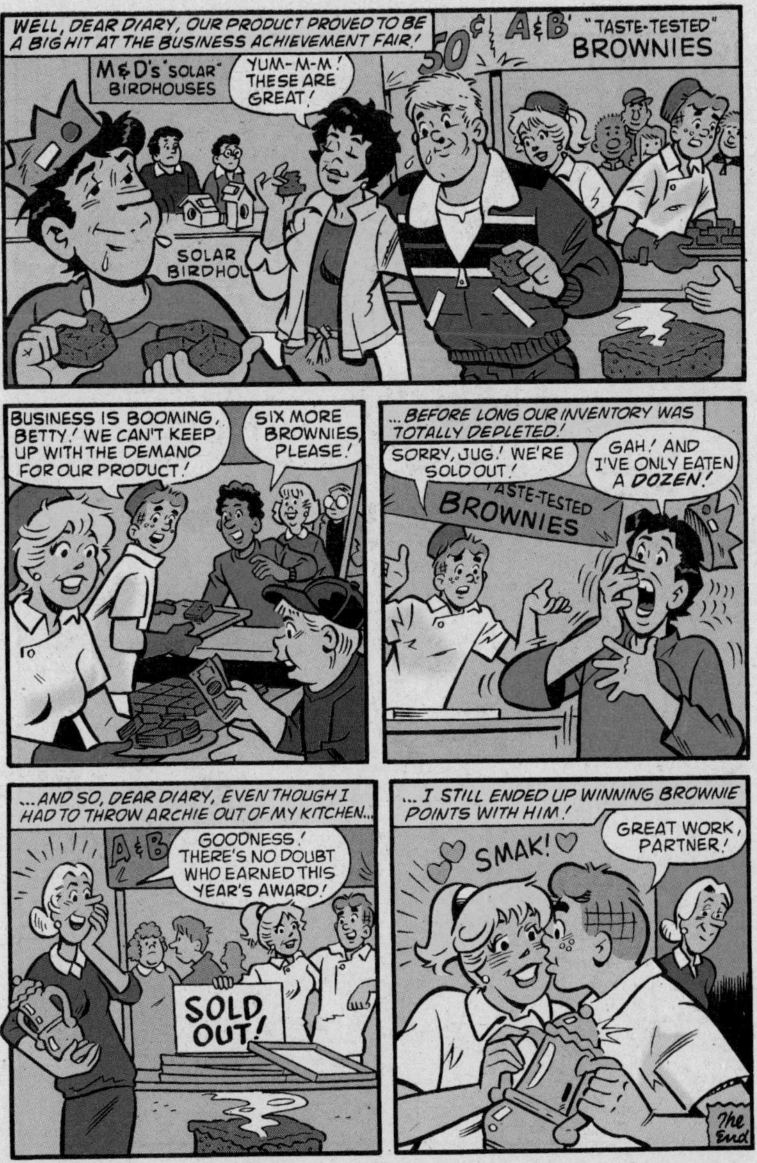
WELL, DEAR DIARY, OUR PRODUCT PROVED TO BE A BIG HIT AT THE BUSINESS ACHIEVEMENT FAIR!
50¢
A&B' "TASTE-TESTED" BROWNIES
M&D's "SOLAR" BIRDHOUSES
YUM-M-M! THESE ARE GREAT!
SOLAR BIRDHOU
BUSINESS IS BOOMING, BETTY! WE CAN'T KEEP UP WITH THE DEMAND FOR OUR PRODUCT!
SIX MORE BROWNIES, PLEASE!
...BEFORE LONG OUR INVENTORY WAS TOTALLY DEPLETED!
SORRY, JUG! WE'RE SOLD OUT!
GAH! AND I'VE ONLY EATEN A DOZEN!
TASTE-TESTED BROWNIES
...AND SO, DEAR DIARY, EVEN THOUGH I HAD TO THROW ARCHIE OUT OF MY KITCHEN...
A&B
GOODNESS! THERE'S NO DOUBT WHO EARNED THIS YEAR'S AWARD!
SOLD OUT!
...I STILL ENDED UP WINNING BROWNIE POINTS WITH HIM!
SMAK!
GREAT WORK, PARTNER!
The End

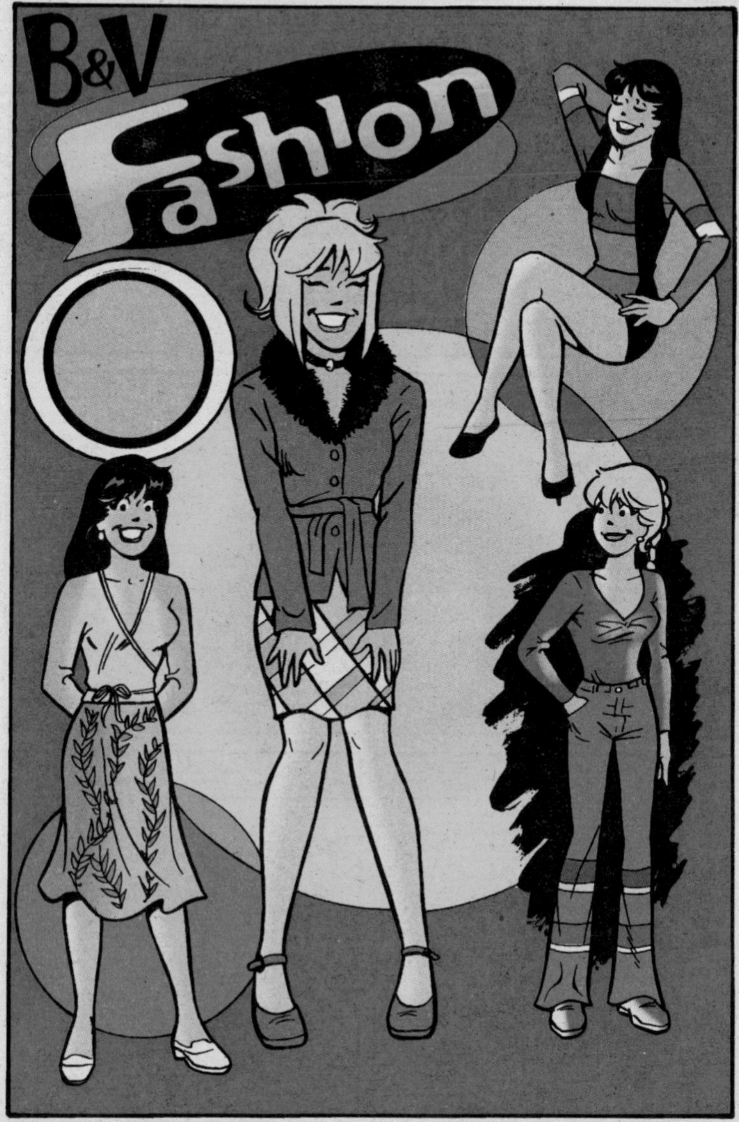
B&V
Fashion

Betty's FASHION WORD FIND!

HI, KIDS! I JUST STARTED A NEW FASHION CLASS IN SCHOOL! THE FIRST DAY, THE TEACHER GAVE US A LOT OF NOTES ON THE BASICS OF THE FASHION BUSINESS! BOY, WAS IT CONFUSING...ESPECIALLY FOR VERONICA! SEE IF YOU CAN FIND THE **20 FASHION WORDS** IN THE WORD FIND BELOW!

```
B A I S T E B I L M L Y
D I E E S U O L B P A I S
K C B E R H S A W D A T O T
S O R E T S E Y L O P T E N I
L N S K I R T J O A S T R C H
E O E H N A T H N W A E I R R
C L W F A H I M N E Y R A D E
O C K S K O N O F T H N L N N
A B L N L O D L T A S T E G
R A T I S I E S O K R B R I
L B E T R T L E S C A P T S
K L E I E S O E T S A B L E
N E E D L E X D I S T R E D
S K R C O L O R N S E T H S
Y L A K H O G A Y G A E P E E S T R O H D
C A M R I C A E L R S G Y G S E L U I G A
Y C S T I T C H L E T L I G S A H T T S E
O L T O R G O R G U Y M B Y T M S X B L R
M N E M E H D E S I L S H A C N E E D E H
A M O N F R E X T Y E A W K Y X S T S I T
```

FASHION WORD LIST (NO PEEKING)

1. SKIRT 2. SEW 3. COLOR 4. DRESS 5. THREAD 6. HEM 7. MATERIAL 8. NEEDLE 9. TEXTURE 10. STITCH 11. STYLE 12. MODEL 13. TREND 14. BLOUSE 15. BASTE 16. PATTERN 17. DESIGNER 18. INSEAM 19. KNIT 20. POLYESTER

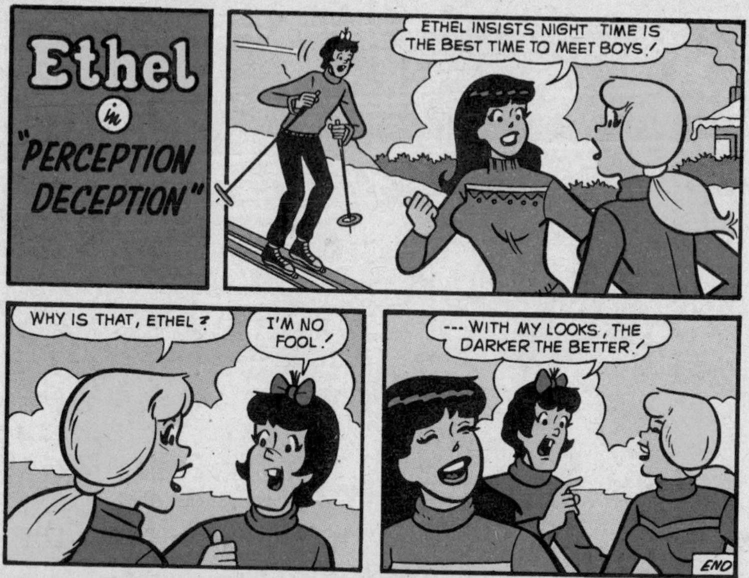
Ethel
in
"PERCEPTION DECEPTION"
ETHEL INSISTS NIGHT TIME IS THE BEST TIME TO MEET BOYS!
WHY IS THAT, ETHEL?
I'M NO FOOL!
--- WITH MY LOOKS, THE DARKER THE BETTER!
END

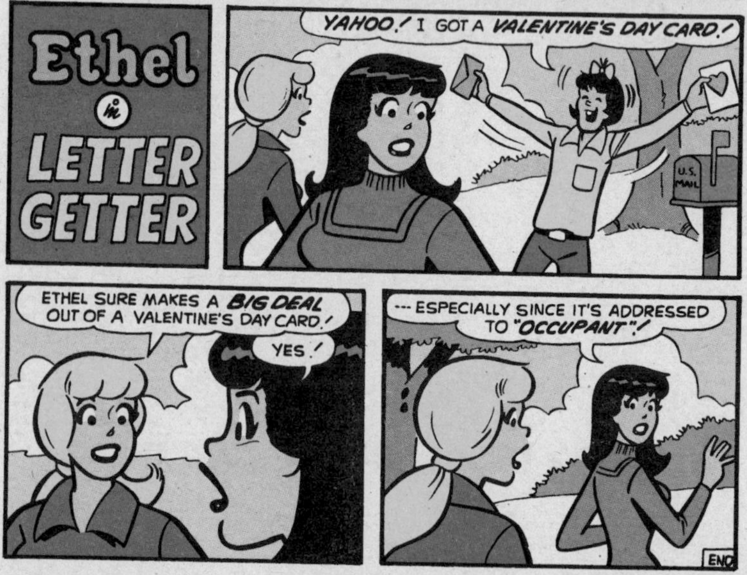
Ethel
in
LETTER GETTER
YAHOO! I GOT A VALENTINE'S DAY CARD!
U.S. MAIL
ETHEL SURE MAKES A BIG DEAL OUT OF A VALENTINE'S DAY CARD!
YES!
--- ESPECIALLY SINCE IT'S ADDRESSED TO "OCCUPANT"!
END

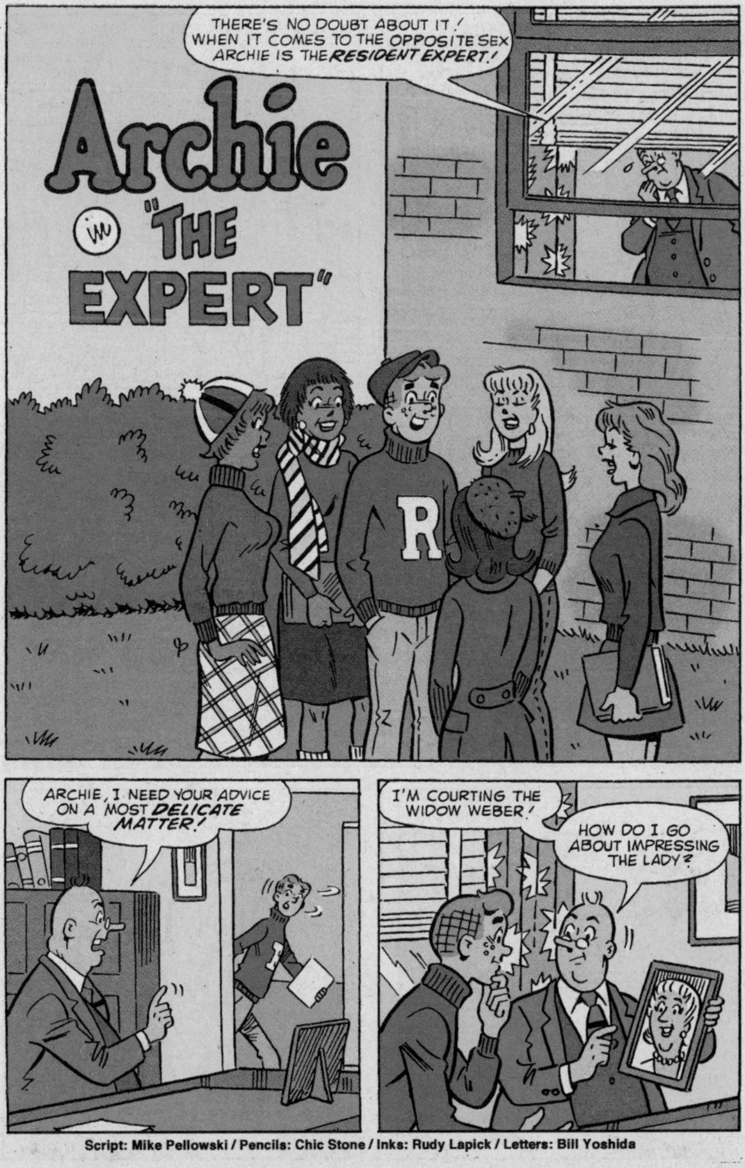
THERE'S NO DOUBT ABOUT IT! WHEN IT COMES TO THE OPPOSITE SEX ARCHIE IS THE RESIDENT EXPERT!
Archie
in "THE EXPERT"
ARCHIE, I NEED YOUR ADVICE ON A MOST DELICATE MATTER!
I'M COURTING THE WIDOW WEBER!
HOW DO I GO ABOUT IMPRESSING THE LADY?

Script: Mike Pellowski / Pencils: Chic Stone / Inks: Rudy Lapick / Letters: Bill Yoshida

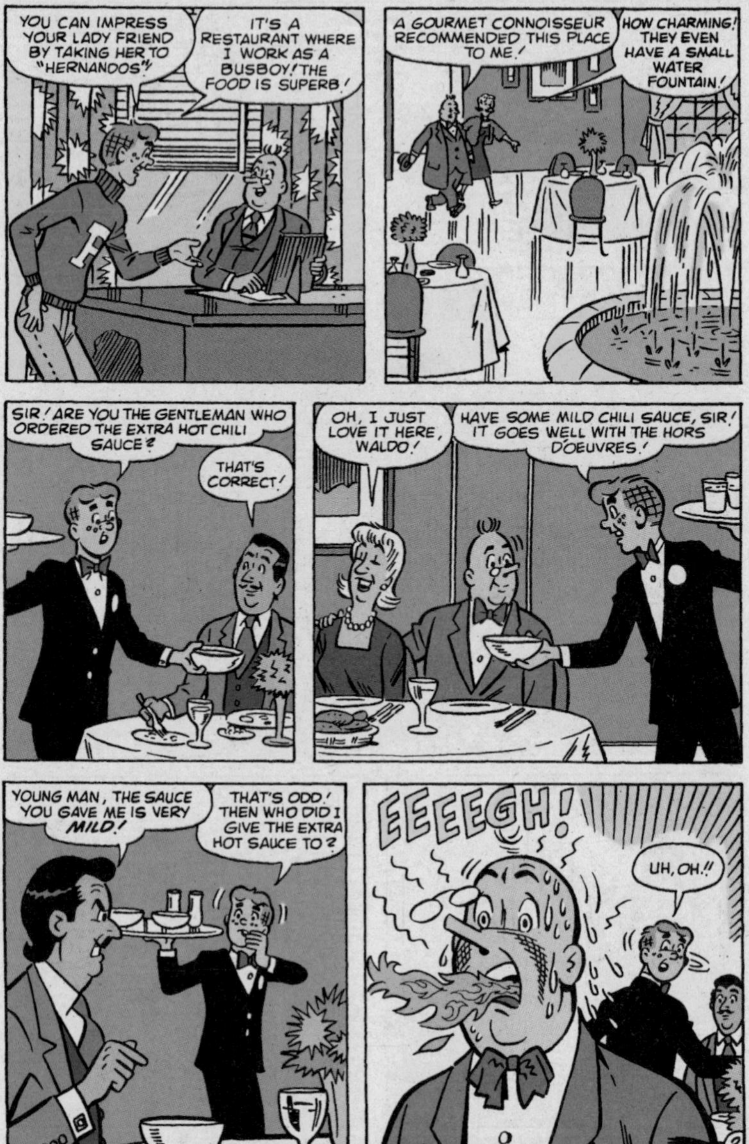

YOU CAN IMPRESS YOUR LADY FRIEND BY TAKING HER TO "HERNANDOS"!
IT'S A RESTAURANT WHERE I WORK AS A BUSBOY! THE FOOD IS SUPERB!
A GOURMET CONNOISSEUR RECOMMENDED THIS PLACE TO ME!
HOW CHARMING! THEY EVEN HAVE A SMALL WATER FOUNTAIN!
SIR! ARE YOU THE GENTLEMAN WHO ORDERED THE EXTRA HOT CHILI SAUCE?
THAT'S CORRECT!
OH, I JUST LOVE IT HERE, WALDO!
HAVE SOME MILD CHILI SAUCE, SIR! IT GOES WELL WITH THE HORS D'OEUVRES!
YOUNG MAN, THE SAUCE YOU GAVE ME IS VERY MILD!
THAT'S ODD! THEN WHO DID I GIVE THE EXTRA HOT SAUCE TO?
EEEEGH!
UH, OH!!
2

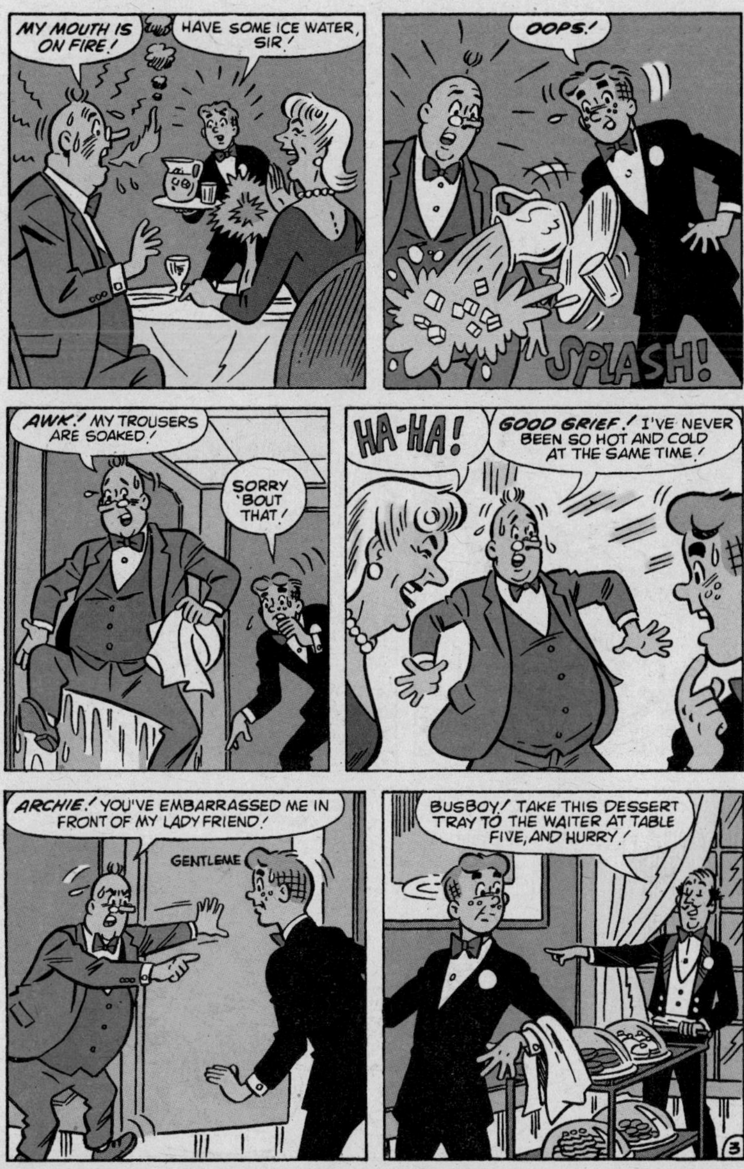
MY MOUTH IS ON FIRE!
HAVE SOME ICE WATER, SIR!
OOPS!
SPLASH!
AWK! MY TROUSERS ARE SOAKED!
SORRY 'BOUT THAT!
HA-HA!
GOOD GRIEF! I'VE NEVER BEEN SO HOT AND COLD AT THE SAME TIME!
ARCHIE! YOU'VE EMBARRASSED ME IN FRONT OF MY LADY FRIEND!
GENTLEME
BUSBOY! TAKE THIS DESSERT TRAY TO THE WAITER AT TABLE FIVE, AND HURRY!
3

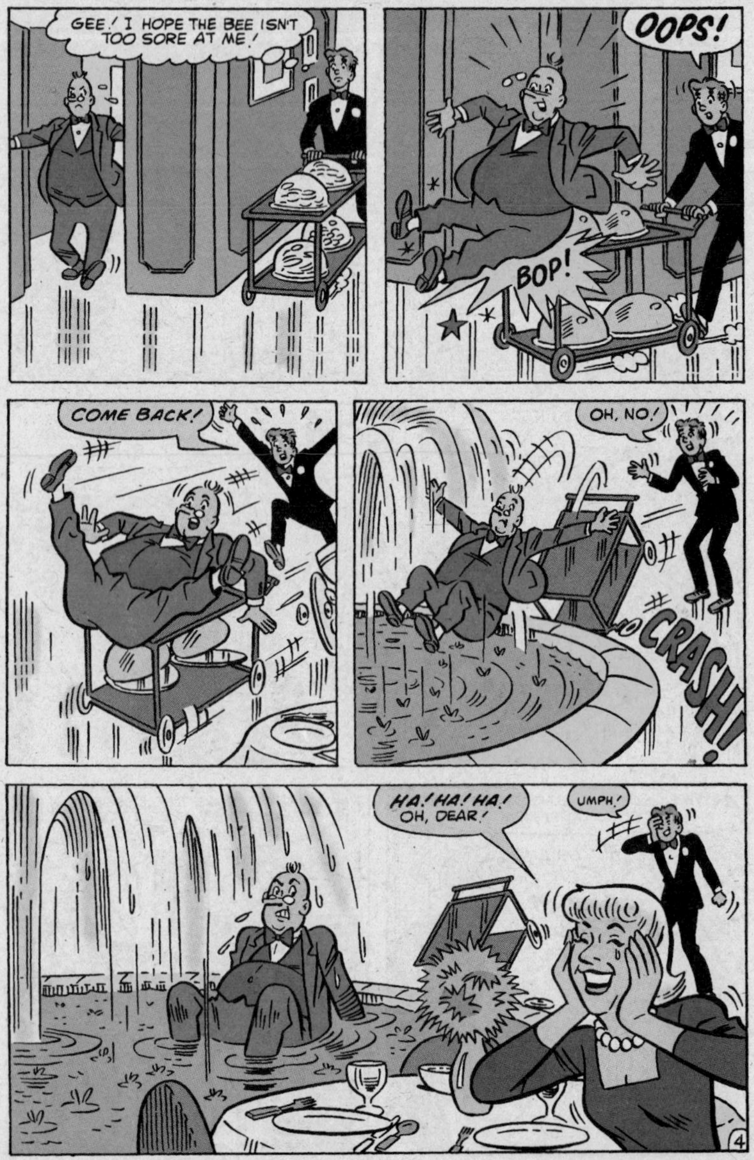
GEE! I HOPE THE BEE ISN'T TOO SORE AT ME!
OOPS!
BOP!
COME BACK!
OH, NO!
CRASH!
HA! HA! HA! OH, DEAR!
UMPH!
4

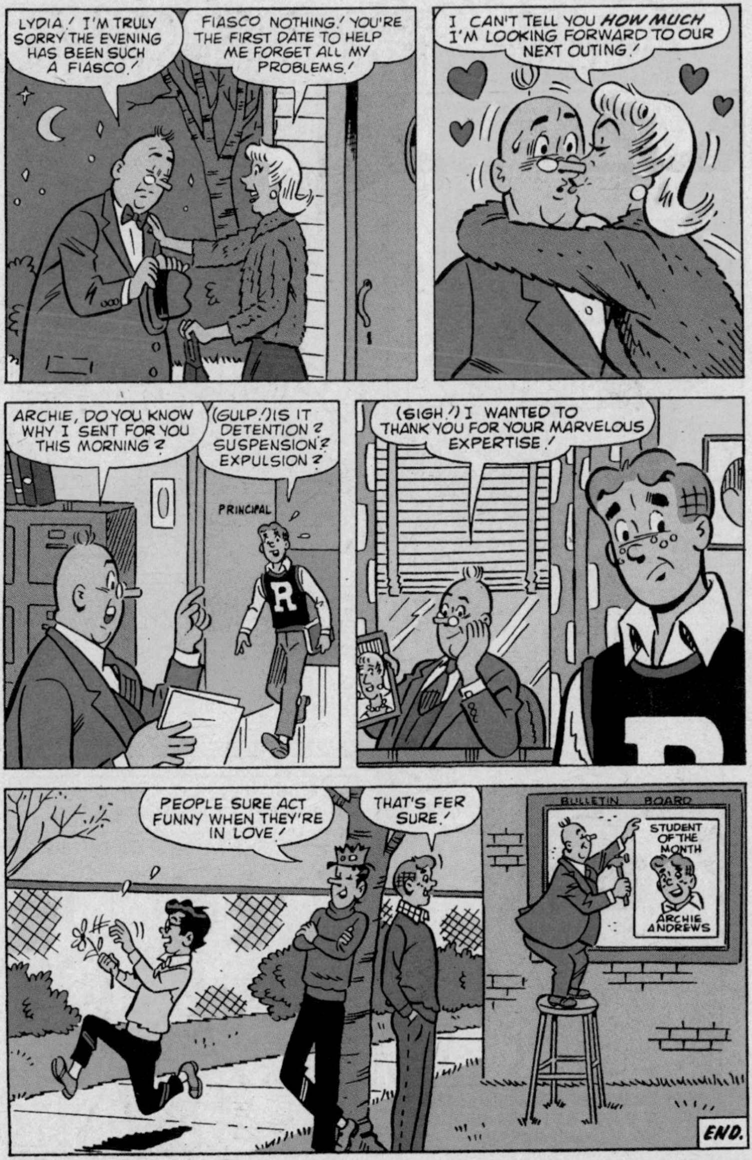
LYDIA! I'M TRULY SORRY THE EVENING HAS BEEN SUCH A FIASCO!
FIASCO NOTHING! YOU'RE THE FIRST DATE TO HELP ME FORGET ALL MY PROBLEMS!
I CAN'T TELL YOU HOW MUCH I'M LOOKING FORWARD TO OUR NEXT OUTING!
ARCHIE, DO YOU KNOW WHY I SENT FOR YOU THIS MORNING?
(GULP!) IS IT DETENTION? SUSPENSION? EXPULSION?
PRINCIPAL
(SIGH!) I WANTED TO THANK YOU FOR YOUR MARVELOUS EXPERTISE!
PEOPLE SURE ACT FUNNY WHEN THEY'RE IN LOVE!
THAT'S FER SURE!
BULLETIN BOARD
STUDENT OF THE MONTH
ARCHIE ANDREWS
END.

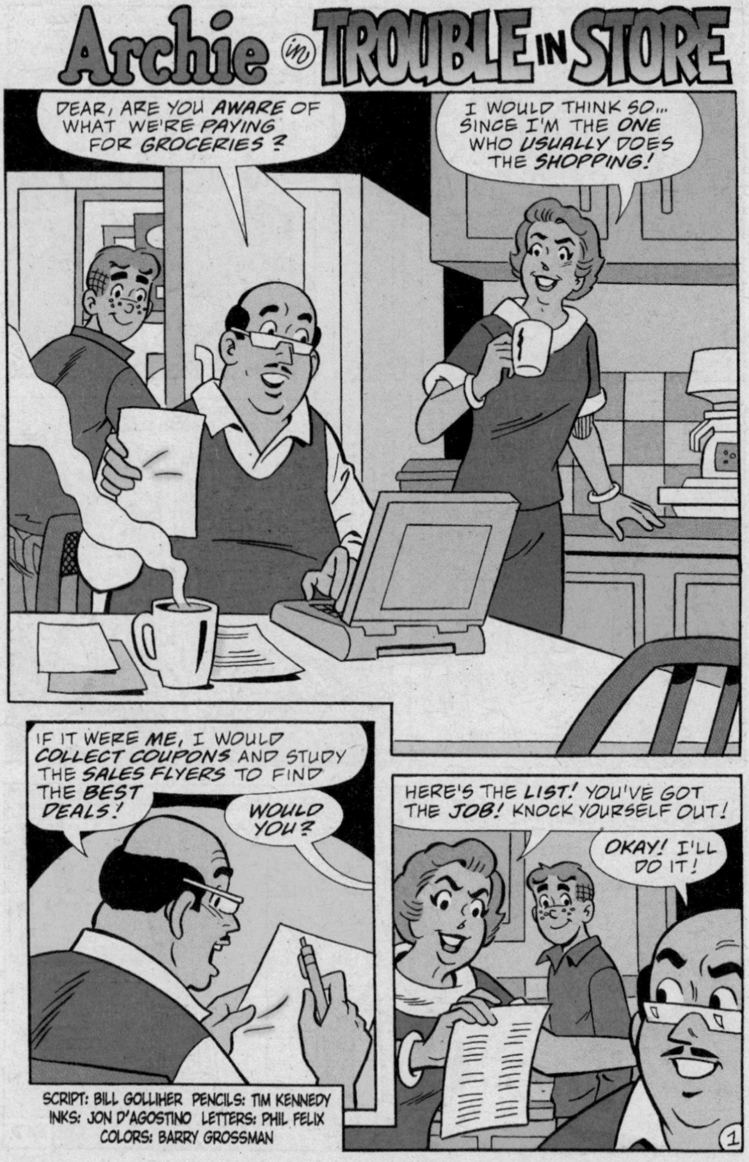
Archie in TROUBLE IN STORE
DEAR, ARE YOU AWARE OF WHAT WE'RE PAYING FOR GROCERIES?
I WOULD THINK SO... SINCE I'M THE ONE WHO USUALLY DOES THE SHOPPING!
IF IT WERE ME, I WOULD COLLECT COUPONS AND STUDY THE SALES FLYERS TO FIND THE BEST DEALS!
WOULD YOU?
HERE'S THE LIST! YOU'VE GOT THE JOB! KNOCK YOURSELF OUT!
OKAY! I'LL DO IT!
SCRIPT: BILL GOLLIHER PENCILS: TIM KENNEDY
INKS: JON D'AGOSTINO LETTERS: PHIL FELIX
COLORS: BARRY GROSSMAN
1

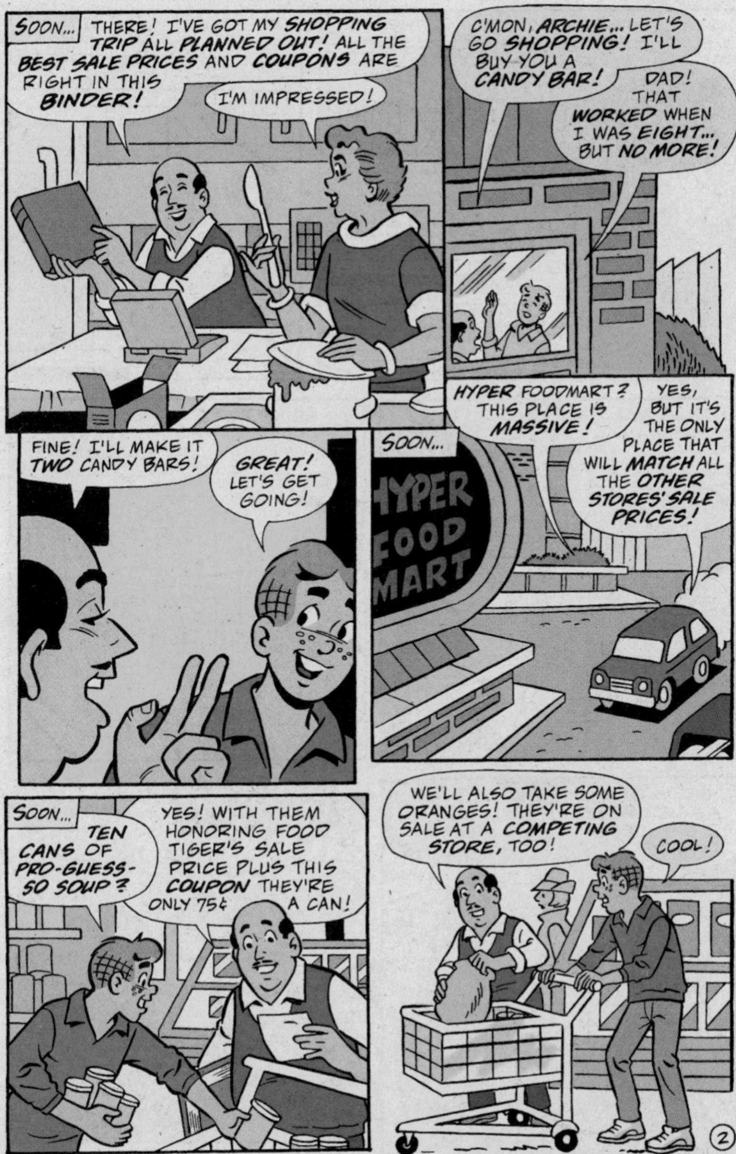
SOON...
THERE! I'VE GOT MY SHOPPING TRIP ALL PLANNED OUT! ALL THE BEST SALE PRICES AND COUPONS ARE RIGHT IN THIS BINDER!
I'M IMPRESSED!
C'MON, ARCHIE... LET'S GO SHOPPING! I'LL BUY YOU A CANDY BAR!
DAD! THAT WORKED WHEN I WAS EIGHT... BUT NO MORE!
FINE! I'LL MAKE IT TWO CANDY BARS!
GREAT! LET'S GET GOING!
SOON...
HYPER FOOD MART
HYPER FOODMART? THIS PLACE IS MASSIVE!
YES, BUT IT'S THE ONLY PLACE THAT WILL MATCH ALL THE OTHER STORES' SALE PRICES!
SOON...
TEN CANS OF PRO-GUESS-SO SOUP?
YES! WITH THEM HONORING FOOD TIGER'S SALE PRICE PLUS THIS COUPON THEY'RE ONLY 75¢ A CAN!
WE'LL ALSO TAKE SOME ORANGES! THEY'RE ON SALE AT A COMPETING STORE, TOO!
COOL!

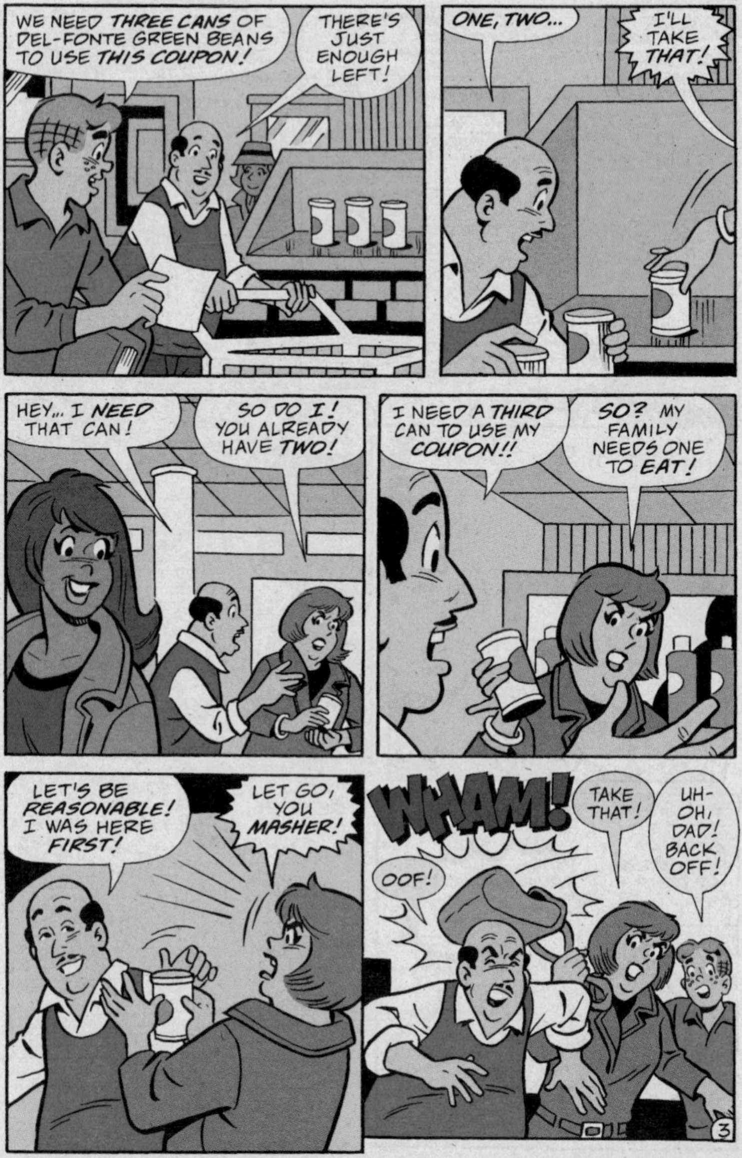
WE NEED THREE CANS OF DEL-FONTE GREEN BEANS TO USE THIS COUPON!
THERE'S JUST ENOUGH LEFT!
ONE, TWO...
I'LL TAKE THAT!
HEY... I NEED THAT CAN!
SO DO I! YOU ALREADY HAVE TWO!
I NEED A THIRD CAN TO USE MY COUPON!!
SO? MY FAMILY NEEDS ONE TO EAT!
LET'S BE REASONABLE! I WAS HERE FIRST!
LET GO, YOU MASHER!
WHAM!
TAKE THAT!
UH-OH, DAD! BACK OFF!
OOF!
3

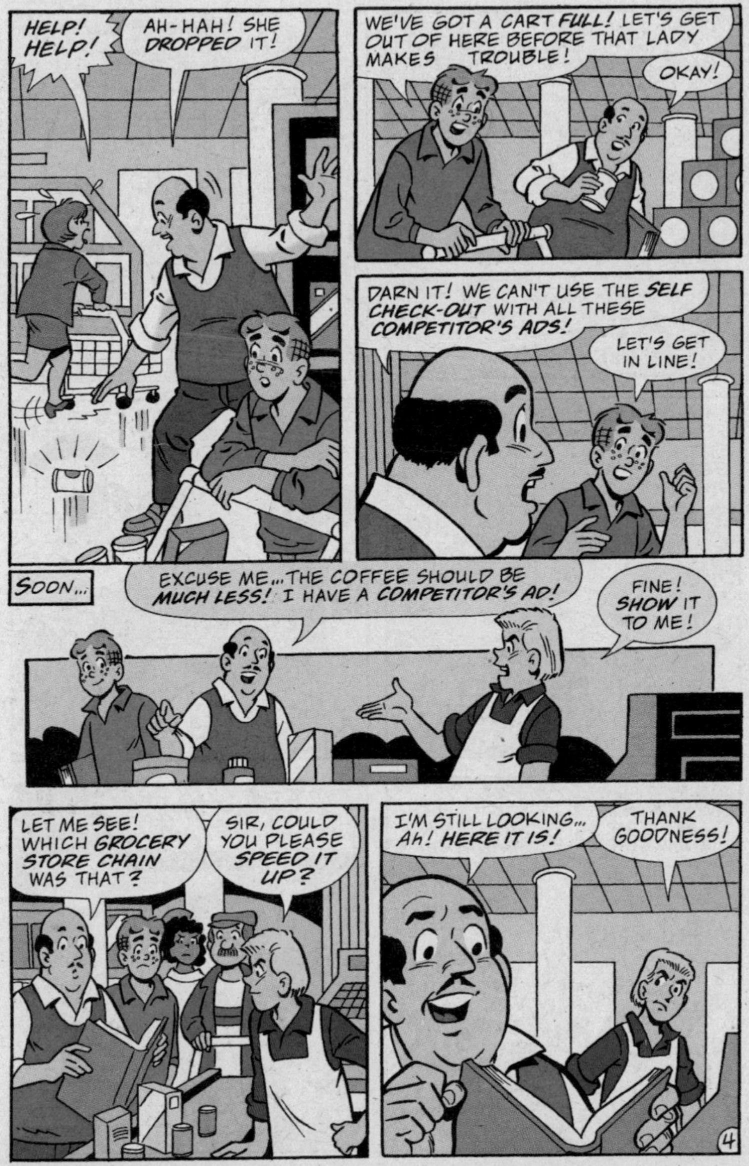
HELP! HELP!
AH-HAH! SHE DROPPED IT!
WE'VE GOT A CART FULL! LET'S GET OUT OF HERE BEFORE THAT LADY MAKES TROUBLE!
OKAY!
DARN IT! WE CAN'T USE THE SELF CHECK-OUT WITH ALL THESE COMPETITOR'S ADS!
LET'S GET IN LINE!
SOON...
EXCUSE ME... THE COFFEE SHOULD BE MUCH LESS! I HAVE A COMPETITOR'S AD!
FINE! SHOW IT TO ME!
LET ME SEE! WHICH GROCERY STORE CHAIN WAS THAT?
SIR, COULD YOU PLEASE SPEED IT UP?
I'M STILL LOOKING... Ah! HERE IT IS!
THANK GOODNESS!
4

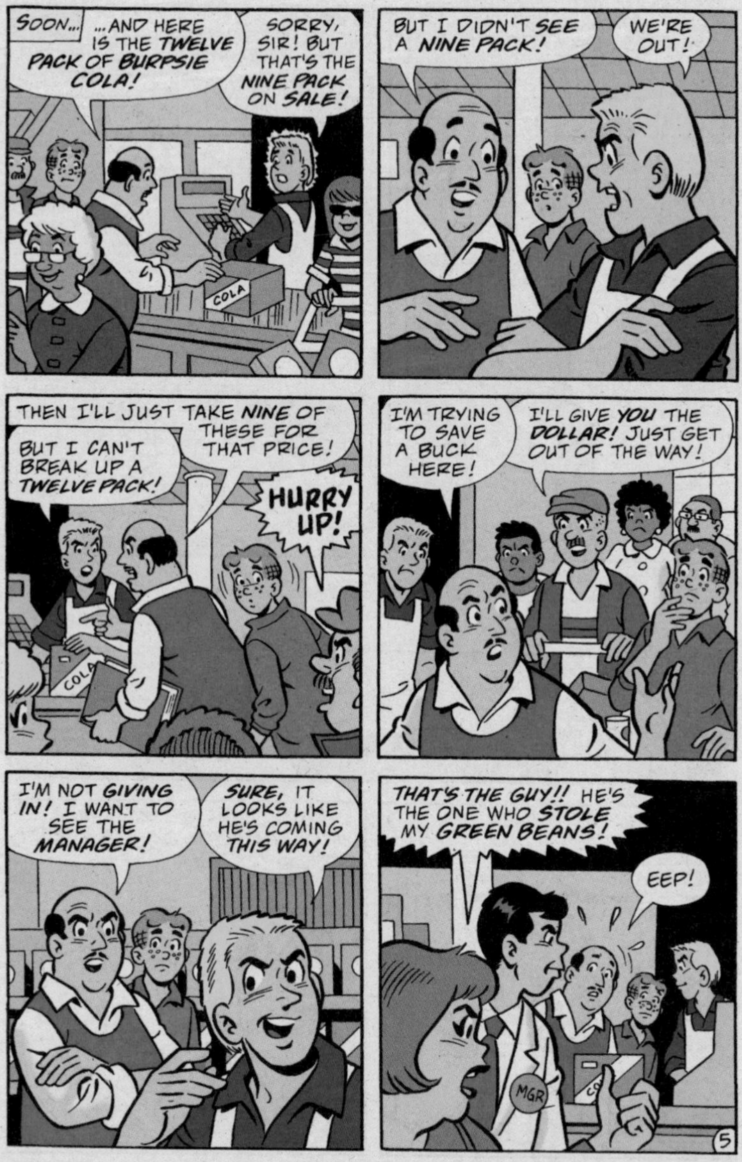
SOON...
...AND HERE IS THE TWELVE PACK OF BURPSIE COLA!
SORRY, SIR! BUT THAT'S THE NINE PACK ON SALE!
COLA
BUT I DIDN'T SEE A NINE PACK!
WE'RE OUT!
THEN I'LL JUST TAKE NINE OF THESE FOR THAT PRICE!
BUT I CAN'T BREAK UP A TWELVE PACK!
HURRY UP!
COLA
I'M TRYING TO SAVE A BUCK HERE!
I'LL GIVE YOU THE DOLLAR! JUST GET OUT OF THE WAY!
I'M NOT GIVING IN! I WANT TO SEE THE MANAGER!
SURE, IT LOOKS LIKE HE'S COMING THIS WAY!
THAT'S THE GUY!! HE'S THE ONE WHO STOLE MY GREEN BEANS!
EEP!
MGR
5

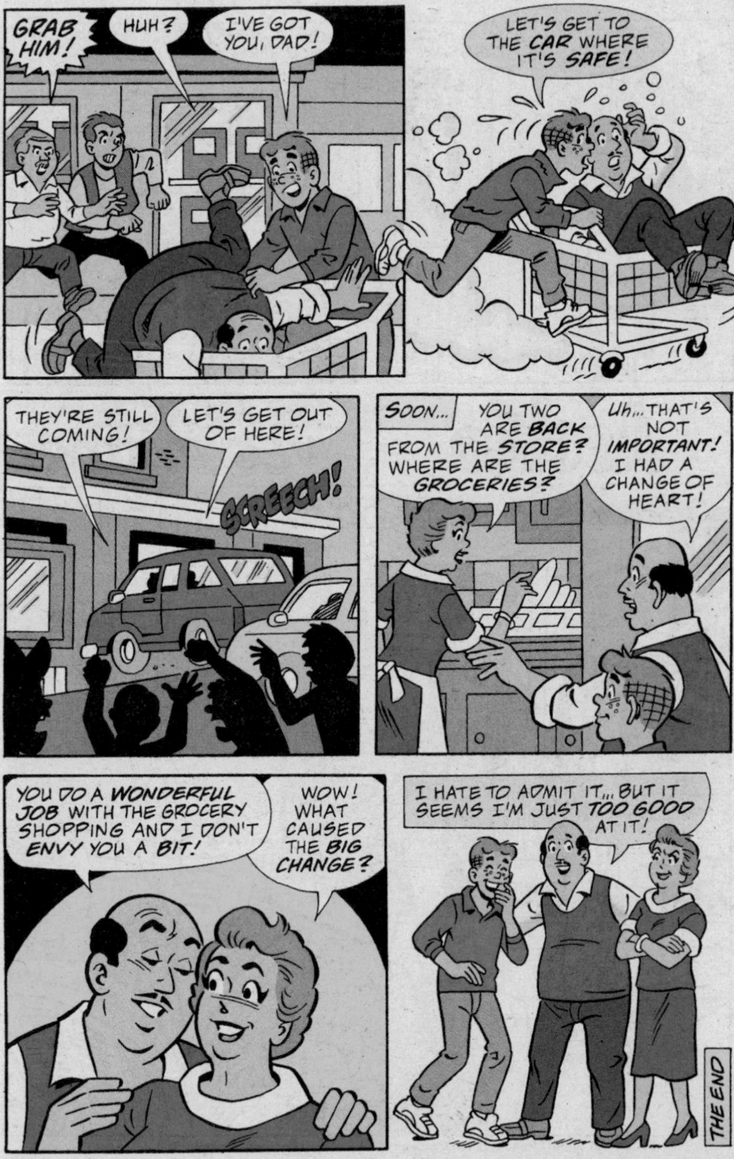
GRAB HIM!
HUH?
I'VE GOT YOU, DAD!
LET'S GET TO THE CAR WHERE IT'S SAFE!
THEY'RE STILL COMING!
LET'S GET OUT OF HERE!
SCREECH!
SOON...
YOU TWO ARE BACK FROM THE STORE? WHERE ARE THE GROCERIES?
Uh... THAT'S NOT IMPORTANT! I HAD A CHANGE OF HEART!
YOU DO A WONDERFUL JOB WITH THE GROCERY SHOPPING AND I DON'T ENVY YOU A BIT!
WOW! WHAT CAUSED THE BIG CHANGE?
I HATE TO ADMIT IT... BUT IT SEEMS I'M JUST TOO GOOD AT IT!
THE END

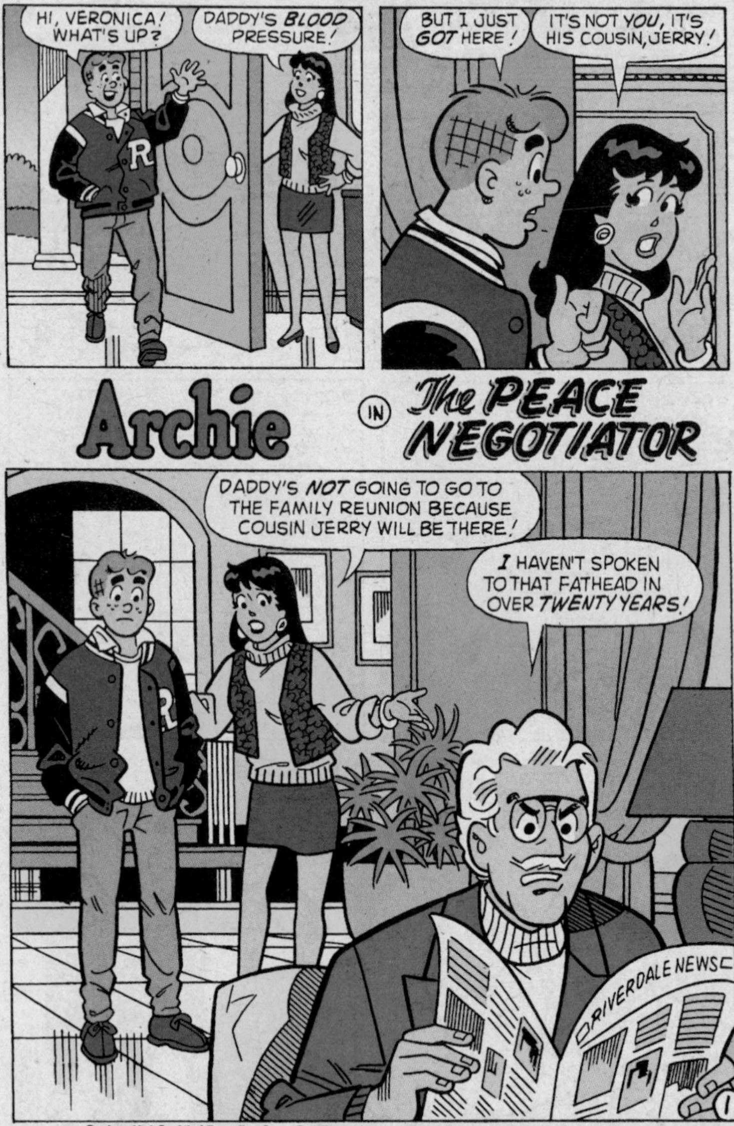
HI, VERONICA! WHAT'S UP?
DADDY'S BLOOD PRESSURE!
BUT I JUST GOT HERE!
IT'S NOT YOU, IT'S HIS COUSIN, JERRY!
Archie IN The PEACE NEGOTIATOR
DADDY'S NOT GOING TO GO TO THE FAMILY REUNION BECAUSE COUSIN JERRY WILL BE THERE!
I HAVEN'T SPOKEN TO THAT FATHEAD IN OVER TWENTY YEARS!
RIVERDALE NEWS
1

Script: Hal Smith / Pencils: Stan Goldberg / Inks: Henry Scarpelli / Letters: Bill Yoshida

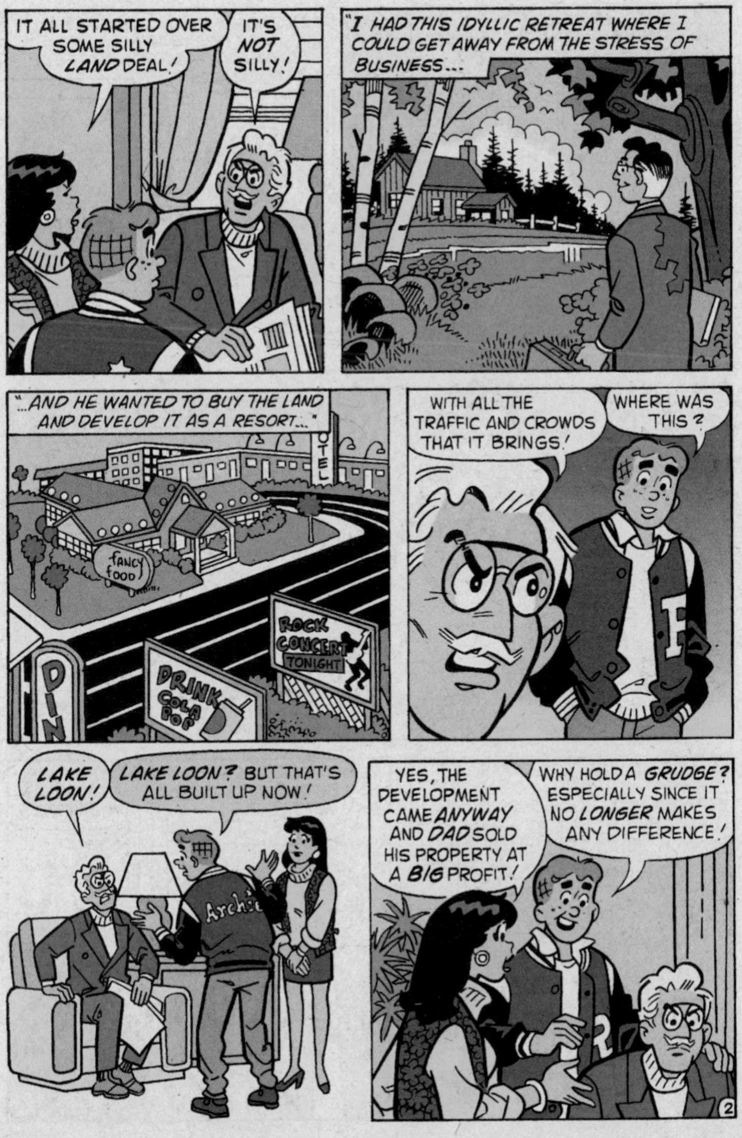
IT ALL STARTED OVER SOME SILLY LAND DEAL!
IT'S NOT SILLY!
"I HAD THIS IDYLLIC RETREAT WHERE I COULD GET AWAY FROM THE STRESS OF BUSINESS...
"...AND HE WANTED TO BUY THE LAND AND DEVELOP IT AS A RESORT..."
OTEL
FANCY FOOD
ROCK CONCERT TONIGHT
DRINK COLA POP
DIN
WITH ALL THE TRAFFIC AND CROWDS THAT IT BRINGS!
WHERE WAS THIS?
LAKE LOON!
LAKE LOON? BUT THAT'S ALL BUILT UP NOW!
Archie
YES, THE DEVELOPMENT CAME ANYWAY AND DAD SOLD HIS PROPERTY AT A BIG PROFIT!
WHY HOLD A GRUDGE? ESPECIALLY SINCE IT NO LONGER MAKES ANY DIFFERENCE!
2

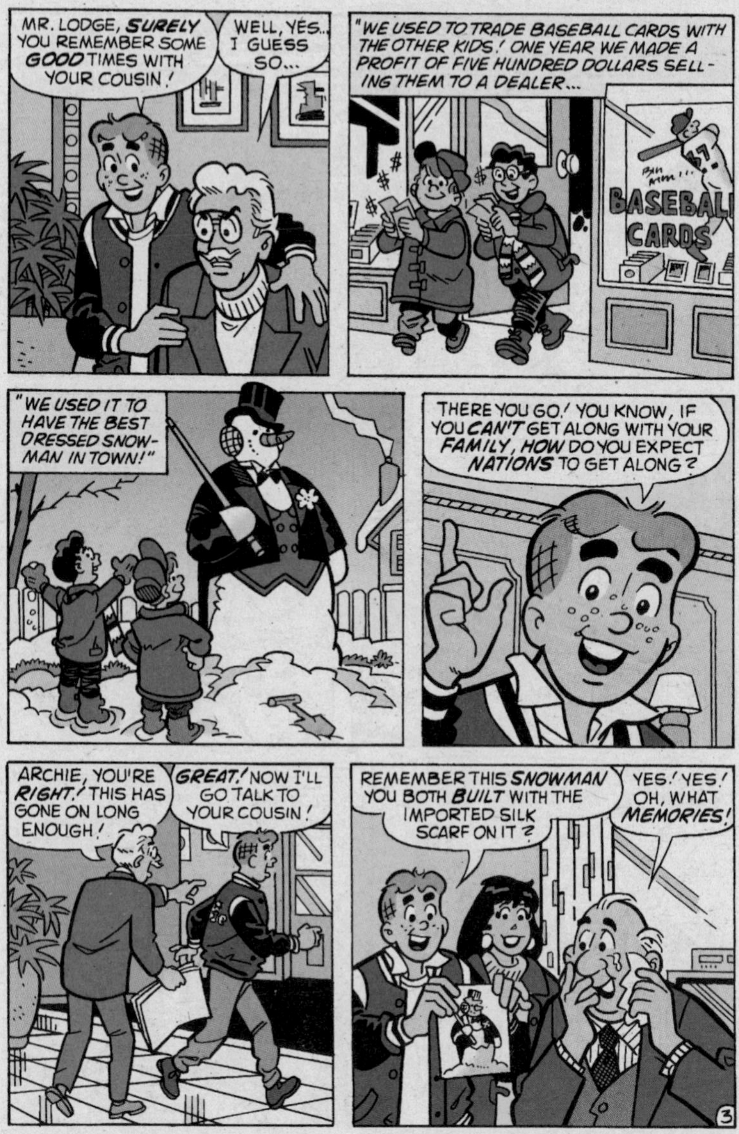

MR. LODGE, SURELY YOU REMEMBER SOME GOOD TIMES WITH YOUR COUSIN!
WELL, YES... I GUESS SO...
"WE USED TO TRADE BASEBALL CARDS WITH THE OTHER KIDS! ONE YEAR WE MADE A PROFIT OF FIVE HUNDRED DOLLARS SELL-ING THEM TO A DEALER...
BASEBALL CARDS
"WE USED IT TO HAVE THE BEST DRESSED SNOW-MAN IN TOWN!"
THERE YOU GO! YOU KNOW, IF YOU CAN'T GET ALONG WITH YOUR FAMILY, HOW DO YOU EXPECT NATIONS TO GET ALONG?
ARCHIE, YOU'RE RIGHT! THIS HAS GONE ON LONG ENOUGH!
GREAT! NOW I'LL GO TALK TO YOUR COUSIN!
REMEMBER THIS SNOWMAN YOU BOTH BUILT WITH THE IMPORTED SILK SCARF ON IT?
YES! YES! OH, WHAT MEMORIES!
3

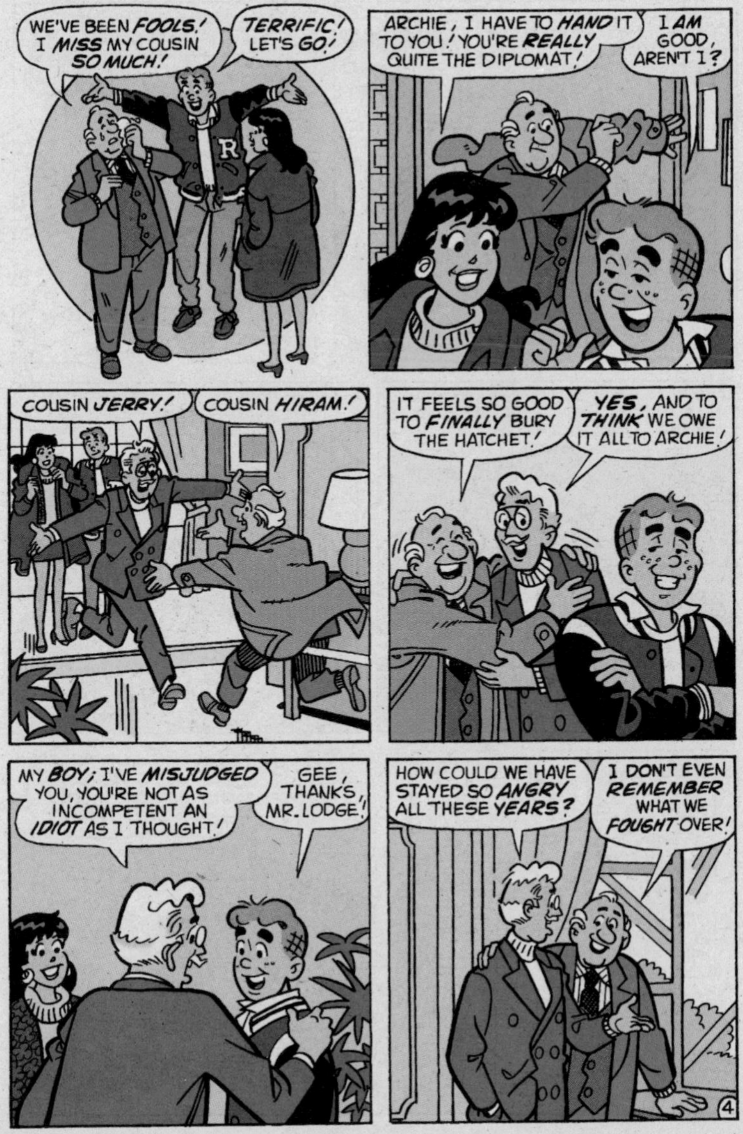
WE'VE BEEN FOOLS! I MISS MY COUSIN SO MUCH!
TERRIFIC! LET'S GO!
ARCHIE, I HAVE TO HAND IT TO YOU! YOU'RE REALLY QUITE THE DIPLOMAT!
I AM GOOD, AREN'T I?
COUSIN JERRY!
COUSIN HIRAM!
IT FEELS SO GOOD TO FINALLY BURY THE HATCHET!
YES, AND TO THINK WE OWE IT ALL TO ARCHIE!
MY BOY; I'VE MISJUDGED YOU, YOU'RE NOT AS INCOMPETENT AN IDIOT AS I THOUGHT!
GEE, THANKS, MR. LODGE!
HOW COULD WE HAVE STAYED SO ANGRY ALL THESE YEARS?
I DON'T EVEN REMEMBER WHAT WE FOUGHT OVER!
4

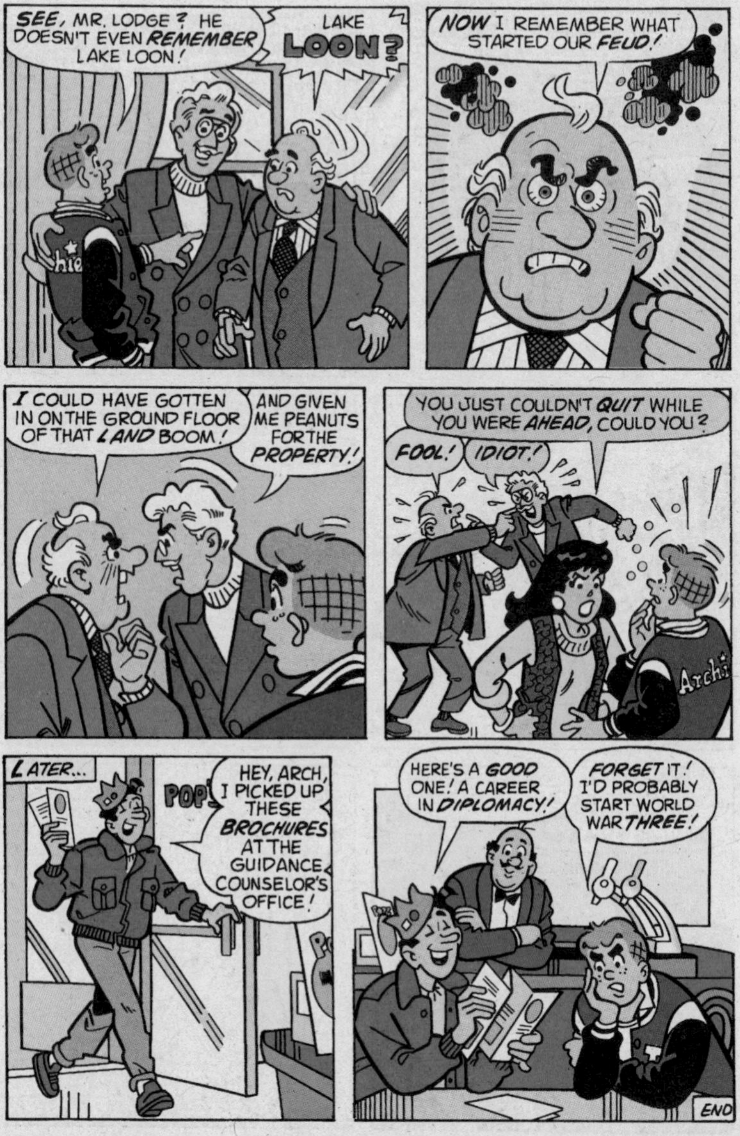
SEE, MR. LODGE? HE DOESN'T EVEN REMEMBER LAKE LOON!
LAKE LOON?
NOW I REMEMBER WHAT STARTED OUR FEUD!
I COULD HAVE GOTTEN IN ON THE GROUND FLOOR OF THAT LAND BOOM!
AND GIVEN ME PEANUTS FOR THE PROPERTY!
YOU JUST COULDN'T QUIT WHILE YOU WERE AHEAD, COULD YOU?
FOOL!
IDIOT!
LATER...
POP'S
HEY, ARCH, I PICKED UP THESE BROCHURES AT THE GUIDANCE COUNSELOR'S OFFICE!
HERE'S A GOOD ONE! A CAREER IN DIPLOMACY!
FORGET IT! I'D PROBABLY START WORLD WAR THREE!
END

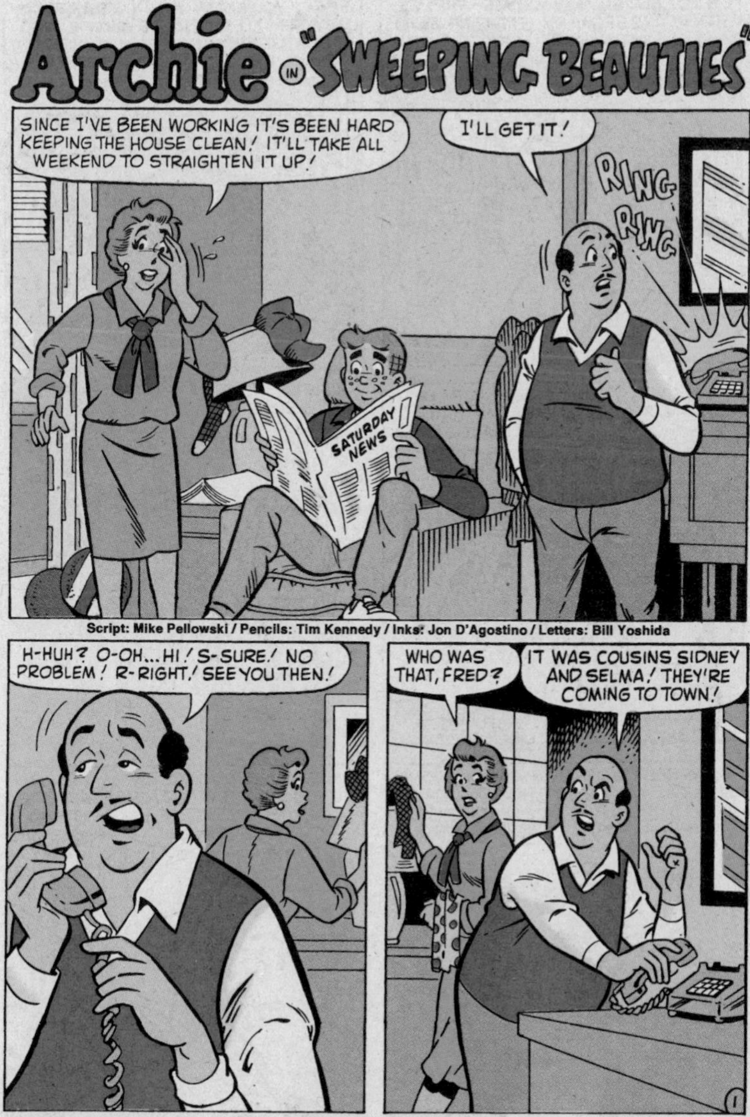
Archie in "SWEEPING BEAUTIES"
SINCE I'VE BEEN WORKING IT'S BEEN HARD KEEPING THE HOUSE CLEAN! IT'LL TAKE ALL WEEKEND TO STRAIGHTEN IT UP!
I'LL GET IT!
RING RING
SATURDAY NEWS
Script: Mike Pellowski / Pencils: Tim Kennedy / Inks: Jon D'Agostino / Letters: Bill Yoshida
H-HUH? O-OH... HI! S-SURE! NO PROBLEM! R-RIGHT! SEE YOU THEN!
WHO WAS THAT, FRED?
IT WAS COUSINS SIDNEY AND SELMA! THEY'RE COMING TO TOWN!
1

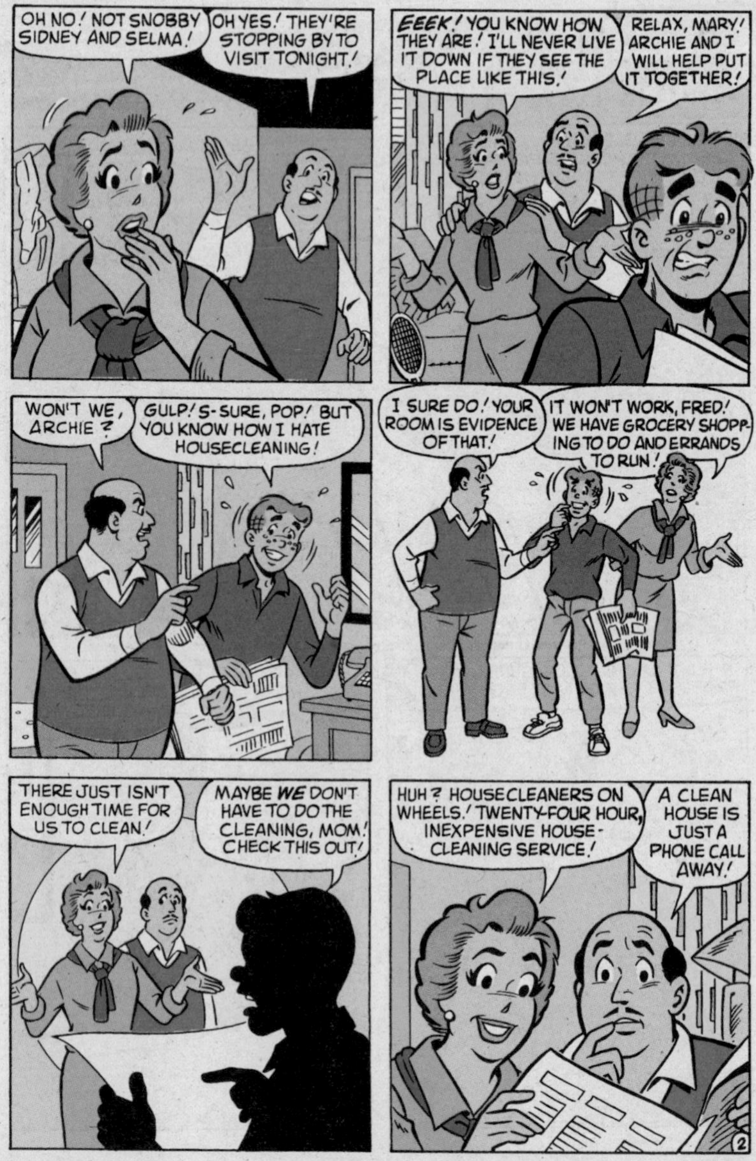

OH NO! NOT SNOBBY SIDNEY AND SELMA!
OH YES! THEY'RE STOPPING BY TO VISIT TONIGHT!
EEEK! YOU KNOW HOW THEY ARE! I'LL NEVER LIVE IT DOWN IF THEY SEE THE PLACE LIKE THIS!
RELAX, MARY! ARCHIE AND I WILL HELP PUT IT TOGETHER!
WON'T WE, ARCHIE?
GULP! S-SURE, POP! BUT YOU KNOW HOW I HATE HOUSECLEANING!
I SURE DO! YOUR ROOM IS EVIDENCE OF THAT!
IT WON'T WORK, FRED! WE HAVE GROCERY SHOPP-ING TO DO AND ERRANDS TO RUN!
THERE JUST ISN'T ENOUGH TIME FOR US TO CLEAN!
MAYBE WE DON'T HAVE TO DO THE CLEANING, MOM! CHECK THIS OUT!
HUH? HOUSECLEANERS ON WHEELS! TWENTY-FOUR HOUR, INEXPENSIVE HOUSE-CLEANING SERVICE!
A CLEAN HOUSE IS JUST A PHONE CALL AWAY!
2

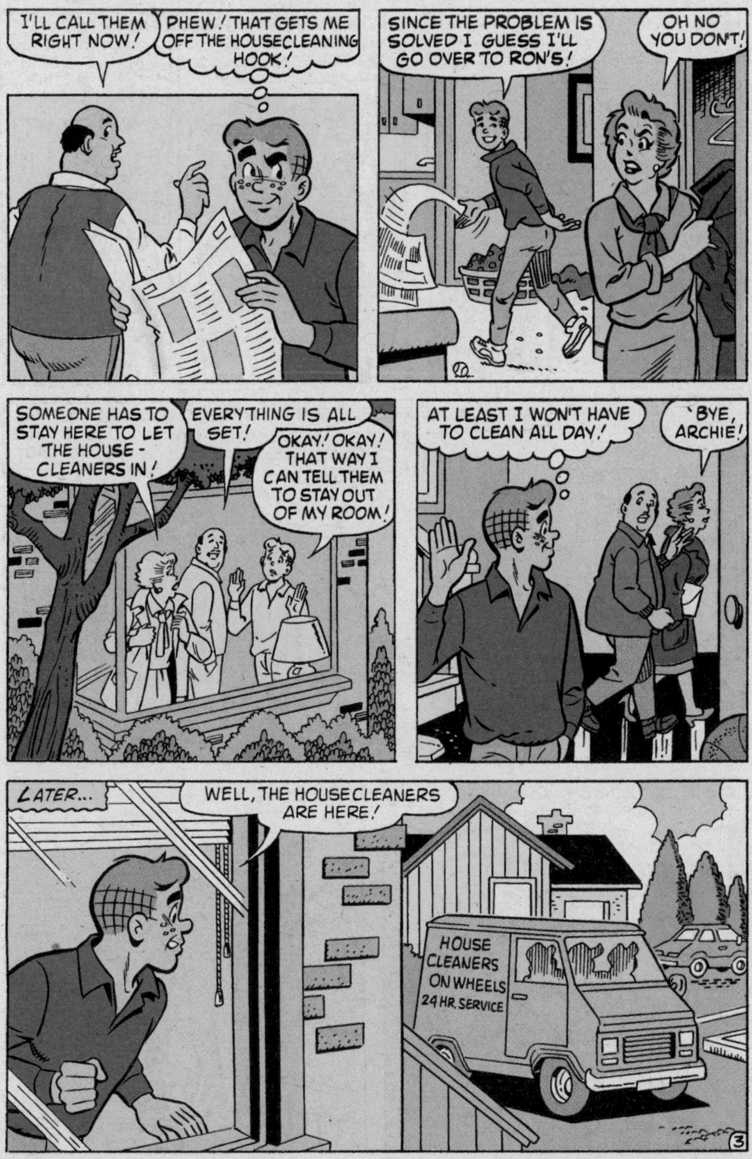
I'LL CALL THEM RIGHT NOW!
PHEW! THAT GETS ME OFF THE HOUSECLEANING HOOK!
SINCE THE PROBLEM IS SOLVED I GUESS I'LL GO OVER TO RON'S!
OH NO YOU DON'T!
SOMEONE HAS TO STAY HERE TO LET THE HOUSE-CLEANERS IN!
EVERYTHING IS ALL SET!
OKAY! OKAY! THAT WAY I CAN TELL THEM TO STAY OUT OF MY ROOM!
AT LEAST I WON'T HAVE TO CLEAN ALL DAY!
'BYE, ARCHIE!
LATER...
WELL, THE HOUSECLEANERS ARE HERE!
HOUSE CLEANERS ON WHEELS 24 HR. SERVICE
3

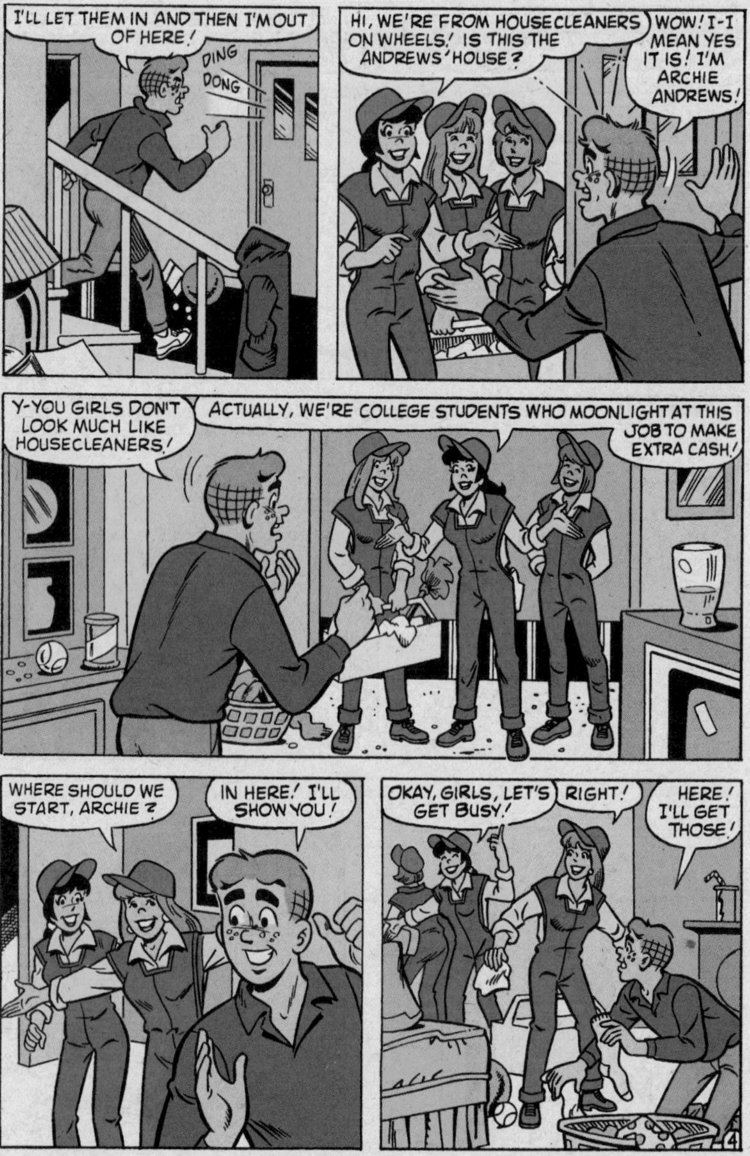

I'LL LET THEM IN AND THEN I'M OUT OF HERE!
DING DONG
HI, WE'RE FROM HOUSECLEANERS ON WHEELS! IS THIS THE ANDREWS' HOUSE?
WOW! I-I MEAN YES IT IS! I'M ARCHIE ANDREWS!
Y-YOU GIRLS DON'T LOOK MUCH LIKE HOUSECLEANERS!
ACTUALLY, WE'RE COLLEGE STUDENTS WHO MOONLIGHT AT THIS JOB TO MAKE EXTRA CASH!
WHERE SHOULD WE START, ARCHIE?
IN HERE! I'LL SHOW YOU!
OKAY, GIRLS, LET'S GET BUSY!
RIGHT!
HERE! I'LL GET THOSE!
4

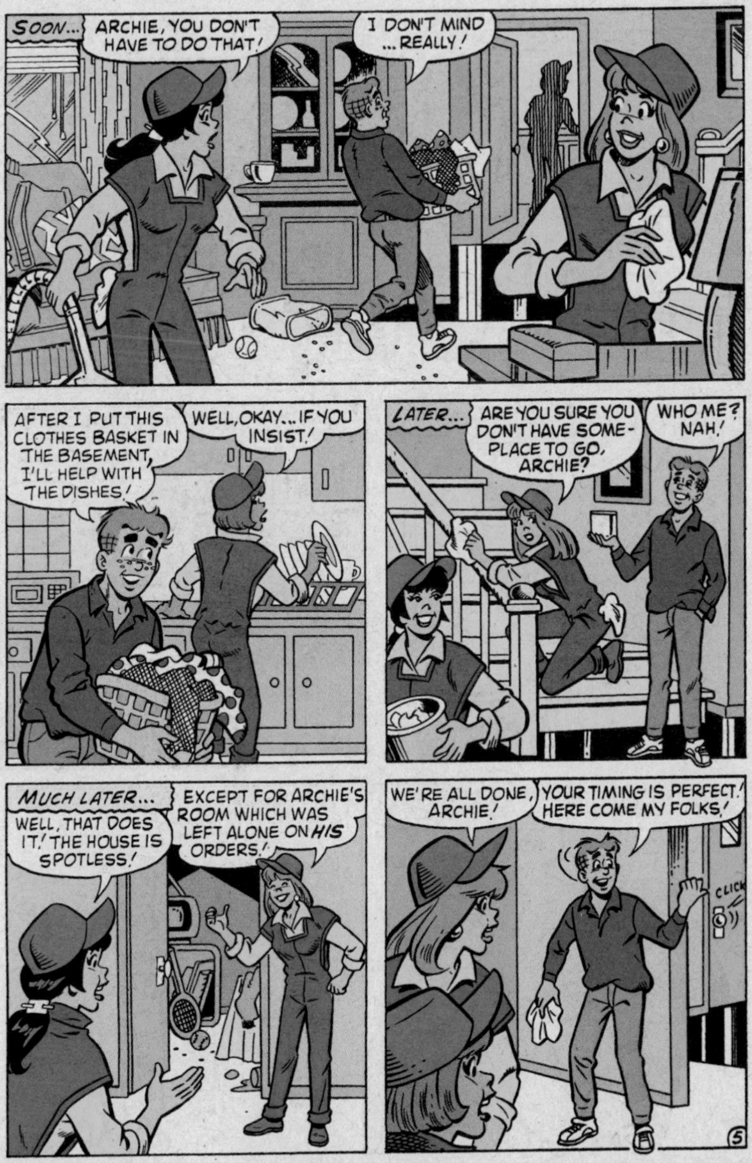
SOON...
ARCHIE, YOU DON'T HAVE TO DO THAT!
I DON'T MIND ... REALLY!
AFTER I PUT THIS CLOTHES BASKET IN THE BASEMENT, I'LL HELP WITH THE DISHES!
WELL, OKAY... IF YOU INSIST!
LATER...
ARE YOU SURE YOU DON'T HAVE SOME-PLACE TO GO, ARCHIE?
WHO ME? NAH!
MUCH LATER...
WELL, THAT DOES IT! THE HOUSE IS SPOTLESS!
EXCEPT FOR ARCHIE'S ROOM WHICH WAS LEFT ALONE ON HIS ORDERS!
WE'RE ALL DONE, ARCHIE!
YOUR TIMING IS PERFECT! HERE COME MY FOLKS!
CLICK
5

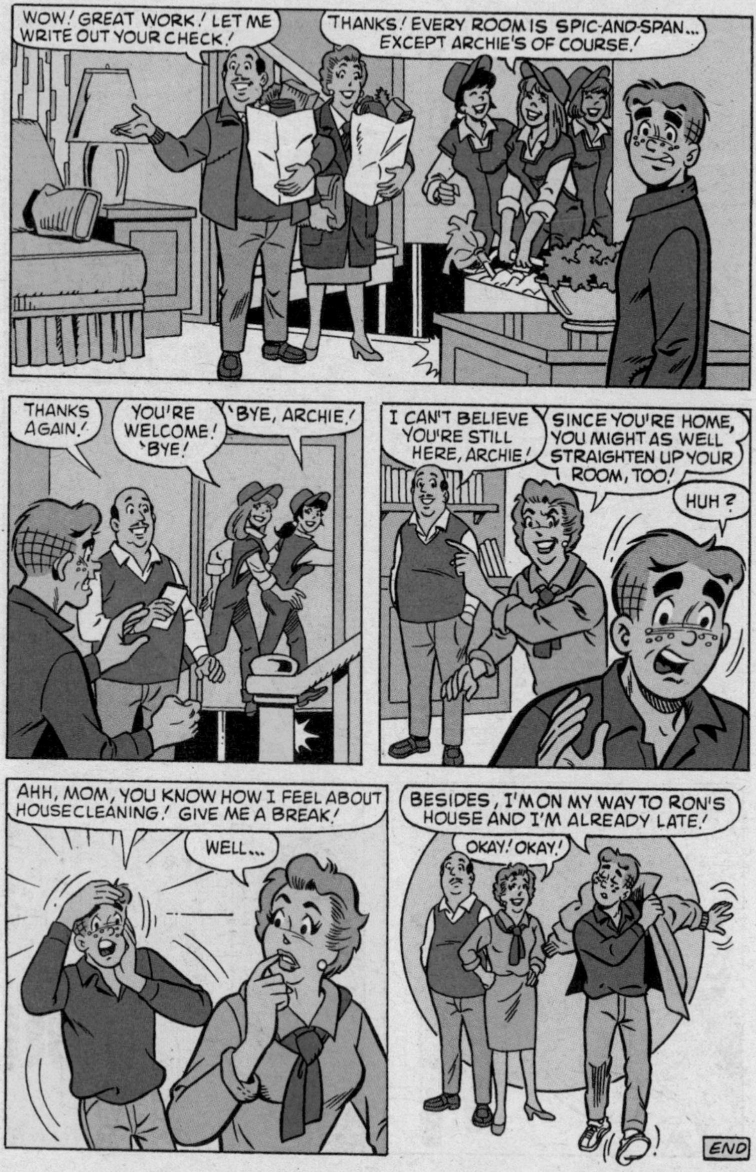
WOW! GREAT WORK! LET ME WRITE OUT YOUR CHECK!
THANKS! EVERY ROOM IS SPIC-AND-SPAN... EXCEPT ARCHIE'S OF COURSE!
THANKS AGAIN!
YOU'RE WELCOME! 'BYE!
'BYE, ARCHIE!
I CAN'T BELIEVE YOU'RE STILL HERE, ARCHIE!
SINCE YOU'RE HOME, YOU MIGHT AS WELL STRAIGHTEN UP YOUR ROOM, TOO!
HUH?
AHH, MOM, YOU KNOW HOW I FEEL ABOUT HOUSECLEANING! GIVE ME A BREAK!
WELL...
BESIDES, I'M ON MY WAY TO RON'S HOUSE AND I'M ALREADY LATE!
OKAY! OKAY!
END

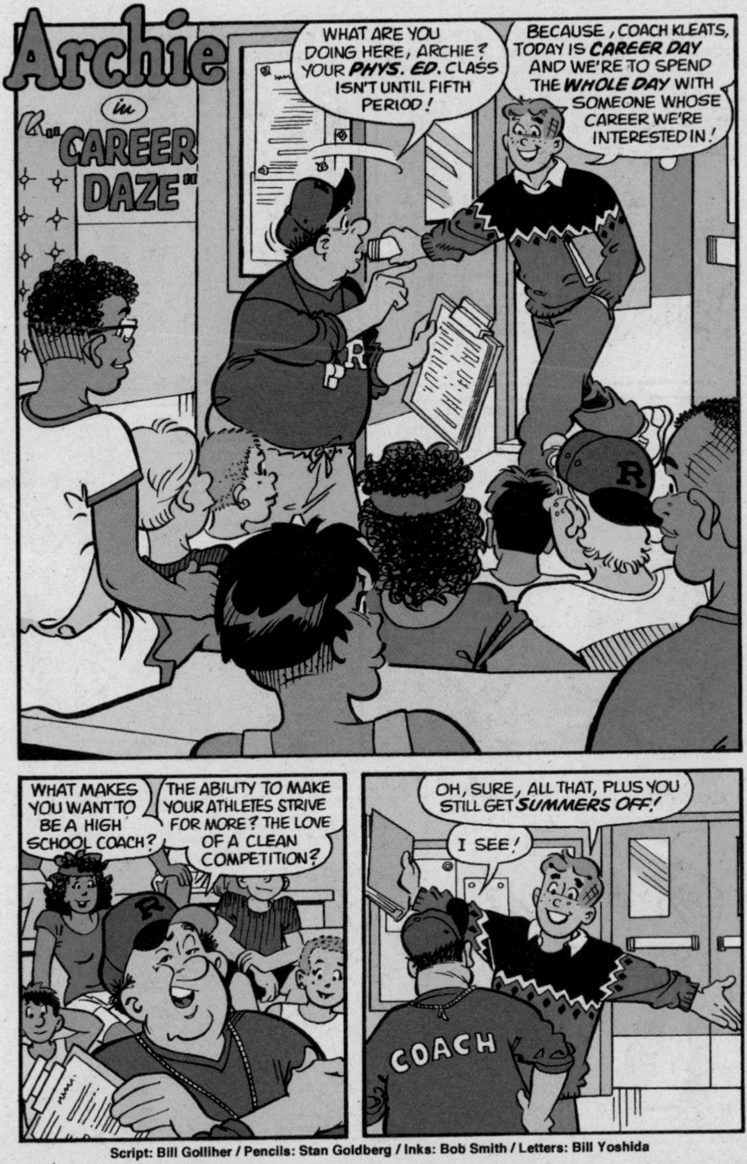
Archie
in
"CAREER DAZE"
WHAT ARE YOU DOING HERE, ARCHIE? YOUR PHYS. ED. CLASS ISN'T UNTIL FIFTH PERIOD!
BECAUSE, COACH KLEATS, TODAY IS CAREER DAY AND WE'RE TO SPEND THE WHOLE DAY WITH SOMEONE WHOSE CAREER WE'RE INTERESTED IN!
WHAT MAKES YOU WANT TO BE A HIGH SCHOOL COACH?
THE ABILITY TO MAKE YOUR ATHLETES STRIVE FOR MORE? THE LOVE OF A CLEAN COMPETITION?
OH, SURE, ALL THAT, PLUS YOU STILL GET SUMMERS OFF!
I SEE!
COACH

Script: Bill Golliher / Pencils: Stan Goldberg / Inks: Bob Smith / Letters: Bill Yoshida

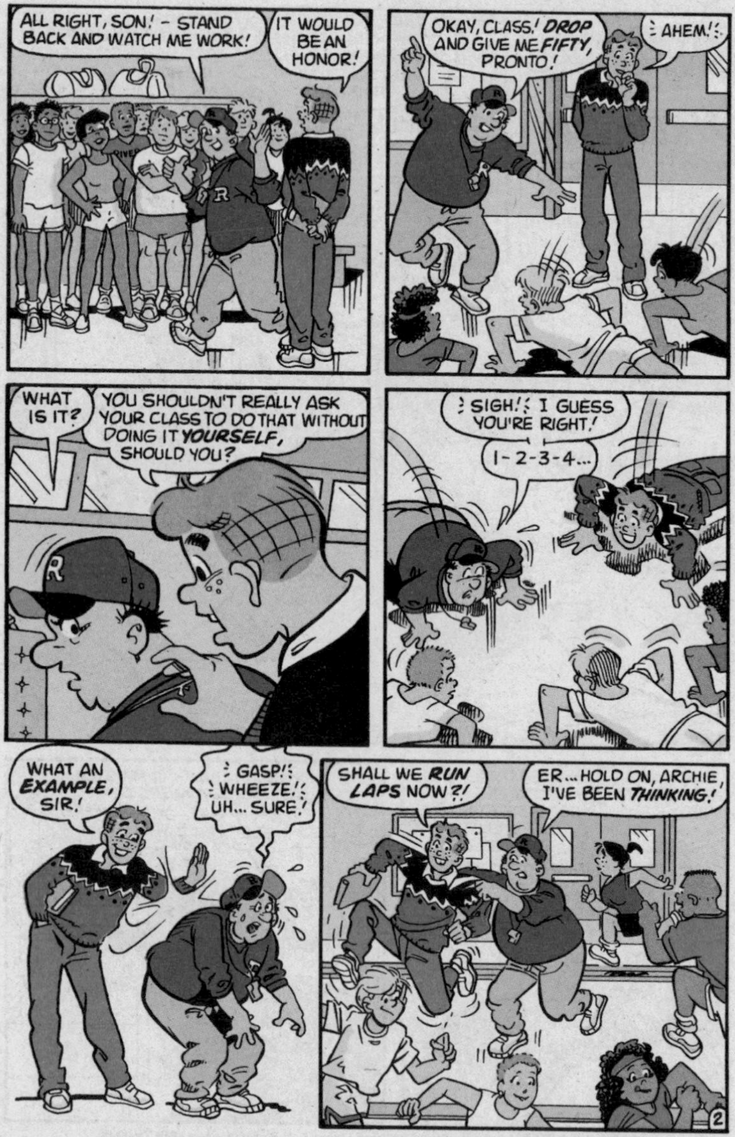
ALL RIGHT, SON! - STAND BACK AND WATCH ME WORK!
IT WOULD BE AN HONOR!
OKAY, CLASS! DROP AND GIVE ME FIFTY, PRONTO!
AHEM!
WHAT IS IT?
YOU SHOULDN'T REALLY ASK YOUR CLASS TO DO THAT WITHOUT DOING IT YOURSELF, SHOULD YOU?
SIGH! I GUESS YOU'RE RIGHT!
1-2-3-4...
WHAT AN EXAMPLE, SIR!
GASP! WHEEZE! UH... SURE!
SHALL WE RUN LAPS NOW?!
ER... HOLD ON, ARCHIE, I'VE BEEN THINKING!
2

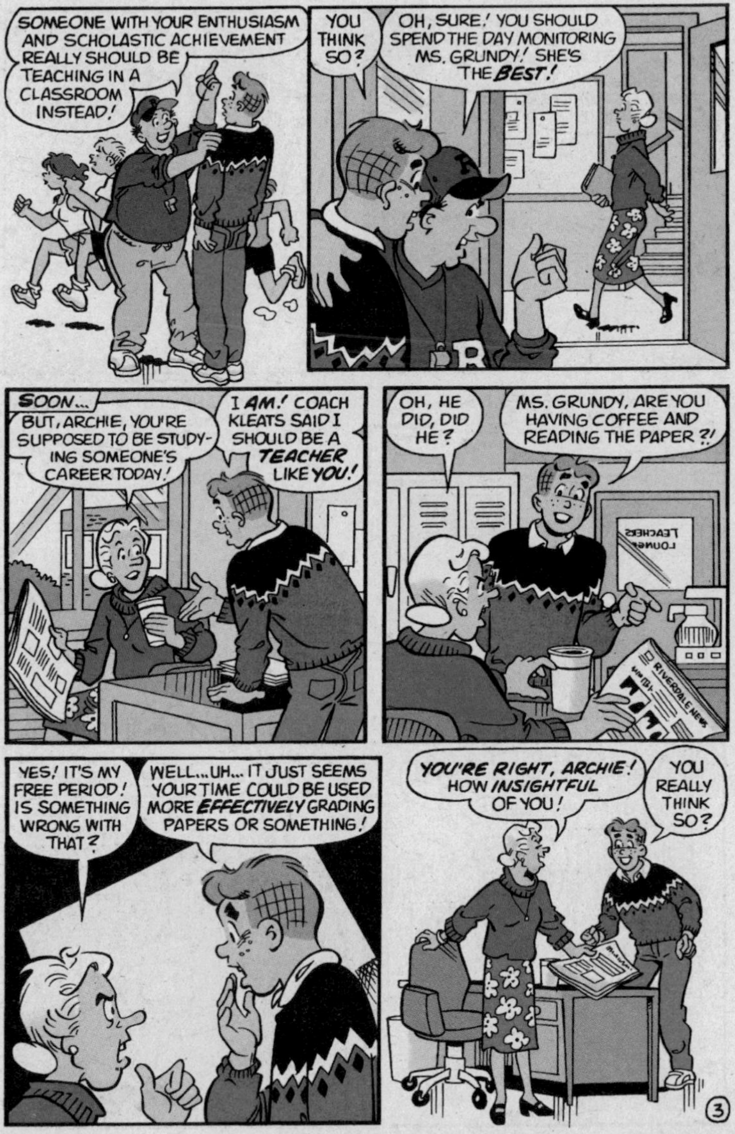
SOMEONE WITH YOUR ENTHUSIASM AND SCHOLASTIC ACHIEVEMENT REALLY SHOULD BE TEACHING IN A CLASSROOM INSTEAD!
YOU THINK SO?
OH, SURE! YOU SHOULD SPEND THE DAY MONITORING MS. GRUNDY! SHE'S THE BEST!
SOON...
BUT, ARCHIE, YOU'RE SUPPOSED TO BE STUDYING SOMEONE'S CAREER TODAY!
I AM! COACH KLEATS SAID I SHOULD BE A TEACHER LIKE YOU!
OH, HE DID, DID HE?
MS. GRUNDY, ARE YOU HAVING COFFEE AND READING THE PAPER?!
RIVERDALE NEWS
YES! IT'S MY FREE PERIOD! IS SOMETHING WRONG WITH THAT?
WELL...UH... IT JUST SEEMS YOUR TIME COULD BE USED MORE EFFECTIVELY GRADING PAPERS OR SOMETHING!
YOU'RE RIGHT, ARCHIE! HOW INSIGHTFUL OF YOU!
YOU REALLY THINK SO?
3

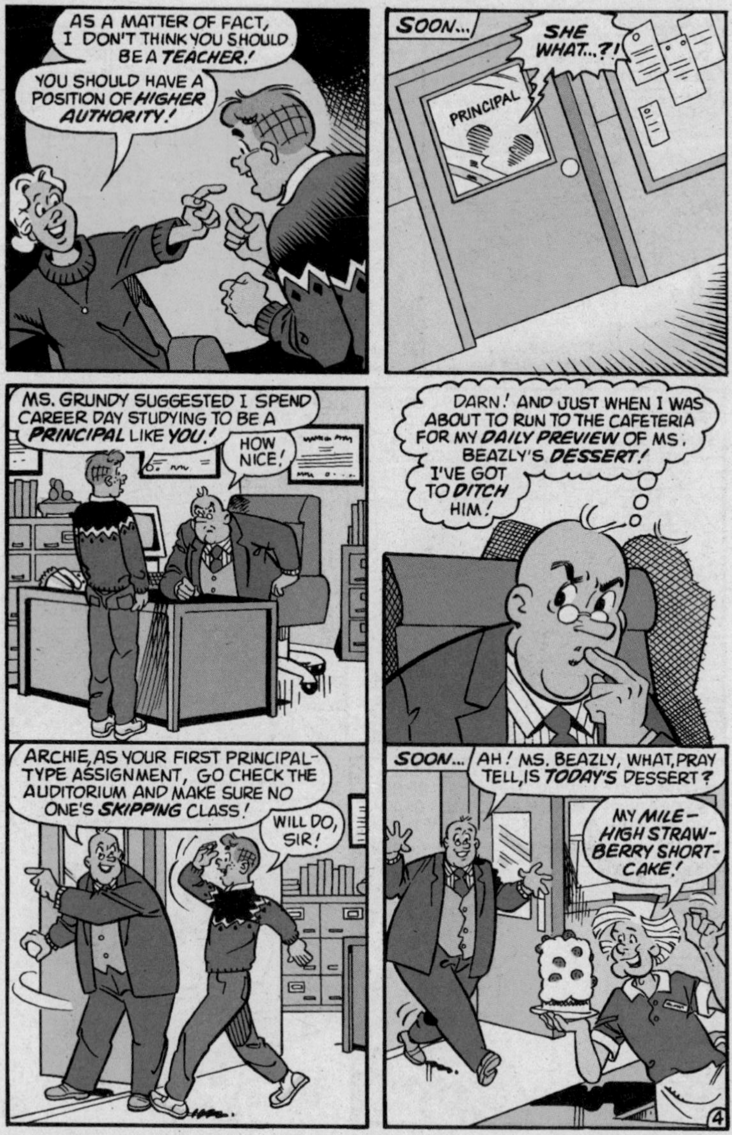

AS A MATTER OF FACT, I DON'T THINK YOU SHOULD BE A TEACHER!
YOU SHOULD HAVE A POSITION OF HIGHER AUTHORITY!
SOON...
SHE WHAT...?!
PRINCIPAL
MS. GRUNDY SUGGESTED I SPEND CAREER DAY STUDYING TO BE A PRINCIPAL LIKE YOU!
HOW NICE!
DARN! AND JUST WHEN I WAS ABOUT TO RUN TO THE CAFETERIA FOR MY DAILY PREVIEW OF MS. BEAZLY'S DESSERT!
I'VE GOT TO DITCH HIM!
ARCHIE, AS YOUR FIRST PRINCIPAL-TYPE ASSIGNMENT, GO CHECK THE AUDITORIUM AND MAKE SURE NO ONE'S SKIPPING CLASS!
WILL DO, SIR!
SOON...
AH! MS. BEAZLY, WHAT, PRAY TELL, IS TODAY'S DESSERT?
MY MILE-HIGH STRAWBERRY SHORTCAKE!
4

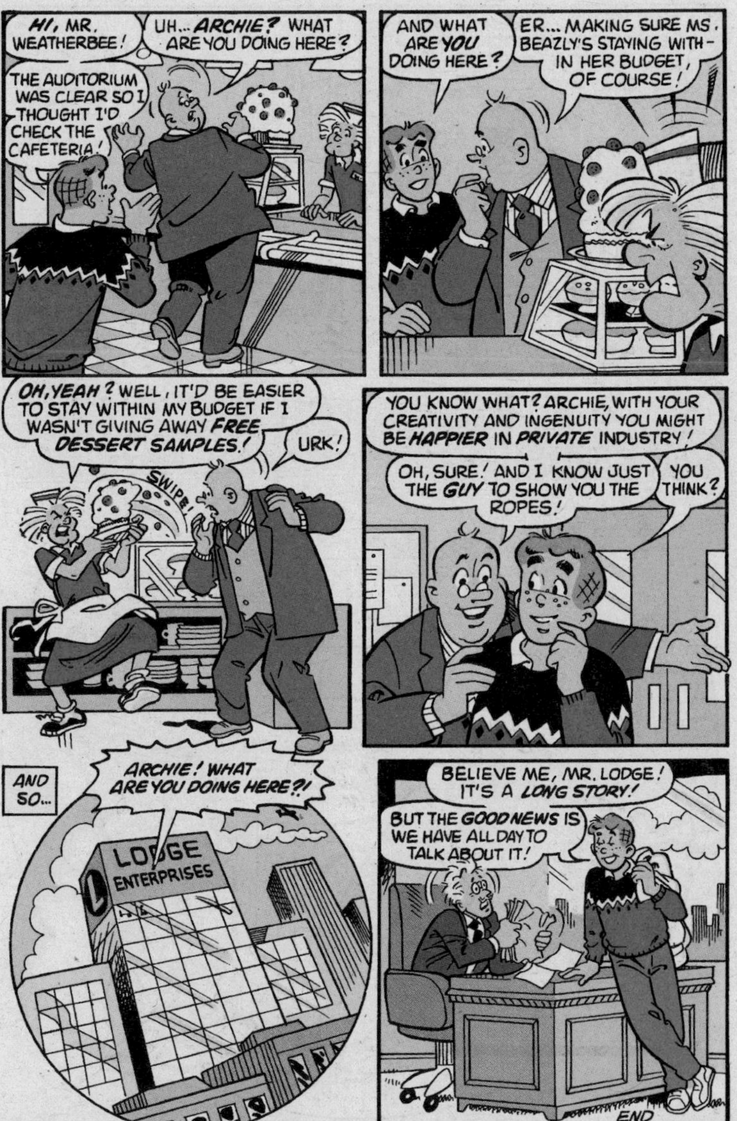
HI, MR. WEATHERBEE!
UH... ARCHIE? WHAT ARE YOU DOING HERE?
THE AUDITORIUM WAS CLEAR SO I THOUGHT I'D CHECK THE CAFETERIA!
AND WHAT ARE YOU DOING HERE?
ER... MAKING SURE MS. BEAZLY'S STAYING WITHIN HER BUDGET, OF COURSE!
OH, YEAH? WELL, IT'D BE EASIER TO STAY WITHIN MY BUDGET IF I WASN'T GIVING AWAY FREE DESSERT SAMPLES!
URK!
SWIPE!
YOU KNOW WHAT? ARCHIE, WITH YOUR CREATIVITY AND INGENUITY YOU MIGHT BE HAPPIER IN PRIVATE INDUSTRY!
OH, SURE! AND I KNOW JUST THE GUY TO SHOW YOU THE ROPES!
YOU THINK?
AND SO...
ARCHIE! WHAT ARE YOU DOING HERE?!
LODGE ENTERPRISES
BELIEVE ME, MR. LODGE! IT'S A LONG STORY!
BUT THE GOOD NEWS IS WE HAVE ALL DAY TO TALK ABOUT IT!
END

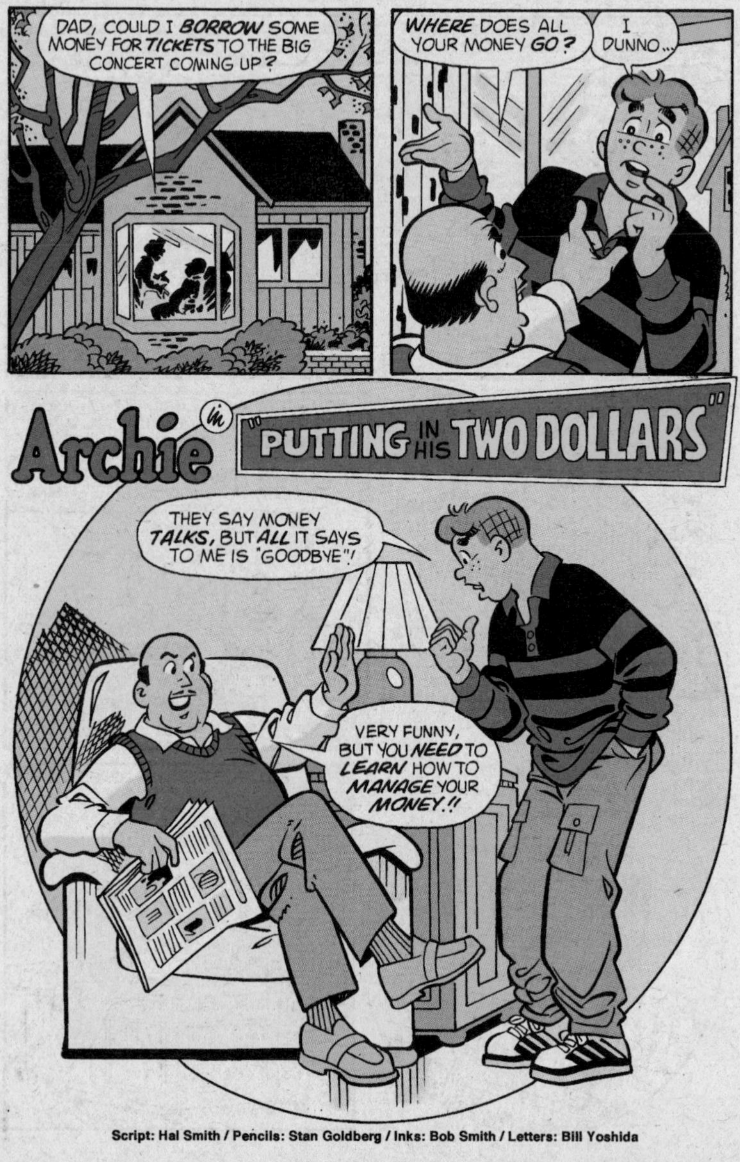

DAD, COULD I BORROW SOME MONEY FOR TICKETS TO THE BIG CONCERT COMING UP?
WHERE DOES ALL YOUR MONEY GO?
I DUNNO...
Archie in
"PUTTING IN HIS TWO DOLLARS"
THEY SAY MONEY TALKS, BUT ALL IT SAYS TO ME IS "GOODBYE"!
VERY FUNNY, BUT YOU NEED TO LEARN HOW TO MANAGE YOUR MONEY!!

Script: Hal Smith / Pencils: Stan Goldberg / Inks: Bob Smith / Letters: Bill Yoshida

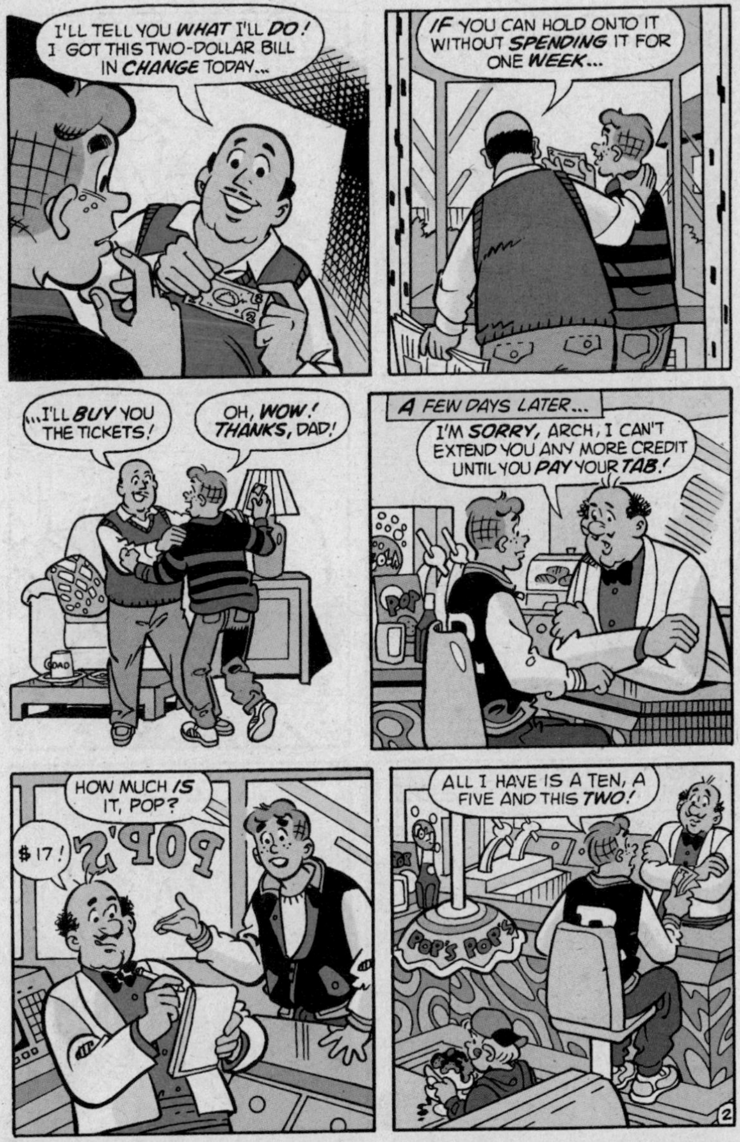
I'LL TELL YOU WHAT I'LL DO! I GOT THIS TWO-DOLLAR BILL IN CHANGE TODAY...
IF YOU CAN HOLD ONTO IT WITHOUT SPENDING IT FOR ONE WEEK...
...I'LL BUY YOU THE TICKETS!
OH, WOW! THANKS, DAD!
DAD
A FEW DAYS LATER...
I'M SORRY, ARCH, I CAN'T EXTEND YOU ANY MORE CREDIT UNTIL YOU PAY YOUR TAB!
POP
HOW MUCH IS IT, POP?
$17!
POP'S
ALL I HAVE IS A TEN, A FIVE AND THIS TWO!
POP'S POP'S
2

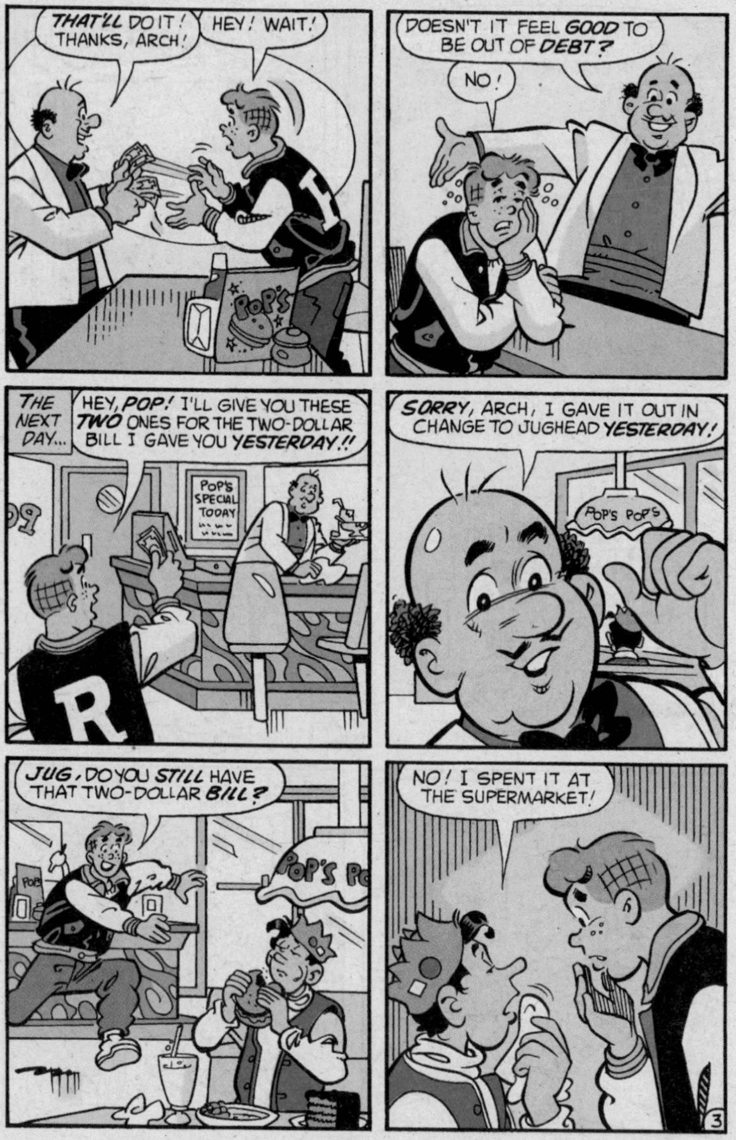
THAT'LL DO IT! THANKS, ARCH!
HEY! WAIT!
POP'S
DOESN'T IT FEEL GOOD TO BE OUT OF DEBT?
NO!
THE NEXT DAY...
HEY, POP! I'LL GIVE YOU THESE TWO ONES FOR THE TWO-DOLLAR BILL I GAVE YOU YESTERDAY!!
POP'S SPECIAL TODAY
SORRY, ARCH, I GAVE IT OUT IN CHANGE TO JUGHEAD YESTERDAY!
POP'S POP'S
JUG, DO YOU STILL HAVE THAT TWO-DOLLAR BILL?
NO! I SPENT IT AT THE SUPERMARKET!
3

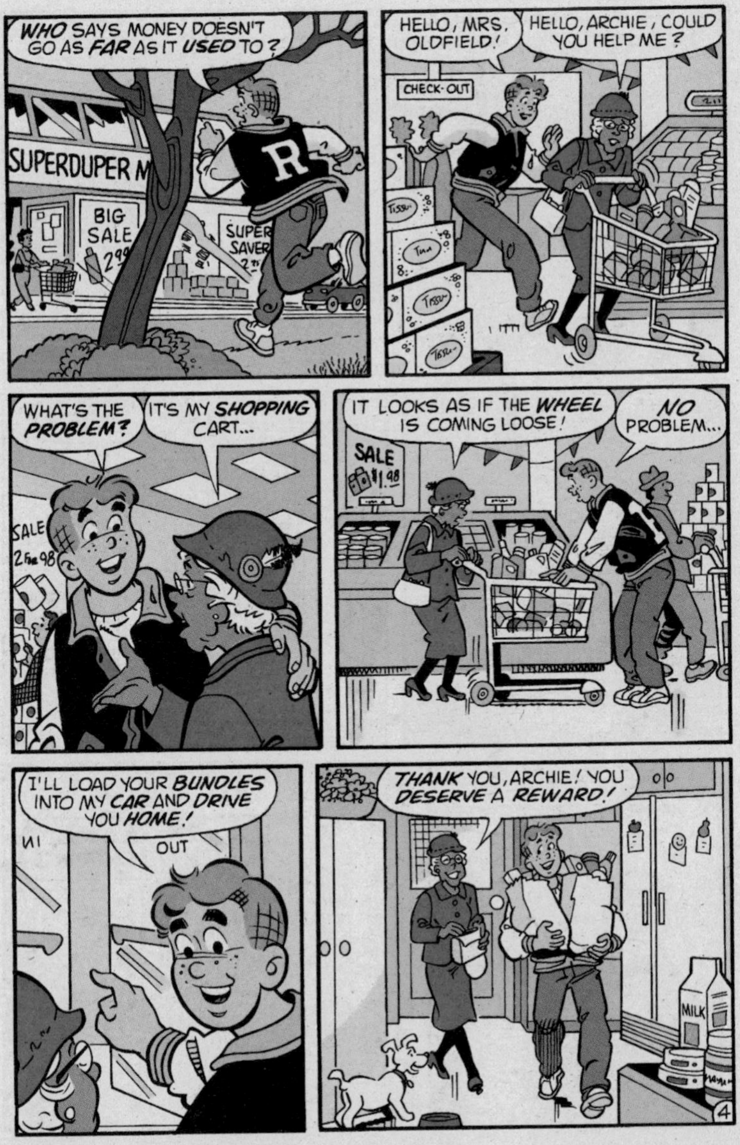
WHO SAYS MONEY DOESN'T GO AS FAR AS IT USED TO?
SUPERDUPER M
BIG SALE 2.99
SUPER SAVER
HELLO, MRS. OLDFIELD!
HELLO, ARCHIE, COULD YOU HELP ME?
CHECK-OUT
WHAT'S THE PROBLEM?
IT'S MY SHOPPING CART...
SALE 2 For 98
IT LOOKS AS IF THE WHEEL IS COMING LOOSE!
NO PROBLEM...
SALE $1.98
I'LL LOAD YOUR BUNDLES INTO MY CAR AND DRIVE YOU HOME!
OUT
THANK YOU, ARCHIE! YOU DESERVE A REWARD!
MILK
4

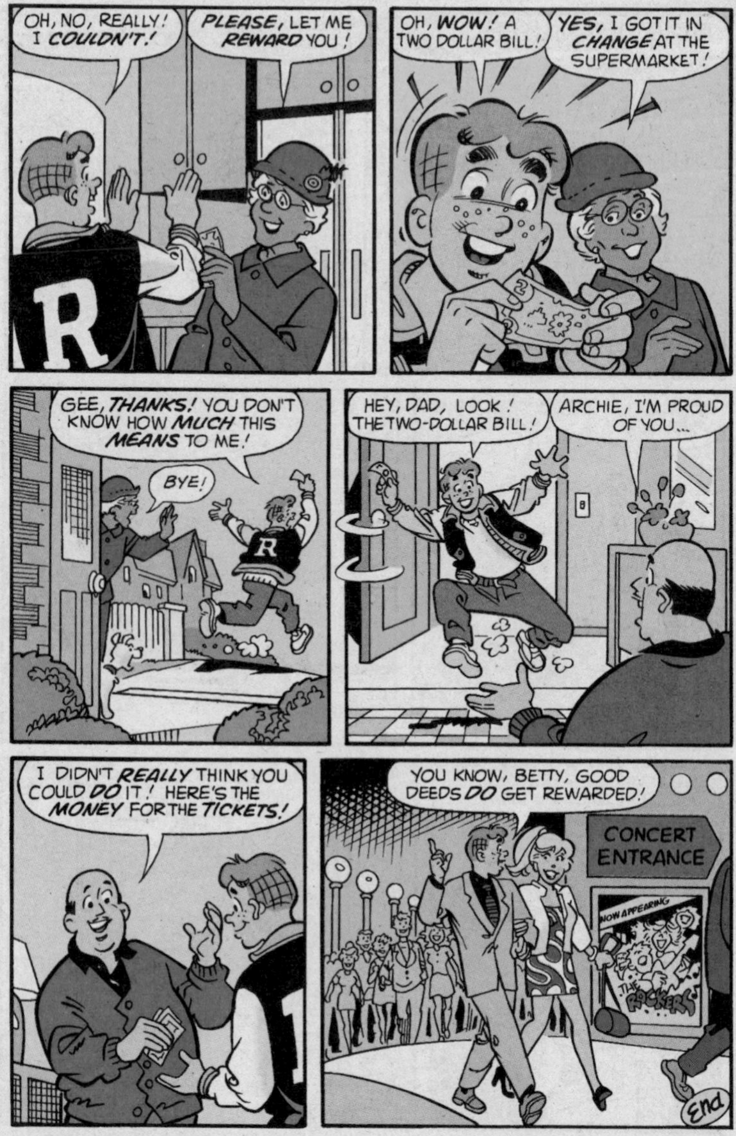
OH, NO, REALLY! I COULDN'T!
PLEASE, LET ME REWARD YOU!
OH, WOW! A TWO DOLLAR BILL!
YES, I GOT IT IN CHANGE AT THE SUPERMARKET!
GEE, THANKS! YOU DON'T KNOW HOW MUCH THIS MEANS TO ME!
BYE!
HEY, DAD, LOOK! THE TWO-DOLLAR BILL!
ARCHIE, I'M PROUD OF YOU...
I DIDN'T REALLY THINK YOU COULD DO IT! HERE'S THE MONEY FOR THE TICKETS!
YOU KNOW, BETTY, GOOD DEEDS DO GET REWARDED!
CONCERT ENTRANCE
NOW APPEARING
THE ROCKERS
End

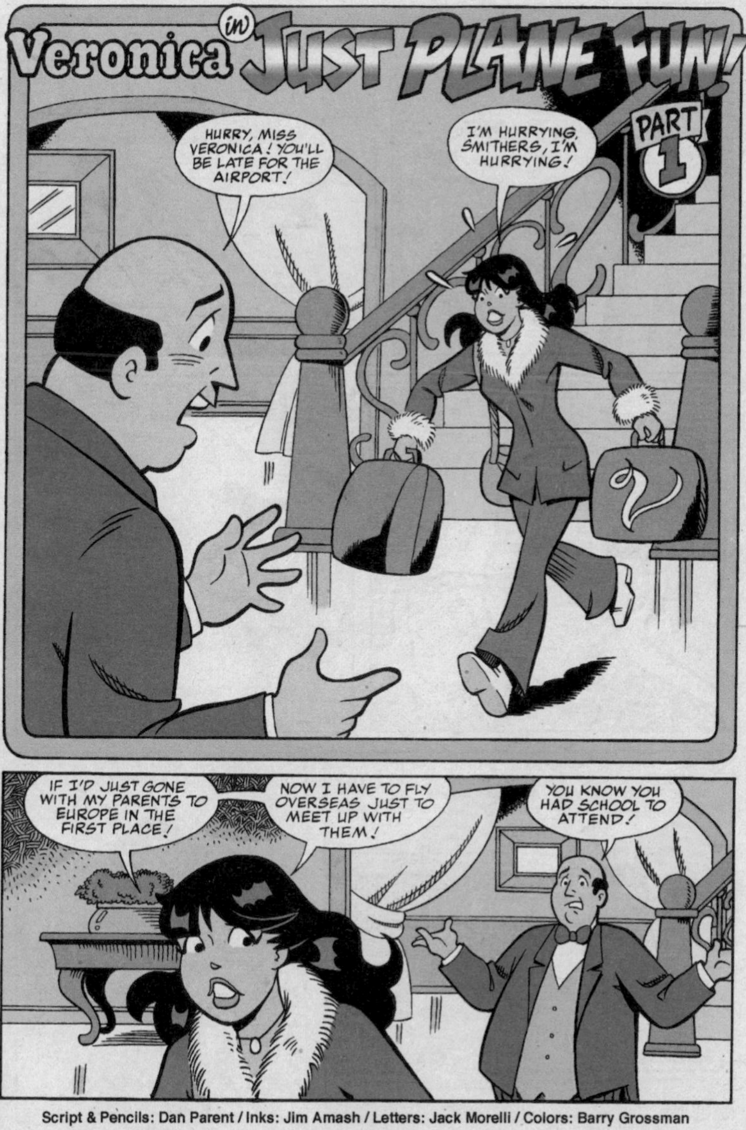
Veronica in JUST PLANE FUN!
PART 1
HURRY, MISS VERONICA! YOU'LL BE LATE FOR THE AIRPORT!
I'M HURRYING, SMITHERS, I'M HURRYING!
IF I'D JUST GONE WITH MY PARENTS TO EUROPE IN THE FIRST PLACE!
NOW I HAVE TO FLY OVERSEAS JUST TO MEET UP WITH THEM!
YOU KNOW YOU HAD SCHOOL TO ATTEND!

Script & Pencils: Dan Parent / Inks: Jim Amash / Letters: Jack Morelli / Colors: Barry Grossman

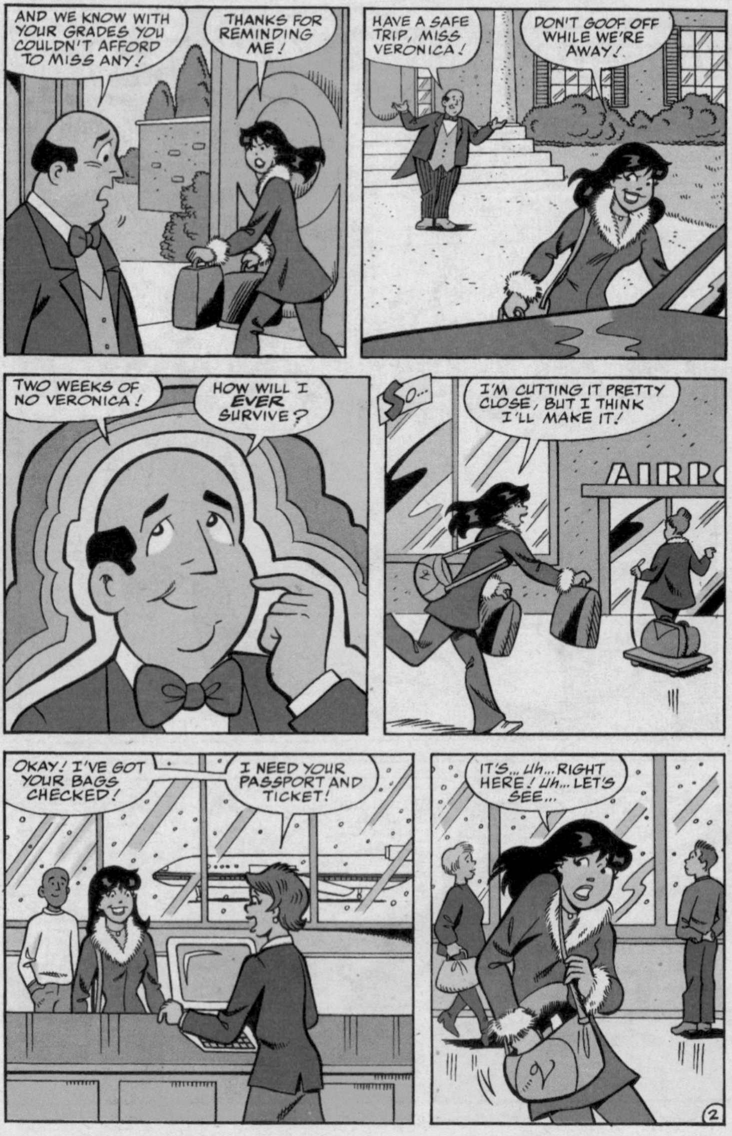
AND WE KNOW WITH YOUR GRADES YOU COULDN'T AFFORD TO MISS ANY!
THANKS FOR REMINDING ME!
HAVE A SAFE TRIP, MISS VERONICA!
DON'T GOOF OFF WHILE WE'RE AWAY!
TWO WEEKS OF NO VERONICA!
HOW WILL I EVER SURVIVE?
SO...
I'M CUTTING IT PRETTY CLOSE, BUT I THINK I'LL MAKE IT!
AIRP
OKAY! I'VE GOT YOUR BAGS CHECKED!
I NEED YOUR PASSPORT AND TICKET!
IT'S... UH... RIGHT HERE! UH... LET'S SEE...
2

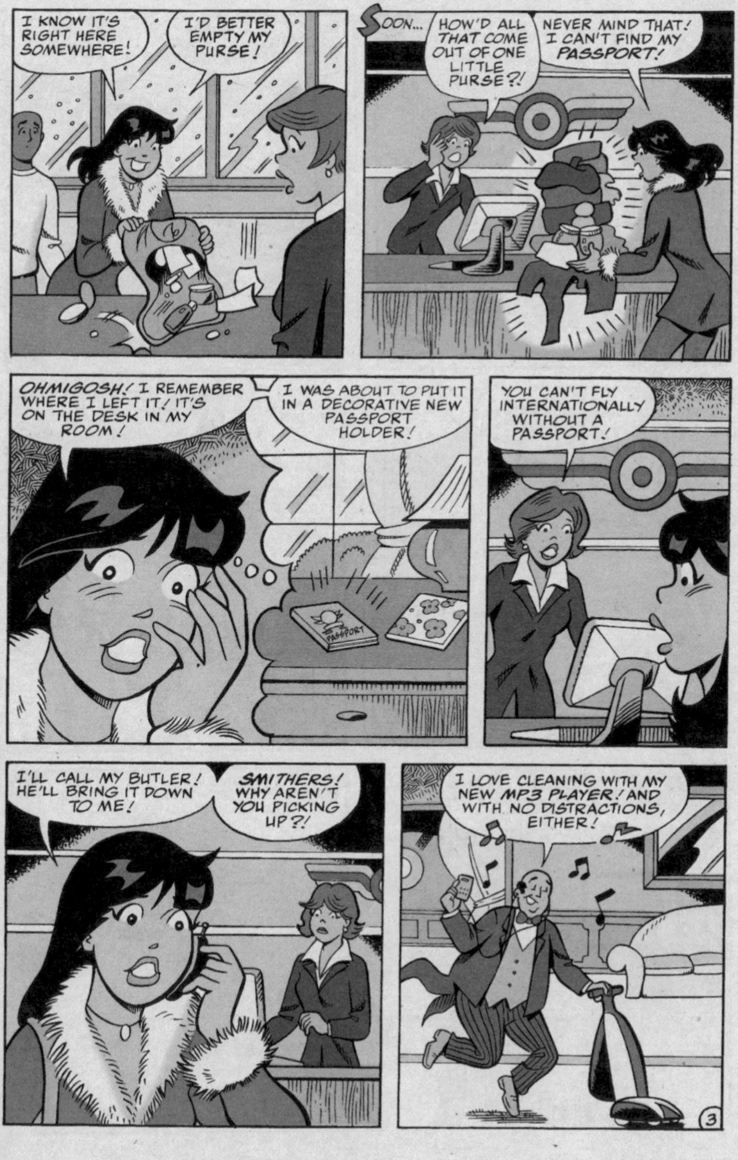
I KNOW IT'S RIGHT HERE SOMEWHERE!
I'D BETTER EMPTY MY PURSE!
SOON...
HOW'D ALL THAT COME OUT OF ONE LITTLE PURSE?!
NEVER MIND THAT! I CAN'T FIND MY PASSPORT!
OHMIGOSH! I REMEMBER WHERE I LEFT IT! IT'S ON THE DESK IN MY ROOM!
I WAS ABOUT TO PUT IT IN A DECORATIVE NEW PASSPORT HOLDER!
PASSPORT
YOU CAN'T FLY INTERNATIONALLY WITHOUT A PASSPORT!
I'LL CALL MY BUTLER! HE'LL BRING IT DOWN TO ME!
SMITHERS! WHY AREN'T YOU PICKING UP?!
I LOVE CLEANING WITH MY NEW MP3 PLAYER! AND WITH NO DISTRACTIONS, EITHER!
3

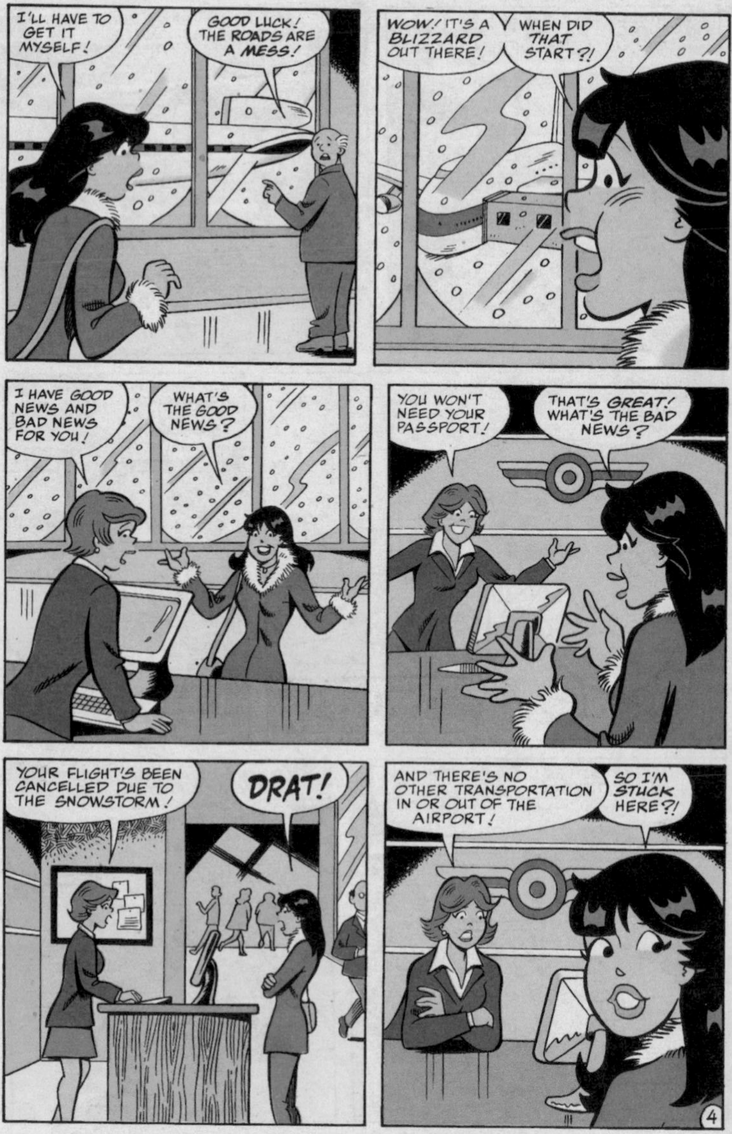
I'LL HAVE TO GET IT MYSELF!
GOOD LUCK! THE ROADS ARE A MESS!
WOW! IT'S A BLIZZARD OUT THERE!
WHEN DID THAT START?!
I HAVE GOOD NEWS AND BAD NEWS FOR YOU!
WHAT'S THE GOOD NEWS?
YOU WON'T NEED YOUR PASSPORT!
THAT'S GREAT! WHAT'S THE BAD NEWS?
YOUR FLIGHT'S BEEN CANCELLED DUE TO THE SNOWSTORM!
DRAT!
AND THERE'S NO OTHER TRANSPORTATION IN OR OUT OF THE AIRPORT!
SO I'M STUCK HERE?!
4

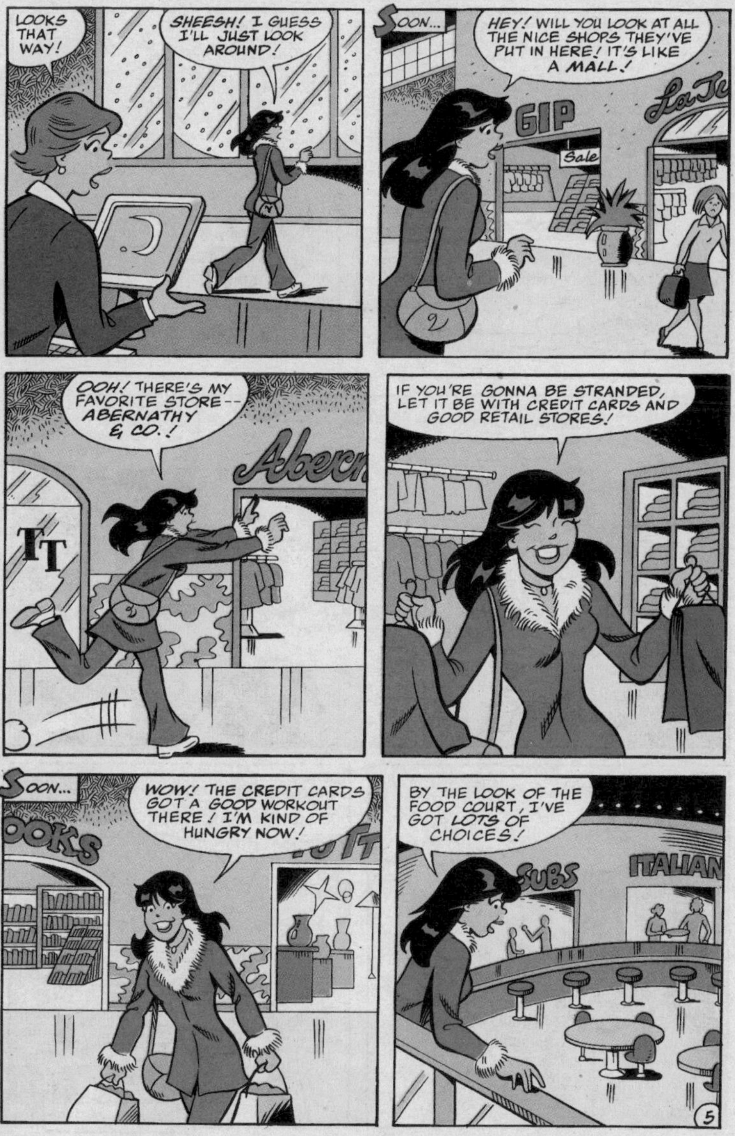
LOOKS THAT WAY!
SHEESH! I GUESS I'LL JUST LOOK AROUND!
SOON...
HEY! WILL YOU LOOK AT ALL THE NICE SHOPS THEY'VE PUT IN HERE! IT'S LIKE A MALL!
GIP
Sale
OOH! THERE'S MY FAVORITE STORE-- ABERNATHY & CO.!
IF YOU'RE GONNA BE STRANDED, LET IT BE WITH CREDIT CARDS AND GOOD RETAIL STORES!
SOON...
WOW! THE CREDIT CARDS GOT A GOOD WORKOUT THERE! I'M KIND OF HUNGRY NOW!
BY THE LOOK OF THE FOOD COURT, I'VE GOT LOTS OF CHOICES!
SUBS
ITALIAN
5

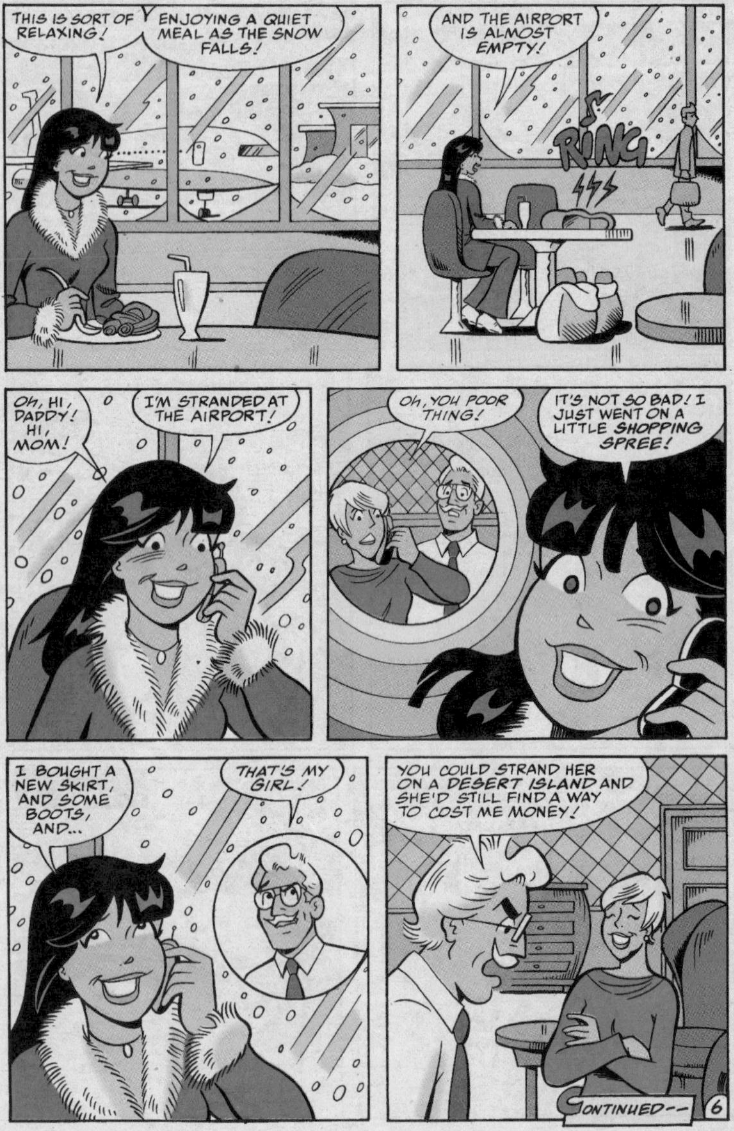

THIS IS SORT OF RELAXING!
ENJOYING A QUIET MEAL AS THE SNOW FALLS!
AND THE AIRPORT IS ALMOST EMPTY!
RING
Oh, HI, DADDY! HI, MOM!
I'M STRANDED AT THE AIRPORT!
Oh, YOU POOR THING!
IT'S NOT SO BAD! I JUST WENT ON A LITTLE SHOPPING SPREE!
I BOUGHT A NEW SKIRT, AND SOME BOOTS, AND...
THAT'S MY GIRL!
YOU COULD STRAND HER ON A DESERT ISLAND AND SHE'D STILL FIND A WAY TO COST ME MONEY!
CONTINUED--
6

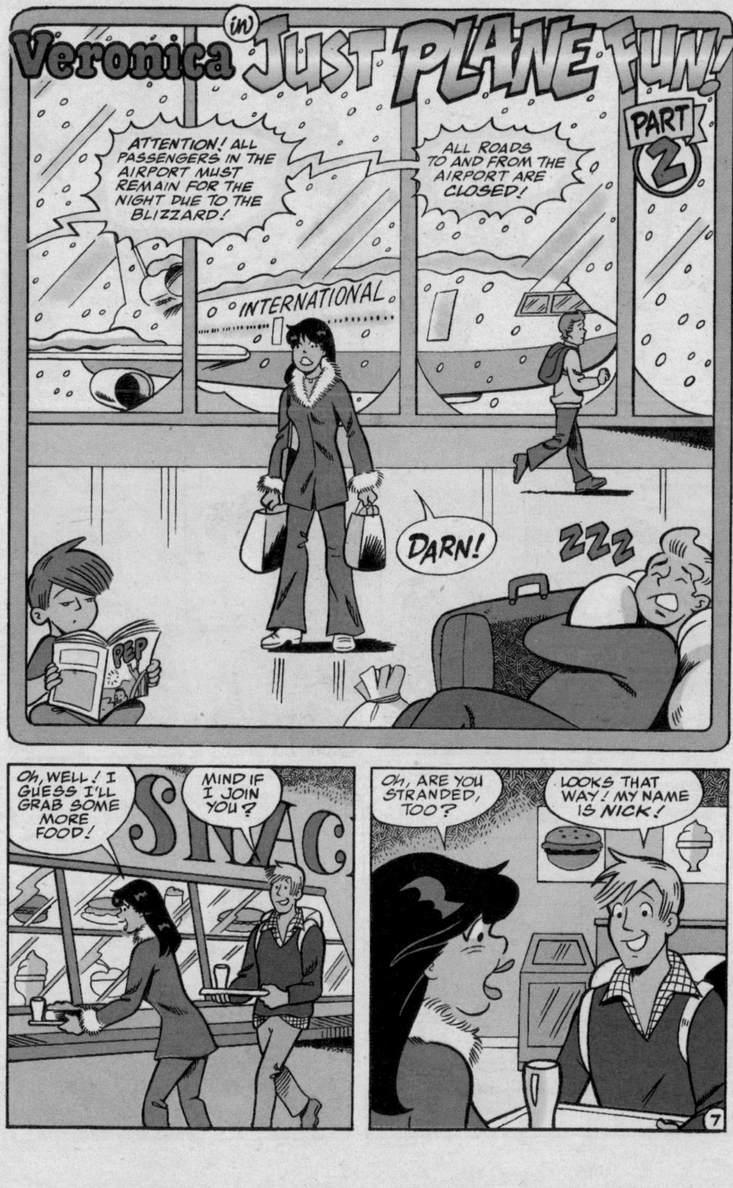
Veronica in JUST PLANE FUN!
PART 2
ATTENTION! ALL PASSENGERS IN THE AIRPORT MUST REMAIN FOR THE NIGHT DUE TO THE BLIZZARD!
ALL ROADS TO AND FROM THE AIRPORT ARE CLOSED!
INTERNATIONAL
DARN!
ZZZ
PEP
Oh, WELL! I GUESS I'LL GRAB SOME MORE FOOD!
MIND IF I JOIN YOU?
Oh, ARE YOU STRANDED, TOO?
LOOKS THAT WAY! MY NAME IS NICK!
7

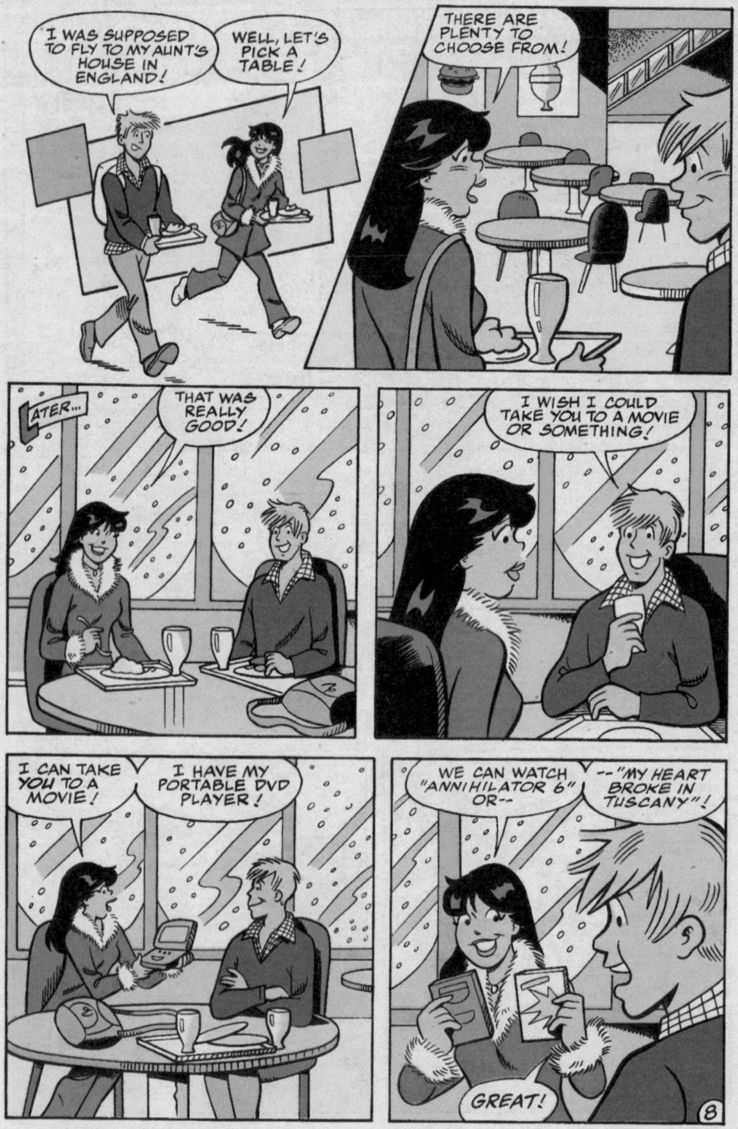
I WAS SUPPOSED TO FLY TO MY AUNT'S HOUSE IN ENGLAND!
WELL, LET'S PICK A TABLE!
THERE ARE PLENTY TO CHOOSE FROM!
LATER...
THAT WAS REALLY GOOD!
I WISH I COULD TAKE YOU TO A MOVIE OR SOMETHING!
I CAN TAKE YOU TO A MOVIE!
I HAVE MY PORTABLE DVD PLAYER!
WE CAN WATCH "ANNIHILATOR 6" OR--
--"MY HEART BROKE IN TUSCANY"!
GREAT!
8

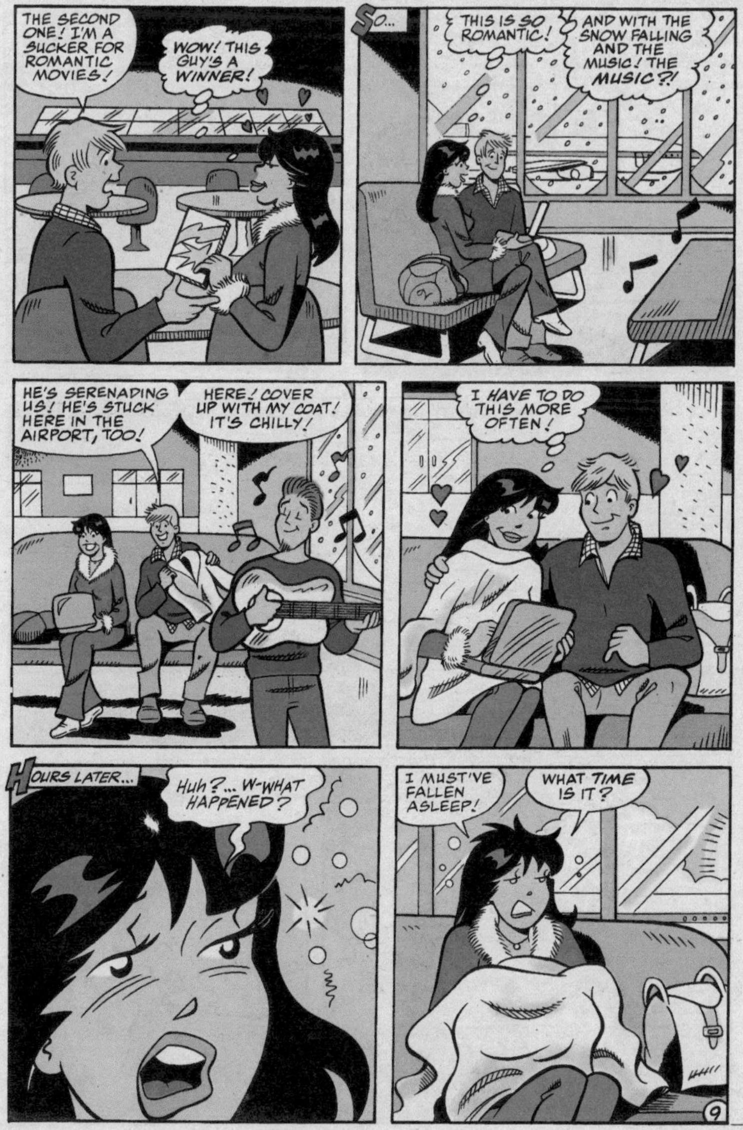
THE SECOND ONE! I'M A SUCKER FOR ROMANTIC MOVIES!
WOW! THIS GUY'S A WINNER!
SO...
THIS IS SO ROMANTIC!
AND WITH THE SNOW FALLING AND THE MUSIC! THE MUSIC?!
HE'S SERENADING US! HE'S STUCK HERE IN THE AIRPORT, TOO!
HERE! COVER UP WITH MY COAT! IT'S CHILLY!
I HAVE TO DO THIS MORE OFTEN!
HOURS LATER...
Huh?... W-WHAT HAPPENED?
I MUST'VE FALLEN ASLEEP!
WHAT TIME IS IT?

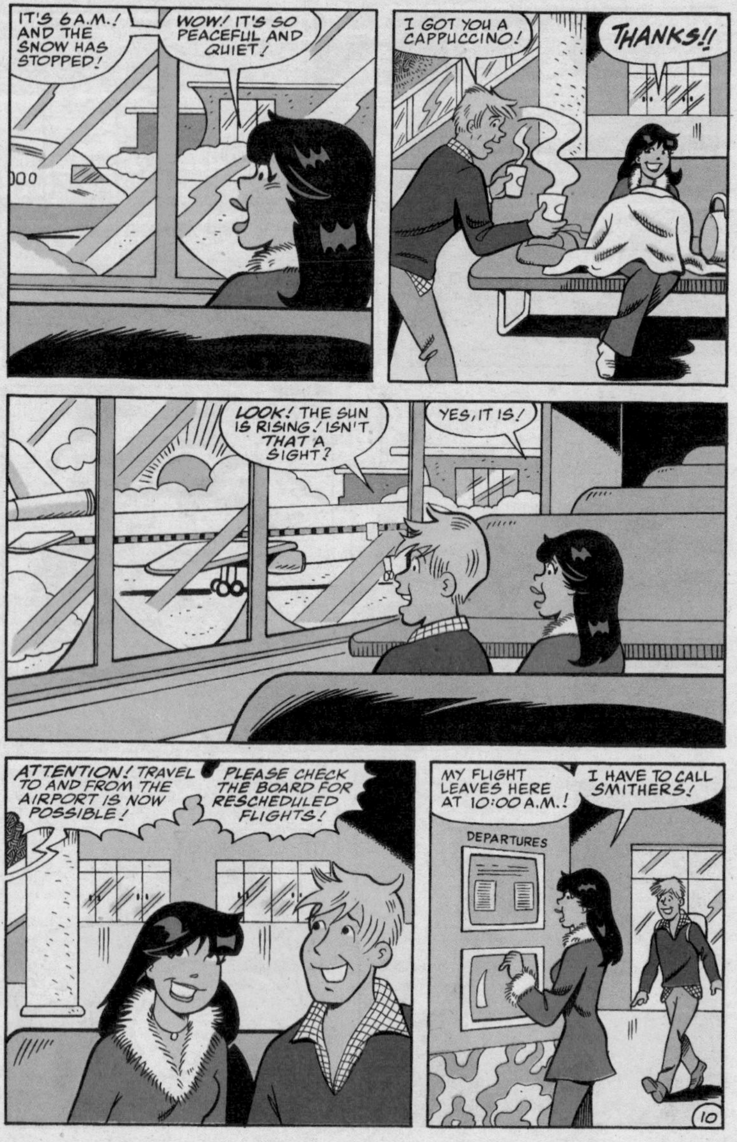
IT'S 6 A.M.! AND THE SNOW HAS STOPPED!
WOW! IT'S SO PEACEFUL AND QUIET!
I GOT YOU A CAPPUCCINO!
THANKS!!
LOOK! THE SUN IS RISING! ISN'T THAT A SIGHT?
YES, IT IS!
ATTENTION! TRAVEL TO AND FROM THE AIRPORT IS NOW POSSIBLE!
PLEASE CHECK THE BOARD FOR RESCHEDULED FLIGHTS!
MY FLIGHT LEAVES HERE AT 10:00 A.M.!
I HAVE TO CALL SMITHERS!
DEPARTURES
10

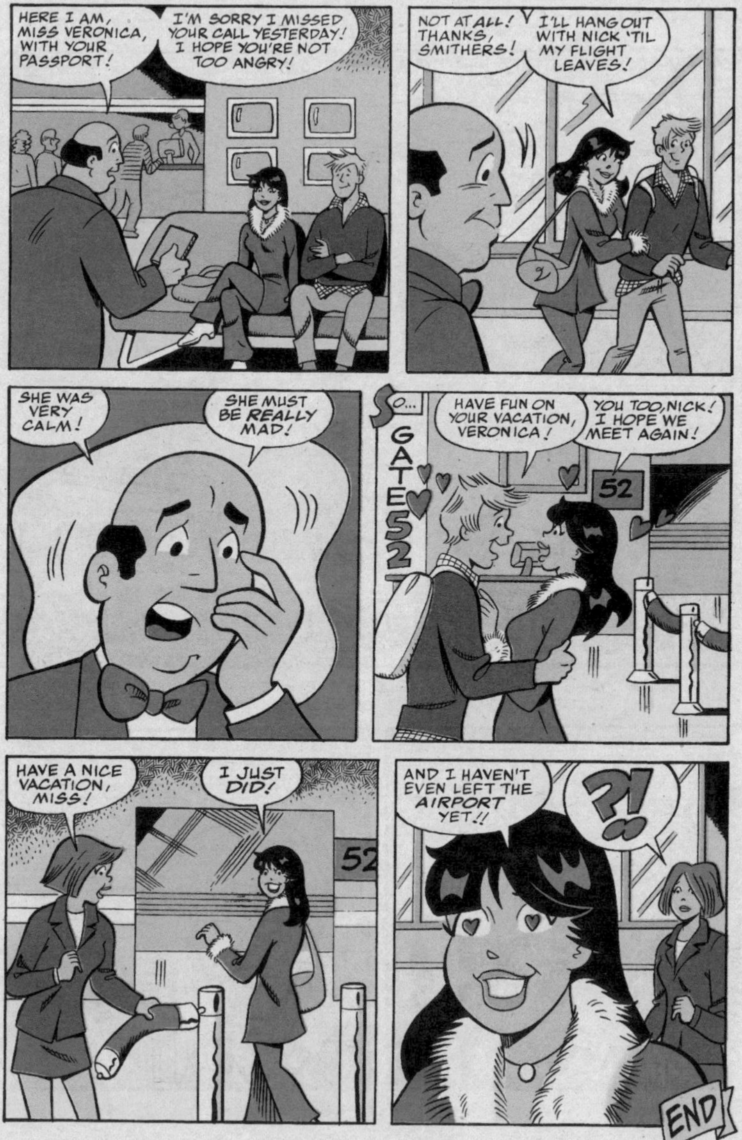
HERE I AM, MISS VERONICA, WITH YOUR PASSPORT!
I'M SORRY I MISSED YOUR CALL YESTERDAY! I HOPE YOU'RE NOT TOO ANGRY!
NOT AT ALL! THANKS, SMITHERS!
I'LL HANG OUT WITH NICK 'TIL MY FLIGHT LEAVES!
SHE WAS VERY CALM!
SHE MUST BE REALLY MAD!
SO...
GATE 52
HAVE FUN ON YOUR VACATION, VERONICA!
YOU TOO, NICK! I HOPE WE MEET AGAIN!
52
HAVE A NICE VACATION, MISS!
I JUST DID!
52
AND I HAVEN'T EVEN LEFT THE AIRPORT YET!!
?!
END

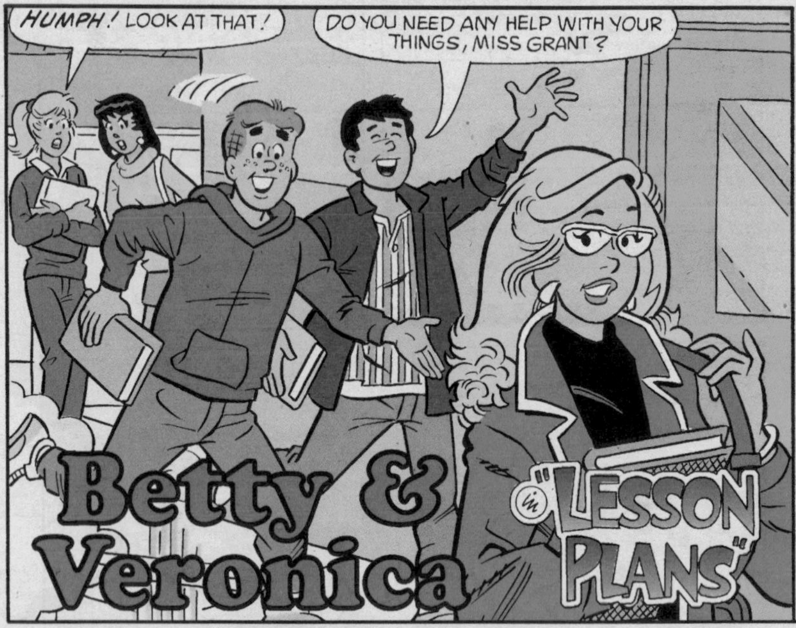
HUMPH! LOOK AT THAT!
DO YOU NEED ANY HELP WITH YOUR THINGS, MISS GRANT?
Betty & Veronica
in "LESSON PLANS"

SCRIPT: MIKE PELLOWSKI PENCILS: TIM KENNEDY INKS: RUDY LAPICK
COLORS: BARRY GROSSMAN LETTERS: BILL YOSHIDA

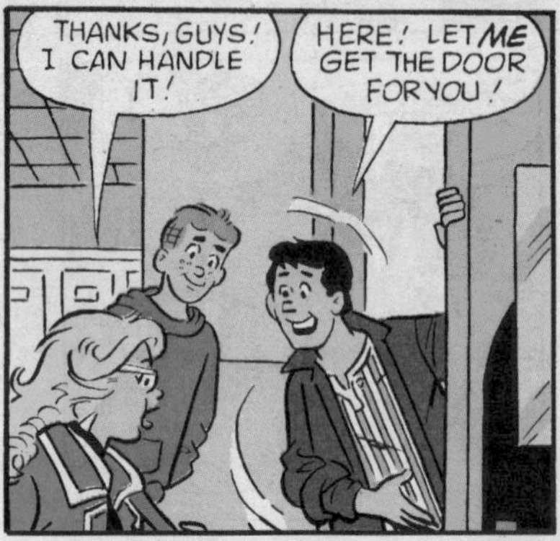
THANKS, GUYS! I CAN HANDLE IT!
HERE! LET ME GET THE DOOR FOR YOU!

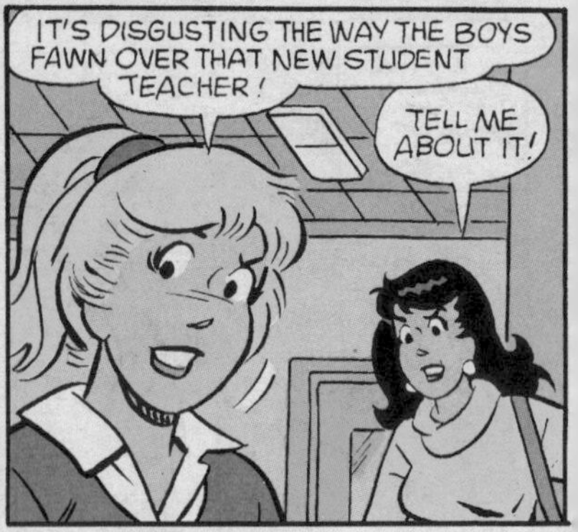
IT'S DISGUSTING THE WAY THE BOYS FAWN OVER THAT NEW STUDENT TEACHER!
TELL ME ABOUT IT!

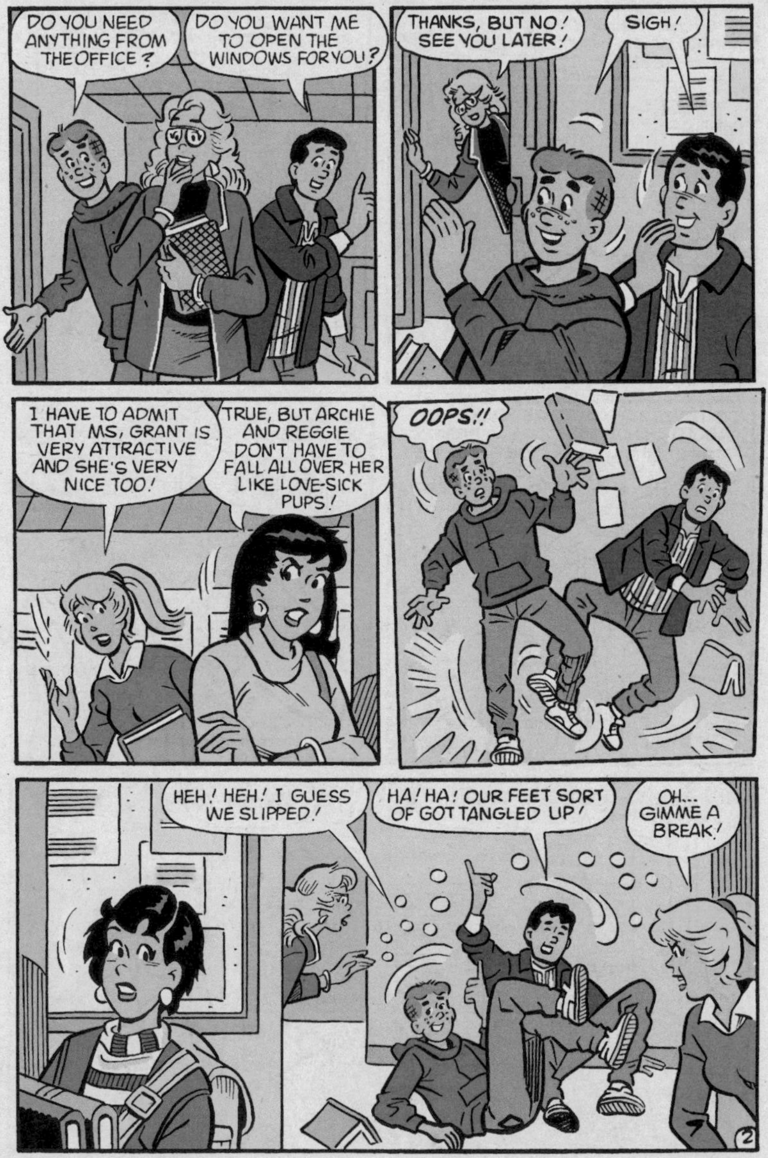
DO YOU NEED ANYTHING FROM THE OFFICE ?
DO YOU WANT ME TO OPEN THE WINDOWS FOR YOU ?
THANKS, BUT NO ! SEE YOU LATER !
SIGH !
I HAVE TO ADMIT THAT MS. GRANT IS VERY ATTRACTIVE AND SHE'S VERY NICE TOO !
TRUE, BUT ARCHIE AND REGGIE DON'T HAVE TO FALL ALL OVER HER LIKE LOVE-SICK PUPS !
OOPS !!
HEH ! HEH ! I GUESS WE SLIPPED !
HA ! HA ! OUR FEET SORT OF GOT TANGLED UP !
OH... GIMME A BREAK !
2

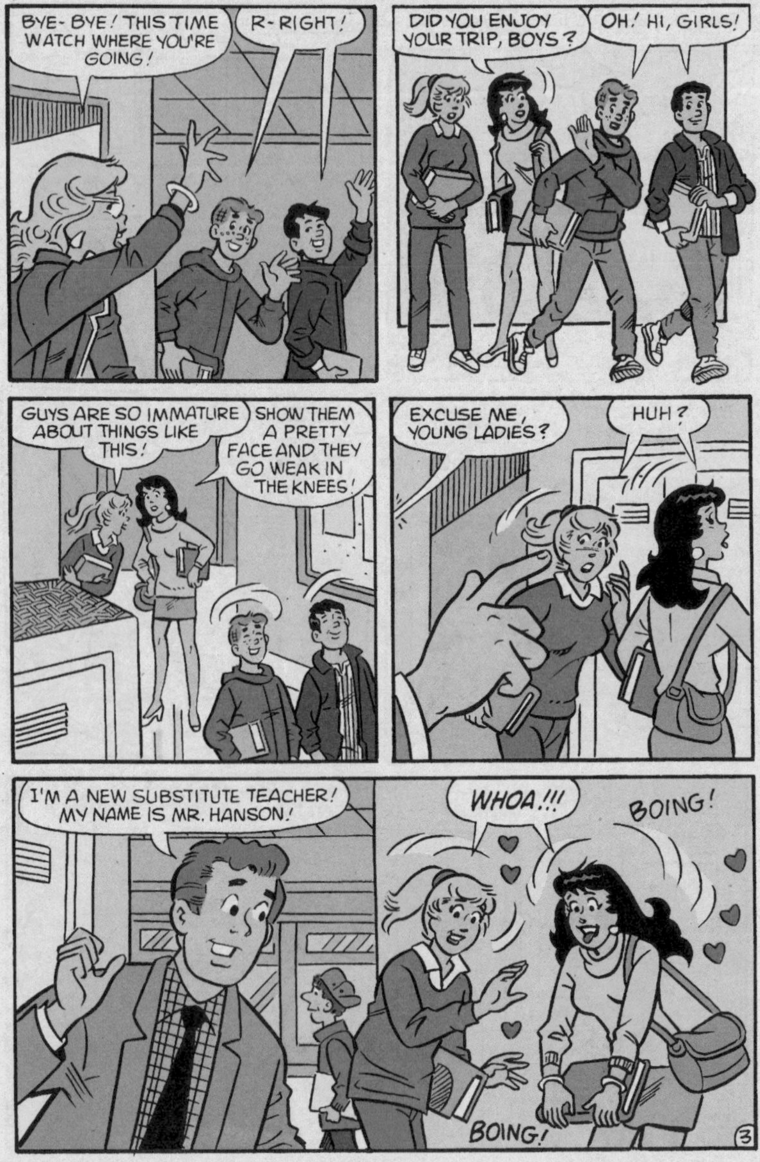
BYE-BYE! THIS TIME WATCH WHERE YOU'RE GOING!
R-RIGHT!
DID YOU ENJOY YOUR TRIP, BOYS?
OH! HI, GIRLS!
GUYS ARE SO IMMATURE ABOUT THINGS LIKE THIS!
SHOW THEM A PRETTY FACE AND THEY GO WEAK IN THE KNEES!
EXCUSE ME, YOUNG LADIES?
HUH?
I'M A NEW SUBSTITUTE TEACHER! MY NAME IS MR. HANSON!
WHOA!!!
BOING!
BOING!
3

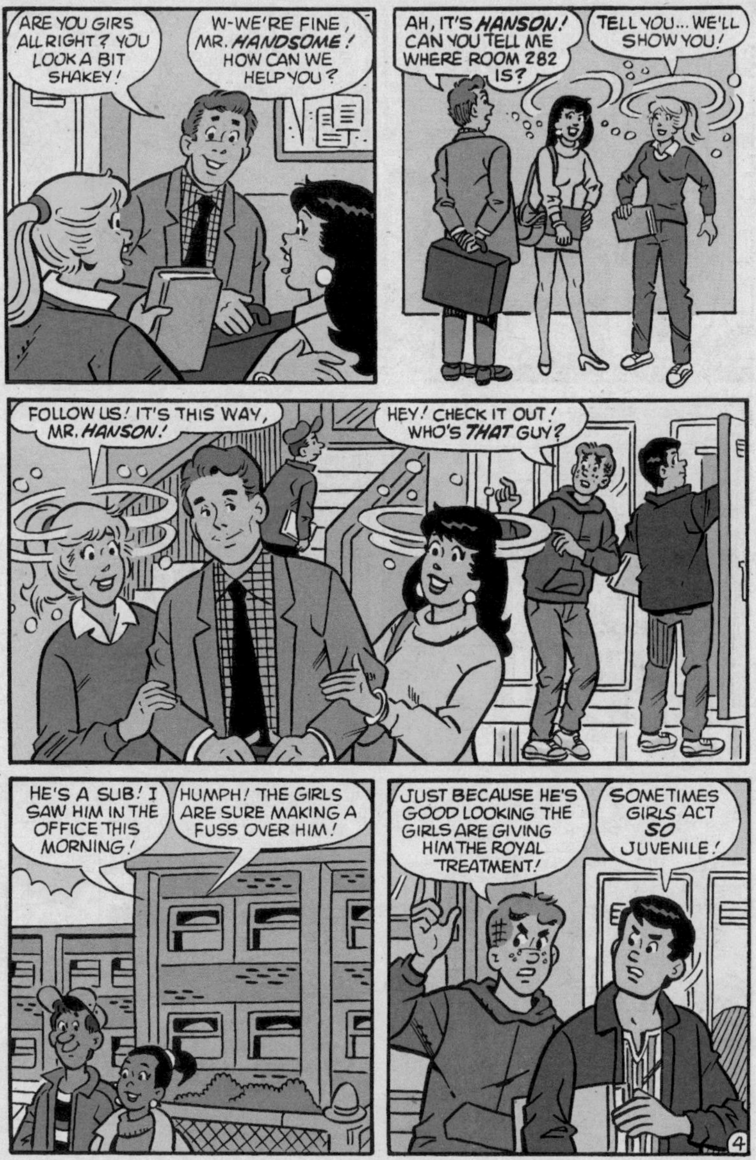
ARE YOU GIRS ALL RIGHT? YOU LOOK A BIT SHAKEY!
W-WE'RE FINE, MR. HANDSOME! HOW CAN WE HELP YOU?
AH, IT'S HANSON! CAN YOU TELL ME WHERE ROOM 282 IS?
TELL YOU... WE'LL SHOW YOU!
FOLLOW US! IT'S THIS WAY, MR. HANSON!
HEY! CHECK IT OUT! WHO'S THAT GUY?
HE'S A SUB! I SAW HIM IN THE OFFICE THIS MORNING!
HUMPH! THE GIRLS ARE SURE MAKING A FUSS OVER HIM!
JUST BECAUSE HE'S GOOD LOOKING THE GIRLS ARE GIVING HIM THE ROYAL TREATMENT!
SOMETIMES GIRLS ACT SO JUVENILE!
4

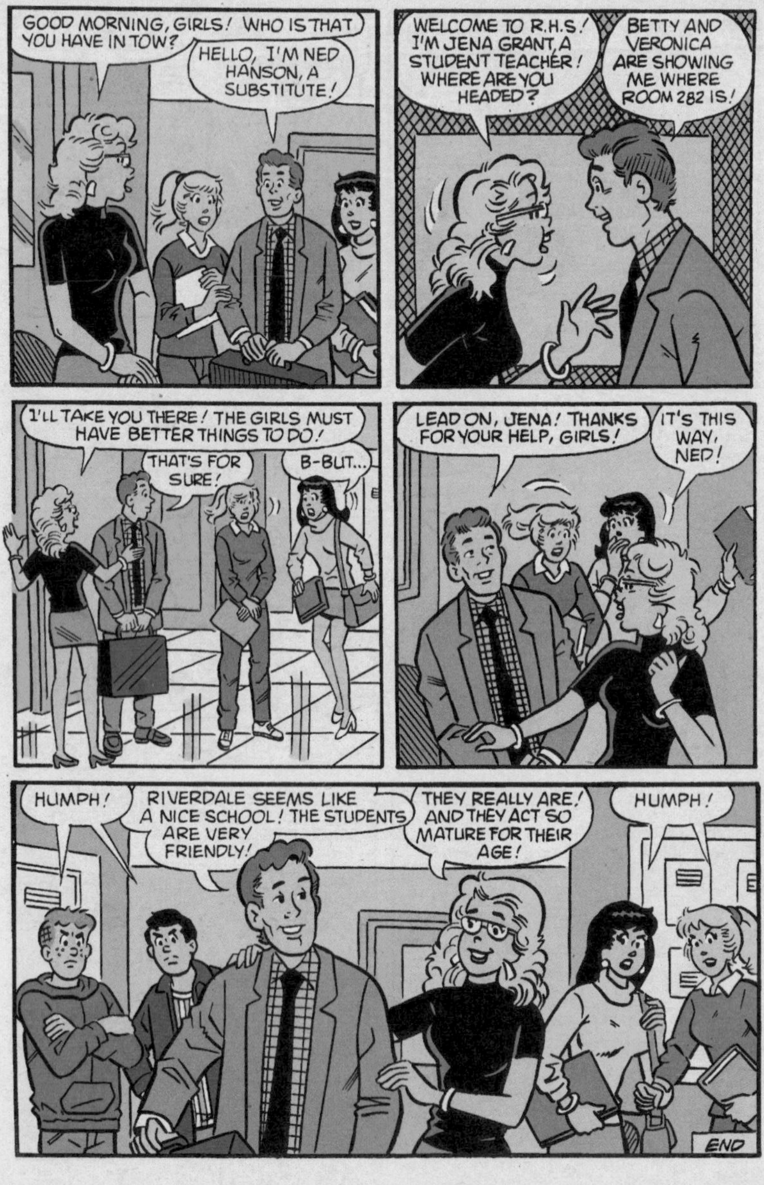
GOOD MORNING, GIRLS! WHO IS THAT YOU HAVE IN TOW?
HELLO, I'M NED HANSON, A SUBSTITUTE!
WELCOME TO R.H.S.! I'M JENA GRANT, A STUDENT TEACHER! WHERE ARE YOU HEADED?
BETTY AND VERONICA ARE SHOWING ME WHERE ROOM 282 IS!
I'LL TAKE YOU THERE! THE GIRLS MUST HAVE BETTER THINGS TO DO!
THAT'S FOR SURE!
B-BUT...
LEAD ON, JENA! THANKS FOR YOUR HELP, GIRLS!
IT'S THIS WAY, NED!
HUMPH!
RIVERDALE SEEMS LIKE A NICE SCHOOL! THE STUDENTS ARE VERY FRIENDLY!
THEY REALLY ARE! AND THEY ACT SO MATURE FOR THEIR AGE!
HUMPH!
END

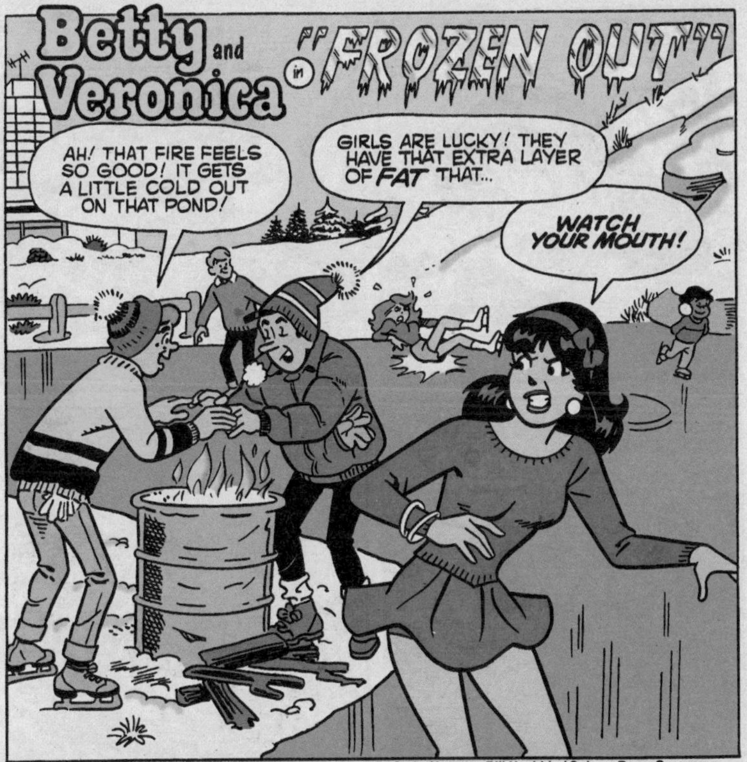
Betty and Veronica
in "FROZEN OUT"
AH! THAT FIRE FEELS SO GOOD! IT GETS A LITTLE COLD OUT ON THAT POND!
GIRLS ARE LUCKY! THEY HAVE THAT EXTRA LAYER OF FAT THAT...
WATCH YOUR MOUTH!

Script: Frank Doyle / Pencils: Dan DeCarlo / Inks: Jimmy DeCarlo / Letters: Bill Yoshida / Colors: Barry Grossman

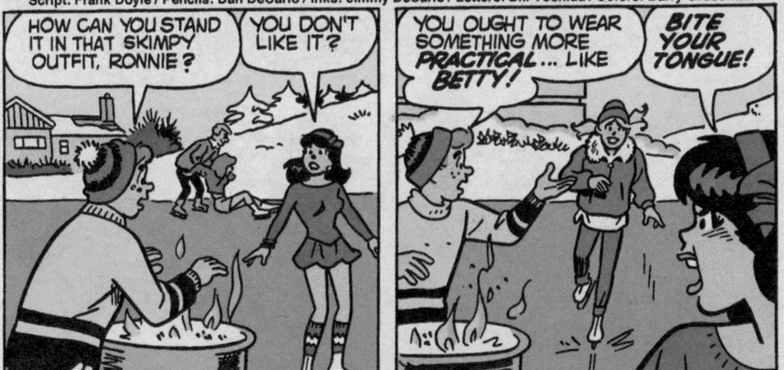
HOW CAN YOU STAND IT IN THAT SKIMPY OUTFIT, RONNIE?
YOU DON'T LIKE IT?
YOU OUGHT TO WEAR SOMETHING MORE PRACTICAL ... LIKE BETTY!
BITE YOUR TONGUE!
1

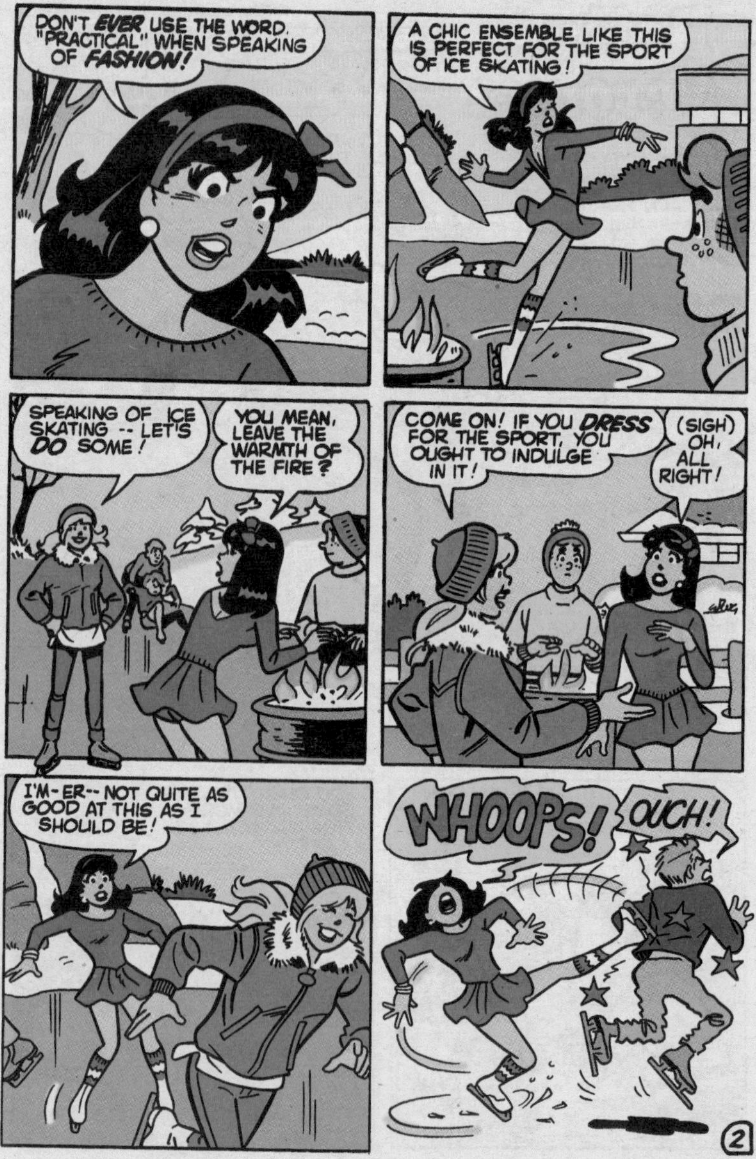
DON'T EVER USE THE WORD "PRACTICAL" WHEN SPEAKING OF FASHION!
A CHIC ENSEMBLE LIKE THIS IS PERFECT FOR THE SPORT OF ICE SKATING!
SPEAKING OF ICE SKATING -- LET'S DO SOME!
YOU MEAN, LEAVE THE WARMTH OF THE FIRE?
COME ON! IF YOU DRESS FOR THE SPORT, YOU OUGHT TO INDULGE IN IT!
(SIGH) OH, ALL RIGHT!
I'M-ER-- NOT QUITE AS GOOD AT THIS AS I SHOULD BE!
WHOOPS!
OUCH!

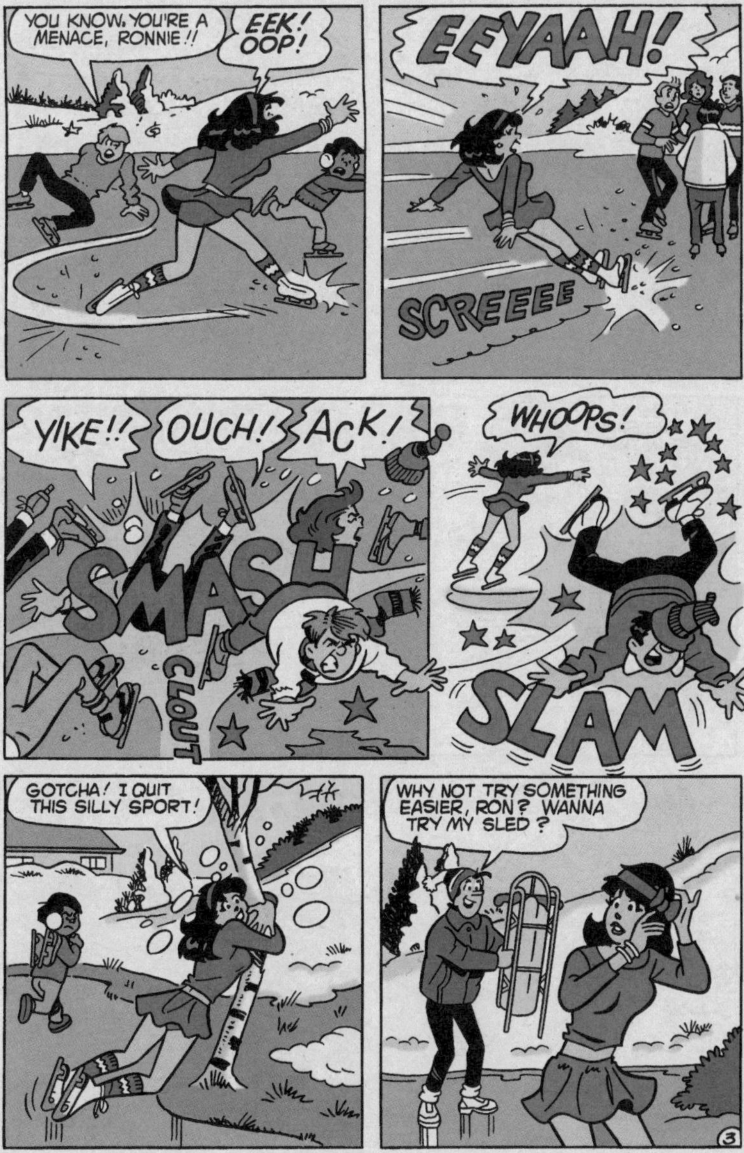
YOU KNOW, YOU'RE A MENACE, RONNIE!!
EEK! OOP!
EEYAAH!
SCREEEEE
YIKE!!
OUCH!
ACK!
SMASH
CLOUT
WHOOPS!
SLAM
GOTCHA! I QUIT THIS SILLY SPORT!
WHY NOT TRY SOMETHING EASIER, RON? WANNA TRY MY SLED?
3

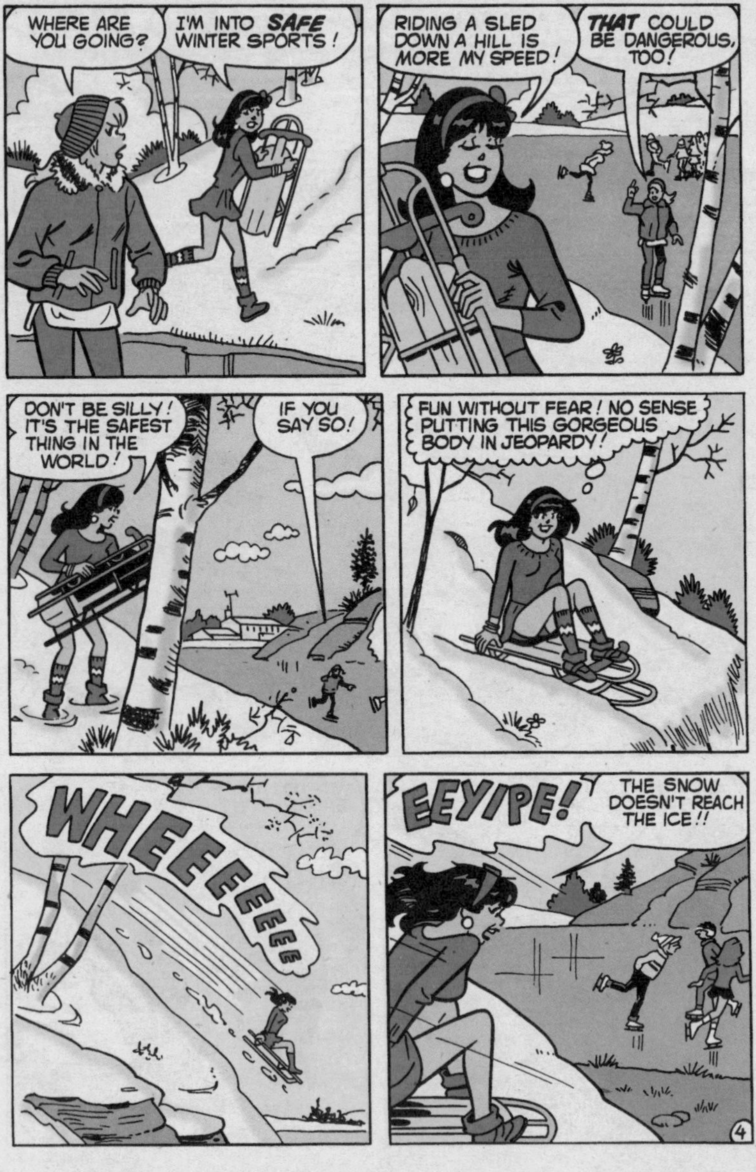

WHERE ARE YOU GOING?
I'M INTO SAFE WINTER SPORTS!
RIDING A SLED DOWN A HILL IS MORE MY SPEED!
THAT COULD BE DANGEROUS, TOO!
DON'T BE SILLY! IT'S THE SAFEST THING IN THE WORLD!
IF YOU SAY SO!
FUN WITHOUT FEAR! NO SENSE PUTTING THIS GORGEOUS BODY IN JEOPARDY!
WHEEEEEEE
EEYIPE!
THE SNOW DOESN'T REACH THE ICE!!
4

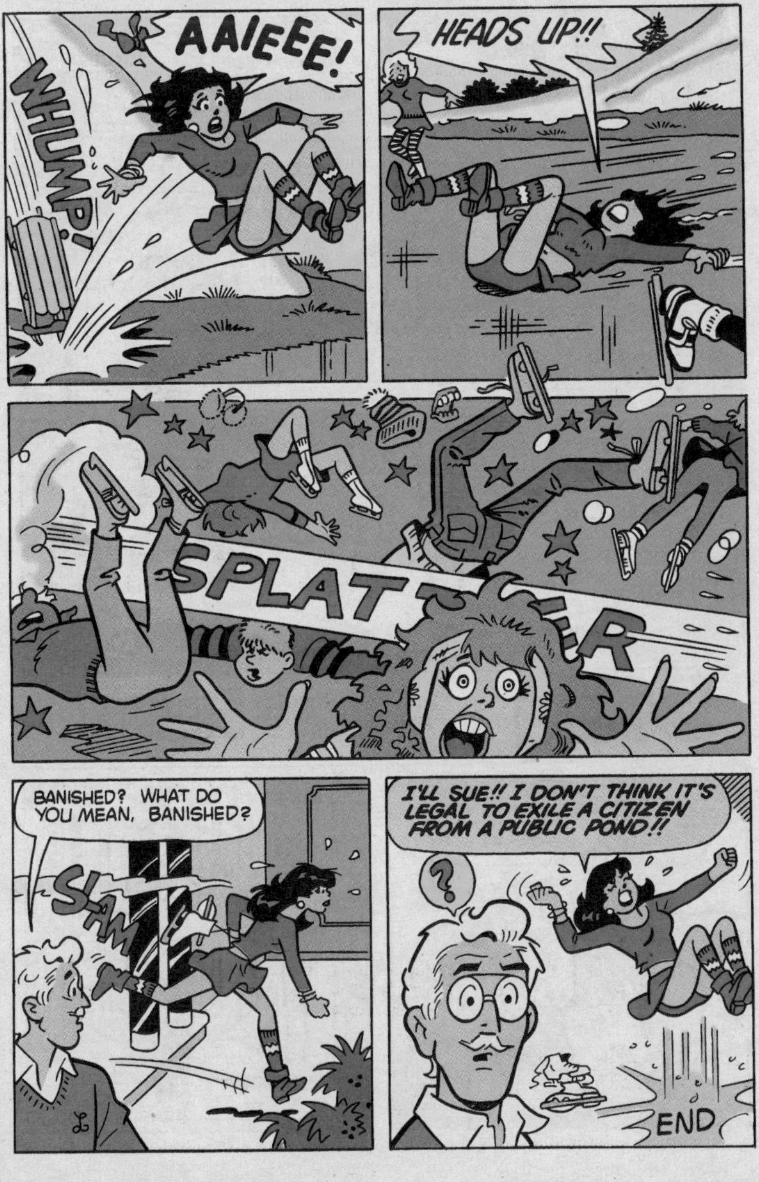
AAIEEEE!
WHUMP!
HEADS UP!!
SPLATTER
BANISHED? WHAT DO YOU MEAN, BANISHED?
SLAM
I'LL SUE!! I DON'T THINK IT'S LEGAL TO EXILE A CITIZEN FROM A PUBLIC POND!!
?
END

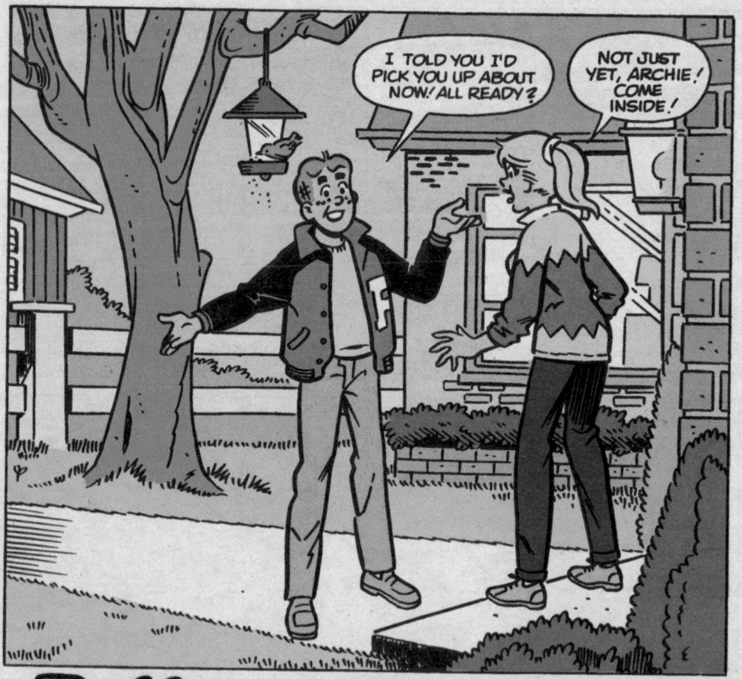
I TOLD YOU I'D PICK YOU UP ABOUT NOW! ALL READY?
NOT JUST YET, ARCHIE! COME INSIDE!

Betty (IN) "THE BIRD FEEDER"

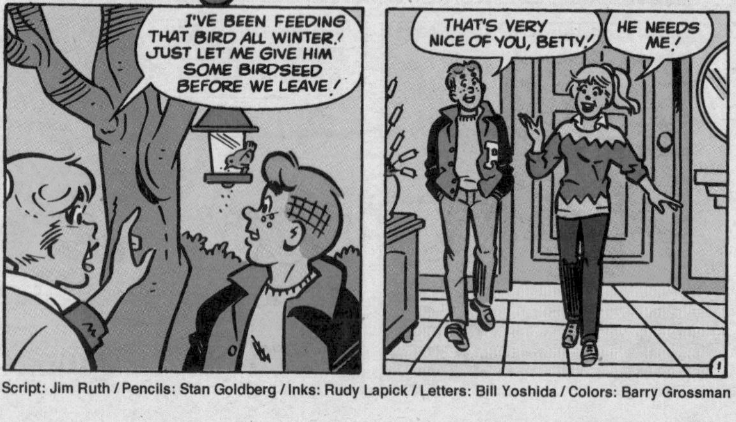
I'VE BEEN FEEDING THAT BIRD ALL WINTER! JUST LET ME GIVE HIM SOME BIRDSEED BEFORE WE LEAVE!
THAT'S VERY NICE OF YOU, BETTY!
HE NEEDS ME!
1

Script: Jim Ruth / Pencils: Stan Goldberg / Inks: Rudy Lapick / Letters: Bill Yoshida / Colors: Barry Grossman

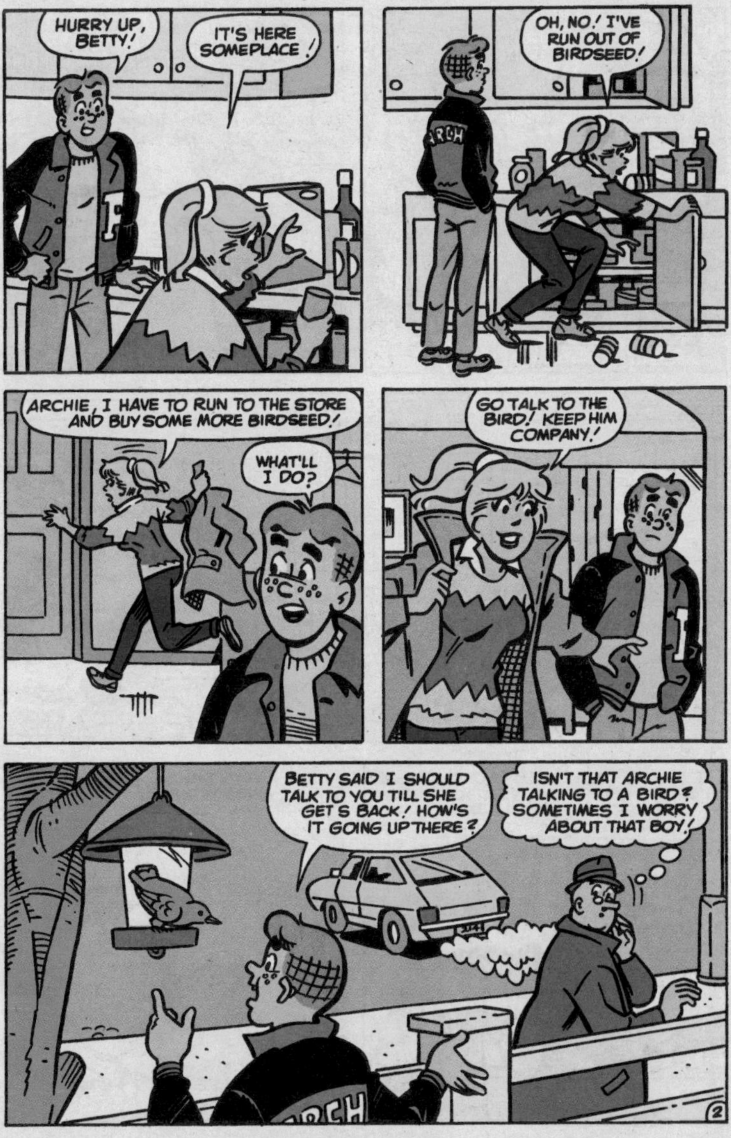
HURRY UP, BETTY!
IT'S HERE SOMEPLACE!
OH, NO! I'VE RUN OUT OF BIRDSEED!
ARCHIE, I HAVE TO RUN TO THE STORE AND BUY SOME MORE BIRDSEED!
WHAT'LL I DO?
GO TALK TO THE BIRD! KEEP HIM COMPANY!
BETTY SAID I SHOULD TALK TO YOU TILL SHE GET S BACK! HOW'S IT GOING UP THERE?
ISN'T THAT ARCHIE TALKING TO A BIRD? SOMETIMES I WORRY ABOUT THAT BOY!
2

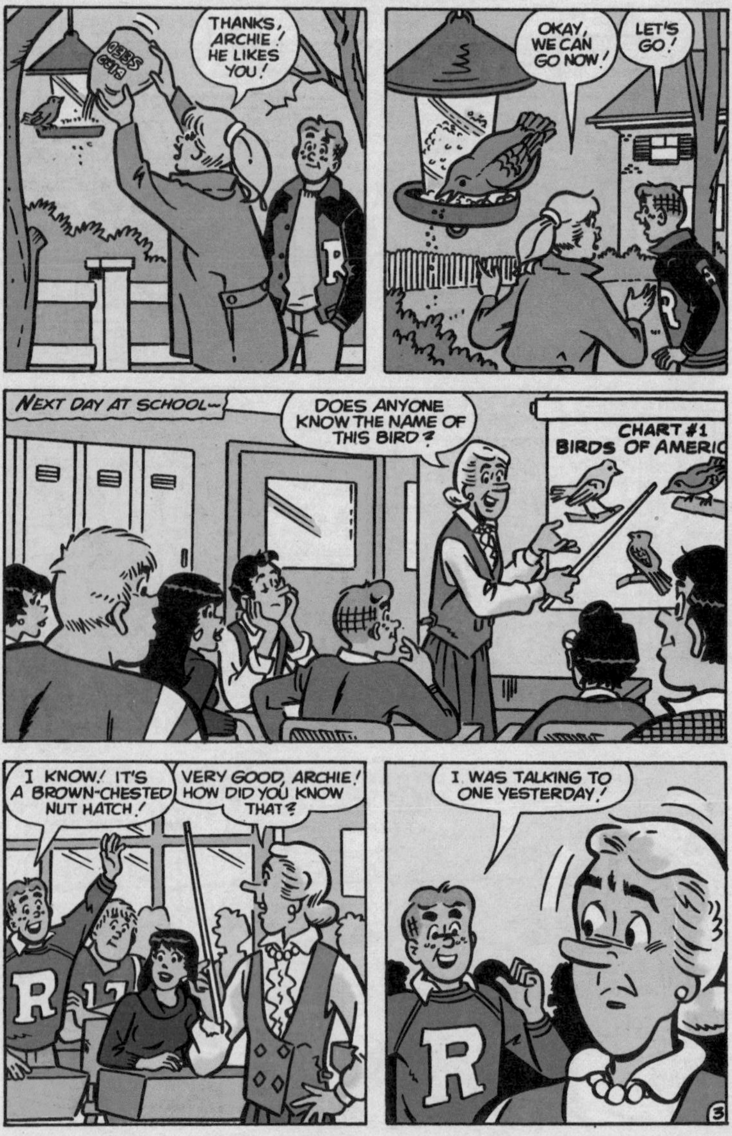

THANKS, ARCHIE! HE LIKES YOU!
BIRD SEED
OKAY, WE CAN GO NOW!
LET'S GO!
NEXT DAY AT SCHOOL--
DOES ANYONE KNOW THE NAME OF THIS BIRD?
CHART #1 BIRDS OF AMERIC
I KNOW! IT'S A BROWN-CHESTED NUT HATCH!
VERY GOOD, ARCHIE! HOW DID YOU KNOW THAT?
I WAS TALKING TO ONE YESTERDAY!
3

LATER:

MR. WEATHERBEE, ARCHIE SAID THE STRANGEST THING BEFORE!

SOMETHING ABOUT TALKING TO BIRDS?

RIVERDALE HIGH NEWS

HOW DID YOU KNOW?

JUST A WILD GUESS!

WHAT ARE WE GOING TO DO?

SEND HIM TO MY OFFICE! I'LL HAVE A TALK WITH HIM!

MR. WEATHERBEE WANTS TO SEE ME?

THE ONE AND ONLY!

PRINC OFFIC

I DON'T KNOW WHAT I'M GOING TO DO WITH THAT BOY!

4

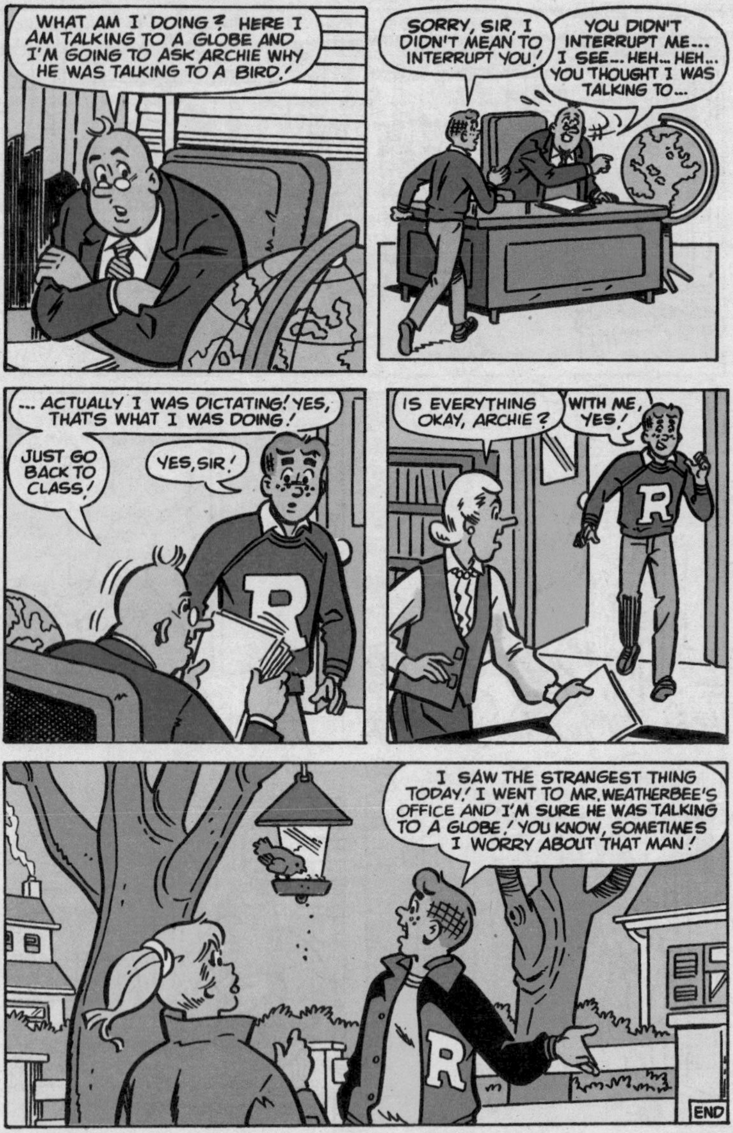
WHAT AM I DOING? HERE I AM TALKING TO A GLOBE AND I'M GOING TO ASK ARCHIE WHY HE WAS TALKING TO A BIRD!
SORRY, SIR, I DIDN'T MEAN TO INTERRUPT YOU!
YOU DIDN'T INTERRUPT ME... I SEE... HEH... HEH... YOU THOUGHT I WAS TALKING TO...
... ACTUALLY I WAS DICTATING! YES, THAT'S WHAT I WAS DOING!
JUST GO BACK TO CLASS!
YES, SIR!
IS EVERYTHING OKAY, ARCHIE?
WITH ME, YES!
I SAW THE STRANGEST THING TODAY! I WENT TO MR. WEATHERBEE'S OFFICE AND I'M SURE HE WAS TALKING TO A GLOBE! YOU KNOW, SOMETIMES I WORRY ABOUT THAT MAN!
END

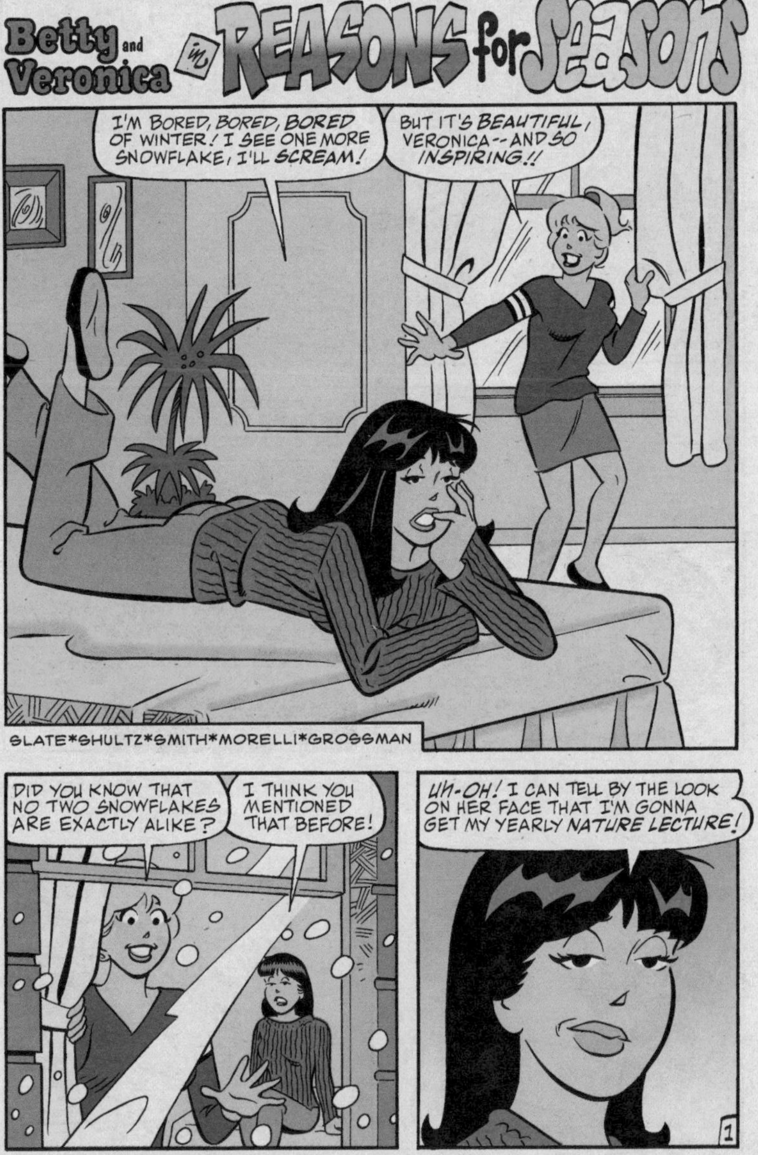
Betty and Veronica
in
REASONS for SEASONS
I'M BORED, BORED, BORED OF WINTER! I SEE ONE MORE SNOWFLAKE, I'LL SCREAM!
BUT IT'S BEAUTIFUL, VERONICA--AND SO INSPIRING!!
SLATE*SHULTZ*SMITH*MORELLI*GROSSMAN
DID YOU KNOW THAT NO TWO SNOWFLAKES ARE EXACTLY ALIKE?
I THINK YOU MENTIONED THAT BEFORE!
UH-OH! I CAN TELL BY THE LOOK ON HER FACE THAT I'M GONNA GET MY YEARLY NATURE LECTURE!
1

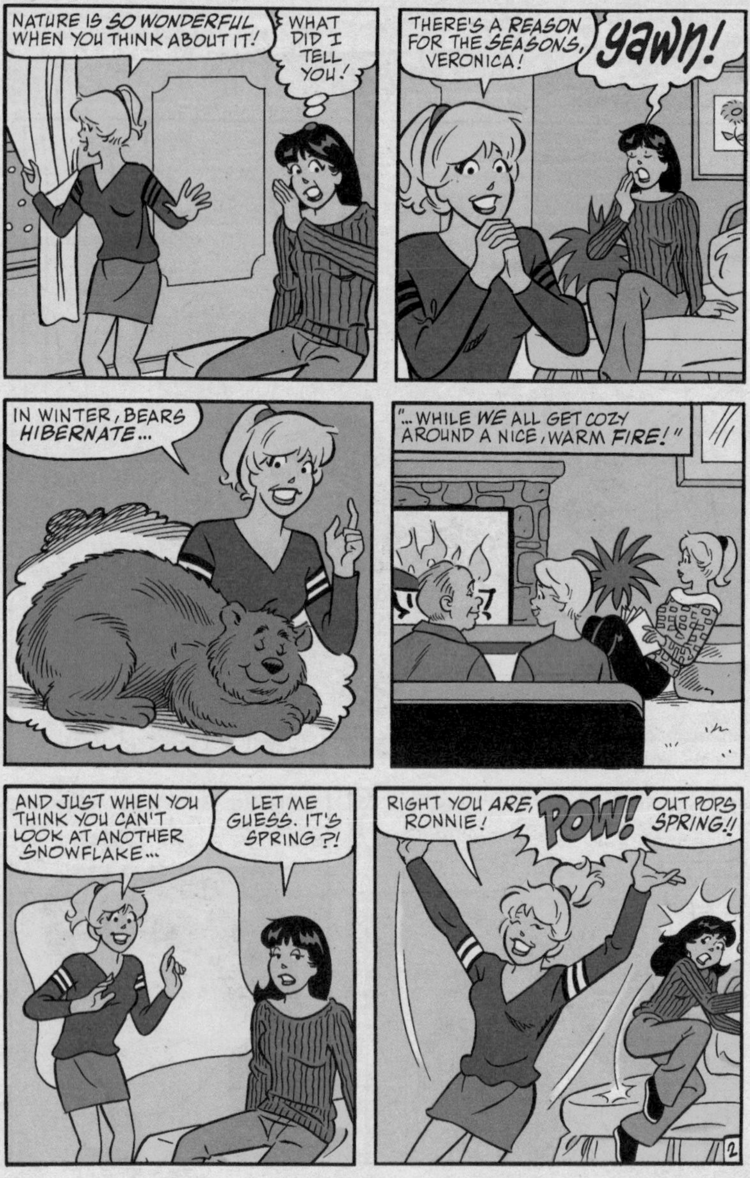
NATURE IS SO WONDERFUL WHEN YOU THINK ABOUT IT!
WHAT DID I TELL YOU!
THERE'S A REASON FOR THE SEASONS, VERONICA!
yawn!
IN WINTER, BEARS HIBERNATE...
"...WHILE WE ALL GET COZY AROUND A NICE, WARM FIRE!"
AND JUST WHEN YOU THINK YOU CAN'T LOOK AT ANOTHER SNOWFLAKE...
LET ME GUESS. IT'S SPRING ?!
RIGHT YOU ARE, RONNIE!
POW!
OUT POPS SPRING!!
2

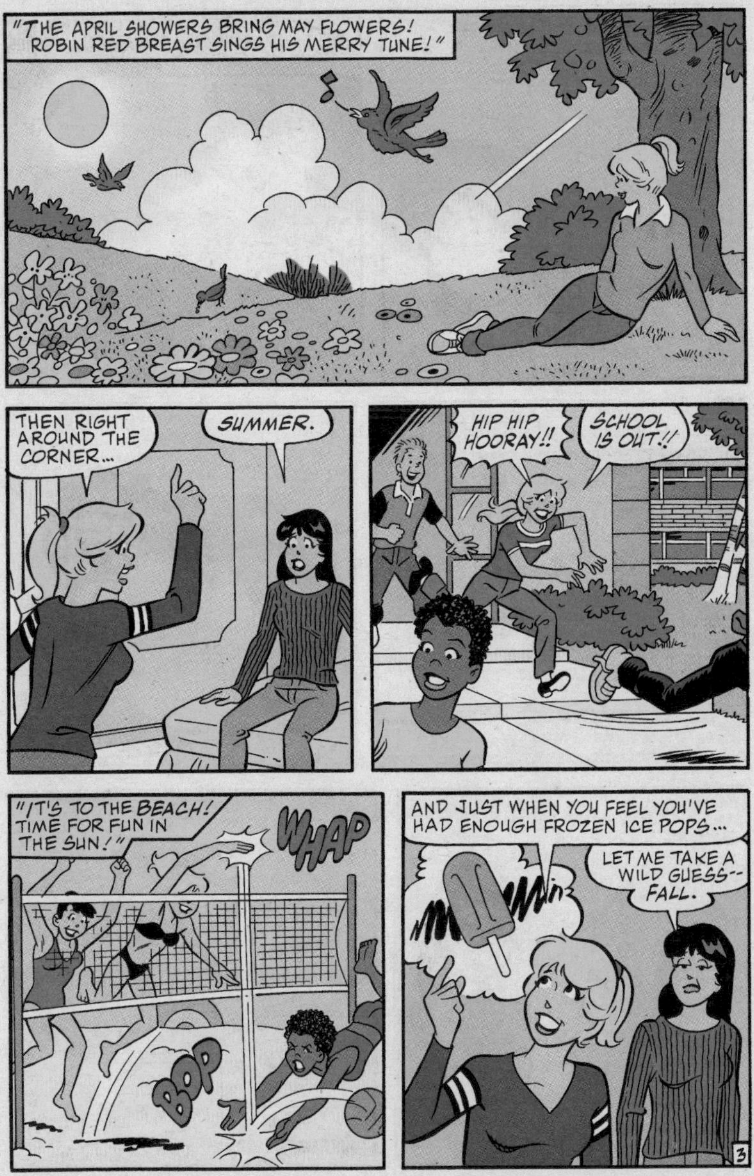
"THE APRIL SHOWERS BRING MAY FLOWERS! ROBIN RED BREAST SINGS HIS MERRY TUNE!"
THEN RIGHT AROUND THE CORNER...
SUMMER.
HIP HIP HOORAY!!
SCHOOL IS OUT!!
"IT'S TO THE BEACH! TIME FOR FUN IN THE SUN!"
WHAP
BOP
AND JUST WHEN YOU FEEL YOU'VE HAD ENOUGH FROZEN ICE POPS...
LET ME TAKE A WILD GUESS-- FALL.
3

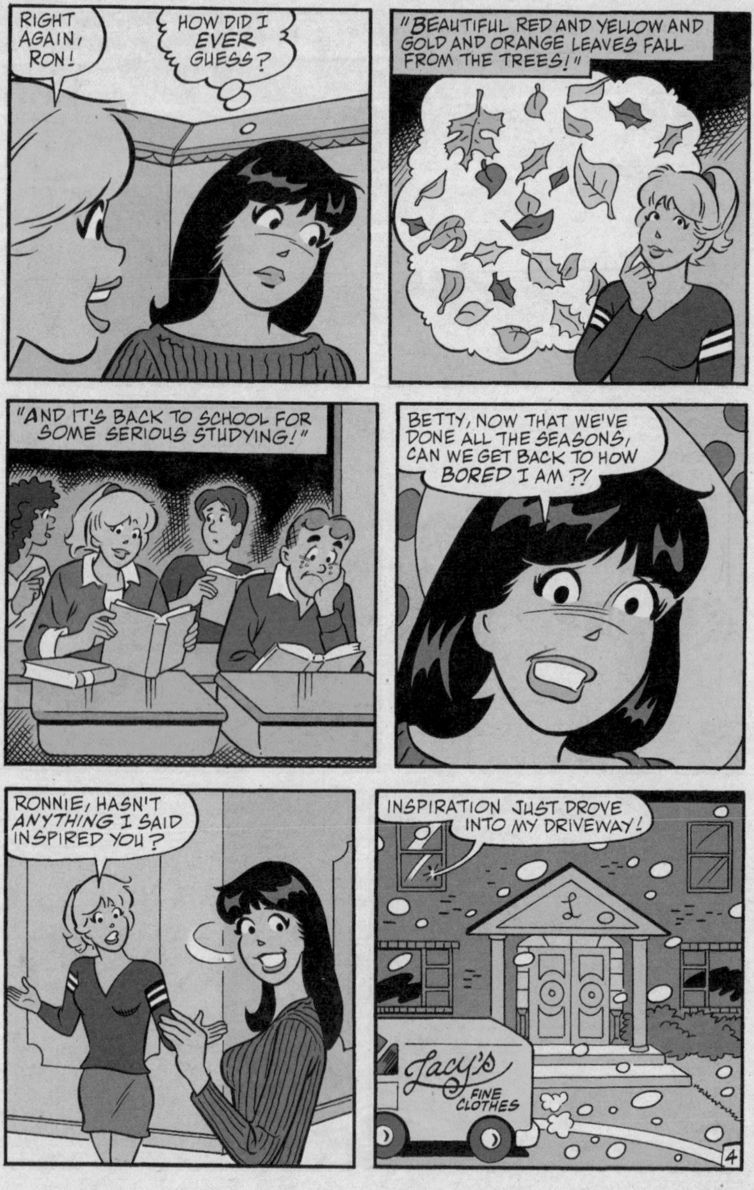
RIGHT AGAIN, RON!
HOW DID I EVER GUESS?
"BEAUTIFUL RED AND YELLOW AND GOLD AND ORANGE LEAVES FALL FROM THE TREES!"
"AND IT'S BACK TO SCHOOL FOR SOME SERIOUS STUDYING!"
BETTY, NOW THAT WE'VE DONE ALL THE SEASONS, CAN WE GET BACK TO HOW BORED I AM?!
RONNIE, HASN'T ANYTHING I SAID INSPIRED YOU?
INSPIRATION JUST DROVE INTO MY DRIVEWAY!
Lacy's FINE CLOTHES
4

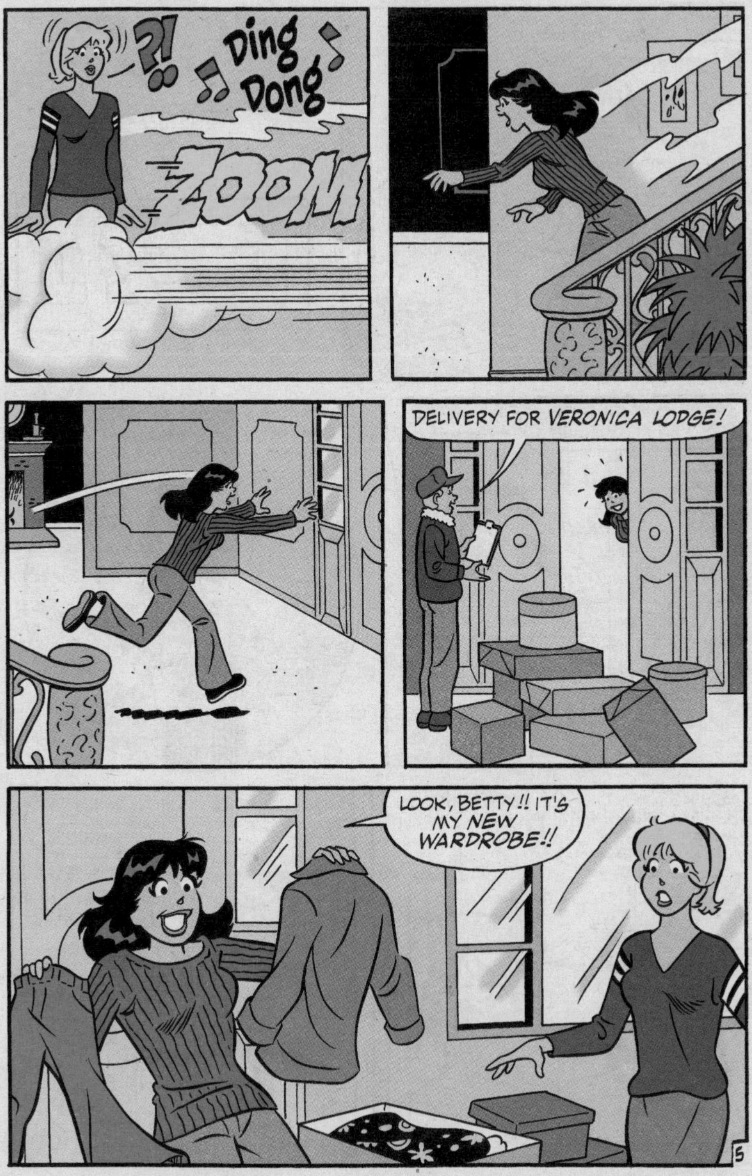
?!
Ding Dong
ZOOM
DELIVERY FOR VERONICA LODGE!
LOOK, BETTY!! IT'S MY NEW WARDROBE!!
5

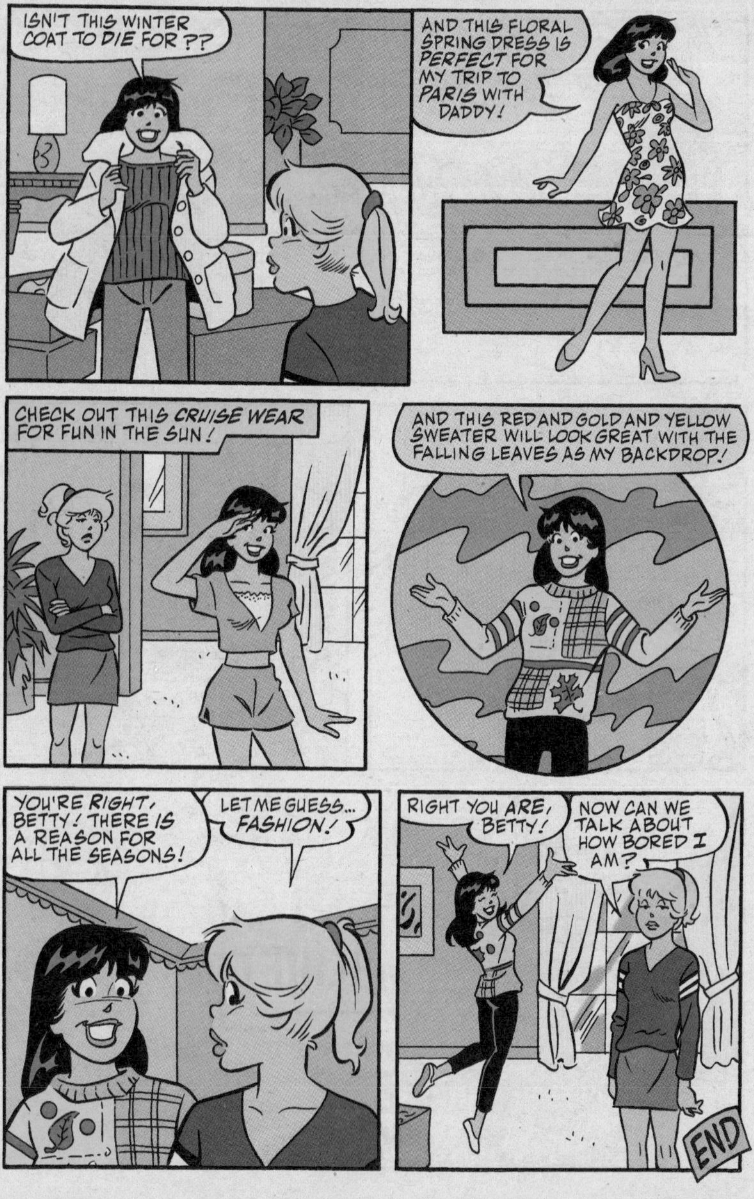
ISN'T THIS WINTER COAT TO DIE FOR ??
AND THIS FLORAL SPRING DRESS IS PERFECT FOR MY TRIP TO PARIS WITH DADDY!
CHECK OUT THIS CRUISE WEAR FOR FUN IN THE SUN!
AND THIS RED AND GOLD AND YELLOW SWEATER WILL LOOK GREAT WITH THE FALLING LEAVES AS MY BACKDROP!
YOU'RE RIGHT, BETTY! THERE IS A REASON FOR ALL THE SEASONS!
LET ME GUESS... FASHION!
RIGHT YOU ARE, BETTY!
NOW CAN WE TALK ABOUT HOW BORED I AM?
END